Joseph II and His Court: A Historical Novel

Joseph II and His Court:
A Historical Novel

Luise Mühlbach

NEW YORK

Joseph II and His Court: A Historical Novel

For information, address:

Cosimo, P.O. Box 416
Old Chelsea Station
New York, NY 10113-0416

or visit our website at:
www.cosimobooks.com

Joseph II and His Court: A Historical Novel originally published by D. Appleton and Company in 1865.

Library of Congress Cataloging-in-Publication Data
A catalog record for this book is available from the Library of Congress

Cover design by www.wiselephant.com

ISBN: 1-59605-761-0

MARIA THERESA.

CONTENTS.

MARIA THERESA.

ISABELLA.

KING OF ROME.

EMPEROR OF AUSTRIA.

MARIE ANTOINETTE.

THE REIGN OF JOSEPH.

ILLUSTRATIONS.

JOSEPH II. AND HIS COURT.

MARIA THERESA.

CHAPTER I.

THE CONFERENCE.

In the council-chamber of the Empress Maria Theresa, the six lords, who composed her cabinet council, awaited the entrance of their imperial mistress to open the sitting.

At this sitting, a great political question was to be discussed; and its gravity seemed to be reflected in the faces of the lords, as, in low tones, they whispered together in the dim, spacious apartment, whose antiquated furniture of dark velvet tapestry corresponded well with the anxious looks of its occupants.

In the centre of the room stood the Baron von Bartenstein and the Count von Uhlefeld, the two powerful statesmen who for thirteen years had been honored by the confidence of the empress. Together they stood, their consequence acknowledged by all, while with proud and lofty mien, they whispered of state secrets.

Upon the fair, smooth face of Bartenstein appeared an expression of haughty triumph, which he was at no pains to conceal; and over the delicate mouth of Von Uhlefeld fluttered a smile of ineffable complacency.

"I feel perfectly secure," whispered Von Bartenstein. "The empress will certainly renew the treaties, and continue the policy which we have hitherto pursued with such brilliant results to Austria."

"The empress is wise," returned Uhlefeld. "She can reckon upon our stanch support, and so long as she pursues this policy, we will sustain her."

While he spoke, there shot from his eyes such a glance of conscious power, that the two lords who, from the recess of a neighboring window, were watching the imperial favorites, were completely dazzled.

"See, count," murmured one to the other, "see how Count Uhlefeld smiles to-day. Doubtless he knows already what the decision of the empress is to be; and that it is in accordance with his wishes, no one can doubt who looks upon him now."

"It will be well for us," replied Count Colloredo, "if we subscribe unconditionally to the opinions of the lord chancellor. I, for my part, will do so all the more readily, that I confess to you my utter ignorance of the question which is to come before us to-day. I was really so preoccupied at our last sitting that I—I failed exactly to comprehend its nature. I think, therefore, that it will be well for us to vote with Count von Uhlefeld—that is, if the president of the Aulic Council, Count Harrach, does not entertain other opinions."

Count Harrach bowed. "As for me," sighed he, "I must, as usual, vote with Count Bartenstein. His will be, as it ever is, the decisive voice of the day; and its echo will be heard from the lips of the empress. Let us echo them both, and so be the means of helping to crush the presumption of yonder crafty and arrogant courtier."

As he spoke he glanced toward the massive table of carved oak, around which were arranged the leathern arm-chairs of the members of the Aulic Council. Count Colloredo followed the glance of his friend, which, with a supercilious expression, rested upon the person to whom he alluded. This person was seated in one of the chairs, deeply absorbed in the perusal of the papers that lay before him upon the table. He was a man of slight and elegant proportions, whose youthful face contrasted singularly with the dark, manly, and weather-beaten countenances of the other members of the council. Not a fault marred the beauty of this fair face; not the shadow of a wrinkle ruffled the polish of the brow; even the lovely mouth itself was free from those lines by which thought and care are wont to mark the passage of man through life. One thing, however, was wanting to this beautiful mask. It was devoid of expression. Those delicate features were immobile and stony. No trace of emotion stirred the compressed lips; no shadow of thought flickered over the high, marble brow; and the glance of those clear, light-blue eyes was as calm, cold, and unfeeling as that of a statue. This young man, with Medusa-like beauty, was Anthony Wenzel von Kaunitz, whom Maria Theresa had lately recalled from Paris to take his seat in her cabinet council.

The looks of Harrach and Colloredo were directed toward him, but he appeared not to observe them, and went on quietly with his examination of the state papers.

"You think, then, count," whispered Colloredo, thoughtfully, "that young Kaunitz cherishes the absurd hope of an alliance with France?"

"I am sure of it. I know that a few days ago the French ambassador delivered to him a most affectionate missive from his friend the Marquise de Pompadour; and I know too that yesterday he replied to it in a similar strain. It is his fixed idea, and that of La Pompadour also, to drive Austria into a new line of policy, by making her the ally of France."

Count Colloredo laughed. "The best cure that I know of for *fixed ideas* is the madhouse," replied he, "and thither we will send little Kaunitz if——"

He ceased suddenly, for Kaunitz had slowly raised his eyes from the table, and they now rested with such an icy gaze upon the smiling face of Colloredo, that the frightened statesman shivered.

"If he should have heard me!" murmured he. "If he——" but the poor count had no further time for reflection; for at that moment the folding-doors leading to the private apartments of the empress were thrown open, and the lord high steward announced the approach of her majesty.

The councillors advanced to the table, and in respectful silence awaited the imperial entrance.

The rustling of silk was heard; and then the quick step of the Countess Fuchs, whose duty it was to accompany the empress to the threshold of her council-chamber, and to close the door behind her.

And now appeared the majestic figure of the empress. The lords laid their hands upon their swords, and inclined their heads in reverence before the imperial lady, who with light, elastic step advanced to the table, while the Countess Fuchs noiselessly closed the door and returned.

The empress smilingly acknowledged the salutation, though her smile was lost to her respectful subjects, who, in obedience to the strict Spanish etiquette which prevailed at the Austrian court, remained with their heads bent until the sovereign had taken her seat upon the throne.

One of these subjects had bent his head with the rest, but he had ventured to raise it again, and he at least met the glance of royalty. This bold subject was Kaunitz, the youngest of the councillors.

He gazed at the advancing empress, and for the first time a smile flitted over his stony features. And well might the sight of his sovereign lady stir the marble heart of Kaunitz; for Maria Theresa was one of the loveliest women of her day. Though thirty-six years of age, and the mother of thirteen children, she was still beautiful, and the Austrians were proud to excess of her beauty. Her high, thoughtful forehead was shaded by a profusion of blond hair, which lightly powdered and gathered up behind in one rich mass, was there confined by a golden net. Her large, starry eyes were of that peculiar gray which changes with every emotion of the soul; at one time seeming to be heavenly-blue, at another the darkest and most flashing brown. Her bold profile betokened great pride; but every look of haughtiness was softened away by the enchanting expression of a mouth in whose exquisite beauty no trace of the so-called "Austrian lip" could be seen. Her figure, loftier than is usual with women, was of faultless symmetry, while her graceful bust would have seemed to the eyes of Praxiteles the waking to life of his own dreams of Juno.

Those who looked upon this beautiful empress could well realize the emotions which thirteen years before had stirred the hearts of the Hungarian nobles, as she stood before them; and had wrought them up to that height of enthusiasm which culminated in the well-known shout of

"MORIAMUR PRO REGE NOSTRO!"

"Our king!" cried the Hungarians, and they were right. For Maria Theresa, who with her husband, was the tender wife; toward her children, the loving mother; was in all that related to her empire, her people, and her sovereignty, a man both in the scope of her comprehension and the strength of her will. She was capable of sketching bold lines of policy, and of following them out without reference to personal predilections or prejudices, both of which she was fully competent to stifle, wherever they threatened interference with the good of her realm, or her sense of duty as a sovereign.

The energy and determination of her character were written upon the lofty brow of Maria Theresa; and now, as she approached her councillors, these characteristics beamed forth from her countenance with such power and such beauty, that Kaunitz himself was overawed, and for one moment a smile lit up his cold features.

No one saw this smile except the imperial lady, who had woke the Memnon into life; and as she took her seat upon the throne, she slightly bent her head in return.

Now, with her clear and sonorous voice, she invited her councillors also to be seated, and at once reached out her hand for the memoranda which Count Bartenstein had prepared for her examination.

She glanced quickly over the papers, and laid them aside. "My lords of the Aulic Council," said she, in tones of deep earnestness, "we have to-day a question of gravest import to discuss. I crave thereunto your attention and advice. We are at this sitting to deliberate upon the future policy of Austria, and deeply significant will be the result of this day's deliberations to Austria's welfare. Some of our old treaties are about to expire. Time, which has somewhat moderated the bitterness of our enemies, seems also to have weakened the amity of our friends. Both are dying away; and the question now before us is, Whether we shall extinguish enmity, or rekindle friendship? For seventy years past England, Holland, and Sardinia have been our allies. For three hundred years France has been our hereditary enemy. Shall we renew our alliance with the former powers, or seek new relations with the latter? Let me have your views, my lords."

With these concluding words, Maria Theresa waved her hand, and pointed to Count Uhlefeld. The lord chancellor arose, and with a dignified inclination of the head, responded to the appeal.

"Since your majesty permits me to speak, I vote without hesitation for the renewal of our treaty with the maritime powers. For seventy years our relations with these powers have been amicable and honorable. In our days of greatest extremity—when Louis XIV. took Alsatia and the city of Strasburg, and his ally, the Turkish Sultan, besieged Vienna—when two powerful enemies threatened Austria with destruction, it was this alliance with the maritime powers and with Sardinia, which, next to the succor of the generous King of Poland, saved the Austrian empire from ruin. The brave Sobieski saved our capital, and Savoy held Lombardy in check, while England and Holland guarded the Netherlands, which, since the days of Philip II., have ever been the nest of rebellion and revolt. To this alliance, therefore, we owe it that your majesty still reigns over those seditious provinces. To Savoy we are indebted for Lombardy; while France, perfidious France, has not only robbed us of our territory, but to this day asserts her right to its possession! No, your majesty—so long as France retains that which belongs to Austria, Austria will neither forgive her enmity nor forget it. See, on the contrary, how the maritime powers have befriended us! It was *their* gold which enabled us first to withstand France, and afterward Prussia—*their* gold that filled your majesty's coffers—*their* gold that sustained and confirmed the prosperity of your majesty's dominions. This is the alliance that I advocate, and with all my heart I vote for its renewal. It is but just tha the princes and rulers of the earth should give example to the world of good faith in their dealings; for the integrity of the sovereign is a pledge to all nations of the integrity of his people."

Count Uhlefeld resumed his seat, and after him rose the powerful favorite of the empress, Count Bartenstein, who, in a long and animated address, came vehemently to the support of Uhlefeld.

Then came Counts Colloredo and Harrach, and the lord high steward, Count Khevenhüller—all unanimous for a renewal of the old treaty. Not one of these rich, proud nobles would have dared to breathe a sentiment in opposition to the two powerful statesmen that had spoken before them. Bartenstein and Uhlefeld had passed the word. The alliance must continue with those maritime powers, from whose subsidies such unexampled wealth had flowed into the coffers of Austria, and—those of the lords of the exchequer! For, up to the times of which we write, it was a fundamental doctrine of court faith, that the task of inquiry into the accounts of the imperial treasury was one far beneath the dignity of the sovereign. The lords of the exchequer, therefore, were responsible to nobody for their administration of the funds arising from the Dutch and English subsidies.

It was natural, then, that the majority of the Aulic Council should vote for the old alliance. While they argued and voted, Kaunitz, the least important personage of them all, sat perfectly unconcerned, paying not the slightest attention to the wise deductions of his colleagues. He seemed much occupied in straightening loose papers, mending his pen, and removing with his finger-tips the tiny specks that flecked the lustre of his velvet coat. Once, while Bartenstein was delivering his long address, Kaunitz carried his indifference so far as to draw out his repeater (on which was painted a portrait of La Pompadour, set in diamonds) and strike the hour! The musical ring of the little bell sounded a fairy accompaniment to the deep and earnest tones of Bartenstein's voice; while Kaunitz, seeming to hear nothing else, held the watch up to his ear and counted its strokes.* The empress, who was accustomed to visit the least manifestation of such inattention on the part of her councillors with open censure—the empress, so observant of form, and so exacting of its observance in others—seemed singularly indulgent to-day; for while Kaunitz was listening to the music of his watch, his imperial mistress looked on with half a smile. At last, when the fifth orator had spoken, and it became the turn of Kaunitz to vote, Maria Theresa turned her flashing eyes upon him, with a glance of anxious and appealing expectation.

As her look met his, how had all coldness and unconcern vanished from his face! How glowed his eyes with the lustre of great and world-swaying thoughts, as, rising from his chair, he returned the gaze of his sovereign with one that seemed to crave forbearance!

But Kaunitz had almost preternatural control over his emotions, and he recovered himself at once.

"I cannot vote for a renewal of our worn-out alliance with the maritime powers," said he, in a clear and determined voice. As he uttered these words, looks of astonishment and disapprobation were visible upon the faces of his colleagues. The lord chancellor contented himself with a contemptuous shrug and a supercilious smile. Kaunitz perceived it, and met both shrug and smile with undisturbed composure, while calmly and slowly he repeated his offend-

* Vide Kormayr, "Austrian Plutarch," vol. xii., p. 352.

ing words. For a moment he paused, as if to give time to his hearers to test the flavor of his new and startling language. Then, firm and collected, he went on:

"Our alliance with England and Holland has long been a yoke and a humiliation to Austria. If, in its earlier days, this alliance ever afforded us protection, dearly have we paid for that protection, and we have been forced to buy it with fearful sacrifices to our national pride. Never for one moment have these two powers allowed us to forget that we have been dependent upon their bounty for money and defence. Jealous of the growing power and influence of Austria, before whose youthful and vigorous career lies the glory of future greatness—jealous of our increasing wealth—jealous of the splendor of Maria Theresa's reign—these powers, whose faded laurels are buried in the grave of the past, have compassed sea and land to stop the flow of our prosperity, and sting the pride of our nationality. With their tyrannical commercial edicts, they have dealt injury to friends as well as foes. The closing of the Scheldt and Rhine, the Barrier treaty, and all the other restrictions upon trade devised by those crafty English to damage the traffic of other nations, all these compacts have been made as binding upon Austria as upon every other European power. Unmindful of their alliance with us, the maritime powers have closed their ports against our ships; and while affecting to watch the Netherlands in our behalf, they have been nothing better than spies, seeking to discover whether our flag transcended in the least the limits of our own blockaded frontiers; and whether to any but to themselves accrued the profits of trade with the Baltic and North Seas. *Vraiment*, such friendship lies heavily upon us, and its weight feels almost like that of enmity. At Aix-la-Chapelle I had to remind the English ambassador that his unknightly and arrogant bearing toward Austria was unseemly both to the sex and majesty of Austria's empress. And our august sovereign herself, not long since, saw fit to reprove the insolence of this same British envoy, who in her very presence spoke of the Netherlands as though they had been a boon to Austria from England's clemency. Incensed at the tone of this representative of our *friends*, the empress exclaimed: 'Am I not ruler in the Netherlands as well as in Vienna? Do I hold my right of empire from England and Holland?'" *

"Yes," interrupted Maria Theresa, impetuously, "yes, it is true. The arrogance of these royal traders has provoked me beyond all bearing. I will no longer permit them to insinuate of my own imperial rights, that I hold them as favors from the hand of any earthly power. It chafes the pride of an empress-queen to be *called* a friend and *treated* as a vassal; and I intend that these proud allies shall feel that I resent their affronts!"

It was wonderful to see the effect of these impassioned words upon the auditors of the empress. They quaked as they thought how they had voted, and their awe-stricken faces were pallid with fright. Uhlefeld and Bartenstein exchanged glances of amazement and dismay; while the other nobles, like adroit courtiers, fixed their looks, with awakening admiration, upon Kaunitz, in whom their experienced eyes were just discovering the rising luminary of a new political firmament.

He, meanwhile, had inclined his head and smiled when the em-

* Coxe, "History of the House of Austria," vol. v., p. 51.

press had interrupted him. She ceased, and after a short pause, Kaunitz resumed, with unaltered equanimity: "Your majesty has been graciously pleased to testify, in your own sovereign person, to the tyranny of our two northern allies. It remains, therefore, to speak of Sardinia alone—Sardinia, who *held Lombardy in check.* No sooner had Victor Amadeus put his royal signature to the treaty made by him with Austria, than he turned to his confidants and said (loud enough for us to hear him in Vienna): 'Lombardy is mine. I will take it, but I shall eat it up, leaf by leaf, like an artichoke.' And methinks his majesty of Sardinia has proved himself to be a good trencherman. He has already swallowed several leaves of his artichoke, in that he is master of several of the fairest provinces of Lombardy. It is true that this royal gourmand has laid aside his crown; and that in his place reigns Victor Emanuel, of whom Lord Chesterfield, in a burst of enthusiasm, has said, that 'he never did and never will commit an act of injustice.' Concede that Victor Emanuel is the soul of honor; still," added Kaunitz with a shake of the head, and an incredulous smile, "still—the Italian princes are abominable geographers—and they are inordinately fond of artichokes.* Now their fondness for this vegetable is as dangerous to Austria as the too-loving grasp of her northern allies, who with their friendly hands not only close their ports against us, but lay the weight of their favors so heavily upon our heads as to force us down upon our knees before them. What have we from England and Holland but their subsidies? And Austria can now afford to relinquish them—Austria is rich, powerful, prosperous enough to be allowed to proffer her friendship where it will be honorably returned. Austria, then, must be freed from her oppressive alliance with the maritime powers. She has youth and vitality enough to shake off this bondage, and strike for the new path which shall lead her to greatness and glory. There is a moral and intangible greatness, of whose existence these trading Englishmen have no conception, but which the refined and elevated people of France are fully competent to appreciate. France extends to us her hand, and offers us alliance on terms of equality. Coöperating with France, we shall defy the enmity of all Europe. With our two-edged sword we shall turn the scales of future European strife, and make peace or war for other nations. France, too, is our natural ally, for she is our neighbor. And she is more than this, for she is our ally by the sacred unity of one faith. The Holy Father at Rome, who blesses the arms of Austria, will no longer look sorrowfully upon Austria's league with heresy. When apostolic France and we are one, the blessings of the Church will descend upon our alliance. Religion, therefore, as well as honest statesmanship, call for the treaty with France."

"And I," cried Maria Theresa, rising quickly from her seat, her eyes glowing with enthusiastic fire, "I vote joyfully with Count Kaunitz. I, too, vote for alliance with France. The count has spoken as it stirs my heart to hear an Austrian speak. He loves his fatherland, and in his devotion he casts far from him all thought of worldly profit or advancement. I tender him my warmest thanks, and I will take his words to heart."

Overcome with the excitement of the moment, the empress

* Kaunitz's own words. Kormayr, "Austrian Plutarch," vol. xi.

reached her hand to Kaunitz, who eagerly seized and pressed it to his lips.

Count Uhlefeld watched this extraordinary scene with astonishment and consternation. Bartenstein, so long the favorite minister of Maria Theresa, was deadly pale, and his lips were compressed as though he were trying to suppress a burst of rage. Harrach, Colloredo, and Khevenhüller hung their heads, while they turned over in their little minds how best to curry favor with the new minister.

The empress saw nothing of the dismayed faces around her. Her soul was filled with high emotions, and her countenance beamed gloriously with the fervor of her boundless patriotism.

"Every thing for Austria! My heart, my soul, my life, all are for my fatherland," said Maria Theresa, with her beautiful eyes raised to heaven. "And now, my lords," added she, after a pause, "I must retire, to beg light and counsel from the Almighty. I have learned your different views on the great question of this day; and when Heaven shall have taught me what to do, I will decide."

She waved her hand in parting salutation, and with her loftiest imperial bearing left the room.

Until the doors were closed, the lords of the council remained standing with inclined heads. Then they looked from one to another with faces of wonder and inquiry. Kaunitz alone seemed unembarrassed; and gathering up his papers with as much unconcern as if nothing had happened, he slightly bent his head and left the room.

Never before had any member of the Aulic Council dared to leave that room until the lord chancellor had given the signal of departure. It was a case of unparalleled violation of court etiquette. Count Uhlefeld was aghast, and Bartenstein seemed crushed. Without exchanging a word, the two friends rose, and with eyes cast down, and faces pale with the anguish of that hour, together they left the council-chamber toward which they had repaired with hearts and bearing so triumphant.

Colloredo and Harrach followed silently to the anteroom, and bowed deferentially as their late masters passed through.

But no sooner had the door closed, than the two courtiers exchanged malicious smiles.

"Fallen favorites," laughed Harrach. "Quenched lights which yesterday shone like suns, and to-day are burnt to ashes! There is to be a *soirée* to-night at Bartenstein's. For the first time in eleven years I shall stay away from Bartenstein's *soirées.*"

"And I," replied Colloredo, laughing, "had invited Uhlefeld for to-morrow. But, as the entertainment was all in his honor, I shall be taken with a sudden indisposition, and countermand my supper."

"That will be a most summary proceeding," said Harrach. "I see that you believe the sun of Uhlefeld and Bartenstein has set forever."

"I am convinced of it. They have their death-blow."

"And the rising sun? You think it will be called Kaunitz?"

"*Will* be? It is called Kaunitz: so take my advice. Kaunitz, I know, is not a man to be bribed; but he has two weaknesses—women and horses. You are, for the present, the favorite of La

Fortina; and yesterday you won from Count Esterhazy an Arabian, which Kaunitz says is the finest horse in Vienna. If I were you, I would present to him both my mistress and my horse. Who knows but what these courtesies may induce him to adopt you as a *protégé?*"

CHAPTER II.

THE LETTER.

FROM her cabinet council the empress passed at once to her private apartments. When business was over for the day, she loved to cast the cares of sovereignty behind, and become a woman—chatting with her ladies of honor over the *on dits* of the court and city. During the hours devoted to her toilet, Maria Theresa gave herself up unreservedly to enjoyment. But she was so impetuous, that her ladies of honor were never quite secure that some little annoyance would not ruffle the serenity of her temper. The young girl whose duty it was to read aloud to the empress and dress her hair, used to declare that she would sooner wade through three hours' worth of Latin dispatches from Hungary, than spend one half hour as imperial hair-dresser.

But to-day, as she entered her dressing-room, the eyes of the empress beamed with pleasure, and her mouth was wreathed with sunny smiles. The little hair-dresser was delighted, and with a responsive smile took her place, and prepared for her important duties. Maria Theresa glided into the chair, and with her own hands began to unfasten the golden net that confined her hair. She then leaned forward, and, with a pleased expression, contemplated the beautiful face that looked out from the silver-framed Venetian glass before which she sat.

"Make me very charming to-day, Charlotte," * said she.

"Your majesty needs no help from me to look charming," said the gentle voice of the little tire-woman. "No hair-dresser had lent you her aid on that day when your Magyar nobles swore to die for you, and yet the world says that never were eyes of loyal subjects dazzled by such beauty and such grace."

"Ah, yes, child, but that was thirteen years ago. Thirteen years! How many cares have lain upon my heart since that day! If my face is wrinkled and my hair grown gray, I may thank that hateful King of Prussia, for he is the cause of it all."

"If he has no greater sins to repent of than those two," replied Charlotte, with an admiring smile, "he may sleep soundly. Your majesty's forehead is unruffled by a wrinkle, and your hair is as glossy and as brown as ever it was."

Brighter still was the smile of the empress, as she turned quickly round and exclaimed: "Then you think I have still beauty enough to please the emperor? If you do, make good use of it to-day, for I have something of importance to ask of him, and I long to find favor in his eyes. To work, then, Charlotte, and be quick, for—"

At that moment, the silken hangings before the door of the dressing-room were drawn hastily aside, and the Countess Fuchs stepped forward.

* Charlotte von Hieronymus was the mother of Caroline Pichler.

2

"Ah, countess," continued the empress, "you are just in time for a cabinet toilet council."

But the lady of honor showed no disposition to respond to the gay greeting of her sovereign. With stiffest Spanish ceremony, she courtesied deeply. "Pardon me, your majesty, if I interrupt you," said she, solemnly, "but I have something to communicate to yourself alone."

"Oh, countess!" exclaimed Maria Theresa, anxiously, "you look as if you bore me sad tidings. But speak out—Charlotte knows as many state secrets as you do; you need not be reserved before her."

"Pardon me," again replied the ceremonious lady, with another deep courtesy, "I bring no news of state—I must speak with your majesty alone."

The eyes of the empress dilated with fear. "No state secret," murmured she; "oh, what can it be, then? Go, Charlotte—go, child, and remain until I recall you."

The door closed behind the tire-woman, and the empress cried out: "Now we are alone—be quick, and speak out what you have to say. You have come to give me pain—I feel it."

"Your majesty ordered me, some time since," began the countess in her low, unsympathizing tones, "to watch the imperial household, so that nothing might transpire within it that came not to the knowledge of your majesty. I have lately watched the movements of the emperor's valet."

"Ah!" cried the empress, clasping her hands convulsively together, "you watched him, and—"

"Yes, your majesty, I watched him, and I was informed this morning that he had left the emperor's apartments with a sealed note in his hands, and had gone into the city."

"No more—just yet," said the empress, with trembling lip. "Give me air! I cannot breathe." With wild emotion she tore open her velvet bodice, and heaving a deep sigh, signed to the countess to go on.

"My spy awaited Gaspardi's return, and stopped him. He was forbidden, in the name of your majesty, to go farther."

"Go on."

"He was brought to me, your majesty, and now awaits your orders."

"So that if there is an answer to the note, he has it," said Maria Theresa, sharply. The countess bowed.

"Where is he?"

"In the antechamber, your majesty."

The empress bounded from her seat, and walked across the room. Her face was flushed with anger, and she trembled in every limb. She seemed undecided what to do; but at last she stopped suddenly, and blushing deeply, without looking at the countess, she said in a low voice, "Bring him hither."

The countess disappeared and returned, followed by Gaspardi.

Maria Theresa strode impetuously forward, and bent her threatening eyes upon the valet. But the shrewd Italian knew better than to meet the lightning glance of an angry empress. With downcast looks and reverential obeisance he awaited her commands.

"Look at me, Gaspardi," said she, in tones that sounded in the valet's ears like distant thunder. "Answer my questions, sir!"

Gaspardi raised his eyes.

"To whom was the note addressed that was given you by the emperor this morning?"

"Your majesty, I did not presume to look at it," replied Gaspardi, quietly. "His imperial majesty was pleased to tell me where to take it, and that sufficed me."

"And whither did you take it?"

"Imperial majesty, I have forgotten the house."

"What street, then?"

"Pardon me, imperial majesty; these dreadful German names are too hard for my Italian tongue. As soon as I had obeyed his majesty's commands, I forgot the name of the street."

"So that you are resolved not to tell me where you went with the emperor's note?"

"Indeed, imperial majesty, I have totally forgotten."

The empress looked as if she longed to annihilate a menial who defied her so successfully.

"I see," exclaimed she, "that you are crafty and deceitful, but you shall not escape me. I command you, as your sovereign, to give up the note you bear about you for the emperor. I myself will deliver it to his majesty."

Gaspardi gave a start, and unconsciously his hand sought the place where the note was concealed. He turned very pale and stammered, "Imperial majesty, I have no letter for the emperor."

"You have it there!" thundered the infuriated empress, as with threatening hand she pointed to the valet's breast. "Deliver it at once, or I will call my lackeys to search you."

"Your majesty forces me then to betray my lord and emperor?" asked Gaspardi, trembling.

"You serve him more faithfully by relinquishing the letter than by retaining it," returned Maria Theresa, hastily. "Once more I command you to give it up."

Gaspardi heaved a sigh of anguish, and looked imploringly at the empress. But in the trembling lips, the flashing eyes, the flushed cheeks that met his entreating glance, he saw no symptoms of relenting, and he dared the strife no longer. His hand shook as he drew forth the letter.

The empress uttered a cry, and with the fury of a lioness snatched the paper and crushed it in her hand.

"Your majesty," whispered the countess, "dismiss the valet before he learns too much. He might—"

"Woe to him if he breathes a word to one human being!" cried the empress, with menacing gesture. "Woe to him if he dare breathe one word to his master!"

"Heaven forbid that I should betray the secrets of my sovereign!" cried the affrighted Gaspardi. "But, imperial majesty, what am I to say to my lord the emperor?"

"You will tell your lord that you brought no answer, and it will not be the first lie with which you have befooled his imperial ears," replied Maria Theresa contemptuously, while she waved her hand as a signal of dismissal. The unhappy Mercury retired, and as he disappeared, the pent-up anguish of the empress burst forth.

"Ah, Margaretta," cried she, in accents of wildest grief, "what an unfortunate woman I am! In all my life I have loved but one man! My heart, my soul, my every thought are his, and he robs me, the mother of his children, of *his* love, and bestows it upon another!"

"Perhaps the inconstancy is but momentary," replied the countess, who burned to know the contents of the letter. "Perhaps there is no inconstancy at all. This may be nothing but an effort on the part of some frivolous coquette to draw our handsome emperor within the net of her guilty attractions. The note would show—"

The empress scarcely heeded the words of her confidante. She had opened her hand, and was gazing upon the crumpled paper that held her husband's secret.

"Oh!" murmured she, plaintively. "Oh, it seems to me that a thousand daggers have sprung from this little paper, to make my heart's blood flow. Who is the foolhardy woman that would entice my husband from his loyalty to me? Woe, woe to her when I shall have learned her name! And I WILL learn it!" cried the unhappy wife. "I myself will take this letter to the emperor, and he shall open it in my presence. I will have justice! Adultery is a fearful crime, and fearful shall be its punishment in my realms. The name! the name! Oh, that I knew the name of the execrable woman who has dared to lift her treasonable eyes toward my husband!"

"Nothing is easier than to learn it, your majesty," whispered the countess, "squat like a toad, close to the ear of Eve"—"the letter will reveal it."

The empress frowned. Oh, for Ithuriel then!

"Dost mean that I shall open a letter which was never intended to be read by me?"

The countess pointed to the paper. "Your majesty has already broken the seal. You crushed it *unintentionally*. There remains but to unfold the paper, and every thing is explained. I will wage that it comes from the beautiful dancer Riccardo, whom the emperor admired so much last night in the ballet, and whom he declared to be the most bewitching creature he had ever seen."

The eyes of the empress dropped burning tears, and, covering her face with her hands, she sobbed aloud. Then she seemed ashamed of her emotion, and raised her beautiful head again.

"It is contemptible so to mourn for one who is faithless," said she. "It is for me to judge and to punish, and that will I! It is my duty as ruler of Austria to bring crime to light. I will soon learn who it is that dares to exchange letters with the husband of the reigning empress. And after all, the speediest, the simplest way to do this, lies before me. I must open the letter, for justice' sake; but I swear that I will not read one word contained within its pages. I will see the name of the writer alone; and then I can be sure that curiosity and personal interest have not prompted me."

And so Maria Theresa silenced her scruples, and persuaded herself that she was compelled to do as the tempter had suggested. She tore open the note; but true to her self-imposed vow, she paused on the threshold of dishonor, and read nothing but the writer's name.

"Riccardo!" cried she, wildly. "You were right, Margaretta; an intrigue with the Riccardo. The emperor has written to her—the emperor, my husband!"

She folded the fatal letter, and oh, how her white hands trembled as she laid it upon the table! and how deadly pale were the cheeks that had flushed with anger when Gaspardi had been by!

The countess was not deceived by this phase of the empress's grief. She knew that the storm would burst, and she thought it better to divide its wrath. She stepped lightly out to call the confessor of her victim.

Maria Theresa was unconscious of being alone. She stood before the table staring at the letter. Gradually her paleness vanished, and the hue of anger once more deepened on her cheeks. Her eyes, which had just been drooping with tears, flamed again with indignation; and her expanded nostrils, her twitching mouth, and her heaving chest, betrayed the fury of the storm that was raging within.

"Oh, I will trample her under foot!" muttered she between her teeth, while she raised her hand as if she would fain have dealt a death-stroke. "I will prove to the court—to the empire—to the world, how Maria Theresa hates vice, and how she punishes crime, without respect of persons. Both criminals shall feel the lash of justice. If my woman's heart break, the empress shall do her duty. It shall not be said that lust holds its revels in Vienna, as at the obscene courts of Versailles and St. Petersburg. No! Nor shall the libertines of Vienna point to the Austrian emperor as their model, nor shall their weeping wives be taunted with reports of the indulgence of the Austrian empress. Morality and decorum shall prevail in Vienna. The fire of my royal vengeance shall consume that bold harlot, and then—then for the emperor!"

"Your majesty will never consent to bring disgrace upon the father of your imperial children," said a gentle voice close by, and, turning at the sound, the empress beheld her confessor.

She advanced hastily toward Father Porhammer. "How!" exclaimed she angrily, "how!—you venture to plead for the emperor? You come hither to stay the hand of justice?"

"I do indeed," replied the father, "for to-day at least, her hand, if uplifted against the emperor, must recoil upon the empress. The honor of my august sovereigns cannot be divided. Your majesty must throw the shield of your love over the fault of your imperial husband."

"Oh, I cannot! I cannot suffer this mortal blow in silence," sobbed the empress.

"Nay," said the father, smiling, "the wife may be severe, though the empress be clement."

"But she, father—must she also be pardoned? she who has enticed my husband from his conjugal faith?"

"As for the Riccardo," replied Father Porhammer, "I have heard that she is a sinful woman, whose beauty has led many men astray. If your majesty deem her dangerous, she can be made to leave Vienna; but let retribution go no further."

"Well, be it so," sighed the empress, whose heart was already softening. "You are right, reverend father, but La Riccardo shall leave Vienna forever."

So saying, she hastened to her *escritoire*, and wrote and signed the order for the banishment of the *danseuse*.

"There," cried she, handing the order to the priest, "I pray you, dear father, remit this to Count Bartenstein, and let him see that she goes hence this very day. And when I shall have laid this evil spirit, perchance I may find peace once more. But, no, no!" continued she, her eyes filling with tears; "when she has gone, some other enchantress will come in her place to charm my husband's love away. Oh, father, if chastity is not in the heart, sin will always find entrance there."

"Yes, your majesty; and therefore should the portals of the heart be ever guarded against the enemy. As watchmen are appointed to guard the property, so are the servants of God sent on earth to extend the protection of Heaven to the hearts of your people."

"And why may I not aid them in their holy labors?" exclaimed the empress, glowing suddenly with a new interest. "Why may I not appoint a committee of good and wise men to watch over the morals of my subjects, and to warn them from temptation, ere it has time to become sin? Come, father, you must aid me in this good work. Help me to be the earthly, as the Blessed Virgin is the heavenly mother of the Austrian people. Sketch me some plan whereby I may organize my scheme. I feel sure that your suggestions will be dictated by that Heaven to which you have devoted your whole life."

"May the spirit of counsel and the spirit of wisdom enligten my understanding," said the father, with solemn fervor, "that I may worthily accomplish the mission with which my empress has intrusted me!"

"But, your majesty," whispered the Countess Fuchs, "in your magnanimous projects for your people, you are losing sight of yourself. The Riccardo has not yet been banished; and the emperor, seeing that no answer is coming to his note, may seek an interview. Who can guess the consequences of a meeting?"

The empress shivered, as the countess probed the wounds herself had made in that poor, jealous heart.

"True, true," returned she, in an unsteady voice. "Go, father, and begin my work of reform, by casting out that wicked woman from among the unhappy wives of Vienna. I myself will announce her departure to the emperor. And now, dear friends, leave me. You, father, to Count Bartenstein. Countess, recall Charlotte, and send me my tire-women. Let the princes and princesses be regally attired to-day. I will meet the emperor in their midst."

The confessor bowed and retired, and the countess opening the door of the inner dressing-room, beckoned to Charlotte, who, in the recess of a deep bay-window, sat wearily awaiting the summons to return.

CHAPTER III.

THE TOILET OF THE EMPRESS.

So dark and gloomy was the face of the empress, that poor Charlotte's heart misgave her, as with a suppressed sigh she resumed her place, and once more took down the rich masses of her sovereign lady's hair. Maria Theresa looked sternly at the reflection of her little maid of honor's face in the glass. She saw how Charlotte's hands trembled, and this increased her ill-humor. Again she raised her eyes to her own image, and saw plainly that anger was unbecoming to her. The flush on her face was not rosy, but purple; and the scowl upon her brow was fast deepening into a wrinkle. Her bosom heaved with a heavy, heavy sigh.

"Ah," thought she, "if I am ever again to find favor in his eyes,

I must always smile; for smiles are the last glowing tints of beauty's sunset. And yet, how can I smile, when my heart is breaking? He said that the Riccardo was the loveliest woman he had ever seen. Alas! I remember the day when he knelt at my feet, and spoke thus of me. Oh, my Franz! Am I indeed old, and no longer lovable?"

In her anxiety to scrutinize her own features, the empress bent suddenly forward, and the heavy mass of puffs and braids that formed the *coiffure* she had seleced for the day, gave way. She felt the sharp points of the hair-pins in her head, and, miserable and nervous as she was, they seemed to wound her cruelly. Starting from her chair, she poured forth a torrent of reproaches upon Charlotte's head, who, pale and trembling more than ever, repaired the damage, and placed among the braids a bouquet of white roses. These white roses deepened the unbecoming redness of the empress's face. She perceived this at once, and losing all self-control, tore the flowers from her hair, and dashed them on the floor.

"You are all leagued against me," cried she, indignantly. "You are trying your best to disfigure me, and to make me look old before my time. Who ever saw such a ridiculous structure as this head-dress, that makes me look like a perambulating castle on a chess-board? Come, another *coiffure*, and let it not be such a ridiculous one as this."

Charlotte, of course, did not remind her mistress that the *coiffure* and roses had been her own selection. She had nothing to do but to obey in silence, and begin her work again.

At last the painful task was at an end. The empress looked keenly at herself in the glass, and convinced that she really looked well, she called imperatively for her tire-women. In came the procession, bearing hooped-skirt, rich-embroidered train, golden-flowered petticoat, and bodice flashing with diamonds. But the empress, usually so affable at her toilet, surveyed both maids and apparel with gloomy indifference. In moody silence she reached out her feet, while her slippers were exchanged for high-heeled shoes. Not a look had she to bestow upon the magnificent dress which enhanced a thousandfold her mature beauty. Without a word she dismissed the maids of honor, all except Charlotte, whose crowning labor it was to give the last touch to the imperial head when the rest of the toilet had been declared to be complete.

Again Maria Theresa stood before that high Venetian glass, and certainly it did give back the image of a regal beauty. For a while she examined her costume from head to foot; and at last—at last, her beautiful blue eyes beamed bright with satisfaction, and a smile rippled the corners of her mouth.

"No," said she, aloud. "No, it is not so. I am neither old nor ugly. The light of youth has not yet fled from my brow. My beauty's sun has not yet set forever. My Franz will love me still; and however charming younger women may be, he will remember the beloved of his boyhood, and we will yet be happy in reciprocal affection, come what may to us as emperor and empress. I do not believe that he said he had never seen so lovely a woman as Riccardo. Poor, dear Franz! He has a tedious life as husband of the reigning sovereign. From sheer *ennui* he sometimes wanders from his wife's heart, but oh! he must, he must return to me; for if I were to lose him, earthly splendor would be valueless to me forever!"

Charlotte, who stood behind her mistress with the comb in her hand, was dismayed at all that she heard; and the plaintive tones of this magnificent empress, at whose feet lay a world of might, touched her heart's core. But she sickened as she thought that her presence had been unheeded, and that the empress had fancied herself alone, while the secrets of her heart were thus struggling into words. The ample train completely screened little Charlotte from view, and a deadly paleness overspread her countenance as she awaited discovery.

Suddenly the empress turned, and putting her hand tenderly on Charlotte's head, she said, in a voice of indescribable melancholy: "Be warned, Charlotte, and if you marry, never marry a man who has nothing to do. Men will grow inconstant from sheer *eunui.*" *

"I never expect to marry, beloved mistress," said the young girl, deeply touched by this confidence. "I wish to live and die in your majesty's service."

"Do you? And can you bear for a lifetime with my impatience, dear child?" asked the empress, kissing the little devotee on the forehead. "You know now, my little Charlotte, why I have been so unkind to-day; you know that my heart was bleeding with such anguish, that had I not broken out in anger, I must have stifled with agony. You have seen into the depths of my heart, and why should I not confide in you, who know every secret of my state-council? No one suspects what misery lies under the regal mantle. And I care not to exhibit myself to the world's pity. When Maria Theresa weeps, let her God and those who love her be the witnesses of her sorrow. Go, now, good little Charlotte, and forget every thing except your sovereign's love for you. Tell the governess of the Archduke Ferdinand to bring him hither. Let the other imperial children await me in my reception-room; and tell the page in the anteroom to announce to his majesty that I request the honor of a visit from him."

Charlotte, once more happy, left the room, her heart filled with joy for herself, and gentle sorrow for her sovereign.

Meanwhile the empress thought over the coming interview. "I will try to recall him to me by love," murmured she, softly. "I will not reproach him, and although as his empress I have a double claim upon his loyalty, I will not appeal to any thing but his own dear heart; and when he hears how he has made his poor Theresa suffer, I know—"

Here her voice failed her, and tears filled her eyes. But she dashed them quickly away, for steps approached, and the governess entered, with the infant prince in her arms.

CHAPTER IV.

HUSBAND AND WIFE.

A HALF an hour later, the princes and princesses of Austria were all assembled in their mother's private parlor. They were a beautiful group. The empress, in their midst, held little Ferdinand in her arms. Close-peeping through the folds of their mother's rich dress, were three other little ones; and a few steps farther were the Archduchesses Christine and Amelia. Near the open harpsichord

* Maria Theresa's words. See Caroline Pichler, "Memoirs of My Life."

stood the graceful form of the empress's eldest child, the Princess Elizabeth, who now and then ran her fingers lightly over the instrument, while she awaited the arrival of her father.

In the pride of her maternity and beauty stood the empress-queen; but her heart throbbed painfully, though she smiled upon her children.

The page announced the coming of the emperor, and then left the room. The empress made a sign to her eldest daughter, who seated herself before the harpsichord. The door opened, and on the threshold appeared the tall, elegant form of the Emperor Francis.

Elizabeth began a brilliant "Welcome," and all the young voices joined in one loud chorus, "Long live our emperor, our sovereign, and our father!" sang the children; but clear above them all were heard the sonorous tones of the mother, exclaiming in the fulness of her love, "Long live my emperor, and my husband!" As if every tender chord of Maria Theresa's heart had been struck, she broke forth into one of Metastasio's most passionate songs; while Elizabeth, catching the inspiration, accompanied her mother with sweetest melody. The empress, her little babe in her arms, was wrapped up in the ecstasy of the moment. Never had she looked more enchanting than she did as she ceased, and gave one look of love to her admiring husband.

The emperor contemplated for a moment the lovely group before him, and then, full of emotion, came forward, and bending over his wife, he kissed the round white arm that held the baby, and whispered to the mother a few words of rapture at her surpassing beauty.

"But tell me, gracious empress," said he, aloud, "to what am I indebted for this charming surprise?"

The eyes of the empress shot fire, but in lieu of a reply, she bent down to the little Archduchess Josepha, who was just old enough to lisp her father's name, and said:

"Josepha, tell the emperor what festival we celebrate to-day." The little one, turning to her father, said, "To-day is imperial mamma's wedding-day."

"Our wedding-day!" murmured the emperor, "and I could forget it!"

"Oh, no! my dear husband," said the empress, "I am sure that you cannot have forgotten this joyous anniversary. Its remembrance only slumbered in your heart, and the presence of your children here, I trust, has awakened that remembrance, and carried you back with me to the happy, happy days of our early love."

The voice of the wife was almost tearful, as she spoke those tender words; and the emperor, touched and humbled at the thought of his own oversight, sought to change the subject. "But why," asked he, looking around, "why, if all our other children are here to greet their father, is Joseph absent from this happy family gathering?"

"He has been disobedient and obstinate again," said the empress, with a shrug of her shoulders, "and his preceptor, to punish him, kept him away."

The emperor walked to the door. "Surely," exclaimed he, "on such a day as this, when all my dear children are around me, my son and the future emperor should be the first to bid me welcome."

"Stay, my husband," cried the empress, who had no intention of allowing the emperor to escape so easily from his embarrassment.

"You must be content to remain with us, without the *future* emperor of Germany, whose reign, I hope I may be allowed to pray, is yet for some years postponed. Or is this a happy device of the future emperor's father to remind me, on my wedding-day, that I am growing old enough to begin to think of the day of my decease?"

The emperor was perfectly amazed. Although he was accustomed to such outbursts on the part of his wife, he searched vainly in his heart for the cause of her intense bitterness to-day. He looked his astonishment; and the empress, mindful of her resolve not to reproach him, tried her best to smile.

The emperor shook his head thoughtfully as he watched her face, and said half aloud: "All is not right with thee, Theresa; thou smilest like a lioness, not like a woman."

"Very well, then," said she sharply, "the lioness has called you to look upon her whelps. One day they will be lions and lionesses too, and in that day they will avenge the injuries of their mother."

The empress, as she spoke, felt that her smothered jealousy was bursting forth. She hastily dismissed her children, and going herself to the door, she called for the governess of the baby, and almost threw him in her arms.

"I foresee the coming of a storm," thought the emperor, as the door being closed, Maria Theresa came quickly back, and stood before him.

"And is it indeed true," said she bitterly, "that you had forgotten your wedding-day? Not a throb of your heart to remind you of the past!"

"My memory does not cling to dates, Theresa," replied the emperor. "What, if to-day be accidentally the anniversary of our marriage? With every beating of my heart, *I* celebrate the hour itself, when I won the proud and beautiful heiress of Austria; and when I remember that she deigned to love *me*, the poor Archduke of Lorraine, my happiness overwhelms me. Come, then, my beautiful, my beloved Theresa; come to my heart, that I may thank you for all the blessings that I owe to your love. See, dearest, we are alone; let us forget royalty for to-day, and be happy together in all the fulness of mutual confidence and affection."

So saying, he would have pressed her to his heart, but the empress drew coldly back, and turned deadly pale. This unembarrassed and confident tenderness irritated her beyond expression. That her faithless spouse should, without the slightest remorse, act the part of the devoted lover, outraged her very sense of decency.

"Really, my husband, it becomes you well to prate of confidence and affection, who have ceased to think of your own wife, and have eyes alone for the wife of another!"

"Again jealous?" sighed the emperor wearily. "Will you never cease to cloud our domestic sky by these absurd and groundless suspicions?"

"Groundless!" cried the empress, tearing the letter violently from her bosom. "With this proof of your guilt confronting you, you will not dare to say that I am jealous without cause!"

"Allow me to inquire of your majesty, what this letter is to prove?"

"It proves that to-day you have written a letter to a woman, of whom yesterday you said that she was the most beautiful woman in the world."

"I have no recollection of saying such a thing of any woman; and I am surprised that your majesty should encourage your attendants to repeat such contemptible tales," replied the emperor, with some bitterness. "Were I like you, the reigning sovereign of a great empire, I should really find no time to indulge in gossip and scandal."

"Your majesty will oblige me by refraining from any comment upon affairs which do not concern you. I alone am reigning empress here, and it is for my people to judge whether I do my duty to them; certainly not for you, who, while I am with my ministers of state, employ your leisure hours in writing love-letters to my subjects."

"I? I write a love-letter?" said the emperor.

"How dare you deny it?" cried the outraged empress. "Have you also forgotten that this morning you sent Gaspardi out of the palace on an errand?"

"No, I have not forgotten it," replied the emperor, with growing astonishment. But Maria Theresa remarked that he looked confused, and avoided her eye.

"You confess, then, that you sent the letter, and requested an answer?"

"Yes, but I received no answer," said the emperor, with embarrassment.

"There is your answer," thundered the enraged wife. "I took it from Gaspardi myself."

"And is it possible, Theresa, that you have read a letter addressed to me?" asked the emperor, in a severe voice.

The empress blushed, and her eyes sought the ground.

"No," said she, "I have not read it, Franz."

"But it is open," persisted he, taking it from his wife's hand. "Who, then, has dared to break the seal of a letter addressed to me?"

And the emperor, usually so mild toward his wife, stood erect, with stormy brow and eyes flashing with anger.

Maria Theresa in her turn was surprised. She looked earnestly at him, and confessed inwardly that never had she seen him look so handsome; and she felt an inexplicable and secret pleasure that her Franz, for once in his life, was really angry with her.

"I broke the seal of the letter, but I swear to you that I did not read one word of it," replied she. "I wished to see the signature only, and that signature was enough to convince me that I had a faithless husband, who outrages an empress by giving her a dancer as her rival!"

"The signature convinced you of this?" asked the emperor.

"It did!"

"And you read nothing else?"

"Nothing, I tell you."

"Then, madam," returned he, seriously, handing the letter back to her, "do me the favor to read the whole of it. After breaking the seal, you need not hesitate. I exact it of you."

The empress looked overwhelmed. "You exact of me to read a love-letter addressed to you?"

"Certainly I do. You took it from my valet, you broke it open, and now I beg you will be so good as to read it aloud, for I have not yet read it myself."

"I will read it, then," cried the empress, scornfully. "And I promise you that I shall not suppress a word of its contents."

"Read on," said the emperor, quietly.

The empress, with loud and angry tone, began:

"To his Gracious Majesty, the Emperor:

"Your majesty has honored me by asking my advice upon a subject of the highest importance. But your majesty is much nearer the goal than I. It is true that my gracious master, the count, led me to the vestibule of the temple of science, but further I have not penetrated. What I know I will joyfully impart to your majesty; and joyfully will I aid you in your search after that which the whole world is seeking. I will come at the appointed hour.

"Your majesty's loyal servant,

"RICCARDO."

"I do not understand a word," said the mystified empress.

"But I do," returned the emperor, with a meaning smile. "Since your majesty has thrust yourself into the portals of my confidence, I must e'en take you with me into the *penetralia*, and confess at once that I have a passion, which has cost me many a sleepless night, and has preoccupied my thoughts, even when I was by your majesty's side."

"But I see nothing of love or passion in this letter," replied Maria Theresa, glancing once more at its singular contents.

"And yet it speaks of nothing else. I may just as well confess, too, that in pursuit of the object of my love, I have spent three hundred thousand guilders, and thrown away at least one hundred thousand guilders' worth of diamonds."

"Your mistress must be either very coy or very grasping," said Maria Theresa, almost convulsed with jealousy.

"She is very coy," said the emperor. "All my gold and diamonds have won me not a smile—she will not yield up her secret. But I believe that she has responded to the love of one happy mortal, Count Saint-Germain."

"Count Saint-Germain!" exclaimed the empress, amazed.

"Himself, your majesty. He is one of the fortunate few, to whom the coy beauty has succumbed; and to take his place I would give millions. Now, I heard yesterday that the confidant of the count was in Vienna; and, hoping to learn something from him, I invited him hither. Signor Riccardo—"

"*Signor* Riccardo! Was this letter written by a man?"

"By the husband of the dancer."

"And your letter was addressed to him?"

"Even so, madame."

"Then this passion of which you speak is your old passion—alchemy."

"Yes, it is. I had promised you to give it up, but it proved stronger than I. Not to annoy you, I have ever since worked secretly in my laboratory. I have just conceived a new idea. I am about to try the experiment of consolidating small diamonds into one large one, by means of a burning-glass."

The empress answered this with a hearty, happy laugh, and went up to her husband with outstretched hands.

"Franz," said she, "I am a simpleton; and all that has been fermenting in my heart is sheer nonsense. My crown does not prevent me from being a silly woman. But, my heart's love, forgive my folly for the sake of my affection."

Instead of responding to this appeal, the emperor stood perfectly still, and gazed earnestly and seriously at his wife.

"Your jealousy," said he, after a moment's silence, "I freely forgive, for it is a source of more misery to you than to me. But this jealousy has attacked my honor as a man, and that I cannot forgive. As reigning empress, I render you homage, and am content to occupy the second place in Austria's realms. I will not deny that such a *rôle* is irksome to me, for I, like you, have lofty dreams of ambition; and I could have wished that, in giving me the *title*, you had allowed me sometimes the privileges of a co-regent. But I have seen that my co-regency irritated and annoyed you; I have, therefore, renounced all thought of governing empires. I have done this, not only because I love you, Theresa, but because you are worthy by your intellect to govern your people without my help. In the world, therefore, I am known as the husband of the reigning empress; but at home I am lord of my own household, and here I reign supreme. The emperor may be subordinate to his sovereign, but the man will acknowledge no superior; and the dignity of his manhood shall be respected, even by yourself."

"Heaven forbid that I should ever seek to wound it!" exclaimed Maria Theresa, while she gazed with rapture upon her husband's noble countenance, and thought that never had he looked so handsome as at this moment, when, for the first time, he asserted his authority against herself.

"You *have* wounded it, your majesty," replied the emperor, with emphasis. "You have dogged my steps with spies; you have suffered my character to be discussed by your attendants. You have gone so far as to compromise me with my own servants; forcing them to disobey me by virtue of your rights as sovereign, exercised in opposition to mine as your husband. *I* gave Gaspardi orders to deliver Riccardo's note to me alone. I forbade him to tell any one whither he went. *You* took my note from him by force, and committed the grave wrong of compelling a servant, hitherto faithful, to disobey and betray his master."

"I did indeed wrong you, dear Franz," said the empress, already penitent. "In Gaspardi's presence I will ask your pardon for my indelicate intrusion, and before him I will bear witness to his fidelity. I alone was to blame. I promise you, too, to sin no more against you, my beloved, for your love is the brightest jewel in my crown. Without it, no happiness would grandeur give to me. Forgive me, then, my own Franz—forgive your unhappy Theresa!"

As she spoke, she inclined her head toward her husband, and looked up to him with such eyes of love, that he could but gaze enraptured upon her bewitching beauty.

"Come, Franz, come!" said she tenderly; "surely, that wicked jest of yours has amply revenged you. Be satisfied with having given me a heartache for jealousy of the coy mistress upon whom you have wasted your diamonds, and be magnanimous."

"And you, Theresa?—will you be magnanimous also? Will you leave my servants and my letters alone, and set no more spies to dog my steps?"

"Indeed, Franz, I will never behave as I have done to-day, while we both live. Now, if you will sign my pardon, I will tell you a piece of news with which I intend shortly to surprise all Austria."

"Out with it, then, and if it is good news I sign the pardon," said the emperor, with a smile.

"It is excellent news," cried the empress, "for it will give new life to Austria. It will bring down revenge upon our enemies, and revenge upon that wicked infidel who took my beautiful Silesia from me, and who, boasting of his impiety, calls it enlightenment."

"Have you not yet forgiven Frederick for that little bit of Silesia that he stole from you?" asked the emperor, laughing.

"No, I have not yet forgiven him, nor do I ever expect to do so. I owe it to him, that, years ago, I came like a beggar before the Magyars to whimper for help and defence. I have never yet forgotten the humiliation of that day, Franz."

"And yet, Theresa, we must confess that Frederick is a great man, and it were well for Austria if we were allies; for such an alliance would secure the blessings of a stable peace to Europe."

"It cannot be," cried the empress. "There is no sympathy between Austria and Prussia, and peace will never come to Europe until one succumbs to the other. No dependence is to be placed upon alliances between incongruous nations. In spite of our allies, the English, the Dutch, and the Russians, the King of Prussia has robbed me of my province; and all the help I have ever got from them was empty condolence. For this reason I have sought for alliance with another power—a power which will cordially unite with me in crushing that hateful infidel, to whom nothing in life is sacred. This is the news that I promised you. Our treaty with England and Holland is about to expire, and the new ally I have found for Austria is France."

"An alliance with France is not a natural one for Austria, and can never be enduring," exclaimed the emperor.*

"It *will* be enduring," cried Maria Theresa, proudly, "for it is equally desired by both nations. Not only Louis XV., but the Marquise de Pompadour is impatient to have the treaty signed."

"That means that Kaunitz has been flattering the marquise, and the marquise, Kaunitz. But words are not treaties, and the marquise's promises are of no consequence whatever."

"But, Franz, I tell you that we have gone further than words. Of this, however, no one knows, except the King of France, myself, Kaunitz, and the marquise."

"How in the world did you manage to buy the good-will of the marquise? How many millions did you pay for the precious boon?"

"Not a kreutzer, dear husband, only a letter."

"Letter! Letter from whom?"

"A letter from me to the marquise."

"What!" cried the emperor, laughing. "*You* write to La Pompadour—*you*, Theresa?"

"With my own hand, I have written to her, and more than once," returned Maria Theresa, joining in the laugh. "And what do you suppose I did, to save my honor in the matter? I pretended to think that she was the wife of the king, and addressed her as '*Madame, ma sœur et cousine.*'"

Here the emperor laughed immoderately. "Well, well!" ex-

* The emperor's own words. Coxe, "History of the House of Austria," vol. v., p. 67.

claimed he. "So the Empress-Queen of Austria and Hungary writes with her own hand to her beloved cousin La Pompadour!"

"And do you know what she calls me?" laughed the empress in return. "Yesterday I had a letter from her in which she calls me, sportively, '*Ma chère reine.*'"

The emperor broke out into such a volley of laughter, that he threw himself back upon a chair, which broke under him, and the empress had to come to his assistance, for he was too convulsed to get up alone. *

"Oh dear! oh dear!" groaned the emperor, still continuing to laugh. "I shall die of this intelligence. Maria Theresa in correspondence with Madame d'Etioles!"

"Well, what of it, Franz?" asked Maria Theresa. "Did I not write to the prima donna Farinelli when we were seeking alliance with Spain? and is the marquise not as good as a soprano singer?" †

The emperor looked at her with such a droll expression that she gave up all idea of defending herself from ridicule, and laughed as heartily as he did.

At this moment a page knocked, and announced the Archduke Joseph and his preceptor.

"Poor lad!" said the emperor; "I suppose he comes, as usual, accompanied by an accuser."

CHAPTER V.

THE ARCHDUKE JOSEPH.

THE emperor was right; Father Francis came in with complaints of his highness. While the father with great pathos set forth the reason of the archduke's absence from the family circle, the culprit stood by, apparently indifferent to all that was being said. But, to any one observing him closely, his tremulous mouth, and the short, convulsive sighs, which he vainly strove to repress, showed the real anxiety of his fast-beating heart. He thrust back his rising tears, for the little prince was too proud to crave sympathy; and he had already learned how to hide emotion by a cold and haughty bearing. From his childhood he had borne a secret sorrow in his heart—the sorrow of seeing his young brother Carl preferred to himself. Not only was Carl the darling of his parents, but he was the pet and plaything of the whole palace. True, the poor little archduke was not gifted with the grace and charming *naïveté* of his brother. He was awkward, serious, and his countenance wore an expression of discontent, which was thought to betray an evil disposition, but which, in reality, was but the reflection of the heavy sorrow which clouded his young heart. No one seemed to understand—no one seemed to love him. Alone in the midst of that gay and splendid court, he was never noticed except to be chided. ‡ The buds of his poor young heart were blighted by the mildew of neglect, so that outwardly he was cold, sarcastic, and sullen, while inwardly he glowed with a thousand emotions, which he dared reveal to no one, for no one seemed to dream that he was capable of feeling them.

* Historical.
† The empress's own words. Coxe, vol. v., p. 69.
‡ Hubner, "Life of Joseph II.," page 15.

To-day, as usual, he was brought before his parents as a culprit; and without daring to utter a word in his own defence, he stood by, while Father Francis told how many times he had yawned over the "Lives of the Martyrs;" and how he had refused to read, longer than one hour, a most edifying commentary of the Fathers on the Holy Scriptures.

The empress heard with displeasure of her son's lack of piety; and she looked severely at him, while he gazed sullenly at a portrait that hung opposite.

"And can it be, my son," exclaimed she, "that you close your heart against the word of God, and refuse to read religious books?"

The boy gave her a glance of defiance. "I do not know," said he, carelessly, "whether the books are religious or not; but I know that they are tiresome, and teach me nothing."

"Gracious Heaven!" cried the empress, with horror, "hear the impious child!"

"Rather, your majesty," said Father Francis, "let us pray Heaven to soften his heart." The emperor alone said nothing; but he looked at the boy with a friendly and sympathizing glance. The child saw the look, and for one moment a flush of pleasure passed over his face. He raised his eyes with an appealing expression toward his father, who could no longer resist the temptation of coming to his relief.

"Perhaps," suggested he, "the books may be dull to a child of Joseph's years."

"No book," returned the empress, "should be dull that treats of God and of His holy Church."

"And the work, your majesty, which we were reading, was a most learned and celebrated treatise," said Father Francis; "one highly calculated to edify and instruct youth."

Joseph turned away from the father, and spoke to the emperor. "We have already gone through five volumes of it, your majesty, and I am tired to death of it. Moreover, I don't believe half that I read in his stupid books."

The empress, as she heard this, uttered a cry of pain. She felt an icy coldness benumb her heart, as she remembered that this unbelieving boy was one day to succeed her on the throne of Austria. The emperor, too, was pained. By the deadly paleness of her face, he guessed the pang that was rending his wife's heart, and he dared say no more in defence of his son.

"Your majesty sees," continued Father Francis, "how far is the heart of his highness from God and the Church. His instructors are grieved at his precocious unbelief, and they are this day to confer together upon the painful subject. The hour of the conference is at hand, and I crave your majesty's leave to repair thither."

"No," said the empress, with a deprecating gesture; "no. Remain, good father. Let this conference be held in the presence of the emperor and myself. It is fitting that we both know the worst in regard to our child."

The emperor bowed acquiescence, and crossing the room, took a seat by the side of the empress.

He rang a little golden bell; and the page who came at the summons, was ordered to request the attendance of the preceptors of his highness the Crown Prince of Austria.

Maria Theresa leaned her head upon her hand, and with a sad and perplexed countenance watched the open door. The emperor, with his arm thrown over the gilded back of the divan, looked earnestly at the young culprit, who, pale, and with a beating heart, was trying his best to suppress his increasing emotion.

"I will not cry," thought he, scarcely able to restrain his tears; "for that would be a triumph for my detestable teachers. I am not going to give them the pleasure of knowing that I am miserable."

And, by dint of great exertion, he mastered his agitation. He was so successful, that he did not move a muscle nor turn his head when the solemn procession of his accusers entered the room.

First, at the head, came Father Porhammer, who gave him lessons in logic and physic; after him walked the engineer Briguen, professor of mathematics; then Herr von Leporini, who instructed him in general history; Herr von Bartenstein, who expounded the political history of the house of Austria; Baron von Beck, who was his instructor in judicature; and finally, his governor, Count Bathiany, the only one toward whom the young prince felt a grain of good-will.

The empress greeted them with grave courtesy, and exhorted them to say without reserve before his parents what they thought of the progress and disposition of the archduke.

Count Bathiany, with an encouraging smile directed toward his pupil, assured their majesties that the archduke was anxious to do right—not because he was told so to do by others, but because he followed the dictates of his own conscience. True, his highness would not see through the eyes of any other person; but this, though it might be a defect in a child, would be the reverse in a man—above all, in a sovereign. "In proof of the archduke's sincere desire to do right," continued Count Bathiany, "allow me to repeat to your majesties something which he said to me yesterday. We were reading together Bellegarde on knowledge of self and of human nature. The beautiful thoughts of the author so touched the heart of his highness, that, stopping suddenly, he exclaimed to me, 'We must read this again; for when I come to the throne I shall need to know, not only myself, but other men also.' "

"Well said, my son!" exclaimed the emperor.

"I cannot agree with your majesty," said the empress, coldly. "*I* do not think it praiseworthy for a child of his age to look forward with complacency to the day when his mother's death will confer upon him a throne. To me it would seem more natural if Joseph thought more of his present duties and less of his future honors."

A breathless silence followed these bitter words. The emperor, in confusion, withdrew behind the harpsichord. The archduke looked perfectly indifferent. While Count Bathiany had been repeating his words, his face had slightly flushed; but when he heard the sharp reproof of his mother, he raised his head, and gave her back another defiant look. With the same sullen haughtiness, he stared first at one accuser, and then at another, while each one in his turn gave judgment against him. First, and most vehement in his denunciations, was Count Bartenstein. He denounced the archduke as idle and inattentive. He never would have any political sagacity whatever. Why, even the great work, in fifteen folios, which he (Count

Bartenstein) had compiled from the imperial archives for the especial instruction of the prince, even *that* failed to interest him! *

Then followed the rest of their professorships. One complained of disrespect; another of carelessness; a third of disobedience; a fourth of irreligion. All concurred in declaring the archduke to be obstinate, unfeeling, and intractable.

His face, meanwhile, grew paler and harder, until it seemed almost to stiffen into marble. Although every censorious word went like a dagger to his sensitive heart, he still kept on murmuring to himself, "I will not cry, I will not cry."

His mother divined nothing of the agony which, like a wild tornado, was desolating the fair face of her child's whole being. She saw nothing beyond the portals of that cold and sullen aspect, and the sight filled her with sorrow and anger.

"Alas," cried she, bitterly, "you are right! He is a refractory and unfeeling boy."

At this moment, like the voice of a conciliatory angel, were heard the soft tones of the melody with which the empress had greeted her husband that morning. It was the emperor, whose hands seemed unconsciously to wander over the keys of the harpsichord, while every head bent entranced to listen.

When the first tones of the heavenly melody fell upon his ear, the young prince began to tremble. His features softened; his lips, so scornfully compressed, now parted, as if to drink in every sound; his eyes filled with tears, and every angry feeling of his heart was hushed by the magic of music. With a voice of love it seemed to call him, and unable to resist its power and its pathos, he burst into a flood of tears, and with one bound reached his father's arms, sobbing—

"Father, dear father, pity me!"

The emperor drew the poor boy close to his heart. He kissed his blond curls, and whispering, said: "Dear child, I knew that you were not heartless. I was sure that you would come when your father called."

The empress had started from her seat, and she now stood in the centre of the room, earnestly gazing upon her husband and her child. Her mother's heart beat wildly, and tears of tenderness suffused her eyes. She longed to speak some word of pardon to her son; but before all things, Maria Theresa honored court ceremony. She would not, for the world, that her subjects had seen her otherwise than self-possessed and regal in her bearing.

With one great effort she mastered her emotions; and before the strength of her will, the mighty flood rolled back upon her heart. Not a tear that glistened in her eyelids fell; not a tone of her clear, silvery voice was heard to falter.

"Count Bathiany," said she, "I perceive that in the education of the archduke, the humanizing influences of music have been overlooked. Music to-day has been more powerful with him than filial love or moral obligation. Select for him, then, a skilful teacher, who will make use of his art to lead my son back to duty and religion." †

* Hormayer says that this book was heavy and filled with tiresome details. (No wonder! In fifteen folios.—TRANS.)

† Maria Theresa's own words. Coxe, "House of Austria," vol. v.

CHAPTER VI.

KAUNITZ.

THREE weeks had elapsed since the memorable sitting at which Maria Theresa had declared in favor of a new line of policy. Three long weeks had gone by, and still no message came for Kaunitz; and still Bartenstein and Uhlefeld held the reins of power.

With hasty steps, Kaunitz paced the floor of his study. Gone was all coldness and impassibility from his face. His eyes glowed with restless fire, and his features twitched nervously.

His secretary, who sat before the writing-table, had been gazing anxiously at the count for some time. He shook his head gloomily, as he contemplated the strange sight of Kaunitz, agitated and disturbed.

Kaunitz caught the eye of his confidant, and coming hastily toward the table, he stood for a few moments without speaking a word. Suddenly he burst into a loud, harsh laugh—a laugh so bitter, so sardonic, that Baron Binder turned pale as he heard the sound.

"Why are you so pale, Binder?" asked Kaunitz, still laughing. "Why do you start as if you had received an electric shock?"

"Your laughing is like an electric shock to my heart," replied the baron. "Its sound was enough to make a man pale. Why, for ten years I have lived under your roof, and never have I heard you laugh before."

"Perhaps you are right, Binder, for in sooth my laugh echoes gloomily within the walls of my own heart. But I could not help it—you had such a droll, censorious expression on your face."

"No wonder," returned Baron Binder. "It vexes me to see a statesman so irresolute and unmanned."

"Statesman!" exclaimed Kaunitz, bitterly. "Who knows whether my *rôle* of statesman is not played out already?"

He resumed his walk in moody silence, while Binder followed him with his eyes. Suddenly Kaunitz stopped again before the table. "Baron," said he, "you have known me intimately for ten years. In all my embassies you have been with me as *attaché*. Since we have lived together, have you ever known me to be faint-hearted?"

"Never!" cried the baron, "never! I have seen you brave the anger of monarchs, the hatred of enemies, the treachery of friends and mistresses. I have stood by your side in more than one duel, and never before have I seen you otherwise than calm and resolute."

"Judge, then, how sickening to me is this suspense, since, for the first time in my life, I falter. Oh! I tremble lest—"

"Lest what?" asked the baron, with interest.

"Binder, I fear that Maria Theresa may prove less an empress than a woman. I fear that the persuasions of the handsome Francis of Lorraine may outweigh her own convictions of right. What if her husband's caresses, her confessor's counsel, or her own feminine caprice, should blind her to the welfare of her subjects and the interest of her empire? Oh, what a giant structure will fall to the earth, if, at this crisis, the empress should fail me! Think what a triumph it would be to dash aside my rivals and seize the helm of state! to gather, upon the deck of one stout ship, all the paltry principalities that call themselves 'Austria;' to band them into one consolidated nation; and then to steer this noble ship into a haven of greatness and glorious peace! Binder, to this end alone I live. I have outlived all human illusions. I have no faith in love—it is bought and sold. No faith in the tears of men; none in their smiles. Society, to me, is one vast mad house. If, in its frenzied walls, I show that I am sane, the delirious throng will shout out, 'Seize the lunatic!' Therefore must I seem as mad as they, and therefore it is that, outside of this study, I commit a thousand follies. In such a world I have no faith; but, Binder, I believe in divine ambition. It is the only passion that has ever stirred my heart—the only passion worthy to fill the soul of a MAN! My only love, then, is ambition. My only dream is of power. Oh! that I might eclipse and outlive the names of my rivals! But alas! alas! I fear that the greatness of Kaunitz will be wrecked upon the shoals of Maria Theresa's shallowness!"

"No, no," said the baron vehemently. "Fear nothing, Kaunitz; you are the man who is destined to make Austria great, and to disperse the clouds of ignorance that darken the minds of her people."

"You may be sure that if ever I attain power, Binder, nor church nor churchman shall have a voice in Austria. Kaunitz alone shall reign. But will Maria Theresa consent? Will she ever have strength of mind to burst the shackles with which silly love and silly devotion have bound her? I fear not. Religion—"

Here the door opened, and the count's valet handed a card to the secretary.

"A visit from Count Bartenstein!" exclaimed the baron triumphantly. "Ah! I knew—"

"Will you receive him here, in the study?"

"I will receive him nowhere," replied Kaunitz coldly. "Say to the count," added he to the valet, "that I am engaged, and beg to be excused."

"What! You deny yourself to the prime minister?" cried Binder, terrified.

Kaunitz motioned to the servant to withdraw.

"Binder," said he exultingly, "do you not see from this visit that *my* day is about to dawn, and that Bartenstein is the first lark to greet the rising sun? His visit proves that he feels a presentiment of his fall, and my rebuff shall verify it. The whole world will understand that when Bartenstein was turned away from my door, I gave old Austria, as well as himself, a parting kick. Away with anxiety and fear! The deluge is over, and old Bartenstein has brought me the olive-branch that announces dry land and safety."

"My dear count!"

"Yes, Binder, dry land and safety. Now we will be merry, and lift our head high up into clouds of Olympic revel! Away with your deeds and your parchments! We are no longer bookworms, but butterflies. Let us sport among the roses!"

While Kaunitz spoke, he seized a hand-bell from the table, and rang vehemently.

"Make ready for me in my dressing-room," said he to the valet. "Let the cook prepare a costly dinner for twenty persons. Let the steward select the rarest wines in the cellar. Tell him to see that the Champagne is not too warm, nor the Johannisberg too cold; the

Sillery too dry, nor the Lachryma Christi too acid. Order two carriages, and send one for Signora Ferlina, and the other for Signora Sacco. Send two footmen to Counts Harrach and Colloredo, with my compliments. Stay—here is a list of the other guests. Send a messenger to the apartments of my sister, the countess. Tell her, with my respects, to oblige me by dining to-day in her own private rooms. I will not need her to preside over my dinner-table to-day."

"But, my lord," stammered the valet, "the countess—"

"Well—what of her?"

"The countess has been de—gone for a week."

"Gone, without taking leave? Where?"

"There, my lord," replied the valet in a low voice, pointing upward toward heaven.

"What does he mean, Binder?" asked Kaunitz, with a shrug.

Binder shrugged responsive.

"The good countess," said he, "had been ill for some time, but did not wish to disturb you. You must have been partially prepared for the melancholy event, for the countess has not appeared at table for three weeks."

"Me? Not at all. Do you suppose that during these last three weeks I have had time to think of her? I never remarked her absence. When did the—the—ceremony take place?"

"Day before yesterday. I attended to every thing."

"My dear friend, how I thank you for sparing me the sight of these hideous rites! Your arrangements must have been exquisite, for I never so much as suspected the thing. Fortunately, it is all over, and we can enjoy ourselves as usual. Here, Philip. Let the house look festive: flowers on the staircases and in the entrance-hall; oranges and roses in the dining-room; vanilla-sticks in the coffee-cups instead of teaspoons. Away with you!"

The valet bowed, and when he was out of hearing Kaunitz renewed his thanks to the baron.

"Once more, thank you for speeding my sister on her journey, and for saving me all knowledge of this unpleasant affair. How glad the signoras will be to hear that the countess has positively gone, never to return! Whom shall I get to replace her? Well, never mind now; some other time we'll settle that little matter. Now to my toilet."

He bent his head to the baron, and with light, elastic step passed into his dressing-room.

CHAPTER VII.

THE TOILET.

WHEN Kaunitz entered his dressing-room, his features had resumed their usual immobility. He walked in, without seeming to be aware of the presence of his attendants, who, ranged on either side of the apartment, awaited his commands.

He went up to his large Venetian mirror, and there surveyed himself at full length. With anxious glance his keen eyes sought out every faint line that told of the four-and-thirty years of his life. The picture seemed deeply interesting, for he stood a long time before the glass. At last the scrutiny was ended, and he turned slightly toward the hair-dresser.

"Is the peruke ready?"

The hair-dresser fluttered off to a bandbox, that lay on the toilet-table: and lifted out a fantastic-looking blond peruke, constructed after "his excellency's own design." Kaunitz was not aware of it, but this wig of his, with its droll mixture of flowing locks before, and prim purse behind, was an exact counterpart of the life and character of its inventor. He had had no intention of being symbolic in his contrivance; it had been solely designed to conceal the little tell-tale lines that were just about to indent the smooth surface of his white forehead. He bent his proud head, while the hair-dresser placed the wonderful wig, and then fell to studying its effect. Here he drew a curl forward, there he gently removed another; placing each one in its position over his eyebrows, so that no treacherous side-light should reveal any thing he chose to hide. Finally the work was done. "Hippolyte," said he, to the hair-dresser, who stood breathlessly by, "this is the way in which my wig is to be dressed from this day forward." *

Hippolyte bowed low, and stepped back to give place to the valets who came in with the count's costume. One bore a rich habit embroidered with gold, and the other a pair of velvet-shorts, red stockings, and diamond-buckled shoes.

"A simpler habit—Spanish, without embroidery, and white stockings."

White stockings! The valets were astounded at such high treason against the court regulations of Vienna. But Kaunitz, with a slight and contemptuous shrug, ordered them a second time to bring him white stockings, and never to presume to bring any other.

"Now, go and await me in the *puderkammer*." †

The valets backed out as if in the presence of royalty, and the eccentric statesman was left with his chief valet. The toilet was completed in solemn silence. Then, the count walked to the mirror to take another look at his adored person. He gave a complaisant stroke to his ruff of richest Alençon, smoothed the folds of his habit, carefully arranged the lace frills that fell over his white hands, and then turning to his valet he said, "Powder-mantle."

The valet unfolded a little package, and, with preter-careful hands, dropped a long white mantle over the shoulders of the ministerial coxcomb. Its light folds closed around him, and, with an Olympian nod, he turned toward the door, while the valet flew to open it. As soon as the count appeared, the other valets, who, with the hair-dresser, stood on either side of the room, raised each one a long brush dipped in hair-powder, and waved it to and fro. Clouds of white dust filled the room; while through the mist, with grave and deliberate gait, walked Kaunitz, every now and then halting, when the brushes all stopped; then giving the word of command, they all fell vigorously to work again. Four times he went through the farce, and then, grave as a ghost, walked back to his dressing-room, followed by the hair-dresser.

At the door, the chief valet carefully removed the powder-mantle, and for the third time Kaunitz turned to the mirror. Then he

* From this time Kaunitz wore his wig in this eccentric fashion. It was adopted by the exquisites of Vienna, and called "the Kaunitz peruke."

† Literally, "powder-room."

carefully wiped the powder from his eyes, and, with a smile of extreme satisfaction he turned to the hair-dresser.

"Confess, Hippolyte, that nothing is more beautifying than powder. See how exquisitely it lies on the front ringlets, and how airily it is distributed over the entire peruke. *Vraiment,* I am proud of my invention."

Hippolyte protested that it was worthy of the godlike intellect of his excellency, and was destined to make an era in the annals of hair-dressing.

"The annals of hair-dressing," replied his excellency, "are not to be enriched with any account of my method of using powder. If ever I hear a word of this discovery breathed outside of these rooms, I dismiss the whole pack of you. Do you hear?"

Down went the obsequious heads, while Kaunitz continued, with his fine cambric handkerchief, to remove the last specks of powder from his eyelids. When he had sufficiently caressed and admired himself, he went to the door. It opened, and two valets, who stood outside, presented him, one with a jewelled snuff-box, the other with an embroidered handkerchief. A large brown dog, that lay couchant in the hall, rose and followed him, and the last act of the daily farce was over.

The count passed into his study, and going at once to the table, he turned over the papers. "No message yet from the empress," said he, chagrined. "What if Bartenstein's visit was *not* a politic, but a triumphant one? What a—"

Here the door opened, and Baron Binder entered. "Your excellency," said he, smiling, "I have taken upon myself to bear you a message which your servants declined to bring. It is to announce a visitor. The hour for reception has gone by, but he was so urgent, that I really could not refuse his entreaties that you might be told of his presence. Pardon my officiousness, but you know how soft-hearted I am. I never could resist importunity."

"Who is your suppliant friend?"

"Count Bartenstein, my lord."

"Bartenstein! Bartenstein back already!" exclaimed Kaunitz, exultingly. "And he begged—he begged for an interview, you say?"

"Begged! the word is faint to express his supplications."

"Then I am not mistaken!" cried Kaunitz, with a loud, triumphant voice; "if Bartenstein begs, it is all over with him. Twice in my anteroom in one day! That is equivalent to a message from the empress." And Kaunitz, not caring to dissimulate with Binder, gave vent to his exceeding joy.

"And you will be magnanimous—you will see him, will you not?" asked Binder, imploringly.

"What for?" asked the heartless statesman. "If he means business, the council-chamber is the place for *that;* if he comes to visit *me*—'I beg to be excused.'"

"But when I beg you, for *my* sake, count," persisted the good-natured baron; "the sight of fallen greatness is such a painful one! How can any one add to it a feather's weight of anguish?"

Kaunitz laid his hands upon the broad shoulders of his friend, and in his eye there kindled something like a ray of affection.

"Grown-up child, your heart is as soft as if it had never been breathed upon by the airs of this wicked world. Say no more about

Bartenstein, and I will reward your interest in his misfortune by making you his successor. You shall be state *referendarius* yourself. Come along, you chicken-hearted statesman, and let us play a game of billiards."

"First," said Binder, sadly, "I must deliver my painful message to Count Bartenstein."

"Bah! the page can be sent to dismiss him."

"But there is no reason why we should keep the poor man waiting."

"Him, the poor man, say you? I remember the day when I waited in *his* anteroom, and as I am an honest man, I shall pay him with interest. Come along, my dear future state *referendarius*."

CHAPTER VIII.

THE RED STOCKINGS.

At Kaunitz's dinner-table on that day revelry reigned triumphant. No jest was too bold for the lips of the men; and if perchance upon the cheeks of their beautiful companions there rose the slightest flush of womanly shame, the knights of the revel shouted applause, and pealed forth their praises in wildest dithyrambics. With glowing faces and eyes of flame they ate their highly-spiced viands, and drank their fiery wines, until all restraint was flung aside, and madness ruled the hour.

The lovely Ferlina, whom Kaunitz had placed next to himself, was beautiful as Grecian Phryne; and Sacco, who was between her adorers, Harrach and Colloredo, was bold and bewitching as Lais.

The odor of flowers—the sound of distant music, every thing that could intoxicate the senses, was there. It was one of those orgies which Kaunitz alone knew how to devise, and into which all the lesser libertines of Vienna longed to be initiated; for once admitted there, they were graduates in the school of vice.

The guests were excited beyond control, but not so the host. He who invoked the demon that possessed the rest, sat perfectly collected. With the coolness of a helmsman he steered the flower-laden bark of voluptuousness toward the breakers, while he befooled its passengers with visions of fatal beauty.

The feast was at an end, and as Kaunitz reviewed the faces of the company, and saw that for the day their passions were weary from indulgence, he said to himself, with diabolical calmness: "Now that they have exhausted every other pleasure, we will sharpen the blunted edge of desire with gambling! When the life of the heart is burnt to ashes, it will still revive at the chink of gold."

"To the gaming-table, friends, to the gaming-table!" cried he. And the dull eyes grew bright, while the guests followed him to the green-covered table, which stood at the farther end of the dining-room.

Kaunitz took from a casket a heap of gold, while La Ferlina gazed upon it with longing sighs. Harrach and Colloredo poured showers from their purses, and Sacco looked from one to the other with her most ineffable smiles. Kaunitz saw it all, and as he threw the dice into the golden dice-box, he muttered, "Miserable worms, ye think yourselves gods, and are the slaves of a little fiend, whose name is Gold!"

As he raised the dice-box, the door opened, and his first valet appeared on the threshold.

"Pardon me, your excellency, that I presume to enter the room. But there is a messenger from the empress, and she begs your excellency's immediate attendance."

With an air of consummate indifference, Kaunitz replaced the dice on the table. "My carriage," was his reply to the valet; and to his guests, with a graceful inclination, he said, "Do not let this interrupt you. Count Harrach will be my banker. In this casket are ten thousand florins—I go halves with the charming Ferlina."

Signora Ferlina could not contain herself for joy, and in the exuberance of her gratitude, she disturbed some of the folds of Kaunitz's lace ruff. Kaunitz was furious; but, without changing a muscle, he went on. "Farewell, my lords—farewell, ladies! I must away to the post of duty."

Another bend of the head, and he disappeared. The valets and hair-dresser were already buzzing around his dressing-room with court-dress and red stocking, but Kaunitz waved them all away, and called Hippolyte to arrange a curl of his hair that was displaced.

The chief valet, who had been petrified with astonishment, now came to life; and advanced, holding in his hand the rich court-dress.

"Pardon, your excellency; but my lord the count is about to have an audience with her imperial majesty?"

"I am," was the curt reply.

"Then your excellency must comply with the etiquette of the empress's court, which requires the full Spanish dress, dagger, and red stockings."

"MUST?" said Kaunitz contemptuously. "Fool! From this day, no one shall say to Count Kaunitz, 'Must.' Bear that in mind. Hand me my muff."

"Muff, my lord?" echoed the valet.

"Yes, fool, my hands are cold."

The valet looked out of the window, where flamed the radiance of a June sun, and with a deep sigh for the waywardness of his master, handed the muff.

Kaunitz thrust in his hands, and slowly left the room, followed by the dog, the valets, and the hair-dresser. Every time his excellency went out, this procession came as far as the carriage-door, to see that nothing remained imperfect in his toilet. With the muff held close to his mouth, for fear a breath of air should enter it, Kaunitz passed through the lofty corridors of his house to his state-carriage. The dog wished to get in, but he waved her gently back, saying:

"No, Phædra, not to-day. I dare not take you there."

The carriage rolled off, and the servants looked after in dumb consternation. At last the first valet, with a malicious smile, said to the others:

"I stick to my opinion—he is crazy. Who but a madman would hope to be admitted to her imperial majesty's presence without red stockings and a dagger?"

Hippolyte shook his head. "No, no, he is no madman; he is only a singular genius, who knows the world, and snaps his fingers at it."

The valet was not far from right. The simple dress, white stockings, and the absence of the dagger, raised a commotion in the palace.

The page in the entrance-hall was afraid to announce the count, and he rushed into the anteroom to consult the marshal of the imperial household. The latter, with his sweetest smile, hastened to meet the indignant count.

"Have the goodness, my lord," said Kaunitz imperiously, "not to detain me any longer. The empress has called me to her presence; say that I am here."

"But, count," cried the horror-stricken marshal, "you cannot seriously mean to present yourself in such a garb. Doubtless you have forgotten, from absence of mind, to array yourself as court etiquette exacts of her majesty's servants. If you will do me the favor to accompany me to my own apartments, I will with great pleasure supply the red stockings and dagger."

Count Kaunitz shrugged his shoulders disdainfully. "Her majesty sent for *me*, not for my red stockings; therefore, please to announce me."

The marshal retreated, in his surprise, several steps. "Never," cried he indignantly, "never would I presume to do so unheard-of a thing! Such a transgression of her majesty's orders is inadmissible."

"Very well," replied Kaunitz coolly, "I shall then have the pleasure of announcing myself."

He passed by the marshal and dismayed page, and was advancing to the door that led to the imperial apartments.

"Hold! hold!" groaned the marshal, whose consternation was now at its height. "That were too presuming! Since her majesty has commanded your attendance, I will do my duty. I leave it to yourself, my lord, to excuse your own boldness, if you can carry it so far as to attempt a justification of your conduct."

He bowed, and passed into the next room; then into the cabinet of the empress, whence he returned with word for Count Kaunitz to enter.

CHAPTER IX.

NEW AUSTRIA.

THE empress received the count with a most gracious smile. "You are late," she said, reaching out her hand for him to kiss.

"I came very near not reaching your majesty's presence at all, for those two wiseacres in the anteroom refused me entrance, because I had neither red stockings nor a dagger."

The empress then perceived the omission, and she frowned. "Why did you present yourself here, without them?" asked she.

"Because, your majesty, I detest red stockings; and I really cannot see why I should be compelled to wear any thing that is so distasteful to me."

Maria Theresa was so surprised, that she scarcely knew what reply to make to the argument; so Kaunitz continued:

"And as for the dagger, that is no emblem of my craft. I am not a soldier, but a statesman; my implement is the crowquill."

"And the tongue," replied the empress, "for you certainly know how to use it. Let us dismiss the dagger and red stockings, then, and speak of your pen and your tongue, for I need them both. I have well weighed the matters under consideration, and have taken counsel of Heaven and of my own conscience. I hope that my decision will be for the best."

Count Kaunitz, courtier though he was, could not repress a slight shiver, nor could he master the paleness that overspread his anxious face.

The empress went on: "I have irrevocably decided. I abide by what I said in council. A new day shall dawn upon Austria—God grant that it prove a happy one! Away, then, with the old alliance! we offer our hand to France, and you shall conduct the negotiations. I appoint you lord high chancellor in the place of Count Uhlefeld. And you owe me some thanks, for I assure you that, to carry out my opposition to my ministers, I have striven with countless difficulties."

"I thank your majesty for resolving upon an alliance with France," said Kaunitz, earnestly; "for I do believe that it will conduce to Austria's welfare."

"And do you not thank me for making you prime minister, or is the appointment unwelcome?"

"I shall be the happiest of mortals if I can accept; but that question is for your majesty to decide."

The empress colored, and looked displeased, while Kaunitz, "himself again," stood composed and collected before her.

"Ah," said she, quickly, "you wish me to beg you to accept the highest office in Austria! Do you think it a favor you do me to become my prime minister, Kaunitz?"

"Your majesty," replied Kaunitz in his soft, calm tones, "I think not of myself, but of Austria that I love, and of you, my honored empress, whom I would die to serve. But I must know whether it will be allowed me to serve my empress and my fatherland as I can and will serve them both."

"What do you mean? Explain yourself."

"If I am to labor in your behalf, my empress, I must have free hands, without colleagues by my side, to discuss my plans and plot against them."

"Ah!" said the empress, smiling, "I understand. You mean Bartenstein and Counts Harrach and Colloredo. True, they are your rivals."

"Oh, your majesty, not my rivals, I hope."

"Well, then, your enemies, if you like that better," said the empress. "I shall not chain you together, then. I will find other places wherewith to compensate them for their past services, and you may find other colleagues."

"I desire no colleagues, your majesty," replied Kaunitz, "I wish to be prime and only minister. Then together we will weld Austria's many dependencies into one great empire, and unite its governments under one head."

"Yours, count?" asked Maria Theresa, in a slight tone of irony.

"Yours, my sovereign. Whatever you may think, up to this moment you have not reigned supreme in Austria. By your side have Bartenstein and Uhlefeld reigned like lesser emperors. Is not

Lombardy governed by its own princes, and does not the Viceroy of Hungary make laws and edicts, which are brought to you for signature?"

"Yes, I am truly hemmed in on every side. But I see no remedy for the evil—I cannot govern everywhere. Hungary and Lombardy have their own constitutions, and must have their own separate governments."

"So long as that state of things lasts, neither Hungary nor Lombardy will be portions of the Austrian empire," said Kaunitz.

"There is no remedy, Kaunitz," returned Maria Theresa; "I have thought these difficulties over and over. My arm is too short to reach to the farthest ends of my realms, and I must be content to delegate some of my power. One hand cannot navigate the ship of state."

"But one head can steer it, your majesty, and one head can direct the hands that work it."

"And will the count be one of my hands?"

"Yes, indeed, your majesty. But the fingers must be subject to this hand, and the hand will then carry out, in all security, the plans of its august head, the empress."

"You mean to say that you wish to be alone as my minister?"

"If I am truly to serve your majesty, it must be so. Let not the sovereignty of Austria be frittered away in multitudinous rivulets; gather it all in one full, fertilizing stream. One head and one hand over Austria's destiny, and then will she grow independent and all-powerful."

"But, man," cried the empress, "you cannot sustain the burden you covet!"

"I will have ample help, your majesty. I will seek ready hands and willing hearts that believe in me, and will do my behests. These must not be my coadjutors, but my subalterns, who think through me, and work for me. If your majesty will grant me this privilege, then I can serve Austria. I know that I am asking for high prerogatives; but for Austria's sake, Maria Theresa will dare every thing; and together we will accomplish the consolidation of her *disjecta membra* into one great empire. The policy which conducts our financial affairs must emanate from yourself, and our foreign policy must be bold and frank, that friends and foes may both know what we mean. We must coffin and bury old Austria with the dead that sleep on the battle-grounds of lost Silesia; and from her ashes we must build a new empire, of which Hungary and Lombardy shall be integral parts. Hand in hand with France, we will be the lawgivers of all Europe; and when, thanks to our thrift and the rich tribute of our provinces, we pay our national debt, then we may laugh at English subsidies and Dutch commerce. And lastly, we will cast our eyes once more upon Silesia, and methinks if France and Austria together should demand restitution of King Frederick, he will scarcely be so rash as to say nay. The ministers of Louis XV., who were adverse to our alliance, are about to retire, and the Duke de Choiseul, our firm friend and the favorite of Mme. de Pompadour, will replace Richelieu. Choiseul seeks our friendship, and the day of our triumph is dawning. Such, your majesty, are my dreams for Austria; it rests with you to make them realities!"

The empress had listened with increasing interest to every word that Kaunitz had spoken. She had risen from her seat, and was pacing the room in a state of high excitement. As he ceased she stopped in front of him, and her large, sparkling orbs of blue glowed with an expression of happiness and hope.

"I believe that you are the man for Austria," said she. "I believe that together we can carry out our plans and projects. God grant that they be righteous and just in His sight! You have read my heart, and you know that I can never reconcile myself to the loss of Silesia. You know that between me and Frederick no harmony can ever exist; no treaty can ever be signed to which he is a party.* I will take the hand of France, not so much for love of herself as for her enmity to Prussia. Will you work with me to make war on Frederick if I appoint you sole minister, Kaunitz? For I tell you that I burn to renew my strife with the King of Prussia, and I would rather give him battle to-day than to-morrow." †

"I comprehend your majesty's feelings, and fully share them. As soon as France and ourselves understand one another, we will make a league against Frederick, and may easily make him strike the first blow; for even now he is longing to appropriate another Silesia."

"And I am longing to cross swords with him for the one he has stolen. I cannot bear to think of going to my fathers with a diminished inheritance; I cannot brook the thought that my woman's hands have not been strong enough to preserve my rights; for I feel that if I have the heart of a woman, I have the head of a man. To see Austria great and powerful, to see her men noble and her women virtuous—that is my dream, my hope, my aim in life. You are the one to perfect what I have conceived, Kaunitz; will you give me your hand to this great work?"

"I will, your majesty, so help me God!"

"Will you have Austria's good alone in view, in all that you counsel as my minister?"

"I will, so help me God!"

"Will you take counsel with me how we may justly and righteously govern Austria, without prejudice, without self-love, without thought of worldly fame, not from love or fear of man, but for the sake of God from whose hands we hold our empire?"

"I will, so help me God!"

"Then," said Maria Theresa, after a pause, "you are my sole minister, and I empower you to preside over the affairs of state, in the manner you may judge fittest for the welfare of the Austrian people."

Kaunitz was as self-possessed a worldling as ever sought to hide his emotions; but he could not suppress an exclamation of rapture, nor an expression of triumph, which lit up his face as nothing had ever illumined it before.

"Your majesty," said he, when he found words, "I accept the trust, and as there is a God above to judge me, I will hold it faithfully. My days and nights, my youth and age, with their thoughts, their will, their every faculty, shall be laid upon the shrine of Austria's greatness; and if for one moment I ever sacrifice your majesty to any interest of mine, may I die a death of torture and disgrace!"

* Maria Theresa's own words.
† Maria Theresa's words. Coxe.

"I believe you; your countenance reflects your heart, and Almighty God has heard your words. One thing remember—that Maria Theresa suffers no minister to dictate to her. She is the reigning sovereign of her people, and will not suffer a finger to be laid upon her imperial rights. Were he a thousand times prime minister, the man that presumed too far with me I would hurl from his eminence to the lowest depths of disgrace. And now that we understand one another, we will clasp hands like men, who are pledged before God to do their duty."

She extended her hand to Kaunitz, who grasped it in his own. "I swear," said he, solemnly, "to do my duty; and never can I forget this hour. I swear to my *sovereign*, Maria Theresa, loyalty unto death; and before my *empress* I bow my knee, and so do homage to the greatest woman of her age."

The empress smiled, while Kaunitz knelt and kissed her fair, jewelled hand. "May God grant that you speak truth, Kaunitz, and may my posterity not have to blush for me! 'Every thing for Austria,' shall be your motto and mine; and this flaming device shall light us on our way through life. Now go, lord high chancellor, and see that the world finds a phœnix in the ashes of the old *régime* which to-day we have consigned to the dust!" *

* From this time, Kaunitz was the sole minister of the empress; and he kept his promise to Binder, who became state *referendarius*, in the place of the once-powerful Bartenstein.

ISABELLA.

CHAPTER X.

THE YOUNG SOLDIER.

KAUNITZ'S prophecy had been fulfilled. No sooner was it known that Austria and France were allies, than Frederick of Prussia, with all haste, made treaties with England. These opposite alliances were the signal for war. For seven years this war held its blood-stained lash over Austria, and every nation in Europe suffered more or less from its effects. Maria Theresa began it with sharp words, to which Frederick had responded with his sharper sword.

The king, through his ambassador, asked the meaning of her extensive military preparations throughout Austria, to which the empress, nettled by the arrogance of the demand, had replied that she believed she had a right to mass troops for the protection of herself and her allies, without rendering account of her acts to foreign kings. Upon the receipt of this reply, Frederick marched his troops into Saxony, and so began the "Seven Years' War," a war that was prosecuted on both sides with bitter vindictiveness.

Throughout Austria the wildest enthusiasm prevailed. Rich and poor, young and old, all rushed to the fight. The warlike spirit that pervaded her people made its way to the heart of the empress's eldest son. The Archduke Joseph had for some time been entreating his mother to allow him to join the army; and, at last, though much against her will, she had yielded to his urgent desire. The day on which news of a victory, near Kunnersdorf, over Frederick, reached the palace, the empress had given her consent, and her son was to be allowed to go in search of laurel-wreaths wherewith to deck his imperial brow.

This permission to enter the army was the first great joy of Joseph's life. His heart, at last freed from its weight of conventional duties, and forced submission to the requirements of court etiquette, soared high into regions of exultant happiness. His countenance, once so cold and impassible, was now full of joyous changes; his eyes, once so dull and weary, glowed with the fire of awakened enthusiasm, and they looked so brilliant a blue, that it seemed as if some little ray from heaven had found its way into their clear, bright depths. The poor boy was an altered creature. He was frolicsome with his friends; and as for those whom he considered his enemies, he cared nothing for their likes or dislikes. He had nothing to lose or gain from them; he was to leave the court, leave Vienna, leave every troublesome remembrance behind, and go, far from all tormentors, to the army.

The preparations were at an end; the archduke had taken formal leave of his mother's court; this evening he was to spend in the imperial family circle; and early on the next morning his journey would begin. He had just written a last note of farewell to a friend. Alone in his room, he stood before a mirror, contemplating with a smile his own image. He was not looking at his handsome face, though happiness was lending it exquisite beauty; the object of his rapturous admiration was the white uniform, which, for the first time, he wore in place of his court-dress. He was no longer the descendant of Charles the Fifth, no longer the son of the empress, he was a soldier—a free, self-sustaining man, whose destiny lay in his own hands, and whose future deeds would prove him worthy to be the son of his great ancestor.

As, almost intoxicated with excess of joy, he stood before the glass, the door opened gently, and a youth of about his own age entered the room.

"Pardon me, your highness," said the youth, bowing, "if I enter without permission. Doubtless your highness did not hear me knock, and I found no one in your anteroom to announce me."

The prince turned around, and reached out his hand, saying, with a laugh: "No, no, you found nobody. I have discharged old Dame Etiquette from my service, and you see before you not his imperial highness, the Archduke Joseph, crown prince of Austria, but a young soldier, brimful of happiness, master of nothing but his own sword, with which he means to carve out his fortunes on the battle-field. Oh, Dominick! I have dropped the rosary, and taken up the sabre; and I mean to twist such a forest of laurels about my head, that it will be impossible for me ever to wear a night-cap again, were it even sent me as a present from the pope himself."

"Do not talk so loud, your highness; you will frighten the proprieties out of their wits."

Joseph laughed. "Dominick Kaunitz," said he, "you are the son of your respected father, no doubt of it; for you behave prettily before the bare walls themselves. But fear not, son of the mighty minister, *my* walls are dumb, and nobody is near to tell tales. We are alone, for I have dismissed all my attendants; and here I may give loud vent to my hallelujahs, which I now proceed to do by singing you a song which I learned not long ago from an invalid soldier in the street."

And the prince began, in a sonorous bass voice, to sing:

"Oh! the young cannon is my bride!
Her orange-wreath is twined with bay,
And on the blood-red battle-field
We'll celebrate our wedding-day.
Trara! trara!
No priest is there
To bless the rites,
No——"

Here young Kaunitz, all etiquette despising, put his hands before the mouth of the prince; and, while the latter strove, in spite of him, to go on with his song, he said, in low but anxious tones:

"For Heaven's sake, your highness, listen to me. You plunge yourself wantonly into danger. Do you suppose that your powerful voice does not resound through the corridors of the palace?"

"Well, if it *is* heard, Dominick, what of it? I bid farewell to my enemies, and this is my 'Hosanna.' You ought to be ashamed of yourself to stop me. My tormentors, you think, have heard the beginning of my song; well, the devil take it, but they shall have the end!"

Once more the archduke began to sing; but Dominick caught his arm. "Do you wish," said he, "to have the empress revoke her permission?"

The archduke laughed. "Why, Dominick, you are crazed with grief for my loss, I do believe; the empress revoke her imperial word, *now*, when all my preparations are made, and I go to-morrow?"

"Empresses do revoke their words, and preparations are often made, to be followed by—nothing," replied Dominick.

The prince looked in consternation at his young friend. "Are you in earnest, dear Dominick?" asked he. "Do you indeed think it possible that I could be hindered from going to the army, on the very eve of my departure?"

"I do, your highness."

The archduke grew pale, and in a tremulous voice said, "Upon what do you found your supposition, my friend?"

"Oh, my dear lord," replied Dominick, "it is no supposition, I fear it is a fact; and I fear, too, that it is your own fault if this disappointment awaits you."

"Good Heaven!" exclaimed the prince, in tones of anguish, "what can I have done to deserve such fearful chastisement?"

"You have displeased the empress by neglect of your religious duties. For more than two weeks you have not entered a place of worship; and, yesterday, when the Countess Fuchs remonstrated with your highness, you replied with an unseemly jest. You said, 'Dearest countess, I hope to prove to you that, although I neglect my mass, I can be pious on the battle-field. There, on the altar of my country, I mean to sacrifice countless enemies, and that will be an offering quite as pleasing in the sight of God.' Were those not your words, prince?"

"Yes, yes, they were—but I meant no impiety. My heart was so full of joy that it effervesced in wild words; but surely my mother cannot mean, for such a harmless jest, to dash my every hope to the earth!"

"Oh, your highness, this is only one offence out of many of which you are accused. I have no time to repeat them now, for my errand here is important and pressing."

"Where learned you all this?" asked the poor archduke.

"Bend down your ear, and I will tell you. My father told me every word of it."

"The lord high chancellor? Impossible!"

"Yes, it would seem impossible that he should repeat any thing, and therefore you may know how seriously the matter affects your highness when I tell you that he sent me to warn you."

A quick, loud knock at the door interrupted him, and before the archduke could say "Come in," the Emperor Francis was in the room. His face looked careworn, and he cast a glance of tender compassion upon his son.

"My child," said he, "I come to speak to you in private, a thing I cannot compass in my own apartments."

Dominick bowed to take leave, but the emperor withheld him. "Stay," said he, "for you may serve us, Dominick. I know you to be Joseph's best friend, and you will not betray him. But I have no time for words. Tell me quickly, Joseph, is there any secret outlet to these apartments? Do you know of any hidden stairway by which you could escape from the palace?"

"I, father! I have secret doors in my apartments? Is this some new device of my enemies to injure me in the eyes of the empress?"

"Hush, hush, Joseph!—How like he is in temperament to his mother!—Answer me at once; there is no question of enemies, but of yourself."

"What would you have me do with secret doors and stairways?" asked Joseph.

The emperor came close to his son, and, in low, cautious tones, whispered, "I would have you, this very hour, leave the palace privately, mount your horse, and speed away from Vienna."

"Fly, my dear father?" cried Joseph. "Has it come to this, that the son must fly from the face of his own mother? Am I a criminal, who must not be told of what crime I am accused? No, your majesty; if death, or imprisonment for life, were here to threaten me, I would not fly."

"Nor would I counsel flight, my son, were you accused of wrong; but this is not a question of crime, of poisoned beaker, or of castle dungeon—it is simply this: Do you wish to join the army, or are you ready to give up your commission and stay at home?"

"Oh, my dear father," cried Joseph, "you well know that I have but one desire on earth—and that is, to go."

"Then, hear me. It has been represented to the empress that your lust for war has made you so reckless, so bloodthirsty, and so impious, that camp-life will prove your ruin. In her excess of maternal love, she has taken the alarm, and has resolved to shield you from danger by withdrawing her consent to your departure."

The archduke's eyes filled with tears. The emperor laid his hand sympathizingly upon his shoulder.

"Do not despair, dear child," said he, tenderly; "perhaps all is not lost, and I may be able to assist you. I can comprehend the nature of your sorrow, for I have suffered the same bitter disappointment. If, instead of leading a useless life, a mere appanage of the empress, I had been permitted to follow the dictates of my heart, and command her armies, I might have—but why speak of my waning career? You are young, and I do not wish to see your life darkened by such early disappointment. Therefore, listen to me. *You* know nothing of the change in your prospects; you have, as yet, received no orders to remain. Write to your mother, that, preferring to go without the grief of taking leave, you have presumed to start to-night without her knowledge, hoping soon to embrace her again, and lay your first-earned laurels at her feet."

The archduke hastened to obey his father, and sat down to write. The emperor, meanwhile, signed to young Kaunitz, who had kept himself respectfully aloof.

"Have you a courser," asked he, "to sell to Joseph, and two good servants that can accompany him until his own attendants can be sent after him?"

"I came hither, your majesty, prepared to make the same proposition, with the fleetest horse in my father's stables, and two trusty servants, well mounted, all of which await his highness at the postern gate."

"Your father's best horse? Then *he* knows of this affair?"

"It was he who sent me to the archduke's assistance. He told me, in case of necessity, to propose flight, and to be ready for it."

"The letter is ready," said the archduke, coming forward.

"I myself will hand it to the empress," said his father, taking it, "and I will tell her that I counselled you to go as you did."

"But dear father, the empress will be angry."

"Well, my son," said the emperor, with a peculiar smile, "I have survived so many little passing storms, that I shall doubtless survive this one. The empress has the best and noblest heart in the world, and its sunshine is always brightest after a storm. Go, then, my child, I will answer for your sin and mine. The empress has said nothing to me of her change of purpose; she looks upon it as a state affair, and with her state affairs I am never made acquainted. Since accident has betrayed it to me, I have a right to use my knowledge in your behalf, and I undertake to appease your mother. Here is a purse with two thousand louis d'ors; it is enough for a few days of *incognito*. Throw your military cloak about you, and away!"

Young Kaunitz laid the cloak upon the shoulders of the archduke, whose eyes beamed forth the gratitude that filled his heart.

"Oh my father and my sovereign," said he in a voice that trembled with emotion, "my whole life will not be long enough to thank you for what you are doing for me in this critical hour. Till now I have loved you indeed as my father, but henceforth I must look upon you as my benefactor also, as my dearest and best friend. My heart and my soul are yours, dear father; may I be worthy of your love and of the sacrifice you are making for me to-day!"

The emperor folded his son to his heart, and kissed his fair forehead. "Farewell, dear boy," whispered he; "return to me a victor and a hero. May you earn for your father on the battle-field the laurels which he has seen in dreams! God bless you!"

They then left the room, Count Kaunitz leading the way, to see if the passage was clear.

"I will go with you as far as the staircase," continued the emperor, "and then—"

At that moment Dominick, who had gone forward into the corridor, rushed back into the room pale and trembling, "It is too late!" exclaimed he in a stifled voice; "there comes a messenger from the empress!"

CHAPTER XI.

THE EMPRESS AND HER SON.

THE young count was not mistaken. It was indeed a message from the empress. It was the marshal of the household, followed by four pages who came to command the presence of the archduke, to whom her majesty wished to impart something of importance.

A deadly paleness overspread the face of the young prince, and his whole frame shivered. The emperor felt the shudder, and drew his son's arm closer to his heart. "Courage, my son, courage!" whispered he: then turning toward the imperial embassy, he said aloud, "Announce to her majesty that I will accompany the archduke in a few moments." And as the marshal stood irresolute and confused, the emperor, smiling, said: "Oh, I see that you have been ordered to accompany the prince yourselves. Come, then, my son, we will e'en go along with the messengers."

Maria Theresa was pacing the floor of her apartment in great excitement. Her large, flashing eyes now and then turned toward the door; and whenever she fancied that footsteps approached, she stopped, and seemed almost to gasp with anxiety.

Suddenly she turned toward Father Porhammer, who, with the Countess Fuchs, stood by the side of the sofa from which she had risen. "Father," said she, in a tremulous voice, "I cannot tell why it is that, as I await my son's presence here, my heart is overwhelmed with anguish. I feel as if I were about to do him an injustice, and for all the kingdoms of the world I would not do him wrong."

"Nay," replied the father, "your majesty is about to rescue that beloved son from destruction; but as your majesty is a loving mother, it afflicts you to disappoint your child. Still, our Lord has commanded if the right eye offend, to pluck it out; and so is it your majesty's duty to pluck from your son's heart the evil growing there, even were his heart's blood to follow. The wounds you may inflict upon your dear child, for God's sake, will soon be healed by His Almighty hand."

"He was *so* happy to become a soldier!" murmured the empress, who had resumed her agitated walk; "his eyes were so bright, and his bearing was so full of joy and pride! My boy is so handsome, so like his dear father, that my heart throbs when I see him, as it did in the days when we were young lovers! A laurel-wreath would well become his fair brow, and I—how proudly I should have welcomed my young hero to my heart once more! Dear, dear boy, must I then wake you so rudely from your first dream of ambition?—I MUST. He would come to evil in the lawless life of the camp; God forgive him, but he is as mad for the fight as Don John of Austria! I should never see him again; he would seek death in his first battle. Oh, I could not survive it; my heart would break if I should have to give up my first-born! Four of my children lie in the vaults of St. Stephen's—I cannot part with my Joseph! Countess," she said, turning suddenly to her lady of honor, "is it not true that Joseph told you he thought that the altar of the battle-field and the sacrifice of his enemies was—"

"His majesty the emperor and his imperial highness, the Archduke Joseph!" said the marshal of the household; and the door was flung open for their entrance.

Maria Theresa advanced, and bowed slightly to the emperor.

"Your majesty's visit at this unusual hour surprises me," said she with emphasis.

"I am aware," replied the emperor graciously, "that I was not expected; but as this is the last day of our son's residence under the parental roof, I am sure that my wife will see nothing strange in my visit. I was with the archduke when your majesty's message reached him, and knowing that you could have no secrets with the son which the father might not hear, I followed the impulse of my affection, and came with him."

"And what signifies this singular and unseemly dress in which my son presents himself before his sovereign?" asked Maria Theresa, angrily surveying the uniform which, nevertheless, she acknowledged in her heart was beyond expression becoming to him.

"Pardon me, your majesty," replied the son, "I had tried on the uniform, and if I was to obey your summons at once, there was no time for a change in my dress."

"And, indeed," said the emperor, "I think the dress becoming. Our boy will make a fine-looking soldier."

The empress being precisely of that opinion herself, was so much the more vexed at her husband for giving it expression. She bit her lip, and her brow contracted, as was usual with her when she was growing angry.

"You held it then as a fact, my son, that you were a soldier?" said she, catching her breath with anxiety.

Joseph raised his fine eyes, with an imploring expression, to the face of his mother. "Your majesty had promised me that I should be a soldier," replied he firmly, "and I have never yet known my mother to break her imperial word to the least of her subjects."

"Hear him!" cried the empress, with a laugh of derision, "he almost threatens me! This young sir will try to make it a point of honor with me to keep my word."

"Pardon me, your majesty," replied Joseph calmly, "I have never allowed myself to doubt your imperial word for one moment of my life."

"Well, then, your highness has my *imperial* permission to doubt it now," cried the empress, severely humiliated by the implied rebuke; "I allow you to doubt whether I will ever hold promises that have been rashly and injudiciously made."

"Why, your majesty," cried the emperor, "surely you will not retract your word in the face of the whole world, that knows of Joseph's appointment!"

"What to me is the opinion of the world?" returned the haughty empress. "To God and my conscience alone I am responsible for my acts, and to them I will answer it that I take back my promise, and declare that Joseph *shall not* go into the army!"

Joseph uttered a cry of anguish. "Mother! mother!" sobbed the unhappy boy, "it cannot be!"

"Why can it not be?" said the empress, haughtily.

"Because it would be a cruel and heartless deed," cried the archduke, losing all control over himself, "so to make sport of my holiest and purest hopes in life; and because I never, never can believe that my own mother would seek to break my heart."

The empress was about to return a scathing reply, when the emperor laid his gentle hand upon her shoulder, and the words died upon her lips.

"I beseech of you, my wife," said he, "to remember that we are not alone. Joseph is no child; and it ill becomes any but his parents to witness his humiliation. Have the goodness, then, to dismiss your attendants, and let us deal with our son alone."

"Why shall I dismiss them?" cried the empress, "they are my trusty confidants; and they have a right to hear all that the future Emperor of Austria presumes to say to his mother!"

"Pardon me," replied the emperor, "I differ with you, and desire that they should not hear our family discussions. In these things I too have my right; and if your majesty does not command them to leave the room, I do."

Maria Theresa looked at the countenance of her husband, which was firm and resolved in its expression. In her confusion she could find no retort. The emperor waited awhile, and seeing that she did not speak, he turned toward the two followers, who stood, without moving, at their posts.

"I request the Countess Fuchs and Father Porhammer to leave the room," said he, with dignity. "Family concerns are discussed in private."

The pair did not go. Father Porhammer interrogated the face of the empress; and the countess, indignant that her curiosity was to be frustrated, looked defiant.

This bold disregard of her husband's command was irritating to the feelings of the empress. She thought that his orders should have outweighed her mere remonstrance, and she now felt it her duty to signify as much.

"Countess Fuchs," said she, "doubtless the emperor has not spoken loud enough for you to hear the command he has just given you. You have not understood his words, and I will take the trouble to repeat them. The emperor said, 'I request the Countess Fuchs and Father Porhammer to leave the room. Our family concerns we will discuss in private.'"

The lady of honor colored, and, with deep inclinations, Father Porhammer and herself left the room.

Maria Theresa looked after them until the door was shut, then she smilingly reached her hand to the emperor, who thanked her with a pressure and a look of deepest affection. The archduke had retired to the embrasure of a window, perhaps to seek composure, perhaps to hide his tears.

"Now," said Maria Theresa, sternly, while her fiery eyes sought the figure of her son, "now we are alone, and Joseph is at liberty to speak. I beg him to remember, that in the person of his mother, he also sees his sovereign, and that the empress will resent every word of disloyalty spoken to the parent. And I hold it to be highly disloyal for my son to accuse me of making sport of his hopes. I have not come to my latest determination from cruelty or caprice; I have made it in the strength of my maternal love to shield my child from sin, and in the rectitude of my imperial responsibility to my people, who have a right to claim from me that I bestow upon them a monarch who is worthy to reign over Austria. Therefore, my son, as empress and mother, I say that you shall remain. That is now my unalterable will. If this decision grieves you, be humble and submissive; and remember that it is your duty, as son and subject, to obey without demurring. Then shall we be good friends, and greet one another heartily, as though you had at this moment returned from the victorious battle-field. There is my hand. Be welcome, my dear and much-beloved child."

The heart of the empress had gradually softened, and as she smiled and extended her hand, her beautiful eyes were filled to overflowing with tears. But Joseph, deathly pale, crossed his arms, and returned her glances of love with a haughty, defiant look, that almost approached to dislike.

"My son," said the emperor, "do you not see your dear mother's hand extended to meet yours?"

"I see it, I see it," cried Joseph, passionately, "but I cannot take it—I cannot play my part in this mockery of a return. No, mother, no, I cannot kiss the hand that has so cruelly dashed my hopes to earth. And you wish to carry your tyranny so far as to exact that I receive it with a smile? Oh, mother, my heart is breaking! Have pity on me, and take back those cruel words; let me go, let me go. Do not make me a byword for the world, that hereafter will refuse me its respect. Let me go, if but for a few weeks, and on the day that you command my return, I will come home. Oh, my heart was too small to hold the love I bore you for your consent to my departure. It seemed to me that I had just begun to live; the world was full of beauty, and I forgot all the trials of my childhood. For one week I have been young, dear mother; hurl me not back again into that dark dungeon of solitude where so much of my short life has been spent. Do not condemn me to live as I have hitherto lived; give me freedom, give me my manhood's rights!"

"No, no! a thousand times no!" cried the exasperated empress; "I see now that I am right to keep such an unfeeling and ungrateful son at home. He talks of his sufferings forsooth! What has he ever suffered at my hands?"

"What have I suffered?" exclaimed Joseph, whose teeth chattered as if he were having a chill, and who was no longer in a state to suppress the terrible eruption of his heart's agony. "What have I suffered, ask you? I will tell you, empress-mother, what I have suffered since first I could love, or think, or endure. As a child I have felt that my mother loved another son more than she loved me. When my longing eyes sought hers, they were riveted upon another face. When my brother and I have sinned together, he has been forgiven, when I have been punished. Sorrow and jealousy were in my heart, and no one cared enough for me to ask why I wept. I was left to suffer without one word of kindness—and you wondered that I was taciturn, and mocked at my slighted longings for love, and called them by hard names. And then you pointed to my caressed and indulged brother, and bade me be gay like him!"

"My son, my son!" cried the emperor, "control yourself; you know not what you say."

"Let him go on, Francis," said the pale mother, "it is well that I should know his heart at last."

"Yes," continued the maddened archduke, "let me go on, for in my heart there is nothing but misery and slighted affection. Oh, mother, mother!" exclaimed he, suddenly changing from defiance to the most pathetic entreaty, "on my knees I implore you to let me go; have mercy, have mercy upon your wretched son!"

And the young prince, with outstretched hands, threw himself upon his knees before his mother. The long-suppressed tears gushed forth, and the wild tempest of his ungovernable fury was spent, and now he sobbed as if indeed his young heart was breaking.

Th emperor could scarcely restrain the impulse he felt to weep with his son; but he came and laid his hand upon the poor boy's head, and looked with passionate entreaty at the empress.

"Dear Theresa," said he, "be compassionate and forgiving. Pardon him, beloved, the hard and unjust words which, in the bitterness of a first sorrow, he has spoken to the best of mothers. Raise him up from the depths of his despair, and grant the boon, for which, I am sure, he will love you beyond bounds."

"I wish that I dared to grant it to yourself, Francis," replied the empress, sadly and tearfully; "but you see that he has made it impossible. I dare not do it. The mother has no right to plead with the empress for her rebellious son. What he has said I freely forgive—God grant that I may forget it! Well do I know how stormy is youth, and I remember that Joseph is my son. It is the wild Spanish blood of my ancestry that boils in his veins, and, therefore, I forgive him with all my heart. But revoke my last sentence—that I cannot do. To do so would be to confirm him in wrong. Rise, my son Joseph—I forgive all your cruel words; but what I have said, I have said. You remain at home."

Joseph rose slowly from his knees. The tears in his eyes were dried; his lips were compressed, and once more he wore the old look of cold and sullen indifference. He made a profound inclination before his mother. "I have heard the empress's commands," said he, in a hoarse and unnatural voice; "it is my duty to obey. Allow me to go to my prison, that I may doff this manly garb, which is no longer suitable to my blasted career."

Without awaiting the answer, he turned away, and with hasty strides left the room.

The empress watched him in speechless anxiety. As the door closed upon him, her features assumed an expression of tenderness, and she said: "Go quickly, Franz—go after him. Try to comfort and sustain him. I do not know why, but I feel uneasy—"

At that moment a cry was heard in the anteroom, and the fall of a heavy body to the floor.

"God help me—it is Joseph!" shrieked the empress; and, forgetting all ceremony, she darted from the room, and rushed by her dismayed attendants through the anteroom, out into the corridor. Stretched on the floor, insensible and lifeless, lay her son.

Without a word the empress waved off the crowd that was assembled around his body. The might of her love gave her supernatural strength, and folding her arms around her child, she covered his pale face with kisses, and from the very midst of the frightened attendants she bore him herself to her room, where she laid him softly upon her own bed.

No one except the emperor had ventured to follow. He stood near, and reached the salts, to which the empress had silently pointed. She rubbed her son's temples, held the salts to his nostrils, and at last, when he gave signs of life, she turned to the emperor and burst into tears.

"Oh, Franz," said she, "I almost wish that he were sick, that day and night I might watch by his bedside, and his poor heart might feel the full extent of a mother's love for her first-born child."

Perhaps God granted her prayer, that these two noble hearts might no longer be estranged, but that each might at last meet the other in the fullest confidence of mutual love.

A violent attack of fever followed the swoon of the archduke. The empress never left his side. He slept in her own room, and she watched over him with gentlest and most affectionate care.

Whenever Joseph awaked from his fever-dreams and unclosed his eyes, there, close to his bedside, he saw the empress, who greeted him with loving words and softest caresses. Whenever, in his fever-thirst, he called for drink, her hand held the cup to his parched lips; and whenever that soft, cool hand was laid upon his hot brow, he felt as if its touch chased away all pain and soothed all sorrow.

When he recovered enough to sit up, still his mother would not consent for him to leave her room for his own. As long as he was an invalid, he should be hers alone. In her room, and through her loving care, should he find returning health. His sisters and brothers assembled there to cheer him with their childish mirth, and his young friend, Dominick Kaunitz, came daily to entertain him with his lively gossip. Altogether, the archduke was happy. If he had lost fame, he had found love.

One day, when, cushioned in his great soft arm-chair, he was chatting with his favorite tutor, Count Bathiany, the empress entered the room, her face lit up with a happy smile, while in her hands she held an *étui* of red morocco.

"What think you I have in this *étui*, dear?" she said, coming forward, and bending over her son to bestow a kiss.

"I do not know; but I guess it is some new gift of love from my mother's dear hand."

"Yes—rightly guessed. It *is* a genuine gift of love, and, with God's grace, it may prove the brightest gift in your future crown. Since I would not let you leave my house, my son, I feel it my duty, at least, to do my best to make your home a happy one. I also wish to show you that, in my sight, you are no longer a boy, but a man worthy to govern your own household. Look at the picture in this case, and if it pleases you, my darling son, I give you, not only the portrait, but the original also."

She handed him the case, in which lay the miniature of a young girl of surpassing beauty, whose large, dark eyes seemed to gaze upon him with a look of melancholy entreaty.

The archduke contemplated the picture for some time, and gradually over his pale face there stole a flush of vague delight.

"Well!" asked the empress, "does the maiden please you?"

"Please me!" echoed the archduke, without withdrawing his eyes from the picture. "'Tis the image of an angel! There is something in her look so beseeching, something in her smile so sad, that I feel as if I would fall at her feet and weep; and yet, mother—"

"Hear him, Franz," cried Maria Theresa to the emperor, who, unobserved by his son, had entered the room. "Hear our own child! love in his heart will be a sentiment as holy, as faithful, and as profound as it has been with us for many happy years! Will you have the angel for your wife, Joseph?"

The archduke raised his expressive eyes to the face of his mother. "If I will have her!" murmured he, sadly. "Dear mother, would she deign to look upon me? Will she not rather turn away from him to whom the whole world is indifferent?"

"My precious child, she will love and honor you, as the world will do, when it comes to know your noble heart." And once more the empress bent over her son and imprinted a kiss upon his pale brow. "It is settled then, my son, that you shall offer your hand to this beautiful girl. In one week you will have attained your nineteenth birthday, and you shall give a good example to your sisters. Do you like the prospect?"

"Yes, dear mother, I am perfectly satisfied."

"And you do not ask her name or rank?"

"You have chosen her for me; and I take her from your hand without name or rank."

"Well," cried the delighted empress, "Count Bathiany, you have ever been the favorite preceptor of the archduke. Upon you, then, shall this honorable mission devolve. To-morrow, as ambassador extraordinary from our court, you shall go in state to ask of Don Philip of Parma the hand of his daughter Isabella for his imperial highness, the crown prince of Austria."

CHAPTER XII.

AN ITALIAN NIGHT.

THE moon is up, but she is hidden behind heavy masses of clouds —welcome clouds that shelter lovers' secrets. The fountains, whose silvery showers keep such sweet time to the murmurings of love, plash gently on, hushing the sound of lovers' voices; on the bosom of yonder marble-cinctured lake, two snow-white swans are floating silently; and, far amid groves of myrtle and olive, the nightingale warbles her notes of love. Not a step echoes through the long avenues of the ducal park, not a light glimmers from the windows of the ducal palace. 'Tis the hour of midnight, and gentle sleep hath come to all.

To all, save two. Stay yet awhile behind the cloud, O tell-tale moon! for there—there are the lovers. See where fair Juliet leans from the marble balcony; while Romeo, below, whispers of plighted vows that naught shall cancel save—death!

"To-morrow, beloved, to-morrow, thou wilt be mine forever?"

"I will be thine in the face of the whole world."

"And wilt thou never repent? Hast thou strength to brave the world's scorn for my sake?"

"Do I need strength to stretch forth my hand for that which is dearer to me than all the world beside? Oh, there is selfishness in my love, Riccardo, for it loses sight of the dangers that will threaten thee on the day when thou callest me wife!"

"There is but one danger, dearest—that of losing thee! I know no other."

"Still, be cautious, for my sake. Remember, we live on Spanish soil, though Italy's skies are overhead; and Spanish vengeance is sharp and swift. Betray not thy hopes by smile or glance—in a few days we will be far away in the paradise where our happiness shall be hidden from all eyes, save those of angels. Be guarded, therefore, dear one—for see! Even now the moon is forth again in all her splendor; and were my father's spies to track thee!—Gracious Heaven, go! Think of Spanish daggers, and let us part for a few short hours."

"Well, I will go, strengthened to turn my eyes from thy beauty, by thoughts of to-morrow's bliss! In the chapel I await thee."

"I will be there. The priest will not betray us?"

"He was the friend of my childhood—we may trust him, Isabella."

"Then, Heaven bless thee! good-night. Hark!—did I not hear something rustle in the thicket?"

"The wind sighing through the pine-trees, love."

"Then, adieu, till morning."

"Adieu, sweet one!"

The moon burst forth in full radiance, and revealed the manly form that hurried through the avenue; while clear as in noonday could be seen the slender white figure that watched his retreating steps.

He is hidden now, but she still lingers, listening enraptured to the fountain's murmur and the nightingale's song; looking upward at the moon as she wandered through heaven's pathless way, and thinking that never had earth or sky seemed so lovely before—

But hark! What sounds are those? A cry, a fearful cry rends the air; and it comes from the thicket where, a moment before, he disappeared from her sight.

She started—then, breathless as a statue, she listened in deadly suspense. Again that cry, that dreadful cry, pierces through the stillness of the night, freezing her young heart with horror!

"His death-wail!" cried the wretched girl; and careless of danger, scarce knowing what she did, heeding nothing but the sound of her lover's voice, she sprang from the balcony, and as though moonbeams had drawn her thither, she swung herself to the ground. For one moment her slight form wavered, then she darted forward and flew through the avenue to the thicket. Away she sped, though the moon shone so bright that she could be distinctly seen, her own shadow following like a dusky phantom behind.

Be friendly, now, fair moon, and light her to her lover, that she may look into his eyes once more before they close forever!

She has reached the spot, and, with a low cry, she throws herself by the side of the tall figure that lies stretched at its length upon the green sward.

Yes, it is he; he whom she loves; the soul of her soul, the life of her life! And he lies cold and motionless, his eyes staring blindly upon the heavens, his purple lips unclosing to exhale his last sighs, while from two hideous wounds in his side the blood streams over the white dress of his betrothed. But he is not dead; his blood is still warm.

She bends over and kisses his cold lips; she tears her lace mantle from her shoulders, and, pressing it to his wounds, tries to stanch the life-blood welling from his side. The mantle grows scarlet with his gore, but the lips are whiter and colder with each kiss. She knows, alas! that there is one nearer to him now than she—Azrael is between her and her lover. He grows colder, stiffer; and—O God!—the death-rattle!

"Take me with thee; take me, take me!" screamed the despairing girl; and her arms clasped frantically around the body, until they seemed as if they were indeed stiffening into one eternal embrace.

"Have pity, Riccardo! My life, my soul, leave me not here without thee! One word—one look, beloved!"

She stared at him in wild despair, and seeing that he made no sign of response to her passionate appeal, she raised her hands to heaven, and kneeling by his side, she prayed.

"O God, merciful God, take not his fleeting life until he has given me one last word—until he has told me how long we shall be parted!"

Her arms sank heavily down, and she sought the face of the dying man, whispering—oh, how tenderly!—"Hear me, my own; tell me when I shall follow thee to heaven!"

She ceased, for suddenly she felt him tremble; his eyes moved until they met hers, and once more a smile flitted across those blanched lips. He raised his head, and slowly his body moved, until, supported in *her* arms, he sat erect. Enraptured, he laid her cheek to his, and waited; for love had called him back to life, and he would speak.

"We shall meet again in three—"

He fell back, and with a last cry expired. Love had struggled hard with death; but death had won the victory.

Isabel shed no tears. She closed her lover's eyes; gave him one long, last kiss; and, as she bent over him, her hair was soaked in his blood. She took the mantle, wet with gore, and pressed it to her heart. "Precious mantle," said she, "we need not part; in three days—or. perchance he said three hours—we shall lie together in the coffin! Until then, Riccardo, farewell!"

Slowly she turned and left the horrible place. Wthout faltering, she came up the long moonlit avenue, her head thrown back, and her large, lustrous eyes fixed upon heaven, as though she sought to find her lover's soul somewhere among the floating clouds.

The moon flung its radiance around her path; and ever, as she walked, it grew brighter, until the poor, stricken child of earth looked like a glorified saint. "God grant that it be three hours!" murmured she; "three days were an eternity!"

She reached the palace, without having thought that there was no door open by which she could enter, when suddenly a form emerged from the shadowed wall, and a woman's voice whispered:

"Quick, for Heaven's sake! the side-door is open, and all in the palace sleep!"

"I, too, in three hours shall sleep!" cried Isabella, triumphantly, and with these words she fell to the ground in a swoon.*

CHAPTER XIII.

ISABELLA OF PARMA.

THE Princess Isabella slept unusually late the next morning. Her little bell, that summoned the ladies of honor, had not yet rung, and the day was far advanced. The first *cameriera* seemed troubled, and whispered her apprehensions that the princess was sick; for she had observed, for some days, she said, that her highness had looked pale.

"But we must go into her room, ladies," added she; "for it is almost time for her highness to visit the duke, and he never forgives an omission of ceremonial. Follow me, then; *I* will undertake to awaken the princess."

She opened the door softly, and entered the sleeping-room of the princess, followed by the other maids of honor.

"She sleeps yet," said the *cameriera;* "but I *must* waken her," murmured she to herself, "it is my duty."

She advanced, and drew aside the heavy folds of the pink-silk curtains that hung around the bed.

"Pardon me, your highness," she whispered; "but—"

She stopped; for, to her great surprise, the princess was awake. She lay in her long white night-dress, with her hands crossed over her

*Caroline Pichler, "Memoirs of My Life." Part I. page 139.

breast, and her head cushioned on the rose-colored pillow that contrasted painfully with the pallor of her marble-white face. Her large eyes were distended, and fixed upon a picture of the blessed Virgin that hung at the foot of the bed. Slowly her looks turned upon her attendants, who, breathless and frightened, gazed upon the rosy pillow, and the pallid face that lay in its midst, dazzling their eyes with its whiteness.

"Pardon me," again whispered the *cameriera*, "it is almost noonday."

"What hour?" murmured the princess.

"It is ten o'clock, your highness."

The princess shivered, and exclaimed, "For three days, then!" And turning away, she began to pray in a low voice, and none but God knew the meaning of that whispered prayer.

Her prayer over, she passed her little white hand over the dark locks that fell around her face and made an effort to rise.

Her maids of honor saw that she was ill, and hastened to assist her. The hour of the princess's toilet was to her attendants the most delightful hour of the day. From her bedchamber all ceremonial was banished; and there, with her young companions, Isabella was accustomed to laugh, jest, sing, and be as merry and as free from care as the least of her father's subjects.

Philip of Parma was by birth a Spaniard, one of the sons of Philip the Fifth. After the vicissitudes of war which wrested Naples and Parma from the hands of Austria, Don Carlos of Spain became king of Naples, and Don Philip, duke of Parma. Isabella, then a child of seven years, had been allowed the privilege of taking with her to Italy her young playmates, who, for form's sake, as she grew older, became her maids of honor. But they were her dear and chosen friends, and with them she was accustomed to speak the Spanish language only.

Her mother, daughter of Louis XV., had introduced French customs into the court of Parma, and during her life the gayety and grace of French manners had rendered that court one of the most attractive in Europe. But the lovely Duchess of Parma died, and with her died all that made court life endurable. The French language was forbidden, and French customs were banished. Some said that the duke had loved his wife so deeply, that in his grief he had excluded from his court every thing suggestive of his past happiness. Others contended that he had made her life so wretched by his jealous and tyrannical conduct, that remorse had driven him to banish, if possible, every reminder of the woman whom he had almost murdered.

In the hearts of her children the mother's memory was enshrined; and the brother and sister were accustomed for her sake, in their private intercourse, to speak *her* language altogether.

At court they spoke the language of the country; and Isabella—who with her friends sang *boleros* and danced the *cachuca;* with her brother, read Racine and Corneille—was equally happy while she hung enraptured upon the strains of Pergolese's music, or gazed entranced upon the pictures of Correggio and the Veronese. The princess herself was both a painter and musician, and no one, more than she, loved Italy and Italian art.

Such, until this wretched morning, had been the life of young Isabella. What was she now? A cold, white image, in whose staring eyes the light was quenched—from whose blanched lips the smile had fled forever!

Her grieved attendants could scarcely suppress their tears, as sadly and silently they arrayed her in her rich robes; while she, not seeming to know where she was, gazed at her own reflected image, with a look of stupid horror. They dressed her beautiful hair, and bound it up in massy braids. They smoothed it over her death-cold forehead, and shuddered to see how like a corpse she looked. At last the task was at an end, and the *cameriera* coming toward her, offered the cup of chocolate which she was accustomed to drink at that hour. Tenderly she besought the unhappy girl to partake of it, but Isabella waved away the cup, saying:

"Dear friend, offer me no earthly food. I pine for the banquet of angels. Let the chaplain be called to bring the *viaticum*. I wish to receive the last sacraments of the dying."

A cry of horror burst from the lips of the maids of honor.

"The chaplain! The last sacraments! For you, my beloved child?" asked the sobbing *cameriera*.

"For me," replied Isabella.

"Heavenly Father!" exclaimed the *aja*. "Have you then presumed to anticipate the will of God, and to go before His presence, uncalled?"

"No, no, death will come to me, I will not seek it. I will endure life as long as God wills, but, in three days, I shall be called hence."

The young girls crowded around her, weeping, and imploring her not to leave them.

Isabella's white lips parted with a strange smile. "You tell me not to die, dear friends; do you not see that I am already dead? My heart is bleeding."

The hand of the *cameriera* was laid upon her arm, and she whispered: "My child, be silent; you know not what you say."

Isabella bowed her head, and then looking tenderly around at her kneeling companions, she said: "Rise and sit by me, my dear girls, and listen to what I am about to say, for we speak together for the last time on earth."

The maidens arose, and obeyed, while Isabella leaned her head for a few moments upon the bosom of her mother's friend, the *cameriera*. There was a pause, during which the poor girl seemed to have received some comfort in those friendly arms; for she finally sighed, and, raising her head again, she spoke solemnly, but not unnaturally.

"I had last night a singular vision," she said. "The spirit of my mother appeared to me, and said that in three days I was to die. I believe in this vision. Do not weep, dear sisters; I go to eternal rest. Life is bitter, death is sweet. Pray for me, that my mother's prophetic words be verified; and you, beloved friend of that mother," added she, kissing the *cameriera's* cheek, "you who know the depths of my heart, and its secret, silent agony, pray for your child, and praying, ask of her heavenly Father—death."

The *aja* made no reply, she was weeping with the others.

Isabella contemplated the group for a moment, while a ray of life lit up her eyes, showing that, even now, it was sad to part from her friends forever. But the expression was momentary. Her face returned to its deadly paleness, as gasping for breath, she stammered: "Now—now—for—my father! Estrella, go to the apartments of the duke, and say that I desire an interview with his royal highness."

The young girl returned in a few moments with an answer. His royal highness had that morning gone some distance in the country on a hunting excursion, and would be absent for several days.

Isabella looked at the *cameriera*, who still stood beside her, and her pale lips quivered. "Did I not know it?" whispered she; "I told you truly, HE did it! God forgive him, I cannot.—And now," continued she, aloud, "now to my last earthly affairs."

So saying, she called for her caskets of jewels and divided them between the young maids of honor; and cutting from her hair one rich, massy lock, she placed it in Estrella's hand, saying, "Share it among you all."

To the *cameriera* she gave a sealed packet, and then bade them leave her to herself; for the ringing of the chapel bell announced the departure of the priest thence, with the blessed sacrament.

The sacred rites were ended. On her knees the Princess Isabella had made her confession, and had revealed to the shuddering priest the horrible secrets of the preceding night. She had received absolution, and had partaken of the holy communion.

"Now, my child," said the priest, in a voice tremulous with sympathy, "you have received the blessing of God, and you are prepared for His coming. May He be merciful to you, and grant your prayer for release from this earth! I, too, will pray that your martyrdom be short."

"Amen!" softly murmured Isabella.

"But the ways of the Lord are inscrutable, and it may be that He wills it otherwise. If, in His incomprehensible wisdom, He should declare that your days shall be long on this earth, promise me to endure your lot with resignation, nor seek to hasten what He has deemed it best to delay?"

"I promise, holy father."

"Make a vow, then, to the Lord, that by the memory of your mother you will fulfil every duty that presents itself to you in life, until God has spoken the word that will call you to Himself."

"I swear, by the memory of my mother, that I will live a life of resignation and of usefulness until God in His mercy, shall free me from my prison."

"Right, dear unhappy child," said the father, smoothing, with his trembling hands, the soft hair that lay on either side of her forehead. "May God reward thee, and in His infinite mercy shorten thy sufferings!"

He stooped, and kissing her pale brow, made the sign of the cross above her kneeling figure. Then, with eyes blinded by tears, he slowly retreated to his own room, where he threw himself upon his knees and prayed that God would give strength to them both to bear the cross of that dreadful secret.

Isabella, too, remained alone. In feverish longing for death, she sat, neither hearing the voices of her friends who begged for admission, nor the pleadings of her brother, who besought her to see him and give him one last embrace. Through the long night that followed, still kneeling, she prayed. When the sun rose, she murmured, "To-morrow!" and through the day her fancy wandered to the verge of madness. Sometimes visions of beckoning angels swarmed around her; then they fled, and in their places stood a hideous skeleton, that, with ghastly smile, held out his fleshless hand, and strove to clasp hers.

Again the night set in, and the next morning at break of day, Isabella rose from her knees, and, hailing the rising sun, cried exultingly, "To-day!"

Exhausted from fasting and such long vigils, her head reeled, and she staggered to her couch. A cold shudder crept over her limbs; all was dark as night about her; she tried to clasp her hands in prayer and could not, for they were numb and powerless. "This is welcome death!" thought she, and her lips parted with a happy smile. Her head fell backward on the pillow, and her senses fled.

CHAPTER XIV.

THE AMBASSADOR EXTRAORDINARY.

THE Princess Isabella opened her eyes, and in their dark and lustrous depths shone returning reason; they glared no more with fever-madness, but were sadder and sweeter than ever.

She gazed at the forms that surrounded her bedside; at the priest, who, with folded hands, was praying at her head; at the *cameriera*, who knelt beside him; at the young girls, who, gathered in a lovely group at her feet, smiled and wept by turns as she looked upon them; and lastly, she felt a kiss upon her hand, and, looking there, she beheld her brother, who wept with joy.

"Where am I?" asked she, feebly.

"You are with those who love you best, darling," said Fernando, joyfully. "With us, who have prayed so long, that the good God has heard and restored you to life."

"I still live, then," said she, sadly. "And how long have I lain here, friends?"

The priest advanced, and blessing her, took her by the hand. "For four weeks, daughter, you have been unconscious of every thing that passed around you. You see, therefore, that your heavenly Father bids you live."

"Four weeks?" whispered the poor girl. "Then, in three months we shall meet again."

She closed her eyes, and lay silent for a while. At length, the priest, bending close to her ear, whispered, "Think, daughter, of the vows, which, by the memory of your mother, you have made to God!"

"I will remember them," murmured she, sadly.

And from this day she mended, until life and strength were restored to her even as before. She thought of her vow, and made no resistance to the will of Heaven; but she hoped for death, and awaited her three months.

Sustained by these hopes, she recovered. But her heart was wounded past all cure; gone were her smiles and her songs. Quietly, sadly, and solemnly glided away the new life to which she had been born through death.

The first day on which she felt able to leave her room, she sent to crave an audience of her father. She had been told that, during her delirium, he had often visited her chamber; but, since her convalescence, he had not sent so much as an inquiry after her health.

He did not, however, deny the interview she sought. He awaited his daughter, said the messenger, in his own apartments.

The princess shuddered, and a deadly faintness came over her.

"My God! my God! will I ever be able to go through this bitter hour? Must I, indeed, look upon him who—"

She closed her eyes to shut out the frightful remembrance. Then, gathering all her strength for the trial, she rose to seek her father, and make one last request of him.

With her head thrown proudly back, and her dark eyes flashing with resolve, she entered his cabinet.

The duke was entirely alone. He had dismissed his attendants, and now stood in the centre of the room, awaiting his daughter in gloomy silence. His cold, stern features had grown more repulsive than ever to the unhappy girl; his piercing eyes more revengeful; his thin, pale lips more cruel. He seemed to her a pitiless stranger, and she could not advance to meet him. Powerless and faint, she stood at the door; all her strength gone.

A few moments of anguish went by, and then the duke, extending his hand, said, in a tone of command, "Come hither, Isabella."

She stepped forward, and almost touched his hand, when, shuddering, her arm dropped heavily down, and, forgetting all caution, she murmured, in tones of deepest agony, "I cannot! I cannot!"

The duke's eyes shot fire, as he, too, dropped his extended hand, and deep, angry folds wrinkled his forehead.

"Why have you desired this interview?" asked he.

"I have a request to prefer, my father," replied Isabella.

He bent his head. "Speak," said he.

"I come to entreat of my father the permission to take the veil."

"And wherefore, I should like to know?" said the duke, carelessly.

"That I may dedicate my few remaining days to the service of the Lord."

"Girlish folly!" said he, with a contemptuous laugh, while he paced up and down the room.

Isabella made no reply, but stood awaiting a more direct answer to her petition. Suddenly, he came up to her, and spoke:

"I cannot grant your request," said he. "I have other plans for you. The grandchild of the King of Spain cannot be permitted to die a penitent in a cloister; if she has atonement to make for crime, let her make it, not under the serge of the nun, but under the purple of the empress."

"I have no ambition," said Isabella, trembling. "Allow me, I entreat you, to enter a convent."

"I repeat that I have other plans for you. I, too, have no ambition for *you*," said the father, coldly, "but I am ambitious for my house, and through you I shall attain my end. One of the greatest monarchs of Europe has sought your hand for the heir of her throne, and I have resolved that you shall become his wife."

"Fate will refuse it to him—Fate, more merciful than my father. I have but a few weeks to live—before a month has elapsed, I shall be in my grave."

"Go there, if it pleases you," cried the duke, "but die with royal robes about you. You shall not die a nun."

"No one on earth, my father, has a right to detain me. If your highness refuse your consent, I will fly to a convent without your permission. And princely though you be, you shall not drag from the altar the bride of the Lord."

"Ah, you rebel against my authority!" cried the duke, with a look that sent a deadly pang to the heart of his daughter. "Know, that I have power to judge you for such treason, and lay your defiant head upon the block!"

"I do not fear death," replied Isabella; "I await it with impatience."

"Ah! you are possessed with a lovesick desire to die! But hear what I have to say, and mark it well. I will relate to you an affair that took place—whilst you were ill. The only son of one of the noblest families in Parma, the pride of his race, and the idol of his parents, conceived a plot against my house, whose treason was equal to parricide. I learned his designs; and with my own eyes and my own ears, I verified his guilt. He was an archtraitor; he had deserved to die on the scaffold. But I had pity on his family, and spared them the disgrace of a public execution. I took his life secretly, and his parents are spared the shame of knowing how he died. Shall I tell you the name of this dead traitor?"

Isabella raised her hand, and parting her blanched lips, she said hoarsely, "No no! in mercy, no!"

"Very well, then I proceed. This traitor, whom I judged, and to whom I dealt his death-stab, had an accomplice. Do you listen?"

Like a broken lily, Isabella's head sank down upon her breast.

"Ah! you listen. The accomplice is placed in a position which makes it inexpedient for me to punish her in her own person. But should she thwart me, should she not fully and cheerfully comply with my demands upon her loyalty, I will see that she suffers more than death in the family of her accomplice. I shall publish the guilt of the dead criminal to the whole world; I will disgrace and dishonor his whole race, and his young sister, with her parents, shall be driven penniless from my realms, to beg or starve in a stranger land."

"Father!" cried the wretched girl, while her every limb quivered with the torture he inflicted, "I am ready to do your will. I will marry whom you choose, and so long as God condemns me to earth, I will obey you in all things. But you shall promise me on your princely honor to shield from all shame or harm the family of—of—the deceased; to befriend his sister, and if she should ever wish to marry, to honor and favor her choice. Promise me this, and as long as I live I submit to your will."

"I promise, on my honor, to do all this, and to forget for their sakes the crime of their son."

"I promise also, on my sacred honor, to accept the husband you have chosen for me. But I will not suffer long, for my life is almost spent."

The duke shrugged his shoulders.

"Your highness," continued his daughter, "will inform me on what day I am to be affianced. I await your commands, and beg your highness's permission to withdraw to my apartments."

"Have you nothing more to say to your father, Isabella?" asked he in a faltering voice.

"Nothing more to say to your royal highness." She courtesied deeply, and, without a glance at her father, left the room.

The duke looked after her with an expression of sorrow. "I have lost her forever!" said he. "When I struck him, I pierced her heart also. Well, so let it be! Better a dead child than a dishonored house!"

He then rang a little golden bell, and ordered preparations to be made for another grand hunt on the morrow.

Isabella accepted her destiny nobly. She resolved to fulfil her promises strictly; but she hoped that God would be satisfied with the sacrifice, and release her before the day of her nuptials.

Finally came the day on which, for the third time, she had hoped to die. She felt a solemn joy steal over her heart, and she desired her maids of honor to deck her in bridal white. Her dark hair was wreathed with orange-blossoms, and in her bosom she wore an orange-bud. She was lovely beyond expression, and her attendants whispered among themselves, though Isabella neither saw nor heard them. She who awaited death took no heed of what was going on around her in the palace.

And yet her stake in that palace was great. On the day before the embassy had arrived, which was to change her fate, and open to her a new life at the court of the Austrian empress.

The duke had received his guests with royal courtesy. But he had besought the count to postpone his interview with the princess until the morrow; for with cruel mockery of his child's sorrow, Philip of Parma had contrived that the day on which she had hoped to meet her dead lover, should be the day of her betrothal to the Archduke of Austria.

Isabella was the only person in the palace who had not heard of the arrival. She had withdrawn into her private cabinet, and there she counted every pulsation of her heart. She dared not hope to die a natural death; she was looking forward to some accident that was to release her from life; something direct from the hand of God she thought would, on that day, make good the prophecy of her lover.

She hoped, watched, prayed. She was startled from her solitude by a knocking at the door, and her father's voice called for admission.

The princes, obedient to her promise, rose and opened the door. Her father surveyed her with a smile of derision. "You have done well," said he, "to deck yourself as a bride; not as the bride of Death, but as the affianced wife of the *living* lover who will one day make you empress of Austria. His ambassador awaits us now in the great hall of state. Follow me into the next room, where your maids of honor are assembled to attend you. Mark me, Isabella! When we arrive in the hall, the ambassador will advance, and in terms befitting the honor conferred, he will request your acceptance of the archduke's hand. I leave it to your tact and discretion to answer him as becomes the princess of a great and royal house."

"And will your highness perform your promise to *me?*" asked Isabella calmly. "Shall his parents live secure in possession of their noble name and estates; and shall his sister be the special object of your highness's protection and favor?"

"I will do all this, provided you give me satisfaction as relates to your marriage."

Isabella bowed. "Then I am ready to accompany your royal highness to the hall of state, and to accept with courtesy the offer of the Austrian ambassador."

Forth went the beautiful martyr and her train through the gorgeous apartments of the palace, until they reached the hall of the throne.

In the centre of the hall the duke left his daughter and her attendants, while he mounted the throne and took his seat upon the ducal chair.

And now advanced Count Bathiany. With all the fervor which her matchless beauty inspired, he begged of the princess her fair hand for his future sovereign the Archduke of Austria. As the count ceased, every eye turned toward the infanta. She had listened with calm dignity to the words of the ambassador, and her large, melancholy eyes had been riveted upon his face while he delivered his errand. There was a pause—a few moments were needed by that broken heart to hush its moanings, and bare itself for the sacrifice. The brow of the duke darkened, and he was about to interpose, when he saw his daughter bow her head. Then she spoke, and every one bent forward to listen to the silvery tones of her voice.

"I feel deeply honored," said she, "by the preference of her imperial majesty of Austria; an alliance with her eldest son is above my deserts; but since it is their desire, I accept the great honor conferred upon me. I regret, however, that their majesties should have directed their choice toward me; for I am convinced that I shall not live long enough to fulfil the destiny to which this marriage calls me." *

When at last the ceremonies of this day of agony were ended; when the infanta had dismissed her ladies of honor, and was once more alone—alone with God and with the past, she threw herself upon her couch, and, with her hands meekly folded across her breast, she lay, looking up, far beyond the palace dome to heaven.

There she prayed until midnight, and when the clock had told the hour, she arose to the new life that awaited her, with its new promises, new expectations, new ties—but no new hopes.

"Heavenly Father," exclaimed she, "it has begun, and I will bear it to the bitter end! I am now the betrothed, and soon will be the wife of another. If I have sinned in my consent to marry one whom I can never love, pardon me, O Lord! and hear me vow that I will faithfully fulfil my duty toward him. I am the affianced of another! Farewell, my beloved, farewell, FOR THREE LONG YEARS!"

CHAPTER XV.

THE DREAM OF LOVE.

THE wedding-festival was over, and Vienna was resting from the fatigue of the brilliant entertainments by which the marriage of the archduke had been followed, both in court and city. And indeed the rejoicings had been conducted with imperial magnificence. For eight days, the people of Vienna, without respect of rank, had been admitted to the palace, to witness the court festivities; while in the city and at Schönbrunn, nightly balls were given at the expense of the empress, where the happy Viennese danced and feasted to their hearts' content.

* The infanta's own words; as veritably historical as is this whole relation of her death-prophecy and its unhappy fulfilment. See Wraxall, "Memoirs of the Courts," etc., and Caroline Pichler.

They had returned the bounty of their sovereign by erecting triumphal arches, strewing the ground with flowers, and rending the air with shouts, whenever the young archduchess had appeared in the streets.

The great *maestro* Gluck had composed an opera for the occasion; and when, on the night of its representation, the empress made her appearance in the imperial *loge*, followed by the archduke and his bride, the enthusiasm of the people was so great that Gluck waited a quarter of an hour, *bâton* in hand, before he could begin his overture.

But now the jubilee was over, the shouts were hushed, the people had returned to their accustomed routine of life, and the exchequer of the empress was minus—one million of florins.

The court had withdrawn to the palace of Schönbrunn, there to enjoy in privacy the last golden days of autumn, as well as to afford to the newly-married pair a taste of that retirement so congenial to lovers.

Maria Theresa, always munificent, had devoted one wing of the palace to the exclusive use of her young daughter-in-law; and her apartments were fitted up with the last degree of splendor. Elegant mirrors, *buhl* and gilded furniture, costly turkey carpets and exquisite paintings, adorned this princely home; and as the princess was known to be skilled both as a painter and musician, one room was fitted up for her as a studio, and another as a music-hall.

From the music-room, a glass door led to a balcony filled with rare and beautiful flowers. This balcony overlooked the park, and beyond was seen the city, made lovely by the soft gray veil of distance, which lends such beauty to a landscape.

On this perfumed balcony sat the youthful pair. Isabella reclined in an arm-chair; and at her feet on a low ottoman sat Joseph, looking up into her face, his eyes beaming with happiness. It was a lovely sight—that of these two young creatures, who, in the sweet, still evening, sat together, unveiling to one another the secrets of two blameless hearts, and forgetting rank, station, and the world, were tasting the pure joys of happily wedded love.

The evening breeze whispered Nature's soft low greeting to them both; and through the myrtle-branches that, hanging over the balcony, clustered around Isabella's head, the setting sun flung showers of gold that lit up her face with the glory of an angel. Bright as an angel seemed she to her husband, who, sitting at her feet, gazed enraptured upon her. How graceful he thought the contour of her oval face; how rich the scarlet of her lovely mouth; what noble thoughts were written on her pale and lofty brow, and how glossy were the masses of her raven black hair! And those wondrous eyes! Dark and light, lustrous and dim, at one moment they flashed with intellect, at another they glistened with unshed tears. Her form, too, was slender and graceful, for Nature had denied her nothing; and the charm of her appearance (above all, to an eye weary of splendor) was made complete by the vapory muslin dress that fell around her perfect figure like a silver-white cloud. The only ornament that flecked its snow was a bunch of pink roses, which the archduke with his own hand had culled for his wife that morning. She wore them in her bosom, and they were the crowning beauty of that simple, elegant dress.

Isabella's head rested amongst the myrtle-branches; her eyes were fixed upon the heavens, with a look of ineffable sadness, and gradually the smile had died from her lips. Her countenance contrasted singularly with that of the archduke. Since his marriage, he had grown handsomer than ever; and from his bright expressive face beamed the silent eloquence of a young and joyful existence.

In his joy he did not see the painful shadows that were darkening his wife's pale beauty. For a while, a deep stillness was about them. Flooded by the gold of the setting sun, lay the park at their feet; farther off glimmered the domes of St. Stephen at Vienna, and faint over the evening air came the soothing tones of the vesper-bell.

"How beautiful is the world!" said Joseph, at length; and, at the sound of his voice, suddenly breaking the stillness that had been so congenial to her reveries, Isabella started. A slight shiver ran through her frame, and her eyes unwillingly came back to earth. He did not see it. "Oh, how lovely is life, my Isabella, now that the music of thy heart replies to mine! Never has earth seemed to me so full of beauty, as it does now that I call thee wife."

Isabella laid her soft hand upon her husband's head, and looked at him for a while. At length she stifled a sigh, and said, "Are you then happy, my husband?"

He drew down the little hand that was resting on his blonde curls, and kissed it fervently. "A boon, my beloved. When we are alone, let us banish Spanish fomality from our intercourse. Be the future empress before the world, but to me be my wife, and call me 'thou.'"

"I will," replied she, blushing. "And I repeat my question, art thou happy, my husband?"

"I will tell thee, dearest. There seems within me such a flood of melody seeking voice, that sometimes, for very ecstasy, I feel as if I must shout aloud all the pent-up joy that other men have frittered away from boyhood, and I have garnered up for this hour. Again I feel intoxicated with happiness, and fear that I am dreaming. I tremble lest some rude hand awake me, and I look around for proof of my sober, waking bliss. I find it, and then breaks forth my soul in hosannas to God. And when, mingling among men, I see a face that looks sad or pale, I feel such sympathy for him who is less happy than I, that I make vows, when I am emperor, to heal all sorrow, and wipe away all tears. Then come great and noble aspirations, and I long to give back to my people the blessings with which they greeted thee, my own Isabella. This is not one feeling, but the meeting of many. Is it happiness, dearest?"

"I cannot tell," replied she; "for happiness is a thing so heavenly in its nature, that one hardly dares to give it a name, lest it take flight, and soar back to its home above the skies. Let us not press it too closely, lest we seek it and it be gone."

"We shall do as it pleases thee," said Joseph, snatching her two hands, and pressing them to his heart. "I know that when thou art by, Happiness is here, and she cannot go back to heaven, unless she take thee too." And again he looked at his wife, as if he would fain have blended their dual being into one.

"I wish to make thee a confession, Isabel," resumed he. "It is a great crime, dearest, but thou wilt give me absolution, I know. As I look back, I can scarce believe it myself, but—hear. When the empress gave me thy miniature, beautiful though it was, I gave my consent to marry, but my heart was untouched. When Count

Bathiany departed on his mission, I prayed that every obstacle might encumber his advance: and oh, my beloved! when I heard that thou wert coming, I almost wished thee buried under Alpine avalanches. When I was told of thy arrival, I longed to fly away from Vienna, from rank and royalty, to some far country, some secluded spot, where no reasons of state policy would force me to give my hand to an unknown bride. Was I not a barbarian, sweetest, was I not an arch-traitor?"

"No, thou wert only a boy-prince, writhing under the heavy load of thy royalty."

"No, I was a criminal; but oh, how I have expiated my sin! When I saw thee my heart leaped into life; and now it trembles lest thou love not *me!* But thou wilt love me, wilt thou not? thou who hast made me so happy that I wish I had a hundred hearts; for one is not enough to contain the love I feel for thee!" *

Isabella was gazing at him with a melancholy smile. "Dreamer!" said she, in a low trembling tone, that sounded to Joseph like heavenly music—"dreamer! the heart that through God's goodness is filled with love is of itself supernaturally magnified; for love is a revelation from heaven."

"Sweet priestess of love! how truly thou art the interpreter of our passion! For it is *ours*, my Isabella, is it not? It is *our* love of which we speak, not *mine* alone. I have confessed to thee; now do the same by me. Tell me, my wife, didst thou hate the man to whom thy passive hand was given, without one thought of thee or of thy heart's predilections?"

How little he guessed the torture he inflicted! He looked into her eyes with such trusting faith, with such calm security of happiness, that her sweet face beamed with tender pity, while her cheeks deepened into scarlet blushes, as she listened to his passionate declarations of love. Poor Isabella!

"No," said she, "no, I never hated thee, Joseph. I had already heard enough to feel esteem for my future husband; and, therefore, I did not hate, I pitied him."

"Pity him, my own, and wherefore?"

"Because without consulting *his* heart, he was affianced to an unknown girl, unworthy to be the partner of his brilliant destiny. Poor Isabella of Parma was never made to be an empress, Joseph."

"She was, she was! She is fit to be empress of the world, for all poetry, all goodness, all intellect and beauty look out from the depths of her lustrous eyes. Oh, look upon me, star of my life, and promise to guide me ever with thy holy light!"

So saying, he took her in his arms, and pressed her to his tender, manly heart.

"Promise me, beloved," whispered he, "promise never to leave me."

"I promise," said the pale wife, "never to forsake thee, until God calls me hence to—"

"Oh!" interrupted Joseph, "may that hour never strike till I be in heaven to receive thee; for love is selfish, Isabella, and my daily prayer is now, that thy dear hand may close my eyes."

"God will not hear that prayer, Joseph," replied Isabella; and as she spoke, her head sank upon his shoulder, and her long hair fell from its fastening, and, like a heavy mourning-veil, shrouded

* These are his own words. Caroccioli "Life of Joseph II."

them both. Her husband held her close to his heart, and as he kissed her, she felt his tears drop upon her cheek.

"I do not know," said he, "why it is, but I feel sometimes as if a tempest were gathering above my head. And yet, the heavens are cloudless, the sun has set; and see, the moon rises, looking in her pale beauty, even as thou dost, my love. She has borrowed loveliness from thee to-night, for, surely, she was never so fair before. But all seems lovely when thou art near, and, I think, that, perchance—thou lovest me. Tell me, Isabella, tell me, dearest, that thou dost love me."

She raised her head, and met his passionate gaze with a look so sad that his heart grew cold with apprehension. Then her eyes turned heavenward, and her lips moved. He knew that she was praying. But why, at such a moment?

"Tell me the truth!" cried he, vehemently—"tell me the truth!"

"I cannot answer thee in words," murmured Isabella, "but thou shalt have music—love's own interpreter. Come, let us go into the music-room."

And, light as a fairy, she tripped before, opening herself the door, though he strove to prevent her.

"No, this is *my* temple, and my hands unclose the doors," said she, once more self-possessed.

Her husband followed her, enchanted. She looked around at the various instruments, and struck a few chords on the piano.

"No. This is too earthly. My own favorite instrument shall speak for me."

So saying, she opened a case that lay on the table, and took from it a violin.

"This," said she to her husband, "is the violin that came with me from Italy."

"How, Isabella," exclaimed he, "dost thou play on my favorite instrument?"

"The violin, to me, is dear above all instruments," replied she; "it alone has tones that respond to those of the human heart." *

With indescribable grace she raised the violin to her shoulder, and began to play. At first her chords were light and airy as the sounds from an Æolian harp; then the melody swelled until it broke into a gush of harmony that vibrated through every chord of the archduke's beating heart. As he stood breathless and entranced, she seemed to him like that picture, by Fiesole, of the angel that comforts the dying. This picture had always been, above all others, the archduke's favorite, and now it stood embodied before him, a living, breathing divinity.

The music died away to his ear, though still she played; but now it seemed to stream from her eyes that shone like luminous stars, and flow from her softly moving lips, that whispered to the spirits which now low, now loud, laughed, sighed, or sobbed out their responses from the magic violin.

Isabella was no longer a woman and his wife. She was a glorified spirit; and now he trembled lest his angel should vanish, and leave him nothing but the memory of a heavenly vision. His eyes filled with tears; a convulsive sigh broke from his breast, and, burying his face in his hands, he sank down upon the sofa.

* The infanta, who played on several instruments, excelled on the violin. Wraxall, vol. ii., page 390.

A light shudder ran through Isabella's frame; her eyes, which had wandered far, far beyond the portals that shut us out from heaven, looked wildly around. Her husband's sigh had awakened her from a blissful dream, and once more her weary heart sank desolate to the earth. But with an expression of tenderest pity she turned toward him and smiled. Then her music changed; it pealed out in rich harmony, fit for mortal ears. She saw her complete mastery over the archduke's soul; his eyes grew bright and joyful once more, and from his countenance beamed the light of perfect contentment.

"Our *epithalamium!*" exclaimed he, overjoyed, and no longer able to control his exultation, he darted from his seat, and clasped the dear musician in his arms.

"I thank thee, my Isabella," said he, with a voice that trembled with excess of happiness. "Yes, this is the voice of love; thou hast answered me with our wedding-song. In this melody is drowned every bitter remembrance of my life; the discords of the past have melted into richest harmony—for thou returnest my love. A thousand times I thank thee; this hour is sacred to me forever.

"Thou hast said that thou lovest me," continued the happy husband, "and now I feel the power and strength of a god. I am ready for the battle of life."

"But I think that I saw the god weep. Poor mortal friend, gods shed no tears—tears are the baptism of humanity."

"Oh, gods must weep for joy, Isabella, else they could not feel its perfection!"

"May Heaven grant that thou weep no other tears!" said the wife, solemnly. "But hear," continued she, raising her little hand, "the palace clock strikes eight, and we promised her majesty to spend this evening with the imperial family circle. We must be punctual, and I have scarcely time to dress."

"Why, wilt thou change that sweet simple dress? Art thou not always the pride of the court? Come—thy muslin and roses will shame all the silk and jewels of my sisters. Come!"

She laid her hand gently upon the arm that drew her forward, and courtesied before him with mock ceremony.

"My lord and husband," said she, laughing, "although your imperial highness has banished Madame Etiquette from our balcony, remember that she stands grimly awaiting us by yonder door, and we must take her with us into the presence of our august empress. Madame Etiquette would never permit me to pass in this simple dress. She would order me indignantly from her sight, and your highness also. Go, therefore, and don your richest Spanish habit. In fifteen minutes I await your highness here."

She made another deep courtesy. The archduke, taking up the jest, approached her, and, kissing her hand, replied:

"I obey your imperial highness, as your loyal husband and loving subject. I shall deck myself with stars and orders; and in princely splendor I shall return, as becomes the spouse of the archduchess of Austria. Your highness's obedient servant."

And in true Spanish fashion, he bent his knee and kissed the hem of her robe. Backing out of her presence he bowed again as he reached the door, but catching her laughing eyes, he suddenly dashed right over Madame Etiquette, and catching his wife in his arms, he gave her a last and a right burgher-like kiss. The archduke was very happy, and the archduchess—well! One day God will reward her!

As the door closed, the expression of her face changed. The smile died from her lips, and her eyes were dim with tears.

"Poor boy!" murmured she, "he loves me, and I—I suffer him to believe that I return his love, while— But I am right," said the devoted girl, and she clasped her hands convulsively together.

"O my Saviour!" cried she, "in mercy give me grace while I live, to be true to the vows, that before thine altar, I have sworn to the Archduke of Austria! It were cruel in me to wound his noble heart—cruel to awake him from his dream of love! Let him at least be happy while I live; and Lord give me strength that I faint not under my burden!"

CHAPTER XVI.

GLUCK.

THE sun had risen, flooding the earth with light, and the people of Vienna had already begun their labors for the day. But the curtains had not yet been drawn from a richly-furnished room, whose walls were lined with books; and in whose centre stood a table covered with papers, whereon the lights, not yet extinguished, were dropping their waxen tears from two lofty silver candelabra. At this table sat a man, looking earnestly at a paper covered with notes of music. He had sat there the whole night long, and his countenance gave no indication of the exhaustion that follows upon night-watching. His large, dark, gray eyes flashed whenever he raised his head thoughtfully, as he frequently did; and when music was born of his thoughts, a smile illuminated his otherwise plain face, and a wonderful light played about his magnificent forehead; the glory of that genius which had made it her dwelling-place.

The form of this man was as striking as his face. Tall and commanding in stature, his wide shoulders seemed proudly to bear the weight of the head that towered above them, and in his lofty bearing there was a dignity that betokened either rank or genius.

He had both; for this man was Christopher von Gluck, son of a huntsman of Prince Eugene, who was born in 1714, in the village of Weidenwang.

This son of the poor huntsman was known throughout all Europe; and in Italy, the nobles in their palaces and the people on the streets sang the melodies of *Phedra*, *Antigone*, *Semiramide*, and *Telemacco*. In Germany he was less known; and in Vienna alone, was he truly appreciated.

There he sat, unconscious of the daylight. On a chair at his side lay a violin and a flute; near them, a violoncello leaned against the wall, and within reach of his hand stood one of those upright pianos just then coming into fashion.

At one moment he wrote rapidly, at another he hummed a melody; again, half declaiming, half singing, he read off a *recitative;* and then bent over and wrote with all his might. The light began to smoke, and the wax dropped over his music, but he saw none of it; neither saw he the daylight that had replaced his candles. He was so absorbed in his work as not to hear a knock at his door.

But now the knock was repeated; and this time so distinctly that it waked him from his dream of harmony, and he frowned. He rose, and striding to the door, withdrew the bolt.

The door opened, and a tall, elegant woman, in a tasteful morning-dress came in. Her fine, regular features were disturbed, and her eyes were red with weeping or watching. When she saw Gluck looking so fresh and vigorous, she smiled, and said, "Heaven be praised, you are alive and well! I have passed a night of anxious terror on your account."

"And why, Marianne?" asked he, his brow unbent, and his face beaming with tenderness; for Gluck idolized his beautiful wife.

She looked at his quiet, inquiring face, and broke into a merry laugh.

"Oh, the barbarian," cried she, "not to know of what he has been guilty of! Why, Christopher, look at those burnt-out wax lights—look at the daylight wondering at you through your curtains. Last night, at ten o'clock, I lit these candles, and you promised to work for only two hours more. Look at them now, and see what you have been doing."

"Indeed, I do believe that I have been here all night," said Gluck, with *naïve* astonishment. "But I assure you, Marianne, that I fully intended to go to bed at the end of two hours. Is it my fault if the night has seemed so short? Twelve hours since we parted? Can it be?"

He went to the window and drew the curtains. "Day!" cried he, "and the sun so bright!" He looked out with a smile; but suddenly his brow grew thoughtful, and he said in a low voice:

"Oh, may the light of day shine upon me also!"

His wife laid her hand upon his arm. "And upon whom falls the light of day, if not upon you?" asked she, reproachfully. "Look back upon your twenty operas, and see each one bearing its laurel-wreath, and shouting to the world your fame! And now look into the future, and see their unborn sisters, whose lips one day will open to the harmony of your music, and will teach all nations to love your memory! And I, Christopher, I believe more in your future than in your past successes. If I did not, think you that I would indulge you as I do in your artistic eccentricities, and sit like a lovelorn maiden outside of this door, my ear strained to listen for your breathing—dreading lest some sudden stroke should have quenched the light of that genius which you overtask—yet daring not to ask entrance, lest my presence should affright your other loves, the Muses? Yes, my dear husband, I have faith in the power of your genius; and for you this glorious sun has risen to-day. Chase those clouds from the heaven of your brow. They are ill-timed."

In the height of her enthusiasm she twined her arms around his neck, and rested her head upon Gluck's bosom.

He bent down and kissed her forehead. "Then, my wife has faith, not in what I have done, but in what I can do? Is it so, love?"

"It is, Christopher. I believe in the power of your genius."

Gluck's face wore an expression of triumph as she said this, and he smiled. His smile was very beautiful, and ever, when she saw it, his wife felt a thrill of happiness. Never had it seemed to her so full of heavenly inspiration.

"Since such is your faith in me, my Egeria, you will then have courage to hear what I have to tell. Tear away the laurel-wreaths from my past works, Marianne—burn them to ashes. They are dust, and to dust they will surely return. Their mirth and their melody, their pomp and their pathos, are all lies. They are not the true children of inspiration—they are impostors. They are the offspring of our affected and falsely sentimental times, and deserve not immortality. Away with them! A new day shall begin for me, or I shall hide my head in bitter solitude, despising my race, who applaud the juggler, and turn away in coldness from the veritable *artiste.*"

"What!" exclaimed Marianne, "those far-famed operas that delight the world—are they nothing more than clever deceptions?"

"Nothing more," cried Gluck. "They did not gush from the holy fount of inspiration; they were composed and arranged to suit the taste of the public and the dexterity of the singers, who, if they trill and juggle with their voices, think that they have reached the summit of musical perfection. But this must no longer be. I have written for time, I shall now work for immortality. Let me interpret what the angels have whispered, and then you shall hear a language which nothing but music can translate. What are the lame efforts of speech by the side of its thrilling tones? Music is a divine revelation, but men have not yet received it in their hearts. *I* have been made its messenger, and I shall speak the message faithfully."

"Ah, Christopher," interposed Marianne, "I fear you will find no followers. If the message be too lofty for the hearers, the messenger will be driven away in disgrace."

"Hear the coward!" cried Gluck vehemently; "see the woman's nature shrinking from the path of honor because it is beset with danger. I did well not to let you know the nature of my last labors, for with your sighs and croakings you would have turned me back again into the highway of falsehood. But you are too late, poltroon. The work is done, and it shall see light." Gluck looked at his wife's face, and the expression he saw there made him pause. He was already sorry, and ready to atone. "No, no! I wrong you, my Egeria: not only are you the wife of my love, but the friend of my genius. Come, dearest, let us brave the world together; and even if that fail us, let us never doubt the might of truth and the glory of its interpreters."

So saying, Gluck reached out his hands; and his wife, with a trusting smile, laid both hers upon them. "How can you doubt me, Christopher?" asked she. "Look back into the past, to the days of our courtship, and say then who was faint-hearted, and who then declared that his little weight of grief was too heavy for those broad shoulders to bear."

"I! I!" confessed Gluck; "but I was in love, and a man in love is always a craven."

"And I suppose," laughed Marianne, "that I was not in love, which will account for my energy and patience on that occasion. To think that my rich father thought me too good for Gluck!—Heaven forgive me, but I could not mourn him as I might have done, had his death not left me free to marry you, you ill-natured giant. Yes! and now that twelve years have gone by, I love you twice as well as I did; and God, who knew there was no room in my heart for other loves, has given me no children, for I long for none. You are to me husband, lover, friend, and—you need not shake your head, sir—you are child, too. Then why have you kept your secrets from me—tell me, traitor, why?"

"Not because you were faint-hearted, my beloved," said Gluck with emotion; "my violent temper wronged us both, when it provoked me to utter a word so false. But genius must labor in secret and in silence; its works are like those enchanted treasures of which we have read—speak of their existence, and lo! they are ashes. Sometimes genius holds an enchanted treasure before the eyes of the *artiste*, who in holy meditation must earn it for himself. One word spoken breaketh the spell, and therefore it was, Marianne, that I spoke not the word. But the treasure is mine; I have earned it, and at my wife's feet I lay it, perchance that she may stand by my side, while the world rejects it as worthless, and heaps obloquy upon my head."

"His will be a bold hand that casts the first stone at the giant!" said Marianne, looking proudly upon the tall and stalwart figure of her husband.

"You call me giant, and that recalls to me a fact which bears upon the subject of our conversation now," said Gluck, with a laugh. "It was the fall of my 'Giant' that first showed me the precipice toward which I, my works, and all my musical predecessors, were hastening."

"You mean your '*Caduta de Giganti*,' which you tried to exhibit before those icy English people?"

"Do not speak against the English, Marianne; they are a good, upright nation. It is not their fault if they are better versed in book-keeping than in music; and I do not know that they are far wrong when they prefer the chink of gold to the strumming and piping which, until now, the world, turning up the whites of its eyes, has called *music*. I, who had been piping and strumming with the rest, suddenly rushed out of the throng, and thrusting my masterpiece in their faces, told them that it was music. Was it their fault if they turned their backs and would not believe me? I think not."

"Oh! you need not excuse the English, Christopher. I know the history of the '*Caduta de Giganti*,' although Master Gluck has never told it me. I know that the young artist met with no favor at English hands; and I know that because his works were not a lame repetition of Italian music and water, the discerning Londoners voted it worthless. I know, too, that Master Gluck, in his distress, took counsel with the great Handel, and besought him to point out the opera's defects. Then said Handel—"

"How, dear prattler, you know what Handel said?"

"I do, Master Gluck. Handel said: 'You have given yourself too much trouble, man. To please the English public you must make a great noise. Give them plenty of brass and sheep-skin.'"

"So he did," cried Gluck, convulsed with laughter. "I followed his advice. I sprinkled the choruses with trumpet and drum, and the second time the opera came out it was a complete success."

Marianne joined in the mirth of her husband.

"But now, if all this is true, why do you like the English?"

"Because my failure in England taught me the utter worthlessness of our present school of music, and inspired me with the desire to reform it."

He drew her arm within his, and seated her on the divan by his side.

CHAPTER XVII.

THE NEW OPERA.

"Now, Marianne," said he, putting his arm around her waist, "hear the secret history of my musical career. I will tell you of the misfortunes which my genius has encountered through life. I begin with England. It is of no use to go back to the privations of my boyhood, though they were many; for hunger and thirst are the tribute that man must pay to fate for the capital which genius gives to him, and which he must increase with all his might and all his strength. Even as a boy, I craved less for bread than for fame; and I consecrated my life and soul to art. I thought that I was in the right way, for I had written eight operas, which the Italians lauded to the skies. But the '*Caduta de Giganti*' was a failure, and 'Artamene' likewise. This double *fiasco* enraged me (you know my bad temper, Marianne). I could not bear to be so misconceived. I was determined to show the English that, in spite of them, I was an *artiste.* I longed to bring them to my feet, as Jupiter did the Titans. So I ordered from one of those poetasters to be found in every land, a sort of *libretto*, called, in theatrical parlance, a lyric drama; and to the words of this monstrosity I arranged the very finest airs of my several operas. When I had completed this musical kaleidoscope I called it 'Pyramus and Thisbe.' I dished up my *olla podrida*, and set it before the hungry English; but they did not relish it. The public remained cold, and, what was far worse, I remained cold myself. I thought over this singular result, and wondered how it was that music which, as a part of the operas for which it was written, had seemed so full of soul, now faded into insipidity when transplanted to the soil of other dramatic situations. I found the answer in the question. It was *because* I had transplanted my music from its native soil, that its beauty had flown. Then it burst upon my mind that the *libretto* is the father of the opera, the music its mother; and so, if the father be not strong and lusty, the mother will bring forth a sickly offspring, which offspring cannot grow up to perfection. Now, my operas are sickly, for they are the children of an unsound father, who is no true poet."

"Still, still, rash man!" whispered Marianne, looking around as though she feared listeners. "Do you forget that the father of your operas is Metastasio?"

"I remember it too well; for many of my works have perished from their union with his weak and sentimental verses. Perished, in *my* estimation, I mean; for to make my operas passable, I have often been obliged to write fiery music to insipid words; and introduce *fioritures* out of place, that the nightingales might compensate to the world for the shortcomings of the poet. Well, my heart has bled while I wrote such music, and I prayed to God to send me a true poet—one who could write of something else besides love; one who could rise to the height of my own inspiration, and who could develop a genuine lyric drama, with characters, not personages, and a plot whose interest should increase unto its end."

"And have you found him?" asked Marianne, with a meaning smile.

"I have. It is—"

"Calzabigi," interrupted she.

"How!" cried the fiery Gluck, "after promising secrecy, has he been unable to curb his tongue?"

"Nonsense, Christopher! he has not said a word to me. I guessed this long ago."

"And how comes it that you never hinted a word of it to *me?*"

"I waited for the hour when you deemed it best to speak, my love; for I fully comprehend the reasons for your silence. I waited therefore until Minerva should come forth, full armed, to challenge Jove's opponents to the strife. Meanwhile I had faith in God and thee, Christopher, and I prayed for Heaven's blessing on thy genius."

"Heaven will hear thy prayer, my better self," cried Gluck, drawing his wife close to his heart. "Oh, how happy I feel to be permitted to speak with thee of my past labors! How gladly shall I listen to thy criticisms or thy approval! both, more to me than those of all the world beside. Come, Marianne, I will begin now."

He sprang up from the divan, and would have hurried to the piano, but Marianne held him back. "*Maestro,*" said she, "before we sacrifice to Apollo, let us give to life and mortality their rights. Prose awaits us in the dining-room, and we shall give her audience before we open the pages of this nameless opera."

"You shall hear its name, Marianne. It is—"

Marianne put her arms around his neck, and whispered, "Hush, my Orpheus!"

"How! You know that also?"

She raised her hand, as if in menace. "Know, Christopher, that little Hymen tolerates no man who has secrets from his wife. You tried to be silent, but betrayed yourself in your sleep. You do not know how often during the night you have called Eurydice in tones of plaintive music. Nor do you know how, as you appealed to the deities of the infernal regions, I shuddered at the power of your weird notes!"

"You heard, then," cried Gluck, enchanted. "And you—"

"My friend Prose, Prose calls with angry voice. Away to the dining-room! A man who has revelled all night with the Muses, needs refreshment in the morning. Nay—you need not frown like Jupiter Tonans—you must go with me to eat earthly food, before I taste your nectar and ambrosia. Come, and to reward your industry you shall have a glass of Lacrimæ Christi from the cellar of the Duke of Bologna."

She drew him from the room, and succeeded in landing him at the breakfast-table.

"Now, I will not hear a word about art," said Marianne, when the servants had brought in the breakfast. "I am the physician, both of body and mind, and condemn you to a silence of fifteen minutes. Then you may talk."

"Of my opera, *carissima?*"

"Heaven forbid! of the wind and weather—nothing else. Now hush, and drink your chocolate."

So Gluck, obedient, drank his chocolate, and ate his biscuit and partridge-wing in silence.

All at once, the comfortable stillness was broken by a loud ringing of the door-bell, and a servant announced Signor Calzabigi.

Gluck darted off from the table, but Marianne, laughing, brought him back again. "First, your glass of Lacrimæ Christi," said she. "Calzabigi will be indulgent and wait for us a moment."

He took the glass, and inclining his head, drank her health.

"Marianne," said he cheerfully, "I have been amiable and tractable as a good child. Enough of Prose, then—give me my freedom now, will you?"

"Yes, *maestro;* you are free; your body is refreshed, and can bear the weight of that strong soul that has no infirmities to impede its flight. Fly, if you list—to Calzabigi!"

CHAPTER XVIII.

RANIERO VON CALZABIGI.

THE door of the drawing-room had scarcely opened before Calzabigi hastened forward to meet Gluck. But, seeing his wife, he stopped, and made a profound inclination.

"Speak out, friend," cried Gluck merrily. "She knows every thing, and think what a treasure of a wife she is! She has known it all along, without betraying herself by a word."

"And does that surprise you?" answered Calzabigi. "It does not me, for well I know that the signora is an angel of prudence as well as of goodness. The signora will allow me to speak before her? Well, then, *maestro*, the die is cast. I am just from the house of Count Durazzo, to whom, at your request, I took the opera yesterday. The count sat up all night to examine it; and this morning, when I was ushered into his room, I found him still in his evening-dress, the score on the table before him."

"Hear, Marianne," exclaimed Gluck, triumphantly, "it is not only the composer who forgets to sleep for the sake of this opera. And what said the theatrical director, Raniero?"

"He said that no intrigue and no opposition should prevent him from representing this magnificent opera. He says that he feels proud of the privilege of introducing such a *chef-d'œuvre* to the world. He has already sent for the transcribers; he has chosen the performers, and begs of the author to distribute the parts. But every thing must be done at once, for the opera comes out in October to celebrate the birthday of the young Archduchess Isabella."

"That is impossible," cried Gluck. "We are in July, and such an opera cannot be learned in three months."

"With good-will, it can be done, Christopher," said Marianne, imploringly. "Do not leave your enemies time to cabal against you; snatch the victory from them before they have time for strategy."

"You do not know what you require at my hands," returned he, passionately. "You do not know how an ill-timed pause or a slighted rest would mar the fair face of my godlike music, and travesty its beauty."

"Hear how he defames himself!" laughed Marianne, "as if it were so easy to desecrate Gluck's masterpiece."

"It is precisely because it *is* my masterpiece that it is easy to travesty," returned Gluck, earnestly. "The lines which distinguish the hand of a Raphael from that of a lesser genius are so delicate as to be almost imperceptible. Slight deviations of the pencil have no effect upon a caricature; but you well know how completely a beautiful face may be disfigured by a few unskilful touches. I will cite as an example the aria of 'Orpheus,' '*Che faro senza Euridice.*' Change its expression by the smallest discrepancy of time or modulation, and you transform it into a tune for a puppet-show. In music of this description a misplaced *piano* or *forte*, an ill-judged *fioriture*, an error of movement, either one, will alter the effect of the whole scene. The opera must, therefore, be rehearsed under my own direction, for the composer is the soul of his opera, and his presence is as necessary to its success as is that of the sun to the creation." *

"Well, I am sure, you can manage the whole *troupe* with that stentor voice of yours," replied Marianne.

"If you do not consent, Gluck," interposed Calzabigi, "they will have to rehearse for the birthday *fête* an opera of Hasse and Metastasio."

"What!" shrieked Gluck, "lay aside my 'Orpheus' for one of Hasse's puny operas? Never! My opera is almost complete. It needs but one last aria to stand out before the world in all its fulness of perfection, and shall I suffer it to be laid aside to give place to one of his tooting, jingling performances? No, no. My 'Orpheus' shall not retire before Hasse's pitiful jeremiades. It shall be forthcoming on the birthday, and I must train the singers by day and by night."

"Right!" exclaimed Marianne, "and we shall crown you with new laurels, Christopher, on that eventful night."

"I am not so sure of that, Marianne. It is easier to criticise than to appreciate, and every thing original or new provokes the opposition of the multitude. In our case, they have double provocation, for Calzabigi's poem is as original as my music. We have both striven for simplicity, nature, and truth; we have both discarded clap-trap of every sort. Oh, Calzabigi, my friend, how happy for me that I have found such a poet! If, through his 'Orpheus,' Gluck is to attain fame, he well knows how much of it is due to the inspiration of your noble poem."

"And never," exclaimed Calzabigi, grasping the extended hand of the composer, "never would the name of poor Calzabigi have been known, had Gluck not borne it along upon the pinions of his own fame. If the world calls me poet, it is because my poem has borrowed beauty from Gluck's celestial music."

"Yes," said Gluck, laughing, "and if your poem fails, you will be equally indebted to Gluck's music. Those half-learned critics, so numerous in the world, who are far more injurious to art than the ignorant, will rave against our opera. Another class of musical pedants will be for discovering carelessness, and, for aught we know, the majority of the world may follow in their wake, and condemn our opera as barbarous, discordant, and overstrained."

"We must try to forestall all these prejudices, and win the critics to the side of truth and real art," said Marianne.

"The signora is right," said Calzabigi. "It is not so much for our own sake, as for the sake of art, that we should strive to have a fair hearing before the world. We have the powerful party of Metastasio and Hasse to gain. But I will deal with them myself. You, *maestro*, speak a word of encouragement to Hasse, and he will

* These are Gluck's own words. Anton Schmid, "Life of Gluck," page 152.

be so overjoyed, that he will laud your opera to the skies. And pray, be a man among men, and do as other composers have done before: pay a visit to the singers, and ask them to bring all their skill to the representation of your great work; ask them to—"

Here, Gluck, boiling over with indignation, broke in upon Calzabigi, so as actually to make the poet start back.

"What!" cried he, in a voice of thunder, "shall I visit the ladies' maids also, and make them declarations of love? Shall I present each singer with a golden snuff-box, while I entertain the *troupe* at a supper, where champagne shall flow like water, and Indian birds'-nests shall be served up with diamonds? Shall I present myself in full court-dress at the anteroom of the tenor, and, slipping a ducat in the hand of his valet, solicit the honor of an interview? Shall I then bribe the maid of the prima donna to let me lay upon her mistress's toilet-table a poem, a dedication, and a set of jewels? Shame upon you, cravens, that would have genius beg for suffrages from mediocrity! Rather would I throw my 'Orpheus' behind the fire, and let every opera I have ever written follow it to destruction. I would bite out my tongue, and spit it in Hasse's face, sooner than go before him with a mouth full of flattering lies, to befool him with praise of that patchwork he has made, and calls AN OPERA! When I was obscure and unknown, I scorned these tricks of trade; and think you that to-day I would stoop to such baseness? Eight years ago, in Rome, a cabal was formed to cause the failure of my '*Trionfo de Camillo*,' Cardinal Albini came to assure me that his influence should put down the plots of my enemies. I thanked him, but refused all protection for my opera: and I told his eminence that my works must depend upon their own worth for success.* And you dare, at this time, to come with such proposals to me? You are not worthy of my friendship. I will have nothing further to say to either of you, you cringing puppets!"

So saying, with his dark-blue dressing-gown flying out like an angry cloud behind him, Gluck strode across the room, and sailed off to his private study.

Marianne, smiling, reached out her hand to the astounded poet.

"Forgive his stormy temper," said she, gently; "he can no more bear contradiction than a spoiled child. His wrath looks formidable; but though there is much thunder, there is no lightning about him. Wait a quarter of an hour, kind friend, and he will be back, suing for pardon, and imploring us to take his hand, just like a naughty child that he is. Then he will smile, and look so ashamed that you will never have the heart to feel resentful."

"I have none already," replied Calzabigi; "his thunder has rolled grandly over our heads, and right noble are its sounds; but the lightning has spared us. We are safe, and—unconvinced. For, indeed, signora," continued Raniero, with earnestness, "we are right. No reliance is ever to be placed upon the justice or good taste of the world, and since the *maestro* refuses to propitiate his judges, I will undertake the task myself. I shall go at once to Metastasio, and after that I shall invite the performers to a supper."

* This is true. Anton Schmid, page 68.

CHAPTER XIX.

THE BIRTHDAY.

It was the birthday of the Archduchess Isabella, and all Vienna was alive with festivity. The passionate love of the archduke for his beautiful young wife was well known, and the people hastened to offer homage to the beloved partner of their future emperor.

From early morning the equipages of the nobility were seen hurrying to the palace, where the archduchess in state, surrounded by the other members of the imperial family, received the congratulations of the court. In an adjoining room, on a table of white marble, were exhibited the rich gifts by which her new relatives had testified their affection; for Isabella was adored by her husband's family.

The Emperor Francis, usually so simple, had presented her with a set of jewels, worth half a million; and the empress, whose joy in the happiness of her son's wedded life knew no bounds, was lavish in her demonstrations of love to the woman who had awakened his heart to gentle emotions.

Not only had every variety of rich costumes been ordered for Isabella from Paris, but the empress had gone so far as to present a set of bridal jewels to her little grand-daughter, a child scarcely a year old. This magnificent *parure* of diamonds, sapphires, and pearls, was the admiration of the whole court. Around it lay the offerings of the young sisters-in-law, all of whom, with one exception, had presented something. The Princess Christina, the dearest friend of Isabella, had painted her miniature, and this beautiful likeness was intended as a present to the Archduke Joseph.* He received it with delight; and while his large blue eyes wandered from the portrait to the original, he testified his pleasure by every possible expression of rapture and gratitude. "And yet," said he, "there is something in this picture which I have never seen in your countenance, Isabella. Your eyes, which to me have always seemed to borrow their light from heaven, here look dark and unfathomable, as if within their melancholy depths there lay a secret full of untold sorrow."

Joseph did not perceive the look of intelligence that passed between his wife and sister as he spoke these words; he still gazed upon the picture, and at last his face, which had been lit up with joy, grew sorrowful and full of thought. Suddenly he laid the miniature down, and placing his hands upon Isabella's shoulders, he looked searchingly at her pale countenance.

"Look at me, my beloved," whispered he, tenderly, "let me see your bewitching smile, that it may give the lie to yonder strange image. I see there your beautiful features, but instead of my loving and beloved wife, my happy, smiling Isabella, I see an angel, but, oh, I see a martyr, too, dying of some secret sorrow. That is not your face—is it my wife? *You* have never looked so wretched, so heart-broken! Speak, Isabella, you are happy, are you not, my own one?"

"Yes, dear husband," whispered she, scarcely moving her blanched lips, "I am happy and contented in your happiness. But see, the

* Wraxall, page 389.

empress beckons to you. She seems about to present some stranger to your notice."

The archduke left to obey the summons, and Isabella and Christina remained together, looking vacantly upon the birthday-table and the splendid gifts that lay in such rich profusion before their eyes.

"Poor brother!" murmured Christina, "he loves as few have ever loved before! And you, dear sister, can you not kindle one spark from the embers of your heart to warm—"

"Why speak of my dead heart?" said Isabella, mournfully. "Did I not long ago confide to you its terrible secret? You, my trusted and dearest friend, have you not seen how I pray Heaven for strength to hold before my husband's eyes the faint ray of light which he mistakes for the sunshine of love? Dear Joseph! His heart is so noble and so rich with love that he sees not the poverty of mine. May God be merciful that his delusion last at least as long as my life! then will I die happy; for I shall have done my duty in the face of a sorrow transcending all other sorrows."

Christina bent her head over the glittering heaps before her, that no one might see her tears. But Isabella saw them as they fell upon the bridal gifts of her little daughter.

She pointed to the jewels. "See, Christina, your tears are brighter than our dear mother's diamonds. Now, were the emperor here—"

"Heaven forbid!" said Christina, as with her gossamer handkerchief she wiped away the fallen tear. "If the empress were to know this, she would be justly displeased, that, on such a day, my tears should dim the splendor of your little daughter's bridal jewels."

"Give yourself no concern for my daughter's jewels, Christina; she will never see her bridal-day."

"How? Do you expect her to be an old maid, like my two eldest sisters?" asked Christina, with assumed playfulness.

Isabella laid her hand on Christina's shoulder. "I believe," said she, solemnly, "or rather I know, that my daughter will ere long be an angel."

"Oh, Isabella," cried Christina, almost impatiently, "is it not enough that you prophesy your own death, to make me wretched, without adding to my grief by predicting that of your child, too?"

"I cannot leave her behind, Christina; I should be unhappy without her. She must follow me—but hush! Here comes the empress—let us be happy for her sake."

And with a sweet smile, Isabella advanced to greet her mother-in-law.

"My dearest daughter," said the empress, "I long for this ceremonial to end, that we may enjoy our happiness *en famille*. We must dine in private, unless you wish it otherwise, for to-day you are empress of all hearts, and your wishes are commands."

Isabella raised the hand of the empress to her lips. "I have but one wish to-day, your majesty," said she; "it is that you love me."

"That wish was granted before it was uttered, my beloved child," replied the empress, tenderly, "for indeed I love you more and more each day of my life; and when I see you and my son together, your happiness seems like the old melody of my own happy bridal so many years ago."

"And yet," said Isabella, "your majesty looks so young—"

"No, child, I am a grandmother," replied the empress, smiling proudly, "but my heart is as young as ever, and it leaps with joy when I look upon the son whom you have made so happy. Why, *his* heart looks out of his great, blue eyes with such—But see for yourself, here he comes!"

At this moment the archduke entered the room, and advanced toward his mother, while at the door, apparently awaiting his return, stood the emperor and the lord high chancellor, Kaunitz.

"Pardon me, your majesty, if I interrupt you," said the archduke. "I have just learned from the marshal of the imperial household that your majesty has declined going to the opera to-night. Can this be possible, when Gluck's new opera has been rehearsing for two months with especial reference to this occasion?"

"It can," replied the empress, "for I do not interdict the representation—I only absent myself from it."

The archduke crimsoned, and he was about to make some hasty reply, when he felt the pressure of his wife's hand upon his arm. He smiled, and controlled himself at once.

"Forgive me, if I venture to remonstrate with your majesty," replied he, good-humoredly. "This new opera of Gluck is a musical gem, and is well worthy your majesty's notice."

"I have been told, on the contrary, that it is very tiresome," exclaimed the empress with impatience. "The *libretto* is heavy, and the music also. It is highly probable that the opera will fail, and it would certainly be unfortunate if, on this day of rejoicing, we should assemble there to witness the failure."

"But your majesty may have been misinformed," persisted Joseph. "Let me beg of you, my dear mother, for the sake of the great *maestro*, who would take your absence sorely to heart, as well as for the sake of the director, Count Durazzo, who has taken such pains to produce this new masterpiece—let me beg you to reconsider your decision."

"And allow me to add my entreaties to those of Joseph," said the emperor, entering the room. "All Vienna awaits the new representation as a high artistic gratification. Without your majesty's presence the triumph of the *maestro* will be incomplete."

"And the emperor, too, opposes me?" said Maria Theresa. "Does he, too, desert the old style, to follow these new-fangled musical eccentricities? Have we not all enjoyed the opera as it exists at present? And if so, why shall this Master Gluck step suddenly forward and announce to us that we know nothing of music, and that what we have hitherto admired as such was nothing more than trumpery? Why does he disdain the poetry of Metastasio, to adopt that of a man whom nobody knows? I will not lend my hand to mortify the old man who for thirty years has been our court-poet. I owe it to him, at least, not to appear at this representation, and that is reason enough for me to refuse my presence there."

"But Calzabigi's poem is of surpassing beauty," remonstrated the emperor; "for Kaunitz himself has seen it, and is in raptures with it."

"Ah, Kaunitz, too, has given his adherence to the new musical caprice of Master Gluck?" said the empress, signing to the count to come forward.

"Yes, your majesty," said Kaunitz, bowing, "I also am for the new and startling, whether in politics or in music. I have learned this lesson from my imperial mistress, whose new line of policy now commands the admiration of all Europe."

The empress received these flattering words with an emotion of visible pleasure; for it was seldom that Kaunitz paid compliments, even to sovereigns.

"You mean, then, that Gluck has not only produced something new, but something of worth, also?"

"Yes, your majesty, music has cut off her queue, and really in her new *coiffure* she is divinely beautiful. Moreover, your majesty has rewarded the seventy years of Metastasio with a rich pension, proof enough to him of the estimation in which his talents are held. Metastasio belongs to the old *régime* you have pensioned off; Calzabigi and Gluck are children of our new Austria. Your majesty's self has created this Austria, and you owe to her children your imperial countenance and favor."

"But I have been told there will be some strife to-night between the rival parties," said the empress.

"And since when has your majesty shunned the battle-field?" asked Kaunitz.

"But the defeat, count, I fear the defeat. The opera is sure to fail."

"No one knows better than your majesty how to console the vanquished. Your majesty was never greater than when, after the defeat of Field-marshal Daun, you went forth to meet him with all the honors which you would have awarded to a victorious general.* If Gluck fails to-day, he will not be the less a great *artiste*, and your majesty will sustain him under his reverses."

The empress laughed. "It is dangerous to contend with Kaunitz, for he slays me with my own weapons. And you, too, my husband, would have me abandon Hasse and Metastasio, who are so pious and so good, for this Gluck, whom I have never met inside of a church? Gluck is not even a Christian."

"But he is a genius," cried out Joseph, "and genius is pleasing in the sight of God. Metastasio and Hasse are old, and having nothing better to do, they go to church. If they were young, your majesty would not meet them so often, I fancy."

The face of the empress grew scarlet while the archduke poured forth these thoughtless words; and all present felt that Gluck and his cause were lost.

But Isabella came to the rescue. Approaching the empress and kissing her hand, she said: "Your majesty has been so good as to say that to-day you would refuse me nothing. I have two requests to make. May I speak?"

"Yes, dear child, you may," replied the empress, already appeased by the gentle voice of her beloved daughter-in-law. "I know so well that you will ask nothing unseemly that I do not fear to grant your requests. What are they?"

"First, your majesty, I beg that my husband and I be permitted to attend the mass that is to be celebrated in your private chapel, that by your side we may beg of God to give peace to Austria, and to bless us, your majesty's own family, with unity and love among ourselves. Will you permit this?"

The empress, in her animated way, drew the archduchess toward her, and kissed her tenderly.

* After the battle of Torgau, which Daun lost.

"You are an angel, Isabella," said she, "and discord ceases at the very sound of your voice. Yes, dearest child, you shall come with Joseph; and side by side we will pray for peace and family concord. For the second boon, I guess it. Is it not that I grant your husband's petition?"

Isabella, smiling, bowed her head, and the empress turned toward the emperor.

"Well, your majesty," continued she, "since my presence is indispensable, I bow to your superior judgment in art, and the court must attend the opera to-night. Are you satisfied, my son?" asked she of the archduke. "Are you satisfied now that I have sacrificed my prejudices to give you pleasure? And on some future occasion will you do as much for me, should I require it?"

"With shame I shall remember your majesty's goodness in pardoning my ungracious behavior to-day," replied the archduke, fervently pressing his mother's hands to his lips.

"I not only forgive but forget it, my son," said Maria Theresa, with one of her enchanting smiles; "this is a day of rejoicing, and no clouds shall darken our happiness. Let us now retire to the chapel, for, believe me, dear son, it is not well to forget our heavenly Father until age forces us to remember our dependence. A great and brilliant destiny is before you, Joseph, and much you need help from Heaven. Watch and pray while you are young, that you may call down the blessing of God upon your career."

CHAPTER XX.

ORPHEUS AND EURYDICE.

On that night, all Vienna sped to the Imperial Opera-house. Not lords and ladies alone, but commoners and artisans with their wives, thronged to hear the wonderful music which for three weeks had divided the Viennese into two bitter factions. On one side stood Metastasio, the venerable court-poet, whose laurels dated from the reign of the empress's father. Linked with his fame was that of Hasse, who for forty years had been called "*Il caro Sassone.*" Hasse, who had composed so many operas, was often heard to say, that, when it came upon him unawares, he did not know his own music.

All Italy had declared for Hasse and Metastasio, and in scornful security the Italians had predicted the discomfiture of the new school of music.

On the other hand were Gluck and his friend Calzabigi, whose partisans disdained the old style, and lauded the new one to the skies. Gluck was perfectly indifferent to all this strife of party. Not once, since the first day of rehearsal, had his countenance lost its expression of calm and lofty security. Resolved to conquer, he receded before no obstacle. In vain had the *prima donna*, the renowned Gabrielle, complained of hoarseness; Gluck blandly excused her, and volunteered to send for her rival, Tibaldi, to take the *rôle* of Eurydice. This threat cured the hoarseness, and Gabrielle attended the rehearsals punctually. In vain had Guadagni attempted, by a few *fioritures*, to give an Italian turn to the severe simplicity of Orpheus's air. At the least deviation from his text, Gluck, with a frown, would recall the ambitious tenor, and do away with his embellishments. In vain had the chorus-singers complained of the impossibility of learning their parts. Gluck instructed them one by one. He had trained the orchestra, too, to fullest precision; and finally, every difficulty overcome, the great opera of "Orpheus and Eurydice" was ready for representation on the birthday of the Archduchess Isabella.

Shortly before the hour of performance, Gluck entered his drawing-room in a rich court-dress, his coat covered with decorations. His wife met him, elegantly attired, and sparkling with diamonds. She held out her hand, and smiled a happy smile.

"Look at me, my hero," said she. "I have arrayed myself in my wedding-jewels. I feel to-night as I did on the day when we plighted our faith to one another before the altar. Then, dear Christopher, our hearts were united; to-day—our souls. Is it not so? And are we not one in spirit?"

"Yes, dearest, yes," replied Gluck, folding her in his arms, "never have I so prized and loved you as in these later days of strife and struggle. Well do I feel what a blessing to man is a noble woman! Often during our rehearsals, when I have encountered the supercilious glances of performers and orchestra, the thought of your dear self has given me strength to confront and defy their scorn. And when, weary in mind and body, I have found my way home, the touch of your hand has refreshed and cooled the fever in my heart. And often when others have pronounced my music worthless, I might have despaired, but for the remembrance of your emotion. I thought of your tears and of your rapture, and hope revived in my sick heart. Your applause, dear wife, has sustained me to the end."

"No, dear Christopher," replied Marianne, "not my applause, but the might of your own inspiration. That which is truly great must sooner or later prevail over mediocrity."

"The world is not so appreciative as you fancy, Marianne! Else had Socrates not drunk of the poisoned beaker, nor Christ, our Lord, been crucified. Mediocrity is popular, because it has the sympathy of the masses. Not only does it come within their comprehension, but it is accommodating;—it does not wound their littleness. I know, dear wife, that my opera is a veritable work of art, and therefore do I tremble that its verdict is in the hands of mediocrity. Poor Marianne! You have arrayed yourself for a bridal, and it *may* happen that we go to the funeral of my masterpiece."

"Well, even so," replied the spirited wife, "I shall not have decked myself in vain; I shall die like the Indian widow, upon the funeral pile of my dear husband's greatness. I will both live and die with you, *maestro;* whether you are apotheosized or stoned, your worth can neither be magnified nor lessened by the world. My faith in your genius is independent of public opinion; and whether you conquer or die, your opera must live."

"How I wish," said Gluck thoughtfully, "that from above, I might look down a hundred years hence and see whether indeed my works will have value on earth, or be thrown aside as antiquated trumpery! But it is useless—an impenetrable cloud covers the future, and we must e'en content ourselves with the verdict of the day. Let me be strong to meet it!—Come, Marianne, the carriage is coming to the door, and we must go. But is all this splendor to be hidden behind the lattice-work of my little stage-box?"

"Oh, no, Christopher," said his wife gayly; "on such a night as this, I have taken another box; from whence I can be a happy witness of my husband's triumph."

"What intrepid confidence the woman possesses!" exclaimed Gluck, catching his wife's gayety. "But how will my brave champion feel, if she has to see as well as hear the hisses that may possibly greet us to-night?"

"I shall feel heartily ashamed of the audience," replied Marianne, "and shall take no pains to conceal my contempt."

"We shall see," answered Gluck, handing her to the carriage, and following her with a merry laugh. "Now, forward!"

Within the theatre all was commotion. On one side, the partisans from the old school, who, from prejudice or custom, adhered to Hasse and Metastasio, predicted failure. This party was composed of Italians, and of all those who had "gone out" with old Austria. New Austria, on the other hand, with all the young *dilettante* of Vienna, were resolved to sustain Gluck, and, if possible, secure to his new opera an unprecedented triumph. The excitement reached even those boxes where sat the *élite* of the Viennese nobility. Even *their* voices were to be heard discussing the merits or demerits of the musical apple of discord. The Gluckites related that Guadagni, who, at first, had been strongly prejudiced against the opera, had finally been moved to tears by its exquisite harmony, and had said to Gluck that he was learning for the first time to what heights of beauty music might soar. The Hasseites replied that the opera was none the less tedious for Guadagni's word. Moreover, if Hasse and Metastasio had not openly condemned Gluck's musical innovations, it was because they were both satisfied that the opera would damn itself, and they were present to witness the discomfiture of its composer.*

Suddenly there was a hush in the theatre. The attention of the disputants was directed toward a small box, in the first tier, the door of which had opened to give entrance to two persons. One was an old man with silver-white hair, which flowed in ringlets on either side of his pale and delicate face. His thin lips were parted with an affable smile, and the glance of his small dark eyes was mild, benevolent, and in keeping with the rest of his countenance. His small, bent figure was clothed in the cassock of an *abbé*, but the simplicity of his costume was heightened by the order of Theresa which, attached to a silk ribbon, hung around his neck.

The other was a tall, gaunt man, in the dress of court *maestro de capello*. His lean face was proud and serious, his large mouth wore an expression of scorn, and his full-orbed, light-blue eyes had a glance of power which accorded well with his lofty stature. The two advanced arm in arm toward the railing, and, at their appearance, a storm of applause arose from the *parterre*, while the partisans of the Italian school cried: "Long live Hasse! Long live Metastasio!"

They bowed, and took their seats. While this was transpiring, the wife of Gluck entered her box. With a quiet smile she listened to the shouts that greeted her husband's rivals.

"He, too," thought she, "will have his greeting and his triumph."

* Anton Schmid, "Ritter von Gluck," page 92.

She was not mistaken. No sooner had Gluck appeared in the orchestra, than, from boxes as well as *parterre*, a thousand voices pealed forth his welcome: "Long live Gluck! long live the great *maestro!*"

Gluck bowed gracefully, while Marianne, happy but tranquil, unfolded her jewelled fan, and leaned back in supreme satisfaction. Metastasio whispered something to Hasse, who nodded his head, and then began to run his fingers through the masses of his bushy, gray hair.

Suddenly were heard these words: "Her majesty the empress, and the imperial court!"

Hushed now was every sound. Every eye was turned toward the box surmounted by the double-headed eagle of Austria. The marshal of the household appeared with his golden wand, the doors of the box flew asunder, the audience rose, and the empress, leaning on the arm of the emperor, entered her box. Magnificently dressed, and sparkling with diamonds, her transcendent beauty seemed still more to dazzle the eyes of her enraptured subjects. She was followed by the archduke, who, in conversation with his wife, seemed scarcely to heed the greetings of his future subjects. Behind them came a bevy of princes and princesses, all of whom, including little Marie Antoinette and Maximilian, the two youngest, had been permitted to accompany the imperial party. It was a family festival, and Maria Theresa chose on this occasion to appear before her people in the character of a mother.

The empress and her husband came forward and bowed. The former then glided gracefully into her large gilt arm-chair, while the latter signed to his children to be seated.

This was the signal of the music to begin. The audience resumed their seats, Gluck raised the leader's staff, and signed to the musicians.

The overture began. In breathless silence the audience listened to that short, earnest overture, whose horns, trumpets, and hautboys seemed to herald the coming of kings and heroes.

The curtain rose, and, in a funeral hall, Orpheus poured forth his grief for the loss of his Eurydice. With this pathetic complaint mingled the voices of the chorus of mourners; then a solo from Orpheus, in which he bewails anew the fate of the noble woman who had died for his sake. The god of love appears, counselling him to descend himself to the infernal regions. Orpheus, strengthened and revived by hope, resolves to tempt the dangerous descent, and calls upon his friends to share his fate.

At the end of the first act the curtain fell amid the profoundest silence. The Hasseites shrugged their shoulders, and even Gluck's warmest adherents felt undecided what to say of this severe Doric music, which disdained all the coquetries of art, and rejected all superfluous embellishment.

"I am glad that Metastasio is here," said the empress, "for his presence will prove to Calzabigi that he is not a pensioned dotard. And what thinks my daughter of the opera?" asked Maria Theresa of the infanta.

But when she saw Isabella's face, her heart grew faint with fear. The archduchess was pale as death, and her countenance wore an expression of grief bordering on despair. Her large, dark eyes, distended to their utmost, were fixed upon the ceiling; and she seemed as if she still heard the wailings of Orpheus and the plaintive chorus of his friends.

Joseph saw nothing of this. He had taken a seat farther back, and was chatting gayly with his little brothers and sisters.

"God help me!" murmured the empress; "she looks as if she were dying! Oh, if she were right with her dismal prophecy of death! What if indeed she is to leave us? Have mercy, O God! I know that I love her too well. She will be taken from me; Heaven will claim from me this sacrifice!" *

Isabella shuddered, and awakened from her horrid dream. Her eyes fell, her cheeks flushed, and once more her lips parted with a gentle smile. With a tender and appealing look, she turned toward the empress and kissed her hand.

"Pardon me, your majesty," whispered she; "the music has entranced and bewildered me. I was in another world, and was lost to the present."

"The music pleases you, then?" asked the empress.

"Oh, your majesty," cried Isabella, "this is no music to give pleasure; it is the sublimest language of truth and love!"

"Then," said the empress tenderly, "if you prize it so highly, dearest, I will prove to you how dearly I love you, for your verdict and mine disagree. Our next festive day will be that on which Joseph is to be crowned King of Rome. And we shall do homage to the taste of the Queen of Rome by ordering that this opera be repeated on the occasion of her coronation."

Isabella shook her head. "I shall not live long enough to be crowned Queen of Rome." †

Maria Theresa was about to murmur a reply, when the curtain rose, and the second act of the opera opened.

The audience, who had been loudly canvassing the music, were silenced, and awaited in breathless expectation the unfolding of the plot. Soon came the wonderful scene between Orpheus and the furies who guard the gates of Avernus. The beseeching tones of Orpheus, and the inexorable "No!" of the furies, made every listener tremble. Even Hasse, overcome by the sublimity of the music, bowed his head with the rest; and Metastasio, enraptured with the words, murmured, "*Ah, che poesia divina!*" Murmurs of applause were heard from every side of the theatre; they grew with every scene, and at last burst forth in wild shouts. It seemed as if the audience were gradually rising to an appreciation of this new and unknown music, until with one accord its matchless beauty burst upon their hearts and overpowered them.

When the curtain fell a second time, the applause knew no bounds. The Gluckites, in triumphant silence, hearkened to the voices of the deeply-moved multitude, who gave full vent to their emotions, and noisily exchanged the thoughts to which the wonderful opera had given birth.

Marianne, supremely happy, listened enraptured, while wreaths fell in showers around the head of her beloved husband. The adherents of Hasse and Metastasio no longer dared to raise their voices in opposition to the public verdict. In this state of excitement the third act began. With increasing delight, the audience listened. When Eurydice, condemned to return to the infernal regions, sang

* The empress's words. Caraccioli, "Life of Joseph II.," page 87.
† Isabella's own words. Wraxall, ii., page 394.

her plaintive aria, sobs were heard throughout the theatre, and murmurs of applause were audible during the whole scene. But when Orpheus concluded his passionate aria "*Che faro senza Eurydice,*" the people could contain their enthusiasm no longer. Exalted, carried away, with beating hearts and tearful eyes, they cried "*Da capo!*" and when Guadagni, in compliance with the call, had repeated his solo, the audience shouted out so often the name of Gluck, that he could resist his joy no longer. He turned, and they saw his noble face scarlet with blushes; then arose another storm. Again and again the "*vivas*" and the clappings were renewed, each time more frantic than before.

Hasse, tired of the spectacle of his rival's triumph, had disappeared. Metastasio, more magnanimous, had remained, and applauded as loudly as any. Marianne, to conceal her tears, had hidden her face behind her open fan; and as the applause of the people increased, until it resembled the shouts of victory, she murmured: "I knew it, I knew it! The true and beautiful must always prevail."

The fire of enthusiasm had spread to the imperial box. The emperor had more than once been heard to call out, "Bravo!" and Maria Theresa had several times felt her eyes grow dim. But she brushed away her tears and exclaimed: "It is beautiful, certainly; but it is a heathen opera, in which not God but gods are invoked!"

Isabella said nothing. She had held up before her face the bouquet which her husband had gathered for her, that her tears might fall unseen among its flowers. Joseph saw those tears shining like dew-drops upon its rose-leaves, and, taking it from her hands, he kissed them away. "Do not weep, my Isabella," whispered he tenderly; "your tears fall like a weight of sorrow upon my heart. Wipe them away, beloved. The day will come when you also shall be an empress, and your people will do you homage as I do now; and then you will have it in your power to heal their sorrows, and wipe away their tears; and they will love and bless you as I—"

A final burst of applause drowned the voice of the archduke. The opera was at an end, and the people were calling again for Gluck, the creator of the lyric drama.

CHAPTER XXI.

"IN THREE YEARS, WE MEET AGAIN."

THE war was over. All Vienna was rejoicing that the struggle which had caused so much bloodshed was at an end, and that Austria and Prussia had made peace.

Neither of the two had gained any thing by this long war, except glorious victories, honorable wounds, and a knowledge of the power and bravery of its enemy. Both had serious burdens to bear, which, for many years to come, would be painful reminders of the past. Austria, to cover the expenses of the war, had invented paper money, and had flooded the empire with millions of coupons. Prussia had coined base money, and all the employés of the state had received notes, which were nicknamed "*Beamtenscheine.*"

After the war these notes were exchanged for this base currency, which soon afterward was withdrawn from circulation as worthless. But Prussia had obtained from Austria full recognition of her rights to Silesia, and she in return had pledged herself to vote for Joseph as candidate for the crown of Rome, and to support the pretensions of the empress to the reversion of the duchy of Modena.

We have said that all Vienna was rejoicing, and turned out to receive the returning army with laurel wreaths and oaken boughs. The people breathed freely once more; they shouted and feasted, and prepared themselves to enjoy to their utmost the blessings of peace.

But while the nation shouted for joy, a cloud was gathering over the imperial palace, and its black shadow darkened the faces of the once happy family.

There wanted now but a few months to complete the third year of the archduke's marriage, and the young princesses seized every opportunity to make schemes of pleasure for the joyous anniversary. Isabella viewed these projects with a mournful smile. Her countenance became sadder and more serious, except when in the presence of her husband. There she assumed an appearance of gayety; laughing, jesting, and drawing from her violin its sweetest sounds. But, with her attendants, or in the company of the other members of the imperial family, she was melancholy, and made her preparations for death, which she foretold would overtake her very soon.

"You believe this terrible presentiment, my daughter?" said the empress to her one day. "Will you indeed forsake us who love you so dearly?"

"It is not that I will, but that I *must* go," replied she. "It is God who calls me, and I must obey."

"But why do you think that God has called you?"

Isabella was silent for a moment, then she raised her eyes with a strange, unspeakable look to the face of the empress. "A dream has announced it to me," said she, "a dream in which I place implicit faith."

"A dream?" said the pious empress to herself. "It is true that God sometimes speaks to men in dreams; sometimes reveals to us in sleep secrets which He denies to our waking, earthly eyes. What was your dream, love?"

"What I saw?" whispered she, almost inaudibly. "There are visions which no words can describe. They do not pass as pictures before the eye, but with unquenchable fire they brand themselves upon the heart. What I saw? I saw a beloved and dying face, a breathing corpse. I lay overwhelmed with grief near the outstretched form of my—my—mother. Oh, believe me, the prayer of despair has power over death itself, and the cry of a broken heart calls back the parting soul. I wept, I implored, I prayed, until the dim eyes opened, the icy lips moved, and the stiffening corpse arose and looked at me, at me who knelt in wild anguish by its side."

"Horrible!" cried the empress. "And this awful dream did not awake you?"

"No, I did not awake, and even now it seems to me that all these things were real. I saw the corpse erect, and I heard the words which its hollow and unearthly voice spoke to me: '*We shall meet again in three—*'"

"Say no more, say no more," said the pale empress, crossing herself. "You speak with such an air of conviction, that for a moment I too seemed to see this dreadful dream. When had you your dream?"

"In the autumn of 1760, your majesty."

The empress said nothing. She imprinted a kiss upon the forehead of the infanta, and hastily withdrew to her own apartments.

"I will pray, I will pray!" sobbed she. "Perhaps God will have mercy upon us."

She ordered her private carriage and drove to St. Stephens, where, prostrate among the tombs of her ancestors, she prayed for more than an hour.

From this day Maria Theresa became sad and silent, anxiously watching the countenance of Isabella, to see if it betokened death. But weeks passed by, and the infanta's prophecy began to be regarded as a delusion only fit to provoke a smile. The empress alone remained impressed by it. She still gazed with sorrowing love at the pale and melancholy face of her daughter-in-law.

"You have made a convert of my mother," said the Archduchess Christina one day to Isabella, "although," added she, laughing, "you never looked better in your life."

"And you, Christina, you do not believe?" said Isabella, putting her arm around Christina's neck. "You, my friend, and the confidante of my sorrows, you would wish to prolong the burden of this life of secret wretchedness and dissimulation?"

"I believe in the goodness of God, and in the excellence of your own heart, dear Isabella. These three years once passed away, as soon as you will have been convinced that this prophecy was indeed nothing but a dream, your heart will reopen to life and love. A new future will loom up before you, and at last you will reward the love of my poor brother, not by noble self-sacrifice, but by veritable affection."

"Would that you spoke the truth!" returned Isabella sadly. "Had my heart been capable of loving, I would have loved him long ago—him, whose noble and confiding love is at once my pride and my grief. Believe me when I tell you that in these few years of married life I have suffered terribly. I have striven with my sorrows, I have tried to overcome the past, I have desired to live and to enjoy life—but in vain. My heart was dead, and could not awake to life—I have only suffered and waited for release."

"Gracious Heaven!" cried Christina, unmoved by the confidence with which Isabella spoke, "is there nothing then that can bind you to life? If you are cold to the burning love of your husband, are you indifferent to your child?"

"Do you think that I will leave my child?" said Isabella, looking surprised. "Oh, no! She will come to me before she is seven years old." *

"Oh, Isabella, Isabella, I cannot believe that you will be taken from us," cried Christina, bursting into tears, and encircling her sister with her arms, as though she fancied that they might shield her from the touch of death. "Stay with us, darling, we love you so dearly!"

Her voice choked by emotion, she laid her head upon Isabella's

* The infanta's own words. This interview of Isabella with Christina is historical, and the most extraordinary part of it is, that the prophecy of her child's death was fulfilled.

shoulder, and wept piteously. The infanta kissed her, and whispered words of tenderness, and Christina's sobs died away. Both were silent. Together they stood with sad hearts and blanched cheeks, two imperial princesses in the prime of youth, beauty, and worldly station, yet both bowed down by grief.

Their lips slightly moved in prayer, but all around was silent. Suddenly the silence was broken by the deep, full sound of a large clock which stood on the mantel-piece. Isabella raised her pale face, and listened with a shudder.

For many months this clock had not struck the hour. The clockmaker, who had been sent to repair it, had pronounced the machinery to be so completely destroyed, that it would have to be renewed. Isabella could not summon resolution to part with the clock. It was a dear memento of home, and of her mother. She had therefore preferred to keep it, although it would never sound again.

And now it struck! Loud, even, and full-toned, it pealed the hour, and its clear, metallic voice rang sharply through the room.

Isabella raised her head, and, pointing to the clock, said, with a shudder: "Christina, it is the signal—I am called!" *

She drew back, as if in fear, while the clock went on with its relentless strokes. "Come, come, let us away!" murmured Christina, with pale and trembling lips.

"Yes, come," sighed Isabella.

She made a step, but her trembling feet refused to support her. She grew dizzy, and sank down upon her knees.

Christina uttered a cry, and would have flown for help, but Isabella held her back. "My end approaches," said she. "My senses fail me. Hear my last words. When I am dead, you will find a letter for you. Swear that you will comply with its demands."

"I swear!" said Christina, solemnly.

"I am content. Now call the physician."

Day after day of anguish went by—of such anguish as the human heart can bear, but which human language is inadequate to paint.

Isabella was borne to her chamber, and the imperial physician was called in. The empress followed him to the bedside, where pale and motionless sat Joseph, his eyes riveted upon the beloved wife who, for the first time, refused to smile upon him, for the first time was deaf to his words of love and sorrow.

The physician bent over the princess, and took her hand. He felt her head, then her heart, while the empress, with folded hands, stood praying beside him; and Joseph, whose eyes were now turned upon *him*, looked into his face, as if his whole soul lay in one long gaze of entreaty.

Van Swieten spoke not a word, but continued his examination. He bade the weeping attendants uncover the feet of the princess, and bent over them in close and anxious scrutiny. As he raised his eyes, the archduke saw that Van Swieten was very pale.

"Oh, doctor," cried he, in tones of agony, "do not say that she will die! You have saved so many lives! Save my wife, my treasured wife, and take all that I possess in the world beside!"

The physician replied not, but went again to the head of the bed, and looked intently at the face of the princess. It had now turned scarlet, and here and there was flecked with spots of purple.

* Historical. Wraxall, p. 387.

Van Swieten snatched from Joseph one of the burning hands which he held clasped within his own.

"Let me hold her dear hands," said he, kissing them again and again.

The doctor held up the little hand he had taken, which, first as white as fallen snow, was now empurpled with disease. He turned it over, looked into the palm, opened the fingers, and examined them closely.

"Doctor, in mercy, speak!" said the agonized husband. "Do you not see that I shall die before your eyes, unless you promise that she shall live!"

The empress prayed no longer. When she saw how Van Swieten was examining the fingers of the archduchess, she uttered a stifled cry, and hiding her head with her hands, she wept silently. At the foot of the bed knelt the attendants, all with their tearful eyes lifted to the face of him who would promise life or pronounce death.

Van Swieten gently laid down the hand of his patient, and opened her dress over the breast. As though he had seen enough, he closed it quickly and stood erect.

His eyes were now fixed upon Joseph with an expression of deep and painful sympathy. "Speak," said Joseph, with trembling lips, "I have courage to hear."

"It is my duty to speak," replied Van Swieten, "my duty to exact of her majesty and of your highness to leave the room. The archduchess has the small-pox."

Maria Theresa sank insensible to the floor. From the anteroom where he was waiting the emperor heard the fall, and hastening at the sound, he bore his wife away.

Joseph, meanwhile, sat as though he had been struck by a thunderbolt.

"Archduke Joseph," cried Van Swieten, "by the duty you owe to your country and your parents I implore you to leave this infected spot."

Joseph raised his head, and a smile illumined his pale face. "Oh," cried he, "I am a happy man; I have had the small-pox! I at least can remain with her until she recovers or dies."

"Yes, but you will convey the infection to your relatives."

"I will not leave the room, doctor," said Joseph resolutely. "No inmate of the palace shall receive the infection through me. I myself will be my Isabella's nurse until—"

He could speak no more; he covered his face with his hands, and his tears fell in showers over the pillow of his unconscious wife.

Van Swieten opposed him no longer. He was suffered to remain, nursing the archduchess with a love that defied all fatigue.

Of all this Isabella was ignorant. Her large, staring eyes were fixed upon her tender guardian, but she knew him not; she spoke to him in words of burning tenderness, such as never before had fallen from her lips; but while she poured out her love, she called him by another name—she called him Riccardo; and while she told him that he was dearer to her than all the world beside, she warned him to beware of her father. Sometimes, in her delirium, she saw a bloody corpse beside her, and she prayed to die by its side. Then she seemed to listen to another voice, and her little hands were clasped in agony, while, exhausted with the horror of the vision, she murmured, "Three years! three years! O God, what martyrdom! In three years we meet again!"

Her husband heeded not her wild language, he listened to the music of her voice. That voice was all that was left to remind him of his once beautiful Isabella; it was still as sweet as in the days when her beauty had almost maddened him—that beauty which had flown forever, and left its possessor a hideous mass of blood and corruption.

On the sixth day of her illness Isabella recovered from her delirium. She opened her eyes and fixed them upon her husband with a look of calm intelligence. "Farewell, Joseph!" said she softly. "Farewell! It is over now, and I die."

"No, no, darling, you will not die," cried he, bursting into tears. "You would not leave me, beloved, you will live to bless me again."

"Do not sorrow for me," said she. "Forgive and forget me." As Joseph, overcome by his emotion, made no reply, she repeated her words with more emphasis: "Forgive me, Joseph, say that you forgive me, for otherwise I shall not die in peace."

"Forgive thee!" cried he. "*I* forgive thee, who for three years hast made my life one long sunny day!"

"Thou wert happy, then," asked she, "happy through me?"

"I was, I *am* happy, if thou wilt not leave me."

"Then," sighed the wife, "I die in peace. He was happy, I have done my duty, I have atoned—"

Her head fell back. A long, fearful silence ensued. Suddenly a shriek—the shriek of a man, was heard. When the attendants rushed in, Isabella was dead, and Joseph had fallen insensible upon the body.*

CHAPTER XXII.

CHE FARO SENZA EURYDICE.

THE funeral rites were ended, and Isabella of Parma slept in St. Stephen's, in the tomb of the kaisers.

Joseph had refused to attend the funeral. From the hour his consciousness had returned to him he had locked himself within his apartments, and night and day he was heard pacing the floor with dull and measured tread. Not even the empress, who had stood imploring at the door, could obtain a word in answer to her entreaties. For two days and nights he remained within. On the third day the emperor knocked at the door, and announced to his son that all was now ready for the funeral, and his presence was indispensable.

Joseph opened the door, and, without a word, leaned upon his father's arm, and traversed the long suite of apartments hung in black, until they reached the room where lay the body of his wife. There, amid burning wax-lights, was the hideous coffin that enclosed

* This extraordinary account of the life and death of the infanta, Isabella of Parma, is no romance; it rests upon facts which are mentioned by historians of the reign of Maria Theresa. Caroline Pichler, whose mother was tire-woman to the empress when the archduchess died, relates the history of the prophecy, wherein Isabella, first in three hours, then in as many days, weeks, months, and years, awaited her death. She also relates the fact of her death at the expiration of three years, "in the arms of her despairing husband." Caroline Pichler, "Memoirs of My Life."

his beloved one, and was about to bear away forever his life, his love, and his happiness. When he saw the coffin, a stifled cry arose from his breast. He darted with open arms toward it, and, bending down, hid his face upon the lid.

At this moment the doors of the room were opened, and the empress entered, attended by her daughters, all in deep mourning. Their faces were wan with weeping, as were those of all who followed the bereaved sovereign. Meanwhile Joseph neither saw nor heard what passed around him. The ceremonies began, but while the priest performed the funeral rites, the archduke murmured words which brought tears to the eyes of his father and mother.

Maria Theresa approached her stricken son. She kissed his hair, and laid her hand lovingly upon his shoulder.

"My son," said she, with quivering lip, "arise and be a man. Her soul is with God and with us; let us give her body to the earth that bore it."

While the empress spoke, the bells of the churches began to toll, and from the streets were heard the beating of muffled drums, and the booming of the cannon that announced to Vienna the moving of the funeral procession.

"Come, my son, come," repeated the empress. "Our time of trial is at hand."

Joseph raised his head from the coffin, and stared wildly around. He saw the priests, the acolytes with their smoking censers, the weeping attendants of his wife; he saw the black hangings, the groups of mourners, and his father and mother standing pale and sad beside him; he heard the tolling of the bells and the dull sound of the funeral drum; and now, now indeed he felt the awful reality of his bereavement, and knew that as yet he had suffered nothing. Tears filled his eyes, and he sank upon his father's breast.

Sobs and wailings filled the funeral hall, while without the inexorable knell went on, the drums still beat, the cannon roared, all calling for the coffin, for whose entrance the imperial vault lay open.

Once more Joseph approached this dreadful coffin. He kissed it, and taking from it one of the roses with which it had been decked, he said, "Farewell, my wife, my treasure; farewell, my adored Isabella!" Then turning toward the empress, he added, "Thank you, dearest mother, for the courage which bears you through this bitter trial; for me, I cannot follow you. Greet my ancestors and say to them that never came a nobler victim to the grave than the one which you bear thither to-day."

"You will not go with us!" said the empress, astounded.

"No, mother, no. Mingle dust with dust, but do not ask me to look into my Isabella's grave."

He turned, and without a word or another look at the coffin, he left the room.

"Let him go," whispered the emperor. "I believe that it would kill him to witness the funeral ceremony."

The empress gave a sign, and the *cortége* moved with the coffin to the *catafalque*, which, drawn by twelve black horses, awaited the body in front of the palace.

Joseph once more retreated to his room, and there, through the stillness of the deserted palace, might be heard his ceaseless tramp, that sounded as though it might be the hammer that was fashioning another coffin to break the hearts of the imperial family. At least it seemed so to the sorrowing empress, who listened to the dull sound of her son's footsteps with superstitious fear. She had gone to him, on her return from the funeral, to console him with her love and sympathy. But the door was locked, and her affectionate entreaties for admission were unanswered.

She turned to the emperor. "Something must be done to bend the obstinacy of this solitary grief," said she anxiously. "I know Joseph. His is a passionate and obdurate nature, strong in love as in hate. He had yielded his whole soul to his wife, and now, alas! I fear that she will draw him with her to the grave. What shall we do, Franz, to comfort him? How shall we entice him from this odious room, which he paces like a lion in his cage?"

"Go once more and command him to open the door. He will not have the courage to defy you," said the emperor.

Maria Theresa knocked again, and cried out, "My son Joseph, I command you, as your sovereign and mother, to open the door."

No answer. Still the same dull, everlasting tread.

The empress stood awhile to listen; then, flushing with anger, she exclaimed, "It is in vain. We have lost all control over him. His sorrow has made him cruel and rebellious, even toward his mother."

"But this is unmanly," cried the emperor with displeasure. "It is a miserable weakness to sink so helpless under grief."

"Think you so?" said the empress, ready to vent upon the emperor her vexation at the conduct of her son. "In your pride of manhood you deem it weak that Joseph grieves for his wife. I dare say that were your majesty placed in similar circumstances, you would know full well how to bear my loss like a man. But your majesty must remember that Joseph has not your wisdom and experience. He is but a poor, artless youth, who has been weak enough to love his wife without stint. This is a fault for which I crave the emperor's indulgence."

"Oh, your majesty," replied the emperor, smiling, "God forbid that he should ever grow less affectionate! I was only vexed that the voice of Maria Theresa should have less power over my son than it has over his father; that silvery voice which bewitched me in youth, and through life has soothed my every pang."

The empress, completely softened, reached out her hand.

"Would you, indeed, mourn for me, Franz?" said she tenderly. "Would you refuse to listen to father or mother for my sake? Yes, dearest, you would, I believe. From our childhood we were lovers, we will be lovers in our old age, and when we part the one that is left will mourn as deeply as Joseph. Let us, then, be lenient with his grief, until our love and forbearance shall have won him to come and weep upon his mother's breast."

"If your majesty permit," said Christina, stepping forward, "I will try to soften his grief."

"What can you do, dear child?" asked the empress of her favorite daughter.

"I have a message for him," replied Christina. "I swore to Isabella that no one but myself should reveal it to Joseph. I know that it will prove consolatory, and Isabella also knew it. For this reason she intrusted it to me."

"Try, then, my daughter, try if your voice will have more power than mine. Meanwhile I will essay the power of music. It overcame him once when he was a boy. We will try him with the music that Isabella loved best."

She called a page and spoke with him in a low voice. In conclusion she said, "Let the carriage go at once and bring him hither in a quarter of an hour."

The page withdrew, and the imperial family were again alone.

"Now, my daughter," said the empress, "see if he will speak to you."

Christina approached the door. "My brother Joseph," said she, "I beseech you open the door to me. I come from Isabella; it is she who sends me to you."

The bolt was withdrawn, and for a moment the pale face of Joseph appeared at the door.

"Come in," said he, waving his hand to Christina. She followed him into the room where so many, many tears had been shed. "Now speak," said he, "what did Isabella say to you?"

His sister looked with pity upon his ghastly face and those hollow eyes grown glassy with weeping. "Poor, poor Joseph!" said she softly, "I see that your love for her was beyond all bounds."

He made a motion of impatience. "Do not pity me," said he. "My grief is too sacred for sympathy. I do not need it. Tell me at once, what said Isabella?"

Christina hesitated. She felt as if the balm she was about to bring would prove more painful than the wounds it was intended to heal.

"Speak, I tell you," cried Joseph angrily. "If you have made use of Isabella's name to gain access to my presence, it is a trick for which I will never forgive you. Why did you disturb me? I was with her," continued he, staring at the divan where so often they had sat together. "She wore her white dress and the pink roses, and she smiled with her enchanting smile. I lay at her feet, I looked into her eyes, I heard the melody of her voice."

"Did she ever say that she loved you?" asked Christina.

He looked at her intently and grew thoughtful. "I do not know," said he after a pause, "whether she ever told me so in words. But there needed no words. I saw her love in every glance, in every smile. Her whole life was love, and oh! I have lost it forever!"

"You have not lost it, for you never possessed it," said Christina.

Joseph drew back and frowned. "What is that?" said he hastily.

Christina approached him, and laying her hand upon his shoulder, she looked into his face until her eyes filled with tears.

"I say," whispered she in a tremulous voice, "do not mourn any longer, dear brother. For she for whom you grieve, she whom you call your Isabella, never loved you."

"That is not true," cried Joseph vehemently. "It is a lie, a wicked lie that you have devised to lessen my grief."

"It is nothing but the truth, and I promised Isabella to tell it to you."

Joseph sank almost insensible upon the divan. Christina seated herself near him, and throwing her arms around him, sobbed, "My brother, my darling brother, think no more of the dead, but turn your heart toward us; for we love you, and Isabella never did. She merely endured your love."

"Endured my love!" murmured Joseph, and his head sank powerless upon Christina's bosom. But suddenly he rose, and looking with a beseeching expression at his sister's beautiful face, he said:

"Bethink you, Christina, of what you do. Think that I love Isabella with all the strength and glow of my heart; think that for me she was the embodiment of all beauty, goodness, and purity. Do not seek to comfort me by destroying my faith in the truth of the only woman I have ever loved. In whom shall I have faith, if not in her? If *her* love was a lie, is there love in this world? Oh, Christina, in mercy say that you have sought to comfort by deceiving me!"

"I have sought to comfort you, by telling you the truth. If you will not believe me, believe her own words."

She drew a paper from her dress and handed it to Joseph. "It is a letter," said she, "which Isabella gave me, and she made me swear that I would fulfil its behests. Read, and be satisfied."

Joseph unfolded the letter. "It is her handwriting," said he to himself, and he tried to read it but in vain; his hand trembled, and his eyes filled with tears.

He gave it back to Christina, who read it aloud:

"My Christina—confidant of my sufferings and sorrow—hear my dying request. To you I leave the task of consoling my husband. His noble tears shall not be shed over the grave of one who is unworthy of them. Tell him the truth, tell him all you know, show him this letter, and bid him not grieve for one who never loved him. Do this for me, it is my last request. ISABELLA."

Suddenly, from the adjoining room, the sweet tones of music were heard; the air was tremulous with melody, which at first soft and low, swelled louder and louder until it filled the room with a gush of harmony that stirred the hearts of those who listened with sweetest and holiest emotions.

Joseph bent eagerly forward. He knew those strains so well! He remembered the night when Isabella's tears had fallen among the rose-leaves, and he had kissed them away. He saw her once more in the pride of her beauty, looking at him from the depths of those glorious dark eyes which he had so madly loved. The music gave life and being to these memories, and its glamour brought back the dead from her grave! He remembered how he had asked her if she loved him, and how, avoiding the words so difficult to speak, she had answered with the witching tones of her violin. Oh, that heavenly evening hour upon the balcony! She had said, "Love has its own language: come and listen." And Christina said *she had not loved!* He could not, would not believe her!

He took the letter from Christina's hand and kissed the paper. "I do not believe you," he said softly. "My trust in her is like my sorrow—for eternity!"

This imperturbable faith had the effect of hardening Christina, and making her cruel. "You shall believe me," said she hastily. "You shall see in her own handwriting that she loved another."

"ANOTHER!" cried the wretched husband. "I will kill him!"

"He died before you ever knew her," said Christina, frightened at the effect of her own heartlessness.

A smile overspread his face. "Dead, before I knew her! Then she forgot him when I loved her." He took up the letter and read it again. "Oh," said he, "see how magnanimous was my Isabella. She has been false to her own heart that she might save me from sorrow. She thought it would dry my tears to think that she did not love me. Oh, beloved, I see through thy noble falsehood—in death as in life I know every working of that unselfish heart!"

Christina said nothing, but she grew more inflexible in her purpose. "He *shall* be convinced," said she to herself. "I will give him her letters to me, and then he will know that he never has been loved."

Again pealed forth the sounds of that heavenly music. Now the violin, mingling with the tones of the harpsichord, glide into a melody of divinest beauty; and the full, rich tones of a woman's voice warbled the complaint of Orpheus: "*Che faro senza Eurydice!*"

Joseph sighed convulsively, and a faint color tinged his pale cheeks. This was Isabella's favorite air; and once more the vision started up before him, once more he saw the tears, he kissed them, and looked into the depths of those starry eyes!

He rose from the divan, and, drawn thither by a power which he could not contend, he left the room, and followed the music that was calling him from madness back to reason.

At the harpsichord sat Ritter Gluck, and by him stood the Archduchess Elizabeth, whose rich and beautiful voice had exorcised the evil spirit.

The emperor and empress, with all their children, came forward to meet the unhappy one, and all with tearful eyes kissed and welcomed him with tender words of love.

Gluck alone seemed not to have seen the archduke. He was chiding Elizabeth for singing falsely, and called upon her to repeat her song. Nevertheless, while he corrected his pupil, the big tears were coursing one another down his cheeks, and fell upon his hands, as they wandered over the instrument, enrapturing every ear.

Elizabeth began again; and again were heard the heart-breaking tones of "*Che faro senza Eurydice!*"

All eyes turned upon the bereaved Orpheus. The empress opened her arms, and completely subdued, he darted to his mother's heart, and cried out, "*Che faro senza Eurydice!*"

Again and again the mother kissed her weeping son. The emperor folded them both to his loving heart. The brothers and sisters wept for mingled grief and joy. Elizabeth's voice failed her, and she sang no more. But Gluck played on, his hands weaving new strains of harmony such as earth had never heard before. His head thrown back, his eyes upturned toward heaven, his face beaming with inspiration, he listened to his music, while from Joseph's anguish was born the wonderful song in Alceste, "*No crudel, no posso vivere, tu lo sai, senza de te.*"

The melody went on, the parents caressed their child, and on his mother's bosom Joseph wept the last tears of his great youthful sorrow. The dream of love was over! Grief had made of him a man.

KING OF ROME.

CHAPTER XXIII.

FATHER PORHAMMER AND COUNT KAUNITZ.

THE empress paced her cabinet with hasty steps. Near the large table, covered with papers of state, stood Father Porhammer.

"Are you sure of what you say?" said Maria Theresa with impatience. "Are you sure that the lord chancellor so far forgets his honor and dignity as to spend his hours of leisure in the company of disreputable actresses? Is it true that his house is the scene of shameful orgies and saturnalian feasts?"

"It is even so, your majesty," replied Porhammer. "It is unhappily true that he whom your majesty has raised to the first place in the empire of—"

"The first place!" echoed the empress angrily. "Know, sir, that the first place in the empire is mine. From God I hold my power and my crown, and I depute them to no man—I alone reign in Austria."

"Your majesty," resumed the father, "did not allow me to finish. I was about to say that he whom your majesty has made your most illustrious subject, he who ought to give to all your subjects an example of moral conduct, is a profligate and libertine. That infamous school of Paris, where reigns the wanton Marquise de Pompadour, the debauched court of Versailles—"

"Hold, father, and remember that France is Austria's dearest ally," interrupted the empress.

The father bowed. "The school of Parisian gallantry, of which the lord chancellor is a graduate, has borne its fruits. Count Kaunitz mocks at religion, chastity, and every other virtue. Instead of giving an honorable mistress to his house, it is the home of Foliazzi, the singer, who holds him fast with her rosy chains."

"We must send her away from Vienna."

"Ah, your majesty, if you send her, Count Kaunitz will go with her. He cannot live without La Foliazzi. Even when he comes hither to your majesty's august presence, La Foliazzi is in his coach, and she awaits his return at the doors of the imperial palace."

"Impossible! I will not believe such scandalous reports. Count Kaunitz never would dare bring his mistresses to my palace doors; he never would have the audacity to treat his official visits to myself as episodes in a life of lasciviousness with an unchaste singer. You shall withdraw your words, Father Porhammer, or you shall prove them."

"I will prove them, your majesty."

Just then the door opened, and a page announced the lord chancellor, Count Kaunitz.

"Admit Count Kaunitz," said the empress, "and you, Father Porhammer, remain."

The father withdrew within the embrasure of a window, while the lord chancellor followed the page into the presence of the empress. The count's face was as fair and his cheeks as rosy as ever; he wore the same fantastic peruke of his own invention, and his figure was as straight and slender as it had ever been. Ten years had gone by since he became prime minister, but nothing had altered *him*. So marble-like his face, that age could not wrinkle, nor care trace a line upon its stony surface.

He did not wait for the imperial greeting, but came forward in his careless, unceremonious way, not as though he stood before his sovereign, but as if he had come to visit a lady of his own rank.

"Your majesty sees," said he, with a courteous inclination of the head, "that I use the permission which has been granted me, of seeking an audience whenever the state demands it. As I come, not to intrude upon your majesty with idle conversation, but to speak of grave and important matters of state, I do not apologize for coming unbidden."

The easy and unembarrassed manner in which Kaunitz announced himself had its effect upon the empress. She who was so accustomed to give vent to the feelings of the moment, overcame her displeasure and received her minister with her usual affability.

"Your majesty, then, will grant an audience to your minister of state?" said Kaunitz, looking sharply at the priest who stood unconcerned at the window.

"Since the lord chancellor comes at such an unusual hour," replied the empress, "I must conclude that his business is of an imperative nature. I am therefore ready to hear him."

Kaunitz bowed, and then turning with an arrogant gesture toward the empress's confessor, he said, "Do you hear, Father Porhammer? the empress will hold a council with me."

"I hear it, my lord," said the priest.

"Then as we are not on the subject of religion, you will have the goodness to leave the room."

"I was ordered by her majesty to remain," replied Father Porhammer quietly.

Kaunitz turned toward the empress, who, with knit and angry brow, was listening to her minister.

"If it be the empress's pleasure," said he, bowing, "I will take the liberty of retiring until her majesty is at leisure for earthly affairs. Religion and politics are not to be confounded together; the former being the weightier subject of the two, I give way."

He bowed again, and was about to leave the room, when the empress recalled him.

"Stay!" said she. "Father Porhammer will leave us for a while."

Without a word, the father bowed and withdrew.

"Now speak, Count Kaunitz," said the empress, hastily, "and let the affair be important that has led you to drive my confessor, in such an uncourteous fashion, from my presence."

"Weighty, most weighty is the news that concerns the imperial house of Austria," said Kaunitz, with his unruffled equanimity. "A courier has brought me tidings of the archduke's election as King of Rome."

"Is that all?" said Maria Theresa. "That is no news. The voice of Prussia decided that matter long ago; and this is the only advantage we have ever reaped from our long and terrible war with Frederick?"

"No, your majesty, no, this is not the only thing we have obtained. This war has yielded us material advantages. It has increased the military strength of the country; it has placed before the eyes of all Europe the inexhaustible nature of Austria's resources; it has brought all the little Germanic principalities under Austria's dominion. It has united Hungary, Sclavonia, Italy, Bohemia, and Lombardy under Austria's flag and Austria's field-marshals. Indeed, your majesty, this war has given us something of far more value than Prussia's vote. The bloody baptism of the battle-field has made Austrians of all those who bled for Austria's rights."

"That does not prevent that abominable man from clinging to my fair domain of Silesia. How will my ancestor, the great Charles, greet me, when I go to my grave, bearing the tidings that under my reign Austria has been shorn of a principality?"

"No such tidings shall your majesty bear to your forefathers," replied Kaunitz, fervently. "Leave Frederick alone with his bit of a principality; more trouble than profit may it be to him! Long before he will have transformed his Silesian Austrians into loyal Prussians, we shall have repaired the damage he has done us by new and richer acquisitions."

"No, no, no!" cried the empress, "let us have no more war. What we do not possess by just right, I never will consent to win with the sword."

"But inheritance and alliance bestow rights," persisted the minister. "Your majesty has marriageable daughters and sons, and it is time to think of negotiating honorable alliances for them."

The eyes of the empress sparkled, and her face beamed with happy smiles. The establishment of her children was her constant thought by night and day, and in broaching this subject, Kaunitz was meeting her dearest wishes. Her displeasure against him melted away like snow before the sun, and she gave herself up entirely to the pleasing discussion.

"It will be difficult to find husbands for my daughters," said she. "All the reigning heads of European families are married, and their sons are too young for Elizabeth and Amelia. I cannot marry my grown-up daughters to boys; nor can I bring a set of insignificant sons-in-law to hang about the court. My husband the emperor would never consent to bestow his daughters upon petty princes, who, instead of bringing influence with them, would derive their reflected consequence from an alliance with us. If we cannot find them husbands worthy of their station, my daughters must remain single, or devote their lives to God."

"If your majesty's eldest daughters choose that holy vocation, politics need not interfere with their inclinations. The boyish heirs of European kingdoms can await the advent of the younger princesses."

"Let them wait," said the empress; "we will train noble queens for them."

"But the Archduke Leopold need not wait," said Kaunitz; "we will begin with him. The Spanish ambassador has received from his sovereign, Carlos IV., a letter directing him to offer his daughter Maria Louisa to your majesty's second son. Knowing that his highness the Archduke Joseph is your majesty's successor, he supposes that the Emperor Francis will bestow upon his second son the grand duchy of Tuscany."

"A very good alliance," returned Maria Theresa, nodding her head. "The women of the house of Bourbon are all estimable. Our lost Isabella was a lovely woman. Well, the grand-daughter of the King of Spain having died, let us renew our connection with him through his daughter; and may God grant to Leopold happier nuptials than were those of my poor Joseph."

"The Archduke Joseph, too, must marry," said Kaunitz.

"Poor Joseph!" sighed the empress; "even now his heart is full of sorrow; and while he mourns his dead, we make plans to marry him to another! But you are right, count; he must marry. We cannot listen to his heart, he must sacrifice himself to duty. Austria must have another heir. But let us give him a little respite."

"He will forget his sorrow when he is crowned King of Rome," said Kaunitz. "Ambition is certain to cure love; and the possession of a crown may well console any man for the loss of a woman."

Maria Theresa was displeased. "Do you deem it, then, so light a thing?" said she, with a frown, "to lose a beloved wife? Do you think it great happiness to wear a crown? You know nothing either of the pains of power or the joys of marriage; but I can tell you that many a time I would have fainted under the burden of my crown, had my Franz not sustained me with his loving and beloved hand. But what know you of love? Your heart is a market-place wherein you seek slaves for your harem, but no honorable woman would make it her home. I have heard scandalous reports concerning your house, Count Kaunitz; I have—"

A light knock was heard at the door, and as the empress gave the word, Father Porhammer entered the room.

CHAPTER XXIV.

MATRIMONIAL PLANS.

FATHER PORHAMMER came forward, while the empress looked at him with a glance of astonishment.

"Forgive me, your majesty, for this intrusion. It is in accordance with your gracious commands, whose fulfilment I have no right to delay. I was ordered by your majesty to prove the fact which I asserted."

"Well, have you the proof?" said the empress, impatiently.

"I have, your majesty. It is in the carriage of the lord chancellor, at the great door of the palace."

The empress made an exclamation; and her face grew scarlet with anger. Her stormy looks rested upon Kaunitz, who, perfectly unconcerned, seemed not to have heard what Porhammer had said. This undisturbed serenity on the part of her minister gave the empress time for recollection. She knew from experience that the lightning of her wrath would play harmlessly about the head of this living statue, and she felt more keenly than she had ever done before, that however Kaunitz's private life might shock her own sense of honor and decency, his vast intellect as minister of state was indispensable to Austria.

With a quick and haughty gesture, she motioned the priest away, and then began to pace up and down the length of the apartment.

Kaunitz remained tranquil near the table, his cold glances resting now on the papers, now on the pictures that hung opposite to him. He was busily engaged arranging his Alençon ruffles, when the empress stopped, and fixed her fiery eyes upon him.

"My lord chancellor, Count Kaunitz, tell me who sits in your carriage before the doors of my palace, awaiting your return from this conference?"

"Who sits in my carriage, your majesty? I was not aware that any one was there whose name it was necessary for me to announce to your imperial majesty."

"I can well believe that you would not dare to pronounce the name of that person in my presence," cried the empress, indignantly: "but let me tell you, sir count, that your behavior is highly displeasing to me, and that I blush to hear the things I do, to the disparagement of your honor and morality."

"Has your majesty any complaint to make of me as minister, or as president of council?" asked Kaunitz, almost roughly. "Have I not fulfilled the vows I made to your majesty ten years ago? Have I discharged my duties carelessly? The ship of state which, in her hour of peril, was confided to my hands, have I not steered her safely through rocks and reefs? Or, have I been unfaithful to my trust? If your majesty can convict me of crime, or even of negligence, then sit in judgment upon the culprit. Tell me of what state offence am I accused?"

"I do not speak of my prime minister," replied the empress somewhat embarrassed. "I have no fault to find with *him*. On the contrary, he has nobly kept the pledge he made to me and to my Austria, and he has been a wise, faithful, and conscientious servant. But this is not enough; there are also duties to perform toward God, toward society, and toward one's self."

"For your majesty, as well as for me, it suffices that I am true to my duties as your subject. As to my duty as a man, this is no place to discuss a matter which lies between God and myself. It would be indecorous for me to raise the veil of my private life before the eyes of your majesty. I came here to speak of Austria's welfare and yours, not of me or mine."

Without giving the empress time to make any reply, Kaunitz resumed the subject which had been interrupted by the visit of Father Porhammer.

"Though your majesty may deem it expedient to postpone the marriage of the Archduke Joseph, still, that need not prevent us from taking the steps that will be necessary to secure an advantageous alliance for the heir to the throne. We can grant a respite to the Archduke of Austria, but the King of Rome must stifle his grief, and attend to the calls of duty. He must silence his heart, for the Emperor of Austria must have a successor."

"At least let us choose him a bride worthy to succeed in his affections the angelic wife he has lost," said the empress, with feeling.

Something like a smile flitted over Kaunitz's sardonic face. "Your majesty must pardon me, but you view this matter entirely too much as a thing of sentiment; whereas, in effect, it is an affair of policy. The main object of the archduke's marriage is to find a princess whose family can advance the interests of the state, and who is in a condition to bear children."

"And have you already found such a wife for my poor child?" asked the empress. "Have you one to propose whom policy will approve, and who will not be distasteful to the eye or the heart?"

"She must be a German princess," said Kaunitz.

"Why MUST?"

"Because the house of Hapsburg must court the good-will of all Germany, which, through this long war and from the divided interests of the German people, it is in danger of losing. Prussia, grown morally strong by the war, is about to become the rival of Austria, and even now she seeks to have a voice in German politics. Northern Germany already inclines to Prussia by its sympathies of creed and opinion. If we allow this to go on, Prussia will divide Germany into two halves. The northern half, that which is Protestant, and in my opinion the wiser half, because free from the prejudices of religion, will belong to enlightened Prussia; the southern half, the bigoted Catholic portion, that which believes in the pope and his Jesuits, may *perhaps* adhere to Austria. Then comes revolution. Prussia will have for her allies, not only northern Germany, but Sweden, England, Holland, Denmark, even Russia. Every step she takes in advance will drive back Austria; and the day may come when Prussia, our powerful enemy, will seek for the Margrave of Brandenburg the crown of the Kaisers."

"Never! never!" exclaimed Maria Theresa, passionately. "To think of this little Burgrave of Nuremberg, the vassal of Rudolf of Hapsburg, growing to be the rival of the stately house of Austria! No, no! Never shall the day dawn when Austria descends to an equality with Prussia! We are natural enemies; we can no more call the Brandenburgs brothers than the eagle can claim kindred with the vulture! You are right, count; the strife of the battle-field is over, let us gird ourselves for that of diplomacy. Let us be wary and watchful; not only the state but the holy church is in danger. I can no longer allow this prince of infidels to propagate his unbelief or his Protestantism throughout my Catholic fatherland. We are the ally and the daughter of our holy father, the pope, and we must be up and doing for God and for our country. Now let us think how we are to check this thirst of Prussia for power."

"There are two expedients," said Kaunitz, calmly interrupting the empress in her torrent of indignation.

"Let us hear them."

"The first one is to strengthen our interest with Germany either by offers of advantages and honors, payment of subsidies, or by matrimonial alliances. For this reason it is that the future King of Rome must choose his wife among the princesses of Germany. Through your majesty's other children we will ally ourselves to the rest of Europe. The Bourbons reign in the south, and they must all be allied to the house of Hapsubrg. Through the marriage of Archduke Leopold with the daughter of the King of Spain, we shall gain a powerful ally; and the archduke himself, as Grand Duke of Tuscany, will represent Austria's interest in Italy. If the Crown

Prince of Parma and the young King of Naples unite themselves to two of your majesty's daughters, then all Italy will be leagued with Austria. When this is accomplished, the word 'Italy' will be a geographical designation, but the country will be an Austrian dependency. Now for Western Europe. For France, we must confirm our alliance with her also. The son of the dauphin, the grandson of Louis XV., is now eleven years old; just three years older than the Archduchess Marie Antoinette."

"Truly, Kaunitz, your plans are great," cried the empress, her face full of smiles and radiant with joy. "The emperor often calls me a match-maker, but I am an insignificant schemer by *your* side. I must say that I approve your plans, and will do all that I can to insure them success."

"The most of them are for the future; before all things we must bestir ourselves about the present. You have seen how later, we can secure the friendship of the south; that of the north must come through the marriage of the King of Rome. His selection of a German princess will incline all Germany toward your majesty's imperial house. Nearest to Prussia are the two important principalities of Bavaria and Saxony."

"And both have unmarried princesses," exclaimed the empress, joyfully. "I wish we might select the daughter of the Elector of Saxony, for that house has suffered so much for Austria, that I would gladly do it this favor. But I have heard that the Princess Mary Kunigunde has very few charms."

"Perhaps Josepha of Bavaria may be handsomer," said Kaunitz dryly.

"She is nevertheless the daughter of Charles VII., and he has never been my friend. I have suffered much from this man, and would you have me accept his daughter as mine?"

"There can be no resentment for bygones in politics," said Kaunitz, deliberately.

"But there may be gratitude for past services," exclaimed the empress, warmly. "I shall never forget how Hungary sustained me when this man would have robbed me of my crown. I never would have worn my imperial diadem but for the help of God, and the sword of St. Stephen, which my brave Magyars drew for me on the battle-field! Without Hungary I would have been dethroned, and shall I now place the crown of St. Stephen's upon the brow of an enemy's daughter! It would be an injustice to my loyal Hungarians. I shall give my voice to Mary of Saxony, but if Joseph prefers Josepha, I will not oppose his choice. And this matter settled, tell me your other plans for strengthening the power of Austria."

"My second plan is to humanize the Hungarian nobles. These nobles reign in Hungary like so many petty sovereigns. There is no such thing as nationality among them. The country is divided into nobles and vassals. The nobles are so powerful that the government is completely lost sight of, and the real sovereigns of Hungary are the Magyars."

"That is in some sense true," answered the empress. "I have often felt how dangerous to my rights was the arrogance of my Hungarian subjects. They lift their haughty heads too near the regions of royalty."

"And your majesty's great ancestor, Charles V., once said that nothing had a right to lift its head in the vicinity of a king. The very trees would he lop, that their branches might not grow too near to heaven; how much more the heads of men, when they were raised too high."

"But such a policy shall never be mine—I will never buy obedience with oppression. Besides, I have already said that I am under obligations to my Hungarian nobles, and I will not injure a hair of their heads."

"There are other ways of conquering besides the sword," said the crafty Kaunitz. "Coercion would but fortify the Magyars in their insolence. These haughty lords must be enticed from their fastnesses to Vienna. They must be greeted with honors, titles, and estates. They must be taught to love splendor, to spend money, to accumulate debts, until they become bankrupt, and their possessions in Hungary fall into the hands of the crown."

"What an infamous policy!" cried the empress.

"Good, nevertheless," said Kaunitz calmly. "Nothing can be done with the Magyars by force. They must be vanquished by pleasure, and also by marriage. They must be made to take home Viennese wives, who will initiate them into the arts of refined life, who will help them to waste their money, and so cut off the wings of their freedom. He who has learned to love pleasure will have no taste for sedition, and he who is in debt is no longer free. Your majesty must bestow gifts and places at court; the Magyars will grow ambitious—they will become hangers-on of princes, and—dissipation, ostentation, and extravagance will do the rest."

While Kaunitz was unfolding his satanic schemes, the empress walked up and down, in visible agitation. When he ceased, she came and stood before him, and with her searching eyes tried to look through the mask of his impenetrable countenance.

"What you have said there," said she, "is a mournful leaf from the book of worldly wisdom which guides your actions, and it is enough to make an honest heart ache to think that good is to be reached by such foul means. My heart struggles against such a course, but my head approves it, and I dare not listen to my womanly scruples, for I am a sovereign. May the wiles of the women of Vienna make loyal subjects of my brave Hungarians! I will bestow honors without end; but for aught else, let it come as it may. Extravagance, debt, and sequestration, they must bring about themselves."

"They will follow; and then sequestered estates must go to Austrian nobles, that our own people may mingle with the Magyars at home, and strengthen the influence of your majesty's house in Hungary."

"Say no more," said the empress, mournfully. "Bring them hither, if you can. But my heart aches, and my ears burn to have heard what you have said. Say no more of Hungary to me—let us speak of our bright plans for my children. It makes me happy to think that so many of them will wear crowns."

"The first will be that of the King of Rome, and I trust that, before his coronation, your majesty will have persuaded him to marry one of the two German princesses of whom we have spoken."

"The Saxon or the Bavarian," said the empress. "I think he will comply—for he will understand as well as ourselves the urgency of the case. When is the coronation to take place?"

"In two weeks, your majesty."

"Then poor Joseph has but fourteen days for his grief. When he returns from Frankfort, I shall remind him of his duty as a sovereign. But hark! It is twelve o'clock—the hour for mass. If the lord chancellor has nothing more to propose, I—"

"Pardon me, your majesty. I have an insignificant petition to present—it concerns myself."

"It is a pleasure to me," said Maria Theresa, "to think that in any way I can gratify you. Speak, then, without fear. What can I do to serve you?"

"It is only for the sake of decorum, your majesty," replied Kaunitz. "You say that I have been useful to the country. I confess that I, too, think that I deserve something from Austria. If I were another man, and Kaunitz stood by, as I reviewed in my mind all that he has done and is trying still to do to make Austria powerful, I would speak thus to your majesty: 'It is in the power of the empress to distinguish merit by elevating it to a position above the common herd. Your majesty has honored Count Kaunitz by calling him your right hand. When the head of a body politic is an empress, it is not enough for the right hand to be called a count.'"

"Shall I call you prince?" laughed Maria Theresa.

"Just what I was about to propose to your majesty," said Kaunitz, as he made a deeper inclination than usual before the empress.

"Then it shall be so," said she, warmly. "From this moment my esteemed minister is Prince Kaunitz, and the letters patent shall be made out this very day."

She extended her hand to the new-made prince, who kissed it fervently.

"I take this title, so graciously bestowed, not because it will confer splendor upon my own name, but because it will prove to the world that those who serve Maria Theresa with fidelity, she delights to honor. And now that this trifling matter is arranged, I beg your majesty's permission to retire."

"Until to-morrow," replied the empress, with a smile.

She waved her hand; but as Kaunitz left the room, he heard her following him into the anteroom. He had already opened the door leading into the hall, but hearing her still advance, he turned again, and made a profound inclination.

"*Au revoir*, my dear prince," said the empress, loud enough for Father Porhammer, who waited to accompany her to the chapel, to hear her greeting.

The father could not withhold some trace of his displeasure from his countenance, while Kaunitz, with a faint, derisive smile, passed on. The empress, at that moment, reopened the door, and came out into the hall. Father Porhammer, advancing to her, said, "Did I not prove to your majesty the truth of my statement concerning the immorality of—"

"The what?" said the empress, with an absent air. "Oh yes, yes. I had forgotten. You wished to prove to me that the lord chancellor had some person in his carriage awaiting his return. I believe you, father—doubtless there is some one in the carriage of the lord chancellor, whom it would be improper to name in my presence. But listen to what I have to say on this subject. It is better for you and for me not to see what goes on either in the lord chancellor's house or in his carriage. Close your eyes, as I shall mine, to whatever is objectionable in his life. I cannot afford to lose his services. So far as I am concerned, he is blameless. His life may be loose, but his loyalty is firm; he is a wise and great statesman, and that, you will allow, is a virtue which may well cover a multitude of sins."

Father Porhammer bowed to the will of his sovereign; Prince Kaunitz went on with his life of debauchery.

"Let us hasten to the chapel," added the empress; and a page throwing open the doors of another apartment, Maria Theresa joined her lords and ladies in waiting, and the imperial court entered the chapel.

But the thoughts of the empress were more of earth than heaven, on that morning. Her heart was filled with maternal cares, and when the services were over, and she had arrived at the door of her cabinet, she dismissed her attendants, and summoned to her presence the marshal of the household, Count Dietrichstein.

As soon as he appeared, Maria Theresa said eagerly: "Come hither, count. I wish to have a confidential conversation with you. You are an old and faithful servant of my family, and I know that I can depend upon your discretion."

"Your majesty well knows that I would sooner die than betray a secret of my imperial mistress," exclaimed good, fat, old Dietrichstein, fervently.

The empress looked kindly at his red, good-humored face. "And you would rather die than tell me an untruth also, is it not so?" said she, smiling.

"That," replied Count Dietrichstein, with another smile, "that is an embarrassing question; for there are cases, when even your majesty's self—"

"Yes, yes; but in this instance I earnestly desire to hear the unvarnished truth."

"If so, your majesty's desire is for me a command, and I will answer truthfully whatever you ask."

"Well, then, listen to me. You have just returned from a tour in Bavaria and Saxony. Of course you have seen the two princesses, Mary Kunigunde and Josepha."

"I know them both," said Dietrichstein, puffing.

"Well, tell me what sort of person is the Princess Mary Kunigunde?"

"She is slender," replied Dietrichstein, shrugging his shoulders; "slender as a bean-pole. If your majesty will pardon me the expression in favor of its truth, her bones rattle as she walks, and if you should chance to touch her by accident, I pity you."

"What for?"

"Because you will retreat from the collision bruised."

"You are a wicked slanderer, count," replied the empress. "You mean to say that the Princess of Saxony is frail and feminine in her appearance."

"If your majesty pleases, so be it; but if you looked into her serene highness's face, you might mistake her for a man, nevertheless."

"Holy Virgin! what does the man mean?" cried the empress, astounded.

"I mean," said the count, with a sort of comic seriousness, "that the frail and feminine princess has a black beard which a cornet might envy."

"Nonsense, count! you saw her at twilight, and mistook a shadow on her face for a beard."

"Pardon me, your majesty, you commanded me to tell the truth. I saw the princess by sunlight as well as by candlelight. Under all circumstances, this black shadow overhung her not very small mouth; and I have strong reason for persisting in my opinion that it was a flourishing beard."

"But Josepha of Bavaria—is she handsomer?"

"Handsomer, your majesty," cried the old count. "It is said that she is a good and estimable person; if this be true, her soul is very, very different from her body. Indeed, her beauty may be said to rival that of the Princess Mary."

"You are a keen critic," sighed the empress. "But suppose you were obliged to marry either one of the princesses, which one would you choose?"

"Your majesty!" exclaimed the old count, horror-stricken. "I never would have the assurance to raise my eyes to thoughts of marriage with a serene highness."

"Well, then," said the empress, "suppose you were a prince and her equal in birth, which one then would you prefer?"

The count looked at the floor, and was silent.

"The truth, the truth!" cried the empress. "Speak out and do not fear. Whatever you say shall be sacred with me. Now tell me, which of the two would you take to wife?"

"Well, then," said Count Dietrichstein, with a grimace of excessive disgust, "since your majesty obliges me to suppose the case, I will tell the truth. If by any artifice I could escape, nothing on earth would induce me to marry either one of them. But if the knife were at my throat, and I had no other way of saving my life, I would take the Princess Josepha, for she—"

"Speak out," said the empress, amused, though sorely disappointed. "You would marry Josepha of Bavaria because—"

"Because," sighed the fat old count, "if she *is* horribly ugly, she has, at least, something like a woman's bosom."

Maria Theresa broke out into a hearty laugh. "You are right," said she, "the reason is a very good one, and has its weight. I thank you for your candor, and will turn over in my mind what you have told me."

"But your majesty has promised not to betray me," protested the count with imploring look.

"And I will keep my promise faithfully," replied the empress, reaching him her hand. "Nevertheless, I cling to the hope that you have exaggerated the defects of the princesses, and that they are not altogether as ugly as you have pictured them to me." *

***This conversation is historical, and the criticism of Count Dietrichstein upon the two princesses, as here related, is almost verbatim. See Wraxall's "Memoirs," vol. ii., page 406.**

CHAPTER XXV.

JOSEPHA OF BAVARIA.

FESTIVITY reigned at the court and throughout the city of Vienna. The weather was cold, but the streets were thronged with people and hung with garlands. Nothing was thought of but balls, illuminations, and dress. Every one was curious to see the splendid spectacle of the day—the entrance of the bride of the King of Rome into Vienna.

The plans of the lord chancellor were beginning to unfold themselves. The Archduke Joseph had been crowned King of Rome at Frankfort, and the empress on his return, had prepared him for his second bridal. He had stoutly refused at first, but finally had yielded to the reasonings of his mother and the persuasions of his father. He had been told to choose between Mary Kunigunde and Josepha.

Not far from Toplitz, as if by accident, he met the Princess Mary out on a hunting party. The princess was on horseback; but she rode awkwardly, and her demeanor was shy and ungraceful. She well knew the object of this *casual* meeting, and when the King of Rome approached to greet her, she turned pale and trembled as she felt the gaze of his large blue eyes. Her paleness did not increase her beauty, nor did her shyness contribute to make her interesting. Joseph was annoyed at her taciturnity and disgusted with her ugliness. After a few brief words he bowed, and galloped off to join his retinue. The princess looked sadly after him, and returned home with a troubled heart. She knew that she had been disdained, and that the King of Rome would never choose her for his bride.

She was right. Joseph preferred the Princess Josepha, whom he had also "met by chance." He, like Count Dietrichstein, having the knife at his throat, selected her for his bride who was minus the flourishing black beard.

It was the 22d of January of the year 1765, and the wedding-day of the King of Rome. From early morning the archduchesses at the palace had been practising a lyric drama from the pen of Metastasio called "*Il Parnasso Confuso.*" The music was by Gluck, and his deep bass was heard accompanying the sweet rich voices of the bridegroom's sisters. They had studied their parts diligently, and felt quite confident of success, as they gathered around the *maestro.* But Gluck was never satisfied, and he kept Apollo and the Muses at their music-lesson until their ladies of honor were obliged to inform them that they must positively retire to their toilets, a courier having arrived to say that the princess had entered the gates of the city.

While all these preparations were going on around him, the King of Rome tarried in his private apartments. He was in the room wherein he had locked himself after the death of Isabella, the room where day and night he had deplored his lost happiness, until Christina had so rudely awakened him from his dream of love and sorrow.

This miserable consolation had had its effect. Joseph wiped away his tears, and having read Isabella's letters and convinced himself that she never had loved him, he had forborne to murmur at her loss.

On this, his bridal-day, he was thinking of the time when alone and heart-broken he had paced this room for three days and nights; and now, surrounded by festivity and splendor, he paced the floor again, awaiting the moment when he should have to mount his horse and meet the princess. He was not with the living bride, but with the dead one; and as he thought of her grace, her smiles, her surpassing beauty, his lip curled with a sneer, and his brow grew dark and stormy.

"And she, too, deceived me," said he; "those smiles, those glances, that love, all were false. While she lay in my arms and listened to my words of love, her heart was in the grave with her murdered lover! Oh, my God! now that I know that *she* deceived me, in whom can I place my trust? Even now, what am I but a dependent boy, the slave of the empress and of her all-powerful minister, who force upon me a woman whom I hate, and bid me make her the mother of my children? Oh, when will my shackles fall, when shall I be free!"

In the distance was heard the dull sound of a cannon. "Already!" cried the unhappy bridegroom. "It is time for me to meet my bride, and to begin the loathsome farce of a second bridal. Verily, if I did not hate this Josepha, I could pity her. She will not find me a loving husband. The Queen of Rome will never be an enviable woman!"

So saying, he threw around his shoulders his velvet cloak edged with ermine, and left the room to join his retinue. They were to meet the princess and accompany her to the castle of Schönbrunn. It was there that the imperial family awaited the bridal party, and there in the chapel the marriage was to be solemnized.

The streets were thronged with people that shouted for joy; the balconies and windows were filled with elegant women, who smiled and waved their hands in greeting to the royal pair. For all the world this was a day of rejoicing, except for the two persons for whose sake the rest rejoiced. These had no part in the universal gayety; and the mirth which was inspired by their presence found no echo in their souls—Joseph's heart was full of dislike and ill-will toward his betrothed, and she was unhappy, fearing the reception that awaited her. She had trembled as she thought of the meeting with Joseph, and then of the proud, powerful, and beautiful woman who was his mother. The fame of her intellect, fascinations, and beauty had reached the court of Munich, and poor Josepha knew very well that *she* was neither handsome, cultivated, nor charming. Her education had been neglected, and if she had attained to the honor of being Queen of Rome and Empress-elect of Austria, it was not that she had any right to a station so exalted, it was that her brother was childless and had promised his inheritance to Austria.

Josepha was sad as she thought of these things, but she could not suppress an emotion of joy when she saw the brilliant *cortége* that was coming from Vienna to meet her. This proud and handsome horseman, whose blue eyes shone like stars, this was her husband, the lord of her destiny! She had seen him once before, and had loved him from that moment. True, he had not chosen her from inclination, but she could not shut her heart to the bliss of being his wife, he who, to-day a king, would in future years place an imperial crown upon her brow.

And now the two cavalcades met; the carriage of the princess drew up, and the King of Rome dismounting, came toward her with a low inclination of the head. Around them stood the noblemen of his suite, whose splendid uniforms and decorations dazzled the eye with their brilliancy. They sprang from their horses and each one reverentially saluted the bride-elect. This done, the King of Rome assisted her to alight, that she might mount the magnificent horse which was now led forward by the empress's chief master of the horse.

When her betrothed held out his hand to her, Josepha, blushing, looked at him with a timid and tender glance, which seemed to implore a return of her love. She could not speak a word, but she pressed his hand.

Joseph, so far from returning the pressure, looked surprised—almost disdainful; and, stepping back, he left to the master of the horse and the other lords in waiting the care of assisting the princess to mount. She sprang into the saddle with perfect confidence, and grasped her reins with so much skill, that although the beautiful animal reared and pranced until his bridle was covered with foam, his rider was perfectly at ease.

"She is, at least, a good horsewoman," said Joseph to himself, as he took his place by her side.

And now the bells chimed merrily, and the cannon proclaimed to all Vienna that the royal pair were about to enter the city.

Silently they rode through the flower-strewn streets, silently they heard the joyous shouts of the multitude, here and there smiling wearily in return, but both tired of splendor, and both longing for rest. Neither spoke to the other; what had they to say to one another—they whom policy had chained together for life?

At the farther end of the city the state-coach of the empress awaited the princess. With an indifferent and careless air, Joseph handed Josepha to the carriage. This time she dared not press his hand; but as the door closed upon herself and her governess, she threw herself back upon the velvet cushions and wept bitterly.

"For the love of Heaven, what mean these tears, your highness?" cried the governess. "Your highness's head-dress will be ruined, and your eyes will be swollen."

"'Tis true," murmured Josepha, "I have no right to weep, as other women do, at such a time. I am nothing but a puppet, that laughs or weeps as etiquette ordains."

"Your highness is excited and does not see your destiny in its true light," replied the lady, with sympathy. "It is one which any woman on earth might envy. You are about to become the wife of the handsomest prince in all Europe, an emperor in prospect, and son of the great Maria Theresa, whose beauty and goodness are the theme of the whole world. And then the lovely and accomplished Archduchesses of Austria—they are to be your sisters-in-law!"

"Yes," said the princess, passionately, "and look at me. You have known me since my infancy, dear friend, therefore you need not flatter me because of my station. Look at me, and tell me if it is not enough to break my heart, that I must appear before this beautiful empress and her daughters, and that I must try to win the affections of this prince, the glance of whose eye is enough to kindle love in the heart of every woman living—oh say, and speak without reserve—tell me if a woman so obscure, so ignorant, and so destitute of charms, can ever hope to be loved or cherished by such a family?"

"Your highness is worthy of all affection, and deserves the choicest of the blessings that are in store for you," replied the lady of honor warmly. "No one knowing your noble heart would say that any station is too exalted for you."

"Oh! who will be troubled with looking into my heart in imperial Vienna?" sobbed the disheartened Josepha. "Externals are every thing in court; and I, unhappy one, who scarcely dare not utter my heart's yearnings to those who encourage me, what will become of me if I meet with cold glances or scornful words? I feel how little I am skilled to win love, and the consciousness of my defects heightens them and renders me still more repulsive."

"Your highness is unjust toward yourself. No one else would ever dream of speaking in such terms of you. Be happy, dear lady, and you will soon grow comely, too."

"Happy!" sighed the princess, looking from the window at the elegant and graceful prince, who, cold and stern as though he had been following the dead, vouchsafed not a look toward the carriage where sat his bride.

With another sigh she turned her head. Her eyes encountered those of the governess, fixed upon her in wondering sympathy. With a bitter smile Josepha laid her hand upon the shoulder of her friend.

"I must tell you something, Lucy," said she—"something terrible and sad. Hear well my words, and mark them! I already love my betrothed beyond power of expression; but he will never return my love. I shall worship him, and I feel that he will hate me!"

Blushing painfully at the sound of her own words, the princess hid her face in her hands.

The carriage stopped, and now the confused and self-tortured girl had to go forward to meet the emperor, who waited at the foot of the great staircase to conduct her to the presence of the empress.

Maria Theresa came gracefully forward, surrounded by her beautiful daughters and a dazzling train of lords and ladies. Josepha's head reeled when she saw them, and almost fainting, she sank down at the feet of the empress.

"Mercy, gracious empress, mercy!" sobbed the poor girl, almost beside herself with terror; while, regardless of all courtly decorum, she covered the hand of Maria Theresa with tears and kisses.

A sneer was perceptible on the faces of the courtiers, and the young archduchesses smiled derisively; but Maria Theresa, whose generous heart beat in sympathetic response to the emotion and fright of the poor young stranger, kindly raised her up, and, kissing her forehead, encouraged her with gracious words.

"Be welcome, my daughter," said she, in her clear and silvery voice. "May all the happiness be yours through life! Come, my children, let us hasten to the chapel."

She made a sign to her husband, and took the arm of the King of Rome. The emperor followed with the Princess Josepha, and now through the splendid halls, that dazzled the eye with festive magnificence, came the long train of courtiers and ladies that graced the pageant of this royal bridal. In the chapel, before the altar, stood Cardinal Megazzi, surrounded by priests and acolytes, all arrayed in the pomp and splendor attendant on a solemn Catholic ceremony.

The princess had not been wedded by proxy; it was therefore necessary that she should be married with the blessings of the church, before she proceeded in state to the throne-room to receive the homage due to her as a queen. No time had therefore been given her to retire before the ceremony, and she was married in her travelling-dress. At the entrance of the chapel stood the new ladies in waiting of the Queen of Rome. One of them relieved her of her hat, which the empress replaced by a wreath of myrtle. Then Maria Theresa, having placed the hand of Josepha in that of her son, the imperial *cortége* approached the altar.

As they stood before the chancel, the King of Rome, overcome by the bitterness of the moment, bowed his head to his unfortunate bride and whispered, "Poor Josepha, I pity you!"

CHAPTER XXVI.

THE MARRIAGE NIGHT.

THE ceremonial was over. The empress herself had conducted the young Queen of Rome to her apartments; and she had stood by her side, while her tire-woman exchanged her dress of golden tissue for a light white *négligée* of finest cambric trimmed with costly lace. With her own hand Maria Theresa unfastened the myrtle-wreath and coronet of diamonds that encircled her daughter-in-law's brow. She then kissed Josepha affectionately, and, bidding her good-night, she besought the blessing of God upon both her children.

And now the princess was alone in this vast apartment. On one side, under a canopy of blue velvet embroidered with gold, was the state-bed of the Queen of Rome. Close by stood the toilet of gold with its wilderness of jewels and *étuis*, all the gifts of the empress. On the walls of blue velvet hung large Venetian mirrors, filling the room with images of that gorgeous bed of state. In the centre, on a marble table, thirty wax-lights in silver candelabra illumined the splendor of the scene. The heavy velvet window curtains were closed; but they threw no shadow, for the park of Schönbrunn was illuminated by two hundred thousand lamps, which far and near lit up the castle on this festive evening with a flood of fiery splendor.*

The Queen of Rome was alone, her bridesmaids and attendants had left her, and she awaited her husband, who would enter her room through a private door which, close to the bed of state, led to his own apartments.

With beating heart and in feverish suspense, trembling with hope and fear, Josepha paced her magnificent room. Heavy sighs broke from her bosom, hot tears fell from her eyes.

"He will come," cried she, wringing her hands, "he will come and look into my face with his heavenly blue eyes, and I—I shall cast down mine like a culprit, and dare not confide my secret to him. O God! O God! I have sworn to conceal my infirmity, for it is not contagious and will harm no one—and yet my heart misgives me when I think that—Oh, no! no! It will soon be over, and

*Hormayer, "Reminiscences of Vienna," vol. v., page 31.

he will never have known it. Were he told of it, it might prejudice him against me, and how could I bear to see those beauteous eyes turned away from me in disgust? I will keep my secret; and after—my love shall atone to him for this one breach of faith. Oh, my God! teach me how to win him! I have nothing to bring to this splendid court save the gushing fountains of my love for him—oh, my father, why have I nothing but this to offer—why have I neither beauty nor grace to please my husband's eyes—for I love him, oh, I love him already more than my life!"

She started, for she heard a sound near the side door. Now the key turned in the lock, and in another moment the king walked in. He still wore the magnificent Spanish court-dress in which he had received the homage of his marriage guests. The order of the Golden Fleece was on his breast, and also the sparkling diamond cross of the imperial house of Hapsburg. Josepha, blushing, recalled to mind her night *négligée*, and dared not raise her eyes.

For a while they stood opposite to one another, Josepha in painful confusion; Joseph, his eyes bent with cold scrutiny upon her person. At length he approached and touched her gently on the arm.

"Why do you tremble so?" asked he kindly. "Raise your head and look at me."

Slowly she lifted her eyes, and looked at him with a gaze of entreaty.

"Now," said he, with a bitter smile, "am I so frightful that you have reason to tremble at my coming?"

"I did not tremble from fear or fright," said she, in a voice scarcely audible.

"Ah, you have no confidence in me," said he, "you wish to hide your emotions from me. And yet madame, let me tell you that nothing but mutual and perfect confidence will help us through this hour and through life. Come, then, Josepha, I will set you the example. I will confide in you without reserve. Give me your hand and let us sit together on yonder divan."

She placed her trembling hand within his, and he led her to the sofa. A flood of deep and silent joy overwhelmed her heart, as alone in that royal apartment, which was hers, she sat by the side of this man whom she had already loved with passion.

"First, madame, let me ask your forgiveness for accepting a hand which was not freely bestowed by yourself, but was placed in mine by the inexorable policy of the destiny that rules kings. In obeying the commands of your brother, you have not only married one whom you did not know, but perhaps you have been forced to stifle other wishes, other inclinations."

"No," cried she, earnestly, "no. I have left nothing to regret, I have made no sacrifice, I—"

"Yes, you have sacrificed your freedom, the most precious boon that Heaven has bestowed on man, to become the galley-slave of policy and princely station. Poor Josepha, I pity you!"

"Do not pity me," said Josepha, tearfully, "pity yourself, whose freedom has been sacrificed to me. You have given your honored hand to a woman whom you do not love, a woman who would be too happy—"

"Had she the power to free herself and me from this compulsory union," interrupted Joseph. "I believe you, for I read in your countenance that your heart is good and noble, and gladly would contribute to the happiness of your fellow-creatures. But we must both accept the destiny which the hand of diplomacy has woven for us. The heads that wear the crowns must also wear the thorns. But we will try to lighten the pain to one another. You have become my *wife* without love, and I, too, have become your *husband* —without love."

Josepha's head fell, she sighed, and murmured something which Joseph could not hear.

He went on: "I do not come to you with vain pretensions of a man who fancies he has won an honorable woman's heart because the priest has bid them love one another. I will not take advantage of the rights which either diplomacy or church has given me over you. Here at least there shall be no dissimulation; here we shall both be privileged to avow honestly and honorably that we are not lovers. Then let us be friends. I come to you in all frankness, offering myself to be to you as a brother. Perhaps it may come to pass that I win your love; perchance your goodness and your worth may win my sad heart back again to life—the day may come when we shall be able to say that we love each other. Let us await this day, and soften the interval by mutual confidence and trust. And should it ever come to us, Josepha, we will then seal with heart-felt embrace the bond which the church has made between us to-day. Take me, then, as brother and friend, and be to me a sister and companion. Will you, Josepha?"

He reached out his hand, and looked at her with a glance of brotherly kindness. She gave him hers with a mournful smile, and her eyes sought the ground.

"Welcome, then, my friend and sister," said Joseph warmly. "Now for unreserved confidence. You promise me that, do you not?"

"I promise," gasped the poor girl.

"And you will open your heart that I may read its every page?"

"I will—I promise to keep nothing from you."

"I promise the same to you, and perhaps this plant of friendship may one day bear the flowers of love. You are inexperienced in the ways of court-life. You will need a pilot to steer you safe amid reefs and breakers. I will be this pilot to you, I will teach you what to suspect and to avoid. Above all, never venture to have an opinion that does not coincide with that of the empress. We are all a pious and well-brought-up family who see with her eyes, and hear with her ears, and never dare confess that we possess sight or hearing in our own persons. Recollect that you, too, must fall in the line of puppets, and give up your senses to the empress."

"But in the depths of my own heart I trust that I may see with the eyes of the King of Rome," replied Josepha with a smile. "For if I am to learn from you, I must surely dare to use my senses."

"Yes; but let no one suspect that you learn any thing from me. In this court we tread on flowers; and if one of our flowers chances to wither we cover it over with a *pater-noster*, and that makes all right again."

"But suppose it will not be made right?" returned Josepha. "Suppose that prayer should fail?"

"Gracious Heaven, what do I hear!" cried Joseph. "What profane doubt are you so bold as to utter! You do not belong to the stupid, pious band, who think that prayer cures all woes? Poor Josepha, let no one but me hear such heresy from your lips--pray, pray; or make believe to pray; no one will ever ask you whether your heart is in it or not. And if any one seeks to know, answer nothing. Pray on, and mistrust every one."

"What! mistrust the generous friend whom kind Providence has given to me this day!" cried Josepha with feeling. "That I can never do. You have encouraged me to confide in you, and even had you not done so, you would have won my confidence unsought."

"I am glad that you think so," returned Joseph. "Let us begin at once, then. Have you a wish that I have it in my power to gratify? Or have you any thing in your heart which you will confide to me as a proof of your faith in my friendship?"

Josepha started, and her cheeks grew white with fear. This question awakened her from her short dream of hope and happiness, and she remembered that she *had* a secret which it was her duty to reveal to her husband. She looked furtively at him. Perhaps he had heard something, and this was a trial of her truth. But no! His face was tranquil and unsuspecting; there was nothing searching in the glance of his deep-blue eyes. No! he knew nothing, and wherefore cloud the brightness of the hour with a confession which might crush its promise of future bliss?

"Well," said Joseph kindly, "is there nothing on your heart that you would confide to your friend?"

"No!" at last said Josepha resolutely. "My life has been dull and uneventful. It is only to-day that I begin to live; the sun of hope is dawning upon my heart; I feel as if I might—"

"Hark!" said Joseph, "I think I hear some one coming. Yes; there is surely a light tap at the door."

The king rose hastily and crossed the room toward the little side-door.

"Is any one there?" asked he in a loud tone of displeasure.

"Yes, your majesty," whispered a trembling voice, "and I pray you earnestly to open the door."

"It is my valet Anselmo," said Joseph to the princess, while he withdrew the bolt.

It was Anselmo, in truth, who, with mysterious mien, beckoned to his lord to come out.

"Will your majesty condescend to step into the corridor, that I may deliver the message with which I am intrusted?" said the valet.

"Is it so weighty, Anselmo, that it cannot lie upon your conscience until morning?"

"Not one moment can I defer it, your majesty, for I was told that your majesty's well-being and health depended upon my speed."

The king stepped outside and closed the door. "Who sent you hither, Anselmo?" asked he.

"I do not know, sire, but I suspect. It was a female form enveloped in a long black cloak, with a hood which concealed her face. She came from the gallery which leads to the apartments of their imperial highnesses, your majesty's sisters, and entered your majesty's own cabinet, which I had left open while I was lighting your majesty hither."

"And what said she?" asked the king impatiently.

"She asked if your majesty had gone into the queen's apartments,

When I told her that you had, she held out this note and said: 'Speed to the king, and as you value his health and welfare, give him this note at once.' She disappeared, and here, your majesty, is the note."

The king took the paper, which by the dim light of the corridor he could not read.

"And who do you think is the mysterious lady, Anselmo?" asked he.

"Sire, I do not know. Perhaps your majesty will recognize the handwriting."

"I wish to know, Anselmo, who *you* think was hidden under that cloak?"

"Well, then, your majesty," said Anselmo, in a whisper scarcely audible, "I think it was the Archduchess Christina."

"I suspected as much," said the king to himself. "It is some intrigue of hers against the Princess Josepha, whom she hates because I selected her in preference to the sister of Christina's lover, the Elector of Saxony." *

Perhaps Anselmo understood a few words of this soliloquy, for he continued: "A courier arrived from Saxony, and I was told by my sister, the tire-woman of her highness, that the Archduchess Christina had received a packet of letters."

"Very well, Anselmo," said the king, "if to-morrow you should be asked whether you delivered the note, say that I tore it up without opening it. Do you hear?"

Dismissing the valet with a wave of the hand, he returned to the princess.

"Pardon me," said he, "for leaving you, and allow me in your presence to read a note which has just been mysteriously delivered into my hands. I wish to give you a proof of my confidence, by intrusting you at once with my secrets."

So saying, he approached the marble centre-table, and opened the letter.

What was it that blanched Josepha's cheek and made her tremble, as Joseph smiled and looked at her? Why did she stare at him while he read, and why did her heart stand still with fright, as she saw his expression change?

He seemed shocked at the contents of the note, and when he raised his eyes and their glance met that of Josepha, she saw them filled with aversion and scorn.

"Madame," said he, and his voice had grown harsh, "madame, I asked you in good faith whether you had anything to confide to my honor. I expressed a desire to win your confidence. You answered that you had nothing to tell. Once more I ask, have you any thing to say? The more humiliating the confession, the more will I appreciate your candor. Speak, therefore."

Josepha answered not a word. Her teeth chattered so painfully that she could not articulate; she trembled so violently that she had to grasp the back of an arm-chair for support.

Joseph saw this, and he laughed a hoarse and contemptuous

* The Princess Christina was in love with the Elector of Saxony; but the Emperor Francis was opposed to the marriage. Christina used all her influence to bring about a marriage between her brother and Mary Kunigunde, the sister of her lover, hoping thereby to pave the way for her own union with the handsome Albert. Failing in this, she beeame the bitter enemy of the unhappy woman to whom Joseph had given the preference.

laugh. She did not ask him why he sneered. She threw herself at his feet, and raised her arms imploringly.

"Mercy," cried the unhappy woman, "mercy!"

He laughed again, and held the paper before her eyes.

"Read, madame, read!" said he rudely.

"I cannot," sobbed she. "I will not read what has been written of me. I will tell you myself all that I know. I will confide my secret to you; I will indeed."

"You have nothing to confide, madame," cried Joseph. "With a sincere and holy desire to perform my duty, I asked for your friendship and your confidence. I cast them both back, for you have allowed the hour of trust to go by! Now it is too late! You are accused. Do not look to me for protection; vindicate yourself if you can. Read this letter, and tell me if the writer speaks the truth."

Josepha still knelt at his feet; but her arms had fallen in despair. She knew that she had nothing more to hope from her husband: she felt that she was about to be sentenced to a life of utter misery.

"You will not read?" said Joseph, as unnoticed, Josepha lay at his feet. "If so, I must read the letter for you myself. It warns me not to come too near to your royal person. It—"

"I will spare you, sire," exclaimed she, as with the energy of despair she rose to her feet. "You will not let me speak, you shall *see* for yourself!"

With a frantic gesture, she tore her dress from her neck and shoulders, and heedless that she stood with arms and bosom exposed, she let it fall to the floor, and bowed her head as if to receive the stroke of the headsman's axe.

"Know my secret," said she, as she folded her hands and stood before her outraged husband. "And now hear me. A few months ago I had a beloved brother, whom I loved the more that he was unfortunate and afflicted. From his childhood he had suffered from a malady which his physicians called leprosy. The very servants deserted him, for it was said that the disease was contagious. I loved my brother with devotion; I went to him, and nursed him until he died. God shielded me, for I did not take the malady. But on my neck and back there came dark spots which, although they are painful, are not contagious. My physicians told me that my strong constitution had rejected the leprosy, and these spots were a regeneration of my skin, which would soon disappear. This, sire, is my fatal secret; and now judge me. It is in your power to make me the happiest of mortals, by granting me a generous pardon; but I will not complain if you condemn and despise me."

"Complain if you choose, it is indifferent to me," cried Joseph, with a hoarse laugh. "Never in this world shall you be my wife. If the hateful tie that binds me to you cannot be unloosed, I will make you answerable for every day of disgust and misery that I am forced to pass under the same roof with you. If I am cursed before the world with the name of your husband, I shall punish you in secret with my everlasting hate."

As if stricken by lightning, she fell to the floor. Her fallen dress exposed to view her beautiful form. Her arms, which were folded above her head, were round and white as those of a Greek statue; and as she lay with her full, graceful shoulders bared almost to the waist, she looked like Niobe just stricken by the wrath of a god.

Joseph was unmindful of this. He had no sympathy with the noble sacrifice which her loving heart had offered to a dying brother. He saw neither her youth nor her grace; he saw but those dark spots upon her back, and he shuddered as she raised her arm to clasp his feet.

"Do not touch me," exclaimed he, starting back. "Your touch is pollution. We are forever divorced. To day the priest joined our hands together, but to-night I part them never more to meet. Farewell."

And hurling at her prostrate form the letter which had betrayed her, he turned and left the room.

CHAPTER XXVII.

AN UNHAPPY MARRIAGE.

It was the morning after the wedding. Maria Theresa had just completed her toilet, and was smiling at her own beautiful image reflected in the looking-glass. She looked every inch an empress in her rich crimson velvet dress, with its long and graceful train, and its border of ermine. Her superb blond hair had been exquisitely dressed by her little favorite Charlotte von Hieronymus. It was sprinkled with gold-powder, and the *coiffure* was heightened by a little cap of crimson velvet, attached to the hair by arrows of gold set with costly brilliants. The complexion of the empress was so lovely, that she never wore *rouge;* and surely such eyes as hers needed none of the "adulteries of art" to heighten their brilliancy or beauty. Although she was in her forty-ninth year, and had given birth to sixteen children, Maria Theresa was still beautiful; not only youthful in appearance, but youthful in heart, and in the strength and greatness of her intellect. She loved the emperor as fondly as she had done twenty-eight years before, and each of her ten living children was as dear to her maternal heart as if each had been an only child.

She had arrayed herself with unusual magnificence to celebrate the entry of the newly-married couple into Vienna. The imperial *cortége* was to stop at the cathedral of St. Stephen, there to witness the bridals of twenty-five young couples, all of whom the empress had dowered in honor of her son's second marriage.

"Surely the prayers of these fifty lovers will bring happiness upon the heads of my son and his wife," said the empress to herself. "They need prayers indeed, for poor Josepha is very unlike our peerless Isabella, and I fear she will not be attractive enough to cause the dead to be forgotten. Still, she seems mild and kind-hearted, and I have already read in her eyes that she is in love with Joseph. I hope this will lead him to love her in return. Sometimes a man will love a woman through pity, afterward through habit."

A nervous and impatient knock at her door interrupted the current of the empress's thoughts: the door was flung open without further ceremony, and the King of Rome entered the room. He was pale and agitated, and to his mother's affectionate welcome he replied by a deep inclination of the head.

The empress perceived at once that something was wrong, and her heart beat rapidly.

"My dear boy," said she, "you do not wear a holiday face, and your young bride—"

"I have no bride," interrupted Joseph, angrily. "I have come to beg of your majesty to discontinue these rejoicings, or at least to excuse *me* from appearing in public at the side of the Princess of Bavaria. She is not my wife, nor ever shall be!"

"What means this?" stammered the empress, bewildered.

"It means that my marriage is null and void; and that no human power shall force me to be husband of a creature tainted with leprosy."

The empress uttered a cry of horror.

"My son, my son!" exclaimed she, "what unheard-of charge is this?"

"A charge which is a miserable truth, your majesty. Do you not remember to have heard that the natural son of Charles of Bavaria had died, not long ago, of leprosy which he had contracted during a journey to the East? Well, his tender and self-sacrificing half-sister volunteered to nurse him, and was with him until he died. Your majesty, no doubt, will look upon this as something very fine and Christian-like. I, on the contrary, would have found it more honorable, if the princess had advised us of the legacy she wears upon her back."

"Woe to her and to the house of Bavaria, if you speak the truth, my son!" cried the empress, indignantly.

"If your majesty will send Van Swieten to her, you may convince yourself of the fact."

A few moments later Van Swieten entered the room. His fame was European. He was well known as a man of great skill and science; added to this, his noble frankness and high moral worth had greatly endeared him to the imperial family. Maria Theresa went hastily forward to meet him.

"Van Swieten," said she, with a voice trembling from agitation, "you have been our friend in many an hour of sorrow, and many a secret of the house of Hapsburg has been faithfully buried in your loyal heart. Help me again, and, above all, let it be in secrecy. The King of Rome says fearful things of his wife. I will not believe them until I hear your verdict. Go at once, I implore you, to the princess, and command her, in my name, to declare her malady."

"But, your majesty, she has not called for my advice," replied Van Swieten, with surprise.

"Then she must take it unasked," said the empress. "The princess will receive you, and you will know how to win her to reveal her condition. As soon as you leave her, return to me."

Van Swieten bowed and left the room. The empress and her son remained together. Neither spoke a word. The King of Rome stood in the embrasure of a window, looking sullenly up at the sky. The empress walked hurriedly to and fro, careless that her violent motions were filling her dress with the gold powder that fell from her head like little showers of stars.

"Christina was right to warn me," said she, after a long pause. "I never should have consented to this alliance with the daughter of my enemy. It is of no use to patch up old enmities. Charles was humbled and defeated by me, and now comes this Josepha to revenge her father's losses, and to bring sorrow to my child. Oh, my son, why did you not follow my counsel, and marry the Princess of Saxony? But it is useless to reproach you. The evil is done—let us consult together how best we may bear it."

"Not at all!" cried Joseph. "We must consult how we may soonest cast it away from us. Your majesty will never require of me the sacrifice of remaining bound to that woman. I obeyed your behest; and in spite of my disinclination to a second marriage, I bent my will before the necessities of diplomacy, and the command of my sovereign. But we are now on a ground where the duty of a subject ends, and the honor of a man stands preëminent. I never will consent to be the husband of this woman whose person is disgusting to me. Far above all claims of political expediency, I hold my right as a man."

"But you hold them with unbecoming language," replied the empress, who did not at all relish the tone of the King of Rome. "And let me tell you, my royal son, that an upright and honorable prince thinks less of his rights as a man than of his duties as a ruler. He strives, while a prince, to be a man; and while a man, to sacrifice his inclinations to the calls of a princely station."

"But not his personal honor," cried Joseph. "Your majesty's code is that of Macchiavelli, who counsels a prince never to let his feelings as a man interfere with his policy as a ruler."

The empress was about to make an angry rejoinder to this remark, when the door opened, and Van Swieten reappeared.

"Ah!" said the empress, "did you see her, Van Swieten?"

"Yes, your majesty," replied Van Swieten, with emphasis, "I have seen the Queen of Rome."

"Do you mean to say that she has no disease that unfits her to be the wife of the King of Rome?" asked Maria Theresa.

"Her only malady is a cutaneous one, which in a short time will be completely cured. Some persons are so happily organized that they throw off disease, even when in contact with it. The princess possesses this sound and healthy organization. The poison which she inhaled by her brother's bedside, has settled upon her skin in a harmless eruption—her constitution is untouched. In a few weeks all trace of it will disappear, and nothing will remain to remind us of her noble disregard of self, save the memory of her heroism and magnanimity. For, indeed, your majesty, it is easier to confront death on the battle-field than to face it in the pestiferous atmosphere of a sick-room."

Maria Theresa turned with a radiant smile toward her son. "You see, my son," said she, "that you have done injustice to your noble wife. Go, then, and entreat her forgiveness."

"No, your majesty," said a soft voice behind them, "it is for me to implore my husband's forgiveness."

The empress turned and beheld her daughter-in-law, splendidly attired, but pale and wan with unmistakable grief.

"Josepha, how came you hither?" asked she.

"I followed Herr van Swieten," replied Josepha. "He told me that your majesty and the King of Rome were here, awaiting his verdict, and I judged from his manner that it would be in my favor. Therefore I came, and having heard his flattering words, which I do not deserve, I am here to inculpate myself. No, Herr van Swieten, if there were any merit in suffering for a brother whom I dearly loved, it would all be effaced by the wrong which I have done to the King of Rome. I feel that I was guilty in not confiding my malady to your majesty, and I bow my head before the justice of my punishment, severe though it may be."

"It shall not be severe, my daughter," said the empress, whose kind heart was completely overcome by Josepha's humility—"I, for my part, forgive you; you are already sufficiently punished."

"I thank your majesty," returned Josepha, kissing her outstretched hand. "It is easy for one so magnanimous, to pardon the guilty; but my husband, will he also forgive me?"

She turned her pale and imploring face toward Joseph, who, with his arms crossed, looked scornfully back.

"No," said she sadly, "no. To obtain his forgiveness, I must make a full confession of my fault."

She approached the window, but her head was cast down so that she did not see with what a look of hate Joseph beheld her advancing toward him.

"To obtain your pardon, sire," said she, "I must say why I deceived you. It was because I preferred perjury to the loss of my earthly happiness—the unspeakable happiness of being your wife. I was afraid of losing my treasure. For I love you beyond all power of expression; from the first moment of our meeting, I have loved you, and this love which, thanks to Almighty God, I have a right to avow before the world—this love it was that misled me. Oh, my husband, have mercy, and forgive the fault that was born of my excessive love for you. A whole life of love and obedience shall atone for my sin. Forgive me, forgive me, for the sake of my love!"

And, overwhelmed by her grief, the princess knelt at the feet of her husband, and raised her hands in supplication for pardon.

The empress looked on with sympathetic heart and tearful eyes; she expected at every moment to see Joseph raise up his wife, and press her to his heart for her touching avowal of love. She expected to hear *him* implore forgiveness; but she was sadly mistaken.

Joseph stood immovable, his eyes flashing scorn and fury at the kneeling princess before him.

This outraged all the pride of Maria Theresa's womanhood. Hastily approaching Josepha, and stretching her arms toward her, she said: "If Joseph has no mercy in his obdurate heart, I at least will not witness such humiliation on the part of his wife. Rise, my daughter, and take shelter under my love; I will not suffer you to be oppressed—not even by my own son."

She would have raised Josepha, but the poor girl waved her gently back. "No, dear lady," said she, sobbing, "let me remain until he forgives me."

"Let her remain, your majesty," cried Joseph with a burst of wrath, "she is in her proper place. But if she means to kneel until she has obtained my forgiveness, let her kneel throughout all eternity! I consented to this marriage for expediency's sake, and I would have done my best to make the burden as light for us both as lay in my power. Your majesty knows how she has deceived me; you have heard her pitiful lie with its pitiful excuse. I might have forgiven her for marrying me, with her disgusting disease, but for being a liar—never!"

"Enough," cried the empress, as much excited by her son's obduracy as by Josepha's touching confession. "This scene must end, and so help me God, it shall never be enacted a second time! You are bound to one another for life, and together you shall remain. Each mortal has his weight of grief to bear. Bear yours in silence, and bear it as becomes your dignity and station. Have the manliness to smile before the world, my son, as beseems a prince who has more regard for his princely duties than for his rights as a man to happiness."

And with that imposing grandeur which Maria Theresa knew so well how to assume, she continued: "Rise, Queen of Rome, and never again forget either your own royal station or the dignity of your womanhood. Give her your hand, my son; if you will not love, you must at least honor and respect your wife. The bells of Vienna even now are pealing your welcome; the people await their sovereigns, and it does not become us to keep them in suspense on such an occasion as this."

Without looking back to see the effect of her words, the empress left the room, and called to her pages to fling wide the palace doors.

"Apprise the court that we are ready to move," said she, in a commanding voice, "and let the carriages approach."

The pages threw open the wide doors; the emperor and the archduchesses entered, and following them came the courtiers and ladies of the imperial household in all the splendor of flashing jewels and costly robes.

The empress, with unruffled serenity, advanced to meet them. Not once were her eyes cast behind toward the unhappy couple, whom she knew perfectly well had yielded to the force of circumstances, and were already throwing the veil of etiquette and courtly decorum over their bleeding hearts.

An hour later the imperial family made its entry into Vienna. In her gilded state-carriage sat the proud and beautiful empress, and at her side was the pale Queen of Rome. On either side of the carriage rode the two husbands, the Emperor Francis of Lorraine and the King of Rome. The people once more shouted for joy, wishing long life to the imperial pair, and joy to the newly-married couple. From one side to another the empress and the queen bowed and smiled to all, while the King of Rome thanked the enraptured Viennese for their welcome. On this day appeared a new color in Vienna, so called in honor of Joseph's deep-blue eyes; it was called "imperial blue."

And the bells chimed; the cannon roared; while in the cathedral the fifty lovers awaited the King and Queen of Rome, whose marriage filled all hearts with joy, and seemed to realize every dream of happiness on earth.

CHAPTER XXVIII.

A STATESMAN'S HOURS OF DALLIANCE.

"ARE there many people in the anteroom?" asked Prince Kaunitz of the state *referendarius*, Baron Binder.

"Yes, your highness," returned Binder, "all waiting impatiently for your appearance."

"Let them wait, the stupid, strutting representatives of littleness! The more insignificant the petty masters, the more conceited are the petty ambassadors. I have no time to see them to-day. We are at peace with the whole world, and our only diplomacy regards marrying and giving in marriage."

"So far you have nothing to boast of in that line," said Binder, laughing. "There are all sorts of stories afloat about the unhappy marriage of the King of Rome. Some go so far as to say that he shows his dislike in public."

"Bah! what matters it whether a prince is a happy husband or not? When a king sets up pretensions to conjugal felicity, he is either an egotist or a fool. If the King of Rome cannot love his good, stupid, ugly wife, he can make love to the dowry she brings him. A goodly inheritance comes with her; what matters it if a woman be thrown into the bargain?"

"Ah, prince, a woman is sometimes harder to conquer than a province; and I think the King of Rome would much rather have won his Bavaria with the sword."

"Because he is a blockhead full of sublime nonsense, who mistakes his love of novelty for wisdom. He would break his head against a wall, this obstinate King of Rome, while I crept safely through a mouse-hole. Walls are not so easily battered down as he supposes; but mouse-holes abound everywhere, as this sapient king will find out some of these days. It was much easier for us to creep into Bavaria with the help of the lovely Josepha, than to flourish our sword in her brother's face. He has not long to live, and we shall come peacefully in possession of his fair province."

"Or rather, the war for its possession will be waged in the king's private apartments."

"On that silly subject again!" exclaimed Kaunitz, impatiently. "If your heart bleeds so freely for the sentimental sorrows of the King of Rome, you may have another opportunity for your sensibilities in the marriage of his brother Leopold; for I assure you that his intended is not one whit handsomer, or more intelligent, than Josepha of Bavaria. So you see that the King of Rome will not be apt to envy his brother."

"Your highness is to escort the Infanta of Spain to Innspruck?"

"Not I, indeed; that honor I do not confer upon insignificant princesses who are nothing but grand-duchesses elect. I go to Innspruck one day sooner than the imperial family, to inspect the preparations for the festivities, and then I shall go as far as the gates of Innspruck—no farther, to receive Donna Maria Louisa."

"That is the reason why your levee is so crowded to-day," replied Binder laughing. "The foreign ministers wish to take leave of their master. And now they have waited long enough for you, prince."

"I shall not see one of them. Austria, thanks to me, is now so powerful, that I need give myself no concern to soothe the anger of a dozen petty envoys, and to-day there are none other in the ante-room."

"The Dutch and Saxon ministers," urged Binder.

"Little nobodies," said Kaunitz, with a shrug. "I will not see them."

"But, indeed, you presume too much upon their littleness. Only yesterday you invited the Hessian ambassador to dine, and then you sat down to table without him."

"He was three minutes behind the time. And do you imagine that Prince Kaunitz waits for a poor little Hessian envoy? I did it on purpose to teach him punctuality."

Here the prince rang a bell, and ordered a page to dismiss the gentlemen in the anteroom.*

Baron Binder looked after the page and shook his head. Kaunitz smiled. "Enough of ambassadors for to-day. The ship of Austria lies proudly and safely in the haven of her own greatness; and would you deprive the pilot of a few hours of relaxation? I shall have to take the helm again to-morrow, when I go to Innspruck, and do you grumble if for a few hours I enjoy life to-day?"

"I was not aware that dismissing one's visitors was a way to enjoy life," said Binder.

"I do not mean that, you old pedant. Do you hear that tapping at the door?"

"Yes, I hear it. It is from the little private door that leads to the corridor."

"Well, that corridor, as you know, leads to a side-entrance of the palace, and if you look out of the window you will see there the equipage of the handsomest, frailest, and most fascinating actress in all Vienna—the equipage of the divine Foliazzi. Hear how the knocking grows louder. My charmer becomes impatient."

"Allow me to retire, then," said Binder, "and leave the field to the prima donna." As he left the room, he muttered: "If Kaunitz were not a great statesman, he would be a ridiculous old fop!"

Kaunitz listened with perfect unconcern to the repeated knocking of his charmer until Binder was out of sight, then he walked up to the looking-glass, smoothed his locks, straightened his ruffles, and drew the bolt of the door. The beautiful Foliazzi, in a coquettish and most becoming morning-costume, radiant with smiles and beauty, entered the room.

Kaunitz greeted her coldly, and answered her rapturous salutation by a faint nod. "Your impatience is very annoying, Olympia," said he; "you beat upon my door like a drum-major."

"Your highness, it is the impatience of a longing heart," said the singer. "Do you know that it seems to me a thousand years since last I was allowed to enter these gates of Paradise! For eight days I have been plunged in deepest sorrow, watching your carriage as it passed by my house, snatching every note from my footman's hands in the hope that it might be one from you—hoping in vain, and at last yielded myself up to fell despair."

"You express yourself warmly," said Kaunitz, unmoved.

"Yes, indeed; for a feeling heart always finds strong expression," answered the signora, showing a row of teeth between her rosy lips that looked like precious pearls. "And now my adored reprobate, why have you banished me from your presence for an eternity? Which of my two enemies have prevailed against me, politics or the Countess Clary? Justify yourself, unkind but beloved prince; say that you have not deceived me, for my heart yearns to forgive you?"

She came very, very near, and with her bewitching smiles looked up into Kaunitz's face.

Kaunitz bent to receive the caress, and laid his hand fondly upon her raven black hair. "Is it true that you have longed for me—very true indeed?" said he.

*Report of the Prussian ambassador Baron Furst to Frederick II.

"I never knew how dear you were to me until I had endured the intolerable pangs of your absence," replied Foliazzi, leaning her head upon the prince's shoulder.

"You love me, then, Olympia? Tell me, dearest, tell me truly?"

"Unjust! You ask me such a question!" cried the signora, putting her arms around the prince's neck. "If I love you? Do you not feel it in every pulsation of my heart? do you not read it in every glance of my eyes? Can you not *feel* that my only thought is of you—my only life, your love?"

"I am really glad to hear it," said Kaunitz, with statue-like tranquillity. "And now I will tell you why I have not sent for you this past week. It was that I might not interrupt your tender interviews with Count Palffy, nor frighten away the poor enamoured fool from the snares you were laying for him."

The signora looked perfectly astounded. "But surely," stammered she, "your highness does not believe—"

"Oh, no! I believe nothing; I know that the Olympia who loves me so passionately, has been for two days the fair friend of the young, rich, and prodigal Count Palffy."

Here the signora laughed outright. "But, your highness, if you knew this, why did you not stop me in my protestations, and tell me so?"

"I only wanted to see whether, really, you were a finished actress. I congratulate you, Olympia; I could not have done it better myself."

"Prince," said the signora, seriously, "I learned the whole of this scene from yourself; and in my relations with you I have followed the example you gave me. While you swore eternal love to me, you were making declarations to the Countess Clary. Oh, my lord, I have suffered at your hands, and the whole world sympathizes with my disappointment! The whole world knows of your double dealings with women, and calls you a heartless young libertine."

"Does it?" cried Kaunitz, for a moment forgetting his coldness, and showing his satisfaction in his face. "Does it, indeed, call me a heartless young libertine?"

"Yes," replied the signora, who seemed not to see his gratification. "And when people see a man who is adored by women, and is false to them all, they say, 'He is a little Kaunitz.'"

When the signora said this, Kaunitz did what he had not done for years, he broke out into a laugh, repeating triumphantly, "A little Kaunitz. But mark you," continued he, "other libertines are called *little* Kaunitzes, but I alone am the *great* Kaunitz."

"True," sighed the signora, "and this great Kaunitz it is who has abandoned me. While I worshipped the air he breathed, he sat at the feet of the Countess Clary, repeating to her the self-same protestations with which an hour before he had intoxicated my senses. Oh, when I heard this, jealousy and despair took possession of my soul. I was resolved to be revenged, and so I permitted the advances of Count Palffy. Ha! while I endured his presence, I felt that my heart was wholly and forever yours! Oh, my adored, my great Kaunitz, say that you love me, and at your feet I throw all the lesser Kaunitzes in token of my fealty!"

The signora would have flung her arms around him, but Kaunitz with a commanding gesture waved her off.

"Very well done, Olympia," said he, nodding his head. "You are as accomplished as you are beautiful; and well I understand how it is that you infatuate by your charms all manner of little Kaunitzes. But now listen to Kaunitz the great. I not only allow, but order you to continue your intrigue with Count Palffy. Take every thing he offers; wring his purse dry; and the sooner you ruin him the better."

"That means that I importune you with my love. Farewell, prince, and may you never repent of your cruelty to poor Olympia."

"Stay," said Kaunitz, coolly. "I have not done with you. Continue your amours with the Hungarian, and love him as much as you choose, provided—"

"Provided?" echoed the singer anxiously, as Kaunitz paused.

"Provided you affect before the world to be still my mistress."

"Oh, my beloved prince," cried Foliazzi, "you will not cast me off!" and in spite of his disinclination she folded Kaunitz to her heart.

The prince struggled to get free. "You have disarranged my whole dress," said he, peevishly. "On account of your folly I shall have to make my toilet again. Hear me, and let me alone. I said that you would *affect* to be my mistress. To this end you will drive as usual to the side-door by which you have been accustomed to enter the palace, and while your carriage stands there for one hour, you shall be treated to a costly breakfast in my little boudoir every morning."

"By your side, my own prince?"

"By yourself, my own Olympia. I have not time to devote an hour to you every day. Your carriage shall stand at my door in the morning. Every evening mine will be for an hour before yours, and while it remains there I forbid you to be at home to any one whatsoever."

"I shall think of nothing but you until that hour," said the signora, fondly.

"*Vraiment*, you are very presuming to suppose that I shall trouble myself to come in the carriage," replied Kaunitz, contemptuously. "It is enough that the coach being there, the world will suppose that I am there also. A man of fashion must have the name of possessing a mistress; but a statesman cannot waste his valuable time on women. You are my mistress, *ostensibly*, and therefore I give you a year's salary of four thousand guilders."

"You are an angel—a god!" cried La Foliazzi, this time with genuine rapture. "You come upon one like Jupiter, in a shower of gold."

"Yes, but I have no wish to fall into the embraces of my Danæ. Now, hear my last words. If you ever dare let it transpire that you are not really my mistress, I shall punish you severely. I will not only stop your salary, but I will cite you before the committee of morals, and you shall be forced into a marriage with somebody."

The singer shuddered and drew back. "Let me go at once into my boudoir. Is my breakfast ready?"

"No—your morning visits there begin to-morrow. Now go home to Count Palffy, and do not forget our contract."

"I shall not forget it, prince," replied the signora, smiling. "I await your coach this evening. You may kiss me if you choose."

She bent her head to his and held out her delicate cheek, fresh as a rose.

"Simpleton," said he, slightly tapping her beautiful mouth, "do you suppose that the great Kaunitz would kiss any lips but those which, like the sensitive mimosa, shrink from the touch of man! Go away. Count Palffy will feel honored to reap the kisses I have left."

He gave her his hand, and looked after her, as with light and graceful carriage she left the room.

"She is surpassingly beautiful," said Kaunitz to himself. "Every one envies me; but each one thinks it quite a matter of course that the loveliest woman in Vienna should be glad to be my mistress. Ah! two o'clock. My guests await me. But before I go I must bring down the Countess Clary from the airy heaven which she has built for herself."

He rang, and a page appeared; for from the time he became a prince, Kaunitz introduced four pages in his household, and kept open table daily for twelve persons.

"Tell the Countess Clary," said he, "that in a few moments I will conduct her to the dining-room. Then await me in my *puder-kammer.*"

CHAPTER XXIX.

PRINCE KAUNITZ AND RITTER GLUCK.

PRINCE KAUNITZ had finished his promenade in the powder-room, and having ascertained by means of his mirror that his peruke was in order, he betook himself to the apartments of the Countess Clary, to conduct her to table.

The young countess, Kaunitz's niece, and a widow scarcely thirty years of age, flew to greet her uncle, radiant with smiles and happiness.

"What an unexpected honor you confer upon me, my dear uncle!" said she, with her sweet low voice. "Coming yourself to conduct me to the table! How I thank you for preparing me a triumph which every woman in Vienna will envy me."

"I came with no intention whatever of preparing you a triumph or a pleasure. I came solely because I wish to have a few words with you before we go to dinner."

"I am all ears, your highness," said the countess, smiling.

Kaunitz looked at his young and lovely niece with uncommon scrutiny. "You have been crying," said he, after a pause.

"No, indeed," said she, blushing.

"Do you suppose that you can deceive me? I repeat it, you have been crying. Will you presume to contradict me?"

"No, dear uncle, I will not."

"And wherefore? No prevarication; I must know."

The young countess raised her soft blue eyes to the face of the haughty prince. "I will tell the truth," said she, again blushing. "I was crying because La Foliazzi was so long with you to-day."

"Jealous, too!" said Kaunitz, with a sneer. "And pray, who ever gave *you* the right of being jealous of me?"

The countess said nothing, but her eyes filled with tears.

"Allow me to discuss this matter with you. I came for this purpose. Our relations must be distinctly understood, if they are to last. You must have the goodness to remember their origin. When you were left a widow you turned to me, as your nearest relative, for assistance. You were unprotected, and your husband had left you nothing. I gave you my protection, not because I was in any way pleased with you, but because you were my sister's child. I invited you hither to do the honors of my house, to give orders to the cooks and steward, to overlook my household arrangements, and to receive my guests in a manner worthy of their host. To insure you the appearance and consideration due to you as my niece and as the lady of my house, I gave you a remuneration of two thousand guilders a year. Were not these my terms?"

"Yes, your highness, they were. They filled me with gratitude and joy; and never will I forget your kindness."

"It seems, however, that you do forget it," replied the heartless uncle. "How does it happen that you take the liberty of being unhappy because La Foliazzi is in my room? What business is it of yours, whom I receive or entertain? Have I ever given you the slightest hope that from my niece I would ever raise you to the eminence of being my wife?"

"Never, never, dear uncle," said the countess, scarlet with shame. "You have never been otherwise to me than my generous benefactor."

"Then oblige me by silencing the absurd rumors that may have led you into the delusion of supposing that I intended to make of you a princess. I wish you to know that I have no idea of marrying again; and if ever I should form another matrimonial alliance, it will either be with an imperial or a royal princess. Will you be so good as to remember this, and to act accordingly?"

"Certainly," replied the countess, her eyes filling with tears. "I assure your highness that I have never been so presuming as to regard you otherwise than as my kinsman and guardian. My feelings of admiration for you are indeed enthusiastic; but I have never felt any thing toward you but the attachment of a daughter."

"Pray do not trouble yourself to feel any thing at all on my account," said Kaunitz, ill-humoredly. "I am not under the necessity of playing the part of a tender father toward you; therefore, dry up the tears you took the trouble to shed on La Foliazzi's account. But enough of this folly. I hope that we understand each other, and that I will not have to repeat this conversation. Be so good as to take my arm. We will go forward to meet our guests."

The young countess took the arm of the prince, and they entered the drawing-room. The guests had long been assembled there, but it never occurred to Kaunitz to make any apology for his late appearance. Nevertheless, his guests were all noble; some of them representatives of princely houses or powerful kingdoms. Kaunitz, however, was not only the all-powerful minister of Maria Theresa; it was well known that his slender, diamond-studded fingers directed the policy of all Europe. No one in that room had the courage to resent his rudeness. All seemed to feel honored as he walked haughtily forward with a slight inclination of his head to the many, and a condescending smile to the few whom it pleased him to distinguish by his notice.*

*Wraxall, "Memoirs," vol. i., page 380.

Prince Kaunitz did not choose to perceive that several distinguished ambassadors, as well as a German prince, himself a reigning sovereign, were present as his guests. He passed them all by to accost a small, graceful man who, seated in a recess, had received no further attention from the high-born company than a condescending nod. Kaunitz gave him his hand, and welcomed him audibly. The honored guest was Noverre, the inventor of the ballet as it is performed to-day on the stage. Noverre blushed with pleasure at the reception given him, while the other guests scarcely concealed their chagrin.

Just then the folding-doors were thrown wide open, and the steward announced in a loud voice that the table of his lord the prince was served. The company arose, and the ladies looked to see which of them was to have the honor of being conducted to the table by the host. Kaunitz feigned neither to see nor to hear. He continued his conversation with Noverre, and when he had quite done, he sauntered carelessly up to his other guests. Suddenly he paused, and his eyes wandered from one to another with a searching glance.

"Good Heaven!" exclaimed he, "of what a rudenesswe were about to be guilty. I had invited Ritter Gluck to meet us to-day, and he has not yet arrived. It shall not be said of me that I was ever wanting in respect to genius as transcendent as his. I must beg of my distinguished guests to await his arrival before going to dinner." *

Hereupon he resumed his conversation with Noverre. The other guests were indignant, for they all felt the insult. The nobles disapproved of the fashion, which had been introduced by Kaunitz, of mingling artists and *savans* of no birth with the aristocracy of Vienna; and the ambassadors felt it as a personal injury that Kaunitz, who yesterday had refused to wait for them, to-day called upon them to wait for a musician.

Kaunitz pretended not to see the displeasure which, nevertheless, his guests were at no great pains to conceal, and he went on talking in an animated strain with Noverre. The poor dancer, meanwhile, gave short and embarrassed answers. He had remarked the discontent of the company, and the prince's over-politeness oppressed him, the more so as he perceived one of the lords gradually approaching, with the intention of addressing the prince. With the deepest respect the dancer attempted to withdraw, but the merciless Kaunitz caught him by one of the buttons of his velvet coat, and held him fast.

"Do not stir," said the prince. "I see the duke quite as well as you do, but he is a liar and a braggart—I dislike him, and he shall not speak with me. Tell me something about the new ballet that you are arranging for the emperor's festival. I hear that Gluck has composed the music. But hush! Here comes the *maestro.*"

Kaunitz walked rapidly forward and met Gluck in the middle of the room. They greeted one another cordially, but proudly—as *two* princes might have done. Around them stood the other guests, frowning to see these two men, both so proud, so conscious of greatness, scarcely seeming aware that others besides themselves were present. Gluck was in full court-dress; at his side a sword; on his breast the brilliant order of the pope. With unembarrassed courtesy

* Swinburne, vol. i., page 80.

he received the greeting of the prince, and made no apology for his tardy appearance.

"Thank Heaven, you have come at last!" exclaimed Kaunitz, in an audible voice. "I was afraid that the gods, angels, and spirits who are the daily associates of the great *maestro* would deprive us poor mortals of the honor of dining with the favorite of the Muses and the Graces."

"The gods, the Muses, and the Graces are the associates of Prince Kaunitz," returned Gluck. "If they are not to be found in their temples, we may be sure that they have taken refuge here."

Kaunitz, who never vouchsafed a civil word in return for compliments, bowed his head, and with a gratified smile turned to his assembled guests.

"Ladies and gentlemen," said he, "let us sit down to dinner."

But the company waited for the signal to rise which would be given when the host offered his arm to the lady whom he complimented by taking her in to dinner.

The prince looked around, and his eyes rested again on Gluck.

"I beg of the Ritter Gluck," said he, graciously, "the honor of conducting him to the table." And with a courteous bow he offered his arm. "Favorite of the Muses, come with me, I am too true a worshipper of your nine lovely mistresses, to resign you to any one else."

Gluck, with a smile appreciative of the honor conferred upon him, took the arm of the prince, and was led into the dining-room.

Behind them came the other guests. All wore discontented faces; for this time the slight had been offered not only to dukes and ambassadors, but to the ladies themselves, who could not help feeling bitterly this utter disregard of all etiquette and good-breeding.

On the day after the dinner Kaunitz started for Innspruck to superintend the festivities preparing for the marriage of the Archduke Leopold. Count Durazzo, the director of the theatre, had preceded the prince by a week. Noverre, with his ballet-dancers, was to follow. The great opera of "Orpheus and Eurydice," whose fame was now European, was being rehearsed at Innspruck, for representation on the first night of the festival.

Although Florian Gassman was a leader of acknowledged skill, Gluck, at the request of the emperor, had gone to Innspruck to direct and oversee the rehearsals.

The furies had just concluded their chorus, and Gluck had given the signal for dismissal, when Prince Kaunitz entered the theatre, and came forward, offering his hand to the *maestro*.

"Well, *maestro*," said he, "are you satisfied with your *artistes?* Are we to have a great musical treat to-morrow?"

Gluck shrugged his shoulders. "My singers are not the angels who taught me this music, but for mortals they sing well. I scarcely think that Donna Maria Louisa has ever heard any thing comparable to the music which is to welcome her to Innspruck."

"I am glad to hear it," said Kaunitz, with his usual composure, although he was inwardly annoyed at Gluck's complacency. "But as I promised the empress to see and hear every thing myself, I must hear and judge of your opera also. Be so good as to have it repeated."

Gluck looked at the prince in amazement.

"What," cried he, "your highness wishes them to go through the whole opera without an audience?"

Prince Kaunitz raised his lofty head in displeasure, and said: "Ritter Gluck, quality has always been esteemed before quantity. I alone am an audience. Let the opera begin, the audience is here." *

Gluck did not answer immediately. He frowned and looked down. Suddenly he raised his head, and his face wore its usual expression of energy and power.

"I will gratify your highness. I myself would like to hear the opera without participating in it. Ladies and gentlemen of the *coulisses*, be so kind as to return! Gentlemen of the orchestra, resume your instruments! Gassman, have the goodness to lead. Do your best. Let us have your highest interpretation of art—for you have an audience such as you may never have again. Prince Kaunitz and Ritter Gluck are your listeners!"

CHAPTER XXX.

AN UNFORTUNATE MEETING.

FESTIVAL followed festival. The streets of the beautiful capital of Tyrol were gay with the multitudes who thronged to the marriage of the empress's second son.

It was the second day after the wedding. On the first evening the opera of "Orpheus and Eurydice" had been triumphantly represented before the *élite* of the city. A second representation had been called for by the delighted audience, although at the imperial palace a magnificent mask ball was to be given, for which two thousand invitations had been issued. It was a splendid confusion of lights, jewels, velvet, satins, and flowers. All the nations of the world had met in that imperial ballroom; not only mortals, but fairies, sylphides, and heathen gods and goddesses. It was a bewildering scene, that crowd of fantastic revellers, whose faces were every one hidden by velvet masks, through which dark eyes glittered, like stars upon the blackness of the night.

The imperial family alone appeared without masks. Maria Theresa, in a dress of blue velvet, studded with golden embroidery, her fair white forehead encircled by a coronet of diamonds and sapphires, walked among her guests with enchanting smiles and gracious words. She leaned upon the arm of the King of Rome, who, looking more cheerful than usual, chatted gayly with his mother or with the crowd around them. Near them were the Grand Duke Leopold and his bride, so absorbed in one another that it was easy to see that they at least were happy in their affections. Behind them flocked the young archduchesses, who were enjoying the ball to the utmost. Whenever the empress approached a group of her guests, they stood in respectful silence while she and her handsome family passed by; but as soon as she had left them, their admiration burst forth in every imaginable form of words. The empress, who overheard these murmured plaudits, smiled proudly upon her young daughters, who, even if they had been no archduchesses, would still have been the handsomest girls in Austria.

* The prince's own words. Swinburne, vol. i., page 362.

While the empress, in the full splendor of her rank and beauty, was representing the sovereign of Austria, the emperor, mingling with the guests, was taking the liberty of amusing himself as ordinary mortals love to do at a masked ball. On his arm hung a mask of most graceful figure, but so completely was she disguised that nothing could be ascertained with regard to her name or rank. Some whispered that it was the emperor's new favorite, the Countess of Auersberg.

As the pair went by, the emperor overheard the conjectures of the crowd, and he turned with a smile to the lady who accompanied him.

"Do not fear," said he; "there is no danger of your being recognized. You are mistaken for another lady. I promised you that you should meet Joseph here, and I will keep my promise. Let us try to make our way through the crowd, that we may join him as soon as possible; for I feel oppressed this evening, I know not why."

"Oh, then, your majesty, let me go back into the anteroom," said the veiled lady. "I begin to feel all the rashness of my undertaking, and although it has the sanction of your majesty and the empress, I feel like a criminal, every moment dreading discovery. Let us go back."

"No, no," replied the emperor, "let us remain until the interview with Joseph is over. I shall feel no better in the anteroom than here. I never shall be well until I leave this beautiful, fearful Tyrol. Its mountains weigh heavily upon my head and my breast. But let us sit down awhile. I love to listen to the people's talk, when the court is not by."

"But while your majesty is present the court is here," said the lady.

"Not so, my dear," whispered the emperor; "the empress and my children are the court, I am but a private nobleman. Ah, there they come! See how beautiful and stately the empress looks! Who would suppose that this grown-up family were her children!—But she, she signs us to approach. Take courage, and await me here."

So saying, the emperor hastened toward his wife, who received him with a loving smile of welcome.

"Now, my son," said she, withdrawing her arm from Joseph, "I give you your freedom. I advise you to mix among the masks, and to go in search of adventures. We have done enough for ceremony, I think we may now enjoy ourselves a little like the rest of mankind. If we were younger, Franzel, we, too, would mix with yonder crowd, and dance awhile. But I suppose we must leave that to our children, and betake ourselves to the card-table or to the opera-house."

"If your majesty leaves me the choice," said the emperor, "I vote for the opera."

The empress took his arm, while she turned to the Countess Lerchenfeld, the governess of the archduchesses. "To the dancing-room, countess," said she; "the archduchesses may dance, but no masks must enter the room. Now, my dear husband, follow me. Adieu, Joseph! To-morrow I expect to hear what fortune has befallen you to-night."

"Your majesty forgets that Fortune is a woman," returned Joseph, smiling, "and you know that I have no luck with women."

"Or you will not have it," said the empress, laughing, and leaving her son to his thoughts.

"Or you will not have it," repeated a soft voice near, and Joseph, turning, saw an elegant-looking woman, veiled and masked.

"Fair mask," said he, smiling, "although you have the qualities of Echo, you have not yet pined away to invisibility."

"Perhaps, sire, my body is only the coffin of my heart, and my heart the unfortunate Echo that has grieved herself to death and invisibility. But perhaps your majesty does not believe in the power of grief, for doubtless you are unacquainted with its pangs."

"And why should you imagine that I am unacquainted with grief?" asked Joseph.

"Because your majesty's station is exalted above that of other men; because God has blessed you with a noble heart, that is worthy of your destiny—the destiny which gives you the power of making other mortals happy."

"How do you know all this?"

"I see it," whispered she, "in your eyes—those eyes that reflect the blue of heaven. Oh, sire, may never a cloud darken that heaven!"

"I thank you for your pious wish," replied the king sadly, "but if you are mortal, you know that in this world there are no such things as cloudless skies. Let us not speak of such serious matters; give me your arm, and let us join in the mirth that is around us."

"If your majesty will permit me, I will while away the hour by relating to you a sad story of life."

"Why a sad story, why not a merry one?"

"Because I came here for no other object than to relate this sad story to yourself. I came to crave your majesty's sympathy and clemency in behalf of a suffering fellow-creature."

"Can I do any thing in the matter?" asked the king.

"From your majesty alone do I hope for succor."

"Very well; if so, let me hear the story. I will listen."

"Sire, my mournful history will ill accord with the merriment of a ballroom. If you will condescend to go with me to one of the boxes in the gallery, I will there confide my secret to your ear, and there I hope to soften your heart. Oh, sire, do not tarry; it is a case of life or death."

"Well," said Joseph, after a pause, "I will go. After all, I am about to have an adventure."

The mask bowed, and made her way through the crowd to a side-door which opened upon the private staircase leading to the boxes. Joseph looked with interest at the light and elegant form that preceded him, and said to himself, "Truly an adventure! I will follow it to the end."

They were now in the galleries, from whence a beautiful view of the ballroom was obtained. The lady entered a box, the king followed. The sound of the music, and the gay voices of the dancers, came with softened murmur to the ears of the king. He thought of the past; but rousing himself to the exigencies of the present, he turned to the lady and said: "Now, fair mask, to your narrative."

"Swear first to hear me to the end! Swear it by the memory of Isabella, whom you so passionately loved!"

"Isabella!" cried Joseph, turning pale. "You are very bold;

madame, to call that name, and call it here! But speak. By her loved memory I will listen."

She took his hand, and pressed it to her lips. Then she begged the king to be seated, and took her place by his side.

"Sire, I wish to relate to you the history of a woman whom God has either blessed or cursed; a woman who, if she were not most unfortunate, would be the happiest of mortals."

"You speak as the Sphinx did before the gates of Thebes. How can one be at the same time blessed and cursed?"

"Sire, it is a blessing to be capable of loving with passion; it is a curse to love, and not be loved in return."

"And a greater curse," murmured Joseph, "to feign love and not to feel it. I have been a victim of such hypocrisy, and never shall I outlive its bitter memories."

"Sire," began the lady, "the woman of whom I speak would willingly give a year of her life if the man she loves would but vouchsafe to her thirsting heart one single glance of love. Think how wretched she must be, when even the appearance of love would satisfy her. But do not suppose, sire, that this woman is the victim of a guilty passion which she dare not own. She is a wife, and the man she adores, and who loves her not, is her husband."

"Why does he not love her?" asked Joseph quickly.

"Because," said the mask, in an agitated voice, "because she has sinned against him. On the day of her marriage, although he nobly invited her confidence, she hid from him a—a—malady. Oh, in mercy, do not go! You *must* hear me," cried she, almost frenzied, "you swore by the memory of Isabella to listen."

Joseph resumed his seat, and said roughly, "Go on, then."

"It was a crime," continued she in a voice of deepest emotion, "but she has paid dearly for her sin. Her husband repulsed her, but her heart was still his; he despised her, and yet she adores him. Her malady has long since disappeared; her heart alone is sick; that heart which will break if her lord refuse to forgive her the offence that was born of her love for him! But oh, sire, he has no pity. When she meets him with imploring looks, he turns away; her letters he sends to her unopened. Oh, he is severe in his wrath; it is like vengeance from Heaven! But still she loves, and still she hopes that one day he will be generous, and forgive her another crime—that of not being blessed with beauty. For months she has longed to tell him that she repents of her faults, that her punishment is just; but, oh! oh! she begs for mercy. She was forbidden to follow him to Innspruck, but she could not stay behind. His parents gave their consent, and she is here at your knees, my lord and king, to plead for mercy. Oh! has there not been enough of cruelty? See me humbled at your feet; reach me your beloved hand, and bid me sit by your side!"

She had sunk to the ground, and now tearing from her face the mask and veil, the King of Rome beheld the death-like countenance of his despised wife.

Joseph rose from his seat and looked at her with inexorable hate. "Madame," said he, "thanks to the name which you used to force me into compliance, I have heard you out. I married you without affection, and you had been my wife but a few short hours when you turned my indifference into undying hate. You come and whine to me for my love; and you inform me that you are lovesick on my account. If so, I dare say that Van Swieten, who cured you of leprosy, can also cure you of your unfortunate attachment. If you never knew it before, allow me to inform you that *your* love gives you no claim to *mine;* and when a woman has the indelicacy to thrust herself upon a man who has never sought her, she must expect to be despised and humbled to the dust. And now, madame, as I still have the misfortune to be your husband, listen to my commands. You came here in spite of my prohibition; as you pass in the world for my wife, you shall at least be obedient to my will. Go back this night to Vienna, and never again presume to entrap me into another interview like this!"

Without vouchsafing a look at the fainting woman who lay at his feet, Joseph left the box, and descended to the ballroom.

But what wail was that, which, coming from the imperial banqueting-hall, hushed every sound of music and mirth, and drove the gay multitude in terror from the ballroom?

The King of Rome was hastily making his way through the terrified crowd, when he was met by one of his own officers.

"I have been seeking your majesty," said he in a trembling voice. "The emperor—"

"In Heaven's name, what of the emperor?"

"He is very ill, your majesty. On leaving the theatre, he was struck down by apoplexy."

The king made no reply. He dashed on from room to room until he reached his father's sleeping-apartment.

And there on the bed, that white, motionless body; that cold, insensible piece of clay; that marble image without breath—was all that earth now held of the Emperor Francis of Lorraine.

He was dead, and his wish had been granted. He had gone forever from the "beautiful, fearful Tyrol;" and its mountains lay no longer heavily on his breast.

CHAPTER XXXI.

MOURNING.

THE sound of rejoicings was hushed. The people of Innspruck had hastened to remove from the streets every symbol of festivity. The flowers and flags, the triumphal arches, and the wreathed arcades had disappeared. The *epithalamium* had been followed by the dirge.

Night had set in—the first night of the emperor's death. The corpse still lay on the bed where its last breath had been drawn, and no one was with the deceased sovereign except two night-watchers, whose drowsy heads were buried in the arm-chairs wherein they sat. Death had banished ceremony. In the presence of their dead emperor, his attendants were seated and slept. In the centre of the room stood the coffin that awaited the imperial remains; for on the morrow the funeral ceremonies were to begin. But the empress had ordered that on this night all ceremony should be suspended.

Deep silence reigned throughout Innspruck. The citizens, worn out with the excitement of the day, had all retired to rest. Even the children of the deceased had forgotten their sorrow in sleep. Maria Theresa alone sought no rest.

All that day she had been overwhelmed by grief; even prayer seemed to bring no relief to her heart. But now she was tranquil, she had thrust back her tears; and the empress-widow, all etiquette forgetting, was making her husband's shroud.

As a woman, she grieved for the partner of her joys and sorrows; as a woman, she wished to pay the last sad honors to the only man whom she had ever loved. She whose hands were accustomed to the sceptre, now held a needle, and to all offers of assistance she made but one reply.

"None of you are worthy to help me in this holy work, for none of you loved him. For you, he was the beneficent and honored sovereign; but for me, he was the joy, the light, the air of my life. I, who loved him, have alone the right to work upon his shroud."

"Oh, your majesty," cried the Countess Daun, while her eyes filled with sympathizing tears, "would that the world could see with what devotion the great Maria Theresa sits in the stillness of the night, and with her own hands prepares her husband's shroud!"

The empress quickly raised her head, and, with something like her accustomed imperiousness, said: "I forbid any one of you to speak of what you have seen to-night. In the simplicity of my grief, I do what my heart urges me to do; but let not my sorrow become the subject of the world's idle gossip. When the husband dies his wife, be she empress or beggar, is nothing but a sorrowing widow. Ah! I am indeed beggared of all my wealth, for I have lost the dearest treasure I possessed on earth. All my joys will die with him."

The empress's sobs choked her utterance; and burying her face in the shroud, she wept aloud.

"In the name of Heaven, your majesty, do not let your tears fall upon the shroud!" cried the Countess Daun, while she tried with gentle force to wrest the cloth from the empress's hands. "I have heard it said that what is laid in the coffin bedewed with tears, draws after it to the grave the one who sheds them."

"Would it were true!" exclaimed the empress, who had already resumed her work. "Would that my Francis could open his arms to receive me, that I might rest by his side from the cares of life! Would that I were with him, who was my lover from earliest childhood; for cold and cheerless will be the life that is no longer lit up by his smile."

She bent over her work, and nothing further was said; but her ladies of honor gazed with tearful eyes upon the high-born mourner, who, in her long, black dress, was making a shroud for her lost husband.

At last the task was completed, and she rose from her seat. With a sad smile she threw the shroud over her head, and it fell around her majestic form like a white veil.

"My veil of eternal widowhood!" said she. "Let me warm it with my love, that it may not lie too cold upon my darling's breast. Now, my friends, go and rest. Pray for the emperor, and for his heart-broken wife."

"Surely," said the Countess Daun, "your majesty will not send us away until we have attended to your wants. Let us remain; we will watch by your bedside."

"No, countess, I will dispense with your services to-night. Charlotte von Hieronymus will stay with me."

Turning to her beloved little tire-woman she said: "I want your attendance yet awhile, Charlotte; you are to dress my hair to-night as becomes a widow. Good-night, ladies."

The ladies of honor, with deep courtesies, left the room.

As the door closed behind them, she said to Charlotte: "Now, Charlotte, dear child, you shall go with me on my last visit to the emperor. Take a pair of scissors, and come."

"Scissors, your majesty?" said Charlotte.

"Yes, my dear," replied she, as she advanced to her work-table from whence she took up a silver candelabrum, and signed to Charlotte to follow.

Wrapping the shroud close about her, the empress went forward through the long suite of magnificent but dark and empty rooms, that lay between her and her husband. Her tall white figure, enveloped in the shroud, looked in the gloom of night like a ghost. The light which she carried, as it flashed across her face gave it a weird aspect; and as the two wanderers went flitting by the large mirrors that here and there ornamented the rooms, they looked like a vision which had started up for a moment, then vanished into utter darkness.

At last they came to a door which stood ajar, through which a light was visible.

"We are here," said the empress, leaning against the door for support. "Step lightly, Charlotte, and make no noise, for the emperor sleeps."

There on the bed, with its yellow, sunken face, was the corpse that had been her husband—the only man she had ever loved. And that hideous black coffin, which looked all the gloomier for the wax-lights that burned around it, was his last resting-place.

Maria Theresa shuddered when she saw all this; but her strong will came to her help, and she went steadily forward until she reached the night-watchers. She awoke them and said, "Go, wait in the next room until I call you." Charlotte was already on her knees, praying.

The empress stood once more irresolute, then rushing forward with a cry she leaned over the body.

Presently she laid her hand lovingly upon the staring eyes of the corpse, and looked long and tenderly at the face.

"Shut your eyes, my Franz," said she softly, "shut your eyes, for never have they looked so coldly upon me before. Do not forget me in heaven, my beloved; but leave your heart with me; mine has been with you for so many years! First I loved you as a child—then as a maiden—and lastly, I loved you as a wife and the mother of your children. And I will ever love you, my own one. I was true as your wife, and I will be true as your widow. Farewell, my beloved, farewell!"

She bent over and kissed the emperor's mouth, and for a moment laid her head upon his cold, still bosom. Then again she drew her hand softly across his eyes, and tried to close them. A proud smile flitted over her wan face, for the eyes of the corpse closed. The loving hand of the wife had prevailed where every other effort had failed. True to her wishes in death as in life, the dead emperor had shut his eyes to earth forever.

"Come, Charlotte, come," cried the empress, almost joyfully, "see how my emperor loves me! He hears me still, and has granted my last request. I will mourn no more, but will think of the day when I shall go to him again and share his home in heaven. Until then, my Franz, farewell!"

She bent her head, and taking the shroud from her shoulders, she spread it carefully over the coffin, smoothing every wrinkle with her hands, until it lay as perfect as the covering of a couch.

"Call the valets, Charlotte," said she; and as they entered the room, she motioned them to advance. "Help me to lay the emperor on yonder bed," said she. "Take the feet and body, and I will bear his head."

With her strong arms, she raised him as a mother would move her sleeping child, and, with the help of the valets, she laid her husband in his coffin. This done, she again sent away the attendants, and then wrapped the body in the shroud as though she had been protecting it from the cold.

"Come hither, Charlotte," said she, "with your scissors." Charlotte approached noiselessly. "Cut off my hair," continued she, taking out her comb, and letting down the rich masses until it fell about her person like another shroud.

"No, your majesty, no," cried Charlotte, bursting into tears. "I never can cut off that magnificent hair."

"Good child," said the empress, "many a weary hour has that magnificent hair cost you, and do you ask to have it spared? It shall give you no more trouble. Take the scissors and cut it off!"

"Has your majesty then forgotten," pleaded Charlotte, "how dearly the emperor loved this hair?"

"No, Charlotte, and therefore he must have it. 'Tis the last love-token I have to give him. I cannot die with him like an Indian wife; but religion does not forbid me to lay this offering at least in his coffin. He used so often to pass his hands through it—he was so proud of its beauty, that now he is gone, no one else shall see it. Say no more, Charlotte, but cut it off."

The empress bent her head, while Charlotte, with a heart-felt sigh and trembling hands, cut off the long and beautiful blond hair which Maria Theresa laid as a love-token in the coffin of her husband.*

CHAPTER XXXII.

THE IMPERIAL ABBESS.

THE funeral rites were over. In the crypt of the church of the Capuchins, under the monument which, twenty years before, the empress had built for herself and her husband, lay the body of Emperor Francis. In this vault slept all the imperial dead of the house of Hapsburg. One after another, with closed eyes and folded hands, their marble effigies were stretched across their tombs, stiff and cold as the bones that were buried beneath. The eternal night of death reigned over those couchant images of stone and bronze.

But Maria Theresa and her emperor had conquered death. Both rising from the tomb, their eyes were fixed upon each other with an expression of deepest tenderness; while Azrael, who stood be-

*Caroline Pichler, "Memoirs," vol. i., p. 28.

hind with a wreath of cypress in his hands, seemed to have transformed himself into an angel of love that sanctified their union even beyond the tomb.

All had left the vault save the widowed empress; she had remained behind to weep and pray. Her prayers ended, she drew her long black cloak around her and strode through the church, unmindful of the monks, who, on either side of the aisle, awaited her appearance in respectful silence. She heeded neither their inclined heads nor their looks of sympathy; stunned by grief, she was unmindful of externals, and scarcely knew that she had left the vault, when her coach stopped before the imperial palace.

Once there, Maria Theresa passed by the splendid apartments which she had inhabited during her husband's life, and ascending the staircase to the second story of the palace, she entered upon the dwelling which had been prepared for her widowhood. It was simple to coldness. Hung with black, nothing relieved the gloom of these rooms; neither mirror, picture, gilding, nor flowers were there. The bedroom looked sad in the extreme. The walls were hung in gray silk; gray velvet curtains were drawn in front of the small widow's bed; the floor was covered with a gray carpet studded with white lilies, and the furniture was like the curtains, of dim, dull gray velvet.*

As the empress entered this dismal room she saluted her ladies of honor who had followed her, and now stood awaiting her commands at the door.

"Bring all my dresses, shawls, laces, and jewels to me in the reception-room, and send a messenger to Prince Kaunitz to say that I await his presence."

The ladies of honor left the room silently, and the empress, closing the door, began again to weep and pray. Meanwhile her attendants were occupied bringing up the costly wardrobe of their imperial mistress. In a little while the dark rooms were brightened with velvet and silk of every color, with gold and silver, with jewels and flowers.

The ladies looked with eager and admiring eyes at the magnificence which had transformed this funereal apartment into a bazaar of elegance and luxury, scarcely daring to speak the hopes and wishes that were filling all their hearts. Suddenly their curious eyes sought the ground, for the empress appeared and entered the room. What a contrast between this pale figure, clad in simplest mourning, and the rich costumes which in the days of her happiness had heightened her beauty; those days which seemed to lie so far, far away from the bitter present!

The empress laid her hand upon her heart, as if to stifle a cry of anguish; then approaching the black marble table, she took up some of the dresses that lay upon it.

With a voice softer and more pathetic than ever they had heard before, she begged the companions of her happier days to accept and wear these costly things as a legacy from the emperor. She then divided them as she thought best; assigning to each lady what best became her and was most appropriate.

Her ladies stood weeping around, while Maria Theresa besought each one to pardon the trouble she had given in her joyous days, for the sake of the misery she now endured. And as she entreated

* Caroline Pichler, "Memoirs," vol. i., p. 20.

them to forget that she had been imperious and exacting, they knelt weeping at her feet, and earnestly implored her not to leave them.

The empress sadly shook her head. "I am no longer an empress," said she, "I am a poor, humbled woman, who needs no more attendance, whose only aim on earth is to serve God and die in His favor! Pray for the emperor, dear friends, and pray for me also."

Slowly turning away, she left the room and entered her cabinet, which opened into the gray bedroom.

"And now to my last worldly task," said she, as ringing a silver hand-bell she bade a page conduct Prince Kaunitz to her presence.

The page opened the door, and the prince came in.

The empress greeted him with a silent bend of her head, and exhausted, sank into an arm-chair that stood before her writing-desk. Kaunitz, without awaiting permission, took a seat opposite.

There was a long pause. At length Kaunitz said: "Your majesty has honored me by commanding my presence hither."

"Yes, I sent for you because I have something of great importance to say," replied the empress.

"I am all attention," replied the minister. "For it is worthy of your noble self so soon to stifle your grief and to attend to the duties of your crown. You have sent for me that we may work. And your majesty has done well, for much business has accumulated on our hands since we last held a cabinet council."

The empress shook her head. "Business no longer troubles me," replied she; "I have sent for you to say that we are no longer to work together."

"Does that mean that your majesty is about to dismiss me in disgrace? Are you no longer satisfied with your minister?" asked Kaunitz.

"No, prince. It means that I myself must retire from the bustle and vanities of this world. My hands are no longer fit to wield a sceptre; they must be folded in prayer—in prayer for my emperor, who was called away without receiving the sacraments of the church. My strength is gone from me; my crown oppresses me; I can no longer be an empress."

"Were you made a sovereign by any power of yours?" asked Kaunitz. "Had you the choice of becoming an empress or remaining an archduchess? What did your majesty say to me when the insolent Charles of Bavaria tried to wrest your imperial crown from your head?—'I received my crown from the hands of God, and I must defend my divine right!' Floods of noble blood were spilled that Maria Theresa might preserve her right; and does she now intend to dim the glory of her crown by sacrificing it to her sorrow as a wife?"

"I am tired of life and of the world, and I intend to take refuge from their troubles in a cloister. Say no more! I am resolved to go, and the palace at Innspruck shall be my convent. There, on the spot where he died, will I make my vows; and as an abbess will I spend my life praying that God may give him eternal rest. My vocation as a sovereign is at an end; I resign my sceptre to my son."*

"That means that your majesty will destroy with your own hands the structure you had commenced; that you have grown faint-hearted, and are unfaithful to your duty and to your subjects."

* Coxe, "History of the House of Austria," vol. v., page 188.

"I will follow the steps of my great ancestor, Charles V.," cried the empress with energy. "I lay down my earthly dignity to humble myself before God."

"And your majesty will be quite as unhappy as your ancestor. Do you suppose that the poor monk ever was able to forget that he had been a great prince?"

"And yet Charles V. remained for several years in a cloister."

"But what a life, your majesty! A life of regret, repentance, and despair. Believe me, it is far better like Cæsar to die pierced by twenty daggers on the steps of a throne, than voluntarily to descend from that throne to enter the miserable walls of a cloister."

"Better perhaps for those who have not renounced the world and its pomps," cried the empress, raising her beautiful eyes to heaven. "But it is neither satiety nor weariness of grandeur that has driven me to a cloister. It is my love for my emperor, my yearning to be alone with God and the past."

"But, your majesty," said Kaunitz with emphasis, "you will not be alone with the past; the maledictions of your people will follow you Will they hold you guiltless to have broken your faith with them?"

"I shall not have broken my faith; I shall have left to my people a successor to whom sooner or later they will owe the same allegiance as they now owe me."

"But a successor who will overturn all that his mother has done for Austria's welfare. Your majesty laid the foundations of Austria's greatness. To that end you called me to the lofty station which I now occupy. Remember that together we pledged our lives and love to Austria. Be not untrue to the covenant. In the name of that people which I then represented, I claim from their *emperor*, Maria Theresa, the strict fulfilment of her bond. I call upon her to be true to her duty as the ruler of a great nation, until the hand of God releases her from her crown and her life."

While Kaunitz spoke, Maria Theresa walked up and down the room with troubled brow and folded arms. As he ceased, she came and stood before him, looking earnestly into his face, which now had cast aside its mask of tranquillity, and showed visible signs of agitation.

"You are a bold advocate of my people's claims," said she; "a brave defender of my Austria. I rejoice to know it, and never will take umbrage at what you have so nobly spoken. But you have not convinced me; my sorrow speaks louder than your arguments. You have termed me 'your emperor.' I know why you have once more called me by that flattering title. You wish to remind me that in mounting the throne of my ancestors I lost the right to grieve as a woman, and pledged myself to gird on the armor of manhood. Hitherto I have made it my pride to plan, to reign, to fight like a man. I have always feared that men might say of me that my hand was too weak to grasp the reins of power. But God, who perhaps gave me the head of a man while leaving me the heart of a woman, has punished me for my ambition. He has left me to learn that, alas! I *am* but a woman—with all the weakness of my sex. It is that womanly heart which, throbbing with an anguish that no words can paint, has vanquished my head; and loud above all thoughts of my duty as an empress is the wail of my sorrow as a widow! But I will show you, Kaunitz, that I am not stubborn. I shall communicate my intentions to no one. For four weeks I will retire to my cloister. Instead of naming Joseph my successor, I will appoint him co-regent. If, after four weeks of probation, I still feel that I can without guilt retire from the world, shall I then be absolved from my oath, and suffered to lay down my crown without reproach from my faithful minister?"

"If, after four weeks of unlimited power delegated to the Emperor Joseph, your majesty still thinks that you have a right to abdicate," replied Kaunitz, "I shall make no opposition to your majesty's choice of a private vocation, for I shall feel that after that time remonstrance with you would be useless."

"Well, then, my novitiate shall begin to-morrow. Apprise the court and the foreign representatives that I wish to meet them in the throne-room, where in their presence I will appoint my son emperor co-regent."

CHAPTER XXXIII.

THE CO-REGENT.

Maria Theresa had kept her word. She had appointed her son co-regent, investing the young emperor with full power to reign, to make laws, to punish, to reward, and to govern her people, while she retired to the palace of Innspruck. There she dwelt in strictest privacy, scarcely seeing her children, and restricting her intercourse to the first lady of honor, her confessor, and a few chosen friends, whom she sometimes admitted to her mournful rooms.

Joseph, the young emperor of four-and-twenty years, was now monarch of all Austria, Hungary, Lombardy, and the Netherlands. He had reached the goal of his longings for power, and now he could begin to think about the happiness of his people.

Since the intoxicating moment when Maria Theresa, in the presence of the whole court, had named him co-regent, and delivered over to his hands her vast empire, Joseph felt as if he had suddenly been transported to a world of enchantment. He had, together with her ministers, dissuaded the empress from her resolution of retiring to Innspruck; but even as he joined his voice to theirs, his heart was trembling with fear lest she should yield. He felt that if she revoked the power she had conferred, he would almost die with disappointment. But the empress remained firm, and her son was triumphant.

She had gone from the throne to the solitude of her own apartments, and left him lord and emperor of Austria! He would no longer be obliged to conceal his thoughts; they should come out into the broad day as deeds, for he was sovereign there!

A day and night had passed by since his mother had renounced her rights to him. He could not sleep. His head was full of plans, his heart of emotion. He *dared* not sleep—he who was the guardian of millions of his fellow-beings—he who felt ready to shed his heart's blood for their good.

On the first day, Joseph had been in council with the ministers of state. The will of the deceased emperor had been opened, and his son now learned, that while his mother was conferring upon him

JOSEPHUS SECUNDUS D. G. ROMANORUM REX

power, his father had left him boundless wealth. The Emperor Francis had left his eldest son sole heir to his estates in Hungary and Galicia, to his jewels and treasures, and also to the millions of money which he had accumulated through manufactures and trade. He had also left to his eldest son the twenty-two millons of coupons which he had taken for the gold which he had advanced to the state for the prosecution of the Seven Years' War. Joseph was therefore the richest prince in all Germany, for his father's vast estates amounted to one hundred and fifty-nine millions of guilders.* But he who had been so intoxicated with joy at his mother's gift, seemed scarcely moved at all as he received the tidings of his vast inheritance.

"I wish that my father had bought all the coupons that were issued, and that they were all mine," said he, with a sigh.

"Your majesty would be no gainer thereby," replied the lord keeper of the finances, Von Kinsky. "These coupons bear but little interest, and paper money is not gold. Its value is nominal."

"But it has one merit," replied the emperor, smiling; "it can be burned. Oh, what a miserable invention is this paper money, which represents value, but possesses none! Suppose that all the holders of these coupons were to come in this morning and ask for their redemption, could the imperial coffers meet their obligations?"

"Not if they all came at once, your majesty."

"But the people have a right to call for them," said the emperor. "In lending their money, they showed their confidence in the government, and this confidence must not be betrayed. Let the twenty-two millions of coupons be put in a package and brought to my private apartments. I wish to dispose of them."

Throughout this day Joseph was so absorbed by business, both private and official, that he had no opportunity of exhibiting himself in his new character, either to his family or his subjects.

But, on the second day of his co-regency, the young emperor appeared in public. On this day, the Viennese celebrated the deliverance of Vienna from the Turks by John Sobieski and his brave Polish legions. The mourning of the female members of the imperial family did not permit them to mingle as usual with the people on this favorite festival; but the emperor resolved to show himself on this occasion in the character of a sovereign. All Vienna was eager to see him as soon as it became rumored that he would certainly attend the mass in honor of the day at the cathedral of St. Stephen.

Meanwhile, the young emperor was in his palace. The anterooms were filled with petitioners of every sort, who, through bribes offered to the members of the imperial household, had penetrated thus far, and were now awaiting the appearance of the emperor. The anterooms of Maria Theresa had always been thronged with these petitioners, and now they jostled each other without ceremony, each one hoping to be remarked by the emperor as he passed on to his carriage.

Suddenly the commotion ceased and took the form of a panic as the door opened and the valets of the emperor came forward, their hands filled with the petitions which they had just taken in. They had all been refused!

A few moments afterward the door opened again, and the lord

* Hubner, "Life of Joseph II.," vol. i., page 28.

chamberlain, Count Rosenberg, advanced to the centre of the room. There was no necessity for the pages to order silence, for the crowd were breathless with expectation, and the deepest stillness reigned throughout the thronged rooms while Count Rosenberg read the first greeting of the emperor to his people.

It was sharp, and to the point. It forbade, in strongest terms, all indirect efforts to obtain promotion or pensions; and it declared once for all that merit alone would be the test of all applications presented to the Emperor Joseph II.

When the count had done reading the proclamation, the valets laid the petitions upon a table, that each man might select and remove his own paper.

"Your majesty has made some enemies to-day," said Count Rosenberg, as he reëntered the cabinet of the emperor. "I saw many a scowl in the anteroom as I passed by the disappointed multitude that thronged my way."

"I do not wish the friendship of intriguers and flatterers," replied the emperor with a merry laugh. "If my proclamations make me enemies, I think they will also make me friends. The good shall be satisfied with my rule; for, during my mother's reign, I have observed much and thought much. And now the day has come when the power is mine to reward virtue and punish vice."

"May Heaven grant that your majesty's day draw to a close without clouds or storms!" said Rosenberg.

The emperor laughed again. "What do you fear, my friend?" asked he. "Have you so long shared with me my burden of dissimulation, that you are frightened to see our shackles fall? Are you afraid of the fresh air, because we wear our masks no longer? Patience, Rosenberg, and all will be well with us. Our dreams are about to be fulfilled: what we have whispered together in the twilight of mutual trust, we may now cry out with free and joyous shouts—'Reform! reform!' My people have prayed quite enough, they shall now learn to do something better—they shall think; they have been long enough led by faith, like little children. I will give them confirmation, and they shall enter upon the responsibilities of manhood. I mean to be a blessing to the virtuous, and a terror to the vicious."

"Unhappily, there is more evil than good in this world," said Count Rosenberg, sighing, "and a man, though he can seldom count his friends, is never at a loss to count his enemies."

"I do not understand you," said Joseph, smiling. "I intend to draw out the fangs of the wicked, so that they shall have power to injure no one."

"Your majesty will do this if time be granted you," said the count. "If—"

"What do you mean?" cried the emperor, impatiently, as Rosenberg hesitated. "Speak on. What do you fear?"

"I fear," whispered the count, "that your day will be darkened by bigots and priests. I fear that the empress will not leave you freedom to carry out your reformation. I fear that your enemies will dry up her tears, and unclasp her folded hands, to force within their grasp the sceptre to which your manhood gives you exclusive right. I fear the influence of her confessor, Father Porhammer; try to conciliate him. It is far better to win over our opponents by forbearance, than to exasperate them by open warfare."

"But open warfare is my right," cried Joseph, "and I am powerful enough to despise all opponents, as well as strong enough to pursue my way without regard to the wickedness of all the bigots in Christendom. Face to face shall we stand, and I defy them all! We have had enough, too, of Spanish etiquette and Italian mummery here. Now we shall have honest German customs; we shall be Germans in thought, in speech, and in sentiment. This is my dream, my bright and beautiful dream! Austria shall one day be Germanized; the kingdoms and provinces which compose my dominions shall no longer be separate nationalities, but all shall be the branches of one lofty tree. The limbs shall lose their names, and be called by that of the trunk; and the trunk shall bear the name of Germany. High above the boughs of this noble tree, which shall extend from France to Poland, I will place my banner and my crown, and before their might all Europe shall bow. This is my dream, Rosenberg, my dream of future greatness!"

"While I listen and look upon your majesty's countenance, bright with inspiration, I, too, bow before the grandeur of your thought, and feel as if this godlike dream must surely become a glorious truth."

"It shall be glorious truth, Rosenberg," exclaimed the emperor. "Why should Germany be severed into many parts, when France and Spain are each a kingdom in itself? Why is England so powerful? Because Scotland and Ireland have lost their identity in hers. Sweden and Norway, are they not, or rather ought they not to be, one? And Russia, how many different races own the sway of the mighty Czar? My empire, too, shall become strong through unity, and I shall be not only emperor of Austria, but, in very deed and truth, emperor of all Germany!"

Rosenberg shook his head, and sighed. "Ah, your majesty," said he, "you are so young that you believe in the realization of mortal dreams."

"I do, and I intend to work out their realization myself. I shall begin by being German myself. I intend to do away with ceremony, priestcraft, and foreign influence. To that intent, my lord chamberlain, you will see that all foreigners are dismissed from the palace, and their places supplied by Germans. My two Italian valets I make over to Porhammer. Nothing but German shall be spoken at court. I will have neither French nor Italian actors here. Count Durazzo shall dismiss his foreign *troupes* and employ Germans in their stead.* Let him see that the German stage flourishes and does honor to the metropolis of the German empire."

"This is an ordinance that will enchant the youths of Vienna," replied the count, gayly.

"Here is another which will equally rejoice their hearts as well as those of all the pretty women in Vienna," added the emperor.

"Your majesty means to revoke the power of the committee on morals?"

"Not quite. I dare not fly so soon in the face of my lady-mother's pet institutions," returned Joseph, laughing; "but I shall suspend them until further notice. Now the pretty sinners may all go to sleep in peace. Now the young girls of Vienna may walk the streets without being asked whither they go, or whence they come. Reform! reform! But hark! there are the church-bells; I go to exhibit myself to my subjects. Come, let us away."

*Gross-Hoffinger, "History of Joseph II.," vol. i., p. 91.

"But your majesty has not made your toilet. The valets are now waiting with your Spanish court-dress in your dressing-room."

"I make them a present of it," said the emperor. "The day of Spanish court-dresses is over. The uniform of my reigment shall be my court-dress hereafter, so that you see I am dressed and ready."

"Then allow me to order that the carriage of state be prepared for your majesty."

"Order that the carriage of state be left to rot in the empress's stables," returned Joseph. "The day of etiquette, also, is over. I am a man like other men, and have as much use of my limbs as they. Let cripples and dotards ride—I shall go to church on foot."

"But your majesty," remonstrated Rosenberg, "what will the people say when they see their emperor stripped of all the pomp of his high station? They will think that you hold them too cheaply to visit them in state."

"No, no. My people will feel that I come among them, not with the cold splendor of my rank, but with the warmth of human sympathy and human nature, and they will greet me with more enthusiasm than if I came in my carriage of state."

The emperor was right. The people who had thronged every street through which he was to pass, shouted for joy, when they saw the ruler of all Austria on foot, accompanied by a few of his friends, making his way among them with as much simplicity as a burgher.

At first astonishment had repressed the enthusiasm of the Viennese, but this momentary reticence overcome, the subjects of Joseph the Second rent the air with their cries of welcome, and pressed around his path, all eager to look into the face of the sovereign who walked among his people as an equal and a man.

"See him! see him!" cried they. "See the German prince who is not ashamed to be a German! See our emperor in the uniform of the German infantry! Long live the emperor! Long live our fatherland! Long live the emperor!" shouted the multitude, while Joseph, his heart overflowing with joy, made his way at last to the cathedral of St. Stephen.

And now the trumpets sounded, and the mighty organ thundered forth a welcome, while cardinals and priests lifted their voices, and the clergy sang the "*Salvum fac imperatorum nostrum.*"

And ever and anon, through the open windows of the cathedral, the people shouted, "Long live the emperor! Long live our fatherland!"

Overcome by the ovation, Joseph sank down upon his knees, and his heart softened by the scene, the circumstances, and the sublime chants of the church, he prayed. Clasping his hands, he prayed that God might give him strength to do his duty to his subjects, and to make them happy.

The "*Salvum fac imperatorum*" over, the mass for the repose of the soul of Sobieski and his twelve thousand Poles was intoned. The emperor prayed for them, and thanked the Almighty Ruler of all things for the rescue they had brought to Vienna in her hour of danger from the infidel.

This was the first public act of Joseph's reign as co-regent.

The mass over, the people witnessed another public act of the young emperor's reign. While Joseph, smiling and bending his head to the crowds that pressed around him, was quietly pursuing his way back to the palace, a procession was seen coming through the streets which attracted the attention of the multitude, and called forth their wonder.

First came a file of soldiers, with shouldered carbines, then an open vehicle drawn by horses from the imperial stables, then another file of soldiers. Within the wagons sat several officers of the emperor's household, with large rolls of paper in their hands, and behind it was a detachment of cavalry with drawn sabres.

"What means this pageant?" asked the people of one another.

For all answer to this question, the multitudes pressed forward and fell in with the mysterious procession.

The train moved on, until it arrived at an open market-place, where it halted. In the centre of the square was a heap of fagots, near which stood two men with lighted torches in their hands.

"An execution!" cried the terror-stricken multitude. "But what an execution! Who was to be burnt at the stake?"

While the crowd were murmuring within themselves, the officers of the emperor's household advanced to the pile, and laid the rolls of papers which they had brought, upon it. They then signed to the people for silence, and one of the officers addressed the crowd.

"The Emperor Joseph, co-regent with the Empress Maria Theresa, sends greeting to his subjects," cried he in a clear, loud voice. "To-day, the first of his reign, and the festival of John Sobieski the deliverer of Vienna, he wishes to prove to his people how much he loves them. In testimony whereof, he presents to them twenty-two millions of coupons, bequeathed to him by his father the late Emperor Francis. These papers are the coupons. In the name of the Emperor Joseph approach, ye torch-bearers, and kindle the pile, that the people of Austria, made richer by twenty-two millions, may recognize, in this sacrifice, the love of their sovereign."

The torches were applied, and high in the air soared the flames that were consuming the emperor's bequest, while the faces of the multitude around were lit up by the glare of the burning pile.

The bells of the churches began to chime, the flames soared higher and higher, and the people looked on in wondering gratitude at the twenty-two millions of consuming guilders, which were the first offering of Joseph II. to his subjects.*

CHAPTER XXXIV.

HAROUN AL RASCHID.

THE emperor was alone in his dressing-cabinet. He stood before a mirror, covering his rich blond curls with a large wig, which fell in long ringlets over his shoulders, and completed the very singular costume in which it had pleased his majesty to array himself.

The emperor surveyed himself with evident satisfaction, and broke out into a hearty laugh. "I think," said he, "that in this dark-haired fop, with his fashionable costume, no one will recognize the emperor. I suppose that in this disguise I may go undetected in search of adventures. If I am to be of use as a prince, I must see all things, prove all things, and learn all things. It is written, 'Prove all things, and hold fast to that which is good.' I

* Hormayer, "Austrian Plutarch," vol. i., p. 129.

am afraid that I shall not hold fast to much that comes under my observation."

He drew back from the mirror, threw over his shoulders a little cloak, bordered with fur, set a three-cornered hat upon the top of his wig, took up a small gold-headed cane, and then returned to survey himself a second time.

"A fop of the latest style—that is to say, a fool of the first water—looks out upon himself from this looking-glass," said he, laughing. "It would be an affront to my majesty if any one were to presume to suspect the emperor under this absurd disguise. I hope I shall be as successful in the way of adventures as was my predecessor Haroun al Raschid."

He drew his cloak close around him, and stepped from a little private door that opened from his dressing-room into the corridor which led to the apartments of his wife. Retired and unobserved, the Empress Josepha lived within these rooms, which, from the first night of their marriage, her husband had never reëntered. The corridor was empty. Joseph could therefore pass out unobserved, until he reached a private staircase leading to the lower floor of the palace. Once there, he raised his head, and stepped boldly out into the hall. The porters allowed him to pass without suspicion, and, unrecognized, the young adventurer reached the public thoroughfares.

"Now," thought he, with a sensation of childish delight, "now I am free, a man just like other men. I defy any one to see my divine right upon my brow, or to observe any difference between the 'imperial blue' of my eyes, and the ordinary blue of those of my subjects."

"Halt, there!" cried a threatening voice to the careless pedestrian. "Out of the way, young coxcomb; do you suppose that I must give way to you?"

"Not at all, your worship," replied Joseph, smiling, as with an active bound he cleared the way for a colossal carman, who, covered with sweat and dust, was wheeling a load of bricks in a barrow.

The carman stopped, and surveying the emperor angrily, cried out in a voice of thunder, "What do you mean by calling me 'your worship?' Do you mean to insult me because you are wasting your father's money on your pretty person, decked out like a flower-girl on a holiday?"

"Heaven forbid that I should seek to insult you!" replied the emperor. "The size of your fists is enough to inspire any one with respect. For all the world I would not offend their owner."

"Well, then, go your way, you whippersnapper," muttered the carman, while the emperor congratulated himself upon having gotten out of the scrape without detection.

"It would have been a prettty anecdote for the history of the Emperor Joseph, had he been discovered in a street brawl with a carman," said he to himself. "A little more, and my imperial face would have been pounded into jelly by that Hercules of a fellow! It is not such an easy matter as I had supposed, to mix on equal terms with other men! But I shall learn by bitter experience how to behave."

At this moment Joseph heard the sounds of weeping. Turning, he beheld coming toward him a young girl of about sixteen, whose slight figure, in spite of the cool autumn day, was scarcely covered by a thin, patched dress of dark stuff. An old, faded silk handkerchief was thrown over her shoulders; her sweet, pale face was bedewed with tears, and her lips were murmuring gentle complaints, though no one stopped to listen. On her right arm she carried a bundle, which every now and then she watched, as if afraid that some one might rob her of its treasures.

Suddenly a kind voice whispered, "Why do you weep, my child?"

The young girl started and met the gaze of a young man, whose blue eyes were fixed upon her with an expression of tenderest sympathy.

"I weep," said she, "because I am unhappy," and she quickened her steps that she might leave him behind. But the emperor kept pace with her.

"Why do you walk so fast? are you afraid of me?"

"I fear the committee of morals," said she, blushing. "If they should see me with you, I might be mistaken for—"

"Have you ever been suspected by them?"

"Yes, sir, although I have always tried, when I was in the streets, to avoid observation. Go, sir, go. Do not heed my tears. I am accustomed to misfortune."

"But it is said that the emperor has suspended the office of that committee."

"I am glad of it," replied the girl, "for good and evil are alike exposed to suspicion; and I would like to walk the streets without fear of being taken for what I am not."

"Where are you going, child?"

"I am going," replied she, with a fresh burst of tears, "to sell the clothes I carry in this bundle."

"What clothes, child?"

"The last decent covering that my poor mother owns," sobbed the girl.

"You are, then, very poor?" asked the emperor, softly.

"Very poor. We are often hungry, and have no food but our own bitter tears. These are the last clothes we have, but they must go for bread, and then perhaps we shall perish of cold."

"Poor girl! have you no father?"

"My father died in defence of Austria and the empress, and as a reward of his devotion to his sovereign, his wife and child have been left to die of want."

"Your father was a soldier?" asked the emperor, much affected.

"He was an officer, who served with distinction in the Seven Years' War. But he never was promoted. He died for Maria Theresa, and his widow and child will soon follow him to the grave."

"Why have you never applied to the empress for relief? Her purse is always open to the wants of the needy."

"To obtain any thing from royalty, sir, you know that one must have influence," replied the girl, bitterly. "We have no influence, nor would we know how to intrigue for favor."

"Why, then, do you not go to the emperor? He at least has no fancy for intriguers and flatterers. You should have gone to him."

"To be haughtily repulsed?" said she. "Oh, sir, the new emperor is a man whose only love is a love of power, and whose only pleasure is to make that power felt by others. Has he not already refused to listen to any petition whatever? Did he not forbid his people to come to him for favors?"

"He did that," replied Joseph, "because he wished to do justice to all; and for that reason he has done away with all presentation of petitions through courtiers or other officers of his household. But he has appointed an hour to receive all those who present their petitions in person."

"So he has said," returned the girl, "but no one believes him. His guards will turn away all who are not richly dressed, and so the emperor will have promised to see the people, though the people will never be allowed to come into his presence."

"Have the Austrians so little faith in the sincerity of the emperor?" asked Joseph. "Do they think that his heart—"

"His heart!" exclaimed the girl. "The emperor is without a heart. Even toward his mother he is said to be undutiful and obstinate. He hates his wife, and she is as mild as an angel. He whose pleasure it is to see an empress at his feet, do you suppose that he can sympathize with the misfortunes of his subjects? No, no; he has already stopped all pensions which the generous empress had given from her private purse."

"Because he intends to bestow them upon worthier objects."

"No, no; it is because he is a miser."

"He a miser!" cried Joseph. "Did he not some days ago burn up twenty-two millions of coupons?"

"It was said so; but no one saw them; and it is whispered that the twenty-two millions were nothing but pieces of waste paper."

The emperor was speechless. He looked at this young traducer with an expression of real horror.

"How!" at length said he, in a voice choked by emotion, "the emperor is suspected of such baseness!"

"He is known to be selfish and miserly," replied his tormentor.

Joseph's eyes flashed with anger; but conquering his bitterness, he constrained himself to smile.

"My child," said he, "you have been deceived. If you knew the emperor, you would find that he is generous and ready to do justice to all men. Go home and write your petition; and come to-day at noon to the imperial palace. The guards will allow you to pass, and a servant will be there to conduct you to me. I, myself, will present your petition, and I know that the emperor will not refuse a pension to the widow and child of a brave Austrian officer."

The girl's eyes filled with tears, as she attempted to thank her unknown benefactor.

But the emperor, who had allowed her to abuse him without interruption, would not listen to her praises.

"Your mother is sick, and needs care," said he. "Go home, and do not sell your clothes, for you will need them to visit the emperor. How much did you expect to get for them?"

"I expected seven ducats, for a portion of this clothing is my mother's wedding-dress."

"Then, my child, let me beg you to accept twelve," said he, drawing out his purse. "I hope they will suffice for your wants until the emperor fills them all."

The young girl bent over and kissed Joseph's hand. "Oh, sir," said she, "you save us from death, and we have nothing to offer in return but our poor prayers."

"Pray for the emperor," said he, gently. "Pray God that he

may win the love of his people. Farewell! I shall wait for you to-day, at noon."

With these words, Joseph quickened his pace, and was soon lost to view.

"My second adventure," thought he. "I must confess that it is not very flattering to walk *incognito* about the streets and hear the sentiments of one's own subjects. How often do kings mistake the murmurings of discontent for the outpourings of joy! It is so pleasant to believe in the love of our subjects, and to shut our eyes to all doubts of their loyalty! But I am resolved to see and judge of the people for myself. My path will often be beset with thorns, but Fate has not made me a monarch for my own good; I am an emperor for the good of others. That child has revealed some painful truths to me; it would seem as if I were fated forever to be misjudged."

CHAPTER XXXV.

THE DISGUISE REMOVED.

At mid-day the emperor reëntered the palace gates. This time he came through the principal entrance, feeling quite secure in his disguise.

He proceeded at once to the hall of reception, wondering whether his young *protégée* would present herself as he had requested her to do.

The sentries allowed him to pass, supposing him to be one of those about to seek an audience with the emperor. Unsuspected he reached the hall.

Yes, there was his little accuser. She stood trembling and blushing in one corner of the room, holding in her hand a paper. As she recognized her unknown protector, she hastened to meet him, and timidly gave him her hand.

"Oh, sir," said she, "you have been true to your word. I was so afraid you would forget me, that I was several times on the point of leaving this grand place. I feel lonely and ashamed; for you see that no one is here but myself. Nobody trusts the emperor. And I, who am here, will surely be repulsed; he never will be as kind as you have been to a poor, friendless girl. My mother has no hope; and if she has sent me to the palace, it was that I might see *you* again, and once more pour forth my gratitude for your kindness. If you would add another to the generous gift you have already bestowed, tell me your name, that my mother and I may beg God's blessing upon it, and then let me go, for I feel that my visit here will be vain!"

"My dear child," said Joseph, laughing, "if all the emperor's opponents were as headstrong as you, the poor man would have but little hope of ever gaining the good-will of his subjects. But I intend to prove to you that you are unjust. Give me your petition. I myself will present it for you. Wait awhile, until I send a messenger who will conduct you to the emperor. Follow him and fear nothing, for I shall be there, too, and there I will tell you my name. *Au revoir.*"

The young girl looked anxiously after him as he disappeared, and once more betook herself to the window. Gradually the room filled with a sad, humble, and trembling crowd, such as often throngs the anterooms of princes and nobles—a crowd which, with tearful eyes and sorrowing hearts, so often returns home without succor and without hope.

But the people who were assembled in this hall of reception seemed more sanguine than is usual with petitioners for imperial favor. They chatted together of their various expectations; they spoke of the emperor's benevolence; and all seemed to hope that they would be heard with patience, and favorably answered.

A door opened, and an officer entered. He looked sharply around the room, and then went directly to the window, where the young girl, with a beating heart, was listening to the praises of that emperor whom in her soul she believed to be a tyrant.

"The emperor will be here presently," said the officer, in answer to a storm of inquiries from every side. "But I have been ordered first to conduct this young lady, the daughter of a deceased officer, to his majesty's presence."

She followed him, silent and anxious. They went through suites of splendid rooms, whose costly decorations struck the child of poverty with new dismay. At last they stopped in a richly gilded saloon, covered with a carpet of Gobelin, and hung with the same rich tapestry.

"Remain here," said the officer, "while I announce you to his majesty."

He disappeared behind the velvet *portière*, and the frightened girl remained with a crowd of richly-dressed nobles, whose embroidered court-dresses and diamond crosses, almost blinded her with their splendor.

Once more the *portière* was drawn aside, and the officer beckoned the girl to advance. She did so with trembling limbs and throbbing heart. The hangings fell, and she was in the dread presence of the emperor. He stood near a window with his back toward her—a tall, graceful man, in a white uniform.

The poor girl felt as if she would cease to breathe, for this was the decisive moment of her young life. The emperor could either consign her to misery, or raise her to comfort, and wipe away the tears of her dear, suffering mother.

He turned and looked at her with a benevolent smile. "Come hither, my child," said he. "You would speak with the emperor. I am he."

The girl uttered a stifled cry, and falling on her knees, she hid her death-like face in her hands. For she had recognized her unknown protector. Yes, this noble man, who had proffered help and promised protection, this was the emperor, and to his face she had called him miser and tyrant!

She never for one moment thought whether he would punish her insolence; she had but one feeling, that of unspeakable anguish for having wounded a noble and generous heart. This alone caused her shame and grief.

The emperor approached, and looked with tenderness at the kneeling maiden, through whose fingers her tears were flowing in streams.

"I have read your petition, and have found that you spoke the truth. From this day your father's pay falls to your mother; and at her death it shall revert to you. I beg you both to forgive the tardiness of this act of justice; for neither the empress nor I had ever heard that your father had any family. Once more forgive us for all that you have endured since his death. And now, my child, rise from your knees; for human beings should kneel before God alone. Dry your tears, and hasten to your mother. Tell her that the emperor is not as heartless as he has been pictured to her by his enemies."

"No, no," cried she, "I cannot rise until my sovereign has forgiven my presumption and my calumnies."

"They are forgiven; for what could you know of me, you poor child, but what you had been told? But now you know me yourself; and for the future if you hear me traduced, you will defend me, will you not?" * He reached out his hand, which she kissed and bedewed with her tears.

The emperor raised her tenderly. "Be comforted; for if you cry so bitterly my courtiers will think that I have been unkind to you. You told me just now that you wished to know the name of your protector that you might pray for him. Well, my child, pray for me—my name is Joseph."

CHAPTER XXXVI.

ROSARY AND SCEPTRE.

THE four weeks to which Maria Theresa had limited her novitiate had almost expired. She still secluded herself from the world, and, in the deep retirement of her palatial cloister, would suffer no mention of worldly affairs in her presence.

In vain her confessor and her attendants strove to awaken her interest to the dissatisfaction of the people with the wild projects of reform that threatened the subversion of all social order. From the day of her retirement, Maria Theresa had forbidden the slightest allusion to politics. Her confesser had on one occasion ventured a hint on the subject of the changes which were being made by the emperor, but the empress had turned her flashing eyes upon him, and had reminded him that, as the servant of the Lord, he was there to exhort and to pray, not to concern himself about the trivialities of this world.

On another occasion the Countess Fuchs had presumed to mention the changes in the imperial household. The empress interrupted her coldly, saying that if she had not lost her relish for the vanities of the court, the countess must absent herself until further orders.

This severity had put an end to all plans for inducing the empress to resume the cares of empire. She was now at liberty to weep and pray without distraction. Even her children, who came daily to kiss her hand, were allowed no conversation but that which turned upon religion. When the morning services were ended, they silently withdrew to their rooms.

For a few days past, the Archduchess Christina had absented herself from this mournful levee. On the first day of her non-appearance the empress had not appeared to remark her absence.

* Historical.

But on the second day her eyes wandered sadly from her prayer-book to her children, and her lips seemed ready to frame some question. Instead of speaking, she bent her head over her rosary, and strove to pray with more devotion than usual.

Finally came a third day, and still Christina was absent. The empress could no longer master her maternal anxiety, and as the Archduchess Elizabeth approached to kiss her hand, she spoke.

"Where is Christina? Why is she not with you?"

"My sister is sick, your majesty," replied the archduchess.

And as though she feared to displease her mother by further speech, she bent her head and withdrew.

The next day when the imperial children entered their mother's apartment, her prayer-book was lying on the table, while she, pale and agitated, was pacing the room with hasty steps. She received her family with a slight motion of her head, and looked anxiously toward the door, until it had closed after the entrance of little Marie Antoinette. Then the empress sighed, and turned away her head lest her children should see the tears that were gushing from her eyes.

But when mass was over, and little Marie Antoinette approached her mother, she took the child up in her arms, and tenderly kissing her cheek, said: "How is Christina, my darling?"

"Sister Christina is very sick, imperial mamma," replied the child, "and she cries all day long. But she loves you very dearly, and longs to see you."

The empress put down her little daughter without a word, and as if she thought to mortify her worldliness, she signed to all present to withdraw, and falling upon her knees, prayed long and fervently.

An hour or two after she sent for her confessor. As he left her room and passed through the anteroom, the attendants saw that his countenance looked joyous in the extreme. They flocked to hear if there was any hope of convincing the empress of the necessity of her return to the world.

"I think there is much," replied the father. "God be thanked, her maternal love has overcome the dangerous lethargy into which sorrow had plunged our beloved sovereign. For a time she was overcome by her grief as a widow; but she begins to feel that her children have a right to her counsels and care. Later she will recognize the claims of her people, and Austria will be saved from the mad schemes of that unbelieving dreamer, her son."

"Do you really believe that her majesty will return to the throne?" asked the countess.

"I do. She besought me in trembling tones to tell her something of her beloved child—and I did nothing to tranquillize her, for she has no right to seclude herself from her people. Maria Theresa is a greater sovereign than her son will ever be, and Austria cannot afford to lose her now. She will visit her daughter to-day. Tell the archduchess not to fear her brother's opposition; for her mother, once resolved to return to her people, will see that her own daughters are not made wretched by a tyrannical brother. The princess will marry her lover."

"I hasten. How soon may we expect the empress?"

"She will surely be there before many hours. Solitude is not congenial to Maria Theresa's heart; her active mind craves occupation, and her grief requires it. Let us appeal to her affections through the illness of her child, and complete reaction will ensue. If once we can persuade her to quit her seclusion, the cloister-dream is over. Let us all work in concert to restore her to the world. It is not the sovereign of a great nation who has a right like Mary to sit at the feet of Jesus. Go at once, Count Bathiany, and may God bless the efforts we are making to restore our empress to her sense of duty. Church and state are alike endangered by the fatal step she has taken."

CHAPTER XXXVII.

THE DIFFERENCE BETWEEN AN ABBESS AND AN EMPRESS.

It was the hour of dinner. Complete silence reigned throughout the imperial palace, except in the halls and stairways that led from the imperial dining-hall to the kitchens below. Both lay far from the apartments of the empress-abbess. She, therefore, felt that she could visit her child without fear of observation. She had just concluded her own solitary dinner, and was trying to collect her thoughts for prayer. In vain. They *would* wander to the sick-bed of her daughter, whom fancy pictured dying without the precious cares that a mother's hand alone is gifted to bestow. Maria Theresa felt that her heart was all too storm-tossed for prayer. She closed her book with a pang of self-reproach, and rose from her arm-chair.

"It is useless," said she, at last. "I must obey the call of my rebellious heart, and tread once more the paths of earthly love and earthly cares. I cannot remain here and think that my Christina longs for her mother's presence, and that I may not wipe her tears away with my kisses. It is my duty to tend my sick child. I am not in the right path, or a merciful God would strengthen me to tread it courageously. I must replace their father to my children. Poor orphans! They need twice the love I gave before, and, God forgive me, I was about to abandon them entirely. It is no injury to the memory of my Francis, for, through his children, I shall but love him the more. How I long once more to press them to my heart! Yes, I must go, and this is the hour. I will pass by the private corridors, and surprise my Christina in her solitude."

With more activity than she had been able to summon to her help since the emperor's burial, Maria Theresa hastened to her dressing-room, and snatching up her long, black cloak, threw it around her person. As she was drawing the hood over her face, she caught a glimpse of herself in a mirror close by. She was shocked at her own image; her face so corpse-like, her cloak so like a hideous pall.

"I look like a ghost," thought the empress. "And indeed I am dead to all happiness, for I have buried my all! But Christina will be shocked at my looks. I must not frighten the poor child."

And actuated partly by maternal love, partly by womanly vanity, Maria Theresa slipped back the ugly hood that hid her white forehead, and opened the black crape collar which encircled her neck, so that some portion of her throat was visible.

"I will always be my Franz's poor widow," said the empress, while she arranged her toilet, "but I will not affright my children by my dress—now I look more like their mother. Let me hasten to my child."

And having again flung back the hood so that some portions of her beautiful hair could be seen, she left the room. She opened the door softly and looked into the next apartment. She had well calculated her time, for no one was there; her ladies of honor had all gone to dinner.

"That is pleasant," said she. "I am glad not to meet their wondering faces; glad not to be greeted as an empress, for I am an empress no longer. I am a poor, humble widow, fulfilling the only earthly duties now left me to perform."

She bent her head and went softly through the second anteroom to the hall. Again, all was empty and silent; neither page, nor sentry, nor lackey to be seen. She knew not why, but a feeling of desolation came over her. She had bidden adieu to the etiquette due to her rank, but this, she thought, was carrying the point too far.

"If I had had the misfortune to fall suddenly ill," said she, "I must have called in vain for succor. No one is by to hear my voice. But at least there must be sentries in the other hall."

No! That hall too was empty. No lackeys were there, no guards! For the first time in her life, Maria Theresa was out of hearing of any human being, and she felt a pang of disappointment and humiliation. She started at the sound of her own footsteps, and walked faster, that she might come within sight of some one—any one. Suddenly, to her joy, she heard the sound of voices, and paused to listen.

The door of the room whence the voices were heard was slightly ajar, and the empress overheard the following conversation. The speakers were Father Porhammer and the Countess Fuchs.

"Do not despair," said the father; "the empress is forgiving and magnanimous; and when she shall have admitted you again to her presence, it will be your duty to aid all those who love Austria, by using your influence to recall her majesty to the throne. Woe to Austria if she persists in elevating her grief above her duty as a sovereign! Woe to the nation if her son, that rebellious child of the church, reign over this land! His insane love of novelty—"

"For Heaven's sake, father," replied the countess, "say nothing against the emperor! His mother's will has placed him on the throne, and we must submit."

The empress heard no more. With noiseless tread she hurried on, until she turned the corner of a side-hall, and then she relaxed her pace. She pondered over what she had just heard, and it did not contribute to tranquillize her mind.

"What can he be doing?" thought she. "What are those mad schemes of which my friends have tried to apprise me? He was ever self-willed and stubborn; ever inclined to skepticism. Alas! alas! I foresee sad days for my poor Austria!"

At that moment the empress had gained a small landing which led to a staircase which she had to descend. She was about to proceed on her way when she perceived a man, whose back was turned toward her, seated on the topmost step. He was so quiet that she thought he was asleep. But as her foot touched him he turned carelessly round, and perceiving the empress, rose slowly, and bent his head as though to any lady whom he might pass.

Maria Theresa was astonished. She knew not what to think of the irreverent bearing of this man, who was no other than Stockel, one of the servants whose duty it had been, for thirty years, to light the fires in her dressing-room.

He had been accustomed every morning to appear before his imperial lady, in winter, to see that her fires were burning; in summer, to distribute her alms. Stockel was from Tyrol; he had been a favorite servant of the empress; and being an upright and intelligent man, his word was known to have some weight with her.* Stockel had been the most respectful and loyal of servants; the appearance alone of the empress had always made his old wrinkled face light up with joy. How did it happen that now, when he had been parted from her for four weeks, he seemed indifferent?

"He is offended because I have never sent for him," thought the kind-hearted empress; "I must try to appease him."

"I am glad to see you, Stockel," said she, with one of her own bewitching smiles; "it is long since you have visited me in my room. I am such a poor, sorrowing widow, that I have not had heart enough to think of the poverty of others."

Stockel said nothing. He turned and slightly shrugged his shoulders.

"How?" said Maria Theresa good-humoredly, "are you offended? Have you the heart to be angry with your empress?"

"Empress?" returned Stockel; "I took your highness for a pious nun. The whole world knows that Maria Theresa is no longer an empress; she no longer reigns in Austria."

Maria Theresa felt a pang as she heard these words, and her cheeks flushed—almost with anger. But overcoming the feeling she smiled sadly and said: "I see that you are really angry, poor Stockel. You do not like to see my palace made a cloister. You think, perhaps, that I have done wrong?"

"I do not pretend to judge of the acts of the rulers of earth," replied he gloomily. "Perhaps the deeds which in ordinary people would be called cowardly, may with them be great and noble. I know nothing about it; but I know what my beloved empress once said to me. She was then young and energetic, and she had not forgotten the oath she had taken when the archbishop crowned her at St. Stephen's—the oath which bound her to be a faithful ruler over her people until God released her."

"What said your empress then?"

"I will tell your highness. I had lost my young wife, the one I loved best on earth, and I came to beg my discharge; for my longing was to go back to my native mountains and live a hermit's life in Tyrol. My empress would not release me. 'How!' said she, 'are you so weak that you must skulk away from the world because Almigthy God has seen fit to bereave you of your wife? He tries your faith, man, and you must be firm, whether you face the storm or bask in the sunshine. Did you not promise to serve me faithfully, and will you now cast away your useful life in vain sorrow? What would you think of me were I so lightly to break my oath to my people—I who must lift my head above every tempest of private sorrow, to fulfil my vow until death?' Thus spoke my empress; but that was many years ago, and she was then sovereign of all Austria."

Maria Theresa looked down, and the tear-drops that had been gathering in her eyes fell upon her black dress, where they glistened like diamonds.

*Thiebault, "Mémoires de Vingt Ans."

"It is true," whispered she, "I was sovereign of all Austria."

"And what prevents you from being sovereign to-day?" asked Stockel eagerly. "Have your people released you?"

The empress waved her hand impatiently. "Enough," said she, "let me go my way!"

"But I have a petition to make, and as it is the last favor I shall ever ask, I hope your majesty will not deny me."

"Speak your wish," replied Maria Theresa hastily.

"I beg of your majesty to allow me to quit your service," replied the man moodily. "I cannot forget the words of Maria Theresa. I will not skulk away from the world while I have strength to work. I am tired of the idle life I lead. It is summer, and there is no fire to kindle. As for the poor unfortunates whom I used to visit, I can do them no good; their benefactress is no more. I must do something, or life will be a burden; and if your majesty will condescend to give me leave, I shall seek another place."

"Another place, Stockel!" said the empress. "What other place?"

"A place in the household of the *reigning* empress," answered Stockel with a low inclination.

Maria Theresa raised her head, and her astonishment was visible in her large, open eyes.

"The reigning empress?" said she musing. "Who can that be?"

"The wife of the reigning emperor, your majesty," said Stockel grimly.

The empress threw back her proud head, and drew her mantle convulsively around her.

"It is well," said she. "Come to me to-morrow, and you shall hear my decision."

CHAPTER XXXVIII.

THE REIGNING EMPRESS.

THE empress went slowly down the staircase. This staircase led to the left wing of the palace, where the apartments of the imperial children were situated. From earliest childhood the daughters of Maria Theresa had had each one her separate *suite*. Each one had her governess, her ladies of honor, and her train of servants, and lived as if in a miniature court.

On great festivals, national or domestic, the younger members of the imperial family were invited to the table of the empress; otherwise they ate in private with their retinue, and each child had a separate table.

It was now the dinner-hour, and Maria Theresa had selected it, because she felt sure that all the attendants of her children were at table, and no one would know of her visit to Christina. But she was mistaken. As she passed by the anteroom leading to the apartments of her children, she heard the voices of the lords and ladies in waiting, and through the half-opened door, saw them chatting together in groups. They did not seem to observe their ex-sovereign; they went on conversing as if nothing had happened. But as the empress was passing the apartments of little Marie Antoinette, her governess appeared, and, with a cry of joy, threw herself at Maria Theresa's feet, and covered her hand with kisses.

The empress smiled. A thrill of pleasure ran through her frame, as she received the homage to which from her birth she had been accustomed.

"Rise, countess," said she, kindly, "and do not let Marie Antoinette know that I am near. But, tell me, how comes it that at this hour I find the retinue of my children at leisure, while they are at table?"

"We are at leisure, your majesty," replied the countess, "because we are waiting for their highnesses to rise from the table."

"Is it then a festival, that my children should be dining at the imperial table?"

"Please your majesty, the reigning emperor has abolished the private tables of their highnesses your children. He finds it cheaper and more convenient for all the members of the imperial faimly to be served at once and at one table."

"Where, then, do my children dine?" asked the empress, with asperity.

"*En famille*, with her imperial majesty, the reigning empress."

"The reigning empress!" echoed Maria Theresa, with a frown. "But how comes it that my children leave their rooms without a retinue? Have you, then, already forgotten that I never permit a breach of court-ceremonial on any account?"

"Please your majesty, the emperor dislikes etiquette, and he has strictly forbidden all Spanish customs as laughable and ridiculous. He has forbidden all attendance upon the imperial family, except on new year's day. He has also forbidden us to kneel before his majesty, because it is an outlandish Spanish custom, and a homage due to God alone. All the French and Italian servants of the palace are dismissed, and their places are supplied by natives. The emperor wishes to have every thing at his court essentially German. For that reason he has ordered the mass to be translated and celebrated in the German language."

The empress heaved a sigh, and drew her mantilla over her face, as if to shut out the future which was unrolling itself to her view. She felt sick at heart; for she began to comprehend that her successor was not only creating a new order of things, but was speaking with contempt of his mother's reign. But she would not comtemplate the sad vision; she strove to turn back her thoughts to the present.

"But if you no longer have your private table," continued she, "why not accompany the princesses?"

"Because the emperor deems it fitting that the imperial family should dine alone. We, ladies in waiting, dine in a small room set apart for us, and then return to our apartments to await their highnesses."

"But the lords in waiting, do they not dine with you?"

"No, your majesty, they have received orders at one o'clock to go to their own houses, or to their former lodgings, to dine. The court table is abolished, and the emperor finds that by so doing he has economized a very considerable sum."

A deep flush of anger passed over the face of Maria Theresa, and her lip curled contemptuously. Economy was one of the few virtues which the profuse and munificent empress had never learned to practise. She considered it beneath the dignity of a sovereign to count the cost of anything."

"Enough," said she, in a constrained voice, "I will go to Christina. Let no one know of my visit. I desire to see my sick daughter alone."

She bent her lofty head, and walked rapidly away. With a beating heart she opened the door that led to the sleeping-room of the princess. There, on a couch, lay a pale, weeping figure, the empress's darling, her beautiful Christina.

She stopped for a moment on the threshold, and looked lovingly at the dear child, whom, for four days, she had not seen; then a thrill of unutterable joy pervaded her whole being.

At this moment Christina raised her languid eyes; her glance met that of her mother; and with a piercing cry, she sprang from the couch. But, overcome by weakness and emotion, she faltered, grew paler, and sank to the floor.

The empress darted forward and caught her fainting daughter in her arms. She carried her to the divan, laid her softly down, and, with quivering lip, surveyed the pale face and closed eyes of the princess.

She recovered slowly, and at length, heaving a deep sigh, unclosed her eyes. Mother and child contemplated each other with loving glances, and as the archduchess raised her arms and clasped them around her mother's neck, she whispered feebly: "Oh, now, all is well! I am no longer desolate; my dear, dear mother has returned to me. She has not forsaken us; she will shield us from oppression and misfortune."

Like a frightened dove Christina clung to the empress, and burying her face in her mother's breast, she wept tears of relief and joy.

The empress drew her close to her heart. "Yes, darling," said she, with fervor, "I am here to shield you, and I will never forsake you again. No one on earth shall oppress you now. Tell me, dear child, what goes wrong with you?"

"Oh, mother," whispered Christina, "there is one in Austria, more powerful than yourself, who will force me to his will. You cannot shield me from the emperor, for you have given him the power to rule over us; and, oh, how cruelly he uses his right!"

"What I have given, I can recall," cried the empress. "Mine are the power and the crown, and I have not yet relinquished them. Now speak, Christina; what grieves you, and why are your eyes so red with weeping?"

"Because I am the most unhappy of mortals," cried Christina, passionately. "Because I am denied the right which every peasant-girl exercises; the right of refusing a man whom I do not love. Oh, mother, if you can, save me from the detested Duke of Chablais, whom my cruel brother forces upon me as a husband."

"Is that your sorrow, my child?" exclaimed the empress. "Joseph is like his father; he loves wealth. The emperor had proposed this half-brother of the King of Sardinia for you, Christina, but I refused my consent; and, now without my knowledge, Joseph would force him upon you, because of his great riches. But patience, patience, my daughter. I will show you that I am not so powerless as you think; I will show you that no one in Austria shall give away my Christina without her mother's approbation."

While the empress spoke, her cheeks flushed, and her eyes glowed with a proud consciousness of might not yet renounced forever. The sorrowing widow was being once more transformed into the stately sovereign, and the eyes, which had been so dimmed by tears, were lit up by the fire of new resolves.

"Oh, mother, my own imperial mother," said Christina, "do not only free me from the man whom I detest, but bless me with the hand of the man I love. You well know how long I have loved Albert of Saxony, you know how dear I am to him. I have sworn never to be the wife of another, and I will keep my oath, or die! Oh, mother, do not make me the sport of policy and ambition! Let me be happy with him whom I love. What are crowns and sceptres and splendor, when the heart is without love and hope? I am willing to lead a simple life with Albert—let me be happy in my own way. Oh, mother! I love him so far above all earthly creatures, that I would rather be buried with him in the grave than be an empress without him."

And she fell upon her knees and wept anew. The empress had listened musingly to her daughter's appeal. While Christina was speaking, the glamour of her own past love was upon her heart. She was a girl again; and once more her life seemed bound up in the love she bore to young Francis of Lorraine. Thus had she spoken, so had she entreated her father, the proud emperor, until he had relented, and she had become the wife of Christina's own father! Not only maternal love, but womanly sympathy pleaded for her unhappy child.

She bent over her, and with her white hand fondly stroked the rich masses of Christina's golden-brown hair.

"Do not weep, my daughter," said she tenderly. "True, you have spoken words most unseemly for one of your birth; for it is the duty of a princess to buy her splendor and her rank with many a stifled longing and many a disappointment of the affections. Kind fate bestowed upon me not only grandeur, but the husband of my love, and daily do I thank the good God who gave me to my best beloved Franz. I do not know why you, too, may not be made a happy exception to the lot of princesses. I have still four beautiful daughters for whom state policy may seek alliances. I will permit one of my children to be happy as I have been. God grant that the rest may find happiness go hand in hand with duty."

The princess, enraptured, would have thrown her arms around her mother's neck; but suddenly her face, which had grown rosy with joy, became pale again, and her countenance wore an expression of deep disappointment.

"Oh, mother," cried she, "we build castles, while we forget that you are no longer the sovereign of Austria. And while you weep and pray in your dark cell, the emperor, with undutiful hand, overturns the edifice of Austria's greatness—that edifice which you, dearest mother, had reared with your own hands. He is like Erostratus; his only fame will be to have destroyed a temple which he had not the cunning to build."

"We will wrest the fagots from his sacrilegious hands," cried the empress.

The archduchess seemed not to have heard her mother's words She threw her arms around the empress, and, clinging convulsively to her, exclaimed, "Oh, do not forsake me, my mother and my empress. That horrible woman, who was dragged from her obscurity to curse my brother's life; that tiresome, hideous Josepha—do not suffer her to wear your title and your crown. O God! O God! Must I live to see Maria Theresa humbled, while Josepha of Bavaria is the reigning empress of Austria?"

The empress started. This was the third time she had heard these words, and each time it seemed as if a dagger had pierced her proud heart.

"Josepha of Bavaria the reigning empress of Austria!" said she scornfully. "We shall see how long she is to bear my title and wear my crown! But I am weary, my daughter. I must go to my solitude, but fear nothing. Whether I be empress or abbess, no man on earth shall oppress my children. The doors of the cloister have not yet closed upon me; I am still, if I choose to be, the reigning empress of Austria."

She pressed a kiss upon Christina's forehead, and left the room.

On her return she encountered no one, and she was just about to open the door of her own anteroom, when she caught the sound of voices from within.

"But I tell you, gentlemen," cried an angry voice, "that her majesty, the ex-empress, receives no one, and has no longer any revenues. She has nothing more to do with the administration of affairs in Austria."

"But I must see the empress," replied a second and a deprecating voice. "It is my right, for she is our sovereign, and she cannot so forsake us. Let me see the empress. My life depends upon her goodness."

"And I," cried a third voice, "I too must see her. Not for myself do I seek this audience, but for her subjects. Oh, for the love of Austria, let me speak with my gracious sovereign!"

"But I tell you that I dare not," cried the ruffled page. "It would ruin me not only with her majesty, but with the reigning emperor. The widowed empress has no more voice in state affairs, and the emperor never will suffer her to have any, for he has all the power to himself, and he never means to yield an inch of it."

"Woe then to Austria!" cried the third speaker.

"Why do you cry, 'Woe to Austria?'" asked a voice outside; and the tall, majestic form of the empress appeared at the door.

"Our empress!" cried the two petitioners, while both fell at her feet and looked up into her face with unmistakable joy.

The empress greeted them kindly, but she added: "Rise, gentlemen. I hear that my son, the emperor, has forbidden his subjects to kneel to him; they shall not, therefore, kneel to me, for he is right. To God alone belongs such homage. Rise, therefore, Father Aloysius; the brothers of the holy order of Jesus must never kneel to fellow-mortal. And you, Counsellor Bündener, rise also, and stand erect. Your limbs have grown stiff in my service; in your old age you have the right to spare them. You," added she, turning to the page, "return to your post, and attend more faithfully to your duty than you have done to-day. When I left this room, no one guarded the entrance to it."

"Your majesty," stammered the confused page, "it was the dinner-hour, and I had never dreamed of your leaving your apartments. His majesty the emperor has reduced the pages and sentries to half their number, and there are no longer enough of us to relieve one another as we were accustomed to do under the reign of your majesty."

"It is well," said the empress haughtily. "I will restore order to my household before another day has passed. And now, gentlemen, what brings you hither? Speak, Father Aloysius."

"My conscience, your majesty," replied Father Aloysius, fervently. "I cannot stand by and see the hailstorm of corruption that devastates our unhappy country. I cannot see Austria flooded with the works of French philosophers and German infidels. What is to become of religion and decency if Voltaire and Rousseau are to be the teachers of Austrian youth!"

"It rests with yourself, my friend," replied the empress, "to protect the youth of Austria from such contaminating influences. Why do those whom I appointed censors of the press permit the introduction of these godless works in my realms?"

"Your majesty's realms!" replied the father sadly. "Alas, they are no longer yours. Your son is emperor and master of Austria, and he has commanded the printing and distribution of every infidel work of modern times. The censors of the press have been silenced, and ordered to discontinue their revision of books."

"Has my son presumed so far?" cried the empress, angrily. "Has he dared to overthrow the barriers which for the good of my subjects I had raised to protect them from the corrupt influences of French infidelity? Has he *ordered* the dissemination of obscene and ungodly books? O my God! How culpable have I been to the trust which thou hast placed in my hands! I feel my guilt; I have sinned in the excess of my grief. But I will conquer my weak heart. Go in peace, father. I will ponder your words, and to-morrow you shall hear from me."

The father bowed and retired, while the empress turned toward Counsellor Bündener and inquired the cause of his distress.

"Oh, your majesty," cried the old man in accents of despair, "unless you help me I am ruined. If you come not again to my assistance my children will starve, for I am old and—"

"What!" interrupted the empress, "your children starve with the pension I gave you from my own private purse?"

"You did, indeed, give me a generous pension," replied Bündener, "and may God bless your majesty, for a more bountiful sovereign never bore the weight of a crown. But desolation and despair sit in the places where once your majesty's name was mingled each day with the prayers of those whom you had succored. The emperor has withdrawn every pension bestowed by you. He has received a statement of every annuity paid by your majesty's orders, and has declared his intention of cleaning out the Augean stables of this wasteful beneficence." *

The empress could not suppress a cry of indignation. Her face grew scarlet, and her lips parted. But she conquered the angry impulse that would have led her to disparage her son in the presence of his subject, and her mouth closed firmly. With agitated mien she paced her apartment, her eyes flashng, her breast heaving, her whole frame convulsed with a sense of insulted maternity. Then she came toward the counsellor, and lifting her proud head as though Olympus had owned her sway, she spoke:

"Go home, my friend," said she imperiously, "and believe my

* Hubner, "Life of Joseph II.," vol. i., p. 28.

royal word when I assure you that neither you nor any other of my pensioners shall be robbed of your annuities. Princely faith shall be sacred above all consideration of thrift, and we shall see who dares impeach mine!"

So saying, Maria Theresa passed into her-dressing-room, where her ladies of honor were assembled. They all bent the knee as she entered, and awaited her commands in reverential silence. At that moment the flourish of trumpets and the call of the guards to arms were heard. The empress looked astounded, and directed an inquiring glance toward the window. She knew full well the meaning of that trumpet signal and that call to arms; they were heard on the departure or the return of one person only in Austria, and that person was herself, the empress.

For the third time the trumpet sounded. "What means this?" asked she, frowning.

"Please your majesty," answered a lady of the bedchamber, "it signifies that her imperial majesty, the reigning empress, has returned from her walk in the palace gardens."

Maria Theresa answered not a word. She walked quickly past her attendants and laid her hand upon the lock of the door which led into her private study. Her head was thrown back, her eyes were full of flashing resolve, and the tone of her voice was clear, full, and majestic. It betokened that Maria Theresa was "herself again."

"Let Prince Kaunitz be summoned," said she. "Send hither the Countess Fuchs and Father Porhammer. Tell the two latter to come to my study when the prince leaves it."

CHAPTER XXXIX.

THE CO-REGENT DEPOSED.

SCARCELY a quarter of an hour had elapsed since the empress's orders had been issued, when a page announced Prince Kaunitz.

Maria Theresa went forward to receive him. Her whole being seemed filled with a feverish excitement which contrasted singularly with the unaltered demeanor of her prime minister, who, cold and tranquil as ever, advanced to meet his sovereign, and bowed with his usual phlegm.

"Well," said Maria Theresa, after a pause, "every thing has not changed in the four weeks of my retirement from court. You at least are the same in appearance. Let me hope that you are the same in spirit and in mind."

"Please your majesty," replied Kaunitz, "four weeks have not yet gone by since I had the honor of an interview with you."

"What do you mean by that?" asked the empress, impatiently. "Do you wish to remind me that I had resolved to wait four weeks before I decided upon a permanent course of action?"

"Yes, your majesty," said Kaunitz. "I am somewhat vain, as everybody knows, and I have already seen my triumph in your majesty's face. I read there that my noble empress has proved me a true prophet. She has not yet been away from her subjects four weeks, and already her head has silenced the weakness of her heart. Three weeks have sufficed to bring Maria Theresa once more to her sense of duty."

"Ah!" said the empress, "are you then so sure that my novitiate wil not end in a cloister?"

"I am convinced of it. For never shall I forget the day on which your majesty swore to be a faithful ruler over Austria as long as you lived. I am convinced of it, too, because I know that, although my empress has the heart of a woman, she has the head of a man, and in all well-ordered unions the head rules the household."

The empress smiled faintly, but said nothing. Her arms were crossed over her breast, her head was bent in thought, and she went slowly back and forth from one end of her study to the other. Kaunitz followed her with his large, tranquil eyes, which seemed to penetrate to the remotest regions of her throbbing heart.

Suddenly she stood before him, and for a moment gazed earnestly in his face.

"Kaunitz," said she, "I have not only considered you for many years as a wise and great statesman, but, what is better yet, I have esteemed you as a man of honor. I exact of you that you act honorably and openly toward me in this hour. Do you promise?"

"An honorable man, your majesty, need not promise to do that which honor requires of him."

"True, true. But you might pay unconscious deference to my rank or to my sex. Courtesy might mislead you. This is precisely what I warn you to avoid. I wish you to speak candidly without thought or consideration for empress or woman. Remember how you pledged your life to Austria's good—and, forgetting all else, answer me truthfully and without fear. Will you, Kaunitz?"

"I will, your majesty. Ask, and you shall be truthfully answered—so help me God."

"Then, tell me, which of us is better calculated to reign in Austria—Joseph or myself? Which of us will best promote the welfare of the Austrian people? Do not answer me at once. Take time to reflect upon the subject, for a weighty question lies in the balance of this hour. I cannot trust myself in this decision, for I have wept so many tears that I have not the strength to see wherein my duty lies. I cannot even trust my own misgivings, for pride or vanity may have blinded my eyes to truth. I am not sure that I view things in their proper light. It is useless, therefore, for me to speak. I desire to hear no one but yourself. I swear to you, by the memory of Charles V., that, whatever you say shall be sacred; for I have exacted of you candor—and say what you will, your candor shall not offend. Who, then, is best fitted to reign, Joseph or I?"

"Your majesty, I have had full time to reflect upon this weighty question; for since first you announced your intention to resign the throne, I have thought of nothing else. In politics we know neither predilection nor prejudice. Necessity and interest decide all things. Your majesty has so often called me a good politician, that I have ended by believing myself to be one. It follows thence that, in deliberating upon this great question, I have laid aside all personal inclination and sympathy, and have had in view the welfare of Austria alone. But for this, the matter would have required no thought, for the Emperor Joseph and I have nothing in common. He fears me, and I do not love him.* We never could be made to

* Kaunitz's own words. Wraxall, vol. ii., p. 490.

understand one another; for the language of the heart is not to be forced by edicts, as is the language of the court. The emperor has forbidden all tongues in Germany, save one. If he persist in this, he will alienate his subjects, and Austria will soon lose her greatness. When a man intends to force his people to forget their mother-tongue, he must do it by degrees; and if he succeeds, he will be a skilful teacher. The best reforms are to be introduced through the byways of life. If we trust them on the highway, they shock and terrify the people. The young emperor, regardless of these considerations, has violently suppressed whatever seemed injudicious to him in your majesty's administration. Perhaps you had done too much; your son, certainly, does too little. I hear everywhere of interdicts, but nowhere of concessions. Old things destroyed, but nothing created to replace them. What will be the result of this? Austria must soon be reduced to a mass of ruins, and your son will go down to posterity with a fame like that of Attila. Save Austria! save him from the curse that threatens both. We have not yet completed the noble edifice of which eleven years ago we laid the foundations. We must finish the structure, and so solid must be its walls that our thoughtless young reformer shall not have strength to batter them down. Your majesty must remain the reigning Empress of Austria. You cannot resign your empire to your son. Duty and the welfare of your subjects forbid it."

The empress inclined her head approvingly. "I believe that you are right, Kaunitz," replied she. "It is not in the pride, but in the deep humility of my heart, that I reassume the crown which God himself placed upon my head. I have no right to say that the load is too heavy since He wills me to bear it. Indeed I feel that He will give me strength to accomplish His will in me, and I am now ready to say, 'Behold the handmaid of the Lord; be it done to me according to His word.' I will never again lift my treasonable hand against that crown which I pray Heaven I may wear for the good of my people. But you, prince, you must be at my side; together we have planned for Austria, together we must complete the noble structure of her greatness."

"I remain, your majesty, and will never cease to labor until the banner of the Hapsburg floats proudly from its battlements. But we must decorate as well as strengthen. We have beautiful young princesses whose alliances will bring wealth and splendor to our imperial edifice. Within, we shall have solid walls that will insure the durability of our structure; without, we shall have brilliant alliances that will perfect its beauty."

"You have a marriage to propose?" said the empress, smiling.

"I have, your majesty, a marriage with the young King of Naples."

"For which of my daughters?" asked Maria Theresa uneasily.

"For the one your majesty shall select."

"Then it shall be Johanna. She is very beautiful, and has a proud and ambitious heart which craves less for love than for rank and splendor. But if I give one of my daughters to diplomacy, you must leave me another for domestic happiness. Christina has undertaken to think that she must marry for love, and I think we ought to make her happy in her own modest way. We owe amends to Albert of Saxony for having declined an alliance with his sister; we also owe him something for his fidelity and good faith as an ally. Let the young lovers be united, then; we have gold and daughters enough to tolerate *one* marriage of inclination in our imperial house."

"But your majesty will give up the youngest, Marie Antoinette, to diplomacy, will you not?"

"You destine her to the throne of France, prince—is it not so?"

"Yes, your majesty. The son of the dauphin is a noble youth, and although his father was unfriendly to Austria, Choiseuil and La Pompadour are for us. Marie Antoinette, therefore, is to be Queen of France. This, however, must be a profound secret between ourselves. While her little highness is being fashioned for her future dignity, we must marry her elder sisters, if not so brilliantly, at least as advantageously as we can. First, then, upon the list is the Archduchess Christina. We must find some suitable rank for herself and her husband, and your majesty will of course bestow a dowry worthy of your daughter's birth and station."

"I will present them the duchy of Teschen as a wedding-gift, and it must be your care, prince, to find an appointment for the Elector of Saxony that will be worthy of my son-in-law."

"Let us name him Captain-General and Stadtholder of Hungary. That will be an effectual means of converting the Hungarians into Austrians, and the appointment is in every way suitable to the elector's rank."

The empress nodded, smiling acquiescence. "Your head," said she, "is always in the right place; and sometimes I cannot help thinking that your heart is better than the world believes it to be, else how could you so readily divine the hearts of others? How quickly have you devised the best of schemes to promote my daughter's happiness, without compromising her imperial station! Christina shall be Stadthalterin of Hungary; and in her name and my own I thank you for the suggestion. One thing, however, lies heavy on my heart. It is the thought of the blow I am about to inflict upon my poor Joseph. How will he bear to be deprived of his sovereignty?"

"I think your majesty named him co-regent only," said Kaunitz.

"I did," replied the empress, "and in very truth I withdraw nothing but a temporary privilege. As empress I know my right to resume the reins of power; but it grieves my maternal heart to exercise it. I think I see him now, poor boy, with his great blue eyes fixed in despair upon me. I never shall have the courage to announce my return to him."

"There will be no need to restrict him in his co-regency. He can be removed to th war department, where he may reign unfettered."

"He shall have unlimited power there," exclaimed the empress, joyfully. "It is the proper province of a man, and Joseph will fill the station far better than I have ever done. I promise not to interfere with him in the field. For other state affairs, I shall attend to them myself, and I do not think that I will ever delegate my power a second time. You had best inform Joseph of my resumption of the throne, and let the Frau Josepha also be advised that she is no longer reigning empress of Austria. For me, I must always remain at heart a sorrowing widow. My sorrows I can never overcome;

my widow's weeds I shall never lay aside.* But above the weeds I will wear the mantle of royalty; and since you have so determined for me, Austria shall once more own the sway of Maria Theresa."

CHAPTER XL

MOTHER AND SON.

THE dream was over—the blessed dream of philanthropy and reform! The reins of power had been snatched from his hands, and Joseph was once more consigned to a life of insignificant inactivity. Like a wounded bird, whose broken wing no longer bears him aloft, his heart fluttered and fell—its high hopes dashed to earth. The old influences which he hated, were at work again, and he had no recourse but absolute silence. His deep humiliation, he was constrained to hide under a mask of serenity; but he knew that his spirit was crushed, and night fell over his stricken soul. Still, he struggled against the chill of his despair, and with all the strength of his being he strove against misfortune.

"I will not succumb," thought he, "I will not be vanquished by this secret grief. I will not be a cause of sorrow to my friends and of triumph to my enemies—I will live and overpower misfortune. Since all in Vienna is so dark, let me seek sunshine elsewhere—I will travel!—Away from this stifling court, to breathe the free air of heaven! Here I am an emperor without an empire; there at least I shall be a man, to whom the world belongs, wherever his steed has strength and speed to bear him. Yes, let me travel, that I may gird up my loins for the day when the sun of royalty shall rise for me. It will come! it will come! And when it dawns, it must find me strong, refreshed, and ready for action."

The emperor made his preparations to depart, and then, in compliance with the requisitions of court etiquette, he sought his mother, to obtain her consent to his journey. Maria Theresa received her son with that half-mournful tenderness which lent such an indescribable fascination to her appearance and manners. She looked at him with a smile so winning and affectionate, that Joseph, in spite of himself, felt touched and gladdened; and the hand which his mother held out was most fervently pressed to his lips. It was the first time they had met in private since the empress had reascended her throne, and both felt the embarrassment and significance of the hour.

"I have longed for this moment with anxious and beating heart, my son," said the mother, while she drew him toward her. "I know, my child, that your heart is embittered toward me. You think that I would have been wiser as well as kinder had I never left my widow's cloister. But reflect, my dear son, as I have done, that my sceptre was given me by the hand of God, and that it would be sinful and cowardly in me to give it into the hands of another until He, in His wisdom, releases me from durance."

*She kept her word. Every month, on the day of her husband's death, she spent the day in solitary prayer and on every yearly anniversary of her widowhood, she knelt for hours by the side of the emperor's tomb, praying for the repose of his soul. Her private apartments were ever after hung with gray, and her coaches and liveries were of the same sad hue.—Caroline Pichler, "Memoirs."

Joseph looked with genuine emotion at the agitated countenance of his mother. He saw the tears gather and fall from her eyes; he saw the quivering lip, the trembling frame: he felt that her integrity was beyond suspicion, her love for him beyond all question. The icy barriers that had closed upon his heart, gave way; he felt the warm and sunny glow of a mother's unspeakable love, and, yielding to the impulse of the moment, he flung his arms around the empress's neck, while he covered her face with kisses. "Mother, my dear mother!" sobbed he; and as if these words had opened the floodgates of all the love which filled his heart, he leaned his head upon her bosom, and was silent.

She smiled fondly upon him as he lay there; she returned his kisses, and stroked his fair, high forehead with her loving hand.

"Have you come back once more to your mother's heart, my darling?" whispered she. "Have you found your way back to the nest whence you have wandered away so long, you stray birdling? Do you feel, my son, that the mother's bosom is the resting-place for her children? Oh! promise me, my heart's treasure, to trust and love me from this hour? We are human, and therefore we are sinful and erring. I well know, dear boy, that I have many failings. From my heart I regret them; and if in your short life, as boy or man, I have grieved you, pardon me, dearest, for I have not meant it in unkindness."

"No, mother," said Joseph, "it is I who should sue for pardon. My heart is wild and stubborn; but I believe that it beats with a love as true and warm for my empress as that of any other man in Austria. Have patience with me, then, my mother, for I am indeed a wandering bird; and, in my wild flight, the shafts of this life have wounded and maimed me. But let us not speak of life—mine is a blasted one."

"Yes, my son, let us speak of your life, and of its misfortunes; for I know that Josepha of Bavaria is its chiefest sorrow. I have heard something of your unhappiness as a husband, and I pity you both."

"You pity her!" cried Joseph, hastily. "How does *she* deserve my mother's compassion?"

The empress laid her hand gently upon her son's shoulder. "She loves you, Joseph," said she, "and I cannot refuse my sympathy to a woman who loves without hope of return."

"She loves me!" exclaimed Joseph, with a laugh of derision. "Yes—and her love is my abhorrence and my shame. Her ogling glances make me shudder with disgust. When she turns upon me her blotched and pimpled face, and calls me by the name of husband, the courtiers sneer, and I—I feel as if I would love to forget my manhood and fell her to the earth."

"She is certainly ugly," said the empress, shaking her head, "but uglier women than she have inspired love. And remember, Joseph, that you chose her yourself. Besides, she has an excellent heart, if you would but take the trouble to explore its unknown regions. Moreover, you will one day be sole Emperor of Austria, and you should seek to give an heir to your throne. If Josepha were the mother of your children, you would no longer think her ugly."

"*She* the mother of my children!" cried Joseph, with such keenness of hate, that the empress shuddered. "Do you think me capable of such a degradation? You have not seen Van Swieten lately, or he would have told you that this woman, in addition to her other attractions, is troubled with a new malady."

"Van Swieten did not mention it to me."

"Well, then, your majesty, I will mention it. This so-called empress has the scurvy."

"Oh, my son, my poor boy!" cried the empress, putting her arm around Joseph's neck as though she would have shielded him from infection. "That is a disgusting malady, but Van Swieten's skill will soon conquer it."

"Yes; but neither he nor you will ever conquer my hate for *her*. Not all the world could make me forgive the deception that was practised upon me when she was allowed to become my wife. *This* woman the mother of my children! No! No one shall ever force me to be the father of any thing born of Josepha of Bavaria!"

The empress turned away and sighed. It was in vain. This was hatred strong as death. "May God comfort you both!" said she, mournfully.

"Then He must put us asunder!" cried out Joseph, almost beside himself. "Believe me, mother," continued he, "death alone can bring us consolation; and may God forgive me when I pray that this atoning angel may come to my relief! She or I! No longer can I bear this ridicule of hearing this leper called an empress!"

"Travel, then, my dear son," said his mother. "Travel and try to enjoy life away from Vienna. Perchance when you will have seen how little true happinesss there is on earth, experience may come to your help, and teach you to be less unhappy."

The emperor shook his head. "Nothing," replied he, moodily, "can ever console me. Wherever I go, I shall hear the rattle of my prisoner's chain. Let us speak of it no more. I thank your majesty for the permission to leave Vienna, and I thank you for this bright and sacred hour, whose memory will bless me as long as I live. You have been to me this day a tender and sympathizing mother. May I henceforward be to you a grateful and obedient son."

"You have not yet told me whither you desire to travel," said the empress, after a pause.

"With your majesty's permission, I would wish to travel in Bohemia and Moravia, and then I wish to visit the courts of Dresden and Munich. Both sovereigns, through their ambassadors, have sent me urgent invitations."

"It would be uncourteous to refuse," said the empress, earnestly. "It is politic for us, as far as possible, to bind all the German princes to us by interchange of kindness."

"Since this is your majesty's opinion, I hope that you will also consent to my acceptance of a third invitation. The King of Prussia has requested to have an interview with me at Torgau."

The brow of the empress darkened.

"The King of Prussia?" said she, almost breathless.

"Yes, your majesty; and, to be frank with you, it is of all my invitations the one which I most desire to accept. I long to see face to face the king whom all Europe, friend or foe, unites in calling 'Frederick the Great'—great not only as a hero, but also as a lawgiver."

"Yes," cried the empress, with indignation, "the king whom

infidels delight to honor. I never supposed that *he* would presume to approach my son and heir as an equal. The Margrave of Brandenburg has a right to hold the wash-basin of the Emperor of Germany, but methinks he forgets his rank when he invites him to an interview."

"Ah, your majesty," replied Joseph, smiling, "the Margrave of Brandenburg, to our sorrow and our loss, has proved himself a king; in more than one battle has he held the wash-basin for Austria's sovereign, but it was to fill it with Austrian blood."

Maria Theresa grew more and more angry as she heard these bold words. "It ill becomes my son," said she, "to be the panegyrist of the victor whose laurels were snatched from his mother's brow."

"Justice impels me to acknowledge merit, whether I see it in friend or foe," answered the emperor. "Frederick of Prussia is a great man, and I only hope that I may ever resemble him."

The empress uttered an exclamation, and her large eyes darted lightning glances.

"And thus speaks my son of the man who has injured and robbed his mother!" exclaimed she indignantly. "My son would press his hand who has spilled such seas of Austrian blood—would worship as a hero the enemy of his race! But so long as I reign in Austria, no Hapsburger shall condescend to give the hand to a Hohenzollern. There is an old feud between our houses; it cannot be healed."

"But if there is feud, your majesty perceives that it is not the fault of the King of Prussia, since he holds out the right hand of friendship. I think it much more Christian-like to bury feuds than to perpetuate them. Your majesty sees, then, how Frederick has been calumniated, since he follows the Christian precept which commands us to forgive our enemies."

"I wish to have nothing to do with him," said the empress.

"But, as I had the honor of saying before, the king has sent me a pressing invitation, and you said just now that it would be uncourteous to refuse."

"Not the invitation of Frederick. I will not consent to that."

"Not even if I beg it as a favor to myself?' asked Joseph fervently. "Not even if I tell you that I have no wish so near at heart as that of knowing the King of Prussia? Think of this day, so brightened to me by the sunshine of your tenderness! Let the mother plead for me with the sovereign; for it is not to my empress, it is to my mother that I confide my hopes and wishes. Oh, do not drown the harmony of this hour in discord! Do not interpose a cloud between us now."

The empress threw back her head. "You threaten me, sir, with your displeasure? If there are clouds between us, see that they disperse from your own brow, and show me the face of a loyal subject and a respectful son. I will not consent to this visit to the King of Prussia; the very thought of it is galling to my pride."

"Is that your majesty's last word?"

"It is my last."

"Then I have nothing further to say, except that, as in duty bound, I will obey the orders of my sovereign," replied Joseph, turning deathly pale. "I shall refuse the invitation of the King of Prussia, and beg leave to retire."

Without awaiting the answer of his mother, he bowed, and hastily left the room.

"Dismissed like a school-boy," muttered he, while tears of rage flowed down his cheeks. "Two chains on my feet—the chains of this accursed marriage, and the chains of my filial duty, impede my every step. When I would advance, they hold me back and eat into my flesh. But it is of no use to complain, I must learn to bear my fate like a man. I cannot rebel openly, therefore must I be silent. But my time will come!

He raised his head proudly, and with a firm step took the way to his private apartments. He went at once into his study, where, on his writing-desk, lay the letter of the King of Prussia.

The emperor seated himself at the desk, and, with a heavy sigh, took up his pen. "Tell the king, your master," wrote he, "that I am not yet my own master; I am the slave of another will. But I will find means some day to atone for the rudeness which I have been forced to offer him in return for his kindness." *

CHAPTER XLI.

DEATH THE LIBERATOR.

THE cruel enemy which had laid low so many branches of the noble house of Hapsburg, had once more found entrance into the imperial palace at Vienna. This terrific invisible foe, which, from generation to generation, had hunted the imperial family with such keen ferocity, was the small-pox. Emperors and Empresses of Austria had been its victims, and almost every one of Maria Theresa's children bore, sooner or later, its brand upon their faces. This fiend had robbed them of the fair Isabella; and now its envenomed hand was laid upon the affianced bride of the King of Naples. The beautiful young Johanna was borne to the vaults of the Capuchins, while in the palace its inmates were panic-stricken to hear that Josepha of Bavaria, too, had taken the infection.

With such lightning swiftness had the venom darted through the veins of the unhappy empress, that her attendants had fled in disgust from the pestiferous atmosphere of her chamber.

And there, with one hired nurse, whom the humane Van Swieten had procured from a hospital, lay the wife of the Emperor of Austria.

No loving hand smoothed the pillow beneath her burning head, or held the cooling cup to her blood-stained lips; no friendly voice whispered words of sympathy; no familiar face bent over her with looks of pity.

Alone and forsaken, as she had lived, so must she die! At his first wife's bedside Joseph had watched day and night; but Josepha's he did not approach. In vain had she sent each day, through Van Swieten, a petition to see him, if only once; Joseph returned, for all answer, that his duty to his mother and sisters forbade the risk.

And there lay the woman whose princely station mocked her misery; there she lay, unpitied and unloved. The inmates of the palace hurried past the infected room, stopping their breathing as they ran: the daughters of Maria Theresa never so much as inquired whether their abhorred sister-in-law were living or dead.

But the poor dying empress was not even alone with her misery.

* Hubner, "Life of Joseph II.," vol. i., p. 87.—Gross-Hoffinger, vol. i., p. 116.

Memory was there to haunt her with mournful histories of her past life: pale, tearful, despairing were these ghosts of an existence uncheckered by one ray of happiness. Ah, with what a heart full of trembling hope had she entered the walls of this palace, which to her had proved a prisoner's cell! With what rapture had she heard the approaching step of that high-born emperor, her husband, on their wedding-night; and oh, how fearful and how swift had fallen the bolt of his vengeance upon her sin! Memory whispered her of this.

She thought of the Emperor Francis, of his tender sympathy with her sorrow; she remembered how he had conspired with her on that fatal night at Innspruck. Then she remembered her husband's scorn, his withering insults, and her loss of consciousness. She thought how she had been found on the floor, and awakend by the terrifying intelligence of the emperor's sudden death. Her tears, her despair, she remembered all; and her wail of sorrow at the loss of her kindest friend.* Memory whispered her of this.

She thought of her dreary life from that day forward: forever the shrinking victim of Christina's sneers, because she, and not the sister of Albert of Saxony, had become the emperor's wife. Even the kind-hearted Maria Theresa had been cold to her; even she, so loving, so affectionate, had never loved Josepha. And the wretched woman thought how one day when the imperial family had dined together, and her entrance had been announced as that of "Her majesty, the reigning empress," the archduchesses had sneered, and their mother had smiled in derision. Memory whispered her of this.†

She thought how her poor, martyred heart had never been able to give up all hope of love and happiness; how day by day she had striven, through humility and obedience, to appease her husband's anger. But he had always repulsed her. One day she had resolved that he *should* see her. She knew that the emperor was in the daily habit of sitting on the balcony which divided her apartments from his. She watched his coming, and went forward to meet him. But when he saw her, in spite of her tears and supplications, with a gesture of disgust, he left the balcony and closed the window that led to it. The next day, when she ventured a second time on the balcony, she found it separated by a high partition, shutting out all hope of seeing her husband more. And she remembered how, one day afterward, when she stepped out upon it, and her husband became aware of her presence, he had, in sight of all the passers-by, started back into his room, and flung down his window with violence.‡ Memory whispered her of this.

But now that she had expiated her first fault by two years of bitter repentance, now that death was about to free him from her hated presence forever, surely he would have mercy, and forgive her the crime of having darkened his life by their unahppy union.

Oh, that once more she could look into the heaven of those deep-blue eyes! That once more before she died she could hear the music of that voice, which to her was like the harmony of angels' tongues!

In vain! Ever came Van Swieten with the same cold message—"The emperor cannot compromise the safety of his relatives."

* Wraxall, vol. ii., page 411.
† Hubner, "Life of Joseph II.," p. 27.
‡ Caroline Pichler, "Memoirs," vol. i., p. 182.

At last, in the energy of despair, Josepha sat erect in her bed, and with her livid, bloody hands, wrote a letter which Van Swieten, at her earnest entreaty, delivered to the emperor.

When, after a short absence, he returned with another denial, she gave such a shriek of anguish that it was heard throughout the palace.

Van Swieten, overwhelmed by pity for the poor martyr, felt that he must make one more effort in her behalf. He could do nothing for her: bodily, she was beyond his power to heal; but he was resolved to be the physician of her broken heart, and, if it lay within the power of man, to soothe and comfort her dying moments.

With the letter which Joseph had returned to him, he hastened to the Empress Maria Theresa. To her he pictured the agony of her dying daughter-in-law, and besought her to soften the emperor's heart.

The empress listened with deep emotion to the long-tried friend of her house. Tears of sympathy gathered in her eyes, and fell over her pale cheeks.

"Joseph will not grant her request, because he fears the infection for us?" asked she.

"Yes, your majesty, that is his pretext."

"He need not fear for me, and he can remain at a distance from the other members of the family," said Maria Theresa. "But I know what are his real sentiments. He hates Josepha, and it is his hatred alone that prevents him from granting her petition. He has a hard, unforgiving heart; he never will pardon his wife—not even when she lies cold in her grave."

"And she will not die until she has seen him," returned Van Swieten, sadly. "It seems as if she had power to keep off death until the last aim of her being has been reached. Oh, it is fearful to see a soul of such fire and resolution in a body already decaying."

The empress shuddered. "Come, Van Swieten," said she, resolutely, "I know how to force Joseph to the bedside of his poor, dying wife."

She rose, and would have gone to the door, but Van Swieten, all ceremony forgetting, held her back.

"I will call the emperor myself," said he; "whither would your majesty go?"

"Do not detain me," cried the empress, "I must go to the emperor."

"But what then?" asked Van Swieten, alarmed.

The empress, who had already crossed her anteroom, looked back with a countenance beaming with noble energy.

"I will do my duty," replied she. "I will do what Christian feeling prompts. I will go to Josepha."

"No, your majesty, no," cried Van Swieten, again laying hands upon his sovereign. "You owe it to your people and your children not to expose yourself to danger."

The empress smiled sadly. "Doctor, where did Isabella and Johanna take the infection? God called them to Himself, and God has shielded me. If it pleases Him that I also shall suffer this fearful scourge, it will not be from contagion. It will be from His divine hand."

"No, no, your majesty, it will be my fault," cried Van Swieten. "On my head will be the sin."

"I free you from all responsibility," replied she, "and say no more; for it is my duty to visit this deserted woman's death-bed. I have been less kind to her than I should have been, and less indulgent than on *my* death-bed I will wish to have been. I have not been a tender mother to her, living—let me comfort her, at least, now that she is dying."

"But she has not asked for your majesty," persisted Van Swieten. "Wherefore—"

But suddenly he stopped, and a cry of horror was stifled between his lips. He had seen upon the forehead and cheeks of the empress those small, dark spots which revealed to his experienced eye that it was too late to shield her from infection.

Maria Theresa was too excited to remark the paleness of Van Swieten. She continued:

"Go to Joseph, and tell him that I await him at the death-bed of his wife. He will not dare refuse her now. Go, doctor, we must both do our duty."

Van Swieten stepped aside, for he had blocked the door.

"Go, your majesty," said he, almost inaudibly. "I will not detain you, but will see the emperor." He turned away, sick at heart. "One empress dying, and another!—O God! grant me help that I may save my beloved Maria Theresa!"

Meanwhile the empress hurried through the deserted halls of the palace to the room of the unhappy Josepha. As she approached the door, she heard her voice in tones of bitterest anguish. The sound filled the heart of Maria Theresa with deepest sympathy and sorrow.

For one moment she stood irresolute; then, gathering all her strength, she opened the door, and went in. At the foot of the bed knelt two Ursuline nuns, those angels of mercy who are ever present to comfort the dying. The entrance of the empress did not interrupt their prayers. They knew that no one could rescue the dying woman; they were praying Heaven to comfort her departing soul.

But was she comforted? She ceased her lamentations, and now lay still. She had heard the door open, and had struggled to rise; but she was too weak, and sank back with a groan.

But she had seen the empress, who, with the courage of a noble spirit, had conquered her disgust, and advancing to the bed, bent over Josepha with a sweet, sad smile. Josepha saw it, and the empress looked more beautiful to her dying eyes than she had ever looked before.

"God bless you, my poor daughter," whispered she, in broken accents. "I come to give you a mother's blessing, and to beg of Almighty God to give you peace."

"Peace, peace!" echoed the sufferer, while the empress, with a shudder surveyed her black and bloated face.

Suddenly she uttered a cry, and opened her arms. "He comes! he comes!" cried she; and her dying eyes unclosed with a ray of joy.

Yes, he came—he, whom she had so longed to see.

When Van Swieten told him that the empress had gone to Josepha's room, he started from his seat, and hurried through the corridor with such wild speed that the physician had been unable to follow him.

Hastily approaching the bed, he put his arms gently around his mother, and sought to lead her away.

"Mother," said he, imploringly, "leave this room. It is my duty to be here, not yours. Bid adieu to the Empress Josepha, and go hence."

"Oh, oh!" groaned Josepha, falling back upon her pillow, "he does not come for my sake, but for his mother's."

"Yes, Josepha," replied Joseph, "I am here for your sake also, and I shall remain with you."

"I also will remain," said Maria Theresa. "This sacred hour shall unite in love those who so long have been severed by error and misapprehension. Life is a succession of strivings to do well, and relapses into wrong. We feel that we have erred toward you, and we come with overflowing hearts to crave forgiveness. Forgive us, Josepha, as you hope to be forgiven!"

"Forgive me also, Josepha," said Joseph, with genuine emotion. "Let us part in peace. Forgive me my obduracy, as from my soul I forgive you. We have both been unhappy—"

"No," interrupted Josepha, "I have not been unhappy; for I—I have loved. I die happy; for he whom I love no longer turns abhorrent from my presence. I shall die by the light of your pardoning smile. Death, that comes every moment nearer, death, to me, brings happiness. He comes with his cold kiss, to take my parting breath—the only kiss my lips have ever felt. He brings me love and consolation. He takes from my face the hideous mask which it has worn through life; and my soul's beauty, in another world, shall win me Joseph's love. Oh death, the comforter! I feel thy kiss. Farewell, Joseph, farewell!"

"Farewell!" whispered Joseph and Maria Theresa.

A fearful pause ensued—a slight spasm—a gasp—and all was over.

"She is released!" said Van Swieten. "May her soul rest in peace!"

The Ursulines intoned the prayers for the dead, and Maria Theresa, in tears, clasped her hands and faltered out the responses. Suddenly she reeled, heaved a sigh, and fell back in the emperor's arms.

"My mother, my dear mother!" cried he, terrified.

Van Swieten touched him lightly. "Do not arouse her. Yonder sleeps the one empress in death—her pains are past; but this one, our beloved Maria Theresa, has yet to suffer. May God be merciful and spare her life!"

"Her life!" cried Joseph, turning pale.

"Yes, her life," said Van Swieten, solemnly. "The empress has the small-pox." *

CHAPTER XLII.

THE MIRROR.

SIX fearful weeks had gone by—six weeks of anxiety, suspense, and care, not only for the imperial family, but for all Austria.

Like the lightning's flash, intelligence had gone through the

*The Empress Josepha died May 28, 1767, at the age of twenty-nine years. Her body was so decayed by small-pox, that, before her death the flesh fell from her in pieces. It was so completely decomposed, that it was impossible to pay it the customary funeral honors. It was hurriedly wrapped up in a linen cloth, and coffined. From these circumstances a rumor prevailed in Bavaria that she had not died, but had been forced into a cloister by her husband.

land that the empress was in danger, and her subjects had lost interest in every thing except the bulletins issued from the palace where Van Swieten and Von Störck watched day and night by the bedside of their beloved sovereign. Deputations were sent to Vienna, sympathizing with the emperor, and the avenues to the palace were thronged with thousands of anxious faces, each waiting eagerly for the bulletins that came out four times a day.

At last the danger passed away. Van Swieten slept at home, and the empress was recovering.

She had recovered. Leaning on the arm of the emperor, and surrounded by her happy children, Maria Theresa left her widow's cell to take up her abode in the new and splendid apartments which, during her convalescence, Joseph had prepared for her reception.

She thanked her son for his loving attention, so contrary to his usual habits of economy, and therefore so much the more a proof of his earnest desire to give pleasure to his mother. She, in her turn, sought to give strong expression to her gratitude, by admiring with enthusiasm all that had been done for her. She stopped to examine the costly Turkey carpets, the gorgeous Gobelin tapestries on the walls, the tables carved of precious woods, or inlaid with jewels and Florentine mosaic, the rich furniture covered with velvet and gold, the magnificent lustres of sparkling crystal, and the elegant trifles which here and there were tastefully disposed upon *étagères* or *consoles*.

"Indeed, my son," cried the empress, surveying the beautiful *suite*, "you have decorated these rooms with the taste and prodigality of a woman. It adds much to my enjoyment of their beauty to think that all this is the work of your loving hands. But one thing has my princely son forgotten; and therein he betrays his sex, showing that he is no woman, but in very truth a man."

"Have I forgotten something, your majesty?" asked Joseph.

"Yes; something, my son, which a woman could never have overlooked. There are no mirrors in my splendid home."

"No mirrors!" exclaimed Joseph, looking confused. "No—yes—indeed, your majesty is right, I had forgotten them. But I beg a thousand pardons for my negligence, and I will see that it is repaired. I shall order the costliest Venetian mirrors to be made for these apartments."

While Joseph spoke, his mother looked earnestly at his blushing face, and perfectly divined both his embarrassment and its cause. She turned her eyes upon her daughters, who, with theirs cast down, were sharing their brother's perplexity.

"I must wait then until my mirrors are made," said the empress, after a pause. "You must think that I have less than woman's vanity, my son, if you expect me to remain for weeks without a greeting from my looking-glass. Of course the small-pox has not dared to disfigure the face of an empress; I feel secure against its sacrilegious touch. Is it not so, my little Marie Antoinette? Has it not respected your mother's comeliness?"

The little archduchess looked frightened at the question, and timidly raised her large eyes. "My imperial mamma is as handsome as ever she was," said the child, in a trembling voice.

"And she will always be handsome to us, should she live until old age shall have wrinkled her face and paled her cheeks," cried Joseph warmly. "The picture of her youthful grace and beauty is engraved upon our hearts, and nothing can ever remove it thence. To the eyes of her children a noble and beloved mother is always beautiful."

The empress said nothing in reply. She smiled affectionately upon her son, and inclining her head kindly to the others, retired to her sitting-room. She walked several times up and down, and finally approached her mirror. In accordance with an old superstition, which pronounces it ill-luck to allow a looking-glass in the room of a sick person, this large mirror had been covered with a heavy silk curtain. The empress drew it back; but instead of her looking-glass, she was confronted by a portrait of her late husband, the emperor. She uttered an exclamation of surprise and joy, and contemplated the picture with a happy smile. "God bless thee, my Franz, my noble emperor!" whispered she. "Thou art ever the same; thy dear smile is unaltered, although I am no longer thy handsome bride, but a hideous and disfigured being, from whom my children deem it fit to conceal a looking-glass. Look at me with thy dear eyes, Franz; thou wert ever my mirror, and in thy light have I seen my brightest day of earthly joy. My departed beauty leaves me not one pang of regret, since thou art gone for whom alone I prized it. Maria Theresa has ceased to be a woman—she is nothing more than a sovereign, and what to her are the scars of the smallpox? But I must see what I look like," said she, dropping the curtain. "I will show them that I am not as foolish as they imagine."

She took up her little golden bell and rang. The door of the next room opened, and Charlotte von Hieronymus entered. The empress smiled and said: "It is time to make my toilet. I will dine to-day *en famille* with the emperor, and I must be dressed. Let us go into my dressing-room."

The maid of honor courtesied and opened the door. Every thing there was ready for the empress. The tire-woman, the mistress of the wardrobe, the maids of honor were all at their posts; and Charlotte hastened to take her place behind the large arm-chair in which the empress was accustomed to have her hair dressed.

But Maria Theresa saw that she had not been expected in her dressing-room, for her cheval-glass was encumbered with shawls, dresses, and cloaks. She took her seat, smilingly saying to herself, "I shall see myself now, face to face."

Charlotte passed the comb through the short hair of the empress, and sighed as she thought of the offering that had been laid in the emperor's coffin; while the other maids of honor stood silent around. Maria Theresa, usually so familiar and talkative at this hour, spoke not a word. She looked sharply at the cheval-glass, and began carelessly, and as if by chance, to remove with her foot, the dresses that encumbered it; then, as if ashamed of her artifice, she suddenly rose from the chair, and with an energetic gesture unbared the mirror.

No mirror was there! Nothing greeted the empress's eyes save the empty frame. She turned a reproachful glance upon the little *coiffeuse*.

Charlotte fell upon her knees, and looked imploringly at the empress. "It is my fault, your majesty," said she, blushing and tembling; "I alone am the culprit. Pardon my maladroitness, I pray you?"

"What do you mean, child?" asked the empress.

"I—I broke the looking-glass, your majesty. I stumbled over it in the dark, and shivered it to pieces. I am very, very awkward—I am very sorry."

"What! You overturned this heavy mirror!" said Maria Theresa. "If so, there must have been a fearful crash. How comes it that I never heard any thing—I who for six weeks have been ill in the adjoining room?"

"It happened just at the time when your majesty was delirious with fever; and—"

"And this mirror has been broken for three weeks!" said Maria Theresa, raising her eyebrows and looking intently at Charlotte's blushing face. "Three weeks ago! I think you might have had it replaced, Charlotte, by this time; hey, child?"

Charlotte's eyes sought the floor. At length she stammered, in a voice scarcely audible, "Please your majesty, I could not suppose that you would miss the glass so soon. You have made so little use of mirrors since—"

"Enough of this nonsense," interrupted the empress. "You have been well drilled, and have played your part with some talent, but don't imagine that I am the dupe of all this pretty acting. Get up, child; don't make a fool of yourself, but put on my crape cap for me, and then go as quickly as you can for a looking-glass."

"A looking-glass, your majesty?" cried Charlotte in a frightened voice.

"A looking-glass," repeated the empress emphatically.

"I have none, your majesty."

"Well, then," said Maria Theresa, her patience sorely tried by all this, "let some one with better eyes than yours look for one. Go, Sophie, and bid one of the pages bring me a mirror from my old apartments below. I do not suppose that there has been a general crashing of all the mirrors in the palace. In a quarter of an hour I shall be in my sitting-room. At the end of that time the mirror must be there. Be quick, Sophie; and you, Charlotte, finish the combing of my hair. There is but little to do to it now, so dry your tears."

"Ah!" whispered Charlotte, "I would there were more to do. I cannot help crying, your majesty when I see the ruins of that beautiful hair."

"And yet, poor child, you have spent so many weary hours over it," replied the empress. "You ought to be glad that your delicate little hands are no longer obliged to bear its weight.—Charlotte," said she suddenly, "you have several times asked for your dismissal. Now, you shall have it, and you shall marry your lover, Counsellor Greiner. I myself will give you away, and bestow the dowry."

The grateful girl pressed the hand of the empress to her lips, while she whispered words of love and thanks.

Maria Theresa smiled, and took her seat, while Charlotte completed her toilet. Match-making was the empress's great weakness, and she was in high spirits over the prospect of marrying Charlotte.

The simple mourning costume was soon donned, and the empress rose to leave her dressing-room. As she passed the empty frame of the Psyche, she turned laughing toward her maid of honor.

"I give you this mirror, Charlotte," said she. "If the glass is really broken, it shall be replaced by the costliest one that Venice can produce. It will be to you a souvenir of your successful *début* as an actress on this day. You have really done admirably. But let me tell you one thing, my child," continued Maria Theresa, taking Charlotte's hand in hers. "Never be an actress with your husband; but let your heart be reflected in all your words and deeds, as yonder mirror will give back the truthful picture of your face. Let all be clear and bright in your married intercourse; and see that no breath of deception ever cloud its surface. Take this wedding-gift, and cherish it as a faithful monitor. Truth is a light that comes to us from Heaven; let us look steadily at it, for evil as well as for good. This is the hour of *my* trial—no great one—but still a trial. Let me now look at truth, and learn to bear the revelation it is about to make."

She opened the door, and entered her sitting-room. Her commands had been obeyed; the mirror was in its place. She advanced with resolute step, but as she approached the glass her eyes were instinctively cast down, until she stood directly before it. The decisive moment had arrived; she was to see—what?

Slowly her eyes were raised, and she looked. She uttered a low cry, and started back in horror. She had seen a strange, scarred, empurpled face, whose colorless lips and hard features had filled her soul with loathing.

But with all the strength of her brave and noble heart, Maria Theresa overcame the shock, and looked again. She forced her eyes to contemplate the fearful image that confronted her once beautiful face, and long and earnestly she gazed upon it.

"Well," said she at last, with a sigh, "I must make acquaintance with this caricature of my former self. I must accustom myself to the mortifying fact that this is Maria Theresa, or I might some of these days call for a page to drive out that hideous old crone! I must learn, too, to be resigned, for it is the hand of my heavenly Father that has covered my face with this grotesque mask. Since He has thought fit to deprive me of my beauty, let His divine will be done."

For some moments she remained silent, still gazing intently at the mirror. Finally a smile overspread her entire countenance, and she nodded at the image in the glass.

"Well! you ugly old woman," said she aloud, "we have begun our acquaintance. Let us be good friends. I do not intend to make one effort to lessen your ugliness by womanly art; I must seek to win its pardon from the world by noble deeds and a well-spent life. Perhaps, in future days, when my subjects lament my homeliness, they may add that nevertheless I was a *good*, and—well! in this hour of humiliation we may praise one another, I think—perchance a *great* sovereign."

Here the empress turned from the mirror and crossing over to the spot where the emperor's portrait hung, she continued her soliloquy. "But Franz, dear Franz, you at least are spared the sight of your Theresa's transformation. I could not have borne this as I do, if you had been here to witness it. Now! what matters it? My people will not remind me of it, and my children have already promised to love me, and forgive my deformity. Sleep, then, my beloved, until I rejoin you in heaven. There, the mask will fall for me, as for poor Josepha, and there we shall be glorified and happy."

The empress then returned to the dressing-room, where her attendants, anxious and unhappy, awaited her reappearance. What was their astonishment to see her tranquil and smiling, not a trace of discontent upon her countenance!

"Let the steward of the household be apprised that I will have mirrors in all my apartments. They can be hung at once, and may be replaced by those which the emperor has ordered, whenever they arrive from Venice. Let my page Gustavus repair to Cardinal Migazzi and inform him that to-morrow I make my public thanksgiving in the cathedral of St. Stephen. I shall go on foot and in the midst of my people, that they may see me and know that I am not ashamed of the judgments of God. Let Prince Kaunitz be advised that on to-morrow, after the holy sacrifice, I will receive him here. Open my doors and windows, and let us breathe the free air of heaven. I am no longer an invalid, my friends; I am strong, and ready to begin life anew."

CHAPTER XLIII.

THE INTERVIEW WITH KAUNITZ.

FROM earliest morning the streets of Vienna had been thronged by a joyous multitude, eagerly awaiting the sight of their restored sovereign. All Vienna had mourned when the empress lay ill; all Vienna now rejoiced that she had recovered. Maria Theresa's road to the church was one long triumph—the outpouring of the sincere love which filled the hearts of her subjects. The empress had done nothing to court this homage; for the notice given to the cardinal had been as short as it possibly could be; but the news of the thanksgiving had flown from one end of Vienna to the other; and every corporation and society, the students of every college, and every citizen that was at liberty to leave home, flocked to congratulate the well-beloved sovereign. The streets through which she had to pass were lined with people bearing flags, banners, and emblems, while near them stood the children of the educational and orphan asylums, which had been endowed by the munificence of the empress. Lofty and lowly, rich and poor, stood in friendly contact with each other; even the nobles, imitating Maria Theresa's affability, mixed smiling and free among the people. All sense of rank and station seemed lost in the universal joy of the hour.

The bells chimed, and the people rent the air with shouts; for this was the signal of the empress's *sortie* from the palace, and her people knew that she was coming to meet them. At last they saw her; leaning on the arm of the emperor, and followed by her other children, she came, proud and resolute as ever. It was a beautiful sight, this empress with her ten lovely sons and daughters, all joyful and smiling, as like simple subjects they walked through the streets toward the church, to thank God for her recovery.

Inexpressible joy beamed from Maria Theresa's eyes—those superb eyes whose light the small-pox could not quench. Her great and noble soul looked out from their azure depths, and her head seemed encircled by a glory. In this hour she was no "ugly old crone," she was the happy, proud, triumphant empress, who in the eyes of her people was both beautiful and beloved. For the moment her widow's sorrows were forgotten; and when surrounded by so many loyal hearts, she sank on her knees before the altar of St.

Stephen, she thanked God for the joy of this hour, and made a vow that her whole life should be devoted to the welfare of the people who on this day had given her so touching a welcome.

Exhausted not only by emotion, but by the heat of the July sun which shone on her head as she returned, the empress at last reached her own rooms. Her tire-women hastened to relieve her of her coverings and to dry her moistened hair and face. But she waved them back.

"No, no, my friends, let me refresh myself in my own way. The air is more skilful than your hands, and is softer than your napkins. Open the doors and the windows, and place my arm-chair in the middle of the room."

"But, your majesty," remonstrated one of the maids of honor, "you forget your condition. The draught will do you injury."

"I do not know what such fastidious people mean by a draught," replied the empress, laughing and taking her seat; "but I know that the good God has sent this air from heaven for man's enjoyment; and when I feel its cool kiss upon my cheek, I think that God is nigh. I have always loved to feel the breath of my Creator, and therefore it is that I have always been strong and healthy. See! see! how it blows away my mantle! You are right, sweet summer wind, I will throw the burden away."

She let fall her mantle, and gave her bare shoulders to the wind, enjoying the breeze, and frightening her maids of honor out of their propriety.

"Now, let me have some refreshment," cried she. Away sped two or three of the ladies, each one anxious to escape from the gust that was driving every thing before it in the empress's rooms.

A page brought in a tray, and there, in the centre of the room, the empress, although yet overheated, ate a plate of strawberries, and drank a glass of lemonade, cooled in ice.*

She was interrupted, in the midst of all this comfort, by another page, who announced Prince Kaunitz. Maria Theresa rose hastily from her seat. "Shut all the doors and windows," exclaimed she, "do not let him scent the draught." †

While her orders were being obeyed, she looked around to convince herself that every avenue was closed through which the wind might penetrate, and that done, she ordered the door to be thrown open, and the prince admitted.

Prince Kaunitz approached with his usual serious and tranquil demeanor. He bowed low, and said: "I congratulate your majesty and the Austrian empire, upon your happy recovery. I, who have no fear of any other enemy, have trembled before this deadly foe of your imperial house. For all other dangers we have craft and valor; but against this one no bravery or statesmanship can avail."

"But skill has availed; and to Van Swieten, under Providence, I am indebted for my life," cried the empress, warmly. "I know, Kaunitz, that you have but little faith in heavenly or earthly physicians; and I pray God that you may never acquire it through the bitter experience of such suffering as I have but lately endured!

* Caroline Pichler, "Memoirs," vol i., pp. 18, 19. Maria Theresa supported without pain extreme degrees of heat and cold. Summer and winter her windows stood open, and often the snow-flakes have been seen to fall upon her *escritoire* while she wrote. In winter, the Emperor Joseph always came into his mother's rooms wrapped in furs.

† Wraxall, vol. ii., p. 380.

Often during my sleepless nights I have longed for a sight of your grave face, and it grieved me to think that perchance we might never meet again to talk of Austria, and plan for Austria's welfare."

"But I knew that your majesty would recover," said Kaunitz, with unusual warmth; "I knew it, for Austria cannot spare you, and as long as there is work for you here below, your strong mind will bid defiance to death."

Maria Theresa colored with pleasure. It was so seldom that Kaunitz gave utterance to such sentiments, that his praise was really worth having.

"You think, then, that Austria needs me?" said she.

"I do, indeed, your majesty."

"But if God had called me to Himself, what would you have done?"

"I would still have labored, as in duty bound, for my country; but I would have owed a lifelong grudge to Providence for its want of wisdom."

"You are a scoffer, Kaunitz," said the empress. "Your Creator is very merciful to allow you time to utter the unchristian sentiments which are forever falling from your lips. But God sees the heart of man, and He knows that yours is better than your words. Since the loving, all-suffering Lord forgives you, so will I. But tell me, how has my empire fared during these six long weeks?"

"Well, your majesty. Throughout the day I worked for myself, throughout the night for you, and nothing is behindhand. Each day adds to our internal strength, that gives us consideration abroad, and soon we shall hold our own as one of the four great European powers, mightier than in the days when the sun never set upon Austrian realms. The empire of Charles V. was grand, but it was not solid. It resembled a reversed pyramid, in danger of being crushed by its own weight. The pyramid to-day is less in size, but greater in base and therefore firmer in foundation.* Strength does not depend so much upon size as upon proportion; and Austria, although her territory has been vaster, has never been so truly powerful as she is in this, the reign of your majesty."

"If Silesia were but ours again! As for Naples and Alsatia, they were never more than *disjecta membra* of our empire; and they were always less profit than trouble. But Silesia is ours—ours by a common ancestry, a common language, and the strong tie of affection. I shall never recover from the blow that I received when I lost Silesia."

"We shall have restitution some of these days, your majesty," said Kaunitz.

"Do you mean to say that I shall ever recover Silesia?" asked the empress, eagerly.

"From the King of Prussia? No—never! He holds fast to his possessions, and his sharp sword would be unsheathed to-morrow, were we to lay the weight of a finger upon his right to Silesia. But we shall be otherwise revenged, in the day when we shall feel that we have attained the noontide of our power and strength."

"You do not intend to propose to me a war of aggression!" said the empress, shocked.

"No, your majesty, but if we should see two eagles tearing to pieces a lamb which is beyond hope of rescue, our two-headed eagle

* "Letters of a French Traveller," vol. i., p. 421.

must swoop down upon the robbers, and demand his share of the booty. I foresee evil doings among our neighbors. Catharine of Russia is bold and unscrupulous; Frederick of Prussia knows it, and he already seeks the friendship of Russia, that he may gain an accomplice as well as an ally."

"God forbid that I should follow in the wake of the King of Prussia!" cried Maria Theresa. "Never will I accept, much less seek an alliance with this cruel woman; whose throne is blood-stained and whose heart is dead to every sentiment of womanly virtue and honor!"

"Your majesty need have no intercourse with the *woman;* you have only to confer with the sovereign of a powerful neighboring empire."

"Russia is not a neighboring empire," exclaimed the empress. "On one occasion I wrote to the Empress Elizabeth, 'I will always be your friend, but with my consent you shall never be my neighbor.' * Poland lies between Russia and Austria."

"Yes," said Kaunitz, with one of his meaning smiles, "but how long will Poland divide us from Russia?"

"Man!" exclaimed Maria Theresa with horror, "you do not surely insinuate that we would dare to lay a hand upon Poland?"

"Not we, but the Empress of Russia will—"

"Impossible! impossible! She dare not do it—"

Kaunitz shrugged his shoulders. "*Dare*, your majesty? Some things we dare not attempt because they are difficult; others are difficult because we dare not attempt them. † The Empress of Russia dares do any thing; for she knows how to take things easily, and believes in her own foresight. Despots are grasping, and Catharine is a great despot. We must make haste to secure her good-will, that when the time comes we may all understand one another."

"I!" exclaimed the empress, "I should stoop so low as to seek the good-will of this wicked empress, who mounted her throne upon the dead body of her husband, while her lovers stood by, their hands reeking with the blood of the murdered emperor! Oh, Kaunitz! you would never ask me to do this thing?"

"Your majesty is great enough to sacrifice your personal antipathies to the good of your country. Your majesty once condescended to write to Farinelli, and *that* act won us the friendship of the King of Spain and of his sons; *that* letter will be the means of placing an Archduchess of Austria on the throne of Naples."

"Would have been," said Maria Theresa, heaving a sigh. "The bride of the King of Naples is no more! My poor Johanna! My beautiful child!"

"But the Archduchess Josepha lives, and I had intended to propose to your majesty to accept the hand of the King of Naples for her highness."

"Is the house of Naples then so desirous of our alliance that it has already offered its heir to another one of my daughters? I am sorry that we should be obliged to accept, for I have heard of late that the king is an illiterate and trifling fellow, scarcely better than the lazzaroni who are his chosen associates. Josepha will not be happy with such a man."

"Your majesty, her highness does not marry the young igno-

* Historical.
† Kaunitz's own words. Hormayer, "Plutarch," vol. xii., p. 271.

ramus who, to be sure, knows neither how to read nor write—she marries the King of Naples; and surely if any thing can gracefully conceal a man's faults, it is the purple mantle of royalty."

"I will give my child to this representative of royalty," said Maria Theresa sadly, "but I look upon her as a victim of expediency. If she is true to her God and to her spouse, I must be content, even though, as a woman, Josepha's life will be a blank."

"And this alliance," said Kaunitz, still pursuing the object for which he was contending, "this marriage is the result of one letter to Farinelli. Your majesty once condescended to write to La Pompadour. *That* letter won the friendship of France, and its fruits will be the marriage of the Archduchess Marie Antoinette, and her elevation to the throne of France. Your majesty sees then what important results have sprung from two friendly letters which my honored sovereign has not disdained to write. Surely when wise statesmanship prompts your majesty to indite a third letter to the Empress of Russia, you will not refuse its counsels and suggestions. The two first letters were worth to us two thrones; the third may chance to be worth a new province."

"A new province!" exclaimed the empress, coming closer to Kaunitz, and in her eagerness laying her hand upon his shoulder. "Tell me—what wise and wicked stratagem do you hatch within your brain to-day?"

"My plans, so please your majesty," said the prince, raising his eyes so as to meet those of the empress, "my plans are not of to-day. They—"

But suddenly he grew dumb, and gazed horror-stricken at the face of Maria Theresa. Kaunitz was short-sighted, and up to this moment he had remained in ignorance of the fearful change that had forever transformed the empress's beauty into ugliness. The discovery had left him speechless.

"Well?" cried the empress, not suspecting the cause of his sudden silence. "You have not the courage to confide your plans to me? They must be dishonorable. If not, in the name of Heaven, speak!"

The prince answered not a word. The shock had been too great; and as he gazed upon that scarred and blotched face, once so smooth, fair, and beautiful, his presence of mind forsook him, and his diplomacy came to naught.

"Forgive me, your majesty," said he, as pale and staggering he retreated toward the door. "A sudden faintness has come over me, and every thing swims before my vision. Let me entreat your permission to retire."

Without awaiting the empress's reply, he made a hasty bow, and fled from the room.

The empress looked after him in utter astonishment. "What has come over the man?" said she to herself. "He looks as if he had seen a ghost! Well—I suppose it is nothing more than a fit of eccentricity."

And she flung back her head with a half-disdainful smile. But as she did so, her eyes lit accidentally upon the mirror, and she saw her own image reflected in its bright depths.

She started; for she had already forgotten the "ugly old woman" whom she had apostrophized on the day previous. Suddenly she burst into a peal of laughter, and cried out, "No wonder poor

Kaunitz looked as if he had seen something horrible! HE SAW ME—and I am the Medusa that turned him into stone. Poor, short-sighted man! He had been in blissful ignorance of my altered looks until I laid my hand upon his shoulder. I must do something to heal the wound I have inflicted. I owe him more than I can well repay. I will give him a brilliant decoration, and that will be a cure-all; for Kaunitz is very vain and very fond of show."

While the empress was writing the note which was to accompany her gift, Kaunitz, with his handkerchief over his mouth, was dashing through the palace corridors to his carriage. With an impatient gesture he motioned to his coachman to drive home with all speed.

Not with his usual stateliness, but panting, almost running, did Kaunitz traverse the gilded halls of his own palace, which were open to-day in honor of the empress's recovery, and were already festive with the sound of the guests assembling to a magnificent dinner which was to celebrate the event. Without a word to the Countess Clary, who came forward elegantly attired for the occasion, Kaunitz flew to his study, and sinking into an arm-chair, he covered his face with his hands. He felt as if he had been face to face with death. That was not his beautiful, majestic, superb Maria Theresa; it was a frightful vision—a messenger from the grave, that forced upon his unwilling mind the dreadful futurity that awaits all who are born of woman.

"Could it be? Was this indeed the empress, whose beauty had intoxicated her subjects, as drawing from its sheath the sword of St. Stephen, she held it flashing in the sun, and called upon them to defend her rights? Oh, could it be that this woman, once beautiful as Olympian Juno, had been transformed into such a caricature?"

A thrill of pain darted through the whole frame of the prince, and he did what since his mother's death he had never done—he wept.

But gradually he overcame his grief, the scanty fountain of his tears dried up, and he resumed his cold and habitual demeanor. For a long time he sat motionless in his chair, staring at the wall that was opposite. Finally he moved toward his *escritoire* and took up a pen.

He began to write instructions for the use of his secretaries. They were never to pronounce in his presence the two words DEATH and SMALL-POX. If those words ever occurred in any correspondence or official paper that was to come before his notice, they were to be erased. Those who presented themselves before the prince were to be warned that these fearful words must never pass their lips in his presence. A secretary was to go at once to the Countess Clary, that she might prepare the guests of the prince, and caution them against the use of the offensive words.*

When Kaunitz had completed these singular instructions, he rang, and gave the paper to a page. As he did so, a servant entered with a letter and a package from her majesty the empress.

The package contained the grand cross of the order of St. Stephen, but instead of the usual symbol, the cross was composed of costly brilliants. The letter was in the empress's own hand—a worthy answer to the "instructions" which Kaunitz was in the act of sending to his secretaries.

* Hormayer, "Austrian Plutarch," vol. xii., p. 274.

The empress wrote as follows: "I send you the grand cross of St. Stephen; but as a mark of distinction you must wear it in brilliants. You have done so much to dignify it, that I seize with eagerness the opportunity which presents itself to offer you a tribute of that gratitude which I feel for your services, and shall continue to feel until the day of my death.*

"MARIA THERESA."

CHAPTER XLIV.

THE ARCHDUCHESS JOSEPHA.

THE plan of the empress and her prime minister approached their fulfilment; Austria was about to contract ties of kindred with her powerful neighbors.

Maria Theresa had again consented to receive the King of Naples as her son-in-law, and he was the affianced husband of the archduchess Josepha. The palace of Lichtenstein, the residence of the Neapolitan ambassador was, in consequence of the betrothal, the scene of splendid festivities, and in the imperial palace preparations were making for the approaching nuptials. They were to be solemnized on the fifteenth of October, and immediately after the ceremony the young bride was to leave Vienna for Naples.

Every thing was gayety and bustle; all were deep in consultation over dress and jewels; and the great topic of court conversation was the *parure* of brilliants sent by the King of Spain, whose surpassing magnificence had called forth an expresson of astonishment from the lips of the empress herself.

The *trousseau* of the archduchess was exposed in the apartments which had once been occupied by the empress and her husband; and now Maria Theresa, followed by a bevy of wondering young archduchesses, was examining her daughter's princely wardrobe, that with her own eyes she might be sure that nothing was wanting to render it worthy of a queen-elect. The young girls burst into exclamations of rapture when they approached the table where, in its snowy purity, lay the bridal dress of white velvet, embroidered with pearls and diamonds.

"Oh!" cried little Marie Antoinette, while she stroked it with her pretty, rosy hand, "oh, my beautiful Josepha, you will look like an angel, when you wear this lovely white dress."

"Say rather, like a queen," returned Josepha, smiling. "When a woman is a queen, she is sure to look like an angel in the eyes of the world."

"It does not follow, however, that because she is a queen, she shall be as happy as an angel," remarked the Archduchess Maria Amelia, who was betrothed to the Duke of Parma.

"Nevertheless, I would rather be the unhappy queen of an important kingdom than the happy wife of a poor little prince," replied Josepha, as, raising her superb diadem of brilliants, she advanced to a mirror and placed it upon her brow. "Do you think," asked she proudly, "that I can be very miserable while I wear these starry gems upon my forehead? Oh no! If it were set with thorns

* Wraxall, vol. ii., p. 479.

that drew my blood, I would rather wear this royal diadem than the light coronet of an insignificant duchess."

"And I," exclaimed Amelia, "would rather wear the ring of a beggar than be the wife of a king who neither reads nor writes, and throughout all Europe is known by the name of a lazzarone."

"Before whom millions of subjects must, nevertheless, bend the knee, and who, despite of all, is a powerful and wealthy monarch," returned Josepha, angrily.

"That is, if his master, the Marquis Tannucci allows it," cried the Archduchess Caroline, laughing. "For you know very well, Josepha, that Tannucci is the king of your lazzaroni-king, and when he behaves amiss, puts him on his knees for punishment. Now when you are his wife, you can go and comfort him in disgrace, and kneel down in the corner by his side. How interesting it will be!"

Upon this the Archduchess Amelia began to laugh, while her sisters joined in—all except Marie Antoinette, who with an expression of sympathy, turned to Josepha.

"Do not mind them, my Josepha," said she; "if your king can not read, you can teach him, and he will love you all the better, and in spite of every thing, you will be a happy queen in the end."

"I do not mind them, Antoinette," returned Josepha, her eyes flashing with anger, "for I well know that they are envious of my prosperity, and would willingly supplant me. But my day of retaliation will come. It will be that on which my sisters shall be forced to acknowledge the rank of the Queen of Naples, and to yield her precedence!"

A burst of indignation would have been the reply to these haughty words, had the Archduchess Caroline not felt a hand upon her shoulder, and heard a voice which commanded silence.

The empress, who, at the beginning of this spicy dialogue, had been absent on her survey in a neighboring apartment, had returned, and had heard Josepha's last words. Shocked and grieved, she came forward, and stood in the midst of her daughters.

"Peace!" exclaimed the imperial mother. "I have heard such words of arrogance fall from your lips as must be expiated by humble petition to your Creator. Sinful creatures are we all, whether we be princesses or peasants; and if we dare to lift our poor heads in pride of birth or station, God will surely punish us. With a breath He overturns the sceptres of kings—with a breath He hurls our crowns to earth, until, cowering at His feet, we acknowledge our unworhthiness. It becomes a queen to remember that she is a mortal, powerless without the grace of God to do one good action, and wearing under the purple of royalty the tattered raiment of humanity. But it is these absurd vanities that have stirred up the demon of pride in your hearts," continued the empress, giving a disdainful toss to the velvet wedding-dress; "let us leave these wretched gew-gaws and betake ourselves to the purer air of our own rooms."

She waved her hand, and motioning to her daughters, they followed her, silent and ashamed. All had their eyes cast down, and none saw the tears that now fell like rain from Josepha's eyes. She was thoroughly mortified and longed to escape to her room; but as she bent her head to take leave of the empress, the latter motioned her to remain.

"I have as yet a few words to speak with you, my daughter," said Maria Theresa, as she closed the door of her dressing-room. "Your haughty conduct of this day has reminded me that you have a sacred duty to perform. The vanities of the world will have less weight with you when you return from the graves of your ancestors. Go to the imperial vault, and learn from the ashes of the emperors and empresses who sleep there, the nothingness of all worldly splendor. Kneel down beside your dear father's tomb, and pray for humility. Tell him to pray for me, Josepha, for my crown weighs heavily upon my brow, and I fain would be at rest."

Josepha made no answer. She stared at her mother with an expression of horror an incredulity, as though she meant to ask if she had heard her words aright.

"Well, my daughter!" cried Maria Theresa, surprised at Josepha's silence. "Why do you linger? Go—go, child, and recalling the sins of your life, beg pardon of God, and the blessing of your deceased father."

"Give me that blessing yourself, dear mother," faltered the princess, clasping her hands, and looking imploringly at the empress. "My father's spirit is here, it is not in that fearful vault."

The empress started. "I cannot believe," said she, with severity, "that my daughter has cause to tremble before the ashes of her father. The guilty alone fear death; innocence is never afraid!"

"Oh, mother, mother! I have no sin upon my soul, and yet I—"

"And yet," echoed the empress as Josepha paused.

"And yet I shiver at the very thought of going thither," said the archduchess. "Yes, your majesty, I shiver at the thought of encountering the black coffins and mouldering skeletons of my forefathers. Oh, mother, have pity on my youth and cowardice! Do not force me to that horrid place!"

"I have no right to exempt you from the performance of this sacred duty, Josepha," replied the empress firmly. "It is a time-honored custom of our family, that the princesses of Austria, who marry kings, should take leave of the graves of their ancestors. I canonot release the Queen of Naples from her duty. She is to wear the crown, she must bear the cross."

"But I dread it! I dread it so!" murmured Josepha. "I shudder at the thought of Josepha's corpse. I never loved her, and she died without forgiving me. Oh, do not force me to go alone in the presence of the dead!"

"I command you to go into the vault where repose the holy ashes of your fathers," repeated the empress sternly. "Bend your lofty head, my daughter, and throw yourself with humility upon the graves of your ancestors, there to learn the vanity of all human greatness and human power."

"Mercy, mercy!" cried the terrified girl. "I cannot, I cannot obey your dreadful behest."

"Who dares say 'I cannot,' when duty is in question?" exclaimed the empress. "You are my daughter and my subject still, and I will see whether you intend to defy my authority."

So saying, she rose and rang her little golden bell. "The carriage of the Archduchess Josepha," said she to the page who answered the summons. "Let a courier be dispatched to the Capuchin fathers to inform them that in a quarter of an hour the princess will visit the imperial vault. Now, princess," continued the empress as the page left the room, "you will not surely have the hardihood to say again, 'I cannot?'"

"No," faltered Josepha, "I will obey. But one thing I must ask. Does your majesty wish to kill me?"

"What do you mean, child?"

"I mean that I will die, if you force me to this vault," replied Josepha, pale as death. "I feel it in the icy chill that seizes my heart even now. I tell you, mother, that I will die, if you send me to the fearful place where Josepha's corpse infects the air with its death-mould. Do you still desire that I shall go?"

"You need not seek to frighten me, Josepha; stratagem will avail you nothing," replied the empress, coldly. "It is not given to mortals to know the hour of their death, and I cannot allow myself to be influenced by such folly. Go, my child, there is nothing to fear; the spirits of your forefathers will shield you from harm," added she kindly.

"I go," replied Josepha; "but my mother has sentenced me to death."

She bent her head and left the room. The empress looked after her daughter as she went, and a sudden pang shot through her heart. She felt as though she could not let her go—she felt as if she *must* call her back, and pressing her to her heart, release her from the ordeal which tried her young soul so fearfully.

Just then the princess, who had reached the door, turned her large dark eyes with another look of entreaty. This was enough to restore the empress to her self-possession.

She would not call her back. She saw rather than heard the trembling lips that strove to form a last appeal for mercy, and the graceful figure vanished.

When she was out of sight, all the tenderness, all the anxiety of the empress returned. She rushed forward, then suddenly sood still and shaking her head, she murmured, "No! no! It would be unpardonable weakness. I cannot yield. She must go to the grave of her fathers."

CHAPTER XLV.

THE DEPARTURE.

THE messenger had returned, the carriage waited, and Josepha had no longer a pretext for delaying her visit to the vault. She *must* obey her mother's behest—she *must* perform the horrible pilgrimage! Pale and speechless she suffered her attendants to throw her mantle around her, and then, as if in obedience to some invisible phantom that beckoned her on, she rose from her seat and advanced rigidly to the door. Suddenly she paused, and, turning to her maid of honor, she said, "Be so kind as to call my sister Antoinette, I must bid her farewell."

A few moments elapsed, when the door opened and the Archduchess Marie Antoinette flew into her sister's arms. Josepha pressed her closely to her heart.

"I could not go, my darling," whispered she, "without once more seeing you. Let me look, for the last time, upon that sweet face, and those bright eyes that are lit up with the blue of heaven. Kiss me, dear, and promise not to forget me."

"I can never forget, never cease to love you, sister," replied the child, returning Josepha's caresses. "But why do you say farewell? Why are you crying? Are you going to leave us already for that young king who is to take you away from us? Oh, Josepha, how can you love a man whom you have never seen?"

"I do not love the King of Naples, dear child," said Josepha, sadly. "Oh, Antoinette! would you could understand my sorrows!"

"Speak, dear sister," replied Antoinette, tenderly. "Am I not twelve years old, and does not the Countess Lerchenfeld tell me, every time I do wrong, that I am no longer a child? Tell me, then, what grieves you? I will keep your secret, I promise you."

"I weep," said Josepha, "because it is so sad to die before one has known the happiness of living."

"Die!" exclaimed Antoinette, turning pale. "Why do you speak of dying, you who are about to become a queen?"

"I shall never live to be a queen, my sister. The empress has commanded me to visit the imperial vault. I *go* thither to-day; in a few days I shall be *carried* thither, never to return.* Farewell, Antoinette; I leave you to-day, but I leave you for the grave."

"No, no, no!" screamed the child. "You shall not go. I will throw myself at the feet of the empress, and never rise until she has released you, dear sister."

"Have you yet to learn that the empress never retracts her words? It is useless. I must go, and my death-warrant is signed."

"It shall not be!" cried Antoinette, beside herself with grief. "Wait dear, Josepha, until I return. I go to obtain your release."

"What can you say to the empress, my poor little one?"

"I will beg for mercy, and if she will not listen, I shall rise and tell her fearlessly, 'Your majesty, Josepha says that you have sentenced her to death. No mortal has power over the life of an imperial princess; God alone has that power. My sister must not go into the vault, for if she does, she dies, and that by *your* hand.'"

And as the child spoke these words, she threw back her head, and her eyes darted fire. She looked like her mother.

"I see, Antoinette," said Josepha, with a smile, "that you would not submit tamely to death. You have a brave soul, my little sister, and will know how to struggle against misfortune. But I—I have no spirit, I can only suffer and obey; and before I die, I must open my heart to you—you shall receive my last thoughts."

Marie Antoinette looked with tearful eyes at her sister, and sank, white as a lily, on her knees.

"I am ready," said she, folding her hands, while Josepha bent forward, and laid her hand, as with a blessing, upon Antoinette's soft blond hair.

"When I am dead," said Josepha, "go to my sisters, and beg them to forgive my unkind words. Tell them that I loved them all dearly. Say to Maria Amelia that she must pardon my unsisterly conduct. It arose, not from haughtiness, but from despair. For, Antoinette, I hated the King of Naples, and well I knew what a miserable fate awaited me as his queen. But there was no rescue for me, that I knew; so I tried to hide my grief under the semblance of exultation. Tell her to forgive me for the sake of the tears I have shed in secret over this hated betrothal. How often

*The princess's own words. See "Mémoires sur la Vie Privée de Marie Antoinette," par Madame Campan, vol i., p. 38.

have I called upon death to liberate me! and yet, now that the dark shadow of Azrael's icy wing is upon me, I fear to die."

"Let me die for you, sister!" exclaimed Antoinette, resolutely. "Give me the hood and mantle. I will cover my face, and no one will know that it is I, for I am almost as tall as you. If I never return from the vault alive, the empress will pardon you for my sake. Oh, I should die happy, if my death would rescue you, Josepha."

And Antoinette attempted to draw off her sister's mantle, and put it around her own shoulders. But Josepha withheld her.

"Dear child," said she, kissing her, "is it possible that you are willing to die for me, you who are so young and happy?"

"For that very reason, Josepha," said Antoinette, "it might be well to die. Who knows what sorrows the world may have in reserve for me? Let me die to-day, dear sister, let me—"

At that moment the door opened, and the maid of honor of the Archduchess Josepha appeared.

"Pardon me, your highness," said she deprecatingly. "A page of her majesty is here to know if you have gone to the imperial vaults."

"Apprise her majesty that I am about to leave," replied Josepha, with dignity. Taking Antoinette in her arms, she said, in a whisper: "You see, it is I who must die. Farewell, dearest; may you live and be happy!"

So saying, she tore herself away from the weeping child and hastened to her carriage. Antoinette, with a shriek, rushed forward to follow, but Josepha had fastened the door. The poor child sank on her knees and began to pray. But prayer brought no consolation. She thought of her sister dying from terror, and wrung her hands while she cried aloud.

Suddenly she ceased, started to her feet, and the blood mounted to her pale face.

"The secret door!" exclaimed she. "I had forgotten it." She crossed the room toward a picture that hung on a wall opposite, and touching a spring in its frame, it flew back and revealed a communication with one of the state-apartments. She sprang through the opening, her golden hair flying out in showers behind her, her cheeks glowing, her eyes flashing, and her heart beating wildly as she sped through the palace to the empress's apartments. The sentry would have stopped her; but throwing him off with an imperious gesture, she darted through the door, and all ceremony forgetting, flew to the sittting-room of the empress, and threw herself at her mother's feet.

CHAPTER XLVI.

INOCULATION.

MARIA THERESA was standing in the embrasure of a window, and she scarcely turned her head as she heard the rustling behind her. She took no notice of the breach of etiquette of which Antoinette was guilty, in rushing unannounced upon her solitude. Her eyes were fixed upon the chapel of the Capuchins in whose vaults lay so many whom she had loved. Her heart and thoughts were within those gray walls, now with her husband and her dead children, now with Josepha, for whom she felt pang after pang of anxiety. In an absent tone she turned and said:

"What brings you hither, little Antoinette?"

"Josepha, dear mother. Have pity on Josepha!"

The empress, with a thrill of joy at her heart, replied, "She did not go, then?"

"Yes, yes, she went because you forced her to go, but she went with a broken heart. Oh, mamma, Josepha says that the dead are waiting to take her with them! May I not order my carriage and fly to bring her back?"

Maria Theresa said nothing. Her eyes turned first upon the beautiful little suppliant at her feet, then they wandered out through the evening haze, and rested on the dark towers of the Capuchin chapel.

"Oh, dear mamma," continued Antoinette, "if I may not bring her back, at least let me share her danger. Be good to your poor little Antoinette. You promised, if I behaved well, to do something for me, mamma, and now I deserve a reward, for Count Brandeis says that I have been a good girl of late. Do not shake your head, it would make me better if I went to pray with Josepha. You do not know how vain and worldly I am. When I saw Josepha's beautiful jewels I was quite envious of her; and indeed, mamma, no one needs solitude and prayer more than I. Let me go and pray for grace by the grave of my father."

The empress laid her hand upon her daughter's head, and looked at her beautiful countenance with an expression of deepest tenderness.

"You are a noble-hearted child, my Antoinette," said she. "With such sensibility as yours, you are likely to suffer from the faults and misconceptions of the world; for magnanimity is so rare that it is often misunderstood. You would share your sister's danger, while believing in its reality. No, no, darling, I cannot accept your generous sacrifice. It would be useless, for Josepha's terror will shorten her prayers. Before you could reach the chapel, she will have left it—"

Maria Theresa paused, and again looked out from the window. The rolling of carriage-wheels was distinctly heard coming toward the palace. Now it ceased, and the sentry's voice was heard at the gates.

"Ah!" cried the empress, joyfully, "I was right. It is Josepha. Her devotions have not been long; but I will confess to you, Antoinette, that a weight is lifted from my heart. I have not breathed freely since she left my presence. Oh, I will forgive her for her short prayers, for they have shortened my miserable suspense!"

"Let me go and bring her to you, mamma," cried Antoinette, clapping her hands and darting toward the door. But the empress held her back.

"No, dear, remain with me. Josepha's heart will reveal to her that her mother longs to welcome her back."

At that moment a page announced the Countess Lerchenfeld.

"It is not my child!" cried the empress, turning pale.

The countess, too, was very pale, and she trembled as she approached the imperial mother.

"She is dead!" murmured Marie Antoinette, sinking almost fainting to the floor.

But the empress called out, "Where is my child? In mercy, tell me why you are here without her?"

"Please your majesty," replied the countess, "I come to beg that you will excuse her highness. She has been suddenly taken sick. She was lifted insensible to the carriage, and has not yet recovered her consciousness."

Maria Theresa reeled, and a deathly paleness overspread her countenance. "Sick!" murmured she, with quivering lip. "What—what happened?"

"I do not know, your majesty. Accordng to your imperial command I accompanied her highness to the chapel. I went as far as the stairway that leads to the crypts. Her highness was strangely agitated. I tried to soothe her, but as she looked below, and saw the open door, she shuddered, and clinging to me, whispered: 'Countess, I scent the loathesome corpse that even now stirs in its coffin at my approach.' Again I strove to comfort her, but all in vain. Scarcely able to support herself, she bade me farewell, and commended herself to your majesty. Then, clinging to the damp walls, she tottered below, and disappeared."

"And did you not hold her back!" cried Marie Antoinette. "You had the cruelty to leave her—"

"Peace, Antoinette," said the empress, raising her hand, imploringly. "What else?" asked she, hoarsely.

"I stood at the head of the stairway, your majesty, awaiting her highness's return. For a while all was silent; then I heard a piercing shriek, and I hastened to the vault—"

"Was it my child?" asked the empress, now as rigid as a marble statue.

"Yes, your majesty. I found her highness kneeling, with her head resting upon the tomb of the emperor."

"Insensible?"

"No, your majesty. I approached and found her icy cold, her eyes dilated, and her face covered with drops of cold sweat. She was scarcely able to speak, but in broken accents she related to me that, as she was making her way toward the altar at the head of the emperor's tomb, she suddenly became sensible that something was holding her back. Horror-stricken, she strove to fly, but could not. When, as she turned her head, she beheld the coffin of the Empress Josepha, and saw that from thence came the power that held her back. With a shriek she bounded forward, and fell at the foot of the emperor's tomb. I supported her until we reached the chapel-door, when she fainted, and I had to call for help to bear her to her carriage."

"And now?" asked the empress, who was weeping bitterly.

"She is still unconscious, your majesty. Herr van Swieten and the emperor are at her bedside."

"And I," cried the unhappy empress, "I, too, must be with my poor, martyred child."

Marie Antoinette would have followed, but her mother bade her remain, and hastening from the room, Maria Theresa ran breathless through the corridors until she reached her daughter's apartments.

There, like a crushed lily, lay the fair bride of Naples, while near her stood her brother in speechless grief. At the foot of the bed Van Swieten and one of the maids of honor were rubbing her white feet with stimulants.

The empress laid her hand upon Josepha's cold brow, and turning to Van Swieten, as though in his hands lay the fate of her child, as she asked:

"Will she die?"

"Life and death," replied the physician, "are in the hands of the Lord. As long as there is life, there is hope."

Maria Theresa shook her head. "I have no hope," said she, with the calmness of despair. "'Tis the enemy of our house. Is it not, Van Swieten? Has she not the small-pox?"

"I fear so, your majesty."

"She must die, then—and it is I who have murdered her!" shrieked the empress, wildly; and she fell fainting to the floor.

On the fifteenth of October, the day on which Josepha was to have given her hand to the King of Naples, the bells of Vienna tolled her funeral knell.

Not in her gilded carriage rode the fair young bride, but cold and lifeless she lay under the black and silver pall on which were placed a myrtle-wreath and a royal crown of gold.

Another spouse had claimed her hand, and the marriage-rites were solemnized in the still vaults of the chapel of the Capuchins.

The empress had not left her daughter's room since the fatal day of her return from the chapel. With all the tenderness of her affectionate nature she had been the nurse of her suffering child. Not a tear was in her eye, nor a murmur on her lips. Silent, vigilant, and sleepless, she had struggled with the foe that was wresting yet another loved one from her house.

Day by day Josepha grew worse—until she lay dying. Still the empress shed no tear. Bending over her daughter's bed, she received her last sigh. And now she watched the corpse, and would not be moved, though the emperor and Van Swieten implored her to seek rest.

When the body was removed, the poor, tearless mourner followed it from the room through the halls and gates of the palace until it was laid in the grave.

Then she returned home, and, without a word, retired to her own apartments. There, on a table, lay heaps of papers and letters with unbroken seals. But the empress heeded nothing of all this. Maternity reigned supreme in her heart—there was room in it for grief and remorse alone. She strode to the window, and there, as she had done not many days before, she looked out upon the gray towers of the chapel, and thought how she had driven her own precious child into the dismal depths of its loathsome vaults.

The door was softly opened, and the emperor and Van Swieten were seen with anxious looks directed toward the window where the empress was standing.

"What is to be done?" said Joseph. "How is she to be awakened from that fearful torpor?"

"We must bring about some crisis," replied Van Swieten, thoughtfully. "We must awake both the empress and the mother. The one must have work—the other, tears. This frozen sea of grief must thaw, or her majesty will die."

"Doctor," cried Joseph, "save her, I implore you. Do something to humanize this marble grief."

"I will try, your majesty. With your permission I will assemble the imperial family here, and we will ask to be admitted to the presence of the empress. The Archduchess Marie Antoinette and the Archduke Maximilian I shall not summon."

Not long after, the door was once more softly opened, and the Emperor Joseph, followed by his sisters and the doctor, entered the empress's sitting-room.

Maria Theresa was still erect before the window, staring at the dark towers of the chapel.

"Your majesty," said Joseph, approaching, "your children are here to mourn with you."

"It is well," replied Maria Theresa, without stirring from her position. "I thank you all. But leave me, my children. I would mourn alone."

"But before we go, will not your majesty vouchsafe one look of kindness?" entreated the emperor. "May we not kiss your hand? Oh, my beloved mother, your living children, too, have a right to your love! Do not turn away so coldly from us. Let your children comfort their sad hearts with the sight of your dear and honored countenance."

There was so much genuine feeling in Joseph's voice, as he uttered these words, that his mother could not resist him. She turned and gave him her hand.

"God bless you, my son," said she, "for your loving words. They fall like balsam upon my sore and wounded heart. God bless you all, my children, who have come hither to comfort your poor, sorrowing mother."

The archduchesses flocked, weeping to her side, and smiled through their tears, as they met her glance of love. But suddenly she started, and looked searchingly around the room.

"Where are my little ones?" said she anxiously.

No one spoke, but the group all turned their eyes upon Van Swieten, whose presence, until now, had been unobserved by the empress.

Like an angry lioness, she sprang forward to the threshold, and laid her hand upon Van Swieten's shoulder.

"What means your presence here, Van Swieten?" cried she loudly. "What fearful message do you bear me now? My children! my children! where are they?"

"In their rooms, your majesty," replied Van Swieten, seriously. "I came hither expressly to apologize for their absence. It was I who prevented them from coming."

"Why so?" exclaimed the empress.

"Because, your majesty, they have never had the small-pox; and contact with you would be dangerous for them. For some weeks they must absent themselves from your majesty's presence."

"You are not telling me the truth, Van Swieten!" cried Maria Theresa, hastily. "My children are sick, and I must go to them."

"Your majesty may banish me forever from the palace," said he, "but as long as I remain, you cannot approach your children. It is my duty to shield them from the infection which still clings to your majesty's person. Would you be the probable cause of their death?"

The earnest tone with which Van Swieten put this question so overcame the empress, that she raised both her arms, and cried out in a voice of piercing anguish: "Ah! it is I who caused Josepha's death!—I who murdered my unhappy child!"

These words once uttered, the icy bonds that had frozen her heart gave way, and Maria Theresa wept.

"She is saved!" whispered Van Swieten to the emperor. "Will your majesty now request the archduchesses to retire? The empress does not like to be seen in tears; and this paroxysm once over, the presence of her daughters will embarrass her."

The emperor communicated Van Swieten's wish, and the princesses silently and noiselessly withdrew. The empress was on her knees, while showers of healing tears were refreshing her seethed heart.

"Let us try to induce her to rise," whispered Van Swieten. "This hour, if it please God, may prove a signal blessing to all Austria."

The emperor approached, and tenderly strove to lift his mother, while he lavished words of love and comfort upon her. She allowed him to lead her to a divan, where gradually the tempest of her grief gave place to deep-drawn sighs, and, finally, to peace. The crisis, however, was long and terrible, for the affections of Maria Theresa were as strong as her will; and fierce had been the conflict between the two.

For some time a deep silence reigned throughout the room. Finally, the empress raised her eyes and said, "You will speak the truth, both of you, will you not?"

"We will, your majesty," replied the emperor and Van Swieten.

"Then, Joseph, say—are my children well and safe?"

"They are, my dearest mother, and but for the doctor's prohibition, both would have accompanied us thither."

Maria Theresa then turned to the physician. "Van Swieten," said she, "you, too, must swear to speak the truth. I have something to ask of you also."

"I swear, your majesty," replied Van Swieten.

"Then say if I am the cause of my daughter's death. Do not answer me at once. Take time for reflection, and, as Almighty God hears us, answer me conscientiously."

There was a pause. Nothing was heard save the heavy breathing of the empress, and the ticking of the golden clock that stood upon the mantel. Maria Theresa sat with her head bowed down upon her hands; before her stood Joseph, his pale and noble face turned toward the physician, and his eyes fixed upon him with an expression of deepest entreaty. Van Swieten saw the look, and answered it by a scarcely perceptible motion of his head.

"Now, speak, Van Swieten," said the empress, raising her head, and looking him full in the face. "Was Josepha's visit to the chapel-vault the cause of her death?"

"No, your majesty," said the physician gravely. "In *this sense* you were not guilty of her highness's death; for the body, in small-pox, is infected long before it shows itself on the surface. Had her highness received the infection in the crypts of the chapel, she would be still living. Her terror and presentiment of death were merely symptoms of the disease."

The empress reached out both her hands to Van Swieten, and said: "Thank you, my friend. You surely would not deceive me with false comfort; I can, therefore, even in the face of this great sorrow, find courage to live and do my duty. I may weep for my lost child, but while weeping I may feel that Heaven's will, and not my guilt, compassed her death. Thank you, my dear son, for your sympathy and tenderness. You will never know what comfort your love has been to me this day."

So saying, she drew the emperor close to her, and putting both her arms around his neck, kissed him tenderly.

"Van Swieten," said she, then, "what do you mean by saying that 'in this sense' I was not guilty of Josepha's death."

"I think, your majesty," replied the emperor, "that I can explain those words. He means to say that had you yielded to his frequent petitions to make use of inoculation as a safeguard against the violence of the small-pox, our dear Josepha might have survived her attack. Is it not so, Van Swieten?"

"It is, your majesty. If the empress would consent to allow the introduction in Austria of inoculation for the small-pox, she would not only shield her own family from danger, but would confer a great blessing on her subjects."

"Indeed, Van Swieten," replied the empress, after a pause, "what you propose seems sinful to me. Besides, I have heard that many who were inoculated for small-pox have died of its effects. But for this, they might have lived for many years. How can I reconcile it to my conscience to assume such an awful responsibility?"

"But," urged Van Swieten, "thousands have been rescued, where two or three have perished. I do not say that the remedy is infallible; but I can safely say that out of one hundred cases, ninety, by its use, are rendered innoxious. Oh, your majesty! when you remember that within ten years five members of your family have been victims to this terrific scourge—when you remember how for weeks Austria was in extremest sorrow while your majesty lay so ill, how can you refuse such a boon for yourself and your people?"

"It is hard for me to refuse any thing to the one whose skilful hand restored me to life," replied the empress, while she reached her hand to Van Swieten.

"My dear, dear mother!" exclaimed Joseph, "do not refuse him! He asks you to save the lives of thousands. Think how different life would have been for me had my Isabella lived! Think of my sisters—think of Antoinette and Maximilian, who long to be with you and cannot."

"Doctor," said the empress, "if my children were inoculated, how long would it be before I could see them?"

"In two hours, your majesty; for in that time the poison would have permeated their systems."

By this time the empress had resumed her habit of walking to and fro when she was debating any thing in her mind. She went on for some time, while Van Swieten and the emperor followed her movements with anxious looks.

Finally she spoke. "Well, my son," said she, coming close to Joseph, and smiling fondly upon him, "I yield to you as co-regent of Austria. You, too, have some right to speak in this matter, and your wishes shall decide mine. To you, also, Van Swieten, I yield in gratitude for all that you have done for me and mine. Let Austria profit by this new discovery, and may it prove a blessing to us all! Are you satisfied, Joseph?"

"More than satisfied," exclaimed he, kissing his mother's hand.

"Now, Van Swieten," continued Maria Theresa, "hasten to inoculate my children. I long to fold them to my poor aching heart.

Remember, you have promised that I shall see them in two hours!"

"In two hours they shall be here, your majesty," said Van Swieten, as he hurried away.

"Stop a moment," cried Maria Theresa. "As you have been the instigator of this thing; upon your shoulders shall fall the work that must arise from it. I exact of you, therefore, to superintend the inoculation of my subjects, and your pay as chief medical inspector shall be five thousand florins. I also give my palace at Hetzendorf as a model hospital for the reception of the children of fifty families, who shall there be inoculated and cared for at my expense. This is the monument I shall erect to my beloved Josepha; and when the little ones who are rescued from death thank God for their recovery, they will pray for my poor child's departed soul. Does this please you, my son?"

The emperor did not answer—his heart was too full for speech. The empress saw his agitation, and opening her arms to clasp him in her embrace, she faltered out, "Come, dear child, and together let us mourn for our beloved dead." *

CHAPTER XLVII.

AN ADVENTURE.

It was a lovely day in June—one of those glorious days when field and wood are like a lofty cathedral, where the birds are the choir, and the wind stirring the censers of the forest perfume, is the organ; while man, in ecstasy with nature's beauty, glances enraptured from heaven to earth—from earth again to heaven.

But pleasantest of all on such a day are the reveries that come and go over the heart, under the shade of a noble oak that lifts its crowned head to the clouds, while birds twitter love-songs among its branches, and lovers lie dreaming on the green sward below.

So thought a young man as he reclined under the shadow of a tall beech-tree that skirted the green border of a meadow, somewhere near the woods around Schönbrunn. He had fastened his horse to a tree not far off, and while the steed cropped the fresh grass, its owner revelled in the luxury of sylvan solitude. With an expression of quiet enjoyment he glanced now upon the soft, green meadow, now at the dim, shady woods, and then at the blue and silver sky that parted him from heaven.

"Oh! how delightful it is," thought he, "to drop the shackles of royalty, and to be a man! Oh, beautiful sky, with livery of 'kaiser blue,' change thy hue, and hide me in a dark cloud that I may be safe from the homage of courtiers and sycophants! If they knew that I was here, how soon would they pursue and imprison me again in my gilded cage of imperial grandeur!"

Just then, in the distance, was heard the sound of a hunting-

* The institution founded on that day by the empress, went very soon into operation. Every spring the children of fifty families among the nobles and gentry were received at the hospital of Hetzendorf. The empress was accustomed to visit the institution frequently; and at the end of each season, she gave its little inmates a splendid ball, which was always attended by herself and her daughters. The festivities closed with concerts, lotteries, and a present to each child. Caroline Pichler, "Memoirs," vol. i., p. 63. Coxe, "History of the House of Austria," vol. v. p. 188.

horn, and the emperor's soliloquy was cut short. An expression of annoyance was visible on his features, as he listened. But instead of advancing, the sounds receded until finally they were lost in the sighing of the wind among the forest-trees.

"They have passed by," exclaimed he joyfully. "This day is mine, and I am free. What a charm is in that word *freedom!* I feel it now; no emperor am I, but a man, to whom the animals will turn their backs, without suspecting that they refuse to look upon an anointed sovereign. But hark! what is that? A doe—a timid doe—perhaps an enchanted princess who can resume her shape at the bidding of a prince only. Here am I, sweet princess—ready, as soon as you become a woman, to leap into your arms."

The emperor grasped his fowling-piece that was leaning against the beech. But the doe caught the sound, raised her graceful head, and her mild eye sought the enemy that threatened her. She saw him, and as he raised the gun to take aim, she cleared the road with one wild bound, and in a few moments was lost in a thicket.

The emperor leaped on his horse, exclaiming, "I must catch my enchanted princess;" and giving his steed the rein, away they flew on the track of the doe; away they flew over fallen trunks and through brier and copse, until the panting steed would have recoiled before a wide hedge—but the emperor cried, "Over it! over it! The princess is beyond!" and the foaming horse gathered up his forelegs for the leap. He made a spring, but missed, and with a loud crash, horse and rider fell into the ditch on the farther side of the hedge.

The emperor fell under the horse, who, in its efforts to rise, inflicted dreadful suffering upon its master. He felt that his senses were leaving him, and thought that he was being crushed to death. The load upon his breast was insufferable, and in his ears there came a sound like the roaring of the ocean. He uttered one cry for help, commended himself to Heaven, and fainted.

How long he lay there, he never knew. When he opened his weary eyes again, he lay on the sward near the hedge, with his head resting upon the lap of a beautiful girl, who was contemplating him with looks of tenderest pity. By her side knelt another young girl, who was bathing his temples with water.

"Look, Marianne," exclaimed she joyfully, "he begins to move. Oh, dear sister, we have saved his life."

"Still, Kathi," whispered the other. "He has not yet his senses. He looks as if he were dreaming of angels. But he will soon awake."

"I don't wonder that he dreams of angels, Marianne, when he looks at you," said Kathi, contemplating her beautiful sister. "But now that he is safe, I will go and look after his horse. Poor animal! he trembles yet with fright, and I think he has lamed his leg. I will lead him to the spring where he can drink and cool his foot. You know the curate says that water is a great doctor for man and beast."

So saying she took up the bridle, and coaxing the horse gently, he followed her, although he shuddered with the pain of his limb.

She disappeared behind a little grove of trees, while her sister contemplated their handsome patient. He lay perfectly quiet, his eyes open, but feeling too weary for speech. He felt uncertain whether he waked or dreamed, nor did he care; for the present moment was unutterably sweet. His pain was slight, and with his head pillowed upon the lap of the lovely girl whose face was beautiful as that of Eve in the groves of Eden, the emperor gazed on in rapture.

Marianne became gradually aware that his glances spoke admiration, for her color slowly deepened, until it glowed like the petals of a newly-opened rose. The emperor smiled as he watched her blushes. "Do angels then blush?" asked he softly.

"He still dreams," said Marianne, shaking her head. "I thought just now that his senses were returning."

"Nò, child," replied Joseph, "I do not dream. I see before me the loveliest vison that ever blessed the eyes of man, or else—I have overtaken the enchanted princess. Oh, princess! it was cruel of you to lure one over that treacherous hedge!"

Marianne looked alarmed. "Poor, poor young man!" murmured she in a low voice, "he is delirious. I must moisten his head again."

She extended her hand to the little pail that held the water, but Joseph caught it, and pressed it warmly to his lips.

Marianne blushed anew, with painful embarrassment, and sought to withdraw her hand.

The emperor would not yield it. "Let me kiss the hand of the angel that has rescued me from death," said he. "For 'tis you, is it not, who saved my life?"

"My sister and I, sir, were coming through the wood," replied Marianne, "when we saw your horse galloping directly toward the hedge. We knew what must happen, and ran with all our might toward you, but before we reached you, the horse had made the leap. Oh, I shudder when I think of it!"

And her face grew white again, while her lustrous eyes were dimmed with tears.

"Go on, go on, my—. No, I will not call you princess lest you should think me delirious. I am not delirious, beautiful Marianne! but I dream, I dream of my boyhood and almost believe that I have come upon enchanted ground. Your sweet voice—your lovely face —this delicious wood—it all seems like fairy-land! But speak on; where did you find me?"

"Under the horse, sir; and the first thing we did was to free you from its weight. We took the rein, and, after some efforts, we got him to his feet. Kathi led him away, and I—I—"

"You, Marianne! tell me—what did you do?"

"I," said she, looking down—"I bore you as well as I was able to this spot. I do not know how I did it, but fright gives one very great strength."

"Go on, go on!"

"We had been gathering mushrooms in the woods, when we saw you. As soon as Kathi had tied the horse, she ran for her little pail, poured out the mushrooms, and filling it with water, we bathed your head until you revived. This, sir, is the whole history, and now that you have recovered, I will help you to rise."

"Not yet, not yet, enchantress. I cannot raise my head from its delicious pillow. Let me dream for a few moments longer. Fairy-land is almost like heaven."

Marianne said no more, but her eyes sought the ground, and her face grew scarlet. The emperor still gazed upon her wonderful beauty, and thought that nothing he had ever seen in gilded halls could approach this peasant-girl, whose red dress and black bodice were more dazzling to his eyes than the laces and diamonds of all Vienna assembled.

"Where," asked he, observing that her snowy shoulders were bare, "where did you get a kerchief to bathe my head?"

Marianne started and laid her hands upon her neck. "Good Heaven!" murmured she to herself; "it was the kerchief from my own bosom!" Unconsciously she reached her hand to take it from the pail.

"What!" said Joseph, stopping her; "would you wear that dripping kerchief? No, no! let the sky, the birds, and the wood-nymphs look at those graceful shoulders; and if *I* may not look, I will shut my eyes."

"Oh! do not shut your eyes; they are blue as the sky itself!" replied Marianne. But as she spoke she drew forward the long braids that trailed behind her on the ground, and quickly untwisting them, her hair fell in showers around her neck and shoulders, so that they were effectually concealed.

"You are right," said the emperor. "Your hair is as beautiful as the rest of your person. It surpasses the sables of a Russian princess. You know perfectly well how to adorn yourself, you bewitching child."

"I did not mean to adorn myself, sir," said Marianne.

"Why, then, did you cover yourself with that superb mantle?"

"Because, sir, I—I was cold."

"Are you so icy, then, that you freeze in midsummer?"

She said nothing, but bent her head in confusion. Luckily, at that moment, Kathi came in sight with the horse.

"Now, sir," exclaimed Marianne, "you can rise, can you not?"

"Not unless you help me, for my head is yet very light."

"Well, sir, if that be so, then stay where you are, and try to sleep, while I pray to the blessed Virgin to protect you."

Meanwhile Kathi came forward, and, when she saw the emperor, nodded her head.

"God be praised, sir," cried she, "you have your senses once more! You have gotten off cheaply with nothing but a black eye. But, bless me! how quiet you are, Marianne! Who would think, that while the gentleman was out of his senses, you were crying as if he had been your sweetheart! Why, sir, her tears fell upon your face and waked you."

"Pardon me," whispered Marianne, "I wiped them away with the kerchief."

"Why did you deprive me of those sweet tears?" whispered the emperor. But Kathi was talking all the while.

"Now," continued she, "try to get up. Put one arm around me, and the other around Marianne, and we will set you upon your legs, to find out whether they are sound. Come—one, two, three; now!"

With the help of the strong peasant-girl, the emperor arose and stood erect. But he complained of dizziness, and would have Marianne to sustain him.

She approached with a smile, while he, drawing her gently to his side, looked into her eyes. The poor girl trembled, she knew not why, for assuredly she was not afraid.

Kathi, who had gone back for the horse, now came up, leading him to his master. "Now," said she, "we are all ready to go. Your horse is a little lame, and not yet able to bear you. Whither shall we lead you, sir? Where is your home?"

"My home!" exclaimed the emperor, with troubled mien. "I had forgotten that I had a home." This question had awakened him from his idyl.

"Where is my home?" echoed he sadly. "It is in Vienna. Can you put me on the road thither?"

"That can we, sir; but it is a long way for such a gentleman as you to travel on foot."

"Let us go, then, to the highway, and perhaps I may there find some conveyance."

"Well, then," cried the gleeful Kathi, "forward, march!"

"Not yet, Kathi. Not until I have thanked you for the great service you have rendered me. Let me give you some testimony of my gratitude. Before we part, let me gratify some wish of yours. Speak first, Kathi."

"H'm," said Kathi, "I have many wishes. It is not so easy to say what I want."

"Well, take time, and think for a moment, child."

Kathi looked as if she were making a bold resolve.

"That ring upon your finger—it is the prettiest thing I ever saw. Will you give it to me?"

"Kathi!" exclaimed Marianne, "how can you ask such a thing?"

"Why not?" returned Kathi, reddening; "did he not tell me to say what I wanted?"

"Yes," said Marianne in a low voice, "but it may be a gift—perhaps it is from his sweetheart!"

"No, Marianne," replied the emperor sadly, "I have no sweetheart. No one cares whether I give or keep the ring. Take it, Kathi."

Kathi held out her hand, and when it had been placed upon her finger she turned it around to see it glisten, and laughed for joy.

"And you, Marianne," said Joseph, changing his tone as he addressed the beautiful creature who stood at his side, "tell me your wish. Let it be something hard to perform, for then I shall be all the happier to grant it."

But Marianne spoke not a word.

"Why, Marianne," cried Kathi impatiently, "do you not see that he is a rich and great lord, who will give you any thing you ask? Why do you stand so dumb?"

"Come, dear Marianne," whispered the emperor, "have you no wish that I can gratify?"

"Yes, sir," cried Marianne, in a voice scarcely audible.

"Speak it, then, sweet one, and it shall be granted."

"Then, sir," said Marianne, her cheeks glowing, though her eyes were still cast down, "my father's house is hard by. Come and rest awhile under his roof, and let me give you a glass of milk, and to your horse some fresh hay."

The emperor seemed to grow very weak while Marianne spoke, for he clung to her as though he had been afraid to fall.

"Yes, Marianne," replied he, "and God bless you for the kind suggestion! Let me for once forget the world and imagine that I, too, am a peasant, with no thought of earth beyond these enchanted woods. Take me to the cottage where your father lives, and let me eat of his bread. I am hungry."

And the emperor, with his strange suite, set off for the cottage of Conrad the peasant.

CHAPTER XLVIII.

THE JUDGMENT OF SOLOMON.

OLD Conrad stood in his doorway, shading his old eyes from the sunbeams, while he looked anxiously down the road that led to the village. It was noonday, and yet the hearth of the kitchen was empty and cold. No kettle was on the hob, no platter upon the table. And yet his daughters had started early for the woods, and surely they must have gathered their mushrooms hours ago.

The old peasant began to be anxious. If it had been Kathi alone, it would have been easy enough to guess at the delay. She was gossiping with Valentine, and forgetting that she had father or sister, home or dinner. But Marianne was along, and she never flirted or loitered. What could be the matter? But—what was that coming up the road? Marianne! Yes, truly, Marianne with a fine lord at her side, who seemed closer to her than propriety seemed to allow.

"Gracious Heaven!" thought the old man, "what has come over my bashful Marianne? What would the villagers say if they should see her now? And what comes behind? Kathi, with a horse. Are the maidens bewitched?"

They came nearer; and now Kathi, from the top of her voice, bade him good-day.

"Are we not fine, father?" cried she, with a loud laugh. But Marianne, coming forward with the emperor, bent gracefully before her old father.

"See, dear father," said she in her soft, musical tones, "we bring you a guest who to-day will share our humble dinner with us."

"A guest whose life has been saved by your daughters," added Joseph, extending his hand.

"And a very rich somebody he must be, father," cried Kathi, "for see how he has paid us for our help. Look at this brave ring, how it glistens! It is mine; and Marianne might have had as much if she had chosen. But what do you think she asked him?—to come home and get a glass of milk!"

"That was well done of my Marianne," said the father, proudly. "It would have been a pity not to let me see the brave gentleman, if indeed you have been so happy as to save his life. Come in, my lord, come in. You are welcome. What we have we give cordially."

"And therefore what you give will be gratefully received," replied the emperor, entering and seating himself.

"Now, sir," said Marianne, "I will go and prepare the dinner." So saying, she passed into the cottage kitchen.

"That is a beautiful maiden," said Joseph, looking wistfully after the graceful figure as it disappeared.

"They are my heart's joy, both of them," replied Conrad. "They are brisk as fawns, and industrious as bees. And yet I am often sad as I look at them."

"Why so?"

"Because I am old and poor. I have nothing to leave them, and when I die, they will have to go to service. That frets me. It is because I love the maidens so dearly that I am troubled about them."

"Let their poverty trouble you no longer, my friend. I will provide for them. I have it in my power to make them both comfortable, and that they shall be, I promise you."

The old man spoke his thanks, and presently came Marianne to announce the dinner. It was served in an arbor covered with honeysuckles and red beans, and the emperor thought that he had never had a better dinner in his imperial palace. The shackles of his greatness had fallen from him, and he drank deeply of the present hour, without a thought for the morrow. Marianne was at his side, and as he looked into the lustrous depths of her dark eyes, he wished himself a peasant that he might look into them forever.

Meanwhile Kathi and her father walked together in the garden. They were both examining the diamond ring, and the hearts of both were filled with ambitious thoughts and hopes.

"He must be very rich," said Kathi, in a low voice. "He has fallen in love with Marianne, 'tis plain, and she has only to ask and have any thing she likes. Look, father, he is kissing her! But don't let them see you. The more he loves her, the more he will give us. But you must speak to Marianne, father. She is as silly as a sheep, and doesn't care whether we are poor or rich. Call her here, and tell her that she *must* ask for a great sum of money—enough for us to buy a fine farm. Then Valentine will marry me at once, and I shall be able to give a wedding-dress to all the other maidens in the village."

"But suppose that the lord should want Marianne?" asked Conrad, turning pale.

Kathi still held up her ring, and she turned toward the sun until it seemed to be in a blaze. "Look, father," said she, in a low tone, "look."

The eyes of the old man were fixed upon the jewel; and strange hopes, with which, until now, he had been unacquainted, stirred his heart. The serpent had found its way into Eden, and it spoke to both in the glitter of this unhappy ring.

"Father," said Kathi, at length, "if Marianne had such a ring as this on her finger she would find many hundred wooers who would forgive her for having had *one* before them."

"Silence!" cried the old man. "If your mother were alive to hear these guilty words, she would think that you were no longer innocent yourself. How I wish she were here in this trying hour! But since you have no parent but me, I must protect you from shame."

With these words the old man walked resolutely to the arbor, followed by Kathi, who implored him not to ruin their fortunes.

"My lord," said Conrad, "the day wanes. If you intend to reach Vienna to-night, you have no time to lose."

"Alas!" thought Joseph, "my dream is over. You are right," said he to the peasant, "unless you will shelter me to-night."

"I have but one bed in my house, sir," replied Conrad, "and that is in the little room of my daughters."

"Then let me sleep there," said Joseph, with the arrogance of one accustomed to command.

"Oh!" faltered Marianne, springing to her father's side, as though she would seek protection from these ensnaring words.

But Kathi shook her sister's arm, and surveying her blushing face, exclaimed with a loud laugh, "You are a fool. What harm can it do us, if the gentleman sleeps in our room? We can make ourselves a bed of hay on the floor, and give him the bedstead. No one will ever think any the less of us."

"I think so, too," said Joseph, who was now resolved to see of what stuff the peasant was made. "Do not hesitate so. Let me sleep in your daughters' room, and I will give you a handful of gold for my lodging."

Kathi gave a cry of delight, and going close to her father, she whispered, "Father, you will not refuse! Think—a handful of gold! We will be the richest farmers in the village! There are two of us—there can be no danger."

"Well!" asked Joseph, impatiently, "have you decided? Did you not tell me that you were poor? and is this not an opportunity I offer you to enrich your daughters?"

"Sir," replied the old man, solemnly, "I do not know whether this opportunity may not be for evil, instead of good. I am a poor and simple farmer, and cannot decide for myself whether the mere fact of your sleeping in the same room with my daughters is right or not. Our curate is a very holy man; I will apply to him for advice."

"Very well," said Joseph, "go and fetch him, he shall decide."

Old Conrad left the garden, followed again by Kathi, who was resolved to leave the great lord alone with her sister. Marianne, who before had been so happy and unembarrassed, now started forward with the intention of going with her father. But the emperor would not allow it. He caught her by both hands and held her fast. "Stay, frightened doe," said he softly. "You are right, dear child, to tremble before men, for they are full of deceit; but do not be afraid of me; I will not harm you."

Marianne raised her dark, tearful eyes to his face, and gradually a smile lit up her lovely features.

"I believe you, my lord," said she. "You have, perhaps, already seen that I would do any thing on earth for you, were it even to give up my life; but for no one would I do that which my mother would blame if she were living—on no account would I do that which I might not tell in prayer to my heavenly Father."

The emperor looked once more at her lovely face.

"Oh, Marianne! why are you a peasant!" exclaimed he. Then raising his eyes to heaven. "Almighty God," continued he, "shield her from harm. In Thy presence I swear to protect her honor—even from myself."

At that moment old Conrad appeared in the road. At his side was a little old man in a faded cassock, whose spare white hair scarcely covered his bald head.

Joseph came forward, holding Marianne by the hand. Kathi darted from the house, laughing vociferously. The priest advanced, his eyes fixed upon the face of the stranger. All at once, pointing with his finger to Joseph, he cried out:

"Conrad, a great honor has befallen your house. Your guest is the emperor!"

"The emperor!" exclaimed three voices—two in joyous notes, the third with the cry of despair.

Conrad and Kathi were on their knees; Marianne leaned deathly pale against the arbor.

"Yes, father," replied Joseph, mastering his annoyance at the revelation; "yes, I am the emperor. But, my friends, do not offer me such homage as belongs to God alone. Rise, Conrad. Old men should not kneel before young ones. Rise, Kathi. Men should kneel before pretty maidens, no matter whether they be princesses or peasants. And now, father, hear my petition. I am tired and suffering. I have had a fall from my horse, and I do not wish to go to-night to Vienna. I have offered this old man a handful of gold to give me his only bed—the one in his daughters' room. But he will not give his consent without your approval. Decide between us, and remember who it is that asks for lodging here."

The head of the old priest sank upon his breast.

"Oh," thought Kathi, "I hope he will say yes."

Marianne made not a movement, while her father looked anxiously toward the priest.

"Well, father, well," cried Joseph. "You say nothing—and yet I have told you that the emperor craves a night's lodging in the room of these young girls. You see that I ask where I might command. I should think that the lord of the whole land is also lord of the little room of two peasant-girls."

"Yes, your majesty. You are lord of the room, but not of the honor of these peasant-girls," replied the curate, raising his eyes, and steadily meeting those of Joseph.*

"Nobly answered, father," replied the emperor, taking the old priest's hand, and pressing it between his own. "Had you decided otherwise, I would not have forgiven you. Before the servant of the Lord, the claims of the sovereign are on an equality with those of his subject. Pardon me, Conrad, for testing your honor as I did, and accept my horse as a token of my respect. If you should ever wish to sell him, bring him to the imperial stables, and he will be ransomed by me for a thousand florins."

"Oh, your majesty," said the happy old man, "I shall die content—for my children are provided for."

"Now we are rich," cried Kathi, "the best match in the village will be proud to marry either one of us."

The emperor, meanwhile, took out his pocket-book, and, tearing out a leaf, wrote some words upon it.

Folding the paper, he advanced to Marianne, and handing it to her, said:

"My dear child, when your father presents this paper to the marshal of my household, Count Rosenberg, he will give him in return for you five hundred florins."

"Five hundred florins!" exclaimed Kathi, with envious looks.

"Take the paper, Marianne," pleaded the emperor. "It is your dowry."

Marianne raised her tearful eyes, but her hands did not move to take the gift. She reflected for a moment, and then spoke.

"Five hundred florins," echoed she, "is not that a large sum?"

"It is, my child," replied Joseph.

"More than the value of the ring you gave my sister, is it not?" asked she.

The emperor looked disappointed. "Yes, Marianne," replied he,

* "Life of Joseph II., Emperor of Austria," vol iii., p. 89.

with a sigh. "You have no reason to envy your sister. Kathi's ring is not worth more than a hundred florins."

He still held the paper in his hands. Suddenly Marianne took it from him, and crossed over to her sister.

"You hear, Kathi," said she, "you hear what the emperor says. This paper is worth five times as much as your ring. Let us exchange."

So saying, she held out the paper, while Kathi with a scream of delight, snatched it from her hand, and as quick as thought, drew the ring from her own finger.

"If you repent your bargain, Marianne," said she, "so much the worse for you. The dowry is mine—and mine it shall remain."

Marianne did not listen. She placed the ring upon her own hand, and contemplated it with a smile of satisfaction. Then going up to the priest, she addressed him with a grace that would have been winning in a countess.

"Father," said she, "you have heard the exchange that Kathi and I have made. The dowry is hers—the ring is mine. As long as I live, I shall wear this token of my emperor's condescending goodness. And when I die, father, promise me that my ring shall go with me to the grave."

The emperor, all etiquette forgetting, made a step forward, with his arms extended. But recovering himself, he stopped; his arms dropped heavily to his side, and he heaved a deep, deep sigh.

Instead of approaching Marianne, he drew near to the priest.

"Father," said he, "my mother will perhaps feel some anxiety on my account. Will you be so kind as to accompany me to the post-house, where I may perhaps be able to procure some vehicle for Vienna."

"I am ready, your majesty," replied the curate; "and if it pleases you, we will set out at once."

"So be it," sighed Joseph. "Farewell, Conrad," continued he; "hearken to the counsels of your excellent pastor, for he is a faithful servant of God. Farewell, Kathi; now that you have a dower, you will speedily find a husband. Let me be godfather to the first baby."

Kathi blushed and laughed, while the emperor turned to the pale Marianne. He took her hand, and, pressing it to his lips, he said to the priest, who was looking on with anxious eyes—

"A man has the right to kiss the hand of a lovely and innocent girl like this, even though he have the misfortune to be born an emperor. Has he not, father?"

Without waiting for an answer, Joseph dropped the poor little cold hand, and turned away.

The old priest followed, while Conrad and his daughters looked on, scarcely crediting the evidence of their senses.

The emperor had reached the cottage-gate, when suddenly he turned, and spoke again.

"Marianne, one last request. Will you give me the kerchief with which you were bathing my head to-day? The evening air is cool about my throat. I am subject to hoarseness."

Marianne was trembling so that she could not answer. But Kathi came forward, and taking the kerchief from a rosebush where it had been hung to dry, she ran forward, and gave it into the emperor's hands.

He bowed, and continued his way.

Marianne gazed wistfully down the road at the tall and noble form that was disappearing from her sight—perhaps forever.

CHAPTER XLIX.

TWO AFFIANCED QUEENS.

THERE was great activity in the private apartments of the empress. Maria Theresa, whose forenoons were usually dedicated to business of state, was now engaged in giving audience to jewellers, milliners, and mantuamakers.

For whom were these preparations? No one knew, although every one desired to know. The secret seemed especially to interest the two young Archduchesses Caroline and Marie Antoinette. These silks, satins, laces, and jewels signified—marriage. Of that, there could be no doubt. But who was to be the bride? The Archduchess Elizabeth was past thirty. Could it be that there was any truth in the rumor of a projected marriage between herself and the old King of France? She was tired of life at the court of Austria, and would have welcomed the change, had the negotiations which were pending on that subject ever come to any thing. But they did not.*

Caroline and Marie Antoinette were very incredulous when it was hinted that their mother's preparations were intended for their eldest sister. They laughed at the absurdity of Elizabeth's faded pretensions.

"It must be that I am about to be married," said Caroline, as she entered her little sister's room one morning, in full dress. "The empress has commanded my presence in her cabinet to-day, and that betokens something unusual and important. But bless me! you, too, are in full dress?"

"Yes," said Marie Antoinette, laughing, and echoing her sister's words, "it must certainly be *myself* that is about to be married, for the empress has commanded *my* presence in her cabinet, and, of course, she has something of great importance to communicate."

"How! You also?" exclaimed Caroline. "At what hour?"

"At twelve exactly, your highness," answered Marie Antoinette, with a deep courtesy.

"The same hour. Then we must go together. I suppose that the empress intends to propose a husband for me, and a new tutor for you, Antoinette."

"Pray, why not a husband?" laughed Marie Antoinette.

"Because, you saucy child," replied her sister, "husbands are not dolls for little girls to play with."

Marie Antoinette tossed her pretty head, saying, "Let me tell you, Caroline, that little girls are sometimes as wise as their elders, and I shall give you a proof of my superior wisdom, by not returning irony for irony. Perhaps it may be you who is to be married—perhaps it may be both of us. There are more crowns in Europe than one. But hark! there sounds the clock. The empress expects us."

* They were frustrated by the Countess du Barry, who never forgave the Duke de Choiseul for entertaining the project. Du Barry prevailed upon the king to say that he was too old to marry, and she revenged herself on Choiseul by bringing about his disgrace. Alex. Dumas, "History of Louis XV."

She gave her hand to her sister, and the two princesses went laughing together to their mother's room.

The empress received them with an affectionate smile, and although her daughters were accustomed to stand in her presence, to-day she told them to sit on either side of her.

They were both beautiful, and their mother surveyed them with pride and pleasure.

"Come, dear children," said she, "we will banish etiquette for a while. To-day I am no empress, I am but a mother. But why do you both smile so significantly at one another? Are you guessing at what is to be the subject of our interview?"

"What can it be, your majesty," said Caroline gayly, "but the explanation of the riddle that has been puzzling all the brains in the palace for a month past?"

"You have guessed," answered Maria Theresa, laughing. "It is of your own marriage that I would speak. I have accepted a crown for you, my Caroline, and the ambassador who will conduct you to your kingdom is already on his way. Your *trousseau* is magnificent and worthy of a queen. Your fair brow was made for a royal diadem, and in yonder room lies one that is made up of a constellation of diamonds."

"But the king—the man—who is he?" asked Caroline anxiously. "Tell me, your majesty, to whom I am affianced?"

The empress's brow grew ruffled.

"My daughter," said she, "a princess marries not a king, but a kingdom. It is given to few mortals wearing crowns to add to their royalty domestic happiness. It becomes you more to ask whether you are to be a great and powerful queen, than the name of the man who is to place his crown upon your head."

The princess was silent, but she said to herself, "If she means to hand me over to the horrid old King of France, I shall say emphatically—No!"

The empress went on. "Diplomacy is the wooer of royal maidens, and diplomacy has chosen you both. For you, too, my little Antoinette, are promised to the heir of a crown."

Marie Antoinette nodded to Caroline. "I told you so," said she. "Mamma did not call me hither to propose a new tutor."

"Yes, my dear," said the empress, laughing, "I did call you hither for that object also. A little girl who is destined to reign over one of the greatest nations in the world, must prepare herself conscientiously to fill her station worthily. You have a noble mission, my child; through your marriage the enmity so long subsisting between Austria and France shall be converted into amity and concord."

"France!" screamed Antoinette. "Your majesty would surely not marry me to the horrid old Louis XV.!"

"Oh no!" replied the empress, heartily amused. "You are affianced to his grandson, who one of these days will be called Louis XVI."

Marie Antoinette uttered a cry and started from her seat. "Oh, my God!" exclaimed she.

"What—what is the matter?" cried Maria Theresa. "Speak, my child, what ails you?"

"Nothing," murmured Antoinette, shaking her head sadly. "Your majesty would only laugh."

"What is it? I insist upon knowing why it is that you shudder at the name of Louis XVI.? Have you heard aught to his disadvantage? Has your brother the emperor—"

"No, no," interrupted Marie Antoinette, quickly, "the emperor has never mentioned his name to me. No one has ever spoken disparagingly of the dauphin in my presence. What made me shudder at the mention of his title, is the recollection of a fearful prophecy which was related to me yesterday, by my French teacher, as we were reading the hisory of Catherine de Medicis."

"Tell it to me, then, my daughter."

"Since your majesty commands me, I obey," said the young girl, gracefully inclining her head. "Catherine de Medicis, though she was very learned, was a very superstitious woman. One of her astrologers owned a magic looking-glass. He brought it before the queen, and she commanded him to show her in the mirror the destiny of her royal house. He obeyed, and drew back the curtain that covered the face of the looking-glass."

"And what did she see there?" asked the empress, with interest.

Marie Antoinette continued: "She saw the lily-decked throne of France; and upon it appeared, one after another, her sons, Henry, Francis, and Charles. Then came her hated son-in-law, Henry of Navarre; after him, Louis XIII.—then his grandson, Louis XIV., then Louis XV."

"And what then?"

"Then she saw nothing. She waited a few moments after Louis XV. had disappeared, and then she saw a figure with a crown upon his head, but this figure soon was hidden by a cloud; and, in his place, the throne was filled with snakes and cats, who were tearing each other to pieces."

"Fearful sight!" said Maria Theresa, rising from her seat and walking about the room.

"It was fearful to Catherine de Medicis, your majesty, for she fainted. Now you know why I dread to be the bride of the one who is to be called Louis XVI."

The empress said nothing. For a while, she went to and fro through the room; then she resumed her seat, and threw back her proud head with a forced smile.

"These are silly fables," said she, "tales with which nurses might frighten little children, but only fit to provoke laughter from rational beings."

"Pardon me, your majesty," interposed Antoinette "but Louis XV. is not too rational to be affected by them."

"How do you know that, child?"

"I know it, your majesty, because Monsieur le Maître, who published this prophecy in his journal '*L'Espion Turc*,' was imprisoned for fifteen years in the Bastile, on account of it. He is still there, although he has powerful friends who have interceded for him in vain."*

"And Aufresne told you all this?"

"Yes, your majesty."

"He ought to go to the Bastile with Le Maître, then. But I hope that my little Antoinette has too much sense to be affected by Aufresne's nonsense, and that she will accept the husband whom her sovereign and mother has chosen for her. It is a bright destiny,

*Swinburne, p. 60.

that of a Queen of France; and if snakes and cats should come near your throne, you must tread them under foot. Look up, my child, and have courage. In two years you will be the bride of the dauphin. Prepare yourself meanwhile to be a worthy representative of your native Austria. The Queen of France must, as far as she is able, assimilate herself to the customs and language of her people. With that intention, Prince Kaunitz has commissioned the Duke de Choiseul to select you a new teacher. He will be accompanied by two French ladies of honor. These people, my dear, are to form your manners according to the requirements of court etiquette in France; but in your heart, my child, I trust that you will always be an Austrian. That you may not be *too* French, Gluck will continue to give you music lessons. I flatter myself that the French cannot compete with us in music. Study well, and try to deserve the brilliant destiny in store for you."

She drew Antoinette close to her and kissed her fondly.

"I will obey your majesty in all things," whispered the child, and sadly she resumed her seat.

"Now, Caroline," continued the empress, a word with you. You see with what modesty and submission your sister has accepted her destiny. Follow her example, and prepare yourself to receive your affianced husband, Ferdinand of Naples."

It was Caroline, now, who turned pale and shuddered. She uttered a cry of horror, and raised her hands in abhorrence. "Never! Never, your majesty," cried she, "I cannot do it. You would not be so unnatural as to—"

"And why not?" asked the empress, coldly.

"Because God Himself has declared against our alliance with the King of Naples. He it is who interposed to save my sisters from this marriage. In mercy, my mother, do not sentence *me* also to death!"

The empress grew pale, and her lip quivered. But Maria Theresa was forever warring with her own emotions, so that nothing was gained for Caroline by this appeal to her maternal love.

"What!" exclaimed she, recovering her self-possession, "do *you* also seek to frighten me? I am not the cowardly simpleton for which you mistake me. As if the King of Naples were a vampire, to murder his wives at dead of night! No, Caroline, no! If it has pleased the Almighty to afflict me, by taking to Himself the two dear children who were to have been Queens of Naples, it is a sad coincidence—nothing more."

"But I cannot marry him!" cried Caroline, wringing her hands; "I should be forever seeing at his side the spectral figures of my dead sisters. Mother, dear mother, have pity on me!"

"Have pity on her!" echoed Antoinette, kneeling at the empress's feet.

"Enough!" exclaimed Maria Theresa, in a commanding voice. "I have spoken, it is for you to obey; for my word has been given, and I cannot retract. If, as your mother, I feel my heart grow weak with sympathy for *your* weakness, as your empress, I spurn its cowardly promptings; for my imperial word shall be held sacred, if it cost me my life. Rise, both of you. It ill becomes the Queens of France and Naples to bow their knees like beggars. Obedience is more praiseworthy than humiliation. Go to your apartments; pray for courage to bear your crosses, and God's blessing will shield you from all evil."

"I will pray God to give me grace to die in His favor," faltered Caroline.

"I will pray Him to take my life at once, rather than I should live to share the destiny of Louis XVI.!" whispered Antoinette, while the two imperial martyrs bowed low before their mother, and retired each to her room.

Maria Theresa looked after their sweet, childish figures, and when the door had closed upon them, she buried her face in the cushions of the sofa where they had been sitting together, and wept.

"My children! my children! Each a queen, and both in tears! Oh, Heavenly Father, grant that I may not have erred, in forcing this weight of royalty upon their tender heads. Mother of God, thou hast loved a child! By that holy love, pray for those who would faint if their crowns should be of thorns!"

EMPEROR OF AUSTRIA.

CHAPTER L.

THE DINNER AT THE FRENCH AMBASSADOR'S.

PRINCE KAUNITZ sat lazily reclining in his arm-chair, playing with his jewelled snuff-box and listening with an appearance of unconcern to a man who, in an attitude of profoundest respect, was relating to him a remarkable story of a young emperor and a beautiful peasant-girl, in which there was much talk of woods, diamonds, milk, and an Arabian steed.

The smile that was upon the face of the minister might either betoken amusement or incredulity.

The detective was at that period of his story where the emperor parted from old Conrad and his daughters. He now paused to see the effect of his narration.

"Very pretty, indeed," said the prince, nodding his head, "but romances are out of fashion. In these days we prefer truth."

"Does your highness suppose I am not speaking truth?" said the man.

Kaunitz took a pinch of snuff, and replied coldly, "I suppose nothing about it. Somebody, I know, has been playing upon your love of the marvellous. I know that you are not telling me the truth."

"Your highness!" exclaimed Eberhard, with the air of an injured man, "no one can impose upon my credulity, for I believe nothing but that which I see. I had this adventure from old Conrad himself, and I saw him receive a thousand ducats for the horse. In the joy of his foolish old heart, he told me the whole story; and as he saw the deep interest which I felt in the tale, he invited me to his house, where I saw the beautiful Marianne, with her diamond on her finger."

"Then you acted like a fool: for the emperor knows you as well as all Vienna does, and he will be furious when he discovers that we have been watching his pastoral amours."

"Indeed, your highness is right, I would be a poor fool to go there without great precaution; for, as you very justly remarked, I am well known in Vienna. But when I made the old peasant's acquaintance I was disguised, and I defy anybody to know me when I choose to play *incognito*. I wore a gray wig and a black patch over one eye. In this dress I visited them, and had the story all over again, with variations, from that coquettish village beauty, Kathi."

"How long ago?"

"Three weeks, your highness."

"How many times since then has the emperor visited his *inamorata?*"

"Six times, your highness. Old Conrad has bought a farm, where he lives in a handsome house, in which each of his daughters now has a room of her own. Marianne's room opens on the garden, where the emperor drinks his milk and enjoys the privilege of her society?"

"Have the girls any lovers?"

"Of course, your highness; but they have grown so proud that Kathi will have nothing to say to her sweetheart, Valentine; while Marianne, it is said, has never encouraged any of the young men in the village. Indeed, they are all afraid of her."

"Because they know that the emperor honors her with his presence?"

"No, your highness, the emperor has not allowed the family to whisper a word of his agency in their newly-gotten wealth. They give out that it is a legacy."

"Do the emperor and Marianne see one another in secret, without the curate and the father's knowledge?"

Eberhard shrugged his shoulders. "Day before yesterday, Marianne went alone to the woods to gather mushrooms, and never came home until dusk. She had been lost in the woods. It was the day on which the emperor was to visit the farm, but he did not come. Perhaps he got lost too. To-morrow, Marianne is to gather mushrooms again. I, too, shall go—to cut wood."

"Is that all?" asked Kaunitz.

"That is all, for to-day, your highness."

"Very well. Go home and invent a continuation of your story. Let no one know of it meanwhile except myself. You can boast of more than some poets and *literati* can say, for you have amused me, and I will reward you. Here are two gold ducats for you."

Eberhard bowed low as he received them, but when he had left the room, and was out of sight of Kaunitz, he turned toward the door muttering, "As if I were such a fool as to sell my precious secret to *you* for two paltry ducats! I know of others who will pay me for my news, and they shall have it."

Meanwhile Kaunitz, buried in his arm-chair, was revolving the story in his mind.

"An emperor, a widower of two wives," said he to himself, "and he treats us to an idyl of the genuine Gessner stamp! An imperial Damon who spends his time twining wreaths of roses with his Phillis! Well—he had better be left to play the fool in peace; his pastoral will keep him from meddling in state affairs. Men call me the coachman of European politics; so be it, and let no one meddle with my coach-box. That noble empress is of one mind with me, but this emperor would like to snatch the reins, and go careering over the heavens for himself. So much the better if he flirts and drinks milk with a dairy-maid. But how long will it last? Eberhard, of course, has gone to Porhammer, who being piously disinclined to such little pastimes, will go straight to the empress; and then Damon will be reproved, and I—I may fall under her displeasure for having known and concealed her son's intrigue. What shall I do? Shall I warn the emperor so that he can carry off his Semele, and go on with his amours? Or shall I—bah! Let things shape themselves. What do I care for them all? I am the coachman of Europe, and they are my passengers."

So saying, Kaunitz threw back his head, and, being alone, indulged himself in a chuckle. It was speedily smothered, however, for three taps at the door announced the approach of the minister's valet.

"The fool intends to remind me that it is time to dress," said he to himself. "There must be some important engagement on hand to make him so audacious. Come in, Hippolyte!—Any engagement for dinner?" asked he, as Hippolyte made his appearance.

"So please your highness, you dine to-day with the French ambassador."

"What o'clock is it?"

"Three o'clock, your highness."

"It is time. Tell the cook to send my dinner to the palace of the French ambassador. His excellency knows the terms on which I dine out of my own house?"

"I had the honor to explain them fully, your highness."

"And he acceded to them?"

"He did, your highness. Your highness, he said, was welcome to bring your dinner, if you preferred it to his. He had one request, however, to make, which was that you would not bring your post-dessert; a request which I did not understand."

"I understand it perfectly. The Count de Breteuil means that he would like me to leave my mouth-cleaning apparatus at home. Come, since it is time, let us begin to dress."

So saying, he rose, and presently he was walking to and fro in the powder-room, buried in his white mantle, while the servants waved their powder-brushes, and the air was dense with white clouds.

"Order the carriage," said the prince, when Hippolyte had presented the snuff-box and the handkerchief of cobweb cambric and lace. "Three footmen to stand behind my chair."

Hippolyte went to order the footmen to the hotel of the Count de Breteuil, while his master slowly made his way to the anteroom where six lackeys awaited him, each one bearing aloft a long silk cloak.

"What says the thermometer to-day?" asked he.

The lackey with the first cloak stepped to a window and examined the thermometer that was fastened outside.

"Sixty degrees, your highness—temperate," said the man.

"Cold! Four cloaks," said Kaunitz; and stepping through the row of servants, one after the other laid cloak upon cloak over his shoulders. When the fourth one had been wrapped around him, he ordered a fifth for his return, and putting his handkerchief to his mouth for fear he might swallow a breath of air, the coachman of Europe proceeded to his carriage, where Hippolyte was ready to help him in.

"Is my mouth-cleaning apparatus in the rumble?" asked the prince, as he sank back in the soft cushions.

"Your highness said that his excellency had requested—"

"Yes, but I did not say that I should heed his excellency's request. Quick, and bring it hither! Cups, brushes, essences, and every thing!"

Off started Hippolyte, and Kaunitz drew his four cloaks around his precious person while he muttered to himself, "I shall show my lord, Count de Breteuil, that the man who has the honor of receiving Kaunitz at his table, makes no conditions with such a guest.

The French ambassador grows arrogant, and I must teach him that the rules of etiquette and customs of society are for him and his compeers, but not for me. Whatever Kaunitz does is becoming and *en règle. Voilà tout.*—Forward!"

Meanwhile the Count de Breteuil was receiving his distinguished guests. After the topics of the day had been discussed, he informed them that he was glad to be able to promise that Prince Kaunitz would come to dinner *without* his abominable apparatus.

"Impossible!" exclaimed the ladies.

"Not at all," replied the count. "I have complied with one of his absurd conditions—he brings his dinner; but I made it my especial request that he would omit his usual post-dessert."

"And he agreed?"

"It would appear so, since he has accepted. It must be so, for see, he is here."

The count went forward to meet the prince, who deigned not the smallest apology for having kept the guests waiting a whole hour.

They repaired to the dining-room, where a costly and luxurious dinner made amends to the company for their protracted fast.

Kaunitz, however, took no notice of these delicate viands. He ate his own dinner, and was served by his own lackeys.

"Your highness," said his neighbor, the Princess Esterhazy, "you should taste this *pâté à la Soubise*, it is delicious."

"Who knows what abominable ingredients may not have gone into its composition?" said Kaunitz. "I might poison myself if I tasted the villanous compound. It is all very well for ordinary people to eat from other men's kitchens. If they die, the ranks close up and nobody misses them; but I owe my life to Austria and to Europe. Eat your *pâté à la Soubise*, if it suit you; *I* eat nothing but viands *à la Kaunitz*, and I trust to no cook but my own."

It was the same with the Tokay, the Johannisberg and the Champagne. Kaunitz affected not to see them, while one of his lackeys reached him a glass of water on a golden salver. Kaunitz held it up to the light. "How dare you bring me water from the count's fountain?" said he, with a threatening look.

"Indeed, your highness," stammered the frightened servant, "I drew it myself from your highness's own fountain."

"How," laughed the Princess Esterhazy, "you bring your water, too?"

"Yes, madame, I do, for it is the purest water in Vienna, and I have already told you that my health is of the first importance to Austria. Bread, Baptiste!"

Baptiste was behind the chair, with a golden plate, on which lay two or three slices of bread, which he presented.

"And bread, too, from his house," cried the princess, laughing immoderately.

"Yes, madame," replied Kaunitz, gravely, "I eat no bread but that of my own baker."

"Oh," replied the gay young princess. "I am not surprised at your taking such wondrous good care of yourself; what astonishes me is, that you should be allowed to enjoy such privileges in a house that is not your own. Why, Louis XIV. could not have been more exacting when he condescended to dine with a subject!"

Kaunitz raised his cold blue eyes so as to meet the look of the bold speaker. "Madame," said he, "Louis XIV. was Louis XIV., and I am Kaunitz."

So saying, he took a glass of water from *his* fountain, and ate a piece of bread from *his* baker. He then leaned back in his chair and took an animated part in the conversation.

This was only because thereby he knew that he would dazzle his hearers by speaking English, French, Italian, or Spanish, as occasion required.

The dinner was at an end and dessert came on the table. Of course Kaunitz refused to partake of it; but while the other guests were enjoying their confections, he took advantage of a pause in the conversation, to say to his pretty neighbor:

"Now, princess, that the company have enjoyed *their* dessert, I shall take the liberty of ordering *mine.*"

"Ah! you have your own dessert?" asked the princess, while the guests listened to hear what was coming.

"I have," said Kaunitz. "I have brought my dessert, of course. Hippolyte, my *étui.*"

Hippolyte brought the offensive *étui* and laid it on the dinner-table, while Baptiste approached with a glass of water. Kaunitz opened the case with quiet indifference and examined its contents. There were several small mirrors, various kinds of brushes, scissors, knives, a whet-stone, and a pile of little linen napkins.*

While Kaunitz examined and took out his disgusting little utensils the ladies looked at Count Breteuil, who could scarcely credit the evidence of his senses. But as Kaunitz set a looking-glass before him, raised his upper lip, and closed his teeth, preparatory to a cleaning, the count rose indignant from his seat.

"Ladies and gentlemen," said he, "we will return to the drawing-room for coffee; Prince Kaunitz desires *this* room to himself."

The company departed, leaving Kaunitz alone. He did not look as if he had heard or seen any thing. He went on grinning, brushing his teeth, drying them in and out with his napkins, and finished off with washing his hands and cleaning his nails. This done, he walked deliberately back to the drawing-room, and, going immediately toward the host, he said:

"Count, I am about to return home. You have taken very great pains to prepare a dinner for me, and I shall make you a princely return. From this day forward I dine no more from home; *your* dinner, therefore, will be immortal, for history will relate that the last time Prince Kaunitz dined away from his own palace, he dined at that of the French ambassador."

With this he bowed, and slowly left the room.

CHAPTER LI.

MARIANNE'S DISAPPEARANCE.

KAUNITZ remained true to his policy in the drama of "The Emperor and the Dairy-Maid." He allowed things to run their course. Twice a week, Eberhard came with additional information, to

* Swinburne, vol i., page 353.

which the minister listened with deep interest, but his interest never took the shape of action. What did *he* care?

"This imperial idyl is a disease," thought he. "It will have its crisis by and by, like a cutaneous eruption. Let it come. Why should I help the patient when I have not been called in?"

Not long after, however, he *was* called in. One morning he was lying in his dressing-gown on a divan, his head bound up in half a dozen silk handkerchiefs, and his whole person in the primeval disorder of a slovenly *négligé,* when his valet announced—the Emperor Joseph.

Kaunitz half rose, saying with a yawn, "Show his majesty to the state reception-room, and beg him to await me there."

"I have no time to wait, my dear prince," said a soft and melancholy voice behind him; and, as Kaunitz turned round, he saw the emperor who was already at his side.

The prince motioned to Hippolyte to leave the room. He went out on tiptoe, and, as he reached the threshold, the emperor himself closed the door and locked it. Kaunitz, who had risen, stood in the middle of the room, looking as indifferent to the visit of an emperor as to that of a tailor.

"Prince," said Joseph, returning and offering his hand, "we have not hitherto been good friends, but you see that I hold you in esteem, for I come to claim your assistance."

"I expected your majesty," replied Kaunitz.

The emperor cast his eyes over the velvet dressing-gown and the half dozen head handkerchiefs, and looked his astonishment. The prince understood the glance, and replied to it.

"I did not expect your majesty quite so soon. A few hours later I would have been ready to receive you. Will you permit me to retire for a few moments, that I may at least make my head, if not the rest of my person, presentable?"

The emperor took the hand of the prince and led him back to the divan. "My dear Kaunitz," said he, "when a man's head is in such a maze as mine to-day, he concerns himself very little about the looks of other men. Sit down again, and I will take this armchair by you."

He drew Kaunitz, with gentle force, upon the divan, and then seated himself at his side.

"Do you know what brings me to you?" said Joseph, blushing.

"I believe that I do, your majesty. It is no state affair, for on state affairs, unhappily, we are ever at variance."

The emperor laughed a sardonic laugh. "What need have I of a state councillor, I who am but a puppet in the hands of my mother, I who must stand, with shackled arms, and look on while she reigns? But it is in vain to murmur. I watch and wait; and while I wait, I find myself inclining fast to *your* policy. I believe you to be an honorable statesman, and I believe also that the course you have pursued, you have chose because you are convinced that it is wise."

"Your majesty means the French alliance," said Kaunitz. "You, like your deceased father, have always opposed it, and but for the firmness of and wisdom of the empress, it would have failed. But we need not discuss this matter to-day; I owe the honor conferred upon me to another question."

"Then you know why I am here?"

"I believe that I know," replied Kaunitz, playing with the silk tassels of his dressing-gown. "I have lately heard a tale about an emperor who was lost in a forest and rescued by a peasant-girl. The sovereign was grateful, as a matter of course, and the damsel forthwith melted away with love at the sight of him, as Semele did for Jupiter. That, too, may be very natural; but let me tell your majesty, it is dangerous, for the committee on morals do not approve of such pastorals, and the empress—"

"That accursed committee!" cried Joseph. "It is they who discovered it, and you who betrayed me."

Kaunitz slightly elevated his shoulders, and his eyes rested, unmoved, upon the emperor's glowing face. "I have never yet," said he, "descended to the office of an informer. Had your majesty addressed me on this subject some weeks ago, I should have said to you, 'You are dreaming a very pretty dream of innocence, moonshine, and childishness. If you do not wish to be roughly awakened, go and dream at a distance from Vienna; for here there are certainly some people who will think it their duty to disturb you!'"

"Why did you not warn me, Kaunitz?"

"I did not wish to have the appearance of forcing myself into your majesty's confidence. I had not been intrusted with your secret, and had no right to warn you."

"No, you warned the empress instead," said Joseph, bitterly.

"I warned nobody, your majesty. I said to myself, 'He is an enviable man to be able, in the midst of an artificial life, to enjoy the sweets of rural intercourse.' I foresaw what must inevitably happen; and pitied the innocent Eve, who will, ere long, be exiled from paradise."

"She *is* exiled!" cried the emperor. "She has been removed, I know not where. She has disappeared, and no trace of her can I find."

"Disappeared!" exclaimed Kaunitz, astonished. "Then I have not heard the whole truth. I did not even know that she was to be removed; I only suspected it."

"Tell me the truth!" cried the emperor, sharply.

"Sire," said Kaunitz, proudly, "there may be times when it is the part of wisdom to be silent; but it is never permitted to a man of honor to be untruthful. I know nothing of this girl's disappearance. The most that I anticipated was a forced marriage. This, I knew, would occasion new differences between the empress and your majesty, and I had supposed that you were coming to me to call for my mediation."

"I must believe you," sighed the emperor. "But prove your integrity by helping me to find her. Oh, Kaunitz, I beseech of you, help me, and earn thereby my gratitude and undying regard!"

"Have I waited so long for your majesty's regard, to earn it on account of a silly peasant?" said Kaunitz, with a bitter smile. "I hope that I shall have a niche in the temple of the world's esteem, even if I do fail in finding the daughter of Conrad the boor. If your majesty has never esteemed me before, you will not begin to do so to-day; and as regards your promised gratitude, the whole world knows, and your majesty also knows, that I am not to be bribed; but I am ready, from the depths of my own attachment to you, to do all that I can to help you."

"Kaunitz," said the emperor, offering him his hand, "you intend to force me to love you."

"If I ever did force your majesty to love me," replied Kaunitz, with animation, "I should count it the happiest day of my life. If I ever succeed in winning your confidence, then I may hope to complete the work I have begun—that of uniting your majesty's dominions into one great whole, before which all Europe shall bow in reverence."

"Let us speak of other things," interrupted the emperor. "Help me to find Marianne."

"Allow me one question, then—am I the only person to whom your majesty has spoken on this subject?"

"No, I have spoken to one other man. I have consulted the shrewdest detective in all Vienna, and have promised him a large reward if he will serve me. He came to me this morning. He had discovered nothing, but gave me to understand that it was you who had betrayed me to the empress."

"What is his name, your majesty?"

"Eberhard. He has sworn to unravel the mystery for me."

"Then it certainly will be unravelled, for he it is who has been tracking your majesty, and who has been the means of betraying you to the empress. I, too, have been giving him gold, with this difference, that your majesty trusted him, and I did not. He is at the bottom of the whole plot."

The emperor sprang from his seat, and hastened to the door. Kaunitz followed, and ventured to detain him.

"I must go," cried Joseph, impatiently. "I must force Eberhard to tell me what has been done with Marianne."

"You will not find him. He, too, has disappeared."

"Then I must go to the empress to beg her to be merciful to that poor child who is suffering on my account. I will exact it of her."

"That will only make the matter worse."

Joseph stamped his foot, and uttered a cry of fury.

"What must I do, then?" exclaimed he.

"Be silent and affect indifference. As soon as the empress believes that you have grown careless on the girl's account, she will begin to think that she has taken the matter too seriously to heart. Conrad must sell his farm, and remove far away from Vienna. Once settled, let *him* come and claim his daughter, and the empress will be very glad to be rid of her. Do this, and all will be right."

Joseph frowned, and seemed reluctant to follow this advice. Kaunitz saw his unwillingness, and continued:

"This is the only means of restoring the girl to peace of mind, and your majesty owes her this reparation. The poor thing has been rudely precipitated from the clouds; and as the comedy is over, the best thing we can do for her is to convince her that it *is* a comedy, and that the curtain has fallen. Your majesty, however, must not again lay your imperial hand upon the simple web of her destiny: leave it to your inferiors to gather up its broken threads. Go away from Vienna; travel, and seek recreation. Leave Marianne to me, and I swear to you that I will rescue and befriend her. When you have gone, I shall go to the empress and relate the whole story. I shall tell all the truth; Maria Theresa has a noble, generous heart; and she will not do any injury to the one who was instrumental in saving the life of her darling son. She will do any thing for her happiness, provided it do not compromise the honor of her imperial house. And she is right. But you must go, and once gone, Marianne shall be free."

"Free not only from others, but from me also," said the emperor, deeply affected. "I feel I have erred toward this innocent young girl. I have deeply sinned; for, regardless of her peace of mind, I have allowed myself to dream of a love that could bring naught but misery to both. For I will not conceal from you, my friend, how much it costs me to renounce this sweet creature, and to promise that I will see her no more. My intercourse with her was the last dying sigh of a love which has gone from my heart forevermore. But—it must be sacrificed. Rescue her, and try to make her happy, Kaunitz; try to efface from her heart the memory of my blasting love."

"I promise to free her, but I cannot promise to rescue her from the memory of your majesty's love. Who knows that from the ring which she has sworn to wear forever, she may not have inhaled a poison that will shorten her young life? To rescue her from such a fate lies not in the power of man. Time—the great comforter—may heal her wounds, but your majesty must promise never to ask whither she has gone. For you she must be dead."

"I promise, on my imperial honor, never to see her again," said Joseph, in a faltering voice. "I will leave to-morrow. Thank God, the world is wide; and, far away from Vienna, I, too, can seek for oblivion, and, perchance, for another ray of earthly happiness."

And so ended the pastoral of the emperor and the village maid.

CHAPTER LII.

COUNT FALKENSTEIN.

"AWAY with care and sorrow! Away with royalty and state!" cried the emperor, as the long train of wagons, which had accompanied him from Vienna, were disappearing in the distance.

The empress had caused preparation for her son's journey to be made with imperial pomp. A brilliant *cortége* of nobles and gentleman had followed the emperor's *calèche*, and behind them came twleve wagons with beds, cooking utensils, and provisions—the whole gotten up with true princely magnificence.

The emperor had said nothing, and had left Vienna amid the chiming of bells and the loud greetings of the people. For two days he submitted to the tedious pageants of public receptions, stupid addresses, girls in white, and flower-decked arches; but on the morning of the third day, two couriers announced not only to the discomfited gentlemen composing his *suite*, but to the conductors of the provision-train, that the emperor would excuse them from further attendance.

Everybody was astonished, and everybody was disappointed. The emperor, meanwhile, stood by laughing, until the last wagon was out of sight.

"Away with sorrow and care!" cried he, approaching his two carriage companions, Counts Rosenberg and Coronini. "Now, my friends," exclaimed he, putting a hand upon the shoulder of each one, "now the world is ours! Let us enjoy our rich inheritance! But—bless me, how forlorn you both look! What is the matter?

have I been mistaken in supposing you would relish my plan of travel?"

"No, your majesty," replied Rosenberg, with a forced smile, "but I am afraid you will scarcely relish it yourself. You have parted with every convenience that makes travelling endurable."

"Your majesty will have to put up with many a sorry dinner and many an uncomfortable bed," sighed Coronini.

"I am tired of comforts and conveniences," rejoined the emperor, laughing, "and I long for the variety of privation. But, in my thoughtlessness, I had taken it for granted that you, too, were weary of grandeur, and would like to get a taste of ordinary life. If I am mistaken, you are free to return with my discharged *cortége;* I force no one to share my hardships. Speak quickly, for there is yet time for me to select other fellow-travellers."

"No, no, your majesty," said Rosenberg gayly, "I will go whither you go, and share your privations!"

"Here I stay, to live and die at your majesty's side!" cried Coronini, with comic fervor.

The emperor nodded. "Thank you both, my friends; I had counted upon you, and would have regretted your refusal to go with me. Thank Heaven, we are no longer under the necessity of parading our rank about the world! I cannot express to you the joy I feel at the prospect of going about unnoticed, like any other man."

"That joy will be denied your majesty," said Rosenberg, with a slight inclination. "The Emperor Joseph can never go unnoticed, like ordinary men."

"Do not hope it, your majesty!" cried Coronini. "Your majesty's rank is stamped upon your brow, and you cannot hide it."

The emperor looked down on the sandy hillock on which they stood, then upward at the bright-blue sky above their heads.

"Are we then under the gilded dome of my mother's palace," said he, after a pause, "that I should still hear the language of courtly falsehood? Awake, my friends, for this is not Austria's imperial capital! It is the world which God created, and here upon our mother earth we stand as man to man. A little shining beetle is creeping on my boot as familiarly as it would on the *sabot* of a base-born laborer. If my divine right were written upon my brow, would not the insects acknowledge my sovereignty, as in Eden they acknowledged that of Adam? But no!—The little creature spreads its golden wings and leaves me without a sign. Happy beetle! Would that I too had wings, that I might flee away and be at rest!"

The emperor heaved a sigh, and his thoughts evidently wandered far away from the scene before him. But presently recalling himself, he spoke again. Pointing to the sky, he said:

"And now, friends, look above you where the heavens enthrone a Jehovah, in whose sight all men are equal; and so long as we dwell together under the open sky, remember him who has said, 'Thou shalt have no other gods before me!'"

"But, your majesty—"

"Majesty! Where is any majesty here? If I were a lion, to shake the forests with my roar, I might pretend to majesty among the brutes; but you see that I am, in all things, like yourself—neither nobler nor greater than you. In Vienna I am your sovereign: so be it; but while we travel, I am simply Count Falkenstein. I beg you to respect this name and title, for the Falkensteins are an older race of nobles than the Hapsburgs, and the turreted castle of my ancestors, the counts, is one of the oldest in Germany. Away, then, with royalty! I ask for admittance into your own rank. Will you accept me, and promise that we shall be on terms of equality?"

He offered a hand to each of his friends, and would not permit them to do otherwise than press it, in token of assent.

"Now let me tell you my plans. We travel like three happy fellows, bent upon recreation alone. We go and stay as it best suits us; when we are hungry, we will dine; when we are tired, we will sleep. A little straw will make our beds, and our cloaks shall keep us warm.* In Florence I shall be forced to play the emperor, as the reigning duke is my brother; but he, too, will join us, and then we shall all go on travelling *incognito.* First we visit Rome, then Naples. We must find out whether our sister Caroline has taught her lazzaroni-king to read and write; and when we shall have learned something of her domestic life, we will turn our faces homeward. In Milan I must again play the emperor, for Lombardy needs my protection, and I must give it. From Lombardy I return to Vienna. Does the route please you?"

"Exceedingly, count," replied Rosenberg.

"It does, indeed, your highness," added Coronini.

"And why, my highness?" asked Joseph, laughing.

"Because the Counts of Falkenstein were princes, and the title being appropriate, I hope your majesty will allow me to use it."

"I regret very much, most worthy master-of-ceremonies-itinerant, that I cannot do so. Pack up your court-manners, Coronini, and carry them in your trunk until we get back to Vienna."

"So be it, then," sighed Coronini, "since your m——, I mean my lord count, will have it so, we must be content to have you hidden under a cloud, like Jupiter, when he made acquaintance with Io."

"By Jupiter, Coronini, you are ambitious in your similes," replied the emperor, laughing. "You look very much like Io, do you not?"

"I hope we may be as lucky as the gods," interrupted Rosenberg, "for every time they visited the earth they were sure to fall in with all the pretty women."

"True; but mythology teaches that the women who aspired to love gods, forfeited both happiness and life," replied the emperor, with a touch of sadness in his voice. "But pshaw!" continued he, suddenly, "what do I say? Away with retrospection! Let us come out of the clouds, and approach, both of you, while I intrust you with a great secret—I am hungry."

The two counts started in breathless haste for the carriage, near which the emperor's valet and the postilion were in earnest conversation; but they returned with very long faces.

"Count," said Rosenberg, sadly, "we have nothing to eat."

"The valet says that Count Falkentstein ordered every thing to be sent back to Vienna except our trunks," sighed Coronini. "All the wine, bread, game, and delicacies remained in the wagons."

"Very well," cried the emperor, laughing heartily at the *contretemps*, "let us go and ask for dinner in yonder village behind the wood."

*The emperor, during his tour as Count Falkenstein, repeatedly slept on straw, over which a leathern cover was spread. Hubner, i, p. 43.

"The postilion says that there is not a public house anywhere about," continued Coronini, in great distress. "He says that we will find nothing to eat in the village."

Instead of making a reply, the emperor walked to the hillock, and questioned the postilion himself.

"What is the name of the village beyond the forest?" asked he.

"Wichern, your majesty."

"Do we change horses there?"

"No, your majesty, we harness up at Unterbergen."

"Can we get any breakfast at Wichern, think you?"

"No, no, your majesty, not a morsel of any thing—none but peasants live in the village."

"Well, my friend, do the peasants live without eating?"

"Oh, your majesty, *they* eat any thing! They live on bread, bacon, eggs, and milk, with sometimes a mess of cabbage or beans."

"And you call that having nothing to eat?" exclaimed Joseph, hastening joyfully back to his friends. "Come, come; we shall find dinner at Wichern, and if nobody will cook for us, we will cook for ourselves."

Coronini opened his eyes like full moons.

"Why do you stare so, Coronini? Are not all soldiers cooks? I, at least, am resolved to learn, and I feel beforehand that I shall do honor to myself. Cook and butler, I shall fill both offices. Come, we are going to enjoy ourselves. Thomas, tell the postilion to drive as far as the entrance of the village. We will forage on foot."

The emperor bounded into the carriage, the two noblemen followed, the postilion cracked his whip, and they were soon at Wichern.

CHAPTER LIII.

WHAT THEY FOUND AT WICHERN.

THE carriage stopped, and before the valet had had time to open the door, the emperor leaped to the ground.

"Come," said he, merrily, "come and seek your fortunes. Thomas, you remain with the carriage. Drive under the shade of that tree and wait for our return. Before all things, I forbid you to tell anybody who we are. From this day forward, my name is Count Falkenstein. Mark me! I expect you to preserve my *incognito.*"

"I will obey you, my lord count," said the valet, with a bow.

The emperor with his two companions walked toward the village. Nothing very hopeful was to be seen as they looked up the dirty little streets. The wretched mud cottages stood each one apart, their yards separated by scraggy willow-hedges, upon which ragged old garments were hanging in the sun to dry. Between the hedges were muddy pools, over which the ducks were wrangling for the bits of weed that floated on the surface of the foul waters. On their borders, in the very midst of the rubbish and kitchen-offal that lay about in heaps, dirty, half-naked children, with straw-colored hair, tumbled over one another, or paddled in the water. In the farm-yards around the dung-heaps, the youngest children of the cottagers kept company with the sow and her grunting pigs.

Before the slovenly entrances of the huts here and there sat dirty, unseemly old men and women, who stared at the three strangers as they surveyed the uninviting picture before them.

"I congratulate the emperor that he is not obliged to look upon this shocking scene," said Joseph. "I am glad that his people cannot cry out to him for help, since help for such squalor as this there is none on earth."

"They are not as wretched as you suppose," said Rosenberg. "These people are scarcely above the brute creation; and they know of nothing better than the existence which is so shocking to you. They were born and bred in squalor, and provided their pastures yield forage, their hens lay eggs and their cows give milk, they live and die contented."

"If so, they are an enviable set of mortals," replied Joseph, laughing, "and we, who require so much for our comfort, are poorer than they. But as there is no help for our poverty, let us think of dinner. Here are three streets; the village seems to have been divided for our especial accommodation. Each one shall take a street, and in one hour from now we meet at the carriage, each man with a dish of contribution. *En avant!* I take the street before me; you do the same. Look at your watches, and be punctual."

So saying, he waved his hand and hastened forward. The same solitude and misery met his view as he walked on; the same ducks, hens, sows, and tumbling children; with now and then the shrill treble of a scolding woman, or the melancholy lowing of a sick cow.

"I am curious now," thought the emperor, "to know how and where I am to find my dinner. But stay—here is a cottage less slovenly than its neighbors; I shall tempt my fortunes there."

He opened the wicker gate and entered the yard. The lazy sow that lay on the dunghill grunted, but took no further notice of the imperial intruder. He stopped before the low cottage door and knocked, but no one came. The place seemed silent and deserted; not the faintest hum of life was to be heard from within.

"I shall take the liberty of going in without awaiting an invitation," said the emperor, pushing open the door and entering the cottage. But he started at the unexpected sight that met his view as he looked around the room. It was a miserable place, cold and bare; not a chair or any other article of household furniture was to be seen; but in the centre of the room stood a small deal coffin, and in the coffin was the corpse of a child. Still and cold, beautiful and tranquil, lay the babe, a smile still lingering around its mouth, while its half-open eyes seemed fixed upon the white roses that were clasped in its little dimpled hands. The coffin lay in the midst of flowers, and within slept the dead child, transfigured and glorified.

The emperor advanced softly and bent over it. He looked with tender sympathy at the little marble image which yesterday was a poor, ragged peasant, to-day was a bright and winged angel. His thoughts flew back to the imperial palace, where his little motherless daughter was fading away from earth, and the father prayed for his only child. He took from the passive hands a rose, and softly as he came, he left the solitary cottage, wherein an angel was keeping watch.

He passed over to the neighboring yard. Here, too, everything seemed to be at rest; but a savory odor saluted the nostrils of the noble adventurer which at least betokened the presence of beings who hungered and thirsted, and had some regard for the creature comforts of life.

"Ah!" said the emperor, drawing in the fragrant smell, "that savors of meat and greens," and he hurried through the house to the kitchen. Sure enough, there blazed a roaring fire, and from the chimney-crane hung the steaming pot whence issued the delightful aroma of budding dinner. On the hearth stood a young woman of cleanly appearance, who was stirring the contents of the pot with a great wooden spoon.

"Good-morning, madame," said the emperor, in a loud, cheerful voice. The woman started, gave a scream, and turned her glowing face to the door.

"What do you mean by coming into strange people's houses and frightening them so?" cried she, angrily. "Nobody asked you in, I am sure."

"Pardon me, madame," said the emperor. "I was urgently invited."

"I should like to know who invited you, for nobody is here but myself, and *I* don't want you."

"Yes, madame; but your steaming kettle, I do assure you, has given me a pressing invitation to dine here."

"Oh! you are witty, are you? Well, carry your wits elsewhere; they won't serve you here. My kettle calls nobody but those who are to eat of my dinner."

"That is the very thing I want, madame. I want to eat of your dinner." As he spoke, the emperor kept advancing until he came close upon the kettle and its tempting contents; but the peasant-woman pushed him rudely back, and thrusting her broad person between himself and the coveted pot, she looked defiance at him, and broke out into a torrent of abuse.

The emperor laughed aloud. "I don't wish to rob you," said he. "I will pay you handsomely if you will only let me have your dinner. What have you in that pot?"

"That is none of your business. With my bacon and beans you have no concern."

"Bacon and beans! Oh, my craving stomach! Here, take this piece of gold and give me some directly."

"Do you take me for a fool, to sell my dinner just as the men will be coming from the field?"

"By no means for a fool," said the emperor, soothingly; "but if you show the men that golden ducat they will wait patiently until you cook them another dinner. Your husband can buy himself a fine holiday suit with this."

"He has one, and don't want two. Go your way; you shall not have a morsel of my dinner."

"Not if I give you *two* gold pieces? Come, do be accommodating, and give me the bacon and beans."

"I tell you you shall not have them," screamed the termagant. "I have no use for your gold, but I want my dinner. So be off with you! you will get nothing from me if you beg all day long."

"Very well, madame; I bid you good-morning," said Joseph, laughing, but inwardly chagrined at his *fiasco*. "I must go on, however," thought he; and he entered the yard of the next house. Before the door sat a pale young woman, with a new-born infant in her arms. She looked up with a languid smile.

"I am hungry," said Joseph, after greeting her with uncovered head. "Have you any thing good in your kitchen?"

She shook her head sadly. "I am a poor, weak creature, sir, and cannot get a meal for my husband," replied she; "he will have to cook his own dinner when he comes home."

"And what will he cook to-day, for instance?"

"I suppose he will make an omelet; for the hens have been cackling a great deal this morning, and an omelet is made in a few minutes."

"Is it? So much the better, then; you can show me how to make one, and I will pay you well."

"Go in the hen-coop, sir, and see if you find any eggs. My husband will want three of them; the rest are at your service."

"Where is the hen-coop?" asked Joseph, much pleased.

"Go through the kitchen out into the yard, and you will see a little room with a wooden bolt; that is the hen-coop."

"I go," cried Joseph merrily. Presently great commotion was heard among the hens, and the emperor returned with a glowing face, his hair and coat well sprinkled with straw. He came forward with both hands full of eggs.

"Here are eight," said he. "Three for your husband, and five for me. Now tell me how I must cook them."

"You will have to go to the kitchen, sir. There you will find a flitch of bacon. Cut off some slices, put them in a pan you will see there, and set it on the fire. My neighbor has just now made some for poor John. Then look on the dresser and take some milk and a little flour. Make a batter of them with the eggs, pour it upon your bacon, and when the eggs are done, the omelet is made. It is the easiest thing in the world."

"My dear good woman, it will be a desperately hard task for me," said the emperor with a sigh. "I'm afraid I shall make a very poor omelet. Won't you come into the kitchen and make it for me? Do, I will pay you well."

"Dear gentleman," said the young woman, blushing, "do you think I am so idle as to sit here, if I could get up and help you? I was brought to bed yesterday of this baby; and I am such a poor, sickly thing that I shall not be able to get up before two days. As the day was bright, dear John brought me and the baby out here, because it was more cheerful on the door-sill than within. I am a weak, useless creature, sir."

"Weak! useless!" cried the emperor, astounded; "and you expect to be up in three days after your confinement? Poor little thing! Have you no physician and no medicine?"

"The Lord is my physician, sir," said the simple creature, "and my medicine is the fresh air. But let me think of your omelet. If you cannot make it yourself, just step to the cottage on the left, and call my neighbor. She is very good to me, and she will make your omelet for you with pleasure."

"A thousand thanks," said the emperor, hastening to follow the directions. He returned in a few moments with a good-humored, healthy young woman, who went cheerfully to work, and the omelet was soon made.

One hour after he had parted from his friends, the emperor was seen coming along the street with a platter in his hand and a little bucket on his arm. He walked carefully, his eyes fixed upon his precious dish, all anxiety lest it should fall from his hands.

Thomas was thunderstruck. An emperor carrying an earthen platter in his hand! He darted forward to receive it, but Joseph motioned him away.

"Don't touch me, Thomas," said he, "or I shall let it fall. I intend to place it with my own hands. Go, now, and set the table. Pile up some of those flat stones, and bring the carriage cushions. We will dine under that wide-spreading oak. Make haste, I am very hungry."

Off went Thomas, obedient, though bewildered; and he had soon improvised a table, over which he laid a shining damask cloth. Luckily, the emperor's camp-chest had not been put in the baggage-wagon, or his majesty would have had to eat with his fingers. But the golden service was soon forthcoming, with goblets of sparkling crystal, and three bottles of fine old Hungarian wine.

"Now," said Joseph triumphantly, "let me place my dishes." With these words he put on his platter and basket, with great ceremony and undisguised satisfaction.

A curious medley of wealth and poverty were these golden plates and forks, with the coarse red platter, that contained the hard-earned omelet. But the omelet was smoking and savory, and the strawberries were splendid.

While the emperor was enjoying the result of his foraging expedition, Rosenberg and Coronini were seen approaching, each with his earthen platter in his hand.

"The hour is up and we are here," said Coronini. "I have the honor of laying my dish at your m—— feet, count."

"Potatoes! beautiful roasted potatoes!" cried Joseph. "Why, count, you have brought us a treat."

"I rejoice to hear it, my lord count; for I was threatened with a broomstick when I tore it from the hands of the woman, who vowed I should not have a single potato. I dashed two ducats at her feet and made off with all speed; for the hour was almost up, and I had exhausted all my manners in the ten houses, which I had visited in vain, before my successful raid upon hers."

"And will not my lord count cast an eye upon my dish?" asked Rosenberg.

"He has obtained that for which I sued in vain!" cried Joseph. "He has actually brought bacon and beans."

"But I did not sue; I stormed and threatened. Neither did I waste my gold to obtain my end. I threw the woman a silver thaler and plenty of abuse in the bargain."

"Let us be seated!" said the emperor, "and pray admire my omelet and my strawberries. Now, Coronini, the strawberries are tempting, but before you taste them, I must tell you that they are tainted with treason: treason toward my own sacred person. Reflect well before you decide to eat them. What I am going to relate is as terrible as it is true. While my omelet was cooking, I strolled out into the road to see if there was any thing else in Wichern besides poultry, pigs, and dirty children. Coming toward me I perceived a pretty little barefoot boy, with a basket full of red, luscious strawberries. I asked where he was going. He said to the neighboring village to sell his strawberries to the farmer's wife, who had ordered them. I offered to buy them, but my gold could not tempt the child—he refused peremptorily to sell them to me at any price. I argued, pleaded, threatened; all to no purpose. At length, seeing there was no other alternative, I snatched his strawberries away, threw him a ducat, and walked off with the prize. He picked up the gold, but as he did so, he saluted my imperial ears with an epithet—such an epithet! Oh, you will shudder when you hear what language the little rascal used to his sovereign! You never will be able to bear it, Coronini: you, whose loyalty is offended every time you address me as Count Falkenstein. I only wonder that the sun did not hide its head, and the earth tremble at the sacrilege! What do you suppose he called me?—An ass! He did, I assure you. That little bare-legged boy called his emperor an ass! Now, Coronini, do you think you can taste of the strawberries that were gathered by those treacherous little hands?"

"If my lord count allows it, I will venture to eat," replied Coronini, "for I really think there was no treason committed."

"Why! not when he called me an—"

"Pray do not say it again," entreated Coronini, raising his hands deprecatingly; "it cuts me to the heart. But Count Falkenstein had already proclaimed that no majesty was by, and when no majesty was there, no majesty could be insulted."

"Oh, you sophist! Did you not say that I wore my title upon my brow? Did you not tell me that I could not hide my majesty from the sons of men? But I forgive you, and the boy also. Let us drink his health while we enjoy his strawberries. Fill your glasses to the brim, and having done honor to those who furnished our repast, allow me to propose—ourselves: To the health of those who are about to eat a dinner which they have earned by the sweat of their brow."

So saying, the emperor touched the glasses of his friends.

"Now, postilion," cried he, before they drank, "blow us a blast on your horn—a right merry blast!"

The postilion put the horn to his lips, and while he blew the glasses clinked gayly: and the friends laughed, jested, and ate their dinner with a relish they had seldom known before.*

CHAPTER LIV.

THE SOMNAMBULIST.

THE policy instituted by Kaunitz, when he became sole minister of the empress, had now culminated in the alliance of Austria with France, through the solemn betrothal of the childish Marie Antoinette with the dauphin. The union was complete—it was to be cemented by the strong tie of intermarriage; and now, that success had crowned the schemes to which she had yielded such hearty consent, Maria Theresa was anxious, restless, and unhappy. Vainly she strove to thrust from her memory the prophecy which had been foretold in relation to the destinies of France. With anguish she remembered the cry of Marie Antoinette; with horror she recurred to the vision which had overcome Catherine de Medicis.

"It is sinful in me," thought the empress, as one morning she left her pillow from inability to sleep. "God alone is Lord of

* Hubner, "Life of Joseph II.," vol. i., page 49.

futurity, and no human hand dare lift its black curtain! But stay," cried she, suddenly springing up, and in her eager haste beginning to dress without assistance. "There is in Vienna a holy nun, who is said to be a prophetess, and Father Gassner, to whom I have extended protection, he, too, is said at times to enjoy the privilege of God's prophets of old. Perhaps they have been sent in mercy to warn us, lest, in our ignorance of consequences, we stumble and sin."

For some time the empress walked up and down her room, undecided whether to turn the sibylline leaves or not. It might be sinful to question, it might be fatal to remain ignorant. Was it, or was it not the will of God, that she should pry into the great mystery of futurity? Surely it could not be sinful, else why should He have given to His servants the gift of prophecy?

"I will go to the Ursuline nun," concluded she, "and Father Gassner shall come to me."

She rang, and ordered a carriage, with no attendant but her first lady of honor. "No footman, no outriders, but a simple court equipage; and inform Father Gassner that in one hour I shall await him in the palace."

In less than half an hour the carriage of the empress was at the gate of the Ursuline Convent. Completely disguised in a long black cloak, with her face hidden under a thick veil, Maria Theresa leaped eagerly to the ground.

Her attendant was about to follow, but the empress motioned her to remain. "Await me here," said she, "I do not wish to be known in the convent. I am about to imitate my son, and visit my subjects *incognito*."

The porteress, who had recognized the imperial liveries, made no opposition to the entrance of the tall, veiled figure. She supposed her to be some lady of the empress's household, and allowed her to pass at once into the hall, following her steps with undisguised curiosity.

She had already ascended the staircase, when she turned to the porteress.

"In which cell is the invalid nun?" asked she.

"Your highness means Sister Margaret, the somnambulist?" asked the porteress. "She has been taken to the parlor of the abbess, for the convenience of the many who visit her now."

"Does she pretend to reveal the future?"

"It would make your highness's hair stand on end to hear her! She has been asleep this morning, and do you know what she said in her sleep. She prophesied that the convent would be honored by a visit from the empress on this very day."

"Did she, indeed?" faltered Maria Theresa. "When? How long ago?"

"About two hours ago, your highness. And as she is never mistaken, the abbess has prepared all things for her majesty's reception. Doubtless your ladyship has been sent to announce her?"

"You really feel sure that she will come?"

"Certainly. Sister Margaret's visions are prophetic—we cannot doubt them."

The empress shuddered, and drew her cloak close around her. "Gracious Heaven!" thought she, "what if she should prophesy evil for my child?—It is well," added she, aloud; "where shall I find her?"

"Your highness has only to turn to the left; the last door leads into the parlor of the abbess."

A deep silence reigned throughout the convent. The empress went on through the dim, long corridor, now with hurried step and wildly-beating heart, now suddenly pausing, faint and irresolute, to lean against a pillar, and gather courage for the interview. As she turned the corner of the corridor, a flood of light, streaming through an oriel window, revived and cheered her. She stepped forward and looked. The window opened upon the chapel, where the lights were burning upon the altar, and high mass was about to begin; for Sister Margaret had said that the empress was very near.

"It is true. They are waiting for me. Oh, she must be a prophetess, for, two hours ago, I had not dreamed of coming hither! I feel my courage fail me. I will go back. I dare not hear, for it is too late."

The empress turned and retraced her steps; then once more calling up all her fortitude, she returned. "For," thought she, "if God permits me to see, why should I remain blind? He it is who has sent me to this holy prophetess. I *must* listen for my Antoinette's sake."

A second time she went forward, reached the parlor, and opened the door. She had scarcely appeared on the threshold, cloaked and screened by her thick black veil, when a clear voice, whose tones were preterhuman in their melody, addressed her. "Hail, Empress of Austria! All hail to her who cometh hither!"

"She is indeed a prophetess!" murmured the empress. "She knows me through my disguise."

She approached the bed and bent over it. The nun lay with closed eyes; but a heavenly smile was upon her lips, and a holy light seemed to play around her pale but beautiful face. Not the least tinge of color was on her cheeks; and but for the tint of carmine upon her lips—so unearthly, so seraphic was her beauty—that she might have been mistaken for a sculptor's dream of Azrael, the pale angel of death.

While the empress gazed awe-stricken, the abbess and the nuns, who had been kneeling around the bed, arose to greet their sovereign.

"Is it indeed our gracious empress?" asked the abbess.

Maria Theresa withdrew her hat and veil, and revealed her pale, agitated face.

"I am the empress," said she, "but I implore you let there be no ceremony because of my visit. In this sacred habitation, God alone is great, and His creatures are all equal before Him. We are in the presence of the servant to whom He has condescended to speak, while to the sovereigns of earth He is silent. To Him alone belongs homage."

"Gracious empress, Sister Margaret had announced your majesty's visit, and we were to have greeted you as becomes Christian subjects. The chapel is prepared, the altar is decked."

"I will repair later to the church, mother. At present, my visit is to Sister Margaret."

"If so, your majesty must not delay. She sleeps but three hours at a time, and she will soon awake. She has the gift of prophecy in her sleep only."

"Then go, holy mother, and leave me alone with her. Go and await me in the church."

The abbess glanced at the clock on the wall. "She will awake in ten minutes," said she, and with noiseless steps the nuns all left the room.

The empress waited until the door was closed and the sound of their light footfall had died away; then again approaching the bed, she called, "Sister Margaret."

The nun trembled, and her brow grew troubled. "Oh," said she, "the angels have flown! Why have you come with your sad notes of sorrow to silence the harmony of my heavenly dreams?"

"You know then that I am sad?" asked the empress.

"Yes, your heart is open to me. I see your anguish. The mother comes to me, not the empress."

Maria Theresa feeling herself in the presence of a supernatural being, glided down upon her knees. "You are right," said she, "it is indeed a sorrowing mother who kneels before you, imploring you, in the humility of my heart, to say what God hath revealed of her daughter s fate!"

"Oh!" cried the nun, in a voice of anguish.

But the empress went on. "My soul trembles for Marie Antoinette. Something seems to warn me not to trust my child to the foul atmosphere of that court of France, where Du Barry sits by the side of the king, and the nobles pay her homage as though she were a virtuous queen. Oh! tell me, holy sister, what will become of my Antoinette in France?"

"Oh! oh!" wailed the nun, and she writhed upon her bed.

"She is so sweet, so pure, so innocent!" continued the empress. "My spotless dove! Will she soil her wings? Oh, sister, speak to me!"

"Oh!" cried the nun, for the third time, and the empress trembled, while her face grew white as that of the prophetess.

"I am on my knees," murmured she, "and I await your answer. Sister Margaret! Sister Margaret! in the name of God, who has endowed you with superhuman wisdom, tell me what is to be the fate of Marie Antoinette?"

"Thou hast called on the name of God," said the nun, in a strange, clear voice, "and I am forced to answer thee. Thou wouldst know the fate of Marie Antoinette? Hear it: *She will live through much evil, but will return to virtue.*"*

"She will then cease to be virtuous," cried the empress, bursting into tears.

"She will learn much evil," repeated the nun, turning uneasily on her bed. "She will endure—poor Marie Antoinette! Unhappy Queen of France! Woe! woe!"

"Woe unto me!" cried the wretched mother. "Woe unto her who leadeth her children into temptation!"

"She will return to virtue!" murmured the nun, indistinctly. "Poor Queen—of—France!"

With a loud cry she threw out her arms, and sat upright in the bed. Her eyes opened, and she looked around the room.

"Where is the reverend mother?" cried she. "Where are the sisters?"

Suddenly her eyes rested upon the black and veiled figure of the empress.

"Who are you?" exclaimed she. "Away with you, black

* Swinburne, vol. i., p. 351.

shadow! I am not yet dead! Not yet! Oh, this pain! this pain!" and the nun fell back upon her pillow.

Maria Theresa rose from her knees, and, wild with terror, fled from the room. Away she sped through the long, dark corridor to the window that overlooked the chapel, where the nuns were awaiting her return—away down the wide stone staircase, through the hall, out into the open air. She hurried into the carriage, and, once seated, fell back upon the cushions and wept aloud.

CHAPTER LV.

THE PROPHECY.

THE empress spoke not a word during the drive to the palace. She was so absorbed in her sorrow as to be unconscious of the presence of another person, and she wept without restraint until the carriage stopped. Then, stifling her sobs and hastily drying her tears, she dropped her veil and walked with her usual majestic gait through the palace halls. In her anteroom she met a gentleman in waiting coming toward her.

"Father Gassner, your majesty."

"Where is he?"

"Here, so please your majesty."

"Let him follow me into my cabinet," said the empress, going forward, while the courtier and the priest came behind. When she reached the door of her cabinet she turned. "Wait here," said she. "When I ring, I beg of you to enter, father. The count will await your return in this room."

She entered her cabinet and closed the door. Once more alone, she gave vent to her sorrow. She wept aloud, and in her ears she seemed to hear the clear, metallic voice of the sick nun pealing out those dreadful words: "*She will live through much evil, but will return to virtue.*"

But Maria Theresa was no coward. She was determined to master her credulity.

"I am a simpleton," thought she. "I must forget the dreams of a delirious nun. How could I be so weak as to imagine that God would permit an hysterical invalid to prophesy to a sound and strong woman like myself? I will speak with Father Gassner. Perhaps he may see the future differently. If he does, I shall know that they are both false prophets, and their prophecies I shall throw to the winds."

Strengthened by these reflections, the empress touched her bell. The door opened, and Father Gassner entered the room. He bowed, and then drawing his tall, majestic figure to its full height, he remained standing by the door, with his large, dark-blue eyes fixed upon the face of the empress. She returned the glance. There seemed to be a strife between the eyes of the sovereign, who was accustomed to see others bend before her, and those of the inspired man, whose intercourse was with the Lord of lords and the King of kings. Each met the other with dignity and composure.

Suddenly the empress strode haughtily up to the priest and said, in a tone that sounded almost defiant:

"Father Gassner, have you the courage to look me in the face and assert yourself to be a prophet?"

"It requires no courage to avow a gift, which God, in the superabundance of His goodness, has bestowed upon one who does not deserve it," replied the father, gently. "If my eyes are opened to see, or my hand to heal, glory be to God who has blessed them! The light, the grace are not mine, why should I deny my Lord?" *

"Then, if I question you as to the future, you will answer?"

"If it is given to me to do so, I will answer."

"Tell me, then, whether Antoinette will be happy in her marriage?"

The priest turned pale, but he said nothing.

"Speak, speak; or I will denounce you as a false prophet!"

"Is this the only thing your majesty has to ask of me?"

"The only one."

"Then denounce me—for I cannot answer your majesty."

Gassner turned, and his hand was upon the lock of the door.

"Stay!" cried the empress, haughtily. "I command you, as your sovereign, to speak the truth."

"The truth?" cried Gassner, in a voice of anguish, and his large eyes opened with an expression of horror.

What did he see with those eyes that seemed to look far out into the dim aisles of the terrible future?

"The truth!" echoed the unhappy mother. "Tell me, will my Antoinette be happy?"

Deep sighs convulsed the breast of the priest, and, with a look of inexpressible agony, he answered, solemnly:

"Empress of Austria, WE HAVE ALL OUR CROSS TO BEAR!" †

The empress started back, with a cry.

"Again, again!" murmured she, burying her face in her hands. But suddenly coming forward, her eyes flaming like those of an angry lioness, she said:

"What mean these riddles? Speak out at once, and tell me, without equivocation—what is to be the fate of Antoinette?"

"WE HAVE ALL OUR CROSS TO BEAR," repeated the priest, "and the Queen of France will surely have hers."

With these words he turned and left the room.

Pale and rigid, the empress stood in the middle of the room, murmuring to herself the two fearful prophecies: "She will live through much evil, but will return to virtue."—"We have all our cross to bear, and the Queen of France will surely have hers."

For a while Maria Theresa was overwhelmed by the double blow she had received. But it was not in her nature to succumb to circumstances. She must overrule them.

She rang her bell, and a page entered the room.

"Let a messenger be dispatched to Prince Kaunitz, I wish to see his highness. He can come to me unannounced."

Not long after the prince made his appearance. A short sharp

*Father Gassner was one of the most remarkable thaumaturgists of the eighteenth century. He healed all sorts of diseases by the touch of his hand, and multitudes flocked to him for cure. His extraordinary powers displeased the bishop of his diocese, and, to avoid censure, Father Gassner sought protection from the empress, who held him in great reverence. His prediction concerning the fate of Marie Antoinette was generally known long before its accomplishment. It was related to Madame Campan, by a son of Kaunitz, years before the Revolution.

† Mémoires de Madame Campan," vol. ii., p. 14.

glance at the agitated mien of the empress showed to the experienced diplomatist that to-day, as so often before, he must oppose the shield of indifference to the storm of passion with which he was about to contend.

"Your majesty," said he, "has sent for me, just as I was about to request an audience. I am in receipt of letters from the emperor. He has spent a day with the King of Prussia."

He attempted to give the letters into the hands of the empress, but she put them back with a gesture of impatience.

"Prince Kaunitz," said she, "it is you who have done this—you must undo it. It cannot, shall not be."

"What does your majesty mean?" asked Kaunitz, astonished.

"I speak of that which lies nearest my heart," said the empress, warmly.

"Of the meeting of the emperor with the King of Prussia," returned Kaunitz, quietly. "Yesterday they met at Neisse. It was a glorious interview. The two monarchs embraced, and the emperor remarked—"

"Enough, enough!" cried Maria Theresa, impatiently. "You affect to misunderstand me. I speak of Antoinette's engagement to the dauphin. It must be broken. My daughter shall not go to France."

Kaunitz was so completely astounded, so *sincerely* astounded, that he was speechless. The paint upon his face could not conceal the angry flush that colored it, nor his pet locks cover the wrinkles that rose up to disfigure his forehead.

"Do not stare at me as if you thought I was parting with my senses," cried the empress. "I know very well what I say. I will not turn my innocent Antoinette into that den of corruption. She shall not bear a cross from which it is in my power to save her."

"Who speaks of crosses?" asked Kaunitz, bewildered. "The only thing of which I have heard is a royal crown wherewith her brow is to be decked."

"She shall not wear that crown!" exclaimed Maria Theresa. "God himself has warned me through the lips of His prophets, and not unheeded shall the warning fall."

Kaunitz breathed more freely, and his features resumed their wonted calmness.

"If that is all," thought he, gayly, "I shall be victorious. An ebullition of superstition is easily quieted by a little good news."

"Your majesty has been following the new fashion," said he, aloud; "you have been consulting the fortune-tellers. I presume you have visited the nun who is subject to pious hysterics; and Father Gassner, I see, has been visiting your majesty, for I met him as I was coming to the palace. I could not help laughing as I saw his absurd length of visage."

Maria Theresa, in reply to this irony, related the answers which had been made to her questions.

Kaunitz listened with sublime indifference, and evinced not a spark of sympathy. When the empress had concluded her story, he merely said:

"What else, your majesty?"

"What else!" echoed the empress, surprised.

"Yes, your majesty. Surely there must be something more than a pair of vague sentences, a pair of 'ohs' and 'ahs,' and a sick nun and a silly priest. These insignificant nothings are certainly not enough to overturn the structure which for ten years we have employed all our skill to build up."

"I well know that you are an infidel and an unbeliever, Kaunitz," cried the empress, vexed at the quiet sneers of her minister. "I know you believe that only which you can understand and explain."

"No, your majesty, I believe all that is reasonable. What I cannot comprehend is unreasonable."

The empress glanced angrily at his stony countenance. "God sometimes speaks to us through the mouths of His chosen ones," cried she; "and, as I believe in the inspiration of Sister Margaret and Father Gassner, my daughter shall not go to France."

"Is that your majesty's unalterable resolution?"

"It is."

"Then," returned Kaunitz, bowing, "allow me to make a request for myself."

"Speak on."

"Allow me at once to retire from your majesty's service."

"Kaunitz!" exclaimed Maria Theresa, "is it possible that you would forsake me?"

"No, your majesty; it is you who forsake me. You are willing, for the sake of two crazy seers, to destroy the fabric which it has been the work of my life to construct. Your majesty desires that *I* should remain your minister, and with my own hand should undo the web that I have woven with such trouble to myself? All Europe knows that the French alliance is my work. To this end I have labored by day and lain awake by night; to this end I have flattered and bribed; to this end I have seen my friend De Choiseul disgraced, while I bowed low before his miserable successor, that I might win him and that wretched Du Barry to my purpose!"

"You are irretrievably bent upon this alliance?" asked the empress, thoughtfully. "It was then not to gratify me that you sought to place a crown upon my dear child's head?"

"Your majesty's wishes have always been sacred to me, but I should never have sought to gratify them, had they not been in accordance with my sense of duty to Austria. I have not sought to make a queen of the Archduchess Maria Antoinette. I have sought to unite Austria with France, and to strengthen the southwestern powers of Europe against the infidelity and barbarism of Prussia and Russia. In spite of all that is taking place at Neisse, Austria and Prussia are, and ever will be, enemies. The king and the emperor may flatter and smile, but neither believes what the other says. Frederick will never lose an opportunity of robbing. He ogles Russia, and would gladly see her our 'neighbor,' if by so doing he were to gain an insignificant province for Prussia. It is to ward off these dangerous accomplices that we seek alliance with France, and through France, with Spain, Portugal, and Italy. And now, when the goal is won, and the prize is ours, your majesty retracts her imperial word! You are the sovereign, and your will must be done. But I cannot lend my hand to that which my reason condemns as unwise, and my conscience as dishonorable. I beg of your majesty, to-day and forever, to dismiss me from your service!"

The empress did not make any reply. She had risen, and was walking hastily up and down, murmuring low, inarticulate words, and heaving deep, convulsive sighs. Kaunitz followed her with the eye of a cool physician, who watches the crisis of a brain-fever. He looked down, however, as the empress, stopping, raised her dark, glowing eyes to his. When he met her glance his expression had changed; it had become as usual.

"You have heard the pleadings of the mother," said she, breathing hard, "and you have silenced them with your cold arguments. The empress has heard, and she it is who must decide against herself. She has no right to sacrifice her empire to her maternity. May God forgive me," continued she, solemnly clasping her hands, "if I err in quelling the voice of my love which cries so loudly against this union. Let it be accomplished! Marie Antoinette shall be the bride of Louis XVI."

"Spoken like the noble Empress of Austria!" cried Kaunitz, triumphantly.

"Do not praise me," returned Maria Theresa sadly; "but hear what I have to say. You have spoken words so bold, that it would seem you fancy yourself to be Emperor of Austria. It was not you who sought alliance with France, but myself. You did nothing but follow out my intentions and obey my commands. The sin of my refusal, therefore, was nothing to you or your conscience—it rested on *my* head alone."

"May God preserve your majesty to your country and your subjects! May you long be Austria's head, and I—your right hand!" exclaimed Kaunitz.

"You do not then wish to retire?" asked she, with a languid smile.

"I beg of your majesty to forgive and retain me."

"So be it, then," returned the empress, with a light inclination of the head. "But I cannot hear any more to-day. You have no sympathy with my trials as a mother. I have sacrificed my child to Austria, but my heart is pierced with sorrow and apprehension. Leave me to my tears. I cannot feel for any one except my child—my poor, innocent child!"

She turned hastily away, that he might not see the tears that were already streaming down her face. Kaunitz bowed, and left the cabinet with his usual cold, proud step.

The minister once gone, Maria Theresa gave herself up to the wildest grief. No one saw her anguish but God; no one ever knew how the powerful empress writhed and wrung her hands in her powerless agony; no one but God and the dead emperor, whose mild eyes beamed compassion from the gilt frame in which his picture hung, upon the wall. To this picture Maria Theresa at last raised her eyes, and it seemed, to her excited imagination, that her husband smiled and whispered words of consolation.

"Yes, dear Franz, I hear you," said she. "You would remind me that this is our wedding-day. Alas, I know it! Once a day of joy, and from this moment the anniversary of a great sorrow! Franz, it is *our* child that is the victim! The sweet Antoinette, whose eyes are so like her father's! Oh, dear husband, my heart is heavy with grief! Why may I not go to rest too? But thou wilt not love me if my courage fail. I will be brave, Franz; I will work, and try to do my duty."

She approached her writing-table, and began to overlook the heaps of papers that awaited her inspection and signature. Gradually her brow cleared and her face resumed its usual expression of deep thought and high resolve. The mother forgot her grief, and the empress was absorbed in the cares of state.

She felt so strongly the comfort and sustenance derived from labor, that on that day she dined alone, and returned immediately to her writing-desk. Twilight came on, and still the empress was at work. Finally the rolling of carriages toward the imperial theatre was heard, and presently the shouts of the applauding audience. The empress heard nothing. She had never attended the theatre since her husband's death, and it was nothing to her that to-night Lessing's beautiful drama, "Emilia Galotti," was being represented for the first time in Vienna.

Twilight deepened into night, and the empress rang for lights. Then retiring to her dressing-room, she threw off her heavy court costume, and exchanged it for a simple *peignoir*, in which she returned to her cabinet and still wrote on.

Suddenly the stillness was broken by a knock, and a page entered with a golden salver, on which lay a letter.

"A courier from Florence, your majesty," said he.

Maria Theresa took the letter, and dismissed the page. "From my Leopold," said she, while she opened it. "It is an extra courier. It must announce the *accouchement* of his wife. Oh, my heart, how it beats!"

With trembling hands she held the missive and read it. But at once her face was lighted up with joy, and throwing herself upon her knees before the portrait of the emperor, she said, "Franz, Leopold has given us a grandson. Do you hear?"

No answer came in response to the joyful cry of the empress, and she could not bear the burden of her joy alone. Some one must rejoice with her. She craved sympathy, and she must go out to seek it.

She left her cabinet. Unmindful of her dress, she sped through the long corridors, farther and still farther, down the staircase and away to the extremest end of the palace, until she reached the imperial theatre.

That night it was crowded. The interest of the spectators had deepened as the play went on. They were absorbed in the scene between Emilia and her father, when a door was heard to open and to shut.

Suddenly, in the imperial box, which had so long been empty, a tall and noble figure bent forward, far over the railing, and a clear, musical voice cried out:

"Leopold has a son!"

The audience, as if electrified, rose with one accord from their seats. All turned toward the imperial box. Each one had recognized the voice of the adored Maria Theresa, and every heart overflowed with the joy of the moment.

The empress repeated her words:

"Leopold has a son, and it is born on my wedding-day. Wish me joy, dear friends, of my grandson!"

Then arose such a storm of congratulations as never before had been heard within those theatre walls. The women wept, and the men waved their hats and cheered; while all, with one voice, cried out, "Long live Maria Theresa! Long live the imperial grandmother!"

CHAPTER LVI.

THE GIFT.

ALL prophecies defying, Maria Theresa had given her daughter to France. In the month of May, 1770, the Archduchess Marie Antoinette was married by proxy in Vienna; and amid the ringing of bells, the booming of cannon, and the shouts of the populace, the beautiful young dauphiness left Austria to meet her inevitable fate.

Meanwhile, in the imperial palace, too, one room was darkening under the shadow of approaching death. It was that in which Isabella's daughter was passing from earth to heaven.

The emperor knew that his child was dying; and many an hour he spent at her solitary bedside, where, tranquil and smiling, she murmured words which her father knew were whispered to the angels.

The emperor sorrowed deeply for the severance of the last tie that bound him to the bright and beautiful dream of his early married life. But he was so accustomed to sorrow, that on the occasion of his sister's marriage, he had gone through the forms required by etiquette, without any visible emotion.

But the festivities were at an end. The future Queen of France had bidden farewell to her native Vienna, and the marriage guests had departed; while darker and darker grew the chamber of the dying child, and sadder the face of the widowed father. The emperor kissed his daughter's burning forehead, and held her little transparent hand in his. "Farewell, my angel," whispered he; "since thy mother calls thee, go, my little Theresa. Tell her that she was my only love—my first and last. Go, beloved, and pray for thy unhappy father."

Once more he kissed her, and when he raised his head, her face was moistened with his tears. He turned hastily away and left the room.

"And now," thought he, "to my duty. I must forget my own sorrows that I may wipe away the tears of my sorrowing people. There is so much grief and want in Austria! Oh, my child, my little one! Amid the blessings of the suffering poor shalt thou stretch forth thy wings and take thy flight to heaven!"

He was on his way to seek an audience of his mother. Maria Theresa was in her cabinet, and was somewhat surprised to see her son at this unusual hour of the day.

"I come to your majesty to beg a boon," said Joseph, with a sad smile. "Yesterday you were distributing Antoinette's wedding-gifts to your children; I alone received nothing. Is there nothing for me?"

"Nothing for you, my son!" exclaimed Maria Theresa, astonished. "Why, every thing is yours, and therefore I have nothing to give. Where your right is indisputable, my presents are superfluous."

"Yes, mother; but it does not become one so generous as you, to let her eldest son wait for an inheritance, when she might make him a handsome present of her own free will. Be generous, then, and give me something, too. I wish to be on an equality with the other children."

"Well, then, you grown-up child, what will you have?" asked the empress, laughing. "Of course you have already chosen your gift, and it is mere gallantry on your part to beg for what you might take without leave. But let us hear. What is it? You have only to ask and have."

"Indeed! May I choose my wedding-gift?"

"Yes, you imperial beggar, you may."

"Well, then, give me the government claims upon the four lower classes."

The empress looked aghast. "Is it money you desire?" said she. "Say how much, and you shall have it from my private purse. But do not rob the poor! The claim that you covet the tax levied upon all the working classes, and you know how numerous they are."

"For that very reason, I want it. It is a princely gift. Shall I have it?"

The empress reflected for a few moments. "I know," said she, looking up with one of her sweetest smiles, "I know that you will not misuse your power; for I remember the fate of your father's legacy, the three millions of coupons. You shall have the claim, my son. It is yours."

"Will your majesty draw out the deed of gift?"

"I will, my son. It is *your* wedding-gift from our darling Antoinette. But you will acquaint me, from time to time, with the use you are making of your power over the poor classes?"

"I will render my account to your majesty. But first draw out the deed."

The empress stepped to her *escritoire* and wrote a few lines, to which she affixed the imperial signature and seal.

"There it is," said she. "I bestow upon my son, the emperor, all the government claims to the impost levied upon the four lower classes. Will that do?"

"It will, and from my heart I thank my dear mother for the gracious gift."

He took the hand of the empress to kiss it, but she held his fast in her grasp, and looked at him with an expression of tenderness and anxiety.

"You are pale, my son," said she, affectionately. "I see that your heart is sad."

"And yet," replied Joseph, with quivering lip, "I should rejoice, for I am about to have an angel in heaven."

"Poor little Theresa!" murmured the empress, while the tears rose to her eyes. "She has never been a healthy child. Isabella calls her hence."

"Yes," replied Joseph, bitterly; "she calls my child away, that she may break the last link that bound her to me."

"We must believe, my child, that it is for the best. The will of God, however painful its manifestations, is holy, wise, and merciful. Isabella declared to us that she would call the child when it had reached its seventh year; she goes to her mother. And now that this bitter dream of your early love is past, perhaps your heart may awaken once more to love. There are many beautiful princesses in Europe, and not one of them would refuse the hand of the Emperor of Austria. It is for you to choose, and no one shall dictate your choice."

"Would your majesty convert me into a bluebeard?" cried

Joseph, coloring. "Do you not see that I murder my wives? Enough, that two of them are buried in the chapel of the Capuchins, and that to-morrow, perhaps, my child will join them. Leopold has given an heir to my throne, and I am satisfied."

"Why do you talk of a successor, my son?" said the empress, "you, who are so young?"

"Your majesty, I am old," replied Joseph, mournfully—"so old that I have no hope of happiness on earth. You see that to-day, when you have been so gracious, I am too wretched to do aught but thank you for your splendid gift. Let me retire, then, to my unhappy solitude; I am not fit to look upon your sweet and honored countenance. I must exile myself until my trial is past."

He left the room, and hastening to his cabinet, "Now," exclaimed he, "now for my mother's gift."

He sat down and wrote as follows:

"MY DEAR PRINCE KAUNITZ: By the enclosed, you will see that the empress, my mother, has presented me with all the government claims upon the working-classes. Will you make immediate arrangements to acquaint the collectors with the following:

"'No tax shall be collected from the working-classes during the remainder of my life.'

"JOSEPH." *

"Now," thought he, as he laid aside his pen, "this document will gladden many a heart, and it will, perchance, win forgiveness for my own weakness. But, why should monarchs have hearts of flesh like other men, since they have no right to feel, to love, or to grieve? Be still, throbbing heart, that the emperor may forget himself, to remember his subjects! Yes, my subjects—my children—I will make you happy! I will—"

There was a light tap at the door, and the governess of the little Archduchess Maria Theresa entered the room.

"I have come," said she, in a faltering voice, "to announce to your majesty that the princess has breathed her last."

The emperor made no reply. He motioned the lady to retire, and bowing his head, gave way to one long burst of grief.

For hours he sat there, solitary and broken-hearted. At length the paroxysm was over. He raised his head, and his eyes were tearless and bright.

"It is over!" exclaimed he, in clear and unfaltering tones. "The past is buried; and I am born anew to a life whereof the aim shall be Austria's greatness and her people's welfare. I am no more a husband, no more a father. Austria shall be my bride, and every Austrian my child."

CHAPTER LVII.

THE CONFERENCE.

GREAT excitement prevailed at Neustadt. All work was suspended, all the shops were shut, and although it was not Sunday, the people, in their holiday attire, seemed to have cast away all thought of the wants, cares, and occupations of every-day life.

For, although it was not Sunday, it was a holiday—a holiday for

* Historical. Hubner, vol. ii., p. 85.

Neustadt, since this was the birthday of Neustadt's fame. For hundreds of years the little village had existed in profound obscurity, its simple inhabitants dreaming away their lives far from the clamor of the world and its vicissitudes. Their slumbers had been disturbed by the Seven Years' War, and many a father, son, husband, and lover had fought and fallen on its bloodthirsty battle-field. But with the return of peace came insignificance, and villagers of Neustadt went on dreaming as before.

To-day, however, on the 3d of September, in the year 1770, they were awakened by an event which gave to Neustadt a place in history. The two greatest potentates in Germany were to meet there, to bury their past enmity, and pledge to each other the right hand of fellowship.

These two potentates were the Emperor of Austria and the King of Prussia. It was, therefore, not surprising that all Neustadt should be out of doors to witness the baptism of Neustadt's celebrity.

The streets were thronged with well-dressed people, the houses were hung with garlands and wreaths, the church-bells were ringing, and all the dignitaries of the town had turned out to witness the pageant.

And now the moment had arrived. The thunder of cannon, the shouts of the people who thronged the avenue that led to the palace, and the clang of martial music, announced the approach of the emperor, whom his people were frantic to welcome.

He came, a young man, on a jet-black Arabian, who rode ahead of those glittering nobles—this was the Emperor Joseph, the hope of Austria.

A thousand voices rent the air with shouts, while Joseph smiled, and bowed, and raised his eyes to the balconies, whence showers of bouquets were falling around him.

He was inclining his head, when a wreath of red roses and orange-flowers, aimed by some skilful hand, fell directly upon his saddle-bow. He smiled, and taking up the wreath, looked around to see whence it came. Suddenly his eye brightened, and his countenance expressed increased interest, while he reined in his horse that he might look again at a lady who was leaning over a balcony just above him. Her tall and elegant figure was clothed in a dress of black velvet, closed from her white throat to her round waist by buttons of large and magnificent diamonds, whose brilliancy was almost dazzling. Her youthful and beautiful face was colorless, with that exquisite and delicate pallor which has no affinity to ill-health, but resembles the spiritual beauty of a marble statue. Her glossy black hair defined the exquisite oval of that fair face, as a rich frame sets off a fine painting. On her head she wore a diadem of brilliants, which confined a rich black-lace veil, that fluttered like a dark cloud around her graceful figure. Her countenance wore an expression of profound sadness, and her large, lustrous eyes were riveted with an earnest gaze upon the emperor.

He bowed to his saddle-bow, but she did not seem to recognize the compliment, for her glance and her sadness were unchanged.

"The wreath is not from her," thought Joseph, with a feeling of disappointment; but as he turned for one more look at her lovely face, he remarked a bouquet which she wore in her bosom. It was similar to the wreath which he held. The same white orange-blossoms and red roses, fastened together by the same white and red ribbon, whose long streamers were now fluttering in the wind.

A triumphant smile overspread the features of the emperor, as blushing, he bowed again and passed on. But his face no longer wore its expression of careless gratification. He grew absent and thoughtful; he forgot to return the greetings of the people; and vainly the ladies, who crowded window and balcony, threw flowers in his way, or waved their handkerchiefs in greeting. He saw nothing but the beautiful vision in the black veil, and wondered whence she came and what could be the hidden meaning of the red and white flowers which she wore and gave to him.

He was glad when the pageant of his entry into Neustadt was over, and, dismounting quickly, he entered the palace, followed by Field-Marshal Lacy and Count Rosenberg.

The people looked after them and shouted anew. But their attention was directed from the emperor to a carriage, drawn by four horses, which, advancing in the very centre of the brilliant *cortége*, seemed to contain some imperial personage, for the staff were around it, as though forming its escort. The curtains of the carriage were all drawn, so that nothing could be seen of its occupant.

Who could it be? A woman, of course; since no man would dare to be driven, while the Emperor of Austria rode. It could be no other than the Empress Maria Theresa, who had taken the journey to Neustadt, that she might look, face to face, upon her celebrated opponent, and offer him her own hand in pledge of future good understanding.

While the populace hoped and speculated, the mysterious equipage arrived before the palace gates. The rich-liveried footmen sprang from the rumble, and stationed themselves at the door of the coach. The two others, who were seated on the box, did likewise; bringing with them, as they alighted on the ground, a roll of rich Turkey carpeting, which they laid, with great precision, from the carriage to the palace steps.

Then the people were convinced that it was the empress. Who but the sovereign lady of Austria and Hungary would walk the streets upon a carpet of such magnificence? And they thronged nearer, eager to catch the first glance of their beloved and honored empress.

The carpet was laid without a wrinkle. One of the footmen opened the carriage door, while another approached the fore-wheel.

"She comes! she comes!" cried the populace, and they crowded around in eager delight.

One foot was put forward—not a foot encased in a satin slipper, but a foot in a buckled shoe, which, glistening though it was with diamonds, was not that of an empress. The occupant of the carriage was a man!

"A man!" exclaimed the bystanders, astounded. Yes. Here he came, wrapped up in a bearskin, which, on this warm summer day, was enough to dissolve an ordinary human being into vapor. Not content with his wrapping, his hands were encased in a huge muff, which he held close to his face, that he might not inhale one single breath of the air that was refreshing everybody else. His head was covered by a hood which concealed his face, of which nothing was visible save a pair of light-blue eyes.

When he had disappeared within the palace doors, the footmen rolled up the carpet and replaced it on the coach-box.

The populace, who had been looking on in speechless wonder, now began to laugh and whisper. Some said it was the King of the North Pole; others declared it was an Arctic bear; others again thought the gentleman had started for Siberia and had lost his way. Finally the desire to know who he was grew uncontrollable, and, thronging around his lackeys, the people shouted out:

"Who is he? Tell us, who is he?"

The lackeys, with the gravity of heralds-at-arms, shouted out in return:

"This is his highness Prince Kaunitz, prime minister of their majesties the Empress Maria Theresa and the Emperor Joseph of Austria!"

CHAPTER LVIII.

KAUNITZ.

"WHAT an abominable idea!" exclaimed Prince Kaunitz, as, perfectly exhausted from his journey, he fell into an arm-chair in his own room. "What an abominable idea to undertake this journey! These German roads are as rough and uncouth as the Germans themselves, and I only wonder that we have arrived without breaking our ribs!"

"It would certainly have been more convenient," said Baron Binder, "if the King of Prussia had visited us in Vienna."

Kaunitz turned his large eyes full upon his friend.

"I suppose," said he, "that you jest, Binder; for you *must* know that it is never safe to have your enemy under your own roof."

"Your highness, then, has no confidence in the protestations of love that are going on between the emperor and the king?"

The prince made no reply. He was looking at himself in a mirror, criticising his toilet, which had just been completed by the expert Hippolyte. Apparently it was satisfactory, for he looked up and spoke:

"You are a grown-up child, Binder; you stare, and believe every thing. Have you not yet learned that statesmanship recognizes nothing but interests? To-day it is to the interest of Frederick to squeeze our hands and protest that he loves us; to-morrow (if he can), he will put another Silesia in his royal pocket. We, too, have found it convenient to write him a love-letter or two; but to-day, if we would, we would pluck off his crown, and make him a little margrave again! Our intimacy reminds me of a sight I once saw while we were in Paris. It was a cage, in which animals, naturally antagonistic, were living in a state of perfect concord. A dog and cat were dining sociably together from one plate, and, not far off, a turkey-hen was comfortably perched upon the back of a fox, who, so far from betraying any symptom of appetite for the turkey, looked quite oblivious of her proximity. I gave the keeper a louis d'or, and he told me his secret. The dog's teeth were drawn, and the cat's claws were pared off; this, of course, forced both to keep the peace. As for the turkey-hen, she was fastened to the back of the fox with fine wire, and this was the secret of her security."

"Ah!" cried Binder, laughing, "this is the history of many a human alliance. How many foxes I have known who carried their hens upon their backs and made believe to love them, because they dared not do otherwise!"

"Peace, Binder, my story is not yet ended. One morning the dog and the cat were found dead in *their* corner; and in the other, the fox lay bleeding and moaning; while of the hen, nothing remained save her feathers. Time—the despot that rules us all, had outwitted the keeper and asserted the laws of Nature. The cat's claws had grown out, and so had the dog's teeth. The fox, after much pondering over his misfortunes, had discovered the reason why he could not reach the hen; and this done, he worked at the wires until they broke. Of course he revenged himself on the spot by gobbling her up; but in his wrath at the wires, he had thrust them so deeply into his own flesh that the wounds they made upon his body caused his death. And so ended the compulsory alliance of four natural enemies."

"Does your highness apply that anecdote to us?" asked Binder. "Are we to end like the cat and the dog?"

"For the present," said Kaunitz, thoughtfully, "our teeth and claws are harmless. We must wait until they have grown out again!"

"Your highness, then, assigns us the *rôle* of the dog?"

"Certainly. I leave it to Prussia to play the cat—she has scratched us more than once, and even to-day, when she covers her paws with velvet, I feel the claws underneath. I came hither to watch her. I am curious to know what it is in Frederick that has so bewitched the young Emperor of Austria."

"It would appear that his majesty of Prussia has extraordinary powers of fascination. No one can resist him."

"*I* shall resist him," said Kaunitz, "for against his fascinations I am defended by the talisman of our mutual hate."

"Do not say so, your highness. The King of Prussia may fear, but he cannot hate you. And did he not make it a special request that you should accompany the emperor?"

"He did; and however disinclined I might be to accept his invitation, I have come lest he should suppose that I am afraid to encounter his eagle eyes.* I fear *him! He* intimidate me! It is expedient for the present that Austria and Prussia should be *quasi* allies, for in this way peace has been secured to Europe. But my system of diplomacy, which the empress has made her own, forbids me to make any permanent alliance with a prince who lives politically from hand to mouth, and has no fixed line of policy.† No—I do not fear him; for I see through his hypocritical professions, and in spite of his usurped crown I feel myself to be more than his equal. If he has won thirteen victories on the battle-field, I have fought twice as many in the cabinet, where the fight is hand to hand, and the victor conquers without an army. On this field he will scarcely dare to encounter me. If he does, he will find his master for once!

"Yes," repeated Kaunitz emphatically, "he will find his master in me. I have never failed to make other men subservient to my schemes, and the King of Prussia shall grace my triumph with the rest. He is the vassal of Austria, and I will be the one to force him

* Ferrand, "History of the Dismemberment of Poland," vol. i., p. 103.
† Kaunitz's own words. See Ferrand, vol. i., p. 69.

back to his allegiance. It is scandalous that this petty king should have been suffered to play an important part in European affairs. I will drive him from his accidental grandeur, and he shall return to his duty. I will humble him if I can; for this King of Prussia is the only man in Europe who has denied me the honors and consideration due me as a politician and a prince." *

While Kaunitz spoke, his marble face grew animated, and his eyes glowed with the fire of hate.

"Nay, prince!" exclaimed Binder, anxious to subdue the fiend that was rising in his friend's heart, "everybody knows that you are the coachman of Europe, and that it is in the power of no man to wrest the reins from your hands."

"May this Prussian ride behind as my footman!" cried Kaunitz, gnashing his teeth. "Oh, I know him! I know why he pays a million of subsidy annually to his accomplice, the virtuous Catharine, that she may continue her assaults upon Poland and Turkey! I know whither his longings travel; but when he stretches his hand out for the booty, we too will be there to claim our share, and he shall yield it."

"Your highness speaks in riddles," said Binder, shrugging his shoulders. "I am accustomed, as you know, to look through your political spectacles; and I beg you to explain, for I am perfectly at a loss to understand you."

The countenance of Kaunitz had resumed its impassible look. He threw back his head, and fixed his cold, heartless blue eyes upon the baron.

"Do you know," said he, "what William the Silent once said of himself? 'If I knew that my night-cap had found out my thoughts I would throw it in the fire.' Now, Binder, do not aim to be my night-cap, or I shall burn you to a cinder.—But enough of this. It would seem that the Emperor Joseph expects me to wait upon him. Well—if it please him that I should make the first visit, I will humor him. When a man feels that he is lord and master of another, he can afford to be condescending! I will indulge the emperor's whim."

He rang, and one of his valets entered the room.

"Is his majesty in the castle?"

"Yes, your highness. His majesty has been reviewing the troops."

"Where is his majesty now?"

"He is with his suite in the parlor that overlooks the square."

"Is it far from this room?"

"No, your highness. It is close by."

"Then reach me a cloak and muff, and woe to you if I encounter a draught on my way!"

CHAPTER LIX.

SOUVENIR D'EPÉRIES.

THE emperor stood in the centre of the room, in lively conversation with the gentlemen of his suite. As Kaunitz entered, he stopped at once, and coming forward, received the prince with a cordial welcome.

* Kaunitz's own words. Ferrand, vol. i., p. 104.

Kaunitz replied by a low bow, and nodded slightly to Prince de Ligne and General Lacy.

"Your highness is just in time," said the emperor. "These gentlemen need encouragement. They have been blushing and trembling like two young *débutantes.*"

"Before whom, your majesty?"

"Oh!—before the great Frederick, of course. And De Ligne, who is considered the most elegant man in Vienna, actually trembled more than anybody else."

"Actors trembling before their manager!" said Kaunitz, with a slight shrug. "Compose yourselves, gentlemen; the King of Prussia is too much absorbed in his own *rôle* to take any notice of you."

"That is right," cried the emperor. "Encourage the *débutantes,* prince!"

"I scarcely think that the prince will succeed where your majesty has failed," said General von Lacy proudly.

"And his highness will hardly have any time to devote to us, for doubtless he too is practising the *rôle* which he must play before the King of Prussia," added De Ligne.

"I beg to impress upon the Prince de Ligne," interrupted Kaunitz, "that the verb 'must' is one which I am well accustomed to conjugate for others, but never allow others to conjugate for me."

"I for one have had it conjugated for *me* by your highness," said the emperor, laughing. "Nobody in Austria knows it in all its moods and tenses better than I. But I have always recognized you as my teacher, and hope always to remain your faithful pupil."

The clouds which were gathering on Kaunitz's brow now shifted to the faces of Lacy and De Ligne.

"I have nothing to teach your majesty," replied Kaunitz, almost smiling; "but allow me as a faithful servant to offer you a suggestion. Present to the King of Prussia that beautiful wreath which you hold in your hand, as an emblem of the friendship which to-day we pledge to Prussia."

"Not I," cried Joseph, while he held up his wreath and admired its white and red roses. "I shall keep my bouquet, were it only for the sake of the beautiful donor. You, prince, who penetrate all things, have pity on me, and find out her name."

"Your majesty saw her, then?"

"Saw her? Yes, by Aphrodite, I did; and never in my life did I see a lovelier woman. She stood there in her velvet dress and veil, looking for all the world like the queen of night, of starry night. You see how she has impressed me, since I, who am so prosaic, launch out into extravagance of speech to describe her."

"She was in mourning?" asked Kaunitz thoughtfully.

"Clothed in black, except the diamonds that sparkled on her bodice, and the bouquet (a match to mine) which she wore in her bosom. Ah, your highness, how you look at my poor flowers, as if treason were lurking among their leaves!"

"It is a beautiful bouquet," said Kaunitz, eying it critically, "and very peculiar. Will your majesty allow me to examine it?"

The emperor handed over the wreath. "Take it," said he, "but be merciful to my pretty delinquents."

Kaunitz took the flowers and looked at them as he would have done at any other thing that might be the links in a chain of evidence, and passed his slender, white fingers through the long ribbons that fastened them together.

"The lady who threw these flowers is a Pole," said he, after a pause.

"How do you know that?" cried the emperor.

"It is certainly not accidental that the wreath should be composed of white and red roses, and tied with a knot of white and red ribbons. White and red, you remember, are the colors of the so-called Republic of Poland."

"You are right!" exclaimed Joseph, "and she wears mourning because a noble woman must necessarily grieve for the sufferings of her bleeding country."

"Look," said Kaunitz, who, meanwhile, was opening the leaves and searching among them, "here is a paper. Does your majesty permit me to draw it out?"

"Certainly. I gave you the wreath to examine, and you shall have the benefit of all that you discover."

Kaunitz bowed his thanks, and began to untwist the stems of the flowers. The emperor and the two courtiers looked on with interest.

The prince drew forth a little folded paper, and reached it over to the emperor.

"Have the goodness, your majesty, to read it yourself. A declaration of love from a lady is not intended for my profane eyes."

The emperor sighed. "No," said he, "it is no declaration for me. I am not so happy. Read, your highness, read it aloud."

Kaunitz unfolded the paper, and read, "*Souvenir d'Epéries.*"

"Nothing more?" asked Joseph.

Kaunitz replied by handing him the note.

"How strange! Only these words, and no explanation. I cannot understand it."

"These words prove my supposition, your majesty. The donor is a Polish lady and one of the Confederates."

"You think so?"

"I am convinced of it. When your majesty was travelling in Hungary, did you not spend a day at Epéries, and honor the Confederates by receiving them both publicly and privately?"

"I did," replied Joseph, warmly. "And it gladdened my heart to assure these brave, struggling patriots of my sympathy."

"Did not your majesty go so far as to promise them mediation with Prussia and Russia?" *

"I did," replied the emperor, with a faint blush.

"Well, then, this female confederate meant to remind you of your promise on the day when you are to hold a conference with Frederick," said Kaunitz, allowing the wreath to slip through his fingers to the floor. "There, your majesty," continued he, "your beautiful Pole is at your feet. Will you rescue her, or unite in crushing her to the earth?"

"Oh, I will rescue her," replied Joseph, "that she may not fall into the hands of ambitious Catharine. It would give her great pleasure to deck her Muscovite head with these sweet Polish roses; but she shall not have them."

With these words, and before his courtiers could anticipate his action, the emperor stooped and picked up the wreath.

"Have a care, your majesty," said the wary Kaunitz, "how you

* Ferrand, vol. i., p. 79.

espouse Polish quarrels. The Poles are unlucky. They can die like men, but they do not live like men. Beware of Polish roses, for their perfume is not wholesome."

Just then a shout was heard in the distance, and the emperor hastened to the window.

"It is the King of Prussia!" cried he, joyfully, and he walked toward the door.

Prince Kaunitz took the liberty of going immediately up and interposing his tall person between Joseph and the doorway.

"Your majesty," said he, reproachfully, "what are you about to do?"

"I am about to go forward to meet the King of Prussia. He is just descending from his carriage. Do not detain me," replied Joseph, hastily.

"But has your majesty forgotten that at Neisse, when the King of Prussia was the host, he came no farther than the stairway to meet you? It is not seemly that Austria should condescend to Prussia."

"My dear prince," said the emperor, with a peculiar laugh, "it is your business to respect these conventions. It is mine to regulate them. As the *little* sovereign of Austria I hasten to do homage to the *great* King of Prussia."

And gently putting the minister aside, the emperor walked rapidly out, followed by his suite.

Kaunitz looked after him with stormy brow.

"Incorrigible fanatic!" said he to himself. "Will you never cease to butt your empty head against the wall? You will butt in vain as long as *I* have power and life. Go. It befits such a little emperor as you to humble yourself before your great king; but Austria is represented in *my* person, and I remain here!"

He looked around the room, and his eyes fell upon the wreath, which the emperor had laid by the side of his hat, on the table. A sneer overspread his countenance as he went toward it, and shook off some of the leaves which were already fading.

"How soon they fall!" said he. "I think that the glorious republic will be quite as short-lived as they. Meanwhile I shall see that the '*Souvenir d'Epéries*' lives no longer than roses have a right to live."

He left the room, resolved to find out who it was that had bestowed the wreath. "For," thought he, "she may prove a useful instrument with which to operate on either side."

CHAPTER LX.

FREDERICK THE GREAT.

WITH youthful ardor, unconscious that his head was uncovered, the emperor hurried down the staircase into the street. Looking neither to the right nor to the left, his eyes fixed upon the spot whence the king was advancing, the emperor rushed onward, for the first time in his life slighting the people who thronged around, full of joy at sight of his elegant and handsome person.

Frederick was coming with equal rapidity, and now, in the very centre of the square, the monarchs met.

At this moment all was quiet. The military, ranged in lines around, were glistening with gold lace and brightened arms. Behind them came the people, who far and near were seen flowing in one great stream toward the square, while on the balconies and through the open windows of the houses around richly-dressed matrons and beautiful maidens enclosed the scene, like one long wreath of variegated flowers.

They met; and in the joy of his youthful enthusiasm, the emperor threw himself into the arms of the King of Prussia, and embraced him with a tenderness that was almost filial. The king returned the caress, and pressed the young monarch to his heart.

While the King of Prussia had been advancing, the people in silence were revolving in their minds the blood, the treasure, the long years of struggle which Austrians had owed to this warlike Frederick. But when they saw how Joseph greeted him, they forgot every thing, and he now seemed to their excited imaginations to come like a resplendent sun of peace, whose rays streamed far into the distance of a happy and prosperous futurity.

It was peace! peace!—the hopes of peace that filled every eye with tears, and bowed every unconscious knee in prayer to Almighty God.

From the midst of the kneeling multitude, a voice was heard to cry out, "Long live peace!" A thousand other voices echoed the words, "Long live peace!"

"Long live the emperor and the king!" cried the same voice; and now the air was rent with shouts, while from street and square, and from every house, the cry went up to heaven, "Long live the emperor! Long live the king!"

Frederick withdrew from Joseph's embrace, and bowed to the multitude with that bright and fascinating smile which no one was ever known to resist.

He then turned to the emperor, and presenting the young Prince of Prussia and the two Princes of Brunswick, he pointed to the white uniforms which they wore, and said: "Sire, I bring you some new recruits.* We are all desirous of serving under your banner. And we feel that it would be an honor," continued he, looking around the square, "to be the companions-in-arms of your majesty's soldiers, for each man looks like a true son of Mars."

"If so," replied the emperor, "they have reason to rejoice, since to-day they are permitted, for the first time, to do homage to their father."

Frederick smiled, and taking Joseph's arm, they walked together to the palace. The king was conducted at once to the apartments prepared for his occupation, whence he shortly emerged to join the noble company assembled in the hall that led into the dining-room.

The brilliant suite of the emperor were awaiting the princely pair, and when they entered the hall together, followed by the *cortége* of Prussia, every head bowed with deferential awe, and every eye sought the ground. One head only bent slightly, and one pair of eyes looked boldly into the face of Frederick the Great.

The eagle eye of the king remarked him at once, and with an affable smile he approached the haughty minister.

"I rejoice, at last, to meet Prince Kaunitz face to face," said he,

*The king wore the Austrian uniform, embroided with silver. The princes and the king's suite also wore it.

17

in his soft and musical voice. "We need no introduction to one another. I am not such a barbarian as to require that he should be pointed out to me whom all Europe knows, admires, and respects."

Something happened to which Kaunitz was totally unaccustomed—he blushed. In spite of himself, he smiled and bowed very, very low; but he found no words wherewith to reply to Frederick's flattering address.

"Sire," said the emperor, coming to the rescue, "you are making the most self-possessed men in Austria grow speechless with ecstasy. Even Kaunitz is at a loss to answer you; and as for poor De Ligne, he is completely dazzled. But by an by, he will get accustomed to the sun's splendor, and then he will recover his accustomed address."*

"I know him well," said Frederick, with another bewitching smile. "I have read your letter to Jean Jacques Rousseau, prince; and I know it to be genuine, for it is too beautiful to be a forgery."

"Ah, sire!" replied De Ligne, "I am not of such renown that obscure writers should seek to forge *my* name."†

The king bowed, and turned to Field-Marshal von Lacy.

"Your majesty need not present this man either," said he, laying his hand upon Lacy's shoulder, "he has given me entirely too much trouble for me not to be familiar with his features. I have good reason to remember Von Lacy, and to rejoice that he is not quartermaster-general to-day; for in that capacity, I and my soldiers have suffered enough from him."

"But where is Loudon?" asked the emperor. "He is very late to-day."

"That is not his habit," replied Frederick, quickly, "I have seldom been able to come upon the field as soon as he. But, sire, we have done him injustice, for he is here, punctual as though he waited his enemies, not his friends."

Crossing over to Loudon, and disregarding his stiff demeanor, Frederick took his hand, and greeted him with the most cordial expressions of regard.

"If it be agreeable to your majesty," said the emperor, as the doors were flung open, "we will proceed to dinner." And he offered his arm.

Frederick took it, but he still kept his eyes upon Loudon.

"Sire," said he to Joseph, "if I am to have the honor of sitting beside your majesty at the table, pray, let me have Loudon on the other side. I would much rather have him there than opposite—I feel safer."

So saying, the king walked on, and the company passed into the dining-room.

"If he turns the heads of all the court with his flattery," muttered Kaunitz, following just after the princely pair, "he shall not succeed with me. What fine things, to be sure! But flattery indiscriminately bestowed leaves a bitter taste in the mouth. He wishes Loudon for his neighbor, forsooth, as if a man could have any rational intercourse with such an ignorant, ill-bred, awkward dolt as he is."

And Kaunitz, who was secretly chagrined at the choice of the

*The emperor's words. "Conversations with Frederick the Great," by Prince de Ligne, p. 11.

†Not long before this, a letter had been written to Jean Jacques, and signed with the king's name. The writer of this letter was Horace Walpole.

king, took the seat which had been assigned to him by the emperor. It was at Joseph's own table, directly opposite the two sovereigns.

"Ah!" exclaimed Frederick, laughing and nodding to Kaunitz, "now I am satisfied. If I would rather have Loudon beside me, I would rather have the greatest statesman in Europe before me, for it is only when I can see him that I feel quite safe from his diplomatic grasp. I take shelter under your highness's eye. Be indulgent to an old soldier, whose sword has so often been struck from his hands by your magic pen."

"Your majesty's pen is as sharp as your sword," replied Kaunitz, "and the world has learned to fear and admire the one as much as the other. We offer resistance to neither; but pay willing homage to the prince who is at once a statesman, an author, and a warrior."

The emperor whispered to Frederick: "Sire, a compliment from Kaunitz is like the flower upon the aloe—it blooms once in a century."

CHAPTER LXI.

THE PRIMA DONNA.

THE festivities of the first day were concluded with a ballet. Great preparations had been made for the reception of the King of Prussia. Noverre with his dancers, and Florian Gassman with his opera corps had been summoned to Neustadt. They came in twenty wagons laden with scenery, *coulisses*, machinery, and costumes, all of which was intended to prove to Frederick that, although the court of Berlin was the acknowledged seat of literature and the fine arts, Vienna was not altogether forsaken by the Muses.

"Your majesty must be indulgent to our theatrical efforts," said the emperor, as they took their seats in the box which had been prepared for their occupation. "We all know that in Berlin the Muses and Graces have their home; they seldom visit Vienna, for they are loyal and love to sit at the feet of their master."

"Ah, sire, you speak of the past. Time was when the Muses were not unpropitious; but now that I am an old man, they have proved inconstant, and have fled from Sans-Souci forever. The Muses themselves are young, and it is but natural that they should seek your majesty's protection. I am thankful, through your intervention, to be admitted once more to Parnassus."

Just as the king was about to seat himself he remarked Kaunitz, who, with his usual grave indifference, was advancing to a chair not far off.

Frederick turned smilingly to Joseph. "Your majesty and I," said he, "might stand to-night as representatives of youthful and aged sovereignty. We both need wisdom in our councils. Let us invite Prince Kaunitz to sit between us."

The emperor bowed, and beckoned to the prince, who, having heard distinctly what had been intended for his ears, could not suppress a momentary expression of exultation. Never in his life had he made a bow so profound as that with which he took the seat which a king had resigned to him. He was so exultant that in the course of the evening he was actually heard to laugh. The ballet began. Gods and goddesses fluttered about the stage, Muses and

Graces grouped themselves together in attitudes of surpassing beauty; and finally, with one grand tableau, composed of all the dancers, the curtain fell.

After the ballet came a concert. It was to open with an air from Gluck's opera of "Alceste," sung in costume by the celebrated Bernasconi.

The orchestra played the introduction, and the curtain rose—but the prima donna did not appear. The leader looked toward the *coulisses*, but in vain; and the audience began to express their impatience in audible murmurs.

The curtain fell slowly, and the marshal of the emperor's household, coming forward, spoke a few words to Joseph, in a low voice.

He turned to the king. "Sire, I have to apologize to you for this unlucky *contretemps*. Signora Bernasconi has been taken suddenly sick."

"Oh!" replied Frederick, laughing, "I am quite *au fait* to the sudden illness of prima donnas. But since I have ordered a half month's salary to be withdrawn from every singer who falls sick on a night of representation, my *cantatrices* at Berlin enjoy unprecedented health."

"Bernasconi must have been made sick by her anxiety to appear well in your majesty's critical eyes."

"Do not believe it. These princesses of the stage are more capricious than veritable princesses. Above all, the Italians."

"But Bernasconi," said Kaunitz, "is not an Italian. She belongs to a noble Polish family."

"So much the worse," laughed Frederick. "That Polish blood is forever boiling over. I am surprised that your highness should permit your director to give to a Polish woman a *rôle* of importance. Wherever the Poles go, they bring trouble and strife."

"Perhaps so, sire," replied Kaunitz; "but they are excellent actors, and no people understand better how to represent heroes." As he said this, Kaunitz drew out his jewelled snuff-box, enriched with a medallion portrait of his imperial mistress, Maria Theresa.

"To *represent* heroes, I grant you; but just as we are beginning to feel an interest in the spectacle of their heroism, lo! the stage-armor falls off, the tin sword rattles, and we find that we were wasting our sympathies upon a band of play-actors."

"Perhaps," said Kaunitz, as he dipped his long, white fingers into the snuff-box, "perhaps we may live to see the stage break under them, and then they may cease to be actors, and become lunatics."

Frederick's eagle eyes were fixed upon Kaunitz while he spoke, but the minister still continued to play with his snuff-box.

"Prince," said he, laughing, "we have been antagonists for so many years that we must celebrate our first meeting by a pledge of future good-will. The Indians are accustomed at such times to smoke the calumet of peace. Here we have tobacco under another form. Will you allow me a pinch from your snuff-box?"

This was a token of such great condescension that even the haughty Kaunitz was seen to blush with gratified vanity. With unusual eagerness, he presented his snuff-box to the king.

The king took the snuff and as he did so, remarked, "This is the first time I have ever taken snuff from another man's box."

"Pardon me, your majesty," replied Kaunitz, quickly. "Silesia was a pinch from our snuff-box."

"True," said Frederick, laughing, "but the tobacco was so strong that it has cost me many an uncomfortable sneeze; and nobody has ever been civil enough to say, 'Heaven bless you.'"

While the king and Kaunitz jested together, Signor Tobaldi had been singing his aria; and now that he ceased, Frederick, for the first time, became aware that any music had been going on.

"Your majesty," said the emperor, "has done injustice, for once, to a prima donna. Bernasconi is really sick, but she has sent a substitute."

"These substitutes," said Frederick, "are always on the look-out for such opportunities of sliding into notice; but unhappily they are not often equal to the tasks they are so eager to perform."

"This substitute," said Joseph, "is no rival opera-singer. She is a dear friend of Bernasconi's, who speaks of her singing with enthusiasm."

"Is that possible? Does one singer go into raptures over another? By all means let us hear the phœnix."

The king looked toward the stage, and his countenance assumed at once an expression of genuine interest.

Once more the orchestra began the introduction to Gluck's beautiful aria. Meanwhile a tall and elegant person was seen to advance toward the foot-lights. Her pure Grecian robe, half covered with a mantle of purple velvet, richly embroidered in gold, fell in graceful folds from her snowy shoulders. Her dark hair, worn in the Grecian style, was confined by a diadem of brilliants; and the short, white tunic which she wore under her mantle, was fastened by a girdle blazing with jewels.

She was so transcendently beautiful that Frederick could not resist the temptation of joining in the applause which greeted her entrance. She seemed unconscious of the effect she produced, so earnestly and anxiously were her large, lustrous eyes fixed upon the spot where Frederick and Joseph were sitting together. She raised her graceful arms as she began the prayer of Alceste; but her looks were riveted upon the sovereigns, who represent divinity on earth. When she sang, the tones of her glorious voice sank deep into the hearts of all who listened. Now it was clear, pure, and vibrating, wooing the air like a clarionet—now it caressed the ear like a speaking violin—and anon it poured forth volumes of harmony that filled all space, as the booming organ fills the aisles of a vast and lofty cathedral. Gluck, the hypercritical Gluck, would have been ravished to hear his music as she sang it; and Frederick, who, up to this hour, had refused to acknowledge the genius of the great German, now sat breathless with rapture, as he listened to such music and such interpretation of music as never had been heard before.

The Emperor Joseph was unmindful of it all. He had a vague idea of celestial sounds that seemed to drown him in an ocean of melody; but he heard not a note of Alceste's prayer. Every sense was stunned save one—and that one was sight.

"It is she," murmured he, as the siren ceased to sing; "it is she, the beautiful Pole. How resplendent she is to-night!" Then turning to Kaunitz, whose observing eyes had been watching his face and whose sharp ears had caught his words, he whispered:

"Do you remember the bouquet that was thrown to me this morning?"

"I forget nothing your majesty deigns to communicate to me," replied Kaunitz.

"This is she. Who can she be?"

"Ah!" exclaimed Kaunitz, slightly elevating his eyebrows. "The '*Souvenir d'Epéries.*' Now I comprehend Bernasconi's illness. She felt ill through patriotism, that this adroit countrywoman of hers might have the opportunity of being remarked by your majesty. I would not be at all surprised if she went out of the way of prima donnas to attract your majesty's attention. These Polish women are fanatics in their love of country."

The emperor said nothing in reply. He scarcely listened. His eyes were still upon the descending curtain that hid the mysterious beauty from his sight. If her object had been to attract him, she had certainly succeeded.

The audience were waiting for some signal from either Joseph or Frederick that they might give vent to their admiration. The king understood the general feeling, and began to applaud with his hands. In a moment the applause became vociferous, and it did not cease until the curtain drew up a second time, and the prima donna came forward to receive her ovation.

For one moment they surveyed the enchanting singer, and then broke out into another wild storm, in which the emperor joined so heartily that his voice was heard above the din, crying out, "*Brava! bravassima!*"

The singer sought his glance, and meeting it, blushed deeply. Then, coming forward a few steps, she began once more to sing.

Her song was a passionate appeal to the two princes, whom she addressed openly, in behalf of Poland.

It was over, and not a sound was heard in the theatre. The audience hung, in breathless anxiety, upon the verdict that must come from those who had been addressed. They were so intent upon Frederick and Joseph that they did not see the singer leave the stage. They were not destined, however, to be enlightened or relieved, for no demonstration was made in the imperial box.

But Joseph, rising from his seat, signed to the marshal of the household to approach.

"Go, count," said he, "go quickly, and ask her name. Tell her it is the emperor who desires to know her."

"Her name is Poland," said Kaunitz, in an absent tone. Then, addressing Joseph, he continued: "Did I not tell your majesty that your adventure was not to end with the throwing of a bouquet? I know these Polish women; they coquette with every thing—above all, with the throes of their dying fatherland."

The emperor smiled, but said nothing. He was watching the return of the marshal of the household.

"Well, count, what is her name?" cried he earnestly.

"Sire, I am unable to find it out. The lady has left the theatre, and no one here, not even the director, knows her name."

"Strange," said the emperor. "Let a messenger, then, be sent to Bernasconi: she, of course, must know."

"Pardon me, your majesty, I have been to Bernasconi. She is here, preparing to sing her second air. She has suddenly recovered and will have the honor of appearing before your majesties in a few moments."

"But what said Bernasconi of the Polish singer?"

"She does not know her name, your majesty. She showed me a letter from Colonel Dumourriez, the French plenipotentiary to the Polish Republic. He designates her only as a Polish lady of noble birth, whose remarkable vocal powers were worthy of your majesty's admiration."

"Do you hear that?" said Frederick to Kaunitz. "Do you hear that? The French plenipotentiary sends this prima donna to sing before the emperor. *Vraiment*, it seems that France is disgusted with war, and intends to try her hand at sentiment. Petticoat-government is so securely established there, that I suppose the French are about to throw a petticoat over the heads of their allies. France and Poland are two *femmes galantes.*"

"Yes, sire," replied Kaunitz, "but one of them is old and ugly. *Madame La Pologne* is an old coquette, who puts on youthful airs, and thinks she hides her wrinkles with paint."

"Does your highness, then, believe that her youth is forever past? Can she never be rejuvenated?" asked Frederick, with a searching look at Kaunitz's marble features.

"Sire, people who waste their youth in dissipation and rioting, have no strength when the day of real warfare dawns."

"And it would seem that the Empress of Russia has some intention of making a serious attack upon the poor old lady," said Frederick, while for the second time he took a pinch from the snuff-box of the crafty Austrian.

Meanwhile the concert was going on. Bernasconi, completely restored, sang the beautiful air from "Orpheus and Eurydice," and Frederick applauded as before. But the emperor sat silent and abstracted. His thoughts were with that Polish woman, whose love of country had brought her to Neustadt to remind him of the promises he had made to the Confederates at Epéries.

"How enthusiastically she loves Poland!" said he to himself. "She will of course find means to cross my path again, for she seeks to interest me in the fate of her fatherland. The next time she comes, I will do like the prince in the fairy-tale, I will strew pitch upon the threshold, that she may not be able to escape from me again."

Kaunitz, too, was preoccupied with thoughts of the bewitching Confederate, but the fact that she would be sure to come again was not quite so consoling to him as to Joseph.

As soon as he returned home, he called for his private secretary, who was one of the most dexterous detectives in Vienna.

"You will make inquiries at once as to the whereabout of the prima donna who sang before me and their majesties to-night. To-morrow at nine o'clock I must know who she is, where she lodges, and what is her business here."

CHAPTER LXII.

FREDERICK THE GREAT AND PRINCE KAUNITZ.

THE great review, which had been gotten up in honor of the King of Prussia, was over. In this review Frederick had become acquainted with the strength of the Austrian army, the superiority of its cavalry, and the military capacity of the emperor who was its commander-in-chief.

The king had been loud in his praises of all three, and had embraced the emperor in presence of the whole army.

Immediately after the review, Frederick sent a page to announce to Prince Kaunitz that he would be glad to see him in his own private apartments.

Kaunitz at once declared his readiness to wait upon the king, and to the unspeakable astonishment of his valet, had actually shortened his toilet and had betrayed some indifference to the arrangement of his peruke. As he left the room, his gait was elastic and active, and his countenance bore visible marks of the excitement with which he was looking forward to the coming interview.

But Kaunitz himself became suddenly aware of all this, and he set to work to force back his emotion. The nearer he came to the king's suite of rooms, the slower became his step and the calmer his mien. At last it was tranquillized, and the minister looked almost as cold and indifferent as ever.

Arrived at the door of the antechamber, he looked around, and having convinced himself that no one was in sight, he drew from his breast-pocket a small mirror which he always wore about his person. Sharply he viewed himself therein, until gradually, as he looked, his face resumed the stony aspect which like a thickening haze concealed his emotions from other men's eyes.

"It is really not worth my while," thought he, "to get up an excitement because I am about to have a conference with that small bit of royalty, Frederick. If he should discover it, he might suppose that I, like the rest of the world, am abashed in the presence of a king because he has some military fame. No—no—what excites me is the fact that I am about to write a bit of history; for this interview between Prussia and Austria will be historical. It is the fate of Europe—that fate which I hold in my hands, that stirs me with such unwonted emotion. This King of Prussia has nothing to do with it. No doubt he hopes to hoodwink me with flattery, but I shall work him to *my* ends, and force him to that line of policy which I have long ago laid down for Austria's welfare."

Here the mirror was returned to his pocket, and he opened the door of the anteroom. The sweet sounds of a flute broke in upon his ear as he entered. The king's aide-de-camp came up and whispered that his sovereign was accustomed to play on the flute daily, and that he never failed even when in camp to solace his solitude with music.

Prince Kaunitz answered with a shrug, and pointing to the door, said, "Announce me to his majesty."

The aide-de-camp opened the door and announced his highness Prince Kaunitz.

The flute ceased, and the rich, musical voice of Frederick was heard to say, "He can enter."

Kaunitz was not much pleased to receive a permission where he fancied himself entitled to an invitation; but he had no alternative, so he walked languidly forward while the officer held the door open.

"Shut the door, and admit no one during the visit of Prince Kaunitz," said the king. Then turning to the prince, he pointed to his flute. "I suspect you are amused to see such an old fellow as I coquetting with the fine arts; but I assure you that my flute is one of my trustiest friends. She has never deceived me, and keeps my secrets faithfully. My alliance with her is for life. Ask her, and she will tell you that we live on terms of truest friendship."

"Unhappily, I do not understand the language of your lady-love. Your majesty will perhaps allow me to turn my attention to another one of your feminine allies, toward whom I shall venture to question your majesty's good faith."

"Of what lady do you speak?" cried Frederick, eagerly.

"Of the Empress Catharine," replied Kaunitz, slightly inclining his head.

"Oh!" said the king, laughing, "you dart like an arrow to the point, and transfix me at once upon the barb of politics. Let us sit down, then. The arm-chair which you are taking now, may boast hereafter that it is the courser which has carried the greatest statesman in Europe to a field where he is sure to win new victories."

Kaunitz was careful to seat himself at the same time as the king, and they both sat before a table covered with charts, papers, and books.

A short pause ensued. Both were collecting their energies for the strife. The king, with his eagle eye, gazed upon the face of the astute diplomatist, while he, pretending not to see it, looked perfectly oblivious of kings or emperors.

"So you will ask of Catharine whether I am a loyal ally or not?" asked the king at last.

"Yes, sire, for unluckily the Empress of Russia is the one who can give me information."

"Why unluckily?"

"Because I grieve to see that a German prince is willing to form alliances with her, who, if she could, would bring all Europe under her yoke, and make every European sovereign her vassal. Russia grows hourly more dangerous and more grasping. She foments discord and incites wars, for she finds her fortune in the dissensions of other nations, and at every misunderstanding between other powers, she makes a step toward the goal whither she travels."

"And what is that goal?"

"The subjugation of all Europe," cried Kaunitz, with unusual warmth. "Russia's policy is that of unprincipled ambition; and if so far she has not progressed in her lust of dominion, it is Austria, or rather the policy which I dictate to Austria, that has checked her advance. It is I who have restored the balance of power, by conquering Austria's antipathy to France, by isolating haughty England, and hunting all Europe against rapacious Russia. But Russia never loses sight of the policy initiated by Peter the Great; and as I have stemmed the tide of her aggression toward the west, it is overflowing toward the south and the east. All justice disregarding. Russian armies occupy Poland; and before long the ships of

Russia will swarm in the Black Sea and threaten Constantinople. Russia is perforce a robber, for she is internally exhausted, and unless she seeks new ports for her commerce, and new sources of revenue, she is ruined."

"You err, I assure you," cried Frederick, eagerly. "Russia is in a condition to sustain any burden; her revenues this year show an increase over the last of five hundred thousand rubles."

"Then this increase comes probably from the million of subsidy which your majesty has agreed to pay to Russia," said Kaunitz, bowing.* "Such rich tribute may well give her strength to attempt any thing; but every thaler which your majesty pays into her treasury is a firebrand which will one day consume all Europe. If indeed, as you say, Russia is strong and formidable, it is for your majesty to hold her in check; if she is exhausted, her alliance is not worth having." †

"Your highness seems eager to have me break off my connection with Russia," said the king, while a cloud passed over his face. "You wish to prove that Russia is a power whose friendship is worthless and whose enmity is to be despised. And yet it is well known to me how zealously the Austrian ambassador was intriguing not long ago to induce Russia to cast me aside and enter into an alliance with you. Your highness must excuse me if I throw aside the double-edged blade of courtly dissimulation. I am an old soldier and my tongue refuses to utter any thing but unvarnished truth."

"If your majesty permits," replied Kaunitz with some warmth, "I, too, will speak the unvarnished truth. You are pleased to charge me with seeking to alienate Russia from Prussia while striving to promote an alliance of the former with Austria. Will your majesty allow me to reply to this accusation in full without interruption?"

"I will," replied Frederick, nodding his head. "Speak on, I shall not put in a word."

CHAPTER LXIII.

RUSSIA A FOE TO ALL EUROPE.

PRINCE KAUNITZ remained silent for a time, as though he were turning over in his mind what he should say to the king. Then slowly raising his head, he met the scrutinizing glance of Frederick with perfect composure, and spoke as follows:

"At the conclusion of the unhappy war which desolated both Austria and Prussia, I had to consider what course for the future was likely to recuperate the prostrate energies of Austria. I resolved in my mind various schemes, and laid them before her imperial majesty. The one which I advocated and which was adopted by the empress, had mainly for its object the pacification of all European broils, and the restoration of the various Austrian dependencies to order and prosperity. For some time I waited to see whether your majesty would not seek to conciliate France, and renew your old league of friendship with her king. But the policy pursued by

* Ferrand, "History of the Dismemberment of Poland," vol. i., p. 84.
† Kaunitz's own words. Ferrand, vol. i., p. 108.

your majesty at the court of Russia convinced me that you were thinking exclusively of securing your provinces in the east. This once understood, it became the interest of Austria to rivet the links which bound her to France; for an alliance with her offered the same advantages to us as that of Russia did to Prussia. Moreover, it was Austria's opinion that Prussia was now too closely bound to Russia for her ever to seek an alliance with France. It therefore appeared that our good understanding with the latter would conduce to preserve the balance of power among European nations, and that it would meet with the favor of all those potentates who were anxious for peace. It follows thence that the court of Vienna is perfectly content with her relations toward France; and I expressly and distinctly declare to your majesty that we never will seek to alienate Russia from Prussia, that we never will encourage any advances from Russia, and that your majesty may rest assured that we never will deviate from our present line of policy. This was what I desired to explain, and I thank your majesty for the courtesy with which you have listened to me." *

The face of the king, which at first had looked distrustful, was now entirely free from suspicion. He rose from his chair, and giving his hand to Kaunitz, said with a cordial smile:

"This is what I call noble and candid statesmanship. You have not spoken as a diplomatist, but as a great minister, who, feeling his strength, has no reason to conceal his actions. I will answer in the same spirit. Sit down again and hear me. You fear Russia, and think that if she gains too great an ascendency among nations, she will use it to the detriment of all Europe. I agree with you, and I myself would view the aggrandizement of Russia under Catharine with disapprobation and distrust. You are right, and I feel the embarrassment of my present political condition. At the commencement of this Turkish war, I would have used my honest endeavors to check the usurping advances of Russia, not only in Turkey but also in Poland. But I myself was in a critical position. You, who had been represented to me as the most rapacious of diplomatists, you had prejudiced all Europe against me, so that for seven long years my only allies were my rights and my good sword. The only hand reached out to me was that of Russia; policy constrained me to grasp and retain it. It is both to my honor and my interest that I keep faith with Russia, and eschew all shifts and tergiversations in my dealings with her. Her alliance is advantageous to Prussia, and therefore I pay her large subsidies, give her advice, allow my officers to enlist in her armies, and finally I have promised the empress that should Austria interfere in behalf of the Turks, I will use all my influence to mediate between you." †

"Does that mean that if Russia and Austria should go to war, your majesty will stand by the former?"

"It means that I will make every effort to prevent a war between Russia and Austria. If, in spite of all that I could do, there should be war between you, it would not be possible for Prussia to remain neutral. Were she to do so, she would deserve the contempt both of friend and foe. I would fulfil my obligations to Russia, that I might secure the duration of our alliance. But I sincerely hope

* This discourse of Kaunitz is historical. It is found in Ferrand's "Histoire des Trois Démembrements de la Pologne," vol. i., p. 112.

† Dohm, "Memoirs of My Times," vol. i., p. 456.

that it may be my good fortune to mediate with such results as will spare me the espousal of either party's quarrel."

"If so, Russia must abandon her ambitious projects in Turkey, and she must speedily consent to secure peace to Poland," replied Kaunitz warmly.

The king smiled, and taking from the table a sealed packet, he presented it to Kaunitz.

"A letter for me!" exclaimed the minister, surprised.

"Yes, your highness. A few moments before you came hither, a courier arrived from Constantinople with dispatches for you and for me."

"Does your majesty allow me to open them?"

"I request you to read them while I read mine, which are, as yet, unopened. I have only read the report of my ambassador at Constantinople. Let us see what news we have."

The king, with a smiling inclination of the head, settled himself in his arm-chair, and began to read.

A long pause ensued. Both tried to seem absorbed in the dispatches from Turkey, yet each one gave now and then a hasty, furtive glance at the other. If their eyes met, they were quickly cast down again, and so they continued to watch and read, until there was no more excuse for silence.

"Bad news from Turkey," said Frederick, speaking first, and putting down his letters.

"The Porte has been unfortunate," said Kaunitz, shrugging his shoulders and looking perfectly indifferent. "Russia has not only gained a great victory on land, but has defeated him at sea, and has burnt his fleet."

"The consequence of all this is, that Turkey now turns to Austria and Prussia for help," replied the king. "Upon our intervention now, hangs the peace of all Europe. We have a most important mission to perform."

"Your majesty intends to undertake it?" asked Kaunitz, carelessly.

"I am resolved to do all that I can to prevent war. It is such a terrible scourge, that no nation has a right to fold her hands and see its horrors, if by any step of hers it can be averted or stopped. Turkey asks for intervention, that she may be restored to the blessings of peace. Shall we refuse her?"

"Austria cannot mediate in this affair unless Russia first proposes it," said Kaunitz, in a listless tone. "The court of Vienna cannot make propositions to Russia. It therefore rests with your majesty to induce the Empress Catharine to make the same request of Austria, as Turkey has made of us both."

"I will propose it to the empress," said the king eagerly; "and I feel sure that she will agree to do so."

Kaunitz bowed loftily. "Then," replied he, "Austria will mediate; but let it be understood that the peace is to be an honorable one for Turkey, and that Russia ceases any further aggression in that quarter."

"The Porte will be under the necessity of making some concessions," said the king, "since he it is whose arms have sustained reverses. But Turkey may still remain a second-rate power, for I think that Russia will be satisfied with the Crimea and the Black Sea for herself, and a guaranty of independent sovereigns for Wallachia and Moldavia."

"Independent princes appointed by Russia!" cried Kaunitz. "My imperial sovereign will never consent to have a Russian province contiguous to Austria; and should Moldavia and Wallachia be governed by hospodars and petty despots, their pretended independence would soon melt away into a Russian dependency. Austria, too, would esteem it a great misfortune if Russia should come into possession of the Crimea and the Black Sea. Her dominion over the Black Sea would be more dangerous to Europe than an extension of her territory. Nothing, in short, would be so fatal to that independence which is dear to all nations, as the cession of this important outlet to Russia." *

"Your highness may be right," said the king; "and Austria has more to fear from this dominion than Prussia; for the Danube is a finger of the Black Sea, which might be used to seize some of your fairest provinces. We will keep this in view when we enter upon our negotiations with Russia."

"Before we begin them at all, we must exact of Russia to restore peace to Poland."

"Ah, you wish to draw Poland into the circle of intervention?" said Frederick, laughing.

"The court of Vienna cannot suffer Russia to oppress this unfortunate people as she has hitherto done. Not only has she forced Stanislaus Augustus upon them, but she has also compelled them to alter their constitution, and, in the face of all justice, her armies occupy Poland, devastating the country, and oppressing both royalists and republicans."

"You are resolved to speak of Poland," said Frederick, again taking so large a pinch of snuff that it bedaubed not only his face, but his white Austrian uniform. He brushed it off with his fingers, and shaking his head, said: "I am not neat enough to wear this elegant dress. I am not worthy of wearing the Austrian livery." † He then resumed: "You interest yourself in Poland. *I* thought that Polish independence had been thrown to the winds. I thought, also, that your highness was of the same opinion on this question as the Empress Catharine, who says that she neither knows where Polish territory begins nor where it ends. Now I am equally at a loss to know what is and what is not Poland, for in Warsaw a Russian army seems to be perfectly at home, and in the south of Poland an Austrian regiment affirms that they occupy Polish ground by command of the Austrian government."

"Your majesty is pleased to speak of the county of Zips. Zips has always belonged to Hungary. It was mortgaged by the Emperor Sigismund to his brother-in-law Wladislaw Jagello for a sum of money. Hungary has never parted with her right to this country; and, as we have been compelled to send troops to our frontier to watch Russia, the opportunity presents itself for us to demonstrate to Poland that Austria can never consent to regard a mortgaged province as one either given or sold. Zips belongs to Austria, and we will pay back to the King of Poland the sum for which it was mortgaged. That is all."

"Yes, but it will be difficult not only for Poland, but for all Europe, which is accustomed to consider Zips as Polish territory, to remember your highness's new boundaries. I, for my part, do not

* The prince's own words. Ferrand, i., p. 112.
† The king's own words. Ferrand, p. 112.

understand it, and I will be much obliged to you if, according to your new order of things, you will show me where Hungary ends and Poland begins."

"Where the county of Zips ends, and where the boundaries of Hungary began in olden times, there the line that separates Austria from Poland should be drawn."

"Ah!" sighed the king, "you speak of the olden time. But we must settle all these things now with regard to the present. I happen, by chance, to have a map of Poland on my table. Oblige me now by showing me Poland as your highness understands its boundaries."

The king stood up, and unfolding a map, laid it on the table. Kaunitz also rose, and stood on the opposite side.

"Now," said Frederick, "let me see the county of Zips."

CHAPTER LXIV.

THE MAP OF POLAND.

"HERE, your majesty, is Zips," said Kaunitz, as he passed his delicate white finger over the lower part of the map.

The king leaned over, and looked thoughtfully at the moving finger. For some time he kept silence, then he raised his head, and met the gaze of the prince.

"A very pretty piece of land which Austria takes from her neighbor," said he, with a piercing glance at Kaunitz.

"Austria takes nothing from her neighbor, sire, except that which belongs to her," replied Kaunitz, quietly.

"How very fortunate it is that this particular piece of land should belong to Austria!" said the king, with a slight sneer. "You see that Poland, who for so many centuries had supposed herself to be the rightful owner of the Zips, has, in virtue of such ownership, projected beyond the Carpathian Mountains quite to the interior of Hungary. Now a wedge of that sort is inconvenient, perhaps dangerous, and it is lucky for Austria that she has found out her right of possession in that quarter. It not only contracts her neighbor's domains, but essentially increases her own. It now concerns Austria to prove to Europe her right to this annexation, for Europe is somewhat astonished to hear of it."

"In the court-chancery, at Vienna, are the documents to prove that the Zips was mortgaged by the Emperor Sigismund to his brother-in-law Wladislaw, in the year 1412, for the sum of thirty-seven thousand groschen."

"Since 1412!" cried Frederick. "Three hundred and fifty-five years' possession on the part of Poland has not invalidated the title of Austria to the Zips! My lawful claim to Silesia was of more modern date than this, and yet Austria would have made it appear that it was superannuated."

"Your majesty has proved, conclusively, that it was not so," replied Kaunitz, with a slight inclination of the head.

"Will Austria take the course which I pursued to vindicate my right?" asked the king, quickly.

"Stanislaus will not allow us to proceed to extremities," replied the Prince. "True, he complained at first, and wrote to the empress-queen to demand what he called justice."

"And will your highness inform me what the empress-queen replied in answer to these demands?"

"She wrote to the King of Poland that the time had arrived when it became incumbent upon her to define the boundaries of her empire. That, in her annexation of the Zips to Austria, she was actuated, not by any lust of territorial aggrandizement, but by a conviction of her just and inalienable rights. She was prepared, not only to assert, but to defend them; and she took this opportunity to define the lines of her frontier, for the reason that Poland was in a state of internal warfare, the end of which no man could foresee." *

"If I were King of Poland, such plain language as this would put me on my guard."

"Sire, if you were King of Poland, no foreign power would employ such language toward you," said Kaunitz, with a half smile.

"That is true," replied the king, shaking his head. "The King of Poland is a weak, good-natured fellow. He cannot forget that he has been the lover of Catharine of Russia, and I verily believe, that if she were to make a sign, he would lay, not only himself, but all Poland, at her feet."

"Austria would never suffer her to accept it," cried Kaunitz.

The king shrugged his shoulders. "And yet, it would appear that when Zips lay at her feet, the Empress of Austria was ready to embrace it. But everybody grows eccentric when Poland is in question. My brother Henry, who is in St. Petersburg, was one day discussing this matter of the annexation of Zips with the empress. As Catharine, like myself, has never had the privilege of examining the records in the court of chancery at Vienna, she expressed some doubt as to the justice of Austria's appropriation in that quarter. 'It seems,' said she, 'as if one had nothing to do but stoop down to pick up something in Poland.' † Now, when proud Austria and her lofty Kaunitz condescend to stoop and pick up, why shall not other people follow their example? I, too, shall be obliged to march my troops into Poland, for every misfortune seems about to visit this unhappy land. Who knows that in the archives at Berlin there may not be some document to prove that I, also, have a right to extend the lines of my frontier?"

While Frederick spoke, he kept his eyes fixed upon the face of Prince Kaunitz, as though he would have read to the very bottom of his soul. The latter pretended not to be aware of it; he looked perfectly blank, while he affected to be still interested in examining the map.

"It would be fortunate if your majesty could discover such documents in *your* archives," replied he, coolly. "I have been told that you have, heretofore, sought for them in Warsaw; unhappily, without being able to find any."

The king could not repress a slight start as he heard this revelation of his own machinations. Kaunitz again affected to see nothing, although he was looking directly in the king's eyes.

"I say," continued Kaunitz, "that it would be most fortunate if, *just at this time*, your majesty could recover your titles to that por-

* Ferrand, i., p. 94.

† Rulhière's "History of Poland," vol. iv., p. 210.

tion of Poland which lies contiguous to Russia. Austria, I assure you, will place no difficulties in the way."

"Really," replied the king, "I must say that these lines form a better natural frontier than my present boundaries." Here he passed his hand somewhere through the north-western provinces of Poland, while he continued: "Would my word suffice if I were to say to Austria that the documents, proving my right to this territory, are to be found in the archives at Berlin?"

"Your majesty's word, as regards this question, is worth more than the documents," said Kaunitz, deliberately.

"But what would Catharine say?—she who looks upon Poland as her own?"

"If she says any thing, it is high time she were undeceived in that respect," said Kaunitz, hastily. "She must be satisfied to share equally with others. Your majesty was pleased to relate to me a portion of the conversation between the empress and Prince Henry. The empress said, 'It seems as if one had nothing to do but stoop down to pick up something in Poland.' But you forgot the sequel. She added these words: 'If the court of Vienna begins the dismemberment of Poland, I think that her neighbors have a right to continue it.'" *

"*Vraiment*, your highness has trusty reporters, and your agents serve you admirably!" exclaimed the king.

Kaunitz bowed haughtily.

"We are your majesty's imitators," replied he. "First during the Silesian war, then at the court of Dresden, we learned from you the value of secret information.† Having been apprised of the remarkable words of the empress, I began to fear that she might encroach upon Poland without regard to the claims of Austria. Your majesty is aware that the Russian army occupy Warsaw, and that a cordon of Russian troops extend as far as the frontiers of Turkey."

"And if I draw my cordon beyond the district of Netz," cried the king, drawing his finger across the map as if it had been a sword, "and Austria extends her frontier beyond Galicia and the Zips, the republic of Poland will occupy but a small space on the map of Europe."

"The smaller the better; the fewer Poles there are in the world the less strife there will be. The cradle of the Poles is that apple of discord which Eris once threw upon the table of the gods; they were born of its seeds, and dissension is their native element. As long as there lives a Pole on the earth, that Pole will breed trouble among his neighbors."

"Ah!" said the king, taking a pinch of snuff, "and yet your highness was indignant at Catharine because she would force the Poles to keep the peace. She appears to *me* to be entirely of one mind with yourself. She, too, looks upon Poland as the apple of Eris, and she has found it so over-ripe that it is in danger of falling from the tree. She has stationed her gardener, Stanislaus, to guard it. Let him watch over it. It belongs to him, and if it come to

* La Roche Aymon, "Vie du Prince Henri," p. 171.

† Through his ambassador at Dresden, Frederick had bribed the keeper of the Saxon archives to send him copies of the secret treaties between Austria and Saxony. He did even worse, for the *attaché* of the Austrian embassy at Berlin was in his pay, and he sent the king copies of all the Austrian dispatches.—L. Mühlbach, "Life of Frederick the Great."

the ground, he has nobody to blame but himself. Meanwhile, should it burst, we will find means to prevent it from soiling *us*. Now let us speak of Turkey. That unlucky Porte must have something done for him, and while we mediate in his behalf, I hope to bring about a good understanding between Austria and Russia. Let us do our best to promote a general peace. Europe is bleeding at every pore; let us bind up her wounds, and restore her to health."

"Austria is willing to promote the general welfare," replied Kaunitz, following the king's example and rising from his chair, "but first Russia must conclude an honorable peace with Turkey, and she must abandon her rapacious designs upon the rest of Europe. But should the Empress of Russia compel us to war with her on this question we will not have recourse to arms until we have found means to alienate from her the most formidable of her allies."

The king laughed. "I approve your policy," said he, "but I am curious to know how you would manage to prevent me from keeping my word. I am certainly pledged to Russia, but I hope that the negotiations into which we are about to enter will end in peace. I shall send a *résumé* of our conference to the empress, and use every effort to establish friendly relations between you."

"Will your majesty communicate her reply to me?" asked Kaunitz.

"I certainly will; for I am a soldier, not a diplomatist, and I am so much in love with truth that I shall be her devotee until the last moment of my life."

"Ah, sire, a man must be a hero like yourself to have the courage to love so dangerous a mistress. Truth is a rose with a thousand thorns. He who plucks it will be wounded, and woe to the head of him who wears it in his crown!"

"You and I have fought and bled too often on the field of diplomacy to be tender about our heads. Let us, then, wear the crown of truth, and bear with its thorns."

So saying, the king reached out his hand, and Kaunitz took his leave.

After the prince had left the room, Frederick remained for a few minutes listening, until he heard the door of the farther anteroom closed.

"Now, Hertzberg," cried he, "come out—the coast is clear."

A gigantic screen, which divided the room in two, began to move, and forth came Count Hertzberg, the king's prime minister.

"Did you hear it all?" asked Frederick, laughing.

"I did, so please your majesty."

"Did you write it down, so that I can send its *résumé* to the Empress Catharine?"

"Yes, your majesty, as far as it was possible to do so, I have written down every word of your conference," said Hertzberg, with a dissatisfied expression of countenance.

The king raised his large eyes with an inquiring look at the face of his trusty minister. "Are you not satisfied, Hertzberg? Why do you shake your head? You have three wrinkles in your forehead, and the corners of your mouth turn down as they always do when something has displeased you. Speak out, man. Of what do you complain?"

"First, I complain that your majesty has allowed the old fox to perceive that you, as well as himself, entertain designs upon Poland, and that in a manner you are willing to guarantee to Austria her theft of the Zips. I also complain that you have consented to induce Russia, through the intervention of Austria, to make peace with Turkey."

"Is that all?" asked the king.

"Yes, your majesty; that is all."

"Well, then, hear my defence. As regards your first complaint, I allowed the old fox (as you call him) to scent my desire for Polish game, because I wished to find out exactly how far I could venture to go in the matter."

"Yes, sire, and the consequences will be, that Austria, who has already appropriated the Zips, will stoop down to pick up something else. She has already had her share of the booty, why should she divide with your majesty?"

"Let Austria have her second share," cried the king, laughing. "It will earn for her a double amount of the world's censure.* As regards your second complaint, let me tell you, that at this moment peace is indispensable to us all, and for this reason I desire to bring Russia and Austria into friendly relations with one another. I think it not only wiser but more honorable to pacify Europe than to light the torch of war a second time. It is not an easy matter to secure a general peace, and we must all make some concessions to achieve a result so desirable. Do you suppose that it is as easy to conciliate unfriendly powers as it is to write bad verses? I assure you, Hertzberg, that I would rather sit down to render the whole Jewish history into madrigals, than undertake to fuse into unanimity the conflicting interests of three sovereigns, when two out of the three are women! But I will do my best. When your neighbor's house is on fire, help to put it out, or it may communicate and burn down your own." †

CHAPTER LXV.

THE COUNTESS WIELOPOLSKA.

"YOU really think that he will come, Matuschka?" asked the Countess Wielopolska of her waiting-woman, who, standing behind the chair, was fastening a string of pearls in her lady's dusky hair.

"I know he will come, your ladyship," replied Matuschka.

"And you have seen the emperor and spoken to him!" exclaimed the countess, pressing her delicate white hands upon her heart, as though she strove to imprison its wild emotions.

"Indeed I have, my lady."

"Oh, tell me of it again, Matuschka; tell me, that I may not fancy it a dream!" cried the countess, eagerly.

"Well, then, my lady, I took your note to the palace, where the emperor has given positive orders that every one who wishes it shall be admitted to his presence. The guard before the door let me pass into the antechamber. One of the lords in waiting told me that the emperor would be there before a quarter of an hour. I had not waited so long when the door opened and a handsome young man in

* The king's own words. Coxe, "History of Austria, vol. v., p. 20.
† The king's own words. "Œuvres Posthumes," vol. ii., p. 187.

a plain white uniform walked in. I should never have taken him for the emperor, except that the lord stood up so straight when he saw him. Then I knelt down and gave the letter. The emperor took it and said: 'Tell your lady that I am not prepared to receive ladies in my palace; but since she wishes to see me, I will go to her. If she will be at home this evening, I will find time to call upon her myself.'"

"Ah!" cried the countess, "he will soon be here. I shall see him —speak to him—pour out the longings of my bursting heart! Oh, Matuschka, as the moment approaches, I feel as if I could fly away and plunge into the wild waters of the Vistula that bear my husband's corpse, or sink lifeless upon the battle-field that is reddened with the blood of my brothers."

"Do not think of these dreadful things, dear lady," said Matuschka, trying to keep back her tears; "it is twilight, and the emperor will soon be here. Look cheerful—for you are as beautiful as an angel when you smile, and the emperor will be much more apt to be moved by your smiles than by your tears."

"You are right, Matuschka," cried the countess, rising hastily from her seat. "I will not weep, for I must try to find favor in the emperor's eyes."

She crossed the room and stood before a Psyche, where for some time she scrutinized her own features; not with the self-complacency of a vain woman, but with the critical acuteness of an artist who contemplates a fine picture. Gradually her eyes grew soft and her mouth rippled with a smile. Like a mourning Juno she stood in the long black velvet dress that sharply defined the outlines of her faultless bust and fell in graceful folds around her stately figure. Her bodice was clasped by an *agraffe* of richest pearls; and the white throat and the jewel lay together, pearl beside pearl, each rivalling the snowy lustre of the other. Had it not been for those starry eyes that looked out so full of mournful splendor, her face might have seemed too statuesque in its beauty; but from their dark depths all the enthusiasm of a nature that had concentrated its every emotion into one master-passion, lit up her face with flashes that came and went like summer lightning.

"Yes, I am beautiful," whispered she, while a sad smile played around her exquisite mouth. "My beauty is the last weapon left me wherewith to battle for Poland. I must take advantage of it. Life and honor, wealth and blood, every thing for my country!"

She turned to her waiting-woman as a queen would have done who was dismissing her subjects.

"Go, Matuschka," said she, "and take some rest. You have been laboring for me all day, and I cannot bear to think that the only friend left me in this world should be overtasked for me. Sometimes you look at me as my mother once did; and then I dream that I feel her hand laid lovingly upon my head, and hear her dear voice exhorting me to pray that God would bless me with strength to do my duty to my bleeding country."

Matuschka fell upon her knees and kissed the hem of her mistress's robe.

"Do not give way," sobbed she, "do not grieve now."

The countess did not hear. She had thrown back her head and was gazing absently above. "Oh, yes, I am mindful of my duty," murmured she. "I have not forgotten the vow I made to my mother and sealed upon her dying lips with my last kiss! I have been a faithful daughter of my fatherland. I have given every thing—there remains nothing but myself, and oh, how gladly would I give my life for Poland! But God has forsaken us; His eyes are turned away!"

"Accuse not the Lord, dear lady," prayed Matuschka. "Put your trust in Him, and take courage."

"It is true. I have no right to accuse my Maker," sighed the countess. "When the last drop of Polish blood is spent and the last Polish heart is crushed beneath the tramp of the enemy's hosts, then it will be time to cry to Heaven! Rise, Matuschka, and weep no more. All is not yet lost. Let us hope, and labor that hope may become reality, and Poland may be free!"

She reached her hand to Matuschka and passed into an adjoining room. It was the state apartment of the inn, and was always reserved for distinguished guests. It had been richly furnished, but the teeth of time had nibbled many a rent in the old-fashioned furniture, the faded curtains, and the well-worn carpet. Matuschka, however, had given an air of some elegance to the place. On the carved oak table in the centre stood a vase of flowers; and, that her dear mistress might have something to remind her of home, Matuschka had procured a piano, to which the countess, when weary of her thoughts, might confide the hopes and fears that were surging in her storm-tossed heart.

The piano was open, and a sheet of music lay on the desk. As the countess perceived it, she walked rapidly toward the instrument and sat down before it.

"I will sing," said she. "The emperor loves music, above all things the music of Gluck."

She turned over the leaves, and then said, softly:

"'Orpheus and Eurydice!' La Bernasconi told me that this was his favorite opera. Oh, that I knew which aria he loved the best?"

She struck a few chords, and in a low voice began to sing. Gradually her beautiful features lost their sadness, she seemed to forget herself and her sorrows, and to yield up her soul to the influence of Gluck's heavenly music. And now, with all the power, the melody, the pathos of her matchless voice, she sang, "*Che faro senza Eurydice!*"

The more she sang, the brighter grew her lovely face. Forgetful of all things around, she gave herself wholly up to the inspiration of the hour, and from its fountains of harmony she drew sweetest draughts of consolation and of hope.

The door had opened, and she had not heard it. On the threshold stood the emperor, followed by Matuschka, while the countess, all unmindful, filled the air with srains so divine, that they might have been the marriage-hymns of Love wedded to Song.

The emperor had stopped for a moment to listen. His face, which at first had worn an expression of smiling flippancy, now changed its aspect. He recognized the music, and felt his heart beat wildly. With a commanding gesture, he motioned Matuschka to withdraw, and noiselessly closed the door.

CHAPTER LXVI.

THE EMPEROR AND THE COUNTESS.

THE countess continued to sing, although Joseph had advanced as far as the centre of the room. The thickness of the carpet made his footfall inaudible. He stood with his right hand resting upon the oak table, while he leaned forward to listen, and one by one the dead memories of his youthful love came thronging around his heart, and filling it with an ecstasy that was half joy and half sorrow.

More and more impassioned grew the music, while the air was tremulous with melody. It softened and softened, until it melted away in sobs. The hands of the enchantress fell from the keys; she bowed her head, and leaning against the music, burst into tears.

The emperor, too, felt the tear-drops gather in his eyes; he dashed them away, and went rapidly up to the piano.

"Countess," said he, in his soft, mellow tones, "I felt it no indiscretion to listen unseen to your heavenly music, but no one save God has a right to witness your grief."

She started, and rising quickly, the emperor saw the face of the lady who had thrown him the wreath.

"It is she!" cried he, "the beautiful Confederate! I thank you from my heart for the favor you have done me, for I have sought you for some days in vain."

"Your majesty sought me?" said she, smiling. "Then I am sure that you are ready to sympathize with misfortune."

"Do you need sympathy?" asked he, eagerly.

"Sire, I am a daughter of Poland," replied she.

"And the Wielopolskas are among the noblest and richest of Poland's noble families."

"Noble! Rich! Our castles have been burned by the Russians, our fields have been laid waste, our vassals have been massacred, and of our kinsmen, some have died under the knout, while others drag out a life of martyrdom in Siberia."

"One of the Counts Wielopolska was a favorite of the king, was he not?" asked Joseph, much moved.

"He was my husband," replied she, bitterly. "Heedless of his countrymen's warnings, he believed in the patriotism of Stanislaus. When he saw his error, he felt that he merited death, and expiated his fault by self-destruction. His grave is in the Vistula."

"Unhappy wife!" exclaimed the emperor. "And had you no other kinsman?"

"I had a father and three brothers."

"You had them?"

"Yes, sire, but I have them no longer. My brothers died on the field of battle; my father, oh, my father!—God grant that he be no more among the living, *for he is in Siberia!*"

The emperor raised his hands in horror; then extending them to the countess, he took hers, and said in a voice of deepest sympathy: "I thank you for coming to me. Tell me your plans for the future, that I may learn how best I may serve you."

"Sire, I have none," sighed she. "Life is so mournful, that I long to close my eyes forever upon its tragedies, but—"

"But what?"

"I should then be robbed of the sight of him who has promised succor to my fatherland," cried she, passionately, while she sank upon her knees and clasped her hands convulsively together.

Joseph bent over, and would have raised her from the floor. "It ill becomes such beauty to kneel before me," said he, softly.

"Let me kneel, let me kneel!" exclaimed she, while her beautiful eyes suffused with tears. "Here, at your feet, let me implore your protection for Poland! Have mercy, sire, upon the Confederates, whose only crime is their resistance to foreign oppression. Reach out your imperial hand to *them*, and bid them be free, for they must either be slaves, or die by their own hands. Emperor of Austria, save the children of Sobieski from barbarous Russia!"

"Do not fear," replied Joseph, kindly. "I promised the Confederates that Austria would recognize their envoy, and I will redeem my word. Rise, countess, I implore you, rise, and may the day not be distant when I shall extend my hand to Poland as I now do to you. You have a pledge of my sincerity, in the fact that we have both a common enemy, and it will not be my fault if I do not oppose her, sword in hand. Still, although men call me emperor, I am the puppet of another will. The crown of Austria is on my mother's head; its shadow, alone, is upon mine. I speak frankly to you; but our acquaintance is peculiar, and, by its nature, has broken down the ordinary barriers of conventional life. Your songs and your tears have spoken directly to my heart. recalling the only happy days that I have ever known on earth. But I am growing sentimental. You will pardon me, I know, for you are a woman, and have known what it is to love."

She slowly shook her head. "No, sire," replied she, "I have never known what it was to love."

The emperor looked directly in her eyes. *She!* Beautiful and majestic as Hera,—*she*, not know what it was to love! "And your husband—" asked he.

"I was married to him as Poland was given to Stanislaus. I never saw him until he became my husband."

"And your heart refused allegiance?"

"Sire, I have never yet seen the man who was destined to reign over my heart."

"Ah, you are proud! I envy him who is destined to conquer that enchanting domain."

She looked for one moment at the emperor, and then said, blushing: "Sire, my heart will succumb to him who rescues Poland. With rapture it will acknowledge him as lord and sovereign of my being."

The emperor made no reply. He gazed with a significant smile at the lovely enthusiast, until she blushed again, and her eyes sought the ground.

"Ah, countess," said Joseph, after a pause, "if all the women of Poland were of your mind, a multitudinous army would soon flock to her standard."

"Every Polish woman is of one mind with me. We are all the daughters of one mother, and our love for her is stronger than death."

The emperor shook his head. "Were this true," replied he, "Poland would never have fallen as she has done. But far be it from me to heap reproaches upon the unfortunate. I will do what it lies in my power to do for the Poles, provided they are willing to second my efforts for themselves. If they would have peace, however, with other nations, they must show strength and unity of purpose among themselves. Until they can stand before the world in the serried ranks of a national unanimity, they must expect to be assailed by their rapacious neighbors. But let us forget politics for a moment. I long to speak to you of yourself. What are your plans? How can I serve you?"

"Sire, I have no plans. I ask nothing of the world but a place of refuge, where I can sorrow unseen."

"You are too young, and, pardon me, if I add, too beautiful, to fly from the world. Come to Vienna, and learn from me how easy it is to live without happiness."

"Your majesty will allow me to go to Vienna?" cried the countess, joyfully. "Ever since I have felt that I could do nothing for Poland, I have longed to live in Vienna, that I might breathe the same atmosphere with your majesty and the Empress Maria Theresa. You are the only sovereigns in Europe who have shown any compassion for the misfortunes of my country, and before your generous sympathy my heart bows down in gratitude and admiration."

"Say you so, proud heart, that has never bowed before?" exclaimed the emperor, smiling, and taking the countess's white hand in his. "Come, then, to Vienna, not to do homage, but to receive it, for nothing becomes your beauty more than pride. Come to Vienna, and I will see that new friends and new ties awaken your heart to love and happiness."

"I have one relative in Vienna, sire, the Countess von Salmour."

"Ah! one of the empress's ladies of honor. Then you will not need my protection there, for the countess is in high favor with the empress; and I may say, that she has more influence at court than I have."

"Sire," said the countess, raising her large eyes with an appealing look, "I shall go to Vienna, if I go under your majesty's protection and with your sanction."

"You shall have both," replied Joseph, warmly. "I will write to my mother to-day, and you shall present my letter. When will you leave? I dare not ask you to tarry here, for this is no place for lovely and unprotected women. Moreover, the King of Prussia has no sympathy with Poland, and he will like you the less for the touching appeal you made in her behalf when you sang at the concert. Greet the empress for me, and let me hope that you will stir her heart as you have stirred mine. And now farewell. My time has expired: the King of Prussia expects me to supper. I must part from you, but I leave comforted, since I am enabled to say in parting, '*Au revoir.*'"

He bowed, and turned to quit the room. But at the door he spoke again.

"If I ever win the right to claim any thing of you, will you sing for me the aria that I found you singing to-night?"

"Oh! your majesty," said the countess, coming eagerly forward, "you have already earned the right to claim whatsoever you desire of me. I can never speak my gratitude for your condescension; perhaps music will speak for me. How gladly, then, will I sing when you command me!"

"I shall claim the promise in Vienna," said he, as he left the room.

The countess remained standing just where he had met her, breathlessly listening to his voice, which for a while she heard in the anteroom, and then to the last echoes of his retreating steps.

Suddenly the door was opened, and Matuschka, with joyful mien, came forward with a purse in her hand.

"Oh, my lady," exclaimed she, "the emperor has given me this purse to defray our expenses to Vienna!"

The countess started, and her pale face suffused with crimson shame.

"Alms!" said she, bitterly. "He treats me like a beggar!"

"No, lady," said Matuschka abashed; "the emperor told me that he had begged you to go to Vienna for business of state, and that he had a right to provide the expenses of our journey there. He said—"

The countess waved her hand impatiently. "Go back to the emperor," said she haughtily. "Tell him that you dare not offer this purse to your lady, for you know that she would rather die than receive alms, even from an emperor."

Matuschka cast down her eyes, and turned away. But she hesitated, and looked timidly at her mistress, whose great, glowing eyes were fixed upon her in unmistakable displeasure.

"My lady," said she, with embarrassment, "I will do your bidding, but you who have been so rich and great, know nothing of the troubles of poverty. Your money is exhausted. I would rather melt my own heart's blood into gold than tell you so; but indeed, dear lady, if you refuse the emperor's gift you will be without a kreutzer in your purse."

The countess raised her hands to her hair and unfastened the pearl wreath with which Matuschka had decorated it in anticipation of the emperor's visit.

"There—take this and sell it. You will readily find a jeweller who understands its value, and if he pays us but the half, it will be twice the sum which you hold in the emperor's purse."

"My lady, would you sell your family jewels? Have you forgotten that your family are pledged not to sell their heirlooms?"

"God will forgive me if I break my vow. It is more honorable to part with my ancestral jewels than to receive alms. I have no heirs, and no one will be wronged by the act. I have but my mother—Poland. For her I am ready to sacrifice the little I possess, and when nothing else remains, I shall yield my life. Go, Matuschka, go!"

Matuschka took the wreath and wept. "I go, lady," sobbed she. "This will last you for half a year, and then the armlets, then the diadem of brilliants, the bracelets, and the necklace, must all go. God grant you may live so long on these family treasures, that old Matuschka may be spared the humiliation of selling the rest! I have lived too long, since I must chaffer with a base-born tradesman for the jewels that were the royal gift of John Sobieski to my lady's noble ancestors."

She raised the countess's robe to her lips, and left the room. Her mistress looked after her, but her thoughts were wandering elsewhere. Slowly sinking on her knees, she began to pray, and the burden of her prayer was this:

"Oh, my God, grant that I may win his love!"

CHAPTER LXVII.

MARIA THERESA.

THE pearls were sold, the countess had arrived in Vienna, and she was in the presence of the empress, whom, although they had never met before, she had so long regarded with affectionate admiration.

"I rejoice to see you," said Maria Theresa, graciously extending her hand. "It gives me pleasure to receive a relative of the Countess von Salmour. But you have another claim upon my sympathy, for you are a Polish woman, and I can never forget that, but for John Sobieski, Vienna would have been a prey to the infidel."

"Upon your majesty's generous remembrance of Sobieski's alliance rests the last hope of Poland!" exclaimed the countess, kneeling and kissing the hand of the empress. "God has inclined to her redemption the heart of the noblest woman in Europe, and through her magnanimity will the wicked Empress of Russia receive her check. Oh, your majesty, that woman, in the height of her arrogance, believes to-day that you are only too willing to further her rapacity and participate in her crimes!"

"Never shall it be said that she and I have one thought or one object in common!" cried Maria Theresa, her face glowing with indignation. "Let her cease her oppression of Poland, or the Austrian eagle will seize the Russian vulture!"

The face of the countess grew radiant with joy. Raising her beautiful arms to heaven, she cried out exultingly: "King of kings, Thou hast heard! Maria Theresa comes to our help! Oh, your majesty, how many thousand hearts, from this day, will bow down in homage before your throne! Hereafter, not God, but Maria Theresa, will be our refuge!"

"Do not blaspheme," cried the empress, crossing herself. "I am but the servant of the Lord, and I do His divine will on earth. God is our refuge and our strength, and He will nerve my arm to overcome evil and work out good. I will countenance and uphold the Confederates, because it is my honest conviction that their cause is just, and that they are the only party in Poland who act in honor and good faith." *

"Hitherto, they would have died to vindicate that honor and that faith; now they will live to defend it from their oppressors. Oh, your majesty, pardon me, if, in my rapture at your goodness, I forget what is due to your exalted station. My heart will burst if I may not give utterance to my joy. I am a lonely creature, with no tie but that which binds me to my unhappy mother, Polonia!"

"So young, and without home or kindred!" said the empress, kindly. "I have already heard of your misfortunes, poor child, from my son the emperor."

At the name of the emperor, the countess's pale face was tinged with a faint rosy color. The empress did not remark it, for she was already thinking what a pity it was that such a surpassingly beautiful woman should be a widow; that such an enchanting creature should be unloved and unwedded.

"You are too handsome," said she, "to remain single. Woman

*The empress's own words. See Ferrand, i., p. 79.

was made for love and marriage. Happy is she who can devote her whole heart to the sweet responsibilities of domestic life, and who is not called upon to assume the duties that weigh down the head of royalty."

While the empress spoke, her eyes were fixed upon the portrait of the Emperor Francis, which still hung between the windows in the place of the mirror, which had been removed from its frame. The Countess Wielopolska had been admitted to the gay sitting-room.

"Earthly grandeur," continued she, "is beset with pains and cares; but the happy wife, whose subjects are her own dear children, is one degree removed from the bliss of angels. You must marry, my dear, and I will find for you a brilliant *parti.*"

"I am poor, your majesty, and am too proud to enter a rich man's palace without a dowry."

"You shall have your dowry. I shall instruct my ambassador at St. Petersburg to demand the return of your estates. It will be one good deed by which that woman* may expiate some of her many crimes. Your estates once restored, you will be an equal match for any nobleman in Europe."

"If I should receive my estates through your majesty's intercession," replied the countess, "my home would be an asylum for all the unfortunate Poles. I should think it treason to dream of personal happiness, while Poland lies shackled and bleeding."

"But Poland shall be free!" cried the empress, with enthusiasm. "With the coöperation of France, the voice of Austria will be so loud that Russia will hear, and withdraw her unjust claims. We will strike off the fetters of Poland, while we forge a gentle chain for the Countess Wielopolska; a chain that falls so lightly upon woman, that its burden is sweeter than freedom."

"Your majesty must forgive me," reiterated the countess; "I have sworn, on my mother's grave, that as long as I can be useful, I will live for Poland. Should she regain her freedom, I will retire to a convent, where every breath I draw shall be a thanksgiving to God. Should she be doomed to slavery, she will need her sons and daughters no more, and then I will die. Your majesty sees that I am already betrothed. I shall soon be the bride of Heaven, or the bride of Death."

"The bride of Heaven!" repeated the empress, her eyes swimming with tears. "Then be it so; it is not I who would entice Mary from her Master's feet. The world is full of Marthas, troubled about many things. Go, choose the better part, sweet enthusiast, and I will see that you have cause for thanksgiving."

She reached her hand to the countess, who kissed it and withdrew. As she opened the door, she felt the bolt turn from the outside.

"His highness Prince Kaunitz," cried a page; and as the countess was making one last inclination of the head, the tall, slender form of Kaunitz filled the space behind her.

"Have I permission to enter, your majesty?" said the minister.

"You are always welcome, prince," replied the empress.

Kaunitz bowed slightly, and as he raised his cold eye to the face of the countess, a faint smile flitted over his features, but it was

*The words by which Maria Theresa always designated Catharine.

followed by a sneer. Without acknowledging her presence by the smallest courtesy, he advanced to the empress, and the door closed upon Poland forever.

CHAPTER LXVIII.

MARIE ANTOINETTE AND COURT ETIQUETTE.

"LETTERS from France, your majesty," said Kaunitz, and the face of the empress grew bright as she recognized the handwriting of her daughter.

"The dauphiness is well?" said she. "Next to her dear self, I love to see her writing. Ah, I have grown very lonely since my little Antoinette has left me! One by one my children go; one dear face alone remains," continued she, pointing to the portrait of the emperor. Then looking at the letters in the hands of the prince, she said:

"Have you good news?"

"Yes, your majesty. The dauphiness is adored by the French people. They repeat her *bon mots*, write odes and madrigals to her beauty, and hang up her portrait in their houses. When she drives out in her *calèche* they impede its progress with their welcomes; and when she appears at the theatre, the prima donnas are forgotten. Half a year ago, when she made her entry into Paris and more than a hundred thousand people went out to meet her, the Duke de Brissac said, 'Madame, you have one hundred thousand lovers, and yet the dauphin will never be jealous of them.' * The dear old Duke! He little knew what literal truth he spoke of the dauphin on that occasion."

"What do you mean?" asked the empress, hastily. "I know by the expression of your face that you have something unpleasant to tell."

"I mean to say the dauphin is not jealous, because he is the only man in France who is not in love with the dauphiness."

The empress turned scarlet. "This is a serious charge which you presume to make against the dauphin," said she, frowning.

"It is unhappily true," replied Kaunitz, coolly.

"The dauphiness makes no mention of such a state of things in her letter. It does not breathe a word of complaint."

"Perhaps the dauphiness, in the innocence of her heart, has no idea of the grounds which she has for complaint."

The empress looked displeased. "Do you know that your language is offensive?" said she. "You assert that the dauphin is insensible to the charms of his beautiful young wife."

"Your majesty well knows that I never assert a falsehood. The dauphin is not in love with his wife, and I do not believe that she has an advocate at the court of Louis XV. Since the shameless partisans of Du Barry have triumphed over the noble Duke of Choiseul, the dauphiness is without a friend. The Duke d'Arguillon is anti-Austrian, and your majesty knows what an enemy to Austria was the father of the dauphin."

"Why do you seek to torture me, Kaunitz?" said the empress,

*"Memoirs of Madame de Campan," vol. i., p. 60.

impatiently. "You are not telling me all this for nothing. Say at once what you have to say."

"Your majesty has not yet read the letter which I had the honor of handing to you just now, I believe," said Kaunitz.

Maria Theresa took up the letter from the *guéridon* on which she had laid it, and began to look it over.

"It is true," sighed she. "The dauphiness complains of solitude. 'Since the Duke de Choiseul has left,' writes she, 'I am alone, and without a friend.' You are right. The dauphiness is in danger. She writes that her enemies are intriguing to part her from the dauphin. They attempted in Fontainebleau to assign her a suite of apartments remote from those of her husband."

"Yes, the anti-Austrian party, seeing that he is indifferent to her, are doing their best to convert this indifference into dislike. But the dauphiness saw through the affair, and complained to the king."

"That was right and bold!" cried the empress, joyfully.

"Yes, it was bold, for it gained another enemy for the dauphiness. She should have spoken to the king through the Duke d'Arguillon, instead of which she applied to his majesty herself. The duke will never forgive her; and when the Duchess de Noailles reproved the dauphiness, she replied that she would never take counsel of etiquette where her family affairs were concerned. The consequence is that the duchess also has gone over to the enemy."

"To the enemy?" exclaimed the empress, anxiously. "Has she, then, other enemies?"

"Madame de Marsan, the governess of the sisters of the dauphin, will never forgive her for having interfered in the education of the young princesses."

"But surely the daughters of the king will be kind to my poor Marie Antoinette!" exclaimed the empress, ready to burst into tears. "They promised to love her; and it is but natural and womanly that they should shun the party which upholds the profligate woman who rules the King of France!"

Prince Kaunitz slightly elevated his shoulders. "Madame Adelaide, the eldest, until the marriage of the dauphin, held the first place at court. Now, the dauphiness has precedence of her, and the court card-parties are held in her apartments. Madame Adelaide, therefore, has refused to be present, and retires to her own rooms, where she holds rival card-parties which are attended by the anti-Austrians, who are opposed to Du Barry. This is the second party who intrigue against the dauphiness.—Madame Sophie perchance remembers her in her prayers; but she is too pious to be of use to anybody. Madame Victoire, who really loves the dauphiness, is so sickly, that she scarcely ever leaves her room. For a while she held little reunions there, which, being very pleasant, were for a while attended by the dauphiness; but Madame de Noailles objected, and court etiquette required that they should be discontinued."

The empress had risen and was pacing the floor in great agitation. "So young, so lovely, and slighted by her husband!" murmured she, bitterly, while large tear-drops stood in her eyes. "The daughter of the Cæsars in strife with a king's base-born mistress and a vile faction who hate her without cause! And I—her mother—an empress, am powerless to help her!"

"No, your majesty," said Kaunitz, "not altogether powerless.

You cannot help her with armies, but you can do so with good advice, and no one can advise her as effectually as her mother."

"Advise her? What advice can I give?" cried the empress, angrily. "Shall I counsel her to attend the *petits soupers* of the king, and truckle to his mistress? Never! never! My daughter may be unhappy, but she shall not be dishonored!"

"I should not presume to make any such proposition to the dauphiness," said Kaunitz, quietly. "One cannot condescend to Du Barry as we did to La Pompadour. The latter was at least a woman of mind, the former is nothing more than a vulgar beauty. But there is another lady whose influence at court is without limit—one whom Du Barry contemns, but whom the dauphiness would do well to conciliate."

"Of what lady do you speak, Kaunitz?"

"I speak of Madame Etiquette, your majesty. She is a stiff and tiresome old dame, I grant you, but in France she presides over every thing. Without her the royal family can neither sleep nor wake; they can neither take a meal if they be in health, nor a purge if they be indisposed, without her everlasting *surveillance*. She directs their dress, amusements, associates, and behavior; she presides over their pleasures, their weariness, their social hours, and their hours of solitude. This may be uncomfortable, but royalty cannot escape it, and it must be endured."

"It is the business of Madame de Noailles to attend to the requisitions of court etiquette," said the empress, impatiently.

"And of the dauphiness to attend to her representations," added Kaunitz.

"She will certainly have enough discretion to conform herself to such obligations!"

"Your majesty, a girl of fifteen who has a hundred thousand lovers is not apt to be troubled with discretion. The dauphiness is bored to death by Madame de Noailles's eternal sermons, and therein she may be right. But she turns the mistress of ceremonies into ridicule, and therein she is wrong. In an outburst of her vexation the dauphiness one day called her 'old Madame Etiquette,' and, as the *bons mots* of a future queen are apt to be repeated, Madame de Noailles goes by no other name at court. Again—not long ago the dauphiness gave a party of pleasure at Versailles. The company were mounted on donkeys."

"On donkeys!" cried the empress with horror.

"On donkeys," repeated Kaunitz, with composure. "The donkey on which the dauphiness rode was unworthy of the honor conferred upon it. It threw its royal rider."

"And Antoinette fell off?"

"She fell, your majesty—and fell without exercising any particular discretion in the matter. The Count d'Artois came forward to her assistance, but she waved him off, saying with comic earnestness, 'Do not touch me for your life! Send a courier for Madame Etiquette and wait until she has prescribed the important ceremonies with which a dauphiness is to be remounted upon the back of her donkey.' Every one laughed of course, and the next day when the thing was repeated, everybody in Paris was heartily amused—except Madame de Noailles. She did not laugh."

Neither could the empress vouchsafe a smile, although the affair was ludicrous enough. She was still walking to and fro, her face scarlet with mortification. She stopped directly in front of her unsympathizing minister, and said: "You are right. I must warn Antoinette that she is going too far. Oh, my heart bleeds when I think of my dear, inexperienced child cast friendless upon the reefs of that dangerous and corrupt court of France! My God! my God! why did I not heed the warning I received? Why did I consent to let her go?"

"Because your majesty was too wise to be guided by lunatics and impostors, and because you recognized, not only the imperative necessity which placed Marie Antoinette upon the throne of France, but also the value and the blessing of a close alliance with the French."

"God grant it may prove a blessing!" sighed the empress. "I will write to-day, and implore her to call to aid all her discretion—for Heaven knows it is needed at the court of France!"

"It is not an easy thing to call up discretion whenever discretion is needed," said Kaunitz, thoughtfully. "Has not your majesty, with that goodness which does so much honor to your heart, gone so far as to promise help to the quarrelsome Poles?"

"Yes," said the empress, warmly, "and I intend to keep my promise."

"Promises, your majesty, are sometimes made which it is impossible to keep."

"But I make no such promises, and therefore honor requires that I fulfil my imperial pledge. Yes, we have promised help and comfort to the patriotic Confederates, the defenders of liberty and of the true faith, and God forbid that we should ever deceive those who trust to us for protection!"

Kaunitz bowed. "Then your majesty will have the goodness to apprise the emperor that the army must be put upon a war footing; our magazines must be replenished, and Austria must prepare herself to suffer all the horrors of a long war."

"A war? With whom?" exclaimed the astounded empress.

"With Russia, Prussia, Sweden, perchance with all Europe. Does your majesty suppose that the great powers will suffer the establishment of a republic here, under the protection of Austria?—a republic upon the body politic of a continent of monarchies, which, like a scirrhous sore, will spread disease that must end in death to all?"

"Of what republic do you speak?"

CHAPTER LXIX.

THE TRIUMPH OF DIPLOMACY.

"I SPEAK of Poland," said Kaunitz, with his accustomed indifference. "I speak of those insolent Confederates, who, emboldened by the condescension of your majesty and the emperor, are ready to dare every thing for the propagation of their pernicious political doctrines. They have been pleased to declare Stanislaus deposed, and the throne of Poland vacant. This declaration has been committed to writing, and with the signatures of the leading Confederates attached to it, has been actually placed in the king's hands, in his own palace at Warsaw. Not content with this, they have distributed thousands of these documents throughout Poland, so that the question to-day, in that miserable hornets' nest, is not whether the right of the Confederates are to be guaranteed to them, but whether the kingdom of Poland shall remain a monarchy or be converted into a republic."

"If this be true, then Poland is lost, and there is no hope for the Confederates," replied the empress. "I promised them protection against foreign aggression, but with their internal quarrels I will not interfere."

"It would be a dangerous precedent if Austria should justify those who lay sacrilegious hands upon the crown of their lawful sovereign; and, for my part, my principles forbid me to uphold a band of rebels, who are engaged in an insolent conspiracy to dethrone their king."

"You are right, prince; it will never do for us to uphold them. As I have openly declared my sympathy with the Confederates, so I must openly express to them my entire disapprobation of their republican proclivities."

"If your majesty does that, a war with France will be the consequence of your frankness. France has promised succor to the Con federates, and has already sent Dumouriez with troops, arms, and gold. France is longing to have a voice in the differences between Russia and Turkey, and she only awaits coöperation from Austria to declare openly against Russia. She will declare against ourselves, if, after your majesty's promises, we suddenly change front and take part against the seditious Poles."

"What can we do, then, to avert war?" cried the empress, anxiously. "Ah, prince, you see that the days of my youth and my valor are past! I shudder when I look back upon the blood that has been shed under my reign, and nothing but the direst necessity will ever compel me to be the cause of spilling another drop of Austrian blood.* How, then, shall we shape our course so as to avoid war?"

"Our policy," said Kaunitz, "is to do nothing. We must look on and be watchful, while we carefully keep our own counsel. We propitiate France by allowing her to believe in the continuance of our sympathy with the Poles, while we pacify Russia and Prussia by remaining actually neutral."

"But while we temporize and equivocate," cried the empress, with fervor, "Russia will annihilate the Poles, who, if they have gone too far in their thirst for freedom, have valiantly contended for their just rights, and are now about to lose them through the evils of disunion. It grieves me to think that we are about to abandon an unhappy nation to the oppression of that woman, who stops at nothing to compass her wicked designs. She who did not shrink from the murder of her own husband, do you imagine that she will stop short of the annexation of Poland to Russia?"

"We will not suffer her to annex Poland," said Kaunitz, slowly nodding his head. "As long as we are at peace with Russia, she will do nothing to provoke our enmity; for France is at our side, and even Prussia would remonstrate, if Catharine should be so bold as to appropriate Poland *to herself alone.*"

"You are mistaken. The King of Prussia, who is so covetous

* The empress's own words. F. V. Raumor, "Contributions to Modern History," vol. iv., p. 419.

of that which belongs to others, will gladly share the booty with Russia."

"Austria could never suffer the copartnership. If such an emergency should arise, we would have to make up our minds to declare war against them both, or—"

"Or?" asked the empress, holding her breath, as he paused.

"Or," said Kaunitz, fixing his cold blue eye directly upon her face, "or we would have to share with them."

"Share what?"

"The apple of discord. Anarchy is a three-headed monster; if it is to be destroyed, every head must fall. It is now devouring Poland; and I think that the three great powers are strong enough to slay the monster once for all."

"This is all very plausible," said Maria Theresa, shaking her head, "but it is not just. You will never convince me that good can be born of evil. What you propose is neither more nor less than to smite the suppliant that lies helpless at your feet. I will have nothing in common with the Messalina who desecrates her sovereignty by the commission of every unwomanly crime; and as for Frederick of Prussia, I mistrust him. He has been my enemy for too many years for me ever to believe that he can be sincerely my friend."

"France was our enemy for three hundred years, and yet we are allied by more than ordinary ties."

"Our alliance will soon come to naught if we walk in the path to which you would lead us, prince. France will not be deaf to the misery of Poland. She will hear the death-cry, and come to the rescue."

"No, your majesty, France will wait to see what we propose to do until it is too late, and she will perceive that a resort to arms will in no wise affect a *fait accompli*. I, therefore, repeat that the only way to prevent the Polish conflagration from spreading to other nations, is for us to preserve a strict neutrality, taking part with neither disputant."

"War must be averted," exclaimed Maria Theresa, warmly. "My first duty is to Austria, and Austria must have peace. To preserve this blessing to my subjects, I will do any thing that is consistent with my honor and the dictates of my conscience."

"Ah, your majesty, diplomacy has no conscience; it can have but one rule—that of expediency."

"You concede, then, that the policy you advocate is not a conscientious one?"

"Yes, your majesty; but it is one which it is imperative for us to follow. Necessity alone decides a national course of action. A good statesman cannot be a cosmopolitan. He looks out for himself, and leaves others to do the same. If Poland succumbs, it will be because she has not the strength to live. Therefore, if her hour be come, let her die. We dare not go to her relief, for, before the weal of other nations, we must have peace and prosperity for Austria."

"But suppose that France should insist that we define our position?"

"Then we can do so—in words. It is so easy to hide one's thoughts, while we assure our allies of our 'distinguished consideration!'"

The empress heaved a deep sigh.

"I see," said she, "that clouds are gathering over the political horizon, and that you are resolved to shield your own house, while the tempest devastates the home of your neighbor. Be it so. I *must* have peace; for I have no right to sacrifice my people before the altars of strange gods. This is my first great obligation, and all other claims must give way to it.—

"*They must give way,*" continued the empress, slowly communing with herself, "but oh! it seems cruel. I scarcely dare ask myself what is to be the fate of Poland? Heaven direct us, for all human wisdom has come to naught!"

Then, turning toward Kaunitz, she held out her hand.

"Go, prince," said she, "and be assured that what we have spoken to each other to-day shall remain sacred between us."

The prince bowed, and left he room.

The empress was alone. She went to and fro, while her disturbed countenance betrayed the violent struggle that was raging in her noble, honest heart.

"I know what they want," murmured she. "Joseph thirsts for glory and conquest, and Kautnitz upholds him. They want their share of the booty. And they will overrule my sympathy, and prove to me that I am bound to inaction. Poland will be dismembered, and I shall bear my portion of the crime. I shudder at the deed, and yet I cannot raise my hand without shedding my people's blood. I must take counsel of Heaven!"

She rang, and commanded the presence of her confessor.

"Perhaps he will throw some light upon this darkness, and the just God will do the rest!"

CHAPTER LXX.

GOSSIP.

THE Countess Wielopolska was alone in her room. She walked to and fro; sometimes stopping before a large pier-glass to survey her own person, sometimes hastening to the window, at the sound of a carriage passing by; then retiring disappointed as the vehicle went on.

"He comes late," thought she. "Perhaps he has forgotten that he promised to come. Gracious Heaven! what, if he should be proof against the blandishments of woman! I fear me he is too cold—and Poland will be lost. And yet his eye, when it rests upon me, speaks the language of love, and his hand trembles when it touches mine. Ah! And I—when he is by, I sometimes forget the great cause for which I live, and—no, no, no!" exclaimed she aloud, "it must not, *shall* not be! My heart must know but one love—the love of country. Away with such silly, girlish dreaming! I am ashamed—"

Here the countess paused, to listen again, for this time a carriage stopped before the door, and the little French clock struck the hour.

"He comes," whispered she, scarcely breathing, and she turned her bright smiling face toward the door. It opened, and admitted a young woman whose marvellous beauty was enhanced by all the auxiliaries of a superb toilet and a profusion of magnificent jewels.

"Countess Zamoiska," exclaimed the disappointed hostess, coming forward, and striving to keep up the smile.

"And why such a cold reception, my dear Anna," asked the visitor, with a warm embrace. "Am I not always the same Luschinka, to whom you vowed eternal friendship when we were school-girls together?"

"We vowed eternal friendship," sighed the Countess Wielopolska, "but since we were happy school-girls, six years have gone by, and fearful tragedies have arisen to darken our lives and embitter our young hearts."

"Pshaw!" said the lady, casting admiring glances at herself in the mirror. "I do not know why these years should be so sad to you. They have certainly improved your beauty, for I declare to you, Anna, that you were scarcely as pretty when you left school as you are to-day. Am I altered for the worse? My heart, as you see, has not changed, for as soon as I heard you were in Vienna, I flew to embrace you. What a pity, your family would mix themselves up in those hateful politics! You might have been the leader of fashion in Warsaw. And your stupid husband, too, to think of his killing himself on the very day of a masked ball, and spoiling the royal quadrille!"

"The royal quadrille," echoed the countess, in an absent tone; "yes, the king, General Repnin, he who put to death so many Polish nobles, and the brutal Branicki, whose pastime it is to set fire to Polish villages, they were to have been the other dancers."

"Yes, and they completed their quadrille, in spite of Count Wielopolska. Bibeskoi offered himself as a substitute, and sat up the whole night to learn the figures. Bibeskoi is a delightful partner."

"A Russian," exclaimed the countess.

"What signifies a man's nation when he dances well?" laughed the lady. "*Dis donc, ma chère*, are you still mad on the subject of politics? And do you still sympathize with the poor crazy Confederates?"

"You know, Luschinka, that Count Pac was my father's dearest friend."

"I know it, poor man; he is at the top and bottom of all the trouble. I beseech you, *chère Anna*, let us put aside politics; I cannot see what pleasure a woman can find in such tiresome things. *Mon Dieu*, there are so many other things more pleasing as well as more important! For instance: how do people pass their time in Vienna? Have you many lovers? Do you go to many balls?"

"Do you think me so base that I could dance while Poland is in chains?" said the countess, frowning.

The Countess Zamoiska laughed aloud. "*Voyons*—are you going to play Jeanne d'Arc to bring female heroism into fashion? Oh, Anna! We have never had more delightful balls in Warsaw than have been given since so many Russian regiments have been stationed there."

"You have danced with those who have murdered your brothers and relatives?—danced while the people of Poland are trodden under foot!"

"*Ah, bah! Ne parlez pas du peuple!*" cried the Countess Zamoiska, with a gesture of disgust. "A set of beastly peasants, no better than their own cattle, or a band of genteel robbers, who have made it unsafe to live anywhere on Polish soil, even in Warsaw."

"You are right," sighed the Countess Wielopolska, "let us drop politics and speak of other things."

"*A la bonne heure.* Let us have a little *chronique scandaleuse. Ah, ma chère,* I am at home there, for we lead an enchanting life in Warsaw. The king is a handsome man, and, in spite of the Empress Catharine, his heart is still susceptible of the tender passion. You remember his *liaison* with the Countess Kanizka, your sister-in-law?"

"A base, dishonored woman, who stooped to be the mistress of the man who has betrayed her country!"

"A king, nevertheless, and a very handsome man; and she was inconsolable when he ceased to love her."

"Ah! she was abandoned, then, was she?" cried the Countess Wielopolska.

"Oh no, dear Anna! Your sister-in-law was not guilty of the *bétise* of playing Queen Dido. As she felt quite sure that the king would leave her soon or late, she anticipated the day, and left him. Was it not excellent? She went off with Prince Repnin."

"Prince Repnin!" exclaimed the countess with horror. "The Russian ambassador!"

"The same. You should have seen the despair of the king. But he was amiable even in his grief. He tried all sorts of lover's stratagems to win back the countess; he prowled around her house at night singing like a Troubadour; he wrote her bushels of letters to implore an interview. All in vain. The *liaison* with Repnin was made public, and that, of course, ended the affair. The king was inconsolable.* He gave ball after ball, never missed an evening at the theatre, gambled all night, gave sleighing parties, and so on, but it was easy to see that his heart was broken; and had not Tissona, the pretty *cantatrice*, succeeded in comforting him, I really do believe that our handsome king would have killed himself for despair."

"Ah, he is consoled, is he?" said the countess with curling lips. "He jests and dances, serenades and gambles, while the gory knout reeks with the noblest blood in Poland, and her noblest sons are staggering along the frozen wastes of Siberia! Oh, Stanislaus! Stanislaus! A day of reckoning will come for him who wears the splendor of royalty, yet casts away its obligations!"

"*Vraiment*, dear Anna, to hear your rhapsodies, one would almost believe you to be one of the Confederates who lately attempted the life of the king," cried the Countess Zamoiska, laughing.

"Who attempted the king's life?" said the countess, turning pale.

"Why three robbers: Lukawski, Strawinski, and Kosinski."

"I never heard of it," replied the countess, much agitated. "Tell me what you know of it, if you can, Luschinka."

"It is an abominable thing, and long too," said Luschinka, with a shrug. "The conspirators were disguised as peasants, and actually had the assurance to come to Warsaw. There were thirty of them, but the three I tell you of were the leaders. The king was on his way to his uncle's palace, which is in the suburbs of Warsaw. They had the insolence to fall upon him in the streets, and his attendants

* Wraxall, "Memoirs of the Court of Vienna," vol. ii., p. 96.

got frightened and ran off. Then the conspirators tore the king from his coach and carried him off, swearing that if he uttered one cry they would murder him. Wasn't it awful? Do you think that the dear king didn't have the corurage to keep as quiet as a mouse while they took him off with them to the forest of Bielani? Here they robbed him of all he had, leaving him nothing but the ribbon that belonged to the order of the White Eagle. Then they dispersed to give the news of his capture to their accomplices, and Kosinski was left to dispatch him. Did you ever!"

"Further, further!" said the countess, scarcely able to speak, as her old school-mate paused in her narrative.

Luschinka laughed. "Doesn't it sound just like a fairy tale, Anna? But it is as true as I live, and happened on the third of November of this blessed year 1771. So Kosinski and six others dragged and dragged the king until he lost his shoes, and was all torn and scratched, and even wounded. Whenever the others wanted to stop and kill the king, Kosinski objected that the place was not lonely enough. All at once they came upon the Russian patrol. Then the five other murderers ran off, leaving the king and Kosinski alone."

"And Kosinski?" asked the countess, with anxiety.

"Kosinski went on with his sword drawn over the king's head, although he begged him for rest. But the king saw that Kosinski looked undecided and uneasy, so as they came near to the Convent of Bielani, he said to Kosinski, 'I see that you don't know which way to act, so you had better let me go into the convent to hide, while you make your escape by some other way.' But Kosinski said no, he had sworn to kill him. So they went on farther, until they came to Mariemont, a castle belonging to the Elector of Saxony. Here the king begged for rest, and they sat down and began to talk. Then Kosinkski told the king he was not killing him of his own will, but because he had been ordered to do so by others, to punish the king for all his sins, poor fellow! against Poland. The king then said it was not his fault, but all the fault of Russia, and at last he softened the murderer's heart. Kosinski threw himself at the king's feet and begged pardon, and promised to save him. So Stanislaus promised to forgive him, and it was all arranged between them. They went on to a mill near Mariemont, and begged the miller to let in two travellers who had lost their way. At first the miller took them to be robbers, but after a great deal of begging, he let them in. Then the king tore a leaf out of his pocket-book, and wrote a note to General Cocceji. The miller's daughter took it to Warsaw, not without much begging on the king's part; and you can conceive the joy of the people when they heard that the king was safe, for everybody seeing his cloak in the streets, and his hat and plume on the road, naturally supposed that he had been murdered. Well, General Cocceji, followed by the whole court, hurried to the mill; and when they arrived, there was Kosinski standing before the door with a drawn sword in his hand. He let in the general, and there on the floor, in the miller's shirt, lay the king fast asleep. So Cocceji went down on his knees and kissed his hand, and called him his lord and king, and the people of the mill, who had never dreamed who it was, all dropped on their knees and begged for mercy. So the king then forgave everybody, and went back to Warsaw with Cocceji. This, my dear, is a true history of the attempt that was made by the Confederates on the life of the handsomest man in Poland!" *

"A strange and sad history," said the Countess Anna. "However guilty the king may be, it would be disgraceful if he were murdered by his own subjects."

"Oh, my love, these Confederates refuse to acknowledge him for their king! Did you not know that they had been so ridiculous as to depose him?"

"What have the Confederates to do with a band of robbers who plundered the king and would have murdered him?" asked Anna indignantly. "Are they to be made answerable for the crimes of a horde of banditti?"

"*Ma chère*, the banditti were the tools of the Confederates. They have been taken, and every thing has been discovered. Pulawski, their great hero, hired the assassins and bound them by an oath. Letters found upon Lukawski, who boasts of his share in the villany, shows that Pulawski was the head conspirator, and that the plot had been approved by Zaremba and Pac!"

"Then all is lost!" murmured Anna. "If the Confederates have sullied the honor of Poland by consenting to crime as a means to work out her independence, Poland will never regain her freedom. Oh, that I should have lived to see this day!"

She covered her face with her hands, and sobbed aloud.

"*Vraiment*, Anna," said the Countess Zamoiska pettishly, "I cannot understand you. Instead of rejoicing over the king's escape, here you begin to cry over the sins of his murderers. All Poland is exasperated against them, and nothing can save them.† So, dear Anna, dry your eyes, or they will be as red as a cardinal's hat. Goodness me, if I hadn't wonderful strength of mind, I might have cried myself into a fright long ago; for you have no idea of the sufferings I have lived through. You talk of Poland, and never ask a word about myself. It shows how little interest you feel in me, that you still call me by the name of my first husband."

"Are you married a second time?" asked Anna, raising her head.

"*Ah, ma chère*, my name has not been Zamoiska for four years. Dear me! The king knows what misery it is to be tied to a person that loves you no longer; and luckily for us, he has the power of divorce. He does it for the asking, and every divorce is a signal for a succession of brilliant balls; for you understand that people don't part to go off and pout. They re-marry at once, and, of course, everybody gives balls, routs, and dinners, in honor of the weddings."

"Have you married again in this way?" asked the countess, gravely.

"Oh yes," replied the unconscious Luschinka; "I have been twice married and twice divorced; but it was not my fault. I loved my first husband with a depth of passion which he could not appreciate, and I was in an agony of despair when six months after our marriage he told me that he loved me no longer, and was dying for the Countess Luwiendo. She was my bosom friend, so you can imagine my grief; *mais j'ai su faire bonne mine à mauvais jeux.* I invited the countess to my villa, and there, under the shade of the old trees in the park, we walked arm in arm, and arranged with my

*Wraxall, "Memoirs," vol. ii., p. 76.

† Lukawski and Strawinski were executed. They died cursing Kosinski as a traitor. Wraxall, vol. ii., p. 83.

husband all the conditions of the separation. Every one praised my generous conduct; the men in particular were in raptures, and Prince Lubomirski, on the strength of it, fell so desperately in love with me, that he divorced his wife and offered me his hand."

"You did not accept it!" exclaimed Countess Anna.

"What a question!" said the ex-countess, pouting. "The prince was young, rich, charming, and a great favorite with the king. We loved each other, and, of course, were married. But, indeed, my dear, love does seem to have such butterfly wings that you scarcely catch it before it is gone! My second husband broke my heart exactly as my first had done; he asked me to leave him, and of course I had to go. Men are abominable beings, Anna: scarcely were we divorced before he married a third wife." *

"Poland is lost—lost!" murmured the Countess Anna. "She is falling under the weight of her children's crimes. Lost! O Poland, my unhappy country!"

"*Au contraire, ma chère*, Warsaw was never gayer than it is at present. Did I not tell you that every divorce was followed by a marriage, and that the king was delighted with the masquerades and balls, and all that sort of thing? Why, nothing is heard in Warsaw at night but laughter, music, and the chink of glasses."

"And nevertheless you could tear yourself away?" said the countess ironically.

"I had to go," sighed the princess. "I am on my way to Italy. You see, *ma chère*, it would have been *inconvenant* and might have made me ridiculous to go out in society, meeting my husbands with their two wives, and I—abandoned by both these faithless men. I should have been obliged to marry a third time, but my heart revolted against it."

"Then you travel alone to Italy?"

"By no means, *mon amour*, I am travelling with the most bewitching creature!—my lover. Oh, Anna, he is the handsomest man I ever laid my eyes upon; the most delightful! and he paints so divinely that the Empress Catharine has appointed him her court painter. I love him beyond all expression; I adore him! You need not smile, Anna, *que voulez-vous? Le cœur toujours vierge pour un second amour.*"

"If you love him so dearly, why, then, does your heart revolt against a marriage with him?" asked the Countess Anna.

"I told you he was a painter, and not a nobleman," answered the ex-princess, impatiently. "One loves an artist, but cannot marry him. Do you suppose I would be so ridiculous as to give up my title to be the respectable wife of a painter? The Princess Lubomirski a Madame Wand, simple Wand! Oh, no! I shall travel with him, but I will not marry him."

"Then go!" exclaimed the Countess Anna, rising, and casting looks of scorn upon the princess. "Degenerate daughter of a degenerate fatherland, go, and drag your shame with you to Italy! Go, and enjoy your sinful lusts, while Poland breathes her last, and vultures prey upon her dishonored corpse. But take with you the contempt of every Polish heart, that beats with love for the land that gave you birth!"

She turned, and without a word of farewell, proudly left the room. The princess raised her brow and opened her pretty mouth

* Wraxall, ii., p. 110.

in bewilderment; then rising, and going up to the mirror, she smoothed her hair and began to laugh.

"What a pathetic fool!" said she. "Anybody might know that her mother had been an actress. To think of the daughter of an *artiste* getting up a scene because a princess will not stoop to marry a painter! *Quelle bétise!*"

With these words she went back to her carriage and drove off.

CHAPTER LXXI.

AN EXPLANATION.

THE Countess Anna, meanwhile, had retired to her room. Exhausted by her own emotions, she sank into a chair, and clasping her hands convulsively, she stared, with distended eyes, upon the blank wall opposite.

She was perfectly unconscious that, after a time, the door had opened and Matuschka stood before her. It was not until the old woman had taken her hand and raised it to her lips, that she started from her mournful reverie.

"What now, Matuschka?" said she, awakening from her dream.

"My lady, I come to know what we are to do. The pearl necklace and wreath are sold, and they have maintained the Countess Wielopolska as beseems her rank; but we live upon our capital, and it lessens every day. Oh, my lady, why will you conceal your poverty, when the emperor—"

"Peace!" interrupted the countess. "When we speak of our poverty don't name the emperor. If there is no more money in our purse, take the diadem of brilliants, sell the diamonds and replace them with false stones. They will bring a thousand ducats, and that sum will last us for a whole year."

"And then?" sobbed Matuschka.

"And then," echoed the countess, thoughtfully, "then we will either be happy or ready for death. Go, Matuschka, let no one know that I am selling my diamonds; but replace them by to-morrow morning; for I must wear them at the emperor's reception."

"Your whole set, pearls and diamonds, are now false," said the persevering servant. "What will the emperor say when he hears of it?"

"He must never know of it. Now go, and return quickly."

Matuschka, looking almost angrily at her lady, left the room. In the anteroom stood a man wrapped in a cloak. She went quickly up to him with the open *étui*.

"The diamond coronet," whispered she. "I am to sell the jewels and have their places filled with false ones. It is to be done before to-morrow."

"How much does she expect for it?" asked the visitor in a low voice.

"A thousand ducats, sire."

"I will send the sum to-night. Hide the coronet until to-morrow, and then return it to her. Where is she?"

"In her cabinet, your majesty."

"Let no one enter until I return."

He then threw down his cloak, and without knocking opened the door. The countess was still lost in thought. She still gazed at the blank wall, still heard the flippant voice which had poured out its profanity as though life had been a jest and immorality a dream.

The emperor stopped to contemplate her for a moment, and his large, loving eyes rested fondly on her noble form.

"Countess Anna," said he, softly.

"The emperor!" exclaimed she, rising and coming joyfully forward, while a deep blush overspread her face.

"What! Will you not respect my *incognito?* Will you not receive me as Count Falkenstein?"

"Is not the name of the emperor the first that is pronounced by the priest when he prays before the altar for his fellow-creatures?" replied she, with an enchanting smile. "Think of my heart as a priest, and let that name be ever the first I speak in my prayers to Heaven."

"By heaven, if priests resembled you, I should not hate them as I do. Come, my lovely priestess, then call me emperor if you will, but receive me as Count Falkenstein."

"Welcome, count," replied she, cheerfully.

"God be praised, then, my royalty has disappeared for a while," said Joseph.

"And yet, my lord and emperor, it is the privilege of royalty to heal all wounds, to wipe away all tears, and to comfort all sorrow. What a magnificent prerogative it is to hold in one's own hand the happiness of thousands?"

"What is happiness, sweet moralist?" cried Joseph. "Mankind are forever in search of it, yet no man has ever found it."

"What is happiness!" exclaimed she, with enthusiasm. "It is to have the power of ruling destiny—it is to stand upon the Himalaya of your might; when, stretching forth your imperial hand, you can say to the oppressed among nations, 'Come unto me, ye who strive against tyranny, and I will give you freedom!'"

"In other words," replied the emperor, with an arch smile, "it is to march to Poland and give battle to the Empress of Russia."

"It is, it is!" cried she, with the fervor of a Miriam. "It is to be the Messiah of crucified Freedom, to redeem your fellows from bondage, and to earn the blessings of a people to whom your name, for all time, will stand as the type of all that is great in a sovereign and good in a man! Oh, Emperor of Austria, be the generous redeemer of my country!"

And scarcely knowing what she said, she took his hand and pressed it to her heart.

Joseph withdrew it gently, saying, "Peace, lovely enthusiast, peace! Give politics to the winds! She is an abominable old hag, and the very rustling of her sibylline leaves as she turns them over in the cabinet of the empress makes me shudder with disgust. Let us drive her hence, then. I came hither to taste a few drops of happiness at *your* side, sweet Anna."

The countess sighed wearily as the emperor drew her to his side; and her pale, inspired face was turned upon him with a look of unutterable anguish.

The emperor saw it, and leaned his head back upon the cushion of the sofa. After a pause he said: "How sweet it is to be here!"

"And yet you came late," whispered she, reproachfully.

"Because I travelled by a circuitous route; got into one hackney-coach and out of another; drove hither, thither, and everywhere, to baffle my mother's spies. Do you suppose that any one of her bigoted followers would believe in a chaste friendship like ours? Do you suppose they would understand the blameless longings I have to see your lovely face, and to listen to the melody of your matchless voice? Tell me, Countess Anna, how have I deserved the rich boon of your friendship?"

"Nay, Count Falkenstein," replied she, with a bewitching smile, "tell me how I have earned yours? Moreover, who tells you that I am disinterested in my sentiments? The day may come when you will understand how entirely I rely upon you for assistance."

"But you have not given your friendship exclusively for the sake of the day that may come? Have you?" said the emperor, with a piercing glance at her beautiful pale face.

The countess cast down her eyes and blushed. "Do you mistrust me?" asked she, in a low, trembling voice.

"Give me a proof of your confidence in me," said Joseph, rising and taking both her hands in his. "You call me friend—give me, then, the right of a friend. Let me in some degree replace to you the fortune of which the Russian empress has robbed you."

"You are mistaken, sire," said the countess, proudly; "the Russian did not rob me of every thing. She took my lands, but I have invested funds in foreign securities which yield me an ample income. I have also my family jewels, and as long as you see me wearing them you may feel sure that I have other means of support."

The emperor shook his head. "You are not wearing your family jewels, Anna," said he.

"How, sire!" exclaimed she, blushing.

He leaned over, and in a low voice said, "Your jewels are false, your pearls are imitation, and there is not a single diamond in that coronet you intend to wear at my mother's reception to-morrow."

The cheeks of the countess grew scarlet with confusion, and her head dropped with shame. The emperor laid his hand upon her arm. "Now, Anna," said he, tenderly, "now that I know all, grant me the happiness of relieving you from your temporary embarrassments. Gracious Heaven! You who are not ashamed to confide your distress to pawnbrokers and jewellers, you refuse to trust *me!*"

"I would rather be under obligations to a stranger than to a friend," returned the countess, in a voice scarcely audible.

"But, Anna," cried the emperor, with a sudden burst of feeling, "you would rather be obliged to the man whom you loved than to a stranger. Oh, if you but loved me, there would be no question of 'mine or thine' between us! It is said—I have betrayed myself, and I need stifle my passion no longer; for I love you, beautiful Anna, I love you from my soul, and, at your feet, I implore you to give me that which is above all wealth or titles. Give me your love, be mine. Answer me, answer me. Do you love me?"

"I do," whispered she, without raising her head.

The emperor threw his arm around her waist. "Then," said he, "from this hour you give me the right to provide for you. Do you not?"

"No, sire, I can provide for myself."

"Then," cried Joseph, angrily, "you do not love me?"

"Yes, sire, I love you. You predicted that my heart would find its master. It has bowed before you and owns your sway. In the name of that love I crave help for Poland. She cries to Heaven for vengeance, and Heaven has not heard the cry. She is threatened by Russia and Prussia, and if noble Austria abandon her, she is lost! Oh, generous Austria, rescue my native land from her foes!"

"Ah!" exclaimed the emperor, sarcastically, "you call me Austria, and your love is bestowed upon my station and my armies! It is not I whom you love, but that Emperor of Austria in whose hand lies the power that may rescue Poland."

"I love *you;* but my love is grafted upon the hope I so long have cherished that in you I recognize the savior of my country."

"Indeed!" cried the emperor, with a sneer.

The countess did not hear him. She continued: "Until I loved you, every throb of my heart belonged to Poland. She, alone, was the object of my love and of my prayers. But since then, sire, the holy fire that burned upon the altar is quenched. I am faithless to my vestal vow, and I feel within my soul the tempest of an earthly passion. I have broken the oath that I made to my dying mother, for there is one more dear to me than Poland now, and for him are the prayers, the hopes, the longings, and the dreams that all belonged to Poland! Oh, my lord and my lover, reconcile me to my conscience! Let me believe that my loves are one; and on the day when your victorious eagles shall have driven away the vultures that prey upon my fatherland, I will throw myself at your feet, and live for *your* love alone."

"Ah, indeed," said the emperor, with a sardonic laugh, "you will go to such extremity in your patriotism! You will sell yourself, that Poland may be redeemed through your dishonor. I congratulate you upon your dexterous statesmanship. You sought me, I perceive, that by the magic of your intoxicating beauty, you might lure me to sacrifice the lives of *my* people in behalf of *yours*. Your love is a stratagem of diplomacy, nothing more."

"Oh, sire," cried she, in tones of anguish, "you despise me, then?"

"Not at all; I admire your policy, but unhappily it is only partially successful. You had calculated that I would not be proof against your beauty, your talents, your fascinations. You are right; I am taken in the snare, for I love you madly."

"And do I not return your love from my heart?" asked she.

"Stay," cried Joseph, "hear me out. One-half your policy, I say, was successful; the other has been at fault. As your lover I will do any thing that man can do to make you happy; but my head belongs to my fatherland, and you cannot rule it, through my heart."

"Sire, I seek nothing that is inconsistent with Austria's welfare. I ask help for Poland."

"Which help might involve Austria in a ruinous war with two powerful nations, and leave her so exhausted that she would have to stand by and witness the partition of Poland without daring to claim a share for herself."

"The partition of Poland!" exclaimed the countess, with a cry of horror. "Avenging God, wilt Thou suffer such culmination of human wickedness! And you, sire, could you share in such a crime? But, no! no! no!—see how misfortune has maddened me, when I doubt the honor of the noble Emperor of Austria! Never would the lofty and generous Joseph stoop to such infamy as this!"

"If Poland must succumb, I will act as becomes my station and responsibilities as the sovereign of a great empire, and I will do that which the wisdom and prudence of my mother shall dictate to her son. But Anna, dear Anna," continued he, passionately, "why should the sweet confession of our love be lost in the turbid roar of these political waters? Tell me that you love me as a woman ought to love, having no God, no faith, no country, but her lover; losing her identity and living for his happiness alone!"

"I love you, I love you," murmured she, with indescribable tenderness; and clasping her hands, she fell upon her knees and raised her eyes to him with a look that made him long to fold her to his heart, and yield up his empire, had she requested it, at his hands. "Help for Poland!" prayed she again, "help for Poland, and I am yours forever!"

Joseph grew angry with himself and with her. "Love does not chaffer," said he, rudely. "When a woman loves, she must recognize her master and bow before his will—otherwise there is no love. For the last time I ask, do you love me?"

"More than life or honor."

"Then be a woman, and yield yourself to me. Away with nationality—it is an abstraction. What are Poland and the world to you? Here, upon my heart, are your country and your altars. Come, without condition and without reserve. I cannot promise to free Poland, but, by the bright heaven above us, I swear to make you happy!"

She shook her head mournfully, and rose from her knees.

"Make me happy?" echoed she. "For me there can be no happiness while Poland sorrows."

"Say that again," thundered the emperor, "and we part forever!"

"I say it again!" said she, with proud tranquillity, but pale as death.

"And yet, if I am not ready to sacrifice my own people for yours, you will not believe in *my* love! You are unwilling to give up an idle dream of Polish freedom; and you ask of me, a man and an emperor, that I shall bring to you the offering of my own honor and of my people's happiness!"

She said nothing.

"It is enough!" cried Joseph, his eyes flashing with anger. "Pride against pride! We part. For the first thing I require of a woman who loves me, is submission. It grieves me bitterly to find you so unwomanly. I would have prized your love above every earthly blessing, had you given it freely. Conditionally I will not accept it; above all, when its conditions relate to the government of my empire. No woman shall ever have a voice in *my* affairs of state. If, for that reason, she reject me, I must submit; although, as at this moment, my heart bleeds at her rejection."

"And mine? *My heart?*" exclaimed the countess, raising her tearful eyes to his.

"Pride will cure you," replied he, with a bitter smile. "Go back to the fatherland that you love so well, and I shall imitate you, and turn to mine for comfort. There is many a mourning heart in Austria less haughty than yours, to which, perchance, I may be able to bring joy or consolation. God grant me some compensation in life for the supreme misery of this hour! Farewell, Countess Wielopolska. To-night I leave Vienna."

He crossed the room, while she looked after him as though her lips were parting to utter a cry.

At the door he turned once more to say farewell. Still she spoke not a word, but looked as though, like Niobe, she were stiffening into marble.

The emperor opened the door, and passed into the anteroom.

As he disappeared, she uttered a low cry, and clasped both her hands over her heart.

"My God! my God! I love him," sobbed she, and reeling backward, she fell fainting to the floor.

CHAPTER LXXII.

FAMINE IN BOHEMIA.

THE cry of distress from Bohemia reached Vienna, and came to the knowledge of the emperor. Joseph hastened to bring succor and comfort to his unhappy subjects.

Their need was great. Two successive years of short harvest had spread want and tribulation throughout all Germany, especially in Bohemia and Moravia, where a terrible inundation, added to the failure of the crops, had destroyed the fruits and vegetables of every field and every little garden.

The country was one vast desert. From every cottage went forth the wail of hunger. The stalls were empty of cattle, the barns of corn. The ploughs lay empty on the ground, for there was neither grain to sow nor oxen to drive. There were neither men nor women to till the soil, for there was no money to pay nor food to sustain them. Each man was alone in his want, and each sufferer in the egotism of a misery that stifled all humanity, complained that no one fed him, when all were fainting for lack of food.

"Bread! bread!" The dreadful cry arose from hundreds of emaciated beings, old and young, who, in the crowded cities, lay dying in the streets, their wasted hands raised in vain supplication to the passers-by.

"Bread! bread!" moaned the peasant in his hut, and the villager at the way-side; as with glaring eyes they stared at the traveller, who, more fortunate than they, was leaving Bohemia for happier climes, and, surely, in gratitude for his own rescue, would throw a crust to the starving wretches whom he left behind.

There they lay, watching for the elegant carriages, the horsemen, the wagons, that were accustomed to pass them on their road to Prague. But now the high-road was empty, for the famine had extended to Prague, and no one cared to go thither.

And yet on either side of the road were hundreds of beings who long ago had left their miserable huts, and now lay in heaps upon the ground, the heavens their only shelter, the wide world their home. These were the inhabitants of the mountains, who had come down to the neighboring villages for help, but had been rudely driven away by those whose sufferings had maddened them, and turned their hearts to stone.

They had lain there for a day, and yet not one trace of a traveller had they seen. The mid-day sun had blistered their foreheads, but they had not felt it, for the fiery pangs of hunger were keener than the sun; and now the evening air that fanned their burning brows, brought no relief, for fiercer and more cruel grew the gnawings of the fiend within.

"There is no help on earth," cried an old woman, the grandmother of a whole generation of stalwart mountaineers who lay stricken around her. There were her son and his wife, once such a stately pair, now reduced to two pale spectres; there were troops of grandchildren, once round-cheeked as the carved angels on the altar of the village chapel, now hollow-eyed and skinny, with their blanched faces upturned imploringly to the parents who were scarcely conscious of their presence there. Hunger had extinguished youth, strength, beauty, and had almost uprooted love. Not only had it destroyed their bodies, but it had even corrupted their souls.

"There is no help on earth," cried the old woman again, with such energy of despair that her voice found its way to the dull ear of every sufferer around. And now from every hollow voice came back the mournful chorus, "There is no help on earth!"

"There is no help in heaven!" shrieked an old man, who with his family was lying in a hollow, whence their moans were heard as though coming from the grave. "There is no God in heaven, else He would hear our cries! There is no God!"

"There is no God!" echoed the maddened wretches, and many a wasted arm was raised in defiance to heaven.

"Peace, peace, my friends!" cried the grandmother, "let us not sin because we starve. We can but die, and the Lord will receive us!" And as she spoke, she raised her trembling body and stretched forth her poor, withered arms, as though she would have calmed the tempest she had raised.

"Peace, Father Martin!" cried she, in a voice of authority. "There is a God above, but He has turned away His face because of our sins. Let us pray to see the light of His countenance. Come, friends, let us gather up all our strength and pray."

She arose and knelt, while, inspired by her example, the multitude knelt also. Old and young, men and women, all with one supreme effort lifted up their hands to heaven.

But the prayer was over, the petitioners fell prostrate to the earth, and still no sign of help from above!

"You see, Mother Elizabeth," groaned Father Martin, "your prayers are all in vain. Heaven is empty, and we must die."

"We must die, we must die!" howled the famishing multitude, and, exhausted by the might of their own despair, they fell to rise no more. A long, fearful silence ensued. Here and there a faint moan struggled for utterance, and a defiant arm was raised as though to threaten Omnipotence; then the poor, puny creatures, whom hunger had bereft of reason, shivered, dropped their hands, and again lay still.

Suddenly the silence was broken by the faint sound of carriage-wheels. Nearer and more near it came, until the horses' heads were to be seen through the clouds of dust that enveloped the vehicle. The poor peasants heard, but scarcely heeded it. They stared in mute despair, or murmured, "It is too late!"

Still the carriage rolled on, the dust grew thicker, and now it hid from the travellers' view the miserable wretches that lay dying around them. But, Heaven be praised, they stop!

There were two carriages, followed by outriders. The first carriage contained three persons, all clad in dark, plain civilian's clothes; but it was easy to recognize, in the youngest of the three, the most important personage of all. It was he who had given the order to halt, and now without waiting for assistance, he leaped from the carriage and walked at once to the foremost group of sufferers. He bent down to the old woman, who, turning her fever-stricken face to him, moaned feebly.

"What is the matter?" said the traveller, in a gentle and sympathizing tone. "How can I help you?"

The old mother made a violent effort and spoke. "Hunger!" said she. "I burn—burn—hunger!"

"Hunger! hunger!" echoed the people around, shaking off their lethargy, and awakening once more to hope.

"Oh, my God, this woman will die before we can succor her!" exclaimed the young man, sorrowfully. "Hasten, Lacy, and bring me some wine."

"We have none," replied Lacy. "Your majesty gave away your last bottle in the village behind."

"But she will die!" exclaimed the emperor, as bending over the poor old woman, he took her skinny hand in his.

"We must die," murmured she, while her parched tongue protruded from her mouth.

"Sire, you are in danger," whispered Lacy.

"Rise, your majesty," interrupted Rosenberg, "these unhappy people have the typhus that accompanies starvation, and it is contagious."

"Contagious for those who hunger, but not for us," replied Joseph. "Oh, my friends," continued he, "see here are three generations all dying for want of food. Gracious Heaven! They have lost all resemblance to humanity. Hunger has likened them to animals. Oh, it is dreadful to think that a crust of bread or a sip of wine might awaken these suffering creatures to reason; but flour and grain can be of no avail here!"

"They may avail elsewhere, sire," said Rosenberg, "and if we can do nothing for these, let us go on and help others."

"It is fearful," said the emperor, "but I will not leave until I have made an effort to save them."

He signed to one of his outriders, and taking out a leaf of his pocket-book, wrote something upon it. "Gallop for your life to Prague," said he, "and give this paper to the lord steward of the palace. He must at once send a wagon hither, laden with food and wine, and that he may be able to do it without delay, tell him to take the stores from the palace and all the viands that are preparing in the kitchen for my reception. This paper will be your warrant. As soon as you shall have delivered your message, fill a portmanteau with old Hungarian wine and gallop back to me. Be here within two hours, if you kill two of my best horses to compass the distance."

The outrider took the paper and, setting spurs to his horse, galloped off to Prague.

"And now, my friends," continued the emperor, "although we have no wine, we have bread and meat. Not much, it is true, but I think it will save these people from death."

The emperor hastened in the direction of his carriage. "Quick, Günther, hand me the camp-chest."

"But your majesty has not eaten a morsel to-day," urged Rosenberg, following him. "I cannot consent to see the food prepared for you, bestowed upon any one. You will lose your health if you fast for such a length of time. You owe it to your mother, the empress, and to your subjects, not to deprive yourself of food."

"Do you think I could eat in the presence of such hunger?" cried the emperor, impatiently. "Come, Günther. come all of you, and help me. Here is a large fowl. Cut it into little morsels, and—oh, what a discovery!—a jar of beef jelly. While you carve the fowl, I will distribute the jelly. Come, Lacy and Rosenberg, take each a portion of this chicken, and cut it up."

"Good Heaven, Lacy, come to my relief!" cried Rosenberg. "The emperor is about to give away his last morsel. We both have had breakfast, but he has not tasted food for a day."

"He is right, our noble emperor," replied Lacy, "in the presence of such suffering he is right to forget himself; if he could not do so, he would not be worthy to be a sovereign."

The emperor heard none of this; he was already with the sufferers, distributing his food. With earnest look, and firm and rapid hand, he put a teaspoonful of jelly between the parched, half-opened lips of the grandmother, while Günther, imitating him, did the same for her son.

For a moment the emperor looked to see the effect of his remedy. He saw an expression of joy flit over the features of the poor old woman, and then her lips moved, and she swallowed the jelly.

"See, see!" cried the emperor, overjoyed, "she takes it. Oh, Günther, this will save them until help comes from Prague! But there are so many of them! Do you think we have a hundred teaspoonfuls of jelly in the jar?"

And he looked anxiously at Günther.

"It is a large jar, your majesty," said Günther, "and I think it will hold out."

"Be sparing of it at any rate, and do not heap up your spoons. And now, not another word! We must go to work."

He stooped down and spoke no more, but his face was lit up by the fire of the Christian charity that was consuming his noble heart. He looked as must have looked his ancestor Rudolph of Hapsburg, who, once meeting a footsore priest bearing the *viaticum* to a dying parishioner, gave up his horse to the servant of God, and continued his way on foot.

While the emperor flew from group to group, resuscitating his expiring subjects, Lacy and Rosenberg were carefully cutting up the fowl that had been roasted for his dinner. A deep silence reigned around, all nature seemed to be at peace, and over the reclining sufferers the evening sun threw long rays of rosy light, that illumined their pallid faces with the hue of hope and returning life.

Gradually there was motion in the scene. Here and there a head arose from the ground, then a body, and presently a gleam of intelligence shot athwart those glaring, bloodshot eyes. The emperor watched them with a happy smile. His errand of mercy was at an end. The jar was empty, but every one had received a share, and all were reviving.

"Now give them a morsel of chicken," said Joseph. "A small piece will suffice, for after their long fast they can only eat sparingly of food; and they will have had enough until help come to us from Prague."

"Then," said Rosenberg, affectionately, "I hope that your majesty, too, will take something. There will certainly be enough left for you to eat your dinner without remorse."

"Never mind me, Rosenberg," laughed the emperor. "I shall not die of starvation, I promise you. When the creature cries out for nourishment, I shall give it; but I think that my Maker will not love me the less for having, voluntarily, felt the pangs of hunger for once in my life. I can never forget this day in Bohemia; it has confirmed my resolution to reign for the good of my people alone, and as God hears me, they shall be happy when I govern them.—But your chicken is ready. To satisfy you, I will go and beg my supper in yonder village, and, as there are enough of you to attend to these poor sufferers, I will take Lacy to keep me company. Come, Lacy."

He took the arm of the field-marshal, and both presently disappeared behind the trees.

CHAPTER LXXIII.

THE BLACK BROTH.

In a quarter of an hour they had reached the village. The same absence of all life struck painfully upon the emperor's heart as they walked along the deserted streets and heard nothing save the echo of their own footsteps. Not the lowing of a cow nor the bleating of a sheep, not one familiar rural sound, broke the mournful stillness that brooded over the air. Occasionally a ghastly figure in tattered garments, from whose vacant eyes the light of reason seemed to have fled, was seen crouching at the door of a hut, wherein his wife and children were starving. This was the only token of life that greeted the eyes of the grave and silent pair.

"Lacy," at last sighed the emperor, "how fearful is this deadly silence! One might fancy that he walked in Pompeii; and Pompeii, alas, is not more lonely. To think that I, an emperor, must look on and give no help!"

"Oh, yes, sire, you can give help," said Lacy, encouragingly. "There must be some means by which this fearful famine can be arrested."

"I have ordered corn from Hungary, where the harvest has been abundant. To encourage the importation of grain in Bohemia, I have promised, besides good prices, a premium of one hundred guilders for each well-laden, four-horse wagon of grain that arrives before the expiration of three weeks."

"But the people will be exhausted before three weeks."

"I have also ordered the commissary store-houses to be opened in Prague, and the grain to be distributed."

"This will last but for a few days," returned Lacy, shaking his head.

"Then what can I do?" exclaimed the emperor, sorrowfully.

"The famine is so great that it can scarcely have arisen from natural causes. Where scarcity is, there will always be found the extortioner, who profits by it. Those who have grain are withholding it for higher prices."

"Woe to them, if I light upon their stores!" exclaimed Joseph, indignantly. "Woe to those who traffic in the fruits of the earth, which God has bestowed for the use of all men!"

"Your majesty will not find them. They will be carefully hidden away from your sight."

"I will seek until I find," replied the emperor. "But look there, Lacy, what a stately dwelling rears its proud head beyond that grove of trees! Is it the setting sun that gilds the windows just now?"

"No, your majesty, the light is from within. I suppose it is the castle of the nobleman, who owns the village."

They walked a few paces farther, when the emperor spoke again. "See, Lacy, here is a hut, from whose chimney I see smoke. Perhaps I shall find something to eat within."

He opened the door of the cottage, and there on the floor, in a heap, lay a woman with four children. Their hollow eyes were fixed without the slightest interest upon the strangers, for they were in the last stage of hunger-typhus, and saw nothing.

Lacy hurried the emperor away, saying, "Nothing can help these except death. I know this terrible fever. I saw it in Moravia in '62."

They stepped from the cottage to the kitchen. A fire was burning in the chimney, and before it stood a man who was stirring the contents of a pot."

"God be praised!" exclaimed the emperor, "here is food."

The man turned and showed a sunken, famished countenance.

"Do you want supper?" said he roughly. "I have a mess in my pot that an emperor might covet."

"He does covet it, my friend," said the emperor, laughing. "What have you there?"

The man threw sinister glances at the well-dressed strangers, who jarred the funeral air of his cottage with untimely mirth.

"Did you come here to mock me?" said he. "Fine folks, like you, are after no good in a poor man's cottage. If you come here to pasture upon our misery, go into the house, and there you will see a sight that will rejoice the rich man's heart."

"No, my friend," replied the emperor, soothingly, "we come to ask for a share of your supper."

The man broke out into a sardonic laugh. "My supper!" cried he. "Come, then, and see it. It is earth and water!"

"Earth and water!" cried the horror-stricken Joseph.

The peasant nodded. "Yes," said he, "the earth gives growth to the corn, and as I have got no corn, I am trying to see what it will do for me! I have already tasted grass. It is so green and fresh, and seems so sweet to our cattle, that we tried to eat the *sweet green grass.*" And he smiled, but it was the smile of a demon.

"Oh, my God!" cried the emperor.

"But it seems," continued the man, as though speaking to himself, "that God loves cattle better than he does men; for the grass which strengthens them, made us so sick, so sick, that it would have been a mercy if we had all died. It seems that we cannot die, however, so now I am going to eat the glorious earth. Hurrah! My supper is ready."

He swung the kettle upon the table and poured the black mass into a platter.

"Now," said he, with a fiendish grin, "now will the great folks like to sup with me?"

"Yes," said the emperor, gravely, "I will taste of your supper."

He stepped to the table, and took the spoon which the bewildered peasant held out to him. Pale with excitement, the emperor put the spoon to his mouth, and tasted. Then he reached it to Lacy.

"Taste it, Lacy" said he. "Oh, to think that these are men who suffer the pangs of starvation!" And completely overcome by his sorrowing sympathy, the emperor's eyes overflowed with tears.

The peasant saw them and said, "Yes, my lord, we are men, but God has forsaken us. He has been more merciful to the cattle, for they have all died."

"But how came this fearful famine among you?" asked Lacy. "Did you not plant corn?"

"How could we plant corn when we had none? For two years our crops have failed, and hunger has eaten our vitals until there is not a man in the village who has the strength to raise a fagot."

"But I saw a castle as we came thither," said Lacy.

"Yes, you saw the castle of the Baron von Weifach. The whole country belongs to him; but we are free peasants. As long as we made any thing, we paid him our tithes. But we have nothing now."

And with a groan he sank down upon the wooden settle that stood behind him.

"The baron does nothing for you, then?"

"Why should he?" said the man, with a bitter laugh. "We pay no more tithes, and we are of no use to him. He prays every day for the famine to last, and God hears his prayers, for God forsakes the poor and loves the rich."

"But how does he profit by the famine?" asked Lacy.

"We have been profitable laborers to him, my lord. For several years past, his corn-fields have been weighed down with golden tassels that made the heart leap with joy at sight of their beauty. He had so much that his barns would not hold it, and he had to put up other great barns, thatched with straw, to shelter it. This year, it is true, he has reaped nothing, but what of that? His barns are still full to overflowing."

"But how comes there such famine, when his barns are full of corn?" asked the emperor, who was listening with intense interest.

"That is a question which does little honor to your head, sir," said the peasant, with a grating laugh. "The famine in Bohemia is terrible precisely because the extortioners hold back their grain and will not sell it."

"But there is a law against the hoarding of grain."

"Yes, there are laws made so that the poor may be punished by them and the rich protected," said the peasant, with a sinister look. "Oh, yes, there are laws! The rich have only to say that they have no corn, and there the law ends."

"And you think that the Baron von Weifach has grain?"

The peasant nodded. "I know it," said he, "and when the time comes, he will put it in the market."

"What time?"

"When the need of the people will be so great that they will part with their last acre of land or last handful of gold for a few bushels of grain. Several years ago, when corn was cheap, he sent his corn abroad to a country where the harvest had been short; but he will not do so this year, for the rich men have speculated so well that corn is dearer here than it is over the frontiers.* But I have enough of your questions. Let me alone, and go about your business."

"Can you buy food with money?" asked the emperor, kindly.

"Yes, indeed, sir," said the peasant, while a ray of hope entered the dark prison of his desponding heart. "If I had money, the housekeeper of the baron would sell me bread, wheat, meat—oh, she would sell me any thing if I had money to pay for it."

"Take this, then," said the emperor, laying several gold pieces on the table. "I hope to bring you more permanent relief, later."

The peasant, with a cry, threw himself upon the gold. He paid no attention whatever to the donor. Shouting for joy at the same time that he was shedding tears in profusion, he darted, with his prize, to his starving wife and children, to bid them live until he brought them food.

Without, stood the emperor and Lacy. "O God!" murmured he to himself, "and I have thought myself a most unhappy man! What is the grief of the heart to such bodily torture as this! Come, Lacy, come. The day of reckoning is here, and, by the eternal God, I will punish the guilty!"

"What means your majesty?" asked Lacy, as the emperor, instead of returning to the village, strode forward toward the path that led to the castle.

"I mean to go at once to yonder castle," cried he, with a threatening gesture, "and my hand shall fall heavily upon the extortioner who withholds his grain from the people."

"But your majesty," urged Lacy, "the word of one discontented peasant is not enough to convict a man. You must have proofs before you condemn him."

"True, Lacy, you are right. I must seek for proofs."

"How, your majesty?"

"By going to the castle. My plan is already laid. As they seem to be feasting to-day, I am likely to find a goodly assemblage of rich men together. I must get an invitation to the feast, and once there, if the charge be just, I promise to furnish the proofs."

"Your majesty's undertaking is not a safe one. I must, therefore, accompany you," said Lacy.

"No, Lacy, I intend that you shall meet me there. Return to the place where we left Rosenberg and the others, take one of the carriages, and drive with him to the castle. When you arrive there, ask for me, and say that you are now ready to proceed on our journey. Günther can remain with the mountaineers, and if our provisions arrive from Prague, he can dispatch a courier to let us know it."

"Shall we ask for your majesty at the castle, sire?"

"Not by my own name. Ask for Baron von Josephi, for by that title I shall introduce myself. Now farewell, and *au revoir.*"

*Gross-Hoffinger, "Life and Reign of Joseph II.," vol. i., p. 138. Carl Ramshorn, "Life and Times of Joseph II.," p. 99.

CHAPTER LXXIV.

THE EXTORTIONERS OF QUALITY.

THE drawing-room of the Freiherr von Weifach was splendidly illuminated. Hundreds of wax lights were multiplied to infinity in the spacious mirrors that lined the walls, and separated one from another the richly-framed portraits of the freiherr's noble ancestors. In the banquet-hall, the dinner-table was resplendent with silver and gold—with porcelain and crystal. Flowers sent out their perfume from costliest vases of Dresden china, and rich old wines sparkled in goblets of glittering glass. Around the table sat a company of richly-dressed ladies and gentlemen of rank. They had been four hours at dinner, and the sense of enjoyment, springing from the satisfaction of appetite, was visible, not only on the flushed faces of the men, but betrayed itself upon the rosy-tinted faces of the elegant women who were their companions.

The dessert was on the table. The guests were indulging themslves in some of those post-prandial effusions which are apt to blossom from heads overheated by wine, and are generally richer in words than in wisdom. The host, with flattering preliminaries, had proposed the health of the ladies, and every goblet sparkled to the brim. Just at that moment a servant entered the room and whispered a few words in his ear. He turned, smiling to his guests, and, apologizing for the interruption, said:

"Ladies and gentlemen, I leave it to you to decide the question just proposed to me. A gentleman has at this moment arrived at the castle, requesting permission to remain until some repairs can be made to his carriage, which has met with an accident in the neighboring village. Shall we invite him to join us while he awaits the return of his vehicle?"

"Let us not be rash in our hospitality," replied the freiherrin, from the opposite side of the table. "In the name of the noble ladies assembled here, I crave to know whether the stranger who comes so *sans façon* to our castle, is worthy of the honor proposed by my husband. In other words, is he a personage of rank?"

"He presents himself as the Baron von Josephi," said the freiherr.

"One of the oldest families in Hungary!" exclaimed one of the guests.

"Then he can be admitted," responded the hostess. "At least, if it be agreeable to the ladies?"

Unanimous consent was given, and the freiherr arose from his seat to convey the invitation to the stranger.

"The Baron von Josephi!" said he, reëntering with the gentleman, and leading him at once to the freiherrin. She received him with smiling courtesy, while the rest of the company directed their glances toward him, anxious to see how he would acquit himself in his rather embarrassing position. He was perfectly self-possessed, and in every gesture showed himself to be a man of the world.

With quiet grace he took his seat at the side of the hostess, and, as he looked around with his large blue eyes, he seemed rather to be criticising than criticised. With a sharp, searching expression, his glances went from one of the company to another, until they in their turn felt not only embarrassed, but harassed and uneasy.

"I do not know why," whispered one of them to the lady who sat next to him, "but this newcomer's face seems very familiar to me. I must have met him somewhere before this."

"You certainly might remember him," replied the lady, "if it were only for his beautiful eyes. I never saw such eyes in my life. His manners, too, are distinguished. I judge that he must have lived at court."

"In other words, you prefer a man who fawns at court to one who reigns like a prince over his own estates," said the first speaker, warmly. "I, for my part—"

"Hush! Let us hear what he is saying," interrupted the lady.

"I am under many obligations for your hospitality," said the Baron von Josephi to the hostess. "For three days that I have travelled in Bohemia, I have met with nothing but poverty and starvation. Thanks to my entrance into your splendid home, I see that plenty still reigns in the castle, although it may have departed from the cottage."

"Yes, thank Heaven, we know how to take care of our own interests here," said the freiherr, laughing.

"And yet you see how things are exaggerated," replied the Baron von Josephi, laughing. "Such dreadful tidings of the famine in Bohemia reached Vienna that the emperor is actually on his way to investigate the matter. I met him not far from Budweis, and he seemed very sad I thought."

"By the saints, he has reason to feel sad," exclaimed one of the guests. "He will find nothing here for his howling subjects. He would have been wiser had he stayed in Vienna!"

"Yes, poor, sentimental little emperor!" cried another with a laugh. "He will find that the stamp of his imperial foot will conjure no corn out of the earth, wherewith to feed his starving boors."

"I do not see why he should meddle with the boors at all," added a third. "Hungry serfs are easy to govern; they have no time to cry for rights when they are crying for bread."

"If the gentlemen are going to talk of politics," said the hostess, rising from her seat, "it is time for ladies to retire. Come, ladies, our cavaliers will join us when coffee is served."

The gentlemen rose, and not until the last lady had passed from the room did they resume their seats.

"And now, gentlemen," said Baron von Josephi, "as our political gossip can no longer annoy the ladies, allow me to say that my presence here is not accidental, as I had led you to suppose."

"And to what are we indebted for the honor?" asked the host.

"I will explain," said the baron, inclining his head. "You have received me with the hospitality of the olden time, without inquiring my rank, lineage, or dwelling-place. Permit me to introduce myself. I have estates in Moravia, and they are contiguous to those of Count Hoditz."

"Then," replied Freiherr von Weifach, "I sympathize with you, for nowhere in Austria has the famine been more severe."

"Severe, indeed! The poor are dying like flies, for they cannot learn to live upon grass."

"Neither will they learn to live upon it in Bohemia," said the freiherr, laughing. "The people are so unreasonable! The noblest race-horse lives upon hay and grass; why should it not be good enough for a peasant of low degree?"

"Mere prejudice on the part of the peasant!" returned the baron. "I have always suspected him of affectation. I have no patience with grumblers."

"You are right, baron," said his neighbor, nodding and smiling. "The people are idle and wasteful; and if we were to listen to their complaints, we would soon be as poor as they."

"And what if a few thousand perish here and there?" interposed another. "They never would be missed, for they multiply like potatoes."

"You say, baron," resumed the host, "that you paid no attention to the complaints of your peasantry?"

"I did like Ulysses, gentlemen; I stopped my ears with wax, that my heart might not grow weak."

"A melodious siren song, to be sure," laughed the company; "a dirge of bread! bread! bread!"

"Ah, you know the song, I perceive," said the Baron von Josephi, joining in the laugh.

"Yes; and we do as you have done, baron. We stop our ears."

"The consequence is," continued Josephi, "that my granaries are full to overflowing. I was on my way to Prague to dispose of it, but the want which I have seen on your estates, freiherr, has touched my heart. Nowhere have I beheld any thing to equal it. Hundreds of starving peasants are on the high-road, not a mile off."

"Did you honor us with your presence to tell me this?" asked the host, with lowering brow. "If so, you might have spared your trouble, for I know it."

"Oh no; I came to you with the best intentions. I have no pity for the peasant, but some for yourself. The health of his workmen is the nobleman's wealth. Now my own people are almost all dead, and as I grieve to see your lands wasted, I offer you my corn."

"Which means that you wish me to buy it," said the freiherr, with a significant smile.

"Yes; and you can have it at once. I know that I might do better by waiting, but I have a tender heart, and am willing to part with it now. I make you the offer."

"How much a *strich?*" * asked the freiherr.

"Twenty florins. You will find it cheap."

Very cheap, forsooth!" cried the host, with a loud laugh, in which his guests all joined. "You wish me to buy your corn for my peasants? Why, it will be worth its weight in gold, and they have none wherewith to pay me."

"You are a humane landlord and a nobleman; and I take it for granted that you will make it a gift to your peasantry."

"Why did you not do as much yourself?" asked the freiherr, scornfully. "Have you not just now said that your people were dying, while your granaries are full? No, no; I want no corn; but when corn has truly risen to twenty florins, then I shall open my granaries, and my crops shall be for sale."

And the freiherr filled his glass and drank a bumper.

"You should not speak so loud," said Josephi, "for you know that the emperor has issued an edict, exacting that all those who have grain shall meet him in Prague, that the government may buy their grain at a reasonable price."

"What fool would heed such an edict?" cried the freiherr. "The

* A *strich*, in Prague, was something more than two bushels.

emperor is not master of our granaries. In the rural districts the nobleman is emperor, and God forbid that it should ever be otherwise!"

"But the emperor has appointed commissioners, who go from place to place, and inspect the crops."

"Yes; they came hither, and they came to all of us—did they not, my lords?"

"Yes, yes!" cried a chorus of merry noblemen.

"But they found nothing—nothing but a few hundred florins that glided, unaccountably, into their hands, and caused them to abscond in a hurry. This people-loving emperor deserves the eternal gratitude of his commissioners, for although they found no corn for him, they found an abundance of gold for themselves."

Josephi colored violently, and his whole frame trembled. His hand clutched the wine-glass which he held, and he seemed to breathe with difficulty.

No one observed it. The company were excited by wine, and their senses were dim and clouded. But for this sumptuous dinner, at which he had indulged himself too far, the freiherr would never have betrayed the secret of his overflowing barns.

Josephi, meanwhile, controlled his indignation, and spoke again. "So, freiherr, you all reject my proposal."

"I do. God be praised, I have enough and to spare!"

"Then, gentlemen," continued the baron, "I offer it to any one of you. You are all from this unhappy district, and some one of you must be in need of grain."

"We are the freiherr's neighbors, and have borrowed his wisdom," said one of the company, "and I can answer for all present that they are well provided."

"There are seven of you present, and none needing grain?" exclaimed Von Josephi.

"Yes. Seven noblemen, all abounding in grain."

"Seven extortioners!" cried Josephi, rising from his seat, and looking as if he would have stricken them to the earth with the lightning of his flashing eyes.

"What means this insolence?" asked the host.

"It means that I have found here seven men of noble birth, who have disgraced their caste by fattening upon the misery of their fellows. But, by the eternal God! the extortioner shall be branded throughout the world. And be he gentle or base-born, he shall feel the weight of my just indignation."

While the emperor spoke, the company had been awaking from the stupor caused by the wine they had been drinking. Gradually their heads were raised to listen, and their eyes shot fire, until, at last, they sprang from their seats, crying out:

"Who dares speak thus to us? By what right do you come to insult us?"

"By what right?" thundered the emperor. "The emperor has given me the right—the little chicken-hearted emperor. whose commissioners you have bribed, and whose subjects you have oppressed, until nothing remains for him but to come among you and drag your infamy to daylight with his own hands."

"The emperor! it is the emperor!" groaned the terror-stricken extortioners, while Joseph looked contemptuously upon their pale and conscience-stricken faces.

Suddenly the host burst into a maudlin laugh.

"Do you not see," said he, "that our facetious guest is making game of us to revenge himself for our refusal to buy his corn?"

"True, true," cried the lords together. "It's a jest—a trick to—"

"Peace!" cried the emperor. "The hour for jesting has passed by, and the hour of retribution is here. I came to Bohemia to feed my starving subjects, and I will feed them! But I shall also punish those who, having bread, have withheld it from the poor. You shall not bribe *me* with your parchments of nobility or with your pride of family. The pillory is for the criminal, and his rank shall not save him."

"Mercy, gracious sovereign, mercy!" cried the freiherr, whose glowing cheeks were now as pale as death. "Your majesty will not condemn us for the idle words we have spoken from excesss of wine?"

"What mercy had you upon the wailing wretches, of whose misery you have made such sport to-day?"

"Your majesty," said one of the noblemen, sullenly, "there is no law to prevent a man from holding his own, and the Bohemian nobleman has his own code of justice, and is amenable to no other."

"The Bohemian nobleman shall enjoy it no longer!" exclaimed the outraged emperor. "Before their earthly judges men shall be equal, as they are before the throne of God."

At that moment the door opened, and the emperor's suite came in.

"Lacy, Lacy!" cried Joseph, "you were right. The famine is not the result of a short harvest. It is due to these monsters of wickedness, whom you see before you in the enjoyment of every luxury that sensuality can crave."

"Mercy, sire, mercy!" cried a chorus of imploring voices, and looking behind him, the emperor saw the ladies, who all sank upon their knees at his feet.

While Joseph had been speaking with Lacy, the lord of the castle had hastened to communicate their disgrace, and to bring the wives of the criminals to their assistance.

The emperor frowned. "Ladies," said he, "we are on the subject of politics, the same subject which banished you hence not long ago. Rise, therefore, and retire—this is no place for you."

"No, sire," cried the Freiherrin von Weifach, "I will not rise until I obtain pardon for my husband. I do not know of what he has been guilty, but I know that our noble emperor cannot condemn the man under whose roof he has come as an invited guest. I know that the emperor is too generous to punish him, who, confiding in him as a man, little suspected that he who came under a borrowed name was the sovereign lord of all Austria."

"Ah, madame, you reproach me with an hour spent at your table, and you expect me to overlook crime in consideration of the common courtesy extended to me as a man of your own rank. I was so fortunate as to overhear the little discussion that preceded my entrance here. Rise, madame, I am not fond of Spanish customs, nor do I like to see women on their knees."

"Mercy for my husband!" reiterated the freiherrin. "Forgive him for thinking more of his own family than of others. What he did was for love of his wife and children."

"Ah!" exclaimed the emperor, "you call that love of his family! You would elevate his cruel avarice into a domestic virtue. I congratulate you upon your high standard of ethics! But rise, I command you. Meanwhile, you are right on one point at least. I have eaten of your salt, and I am too true a nobleman to betray you to the emperor. I will merely tell him that the corn is found, and that his poor people may rejoice. Open your granaries, therefore, my lords. Let each of you this night send a courier to your tenants, proffering grain to all, free of charge, stipulating only that, as a return for the gift, the peasantry shall bestow a portion of their corn upon their mother earth.* You will see how magical is the effect of generosity. Your stores will scatter blessings over this unhappy land, and the poor will bless you as their benefactors. Yes, gentlemen, from this day forward you will be the friends of the needy; for, God be praised, you have corn, and, for the sake of your corn, I forgive you. But see that the future makes full atonement for the past."

No one answered a word. With sullen mien and downcast eyes they stood, while the emperor surveyed them with surprise.

"What!" said he, after a long and painful pause, "not a word of thanks! Joy has made you dumb, I perceive. And no wonder; for to feel (for the first time) the pleasures of benevolence may well make you speechless with happiness. As for you, madame," continued the emperor, addressing his hostess, "I will not deprive you of a share in your husband's generosity. You will be so kind as to call up your servants and bid them load a wagon with the remains of our excellent dinner, not forgetting the wines; and you will then send it, with your greetings, to your tenants in yonder village. Your servants can go from house to house until the store is exhausted."

"I will do what your majesty commands," said the freiherrin, pale with rage.

"I do not doubt it," replied the emperor, laughing. "And as I will be glad to hear how your bounty is received in the village, two of my own attendants will accompany yours. Farewell, my lords, I must leave you, for I have a large company on the high-road whom I have invited to supper. The freiherrin will oblige me by receiving them to-night as her guests. In this stately castle there are, doubtless, several rooms that can be thrown open to these weary, suffering mountaineers. Have I your permission to send them hither?"

"I will obey your majesty's commands," sobbed the lady, no longer able to control her tears.

The emperor bowed, and turning to his attendants, said, "Come, my friends, our messengers have probably arrived before this, and our guests await us."

He advanced to the door, but suddenly stopped and addressed the company. "My lords," said he, "for once your wisdom has been at fault. It is well that the sentimental little emperor did not remain, as you advised, in Vienna; for the stamp of his imperial foot has struck abundance out of the earth, and it will save the lives of his starving boors."

*Gross-Hoffinger, vol. i., p. 141.

CHAPTER LXXV.

DIPLOMATIC ESOTERICS.

PRINCE KAUNITZ was in his cabinet. Baron Binder was reading aloud the secret dispatches which had just come in from the Austrian ambassador at Berlin, the young Baron van Swieten. Meanwhile, Kaunitz was busy with a brush of peacock's feathers, dusting the expensive trifles that covered his *escritoire*, or polishing its ebony surface with a fine silk handkerchief which he kept for the purpose. This furbishing of trinkets and furniture was a private pastime with the all-powerful minister; and many a personage of rank was made to wait in the anteroom, while he finished his dusting or rearranged his *bijouterie*, until it was grouped to his satisfaction.

The dispatches which were being read were of the highest importance; for they related to a confidential conversation with the King of Prussia on the subject of the political apple, at which all were striving for the largest bite. The King of Prussia, wrote the ambassador, had spoken jestingly of the partition of Poland. He had bespoken for himself the district of Netz and Polish Prussia, premising that Dantzic, Thorn, and Cracow were to be left to Poland.

"Very well arranged," said Kaunitz, with his accustomed *sang froid*, while he brightened the jewels of a Sèvres inkstand which had been presented to him by Madame de Pompadour. "*Vraiment* the *naïveté* of this Frederick is prodigious. He appropriates the richest and most cultivated districts of Poland to himself; and then inserts, as an unimportant clause, the stipulation that Cracow, with its adjacent territory, the rich salt mines of Wieliczka, shall *not* belong to Austria."

"Van Swieten would not agree to the arrangement," said Binder, "and he furthermore declared to the king that such a distribution would be prejudicial to Austria. He proposed, however, that Austria might be indemnified by the possession of Bosnia and Servia, which the Porte should be made to yield."

"What a preposterous fool!" exclaimed Kaunitz. "Who gave him the right to make such a proposition—"

"Why, your highness, I suppose he thought—"

"He has no right to think," interrupted Kaunitz. "I ask of no employé of mine to think. My envoys have nothing to do but to work out *my* thoughts, and that without any intervention of their own fancies. It is very presuming in my little diplomatic agents to think what I have not thought, and of their own accord to make propositions to foreign courts. Write and tell him so, Binder, and add, that neither our permanent peaceful relations with Turkey, nor the sentiments of consideration which are entertained by the empress for the Porte, will allow of any attempt to lessen his territory." *

"Then you are really in earnest," and intend to be a firm ally of the Porte?" inquired Binder with astonishment.

"In earnest!" repeated Kaunitz, with a shrug. "You statesman in swaddling-clothes! You do not know the first principles of your

* Wilhelm von Dohm, "Memoirs of My Time," vol. i., 489.

profession; and yet you have lived with me for thirty years! In diplomacy there is no such thing as stability of policy. Policy shapes itself according to circumstances, and changes as they change. The man who attempted to follow fixed principles in international policy, would scon find himself and his government on the verge of a precipice."

"And yet there is no statesman in Europe who adheres so closely to his principles as yourself," exclaimed Binder, with the enthusiasm of true friendship.

Kaunitz majestically inclined his head. "My principles are these: To make Austria rich, great, powerful. Austria shall be *quocunque modo*, the first power in Europe; and in after-years the world shall say that the genius of Kaunitz placed her on the mountain-peaks of her greatness. For this end, it is indispensable that I remain at the head of European affairs. Not only Austria, but all Europe, looks to me to guide her through the storm that is threatening the general peace. I dare not leave the helm of state to take one hour's rest; for what would become of the great continental ship, if, seeking my own comfort, I were to retire and yield her fortunes to some unsteady hand? There is no one to replace me! No one! It is only once in a century that Heaven vouchsafes a great statesman to the world. This makes me fear for Austria when I shall have gone from earth and there is no one to succeed me." *

"May you live many years to rule in Austria!" cried Binder, warmly; "you are indispensable to her welfare."

"I know it," said Kaunitz, gravely. "But there are aspirants for political fame in Austria, who would like to lay their awkward hands upon the web that I weave? No one knows how far the youthful impetuosity and boundless vanity of such ambition may go. It might lead its possessor to entertain the insane idea that he could govern Austria without my guidance."

"You speak of the Emperor Joseph?"

"Yes, I do. He is ambitious, overbearing, and vain. He mistakes his stupid longings to do good for capacity. He lusts for fame through war and conquest, and would change every thing in his mother's empire, for the mere satisfaction of knowing that the change was his own work. Oh, what would become of Austria if I were not by, to keep him within bounds? It will task all my genius to steer between the Scylla of a bigoted, peace-loving empress, and the Charybdis of this reckless emperor; to reconcile their antagonisms, and overrule their prejudices. Maria Theresa is for peace and a treaty with the Porte, who has lately been a good-natured, harmless neighbor—Joseph thirsts for war that he may enlarge his dominions and parade himself before the world as a military genius. If his mother were to die to-morrow, he would plunge headlong into a war with Russia or Turkey, whichever one he might happen to fancy. I am obliged to hold this prospect forever before his eyes to keep him quiet. I must also pay my tribute to the whims of the reigning empress; and if we declare war to pacify Joseph, we must also make it appear to Maria Theresa that war is inevitable."

"By Heaven, that is a delicate web, indeed!" cried Binder, laughing.

"Yes, and let no presuming hand ever touch a thread of it!"

* The prince's own words. See Swinburne, vol. i., p. 230.

replied Kaunitz. "I say as much as I have said to you, Binder, because the greatest minds *must* sometimes find a vent for their conceptions, and I trust nobody on earth except you. Now you know what I mean by 'permanent treaties with the Porte,' and I hope you will not ask any more silly questions. You ignoramus! that have lived so long with Kaunitz and have not yet learned to know him!"

"Your highness is beyond the comprehension of ordinary men," said Binder, with a good-humored smile.

"I believe so," replied Kaunitz, with truthful simplicity; while he carefully placed his paper, pens, lines, and penknife in the drawer wherein they belonged.

The door opened, and a servant announced his excellency Osman Pacha, ambassador of the Ottoman Porte.

"Very well," replied Kaunitz with a nod, "I will see him presently."

"You see," said he to Binder, as the door closed upon the servant, "we are about to begin in earnest with the Porte. I shall receive him in the drawing-room. Meanwhile, remain here, for I shall need you again."

He smiled kindly upon his friend, and left the room. Binder looked after him with tenderest admiration. "He is a very great man," said he to himself, "and he is right. But for him, Austria would fall to the rank of a second power. What if he does know it and boast of it? He is a truthful and candid man. *Voilà tout.*"

And he sat down to write to Van Swieten in Berlin to beware of saying any thing prejudicial to the interests of the Porte.

He had just concluded his letter when Kaunitz returned. His countenance was beaming with satisfaction and his lips were half parting with a smile. "Binder," said he, laying a roll of papers on the *escritoire*, "here are sugar-plums for the emperor. Can you guess what I have in these papers?"

"Not a declaration of war from Russia!" exclaimed Binder.

"Hm; something very like it, I assure you. Listen! It is the secret treaty that our minister at Constantinople, Herr von Thugut, has just concluded with the Porte. The Sultan has already signed it, and to-day I shall present it for signature to the empress. She will do it readily; for although she may not absolutely dote on the infidel, she hates Russia; and the unbelieving Turk is dearer to her than her Christian cousin, the Empress Catharine."

"Then, after all, we are the firm allies of Turkey?" said Binder.

The prince gave a shrug, and trifled with the papers he had brought with him. "We have bound ourselves," said he, reading here and there among the leaves, "to bring about a peace between Russia and Turkey, by which the former shall restore to the latter all the provinces which she has conquered from the Porte; or, if not all, those which are indispensable to preserve the honor of Turkey intact. We have furthermore bound ourselves to secure the independence of the Republic of Poland."

"But, prince, that contradicts all your previous understandings with Prussia and Russia; it contradicts your plans for the partition of Poland. It will certainly lead to war, for our highness has forgotten that Prussia and Russia have already agreed, for the *soi disant* pacification of Poland, to appropriate the greater part of her provinces to themselves."

"I beg you to believe, my verdant friend, that I never forget any thing," said Kaunitz, somewhat haughtily. "I am perfectly *au fait* to the Russo-Prussian treaty; but I have not been invited to the banquet, and I do not intend to go uninvited. When they speak, we will consider their offers. If they say nothing, we go to war. If they speak, we will allow ourselves to be persuaded to share the booty which we cannot restore to its owners. In that way, we are in a manner forced into this coalition, and the opprobrium of the act falls upon those who devised it, while Maria Theresa's scruples will be more easily overcome."

"Prince," said Binder, with a sigh, "I give it up. I never will make a statesman. I listen to your words as to a Delphic oracle, and do not pretend to understand their ambiguous meaning. I understand, however, do I not, that we are the allies of the Sultan? Now we thereby do him a great favor—what does he give in return?"

"Not much, but still something," said Kaunitz, with composure, while his fingers again turned over the leaves. "The Porte, who, like yourself, apprehends war with Russia, understands that if Austria is to befriend him, she must put her army upon a war footing. If Austria is to do this for the sake of Turkey, Turkey of course must furnish the means. The Porte then, in the course of the next eight months, will pay us the sum of twenty thousand purses, each containing five hundred silver piasters. Four thousand purses will be paid down as soon as the treaty is signed." *

"Ten millions of piasters!" exclaimed Binder, with uplifted hands. "By Heaven, prince, you are a second Moses. You know how to strike a rock so that a silver fountain shall gush from its barrenness."

"I shall make good use of it, too. Our coffers need replenishing, and the emperor will rejoice to see them filled with the gold of the infidel. It will enable him to raise and equip a gallant army, and that will give him such unbounded delight that we are sure of his signature. Besides this, the Porte presents us with a goodly portion of Wallachia; he fixes the boundaries of Transylvania to our complete satisfaction, and allows us free trade with the Ottoman empire, both by land and by water."

"But all these concessions will cost us a war with Russia. The rapacious Czarina will be furious when she hears of them."

"She will not hear of them," said Kaunitz, quietly. "I have made it a stringent condition with Osman Pacha that the treaty with Turkey shall be a profound secret. The Sultan and his vizier have pledged their word, and the Mussulman may always be trusted. We will only make the treaty public in case of a war with Russia."

"Whence it follows that as Russia is much more likely to court our friendship than our enmity, the treaty with the Porte is all moonshine."

"With the exception of the ten millions of piasters, which are terrene and tangible. It remains now to see whether Turkey will keep silence or Russia will speak! In either case, the peace of all Europe now lies in Austria's hands. We will preserve or destroy it as is most advantageous to our own interests."

At that moment the door leading to the anteroom was opened, and a page announced Prince Gallitzin, ambassador of her majesty the Empress of Russia.

* Dohm, "Memoirs of My Time," vol. i., p. 471.

This announcement following the subjects which had been under discussion, was so significant, that Kaunitz could not conceal his sense of its supreme importance. He was slightly disturbed; but recovering himself almost instantaneously, he said:

"In five minutes I will receive his highness in this room. Now begone, and open the door punctually."

"What can the Russian minister want to-day?" said Binder.

"He has come to speak at last," replied Kaunitz, taking breath.

"Not of the partition of Poland, but of your Turkish treaty. You will see that he if he gain any thing by talking, the Porte will not keep silence."

"Three minutes gone," said Kaunitz, taking out his watch. "Not another word, Binder. Step behind that screen and listen to our discussion. It will save me the trouble of repeating it to you."

While Binder was concealing himself, Kaunitz was composing his visage before a looking-glass. It soon reached its accustomed serenity, and not a lock of the peruke was out of place.

In five minutes the page reopened the door and announced the entrance of the Russian ambassador.

CHAPTER LXXVI.

RUSSIA SPEAKS.

PRINCE KAUNITZ stood in the centre of the room when the Russian minister made his appearance. He raised his cold blue eyes with perfect indifference to the smiling face of the Russian, who bowed low, while his host vouchsafed him a slight inclination of the head. Prince Gallitzin seemed to be as unconscious of this haughty reception as of the fact that Kaunitz had not moved forward a single step to greet him. He traversed with unruffled courtesy the distance that separated him from Austria, and offered his hand with the grace of a finished courtier.

Kaunitz raised his languidly, and allowed it to rest for a moment in the palm of his cordial visitor.

"See, what a propitious incident," said Prince Gallitzin; "Austria and Russia have given each other the hand."

"Pardon me, your highness," replied Kaunitz gravely, "Russia has offered her hand, and Austria takes it."

"But without returning my cordial pressure," said the Russian.

Prince Kaunitz appeared not to hear this affectionate reproach. He pointed to the arm-chairs on either side of the *escritoire*, saying, "Let us be seated."

Prince Gallitzin waited until Kaunitz had taken his seat, which he did in a most deliberate manner, then he took the chair opposite.

"Your highness has been so good as to look over the new proposals for peace which Russia has offered to Turkey?" asked Prince Gallitzin.

"I have read them," replied Kaunitz, curtly.

"Your highness will then have remarked that, accommodating herself to the wishes of Austria, Russia has retained only such of her conditions as were necessary to the preservation of her dignity before the world. But my imperial mistress has instructed me to say explicitly that her moderation toward Turkey is exclusively the fruit of her consideration for Austria. But for this consideration, Turkey would have felt the full weight of the empress's vengeance; and it might have come to pass that this Porte, who already totters with his own weakness, would have been precipitated by Russia far into the depths of the Black Sea."

"In that case Russia would have learned that Austra is a diver that knows how to fish for pearls. We would have rescued the Porte from the Black Sea, and if he had not been strong enough to sustain himself, we would have exacted a tonic at your hands in the form of more advantageous conditions of peace."

"Then our conditions are not satisfactory?"

"They are of such a nature that Austria cannot entertain them for a moment. Turkey can never consent to the independence of the Crimea and Wallachia, nor will Austria counsel her to such an indiscreet concession. This would be so contrary to the interests of Austria that we would oppose it, even should Turkey be forced by untoward circumstances to yield the point."

"Ah!" cried Gallitzin, laughing, "Austria would find herself in the singular position of a nation warring with another to force that nation to take care of its own interests. Will your highness then tell me, what are the conditions which Austria is willing to accept for Turkey?"

"They are these: that the right of the Sultan to appoint the Khan of the Crimea and the Hospodar of Wallachia remain untouched. If Russia will recognize the sovereignty of the Porte in that quarter, then Austria will induce him to withdraw his pretensions in Tartary."

"And to leave to Russia the territory she has conquered there?" asked Gallitzin with his ineffable smile. "The czarina has no desire to enlarge her vast empire. Russia does not war in the Crimea for herself, but for a noble race of men who feel rich and powerful enough to elect their own rulers. Her struggle in Tartary is simply that of civilization and freedom against barbarism and tyranny."

"How beautiful all this sounds in the mouth of a Russian!" said Kaunitz, smiling. "You will acknowledge that Russia is not always consistent; for instance—in Poland, where she does not perceive the right of a noble race of men to elect their own rulers, but forces upon them a king whom they all despise. I must now declare to you that my sovereign will enter into negotiations with Turkey on one condition only: that the territorial rights of Poland be left untouched, not only by Russia, but by any other European power." *

Prince Gallitzin stared at Kaunitz as he heard these astounding words; but the Austrian met his gaze with perfect unconcern.

"Your highness defends the integrity of Polish territory," said Gallitzin, after a short pause, "and yet you have been the first to invade it. Is not the Zips a portion of the kingdom of Poland?"

"No, your highness, no. The Zips was originally a Hungarian dependency, and was mortgaged to Poland. We intend to resume our property and pay the mortgage in the usual way. This is not at all to the point. We speak of the fate of Poland. As for Austria, *she* aims at nothing but her rights; and as soon as the Empress of Russia withdraws her troops from Polish ground, we will withdraw ours, as well as all pretensions whatever to the smallest portion of Polish territory."

* V. Dohm, "Memoirs," vol. i., p. 492.

"And doubtless your highness intends to restore every thing for which the Poles are now contending. Her ancient constitution, for instance; that constitution which has been thrown upon the political system of Europe like the apple of Eris, threatening discord and conflict without end."

"No," said Kaunitz, quickly, "their constitution must be modified as the interests of their neighbors may require. We must unite on some modifications that are suitable to us, and if Poland refuse to accept them, she must be forced to do it."

"Ah!" cried Gallitzin, much relieved, "if your highness is of this mind we will soon understand one another; and I may, therefore, be permitted to speak with perfect frankness on the part of Russia."

"At last!" exclaimed Kaunitz, taking a long breath. "Russia will speak at last! So far she has only acted, and I confess that her actions have been inexplicable."

"Russia keeps pace with Austria," said Gallitzin. "The court of Vienna says that the integrity of Poland must be respected; nevertheless she is the first to lay her hand upon it."

"Some things we dare not do because they seem too difficult—others only seem to be difficult because we dare not do them. We have taken our slice of Poland because it belonged to us, and the difficulty of the step has not deterred us."

"Ah, your highness, as regards your right to the Zips, there is not a kingdom in Europe that has not some old forgotten right to her neighbor's territory! Russia and—Prussia, too, have similar claims on Poland, so that if it be agreeable to the empress-queen and to—your highness we will meet together to have an understanding on the subject. Some little time may be required to define our several claims, but this once settled, there will be no further difficulty in the way."

"I see," said Kaunitz, with a satisfied air, "that we already understand one another. As Russia has spoken and has made proposals, Austria is ready to respond. But before we attend to our own affairs, let us give peace to Turkey. The court of Vienna will negotiate between you. Let me advise you to be exorbitant in your demands; go somewhat beyond your real intentions, so that Austria may be obliged to decline your proposals."

"And in this way your highness proposes to bring about a peace with Turkey?" asked Prince Gallitzin, astounded.

"Certainly I do. Austria declines the proposals; Russia moderates her demands, that is, she concedes what she never intended to exact, and presents this as her ultimatum. Austria, satisfied with the concessions *now* offered to her ally, is of opinion that he should accept them; and if he prove unreasonable, must force him to do it."

"Your highness is indeed a great statesman!" exclaimed Gallitzin, with enthusiasm.

"When a Russian ambassador says so it must be true," replied Kaunitz, bowing. "As to Poland, the great question there is to preserve the balance of power. I beg, therefore, that Russia and Prussia will make known at once the extent of their claims there, that Austria may shape hers accordingly. I shall enter at once into correspondence with the King of Prussia, to ascertain his views as to the future boundaries of Poland. Two things are indispensable to insure the success of this affair."

"What are they?"

"First: perfect frankness between the three powers who are to act as one; and celerity of action, lest Poland should be quieted before we come in with *our* remedy."

"I agree with you. And second?"

"Second: profound secrecy. If France or England were to scent the affair, there would be troublesome intervention, and we might all be disappointed. Europe must not learn the partition of Poland until it is a *fait accompli.*"

"I promise discretion both for Russia and Prussia," said Gallitzin, eagerly. "Europe shall not hear of it until our troops are on the spot to defend us from outside interference. All that is necessary now is to find three equal portions, so that each claimant shall be satisfied."

"Oh," said Kaunitz carelessly, as he played with the lace that edged his cuffs, "if three equal parts are not to be found on Polish ground, we can trespass upon the property of another neighbor who has too much land; and if he resists, we can very soon bring him to reason."

Prince Gallitzin looked with visible astonishment at the cold and calm face of the Austrian. "Another neighbor?" echoed he, with embarrassment. "But we have no neighbor unless it be the Porte himself."

"Precisely the neighbor to whom I have reference," said Kaunitz, nodding his head. "He is almost as troublesome as Poland, and will be the better for a little blood-letting. I authorize your highness to lay these propositions before your court, and I await the answer."

"Oh!" cried Gallitzin, laughing, while he arose from his chair, "you will always find Russia ready for a surgical operation upon the body of her hereditary enemy. The law, both of nature and of necessity, impels her to prey upon Turkey, and the will of Peter the Great can never be carried out until the foot of Russia rests upon the Sultan's throne at Stamboul."

"Well," said Kaunitz, when Prince Gallitzin had taken his leave, "did you understand our conference, Binder?"

"Understand!" exclaimed Binder, coming from behind the screen. "No, indeed! I must have been drunk or dreaming. I surely did not hear your highness, who, not an hour since, concluded a treaty with Turkey by which the independence of Poland was to be guaranteed—I surely did not hear you agree to a partition between Russia, Prussia, and Austria!"

"Yes, you did. We are driven to accept our share of Poland merely by way of decreasing that of our neighbors."

"Then I *did* understand as regards Poland. But I must have been dreaming when I thought you had told me that we had concluded a treaty with the Porte by which he pays us ten millions of piasters for our good offices with Russia."

"Not at all. I certainly told you so."

"Then, dear prince, I have lost my senses," cried Binder, "for indeed I dreamed that you had proposed to Russia, in case there was not land enough to satisfy you all in Poland, to take some from the Sultan."

"You have heard aright. You are very tiresome with your questions and your stupid, wonder-stricken face. I suppose if a piece of Poland were thrown at your feet, you would pick it up and hand it over to Stanislaus; and if the Porte stood before you with a million of piasters, you would say, 'Not for the world!' It is easy to see what would become of Austria in your dainty hands! An enviable position she would hold, if conscience were to guide her policy!"

"No danger while *you* hold the reins, for there will never be a trace of conscience in your policy," muttered Binder, gathering up his papers and passing into the adjoining room.

Prince Kaunitz shrugged his shoulders and rang his bell.

"My new state-coach," said he to Hippolyte, who, instead of flying off as usual to obey, remained standing at the door.

"Why do you stand there?" asked the Prince.

"Pardon me, your highness, the state-coach is not ready," stammered the valet.

"Not yet ready?" repeated the prince, accenting each word. "Did I not order it to be here at two o'clock?"

"Yes, your highness, but the upholsterer could not understand the drawings which were given him. He began to work by them, but was obliged to undo his work, and this caused the delay."

"The man has the assurance to say that he could not work after the drawings made by my own hand?" asked Kaunitz, with a firey glance of anger in his eyes. "Because he is an ass, does the churl dare to criticise *my* drawings? Let him bring the body of the coach to the palace, and I will show him that he is a bungler and knows nothing of his trade."

And the prince, in his rage, stalked to the door. Suddenly he stopped. "What is the state of the thermometer to-day?" said he.

The valet flew to the window and examined the little thermometer that hung outside.

"Sixty degrees, your highness."

"Sixty degrees!" sighed the prince. "Then I dare not go to the coach-house. Is the coach mounted on the wheels?"

"No, your highness."

"Then let the upholsterer have the carriage brought to my room, with the drawings and his tools. Be off! In ten minutes all must be here!"

Just ten minutes later the door opened, and in came a handbarrow, upon which stood the body of the coach. It was one mass of bronze, plate-glass mirrors, and gilding. Behind it appeared the upholsterer, pale with fright, carrying on one arm a bundle of satin and velvet, and in his right hand holding the drawings of the prince.

"Set it down in the centre of the room," said Kaunitz, imperiously, and then turning a look of wrath upon the unhappy upholsterer, he said, with terrible emphasis: "Is it true that you have the audacity to say that you cannot work after my drawings?"

"I hope your highness will forgive me," stammered the upholsterer, "but there is not room in the inside of the coach for all the bows and rosettes. I would have been obliged to make them so small that the coach would have looked like one of the patterns we show to our customers."

"And you dare tell me that to my face? Do you suppose that I do not know your miserable trade, or do you mean that it is easier to govern an empire than to trim up a coach? I will prove to you that I am a better upholsterer than you are. Open the door, and I will decorate the coach myself."

The upholsterer opened the richly-gilded glass door, and Kaunitz, as much in earnest as when he had been giving and taking a kingdom, entered the coach and seated himself.

"Give me the satin and velvet, and hold up the drawings, that I may work after them. Some of you hand me the nails, and some one have the needle ready. You shall see how Prince Kaunitz, through the stupidity of his upholsterer, is obliged to decorate the interior of his own coach."

The prince began to work; and in the same room where he had signed treaties and received ambassadors, the great Austrian statesman sewed and hammered until he had decorated his carriage to his own satisfaction.

CHAPTER LXXVII.

THE LAST PETITION.

MARIA THERESA paced her cabinet in visible agitation. Her face was sad beyond expression, and her eyes turned anxiously toward the door.

"I tremble," murmured she; "for the first time in my life I mistrust the deed I am about to do. All is not clear in the depths of my conscience; the voice that whispers such misgivings to my heart, is one which shames the worldly wisdom of my councillors. We are about to do a wicked deed, and we shall answer for it before Heaven! Would that my right hand had lost its cunning, ere ever it had been forced to sign this cruel document! Oh, it is an unholy thing, this alliance with an unbelieving king and a dissolute empress! And an alliance for what? To destroy a kingdom, and to rob its unhappy people of their nationality forever!

"But what avails remorse?" continued she, heaving a deep sigh. "It is too late, too late! In a few moments Joseph will be here to exact my signature, and I dare not refuse it. I have yielded my right to protest against this crime, and—ah, he comes!" cried the empress, pressing her hands upon her heart, as she heard the lock of the door turning.

She fell into an arm-chair and trembled violently. But it was not the emperor who appeared as the door opened; it was the Baroness von Salmour, governess to the archduchesses.

"Baroness!" cried the empress, "it must be something of most imminent importance that brings you hither. What is it?"

"I come in the name of misfortune to ask of your majesty a favor," said the baroness, earnestly.

"Speak, then, and speak quickly."

"Will your majesty grant an audience to my unhappy countrywoman, the Countess Wielopolska?"

"The Countess Anna!" said the empress, with a shudder. Then, as if ashamed of her agitation, she added, quickly.

"Admit her. If the emperor comes, let him enter also."

The baroness courtesied and withdrew, but she left the door open; and now was seen advancing the tall and graceful figure of the countess. Her face was pale as that of the dead. She still wore her black velvet dress, and the long veil which fell around her person, hovered about her like a dark, storm-heralding cloud.

"She looks like the angel of death," murmured the empress. "It seems to me that if those pale, transparent hands, which she folds over her breast, were to unclasp, her icy breath would still the beatings of my heart forever!"

The countess glided in like a vision, and the door closed behind her. The empress received her with an affable smile.

"It is very long since I have seen you," said the proud Maria Theresa, with an embarrassment to which her rank had hitherto made her a stranger.

"I was waiting to be summoned by your majesty," replied the countess.

"And as I did not summon you, you came voluntarily. That was kind. I am very glad to see you."

The lady replied to these flattering words by an inclination of the head, and a pause ensued. Each one seemed waiting for the other to speak. As the empress perceived, after a while, that the lips of the pale countess did not move, she resolved to break the irksome silence herself. In her own frank way, scorning all circumlocution, she went at once to the subject nearest their hearts.

"I know why you are here to-day," said she, with a painful blush. "You have heard of the fate which threatens Poland, and you have come to ask if thus I fulfil the promises I made to you! Speak—is it not so? Have I not rightly read the meaning of that lovely but joyless face?"

"It is so," sighed the countess, and her voice trembled with unshed tears. "Yes, from the solitude wherein I had buried my grief since last I saw your majesty, I have heard the fatal tidings of my country's woe, and yet I live! Oh, why should the body survive, when the soul is dead?"

Her words died away upon her lips, and she seemed to grow paler and more pale, as though every drop of blood in her veins had stiffened and turned to ice. But she heaved a sigh and rallied, for hope now touched her heart, and the statue awoke to life.

"Ah, great empress," said she, with fervor, "I come to you, in whose powerful hand lies the issue of my country's fate, whose mighty word can bid us live, or doom us to death."

"Oh, were it so, you would not sue in vain!" cried the empress, sorrowfully. "Had the fate of Poland lain in *my* hands, she would have risen triumphant from the arena, where she has battled so bravely for her sacred rights!"

"Poland's fate lies in your majesty's hand!" exclaimed the countess, vehemently. "You have not yet signed the warrant for my country's execution; you are still innocent of her blood; your hand is still free from participation in the crime of her enemies and yours! Oh, let me kiss that hand, and bless it, while yet it is spotless and pure as your noble heart."

Hurried away by the might of the sorrow that overwhelmed her, the countess darted forward, and throwing herself at the feet of the empress, drew her hand fervently to her lips.

"Rise, dear countess Anna, rise," said the empress, soothingly. "I cannot bear to see you at my feet, when I can do nothing to avert the fate of Poland."

"Who, then, can help her, if not your majesty?" cried the countess. "Oh, I did not come hither to reproach you; I came but to entreat you to speak the word that will disenthrall my country!"

"I cannot do it; as God hears me, I cannot," repeated Maria Theresa, in a voice of anguish. "I have striven against it with all my might. What I have suffered for your countrymen, no one will ever know! The anxious days and wretched nights that I have spent for their sakes, have threatened my life." *

"I CANNOT!" echoed the countess, who seemed to have heard nothing but these few words. "An empress!—an empress! who, with a wave of her hand, sways millions of men, and is responsible for her actions to no earthly power!"

"Save that which resides in the claims of her subjects upon the sovereign, who is bound to reign for their good. I am responsible to my people for the preservation of peace. Too much blood has been shed since I came to the throne; and nothing would induce me to be the cause that the soil of Austria should be crimsoned by another drop." †

"And to spare a drop of Austrian blood, your majesty will deal the blow that murders a whole nation!" cried the countess, rising to her feet and looking defiance at the empress. "In your egotism for Austria, you turn from a noble nation who have as good a right to freedom as your own people!"

"Countess, you forget yourself. By what right do you reprove me?"

"By the right which misfortune gives to truth," replied she, proudly, "and by the right which your imperial word has given me to speak. For now I recall to you that promise, and I ask where is the eagle that was to swoop down upon the vultures which are preying upon Poland?"

"Oh, they have caged the eagle," said the empress, sadly. "God in heaven knows how manfully I have battled for Poland. When I threatened interference, the answer was this: 'We have resolved to dismember Poland, and you shall not prevent us.' What, then, could I do? Declare war? That were to ruin my people. Remain passive, while my enemies enlarged their frontiers, so as to endanger my own? We then had recourse to stratagem. We defended our soil inch by inch, and gave up when resistance became fanaticism. We required for our share more than we desired, hoping to be refused. But no! To my sorrow and disappointment, even more was apportioned than we had claimed. Oh! the whole thing has been so repugnant to my sense of justice, that I refused to take any share in its arrangements, and all the negotiations have been conducted by the emperor, Prince Kaunitz, and Marshal Lacy." ‡

"And these are the ashes of the mighty promises of emperors and empresses!" exclaimed the countess, bitterly. "Oh, empress, think of the time when you shall appear before God, to give account of your deeds! How will you answer, when the record of this day is brought before you? For the last time I am at your feet. Oh, as you hope for mercy above, do not sign the act that dismembers Poland!"

She was again on her knees, her beautiful eyes drowned in tears, and her hands clasped convulsively above her head.

"Oh, my God!" exclaimed the empress, rising to her feet, "she

* The empress's own words. See Raumer, "Contributions to Modern History," vol. iv., p. 539.

† The empress's own words. See Wolf, "Austria under Maria Theresa," p. 527.

‡ This discourse is historical. See Wolf, p. 525. Raumer, vol. iv., p. 540.

does not believe me." Then bending tenderly over the countess, she pressed her hands between her own, and gently raised her to a seat.

"Do you not see how deeply I suffer, when I have no spirit to chide your hard words to me? It is because I comprehend your sorrow, poor child, that I forgive your injustice. And now, to prove my sincerity," added she, going to her *escritoire* and taking from it a letter, "read this! I was about to send it to Prince Kaunitz, when your visit caused me to forget it. Read it aloud, that I may know whether you understand me at last."

The countess unfolded the letter and read:

"When my own empire was threatened, and I knew not where to lay my head; when the sorrows of childbirth were overtaking me, I threw myself upon God and my just rights. But to-day, when humanity, justice, ay—reason itself, cry aloud against our acts, I confess to you that my anxiety transcends all that I have ever suffered in my life before. Tell me, Prince Kaunitz, have you thought of the evil example we are giving to the nations of earth, when, for the sake of a few acres of additional territory, we cast away our reputation, our dignity, and our honor?

"If I yield to-day, it is because I struggle alone, and no longer have the vigor of mind to contend for right, as in years gone by I would have done. I am overpowered, but I surrender with a bleeding heart." *

The countess remained looking at the paper for a time, then she raised her tearful eyes to the face of the empress. "I thank your majesty," said she, deeply moved, "for allowing me to see this letter. It will remain in history as a noble monument of Maria Theresa's rectitude. I have no longer a word of blame for you; and once again, in love and reverence, I kiss this hand, although I know that to-day it must sign the death-warrant of unhappy Poland."

She drew near, and raised the hand of the empress to her lips. But Maria Theresa threw her arms around the countess, exclaiming: "To my heart, dear, unhappy one! I cannot save Poland, but I can weep with her loveliest and noblest daughter!"

The countess, overcome by this unexpected tenderness, leaned upon the bosom of the empress, and wept. Maria Theresa stroked her lustrous black hair, and, as she kissed her marble cheek, the tears that had gathered in her eyes, fell upon the head of the countess, where they glittered like stars upon the darkness of the night.

CHAPTER LXXVIII.

FINIS POLONIÆ.

NEITHER saw the door open; but both heard a soft, melodious voice, saying: "Pardon me, your majesty, I thought you were alone."

The countess uttered a low cry, and trembled from head to foot.

"Do not fear," said the empress, as she gently withdrew her arms, "it is my son the emperor. We need not hide our tears from him, for he knows that this is not the first time his mother has wept for Poland."

* This letter was written by Maria Theresa's own hand. See Hormayer, "Pocket History of Our Native Land," 1831, p. 66.

The emperor said nothing; he stood staring at the pale and trembling Anna. He, too, grew deathly pale as he looked, and now his trembling limbs answered to the agitation that was overpowering her. Suddenly, as though awaking from a painful dream, he approached, and offering his hand, said:

"I rejoice to see you. I have long sought you in vain."

She did not appear to see him. Her arm hung listlessly at her side, while her figure swayed to and fro like a storm-tossed lily.

"I have not been in Vienna," answered she, in a voice scarcely audible. "I had gone to bury my sorrow in solitude."

"But her love for Poland brought her hither," said the empress, putting her arm affectionately around the countess's waist.

"I believe you," returned Joseph, bitterly. "The fate of Poland is the only thing worthy of touching the Countess Wielopolska. She is not a woman, she is a Pole—nothing more."

One low wail struggled from the depths of her breaking heart, but she spoke not a word.

The emperor went on: "The Countess Wielopolska is not a woman. She is a monad, representing patriotism; and he who cannot think as she does, is a criminal unworthy of her regard."

"You are cruel, my son," said the empress, deprecatingly. "If the countess has been bitter in her reproaches to you, we must remember her grief and her right to reproach us. We should be gentle with misfortune—above all, when we can bring no relief."

"Let him go on, your majesty," murmured the wretched Anna, while her eyes were raised with a look of supreme agony upon the stern face of the emperor.

"Your majesty is right. I am nothing but a Pole, and I will die with my fatherland. *Your* hands shall close our coffin-lids, for our fates will not cost you a tear. The dear, noble empress has wept for us both, and the remembrance of her sympathy and of your cruelty we will carry with us to the grave."

The emperor's eyes flashed angrily, and he was about to retort, but he controlled himself and approached the empress.

"Your majesty will pardon me if I interrupt your interesting conversation, but state affairs are peremptory, and supersede all other considerations. Your majesty has commanded my presence that I might sign the act of partition. The courier, who is to convey the news to Berlin and St. Petersburg, is ready to go. Allow me to ask if your majesty has signed?"

The countess, who understood perfectly that the emperor, in passing her by, to treat with his mother of this dreadful act of partition, wished to force her to retire, withdrew silently to the door.

But the empress, hurt that her son should have been so unfeeling, went forward, and led her back to her seat.

"No, countess, stay. The emperor says that you represent Poland. Then let him justify his acts to us both, and prove that what he has done is right. I have suffered such anguish of mind over the partition of Poland, that Joseph would lift a load from my heart, if he could show me that it is inevitable. My son, you have come for my signature. Before God, your mother, and Poland herself, justify our deed, and I will sign the act."

"Justify? There are many things which we may defend without being able to justify them; and stern necessity often forces us to the use of measures which conscience disapproves."

"Prove to me, then, the necessity which has forced us to dismember a country whose people have never injured us," said the empress, authoritatively.

"But whose disunion at home has become dangerous to their neighbors. Poland lies like a sick man in our midst, whose dying breath infects the land. When there is a fire in our neighborhood, we are sometimes obliged to tear down the burning house lest the fire spread to our own."

"Yes," interrupted the countess, "but you do not rob the neighbor of his land. The soil belongs to him who owns the house."

"But the Poles are not worthy to own their soil. What is Poland to-day? A race of slaves and peasants, without law or order, driven hither and thither by a lewd and corrupt aristocracy, who, instead of blushing for the degeneracy of their caste, hold their saturnalia over the very graves of their noble ancestors. And at the head of this degenerate people is their king, the minion of a foreign court, who promulgates the laws which he receives from his imperial Russian mistress. Verily, God has weighed the Polish nation in His balance, and they have been found wanting."

"Enough!" faltered the countess, raising her hand in deprecation. "Why will you vilify a people who are in the throes of death?"

"No, it is not enough," said the emperor, sternly. "The empress says that I must justify the acts of the three powers to Poland—that pale and beautiful statue before me which lives—and yet is not a woman. I say it again: a nation dies by its own corruption! Poland bears within herself the seeds of her destruction. Her people have been false to their antecedents, false to themselves, to their honor, and even to their faith." *

"You accuse, but you bring no proofs!" exclaimed the countess, her eyes now flashing with wounded pride.

"It will not be difficult to collect my proofs," said the emperor, sneering. "Look at what takes place in Poland, since your countrymen have foreseen the fate of their fatherland. What are the Polish diet doing since they anticipate the close of their sittings? Voting themselves pensions, property, and every conceivable revenue, at the expense of the republic, and giving her, with their own parricidal hands, the *coup de grace.* Such shameless corruption has never come to light in the history of any other nation. Freedom and fatherland are in every mouth, but, in reality, no people care less for either than do the Poles. Slaves, who, while they hold out their hands to be manacled, are striving to reign over other slaves! † This is a picture of the Poland whom you love, and through her own crimes she is dying."

"It is not true!" cried the indignant countess. "She dies through the covetousness and greed of her neighbors. It is they who have sown dissension in Poland, while forcing upon her unhappy people a king who is nothing but the despicable tool of their despicable intrigues."

"All this has no reference to Austria," objected the emperor. "We had nothing to do with the selection of the king—nothing to do with the projects of dismemberment. They were resolved upon, with or without our sanction, and the law of self-preservation de-

* Wolf. "Austria under Maria Theresa," p. 535.
† Raumer, "Contributions," vol. iv., p. 551.

mands that if we cannot prevent, we must endeavor to profit by them. I know that the partition of Poland has an appearance of gross outrage which is obvious to every eye; while the stringent necessity which has driven Austria to participate in it is known to few. I confess that I would be grieved if the world should misjudge me on this question; for I try, both in public and private life, to be an honest man; and I believe that honesty in statesmanship is the wisest and soundest policy.* We could not do otherwise than we have done, and now, with the full conviction of the exigency which has called for the act, I repeat my question to your majesty, have you signed the act, or will you be so kind as to sign it now?"

The empress had listened with profound attention to her son's discourse, and her countenance, which before had been pale with anxiety, had assumed an expression of blended serenity and resolution. A pause ensued. Marble-white and speechless the countess, with half-open mouth, started and bent forward, her eyes fixed upon the empress; the emperor, stern and proud, threw back his head and gazed defiantly.

In the midst of this throbbing silence, Maria Theresa went forward and took her seat at the *escritoire*. She dipped her pen in the silver inkstand, and a sob, that sounded like the last death-sigh, escaped from the lips of the countess. The empress turned quickly around; but the glance of her eye was resolute and her hand was firm.

She bent over the parchment and wrote; then, throwing her pen on the floor, she turned to the emperor and pointed with her right hand to the deed. "*Placet*," cried she, with her clear, ringing voice—"*placet*, since so many great and wise men will have it so. When I am dead, the world will learn what came of this violation of all that man holds sacred." †

And either that she might conceal her own emotion, or avoid an outburst of grief from the countess, the empress walked hastily through the room, and shut herself up in her dressing-room.

The countess moaned, and murmuring, "*Finis Poloniæ!*" she, too, attempted to cross the room.

The emperor watched her, his eyes beaming with tenderness, his heart a prey to violent anguish. As she reached the door, he saw her reel and cling to a column for support.

With one bound he reached her, and flinging his arms around her swaying figure, she fell, almost unconscious, upon his bosom. For one bewildering moment she lay there.

"*Finis Poloniæ!*" murmured she again, and, drawing herself up to her full height, she again approached the door.

"Farewell!" said she, softly.

The emperor seized her hand. "Anna," said he, imploringly, "Anna, do we part thus? Is this our last interview? Shall we never meet again?"

She turned, and all the love that she had struggled to conquer was in her eyes as they met his. "We shall meet once more," replied she.

"When?" cried Joseph, frantic with grief.

"When the hour has come for us to meet again, I will send for you. Promise to be there to receive my last farewell."

* The emperor's own words. See Raumer, "Contributions," &c., vol. iv., p. 539.
† The empress's own words.

"I swear to be there."

"Then, farewell."

"Farewell, beloved Anna! Oh, let me touch your hand once more!"

"No!" said she, harshly; and, opening the door, she disappeared, and the emperor was left alone.

CHAPTER LXXIX.

THE MAD COUNTESS.

COUNT STARHEMBERG paced his splendid drawing-room in a state of great excitement. Sometimes he murmured broken sentences, then he sighed heavily, and again he seemed to be a prey to fear. Occasionally, his eyes glanced almost reproachfully toward the figure of a young man, who, with folded arms and smiling countenance, stood in the embrasure of a window watching the old man's agitation.

As the clock on the marble mantel struck the hour, the count stopped before his young visitor, and looked searchingly at his mild and effeminate face.

"The half hour has elapsed, Count Esterhazy," said he, solemnly. "I have told you frankly that my niece, although a beautiful and perchance a good-hearted woman, has a temper which is the terror of my household. She inherits this misfortune from her deceased father, and, unhappily, her lovely and amiable mother did not long survive him. There has been no one, therefore, to control her; and her terrible temper has never been restrained. Do not say to me that *I* might have conquered it! I have dedicated my whole life to her; and lest she should make another being unhappy, I have remained a bachelor, as you perceive. But I had made a solemn promise to her parents that I would be a father to her, and I have kept my promise. It is not my fault if their child is less amiable than other women. She has an energetic character, and I fear that if she marries, she will find means to tyrannize over her husband. I repeat this to you, count, that we may clearly understand each other; and now that the half hour has gone by, do you still urge your suit?"

"Yes, count, I do," replied Esterhazy in a soft, treble voice. "I repeat to you the offer of my hand to the Countess Margaret Starhemberg."

The count bowed. "I have done my duty, and, being cleared of all responsibility in the affair, I give my consent. You must now try to win hers."

"I would like to see the countess in your presence," said Esterhazy, unmoved.

Count Starhemberg rang the bell, and ordered a servant to bear a request to his niece to join him in the drawing-room.

"The countess would have the honor of joining her uncle immediately," was the answer.

"This promises well," said the old count, looking relieved. "She generally practises her music at this hour; and I am surprised that—"

Just then the sharp tones of an angry female voice were heard without, then the jingling of glasses, then a crash, and the fall of some heavy metallic body.

"That is my niece," said the old man with a shiver. "With that *fanfare* she usually announces her coming."

Now the door was flung violently open, and a tall, magnificent woman dashed into the room. Her features, marvellously chiselled as those of the antique Venus, would have been irresistible in beauty, if their expression had corresponded to their symmetry. But in her large black eyes glared the fire of ungoverned passion, and her rosy mouth was curled with contempt.

Her tall figure was of exquisite proportions; and her arms, adorned but not hidden by the lace which fell from the short sleeves of her crimson velvet dress, were as fair and beautiful as those of the Venus of Milo.

Count Esterhazy, intoxicated by the sight of her wondrous beauty, withdrew abashed behind the window-curtain, while the countess, graceful as an angry leopardess, bounded through the room, and stood before her uncle.

"Who has annoyed you, my child?" asked he timidly.

"He is an idiot, an awkward animal, and shall be driven from the house with the lash!" cried she. "Just imagine, uncle, that as I was coming hither, I met him in the anteroom with a plateau of cups and glasses. When he saw me, the fool fell to trembling as if he had seen an evil spirit—the plateau shook; and my dear mother's last gift, the goblet from which she had cooled her dying lips, fell to the floor and was broken."

Her voice, at first so loud and angry, was now soft and pathetic, and her eyes glistened with tears. She shook them off impatiently.

"I can well understand, dear child, how much it must have grieved you to lose this precious relic," said her uncle, soothingly.

She blushed as though she had been surprised in a fault.

"Oh, it was not that," said she, pettishly, "it is all the same to me whether the goblet was a relic or not, for I hate sentiment. But I detest such an awkward fool. He never *could* carry any thing without letting it fall."

"Nay, my child, he has often carried you for hours in his arms, and yet he never let you fall."

"Uncle, your jests are insupportable," cried she, stamping with her little satin-slippered foot upon the carpet. "You excuse this gray-headed dunce merely to vex me, and to remind me that I am an orphan without a home."

"But my dear—"

"Peace! I will not be interrupted. If I am tyrannized over in every other way, I will at least claim the right to speak—I wish to say that this old plague shall not remain here another day to torment my life with his nonsense. This time, however, I made him feel the weight of my hand. His face was as red as my dress after it."

"You struck my faithful old Isidor?" cried the count, shocked.

"Yes, I did," replied she, looking defiantly into her uncle's mild face. "I beat him well, and then I threw the whole waiter of cups and glasses upon the floor. Have you any fault to find with that, my sympathizing uncle?"

"None, none," said the old man. "If it gave you pleasure to break the glasses, we will go out and buy others."

"We! No, indeed, we shall not. Isidor shall pay for them from his wages. It was his fault that I was obliged to break them, and no one shall suffer for it except himself. I claim that as an act of bare justice to myself."

"But, my dear countess—"

She stamped her foot again. "Great God! have you no object in life except that of contradicting and ill-treating me?"

The count sighed and approached the door. She heard him, and an exulting smile lit up her beautiful, stormy face.

"Well, as you will not tell him, I shall do it myself. Yes—I shall do it myself. Do you hear, uncle? You shall not say a word to him."

"I will say nothing, Margaret. Will you now allow me to speak of other things? Is your vehemence—"

"UNCLE!"

"In your just displeasure, you have overlooked the fact that we are not alone."

He pointed to the window where, half hidden by the heavy silk drapery, stood Count Frank Esterhazy. The countess followed her uncle's glance, and as she became aware of the visitor's presence, burst into a merry laugh.

"Do not be frightened, young man," said she then; "you may come out from your corner. I am not a cat, and I don't devour mice. Ah, you have heard our discussion? What a pity you are not a dramatic poet, you have had such an opportunity for depicting a foolish old guardian and his spirited ward!"

"Unfortunately, I am not a poet," said the young count, coming forward and bowing to the floor. "If I were, I could write to-day a hundred sonnets to the eyes of the majestic Hera whose anger heightens her wonderful beauty."

"Uncle," said the countess, suddenly assuming a stately and court-like demeanor, "be so good as to present me this young stranger, who pays such insipid compliments."

"My dear niece, let me introduce Count Frank Esterhazy, a nobleman just returned from Italy, who is in high favor with the empress."

"The latter is no recommendation, uncle, for am I not also a favorite with the empress? Have you not often told me so, when the empress was humbling me with some of her tyrannical condescension?"

"Certainly, my child, I have said so."

"Then you see that it is not necessary to be estimable for one to gain the empress's good-will. For my part, I wish she loved me less, for then she would spare me some of the long sermons with which she edifies me, when I happen to appear at court."

"That, probably, is the reason you appear so seldom," said Count Esterhazy. "I have heard your absence complained of."

"By her majesty?" asked Count Starhemberg.

"No, your excellency, by the emperor."

"What did he say?"

"Dare I repeat his words?" asked Esterhazy, appealing to the countess. She bowed her head, and leaned against the back of an arm-chair.

"I was yesterday at the empress's reception. The emperor was so kind as to do the honors of the court to me. He pointed out the several beauties of Vienna, who were all strangers to me—'But,' said he, 'the most beautiful woman in Austria I cannot show you, for she is not here. The Countess Margaret von Starhemberg has the beauty of Juno and Venus united.'"

The countess said nothing; she stood with downcast eyes. Her cheek had paled, and her lips were firmly compressed together. Suddenly she rallied and said, with a careless laugh:

"I wager that the empress and her ladies made some amiable commentary on the emperor's words. Come, tell me, what said the empress?"

"If you command me, countess, I will tell you. The empress added, with a sigh, 'It is true, she is as beautiful as a goddess, but it is Eris whom she resembles.'"

"Very witty!" exclaimed the countess, with a sneer.

"And the emperor?" inquired the uncle.

"The emperor frowned at the ladies, who began to laugh. 'Your majesty may be right,' said he, 'but Grecian mythology has forgotten to say whether the fierce goddess was ever vanquished by love. Love tames the most turbulent of women.'"

The countess uttered a sharp cry, and caught with both her hands at the back of the arm-chair. Her eyes closed, and a deadly paleness overspread her countenance. Her uncle hastened to put his arm around her, inquiring tenderly, "Dearest child, what ails you?"

She leaned for a while upon his shoulder; then raising her head while deep blushes crimsoned her cheeks, she said, haughtily: "It is nothing. A sudden faintness to which I am subject." With an inclination of the head to Count Esterhazy, she continued:

"You will be so good as not to mention this weakness of mine. It is purely physical, and I hope to conquer it in time. I am rejoiced to think that I have verified the words of the empress and have appeared before you to-day as an Eris. I suppose you came hither to see me out of curiosity."

"No, Countess Margaret, the purport of my visit was any thing but curiosity. I come, with the sanction of your guardian, to offer you my hand."

The black eyes of the countess darted fire at the smiling suitor.

"You do not answer me," said he blandly. "I say that I have won the consent of your uncle, and respectfully solicit yours. It shall be the study of my life to make you happy, and, perhaps, at some future day, my untiring devotion may win a return of my love. Speak, then, countess; say that you will be my wife."

"Never, never!" cried she, stretching forth her arms as though to ward away some threatening evil. "I shall never be the wife of any man. I was not made for marriage, I cannot bow my will before that of any other fellow-mortal."

"I shall not require you to do so," replied the count, as though he had now removed every objection. "You will be in my house as you are here, absolute mistress of all things, and I shall claim nothing but the right of being your humblest and most devoted servant."

"Unhappily for you, you know not what you claim," exclaimed the countess angrily. "Ask my uncle, ask his household, and they will tell you that I am a tyrant, changing my will twenty times an hour; hating to-day the thing I shall love to-morrow. You would aspire to be my husband, would you? Have you no friends to warn you of the reefs upon which you are running that poor little crazy bark of yours? Why the very people, as they see me pass, tell of my frantic doings; and every child in Vienna knows that I beat my servants, rage about my uncle's house like the foul fiend, and dash through the streets on horseback like the Wild Huntsman."

"'Love tames the wildest hearts,' so says the emperor."

Margaret started, and darted a fiery glance at his tranquil face.

"But I do not love you, I tell you; and it is useless to say another word on the subject."

"Nay," said the couut, taking her hand, "it is not useless. I beseech you, do not deny my suit."

At this moment the door opened, and a servant came in with a golden tray, on which lay a letter.

"From her majesty the empress," said the servant, handing it to Count Starhemberg. The count took the letter and went into the embrasure of the window, while the servant retired noiselessly.

"Countess Margaret," said Count Esterhazy, in an imploring voice, "once more I entreat you to accept me as your husband."

She looked at him with withering contempt. "Have I not told you," cried she, passionately, "that I do not love you? A man of honor ceases to importune a woman after such an avowal."

"A man of spirit never gives up; he perseveres, in the hope that, sooner or later, he will reach his goal. No man has the right to expect that he will obtain a treasure without trouble."

"Cant! miserable cant!" And the great glowing eyes that were looking with such scorn at the slight figure of the count, encountered their own image in the glass before which they both were standing.

"Look!" cried she, pointing to the mirror, "yonder reflection gives its answer to your suit. Do you see that tall woman, whose head towers above the blond mannikin that stands beside her? Look at her black hair, her fiery eyes, and resolute bearing! And now look at the little fair-haired puppet, that resembles a man about as much as do the statuettes on my toilet-table. Ah, sir count, if you were the woman and I the man there might be marriage between us! But as it is, you would die of my violence, or I of your insipidity. So, excuse me."

She made a deep courtesy and turned to leave the room. But she felt a touch upon her shoulder, and looking back, she saw her uncle gazing at her with a face of great anxiety.

"My child," said he, in a faltering voice, "do not send Count Esterhazy so rudely away. He is rich, noble, and distinguished, and in every way worthy of my lovely niece. Do not refuse him, Margaret."

"The count has recovered from his stupid delusion, uncle; I have told him how impossible it is for me to accept his hand."

"But, my poor child, you must try to love him. You dare not reject his offer."

"What! *I* dare not reject whom I please!" cried she, in a voice shrill with passion.

"No, you dare not. The empress commands you to accept the hand of Count Esterhazy. Here is the note I have at this moment received from her majesty."

Margaret tore the paper savagely from her uncle's hand. With staring eyes she read its contents, while her whole body trembled violently, and her lips were bloody with the efforts she was making to suppress a scream.

At last she gave it back. "Read it," said she, hoarsely; "the letters swim before my eyes."

The count took the note and read:

"DEAR COUNT STARHEMBERG: It is my desire that your niece, the Countess Margaret, shall become the wife of some honorable man. In this way she may hope to conquer her ungovernable temper, and become a reasonable woman. I have heard that Count Esterhazy intends to become her suitor, and I command her to accept his hand. She has led a life of wild independence, and it is time she were tamed by the cares, duties, and responsibilities of matrimony. I am both her empress and godmother, and I use my double right for her good. The marriage shall take place in one week, or she goes into a convent. That is my ultimatum.

"I remain yours with sentiments of esteem,

"MARIA THERESA."

CHAPTER LXXX.

THE BETROTHAL.

A LONG pause ensued after the reading of the letter. The countess stood with her eyes riveted upon her uncle's face, as though she were waiting for something more. The young count watched her furtively, but he looked determined.

"You see, my child," at last sighed the old count, "it is inevitable. The empress must be obeyed."

"No, no!" screamed the wretched girl, awaking from her stupor, "I will not be the wife of that man."

"Then you will have to go into a convent."

"No!" cried she, her face suddenly lighting up with a flash of hope—"no, I will do neither. There is a means of rescuing me from both."

She turned with a bewitching smile to Count Esterhazy, and in a voice whose softness was music to his ear, she addressed him:

"In your hands lies the power to rescue me from a forced bridal. You have heard that despotic note from the empress. Matchmaking is a monomania with Maria Theresa: it is useless, therefore, for me to appeal to her, for on a question of marriage she is inexorable. But you, Count Esterhazy," continued she, in tones of caressing melody, "you will rescue me, will you not? I cannot be your wife, for I do not love you; I cannot go into a convent, for I have no piety. Go, then, to the empress, and tell her that you do not wish to marry me. You, at least, are free. Refuse to accept me for your wife, and this miserable comedy is at an end."

She had clasped her little white hands, and was looking imploringly in his face.

The young man shook his head. "I cannot say this to the empress," said he, quietly, "for it is she who sent me hither to woo you."

"The empress sent you hither!" cried the countess, springing forward like a lioness. "You came not as a free suitor, but as an obedient slave of the empress."

"I came at the command of the empress," said the young man, mildly.

The countess burst into a loud laugh.

"That, then, was the glowing love which you were describing just now; that your tender wish to live for my happiness alone. Obedient school-boy! You were told to come and ask for my hand, and you came—for fear of being whipped Oh! why am I not a man? By the heaven above! no woman should inflict upon me such contumely!"

"It is true," said Count Esterhazy, taking no note of her words, "that the empress ordered me hither. But since I have seen you, I need no prompting save that of my own heart."

"Peace, fool! nobody believes you. You had consented to woo me, in obedience to your despotic sovereign. But you have seen me; now you know with how much justice I am called 'The Mad Countess,' and now, surely, you have manhood enough to reject a termagant like me. Go, then, and tell the empress that I was willing, but you were not—"

"I would not thus belie you, lovely Margaret."

"What do I care whether you belie me or not, so that I am rid of you?" said she, contemptuously.

"Submit, my dear child," said the old count, with tears in his eyes. "'Tis the first time in your life that you have been thwarted, and therefore it is hard for you to succumb."

"I will not submit!" cried Margaret, flinging back her head. "I will not marry this man. Uncle, dear uncle, leave me one moment with him. I have something to say that he alone must hear."

The count withdrew at once into another room.

"Now, sir, that we are alone, I have a secret to reveal—to God and to yourself. Swear by the memory of your mother that you will not betray me."

"I swear."

She bowed her head, as though accepting the oath. "And now," said she, faltering and blushing, "I will tell you why I can never be your wife. I—" she hesitated, and her head sank upon her bosom, while she stifled a sigh. "I love another," whispered she, almost inarticulately. "Yes, I love another. I love him with every throb of my heart, with all the strength of my being. My every breath is a prayer for him. Every wish, hope, and longing of my soul points to him alone. I would die to give him one hour of joy. Now, that I have made this avowal, you retract your suit, do you not? You will go now to the empress and say that you will not accept me for your wife. You give me my freedom, surely—you give it to me now."

Count Esterhazy smiled compassionately. "This is a fable, countess, which you have invented to escape me. A few moments ago you said that you would never love."

"I said that to disincline you to marry me."

"I do not believe you," said Esterhazy, calmly. "You have invented this story of your love for that end; but it is a falsehood, for you are as cold as an icicle."

"Oh, I wish that I were. For this love is my greatest misfortune. Look at me, count. Does this seem like dissimulation?"

And she raised up to his view a face, scarlet with blushes, and eyes filled with burning tears.

"No, countess," said Esterhazy, after contemplating her earnestly, "I will believe the tears that glisten in your speaking eyes.

But now, answer me one question. Your confidence gives me the right to ask it. Is your love returned?"

She remained silent, as if communing with herself, while every trace of color vanished from her cheeks.

"No," said she, at last, with quivering lips. "No, he does not know it; and if he did, he could not offer me his hand."

"Then," replied Esterhazy, coolly, "your love is no impediment to our marriage. Cherish it, if you choose; raise altars to this unknown god, and deck them with the brightest flowers of devotion. I will not inquire the name of your deity. Your secret is safe, even from myself. I, on the contrary, have never loved. My heart stands with doors and windows open, ready to receive its mistress; and as the empress has selected you, it waits joyfully for you to take possession."

The countess laid her hand upon his arm, and grasped it like a vise.

"You will not recede!" said she, hoarsely. "You still persist in desiring me for your wife?"

"You have told me that your love is hopeless, therefore is mine hopeful. Perhaps one day it may succeed in winning yours."

"But you do not love me," shrieked the maddened girl. "You are here by command of the empress."

"And the Esterhazys have always been the loyal servants of the empress. Whenever she commands, they obey—were it at the cost of life and happiness. Allow me, then, to persevere in my obedience, not only to her desires, but to my own. I once more solicit the honor of your hand."

"Woe to you if, after this, I yield!" cried she, with threatening gesture. "I have stooped to entreat you, and my prayers have been vain. I have withdrawn the womanly veil that concealed my heart's cherished secret, and you have not renounced your unmanly suit. I said that I did not love you. Look at me, and hear me, while I vow eternal hatred, should I be forced to give you my hand."

"There is but one step from hate to love. Allow me to hope that you will think better of it, and take that step."

A fearful cry rang from her lips, her eyes glowed like burning coals, and she raised her clinched hand as though she had hoped it might fell him to the earth. But suddenly it sank helpless to her side, and she looked long and searchingly into Count Esterhazy's face.

A long silence ensued. "It is well," said she, at length, in clear, shrill tones. "You have challenged me to mortal combat, and it may be that you will win. But, oh, believe me when I tell you that victory will bring you no glory! Your strength is not your own; it lies in the imperial hand of Maria Theresa. I swear to you that if I become your wife, my whole life shall be consecrated to hatred and revenge. Count Esterhazy, I hold my word inviolate, whether I pledge it to friend or foe; and when the blight shall fall upon your head that will grow out of this hour we have spent together, remember that had you been a man of honor you might have spared yourself the shame!"

Without another word she lifted her proud head, and, with a look of withering scorn, left the room.

Count Esterhazy's eyes followed her retreating figure, and his placid brow grew troubled. "Beautiful as she is," murmured he, "it is dangerous to woo her. She has the beauty of Medusa. My heart positively seems to petrify under her glance. I would be more than willing to renounce the honor of wedding this beautiful demon, but I dare not refuse."

And he drew out his delicate, embroidered handkerchief to wipe off the big drops of sweat that stood upon his forehead.

"Well?" asked Count Starhemberg, opening the door and putting through his head.

"Pray come in," said Esterhazy, in a piteous tone

"Ah, my niece has left! Well, I suppose that, as usual, she has conquered, and you release her?"

"Not at all," replied the unhappy mannikin; "I still beg for the honor of her hand. The empress has spoken, and I have only to obey."

CHAPTER LXXXI.

FRANZ ANTONY MESMER.

For some weeks great excitement had existed in Vienna. In all assemblies, coffee-houses, and restaurants, in the streets and on the public places, the topic of conversation had been the wonderful cures of the Suabian physician, Mesmer. These cures contravened all past experience, and set at naught all reason. Mesmer made no use of decoction or electuary—he prescribed neither baths nor cataplasms; he cured his patients by the power of his hand and the glance of his large, dark eye. He breathed upon their foreheads, and forthwith they saw visions of far-off lands; he passed the tips of his fingers over their faces, and pain and suffering vanished at his touch. No wonder that physicians denounced him as a charlatan, and apothecaries reviled him as an impostor.

No wonder that the populace, so prone to believe the marvellous, had faith in Mesmer, and reverenced him as a saint. Why should he not perform miracles with his hand, as did Moses with a rod, when he struck the rock? Why should not the power of his eye master disease, as once the glance of the Apostles gave speech to the dumb, and awakened life in the dead?

Mesmer, too, was an apostle—the apostle of a new faith. He bade suffering humanity turn to heaven for relief. "The reflection from the planets," said he, "and the rays of the sun, exercise over the human system a magnetic power. The great remedy for disease lies in this magnetic power, which resides in iron and steel, and which has its highest and most mysterious development in man."

The people believed, and sought his healing hand. He mastered their infirmities, and soothed their sufferings. But the more the world honored and trusted him, the more bitter grew the hatred of the faculty. Each day brought him fresh blessings and fresh imprecations. The physicians, who, in Salzburg, had hurled Paracelsus from a rock, dared not attempt the life of Mesmer; but they persecuted him as an impostor, and proved, by learned and scientific deduction, that his system was a lying absurdity.

Those who affected strength of mind, and refused to believe any thing except that which could be demonstrated by process of reasoning, gave in their adherence to the indignant physicians. Those, on the contrary, who had faith in the mysteries of religion, were disciples of Mesmer; and they reverenced him as a prophet sent from heaven, to prove the supremacy of nature over knowledge.

Mesmer's fame had reached the court, and the empress herself became interested in his extraordinary achievements. In vain Van Swieten and Stork besought her to silence the audacious quack, who was ruining a great profession. She shook her head, and would have nothing to do with the feud.

"I shall wait and see," said she. "His system is harmless, and I shall not fetter him. One thing is certain. His manipulations will never poison anybody, as many a regular physician's prescription has done, and he shall not be molested. He has voluntarily sought an ordeal which will determine his position before the world. If he cures the blindness of my little *protégé*, Therese, I shall give in my adherence with the rest; for he who restores the blind to sight, holds his skill from above."

This young girl was known to all Vienna. In her second year, after an attack of suppressed measles, she had become blind, and all attempts to restore her sight had proved unavailing. But if sight had been denied to her eyes, her soul was lit up by the inspiration of art. When Therese sat before the harpsichord and her dexterous fingers wandered over its keys—when, with undisturbed serenity, she executed the most difficult music that could be written for the instrument, no one who saw her beautiful eyes could have surmised their inutility. Her features were expressive, and those sightless eyes seemed at times to brighten with joy, or to grow dim with sorrow. Nevertheless, Therese von Paradies was wholly blind; her eyes were merely the portals of her soul—they sent forth light, but received none in return.

CHAPTER LXXXII.

THERESE VON PARADIES.

THERESE VON PARADIES was in her room; her mother stood near, for, with the assistance of a maid, she had just completed her daughter's toilet. Therese was elegantly dressed, and she seemed to enjoy her splendor although she was not permitted to see it.

"Say, mother," said she, as the last touch had been given to her dress, "of what material is my gown? It feels as soft as a young girl's cheek."

"It is satin, my child."

"Satin? And the color?"

"White."

"White!" repeated she, softly. "The color without color. How strange that must be! I shudder when I think that I shall see it before long."

"Why should you shudder?" said her mother, tenderly. "You should rejoice, dear child, that the world, with all its beauties, is about to become known to you."

"I do not know," replied Therese, thoughtfully. "I shall enter upon a new world which will astonish and perchance affright me by its strangeness. Now I know you all in my heart, but when I see you I shall no longer recognize you. Oh, mother, why do you wish me to be restored to sight? I am very happy as I am."

"Silly child, you will be still happier when you see. It is absurd for you to dread an event which will add a hundredfold to your enjoyment of life."

"And why absurd, dear mother? Does not the heart of the bride, on her wedding-day, beat half in hope and half in fear? And is not her soul filled with sweet apprehension? I am a bride—the bride of light—and I await my lover to-day."

"Ah, who knows if light will come?" sighed the mother.

"It will come, mother," said Therese, confidently. "I felt it yesterday, when, for a moment, Mesmer removed the bandage from my eyes. It was for a second, but I *saw*, and what I saw cut like a sharp sword athwart my eyes, and I fell, almost unconscious."

"That was a ray of light—the first glance of your bridegroom!" cried the mother, joyfully.

"Then I fear that I shall never be able to bear his presence," replied Therese, sadly. "But tell me, mother, am I dressed as becomes a bride?"

"Yes, Therese, you are beautifully dressed; for to-day we receive a throng of distinguished guests. The empress herself has sent one of her lords in waiting, to bear her the tidings of your restoration to sight. The two great doctors, Van Swieten and Stork, will be here to see the marvel; and princes and princesses, lords and ladies, ministers and generals, will be around you."

"How is my hair dressed?"

"It is dressed as you like it, *à la Matignon*. Pepi has built a tower upon your head at least three quarters of an ell high, and above that is a blue rosette, with long ends."

"It is indeed very high," replied Therese, laughing, "for I cannot reach it with my hands. But I have another question to ask, dear mother. Promise me that it shall be frankly answered."

"I promise."

"Well, then, tell me, is my appearance pleasing? Hitherto every one has been kind to me because of my misfortune; but when I stand upon equal footing with other women, do you think that I am pretty enough to give pleasure to my friends?"

"Yes, my dear, you are very handsome," said the mother, smiling lovingly at her child's simplicity. "Your figure is graceful, your face is oval, your features are regular, and your brow is high and thoughtful. When the light of day shall be reflected from your large, dark eyes, you will be a beautiful woman, my daughter."

"Thank you, dear mother, these are pleasant tidings," said Therese, kissing her.

"I must leave you, dearest," said her mother, softly disengaging herself from Therese's arms. "I have my own toilet to make, and some preparations for our guests. I will send the maid."

"No, dear mother, send no one. I need silence and solitude. I, too, have preparations to make for the heavenly guest that visits me to-day. I must strengthen my soul by prayer."

She accompanied her mother to the door, kissed her again, and returning, seated herself at the harpsichord. And now from its keys came forth sounds of mirth and melancholy, of love and complaint, of prayers and tears. At one time she intoned a hymn of joy; then came stealing over the air a melody that brought tears to the eyes of the musician ; then it changed and swelled into a torrent of gushing harmony.

Suddenly she paused, a tremor ran through her frame, and a blush slowly mantled her cheek. Her hands fell, and her bosom heaved. As if drawn by some invisible power, she rose from her instrument and went toward the door. In the centre of the room she stopped and pressed her hands upon her heart.

"He comes," murmured she, with a smile of ecstasy, "he mounts the staircase, now he is in the corridor, his hand is upon the door."

Yes ; the door opened so softly that the acutest ear could not have detected a sound. But Therese felt it, and she would have gone forward, but her feet were paralyzed, and she remained with outstretched arms. With her heart she had seen him who now appeared upon the threshold. The person, whose coming had so agitated the young girl, was a man of scarcely forty years, of a lofty imposing carriage, and of prepossessing features. His large, blue eyes rested upon Therese with a glance of power, which thrilled through every fibre of her being. He held out his right arm toward her; then slowly lowering it, he pointed to the floor. Therese followed its motion and sank on her knees. A triumphant smile beamed over Mesmer's face, and he raised his hand again. The girl arose, and as though she had seen him open his arms, she darted forward and laid her head upon his breast.

"Mesmer, my friend, my physician," whispered she, softly.

"Yes, it is I," replied Mesmer, in a rich, melodious voice. "Your heart has seen me, your eyes shall see me too, my child."

He led her to a sofa and seated her gently beside him. Then passing his outstretched hand before her, she trembled.

"You are very much excited to-day, Therese," said he, with a slight tone of disapprobation.

"I am excited because you are so, dear friend," said the blind girl. "Your eyes dart beams that threaten to consume the world."

"A world of ignorance and of wickedness," said he, in reply. "Yes, Therese, I will consume it to-day, and in its stead shall arise a supernatural world; yet one to which banished Nature shall return and claim her rights to man. Oh, will I have strengh to say, 'Let there be light!'"

"Dear friend, if you doubt the result, do not expose yourself to the humiliation of failure. I am satisfied with my blindness, for I have a world of light in my heart."

"No!" cried Mesmer, with energy, "the work is begun, it must be completed. You *must* see, Therese, or all for which I have striven will recoil upon my head, and bury me beneath its ruins. This day decides not only your fate, poor child, but mine. To-day must Mesmer prove to the world that the animal magnetism, which physicans deride as a quackery, *savans* deny as impracticable, and the people ignorantly worship as sorcery, is a golden link which binds humanity to heaven. To-day you shall be healed by the magnetic power which binds you to me, and links us both to God."

"Heal me then, dear master!" cried the girl, inspired by his enthusiasm. "Restore me to sight, and, in so doing, give light to those who cannot see your Godlike gift."

He laid his hand upon her shoulder, and gazed earnestly in her face. "You have faith in me then, Therese, have you not?"

"I believe in you, and I comprehend you, master. I know that

I shall see; and when the scales fall from my eyes, the light of conviction will dawn for others. They will then comprehend that there is a power in Nature stronger than the craft of bare human wisdom."

"Oh, you speak my very thoughts, dear Therese," said Mesmer, tenderly. "You see into my mind, and its perceptions find birth upon your lips. Let doctors sneer, and learned skeptics disbelieve, but the day will come when all must acknowledge that magnetism is truth, and all human wisdom lies. Physicians, though, will be its deadliest enemies, for they are travellers, who, having strayed from the right path, go farther and farther from truth, because they will not retrace their steps." *

"But you will show them the path, my master, and the world will honor you above other men."

"If ingratitude do not blind it to truth. It is hard to find daylight in the labyrinth of established faith. I, too, have wandered in this labyrinth, but in all my divarications I sought for Truth. With passionate longing I called her to my help. Far removed from the hum of human imbecility, down among the solitudes of untrodden forests I sought her. Here I was face to face with Nature, and listened for response to the anxious questionings of my restless heart. It was well for me that the trees were the only witnesses of my agitation, for my fellow-men, had they met, would have chained me as a madman."

"Not I, master. I would have understood your noble strife."

Mesmer pressed her hand and went on: "Every occupation became distasteful to me, every moment dedicated to aught else seemed to be treason to truth. I regretted the time which it cost me to translate my thoughts into words, and I formed the singular resolution of keeping silence. For three months I reflected without speaking a word. At the end of this time a new faculty unfolded itself in my mind, and I began to see with rapture that the day of truth had dawned. I knew that henceforth my life would be one long struggle against preconceived error; but this did not affright me. So much the more did I feel the obligation resting upon me to impart to my fellow-beings the gifts I had received. I have suffered much from their prejudices; but most from the sneers of envious physicians, who, sooner than receive a light from other hands, would stumble in the night of their ignorance forever.† But my day of triumph is here. You, Therese, are the evangelist of my new faith, and your restored vision shall announce it to the world!"

"It shall, dear master, it shall; and against their will these infidels shall believe. They will see that we have all been blind together—all but you, who, questioning in faith, have received your answer from on high. Take the bandage from my eyes and let me see the light of day! I tremble no longer with apprehension of its splendor!"

Mesmer held her back as she raised her hands to her head. "Not yet, Therese. Your bandage must be removed in the presence of my enemies."

"Whom do you expect, master?"

"I have told you—I expect my enemies. Professor Barth will be

* Mesmer's own words. See "Franz Anton Mesmer, of Suabia," by Dr. Justinus Kerner, p. 58.

† This whole conversation is in Mesmer's words. See Justinus Kerner, p. 60.

there to sneer at the charlatan who, by an invisible power, has healed the malady which his couching knife would have sought in vain to remove. Doctor Ingenhaus, my bitter rival, will be there, to find out by what infernal magic the charlatan has cured hundreds of patients pronounced by him incurable. Father Hell will be there, to see if the presence of a great astronomer will not affright the charlatan. Oh, yes!—And others will be there—none seeking knowledge, but all hoping to see me discomfited."

"Do not call yourself so often by that unworthy name," said Therese sorrowfully.

"Men call me so; I may as well accept the title."

"Perhaps they have called you so in days gone by; but from this day they will call you 'Master,' and will crave your pardon for the obloquy they have heaped upon your noble head."

"How little you know of the world, Therese! It never pardons those who convict it of error; and above all other hatred is the hatred that mankind feel for their benefactors."

"Gracious Heaven, master, if this is the world which is to open to my view, in mercy leave me to my blindness!"

She stopped suddenly, and sank back upon the cushion of the sofa. Mesmer raised his hands and passed them before her forehead.

"You are too much excited. Sleep!"

"No, no, I do not wish to sleep," murmured she.

"I command you to sleep," repeated Mesmer.

Therese heaved a sigh; her head fell farther back, and her audible, regular breathing soon proved that sleep had come at the bidding of her master.

Mesmer bent over her, and began his manipulations. He approached her lips, and opening her mouth, breathed into it. She smiled a happy smile. He then raised his hands and touching the crown of her head described half-circles in the air; then stooping over her, he again inhaled her breath, and breathed his own into her mouth.

The door opened, and the mother of Therese came in.

"The guests are here," said she.

Mesmer inclined his head. "We are ready."

"Ready and Therese sleeps so soundly?"

"I will awake her when it is time. Where is my harmonicon?"

"In the parlor, where you ordered it to be placed."

"Let us go, then, and thence we will call Therese."

CHAPTER LXXXIII.

THE FIRST DAY OF LIGHT.

THE *élite* of Vienna were assembled in the drawing-room of Herr von Paradies. The aristocratic, the scientific, and the artistic world were represented; and the empress, as before intimated, had sent her messenger to take notes of the extraordinary experiment which was that day to be tried upon the person of her young pensioner. At the request of Mesmer, some of the lower classes were there also, for it was his desire that the cottage as well as the palace should bear testimony to the triumph of animal magnetism over the prejudices of conventional science.

By order of Mesmer, the room had been darkened, and heavy green curtains hung before every window. Seats were arranged around the room, in the centre of which was a space occupied by a couch, some chairs, and a table on which lay a box.

Upon this box the eyes of the spectators were riveted; and Professor Barth himself, in spite of his arrogant bearing, felt quite as much curiosity as his neighbors, to see its contents.

"You will see, Herr Kollege," said he to one who sat beside him, "you will see that he merely wishes to collect this brilliant assemblage in order to perform an operation in their presence, and so make a name for himself. This box of course contains the instruments. Wait and watch for the lancet that first or last is sure to make its appearance."

"What will be the use of his lancet," replied Herr Kollege, "when there is nothing upon which it can operate? The girl is irretrievably blind; for neither knife nor lancet can restore life to the deadened optical nerve."

"If he attempts to use the lancet in *my* presence," said the professor in a threatening tone, "I will prevent him. I shall watch him closely, and woe to the impostor if I surprise him at a trick!"

"The box does not contain surgical instruments," whispered the astronomer Hell. "I know what he has in there."

"What?" asked the others eagerly.

"A planet, my friends. You know he is given to meddling with planets. I hope it is one unknown to science; for if he has carried off any of *my* stars, I shall have him arrested for robbery."

This sally caused much laughter, which was interrupted by the entrance of Mesmer with Frau von Paradies. Without seeming to observe the spectators who now thronged the room, Mesmer advanced to the table where lay the box. His face was pale, but perfectly resolute; and as his eyes were raised to meet those of the guests, each one felt that whatever might be the result, in the soul of the operator there was neither doubt nor fear.

Mesmer opened the box. A breathless silence greeted this act. Every whisper was hushed, every straining glance was fixed upon that mysterious coffer. He seated himself before it, and Professor Barth whispered, "Now he is about to take out his instruments."

But he was interrupted by the sound of music—music so exquisite that the heart of the learned professor himself responded to its pathos. It swelled and swelled until it penetrated the room and filled all space with its thrilling notes. All present felt its power, and every eye was fixed upon the enchanter, who was swaying a multitude as though their emotions had been his slaves, and his music the voice that bade them live or die.

"Ah!" whispered the astronomer, "you made a mistake of a part of speech. The man has not instruments, but *an* instrument."

"True," replied the professor, "and your planet turns out to be an insignificant harmonicon."

"And the lancet," added Ingenhaus, "is a cork, with a whalebone handle."

Mesmer played on, and now his music seemed an entreaty to some invisible spirit to appear and reveal itself to mortal eyes. At least, so it sounded to the ears of his listeners. They started—for responsive to the call, a tall white figure, whose feet seemed scarcely to touch the floor, glided in and stood for a moment irresolute. Mesmer raised his hand and stretching it out toward her, she moved. Still he played on, and nearer and nearer she came, while the music grew louder and more irresistible in its pleadings.

A movement was perceptible among the spectators. Several ladies had fainted; their nerves had given way before the might of that wonderful music.* But no one felt disposed to move to assist them, for all were absorbed by the spell, and each one gazed in speechless expectation upon Mesmer and Therese.

He still played on, but he threw up his head, and his large eyes were directed toward his patient with a look of authority. She felt the glance and trembled. Then she hastened her steps, and smilingly advanced until she stood close beside the table. He pointed to the couch, and she immediately turned toward it and sat down.

"This is well gotten up," said Professor Barth. "The scene must have been rehearsed more than once."

"If the blind are to be restored to sight by harmonicons," whispered Doctor Ingenhaus, "I shall throw my books to the winds, and become an itinerant musician."

"If planets are to be brought down by a wave of the hand," said Hell, "I will break all my telescopes, and offer my services to Mesmer as an amanuensis."

The harmonicon ceased, and the censorious professors were forced to stop their cavilling.

Mesmer arose, and, approaching Therese, made a few passes above her head.

"My eyes burn as if they were pierced with red-hot daggers," said she, with an expression of great suffering.

He now directed the tips of his fingers toward her eyes, and touched the bandage.

"Remove the bandage, and see!" cried he in a loud voice.

Therese tore it off, and pale as death she gazed with wonder at the "Master," who stood directly in front of her. Pointing to him, she said with an expression of fear and dislike:

"Is that a man which stands before me?" †

Mesmer bowed his head. Therese started back, exclaiming, "It is fearful! But where is Mesmer? Show me Mesmer!"

"I am he," said Mesmer, approaching her.

She drew back and looked at him with a scrutinizing expression. "I had supposed that the human face was radiant with joy," said she, "but this one looks like incarnate woe. Are all mankind sad? Where is my mother?"

Frau von Paradies was awaiting her daughter's call; she now came forward, her face beaming with love and joy. But Therese, instead of meeting her with equal fervor, shrank, and covered her face with her hands.

"Therese, my daughter, look upon me," said the mother.

"It is her voice," cried Therese, joyfully, removing her hands. Frau von Paradies stood by, smiling.

"Is this my mother?" continued she, looking up into her face. "Yes—it must be so; those tearful eyes are full of love. Oh, mother, come nearer, and let me look into those loving eyes!"

* It frequently happened that not only women, but men also, fainted, when Mesmer played on the glass-harmonicon. Justinus Kerner, p. 42.

† Therese's own words. Justinus Kerner, p. 63.

Her mother leaned over her, but agan Therese recoiled. "What a frightful thing!" said she, with a look of fear.

"What, Therese? What is frightful?" asked her mother.

"Look at your mother, Therese," said Mesmer. She heard the well-beloved voice, and her hands fell from her eyes.

"Now tell me, what disturbs you," said Frau von Paradies.

Therese raised her hand and pointed to her mother's nose. "It is that," said she. "What is it?"

"It is my nose!" exclaimed her mother, laughing, and her laugh was echoed throughout the room.

"This nose on the human face is horrible," said Therese. "It threatens me as though it would stab my eyes." *

"I will show you the figure of a man who threatens," said Mesmer, assuming an angry air, clinching his fists, and advancing a few paces.

Therese fell upon her knees with a cry. "You will kill me!" exclaimed she, cowering to the floor.

The spectators were thunderstruck. Even Professor Barth yielded to the overwhelming evidence of his senses.

"By Heaven, it is no deception!" exclaimed he. "She sees!"

"Since Professor Barth is convinced, no one will dare dispute the fact," observed Mesmer, loud enough to be overheard by the professor.

Barth frowned, and pretended not to hear. He already repented of what he had said, and would have bought back his own words with a handful of ducats. But it was too late. Every one had heard him, and on every side murmurs of astonishment and of admiration grew into distinct applause.

Meanwhile, Therese was greeting her father and her other relatives. But she, who had always been so affectionate, was now embarrassed and cold.

"I knew it," said she, sadly. "I knew that the gift of sight would not increase my happiness. Imagination had drawn your images, and I loved the pictures she had painted. But now that I see you with the eyes of flesh, my heart recoils from participation in the sad secrets which your careworn faces reveal. Ah, I believe that love, in its highest sense, is known to the blind alone! But where is Bello? Let me see my dog, the faithful companion of my days of dependence."

Bello had been whining at the door, and as Frau von Paradies opened it, he bounded to his mistress, caressing her with his paws, and licking her hands.

Therese bent over him, and the dog raised his eyes to hers. She stroked his glossy, black coat, and, for the first time since she had recovered her sight, she smiled.

"This dog is more pleasing to me than man," said she, communing with herself. "There is truth in his eyes, and his face does not terrify me, like those of my own race." †

"I think we may take our leave," growled Professor Barth, "the comedy is over, and the relations and friends can applaud the author and the actress. I don't feel it my duty to remain for that purpose."

"Nor I," added Doctor Ingenhaus, as he prepared to accompany the professor. "My head is in a whirl with the antics of this devilish doctor."

* These are the exact words of Therese. Justinus Kerner, p 68.

† Therese's own words. Justinus Kerner, p. 63.

"Take me with you," said Father Hell. "I must go and look after my planets. I'm afraid we shall miss another Pleiad."

So saying, the representatives of science took their leave. At the door they met Count von Langermann, the messenger of the empress.

"Ah, gentlemen," said he, "you are hastening from this enchanted spot to announce its wonders to the world. No one will venture to doubt, when such learned professors have seen and believed. I myself am on my way to apprise the empress of Mesmer's success."

"Pray inform the empress, also, that we have seen an admirable comedy, count," said Barth, with a sneer.

"A comedy!" echoed the count. "It is a marvellous reality. Yourself confessed it, professor."

"A careless word, prematurely uttered, is not to be accepted as evidence," growled Barth.

"Such astounding things demand time for consideration. They may be optical delusions," added Ingenhaus.

"Ah, gentlemen, the fact is a stubborn one," laughed Count Langermann. "Therese von Paradies has recovered her sight without couching-knife or lancet, and I shall certainly convey the news of the miracle to the empress."

"What shall we do?" asked the astronomer of his compeers, as Count Langermann bowed and left them.

Professor Barth answered nothing.

"We must devise something to prop up science, or she will fall upon our heads and crush us to death," said Ingenhaus.

"What are we to do?" repeated Barth, slowly, as after an embarrassing silence, the three had walked some distance together down the street. "I will tell you what we must do. Treat the whole thing as a farce, and maintain, in the face of all opposition, that Therese von Paradies is still blind."

"But, my honored friend, unhappily for us all, you have made this impracticable by your awkward enthusiasm."

"I spoke ironically, and the ass mistook sarcasm for conviction."

"Yes, and so did everybody else," sighed Hell. "You will find it difficult to convince the world that you were not in earnest."

"Perhaps to-day and to-morrow I may fail to convince the world, but the day after it will begin to reason and to doubt. If we do not oppose this quack with a strong phalanx of learned men, we shall be sneered at for our previous incredulity. Now I adhere to my text. Therese von Paradies is blind, and no one shall prove to me that she can see. Come to my study, and let us talk this provoking matter over."

Meanwhile, Therese was receiving the congratulations of her friends. She gazed at their unknown faces with a melancholy smile, and frowned when it was said to her, "This is the friend whom you love so much"—"This is the relative whose society has always been so agreeable to you."

Then she closed her eyes, and said they were weary. "Let me hear your voices, and so accustom myself to your strange countenances," said she. "Speak, dear friends; I would rather know you with the heart than with these deceiving eyes."

Suddenly, as one of her female companions came up to greet her, Therese burst into a merry laugh. "What absurd thing is that growing out of your head?" asked she.

"Why, that is the *coiffure*, which you like the best," replied her mother. "It is a *coiffure à la Matignon.*"

Therese raised her hands to her own head. "True, the very same towering absurdity. I never will wear it again, mother."

"It is very fashionable, and you will become accustomed to it."

"No, I shall never be reconciled to such a caricature. Now that I can choose for myself, I shall attend less to fashion than to fitness in my dress. But I have seen mankind—let me see nature and heaven. Mesmer, may I look upon the skies?"

"Come, my child, and we will try if your eyes can bear the full light of day," replied Mesmer, fondly, and taking her arm he led her toward the window.

But Therese, usually so firm in her tread, took short, uncertain steps, and seemed afraid to advance.

"Gracious Heaven!" exclaimed she, clinging anxiously to Mesmer, "see how the windows come toward us! We shall be crushed to death!"

"No, Therese; it is we who advance, not they. You will soon acquire a practical knowledge of the laws of optics, and learn to calculate distances and sizes as well as the rest of us."

"But what is this?" cried she, as they approached the tall mirror that was placed between the windows.

"That is a mirror."

"And who is that man who is so like yourself?"

"That is only the reflection of my person in the mirror."

"And who is that ridiculous being with the *coiffure à la Matignon?*"

"That is yourself."

"I!" exclaimed she, quickly advancing to the mirror. But suddenly she retreated in alarm. "Gracious Heaven! it comes so fast that it will throw me down." Then she stopped for a moment and laughed. "See," said she, "the girl is as cowardly as myself. The farther I step back the farther she retreats also."

"All this is an optical delusion, Therese. The girl is nothing but a reflection, a picture of yourself in the mirror."

"True, I forgot. You told me that just now," replied Therese, drawing her hand wearily across her forehead. "Well, let me contemplate myself. This, then, is my likeness," said she, musing. "My mother was mistaken. This face is not handsome. It is weary and soulless. Come, master, I have enough of it—let me see the heavens."

"Wait until I draw the curtain to see whether you are able to bear the full light of day."

The curtain was lifted, and Therese, giving a scream, hid her eyes.

"Oh, it cuts like the point of a dagger!" cried she.

"I thought so; you will have to become gradually accustomed to it. You shall see the sky this evening. But now you must suffer me to bind up your eyes, for they must have rest." *

* The description of Therese's impressions, and the words she used upon the recovery of her sight, are not imaginary. They are all cited by Justinus Kerner, and were related to him by her own father.

CHAPTER LXXXIV.

DIPLOMATIC STRATEGY.

THE Emperor Joseph was in his cabinet, engaged in looking over the letters and documents of the day, when a page announced his highness Prince Kaunitz. Joseph waved his hand in token of consent, and when the prince appeared at the door, rose to meet him as he entered the room.

"It must be business of state that brings your highness to my study at this early hour," said the emperor.

"It is indeed, sire," said Kaunitz, taking the chair which Joseph himself had just placed for him.

"And it must be a day of rejoicing with you, prince, for I see that you wear every order with which you have been decorated by every court in Europe. What does this display signify?"

"It signifies, sire, that the day has come, which I have awaited for twenty years, the day for which I have schemed and toiled, and which for me shall be the proudest day of my life. I go out to battle, and if I am to be victorious, your majesty must come to my assistance."

"Is it a duel with the empress, in which I am to be your second? I thank you for the honor, but you know that I have no influence with my lady mother. I am an emperor without a sceptre. But tell me, Kaunitz, what is the cause of the trouble?"

"You know it, sire, and I have come to prove to you that I am a man of my word, and keep my promises."

"I do not remember that you ever promised me any thing."

"But I do. I remember a day on which my young emperor came to me to complain of a wrong which had been inflicted upon him at court."

"Marianne!" exclaimed the emperor, with a sigh. "Yes, yes, the day on which I lost sight of her forever."

"Yes, sire. The emperor, worthy of his high vocation, relinquished the girl who had found favor in his eyes, and for this sacrifice I promised him my loyal friendship. Three objects formed the ties that bound us together on that day. Does your majesty remember?"

"Yes. You promised to place Austria at the head of European affairs; you have done so. You promised indemnity for Silesia; we have it in our recent acquisitions in Poland."

"I promised also to crush the priesthood, and to ruin the Jesuits," cried Kaunitz, exultingly, "and I am here to fulfil my promise. The hour has come; for I am on my way to obtain the consent of the empress to the banishment of the Jesuits from Austria."

"You never will obtain it. Attachment to the Order of Jesus is an inheritance with the house of Hapsburg; and my mother styles me a degenerate son because I do not participate in the feeling."

"We will find means to alienate the empress," said Kaunitz, quietly. "I hope so, but I doubt it. Tell me what I am to do, and I am ready to make another charge against them."

Prince Kaunitz opened his pocket-book, and took thence a letter which he handed to the emperor.

"Will your majesty have the goodness to hand this to the empress? It is a letter from Carlos III., in which he earnestly requests his illustrious kinswoman to give protection no longer to the Jesuits, whom he has driven from Spain."

"Indeed?" said the emperor, smiling. "If that is all, the Spanish ambassador might have delivered it quite as well as I."

"No, sire, that is not all. It was the King of Spain's request that your majesty should deliver the letter, and sustain it by every argument which your well-known enmity to the Jesuits might suggest."

"I am more than willing to undertake it; but to-day, as ever, my representations to the empress will be vain."

"Do your best, sire, and I will come to your relief with a reserved force, which will do good service. Only allow me to request that you will not quit the empress until the reserve comes up."

"Then the parts we are to play are distributed and learned by heart?"

"Just so; and Heaven be propitious, that the scenery may work well, and the actors may know their cue!"

"We have accomplices, then?"

"I shall be accompanied by the papal nuncio, and if your majesty permits me, I will go for him at once. In half an hour I shall come to the rescue."

"Go, then, and I fly to the empress," cried Joseph, with exultation.

CHAPTER LXXXV.

DOMINUS AC REDEMPTOR NOSTER.

True to their agreement, the emperor sought an interview with his mother. Not enjoying, like her prime minister, the privilege of entering the empress's presence without formal leave, Joseph was always obliged to wait in her anteroom until the chamberlain returned with her majesty's answer. To-day the empress was propitious, and gave word for her son to be admitted to her private cabinet at once. That he might enter promptly upon the object of his visit, the emperor opened the interview by handing the letter of the King of Spain, and requesting her majesty to read it in his presence.

The empress, surprised at the urgency of the demand, sat before her *escritoire* and read the missive of her royal relative; while her son, with folded arms, stood near a window, and scrutinized her countenance.

He saw how gradually her expression lowered, until heavy folds corrugated her brow, and deep heavings agitated her chest.

"Those are the sea-gulls that announce the coming storm," said he, to himself. "I must be on my guard lest I be engulfed in the foaming waves."

As if she had guessed his thoughts, Maria Theresa raised her eyes from the letter, and darted a look of displeasure at her son.

"Is the emperor aware of the contents of this letter?" asked she.

"I believe so, your majesty," replied he, coming forward and bowing. "It is an urgent request on the part of the King of Spain, to have the Jesuits removed from Austria."

"Nothing less," cried the empress, indignantly. "He expects me to assume all his enmity toward the Jesuits, and urges it in a most unseemly manner. Doubtless, he requested your majesty to present his letter in. person, because it is well known, that in this, as in all other things, your opinions are at variance with those of your mother. I presume this is a new tilt against my predilections, like that in which you overthrew me but a few weeks since, when I signed the act that ruined Poland. Speak out. Are you not here to sustain the King of Spain?"

"I am, your majesty," cried Joseph, reddening. "I would do as the King of Spain has done. I would importune you until the power of the Jesuits is crushed in Austria, as it has been crushed in France and in Spain."

"You will not succeed!" cried the empress, trying to control her rising anger. "I make no protest against the action of the kings of France, Spain, or Portugal, for I presume that they have decided according to their convictions; but in Austria the Jesuits deserve all praise for their enlightened piety, and their existence is so essential to the well-being of the people, that I shall sustain and protect them as long as I live."*

"Then," cried Joseph, passionately, "Austria is lost. If I were capable of hate, I should hate these Jesuits, who, propagating the senile vagaries of an old Spanish dotard, have sought to govern the souls of men, and have striven for nothing on earth or in heaven save the extension of their own influence and authority."

"It appears to me that my son has no reason to lament the softness of his own heart," replied Maria Theresa, bitterly. "If he were absolute sovereign here, the Jesuits would be exiled to-morrow; and the King of Prussia, for whom he entertains such unbounded admiration, would be the first one to offer them shelter. I will answer your vituperation, my son, by reading to you a letter written by Frederick to his agent in Rome. It relates to the rumor now afloat that the pope is about to disperse the holy brotherhood. I have just received a copy of it from Italy, and it rejoices me to be able to lay it before you. Hear your demi-god."

The empress took a paper from her *escritoire*, and unfolding it, read aloud:

"Announce distinctly, but without bravado, that as regards the Jesuits, I am resolved to uphold them for the future, as I have done hitherto. Seek a fitting opportunity to communicate my sentiments on the subject to the pope. I have guaranteed free exercise of religion to my subjects in Silesia. I have never known a priesthood worthier of esteem than the Jesuits. Add to this, that as I am an infidel, the pope cannot dispense me from the obligation of performing my duty as an honorable man and an upright sovereign.

"FREDERICK."*

"Well," asked the empress, as she folded the letter, "shall the infidel shame the Christian? Would you seriously ask of me to be less clement to the priesthood than a Protestant prince? Never, never shall it be said that Maria Theresa was ungrateful to the noble brotherhood who are the bulwarks of order and of legitimate authority."

* Peter Philip Wolf, "General History of the Jesuits," vol. iv., p. 53.

Joseph was about to make an angry retort, when the door opened and a page announced, with great formality :

"His highness Prince Kaunitz, and his eminence the papal nuncio, Monsignore Garampi."

The two ministers followed close upon the announcement, and the nuncio was received by the empress with a beaming smile.

"I am curious to know what has brought Prince Kaunitz and the papal nuncio together," said she. "It is unusual to see the prime minister of Austria in the company of churchmen. It must, therefore, be something significant which has united church and state to-day."

"Your majesty is right," replied Kaunitz, "the visit of the nuncio is so significant for Austria, that the visit of your majesty's minister in his company was imperative."

"Your eminence comes to speak of state affairs?" inquired the empress, surprised.

The nuncio drew from his robe a parchment to which was affixed a ribbon with the papal seal.

"His holiness instructed me to read this document to your apostolic majesty," said Monsignore Garampi, with a respectful inclination of the head. "Will your majesty allow me?"

"Certainly," said the empress, leaning forward to listen.

The nuncio then unfolded the parchment, and amid the breathless attention of all present, read the celebrated document, which in history bears the name of its first words "*Dominus ac Redemptor Noster.*" This letter stated that in all ages the pope had claimed the right to found religious orders or to abolish them. It cited Gregory, who had abolished the order of the Mendicant Friars; and Clement V., who had suppressed that of the Templars. It then referred to the Society of the Brotherhood of Jesus. It stated that this society had hitherto been sustained and fostered by the papal see, on acccount of its signal usefulness and the eminent piety of its members. But of late, the brotherhood had manifested a spirit of contentiousness amongst themselves, as well as toward other orders, organizations, and universities; and had thereby fallen under the displeasure of the princes from whom they had received encouragement and protection.

When the nuncio had read thus far, he paused and raised his eyes to the face of the empress. It was very pale and agitated, while the countenance of the emperor, on the contrary, was flushed with triumph. Joseph tried to meet the glance of Prince Kaunitz's eye, but it was blank as ever; sometimes fixed vacantly upon the nuncio, and then turning with cold indifference toward the speaking countenances of the devoted friend and inveterate enemy of the Order of Jesus.

"Go on, your eminence," at length faltered the empress.

The nuncio bowed and continued in an audible voice: "Seeing that between the Holy See and the kings of France, Spain, Portugal, and the Sicilies, misundertstandings have arisen which are attributable to the influence of the Order of Jesus; seeing that the society at this present time has ceased to bear the rich fruits of its past usefulness; the pope, after conscientious deliberation, has resolved, in the fulness of his apostolic right, to suppress the brotherhood."

A loud cry burst from the lips of the empress, as overwhelmed by these bitter tidings she covered her face with her hands. The emperor approached as though he wished to address her, but she waved him off impatiently.

"Away, Joseph!" said she; "I will listen neither to your condolence nor to your exultation. Let me advise you, too, to moderate your transports, for this is Austrian soil, and no one reigns in Austria but Maria Theresa. The Jesuits have been a blessing to mankind; they have instructed our youth, and have been the guardians of all knowledge; they have encouraged the arts and sciences, and have disseminated the Christian faith in every part of the world. They have been the true and loyal friends of my house; and in their day of adversity, though I may not defend them against their ecclesiastical superiors, I will protect them against malice and insult."

Thus spoke the generous and true-hearted Maria Theresa; but her efforts to sustain the Jesuits, as an organized brotherhood, were fruitless. They were an ecclesiastic fraternity, and as such, their existence was beyond the reach of civil authority. As individuals, they were her subjects; but as a society, they were amenable to the laws of the Church, and by that code alone, they stood or fell.

Bravely she struggled; but the earnest representations of the nuncio, the sharp, cutting arguments of Kaunitz, and her own reluctance to come to a rupture with the pope in a matter essentially within ecclesiastical jurisdiction, all these things united, bore down her opposition; and with the same reluctance as she had felt in acquiescing to the partition of Poland, she consented to the suppression of the Society of Jesus.

"Come hither, my son," said the empress, reaching her hand to Joseph. "Since I have seen fit to give my consent to this thing, I have nothing wherewith to reproach you. As co-regent I hope that what I am about to say will obtain your approbation. Monsignore, you have read to me the order of his holiness, Clement XIV., for the suppression of the Jesuits. For my part, nothing would ever have induced me to expel them from my dominions. But since his holiness sees fit to do so, I feel it to be my duty, as a true daughter of the Church, to allow the order to be put into execution.* Acquaint his holiness with my decision, and remain a few moments that you may witness the promptitude with which his intentions shall be carried out."

She sat down to her *escritoire*, and tracing a few lines upon a piece of paper, handed it to Prince Kaunitz.

"Prince," said she, "here is the order, which, in accordance to strict form, must be in my own handwriting. Take it to Cardinal Migazzi. Let him carry out the intentions of the pope, and himself perform the funeral rites of the devoted Sons of Jesus."

She turned away her head, that none might see the tears which were streaming from her eyes. Then rising from her seat, she crossed the room. Those who had brought this grief upon her, watched her noble form, and as they saw how her step faltered, they exchanged silent glances of sympathy. When she reached the door, she turned, and then they saw her pale, sad face and tearful eyes.

"When the cardinal visits the College of the Jesuits to read the papal order, let an imperial *commissarius* accompany him," said

* The empress's own words. Gross-Hoffinger, vol. i., p. 193.

Maria Theresa in an imperative tone. "Immediately after its promulgation, he shall promise to the Jesuits my imperial favor and protection, if they submit to the will of the pope as becomes true servants of God and of the Church. It shall also be exacted that the proceedings against the Order of Jesus shall be conducted with lenity and due respect; and for the future, I shall never suffer any member of the society to be treated with contumely or scorn." *

She bowed her lofty head, and withdrew.

Complete silence followed the disappearance of the empress. No one dared to violate the significance of the moment by a word. The nuncio bowed low to the emperor and retired; but as Kaunitz was about to follow, Joseph came hastily forward and clasped him in his arms.

"I thank you," whispered he. "You have fulfilled your pledges, and Austria is free. My obligations to you are for life!"

The two ministers then went down together to the great palace gate, where their state-carriages awaited them.

Prince Kaunitz greeted the nuncio with another silent bow; and shrinking from the blasts of a mild September day,† wrapped himself up in six cloaks, and sealed up his mouth with a huge muff of sables. He then stepped into his carriage, and drove off. Once safe and alone within his exhausted receiver, he dropped his muff for a moment, and, wonderful to relate—he smiled.

"Let things shape themselves as they will," said he, thoughtfully. "I am absolute master of Austria. Whether the sovereign be called Maria Theresa, or Joseph, it is all one to me. Both feel my worth, and both have vowed to me eternal gratitude. Poland has fallen—the Jesuits are dispersed; but Kaunitz is steadfast, for he is the pillar upon which the imperial house leans for support!"

Four weeks after the publication of the papal order by Cardinal Migazzi, the great doors of the Jesuit College were opened, and forth from its portals came the brotherhood of the Order of Jesus.

Led by their superior, all in their long black cassocks, with rosaries hanging at their blue girdles, they left the familiar home, which had been theirs for a hundred years. Each one carried in his hands his Bible and breviary. The faces of the brothers were pale and unspeakably sad, and their lips were compressed as though to thrust back the misery that was surging within their hearts.

The multitude were mute as they. Not a word, whether of sympathy or of animosity, greeted the silent procession. On went the noiseless, spectre-like train, until it reached the market-place. There the superior stopped, and the brothers gathered around him in one vast circle.

He uncovered his head, and all followed his example. All bowed their heads in prayer to God who had willed that this great humiliation should befall them. In one last petition to Heaven for resignation, they bade adieu to their glorious past with its glorious memories; and the people, overcome by the simple sublimity of the scene, fell upon their knees and wept, repeating, while they wept, the prayers which they had learned from the teachers with whom they were parting forever.

The prayer was ended, and now the superior went from brother

* The empress's words. Adam Wolf. "Maria Theresa," p. 432.

† The papal order was promulgated in Vienna on September 10, 1773.

to brother, taking the hand of each one. And every man faltered a blessing which their chief returned. So he went from one to another, until he had greeted them all; then passing from the crowd, with a Jesuit on either side, he disappeared.

So ended the dispersion of the Order of Jesus, whom the whole world believed to be crushed forever. But they knew better; for, as crowding around their chief, they had whispered: "Shall we ever be a brotherhood again?" he had returned the pressure of their friendly hands, and had replied with prophetic fervor:

"Yes; whenever it is God's will to reinstate us. Wait patiently for the hour. It will surely come; for Loyola's order, like the soul, is immortal!"

CHAPTER LXXXVI.

HEART-STRUGGLES.

THE week of delay which the empress had granted to the Countess Margaret had passed away, and the eve of her bridal had dawned. During those eight eventful days the countess had been more fitful than ever, and her uncle's household had suffered accordingly.

"She will take her life," whispered the servants among themselves, as each day, like a pale spectre, she glided through the house, to mount her wild Arabian. The two footmen who accompanied her on these occasions, told how she galloped so madly that they could scarcely keep pace with her; and then suddenly checked her horse, and with her head bent over its neck, remained motionless and wept.

Once the emperor had surprised her in tears, and when she became aware of his presence, she started off on a mad run and left him far behind. This occurred twice; but the third time the emperor came upon her so quickly, that before she had time to fly, he had grasped her rein. The footmen declared that they had never heard such a cry as she gave; and they thought that the emperor would be highly offended. But he only laughed, and said:

"Now, countess, you are my prisoner; and I shall not allow my beautiful Amazon to go, until she has told me why we never see her at court."

The countess turned so pale that her servants thought she would fall from her horse, and the emperor cried out: "Good Heaven! what is the matter with you?"

She broke into a loud laugh, and striking her horse with the whip, tried to gallop off again. But the emperor put spurs to his horse, and the two dashed on together. Neck and neck they ran; the countess lashing her Arabian until he made wild leaps into the air, the emperor urging his Barb with whip and spur, until his flanks were white with foam. At last he came so near, that he made a grasp at her rein and caught it, exclaiming, with a merry laugh:

"Caught again!"

The countess turned around with eyes that darted lightning.

"Why do you laugh so immoderately?" said she.

"Because we are enacting such a delightfully comic scene. But do not look so angry; your bright eyes are on fire, and they make a man's heart boil over. Answer my question, and I restore you to freedom. Why do you shun me, and why do you never come to court?"

Now the pale cheeks flushed, and the voice was subdued until its tones were like plaintive music. "Sire, I do not visit the court, because I am a poor, unhappy creature, unfitted for society, and because no one misses me there."

"And why do you fly from me as if I were Lucifer, the son of the morning?"

"Ah, your majesty, grief flies from the light of day, and seeks the cover of friendly night! And now, free my horse, if you would not have me fall dead at your feet!"

Again she turned pale, and trembled from head to foot. When the emperor saw this, he loosed her rein, and bowing to her saddle-bow, galloped away out of sight. The countess turned her horse's head, and went slowly home.

All this Count Starhemberg learned from the footmen, for never a word had his niece spoken to him since the unhappy day of Count Esterhazy's visit. To say the truth, the old man was not sorry that her sorrow had taken the shape of taciturnity; for her pale cheeks and glaring eyes affrighted him; and he hugged himself close in his short-lived security, as each day she declined to appear at table, and was served in the solitude of her own room.

She was served; but her food returned untouched. Neither did she seem to sleep; for at all times of the night she could be heard pacing her room. Then she would sit for hours before her piano; and, although her playing and singing had been equally renowned, her uncle had never suspected the genius that had lain concealed in the touch of her hands and the sound of her voice. It was no longer the "fierce countess," whose dashing execution had distanced all gentler rivals; it was a timid maiden, whose first love was finding utterance in entrancing melody. On the night following her last encounter with the emperor, the music became more passionate in its character. It was less tender, but far more sad; and often it ceased, because the musician stopped to weep.

Her uncle heard her sob, and following the impulse of his affection and compassion, he opened the room, and came softly in.

He called her, and she raised her head. The light from the wax-candles that stood on the harpsichord fell directly upon her face, which was bedewed with tears. Her uncle's entrance seemed neither to have surprised nor irritated her. With an expression of indescribable woe she merely murmured:

"See, uncle, to what the empress has reduced me."

Her uncle took her in his arms, and, like a weary child, she leaned her head upon his shoulder. Suddenly she started, and disengaging herself, she stood before him, and took his hands in hers. "Oh, is it inevitable? Must I bow my head like a slave to this marriage, while my heart proclaims an eternal NO!"

The old count wiped his eyes. "I fear there is no hope, my child. I have done all that I could."

"What have you done?"

"I first appealed to Count Esterhazy; but he declared himself to be too intoxicated by your beauty to resign you. I then tried to interest some of our friends at court; but no one dared to intercede for my darling. The empress has received a severe blow in the expulsion of the Jesuits, and no one has the courage to come between her and her mania for match-making. I then appealed to her majesty myself; but in vain. Her only answer was this: 'You were to marry the count, or go into a convent.' She added, that to-morrow every thing would be prepared in the court chapel for your marriage; that she, herself, would honor you by giving you away; and that, if you did not come punctually, when the imperial state coach was sent for you, she would have you taken instead to a convent."

"Is that all?" asked she, with a painful blush.

"No, Margaret. I saw the emperor also."

"What said he?" asked the countess, in a hoarse voice, pressing so heavily upon the old man's shoulder, that he could scarcely stand under the weight of her hands. "Word for word, tell me what he said."

"I will tell you. The emperor said: 'Dear count, no one would serve you sooner than I. But as regards her mania for marrying people, the empress is inflexible. And, indeed, it seems to me that she has chosen admirably for your beautiful niece. Count Esterhazy is young, handsome, immensely rich, and a favorite at court. You will see, dear count, that she will end by making him an affectionate and obedient wife; for a young girl's hate is very often nothing but concealed love. Those were the emperor's words, my dear. I protested against his interpretation of your dislike to Count Esterhazy—but in vain."

To this, Margaret replied not a word. Her hands had gradually fallen from her uncle's shoulders, until they hung listless at her side. Her graceful head was bowed down by the sharp stroke of the humiliation which had just stricken her, and her whole attitude was that of hopeless disconsolation.

After a few moments she threw back her head with wild defiance. "He will find that he is a false prophet," exclaimed she, with a laugh of scorn. "I promise him that."

"But, my dear girl—" began Count Starhemberg.

"Will you, too, insult me with prophecies of my future *obedience* to this fine young man? Do you, too, wish to prove to me that I am a fortunate—"

"My child, I wish nothing of the sort."

"Then what means the 'but'? Does it mean that I am to be consoled by the splendor that is to attend this—execution? Does it mean that my maidenly blushes—the blushes that betray my secret love—are to be hidden by a veil of priceless lace? Does it mean that the chains, with which your peerless empress will fetter my arms, are to be of gold, secured with diamonds? Have you taken care to provide the myrtle-wreath, the emblem of love, wherewith to deck the bride's bow? O God! O God! May some imperial daughter of this woman suffer worse than death for this!"

The count shuddered, and left the room. He had not dared to say that, in truth, her bridal-dress was all that she had described. It had all been chosen. The rich robe, the costly veil, the golden bracelets, the glittering diamonds, even the myrtle-wreath, the emblem of the humble as well as the high-born bride—all were there, awaiting the morrow.

CHAPTER LXXXVII.

THE FORCED BRIDAL.

THE ceremony was to take place at eleven o'clock. The imperial carriage of state was at the door; and behind it stood the gilded coaches of Counts Esterhazy and Starhemberg. The former had been awaiting the appearance of his bride for two hours; but to all his tender messages she had curtly replied that she would come when she was ready.

"I fear she will play us some dreadful trick," sighed the old count.

"My dear count," returned Esterhazy, "no *man* would be so presuming as to thwart the empress."

"Perhaps not—but my niece has more character than some men."

"What have I done for her to scorn me as she does!" cried the unhappy little bridegroom.

"You have opposed her, that is all. My niece is an Amazon, and cannot bear to give up her heart at another's will. Had she been left free, it might have been otherwise."

"Do you really think she will come to love me?" asked Esterhazy, surveying his diminutive comeliness in the mirror opposite.

"I am quite sure of it, and so is the emperor. Take courage, then; bear with her whims for a while; they are nothing but harmless summer lightnings. Do not heed the storm; think of the flowers that will spring up to beautify your life, when the showers of her tears shall have passed away."

"Oh, I will be patient. She shall exhaust herself."

Here the door opened, and the countess's maid entered with a request that Count Esterhazy would follow her to her lady's apartment.

The count kissed his hand to Count Starhemberg and hurried away. When he entered the countess's sitting-room, she was standing in all the pride of her bridal attire, and seemed more transcendently beautiful than ever. The court-dress, with its long trail, heightened the elegance of her figure, and the silver-spotted veil, that fell to her feet, enveloped her like a white evening cloud.

But how little did her face accord with this superb festive dress! Her cheek was deadly pale; her exquisite mouth was writhing with anguish, and her great, glowing eyes darted glances of fiery hatred.

"You really have the courage to persevere, Count Esterhazy? You will perpetrate the crime of marriage with me?"

"When a man opens his arms to receive the most enchanting woman that ever was sent on earth, do you call that a crime?" said Esterhazy, tenderly.

An impatient shrug was the answer to this attempt at gallantry.

"Have I not told you that you would earn nothing for your reward but my hatred? In the despair of my heart, have I not told you that I love another man? Oh, you have come to tell me that you spare me the sacrifice—have you not? You will not force a helpless girl to marry you, who does so only to escape a convent—will you? Oh, tell me that you have summoned manliness enough to resist the empress, and to give me my freedom!"

"I have summoned manliness enough to resist *you;* and bearing *your* anger, I am resolved to take the bewitching woman to wife whom my generous empress has selected for me."

"You are a contemptible coward!" cried she.

"I forgive you the epithet, because I am in love," replied he, with a smile.

"But if you have no pity for me," cried she wildly, "have pity on yourself. You have seen how I treat my uncle, and yet I love him dearly. Think what your fate will be, since I hate you immeasurably."

"Ah," said he, "can you expect me to be more merciful to myself than to you? No, no! I rely upon my love to conquer your hate. It will do so all in good time."

"As there is a God in heaven, you will rue this hour!" cried Margaret with mingled defiance and despair.

"Come, countess, come. The empress and her son await us in the court-chapel."

Margaret shivered, and drew her veil around her. She advanced toward the door, but as the count was in the act of opening it, she laid her two hands upon his arm, and held him back.

"Have mercy on my soul!" sobbed she. "It is lost if I become your wife. I have a stormy temper, and sorrow will expand it into wickedness. I feel that I shall be capable of crime if you force me to this marriage."

"Gracious Heaven!" cried the count, pettishly, "if you abhor me to such a degree, why do you not go into a convent?"

"I had resolved to do so, for the convent is less repulsive to me than a home in your palace; but I could not bring myself to the sacrifice. No!—Were I to be immured within those convent walls, I should forever be shut out from the sight of him whom I love. Do you hear this? Do you hear that I marry you only to be free to see him, to hear his voice, to catch one glance of his eye as he passes me in the crowd? Oh, you will not take to wife a woman who meditates such perjury as this! You will not give your father's name to her who is going to the altar with a lie upon her lips and a crime upon her soul! Go—tell all this to the empress. Tell her that you will not disgrace your noble house by a marriage with me! Oh, Count Esterhazy, be merciful, be merciful!"

"Impossible, countess, impossible; were it even possible for me to belie you by such language. I shall not see the empress until we stand before the altar together, and then she will be in her oratorium, far beyond my reach."

"Yes, yes, you can reject me at the altar. Oh, see how I humble myself! I am on my knees before you. Spurn me from you in the face of the whole world!"

Count Esterhazy looked thoughtful. Unhappily, the countess on her knees was more beautiful than ever; so that remembering her uncle's words, he said to himself:

"Yes—I will humor her—I must feign to yield."

He stretched out his hands, saying, "Rise, countess. It does not become a sovereign to kneel before her slave. I have no longer the power to oppose your will. Before the altar, I will say 'No' to the priest's question, and you shall be free."

The countess uttered a loud cry of joy, and rose to her feet. And as her pale cheek kindled with hope, and her eyes beamed with happiness, she was more beautiful than she had ever been in her life before, and Count Esterhazy exulted over it.

"God bless you!" exclaimed she, with a heavenly smile. "You have earned my affection now; for my life I vow to love you as a cherished brother. Come, dear, generous, noble friend, come. Let us hasten to the chapel."

It was she now who opened the door. Count Starhemberg awaited them in the drawing-room. Margaret flew to meet him, and embracing him, said:

"Do I not look like a happy bride now? Come, uncle, come, dear Count Esterhazy, let us go to our bridal."

She took Esterhazy's arm, and he placed her in the carriage. The old count followed, in speechless wonder.

At the door of the chapel, they were met by the empress's first lady of honor, who conducted the bride to the altar. The emperor walked by the side of Count Esterhazy. The face of the countess was radiant with happiness, and all who saw her confessed that she was lovely beyond all description.

And now the ceremonial began. The priest turned to Count Esterhazy and asked him if he took the Countess Maragret von Starhemberg for his wedded wife, to love, honor, and cherish her untii death should them divide.

There was a pause, and Margaret looked with a bright smile at the face of her bridegroom. But the eyes of the spectators were fixed upon him in astonishment, and the brow of the empress grew stormy.

"Will you take this woman for your wedded wife?" repeated the priest.

"I will," said Esterhazy, in a loud firm voice.

A cry escaped from the lips of Margaret. She was so faint that she reeled and would have fallen, but for the friendly support of an arm that sustained her, and the witching tones of a voice that whispered: "Poor girl, remember that a cloister awaits you."

She recognized the voice of the emperor; and overcoming her weakness, the courage of despair came to her help.

She raised herself from Joseph's arms and taking the *vinaigrette* that was tendered her by the lady of honor, she inhaled its reviving aroma; then she looked at the priest.

He continued, and repeated his solemn question to her. Etiquette required that before she answered, she should have the sanction of the empress. The countess turned, with a low inclination, to the lady of honor, who, in her turn, courtesied deeply to the empress.

Maria Theresa bowed acquiescence, and the bride, having thanked her with another courtesy, turned once more to the priest and said, "Yes."

The ceremony was over, and the young couple received the congratulations of the court. Even the empress herself descended from the oratorium to meet them.

"I have chosen a very excellent husband for you," said she, smiling, "and I have no doubt you will be a very happy woman."

"It must be so, of course, your majesty," replied the bride; "for had your majesty not ascertained that this marriage had been made in heaven, you would not have ordered it on earth, I presume."

Maria Theresa darted a look of anger at the countess, and turning her back upon such presumption, offered her good wishes to the count.

"What did you say, to irritate the empress so?" whispered Joseph to the bride.

Margaret repeated her words. "That was a bold answer," said he.

"Has your majesty ever taken me for a coward? I think I have shown preter-human courage this day."

"What! Because you have married Count Esterhazy? Believe me, you will be the happiest of tyrants, and he the humblest of your slaves."

"I will show him that slaves deserve the lash!" cried she, with a look of hatred at her husband, who came forward to conduct her to the palace, where the marriage guests were now to be received.

The festivities of the day over, the empress's lady of honor conducted the countess to her new home. It was the duty of this lady to assist the bride in removing her rich wedding-dress, and assuming the costly *négligé* which lay ready prepared for her on a lounge in her magnificent dressing-room.

But the countess imperiously refused to change her dress. "Have the goodness," said she, "to say to her majesty, that you conducted me to my dressing-room. You can say further," added she, hearing the door open, "that you left me with Count Esterhazy."

She pointed to the count, who entered, greeting the ladies with a respectful bow.

"I will leave you, then," said the lady, kissing Margaret's forehead. "May Heaven bless you!"

Count Esterhazy was now alone with his wife. With a radiant smile and both hands outstretched, he came toward her.

"Welcome to my house, beautiful Margaret! From this hour you reign supreme in the palace of the Esterhazys."

The countess stepped back. "Do not dare to touch my hand. A gulf yawns between us; and if you attempt to bridge it, I will throw you, headlong, into its fiery abyss."

"What gulf? Point it out to me, that I may bridge it with my love," cried Esterhazy.

"The gulf of my contempt," said she, coldly. "You are a coward and a liar. You have deceived a woman who trusted herself to your honor; and God in heaven, who would not hear my prayers, God shall be the witness of my vengeance. Oh, you shall repent from this hour to come, that ever you called me wife! I scorn to be a liar like you, and I tell you to beware. I will revenge myself for this accursed treachery."

"I do not fear your revenge, for you have a noble heart. The day will come when I shall be forgiven for my deception. Heaven is always clement toward the repentant sinner; and you are my heaven, Margaret. I await the day of mercy."

"Such mercy as Heaven has shown to me, I shall show to you," cried she. "And now, sir, leave this room. I have nothing more to say to you."

"What, Margaret!" said Esterhazy, with an incredulous smile, "you would deny me the sweet right of visiting your room? Chide, if you will; but be not so cruel. Let me have the first kiss—"

As he attempted to put his arms around her, Margaret uttered a fearful cry. Freeing herself with such violence that Esterhazy reeled backward with the shock, she exclaimed:

"You are worse than a coward, for you would take advantage of rights which my hatred has annulled forever."

"But, Margaret, my wife—"

"Count Esterhazy," said Margaret slowly, "I forbid you ever to use that word in this room. Before the world I must endure the humiliation of being called your wife; but once over the threshold of my own room, I am Margaret Starhemberg, and you shall never know me as any other Margaret. Now go!"

She pointed to the door; and as the count looked into her face, where passion was so condensed that it almost resembled tranquillity, he had not the hardihood to persist. He felt that he had gained his first and last victory.

As soon as he had passed the door, Margaret locked and bolted it; then, alone with the supreme anguish that had been crushed for these long, long hours, she fell upon her knees, and wept until the morning-star looked down upon her agony.

CHAPTER LXXXVIII.

PRINCE LOUIS DE ROHAN.

THE cardinal prince, Louis de Rohan, French ambassador at Vienna, had petitioned the empress for a private audience, and the honor had been granted him. It was the first time, since a year, that he had enjoyed this privilege; and the proud prince had determined that all Vienna should know it, for all Vienna was fully aware of the empress's dislike to him.

Accompanied by a brilliant *cortége*, the prince set out for the palace. Six footmen stood behind his gilded carriage, while inside, seated upon cushions of white satin, the prince dispensed smiles to the women, and nods to the men who thronged the streets to get a glimpse of his magnificence. Four pages, in the Rohan livery, dispensed silver coin to the populace; while behind came four carriages, bearing eight noblemen of the proudest families in France, and four other carriages which bore the household of this haughty prince of church and realm.*

The *cortége* moved slowly, and the people shouted. From every window, burgher's or nobleman's, handsome women greeted the handsome cardinal who was known to be a *connoisseur* in female beauty. The crowd outside followed him to the palace-gates, and when his carriage stopped, they shouted so vociferously, that the noise reached the ears of the empress; and so long, that their shouts had not ceased when the cardinal, leaving his brilliant suite, was ushered into the small reception-room where Maria Theresa awaited him.

She stood by the window, and half turned her head, as the prince, with profoundest salutations, came forward. She received his obsequious homage with a slight inclination of the head.

"Can your eminence tell me the meaning of this din?" asked she, curtly.

"I regret not to be able to do so, your majesty. I hear no din;

*In the beginning of the year 1780, Prince de Rohan was made cardinal and grand almoner of France. Before that time, he had been Archbishop of Strasburg. "Mémoires sur la Vie Privée de Marie Antoinette," vol. i., p. 47.

I have heard nothing save the friendly greetings of your people, whose piety edifies my heart as a priest, and whose welcome is dear to me as a *quasi* subject of your majesty. For the mother of my future queen must allow me the right to consider myself almost as her subject."

"I would prefer that you considered yourself wholly the subject of my daughter; as I doubt whether she will ever find much loyalty in *your* heart, prince. But before we go further, pray inform me what means all this parade attendant upon the visit of the French ambassador here to-day? I am not aware that we are in the carnival; nor have I an unmarried daughter for whom any French prince can have sent you to propose."

"Surely your majesty would not compare the follies of the carnival with the solemnity of an imperial betrothal," said the archbishop, deferentially.

"Be so good as not to evade my question. I ask why you came to the palace with a procession just fit to take its place in a carnival?"

"Because the day on which the mother of the dauphiness receives me, is a great festival for me. I have so long sued for an audience, that when it is granted me, I may well be allowed to celebrate it with the pomp which befits the honor conferred."

"And in such a style that all Vienna may know it, and the rumor of your audience reach the ears of the dauphiness herself."

"I cannot hope that the dauphiness takes interest enough in the French ambassador to care whether he be received at a foreign court or not," replied the cardinal, still in his most respectful tone.

"I request you to come to the point," said Maria Theresa, impatiently. "Tell me, at once, why you have asked for an audience? What seeks the French ambassador of the empress of Austria?"

"Allow me to say that had I appeared to-day before your majesty as the French ambassador, I would have been accompanied by my *attachés* and received by your majesty in state. But your majesty is so gracious as to receive me in private. It follows, therefore, that the Cardinal de Rohan, the cousin of the dauphin, visits the imperial mother of the young dauphiness."

"In other words, you come hither to complain of the dauphiness-consort; again to renew the unpleasant topics which have been the cause of my repeated refusals to see you here."

"No, your majesty, no. I deem it my sacred duty to speak confidentially to the mother of the dauphiness."

"If the mother of the dauphiness-consort will listen," cried the proud empress, sharply emphasizing the word "consort."

"Pardon me, your majesty, the apparent oversight," said De Rohan, with a smile. "But as a prince of the church, it behooves me, above all things, to be truthful, and the Dauphiness of France is not yet dauphiness-consort. Your majesty knows that as well as I do."

"I know that my daughter's enemies and mine have succeeded so far in keeping herself and her husband asunder," said the empress bitterly.

"But the dauphiness possesses, in her beauty, worth, and sweetness, weapons wherewith to disarm her enemies, if she would but use them," said De Rohan, with a shrug. "Unhappily, she makes no attempt to disarm them."

"Come—say what you have to say without so much circumlocution," cried Maria Theresa, imperiously. "What new complaint have the French against my daughter?"

"Your majesty is the only person that can influence the proud spirit of the dauphiness. Marie Antoinette adores her mother, and your majesty's advice will have great weight with her."

"What advice shall I give her?"

"Advise her to give less occasion to her enemies to censure her levity and her contempt of conventional forms."

"Who dares accuse my daughter of levity?" said the empress, her eyes flashing with angry pride.

"Those who, in the corruption of their own hearts, mistake for wantonness that which is nothing more than the thoughtlessness of unsuspecting innocence."

"You are pleased to speak in riddles. I am Maria Theresa—not Œdipus."

"I will speak intelligently," said De Rohan, with his everlasting smile. "There are many things, innocent in themselves, which do not appear so to worldly eyes. Innocence may be attractive in a cottage, but it is not so in a palace. An ordinary woman, even of rank, has the right, in the privacy of her own room, to indulge herself in childish sport; but your majesty's self cannot justify your daughter when I tell you that she is in the habit of playing wild games with the young ladies who have been selected as her companions."

"My poor little Antoinette!" exclaimed the empress, her eyes filling with compassionate tears. "Her enemies, who do not allow her to be a wife, might surely permit her to remain a child! I have heard before to-day, of the harmless diversions which she enjoys with her young sisters-in-law. If there were any sense of justice in France, you would understand that, to amuse half-grown girls, the dauphiness must herself play the child. But I know that she has been blamed for her natural gayety, poor darling; and I know that Madame de Marsan will never forgive her for feeling a sisterly interest in the education of the young princesses of France.* I know that the saloons of Madame de Marsan are a hot-bed of gossip, and that every action of the dauphiness is there distorted into crime.† If my lord cardinal has nothing else to tell me, it was scarcely worth his while to come to the palace in so pompous a manner, with such a solemn face."

"I did not come to your majesty to accuse the dauphiness, but to warn her against her enemies; for unfortunately she *has* enemies at court. These enemies not only deride her private diversions, but, with affectation of outraged virtue, they speak of recreations, hitherto unheard of at the court of France."

"What recreations, pray?"

"The dauphiness, without the sanction of the king, indulges in private theatricals."

"Private theatricals! That must be an invention of her enemies."

"Pardon me, your majesty, it is the truth. The dauphiness and her married sisters-in-law take the female characters, and the brothers of the king the male. Sometimes Monsieur de Campan, the private secretary of the deceased queen, and his son, who fills the same office for the dauphiness, join the actors. The royal

* Madame de Marsan was their governess.

† "Mémoires de Madame de Campan," vol. i., p. 65.

troupe give their entertainments in an empty *entre-sol*, to which the household have no access. The Count of Provence plays the *jeune premier*, but the Count d'Artois also is considered a good performer. I am told that the costumes of the princesses are magnificent, and their rivalry carried to the extreme."

The empress, affecting not to hear the last amiable remark, said: "Who are the audience?"

"There is but one spectator, your majesty, the dauphin himself."

Maria Theresa's face lighted up at once, and she smiled.

The cardinal went on: "The aunts of the dauphin themselves are not admitted to their confidence, lest they might inform the king, and his majesty forbid the indecorous representations."

"I shall write to the dauphiness and advise her to give up these representations," said Maria Theresa, calmly, "not because they are indecorous, but because they are a pretext for her enemies. If she has the approbation of her husband, that of itself ought to suffice to the court; for it is not an unheard thing to have dramatic representations by the royal family. Louis XIV. appeared on the boards as a dancer; and even under the pious Madame de Maintenon, the princes and princesses of France acted the dramas of Corneille and Racine."

"But they had the permission of the king, and none of them were future queens."

"What of that? If the queen approved of the exhibition, the dauphiness might surely repeat it. My daughter is doing no more at Versailles, than she has been accustomed to do at Schönbrunn, in her mother's presence."

"The etiquette of the two courts is dissimilar," said De Rohan, with a shrug. "In Vienna, an archduchess is permitted to do that which, in Paris, would be considered an impropriety."

"Another complaint!" cried the empress, out of patience.

"The dauphiness finds it a bore," continued De Rohan, "to be accompanied wherever she goes, by two ladies of honor. She has, therefore, been seen in the palace, even in the gardens of Versailles, without any escort, except that of two servants."

"Have you come to the end of your complaints?" said the empress, scarcely able to control her passion.

"I have, your majesty. Allow me to add, that the reputation of a woman seldom dies from a single blow—it expires gradually from repeated pricks of the needle. And queens are as liable to such mortality as other women."

"It ill becomes the Prince de Rohan to pass judgment upon the honor of women," cried Maria Theresa, exasperated by his lipmorality. "If the French ambassador presumes to come to me with such trivial complaints as I have heard to-day, I will direct my minister in Paris to make representations to the king of another and a more serious nature."

"Regarding the unpardonable indifference of the dauphin to his wife?" asked the cardinal, with sympathizing air.

"No. Regarding the unpardonable conduct of the French ambassador in Vienna," exclaimed the empress. "If the cardinal is so shocked at a slight breach of etiquette, he should be careful to conceal his own deformities under its sheltering veil. Innocence may sin against ceremony; but he, who leads a dissolute and voluptuous life, should make decorum a shield wherewith to cover his own shame!"

"I thank your majesty for this axiom so replete with worldly wisdom. But for whom can it be intended? Certainly not for the dauphiness."

"No; for yourself, prince and cardinal!" cried the empress, beside herself with anger. "For the prelate who, unmindful of his rank and of its obligations, carries on his shameless intrigues even with the ladies of my court. For the ambassador who, leading a life of Oriental magnificence, is treading under foot the honor of his country, by living upon the credulity of his inferiors. All Vienna knows that your household makes unworthy use of your privileges as a foreign minister, by importing goods free of tax, and reselling them here. All Vienna knows that there are more silk stockings sold at the hotel of the French embassy than in all Paris and Lyons together. The world blames me for having revoked the privilege enjoyed by foreign embassies to import their clothing free of duty. It does not know that the abuse of this privilege by yourself has forced me to the measure."

"Your majesty is very kind to take so much trouble to investigate the affairs of my household. You are more *au fait* to the details than myself. I was not aware, for instance, that silk stockings were sold at the embassy. No more than I was aware that I had had any *amours* with the ladies of the court. I have a very cold heart, and, perhaps, that is the reason why I have never seen one to whom I would devote a second thought. As regards my manner of living, I consider it appropriate to my rank, titles, and means; and that is all that I feel it necessary to say on the subject."

"You dispose of these charges in a summary manner. To hear you, one would really suppose there was not the slightest ground for reproach in your life," said the empress, satirically.

"That this is quite within the range of possibility, is proved by the case of the dauphiness," replied De Rohan. "If your majesty thinks so little of her breaches of etiquette, it seems to me that mine are of still less consequence. And allow me to say, that the French nation will sooner forgive me a thousand intrigues with the ladies of Vienna, than pass over the smallest deviation from court usages on the part of the dauphiness. Marie Antoinette has defied them more than once, and I fear me, she will bitterly repent her thoughtlessness. Her enemies are watchful and—"

"Oh, I see that they are watchful," exclaimed Maria Theresa, "I see it. Do not deny it, you are one of those whose evil eyes see evil doings in every impulse of my dear defenceless child's heart. But have a care, sir cardinal, the friendless dauphiness will one day be Queen of France, and she will then have it in her power to bring to justice those who persecute her now!" *

"I hope that I shall never be accused of such fellowship," said De Rohan, for the first time losing his proud self-possession.

"I, the Empress of Austria, accuse you to-day of it!" cried Maria Theresa, with threatening mien. "Oh, my lord, it does you little honor—you, a royal personage and a prince of the church, to exchange letters with a Du Barry, to whose shameless ears you defame the mother of your future queen!"

* "Mémoires de Madame de Campan," vol. i., p. 47.

"When did I do this? When was I so lost to honor as to speak a disrespectful word of the Empress of Austria?"

"You deny it—do you? Let me tell you that your praise or your blame are all one to me; and if I have granted you this interview, it was to show you how little I am disturbed by your censorious language. I know something of the intriguing at Versailles. I have even heard of the private orgies of the 'Œil de Bœuf,' where Louis entertains his favorites. And I will tell you what took place at the last one. The Countess du Barry was diverting the company with accounts of the hypocrisy of the Empress of Austria; and to prove it, she drew from her pocket-book a letter, saying: 'Hear what the Cardinal de Rohan says about her.' Now, cardinal, do you still deny that you correspond with her?"

"I do deny it," said the prince, firmly. "I deny that I ever have written her a word."

The empress took from her pocket a paper, and read as follows:

"'True, I have seen Maria Theresa weeping over the fate of Poland, but this sovereign, who is such an adept in the art of dissimulation, appears to have tears and sighs at her command. In one hand she holds her pocket-handkerchief, and in the other the sword with which she cuts off a third of that unhappy country.' *

"Now, sir cardinal, upon your sacred honor, did you or did you not write these words?"

The prince turned pale, and grasped the arm of the chair on which he sat.

"Upon your honor and your conscience, before God!" reiterated the empress.

The cardinal raised his eyes slowly, and in a low voice, said:

"I dare not deny it. I wrote them. In an unlucky hour I wrote them—but not to Du Barry."

"To whom, then?"

"To one who has betrayed me to Du Barry. Far be it for me to name him. I alone will bear the weight of your majesty's displeasure. I alone am the culprit."

"I know of no culprit in the matter," replied Maria Theresa, throwing back her stately head. "I stand before God and before the world, and every man has a right to pass sentence upon my actions—even the Cardinal de Rohan. I merely wish to show him that the dauphiness and her mother both know what to expect of his eminence."

"The dauphiness knows of this letter?" cried De Rohan.

"It is she who sent me this copy."

The prince bowed his head down upon his hands.

"I am lost!" murmured he.

The empress surveyed him with mistrust. Such emotion on the part of such a man astonished her, and she doubted its sincerity.

"Why this comedy, prince?" said she. "I have already told you that I am indifferent to your opinion."

"But the dauphiness never will forgive me," said he, uncovering his face. "My contrition is no comedy; for I look with prophetic eyes into the future—and there I see anguish and tears."

"For whom?" said Maria Theresa, scornfully.

"For me, and perchance for the dauphiness. She considers me her enemy, and will treat me as such. But hatred is a two-edged

* "Mémoires de Weber concernant Marie Antoinette," vol. viii., p. 305.

sword which is as apt to wound the one who holds it as the one for whom it is unsheathed. Oh, your majesty, warn the dauphiness! She stands upon the brow of a precipice, and if she do not recede, her enemies will thrust her headlong into the abyss below. Marie Antoinette is an angel of innocence and chastity, but the world in which she lives does not understand the language of angels; and the wicked will soil her wings, that her purity may not be a reproach to their own foulness. Warn the dauphiness to beware of her enemies. But, as God hears me, I am not one of them. Marie Antoinette will never believe me, and, therefore, my fate is sealed. I beg leave of your majesty to withdraw."

Without awaiting the answer, the prince bowed and retired.

Maria Theresa looked thoughtfully after him, and long after he had closed the door, she remained standing in the centre of the room, a prey to the anxious misgivings which his visit had kindled in her heart.

"He is right," said she, after a time. "She wanders upon the edge of a precipice, and I must save her. But, oh my God! where shall I find a friend who will love her enough to brave her displeasure, and, in the midst of the flattery which surrounds her, will raise the honest voice of reproof and censure? Ah, she is so unhappy, my little Antoinette, and I have no power to help her! Oh my God! succor my persecuted child!"

CHAPTER LXXXIX.

THE POLES AT VIENNA.

THE three powers which had lived so long at variance, had united themselves in one common cause—the pacification of Poland. In vain had Stanislaus refused his assent to their friendly intervention. In vain had he appealed to England and France for help. Neither of these powers was willing, for the sake of unhappy Poland, to become involved in a war with three nations, who were ready to hurl their consolidated strength against any sovereign who would have presumed to dispute their joint action.

In vain King Stanislaus began, by swearing, that sooner than consent to the dismemberment of Poland, he would lose his right hand. The three powers, tired of his impotent struggles, informed him, through their envoys at Warsaw, that there were limits to the moderation which decorum prescribed to governments; that they stood upon these limits, and awaited his speedy acquiescence to the act of partition.* The Russian empress added that, if Stanislaus did not call a convention of the Polish Diet to recognize the act, she would devastate his land, so that he would not have a silver spoon left to him.†

The unhappy king had no longer the nerve to brave such terrific threats. He submitted to the will of his tyrants, and came in as a fourth power, eager to obtain as much as he could for his own individual advantage.

The wretched Poles took no notice of the edicts of a king who

* Raumer, "Contributions to Modern History," vol. iv., p. 516.
† Raumer, "Contributions to Modern History," vol. i., p. 507.

had been forced upon them by a strange sovereign. Only a few cowards and hirelings obeyed the call for a convention; so that in all, there were only thirty-six members, who, under the *surveillance* of Austrian and Prussian hussars, signed their names to the act of partition.

The King of Prussia received Pomerelia, and the district of Nantz; Russia took Livonia, and several important waywodeships; and Austria obtained the county of Zips, a portion of Galicia and of Lodomeria, and half of the palatinate of Cracow.

Here and there an isolated voice was raised to protest against the stupendous robbery; but it was lost amidst the clash of arms and the tread of soldiery. Whenever a word was spoken that fretted the sensibilities of Austria or Prussia, Catharine said she was willing to bear all the blame of the thing; and laughing heartily, she called the protests that were sent on the subject, "*moutarde après dîner.*" Frederick resorted to self-deception, proclaiming to the world, "that for the first time the King and the Republic of Poland were established on a firm basis; that they could now apply themselves in peace to the construction of such a government as would tend to preserve the balance of power between proximate nations, and prevent them from clashing." *

The Poles, in silent rancor, submitted to their fate, and took the oath of allegiance to their oppressors. New boundary-lines were drawn, and new names assigned to the sundered provinces of the dismembered fatherland. The citadels were given over to their foreign masters, and now the deed was consummated.

Even Maria Theresa rejoiced to know it, and whether to relieve her burdened heart, or to pretend to the world that she approved of the transaction, she ordered a solemn *Te Deum* to be sung in the cathedral of St. Stephen, in commemoration of the event.

The entire court was to assist at this ceremony, after which the empress was to receive the oath exacted from those of her new subjects who desired to retain possession of their property.

The ladies of the court were in the anteroom, awaiting the entrance of the sovereigns. Their handsome, rouged faces were bright with satisfaction; for they had all suffered from the misery which, for a year past, had been endured by their imperial mistress. Now they might look forward to serene skies and a renewal of court festivities, and they congratulated one another in triumph.

But they were cautious not to give too audible expression to their hopes. They whispered their expectations of pleasure, now and then casting stolen glances at a tall figure in black, which, sorrowful and alone, stood tearfully regarding the crowds in the streets who were hurrying to church to celebrate her country's downfall. This was the Countess von Salmour, governess to the Archduchess Mariana. With the other ladies of the palace, she was to accompany the empress to the cathedral; but it was clear to all beholders that to her this was a day of supreme humiliation.

The great bell of St. Stephen's announced to her people that the empress was about to leave the palace. The folding-doors were flung open, and she appeared leaning on the arm of the emperor, followed by the princes, princesses, generals, and statesmen of her realms. Silently the ladies of honor ranged themselves on either side of the room to let the imperial family pass by. Maria Theresa's

* Raumer, "Contributions," p. 542.

eyes glanced hastily around, and fell upon the pale, wan features of the Countess von Salmour.

All eyes now sought the face of the unhappy lady, whose sad mourning garments were in such striking contrast with the magnificent dresses of the ladies around her.

"Madame von Salmour," said the empress, "I dispense you from your duties for this day. You need not accompany the court to church."

The countess courtesied deeply, and replied: "Your majesty is right to excuse me; for had I gone with the court to church, I might have been tempted to utter treason to Heaven against the oppressors of my country."

The company were aghast at the audacity of the rejoinder, but the empress replied with great mildness:

"You are right; for the temptation would indeed be great, and it is noble of you to speak the truth. I respect your candor."

She was about to pass on, but paused as if she had forgotten something.

"Is the Countess Wielopolska in Vienna?" asked she.

"She arrived yesterday, your majesty."

"Go to her while we are at church," said Maria Theresa, compassionately.

Madame von Salmour glanced toward the emperor, who, with an expression of painful embarrassment, was listening to their conversation.

"Pardon me, your majesty," said the lady, "the Countess Wielo" polska is making preparations for a journey, and she receives no one. We parted yesterday. To-morrow she leaves Vienna forever."

"I am glad that she intends to travel," said Maria Theresa, approvingly. "It will divert her mind;" and with a friendly smile, she took leave of the governess, and passed on.

Joseph followed with wildly throbbing heart; and neither the triumphant strains of the *Te Deum*, nor the congratulatory shouts of his subjects, could bring back serenity to his stormy brow. He knelt before the altar, and with burning shame thought of his first entry into St. Stephen's as Emperor of Austria. It had been the anniversary of the deliverance of Vienna by John Sobieski and his Poles; and in the self-same spot where the emperor had thanked God for this deliverance, he now knelt in acknowledgment of the new principalities which were the fruits of his own ingratitude to Poland.

From these painful and humiliating retrospections, the emperor's thoughts wandered to the beautiful being, who, like a hamadryad, had blended her life with the tree of Polish liberty. He thought of that face whose pallid splendor reminded him of the glories of waning day; and he listened through the long, dim aisles of memory, to the sound of that enchanting voice, whose melody had won his heart long ago on that first, happy evening at Neustadt.

The Countess Wielopolska was leaving Vienna forever, and yet there was no message for him. A longing, that seemed to drown him in the flood of its intensity, rushed over his soul. He would fly to her presence and implore her to forgive the chant of victory that was rejoicing over her country's grave! Oh, the crash of that stunning harmony, how it maddened him, as kneeling, he listened to its last exultant notes!

VIEW OF VIENNA IN THE REIGN OF JOSEPH II.

From an engraving in The Royal Magazine.

It was over, and Joseph scarcely knew where he was, until his mother laid her hand upon his shoulder and motioned him to rise.

In the great reception-room, with all the pomp of imperial splendor, Maria Theresa sat upon her throne and received the homage of her new subjects. Each one, as he passed, knelt before the powerful empress, and as he rose, the chief marshal of the household announced his name and rank. The ceremony over, Maria Theresa descended from the throne to greet her Polish subjects in a less formal manner. No one possessed to a greater degree than herself the art of bewitching those whom she desired to propitiate; and to-day, though her youth and beauty were no longer there to heighten the charms of her address, her elegant carriage, her ever-splendid eyes, and graceful affability, were as potent to win hearts as ever. Discontent vanished from the faces of the Poles, and by and by they gathered into groups, in which were mingled Hungarians, Italians, and Austrians, all the subjects of that one great empress.

The majority of the Poles had adopted the French costume of the day. Few had possessed the hardihood to appear before their new sovereign in their rich national dress. Among these few was an old man of tall stature and distinguished appearance, who attracted the attention of every one present.

While his countrymen unbent their brows to the sunshine of Maria Theresa's gracious words, he remained apart in the recess of a window. With scowling mien and folded arms, he surveyed the company; nor could the empress herself, obtain from him more than a haughty inclination of the head.

The emperor was conversing gayly with two Polish noblemen, whose cheerful demeanor bore evidence to the transitory nature of their national grief, when he observed this old man.

"Can you tell me," said he, "the name of yonder proud and angry nobleman?"

The faces of the two grew scarlet, as following the direction of the emperor's finger, they saw the eyes of the old man fixed, with scorn, upon their smiling countenances.

"That," said one of them, uneasily, "is Count Kannienski."

"Ah, the old partisan leader!" exclaimed the emperor. "As he does not seem inclined to come to me, I will go forward and greet him myself."

So saying, Joseph crossed over to the window where the old count was standing. He received him with a cold, solemn bow.

"I rejoice to meet Count Kannienski, and to express to him my esteem for his character," began the emperor, reaching out his hand.

The count did not appear to perceive the gesture, and merely made a silent bow. But Joseph would not be deterred from his purpose by a *hauteur* which he knew very well how to excuse.

"Is this your first visit to Vienna?" asked he.

"My first and last visit, sire."

"Are you pleased with the Austrian capital?"

"No, your majesty, Vienna does not please me."

The emperor smiled. Instead of being irritated at the haughtiness with which his advances were met, he felt both respect and sympathy for the noble old man who disdained to conceal his discontent from the eyes of the sovereign himself.

"I wonder that you do not like Vienna. It has great attractions for strangers, and you meet so many of your countrymen here just now!—there were never as many Poles in Vienna before."

An angry glance shot athwart the face of the old man. "There were many more when John Sobieski delivered Vienna from the hands of *her* enemies," said he. "But that is almost a hundred years ago, and the memory of princes does not extend so far to the obligations of the past.* But," continued he, more courteously, "I did not come here to speak of my country. We must be resigned to the fate apportioned to us by Providence, and you see how readily my countrymen adapt themselves to the vicissitudes of their national life."

"And yet, count, their smiles are less pleasing to me than your frowns. In spite of the present, I cherish the past, and honor those who mourn over the misfortunes of their native land."

The old man was touched, and looked at the handsome, expressive face of the emperor. "Sire," said he, sadly, "if Stanislaus had resembled you, Poland would have been free. But I have not come hither to-day to whine over the unalterable past. Nor did I come to pay homage to the empress."

"Nevertheless the empress would rejoice to become acquainted with the brave Count Kannienski. Allow me, count, to present you."

Kannienski shook his gray locks. "No, sire, I came to Vienna purely for the sake of a woman who will die under the weight of this day's anguish. I came to console her with what poor consolation I have to bestow."

"Is she a Pole?" asked Joseph, anxiously.

"Yes, sire; she is the last true-hearted Polish woman left on earth, and I fear she is about to die upon the grave of her fatherland."

"May I ask her name?"

"Countess Anna Wielopolska. She it is who sent me to the palace, and I came because she asked of me one last friendly service."

"You bring me a message?" faltered the emperor.

"The countess begs to remind the emperor of the promise he made on the day when the empress signed the act of—"

"I remember," interrupted the emperor.

"She asks, if mindful of his promise, he will visit her to-morrow afternoon at six o'clock."

"Where shall I find her?"

"In the very same room which she occupied before. I have delivered my message. Your majesty will, therefore, permit me to withdraw."

He bowed and turned away. Slowly and proudly he made his way through the giddy crowd, without a word of recognition for the frivolous Poles who saluted him as he passed.

"He is the last Polish hero, as she is the last Polish heroine," sighed the emperor, as he followed the old man with his eyes. "Our destiny is accomplished. She would bid me a last farewell."

* This whole conversation is historical. It was often related by the emperor, who said that he had been so touched by Count Kannienski's patriotism and boldness, that but for the fear of a repulse, he would have embraced him. Swinburne, vol. i., page 349.

CHAPTER XC.

THE LAST FAREWELL.

COUNTESS ANNA WIELOPOLSKA was alone in her room, which, like herself, was decked to receive some great and distinguished guest. A rich carpet covered the floor, flowers bloomed in costly vases, the piano was opened, and the music on the stand showed that the countess still found consolation in her genius. But she herself was strangely altered since the day on which she had thrown her bouquet to the emperor in Neustadt. Nevertheless she wore the same dress of black velvet, the same jewels, and in her bosom the same bouquet of white roses, bound with a long scarlet ribbon.

Her heart beat high, and her anxious eyes wandered to the little bronze clock that stood upon a *console* opposite. The clock struck six, and her pale cheek flushed with anticipated happiness.

"It is the hour," said she. "I shall see him once more." And as she spoke, a carriage stopped, and she heard his step within the vestibule below. Trembling in every limb, she approached the door, and bent her ear to listen.

"Yes, he comes," whispered she, while, with a gesture of extreme agitation, she drew from her pocket a little case, whence she took a tiny flask, containing a transparent, crimson liquid. She held it for a few seconds to the light, and now she could hear the sound of his voice, as he spoke with Matuschka in the anteroom. The steps came nearer and nearer yet.

"It is time," murmured she; and hastily moving the golden capsule that covered the vial, she put it to her lips and drank it to the last drop.

"One hour of happiness," said she, replacing the vial in her pocket, and hastening back to the door.

It was opened, and the emperor entered the room. Anna met him with both hands outstretched, and smiled with unmistakable love as he came forward to greet her. Silent, but with visible agitation, the emperor looked into those eyes, which were already resplendent with the glory of approaching death. Long they gazed upon each other without a word, yet speaking love with eyes and lips.

Suddenly the emperor dropped her hands, and laying his own gently upon her cheeks, he drew down her head, and rested it upon his breast. She left it there, and looked up with a tender smile.

"Do not speak, love," said he. "I am an astrologer, who looks into his heaven to read the secrets there. And, oh," sighed he, after he had gazed for a time, "I see sorrow and suffering written upon that snowy brow. Tears have dimmed the splendor of my stars, but they have not been able to lessen their beauty. I know you again, my queen of the night, as you first appeared to me at Neustadt. You are still the same proud being, Anna."

"No, dearest, no. I am a trembling woman, craving nothing from earth save the glance of my beloved, and the privilege of dying in his embrace."

"She who loves, desires to live for her lover," said he, pressing her again and again to his heart.

"Death is the entrance to eternal life, and she who truly loves will love throughout eternity."

"Speak not of death in this hour of ecstasy, when I have found you once more as I had pictured you in dreams. Oh, Anna, Anna! will you part me from you again? Have you indeed brought me hither to cheat me with visions of love, and then to say farewell, forever!"

"No, Joseph, I bid you eternal welcome. Oh, my lover, my soul has gone forth to meet yours, and nothing shall ever part us again."

"And are you mine at last!" cried Joseph, kissing her passionately. "Has the statue felt the ray of love, and uttered its first sweet sound? Oh, how I longed to hear that sound! I have gone about by day, wearing the weight of sovereignty upon my fainting shoulders; and by night I have wept like a lovesick boy for your sake, Anna; but no one suspected it. No one knew that the emperor was unhappy."

"I knew it," whispered she—"I knew it; for your sorrows have all been mine."

"No, no!" cried Joseph, awaking from his dream of bliss, "you told me that Poland was dearer to you than I. I remember it now! You refused me your hand, and forsook me for the sake of your country."

"But, now, beloved," said she, clinging to him, "now I am but a woman—a woman who abandons her fatherland with all its memories, and asks but one blessing of Heaven—the blessing of living and dying in her lover's arms."

"Oh, if you would not kill me, speak no more of dying, Anna! Now you are mine—mine for life; and my heart leaps with joy as it did when first I heard your heavenly voice. Let me hear it once more. Sing to me, my treasure."

She went to the harpsichord, and the emperor bent over her, smiling as he watched the motion of her graceful hands upon the keys. She struck a few full chords, and then glided into a melody of melancholy sweetness. The emperor listened attentively; then, suddenly smiling, he recognized the song which she had sung before the King of Prussia and himself.

The words were different now. They represented Poland as a beggared queen, wandering from door to door, repulsed by all. She is starving, but she remembers that death will release her from shame and hunger.

The countess was singing these lines—

> "If life to her hath brought disgrace,
> Honor returns with death's embrace——"

when she stopped and her hands fell powerless from the instrument. The emperor raised her head, and saw wtih alarm that her face was distorted by pain. Without a word, he took her in his arms, and, carrying her across the room, laid her gently upon the sofa. She raised her loving eyes to his, and tried to steal her arm around his neck, but it fell heavily to her side. Joseph saw it, and a pang of apprehension shook his manly frame.

"Anna!" groaned he, "what means this?"

"Honor returns with death's embrace," whispered she.

The emperor uttered a savage cry, and raised his despairing arms to heaven. "And it was false," cried he, almost mad with grief—

"it was false! She had not forgotten Poland. Oh, cruel, cruel Anna!" and he sobbed piteously, while she strove to put her trembling hand upon his head.

"Cruel to myself, Joseph, for I have just begun to value life. But I swore to my mother that I would not outlive the disgrace of Poland; and you would have ceased to love me had I violated my oath. Forgive the pain I inflict upon you, dearest. I longed for one single hour of happiness, and I have found it here. With my dying breath I bless you."

"Is there no remedy?" asked he, scarcely able to speak.

"None," said she, with a fluttering smile. "I obtained the poison from Cagliostro. Nay—dear one, do not weep; you see that I could not live. Oh, do not hide your face from me; let me die with my eyes fixed upon yours!"

"And," cried Joseph, "must I live forever?"

"You must live for your subjects—live to be great and good, yet ever mistrusted, ever misunderstood. But onward, my prince, and the blessing of God be upon you! Think, too, that the Poles, my brethren, are among your subjects, and promise me to love and cherish them?"

"I promise."

"Try to reconcile them to their fate—do not return their ill-will; swear to me that you will be clement to my countrymen?"

"I swear! I swear to respect their misfortunes, and to make them happy!"

One last, beaming smile illuminated her face. "Thank you—dearest," said she, with difficulty. "My spirit shall look out from the eye of every Pole, to whom you will have given—one moment—of joy! Oh, what agony! Farewell!"

One more look—one shudder—and all was still.

The emperor fell upon his knees by the body, and prayed long and fervently. The little clock struck seven. The hour of happiness had passed away forever.

The following day, Joseph, pale, but perfectly calm, sought an interview with his mother.

"I come to ask leave of absence of your majesty," said he, languidly.

"Leave of absence, my son? Do you wish to travel again so soon?"

"I *must* travel, your majesty. I must make a journey to Galicia, to become acquainted with our new subjects."

"Perhaps it might be as well for us to show them some consideration at this period. I had already thought of this; but I have been told that Galicia is rather an uncivilized country, and that the people are ill-disposed toward us."

"We cannot expect them to love their oppressors, your majesty."

"No—but it is a dreadful country. No roads—no inns—miles and miles of uninhabited woods, infested by robbers. Oh, my son, postpone your journey to a milder season! I shall be trembling for your safety."

"There is no danger, your majesty. Give me your consent; I am very, very desirous of visiting Poland."

"But no vehicle can travel there at this time of year, my son."

"I will go on horseback, your majesty."

"But where will you get provisions, Joseph? Where will you rest at night?"

"I will rest wherever night overtakes me, either in a cottage, on my horse, or on the ground. And as for food, mother, if there is food for our people, there will be some for me; and if there should be scarcity, it is but just that I should share their hardships. Let me go, I entreat you."

"Go, then, my son, and God's blessing be with you," said the empress, kissing her son's forehead.

"Joseph!" said she, as he was leaving the room, "have you heard that the poor young Countess Anna has committed suicide on account of the troubles in Poland?"

"Yes, your majesty," replied Joseph, without flinching.

"Perhaps you had better defer your journey for a day to attend her funeral. All the Poles will be there; and as we both knew and admired her, I think it would propitiate our new subjects if we gave some public mark of sympathy by following the body to the grave. I have forbidden mention to be made of the manner of her death, that she may not be denied a resting-place within consecrated ground."

How she probed his wound until the flesh quivered with agony!

"The Countess Wielopolska is not to be interred in Austria, your majesty," said he. "Count Kannienski will accompany the body to Poland. Near Cracow there is a mound wherein it is said that Wanda, the first Queen of Poland, was buried. Anna Wielopolska will share her tomb. Her heroic spirit could rest nowhere save in Poland. When I visit Cracow I will go thither to plant flowers upon her grave, that the white roses she loved may grow from the consecrated earth that lies upon her heart."

CHAPTER XCI.

THE CONCERT.

THERESE PARADIES was to give a concert, the first at which she had performed since the restoration of her sight. Of course, the hall was thronged, for in spite of the incontrovertible fact itself, and of its corroboration by the Paradies family, there were two parties in Vienna—one who believed in the cure, and the other who did not. Those who did not, doubted upon the respectable testimony of Professor Barth, Doctor Ingenhaus, and the entire faculty, who, one and all, protested against the shameful imposition which Mesmer was practising upon an enlightened public.

The audience, therefore, was less interested in Therese's music, wonderful as it was, than in her eyes; for her father had announced that during the pauses Therese would prove to the incredulous that her cure was no deception.

Professor Barth, Doctor Ingenhaus, and the astronomer were there in the front row, sneering away the convictions of all who were within hearing. Herr Paradies now appeared, and as he stood reckoning the profits that were to gladden his pockets on that eventful evening, Barth left his seat and approached him.

"You really believe, do you, that your daughter sees?" said the professor.

"She sees as well as I do. Were you not there to witness it yourself when her bandage was removed?"

"I humored the jest to see how far the impudence of Mesmer and the credulity of his admirers would travel together. I hear curious accounts of your daughter's mistakes, granting her the use of her eyesight. It is said that some one presented her a flower, when, looking at it, she remarked, 'What a pretty star!' And did she not put a hair-pin in her mother's cheek while trying to fasten her hair?"

"Yes, she did both these things, but I think they prove her to be making awkward use of a new faculty. She is not likely to know the name of a thing when she sees it for the first time; neither has she learned to appreciate distances. Objects quite close to her she sometimes stumbles upon, and those out of reach she puts out her hand to take. All this will correct itself, and when Therese has become as familiar with prospective illusions as the rest of us, she will go out into the streets, and the world will be convinced."

"You really believe it, then?"

"I am as convinced of it as that I see myself."

"It is very disinterested of you to publish it," said the professor, looking significantly at the happy father. "This acknowledgment will cost you a considerable sum."

"How?" asked Von Paradies, frightened. "I do not understand."

"It is very simple, nevertheless," said the professor, carelessly. "Does the empress give your daughter a pension?"

"Certainly. You know she does, and a handsome one, too."

"Of course it is lost to her," replied Barth, enjoying the sudden paleness which overspread the radiant face of Von Paradies. "A girl who sees has no right to the money which is given to the blind; and I heard Von Stork this very day saying that as soon as it was proved that your daughter could see, he intended to apply to the empress for her pension in behalf of another party."

"But this pension is our chief support; it enables us to live very comfortably. If it were withdrawn, I should be a beggar."

"That would not alter the case. Pensions are granted to those who by their misfortunes have a claim upon the public charity. The claim dies from the moment that your daughter's infirmity is removed. Through the favor of the empress she has become a scientific musician, and this now must be her capital. She can teach music and give concerts."

"But that will not maintain us respectably," urged Von Paradies, with increasing uneasiness.

"Of course it will not maintain you as you live with your handsome pension. But you need not starve. Be that as it may, there is a blind countess who is my patient, for whom Von Stork is to obtain the pension as soon as you can convince the faculty that your daughter is no longer in need of it. This patient, I assure you, will receive it as long as she lives, for it will never enter into her head to fancy that she has been cured by Master Mesmer."

"But, my dear professor," entreated Von Paradies, "have mercy on me and my family! For sixteen years we have received this income, and it had been secured to us during Therese's lifetime."

"Nevertheless, it goes to the countess, if she is not blind, I tell you. The empress (so says Von Stork) has never refused a request of his, because he never asks any thing but that which is just and reasonable."

"We are ruined!" exclaimed Von Paradies, in accents of despair.

"Not unless you prove to us that your daughter *is not deceiving you,*" replied Barth, with sharp emphasis. "If you can show her to be blind, you are saved; and Von Stork would petition the empress, in consideration of the shameful imposition practised upon your paternal love, to increase the pension. Well—this evening's entertainment will decide the matter. Meanwhile, adieu!"

The professor lounged back to his seat, leaving his poisoned arrow behind.

"I think," said Barth, smiling, as he saw the victim writhe, "that I have given him a receipt for his daughter's eyes that will be more potent than Mesmer's passes. It will never do to restore the age of miracles."

"No, indeed; if miracles are to make their appearance upon the stage of this world, what becomes of science?" asked Ingenhaus.

"Let us await the end of the farce," said the professor. "Here she comes."

A murmur went through the hall as Therese entered. The guests rose from their seats to obtain a sight of her. They had known her from infancy; but to-night she was an object of new and absorbing interest, even to the elegant crowd, who seldom condescended to be astonished at any thing.

Therese seemed to feel her position, for whereas she had been accustomd to trip into the concert-room with perfect self-possession, she now came timidly forward, with downcast eyes. The audience had always received her with enthusiasm, for she was a great *artiste;* but now perfect silence greeted her entrance, for nothing was remembered, save the marvel which her appearance there was to attest.

Whether accidentally or intentionally, several chairs were in her way as she passed to the instrument. She avoided them with perfect confidence, scarcely brushing them with the folds of her white satin dress.

"She is cured! She is no longer blind!" murmured the spectators; and with renewed curiosity, they watched her every motion.

There were three people within the concert-room upon whom these murmurs produced profound and dissimilar impressions.

Barth frowned angrily; Von Paradies grew paler and trembled like a coward as he was; while Mesmer, who leaned against a pillar, fixed his eyes upon Therese with a glance of supreme happiness. Therese returned the glance with one of such deep trust and love, that no one who saw it could doubt her power of vision. The audience burst out into one simultaneous storm of applause, and this reminded the young girl that she was not alone with her "master." She raised her eyes for the first time toward the spectators, and met every glance directed toward herself.

The sight of this sea of upturned faces so terrified the poor child, that she felt faint and dizzy. She groped about with her hands, to find a seat, for she could scarcely stand.

The action attracted universal attention. A significant look passed between Von Paradies and Barth, while Mesmer's brow darkened, and his face flushed with disappointment. It was very unfortunate—that faintness of Therese.

She stood irresolute and alone, unable to advance, and too weak to see the chair that stood close at hand.

For some time, the audience surveyed her with breathless interest. Suddenly the silence was broken by a voice in the crowd:

"Will no one take pity upon the girl and lead her to the harpsichord? Do you not see that she is as blind as ever?"

Therese recovered herself when she heard these insulting words, and her eyes flashed strangely for eyes that could not see.

"I am not blind!" cried she, in a clear, firm voice, and as if the sneer had restored her strength and self-possession, she came forward at once, and took her seat.

The audience applauded a second time, and Therese bowed and smiled. While she drew off her gloves, she looked back at Mesmer, who returned the glance with one of affectionate pride.

Scarcely knowing what she did, Therese began to play. She kept her eyes fixed upon Mesmer, and as she felt the power of his magnetic glance, she soared into heights of harmony that ravished the ears of her listeners, and left all her previous performances far behind.

She ended with a sigh, as though awaking from some heavenly dream. Never had she been so enthusiastically applauded as now. This time it was not her vision, but her incomparable skill which had elicited the acclamations of the public; and Therese, happy in her success, bowed, and smiled again upon her admirers.

And now the artistic exhibition was at an end. Herr von Paradies, advancing, informed the public, that they would now proceed to test the genuineness of his daughter's cure. He then came to the edge of the platform, and spoke in a loud, distinct voice: "I request the distinguished company, who have brought books or music for the purpose, to hand them to me, that we may discover whether in truth she sees, or imagines that she sees. I beg so much the more for your attention, ladies and gentlemen," continued he, in a faltering voice, "that this night is to decide a fearful doubt in my own mind. Doctor Mesmer affirms that my daughter's vision has been restored. I, alas! believe that she is yet blind!"

The audience expressed astonishment; Therese uttered a cry of horror, and turned to Mesmer, who, pale and stunned by the shock of her father's cruel words, had lost all power to come to the poor child's assistance.

Barth was laughing behind his pocket-handkerchief. "The remedy works," whispered he to Ingenhaus—"the remedy works."

Two gentlemen arose. One handed a book, the other a sheet of music. As Von Paradies turned the book over to his daughter, she gave him a reproachful look. She opened it and read: "Emilia Galotti, by Gotthold Ephraim Lessing."

"And, now," continued she, "if one of the ladies present will select a passage, and another will look over me as I read, the audience can thus convince themselves that I see."

One of the most distinguished ladies in Vienna approached Therese and stood close by her side, while another, a celebrated actress, requested her to open the book at page 71.

Therese turned over the leaves and found the place.

"That is right, my love," said the countess. "Now read."

Therese began to read, and when she ended, the excitement of the people knew no bounds.

"She sees! She sees!" cried the people. "Who can doubt it?"

And now from the crowd arose a voice:

"We have enough proof. The fact is self-evident, and we may all congratulate the *fraulein* upon the recovery of her sight. Let us have more of her delightful music."

"I am sorry that I cannot agree with Doctor Mesmer's invisible patron," said Von Paradies. "I strive to forget that I am her father, and place myself on the side of the incredulous public, who have a right to demand whether indeed the days of miracles have returned."

"My remedy does wonders," said Barth to the faculty.

Herr von Paradies continued: "This being the case, it is easier for us to suppose that the distinguished actress, who selected the page, has been requested to do so, than to believe that my daughter has seen the words just read; for this lady is known to be a follower of Doctor Mesmer. Perhaps the countess did not remark that the corner of the leaf is slightly turned down."

He took the book and passed the leaves rapidly over his thumb.

"Here it is," said he, holding it up.

"Father!" exclaimed Therese, indignantly, "I saw you turn the leaf a few minutes ago with your own hand."

"SAW!" cried Von Paradies, raising his hands. Then turning to the audience, he continued: "As regards this book, it was handed to me just now by Baron von Horka, one of Mesmer's most devoted adherents. He may have been commissioned to select this particular work, and Therese may be aware of it. If I am thus stringent in my acceptance of the evidence in this case, it is because I long to possess the sweet assurance of my dear child's complete cure."

"Hear him," laughed Barth, touching Ingenhaus on the elbow.

Therese, meanwhile, was growing embarrassed; and, looking to Mesmer for encouragement she lost sight of every thing under the influence of his eyes. Her father held the paper before her, but she was not aware of it. The audience whispered, but Mesmer at that moment, turning away from Therese, she sighed, and, recovering her self-possession, took the paper and placed it before the harpsichord.

"March, from 'Œdipus,'" said she, seating herself before the instrument.

"Why, Therese," cried her father, "you read the title without turning to the title-page."

"I saw the piece when it was handed to you by Ritter Gluck."

"You are acquainted with Gluck?" asked Von Paradies. "He has never been to our house."

"I have seen him at Doctor Mesmer's," replied Therese.

"Ah, indeed! Ritter Gluck, who hands the music, is like Baron von Horka, who brought the book, a friend of Mesmer's," said Von Paradies, with a sneer that affrighted his daughter and made her tremble.

But she placed her hands upon the keys and began to play.

The enraptured audience again forgot her eyes, and, entranced by the music, hung breathless upon her notes, while she executed the magnificent funeral march in "Œdipus." Suddenly, at the conclusion of a passage of exquisite beauty, she ceased, and her hands wandered feebly over the keys. Her father, who was turning the leaves, looked almost scornfully at the poor girl; who, alarmed and bewildered by his unaccountable conduct, grew deadly pale, and finally, with a deep sigh, closed her eyes.

After a few moments she began again. From her agile fingers dropped showers of pearly notes, while, through all the fanciful combinations of sound, was heard the solemn and majestic chant of the funeral march. The audience could scarcely contain their raptures; and yet they dared not applaud for fear of losing a note.

She seemed to be astray in a wilderness of harmony, when her father, with an impatient gesture, laid his hands upon her fingers and held them down.

"You are no longer playing by note!" exclaimed he, with affected surprise. "You are giving us voluntaries from 'Orpheus,' instead of the funeral march. I appeal to the public to say whether my daughter is playing the funeral march?"

There was a pause, then a voice, tremulous with emotion, said, "No, it is no longer the funeral march; it is now a beautiful arrangement from 'Orpheus.'"

Herr von Paradies, with an expression of profoundest anguish, threw his arm around his daughter, exclaiming, "Oh, my beloved child, it is then as I feared! We have been deceived, and you are blind for life."

"Father!" screamed Therese, flinging him off; "father, you know—"

"I know that you are blind," cried he, following her, and again clasping her in his arms. "Come, my poor child, come, and fear nothing! Your father will work for you; and his hand shall guide your faltering steps. Oh, my child! May God forgive those who have brought this bitter disappointment upon my head! My dream of hope is over. You are blind, Therese, hopelessly blind, and your father's heart is broken!"

The audience were deeply moved by this outburst of paternal grief and tenderness. Here and there were heard half-audible murmurs of sympathy, and many of the ladies had their handkerchiefs to their eyes. Everybody was touched except Professor Barth. He, on the contrary, was chuckling with satisfaction, and felt much more inclined to applaud than to commiserate. He looked at Ingenhaus, who, not being in the secret, was divided between sympathy for the father and indignation toward the charlatan. Indeed, he had so far forgotten his own interest in the scene, that he was weeping with the rest.

"Console yourself, my friend," said Barth, "all this is the result of my efforts in behalf of science. I deserve a public vote of thanks for having out-mesmered Mesmer."

He stopped—for Therese's voice was heard in open strife with her father. "Let me go!" cried she, with passion. "I am not blind. As God hears me, I see—but oh, how fearful have been the revelations that sight has made to me this night!"

Poor, poor Therese! The shock of her father's treachery had proved too great for her girlish frame. She reeled and fell back insensible in his arms.

Von Paradies, with simulated anguish, turned to the audience and bowed his stricken head. Then raising his daughter in his arms, he carried her away from the stage.

CHAPTER XCII.

THE CATASTROPHE.

THERESE lay for several hours unconscious, while her mother wept, and watched over her, and her father stood by, sullenly awaiting the result.

At last she heaved a sigh and opened her eyes. "Where am I?" asked she, feebly.

"At home, darling," replied the tender mother, bending over and kissing her.

"No—I am in the fearful concert-room. They stare at me with those piercing daggers which men call eyes; and oh, their glances hurt me, mother! There they sit, heartlessly applauding my misery, because it has shaped itself into music! Let me go; I am strong, and I SEE!"

She attempted to rise, but her father held her back. "Lie still, my child," said he, reproachfully; "it is in vain for you to carry this deception further. Trust your parents, and confess that you are blind. Were it otherwise, you would not mistake your own familiar chamber for the vast concert-room. For Mesmer's sake, you have sought to deceive us, but it is useless, for we know that you are blind."

"You are blind—you are blind!" These oft-repeated words seemed fraught with a power that almost made her doubt her own senses. She saw, and yet she felt as if sight were receding from her eyes.

"Oh, my God! Why will my father madden me!" cried the unhappy girl, rising in spite of all efforts to detain her, and looking around the room. "Ah—now I remember, I fainted and was brought home. Yes, father, yes, I tell you that I see," cried she, wringing her hands, and writhing with the agony he was inflicting upon her. "I see in the window the blue flower-pot which Mesmer brought me yesterday—there opposite stands my harpsichord, and its black and white keys are beckoning me to come and caress them. Two open books lie upon the table, and over it are scattered drawings and engravings. Oh, father, have I not described things as they are?"

"Yes, child—you have long been familiar with this room, and need not the help of eyes to describe it."

"And then," continued she, "I see you both. I see my mother's dear face, tender as it was when first my eyes opened to the light of its love; and, my father, I see you with the same frown that terrified me in the concert-room—the same scowl that to my frightened fancy, seemed that of some mocking fiend who sought to drive me back to blindness! What is it, father? What has changed you so that you love your child no longer, and seek to take the new life that God has just bestowed?"

"God has bestowed nothing upon you, and I will no longer be the tool of an impostor," replied he, morosely. "Am I to be the laughing-stock of Vienna, while men of distinction see through the tricks of the charlatan? I must and will have the strength to confess my folly, and to admit that you are blind."

Therese uttered a cry, and shook as though a chill had seized her. "O God, help me!" murmured the poor girl, sinking in her mother's outstretched arms, and weeping piteously. Suddenly she raised her head and gradually her face brightened, her cheeks flushed, her lips parted with a smile, and her large expressive eyes beamed with happiness. Once more she trembled—but with joy, and leaning her head upon her mother's shoulder, she whispered, "He comes."

The door opened, and Mesmer's tall and commanding figure advanced toward the group. Therese flew to meet him and grasped his hands in hers.

"Come, master, come and shield me! God be thanked, you are here to shelter me. If you leave again, I shall lose my sight."

He passed his hands lightly over her face, and looked earnestly into her eyes.

"You are dissatisfied with me, master," said she anxiously. "You are displeased at my childish behavior. I know that I was silly; but when I saw those multitudinous heads so close together, all with eyes that were fixed on me alone, I began again to feel afraid of my own race. It seemed as if the walls were advancing to meet me—and I retreated in terror."

"What confused you at the harpsichord, child?"

"The sight of the small, dazzling notes, and the singular motions of my own fingers. I am so unaccustomed to see, that hands and notes appeared to be dancing a mad Morrisco, until at last I grew confused and saw nothing."

"All this is so natural," said Mesmer sadly. "for the seat of your infirmity lay in the nerves. And now that they require rest, you are a prey to agitation and to tears. Unhappy Therese, there are some who seek to plunge you back into the darkness from whence I have rescued you!"

She put her arms upon his shoulders and sobbed, "Save me, master, save me—I could not bear blindness now!"

At the other end of the room stood Von Paradies and his wife. She laid her hand upon his arm, saying imploringly:

"What signifies all this mystery, husband? Why do you torture our little Therese so cruelly? You know that she sees; why, then, do you—"

"Peace!" interrupted Von Paradies angrily. "If Therese does not become blind again, we shall lose our pension."

"My poor child," sobbed the mother, "you are lost!"

"I have come to your help, Therese," said Mesmer audibly. "I know all that is passing under this roof," continued he, with a look of scorn at her parents. "They are trying to deprive you of your sight, and they well know that excitement and weeping will destroy it. But my name and honor are linked with your fortunes, child and I shall struggle for both. I have come to take you to the villa with my other patients. You shall be under my wife's care, and will remain with us until your eyes are fortified against nervous impressions. The carriage is at the door."

"I am ready to go," replied Therese, joyfully.

"I will not suffer her to leave the house!" cried Von Paradies, striding angrily forward. "Therese is my daughter, and shall not be torn from her father's protection."

"She goes with me," thundered Mesmer with eyes that flashed lightning, like those of Olympian Zeus. "You gave her to me as a patient, and until she is cured she belongs to her physician."

He took Therese in his arms and carried her toward the door

But Von Paradies, with a roar like that of some wild animal, placed himself before it and defended the passage.

"Let me pass," cried he.

"Go—but first put down Therese."

"No—you shall not deprive her of the sight I have bestowed." With these words, he raised his muscular right arm, and swinging off Von Paradies as if he had been a child, Mesmer passed the opening and stood outside.

"Farewell, and fear nothing," cried he, "for your pension will not be withdrawn. Therese is once more blind. But as God is just, I will restore her again to sight!"

Mesmer, however, was destined to be foiled. His enemies were richer and more influential than he; and Von Paradies, in mortal terror for his pension, sustained them. Von Stork obtained an order, commanding the relinquishment of Therese to her natural guardians; and her father, armed with the document, went and demanded his daughter. Therese flew to Mesmer's arms, and a fearful scene ensued. It shall be described in Mesmer's own words.

"The father of Therese, resolved to carry her away by main force, rushed upon me with an unsheathed sword. I succeeded in disarming him, but the mother and daughter both fell insensible at my feet: the former from terror, the latter because her unnatural father had hurled her against the wall, where she had struck her head with such violence as to lose all consciousness. Madame von Paradies recovered and went home; but poor Therese was in a state of such nervous agony that she lost her sight entirely. I trembled for her life and reason. Having no desire to revenge myself upon her parents, I did all that I could to save her. Herr von Paradies, sustained by those who had instigated him, filled Vienna with the cry of persecution. I became an object of universal contumely, and a second order was obtained by which I was commanded to deliver Therese to her father." *

From this time Therese remained blind, and continued to give concerts in Vienna, as she had done before. Barth and his accomplices were triumphant; and Mesmer, disgusted with his countrymen, left Vienna, and made his home in Paris.

Therese von Paradies then, as her father asserted, was blind. Whether she ever was any thing else, remains to this day an open question. The faculty denied furiously that she had seen: Mesmer's friends, on the contrary, declared solemnly that she had been restored by animal magnetism; but that her cruel father, for the sake of the pension, had persecuted her, and so succeeded in destroying her eyesight forever.

* Justinus Kerner, "Franz Anton Mesmer," p. 70.

MARIE ANTOINETTE.

CHAPTER XCIII.

LE ROI EST MORT, VIVE LE ROI!

It was the evening of the tenth of May, 1774. The palace of Versailles, the seat of royal splendor, was gloomy, silent, and empty. Regality, erst so pleasure-loving and voluptuous, now lay with crown all dim, and purple all stained, awaiting the last sigh of an old, expiring king, whose demise was to restore to it an inheritance of youth, beauty, and strength.

In one wing of the palace royalty hovered over a youthful pair, as the genius of hope; in another it frowned upon the weak old king as the implacable angel of death.

Louis the Fifteenth was balancing the great account of his life—a life of luxury, voluptuousness, and supreme selfishness. Yielding to the entreaties of his daughters, he had sent for the Archbishop of Paris; but knowing perfectly well that the sacraments of the church would not be administered under a roof which was polluted by the presence of Du Barry, the old libertine had banished her to the Chateau de Ruelles.

But Monseigneur de Beaumont required something more than this of the royal sinner. He exacted that he should make public confession of his scandalous life in presence of the court to which he had given such shameful example. The king had struggled against such open humiliation, but the archbishop was firm, and the fear of death predominating over pride, Louis consented to make the sacrifice.

For three days the courtiers had hung about the anteroom, afraid to enter (for the king's disease was small-pox), yet afraid to take flight, lest by some chance he should recover. But now the doors of the royal apartments were flung wide open, and there was great trepidation among the crowd. The archbishop in his canonicals was seen standing by the bed of state; on one side of him stood the grand almoner, and on the other the minister, the Duke d'Aiguillon. At the foot of the bed knelt the daughters of the king, who in soft whispers were trying to comfort their miserable father.

"The king wishes to bid adieu to his friends!" cried the Duke d'Aiguillon, in a loud voice.

Here was a dilemma! Everybody was afraid of the small-pox, for the handsome Marquis de Letorières, whom Louis had insisted upon seeing, had just died of the infection, and nobody desired to follow him. And yet the king *might* outlive this attack, and then—what?

Once more the Duke d'Aiguillon called out for the king's friends; and, trembling from apprehension of results that might follow this latter contingency, they entered the chamber of death. The atmosphere was fearful. Not all the fumes of the incense which was sending its vapory wreaths to the pictured ceilings could overpower the odor of approaching dissolution. In vain the acolytes swung their golden censers—death was there, and the scent of the grave.

Breathless and with compressed lips the king's friends listened to his indistinct mutterings, and looked upon his swollen, livid, blackened face. Each one had hurried by, and now they all were free again, and were preparing to fly as far as possible from the infected spot. But the clear, solemn voice of the archbishop—that voice which so often had stricken terror to their worldly hearts—was heard again, and he bade them stay.

"The king asks pardon of his subjects for the wicked and scandalous life which he has led on earth," said the archbishop. "Although as a man he is responsible to God alone for his deeds, as a sovereign he acknowledges to his subjects that he heartily repents of his wickedness, and desires to live only that he may do penance for the past and make amends for the future."

A piteous groan escaped from the lips of the dying monarch, but his "friends" did not stay to hear it; they fled precipitately from the frightful scene.

While here a trembling soul was being driven from its earthly dwelling, in another wing of the palace the other members of the royal family were in the chapel at prayer. The evening services were over, and the chaplain was reading the "forty hours' prayer," when the sky became suddenly obscured, peal upon peal of thunder resounded along the heavens, and night enveloped the chapel in its dismal pall of black. Livid flashes of lightning lit up the pale faces of the royal supplicants, while to every faltering prayer that fell from their lips the answer came from above in the roar of the angry thunder-clap.

There, before the altar, knelt the doomed pair, the innocent heirs of a selfish and luxurious race of kings, whose sins were to be visited upon their unconscious heads. No wonder they wept—no wonder they shuddered on the dark and stormy night which heralded their reign.

The rites were ended, and the dauphin and dauphiness went silently together to their apartments. The few trusty attendants who were gathered in the anteroom greeted them with faint smiles, and uttered silent orisons in their behalf; for who could help compassionating these two young creatures, upon whose inexperienced heads the thorny crown of royalty was so soon to be placed?

As they entered the door, a flash of lightning, that seemed like the fire which smote the guilty cities of Israel, flashed athwart their paths, and the thunder cracked and rattled above the roof as though it had been riving that palace-dome asunder. The dauphiness cried out, and clung to her husband's arm. He, scarcely less appalled, stood motionless on the threshold.

The violence of the wind at that moment had burst open some outer door. The lights in the chandeliers were almost extinguished, and one solitary wax-light, that had been burning in the recess of a window, went entirely out. Regardless of etiquette, and of the presence of the royal pair, Monsieur de Campan sprang to the chandelier, and, relighting the candle, quickly replaced it in the window.

The dauphin beheld the act with astonishment, for no one at

that court was more observant of decorum than Monsieur de Campan.

"What means that light in the window?" inquired the dauphin, in his clear, touching voice.

"Pardon me, your highness, it is merely a ceremony," replied Monsieur de Campan, confused.

"What ceremony?" asked the dauphin, with surprise.

"Your highness commands me?"

"I request you—if the dauphiness permits," said Louis, turning to his wife, who, almost exhausted, leaned for support against him, and bowed her head.

"Your majesty has given orders, that as soon as the event, which is about to take place, has occurred, the whole court shall leave Versailles for Choisy. Now it would not be possible to issue verbal orders in such a moment as the one which we await; so that the master of the horse and myself had agreed upon a signal by which the matter could be arranged without speech. The *gardes du corps*, pages, equerries, coaches, coachmen, and outriders, are all assembled in the court-yard, their eyes fixed upon this light. As soon as it is extinguished, it will be understood that the moment has arrived when the court is to leave Versailles."

"The disappearance of the light, then, will communicate the tidings of the king's death?"

Monsieur de Campan bowed. Louis drew his wife hurriedly forward, and passed into another room, where, with his hands folded behind him, he walked to and fro.

"God is just," murmured he to himself, "and there is retribution in heaven."

Marie Antoinette, whose large violet eyes had followed her husband's motions, raised them to his face with a look of inquiry. She rose from the divan on which she was sitting, and putting her small, white hand upon the dauphin's shoulder, said:

"What do you mean, Louis?"

"I mean that this solitary light, for whose disappearance these people are waiting, shines in retribution for the fearful death-bed of my father."

"I do not understand."

"No, Antoinette, how should you? You have never heard the tragic story of my father's death, have you?"

"No, my husband," said she, tenderly; "tell it to me now."

"I will, Antoinette. He was one of the best and truest hearts that ever lived, and yet these selfish courtiers all forsook him in his dying hour. He lay alone and abandoned in his room by all save my angelic mother, who nursed him as loving woman alone can nurse. The court was at Fontainebleau, and the dauphin's father announced that as soon as his son had expired, they would all journey to Choisy. My father, who in an arm-chair, was inhaling, for the last time, the balmy breath of spring, saw these hurried preparations for departure from the open window where he sat. He saw carriages, horses, trunks, lackeys, and equerries ready at a moment's warning to move. He saw that the signal for the rushing crowd to depart was to be his death. Turning to his physician, he said, with a sad smile, 'I must not be too long in dying, for these people are becoming impatient.'" *

* Soulavie, "Mémoires," etc., vol. i.

"Shameful!" cried Marie Antoinette, wiping away her tears.

"Ay, more than shameful!" exclaimed Louis. "Now, you see, that the hour of retribution has come, for once more the court grows impatient with the length of a dying sovereign's agony. Oh, would that my noble father were alive! How much more worthy was he to be a king than I."

"From my heart I echo your wish," said Antoinette, fervently. "How was it that he died so young?"

Louis looked searchingly at the face of his young wife. "He died of a malady whose name is an impeachment of the honor of those who survive him," said the dauphin, sternly, "and my mother died of the same disease.* But let us not throw any darker shadows over the gloom of this heavy hour. I am stifled—I have a presentiment of—"

A loud shout interrupted the dauphin. It came nearer and nearer, and now it reached the anteroom, where the crowding courtiers were pouring in to greet King Louis XVI.

The dauphin and his wife were at no loss to understand these shouts. They exchanged glances of fear, and side by side they fell upon their knees while, with tear-streaming eyes, they faltered: "O God have mercy upon us, we are so young to reign!" †

The doors were thrown open, and the mistress of ceremonies of Marie Antoinette appeared. Behind her came a multitude of lords and ladies, their curious eyes peering at what they had never expected to see—a royal couple assuming the purple, not with pomp and pride, but with humility, distrust, and prayer.

They rose, and faced their subjects. Madame de Noailles courtesied so low that she was upon her knees.

"Your majesties will forgive this intrusion," said she, with all the *aplomb* of her dignity. "I come to request that your majesties will repair to the state reception-room to receive the congratulations of your royal relatives, and those of your court, who are all waiting anxiously to do you homage."

Such a request, from the lips of Madame de Noailles, was the exaction of an indispensable form of court-etiquette, which the young couple dared not evade.

Arm in arm they went, Marie Antoinette hiding her tears with her handkerchief, and looking inexpressibly lovely in her childish emotions, while the loud greetings of a magnificent court hailed her as their queen.

While the consorts of the royal princes folded their sister-in-law in their arms, the princes, with courtly decorum, bowed ceremoniously before the king.

"Permit us, sire," began the Count of Provence, "to be the first to lay our homage at your majesty's feet, and to—"

"My brothers, my brothers!" cried Louis, deeply affected, "is my crown to rob me of the dear ties of kindred? Oh, do not call me king, for I cannot afford to lose the dear companions of my childhood."

"Sire," replied the Count of Provence, "you shall not lose them; and for us, our gain is two-fold. We receive from God a gracious

* It was generally believed that the dauphin and his wife were poisoned by a political party, whose leader was the Duke de Choiseul. The royal couple belonged to the anti-Austrian party. "Mémoires de Campan," vol. i., p. 78.

† "Mémoires de Campan," vol. i., p. 78.

king, and retain our much-loved brother." And the count embraced the king, who had opened his arms to receive him.

A quarter of an hour later, the chateau of Versailles was deserted. The courtiers, pages, equerries, and lackeys, had all departed, delighted to leave that infected atmosphere, within whose poisonous influence the iron rules of etiquette had detained them while Louis XV. lived. None of them felt inclined to do homage to departed royalty. Even the Duke de Villequier, first gentleman of the bed-chamber, in his terror, forgot etiquette; and instead of watching the king's corpse, he, too, made ready to go with the rest.

"Monsieur," said the duke to Andouillé, the king's physician, "I leave you that you may be able to open and embalm the body."

Andouillé grew pale, for he knew perfectly well that the performance of such a ceremony as that, was his death-warrant. However, after a pause, he replied, "I am ready, your grace, but you must remain to hold the king's head. It is, as you know, a part of your duty as gentleman of the bedchamber." *

The Duke de Villequier said nothing. He merely bowed and hurried from the room. Andouillé followed his example, but, more considerate than the other attendants of the king, he made some provision for the deserted corpse. He sent for one of the subordinates of the palace, and ordered him to watch by the body. Then, going to his carriage, he saw several hodmen lounging about, who were carrying mortar for some repairs that were being made at the palace. The physician called them, and bade them go tell the lord-steward that the king's coffin must be saturated with spirits of wine, and his winding-sheet also.

Such were the preparations that were made for the obsequies of the defunct king; and his body was watched by a few servants and these hodmen whom Andouillé had employed as messengers.

CHAPTER XCIV.

THE MEMORANDA.

It was early in the morning. The court had accompanied the king and queen to Choisy, and thither had flocked the representatives of every class in Paris, to do homage to the king and wish him a prosperous reign.

The people seemed wild with joy, and nobody vouchsafed a thought to the memory of the "*Bien-aimé*," whose body was even now being taken to its last rest, in the vaults of St. Denis. The funeral train was any thing but imposing. The coffin, placed upon a large hunting-wagon, was followed by two carriages, containing the Duke d'Ayen, the Duke d'Aumont, and two priests. Twenty pages and as many grooms closed the procession, which went along without attracting the notice of anybody. The burial-service was read in the crypt, and the coffin hastily lowered in the vault, which was not only walled up, but cemented also, for fear the infection imprisoned within might escape from the dungeon of the dead and infest the abodes of the living.

Not one of the royal family had followed the body. The king was at Choisy, and all hearts were turned to him. Thousands of men went

* Campan, vol. i., p. 79.

in and out of the palace, each one with his burden of fears, hopes, uneasiness or expectations. Who was now to find favor at court? Would it be the queen, or the aunts of the king? What fate awaited Du Barry? Who would be prime minister?

While these matters were being discussed without, the king, who had not yet made his appearance, was in his cabinet. His disordered mien, tangled hair, and red eyes, as well as the lights that still flickered in the chandeliers, showed plainly that he had not been to bed that night.

He could not sleep. The future lowered dark and threatening before him, and day had not brought comfort to his anxious mind. Great drops of sweat stood upon his brow, and his face, never at the best of times handsome, to-day was less attractive than ever.

"I am so young!" thought he, despondently. "I know of no man at this court, in whose honesty I can confide. Every man of them has curried favor with that shameless woman whose presence has defiled the throne of my ancestors, and disgraced the declining years of my grandfather. To whom shall I turn? Who will give counsel to a poor, inexperienced youth?"

A slight knock was heard at the door. The king rose and opened it.

"Monsieur de Nicolai," said Louis, surprised, as the old man stood before him with head inclined. "What brings you to me?"

"The will of your deceased father, sire."

The king stepped back and motioned him to enter. "Now speak," said he. "I know that you were with my father on his death-bed; and I have often sought to win your friendship, but until now have sought in vain."

"Sire, I was afraid that if I betrayed an interest in your majesty, I might not be allowed to live long enough to fulfil the trust confided to me by your father. I had sworn that on the day you ascended the throne of France I would deliver his will to your majesty."

"And you have preserved it? You have brought it to me?"

"Sire, here it is," said the old nobleman, taking from his breast a sealed package, and laying it in the king's hands.

Louis grasped it eagerly, and deeply moved, read the address: "Papers to be delivered to whichever one of my sons ascends the throne of France."

"Your majesty sees that I have kept my trust," said De Nicolai.

"Oh, why is not my father here to reign in my stead!" exclaimed Louis.

"He died, sire, that he might be spared the sight of the disgrace which has overtaken France. He died that the world might bear witness to the baseness of those who, since his death, have swayed the destinies of France. He did not die in vain. Your majesty's self will profit by his martyrdom."

"Yes, I have heard of it all. I know the invisible hand that dealt the death-blow to my father, my mother, and my grandmother. I know it, and—"

"Sire, your majesty's father forgave his enemies; and, through me, he prays your majesty to do likewise."

"I will obey," said Louis, inclining his head, "and leave the guilty to the vengeance of Heaven."

"And now, sire, that my mission is accomplished, allow me to retire, and let me entreat you to lay your father's words to heart."

"I will do so, I promise you. Can I do aught to serve you?"

"No, your majesty, I have nothing to ask of man."

The king gave him his hand, and followed him with wistful eyes until the door had closed behind him.

"Oh, how beggared seems a king, when he has nothing wherewith to recognize the loyalty and love of his friends!" thought Louis, with a weary sigh.

He took up the packet and read: "Treaty concluded between Louis XV. and Maria Theresa, on the 1st of May, 1756. Arguments to prove that, sooner or later, the Austrian alliance will be an injury to France."

The king turned over the pages and read the following:

"Whichever one of my sons is called to the throne of Louis XV. let him hearken to the warning of his father. Beware, my son, of entanglements with Austria. Never seek the hand of an Austrian princess; for marriages with Austria have brought no blessing to France."

The king sighed heavily, and his head sank upon his breast. "Too late—too late, my father! My fate is decided!" And Louis took up the second memorandum.

"List of persons whom I recommend to my son, the King of France."

"Ah!—this is the guide I was seeking. Let me see. First,—'Monsieur de Maurepas—a statesman who has steadily opposed the policy advocated by La Pompadour.' That is well—I shall recall him from banishment. 'Messieurs de Machault, de Nivernois, de Muy Perigord, de Broglie, d'Estaing, and others—all men of honor.' How far-sighted was my father, in recommending these men! They are the very nobles who have kept aloof from the late king's mistresses. With one exception, I adopt the list; but there is one among them, who stooped to be a flatterer of Du Barry. The Duke d'Aiguillon is certainly a statesman, but he cannot be of my ministry."

Here the king paused, perplexed to know who should be appointed in D'Aiguillon's place. Suddenly his face brightened, and he rose from his chair.

"Marie Antoinette," thought he, "I will advise with her. Though we may not love one another, we are friendly; and she has a right to my confidence. Besides, she is intelligent and principled."

Here the king took up his memoranda, and prepared to seek his wife. He had gotten as far as the door, when his expression changed again, and his face once more wore a look of blank despondency. With a grieved and perplexed mind, he returned to the table.

"No, no," sighed he, falling back into his chair, "that will never do. She is an Austrian; and her policy would be in direct opposition to that of my father."

For some time the poor young king sat in profound discouragement. Finally, with a long, weary sigh, he raised his head, and began to reflect again. At last he solved the difficult problem.

"Ah!—I have it now," thought he, heartily relieved. "I will go to Madame Adelaide. She was my mother's dearest friend and my father's favorite sister. She shall be my counsellor. I believe that, with her assistance, I may succeed in carrying out the policy dictated by my father."

He gathered up his papers, and went into the anteroom, where he ordered a page to go to Madame Adelaide, and say that the king would visit her if she could conveniently receive him.*

CHAPTER XCV.

FRANCE AND AUSTRIA.

WHILE the king was closeted with Madame Adelaide, the queen, on her side, was receiving her royal household. This ceremony over, she had gladly retired to the privacy of her own room, there to restore order to her confused mind.

But her rest was not of long duration, for presently came Monsieur de Campan to announce the visit of the Austrian ambassador.

The queen received him most cordially, rising from her seat, and advancing a few steps to meet him. Madame de Noailles, who, conforming to etiquette, had entered with Monsieur de Campan, and was to remain in the room during the interview, was shocked at the queen, and frowned visibly.

Marie Antoinette paid no attention to her. She reached her hand to Count von Mercy, and allowed him to press it to his lips.

Again Madame de Noailles was horror-stricken. The kissing of the queen's hand was a state ceremonial, and was inadmissible in private.

The queen had forgotten the existence of her mistress of ceremonies. With sparkling eyes and beaming smiles she greeted the old count, who, to her, was the representative of all that she loved—her mother, her sisters, and her native country.

"Have you news for me from Vienna, count?" said she, in a voice whose tones were strikingly like those of her mother.

"I bring to your majesty letters of condolence and of congratulation from the empress and the emperor."

"Why, you must be a conjurer, count. Our reign is not twenty-four hours old yet, and you bring us congratulations from Vienna?"

"I will explain, your majesty," said the old count, with a smile. "You remember, that more than a week ago the king lay in a stupor, which, for some hours, was supposed to be death. During his stupor, my courier started for Vienna, and the messenger sent after him, to stop the dispatches, arrived too late. The answers had been sent, and there are the congratulatory letters."

The count handed his papers, and as the queen cast down her beautiful eyes to read the address, she exclaimed, joyfully:

"My mother's handwriting and my brother's!"

She broke the seal of the empress's letter, and her countenance fell.

"Nothing but official papers," said she, sighing, and putting them on the table. "I know the contents of Joseph's letter without reading it. Have you no news for me from Vienna? Think of something to tell me from home, dear count."

Count von Mercy cast a stolen glance at the mistress of ceremonies, who, stiff and watchful, stood close by the side of the queen's chair. Marie Antoinette understood the look.

* Madame Adelaide, an anti-Austrian, and, therefore, one of the queen's enemies, was, throughout his whole reign, the counsellor of her nephew.

"Madame de Noailles," said she, turning with a smile to address her, "you will not, I hope, think me rude, if I request you to allow me a few moments' interview with Count von Mercy. He has something to say to me that is of a strictly confidential nature."

The mistress of ceremonies did not appear to have heard a word of this address. Marie Antoinette reddened, and threw back her head.

"I request Madame de Noailles," repeated she, changing her tone, "to retire into the reception-room. I wish to speak with Count von Mercy alone."

"I must be permitted to say that your majesty's request cannot be granted," replied Madame de Noailles. "No Queen of France is permitted to receive a foreign ambassador otherwise than in the presence of the court. I shall have to ask his majesty's pardon for a breach of decorum, which I was too late to prevent—the reception of the ambassador here with myself alone to witness the interview."

The queen's eyes flashed with anger as she listened to this presumptuous language.

"You will have to ask pardon of no one but myself, madame, for your unseemly language to your sovereign."

"Excuse me, your majesty, I perform my duty, and this requires of me to see that no one here commits any breach of court etiquette. The laws of etiquette are as binding upon the queen as upon her subjects—and she cannot infringe them."

"I announce to you, madame, that no laws of yours shall be binding upon me. The Queen of France is here to make laws—not to receive them. And for the last time I command you to quit this room, and to leave me alone with the representative of my imperial mother."

Madame de Noailles made a deep courtesy, and backed out of the room.

Marie Antoinette looked after her, until the last traces of her long train had vanished, and the silk *portière* had fallen in its place.

"Ah!" said she, taking a long breath, "at last I have gained a victory. It is now my turn to lecture, and madame has received her first scolding. Well, count, now that she is fairly off, what have you to tell me from Vienna?"

Count von Mercy looked toward the door, and having convinced himself that it was well closed, he drew from his pocket a package, and presented it to the queen.

Marie Antoinette hastily tore open the seals and began to read.

"Oh!" said she, with a disappointed look, "this is no private letter. It is nothing but a letter of instructions, directing me how to win the king's confidence, so as to influence his policy and secure a new ally to Austria. The empress need not remind me that I must look to the interests of the house of Hapsburg. The Queen of France will never forget that she is the daughter of Maria Theresa, and she will do all in her power to promote an alliance between France and Austria. Tell my mother that I never will cease to be her subject, and that her interests shall always be mine. And now for the other mission."

"Good Heaven!" cried she, after opening the letter, "more politics." She looked down the page, and read: "Personages whom I recommend as suitable for the counsellors and household of the king."

This was quite a long list in the empress's handwriting, and at its head stood the name of the Duke de Choiseul. "The Queen of France must use every effort to secure his appointment as minister, for he is sincerely attached to us."

Many other distinguished names were there; but not one of those which had been mentioned by the king's father.

"I will preserve this paper with care," said Marie Antoinette, burying her letters deep in her pocket. "No doubt, you know their contents, count. A postscript says, 'Consult frequently with Mercy;' so let us begin at once."

"Will your majesty not read the letter of the emperor?"

"Why should I read it now? It grieves me to see these political documents from the hands of dear relatives who ought to write to me of home and love. I will put it with the official letter of the empress for the king to read."

"Pardon me, your majesty, but I do not think it is official."

"Read it for me, then," said the queen, throwing herself back in the deep recesses of her arm-chair. "I have confidence enough in you to be willing that you shall see my brother's letter, should it even be a private one."

Count von Mercy bowed, and unfolded the letter, which was as follows:

"MADAME: I congratulate you upon your husband's accession to the throne of France. He will repair the faults of his predecessor's reign, and win the love of his people. The French nation has groaned under the inflictions of a king who not only proscribed parliament, but intrusted every office of state to his favorites. He banished De Choiseul, Malesherbes, and Chalotais; and in their stead elevated the Maurepas, the D'Aiguillons, and that hateful Abbé Terray, who, for rapacity, were none of them better than Du Barry—and thus he ended by losing the love of his subjects. I have often pitied Louis XV. for degrading himself as he did before the eyes of his family, his subjects, and the world.

"Unite your efforts to those of your husband, that you may win the love of the French nation. Leave no stone unturned to secure their affection, for, by so doing, you will prove a blessing to your people.

"Strengthen our alliance with France, and apply yourself to the mission for which you were educated—that of peace-maker between two of the most important powers of Europe.

"I kiss your hands, and remain, with the highest esteem and consideration, your majesty's friend and brother,

"JOSEPH." *

"You are right, count," said the queen, as the ambassador concluded his reading. "This is no official document, but a most significant letter of instructions. I am expected to preserve peace between France and Austria. Ah, I fear that I am not calculated to walk the slippery arena of politics, and I confess to you that I feel in no wise drawn toward it. It does seem to me that a queen of nineteen may be pardoned if she feels some desire to enjoy life. I intend to begin by breaking the fetters which have hitherto made such wretched puppets of the queens of France; and before long

* "Letters of Joseph II., as Characteristic Contributions," etc., p. 20.

you will see the workings of my court revolution. But there is one thing near to my heart, which you must assist me to compass. The Duke de Choiseul must be minister of foreign affairs. I know that he desires it, and I am under obligations to him which deserve some return. I owe it to him that I am Queen of France. Now, if I succeed in elevating Choiseul to the ministry," continued the queen, with an appealing smile, "I hope that Austria will be satisfied, and will allow me to retire from the field. The Duke de Choiseul will be a much abler auxiliary than I, near the king. We must, therefore, have him recalled."

"The duke arrived in Paris from Chanteloup this morning, but does not think it advisable to present himself, until he receives a message from the king."

"I shall see that the message is sent," said Marie Antoinette, confidently. "The king will not refuse me, I know. You shrug your shoulders, count. Do you think it doubtful?"

"Your majesty condescends to speak confidentially with me," said the count, seriously. "I am an old servant of your house, and my hair has grown gray in its service. In consideration, then, of the deep affection which I have ever felt for your majesty, will you allow me to speak with you frankly?"

"I implore you, count, to do so."

"Then, your majesty, let me warn you to be careful. Things do not work at this French court as they ought to do. Your majesty has bitter enemies, who await an opportunity to declare themselves openly. The Count of Provence and the aunts of the king are at the head, and, believe me, they are watchful spies."

"Oh, my God!" cried the poor young queen, "what have I done to earn their enmity?"

"You are an Austrian princess, and that suffices for them. Your marriage was a victory over the anti-Austrian party, for which the Duke de Choiseul never will be forgiven; and as for yourself, if you give them the opportunity, they will not scruple to take revenge upon your own royal person. The Count of Provence has a sharp tongue, and his aunts and himself will spare no means to wound or to injure you. Therefore, pardon me, if again I bid you beware of your enemies. There is Madame de Noailles, for instance, she belongs to the most powerful families in France, and the French nation regard her as the palladium of the queen's honor. Your majesty cannot afford to offend her. It would be a great misfortune for you, if she should resign her office; for her resignation would place on the list of your enemies all the most influential nobles in France."

"Is that all?" asked the queen, with a painful blush.

"Yes, your majesty; and I thank you for your condescension in listening so long."

"Then hear me," said Marie Antoinette, rising and standing proudly before him. "You tell me that I have enemies. Be it so, and may God forgive them! But it were unworthy the daughter of Maria Theresa to stoop to conciliate them. With visor raised, and front exposed, I stand before them. My blameless life shall be my defence, for I will so live that all France shall be my champions. As for Madame de Noailles, I will make no concessions to her. My virtue needs no more protection from etiquette than that of any other woman. Heretofore the Queens of France have been nothing but *Marionettes* in the hands of their high-born *duennas*. I intend to transform the puppets into women, whom the French nation can love and esteem; for I wish my people to know that their queen's virtue is not a thing of form, but the veritable overflowing of a heart aspiring to perfection."

"Right royally spoken!" said a soft voice behind, and the queen starting, beheld the king, who, having opened the door quietly, had heard her last words.

CHAPTER XCVI.

THE KING'S LIST.

MARIE ANTOINETTE, with a happy smile, gave her hand to her husband. He raised it to his lips, and kissed it so fervently that his young wife blushed with pleasure.

"Do you know what brings me to you, Antoinette?" said he gayly. "The deadly anxiety of good Madame Etiquette. She met me in the anteroom, and confessed that she had been guilty of the crime of leaving the queen alone with a foreign ambassador. To relieve her mind, I promised to come hither myself, and put an end to the treason that was hatching between France and Austria."

"Ah!" said Marie Antoinette, with a bewitching pout, "then you came, not to see me, but to save Madame Etiquette a fit of the vapors."

"I made use of her as a pretext to intrude myself upon you," said the king with embarrassment.

"Oh, your majesty well knows that you need no pretext to come in my presence!" said Marie Antoinette, eagerly.

"Certainly, I require it just now, for I have broken up a charming *tête-à-tête*," said the king, bowing to Von Mercy.

"The count has brought me letters from the empress," said Marie Antoinette. "And what do you suppose they were? Congratulations upon our accession to the throne."

The king smiled, but expressed no surprise.

"What, you are not surprised!" said the queen. "Do you take the count for a sorceror?"

"I take him for a true and loyal friend of his sovereign," said Louis, "and I only wish that I possessed one as faithful. But I am not at all astonished to hear of the congratulations, since the courier started off with the news a week ago."

"Your majesty knew it, then?"

"A king must know all things," said he gravely. "Are you not of my opinion, count? Is it not proper that a sovereign should possess a knowledge of every important letter which comes into his kingdom or leaves it?"

"I believe so, your majesty," replied the count, somewhat confused.

"I am convinced of it, and so is the Empress of Austria," said the king, with a laugh. "She is admirably well posted in all that concerns foreign courts, and not a document leaves the French embassy in Vienna of which she has not a copy. Is it not so, Count von Mercy?"

"I do not believe, sire, that there is any person in the French embassy capable of betraying the interests of his country, or of revealing its secrets."

"Then change your creed, count, for in every country there are men open to bribery. But," continued he, turning to the queen, "we have wandered from our subject—your majesty's letters from Vienna. Have you good news?"

"It is merely official, sire," replied the queen, handing the letter to the king.

Louis looked it over; then replacing it upon the table, said, "And the other letters?"

"Which other letters?" asked the queen.

"Did you not tell me there were several?"

"No, sire," replied the queen, reddening.

"What fables men do invent!" exclaimed the king. "A courier has just arrived from the French embassy, in Vienna, with dispatches informing us that Count von Mercy had received for your majesty one official letter from the empress, and two private letters of instruction, one of which contained a list of persons recommended by her majesty; and, finally, a fourth missive, private, from the Emperor Joseph. And all this is pure invention, Count von Mercy?"

"It is, your majesty," said the count, with much embarrassment, while Marie Antoinette cast down her eyes, and blushed.

The king enjoyed their confusion for a while; he seemed to take pleasure in this first triumph of his regal power, and a smile flitted over his rather clumsy features.

"You see, then," continued he, "that I have received false intelligence, and it is evident that Austrians are less corrupt than Frenchmen, for I am told that Count von Mercy and Prince Kaunitz are *au fait* to every thing that transpires in the palace here. Be that as it may, we intend to follow the example of the queen. Our policy shall be so frank and honorable that all the world may know it and welcome. But—it occurs to me that the mistress of ceremonies is in great anguish of mind. She will not recover her equanimity until she sees you again, count."

"In that case, your majesty, I beg leave to retire," replied the count.

The king bowed, and the queen gave him her hand.

As the count was about to raise the *portière*, the king called him back. "Do you send a courier to Vienna to-day?" asked his majesty.

"Yes, sire, in one hour."

"Then let me impart to you a secret which I think will interest her imperial majesty of Austria—my new ministry."

"How! has your majesty already chosen them?" asked Marie Antoinette, anxiously.

The king nodded. "It was my first sacred duty to seek guides for my inexperience, and I have chosen ministers who are able statesmen, and have already served before."

The queen's eyes brightened, and even Count von Mercy seemed surprised and pleased.

"Do, your majesty, let us have their names," said Marie Antoinette.

"First, Monsieur de Maurepas."

The queen uttered an exclamation. "The minister of the regency, who has been banished for forty years!"

"The same. He was a friend of my father. He will be prime

minister; and as I am so unfortunate as to have to bear the weight of royalty at twenty years, I have taken care to select old and experienced men as my counsellors."

"And who is to succeed the Duke d'Aiguillon?" cried Marie Antoinette, "for I presume that your majesty intends to give him his dismissal."

"I would be glad to retain him as my minister," said the king, pointedly, "for his policy is identical with mine. He has the interests of France at heart, and has never suffered himself to be led away by foreign influence. But unluckily, he was too intimate with Du Barry, and on this ground I shall dismiss him."

"And his successor?" asked the queen, scarcely able to restrain her bitter disappointment.

"His successor is the Count de Vergennes."

"De Vergennes!" cried the queen, scornfully. "He who married a slave in Constantinople?"

"Ah, you have heard that ridiculous story, which was invented by Monsieur de Choiseul? Nobody here ever believed it; and let me tell you that the Countess de Vergennes enjoys the esteem and consideration of all who know her. Vergennes himself is a man of talent, and will do me good service. The other ministers are: for the war department, Count de Muy; for the minister of finance, instead of that hateful Abbé Terray—(was not that the emperor's expression?)—I have chosen Count de Clugny."

"Count de Clugny!" said Marie Antoinette, again beginning to hope. "Does your majesty mean the friend of the Duke de Choiseul?"

"Himself, madame," said the king, coolly. "And while you are speaking of Monsieur de Choiseul, I am reminded that this is not the first time his name has been mentioned to-day. You, Count von Mercy, are a friend of his—I am not. You can, therefore, tell me whether it is true that he has left Chanteloup, wither the deceased king had banished him."

"Yes, sire, the Duke de Choiseul arrived this morning in Paris."

"What can he want in Paris?" asked the king, with an unconscious look. "Why did he leave Chanteloup? It seems to me that for the man who is so lucky as to have a landed estate, this is the very time of year to stay there. You had better advise your friend to return to the country. And now, count, you know all that I have to tell, and I will detain you no longer. Madame de Noailles must be in despair. Comfort her by informing her that you left the Queen of France in the company of her husband."

CHAPTER XCVII.

THE FIRST PASQUINADE.

THE court had left Choisy for the Chateau de la Muette, near Paris. Here the queen was to hold her first public levee, and her subjects longed to appear before her, for the Parisians were enthusiastic admirers of grace and beauty. Marie Antoinette had won their hearts by refusing to accept the tax called "*La ceinture de la reine.*" This tax was the perquisite of the Queen of France on her accession to the throne. But having discovered that the nobles had managed to evade it and cast the burden of taxation upon the poor, Marie Antoinette had requested her husband's leave to relinquish her right to it. Like wildfire the news of the young queen's generosity spread throughout Paris; and in all the streets, *cafés*, and *cabarets* the people were singing this couplet:

> "Vous renoncez, charmante souveraine,
> Au plus beau de vos revenus;
> A quoi vous servirait la ceinture de reine,
> Vous avez celle de Vénus."

They sang, they shouted, and made merry, happy in the possession of a young king, and a beautiful queen, casting never a thought toward him who, years before, had been surnamed *Le Bien-aimé.* *

One speculating jeweller, alone, honored the memory of the deceased king, and made his fortune thereby. He manufactured a mourning snuff-box, of black shagreen, whose lid was ornamented with a portrait of the queen. He called his boxes "*La consolation dans le chagrin,*" † and his portrait and pun became so popular, that in less than a week he had sold a hundred thousand of these boxes. ‡

Louis, also, had his share of the national good-will. He renounced the tax called "*Le joyeux avénement;*" and to commemorate the act, another snuff-box made its appearance in Paris as a *pendant* to the "Consolation in Grief." The king's box contained the portraits of Louis XII. and Henry IV. Below these, was his own likeness, with the following inscription: "*Les pères du peuple, XII. et IV. font XVI.*" These boxes were as popular as those of the queen: and Louis and Marie Antoinette were the idols of the Parisians.

"Long live the king!" was the cry from morn till night. Hope brightened every eye, and reigned in every heart. The people dreamed of peace, happiness, and plenty, and the fashions symbolized their state of mind. The women dressed their heads with ears of wheat, and ate their *dragées* from cornucopias. The men poured out their enthusiasm in sonnets and addresses, and every thing in France was *couleur de rose.*

Couleur de rose—with one exception. The anti-Austrian party frowned, and plotted, and hated. Exasperated by the enthusiasm which the beautiful young queen inspired, they watched her every motion, eager to magnify the most trivial imperfection into crime; hoping, sooner or later, to render her obnoxious to the French people, and finally, to compass the end of all their wicked intrigues—a separation between the king and queen, and the disgrace and banishment of Marie Antoinette to Austria.

It was the day of the grand reception, at La Muette, where every lady having a right to appear at court might come uninvited and be presented to the queen. The great throne-room was prepared for the occasion; and although its decorations were black, they were tastefully enlivened with white and silver. The throne itself was covered with black velvet, trimmed with silver and fringe. Hundreds of ladies thronged the room, all with their eyes fixed upon the door through which the queen and her court must make their entrance.

* "Mémoires de Weber," vol. i., p. 43.

† "Mémoires de Madame de Campan," vol. i., p. 91.

‡ This word "*chagrin*," signifies not only grief, but also that preparation of leather, which, in English, is called "shagreen." Hence the pun.

The folding-doors were thrown wide open, and, announced by her mistress of ceremonies, Marie Antoinette appeared.

A murmur of admiration was heard among the crowd. Never had the queen looked so transcendently lovely as she did to-day in her dress of deep mourning. She seemed to feel the solemnity of her position as queen-consort of a great nation, and the expression of her face was tranquil and dignified. No woman ever represented royalty with better grace than Marie Antoinette, and the old coquettes of the regency and of the corrupt court of Louis XV. were awed by her stateliness. They could not but confess that they were in the presence of a noble and virtuous woman: therefore they disliked her, whispering one to the other, "What an actress!"

Marie Antoinette took her seat upon the throne. On her right and left were the royal family, and behind them the ladies of the court. Opposite stood Madame de Noailles, whose duty it was to present those who were unknown to the queen.

The presentation began. Forth in their high-heeled shoes came the noble-born widows, who, old and faded, were loath to forget that in the days of the regency they had been blooming like the queen, and who, in happy ignorance of their crow's feet and wrinkles, were decked in the self-same costumes which had once set off their roses and dimples.

It was a ludicrous sight—these ugly old women, with their jewels and patches, their extraordinary head-dresses, and their deep, deep courtesies, painful by reason of the aching bones of three-score and ten. The young princesses dared not raise their eyes to these representatives of by-gone coquetry, for they were afraid to commit a crime—they were afraid that they might laugh. But the ladies of honor, safe behind the hoops of the queen and her sisters-in-law made merry over the magnificent old ruins. Madame de Noailles was so busy with the front, that she overlooked the rear, where the lively young Marquise de Charente Tounerre, tired of standing, had glided down and seated herself comfortably on the floor. Neither could she see that the marquise, in the exuberance of her youthful spirits, was pulling the other ladies by their skirts, and amusing them with mimicry of the venerable coquettes before mentioned; so that while etiquette and ceremony were parading their ugliness in front of the throne, behind it, youth and beauty were tittering and enjoying the absurd pageant in utter thoughtlessness of all consequences.

The mistress of ceremonies was in the act of presenting one of the most shrivelled and most elaborately dressed of the ancients, when the queen, attracted by the whispering behind, turned her head in the direction of her ladies of honor. There on the floor, sat the Marquise de Charente Tounerre, imitating every gesture of the old *comtesse;* while the others, including the princesses themselves, were pursing up their lips, and smothering their laughter behind handkerchiefs and fans. The drolleries of the marquise were too much for the queen. She turned away in terror, lest they should infect her with untimely levity, and just at that moment the *comtesse* made precisely such a courtesy as the marquise was making behind her.

Marie Antoinette felt that her dignity was departing. She struggled to recall it, but in vain; and instead of the stately inclination which it was her duty to return, she suddenly opened her fan to hide the mirth which she was unable to control.

The gesture was seen not only by the austere mistress of ceremonies, but by the *comtesse* herself, who, furious at the insult, looked daggers at the queen, and omitting her third courtesy, swept indignantly to her place.

A short pause ensued. Madame de Noailles was so shocked that she forgot to give the signal for another presentation. The queen's face was still buried under her fan, and the princesses had followed her example. Discontent was manifest upon the countenances of all present, and the lady whose turn it was to advance did so with visible reluctance.

Marie Antoinette recovered her self-possession, and looked with perfect serenity toward the high and mighty duchess, whose titles were being pompously enumerated by the punctilious mistress of ceremonies. As ill luck would have it, this one was older, uglier, and more strangely bedizened than all the others together. The queen felt a spasmodic twitch of her face; she colored violently, and opening her fan again, it was evident to all that assemblage of censorious dames that for the second time youth and animal spirits had prevailed over decorum.

In vain Marie Antoinette sought to repair the *contretemps*. In vain she went among them with her sweetest smiles and most gracious words. Their outraged grandeur was not to be appeased—she had offended beyond forgiveness.

The Areopagus sent forth its fiat. The queen was a frivolous woman; she had that worst of failings—a taste for satire. She despised all conventionalities, and trampled all etiquette under foot.

On that day the number of her enemies was increased by more than a hundred persons, who attacked her with tongues sharper than two-edged swords. The first thrust was given her on the morning that followed the reception; and the same people who a few days before had been singing her praises on the Pont-neuf, were equally, if not better pleased with the ballad of "*La Reine moqueuse,*" of which the cruel *refrain* was as follows:

"Petite reine de vingt ans
Vous qui traitez si mal les gens,
Vous repasserez la barrière
Laire, laire, laire, lanlaire, lanla." *

CHAPTER XCVIII.

THE NEW FASHIONS.

THE queen had submitted to a state of things which she felt to be irremediable. She had renounced all idea of interceding with the king for De Choiseul, for she felt that interference on her part would be resented; and she could not afford to lessen, by so much as a shade, the kindly feelings which her husband had begun to manifest toward her.

Louis appeared to have no greater happiness than that which he found in his wife's society. They were often seen wandering in the shady walks of the palace gardens, talking, jesting, and laughing

* "Mémoires de Madame de Campan," vol. i., pp. 90, 91.

together, as might have done any other young couple, unencumbered by the burden of royalty. It had even happened to Louis to steal an arm around the graceful form of the queen, and once or twice to bestow a shy kiss upon her ivory shoulders.

The heart of the king was thawing; and Marie Antoinette, who had so longed and pined for his regard, sometimes blushed, while with beating heart she indulged a hope that the king was falling in love.

She sought, by every means in her power, to please him; and she who, hitherto, had seemed indifferent to dress, now bestowed hours of thought upon the toilet of the day.

The anti-Austrian party, the royal aunts, the brothers of the king, and the Orleans family, all her enemies, observed this new taste for dress with secret satisfaction. Not one of them suspected that it was aimed at the heart of the king; and that Marie Antoinette, whom they were deriding as a coquette, was coquetting with her husband, and dressing for him alone. So they flattered and encouraged her, hoping to divert her mind from politics, and urge her on to ruin.

The Duchess of Chartres had mentioned to the queen a Parisian *modiste*, who had instituted a complete revolution in dress. This wonderful *modiste*, whose taste in modes was exquisite, was Mademoiselle Bertin. The duchess had described her dresses, laces, caps, and *coiffures*, with so much enthusiasm, that Marie Antoinette grew impatient with curiosity, ordered her carriage, and sent a message to Madame de Noailles to prepare to accompany her at once to Bertin's establishment.

Madame received this message with indignation, and instead of making ready to obey, went in hot haste to the queen's reception-room.

"I wish to drive to Bertin's to make some purchases," said Marie Antoinette, as her tormentor appeared at the door.

"That is impossible, your majesty," said the guardian of the *inferno* of etiquette. "No Queen of France has ever set foot within the precincts of a shop, or has ever appeared in a public place of that sort. It would be such an egregious breach of etiquette, that I am convinced your majesty will not be guilty of it."

"Well," said the queen, with a scornful laugh, "I will not disturb your virtuous convictions. I will *not* be guilty of that which no Queen of France has ever stooped to do, so that you can have Bertin sent to the palace, and I can examine her goods here."

"Here! Your majesty would receive a *modiste* in your reception-room!" cried De Noailles, rolling up the whites of her eyes. "I beseech your majesty to remember that none but the noble ladies, who have the privilege of the *tabouret*, are allowed to enter the queen's reception-room."

The queen bit her rosy lips. "Well, then, madame," said she, "I will receive Bertin in my own cabinet. I presume there can be no objections to that; and, if there were, I should certainly not heed them."

"The duty of my office, nevertheless, obliges me to remark to your—"

"There is no office at this court which justifies any one in a direct disobedience of the queen's orders. Go, then, madame, and order that Bertin be sent to me in an hour."

"Oh!" murmured Marie Antoinette, as the mistress of ceremonies slowly retreated, "that woman's sole delight in life is to irritate and annoy me!"

An hour later, Mademoiselle Bertin made her appearance before the queen. Four royal lackeys followed her, laden with band-boxes.

"Mademoiselle," said the queen, "have you brought me the latest fashions?"

"No, your majesty," replied Bertin, reverentially, "I bring the materials wherewith to fill your majesty's orders."

"Were you not told to bring your samples of fashions?" asked Marie Antoinette, with surprise.

"Your majesty, there are no new fashions," said Bertin. "Your majesty's word is necessary to create them. A queen does not follow the fashion, it follows her."

"Ah! you intend that I shall invent new fashions?"

"Yes, your majesty. The Queen of France cannot stoop to wear that which has already been worn by others."

"You are right," said the queen, pleased by the flattery of the shrewd *modiste.* "Make haste, and show me your goods, that I may begin at once to set the fashions to the court. It will be quite an amusement to invent new modes of dress."

Mademoiselle Bertin smiled, and, opening her boxes, exhibited her goods. There were the beautiful silken fabrics of Lyons; the shimmering white satin, besprinkled with bouquets that rivalled nature; there were heavy, shining velvets, heightened by embroidery of gold and silver; laces, from Alençon and Valenciennes, whose web was as delicate as though elfin fingers, had spun the threads; muslins, from India, so fine that they could only be woven in water; crapes, from China, with the softness of satin and the sheen of velvet; there were graceful ostrich-plumes from Africa, and flowers from Paris, so wondrous in their beauty that nothing was wanting to their perfection save perfume.

Marie Antoinette flitted from one treasure to another; her white hands at one moment deriving new beauty from the dark velvets upon which they rested; at another, looking lovelier than ever, as they toyed with the transparent laces. There was nothing queenly about her now. She was merely a charming woman, anxious to outshine all other women in the eyes of one man.

When Mademoiselle Bertin took her leave, the queen gave her orders to return to the palace daily. "One thing I shall exact of you, mademoiselle, you shall disclose the secret of my toilet for the day to nobody; and the fashions shall be made public at the end of one week."

Mademoiselle Bertin, with a solemnity befitting the importance of her office, swore that henceforth the hands which had been honored by carrying out the ideas of a queen, should never work for lesser mortals; that her dresses should be made with closed doors, and that she would rather be led to execution than betray to a living soul the mysteries of her royal patroness's toilet.*

* Mademoiselle Bertin, from that day, became an important personage, and received many a rich present from noble ladies anxious to imitate the queen in dress.

CHAPTER XCIX.

THE TEMPLE OF ETIQUETTE.

THE hour for the queen's toilet was one of ravishment to Madame de Noailles; for it was a daily glorification of that etiquette which she worshipped, and which Marie Antoinette abhorred. In that hour, its chains were on her hands and feet. She could neither breathe, speak, nor move, but within the narrow limits of its weary exactions.

The queen's toilet, then, was Madame de Noailles' triumph; and she always made her appearance in the dressing-room with an air of supreme satisfaction.

The first lady of honor poured the water into the golden basin, and Marie Antoinette, who at least had the privilege of washing her own hands, stood patiently waiting until the towel had been passed by a lady of the bedchamber to the same lady of honor who had poured out the water. The latter, on one knee, gave the towel, and the queen wiped her hands.

The second act of the royal toilet began at the solemn moment when the queen changed her richly-embroidered night-chemise for the simpler one she wore during the day. This changing of garments was a sublime ceremonial, not only in the queen's dressing-room, but also in that of the king. At the king's great levee, none but a prince of the blood had the right to reach him his shirt. At the lesser levee, the nobleman whom the king wished to honor, was called upon to fill this high office; and the enviable mortal, thus honored, remained near the king's person for the whole day; was entitled to dine at the royal table, and had a seat in the king's hunting-wagon.

Now, at the toilet of the queen, the ceremonial was different; and, as in all such matters, more onerous for the woman than for the man. The honor of presenting the chemise, devolved upon the lady present whose rank was the highest.

On the particular day to which we allude, it was the privilege of Madame de Noailles. Marie Antoinette had allowed her night-dress to slip from her shoulders, and stood, bare to the waist, awaiting the pleasure of her mistress of ceremonies. She crossed her beautiful arms, and bent her head in readiness to receive the chemise, which the lady of the bedchamber was in the act of passing to Madame de Noailles.

At this moment there was a knock at the door, and the Duchess of Orleans entered the room. A triumphant smile lit up the face of Madame Etiquette, for now the ceremony would be prolonged. It was no longer her duty, it was that of the duchess, to wait upon the queen. But the proud Countess de Noailles could not condescend to pass the garment to the duchess. That was the duty of the aforesaid lady of the bedchamber. The mistress of ceremonies motioned her to approach, and the duchess began to draw off her gloves.

Meanwhile, Marie Antoinette, with folded arms, stood beautiful as one of Dian's nymphs, but very uncomfortable in her beauty; for she was beginning to grow chilly, and her teeth chattered. At last the preparations were made, and the duchess advanced with the coveted garment.

Suddenly she stopped, and stood perfectly still. She had heard the voice of "Madame," the Countess of Provence; and it would have been an unpardonable sin for the Duchess of Orleans to deprive a princess of the blood, of handing the chemise to the queen.

The door opened, and the sister-in-law of Marie Antoinette came in. The duchess retreated—Madame de Noailles aproached slowly and relieved her of the chemise, and with unflinching deliberation, again gave it into the hands of the lady of the bedchamber.

And there stood the queen, shivering and waiting. Scarlet with shame and anger, though trembling from head to foot, she murmured resentful words against her tormentors. The princess saw it all, and hastened to her relief. Without stopping to remove her gloves, she took the chemise, and advancing, in great haste, to throw it over the queen's head, she struck against her high *toupet* and disarranged the head-dress.

"Oh, my dear sister," said the queen, laughing, "my hair will have to be dressed anew."

Madame de Noailles drew down her eyebrows, as she was accustomed to do when irritated by indecorum, and motioned to the second lady of the bedchamber to put on the queen's shoes. The royal toilet now went on more smoothly, and was completed according to form. This done, it became the duty of the victim to pass into her reception-room, attended by her ladies. Madame de Noailles had opened the door and stood before it like a she-cerberus waiting for her prey to pass within, when the queen, still laughing at her disordered *coiffure*, threw herself into a chair before her *cheval*-glass, and said:

"I hope, madame, that etiquette does not require of the Queen of France to appear before her court with dishevelled hair. If I may be permitted to express a preference in the matter, I would like to have my hair in order."

Madame de Noailles closed the door, and turned stiffly to the first lady of the bedchamber.

"Oh, no," said Marie Antoinette, "I will not trouble my good Madame de Campan to-day. Did my secretary fetch the hair-dresser from Paris?"

"Yes, your majesty," said a lady in waiting, "the hair-dresser is in the outer room."

"Go and call him, De Campan. And now, ladies," said Marie Antionette to the princesses, "you shall see one of the demi-gods. Leonard is called in the world of fashion '*le dieu des coiffures.*'"

"Leonard!" exclaimed Madame de Noailles. "And has your majesty then forgotten that the queen is not permitted to be waited upon by any but womanly hands?"

"The queen not *permitted!*" echoed Marie Antoinette, proudly. "We shall see whether the Queen of France asks permission of her subjects to employ a male or female hair-dresser!"

The door opened, and the discussion was stopped by the entrance of Madame de Campan with Leonard.

"Now, ladies," continued the queen, "be so good as to await me in the reception-room." As she saw that the prim lips of De Noailles were about to be opened, she added: "The mistress of ceremonies and the ladies of the bedchamber will remain."

Leonard's skilful hands were soon at work, loosening the queen's hair; and it glistened, as it fell, like glimmering gold. He surveyed it with such looks of enthusiasm as a statuary might bestow upon the spotless block of marble, whence he will fashion, ere long, the statue of a goddess.

Marie Antoinette, from the mirror, saw his complacent face, and smiled. "What style do you intend to adopt for me?" asked she.

"The *coiffure à la Marie Antoinette,*" said Leonard.

"I have never seen it."

Here Leonard sank the subject, and became the *artiste.* His head went proudly back with a look of conscious power.

"Your majesty must not think me so barren of invention that I should deck the head of my queen with a *coiffure* that has been seen before by mortal eyes."

"Then you are about to invent a *coiffure?*"

"If it please your majesty—if your majesty will condescend to leave its fashion to the inspiration of my genius."

"Follow your inspiration by all means," said the queen, highly amused, and Leonard began his work. A long, solemn pause ensued, and all eyes were strained to see the result. He combed the queen's hair over a trellis of fine wire, then he introduced two down cushions, which he had brought in his band-box, and after he had built him a tower of a foot high, he took a long breath and surveyed the structure. Then he glanced at the toilet-table where lay a mass of flowers, feathers, and laces, which Bertin had left.

"May I be allowed to select from these?" asked he.

The queen nodded, and Leonard chose a bunch of white ostrich-feathers, which he prepared to place in her head.

"Feathers!" cried Marie Antoinette. "You surely are not going to put feathers in my hair!"

"Pardon me, your majesty," said Leonard, with an air of supreme wisdom, "if I beg you to allow me to complete my *coiffure,* before you decide upon its merits." And he went to work to fasten the feathers in his tower.

"This is really becoming," said the queen, not reflecting that her beautiful face with its lofty brow and exquisite contour could bear any abomination with which Leonard chose to invest it.

"I adopt the feathers," said she, "and allow you to call the *coiffure* after me. Poor ostriches, they will not thank me! From this day you are in my service, Monsieur Leonard, and my steward will assign you your apartments."

Leonard bowed with the dignity of an artist who feels that in the favor of his sovereign he receives his merited reward.

"Come every morning at this hour, and every evening at seven o'clock," said Marie Antoinette. "Meanwhile, you are at liberty to dress the hair of as many ladies as you choose."

"Pardon me, your majesty," interposed Madame de Noailles. "An old immutable regulation of the French court forbids any person employed by the royal family to serve a subject; and the *coiffeur* of the queen cannot be allowed to dress the hair of any lady in France."

"Nevertheless, I give him permission to dress as many heads as he pleases, when he is not in attendance upon myself. What is the use of a man's taste and talent if it is all to be wasted on one monotonous employment? Let Monsieur Leonard exercise his ingenuity upon different styles of women, that he may have scope for his imagination."

The mistress of ceremonies sighed, and opened the door. Marie Antoinette approached it gayly, for she was all anxiety to test the effect of her *coiffure* upon the ladies in waiting.

CHAPTER C.

THE NEW FASHIONS AND THEIR UNHAPPY RESULTS.

A MURMUR of surprise and admiration was heard among the ladies, when the queen appeared in the reception-room. The Countess of Provence could scarcely retain her discontent, as she surveyed the magnificent costume of her beautiful sister-in-law.

For a few moments the queen enjoyed the pleasure of being sincerely admired. Then, advancing to the princess, she took her hand and said: "Oblige me, dear sister, by dining with the king and myself *en famille*. Let us have a social meal together to-day."

"Certainly, your majesty, I will do so with pleasure; but what you are pleased to call a family-dinner will lose all its charm through the curiosity of your majesty's admirers, who come from Paris, from Versailles, and from all the ends of the earth, to look at the royal family taking their dinner."

"Not at all," said the queen, eagerly. "I look upon this daily exhibition as a tyrannical custom, which must be abolished. It is too hard that we cannot have our meals in private, but must be gazed at like animals, and denied the privilege of confidential intercourse. I have submitted to be stared at for four years, but the queen is not to be ruled as the dauphiness has been. We shall dine to-day *en famille*, and from this time the public have access to our dining-room no more."

"That is delightful news," answered the princess, "but I pity the good people who are coming in expectaton of seeing your majesty at table."

"They will return to their homes," said the queen, slightly raising her shoulders, "and when they reflect coolly on the subject, they will certainly not think less of me because I prefer to dine like the rest of the world. I believe that if we desire popularity with the people, we must show them that we have feeling hearts like themselves, and it is by such means that I hope to gain the love of the French nation."

The princess was secretly vexed at the honesty and purity of the queen's motives, but she forced a smile, and replied: "You have already succeeded in doing so; for the French people adore you; and if they could only see you to-day in that *piquant* head-dress, they would verify the saying of the mayor of Paris: 'Your majesty beholds in us a hundred thousand lovers.' "

Marie Antoinette laughed. "Quite a respectable army," said she, slightly blushing; "but to complete its worth it must be commanded by the king. How surprised he will be to see us dining in private!"

"His majesty has not been consulted?"

"It is a surprise which I have in store for him. He has often bewailed this stupid custom, but dared not complain, for fear of remarks. I am less timid than he, and I am about to give you a proof of the same."

"Madame de Noailles," added she, aloud, "inform the ushers that while the royal family are at dinner no strangers will be admitted to the dining-room. The privilege of entrance shall cease from to-day."

The countess had been awaiting her opportunity to speak.

"Your majesty," said she, with an expression of painful anxiety, "I entreat of you not to revoke that privilege! Believe me when I tell you that it is dangerous to interfere with customs which are so old that the people have grown to look upon them as rights. Ever since the days of Francis I. the royal family has dined in public, and every decently-clad person has enjoyed the privilege of entering the banquet-room. Moreover, allow me to observe to your majesty that this public meal is an express ceremony of the French court, and it is indispensable to its dignity."

"Etiquette, madame," replied Marie Antoinette, "is not *made* for sovereigns, but *regulated* by them. You speak of the people's rights; allow me to claim something for mine. It has ever been the habit of kings and queens to give commands, not to receive them. Let me, therefore, advise you to strike out from your code of etiquette the rule which obliges us to dine in public, and to insert in its stead the following: 'On days of festivals or of public rejoicing, the people will be admitted to the king's dining-room.' And now, sister, let us take a turn in the park."

So saying, the queen took the arm of the princess, and, followed by the ladies in waiting, they went out upon the terrace. Madame de Noailles remained behind in the large, empty reception-room. Her face was pale and troubled, and she leaned despondently against the high back of an arm-chair near that from which the queen had just risen.

"Royalty totters on its throne!" murmured she, in a low voice. "This woman's bold hand is shaking the pillars of her own temple, and when it falls it will bury both king and queen under its fragments. She laughs at etiquette as ridiculous despotism; she does not know that it is the halo that renders her sacred in the eyes of the people. I see the tempest lowering," continued the mistress of ceremonies, after a thoughtful pause. "The queen is surrounded by enemies whom she defies, and those who would be her friends she alienates by her haughtiness. In the innocence of her thoughtless heart, what unhappy precedents has she established this day! They are the dragon's teeth that will grow armed men to destroy their sower. She despises conventionalities and braves old customs. She does not know how dearly she will pay for her milliner, her hair-dresser, and her dinners in private! I have done my duty. I have warned and remonstrated, and will continue to do so as long as my patience and honor can endure the humiliations to which I am exposed—but no longer! By the Heaven that hears me—no longer!"

The countess was right. The apparently trifling incidents of the day were fraught with mournful consequences to the queen. Heretofore she had been remarked for her simplicity of dress; from the introduction of Bertin and Leonard into her household she dressed with rare magnificence. Not only the ladies of the court, but those of the city, followed her extravagance at a distance. They must wear the same jewels, the same flowers, the same costly silks and laces. Ostrich-feathers became the rage, and they were soon so scarce that fabulous prices were paid to import them for the use of the Frenchwomen.

The *trousseau* of a young beauty became as important as her dowry. Mothers and husbands sighed, and at last ended by abusing the queen. It was she who had set the example of this wasteful luxury in dress; she who had bewitched all the women, so that they had gone mad for a feather or a flower. Strife was in every house. Parents were at variance with their children; marriages were broken off through the exactions of the brides; and on all sides the blame of everybody's domestic troubles fell upon the shoulders of the queen.*

CHAPTER CI.

SUNRISE.

THE court had now moved to Marly. Each day brought its variety of sports, and the palace became the very shrine of pleasure. Even the king, fascinated by his wife's grace and gayety, lost his awkward bearing, and became a devoted lover. He was ready to gratify every whim of hers without ever inquiring whether it was consistent with the dignity and station of a queen. True, all her whims were innocent in themselves; but some of them were childish, and therefore inappropriate to her position.

The king grew so bold that he paid graceful compliments to the queen on the subject of her beauty; and in the exuberance of his young, gushing love, he went beyond his courtiers in felicity of expression, so that finally he became more eloquent than D'Artois, more impassioned than De Chartres, and more piquant than De Provence.

Marie Antoinette beheld this transformation with rapture; and her little innocent coquetries with the princes and noblemen of the court had but one aim—that of heightening the effect of her charms upon her royal husband.

"One of these days," thought she, "he will learn to love me. I await this day, as Nature throughout her dark winter nights, awaits the rising of the glorious sun. Oh how happy will I be when the morning of my wedded love has dawned!"

"But,"—added she, interrupting herself and smiling, "what a simpleton I am with my similes; like a blind man enraptured with a color! I talk of sunrise—I, who am such a barbarian that I never saw the day dawn in my life!—And to think that the French are so fond of comparing me to the rising sun! I think I had better make acquaintance with the original of which I hear so often that I am the copy!"

So the queen, full of a new idea, sent for the Countess de Noailles.

"Madame," said she, "can you tell me at what hour the sun rises?"

"When the *sun* rises!" exclaimed madame, who had hardly ever taken the trouble to remember that the sun rose at all.

"Yes, madame, I wish to know at what hour the sun rises; and I hope there is nothing in your code of etiquette which forbids the Queen of France to aspire to a knowledge of that very commonplace fact."

"I regret, your majesty, that I cannot enlighten you, for I have

* Madame Campan, "Memoirs," vol. i., page 96.

never felt any interest in the matter. But if you allow me, I will make the necessary inquiries."

"Do so, if you please, madame."

Madame de Noailles was absent for some time. At last she returned.

"Pardon me, your majesty, that I have been away so long. But no one in the palace could give me the information I sought. Luckily, in passing one of the corridors, I met a gardener coming in with fresh flowers for your majesty's cabinet, and he was able to tell me. The sun rises at present at three o'clock."

"Thank you. Be so good as to make your arrangements accordingly. I shall get up at three o'clock to-morrow morning and go out upon the hillock in the garden to see the dawn of day."

"Your majesty would go out into the garden at three o'clock in the morning?" said madame, almost fainting with horror.

"Yes, madame," said Marie Antoinette, with decision. "Is there any law in France to forbid me a sight of the sun at that hour?"

"No, your majesty, for such an extraordinary demand could never have been presupposed. Since France was a kingdom, no Queen of France has ever been known to indulge a wish to see the sun rise."

"Unhappy queens! I suppose they were so profoundly engaged in the study of your favorite code, that they had no time to admire the works of God. But you see that I am an eccentric queen, and I would go in all humility to adore Him through one of His glorious works. And as, luckily for me, etiquette has never legislated on the subject, you have no grounds for objection, and I shall commit the astounding indiscretion of going out to see the sun rise."

"Still, your majesty must allow me to say that for all extraordinary cases not provided for in the code of etiquette, the queen must have the consent of the king."

"Do not concern yourself about that; I shall express my desire to the king, and that will suffice. My ladies in waiting who keep diaries can then note, with quiet conscience, that on this day the Queen of France, with the consent of her husband, went into the garden to see the sun rise."

Marie Antoinette slightly inclined her head, and passed into her dressing-room, there to put herself in the hands of Monsieur Leonard. The skilful hair-dresser was in his happiest vein; and when he had achieved the great labor of his day, the queen was inexpressibly charming.

Conformably to her wishes, many irksome court-customs had been laid aside at Marly. The strict lines of demarcation between royalty and nobility no longer hampered the daily intercourse of the sovereigns and their subjects. The lords and ladies in waiting were at liberty to join the queen's circle in the drawing-rooms, or to group themselves together as inclination prompted. Some talked over the events of the day, some discussed the new books which lay in heaps upon a table in one of the saloons; others, again, played billiards with the king.

To-day the court was assembled in an apartment opening into the garden; and the queen, who had just made her appearance in all the splendor of her regal beauty, was the cynosure of attraction and of admiration. She stood in the centre of the room, her eyes fixed wistfully upon the setting sun, whose dying rays were flooding park, terrace, and even the spot on which she stood, with a red and golden light. By her side stood the king, his mild countenance illumined with joy and admiration of his young wife's surpassing loveliness. On the other side of the queen were the princes and princesses of the blood; and around the royal group an assemblage of the youngest, prettiest, and sprightliest women of the aristocracy, escorted by their cavaliers, young nobles whose rank, worth, and culture entitled them to all the favor which they enjoyed at court. At the head of the wits were the Count de Provence, the Count d'Artois, and their kinsman, the Duke de Chartres, known years afterward as "Philippe Égalité." De Chartres and the witty Duke de Lauzun were among the most enthusiastic admirers of the queen.

The French court was in the zenith of its splendor. Youth and beauty were the rule, age was the exception; and in the saloons of Marie Antoinette, its solitary representatives frowned through the deep and angry furrows that dented the wrinkled visage of Madame de Noailles.

To-day the high-priestess of etiquette had taken advantage of the liberty allowed to all, and had absented herself. Her absence was a sensible relief to a court where no man was older than the king, and many a woman was as young as the queen.

For a time Marie Antoinette's glance lingered caressingly upon the garden, through whose perfumed alleys the evening wind was rustling with a sweet, low song. The court, following the mood of the queen, kept perfectly silent. Of what were they thinking? that crowd of youthful triflers, so many of whom were hurrying to the bloody destiny which made heroes of coxcombs and heroines of coquettes!

Suddenly the expression of the queen's face, which had been thoughtful and solemn, changed to its usual frankness and gayety. "Ladies and gentlemen," said she, in that clear, rich voice of hers, which always reminded one of little silver bells, "I have a riddle to propose."

"A riddle!" echoed the company, crowding around to hear.

"Yes, a riddle, and woe to those who cannot guess it! They will be sentenced to sit up this whole night long."

"A severe sentence," said the king, with a sigh. "May I not be one of the condemned? Well, then, lovely sphinx, tell us your riddle."

"Listen all!" said Marie Antoinette, "and strain your every faculty to its solution. Princes and princesses, lords and ladies, can you tell me at what hour the sun will rise to-morrow?"

The perplexed company looked at one another. Everybody seemed puzzled except the king. He alone smiled, and watched the countenances of the others.

"Come, gentlemen, you who are fed on the sciences—come, ladies, you so expert to guess—will none of you solve my riddle?" cried the lively queen. "You, brother Philip, who know all things, have you never asked this question of the sun?"

"I interest myself, dear sister, in matters which concern myself, my family, and France," replied the Count de Provence, not overpleased at the appeal. "The sun, which belongs to another world, has no share in my studies or my meditations."

"Condemned," said the queen, with a merry laugh. "No sleep for you to-night. And you, brother d'Artois, who are such a devotee of beauty, have you never worshipped at the shrine of solar magnificence?"

"The sun rose in this room, your majesty, about a quarter of an hour ago," said Count d'Artois, bowing. "I can, therefore, safely say that in the chateau of Marly it usually rises at eight o'clock."

"Compliments will not save you, D'Artois; you shall not go to sleep this night. And what say you, my sisters-in-law, and our dear Elizabeth?"

"Oh, we dare not be wiser than our husbands!" said the Countess de Provence, quickly.

"Then you shall share their fate," returned Marie Antoinette. "And now," continued she, "cousin de Chartres, it is said that your merry-making sometimes lasts until morning. You, then, must be intimately acquainted with the habits of the rising sun."

"*Ma foi,*" said the duke, with a careless laugh, "your majesty is right. My vigils are frequent; but if returning thence, I have ever met with the sun, I have mistaken it for a street-lantern, and have never given a second thought to the matter."

"Nobody, then, in this aristocratic assemblage, knows aught about the rising of the sun," said the queen.

A profound silence greeted the remark. The queen's face grew pensive, and gradually deepened into sadness.

"Ah!" exclaimed she, with a sigh, "what egotists we are in high life! We expect heaven to shield and sustain us in our grandeur, and never a thought do we return to heaven."

"Am I not to be allowed the privilege of guessing, madame?" asked the king.

"You, sire!" said Marie Antoinette. "It does not become the king's subjects to put questions to him, which he might not be able to answer."

"Nevertheless, I request your majesty to give me a trial."

"Very well, sire. Can you read my riddle, and tell me at what hour the sun will rise to-morrow?"

"Yes, your majesty. The sun will rise at three o'clock," said Louis, with a triumphant smile.

Everybody wondered. Marie Antoinette laughed her silvery laugh, and clapped her little white hands with joy. "Bravo, bravo, my royal Œdipus!" cried she, gayly. "The sphinx is overcome; but she will not throw herself into the sea just yet. She is too happy to bend the knee before her husband's erudition."

With bewitching grace, the queen inclined her beautiful head and knelt before the king. But Louis, blushing with gratification, clasped her hands in his, and raised her tenderly to her feet.

"Madame," said he, "if I had the tact and wit of my brother Charles, I would say that the sun, which so lately has risen, must not set so soon upon its worshippers. But answer me one question—what is the meaning of the riddle with which your majesty has been entertaining us?"

"May I answer with another question? Tell me, sire, have you ever seen the sun rise?"

"I? No, your majesty. I confess that I never have."

"And you, ladies and gentlemen?"

"I can answer for all that they have not," laughed D'Artois.

"Now, sire," said the queen, again addressing her husband, "tell me one thing. Is it unseemly for a Queen of France to see the sun rise?"

"Certainly not," answered the king, laughing heartily.

"Then will your majesty allow me to enjoy that privilege?"

"It seems to me, madame, that you have no consent to ask save that of your own bright eyes. If they promise to remain open all night, you have no one to consult on the subject but yourself."

"I thank your majesty," said the queen. "And now, as none of the company were able to solve my riddle, all must prepare to sit up with me. May I hope, sire, that you will be magnanimous enough to relinquish the right you have earned to retire, and afford me the happiness of your presence also?"

Louis looked quite discomfited, and was about to stammer out some awkward reply, when the marshal of the household threw open the doors of the banquet-hall, and approaching the king, cried out, "*Le roi est servi.*"

"Ah!" said he, much relieved, "let us refresh ourselves for the vigil."

Dinner over, the company promenaded in the gardens for an hour, and then returned to the drawing-room to await the compulsory privilege of seeing the sun rise. Marie Antoinette, with the impatience of a child, was continually going out upon the terrace to see how the night waned; but the moon was up, and the gardens of Marly were bathed in a silver light that was any thing but indicative of the dawn of day.

The scene was so calm and lovely, that the young queen returned to the drawing-room in search of the king, hoping to woo him to the enjoyment of the beautiful nature, which was elevating her thoughts far above the kingdoms of earth and peacefully leading her heart to Heaven. But the king was nowhere to be seen, and as she was seeking him first in one room, then in another, she met the Count de Provence.

I am charged, madame," said he, "with an apology from the king. His majesty begs that you will pardon him for making use of his right to retire. He hopes that your majesty will not enjoy your night the less for his absence." *

The queen colored to her brows, and her expressive face gave token of serious annoyance. She was about to dismiss the company, saying that she had changed her mind, but she remembered that by so doing she might become the subject of the ridicule of the court. Her pride whispered her to remain, and smothered her instinctive sense of propriety. She looked anxiously around for Madame de Noailles, but on the first occasion, when her advice might have been welcome, she was absent. She had been told that etiquette had nothing to do with the queen's party of pleasure, and she, like the king, had retired to rest.

Marie Antoinette then motioned to her first lady of honor, the Princess de Chimay, and requested her to say to Madame de Noailles that her presence would be required in the drawing-room at two o'clock, when the court would set out for the hill, from whence they would witness the dawn of the morrow.

"It is an unconscionable time coming," yawned the Countess de Provence. "See, my dear sister, the hand of the clock points to midnight. What are we to do in the interim?" asked she, peevishly.

"Propose something to while away the time," said the queen, smiling.

* Campan, vol. i., p. 98.

"Let us depute D'Artois to do it. He is readier at such things than the rest of us," said the princess.

"Does your majesty second the proposal?" asked D'Artois.

"I do with all my heart."

"Then," said the thoughtless prince, "I propose that we play the most innocent and rollicking of games—blindman's buff." *

A shout of laughter, in which the young queen joined, was the response to this proposition.

"I was charged with the duty of relieving the tedium of the court," continued the prince gravely. "I once more propose the exciting game of blindman's buff." †

"We are bound to accede," replied the queen, forgetting her embarrassment of the moment before. "Let us try to recall the happy days of our childhood. Let us play blindman's buff until the sun rises and transforms the children of the night once more into earnest and reasoning mortals."

CHAPTER CII.

THE FOLLOWING DAY.

THE queen was alone in her cabinet, which she had not left since she had seen the sun rise. She had taken cold in the garden, and as a souvenir of the event, had carried home a fever and a cough. But it was not indisposition alone which blanched her cheeks. Something mightier than fever glowed in her flashing eyes, something more painful than malady threw that deadly paleness over her sweet, innocent face. From time to time she glanced at a paper lying on the table before her, and every time her eye fell upon it her brow grew darker.

There was a knock at the door. She started, and murmuring—"The king!"—she flung her handkerchief over the papers, and throwing back her head, compelled herself to calmness; while her husband, lifting the silken *portière*, advanced toward the table. She tried to rise, but Louis came hastily to prevent it, saying: "I come to make inquiries concerning your health; but if my presence is to disturb you, I shall retire."

"Remain, then, sire—I will not rise," said the queen, with a languid smile.

"Are you still suffering?" said Louis.

"Only from a cold, sire; it will pass away."

"A cold, for which you are indebted to the chill night-air. It would appear that the Queens of France, who lived and died without seeing the sun rise, were not so stupid, after all."

The queen gave a searching look at the king's face, and saw that it was disturbed.

"I went with your majesty's consent."

"I believe that I was wrong to give it," returned he, thoughtfully; "I should have remembered that for a hundred years past the

* Campan, vol. i., p. 98.

† This game was frequently played in the courtly circles, and not only in aristocratic houses, but in all social gatherings. It became the fashion. Madame de Genlis, who was fond of scourging the follies of her day, made this fashion the subject of one of her dramas.

court of France has been so corrupt that unhappily the French nation have lost all faith in chastity and purity of heart. You, madame, must teach them to distinguish the innocence which has nothing to conceal, from the depravity which has lost all shame. But we must be cautious, and so conduct ourselves, that our actions may be beyond misconstruction."

"Your majesty wishes me to infer that my harmless desire to behold one of the glorious works of my Maker, has been misinterpreted?" said the queen, opening her large eyes full upon her husband.

The king avoided her glance.

"No, no," said he, with embarrassment. "I speak not of what has been, but of what might be."

"And this most innocent of wishes has inspired your majesty with these apprehensions?"

"I do not say so, but—"

"But your majesty knows that it *is* so," cried the queen. "It is very generous of you to save my feelings by concealing that which you know must subject me to mortification; but others here are less magnanimous than you, sire. I have already seen the obscene libel to which my pleasure party has given birth. I have read '*Le lever de l'aurore.*'"

"Who has dared to insult you by the sight of it?" asked Louis, indignantly.

"Oh, sire," said Marie Antoinette, bitterly, "there are always good friends, who are ready to wound us with the weapons of others. I found the lampoon on my table this morning, among my letters."

"You shall not be exposed to a repetition of this. Campan shall look over your papers before he presents them."

"Do you think I am likely to find them often, sire? I hope not. But be that as it may, I am no coward. I have courage to face any amount of calumny—for my heart is pure, and my life will vindicate me."

"It will, indeed," said the king, tenderly. "But you must keep aloof from the poisonous atmosphere of slander. We must live less among the multitude."

"Ah, sire, how can we keep aloof from those who have the right to be near us?"

The king started, almost imperceptibly, and his anxious glance rested upon his wife's honest, truthful eyes. Removing her handkerchief, she pointed to a paper.

"This is the envelope in which I found '*Le lever de l'aurore.*' The handwriting is disguised; but tell me frankly if you do not recognize it. *I* do."

"I—really—I may be mistaken," began the king, "but—"

"Nay, you see that it is the hand of the Count de Provence, your own brother, sire. He it is, who enjoys the cruel satisfaction of having forced this indecent libel upon my notice, and I doubt not for one moment that he also is the one who sent it to you."

"Yes, no doubt, he did it to warn us, and we must be grateful and take the warning to our hearts."

The queen laughed scornfully.

"Does your majesty suppose that these drawings were made with the same benevolent intention?" said she, handing him a second paper. "Look at these indecent caricatures, made still more obnoxious by the vulgar observations attached to them. There is no disguise of his handwriting here, for this was not intended for my eye."

"Too true," sighed the king—"the drawings and the writing are both my brother's. But who can have sent you these shameful sketches?"

"I told you just now, sire, that there are always people to be found, who stab their friends with borrowed weapons. The drawings were accompanied by a letter, informing me, that they were executed in the saloons of Madame Adelaide, and that the remarks were the joint productions of your majesty's brother and your aunts."

The king passed his handkerchief over his forehead, to dry the heavy drops of sweat that were gathering there, and rose up, with the paper in his hand.

"Where is your majesty going?" asked the queen.

"To my brother," cried he, indignantly. "I will show him this disgraceful paper, and ask by what right he outrages my wife and his queen! I shall tell him that his actions are those of a traitor and—"

"And when you have told him that, will you punish him as kings punish traitors?"

The king was silent, and the queen continued, with a sad smile.

"You could not punish him; for the traitor who outrages the queen is the brother of the king, and, therefore, he can outrage with impunity."

"He shall not do it with impunity! I will force him to honor and love you."

"Ah, sire, love will not yield to force," said Marie Antoinette, in a tone of anguish. "Were I as pure as an angel, the Count de Provence would hate me for my Austrian birth, and Madame Adelaide would use the *great* influence she possesses over your majesty to rob me of the *little* favor I am gaining in your sight."

"Oh, Antoinette, do you not feel that my whole heart is yours?" said Louis, affectionately. "Believe me, when I say that it is in the power of no human being to sully your sweet image in my eyes. Do not fear the royal family. I am here to protect you, and, soon or late, your worth will overcome their prejudices."

"No, sire, no. Nothing will ever win me their regard. But I am resolved to brave their enmity, satisfied that, in the eyes of the world, my conduct and my conscience both will sustain me."

"Your husband also," said the king, kissing her hand.

"Sire, I hope so," said Marie Antoinette, in a tremulous voice. "And now," continued she, dashing away the tear-drops that were gathering in her eyes, "now give me those caricatures. They have served to convince your majesty that I know my enemies—and defy them. Their mission is accomplished; let us try to forget their existence."

She took the drawings from his hand, and, tearing them to pieces, scattered them over the carpet. The king picked up a few of the fragments.

"Will you allow me to retain these as a *souvenir* of this hour?" said he, gazing fondly upon her sweet face.

"Certainly, sire."

"But you know that princes can never receive a gift without returning one. Therefore, do me the favor to accept this. It is paper for paper."

He drew from his bosom a little package, to which the royal seal was affixed, and Marie Antoinette took it, with a glance of surprise.

"What can it be?" said she, as she unfolded it.

He watched her as she read; and thought how beautiful she was, as, blushing and smiling, she held out her hand to thank him.

"How, sire," said she, joyfully, "you make me this royal gift?"

"If you will accept it. The chateau de Trianon is a small estate, but its mistress may at least find it a home where she will have liberty to enjoy nature without exciting the malevolence of her enemies. No one can watch you there, Antoinette; for your castle is not large enough to lodge your slanderers. It will scarcely accommodate your friends."

"How can I ever thank you, sire?" said she, in grateful accents. "You have understood my heart, and have gratified its weary longings for occasional solitude. This, then, is my own private domain?"

"Certainly."

"And I may rule there without interference from state or etiquette?"

"Assuredly. As *chatelaine* of Trianon, you alone will regulate its customs, and all who visit you, must submit to your rules."

"And no man can enter my chateau without an invitation?"

"Not even the king himself."

Marie Antoinette smiled until the pearls encased within her coral lips dazzled the royal vision.

"How delightful!" said she. "I do not think that the Count de Provence will ever be invited to Trianon."

"Nor I," replied Louis.

"But the king will be asked so often, that he will certainly wish he were the Count de Provence. Still, he must promise not to come until he receives his invitation."

"I promise, beautiful *chatelaine.*"

"And then to come whenever I invite him."

"That I can promise more safely than the other."

"Upon your royal word?"

"Upon my royal word. And thus I seal it with a kiss upon your fair hand."

"Upon my hand only, sire?" asked she, while she turned a cheek, whose hue was like the rosy lining of a sea-shell.

Louis accepted the challenge, and pressed a kiss so passionate upon that cheek, that it flushed to a deep, burning crimson, and the queen's eyes were cast down, till nothing of them was visible except her long, dark lashes.

The royal lover, too, grew very red, and stammered a few inaudible words. Then, bowing, awkwardly, he stumbled over an armchair, and retreated in dire confusion.

Marie Antoinette looked after her clumsy king with a beating heart.

"Am I, indeed, to be blessed with his love?" thought the poor, young thing. "If I am, I shall be the happiest and most enviable of women."

CHAPTER CIII.

THE LAST APPEAL.

THE carriage of the Countess Esterhazy was returning from a ball which the empress had given in honor of her son's departure from Vienna. Joseph was about to visit France, and his lovely young sister was once more to hear the sound of a beloved voice from home.

It was long past midnight; but the Hotel Esterhazy was one blaze of light. It had been one of the countess's first orders to her steward that, at dusk, every chandelier in her palace should be lighted. She hated night and darkness, she said, and must have hundreds of wax-lights burning from twilight until morning. This was one of the whims of the fair Margaret, which, although it amused all Vienna, was any thing but comic to her husband, for it cost him one thousand florins a month.

The hotel, then, from ground-floor to attic, was bright as noonday. Six lackeys, in silvered livery, stood on either side of the entrance, with torches in their hands, to light their lady to the vestibule. From the inner door to the staircase a rich Turkey carpet covered the floor; and, here again, stood twelve more lackeys, performing the office of candelabra to the light-loving countess. At the foot of the stairs stood the steward and the butler of the household, awaiting such orders as she might choose to fling at them on her way; and at the head of the stairs, waiting to receive her, stood a bevy of *dames de compagnie*, and other female attendants.

The countess passed through this living throng without vouchsafing one glance in acknowledgment of their respectful greetings. In profound silence she swept up the stairway; her long, glossy train of white satin following her as she went, like the foaming track that a ship leaves upon the broad bosom of the ocean, and the diamonds that decked her brow, neck, and arms, flinging showers of radiance that dazzled the eye like lightning when the storm is at its height. Her head was thrown back, her large black eyes were starry as ever, and her face was so pale that its pallor was unearthly.

At the landing-place she turned, and speaking to the steward, said:

"Let Count Esterhazy know that in ten minutes I await him in the blue-room." Having said thus much, she continued her way, and disappeared from the eyes of her staring household.

Her disappearance was the signal for the transformation of the candelabra into men.

"Did you hear her?" whispered one. "She has sent for the count."

"Never troubling herself whether he sleeps or wakes," said another. "Poor man! He has been in bed for four hours."

"No wonder he goes to bed early," remarked a third. "It is the only place on earth where he has peace."

"Nevertheless he will be obedient and come; he dare not refuse."

"Oh, no!" was the general response. "In ten minutes he will be here; or his amiable countess will treat us to a scene like some we have witnessed, wherein she flings handfuls of gold out of the windows, and gathers all the people in Vienna before the hotel to see the show."

The servants were right; Count Esterhazy did not disobey his wife. He trembled when he received her message, called nervously for his valet to dress him, and at the end of the ten minutes was on his way to the blue-room.

The countess was there before him, looking like an angry queen about to condemn a recreant vassal to death. And Esterhazy, with the mien and gait of a culprit, came into her presence with a bow that was almost a genuflection.

"You see, countess," said he, "with what haste I obey your commands. I feel so honored at the call, that—"

He paused—for really her fiery eyes seemed to burn him; and her contempt dried up the stream of his commonplace flattery, as the breath of the sirocco parches up the dew-drops.

"Why do you not go on?" said she.

"I am bewildered by my own joy," replied he, blandly. "Remember—it is the first time since our marriage that you have allowed me the privilege of an interview in private; and I may well lose my speech in the intoxication of such a moment."

"It *is* the first time. You have a good memory. Can you also recollect how long it is since we had that interview?"

"Can I recollect? Four long years!"

"Four long years," sighed she, "to the day, and almost to the hour."

"Indeed!" exclaimed the count. "And can you forgive me for having forgotten this charming anniversary?"

"You are happy to have tasted of the Lethe of indifference. I—I have counted the days and the hours of my slavery; and each day and hour is branded upon my heart. Have you forgotten, too, Count Esterhazy, what I swore to you on that wedding-night?"

"Yes, Margaret—I have forgotten all the cruel words you spoke to me in an outburst of just indignation."

"I wonder that you should have forgotten them, for it has been my daily care to remind you of the vow I then made. Have I not kept my word? Have I not crossed your path with the burning ploughshares of my hatred? Have I not cursed your home, wasted your wealth, and made you the laughing-stock of all Vienna?"

"You judge yourself with too much severity, Margaret," said the count, mildly. "True—we have not been very happy; since this is the first time since our marriage-night, that we are face to face without witnesses. I will not deny, either, that our household expenditures have cost several millions, and have greatly exceeded our income. But the lovely Countess Esterhazy has a right to exceed all other women in the splendor of her concerts and balls, and the richness of her dress. Come, make me amends for the past—I forgive you. There is still time to—"

"No!" exclaimed she, "the time went by four years ago. You can never make amends to *me*, nor I to *you*. Look at yourself! You were then a young man, with high hopes and a light heart. Many a woman would have been proud to be called your wife—and yet you chose *me*. Now, that four years of accursed wedded life have gone over your head, you have passed from youth to old age, without ever having known an interval of manhood. And I—O God! What have I become through your miserable cowardice! I might have grown to be a gentle woman, had fate united me to him whom I love; but the link that has bound me to you has unsexed me. Our marriage was a crime, and we have paid its penalty; *you* are as weak as a woman, and *I*—as inflexible as a man."

Two large tears glittered in her eyes, and fell slowly down her pale cheeks. Count Esterhazy approached and caressed her with his hands. She shuddered at his touch, recoiling as if from contact with a reptile. Meanwhile, he was imploring her to begin a new life with him—to give him her hand, to make him the happiest of men.

"No, no, no!" cried she. "In mercy cease, or you will drive me mad. But I will forgive you even your past treachery, if you will grant the request I am about to make."

"You will condescend to ask something of me! Speak, Margaret speak! What can I do to make you happy?"

"You can give me my freedom," replied the countess, in a soft, imploring voice. "Go with me to the empress, and beg her to undo what she has done. Tell her that she has blasted the lives of two human beings—tell her that we are two galley-slaves, pining for liberty."

Count Esterhazy shook his head. "The empress will never allow us to be divorced," said he, "for I have too often assured her that I was happy beyond expression, and she would not believe me if I came with another story."

"Then let us go to the fountain-head," said the countess, wringing her hands. "Let us go to the pope, and implore him to loose the bands of our mutual misery."

"Impossible! That would be a slight which the empress never would forgive. I should fall under her displeasure."

"Oh, these servile hearts that have no life but that which they borrow from the favor of princes!" cried Margaret, scornfully. "What has the favor of the empress been worth to you? For what have you to thank her? For these four years of martyrdom, which you have spent with a woman who despises you?"

"I cannot dispense with the good-will of my sovereign," said the count, with something like fervor. "For hundreds of years, the Esterhazys have been the favorites of the Emperors of Austria; and we cannot afford to lose the station we enjoy therefrom. No—I will do nothing to irritate the empress. She chose you for my wife, and, therefore, I wear my chains patiently. Maria Theresa knows how I have obeyed and honored her commands; and, one of these days, I shall reap the reward of my loyalty. If Count Palfy dies, I am to be marshal of the imperial household; but yet higher honors await us both. If I continue to deserve the favor of the empress, she will confer upon me the title of 'prince.' You refuse to be my wife, Margaret; but you will one day be proud to let me deck that haughty brow with the coronet of a princess."

Margaret looked more contemptuously at him than before.

"You are even more degraded than I had supposed," said she. "Poor, crawling reptile, I do not even pity you. I ask you, for the last time, will you go with me to Rome to obtain a divorce?"

"Why do you repeat your unreasonable request, Margaret? It is vain for you to hope for a divorce. Waste my fortune if you will—I canot hinder you—I will find means to repair my losses; and the empress, herself, will come to my assistance, for—"

"Enough!" interrupted the countess. "Since you will not aid

me in procuring our divorce, it shall be forced upon you. I will draw across your escutcheon such a bar sinister as your princely coronet will not be large enough to hide. That is my last warning to you. Now leave me."

"Margaret, I implore you to forgive me if I cannot make this great sacrifice. I cannot part from you, indeed I cannot," began the count.

"And the empress will reward your constancy with the title of 'prince,'" replied Margaret, with withering scorn. "Go—you are not worthy of my anger—but I shall know where to strike. Away with you!"

Count Esterhazy, with a deep sigh, turned and left the room.

"The last hope to which I clung, has vanished!" said she, "and I must resort to disgrace!"

She bent her head, and a shower of tears came to her relief. But they did not soften her heart. She rose from her seat, muttering, "It is too late to weep! I have no alternative. The hour for revenge has struck!"

CHAPTER CIV.

THE FLIGHT.

THE countess passed into her dressing-room. She closed and locked the door, then, going across the room, she stopped before a large picture that hung opposite to her rich Venetian toilet-mirror. The frame of this picture was ornamented with small gilt rosettes. Margaret laid her hand upon one of these rosettes, and drew it toward her. A noise of machinery was heard behind the wall. She drew down the rosette a second time, and then stepped back. The whirr was heard again, the picture began to move, and behind it appeared a secret door. Margaret opened it, and, as she did so, her whole frame shook as if with a deadly repugnance to that which was within.

"I am here, Count Schulenberg," said she, coldly.

The figure of a young man appeared at the doorway.

"May I presume to enter paradise?" said he, stepping into the room with a flippant air.

"You may," replied she, without moving; but the hue of shame overspread her face, neck, and arms, and it was plain to Count Schulenberg that she trembled violently.

These were to him the signals of his triumph; and he smiled with satisfaction as he surveyed this lovely woman, so long acknowledged to be the beauty *par excellence* of the imperial court at Vienna. Margaret allowed him to take her hand, and stood coldly passive, while he covered it with kisses; but when he would have gone further, and put his arm around her waist, she raised her hands, and receded.

"Not here," murmured she, hoarsely. "Not here, in the house of the man whose name I bear. Let us not desecrate love; enough that we defile marriage."

"Come, then, beloved, come," said he, imploringly. "The coach is at the door, and I have passes for France, Italy, Spain, and England. Choose yourself the spot wherein we shall bury our love from the world's gaze."

"We go to Paris," replied she, turning away her head.

"To Paris, dearest? Why, you have forgotten that the emperor leaves for Paris to-morrow, and that we incur the risk of recognition there."

"Not at all—Paris is a large city, and if we are discovered, I shall seek protection from the emperor. He knows of my unhappy marriage, and sympathizes with my sorrows."

"Perhaps you are right, dearest. Then in Paris we spend our honey-moon, and there enjoy the bliss of requited love."

"There, and not until we reach there," said she, gravely. "I require a last proof of your devotion, count. I exact that until we arrive in Paris you shall not speak to me of love. You shall consider me as a sister, and allow me the privilege of travelling in the carriage with my maid—she and I on one seat, you opposite."

"Margaret, that is abominable tyranny. You expect me to be near you, and not to speak of love! I must be watched by your maid, and sit opposite to you!—You surely cannot mean what you say."

"I do, indeed, Count Schulenberg."

"But think of all that I have endured for a year that I have adored you, cold beauty! Not one single proof of love have you ever given me yet. You have tolerated mine, but have never returned it."

"Did I not write to you?"

"Write; yes. You wrote me to say that you would not consent to be mine unless I carried you away from Vienna. Then you went on to order our mode of travelling as you would have done had I been your husband. 'Be here at such an hour; have your passes for various countries. Describe me therein as your sister. Come through the garden and await me at the head of the secret stairway.' Is this a love-letter? It is a mere note of instructions. For one week I have waited for a look, a sigh, a pressure of the hand; and when I come hither to take you from your home forever, you receive me as if I were a courier. No, Margaret, no—I will not wait to speak my love until we are in Paris."

"Then, Count Schulenberg, farewell. We have nothing more to say to one another."

She turned to leave the room, but Schulenberg darted forward and fell at her feet. "Margaret, beloved," cried he, "give me one single word of comfort. I thirst to know that you love me."

"Can a woman go further than I am going at this moment?" asked Margaret, with a strange, hollow laugh.

"No. I acknowledge my unspeakable happiness in being the partner of your flight. But I cannot comprehend your love. It is a bitter draught in a golden beaker."

"Then do not drink it," said she, retreating.

"I must—I must drink it; for my soul thirsts for the cup, and I will accept its contents."

"My conditions?"

"Yes, since I must," said Schulenberg, heaving a sigh. "I promise, then, to contain my ecstasy until we reach Paris, and to allow that guardian of virtue, your maid, to sit by your side, while I suffer agony opposite. But oh! when we reach Paris—"

"In Paris we will talk further, and my speech shall be different."

"Thank you, beloved," cried the count passionately. "This heavenly promise will sustain me through my ordeal." He kissed the tips of her fingers, and she retired to change her ball-dress for a travelling habit.

When she had closed the door, the expression of Count Schulenberg's face was not quite the same.

"The fierce countess is about to be tamed," thought he. "I shall win my bet, and humble this insolent beauty. Let her rule if she must, until we reach Paris; but there I will repay her, and her chains shall not be light. Really, this is a piquant adventure. I am making a delightful wedding-tour, without the bore of the marriage-ceremony, at the expense of the most beautiful woman in Europe; and to heighten the piquancy of the affair, I am to receive two thousand louis d'ors on my return to Vienna. Here she comes."

"I am ready," said Margaret, coming in, followed by her maid, who held her mistress's travelling-bag.

Count Schulenberg darted forward to offer his arm, but she waved him away.

"Follow me," said she, passing at once through the secret opening. Schulenberg followed, "sighing like a furnace," and looking daggers at the confidante, who in her turn looked sneeringly at him. A few moments after they entered the carriage. The windows of the Hotel Esterhazy were as brilliantly illuminated as ever, while the master of the house slumbered peacefully. And yet a shadow had fallen upon the proud escutcheon which surmounted the silken curtains of his luxurious bed—the shadow of that disgrace with which his outraged wife had threatened him!

CHAPTER CV.

JOSEPH IN FRANCE.

A LONG train of travelling carriages was about to cross the bridge which spans the Rhine at Strasburg, and separates Germany from France. It was the suite of the Count of Falkenstein, who was on his way to visit his royal sister.

Thirty persons, exclusive of Count Rosenberg and two other confidential friends, accompanied the emperor. Of course, the *incognito* of a Count of Falkenstein, who travelled with such a suite, was not of much value to him; so that he had endured all the tedium of an official journey. This was all very proper in the eyes of Maria Theresa, who thought it impossible for Jove to travel without his thunder. But Jove himself, as everybody knows, was much addicted to *incognitos*, and so was his terrene representative, the Emperor of Austria.

The imperial *cortége*, then, was just about to pass from Germany to France. It was evening, and the fiery gold of the setting sun was mirrored in the waves of the Rhine which with gentle murmur were toying with the greensward that sloped gracefully down to the water's edge. The emperor gave the word to halt, and rising from his seat, looked back upon the long line of carriages that followed in his wake.

"Rosenberg," said he, laying his hand upon the count's shoulder, "tell me frankly how do you enjoy this way of travelling?"

"Ah, sire, I have been thinking all day of the delights of our other journeys. Do you remember our hunt for dinner in the dirty little hamlet, and the nights we spent on horseback in Galicia? There was no monotony in travelling then!"

"Thank you, thank you," said the emperor, with a bright smile. "I see that we are of one mind."

He motioned to the occupants of the carriage immediately behind him, and they hastened to obey the signal.

The emperor, after thanking them for the manner in which they had acquitted themselves of their respective duties, proposed a change in their plans of travel.

"Then," replied Herr von Bourgeois, with a sigh, "your majesty has no further use for us, and we return to Vienna."

"Not at all, not at all," said the emperor, who had heard and understood the sigh wafted toward Paris and its thousand attractions. "We will only part company that we may travel more at our ease, and once in Paris, we again join forces. Be so good as to make your arrangements accordingly, and to make my adieux to the other gentlemen of our suite."

Not long after, the imperial *cortége* separated into three columns, each one of which was to go independent of the other, and all to unite when they had reached Paris. As the last of the carriages with which he had parted, disappeared on the other side of the bridge the emperor drew a long breath and looked radiant with satisfaction.

"Let us wait," said he, "until the dust of my imperial magnificence is laid, before we cross the bridge to seek lodgings for the night. Meanwhile, Rosenberg, give me your arm and let us walk along the banks of the Rhine."

They crossed the high-road and took a foot-path that led to the banks of the river. At that evening hour every thing was peaceful and quiet. Now and then a peasant came slowly following his hay-laden wagon, and occasionally some village-girl carolled a love-lay, or softly murmured a vesper hymn.

The emperor, who had been walking fast, suddenly stopped, and gazed with rapture upon the scene.

"See, Rosenberg," said he, "see how beautiful Germany is to-day! As beautiful as a laughing youth upon whose brow is stamped the future hero."

"Your majesty will transform the boy into a hero," said Rosenberg.

The emperor frowned. "Let us forget for a moment the mummery of royalty," said he. "You know, moreover, that royalty has brought me nothing but misery. Instead of reigning over others, I am continually passing under the Caudine Forks of another's despotic will."

"But the day will come when the emperor shall reign alone, and then the sun of greatness will rise for Germany."

"Heaven grant it! I have the will to make of Germany one powerful empire. Oh, that I had the power, too! My friend, we are alone, and no one hears except God. Here on the confines of Germany, the poor unhappy emperor may be permitted to shed a tear over the severed garment of German royalty—that garment which has been rent by so many little princes! Have you observed, Rosenberg, how they have soiled its majesty? Have you noticed the pretensions of these manikins whose domains we can span with our hands? Is it not pitiable that each one in his principality is equal in power to the Emperor of Austria!"

"Yes, indeed," said Rosenberg with a sigh, "Germany swarms with little princes!"

"Too many little princes," echoed Joseph, "and therefore their lord and emperor is curtailed by so much of his own lawful rights, and Germany is an empty name among nations! If the Germans were capable of an enlightened patriotism; if they would throw away their Anglomania, Gallomania, Prussomania, and Austromania, they would be something more than the feeble echoes of intriguers and pedants.* Each one thrusts his own little province forward, while all forget the one great fatherland!"

"But the Emperor Joseph will be lord of all Germany," cried Rosenberg, exultingly, "and he will remind them that they are vassals and he is their suzerain!"

"They must have a bloody lesson to remind them of that," said the emperor, moodily. "Look behind you, Rosenberg, on the other side of the Rhine. There lies a kingdom neither larger nor more populous than Germany; a kingdom which rules us by its industry and caprices, and is great by reason of its unity, because its millions of men are under the sway of one monarch."

"And yet it was once with France as it is to-day with Germany," said Count Rosenberg. "There were Normandy, Brittany, Provence, Languedoc, Burgundy, and Franche-Comté, all petty dukedoms striving against their allegiance to the king. Where are their rulers now? Buried and forgotten, while their provinces own the sway of the one monarch who rules all France. What France has accomplished, Germany, too, can compass."

The emperor placed his hand affectionately upon Rosenberg's shoulder. "You have read my heart, friend," said he, smiling. "Do you know what wild wishes are surging within me now? wishes which Frederick of Prussia would condemn as unlawful, although it was quite righteous for him to rob Austria of Silesia. I, too, have my Silesia, and, by the Lord above me! my title-deeds are not as mouldy as his!"

"Only that your Silesia is called Bavaria," said Rosenberg, with a significant smile.

"For God's sake," cried Joseph, "do not let the rushes hear you, lest they betray me to the babbling wind, and the wind bear it to the King of Prussia. But you have guessed. Bavaria is a *portion* of my Silesia, but only a portion. Bavaria is mine by right of inheritance, and I shall take it when the time comes. It will be a comely patch to stop some of the rents in my imperial mantle. But my Silesia lies at every point of the compass. To the east lie Bosnia and Servia—to the south, see superannuated Venice. The lion of St. Mark is old and blind, and will fall an easy prey to the eagle of Hapsburg. This will extend our dominions to the Adriatic sea. When the Duke of Modena is gathered to his fathers, my brother, in right of his wife, succeeds to the title; and as Ferrara once belonged to the house of Modena, he and I together can easily wrest it from the pope. Close by are the Tortonese and Alessandria, two fair provinces which the King of Sardinia supposes to be his. *They* once formed a portion of the duchy of Milan; and Milan is ours, with every acre of land that ever belonged to it. By Heaven, I will have all that is mine, if it cost me a seven years' war to win it back! This is not all. Look toward the west, beyond the spires of Stras-

* The emperor's own words. See "Joseph II., Correspondence," p. 175.

burg, where the green and fertile plains of Alsatia woo our coming. They now belong to France, but they *shall* be the property of Austria. Farther on lies Lorraine. That, too, is mine, for my father's title was 'Duke of Lorraine.' What is it to me that Francis the First sold his birthright to France? All that I covet I shall annex to Austria, as surely as Frederick wrested Silesia from me."

"And do you intend to let him keep possession of Silesia?" asked Rosenberg.

"Not if I can prevent it, but that may not be optional with me. I will—but hush! Let us speak no more of the future; my soul faints with thirst when I think of it. Sometimes I think I see Germany pointing to her many wounds, and calling me to come and heal her lacerated body. And yet I can do nothing! I must stand with folded arms, nor wish that I were lord of Austria; for God knows that I do not long for Maria Theresa's death. May she reign for many years; but oh! may I live to see the day wherein I shall be sole monarch not only of Austria, but of all Germany. If it ever dawns for me, the provinces shall no longer speak each one its own language. Italians, Hungarians, and Austrians, all shall be German, and we shall have one people and one tongue. To insure the prosperity of my empire, I will strengthen my alliance with France. I dislike the French, but I must secure their neutrality before I step into possession of Bavaria, and assert my claims to my many-sided Silesia. Well—these are dreams; day has not yet dawned for me! The future Emperor of Germany is yet a vassal, and he who goes to France to-day is nothing but a Count of Falkenstein. Come, let us cross the bridge that at once unites France with Germany, and divides them one from the other." *

CHAPTER CVI.

THE GODFATHER.

THERE was great commotion at the post-house of the little town of Vitry. Two maids, in their Sunday best, were transforming the public parlor of the inn into a festive dining-room; wreathing the walls with garlands, decking the long dining-table with flowers, and converting the huge dresser into a *buffet* whereon they deposited the pretty gilt china, the large cakes, the pastries, jellies, and confections, that were designed for the entertainment of thirty invited guests. The landlord and postmaster, a slender little man with an excellent, good-humored face, was hurrying from *buffet* to table, from table to kitchen, superintending the servants. The cook was deep in the preparation of her roasts and warm dishes; and at the kitchen door sat a little maiden, who, with important mien, was selecting the whitest and crispest leaves from a mountain of lettuce which she laid into a large gilt salad-bowl beside her; throwing the others to a delighted pig, who, like Lazarus, stood by to pick up the leavings of his betters. In the yard, at the fountain, stood the man-of-all-work, who, as butler *pro tem.*, was washing plates and glasses; while close by, on the flags, sat the clerk of the post-office, polishing and uncorking the bottles which the host had just brought from the cellar in honor of his friends.

* These are Joseph's own words. See "Letters of Joseph II.," p. 175.

Monsieur Etienne surveyed his notes of preparation, and gave an approving nod. His face was radiant as he returned to the house; gave another glance of satisfaction around the dining-room, and passed into an adjoining apartment. This was the best-furnished room in the post-house; and on a soft lounge, near the window, reclined a pale young woman, beautifully dressed, whose vicinity to a cradle, where lay a very young infant, betokened her recent recovery from confinement.

"Athanasia, my goddess," said Monsieur Etienne, coming in on tiptoe, "how do you feel to-day?"

She reached out her pale hand and answered in a languid voice: "The doctor says that, so far, I am doing pretty well, and, by great precautions, I may be able, in a few weeks, to resume my household duties."

Monsieur Etienne raised his eyebrows, and looked thoughtful. "The doctor is over-anxious, my dear," said he: "he exaggerates your weakness. Our little angel there is already three weeks old, and will be standing on his legs before long."

"The doctor is more sympathizing than you, Monsieur Etienne," began the wife.

"My treasure," interrupted her husband, "no one can wish to spare you premature exertion more than I. But I do entreat of you, my angel, to do your best to remain with the company to-day as long as you can."

"I will do all in my power to oblige you," said Madame Etienne, condescendingly, "and if you require it, I will sit up from first to last."

"It will be a great festival for us, provided no passengers arrive to-day. Good Heaven! if they should come, what could I do with them? Even the best of those we receive here are scarcely fit to introduce among our respectable guests; and then, as for post-horses, I want every one of them for the company. Heaven defend us, then, from passengers, for—oh! oh! is it possible! Can it be!" said Etienne, interrupting himself. "Yes, it is the sound of a post-horn."

"Perhaps it is some of our guests," suggested Madame Etienne.

"No no, for our postilions to-day play but one air, '*Je suis père, un père heureux,*'" said Monsieur Etienne, listening with all his might to the approaching horn.

"It is a passenger," said he, despondingly, "Athanasia, my angel, we are lost!"

So saying, Monsieur Etienne darted out of the room, as if he were rushing off to look for himself; but he stopped as soon as he had reached his front door, for there was no necessity to go farther. A dark *calèche*, with three horses, dashed up to the door, while not far behind came another chaise, whose post-horn was sounding "*Je suis père, un père heureux.*"

"Is it possible?" thought the discomfited postmaster. "Yes, here they come at the very moment when the guests are arriving."

Just then another horn was heard, and "*Je suis père, un père heureux,*" made the welkin ring.

On every side they came, but the unlucky passenger *calèche* blocked up the passage. Monsieur Etienne, following the impulses of his heart, rushed past the strangers, and ran to greet the most important of his guests, the village curate and the pastor of the next market-place. But just then the bewildered little man remembered his duty, and darted back to the passengers.

There were two gentlemen in the carriage, and on the box, near the postilion, a third person, who had the air of a valet.

"The gentlemen wish to go on to the next stage?" said Etienne, without opening the door.

"No, sir," said one of the passengers, raising his dark-blue eyes to the post-house. "Your house looks inviting, and we would like a room and a cosy dinner."

Monsieur Etienne scarcely knew what reply to make to this untimely request. "You wish to dine here—here—you would—"

Down came another post-chaise, thundering on the stones, and louder than ever was the sound of "*Je suis père, un père heureux.*"

Certainly, at that moment, the song was a mockery, for Monsieur Etienne was a most unhappy and distracted father.

"Gentlemen," said he, pathetically, "oblige me by going on to the next town. Indeed—"

"Why, will you not give us dinner?" asked the gentleman who had spoken before. "I see a number of people passing us and entering the house. How is that?"

"Sir, they are—that is—I am," stammered the landlord; then suddenly plunging into a desperate resolve, he said, "Are you a father?"

A shade passed over the stranger's face as he replied, "I *have* been a father. But why such a question?"

"Oh, if you have been a father," answered Etienne, "you will sympathize with me, when I tell you that to-day we christen our first-born child."

"Ah, indeed!" exclaimed the passenger, with a kind smile. "Then these persons are—"

"My guests," interrupted the landlord and postmaster, "and you will know how to excuse me if—"

"If you wish us to the devil," returned the blue-eyed stranger, laughing merrily. "But, indeed, I cannot oblige you, my excellent friend, for I don't know where his infernal majesty is to be found; and if I may be allowed a preference, I would rather remain in the society of the two priests whom I see going into your house."

"You will not go farther, then—"

"Oh, no, we ask to be allowed to join your guests, and attend the christening. The baptism of a first-born child is a ceremony which touches my heart, and yours, also, does it not?" said the stranger to his companion.

"Certainly," replied the other, laughing, "above all, when it is joined to another interesting ceremony—that of a good dinner."

"Oh, you shall have a good dinner!" cried Etienne, won over by the sympathy of the first speaker. "Come in, gentlemen, come in. As the guests of our little son, you are welcome."

CHAPTER CVII.

THE GODFATHER.

"WE accept with pleasure," said the strangers, and they followed the host into the house. The door of the room where the guests were assembled was open, and the strangers, with a self-possession which proved them to be of the aristocracy, walked in and mingled at once in the conversation.

"Allow me, gentlemen," said the host, when he had greeted the remainder of his guests, "allow me to present you to Madame Etienne. She will be proud to receive two such distinguished strangers in her house to-day."

Madame Etienne, with a woman's practised eye, saw at once that these unknown guests, who were so perfectly unembarrassed and yet so courteous, must belong to the very first ranks of society; and she was happy to be able to show off her *savoir vivre* before the rest of the company.

She received the two travellers with much grace and affability; and whereas the curates were to have been placed beside her at table, she assigned them to her husband, and invited the strangers to the seats instead. She informed them of the names and station of every person present, and then related to them how the winter previous, at the ball of the sub-prefect, she had danced the whole evening, while some of the prettiest girls in the room had wanted partners.

The gentlemen listened with obliging courtesy, and appeared deeply interested. The blue-eyed stranger, however, mingled somewhat in the general conversation. He spoke with the burgomaster from Solanges of the condition of his town, with the curates of their congregations, and seemed interested in the prosperity of French manufactures, about which much was said at table.

All were enchanted with the tact and affability of the strangers. Monsieur Etienne was highly elated, and as for madame, her paleness had been superseded by a becoming flush, and she never once complained of over-exertion.

The dinner over, the company assembled for the baptism. It was to take place in the parlor, where a table covered with a fine white cloth, a wax-candle, some flowers, a crucifix, and an improvised font, had been arranged for the occasion.

The noble stranger gave his arm to Madame Etienne. "Madame," said he, "may I ask of you the favor of standing godfather to your son?"

Madame Etienne blushed with pleasure, and replied that she would be most grateful for the honor.

"In this way," thought she, "we shall find out his name and rank."

The ceremony began. The curate spoke a few impressive words as to the nature of the sacrament, and then proceeded to baptize the infant. The water was poured over its head, and at last came the significant question: "What is the name of the godfather?" All eyes were turned upon him, and Madame Etienne's heart beat hard, for she expected to hear the word "count" at the very least.

"My name?" said he. "Joseph."

"Joseph," repeated the priest. "Joseph—and the surname?"

"I thought Joseph would be enough," said the stranger, with some impatience.

"No, sir," replied the priest. "The surname, too, must be registered in the baptismal records."

"Very well, then, Joseph the Second."

"The Second?" echoed the curate, with a look of mistrust. "*The Second!* Is that your surname?"

"Yes, my name is 'The Second.'"

"Well, be it so," returned the curate, with a shrug. "Joseph—

the—Second. Now, what is your profession—excuse me, sir, but I ask the customary questions."

The stranger looked down and seemed almost confused.

The curate mildly repeated his question. "What is your profession, or your station, sir?"

"Emperor of Austria," replied Joseph, smiling.

A cry of astonishment followed this announcement. The pencil with which the priest was about to record the "profession" of the godfather fell from his hands. Madame Etienne in her ecstasy fell almost fainting into an arm-chair, and Monsieur Etienne, taking the child from the arms of the nurse, came and knelt with it at the emperor's feet.

This was the signal for a renewal of life and movement in the room. All followed the example of the host, and in one moment old and young, men and women, were on their knees.

"Your majesty," said Etienne, in a voice choked with tears, "you have made my child famous. For a hundred years the honor you have conferred upon him will be the wonder of our neighborhood, and never will the people of Vitry forget the condescension of your majesty in sitting among us as an equal and a guest. My son is a Frenchman, but at heart he shall also be a German, like our own beautiful queen, who is both Austrian and French. God bless and preserve you both! Long live our queen, Marie Antoinette, and long live her noble brother, the Emperor of Austria!"

The company echoed the cry, and their shouts aroused Madame Etienne, who arose and advanced toward her imperial visitor. He hastened to replace her gently in her arm-chair.

"Where people are bound together by the ties of parent and godfather," said he, "there must be no unnecessary ceremony. Will you do me one favor, madame?"

"Sire, my life is at your majesty's disposal."

"Preserve and treasure it, then, for the sake of my godson. And since you are willing to do me the favor," continued he, drawing from his bosom a snuff-box richly set with diamonds, "accept this as a remembrance of my pleasant visit to you to-day. My portrait is upon the lid, and as I am told that all the lovely women in France take snuff, perhaps you will take your snuff from a box which I hope will remind you of the giver.

"And now," continued the emperor, to the happy Monsieur Etienne, "as I have been admitted to the christening, perhaps you will accommodate me with a pair of horses with which I may proceed to the next stage."

CHAPTER CVIII.

THE ARRIVAL AT VERSAILLES.

THE French court was at Versailles, it having been decided by the king and queen that there they would receive the emperor's visit. A magnificent suite of apartments had been fitted up for his occupation, and distinguished courtiers appointed as his attendants. He was anxiously expected; for already many an anecdote of his affability and generosity had reached Paris.

A courier had arrived to say that the emperor had reached the last station, and would shortly be in Versailles. The queen received this intelligence with tears of joy, and gathered all her ladies around her in the room where she expected to meet her brother. The king merely nodded, and a shade of dissatisfaction passed over his face. He turned to his confidential adviser, Count Maurepas, who was alone with him in his cabinet.

"Tell me frankly, what do you think of this visit?"

The old count raised his shoulders *à la Française*. "Sire, the queen has so often invited the emperor, that I presume he has come to gratify her longings."

"Ah, bah!" said Louis, impatiently. "He is not so soft-hearted as to shape his actions to suit the longings of his family. Speak more candidly."

"Your majesty commands me to be perfectly sincere?"

"I entreat you, be truthful and tell me what you think."

"Then I confess that the emperor's visit has been a subject of much mystery to your majesty's ministers. You are right in saying that he is not the man to trouble himself about the state of his relatives' affections. He comes to Paris for something nearer to his heart than any royal sister. Perhaps his hope is that he may succeed in removing me, and procuring the appointment of De Choiseul in my stead."

"Never! Austria cannot indulge such vain hopes, for her watchful spies must ere this have convinced the Hapsburgs that my dislike toward this duke, so precious in the eyes of Maria Theresa, is unconquerable. My father's shade banished him to Chanteloup, and I will follow this shade whithersoever it leads. If my father had lived (and perchance Choiseul had a hand in his death) there would have been no alliance of France with Austria. I am forced to maintain it, since my wife is the daughter of Maria Theresa; so that neither the Austrian nor the anti-Austrian party can ever hope to rule in France. Marie Antoinette is the wife of my heart, and no human being shall ever dislodge her thence. But my love for her can never influence my policy, which is steadfast to the principles of my father. If Joseph has come hither for political purposes, he might have spared his pains."

"He may have other views besides those we have alluded to. He may come to gain your majesty's sanction to his ambitious plans of territorial aggrandizement. The emperor is inordinately ambitious, and is true to the policy of his house."

"Which, nevertheless, was obliged to yield Silesia," said Louis, derisively.

"That is the open wound for which Austria seeks balsam from Turkey. If your majesty does not stop him, the emperor will light the torch of war and kindle a conflagration that may embrace all Europe."

"If I can prevent war, it is my duty to do so; for peace is the sacred right of my people, and nothing but imperative necessity would drive me to invade that right."

"But the emperor is not of your majesty's mind. He hopes for war, in expectation of winning glory."

"And I for peace, with the same expectation. I, too, would win glory—the glory of reigning over a happy and prosperous people. The fame of the conqueror is the scourge of mankind; that of the legislator, its blessing. The last shall be my portion—I have no object in view but the welfare of the French nation."

"The emperor may endeavor to cajole your majesty through your very love for France. He may propose to you an extension of French territory to reconcile you to his acquisitions in Turkey. He may suggest the Netherlands as an equivalent for Bosnia and Servia."

"I will not accept the bribe," cried Louis hastily. "France needs no aggrandizement. If her boundaries were extended, she would lose in strength what she gained in size; so that Joseph will waste his time if he seeks to awaken in me a lust of dominion. I thirst for conquest, it is true—the conquest of my people's hearts. May my father's blessing, and my own sincere efforts enable me to accomplish the one purpose of my life!"

"You have accomplished it, sire," replied De Maurepas, with enthusiasm. "You are the absolute master of your subjects' hearts and affections."

"If so, I desire to divide my domains with the queen," said Louis, with a searching look at De Maurepas. The minister cast down his eyes. The king went on: "You have something against her majesty—what is it?"

"The queen has something against me, sire. I am an eyesore to her majesty. She thinks I am in the way of De Choiseul, and will try every means to have me removed."

"You know that she would try in vain. I have already told you so. As a husband, I forget that Marie Antoinette is an Archduchess of Austria, but as my father's son—never! It is the same with her brother. I may find him agreeable as a relative; but as Emperor of Austria, he will know me as King of France alone. Be his virtues what they may, he never can wring the smallest concession from me. But hark!—I hear the sound of wheels. You know my sentiments—communicate them to the other ministers. I go to welcome my kinsman."

When the king entered the queen's reception-room, she was standing in the midst of her ladies. Her cheeks were pale, but her large, expressive eyes were fixed with a loving gaze upon the door through which her brother was to enter. When she saw the king, she started forward, and laying both her hands in his, smiled affectionately.

"Oh, sire," said she, "the emperor has arrived, and my heart flutters so, that I can scarcely wait for him here. It seems to me so cold that we do not go to meet him. Oh, come, dear husband, let us hasten to embrace our brother. Good Heaven! It is not forbidden a queen to have a heart, is it?"

"On the contrary, it is a grace that well becomes her royalty," said Louis, with a smile. "But your brother does not wish us to go forward to meet him. That would be an acknowledgment of his imperial station, and you know that he visits us as Count of Falkenstein."

"Oh, etiquette, forever etiquette!" whispered the queen, while she opened her huge fan and began to fan herself. "There is no escape from its fangs. We are rid of Madame de Noailles, but Madame Etiquette has stayed behind to watch our every look, to forbid us every joy—"

Just then the door opened, and a tall, manly form was seen upon the threshold. His large blue eyes sought the queen, and recognizing her, his face brightened with a bewitching smile. Marie Antoinette, heedless of etiquette, uttered a cry of joy and flew into his arms. "Brother, beloved brother!" murmured she, in accents of heartfelt tenderness.

"My sister, my own dear Antoinette!" was the loving reply, and Joseph drew her head upon his breast and kissed her again and again. The queen, overcome by joy, burst into tears, and in broken accents, welcomed the emperor to France.

The bystanders were deeply affected, all except the king—he alone was unmoved by the touching scene. He alone had remarked with displeasure that Marie Antoinette had greeted her brother in their native tongue, and that Joseph had responded. It was a German emperor and a German archduchess who were locked in each other's arms—and near them stood the King of France, for the moment forgotten. The position was embarrassing, and Louis had not tact enough to extricate himself gracefully. With ruffled brow and downcast eyes he stood, until, no longer able to restrain his chagrin, he turned on his heel to leave the room.

At this moment a light hand was laid upon his arm, and the clear, sonorous voice of the queen was heard.

"My dear husband, whither are you going?"

"I am here too soon," replied he, sharply. "I had been told that the Count of Falkenstein had arrived, and I came to greet him. It appears that it was a mistake, and I retire until he presents himself."

"The Count of Falkenstein is here, sire, and asks a thousand pardons for having allowed his foolish heart to get the better of his courtesy," said Joseph, with the superiority of better breeding. "Forgive me for taking such selfish possession of my sister's heart. It was a momentary concession from the Queen of France to the memories of her childhood; but I lay it at your majesty's feet, and entreat you to accept it as your well-won trophy."

He looked at the king with such an expression of cordiality, that Louis could not withstand him. A smile which he could not control, rippled the gloomy surface of the king's face; and he came forward, offering both hands.

"I welcome you with my whole heart, my brother," said he in reply. "Your presence in Versailles is a source of happiness both to the queen and to myself. Let me accompany you to your apartments that you may take possession at once, and refresh yourself from the fatigues of travelling."

"Sire," replied Joseph, "I will follow your majesty wheresoever you please; but I cannot allow you to be inconvenienced by my visit. I am a soldier, unaccustomed to magnificence, and not worthy of such royal accommodation as you offer."

"How!" cried the queen. "You will not be our guest?"

"I will gladly be your guest at table if you allow it," replied the emperor, "but I can dine with you without lodging at Versailles. When I travel, I do not go to castles but to inns."

The king looked astounded. "To inns?" repeated he with emphasis.

"Count Falkenstein means hotels, your majesty," cried the queen, laughing. "My brother is not quite accustomed to our French terms, and we will have to teach him the difference between a hotel and an inn. But to do this, dear brother, you must remain with us. Your apartments are as retired as you could possibly desire them."

"I know that Versailles is as vast as it is magnificent," said Joseph, "but I have already sent my valet to take rooms for me in

Paris. Let us, then, say no more on the subject.* I am very grateful to you for your hospitality, but I have come to France to hear, to see, and to learn. I must be out early and late, and that would not suit the royal etiquette of Versailles."

"I thought you had come to Paris to visit the king and myself," said Marie Antoinette, looking disappointed.

"You were right, dear sister, but I am not so agreeable that you should wish to have me constantly at your side. I wish to become acquainted with your beautiful Paris. It is so full of treasures of art and wonders of industry, that a man has only to use his eyes, and he grows accomplished. I am much in need of such advantages, sire, for you will find me a barbarian for whose lapses you will have to be indulgent."

"I must crave then a reciprocity of indulgence," replied Louis. "But, come, count—give your arm to the queen, and let her show you the way to dinner. To-day we dine *en famille*, and my brothers and sisters are impatient to welcome Count Falkenstein to Versailles."

CHAPTER CIX.

COUNT FALKENSTEIN IN PARIS.

A MODEST hackney-coach stood before the door of the little Hotel de Turenne, in the Rue Vivienne. The occupant, who had just alighted, was about to enter the hotel, when the host, who was standing before the door, with his hands plunged to the very bottom of his breeches pockets, stopped the way, and, not very politely, inquired what he wanted.

"I want what everybody else wants here, and what your sign offers to everybody—lodgings," replied the stranger.

"That is precisely what you cannot have," said mine host, pompously. "I am not at liberty to receive any one, not even a gentleman of your distinguished appearance."

"Then, take in your sign, my friend. When a man inveigles travellers with a sign, he ought to be ready to satisfy their claims upon his hospitality. I, therefore, demand a room."

"I tell you, sir, that you cannot have it. The Hotel de Turenne has been too highly honored to entertain ordinary guests. The Emperor of Austria, brother of the beautiful queen, has taken lodgings here."

The stranger laughed. "If the emperor were to hear you, he would take lodgings with some one more discreet than yourself. He travels *incognito* in France."

"But everybody is in the secret, sir; and all Paris is longing for a sight of Count Fălkenstein, of whom all sorts of delightful anecdotes are circulated. He is affabilitiy itself, and speaks with men generally as if they were his equals."

"And pray," said the stranger, laughing, "is he made differently from other men?"

The host eyed his interrogator with anger and contempt. "This is very presuming language," said he, "and as his majesty is my guest, I cannot suffer it. The French think the world of him, and no wonder, for he is the most condescending sovereign in Europe. He

* "Mémoires de Madame de Campan," vol. i., p. 172.

refused to remain at the palace, and comes to take up his abode here. Is not that magnanimous?"

"I find it merely a matter of convenience. He wishes to be in a central situation. Has he arrived?"

"No, not yet. His valet is here, and has set up his camp-bed. I am waiting to receive the emperor and his suite now."

"Is the valet Günther here?"

"Ah, you know this gentleman's name! Then perhaps you belong to the emperor's suite?"

"Yes," said the stranger, laughing, "I shave him occasionally. Now call Günther."

There was something rather imperious in the tone of the gentleman who occasionally shaved the emperor, and the landlord felt impelled to obey.

"Of course," said he, respectfully, "if you shave the emperor, you are entitled to a room here."

The stranger followed him up the broad staircase that led to the first story of the hotel. As they reached the landing, a door opened, and the emperor's valet stepped out into the hall.

"His majesty!" exclaimed he, quickly moving aside and standing stiff as a sentry by the door.

"His majesty!" echoed the landlord. "This gentleman—this—Your majesty—have I—"

"I am Count Falkenstein," replied the emperor, amused. "You see now that you were wrong to refuse me; for the man whom you took for an ordinary mortal was neither more nor less than the emperor himself."

The landlord bent the knee and began to apologize, but Joseph stopped him short. "Never mind," said he, "follow me, I wish to speak with you."

The valet opened the door, and the emperor entered the room, the frightened landlord following.

"These are my apartments?" continued Joseph, looking around.

"Yes, your majesty."

"I retain four of them—an anteroom, a sitting-room, a bedroom, and a room for my valet. I will keep them for six weeks, on one condition."

"Your majesty has only to command here."

"Well, then, I command you to forget what I am in Austria. In France, I am Count Falkenstein; and if ever I hear myself spoken of by any other name, I leave your house on the spot."

"I will obey your instructions, count."

"You understand, then, that I desire to be received and regarded as an ordinary traveller. Whence it follows that you will take in whatever other guests apply to you for lodging. You have proved to me to-day how unpleasant it is to be turned away, and I desire to spare other applicants the same inconvenience."

"But suppose the Parisians should wish to see Count Falkenstein?"

"They will have to submit to a disappointment."

"Should any one seek an audience of—the count?"

"The count receives visitors, but gives audience to no one. His visitors will be announced by his valet. Therefore you need give yourself no trouble on that head. Should any unfortunate or needy persons present themselves, you are at liberty to admit them."

"Oh!" cried the host, with tears in his eyes, "how the Parisians will appreciate such generosity!"

"They will not have the opportunity of doing so, for they shall not hear a word of it. Now go and send me a barber; and take all the custom that presents itself to you, whether it comes in a chariot or a hackney-coach."

The host retired, and as the door was closing, Count Rosenberg appeared. The emperor took his hand, and bade him welcome.

"I have just been to the embassy," said Rosenberg, "and Count von Mercy says—"

"That I told him I would take rooms at the Hotel of the Ambassadors, but I also reserve to myself this nice little bachelor establishment, to which I may retreat when I feel inclined to do so. The advantage of these double quarters is, that nobody will know exactly where to find me, and I shall enjoy some freedom from parade. At the Hotel of the Ambassadors I shall be continually bored with imperial honors. Here, on the contrary, I am free as air, and can study Paris at my leisure."

"And you intend to pursue these studies alone, count? Is no one to accompany you to spare you inconvenience, perchance to assist you in possible peril?"

"Oh, my friend, as to peril, you know, that I am not easily frightened, and that the Paris police is too well organized to lose sight of me. Monsieur de Sartines, doubtless, thinks that I need as much watching as a house-breaker, for it is presumed at court that I have come to steal the whole country, and carry it to Austria in my pocket."

"They know that to Count Falkenstein nothing is impossible," replied Rosenberg. "To carry away France would not be a very hard matter to a man who has robbed the French people of their hearts."

"Ah, bah! the French people have no hearts. They have nothing but imagination. There is but one man in France who has genuine sensibility—and that one is their poor, timid young king. Louis has a heart, but that heart I shall never win. Heaven grant that the queen have power to make it hers!"

"The queen? If Louis has a heart, it surely cannot be insensible to the charms of that lovely young queen!"

"It ought not to be, for she deserves the love of the best of men. But things are not as they should be here. I have learned *that* in the few hours of my visit to Versailles. The queen has bitter enemies, and you and I, Rosenberg, must try to disarm them."

"What can I do, count, in this matter?"

"You can watch and report to me. Swear to me, as an honest man, that you will conceal nothing you hear to the queen's detriment or to mine."

"I swear it, count."

"Thank you, my friend. Let us suppose that our mission is to free my sister from the power of a dragon, and restore her to her lover. You are my trusty squire, and together we shall prevail over the monster, and deliver the princess."

At that moment a knocking was heard at the door. It was opened, and an elegant cavalier, with hat and sword, entered the room, with a sweeping bow. The emperor stepped politely forward, and inquired his business.

The magnificent cavalier waved his hat, and with an air of proud consciousness, replied:

"I was requested to give my advice regarding the arrangement of a gentleman's hair."

"Ah, the barber," said the emperor. "Then be so good, sir, as to give your advice, and dress my hair."

"Pardon me, sir, that is not my profession," replied the cavalier, haughtily. "I am a physiognomist. Allow me to call in my subordinate."

"Certainly," said the emperor, ready to burst with laughter, as he surveyed the solemn demeanor of the *artiste*. The latter walked majestically to the door, and opened it.

"Jean!" cried he, with the voice of a field-marshal; and a youth fluttered in, laden with powder-purses, combs, curling-tongs, ribbons, pomatum, and the other appurtenances of a first-rate hair-dresser.

"Now, sir," said the physiognomist, gravely, "be so good as to take a seat."

Joseph obeyed the polite command, upon which the physiognomist retired several paces, folded his arms, and contemplated the emperor in solemn silence.

"Be so kind as to turn your head to the left—a little more—so—that is it—I wish to see your profile," said he, after a while.

"My dear sir, pray inform me whether in France it is customary to take a man's portrait before you dress his hair?" asked the emperor, scarcely able to restrain his increasing mirth; while Rosenberg retired to the window, where Joseph could see him shaking, with his handkerchief before his mouth.

"It is not customary, sir," replied the physiognomist, with grave earnestness. "I study your face that I may decide which style becomes you best."

Behind the chair stood the hair-dresser in a fashionable suit of nankeen, with lace cuffs and ruffles, hovering like a large yellow butterfly over the emperor, and ready at the signal to alight upon the imperial head with brush and comb.

The physiognomist continued his study. He contemplated the head of the emperor from every point of view, walking slowly around him, and returning to take a last survey of the front.

Finally his eye rested majestically upon the butterfly, which fluttered with expectation.

"Physiognomy of a free negro," said he, with pathos. "Give the gentleman the Moorish *coiffure*." * And with a courtly salute he left the room.

The emperor now burst into shouts of laughter, in which he was heartily joined by Rosenberg.

Meanwhile the butterfly had set to work, and was frizzing with all his might.

"How will you manage to give me the Moorish *coiffure?*" asked the emperor, when he had recovered his speech.

"I shall divide your hair into a multitude of single locks; curl, friz them, and they will stand out from your head in exact imitation of the negro's wool," answered the butterfly, triumphantly.

"I have no doubt that it would accord charmingly with my physiognomy," said the emperor, once more indulging in a peal of laughter, "but to-day I must content myself with the usual European

* "Mémoires d'un Voyageur qui se Repose," vol. iii., p. 42.

style. Dress my hair as you see it, and be diligent, for I am pressed for time."

The hair-dresser reluctantly obeyed, and in a few minutes the work was completed and the *artiste* had gone.

"Now," said Joseph to Count Rosenberg, "I am about to pay some visits. My first one shall be to Monsieur de Maurepas. He is one of our most active opponents, and I long to become acquainted with my enemies. Come, then, let us go to the hotel of the keeper of the great seal."

"Your majesty's carriages are not here," replied Rosenberg.

"Dear friend, my equipages are always in readiness. Look on the opposite side of the street at those hackney-coaches. They are my carriages for the present. Now let us cross over and select one of the neatest."

Perfect silence reigned in the anteroom of Monsieur de Maurepas. A liveried servant, with important mien, walked forth and back before the closed door of the reception-room, like a bull-dog guarding his master's sacred premises. The door of the first anteroom was heard to open, and the servant turned an angry look toward two gentlemen who made their appearance.

"Ah," said he, "the two gentlemen who just now alighted from the hackney-coach?"

"The same," said the emperor. "Is monsieur le comte at home?"

"He is," said the servant pompously.

"Then be so good as to announce to him Count Falkenstein."

The man shrugged his shoulders. "I am sorry that I cannot oblige you, sir. Monsieur de Taboreau is with the count; and until their conference is at an end, I can announce nobody."

"Very well, then, I shall wait," replied Joseph, taking a seat, and pointing out another to Count Rosenberg.

The servant resumed his walk, and the two visitors in silence awaited the end of the conference.

"Do you know, Rosenberg," said Joseph, after a pause, "that I am grateful to Count de Maurepas for this detention in his anteroom? It is said that experience is the mother of wisdom. Now my experience of to-day teaches me that it is excessively tiresome to wait in an anteroom. I think I shall be careful for the future, when I have promised to receive a man, not to make him wait. Ah! here comes another visitor. We are about to have companions in *ennui*."

The person who entered the room was received with more courtesy than "the gentlemen who had come in the hackney-coach." The servant came forward with eagerness, and humbly craved his pardon while informing him that his excellency was not yet visible.

"I shall wait," replied the Prince de Harrai, advancing to a seat. Suddenly he stopped, and looked in astonishment at Count Falkenstein, who, perfectly unconcerned, was sitting in a corner of the room.

"Great Heaven! his majesty, the emperor!" cried he, shocked, but recovering himself sufficiently to make a deep inclination.

"Can your majesty pardon this unheard-of oversight!"

"Peace, prince," replied the emperor, smiling; "you will disturb the ministers at their conference."

"Why, man, how is it that his excellency is not apprised of his majesty's presence here?" said the Prince de Harrai to the lackey.

"His excellency never spoke to me of an emperor," stammered

the terrified lackey. "He desired me to admit no one except a foreign count, whose name, your highness, I have been so unlucky as to forget."

"Except Count Falkenstein."

"Yes, your highness, I believe—that is, I think it—"

"And you leave the count to wait here in the anteroom!"

"I beg monsieur le comte a thousand pardons. I will at once repair my error."

"Stay," said the emperor, imperatively. Then turning to the Prince de Harrai, he continued good-humoredly: "If your highness is made to wait in the anteroom, there is no reason why the Count of Falkenstein should not bear you company. Let us, then, wait together."

The ministerial conference lasted half an hour longer, but at last the door opened, and Monsieur de Maurepas appeared. He was coming forward with ineffable courtesy to receive his guests, when perceiving the emperor, his self-possession forsook him at once. Pale, hurried, and confused, he stammered a few inaudible words of apology, when Joseph interrupted and relieved him.

He offered his hand with a smile, saying: "Do not apologize; it is unnecessary. It is nothing but right that business of state should have precedence over private visitors." *

"But your majesty is no private individual!" cried the minister, with astonishment.

"Pardon me," said the emperor, gravely. "As long as I remain here, I am nothing more. I left the Emperor of Austria at Vienna; he has no concern with the Count of Falkenstein, who is on a visit to Paris, and who has come hither, not to parade his rank, but to see and to learn where there is so much to be learned. May I hope that you will aid Count Falkenstein in his search after knowledge?"

CHAPTER CX.

THE QUEEN AND THE "DAMES DE LA HALLE."

A BRILLIANT crowd thronged the apartments of the Princess d'Artois. The royal family, the court, and the lords and ladies of high rank were assembled in her reception-rooms, for close by an event of highest importance to France was about to transpire. The princess was giving birth to a scion of royalty. The longings of France were about to be fulfilled—the House of Bourbon was to have an heir to its greatness.

The *accouchement* of a royal princess was in those days an event that concerned all Paris, and all the authorities and corporations of the great capital had representatives in those reception-rooms. It being only a princess who was in labor, and not a queen, none but the royal family and the ministers were admitted into her bedchamber. The aristocracy waited in the reception-rooms, the people in the corridors and galleries. Had it been Marie Antoinette, all the doors would have been thrown open to her subjects. The fishwives of Paris, the laborers, the *gamins*, even the beggars had as much right to see the Queen of France delivered, as the highest dignitary of the land. The people, then, who thronged both palace

*The emperor's own words. Hubner, "Life of Joseph II.," p. 141.

and gardens, were awaiting the moment when the physician should appear upon the balcony and announce to the enraptured populace that a prince or princess had been vouchsafed to France.

From time to time one of the royal physicians came out to report the progress of affairs, until finally the voice of the *accoucheur* proclaimed that the Princess d'Artois had given birth to a prince.

A cry of joy followed this announcement. It was that of the young mother. Raising her head from her pillow, she cried out in ecstasy, "Oh, how happy, how happy I am!" *

The queen bent over her and kissed her forehead, whispering words of affectionate sympathy in her ear; but no one saw the tears that fell from Marie Antoinette's eyes upon the lace-covered pillow of her fortunate kinswoman.

She kissed the princess again, as though to atone for those tears, and with tender congratulations took her leave. She passed through the reception-rooms, greeting the company with smiling composure, and then went out into the corridors which led to her own apartments. Here the scene changed. Instead of the respectful silence which had saluted her passage through the rooms, she encountered a hum of voices and an eager multitude all pressing forward to do her homage after their own rough fashion.

Every one felt bound to speak a word of love or of admiration, and it was only by dint of great exertion that the two footmen who preceded the queen were able to open a small space through which she could pass. She felt annoyed—even alarmed—and for the first time in her life regretted the etiquette which once had required that the Queen of France should not traverse the galleries of Versailles without an escort of her ladies of honor.

Marie Antoinette had chosen to dispense with their attendance, and now she was obliged to endure the contact of those terrible "dames de la halle," who for hundreds of years had claimed the privilege of speaking face to face with royalty, and who now pressed around her, with jokes that crimsoned *her* cheeks while they were rapturously received by the *canaille*.

With downcast eyes and trembling steps, she tried to hurry past the odious crowd of *poissardes*.

"Look, look," cried one, peering in her face, "look at the queen and see her blushing like a rose-bud!"

"But indeed, pretty queen, you should remember that you are not a rose-bud, but a full-blown rose, and it is time that you were putting forth rose-buds yourself."

"So it is, so it is," shouted the multitude. "The queen owes us a rose-bud, and we must have it."

"See here, pretty queen," cried another fish-wife, "it is your fault if we stand here on the staircases and out in the hot sun to-day. If you had done your duty to France instead of leaving it to the princess in yonder, the lackeys would have been obliged to open the doors to us as well as to the great folks, and we would have jostled the dukes and princes, and taken our ease on your velvet sofas. The next time we come here, we must have a tramp into the queen's room, and she must let us see herself and a brave dauphin, too."

* Madame de Campan, vol. i., p. 216. The prince whose advent was a source of such triumph to his mother, was the Duke de Berry, father of the present Count de Chambord. He it was who, in 1827, was stabbed as he was about to enter the theatre, and died in the arms of Louis XVIII., former Count de Provence.

"Yes, yes," cried the fish-wives in chorus, "when we come back we must see the young dauphin."

The queen tried to look as though she heard none of this. Not once had she raised her eyes or turned her head. Now she was coming to the end of her painful walk through the corridors, for Heaven be praised! just before her was the door of her own anteroom. Once across that threshold she was safe from the coarse ribaldry that was making her heart throb and her cheeks tingle; for there the rights of the people ended, and those of the sovereign began.

But the "dames de la halle" were perfectly aware of this, and they were determined that she should not escape so easily.

"Promise us," cried a loud, shrill voice, "promise us that we shall have a young dauphin as handsome as his mother and as good as his father."

"Yes, promise, promise," clamored the odious throng; and men and women pressed close upon the queen to see her face and hear her answer.

Marie Antoinette had almost reached her door. She gave a sigh of relief, and for the first time raised her eyes with a sad, reproachful look toward her tormentors.

Just then a strapping, wide-shouldered huckster, pushed her heavy body between the queen and the door, and barring the entrance with her great brown arms, cried out vociferously: "You do not pass until you promise! We love you and love the king: we will none of the Count de Provence for our king; we must have a dauphin."

The queen still pretended not to hear. She tried to evade the *poissarde* and to slip into her room; but the woman perceived the motion, and confronted her again.

"Be so kind, madame," said Marie Antoinette, mildly, "as to allow me to pass."

"Give us the promise, then," said the fish-wife, putting her arms a-kimbo.

The other women echoed the words, "Give us the promise, give us the promise!"

Poor Marie Antoinette! She felt her courage leaving her—she must be rid of this fearful band of viragos at any price. She would faint if she stood there much longer.

Again the loud cry—"Promise us a dauphin, a dauphin, a dauphin!"

"I promise," at last replied the queen. "Now, madame, in mercy, let me have entrance to my own rooms."

The woman stepped back, the queen passed away, and behind her the people shouted out in every conceivable tone of voice, "She has promised. The queen has promised a dauphin!"

Marie Antoinette walked hurriedly forward through the first anteroom where her footman waited, to the second wherein her ladies of honor were assembled.

Without a word to any of them she darted across the room and opening the door of her cabinet, threw herself into an arm-chair and sobbed aloud. No one was there excepting Madame de Campan.

"Campan," said she, while tears were streaming down her cheeks, "shut the door, close the *portière*. Let no one witness the sorrow of the Queen of France!"

With a passionate gesture, she buried her face in her hands and wept aloud.

After a while she raised her tearful eyes and they rested upon Madame de Campan, who was kneeling before her with an expression of sincerest sympathy.

"Oh, Campan, what humiliation I have endured to-day! The poorest woman on the street is more fortunate than I; and if she bears a child upon her arm, she can look down with compassion upon the lonely Queen of France,—that queen upon whose marriage the blessing of God does not rest; for she has neither husband nor child."

"Say not so, your majesty, for God has smitten your enemies, and with His own tender hand He is kindling the fire of love in the heart of the king your husband."

Marie Antoinette shook her head sadly. "No—the king does not love me. His heart does not respond to mine. He loves me, perhaps, as a sister, but no more—no more!"

"He loves your majesty with the passion and enthusiasm of a lover, but he is very timid, and waits for some token of reciprocity before he dares to avow his love."

"No, he does not love me," repeated Marie Antoinette with a sigh. "I have tried every means to win his heart. He is indulgent toward my failings, and kindly anticipates my wishes; sometimes he seems to enjoy my society, but it is with the calm, collateral affection of a brother for his sister. And I!—oh, my God! my whole heart is his, and craves for that ardent, joy-bestowing love of which poets sing, and which noble women prize above every earthly blessing. Such love as my father gave to my happy mother, I would that the king felt for me."

"The king does not know the extent of his love for your majesty," said De Campan soothingly. "Some fortunate accident or dream of jealousy will reveal it to him before long."

"God speed the accident or the dream!" sighed the queen; and forthwith her tears began to flow anew, while her hands lay idly upon her lap.

Those burning tears at last awakened her from the apathy of grief. Suddenly she gave a start and threw back her head. Then she rose from her seat, and, like Maria Theresa, began to pace the apartment. Gradually her face resumed its usual expression, and her demeanor became, as it was wont to be, dignified and graceful.

Coming directly up to Madame de Campan, she smiled and gave her hand. "Good Campan," said she, "you have seen me in a moment of weakness, of which I am truly ashamed. Try to forget it, dear friend, and I promise that it shall never be repeated. And now, call my tire-women and order my carriage. Leonard is coming with a new *coiffure*, and Bertin has left me several beautiful hats. Let us choose the very prettiest of them all, for I must go and show myself to the people. Order an open carriage, that every one may see my face, and no one may say that the queen envies the maternal joys of the Countess d'Artois. To-night we are to have the opera of 'Iphigenia'—it is one of my magnificent teacher's *chefs-d'œuvre*. The emperor and I are to go together to listen to our divine Gluck's music, and Paris must believe that Marie Antoinette is happy—too happy to envy any woman! Come, Campan, and dress me becomingly."

CHAPTER CXI.

THE ADOPTED SON OF THE QUEEN.

An hour later, the queen entered her carriage in all the splendor of full dress. Leonard had altered her *coiffure.* Instead of the three-story tower, her hair was low, and she wore a most becoming hat, chiefly made up of flowers and feathers. She also wore rouge, for she was very pale; and to conceal the traces of weeping she had drawn a faint dark line below her lower lashes which greatly increased the brilliancy of her eyes.

She ordered her coachman to drive through the town. Wherever the royal outriders announced her coming, the people gathered on either side of the streets to wave their hats and handkerchiefs, and greet her with every demonstration of enthusiasm and love.

Marie Antoinette greatly enjoyed her popularity, she bowed her head, and smiled, and waved her hand in return, calling upon the ladies who accompanied her to sympathize with her happiness.

"Indeed," said she to the Princess de Lamballe,* "the people love me, I do believe. They seem glad to see me, and I, too, like to see them."

"Your majesty sees that in Versailles, as in Paris, you have thousands of lovers," replied the princess.

"Ah," said the queen, "my lovers are there to be seen; but my enemies, who lie concealed, are more active than my friends. And how do I know that they are not now among the crowd that welcomes me! How dreadful it is to wear a mask through life! They, perhaps, who shout 'Long live the queen,' are plotting against her peace, and I, who smile in return, dare not trust them!"

The royal equipage had now reached the gates, and was passing into the country. Marie Antoinette felt a sense of relief at the change. She gazed with rapture upon the rich foliage of the trees, and then looking pensively above for a few moments, she watched the floating clouds of blue and silver, and then followed the flight of the birds that were soaring in such freedom through the air.

"How I wish that I could fly!" said she, sighing. "We mortals are less privileged than the little birds—we must creep along the earth with the reptiles that we loath! Faster, tell the coachman to drive faster!" cried she, eagerly, "I would like to move rapidly just now. Faster, still faster!"

The command went forward, and the outriders dashed ahead at full speed. The carriage whirled past the cottages on the wayside, while the queen, leaning back upon her satin cushions, gave herself up to the dreamy enjoyment which steals over the senses during a rapid drive.

Suddenly there was an exclamation, and the horses were reined in. The queen started from her reverie, and leaned forward.

"What has happened?" cried she of the equerry, who at that moment sprang to the side of the *calèche.*

"Your majesty, a child has just run across the road, and has been snatched from under the horses' feet."

*The Princess de Lamballe was subsequently beheaded, and her head was carried through the streets of Paris on a pike.—Trans.

"A child!" exclaimed the queen, starting from her seat. "Is it killed?"

"No, your majesty. It is luckily unhurt. The coachman reined up his horses in time for one of the outriders to save it. It is unhurt—nothing but frightened. Your majesty can see him now in the arms of the old peasant-woman there."

"She is about to return to the cottage with it," said the queen. Then stretching her arms toward the old woman, she cried out in an imploring voice: "Give me the child—bring it here! Heaven has sent it to me as a comfort! Give it to me, I entreat you."

Meanwhile the old woman, recalled by the equerry, was approaching the carriage. "See," exclaimed the queen to her ladies, "see what a lovely boy!" And, indeed, he was a beautiful child, in spite of his little tattered red jacket, and his bare brown legs, as dark with dirt as with sunburn.

"Where is his mother?" asked Marie Antoinette, looking compassionately at the child.

"My daughter is dead, madame," said the peasant. "She died last winter, and left me the burden of five young children to feed."

"They shall burden you no longer," exclaimed the queen kindly. "I will maintain them all, and this little angel you must give to me. Will you not?"

"Ah, madame, the child is only too lucky! But my little Jacob is so wilful that he will not stay with you."

"I will teach him to love me," returned the queen. "Give him to me now."

She leaned forward and received the child from his grandmother's arms. It was so astounded, that it uttered not a cry; it only opened its great blue eyes to their utmost, while the queen settled it upon her lap.

"See," exclaimed the delighted Marie Antoinette, "he is not at all afraid of me. Oh, we are going to be excellent friends! Adieu, my poor old grandmother. I will send you something for your children as soon as I reach home. And now, Monsieur de Vievigne, let us return to Versailles. Tell your grandmamma good-by, little Jacob. You are going to ride with me."

"Adieu, my little one," said the grandmother. "Don't forget your—"

Her words were drowned in the whirr of the carriage, which disappeared from her wondering eyes in a cloud of dust.

The motion, the noise, and the air brushing his curls into his face, awakened the boy from his stupor. He started from the queen's arms, and looking wildly around, began to yell with all his might. Never had such unharmonious sounds assailed the ears of the queen before. But she seemed to be quite amused with it. The louder little Jacob screamed and kicked, the closer she pressed him to her heart; nor did she seem to observe that his dirty little feet were leaving unsightly marks upon her rich silk dress.

The *calèche* arrived at Versailles, and drew up before the doors of the palace. With her newly acquired treasure in her arms, the queen attempted to leave the carriage, but the shrieks and kicks became so vigorous, that she was obliged to put the child down. The pages, gentlemen, and ladies in waiting, stared in astonishment as her majesty went by, holding the refractory little peasant by the hand, his rosy cheeks covered with many an arabesque, the joint production of tears and dirt. Little cared Jacob for the splendor around him; still less for the caresses of his royal protectress.

"I want to go to my grandmother," shrieked he, "I want my brother Louis and sister Marianne!"

"Oh, dear little one!" cried the queen, "what an affectionate heart he has! He loves his relatives better than all our luxury, and the Queen of France is less to him than his poor old grandmother! —Never mind, darling, you shall be loved as well and better than you ever were at home, and all the more that you have not learned to flatter!"

She bent down to caress him, but he wiped off her kisses with indignation. Marie Antoinette laughed heartily, and led the child into her cabinet, where she placed him on the very spot where she had been weeping a few hours earlier.

"Campan," said she, "see how good God has been to me to-day! He has sent me a child upon whom I can lavish all the love which is consuming my poor, lonely heart. Yes, my little one, I will be a mother to you, and may God and your own mother hear my vow! Now, Campan, let us take counsel together as to what is to be done. First, we must have a nurse, and then his face must be washed, and he must be dressed as becomes my pretty little adopted son."

The child, who had ceased his cries for a moment, now broke out into fresh shrieks. "I want to go home! I won't stay here in this big house! Take me to my grandmother!"

"Hush, you unconscionable little savage!" said Madame de Campan.

"Oh, Campan!" cried the queen deprecatingly, "how can you chide the little fellow! His cries are so many proofs of the honesty of his heart, which is not to be bribed of its love by all that royalty can bestow!" *

CHAPTER CXII.

"CHANTONS, CÉLÉBRONS NOTRE REINE."

THE opera-house was full to overflowing. In the lowest tier were the ladies of the aristocracy, their heads surmounted by those abominable towers of Leonard's invention. Above them sat the less distinguished spectators; and the parquet was thronged by poets, learned men, students, and civil officers of various grades. Almost every class found some representatives in that brilliant assemblage; and each one felt keenly the privilege he enjoyed in being present on that particular occasion. But it was not altogether for the sake of the music that all Paris had flocked to the opera. The Parisians were less desirous to hear "Iphigenia," than to see the emperor, who was to be there in company with his sister.

Since his arrival in the capital, Joseph had been the theme of every conversation. Every one had something to relate of his affa-

* The queen kept her word. The boy was brought up as her own child. He always breakfasted and dined by her side, and she never called him by any other name save that of "my child." When Jacques grew up, he displayed a taste for painting, and of course had every advantage which royal protection could afford him. He was privileged to approach the queen unannounced. But when the Revolution broke out, this miserable wretch, to avoid unpopularity, joined the Jacobins, and was one of the queen's bitterest enemies and most frenzied accusers.

bility, his condescension, or his goodness. His *bon mots*, too, were in every mouth; and the Parisians, who at every epoch have been so addicted to wit, were so much the more enraptured with the impromptu good things which fell from Joseph's lips, that the Bourbons were entirely deficient in sprightliness.

Every man had an anecdote to relate that concerned Joseph. Yesterday he had visited the Hotel-Dieu. He had even asked for admission to the apartments of the lying-in women, and upon being refused entrance by the sisters, he had said, "Do let me see the first scene of human misery." The sisters, struck by the words as well as by the noble bearing of the stranger, had admitted him; and upon taking leave he had remarked to the nun who accompanied him, "The sufferings which you witness in this room, reconcile you without doubt to the vows you have made." It was only after his departure that his rank was discovered, and this by means of the gift he left in the hands of the prioress—a draft upon the imperial exchequer of forty-eight thousand livres.

A few days previous, he had sought entrance to the "Jardin des Plantes;" but the porter had refused to open the gates until a larger number of visitors should arrive. So the emperor, instead of discovering himself, took a seat under the trees and waited quietly until the people had assembled. On his return, he had given eight louis d'ors to the porter; and thus the latter had learned his majesty's rank.

Again—the emperor had called upon Buffon, announcing himself simply as a traveller. Buffon, who was indisposed, had gone forward to receive his guest in a dressing-gown. His embarrassment, as he recognized his imperial visitor, had been very great. But Joseph, laughing, said, "When the scholar comes to visit his teacher, do you suppose that he troubles himself about the professor's costume?"

That was not all. He was equally affable with artists. He talked daily with the painters in the Louvre; and having paid a visit to the great actor Le Kain, whom he had seen the night before in the character of a Roman emperor, he found him like Buffon in a dressing-gown.

When Le Kain would have apologized, the emperor had said, "Surely emperors need not be so fastidious one toward the other!"

"The emperor goes everywhere," cried a voice in the crowd. "Yesterday he paid a visit to one of the tribunals and remained during the sitting. He was recognized, and the president would have assigned him a seat among the council, but the emperor declined and remained in a trellised-box with the other spectators."

"How!" cried another voice, "the emperor sat in a little common trellised-box?"

"Yes," replied the first speaker, "he was in one of those boxes called lanterns. Even Marsorio and Pasquin had something to say on the subject." *

"What did they say? Tell us what said our good friends, Marsorio and Pasquin."

"Here it is. I found it pasted on a corner of the Palais Royal and I tore it down and put it in my pocket. Shall I read it?"

* Marsorio and Pasquin were the anonymous wits of the people, the authors of all the epigrams and pasquinades which were pasted about the streets and originated with—nobody. Marsorio and Pasquin still exist in Rome.

"Yes, yes," cried the multitude; and it was whispered among them that this was Riquelmont, the author of the satires that were sung on the Pont-Neuf, and were attributed to Marsorio and Pasquin.

"Now, gentlemen, listen!"

And with a loud voice, Riquelmont began to read:

> "MARSORIO.—Grand miracle, Pasquin.
> Le soleil dans une lanterne!
> PASQUIN.—Allons donc, tu me bernes!
> MARSORIO.—Pour te dire le vrai, tiens: Diogène en vain
> Cherchait jadis un homme, une lanterne à la main,
> Eh bien, à Paris ce matin
> Il l'eût trouvé dans la lanterne."

"Good, good!" cried the listeners, "the emperor is indeed a wonderful—"

Just then the bell for the curtain was heard, and the crowd pressed into the parterre. Amid the profoundest stillness the opera began. Before the first scene had ended, a slight rustling of chairs was heard in the king's box, and all eyes were turned thither. The whole royal family, with the exception of the king, were there; and in their midst, loveliest of all, appeared the young queen, brilliant with youth, grace, and beauty as she bent her head, and, with bewitching smiles, returned the greetings of her subjects.

The audience broke out into a storm of rapturous applause, and Marie Antoinette, kissing her fair hand, took her seat and prepared to listen to the music.

But the spectators were less interested in "Iphigenia" than in the imperial box. Their eyes were continually seeking the emperor, who, concealed behind the heavy velvet draperies, was absorbed in the performance. At one stage of the representation, Iphigenia is led in triumph through the Greek camp, while a chorus of Thessalians sing—

> "Que d'attraits, que de majesté,
> Que de graces! que de beauté!
> Chantons, célébrons notre reine!"

The audience took the cue and transformed themselves into actors. Every eye and every head turned to the royal box, and for the second time every hand was raised to applaud. From boxes, galleries, and parquet, the cry was, "Da capo, da capo! Again that chorus!"

The singer who represented Achilles comprehended that the enthusiasm of the spectators was not for the music.

Enchanted with the idea of being the mouthpiece of the people, he stepped to the front of the stage, and raising his arm in the direction of the royal box, he repeated the line,

> "Chantons, célébrons notre reine!"

The heart of the young queen overflowed with excess of joy. She leaned toward the emperor, and gently drawing him forward, the brother and sister both acknowledged the graceful compliment. The emperor was saluted with shouts, and the singers began for the second time, "*Chantons, célébrons notre reine!*" The people, with one accord, rose from their seats, and now, on every side, even from the stage, were heard the cries of "Long live our queen! Long live the emperor!"

Marie Antoinette, leaning on her brother's arm, bent forward again, and, for the third time, the singers, and with them the people, sang, "*Chantons, célébrons notre reine!*"

This time, every occupant of the imperial box rose to return acknowledgments, and the audience began for the fourth time,

"Chantons, célébrons notre reine!"

The queen was so overcome, that she could no longer restrain her tears. She tried to incline her head, but her emotion overpowered her, and covering her face with her handkerchief, she leaned upon the shoulder of her brother, and wept.

The applause ceased. The emotion of Marie Antoinette had communicated itself to her worshippers, and many an eye was dimmed with sympathetic tears.

Suddenly, in the *parterre*, a tall, manly form arose from his seat, and, pointing to the queen, recited the following couplet:

"Si le peuple peut espérer
Qu'il lui sera permis de rire,
Ce n'est que sous l'heureux empire
Des princes qui savent pleurer."

This happy impromptu was enthusiastically received. Marie Antoinette had dried her tears to listen, and as she prepared to leave the theatre, she turned to her brother, and said:

"Oh! that I could die now! Death would be welcome, for in this proud moment I have emptied my cup of earthly joy!" *

CHAPTER CXIII.

THE HOTEL TURENNE.

THE host of the Hotel Turenne had punctually obeyed the orders of Count Falkenstein. He had taken every applicant for rooms, whether he came in an ignominious hackney-coach or in a magnificent carriage.

But now every room was taken, and the host, fearful of consequences, was waiting for the emperor to appear, that he might be informed of the important fact.

In ten or fifteen minutes, his imperial majesty was seen coming down the staircase, and Monsieur Louis approached, with a low bow.

"May I have the honor of speaking with Count Falkenstein?"

"Certainly," said the count. "What is it?"

"I wished to inform monsieur le comte, that my hotel is full to the garret. Should monsieur le comte, then, see a traveller leaving my door, he will know that I am not infringing his imp—his orders, I mean. I have not a single room left."

"Your hotel is popular. I congratulate you. But I am not at all surprised, for you make your visitors exceedingly comfortable."

"A thousand thanks, monsieur le comte, but that is not the reason. I have never been so thronged before. It is all owing to the honor conferred upon me by your—, I mean, by monsieur le comte. It will be a heavy disappointment to all who apply to hear that I have no room."

* "Mémoires de Weber," vol. i., p. 48.—Mémoires de Madame de Campan, vol. i., p. 127.—Hubner, "Life of Joseph II.," page 142.

"Monsieur Louis," said the emperor, "you are mistaken. There are two empty rooms, opening into mine."

"But, monsieur le comte, it is impossible for me to let those rooms, for not only every word spoken in your own room can be overheard there, but yourself will be disturbed by hearing all that is said by the occupants. You see that these rooms cannot be occupied, monsieur le comte."

"I see nothing of the sort," said Joseph, laughing. "Not only are you welcome to let those two rooms, but I request you to do so. Let no man be incommoded on my account. I shall know how to submit to the inconvenience which may be entailed upon me."

"Well, he certainly is the most condescending and humane prince that I ever heard of," thought Monsieur Louis, as the emperor's carriage drove off. "And one thing is certain—I shall be careful whom I give him for neighbors. I do not believe a word of what the Count de Provence's valet says, that he wants to take Alsace and Lorraine, and has come to France to change the ministry. The king's brothers are not over-fond of the queen nor of the emperor; but the people love them, and everybody in Paris envies me, now that I have the great emperor as my guest."

And Monsieur Louis, with head erect and hands folded behind him, went up and down his entrance hall, enjoying the sunshine of his favor with princes.

"I do wish nobody else would come here," thought he, in an ecstasy of disinterestedness. "Suppose that the enemies of his majesty should introduce a murderer in my house, and the emperor should lose his life! I should be eternally disgraced. I am really responsible to his majesty's subjects for his safety. I am resolved, since he has commanded me to let these rooms, to allow none but ladies to occupy them."

Filled with enthusiasm at this fortunate idea, the host walked to the door, and shook his fist at mankind in general—above all to that segregate of the male species who might happen to be entertaining thoughts of lodging at the Hotel Turenne.

Presently a tavelling-chariot came thundering to the door. Monsieur Louis peered with his keen, black eyes into the vehicle, and, to his great relief, saw two ladies.

The gentleman who accompanied them asked to be accommodated with two rooms; and the host, in his joy, not only opened the coach door himself, but took the huge silver candelabrum from the butler's hand, and lighted the company himself to their apartments.

As they reached the landing, a carriage stopped before the door, and a manly voice was heard in the vestibule below.

"How lucky for me that these happened to be women," thought Monsieur Louis, "for there is the emperor already returned from the theatre!"

He opened the door of the anteroom, and his guests followed him in silence. Not a word had been spoken by either of the ladies, and nothing was to be seen of their faces through the thick veils which covered them.

"Do the ladies require supper?" inquired the host.

"Certainly," replied the gentleman whom Monsieur Louis took to be the husband of the lady who had seated herself. "The best you can provide; and let it be ready in quarter of an hour."

"Will madame be served in this room?"

"Yes; and see that we have plenty of light. Above all, be quick."

"This gentleman is very curt," thought the host, as he left the room. "What if he should entertain evil designs?—I must be on my guard." Then returning, he added, "Pardon, monsieur, for how many will supper be served?"

The stranger cast a singular glance at the lady in the arm-chair, and said in a loud and somewhat startling voice, "For two only."

"Right," thought the host, "the other one is a lady's maid. So much the worse. They are people of quality, and all that tribe hate the emperor. I must be on my guard."

So Monsieur Louis determined to warn the emperor; but first he attended to his professional duties. "Supper for the guests just arrived!" cried he to the chief butler. "Plenty of light for the chandeliers and candelabra! Let the cook be apprised that he must be ready before fifteen minutes."

Having delivered himself of these orders, the host hastened to inform the emperor's valet, Günther, of his uneasiness and suspicions.

Meanwhile, the *garçons* were going hither and thither preparing supper for the strangers. Scarcely ten minutes had elapsed before the first course was upon the table, and the butler, with a bow, announced the supper.

The singular pair for whom these costly preparations had been made, spoke not a word to each other. The lady, motionless, kept within the privacy of her veil; and the gentleman, who was watching the waiters with an ugly frown, looked vexed and impatient.

"Retire, all of you," said he, imperiously. "I shall have the honor of waiting on madame myself."

The butler bowed, and, with his well-bred subordinates, left the room.

"Now, madame," said the stranger, with a glance of dislike, to the lady's maid, "do *you* leave the room also. Go and attend to your own wants. Good-night."

The maid made no reply, but remained standing in the window as though nothing had been said.

"You seem not to hear," said the stranger. "I order you to leave this room, and, furthermore, I order you to return to your place as a servant, and not to show yourself here in any other capacity. Go, and heed my words!"

The lady's-maid smiled derisively and replied, "Count, I await my lady's orders."

The veiled lady then spoke. "Gratify the count, my good Dupont," said she, kindly. "I do not need you to-night. Let the host provide you with a comfortable room, and go to rest. You must be exhausted."

"At last, at last we are alone," exclaimed the count as the door closed upon his enemy, the lady's maid.

"Yes, we are alone," repeated the lady, and, throwing off her wrappings, the tall and elegant form of the Countess Esterhazy was disclosed to view.

CHAPTER CXIV.

THE DÉNOUEMENT.

FOR a moment they confronted each other; then Count Schulenberg, with open arms, advanced toward the countess.

"Now, Margaret," cried he, "you are mine. I have earned this victory by my superhuman patience. It is achieved—I am rewarded—come to my longing heart!"

He would have clasped her in his arms, but she stepped back, and again, as in her dressing-room at Vienna, her hands were raised to ward him off. "Do not touch me," said she, with a look of supreme aversion. "Come no nearer, Count Schulenberg, for your breath is poison, and the atmosphere of your proximity is stifling me."

The count laughed. "My beautiful Margaret, you seek in vain to discourage me by your charming sarcasm. Oh, my lovely, untamed angel, away with your coldness! it inflames my passion so much the more. I would not give up the triumph of this hour for a kingdom!"

"It will yield you nothing nevertheless, save my contempt. You must renounce your dream of happiness, for I assure you that it has been but a dream."

"You jest still, my Margaret," replied the count, with a forced laugh. "But I tell you that I intend to tame my wild doe into a submissive woman, who loves her master and obeys his call. Away with this mask of reluctance! You love me; for you have given me the proof of your love by leaving kindred and honor to follow me."

"Nay, count. I have given you a proof of my contempt, for I have deliberately used you as a tool. You, the handsome and admired Count Schulenberg—you who fancied you were throwing me the handkerchief of your favor, you are nothing to me but the convenient implement of my revenge. You came hither as my valet, and as I no longer need a valet, I discharge you. You have served me well, and I thank you. You have done admirably, for Dupont told me to-day that you had not yet exhausted the money I gave you for the expenses of our journey. I am, therefore, highly satisfied with you, and will recommend you to any other woman desirous of bringing disgrace upon her husband."

The count stared at her in perfect wonder. He smiled, too—but the smile was sinister and threatened evil.

"How!" said the countess. "You are not yet gone! True—I forgot—a lady has no right to discharge her valet without paying him."

With these words she drew a purse from her pocket and threw it at his feet.

A loud grating laugh was the reply. He set his foot upon the purse, and folding his arms, contemplated the countess with a look that boded no good to his tormentor.

"You do not go, Count Schulenberg?" said she.

"No—and what is more, I do not intend to go."

"Ah!" cried Margaret, her eyes glowing like coals, "you are dishonorable enough to persist, when I have told you that I despise you!"

"My charming Margaret, this is a way that women have of betraying their love. You all swear that you despise us; all the while loving us to distraction. You and I have gone too far to recede. You, because you allowed me to take you from your husband's house; I, because I gave in to your rather exacting whims, and came to Paris as your valet. But you promised to reward me, and I must receive my wages."

"I promised when we should reach Paris to speak the truth, Count Schulenberg; and as you are not satisfied with as much as I have vouchsafed, hear the whole truth. You say that in consenting to accompany you, I gave a proof of love. Think better of me, sir! Had I loved you, I might have died for you, but never would I have allowed you to be the partner of my disgrace. You have shared it with me precisely because I despise you, precisely because there was no man on earth whom I was less likely to love. As the partner of my flight, you have freed me from the shackles of a detested union, to rupture which, I underwent the farce of an elopement. The tyranny of Maria Theresa had compelled me to marriage with a wretch who succeeded in beguiling me to the altar by a lie. I swore to revenge myself, and you have been the instrument of my revenge. The woman who could condescend to leave her home with *you*, is so doubly-dyed in disgrace that Count Esterhazy can no longer refuse to grant her a divorce. And now, count, that I have concealed nothing, oblige me by leaving me—I need repose."

"No, my bewitching Margaret, a thousand times no!" replied the count. "But since you have been so candid, I shall imitate your charming frankness. Your beauty, certainly, is quite enough to madden a man, and embolden him to woo you, since all Vienna knows how the Countess Esterhazy hates her husband. But you seemed colder to me than you were to other men, all of whom complained that you had no heart to win. I swore not to be foiled by your severity, and thereupon my friends staked a large wager upon the result. Fired by these united considerations, I entered upon my suit and was successful. You gave me very little trouble, I must say *that* for you, countess. Thanks to your clemency, I have won my bet, and on my return to Vienna, I am to receive one thousand louis d'ors."

"I am delighted to hear it, and I advise you to go after them with all speed," replied the countess quietly.

"Pardon me if I reject the advice—for, as I told you before, I really love you. You have thrown yourself into my arms, and I would be a fool not to keep you there. No, my enchantress, no! Give up all hope of escaping from the fate you have chosen for yourself. For my sake you have branded your fair fame forever, and you shall be rewarded for the sacrifice."

"Wretch," cried she, drawing herself proudly up to her full height, "you well know that you had no share in the motives of the flight! Its shame is mine alone; and alone will I bear it. To you I leave the ridicule of our adventure, for if you do not quit my room, I shall take care that all Vienna hears how I took you to Paris as my valet."

"And I, Countess Esterhazy, shall entertain all Vienna with the contents of your album, which I have taken the liberty not only of reading, but of appropriating."

The countess gave a start. "True," murmured she, "I have missed it since yesterday."

"Yes, and I have it. I think a lover has a right to his mistress's secrets, and I have made use of my right. I have been reading your heavenly verses to the object of your unhappy attachment, and all Vienna shall hear them. What delicious scandal it will be to tell how desperately in love is the Countess Esterhazy with the son of her gracious and imperial godmother!"

"Tell it then," cried Margaret, "tell it if you will, for I do love the emperor! My heart bows down before him in idolatrous admiration, and if he loved *me*, I would not envy the angels their heaven! He does not return my love—nor do I need that return to make me cherish and foster my passion for him. No scorn of the world can lessen it, for it is my pride, my religion, my life! And now go and repeat my words; but beware of me, Count Schulenberg, for I will have revenge!"

"From such fair hands, revenge would fall quite harmless," exclaimed the count, dazzled by the splendor of Margaret's transcendent beauty; for never in her life had she looked lovelier than at that moment. "Revenge yourself if you will, enchantress, but mine you are doomed to be. Come, then, come!"

Once more he approached, when the door was flung violently open, and a loud, commanding voice was heard:

"I forbid you to lay a finger upon the Countess Esterhazy," exclaimed the emperor.

Margaret uttered a loud cry, the color forsook her cheeks, and closing her eyes she fell back upon the sofa.

CHAPTER CXV.

THE PARTING.

THE emperor hastened to her assistance, but finding her totally insensible, he laid her gently down again.

"She is unconscious," said he; "kind Nature has lulled her to insensibility—she will recover." Then taking the veil from the countess's hat, he covered her face, and turned toward the terrified count, who, trembling in every limb, was powerless to save himself by flight.

"Give me the countess's album!" said the emperor sternly. Count Schulenberg drew it mechanically forth, and, with tottering steps, advanced and fell at the emperor's feet.

Joseph tore the book from his hands, and laid it on the sofa by the countess. Then returning, he cried out in a tone of indignation, "Rise! You have behaved toward this woman like a dishonorable wretch, and you are unworthy the name of nobleman. You shall be punished for your crimes."

"Mercy, sire, mercy," faltered the count. "Mercy for a fault which—"

"Peace!" interrupted Joseph. "The empress has already sent a courier to order your arrest. Do you know what is the punishment in Austria for a man who flies with a married woman from the house of her husband?"

"The punishment of death," murmured the count inaudibly.

"Yes, for it is a crime that equals murder," returned the emperor; "indeed, it transcends murder, for it loses the soul of the unhappy woman, and brands her husband with infamy."

"Mercy, mercy!" prayed the wretch.

"No," said Joseph sternly, "you deserve no mercy. Follow me."

The emperor returned to his own room, and opening the door that led to the anteroom he called Günther.

When the valet appeared, Joseph pointed to the count, who was advancing slowly, and now stopped without daring to raise his head.

"Günther," said the emperor, "I give this man in charge to you. I might require him on his honor not to leave this room until I return; but no man can pledge that which he does not possess; I must, therefore, leave him to you. See that he does not make his escape."

The emperor then recrossed his own room, and closing the door behind him, entered the apartment of the countess. She had revived; and was looking around with an absent, dreamy expression.

"I have been sleeping," murmured she. "I saw the emperor, I felt his arm around me, I dreamed that he was bending over me—"

"It was no dream, Countess Esterhazy," said Joseph softly.

She started, and rose from the sofa, her whole frame tremulous with emotion. Her large, glowing eyes seemed to be searching for the object of her terror, and then her glance rested with inexpressible fear upon the door which led into the emperor's room.

"You were there, sire, and heard all—all?" stammered she, pointing with her hand.

"Yes—God be praised, I was there, and I am now acquainted with the motives which prompted your flight from Count Esterhazy. I undertake your defence, countess; my voice shall silence your accusers in Vienna, and if it becomes necessary to your justification, I will relate what I have overheard. I cannot blame you, for I know the unspeakable misery of a marriage without love, and I comprehend that, to break its fetters, you were ready to brave disgrace, and to wear upon your spotless brow the badge of dishonor The empress must know what you have undergone, and she shall reinstate you in the world's estimation; for she it is who has caused your unhappiness. My mother is too magnanimous to refuse reparation where she has erred."

"Sire," whispered the countess, while a deep blush overspread her face, "do you mean to confide all—all to the empress?"

"All that concerns your relations with your husband and with Count Schulenberg. Pardon me that I overheard the sweet confession which was wrung from you by despair! Never will I betray it to living mortal; it shall be treasured in the depths of my heart, and sometimes at midnight hour I may be permitted to remember it!—Come back to Vienna, countess, and let us seek to console each other for the agony of the past!"

"No, sire," said she mournfully, "I shall never return to Vienna; I should be ashamed to meet your majesty's eye."

"Have you grown so faint-hearted?" said the emperor, gently. "Are you suddenly ashamed of a feeling which you so nobly avowed but a few moments since? Or am I the only man on earth who is unworthy to know it?"

"Sire, the judgment of the world is nothing to me; it is from *your* contempt that I would fly and be forgotten. Let other men judge me as they will—I care not. But oh! I know that you despise me, and that knowledge is breaking my heart. Farewell, then, forever!"

The emperor contemplated her with mournful sympathy, and took both her hands in his. She pressed them to her lips, and when she raised her head, her timidity had given place to strong resolution.

"I shall never see your majesty again," said she, "but your image will be with me wherever I go. I hope for great deeds from you, and I know that you will not deceive me, sire. When all Europe resounds with your fame, then shall I be happy, for my being is merged in yours. At this moment, when we part to meet no more, I say again with joyful courage, I love you. May the blessing of that love rest upon your noble head! Give me your hand once more, and then leave me."

"Farewell, Margaret," faltered the emperor, intoxicated by her tender avowal, and opening his arms, he added in passionate tones, "Come to my heart, and let me, for one blissful moment, feel the beatings of yours! Come, oh, come!"

Margaret leaned her head upon his shoulder and wept, while the emperor besought her to relent and return to Vienna with him.

"No, sire," replied she, firmly. "Farewell!"

He echoed "farewell," and hastily left the room.

When the door had closed upon him, the countess covered her face with her hands and sobbed aloud. But this was for a moment only.

Her pale face resumed its haughty expression as she rose from her seat and hastily pulled the bell-rope. A few minutes later, she unbolted the door, and Madame Dupont entered the room.

"My good friend," said the countess, "we leave Paris to-night."

"Alone?" asked the maid, looking around.

"Yes; rejoice with me, we are rid of him forever. But we must leave this place at once. Go and order post-horses."

"But, dear lady, whither do we journey?"

"Whither?" echoed Margaret, thoughtfully. "Let the will of God decide. Who can say whence we come, or whither we go?"

The faithful servant hastened to her mistress, and taking the hand of the countess in hers, pressed it to her lips. "Oh, my lady," said she, "shake off this lethargy—be your own brave self again."

"You are right, Dupont," returned Margaret, shaking back her long black hair, which had become unfastened and fell almost to her feet, "I must control my grief that I may act for myself. From this day I am without protector, kindred, or home. Let us journey to the Holy Land, Dupont. Perhaps I may find consolation by the grave of the Saviour."

One hour later, the emperor, sitting at his window, heard a carriage leave the Hotel Turenne. He followed the sound until it was lost in the distance; for well he knew that the occupant of that coach was the beautiful and unfortunate Countess Esterhazy.

Early on the following morning, another carriage with blinds drawn up, left the hotel. It stopped before the Austrian embassy, and the valet of the emperor sprang out. He signified to the porter that he was to keep a strict watch over the gentleman within, and then sought the presence of the Count von Mercy.

A quarter of an hour went by, during which the porter had been peering curiously at the pale face which was staring at the windows of the hotel. Presently a secretary and a servant of the ambassador came out equipped for a journey. The secretary entered the carriage; the servant mounted the box, and Count Schulenberg was transported a prisoner to Vienna.*

CHAPTER CXVI.

JOSEPH AND LOUIS.

THE emperor was right when he said that his sister would derive little pleasure from his visit to Paris. Her happiness in his society had been of short duration; for she could not be but sensible of the growing dislike of the king for his imperial brother-in-law. Joseph's easy and graceful manners were in humiliating contrast to the stiff and awkward bearing of Louis; and finally, Marie Antoinette felt many a pang as she watched the glances of aversion which her husband cast upon her brother, at such times as the latter made light of the thousand and one ceremonies which were held so sacred by the royal family of France.

The king, who in his heart had been sorely galled by the fetters of French etiquette, now that the emperor ridiculed it, became its warmest partisan; and went so far as to reprove his wife for following her brother's example, and sacrificing her royal dignity to an absurd longing for popularity.

The truth was, that Louis was envious of the enthusiasm which Joseph excited among the Parisians; and his brothers, the other members of the royal family, and his ministers, took every opportunity of feeding his envy, by representing that the emperor was doing his utmost to alienate the affections of the French from their rightful sovereign; that he was meditating the seizure of Alsace and Lorraine; that he was seeking to reinstate De Choiseul, and convert France into a mere dependency upon Austria.

Louis, who had begun to regard his wife with passionate admiration, became cold and sarcastic in his demeanor toward her. The hours which, until the emperor's arrival in Paris, he had spent with Marie Antoinette, were now dedicated to his ministers, to Madame Adelaide, and even to the Count de Provence—that brother whose enmity to the queen was not even concealed under a veil of courtly dissimulation.

Not satisfied with filling the king's ears with calumnies of his poor young wife, the Count de Provence was the instigator of all those scandalous songs, in which the emperor and the queen were daily ridiculed on the Pont-Neuf; and of the multifarious caricatures which, hour by hour, were rendering Marie Antoinette odious in the eyes of her subjects. The Count de Provence, who afterward wore his murdered brother's crown, was the first to teach the French nation that odiouus epithet of "*l'Autrichienne,*" with which they hooted the Queen of France to an ignominious death upon the scaffold.

The momentary joy which the visit of the emperor had caused to

* Count Schulenberg was sentenced to death; and Maria Theresa, who was inexorable where a breach of morals was concerned, approved the sentence. But Count Esterhazy hastened to intercede for his rival, acknowledging at last that Schulenberg had freed him from a tie which was a curse to him.

his sister had vanished, and given place to embarrassment and anxiety of heart. Even *she* felt vexed, not only that her subjects preferred a foreign prince to their own rightful sovereign, but that Joseph was so unrestrained in his sarcasms upon royal customs in France. Finally she was obliged to confess in the silence of her own heart, that her brother's departure would be a relief to her, and that these dinners *en famille*, to which he came daily as a guest, were inexpressibly tedious and heavy.

One day the emperor came earlier than usual to dinner—so early, in fact, that the king was still occupied holding his daily levee.

Joseph seated himself quietly in the anteroom to await his turn. At first no one had remarked his entrance; but presently he was recognized by one of the marshals of the household, who hastened to his side, and, apologizing, offered to inform the king at once of Count Falkenstein's presence there.

"By no means," returned the emperor, "I am quite accustomed to this sort of thing. I do it every morning in my mother's anteroom at Vienna." *

Just then the door opened, and the king, who had been apprised of the emperor's arrival, came forward to greet him.

"We were not aware that we had so distinguished a guest in our anteroom," said Louis, bowing. "But come, my brother," continued he cordially, "the weather is beautiful. Let us stroll together in the gardens. Give me your arm."

But Joseph, pointing to the crowd, replied, "Pardon me, your majesty, it is not yet my turn; and I should be sorry to interrupt you in your duties as sovereign."

Louis frowned; and all traces of cordiality vanished from his face. "I will receive tnese gentlemen to-morrow," said he, with a slight nod to his courtiers; and they, comprehending that they were dismissed, took their leave.

"Now, count," pursued the king, trying to smile, but scarcely succeeding in doing so, "we are at liberty."

So saying, he bowed, but did not repeat the offer of his arm; he walked by the emperor's side. The usher threw open the doors, crying out in a loud voice:

"The king is about to take a walk!"

"The king is about to take a walk," was echoed from point to point; and now from every side of the palace came courtiers and gentlemen in waiting, to attend their sovereign; while outside on the terrace the blast of trumpets was heard, so that everybody in Versailles was made aware that the king was about to take a turn in his gardens, and his anxious subjects, if so disposed, might pray for his safe return.

The emperor looked on and listened with an amused smile, highly diverted at the avalanche of courtiers that came rushing on them from corridor and staircase. Meanwhile the sovereigns pursued their way in solemn silence until the brilliant throng had descended the marble stairs that led from the terrace to the gardens. Then came another flourish of trumpets, one hundred Swiss saluted the king, and twelve *gardes de corps* advanced to take their places close to the royal promenaders.

"Sire," asked Joseph, stopping, "are all these people to accompany us?"

* Mémoires de Weber, vol. i., p. 48.

"Certainly, count," replied Louis, "this attendance upon me when I walk is prescribed by court etiquette."

"My dear brother, allow me to state that it gives us much more the appearance of state prisoners than of free sovereigns enjoying the fresh air. In the presence of God let us be simple men—our hearts will be more apt to be elevated by the sight of the beauties of nature, than if we go surrounded by all this 'pomp and circumstance' of royalty."

"You wish to go without attendants?" asked Louis.

"I ask of your majesty as a favor to let me act as a body-guard to the King of France to-day. I promise to serve him faithfully in that capacity—moreover, have we not this brilliant suite of noblemen to defend us in case of danger?"

The king made no reply. He merely turned to the captain of the Swiss guard to inform him that their majesties would dispense with military escort. The officer was so astounded that he actually forgot to make his salute.

At the gate of the park the king also dismissed the *gardes de corps*. These were quite as astonished as the Swiss had been before them; for never until that day had a King of France taken a walk in his gardens without one hundred Swiss and twelve body-guards.*

CHAPTER CXVII.

THE PROMENADE AND THE EPIGRAM.

THE royal brothers-in-law then were allowed to promenade alone; that is to say, they were attended by twenty courtiers, whose inestimable privilege it was to follow the king wherever he went.

"It is not then the custom in Austria for princes to appear in public with their escort?" asked the king, after a long pause.

"Oh, yes, we have our body-guards, but they are the people themselves, and we feel perfectly secure in their escort. You should try this body-guard, sire; it is more economical than yours, for its service is rendered for pure love."

"Certainly," replied the king carelessly, "it is a very cheap way of courting popularity; but the price would be too dear for a king of France to pay—he cannot afford to sell his dignity for such small return."

The emperor raised his large blue eyes, and looked full in the king's face. "Do you really think," he said, "that a king compromises his dignity by contact with his subjects? Do you think that to be honored by your people you must be forever reminding them of your 'right divine?' I, on the contrary, believe that the sovereign who shows himself to be a man, is the one who will be most sincerely loved by the men whom he governs. We are apt to become dazzled by the glare of flattery, sire, and it is well for us sometimes to throw off our grandeur, and mix among our fellows. There we will soon find out that majesty is not written upon the face of kings, but resides in the purple which is the work of the tailor, and the crown, which is that of the goldsmith. I learned this not long ago from a shoemaker's apprentice."

"From a shoemaker's apprentice!" exclaimed Louis, with a

* Hubner, i., p. 148.

supercilious smile. "It would be highly edifying to hear from the Count of Falkenstein how it happened that the Emperor of Austria was taught the nothingness of royalty by a shoemaker's lad!"

"It came quite naturally, sire. I was out driving in a plain *cabriolet*, when I remarked the boy, who was singing, and otherwise exercising his animal spirits by hopping, dancing, and running along the road by the side of the vehicle. I was much diverted by his drollery, and finally invited him to take a drive with me. He jumped in without awaiting a second invitation, stared wonderfully at me with his great brown eyes, and in high satisfaction kicked his feet againt the dash-board, and watched the motion of the wheels. Now and then he vented his delight by a broad smile, in which I could detect no trace of a suspicion as to my rank of majesty. Finally I resolved to find out what place I occupied in the estimation of an unfledged shoemaker; so I questioned him on the subject. He contemplated me for a moment, and then said, 'Perhaps you might be an equerry?'—'Guess higher,' replied I.—'Well, a count?'—I shook my head. 'Still higher.'—'A prince?'—'Higher yet.'—'Well, then, you must be the emperor.'—'You have guessed,' said I. Instead of being overcome by the communication, the boy sprang from the *cabriolet*, and pointing at me with a little finger that was full of scorn and dirt, he cried out to the passers-by, 'Only look at him! he is trying to pass himself off for the emperor.'"*

Louis had listened to this recital with grave composure, and as his face had not once relaxed from its solemnity, the faces of his courtiers all wore a similar expression. As Joseph looked around, he saw a row of blank countenances.

There was an awkward pause. Finally the king observed that he could not see any thing diverting in the insolence of the boy.

"I assure your majesty," replied the emperor, "that it was far more pleasing to me than the subservience of a multitude of fawning courtiers." He glanced sharply at the gentlemen of their suite, who knit their brows in return.

"Let us quicken our pace if it be agreeable to you, count," said Louis, with some embarrassment. The attendants fell back, and the two monarchs walked on for some moments in silence. The king was wondering how he should manage to renew the conversation, when suddenly, his voice, tremulous with emotion, Joseph addressed him.

"My brother," said he, "accident at last has favored me, and I may speak to you for once without witnesses. Tell me, then, why do you hate me?"

"My brother," exclaimed Louis, "who has dared—"

"No one has intimated such a thing," returned Joseph, vehemently; "but I see it, I feel it in every look of your majesty's eyes, every word that falls from your lips. Again, I ask why do you hate me? I who came hither to visit you as friend and brother! Or do you believe the idle rumors of your courtiers, that I came to rob aught besides the heart of the King of France? I know that I have been represented as unscrupulous in my ambition, but I entreat of you, dear brother, think better of me. I will be frank with you and confess that I *do* seek for aggrandizement, but not at the expense of my allies or friends. I strive to enlarge my territory, but I shall claim nothing that is not righteously my own. There

* "Characteristics and Anecdotes of Joseph II. and his Times," p. 105.

are provinces in Germany which are mine by right of inheritance, others by the right which Frederick used when he took Silesia from the crown of Austria."

"Or that which Joseph used when he took Galicia from the King of Poland," interrupted Louis, significantly.

"Sire, we did not take Galicia. It fell to us through the weakness of Poland, and by reason of exigencies arising from an alliance between the three powers. My claim to Bavaria, however, is of another nature. It is mine by inheritance—the more so that the Elector of Zweybrücken, the successor of the Elector of Bavaria, is willing to concede me my right to that province. The Bavarians themselves long for annexation to Austria, for they know that it is their only road to prosperity. They look with hope and confidence to Maria Theresa, whose goodness and greatness may compensate them for all that they have endured at the hands of their pusillanimous little rulers. The only man in Germany who will oppose the succession of Austria to Bavaria, is Frederick, who is as ready to enlarge his own dominions as to cry 'Stop thief!' when he sees others doing likewise. But he will not raise a single voice unless he receive encouragement from other powers. If my visit to France has any political significance, it is to obtain your majesty's recognition of my right to Bavaria. Yes, sire, I *do* wish to convince you of the justice of my claim, and to obtain from you the promise of neutrality when I shall be ready to assert it. You see that I speak without reserve, and confide to you plans which heretofore have been discussed in secret council at Vienna alone."

"And I pledge my royal word never to betray your majesty's confidence to living mortal," replied Louis, with undisguised embarrassment and anxiety. "Believe me when I say that every thing you have spoken is as though I had never heard it. I shall bury it within the recesses of my own heart, and there it shall remain."

The emperor surveyed his brother-in-law with a glance of mistrust. He thought that the assurance of his secrecy was given in singular language. He was not altogether satisfied to hear that what he had been saying was to be treated as though it had never been said at all.

"Will your majesty, then, sustain me?" asked he of Louis. This direct question staggered his majesty of France. He scarcely knew what he was saying.

"You ask this question," replied he, with a forced smile, "as if the elector was dead, and our decision were imperative. Fortunately, his highness of Bavaria is in excellent health, and the discussion may be—deferred. Let us think of the present. You were wise, my dear brother, when you remarked that the beauties of Nature were calculated to elevate our minds. What royalty can be compared to hers?"

The emperor made no reply. He felt the full significance of the king's ungracious words, and more than ever he was convinced that Louis regarded him with dislike and ill-will. Again there was a painful silence between the two, and every moment it weighed more heavily upon both.

At last Louis, awaking to a sense of what was due from host to guest, made a desperate resolution, and spoke.

"Have you made any plans for this evening, my brother?" asked he, timidly.

"No!" was the curt reply.

"You would be very amiable if, instead of visiting the theatres, you would join the queen in a game of cards."

"I never play," returned Joseph. "A monarch who loses money at cards, loses the property of his subjects." *

"Since you do not like cards, we have other recreations at hand. How would you relish a hunt in the woods of Meudon?"

"Not at all," said Joseph. "Hunting is no recreation for a monarch. *His* time is too precious to be frittered away in such idle sport."

"Ah," said Louis, whose patience was exhausted, "you imitate your old enemy, the King of Prussia, who for twenty years has been crying out against the sins of hunting and gambling."

The emperor's face grew scarlet, and his eyes flashed. "Sire," replied he, "allow me to observe to you that I imitate nobody, and that I am resolved now as ever to conduct myself as I see fit."

To this the king bowed in silence. He was so weary of his walk that he led the way to a road by which a short-cut might be made to the palace. This road was crossed by an avenue of trees which bordered a large iron gate leading to the front entrance of the palace. Here the people were accustomed to assemble to obtain a view of their sovereigns; and to-day the throng was greater than usual, for they had learned from the Swiss guard that the two monarchs were out together, and thousands of eager eyes were watching for the glittering uniforms of the *gardes de corps*.

Great was their astonishment to see two individuals alone, apparently independent of the courtiers at some distance behind them.

"Who could they be—these two gentlemen advancing together? Certainly not the emperor and the king, for the latter never took a step without his life-guards."

"But it *is* the emperor!" cried a voice in the crowd. "I know his handsome face and his dark-blue eyes."

"And the other is the king!" exclaimed another voice.

"It cannot be," said a third. "The King of France never moves in his own palace without a wall of guards around him—how much less in the open parks, where he is exposed to the danger of meeting his subjects!"

"I suppose we are indebted to the emperor for this bold act of his majesty to-day," said another critic.

"Yes, yes, he it is who has persuaded the king to trust us," cried the multitude. "Let us thank him by a hearty welcome."

The two princes were now quite near, and the crowd took off their hats. The emperor greeted them with an affable smile; the king with several nods, but without a shadow of cordiality. Suddenly the air was rent with shouts, and a thousand voices cried out, "Long live the emperor!"

The king reddened, but dared not give vent to his displeasure. His eyes sought the ground, while Joseph, gently shaking his head, looked at the people and pointed furtively at their sovereign.

They understood him at once, and, eager to repair the inadvertence, they shouted, "Long live the emperor! Long live our king, the father of his people!"

The emperor now smiled and waved his hand; while the king, still displeased, bowed gravely and turned toward Joseph.

* Joseph's own words. Hubner, part i., page 151.

"You are quite right," said he, in sharp, cutting accents, "popularity is a cheap commodity. A king has only to ride about in hackney-coaches and put on the people's garb, to become the idol of the lower classes. The question, however, is, how long will a popularity of this sort last?"

"If it be called forth by a hackney-coach and an ordinary dress, sire, it may be of short duration; but if it is to last, it must be accorded to real worth," replied Joseph, sympathizing with the discontent of the king.

"Which no one would presume to deny in your majesty's case," rejoined Louis with a constrained and awkward bow.

"Oh," exclaimed Joseph, blushing, "I had not understood that your majesty's irony was intended for me, else I should not have answered as I did. I do not strive after popularity. My actions flow naturally from my convictions. These teach me that my natural condition is not that of an emperor, but of a man, and I conduct myself accordingly." *

So saying, the emperor turned once more to salute the people, and then ascended the white marble steps which led to the terrace of the palace. The two monarchs and the glittering courtiers disappeared amid the "*vivas*" of the multitude, and now they became suddenly silent.

In the midst of this silence, the same voice which had so sharply criticised the king, was heard. Again it spoke as follows:

"Marsorio has made another epigram, and mistaking me for Pasquin has just whispered it in my ear!"

"What did he say? Tell us what our good Marsorio says! Repeat the epigram!" saluted the speaker on every side.

"Here it is," returned the voice.

"A nos yeux étonnés de sa simplicité
Falkenstein a montré la majesté sans faste;
Chez nous par un honteux contraste
Qu'a-t'il trouvé? Faste sans majesté." †

CHAPTER CXVIII.

THE DINNER EN FAMILLE.

MEANWHILE the king and the emperor reached the apartment which opened into the private dining-room of the royal family. The princes with their wives were already there; but Marie Antoinette always came at the last moment. She dreaded the sarcasm of the Count de Provence, and the sullen or contemptuous glances of the king. She would have given much to return to the old stiff, public ceremonial which she had banished, but that she could not do. It would have been too great a concession to the court. Her only refuge was to stay away as long as decorum allowed, and after the emperor's arrival she never entered the room until he had been announced.

To-day she was even later than usual; and the king, who like other mortals, was hungry after his walk, began to grow sulky at the delay. When at last she entered the room, he scarcely vouch-

* The emperor's own words. Ramshorn's "Joseph II.," page 146.
† Ramshorn, page 146.

safed her an inclination of the head as he rose to conduct her to the table. The queen seemed not to perceive the omission. She gave him her hand with a sweet smile, and despite his ill-humor, Louis could not suppress a throb as he saw how brilliantly beautiful she was.

"You have made us wait, madame," said he, "but your appearance to-day repays us for your tardiness."

The queen smiled again, for well she knew that she was bewitchingly dressed, and that the new *coiffure* which Leonard had contrived, was really becoming, and would heighten her charms by contrast with the hideous towers that were heaped, like Pelion upon Ossa, over the heads of the princesses.

"I hope that your majesty will forgive me for being late," said she, secure in the power of her fascinations. "My little Jacques is to blame. He is sick to-day, and would have no one to put him to sleep but myself."

"Your majesty should feel flattered," cried the Count de Provence. "You are expected to put off your dinner until a little peasant is pleased to go to sleep."

"Pardon me, your highness," said the queen, coloring, "Jacques is no longer a peasant—he is my child."

"The dauphin, perchance, which your majesty promised not long since to the *dames de la halle?*" answered the king's brother.

The queen blushed so deeply that the flush of her shame overspread her whole face and neck; but instead of retorting, she turned to address her brother.

"You have not a word of greeting for me, Joseph?"

"My dear sister," said the emperor, "I am speechless with admiration at your *coiffure*. Where did you get such a wilderness of flowers and feathers?"

"They are the work of Leonard."

"Who is Leonard?"

"What!" interrupted the Countess d'Artois, "your majesty does not know who Leonard is—Leonard the queen's hair dresser—Leonard the autocrat of fashion? He it is who imagined our lovely sister's *coiffure*, and certainly these feathers are superb!"

"Beautiful indeed!" cried the Countess de Provence, with an appearance of ecstasy.

"Are these the costly feathers which I heard your majesty admiring in the hat of the Duke de Lauzun?" asked the Count de Provence, pointedly.

"That is a curious question," remarked the king. "How should the feathers of the Duke de Lauzun be transported to the head of the queen?"

"Sire, I was by, when De Guéménée on the part of De Lauzun, requested the queen's acceptance of the feathers."

"And the queen?" said Louis, with irritation.

"I accepted the gift, sire," replied Marie Antoinette, calmly. "The offer was not altogether in accordance with court-etiquette, but no disrespect was intended, and I could not inflict upon Monsieur de Lauzun the humiliation of a refusal. The Count de Provence, however, can spare himself further anxiety in the matter, as the feathers that I wear to-day are those which were lately presented to me by my sister, the Queen of Naples."

"Indeed!" exclaimed the emperor, "I was not aware that Caroline gave presents, although I know that she frequently accepts them from her courtiers."

"The etiquette at Naples differs then from that of Paris," remarked the king. "No subject has the right to offer a gift to the Queen of France."

"Heaven be praised!" cried the Count de Provence, "nobody here pays any attention to court-customs! Since Madame de Noailles gave in her resignation we have been free to do all things. This inestimable freedom we owe to our lovely sister-in-law; who, in defiance of all prejudice, has had boldness enough to burst the fetters which for so many hundred years had impeded the actions of the Queens of France."

At that moment the first lady of honor, on bended knee, presented the queen her soup, and this relieved Marie Antoinette from the painful embarrassment which this equivocal compliment occasioned. But the emperor interposed.

"You have reason to be thankful to my sister that she has had the independence to attack these absurdities," said Joseph, warmly. "But pardon me if I ask if etiquette at Versailles approves of the conversion of the corridors, galleries, and staircases of the palace into booths for the accommodation of shopkeepers and tradesmen." *

"It is an old privilege which custom has sanctioned," returned the king, smiling.

"But which violates the sanctity of the king's residence," objected the emperor. "The Saviour who drove the money-changers from the temple, would certainly expel these traders, were he to appear on earth to-day."

This observation was received in sullen silence. The royal family looked annoyed, but busied themselves with their knives and forks. A most unpleasant pause ensued, which was broken by the queen, who turning to her brother, asked him what he had seen to interest him since his arrival in Paris.

"You well know," said he, "that Paris abounds in interesting institutions. Yesterday I was filled with enthusiasm with what I saw in the course of my morning ramble."

"Whither did you go, count?" asked Louis, appeased and flattered by the emperor's words.

"To the *Invalides*; and I confess to you that the sight of this noble asylum filled me with as much envy as admiration. I have nothing in Vienna that will bear comparison with this magnificent offering of France to her valiant defenders. You must feel your heart stir with pride whenever you visit those crippled heroes, sire."

"I have never visited the *Invalides*," said the king, coloring.

"What!" cried Joseph, raising his hands in astonishment, "the King of France has never visited the men who have suffered in his behalf! Sire, if you have neglected this sacred duty, you should hasten to repair the omission."

"What else did you see?" asked the queen, striving to cover the king's displeasure, and the contemptuous by-play of the Count de Provence.

"I visited the Foundling Hospital. To you, Antoinette, this hospital must possess especial interest."

* This custom was subsequently abolished by Marie Antoinette, and the lower classes never forgave her for withdrawing this extraordinary privilege from the hucksters of Paris.

"Oh, yes. I subscribe yearly to it from my private purse," said the queen.

"But surely you sometimes visit the pious sisters upon whom devolves the real burden of this charity, to reward them by your sympathy for their disinterested labors?"

"No, I have never been there," replied the queen, confused. "It is not allowed to the Queens of France to visit public benevolent institutions."

"And yet it is allowable for them to attend public balls at the opera-house!"

Marie Antoinette blushed and looked displeased. This sally of the emperor was followed by another blank pause, which finally was broken by himself.

"I also visited another noble institution," continued he, "that of the deaf mutes. The Abbé de l'Epée deserves the homage of the world for this monument of individual charity; for I have been told that his institution has never yet received assistance from the crown. My dear sister, I venture to ask alms of you for his unfortunate *protégés*. With what strength of love has he explored the dark recesses of their minds, to bear within the light of intelligence and cultivation! Think how he has rescued them from a joyless stupor, to place them by the side of thinking, reasoning and happy human beings! As soon as I return to Vienna, I shall found an institution for the deaf and dumb; I have already arranged with the abbé to impart his system to a person who shall be sent to conduct the asylum I propose to endow."

"I am happy to think that you meet with so many things in France worthy of your approval, count," remarked the king.

"Paris, sire," said Joseph, "is rich in treasures of whose existence you are scarcely aware."

"What are these treasures, then? Enlighten me, count."

"They are the magnificent works of art, sire, which are lying like rubbish in your royal store-houses in Paris. Luckily, as I have been told, etiquette requires that the pictures in your palaces should, from time to time, be exchanged, and thus these masterpieces are sometimes brought to view. In this matter, I acknowledge that etiquette is wisdom."*

"Etiquette," replied Louis, "is often the only defence which kings can place between themselves and importunate wisdom."

"Wisdom is so hard to find that I should think it impossible for her to be importunate," returned Joseph. "I met with her yesterday, however, in another one of your noble institutions—I mean the military school. I spent three hours there, and I envy you the privilege of visiting it as often as you feel disposed."

"Your envy is quite inappropriate," replied Louis, sharply, "for I have never visited the institute at all."

"Impossible!" cried the emperor, warmly. "You are unacquainted with all that is noblest and greatest in your own capital, sire! It is your duty as a king to know every thing that concerns the welfare of your subjects, not only here in Paris, but throughout all France."†

"I disagree with you, and I am of opinion that wisdom is often

* The emperor's words. Campan, vol. i., p. 178.
† The emperor's words. Campan, vol. i., p. 79.

exceedingly offensive," replied the king, frowning, as with a stiff bow, he rose from the table.

Marie Antoinette looked anxiously at Joseph to see the effects of her husband's impoliteness; but the emperor looked perfectly unconscious, and began to discuss the subject of painting with the Count d'Artois.

The queen retired to her cabinet, heartily rejoicing that the *dîner en famille* had come to an end; and almost ready to order that the royal meals should be served in the state dining-room, and the people of Paris invited to resume their old custom of coming to stare at the royal family!

She sat down to her *escritoire,* to work with her treasurer and private secretary; that is, to sign all the papers that he placed before her for that purpose.

The door opened and the emperor entered the room. The queen would have risen, but he prevented her, and begged that he might not feel himself to be an intruder.

"I came, dear sister," said he, "to ask you to accompany me to the theatre to-night. Meanwhile it will give me great pleasure to see you usefully employed."

So the queen went on signing papers, not one of which she examined. The emperor watched her for a time in astonished silence; finally he came up to the *escritoire.*

"Sister," said he, "I think it very strange that you put your name to so many documents without ever looking at their contents."

"Why strange, brother?" asked the queen, opening her large eyes in wonder.

"Because it is a culpable omission, Antoinette. You should not so lightly throw away your royal signature. The name of a sovereign should never be signed without deliberation; much less blindly, as you are signing yours at present." *

Marie Antoinette colored with vexation at this reproof in presence of one of her own subjects. "Brother," replied she hastily, "I admire the facility with which you generalize on the subject of other people's derelictions. Unhappily, your homilies are sometimes misapplied. My secretary, Monsieur d'Augeard, has my full confidence; and these papers are merely the quarterly accounts of my household expenditures. They have already been approved by the auditor, and you perceive that I risk nothing by affixing my signature."

"I perceive further," replied Joseph, smiling, "that you are of one mind with your husband, and find wisdom sometimes very offensive. Forgive me if in my over-anxiety I have hurt you, dear sister. Let us be friends; for indeed, my poor Antoinette, you are sorely in need of friends at this court."

The queen dismissed her secretary, and then came forward and took her brother's hand. "You have discovered then," said she, "that I am surrounded by enemies?"

"I have indeed; and I tremble for your safety. Your foes are powerful, and you—you are not sufficiently cautious, Antoinette."

"What is it in me that they find to blame!" exclaimed she, her beautiful eyes filling with tears.

"Some other day, we must talk of this together. I see that you are threatened; but as yet, I neither understand the cause of your

* The emperor's own words.

danger nor its remedy. As soon as I shall have unravelled the mystery of your position, I will seek an interview with you; and then, dear sister, we must forget that we are sovereigns, and remember but one thing—the ties that have bound us together since first we loved each other as children of one father and mother."

Marie Antoinette laid her head upon her brother's bosom and wept. "Oh, that we were children again in the gardens of Schönbrunn!" sobbed she; "for there at least we were innocent and happy!"

CHAPTER CXIX.

A VISIT TO JEAN JACQUES ROUSSEAU.

BEFORE the door of a small, mean house in the village of Montmorency, stood a hackney-coach from which a man, plainly dressed, but distinguished in appearance, had just alighted. He was contemplated with sharp scrutiny by a woman, who, with arms a-kimbo, blocked up the door of the cottage.

"Does Monsieur Rousseau live here?" asked the stranger, touching his hat.

"Yes, my husband lives here," said the woman, sharply.

"Ah, you are then Therese Levasseur, the companion of the great philosopher?"

"Yes, I am; and the Lord knows that I lead a pitiful life with the philosopher."

"You complain, madame, and yet you are the chosen friend of a great man!"

"People do not live on greatness, sir, nor on goodness either. Jean Jacques is too good to be of any use in this world. He gives away every thing he has, and leaves nothing for himself and me."

The stranger grew sad as he looked at this great, strapping woman, whose red face was the very representative of coarseness and meanness.

"Be so good as to conduct me to Monsieur Rousseau's presence, madame," said he, in rather a commanding tone.

"I shall do no such thing," cried Therese Levasseur, in a loud, rough voice. "People who visit in hackney-coaches should not take airs. Monsieur Rousseau is not to be seen by everybody."

"A curious doctrine that, to be propounded before a philosopher's door!" said the stranger, laughing. "But pray, madame, excuse me and my hackney-coach, and allow me to pass."

"You shall first tell your business. Do you bring music to copy?"

"No, madame, I come merely to visit monsieur."

"Then you can go as you came!" exclaimed the virago. "My husband is not a wild animal on exhibition, and I am not going to let in every idle stranger that interferes with his work, and cuts off my bread. God knows he gives me little enough, without lessening the pittance by wasting his time talking to you or the like of you."

The stranger put his hand in his pocket, and, drawing it out again, laid something in the palm of Therese's broad, dirty hand. He repeated his request.

She looked at the gold, and her avaricious face brightened.

"Yes, yes," said she, contemplating it with a greedy smile, "you shall see Jean Jacques. But first you must promise not to tell him of the louis d'or. He would growl and wish me to give it back. He is such a fool! He would rather starve than let his friends assist him."

"Be at ease—I shall not say a word to him."

"Then, sir, go in and mount the stairs, but take care not to stumble, for the railing is down. Knock at the door above, and there you will find Jean Jacques. While you talk to him I will go out and spend this money all for his comfort. Let me see—he needs a pair of shoes and a cravat—and—well," continued she, nodding her head, "farewell, don't break your neck.

"Yes," muttered she, as she went back to the street, "he wants shoes and cravats, and coats, too, for that matter, but I am not the fool to waste my money upon him. I shall spend it on myself for a new neckerchief; and if there is any thing left, I shall treat myself to a couple of bottles of wine and some fish."

While Therese stalked through the streets to spend her money, the stranger had obtained entrance into the little dark room where sat Jean Jacques Rousseau.

It was close and mouldy like the rest of the house, and a few straw chairs with one deal table was the only furniture there. On the wall hung several bird-cages, whose inmates were twittering and warbling one to another. Before the small window, which looked out upon a noble walnut-tree, stood several glass globes, in which various worms and fishes were leading an uneasy existence.

Rousseau himself was seated at the table writing. He wore a coat of coarse gray cloth, like that of a laborer, the collar of his rough linen shirt was turned down over a bright cotton scarf, which was carelessly tied around his neck. His face was pale, sad, and weary; and his scant gray hairs, as well as the deep wrinkles upon his forehead, were the scroll whereon time had written sixty years of strife and struggle with life. Imagination, however, still looked out from the depths of his dark eyes, and the corners of his mouth were still graceful with the pencillings of many a good-humored smile.

"Pardon me, sir," said the stranger, "that I enter unannounced. I found no one to precede me hither."

"We are too poor to keep a servant, sir," replied Rousseau, "and I presume that my good Therese has gone out on some errand. How can I serve you!"

"I came to visit Jean Jacques Rousseau, the poet and philosopher."

"I am the one, but scarcely the other two. Life has gone so roughly with me, that poetry has vanished long ago from my domicile, and men have deceived me so often, that I have fled from the world in disgust. You see, then, that I have no claim to the title of philosopher."

"And thus speaks Jean Jacques Rousseau, who once taught that mankind were naturally good?"

"I still believe in my own teachings, sir," cried Rousseau warmly. "Man is the vinculum that connects the Creator with His creation, and light from heaven illumes his birth and infancy. But the world, sir, is evil, and is swayed by two demons—selfishness and falsehood.* These demons poison the heart of man, and influence him to actions whose sole object is to advance himself and prejudice his neighbor."

"I fear that your two demons were coeval with the creation of the world," said the stranger, with a smile.

"No, no; they were not in Paradise. And what is Paradise but the primitive condition of man—that happy state when in sweet harmony with Nature, he lay upon the bosom of his mother earth, and inhaled health and peace from her life-giving breath? Let us return to a state of nature, and we shall find that the gates of Paradise have reopened."

"Never! We have tasted of the tree of knowledge, and are forever exiled from Eden."

"Woe to us all, if what you say is true; for then the world is but a vale of misery, and the wise man has but one resource—self-destruction! But pardon me, I have not offered you a chair."

The stranger accepted a seat, and glanced at the heaps of papers that covered the rickety old table.

"You were writing?" asked he. "Are we soon to receive another great work from Rousseau's hands?"

"No, sir," replied Rousseau, sadly, "I am too unhappy to write."

"But surely this is writing," and the stranger pointed to the papers around.

"Yes, sir, but I copy music, and God knows that in the notes I write, there is little or no thought. I have written books that I might give occasion to the French to think, but they have never profited by the opportunity. They are more complaisant now that I copy music. I give them a chance to sing, and they sing."†

"It seems to me that there is great discord in their music, sir. You who are as great a musician as a philosopher, can tell me whether I judge correctly."

"You are right," replied Rousseau. "The dissonance increases with every hour. The voice which you hear is that of the people, and the day will come when, claiming their rights, they will rend the air with a song of such hatred and revenge as the world has never heard before."

"But who denies their rights to the people?"

"The property-holders, the priests, the nobles, and the king."

"The king! what has he done?"

"He is the grandson of that Louis XV., whose life of infamy is a foul blot upon the fame of France; and nothing can ever wash away the disgrace save an ocean of royal blood."

"Terrible!" exclaimed the visitor, with a shudder. "Are you a prophet, that you allow yourself such anticipations of evil?"

"No, sir, I predict what is to come, from my knowledge of that which has gone by."

"What do you mean?"

Rousseau slowly shook his head. "Fate has threatened this unhappy king from the day of his birth. Warning after warning has been sent and disregarded. Truly, the man was a wise one who said, 'Whom the gods destroy, they first blind!'"

* This is not very philosophical. If the fraction man be intrinsically good, how is it that the whole (the world which is made up of nothing but men) is so evil? Is there a demiurge responsible for the introduction of these two demons?

† This is Rousseau's own language. Ramshorn, p. 140.

"I implore you, speak further. What evil omens have you seen that lead you to apprehend misfortune to Louis XVI.?"

"Have you never heard of them? They are generally known."

"No, indeed, I beseech you, enlighten me, for I have good reason for my curiosity."

"Louis was not born like his predecessors, and it is generally believed that he will not die a natural death. Not a single member of the royal family was present at his birth. When, overtaken by the pangs of childbirth, his mother was accidentally alone in the palace of Versailles; and the heir of France, upon his entrance into life, was received by some insignificant stranger. The courier who was sent to announce his birth fell from his horse and was killed on the spot. The Abbé de Saujon, who was called in to christen the infant, was struck by apoplexy while entering the chapel door, and his arm and tongue were paralyzed.* From hundreds of healthy women the physician of the dauphiness chose three nurses for the prince. At the end of a week two of them were dead, and the third one, Madame Guillotine, after nursing him for six weeks, was carried off by small-pox. Even the frivolous grandfather was terrified by such an accumulation of evil omens, and he was heard to regret that he had given to his grandson the title of Duke de Berry, 'For,' said he, 'the name has always brought ill-luck to its possessors.'"†

"But the king has long since outlived the name, and has triumphed over all the uncomfortable circumstances attending his birth, for he is now King of France."

"And do you know what he said when the crown was placed upon his head?"

"No, I have never heard."

"He was crowned at Rheims. When the hand of the archbishop was withdrawn from the crown, the king moaned, and turning deadly pale, murmured, 'OH, HOW IT PAINS ME!'‡ Once before him, a King of France had made the same exclamation, and that king was Henry III."

"Strange!" said the visitor. "All this seems very absurd, and yet it fills me with horror. Have you any thing more of the same sort to point out?"

"Remember all that occurred when the dauphin was married to the Archduchess Marie Antoinette. When she put her foot upon French ground, a tent had been erected, according to custom, where she was to lay aside her clothing, and be attired in garments of French manufacture. The walls of the tent were hung with costly Gobelin tapestry, all of which represented scenes of bloodshed. On one side was the massacre of the innocents, on the other the execution of the Maccabees. The archduchess herself was horror-stricken at the omen. On that night, two of the ladies in waiting, who had assisted the queen in her toilet, died suddenly. Think of the terrible storm that raged on the dauphin's wedding night; and of the dreadful accident which accompanied his entrance into Paris; and then tell me whether death is not around, perchance *before* this unhappy king?"

"But to what end are these omens, since they cannot help us to avert evil?"

* "Mémoires de Madame de Creque," vol. iii., p. 179.
† Creque, vol. iii., p. 180.
‡ Campan, vol. i., p. 115.

"To what end?" asked Rousseau, as with a smile he contemplated the agitated countenance of his guest. "To this end—that the emperor Joseph may warn his brother and sister of the fate which threatens, and which will surely engulf them, if they do not heed the signs of the coming tempest."

"How, Rousseau! you know me?"

"If I had not known you, sire, I would not have spoken so freely of the king. I saw you in Paris at the theatre, and I am rejoiced to be able to speak to your majesty as man to man, and friend to friend."

"Then let me be as frank as my friend has been to me," said Joseph extending his hand. "You are not situated as becomes a man of your genius and fame. What can I do to better your condition?"

"Better my condition?" repeated Rousseau absently. "Nothing. I am an old man whose every illusion has fled. My only wants are a ray of sunshine to warm my old limbs, and a crust of bread to appease my hunger."

At this moment a shrill voice was heard without: "Put down the money and I will fetch the music, for we are sadly pressed for every thing."

"Good Heaven!" exclaimed Rousseau, anxiously. "I am not ready, and I had promised the music to Therese for this very hour. How shall I excuse myself?" Here the unhappy philosopher turned to the emperor. "Sire, you asked what you could do for me—I implore you leave this room before Therese enters it. She will be justly displeased if she finds you here; and when my dear good Therese is angry, she speaks so loud that my nerves are discomposed for hours afterward. Here, sire, through this other door. It leads to my bedroom, and thence by a staircase to the street."

Trembling with excitement, Rousseau hurried the emperor into the next room. The latter waved his hand, and the door closed upon him. As he reached the street Joseph heard the sharp, discordant tones of Therese Levasseur's voice, heaping abuse upon the head of her philosopher, because he had not completed his task, and they would not have a sou wherewith to buy dinner.

CHAPTER CXX.

THE PARTING.

THE visit of the emperor was drawing to a close. He had tasted to its utmost of the enjoyments of the peerless city. He had become acquainted with its great national institutions, its industrial resources, its treasures of art and of science. The Parisians were enthusiastic in his praise; from the nobleman to the artisan, every man had something to say in favor of the gracious and affable brother of the queen. Even the fish-wives, those formidable *dames de la halle,* had walked in procession to pay their respects, and present him a bouquet of gigantic proportions.*

The emperor was popular everywhere except at court. His candor was unacceptable, and his occasional sarcasms had stung the

*On this occasion Madame Trigodin, one of the most prominent of the *poissardes*, made an address on behalf of the sisterhood. Hubner, i., p. 151.

pride of the royal family. The king never pardoned him the unpalatable advice he had bestowed relative to the hospitals, the *Invalides*, and the military schools. The queen, too, was irritated to see that whereas her brother might have expressed his disapprobation of her acts in private, he never failed to do so in presence of the court. The consequence was, that, like the king and the rest of the royal family, Marie Antoinette was relieved when this long-wished-for visit of the emperor was over. This did not prevent her from clinging to his neck, and shedding abundant tears as she felt his warm and loving embrace.

The emperor drew her close to his heart, whispering meanwhile, "Remember that we must see each other in private. Send some one to me to conduct me to the room in the palace which you call your 'asylum.'"

"How!" said the queen with surprise, "you have heard of my asylum? Who told you of it?"

"Hush, Antoinette, you will awaken the king's suspicion, for all eyes are upon us! Will you admit me?"

"Yes, I will send Louis to conduct you this afternoon." And withdrawing herself from her brother's arms, the queen and the royal family took leave of Count Falkenstein.

His carriages and suite had all left Paris, and Joseph, too, was supposed to have gone long before the hour when he was conducted to the queen's "asylum" by her faithful servant Louis. This "asylum" was in an obscure corner of the Tuileries, and to reach it the emperor was introduced into the palace by a side door. He was led through dark passages and up narrow staircases until they reached a small door that Louis opened with a key which he took from his pocket. He clapped his hand three times, and the signal being answered, he made a profound inclination to the emperor.

"Your majesty can enter. The queen is there."

Joseph found himself in a small, simple apartment, of which the furniture was of white wood covered with chintz. On the wall was a hanging *étagère* with books; opposite, an open harpsichord, and in the recess of the window, a table covered with papers. The emperor hastily surveyed this room, and no one coming forward, he passed into another.

Here he found his sister, no longer the magnificent queen whose rich toilets were as proverbial as her beauty; but a lovely, unpretending woman, without rouge, without jewels, clad in a dress of India muslin, which was confined at the waist by a simple sash of pale lilac ribbon.

Marie Antoinette came forward with both hands outstretched. "I am dressed as is my custom," said she, "when the few friends I possess come to visit me here—here in my asylum, where sometimes I am able to forget that I am Queen of France."

"You have no right ever to forget it, Antoinette, and it was expressly to remind you of this that I asked for a private interview with my sister."

"You wished to see this asylum of which you had heard, did you not?" asked the queen with a shade of bitterness. "I have been calumniated to you, as I have been to the king and to the French people. I know how my enemies are trying to make my subjects hate me! I know that about these very rooms, lewd songs are sung on the Pont-Neuf which make the Count de Provence hold his sides with laughter."

"Yes, Antoinette, I have heard these things, and I came hither expressly to visit this 'asylum.'"

"Well, Joseph, it is before you. The room through which you passed, and this one, form my suite. The door yonder leads to the apartments of the Princess de Lamballe, and I have never opened it to enter my retreat except in her company."

"You had never the right to enter it at all. A retreat of this kind is improper for you; and woe to you, Antoinette, if ever another man beside myself should cross its threshold! It would give a coloring of truth to the evil reports of your powerful enemies."

"Gracious God of Heaven!" cried the queen, pale with horror, "what do they say of me?"

"It would avail you nothing to repeat their calumnies, poor child. I have come hither to warn you that some dark cloud hangs over the destiny of France. You must seek means to disperse it, or it will burst and destroy both you and your husband."

"I have already felt a presentiment of evil, dear brother, and for that very reason I come to these little simple rooms that I may for a few hours forget the destiny that awaits me, the court which hates and vilifies me, and in short—my supremest, my greatest sorrow—the indifference of my husband."

"Dear sister, you are wrong. You should never have sought to forget these things. You have too lightly broken down the barriers which etiquette, hundreds of years ago, had built around the Queens of France."

"This from *you*, Joseph, you who despise all etiquette!"

"Nay, Antoinette, I am a man, and that justifies me in many an indiscretion. I have a right to attend an opera-ball unmasked, but you have not."

"I had the king's permission, and was attended by my ladies of honor, and the princes of the royal family."

"An emperor may ride in a hackney-coach or walk, if the whim strike him, but not a queen, Antoinette."

"That was an accident, Joseph. I was returning from a ball with the Duchess de Duras, when our carriage broke, and Louis was obliged to seek a hackney-coach or we would have returned to the palace on foot."

"Let it pass, then. An emperor or a king, were he very young, might indulge himself in a game of blind man's buff without impropriety; but when a queen ventures to do as much, she loses her dignity. Nevertheless, you have been known to romp with the other ladies of the court, when your husband had gone to his room and was sound asleep."

"But who ever went to bed as early as the king?" said Marie Antoinette, deprecatingly.

"Does he go to bed too early, Antoinette? Then it is strange that on one evening when you were waiting for him to retire so that you and your ladies might visit the Duchess de Duras, you should have advanced the clock by half an hour, and sent your husband to bed at half-past ten, when of course he found no one in his apartments to wait upon him.* All Paris has laughed at this mischievous prank of the queen. Can you deny this, my thoughtless sister?"

* Campan, 129.

"I never tell an untruth, Joseph; but I confess that I am astounded to see with what police-like dexterity you have ferreted out every little occurrence of my private life."

"A queen has no private life. She is doomed to live in public, and woe to her if she cannot account to the world for every hour of her existence! If she undertake to have secrets, her very lackeys misrepresent her innocence and make it crime."

"Good Heaven, Joseph!" cried the queen, "you talk as if I were a criminal before my accusers."

"You *are* a criminal, my poor young sister. Public opinion has accused you; and accusation there is synonymous with guilt. But I, who give you so much pain, come as your friend and brother, speaking hard truths to you, dearest, by virtue of the tie which binds us to our mother. In the name of that incomparable mother, I implore you to be discreet, and to give no cause to your enemies for misconstruction of your youthful follies. Take up the load of your royalty with fortitude; and, when it weighs heavily upon your poor young heart, remember that you were not made a queen to pursue your own happiness, but to strive for that of your subjects, whose hearts are still with you in spite of all that your enemies have done or said. Give up all egotism, Antoinette—set aside your personal hopes; live for the good of the French nation; and one of these days you will believe with me, that we may be happy without individual happiness."

The queen shook her head, and tears rolled down her cheeks. "No, no, dear Joseph, a woman cannot be happy when she is unloved. My heart is sick with solitude, brother. I love my husband and he does not return my love. If I am frivolous, it is because I am unhappy. Believe me when I tell you that all would be well if the king would but love me."

"Then, Antoinette, all shall be well," said a voice behind them; and, starting with a cry of surprise and shame, the queen beheld the king.

"I have heard all," said Louis, closing the door and advancing toward Joseph. With a bright, affectionate smile, he held out his hand, saying as he did, "Pardon me, my brother, if I am here without your consent, and let me have a share in this sacred and happy hour."

"Brother!" repeated Joseph, sternly. "You say that you have overheard us. If so, you know that my sister is solitary and unhappy. Since you have no love for her, you are no brother to me; for she, poor child, is the tie that unites us! Look at her, sire; look at her sweet, innocent, tear-stricken face! What has she done that you should thrust her from your heart, and doom her to confront, alone, the sneers and hatred of your cruel relatives? She is pure, and her heart is without a stain. I tell you so—I, who in unspeakable anxiety have watched her through hired spies. Had I found her guilty I would have been the first to condemn her; but Antoinette is good, pure, virtuous, and she has but one defect—want of thought. It was your duty to guide her, for you received her from her mother's hands a child—a young, harmless, unsuspecting child. What has she ever done that you should refuse her your love?"

"Ask, rather, what have I done, that my relatives should have kept us so far asunder?" replied Louis, with emotion. "Ask those who have poisoned my ears with calumnies of my wife, why they should have sought to deny me the only compensation which life can offer to my royal station—the inestimable blessing of loving and being loved. But away with gloomy retrospection! I shall say but one word more of the past. Your majesty has been watched, and your visit here discovered. I was told that you were seeking to identify the queen with her mother's empire—using your influence to make her forget France, and plot dishonor to her husband's crown. I resolved to prove the truth or falsehood of these accusations myself. I thank Heaven that I did so; for from this hour I shall honor and regard you as a brother."

"I shall reciprocate, sire, if you will promise to be kind to my sister?"

The king looked at Marie Antoinette, who, seated on the sofa whence her brother had risen, was weeping bitterly. Louis went toward her, and, taking both her hands in his, pressed them passionately to his lips. "Antoinette," said he, tenderly, "you say that I do not love you. You have not then read my heart, which, filled to bursting with love for my beautiful wife, dared not ask for response, because I had been told that you—you—but no—I will not pain you with repetition of the calumny. Enough that I am blessed with your love, and may at last be permitted to pour out the torrent of mine! Antoinette, will you be my wife?"

He held open his arms, and looked—as lovers alone can look. The queen well knew the meaning of that glance, and, with a cry of joy, she rose and was pressed to his heart. He held her for some moments there, and then, for the first time in their lives, the lips of husband and wife met in one long, burning kiss of love.

"My beloved, my own," whispered Louis. "Mine forever—nothing on earth shall part us now."

Marie Antoinette was speechless with happiness. She leaned her head upon her husband's breast and wept for joy, while he fondly stroked and kissed her shining hair, and left the trace of a tear with every kiss.

Presently he turned an imploring look upon the emperor, who stood by, contemplating the lovers with an ecstasy to which he had long been a stranger.

"My brother," said Louis, "for I may call you so now—seven years ago, our hands were joined together by the priest; but, the policy that would have wounded Austria through me, has kept us asunder. This is our wedding-day, this is the union of love with love. Be you the priest to bless the rites that make us one till death."

The emperor came forward, and, solemnly laying his hands upon the heads of the king and queen, spoke in broken accents:

"God bless you, beloved brother and sister—God give you grace to be true to each other through good and evil report. Be gentle and indulgent one toward the other, that, from this day forward, your two hearts may become as one! Farewell! I shall take with me to Austria the joyful news of your happiness. Oh, how Maria Theresa will rejoice to know it, and how often will the thought of this day brighten my own desolate hearth at Vienna! Farewell!"

CHAPTER CXXI.

DEATH OF THE ELECTOR OF BAVARIA.

A LARGE and brilliant assemblage thronged the state apartments of the imperial palace at Vienna. The aristocracy not only of the capital, but of all Austria, had gathered there to congratulate the emperor upon his safe return.

It was the first of January, 1778, and as New Year's day was the only festival which Joseph's new ordinance allowed, the court took occasion to celebrate it with all the pomp of embroidery, orders, stars, and blazing jewels.

The empress had never thrown off her mourning, so that her dark gray dress with its long train was in striking contrast with the rich, elegant costumes, the flowers and diamonds of the other ladies present. Still, there was something in this tall, noble form which distinguished it above the rest, and spoke to all beholders of the sovereign will that resided there. Maria Theresa was still the majestic empress—but she was now an old woman.

Time as well as disease had marred her beauty, and the cares, anxieties, and afflictions of sixty years had written their inexorable record upon the tablet of her once fair brow. Not only these, but accident also had destroyed the last lingering traces of Maria Theresa's youthful comeliness. Returning from Presburg, she had been thrown from her carriage, and dashed with such force against the stones on the road, that she had been taken up bloody, and, to all appearances, lifeless. Her face had suffered severely, and to her death she bore the deep-red scars which had been left by her wounds. Her figure, too, had lost its grace, and was now so corpulent that she moved slowly and heavily through the rooms, where, in former years, she had stood by the side of her "Francis," the most beautiful woman of her own or of any European court.

Her magnificent eyes, however, had defied time, they were large, flashing, expressive as ever—as quick to interpret anger, enthusiasm, or tenderness as in the days of her youth.

On the evening of which we speak, the empress was at the card-table. But those great, glowing eyes were roving from one side of the room to the other in restless anxiety. Sometimes, for a moment, they rested upon the emperor who was standing near the table in conversation with some provincial nobleman. The cheerful and unconcerned demeanor of her son seemed to reassure the empress, who turned to her cards, and tried to become interested in the game. Not far off, the archduchesses, too, were at cards, and the hum of conversation subsided almost to a whisper, that the imperial party might not be disturbed. Gradually the empress became absorbed in her cards, so that she was unobservant of the entrance of one of the emperor's lords in waiting, who whispered something in Joseph's ear, whereupon the latter left the room in haste.

Not very long after the emperor returned pale and excited, and approached the card-tables. Maria Theresa, at that moment, had just requested Count Dietrichstein to deal for her, and she was leaning back in her chair, awaiting the end of the deal.

The emperor bent over and whispered something in her ear, when she started, and the cards, which she was just gathering, fell from her hands. With unusual agility she rose, and taking the emperor's arm, turned away without a word of apology, and left the room.

The archduchesses had not yet perceived their mother's absence, when Count Dietrichstein, on the part of the emperor, came forward, and whispered a few words to each one of them. Precisely as their mother had done the princesses rose, and without apology retired together.

The company started, and whispered and wondered what could have happened to discompose the imperial family; but no one present was competent to solve the mystery.

Meanwhile Maria Theresa had retired to her cabinet, where she met Prince Kaunitz, furred like a polar bear, by way of protection from the temperature of the palace, which was always many degrees below zero, as indicated by the thermometer of his thin, bloodless veins. The minister was shaking with cold, although he had buried his face in a muff large enough to have been one of his own cubs.

The empress returned his greeting with an agitated wave of her hand, and seated herself in an arm-chair at the large round table that always stood there.

Exhausted by the unusual haste with which she had walked as well as by the excitement, which, in her old age, she was physically inadequate to bear, she leaned back to recover her breath. Opposite stood the emperor, who, with a wave of his hand, motioned to Kaunitz to enter also.

Maria Theresa's large eyes were fixed upon him at once.

"Is it true," said she, "that the Elector of Bavaria is dead?"

"Yes, your majesty," said Kaunitz. "Maximilian reigns no longer in Bavaria. Here are the dispatches from our ambassador at Munich."

He held them out, but the empress put them back, saying:

"I am not sufficiently composed to read them. Give them to my son, and have the goodness to communicate their contents to me verbally."

The face of Kaunitz grew pale, as he turned with the dispatches to the emperor. The latter at once comprehended the prince's agitation, and smiled.

"I beg of your majesty," said he, "to excuse the prince, and to allow me to read to you the particulars of Maximilian's demise. His highness must be fatigued, and, doubtless, your majesty will allow him to retire within the embrasure of yonder window, until I have concluded the perusal of the dispatches."

Kaunitz brightened at once as the empress gave her consent, and he gladly withdrew to the window which was far enough from the table to be out of reach of the emperor's voice.

Joseph could not restrain another smile as he watched the tall, stiff form of the old prince, and saw how carefully he drew the window curtains around him, lest a word of what was going on should reach his ears.

"Pardon me, your majesty," said Joseph, in a low voice, "but you know what a horror Kaunitz has of death and the small-pox. As both these words form the subject of our dispatches, I was glad to relieve the prince from the necessity of repeating their contents."

"That you should have remembered his weakness does honor to your heart, my son," replied Maria Theresa. "In my agitation I had forgotten it. Maximilian, then, must have died of small-pox."

"He did, your majesty, like his sister, my unhappy wife."

"Strange!" said Maria Theresa, thoughtfully. "Josepha has often spoken to me of the presentiment which her brother had that he would die of the small-pox."

"It proves to us that man cannot fly from his destiny. The elector foresaw that he would die of small-pox, and took every precaution to avert his fate. Nevertheless, it overtook him."

The empress sighed and slowly shook her head. "Where did he take the infection?" asked she.

"From the daughter of the marshal of his household, who lived at the palace, and took the small-pox there. Every attempt was made to conceal the fact from the elector, and indeed he remained in total ignorance of it. One day while he was playing billiards, the marshal, who had just left his daughter's bedside, entered the room. The elector, shuddering, laid down his cue, and turning deathly pale, murmured these words: 'Some one here has the small-pox. I feel it.' He then fell insensible on the floor. He recovered his consciousness, but died a few days afterward.* This is the substance of the dispatches. Shall I now read them?"

"No, no, my son," said the empress, gloomily. "Enough that the son of my enemy is dead, and his house without an heir."

"Yes, he is dead," replied Joseph, sternly. "The brother of my enemy—of that wife with whom for two years I lived the martyrdom of an abhorred union! He has gone to his sister, gone to his father, both our bitter, bitter foes. I hated Josepha for the humiliation I endured as the husband of such a repulsive woman; but today I forgive her, for 'tis she who from the grave holds out to me the rich inheritance which is the fruit of our marriage."

The empress raised her eyes with an expression of alarm.

"What!" exclaimed she, "another robbery! Lies not the weight of one injustice upon my conscience, that you would seek to burden my soul with another! Think you that I have forgotten Poland!—No! The remembrance of our common crime will follow me to the bitter end, and it shall not be aggravated by repetition. I am empress of Austria, and while I live, Joseph, you must restrain your ambition within the bounds of justice and princely honor."

The emperor bowed. "Your majesty must confess that I have never struggled against your imperial will. I have bowed before it, sorely though it has humiliated me. But as there is no longer any question of death before us, allow me to recall Prince Kaunitz, that he may take part in our discussion."

Maria Theresa bowed in silence, and the emperor drew the minister from his retreat behind the curtains.

"Come, your highness," whispered Joseph. "Come and convince the empress that Bavaria must be ours. We are about to have a struggle."

"But I shall come out victor," replied Kaunitz, as he rose and returned to the table.

Maria Theresa surveyed them both with looks of disapprobation and apprehension. "I see," said she, in a tremulous voice, "that you are two against one. I do not think it honorable in Kaunitz to uphold my son against his sovereign. Tell me, prince, do you come hither to break your faith, and overthrow your empress?"

"There lives not man or woman in the world who can accuse

* Wraxall, "Memoirs of the Courts of Berlin, Vienna, etc.," vol. i., p. 306.

Kaunitz of bad faith," replied the prince. "I swore years ago to dedicate myself to Austria, and I shall keep my word until your majesty releases me."

"I suppose that is one of your numerous threats to resign," said the empress, with irritation. "If there is difference of opinion between us, I must yield, or you will not remain my minister. But be sure that to the last day of my life I shall retain my sovereignty, nor share it with son or minister; and this conceded, we may confer together. Let the emperor sit by my side, and you, prince, be opposite to us, for I wish to look into your face that I may judge how far your tongue expresses the convictions of your conscience. And now I desire the emperor to explain his words, and tell me how it is that the succession of Bavaria concerns the house of Hapsburg."

"Frankly, then," cried Joseph, with some asperity, "I mean that our troops must be marched into Bavaria at once; for by the extinction of the male line of Wittelsbach, the electorate is open to us as an imperial fief, and—"

"Austria, then, has pretensions to the electorate of Bavaria," interrupted Maria Theresa, with constrained calmness.

The emperor in his turn looked at his mother with astonishment. "Has your majesty, then, not read the documents which were drawn up for your inspection by the court historiographer?"

"I have seen them all," replied the empress, sadly. "I have read all the documents by which you have sought to prove that Austria has claims upon Lower Bavaria, because, in 1410, the Emperor Sigismund enfeoffed his son-in-law, Albert of Austria, with this province. I have read further that in 1614 the Emperor Matthias gave to the archducal house the reversion of the Suabian estate of Mindelheim, which subsequently, in 1706, when the Elector of Bavaria fell under the ban of the empire, was actually claimed by the Emperor of Austria. I have also learned that the Upper Palatinate, with all its counties, by the extinction of the Wittelsbach dynasty, becomes an open feoff, to which the Emperor of Austria thinks that he may assert his claims."

"And your majesty is not convinced of the validity of my claims?" exclaimed the emperor.

Maria Theresa shook her head. "I cannot believe that we are justified in annexing to Austria an electorate which, not being ours by *indisputable* right of inheritance, may be the cause of involving us in a bloody war."

"But which, nevertheless, is the finest province in all Germany," cried Joseph impatiently; "and its acquisition the first step toward consolidation of all the German principalities into one great empire. When the Palatinate, Suabia, and Lower Bavaria are ours, the Danube will flow through Austrian territory alone; the trade of the Levant becomes ours; our ships cover the Black Sea, and finally Constantinople will be compelled to open its harbor to Austrian shipping and become a mart for the disposal of Austrian merchandise. Once possessed of Bavaria, South Germany, too, lies open to Austria, which like a magnet will draw toward one centre all its petty provinces and counties. After that, we approach Prussia, and ask whether she alone will stand apart from the great federation, or whether she has patriotism and magnanimity enough to merge her name and nationality in ours. Oh, your majesty, I implore you do not hesitate to pluck the golden fruit, for it is ours! Think, too, how anxiously the Bavarians look to us for protection against the pretensions of Charles Theodore, the only heir of the deceased elector. The people of Bavaria well know what is to be their fate if they fall into the hands of the elector palatine. Surrounded by mistresses with swarms of natural children, his sole object in life will be to plunder his subjects that he may enrich a progeny to whom he can leave neither name nor crown. Oh, your majesty, be generous, and rescue the Bavarians from a war of succession; for the elector palatine has no heir, and his death will be the signal for new strife."

"Nay, it seems to me that the Duke of Zweibrücken * is the natural heir of Charles Theodore, and I suppose he will be found as willing to possess his inheritance as you or I, or any other pretender," replied Maria Theresa. "But if, as you say, the Bavarians are sighing to become Austrian subjects, it seems to me that they might have character enough to give us some indication of their predilections; for I declare to you both that I will not imitate the treachery of Frederick. I will not bring up mouldy documents from our imperial archives to prove that I have a right to lands which for hundreds of years have been the property of another race; nor will I, for mad ambition's sake, spill one drop of honest Austrian blood."

"And so will Austria lose her birthright," returned Joseph angrily. "And so shall I be doomed to idle insignificance, while history ignores the only man who really loves Germany, and who has spirit to defy the malice of his contemporaries, and in the face of their disapproval, to do that which is best for Germany's welfare. Is it possible that your majesty will put upon me this new humiliation? Do you really bid me renounce the brightest dream of my life?"

"My dear son," said the empress, "I cannot view this undertaking with your eyes; I am old and timid, and I shudder with apprehension of the demon that follows in the wake of ambition. I would not descend to my grave amid the wails and curses of my people—I would not be depicted in history as an ambitious and unscrupulous sovereign. Let me go to my Franz blessed by the tears and regrets of my subjects—let me appear before posterity as an upright and peace-loving empress. But I have said that I am old—so old that I mistrust my own judgment. It may be that I mistake pusillanimity for disinterestedness. Speak, Kaunitz—so far you have been silent. What says *your* conscience to this claim? Is it consistent with justice and honor?"

"Your majesty knows that I will speak my honest convictions even though they might be unacceptable to the ear of my sovereign," replied Kaunitz.

"I understand," said the empress, disconsolately. "You are of one mind with the emperor."

"Yes," replied Kaunitz, "I am. It is the duty of Austria to assert her right to an inheritance which her ancestors foresaw, hundreds of years ago, would be indispensable to her future stability. Not only your majesty's forefathers, but the force of circumstances signify to us that the acquisition is natural and easy. It would be a great political error to overlook it; and believe me that in no science is an error so fatal to him who commits it as in the science of government. Bavaria is necessary to Austria, and your majesty may become its ruler without so much as one stroke of the sword."

* Called in English history, Duke of Deux-ponts.—Trans.

"Without a stroke of the sword!" exclaimed Maria Theresa, impetuously. "Does your highness suppose that such a stupendous acquisition as that, is not to provoke the opposition of our enemies?"

"Who is to oppose us?" asked Kaunitz. "Not France, certainly; she is too closely our relative and ally."

"I do not rely much upon the friendship of France," interrupted the empress. "Marie Antoinette is mistress of the king's affections; but his ministers guide his policy, and they would gladly see our friendly relations ruptured."

"But France is not in a condition to oppose us," continued Kaunitz. "Her finances are disordered, and at this very moment she is equipping an army to aid the American rebellion. We have nothing to fear from Russia, provided we overlook her doings in Turkey, and look away while she absorbs the little that remains of Poland. England is too far away to be interested in the matter, and Frederick knows by dear-bought experience that her alliance, in case of war, is perfectly worthless. Besides, George has quite enough on his hands with his troubles in North America. Who, then, is to prevent us from marching to Bavaria and taking peaceable possession of our lawful inheritance?"

"Who?" exclaimed the empress. "Our greatest and bitterest enemy—the wicked and unprincipled *parvenu* who has cost me so many tears, my people so many lives, and who has robbed me of one of the fairest jewels in my imperial crown."

Kaunitz shrugged his shoulders. "Your majesty is very magnanimous to speak of the Margrave of Brandenburg as a dangerous foe."

"And if he were a dangerous foe," cried Joseph vehemently, "so much the more glory to me if I vanquish him in battle and pluck the laurels from his head!"

Kaunitz looked at the emperor and slightly raised his finger by way of warning. "The King of Prussia," said he, "is no longer the hero that he was in years gone by; he dare not risk his fame by giving battle to the emperor. He rests upon his laurels, plays on the flute, writes bad verses, and listens to the adulation of his fawning philosophical friends. Then why should he molest us in Bavaria? We have documents to prove that the heritage is ours, and if we recognize his right to Bayreuth and Anspach, he will admit ours to whatever we choose to claim."

Maria Theresa was unconvinced. "You make light of Frederick, prince; but he is as dangerous as ever, and after all I think it much safer to fear our enemies than to despise them."

"Frederick of Prussia is a hero, a philosopher, and a legislator," cried Joseph. "Let me give him battle, your majesty, that I may win honor by vanquishing the victor."

"Never will I give my consent to such measures, unless we are forced to adopt them in defence of right."

"Our right here is indisputable," interposed Kaunitz. "Copies of our documents have already been circulated throughout Germany; and I have received from Herr von Ritter, the commissioner of Charles Theodore, the assurance that the latter is ready to resign his pretensions in consideration of the advantages we offer."

"What are these advantages?" asked Maria Theresa.

"We offer him our provinces in the Netherlands, and the privilege of establishing a kingdom in Burgundy," replied Joseph. "We also bestow upon his multitudinous children titles, orders, and a million of florins."

"And shame all virtue and decency!" cried the empress, coloring violently.

"The elector loves his progeny, and cares little or nothing for Bavaria," continued Joseph. "We shall win him over, and Bavaria will certainly be ours."

"Without the shedding of one drop of blood," added Kaunitz, drawing from his coat-pocket a paper which he unfolded and laid upon the table.

"Here is a map of Bavaria, your majesty," said Kaunitz, "and here is that portion of the electorate which we claim, through its cession to Albert of Austria by the Emperor Sigismund."

"We must take possession of it at once," cried Joseph; "at once, before any other claimant has time to interpose."

The empress heaved a sigh. "Yes," said she, as if commur ing with herself, "it all looks smooth and fair on paper. It is very easy to draw boundary lines with your finger, prince. You have traced out mountains and rivers, but you have not won the hearts of the Bavarians; and without their hearts it is worse than useless to occupy their country."

"We shall win their hearts by kindness," exclaimed the emperor. "True, we take their insignificant fatherland, but we give them instead, the rich inheritance of our own nationality; and future history will record it to their honor that theirs was the initiatory step which subsequently made one nation of all the little nationalities of Germany."

The empress answered with another sigh, and looked absently at the outspread map, across which Kaunitz was drawing his finger in another direction.

"Here," said he, "are the estates which the extinct house held in fief from the German emperor."

"And which I, as Emperor of Germany, have a right to reannex to my empire," cried Joseph.

"And here, finally," pursued Kaunitz, still tracing with his finger, "here is the lordship of Mindelheim, of which the reversion was not only ceded to Austria by the Emperor Matthias, but actually fell to us and was relinquished to the Elector of Bavaria by the too great magnanimity of an Austrian sovereign. Surely, your majesty is not willing to abandon your inheritance to the first comer?"

Maria Theresa's head was bent so low that it rested upon the map whereon her minister had been drawing lines of such significance to Austria. Close by, stood the emperor in breathless anxiety; while opposite sat Kaunitz, impassable as ever.

Again a deep sigh betokened the anguish that was rending the honest heart of the empress; and she raised her head.

"Alas for me and my declining energies!" said she, bitterly. "Two against one, and that one a woman advanced in years! I am not convinced, but my spirit is unequal to strife. Should we fail, we will be made to feel the odium of our proceedings; should we triumph, I suppose that the justice of our pretensions will never be questioned. Perhaps, as the world has never blamed Frederick for the robbery of Silesia, it may forgive us the acquisition of Bavaria. In the name of God, then, do both of you what you deem it right to do; but in mercy, take nothing that is not ours. We shall be involved in war; I feel it, and I would so gladly have ended my life in the calm, moon-like radiance of gentle peace." *

"Your majesty shall end your life in peace and prosperity; but far in the future be the day of your departure!" cried Joseph, kissing the hand of the empress. "May you live to see Austria expand into a great empire, and Germany rescued from the misrule of its legions of feeble princes! The first impulse has been given to-day. Bavaria is rescued from its miserable fate, and becomes an integral portion of one of the most powerful nations in Europe."

"May God be merciful, and bless the union!" sighed the empress. "I shall be wretched until I know how it is to terminate, and day and night I shall pray to the Lord that He preserve my people from the horrors of war."

"Meanwhile Kaunitz and I will seek a blessing on our enterprise by taking earthly precautions to secure its success. You, prince, will use the quill of diplomacy, and I shall make ready to defend my right with a hundred thousand trusty Austrians to back me. To-night I march a portion of my men into Lower Bavaria."

"Oh," murmured the unhappy empress, "there will be war and bloodshed!"

"Before your majesty marches to Bavaria," said Kaunitz, inclining his head, "her majesty, the empress, must sign the edict which shall apprise her subjects and the world of the step we meditate. I have drawn it up, and it awaits her majesty's approbation and signature."

The prince then drew from his muff a paper, which he presented to the empress. Maria Theresa perused it with sorrowful eyes.

"It is nothing but a *résumé* of our just claims to Bavaria," said Joseph, hastily.

"It is very easy to prove the justice of a thing on paper," replied Maria Theresa; "may God grant that it prove to be so in deed as well as in word. I will do your bidding, and sign your edict, but upon your head be all the blood that follows my act!"

She wrote her name, and Joseph, in an outburst of triumph, shouted, "Bavaria is ours!"

CHAPTER CXXII.

A PAGE FROM HISTORY.

MARIA THERESA'S worst apprehensions were realized, and the marching of the Austrian troops into Bavaria was the signal for war. While all the petty sovereigns of Germany clamored over the usurpation of Austria, pamphlet upon pamphlet issued from the hands of Austrian jurists to justify the act. These were replied to by the advocates of every other German state, who proved conclusively that Austria was rapacious and unscrupulous, and had not a shadow of right to the Bavarian succession. A terrible paper war ensued, during which three hundred books were launched by the belligerents at each other's heads.† This strife was productive of one good result; it warmed up the frozen patriotism of all the Ger-

* The empress's own sentiments. Wraxall, i., p. 311.

† Schlosser's History of the Eighteenth Century, vol. iv., p. 363.

man races. Bavarians, Hessians, Wurtembergers, and Hanoverians, forgot their bickerings to join the outcry against Austria; and the Church, to which Joseph was such an implacable enemy, encouraged them in their resistance to the "innovator," as he was called by his enemies.

Of all the malcontents, the noisiest were the Bavarians. The elector palatine, whose advent all had dreaded, was greeted upon his entrance into Munich with glowing enthusiasm; and the people forgot his extravagance and profligacy to remember that upon him devolved the preservation of their independence as a nation.

But Charles Theodore was very little edified by the sentiments which were attributed to him by the Bavarians. He longed for nothing better than to relieve himself of Bavaria and the weight of Austrian displeasure, to return to the palatinate, and come into possession of the flesh-pots that awaited his children in the form of titles, orders, and florins. He lent a willing ear to Joseph's propositions, and a few days after his triumphant entrance into Munich, he signed a contract relinquishing in favor of Austria two-thirds of his Bavarian inheritance. Maria Theresa, in the joy of her heart, bestowed upon him the order of the Golden Fleece, and on January 3, 1778, entered into possession of her newly acquired territory.

Meanwhile, in Bavaria, arose a voice which, with the fire of genuine patriotism, protested against the cowardly compliance of the elector palatine. It was that of the Duchess Clemens, of Bavaria. She hastened to give information of his pusillanimity to the next heir, the Duke of Zweibrücken, and dispatched a courier to Berlin asking succor and protection from the crown of Prussia.

The energy of this Bavarian patriot decided the fate of the Austrian claim. The Duke of Zweibrücken protested against the cession of the smallest portion of his future inheritance, and declared that he would never relinquish it to any power on earth. Frederick pronounced himself ready to sustain the duke, and threatened a declaration of war unless the Austrian troops were removed. In vain Maria Theresa sought to indemnify the duke by offers of orders, florins, and titles, which had been so successful with Charles Theodore—in vain she offered to make him King of Burgundy—he remained incorruptible. He coveted nothing she could bestow, but was firm in his purpose to preserve the integrity of Bavaria, and called loudly for Frederick to come to the rescue.

Frederick responded: "He was ready to defend the rights of the elector palatine against the unjust pretensions of the court of Vienna,"* and removed his troops from Upper Silesia to the confines of Bohemia and Saxony. This was the signal for the advance of the Austrian army; and despite her repugnance to the act, Maria Theresa was compelled to suffer it. She was also forced to allow Joseph to take command in person. This time her representations and entreaties had been vain; Joseph was thirsting for military glory, and he bounded like a war-horse to the trumpet's call. The empress felt that her hands were now powerless to restrain him, and she was so much the feebler, that Kaunitz openly espoused the side of the ambitious emperor.

With convulsive weeping Maria Theresa saw her son assume his command, and when Joseph bade her farewell, she sank insensible from his arms to the floor.

* Dohm's Memoirs, vol. i.

CHAPTER CXXIII.

THE EMPEROR AS COMMANDER-IN-CHIEF.

THE Emperor Joseph was pacing the floor of his cabinet. Sometimes he paused before a window, and with absent looks surveyed the plain where his troops were encamped, and their stacked arms glistened to the sun; then he returned to the table where Field-Marshal Lacy was deep in plans and charts.

Occasionally the silence was broken by the blast of a trumpet or the shouts of the soldiery who were arriving at headquarters.

"Lacy," said the emperor, after a long, dreary pause, "put by your charts, and give me a word of consolation."

The field-marshal laid aside his papers and rose from the table. "Your majesty had ordered me to specify upon the chart the exact spot which Frederick occupies by Welsdorf, and Prince Henry by Nienberg."

"I know, I know," answered Joseph impatiently. "But what avails their encampment to-day, when to-morrow they are sure to advance?"

"Your majesty thinks that he will make an attack?"

"I am sure of it."

"And I doubt it. It is my opinion that he will avoid a collision."

"Why then should he have commenced hostilities?" cried Joseph angrily. "Have you forgotten that although the elector palatine is ready to renounce Bavaria, Frederick opposes our claims in the name of Germany and of the next heir?"

"No, sire; but Frederick has spies in Vienna, who have taken care to inform him that Maria Theresa is disinclined to war. He has, therefore, declared against us, because he hopes that the blast of his coming will suffice to scatter the armies of Austria to the winds."

"The time has gone by when the terror of his name could appal us," cried Joseph, proudly throwing back his head. "I hope to convince him ere long that I am more than willing to confront him in battle. Oh, how weary is the inactivity to which my mother's womanish fears condemn me! Why did I heed her tears, and promise that I would not make the attack? Now I must wait, nor dare to strike a blow, while my whole soul yearns for the fight, and I long either to lead my troops to victory or perish on the field of battle."

"And yet, sire, it is fortunate that you have been forced to inactivity. To us time is every thing, for Frederick's army outnumbers ours. He has seventy thousand men with him near the Elbe, and fifty thousand under Prince Henry near Nienberg."

"Yes, but I shall oppose his hundred and twenty thousand men with twice their number," cried Joseph impatiently.

"Provided we have time to assemble our men. But we must have several days to accomplish this. At the end of a week our army will be complete in numbers, and we can then await the enemy behind our intrenchments, and the natural defences afforded us by the steep banks of the Elbe."

"Await—nothing but await," said Joseph scornfully. "Forever condemned to delay."

"In war, delay is often the best strategy, sire. The great Maurice, of Saxony, has said that fighting is an expedient by which incompetent commanders are accustomed to draw themselves out of difficult positions. When they are perplexed as to their next move, they are apt to stumble into a battle. I coincide with the great captain, although I well know that I shall incur your majesty's displeasure thereby. Our policy is to remain upon the defensive, and await an attack. Frederick has been accustomed to win his laurels by bold and rapid moves, but we have now for us an ally who will do better service in the field against him than our expertest generalship."

"Who is that?" asked Joseph, who was listening in no amiable mood to Lacy's dissertation on strategy.

"It is old age, sire, which hourly reminds Frederick that his hand is too feeble to wield a sword or pluck new laurels. Frederick accompanied his army in a close carriage; and yesterday, as he attempted to mount his horse, he was so weak that he had to be helped into the saddle; in consequence of which he reviewed his troops in an ill-humor, cursed the war, and wished Austria to the devil."

"And this is the end of a great military chieftain," said Joseph sadly; "the close of a magnificent career! May God preserve me from such a fate! Sooner would I pass from exuberant life to sudden death, than drag my effete manhood through years of weariness to gradual and ignominious extinction!

"But," continued the emperor, after a pause, "these are idle musings, Lacy. Your picture of the great Frederick has made me melancholy; I cannot but hope that it is overdrawn. It cannot be that such a warrior has grown vacillating; he will surely awake, and then the old lion will shake his mane, and his roar—"

At this moment a horseman at full speed was seen coming toward the house. He stopped immediately before the window. A little behind came another, and both dismounting, spoke several words to the soldiery around, which evidently produced a sensation.

"Lacy," said Joseph, "something has happened; and from the countenances of the men, I fear that these messengers have brought evil tidings. Let us go out and see what has occurred."

As the emperor was about to lay his hand upon the door, it opened, and one of his adjutants appeared.

"Sire," said he, almost breathless, "a courier has arrived from the borders of Bohemia, and he brings startling intelligence."

"Tell us at once what it is," said the emperor.

"The King of Prussia has left the county of Glatz and has marched into Bohemia."

The emperor's face brightened instantaneously. "That is glorious news!" cried he.

"Glorious news, sire?" exclaimed the astounded adjutant. "The courier who brings the intelligence has no words strong enough to depict the terror of the inhabitants. They were gathering their effects and flying to the interior, while the Prussian troops occupied the villages without opposition."

"The count is correct," said Lacy, who just then reëntered the room. "I have spoken with the man who brought the tidings. He is the mayor of his village, and he fled as the staff of the king entered the place."

"I must speak with him myself," cried Joseph quickly ; and the adjutant opening the door, the villager was introduced into the room.

"Did you see the King of Prussia?" asked the emperor.

"Yes, sire, I saw him," replied the man, gloomily. "I heard him order his men to forage their horses from our barns, and to strip our gardens of their fruit and vegetables. I heard him give orders to spare nothing ; for, said he, 'the people must be made to feel that the enemy is in their midst.' " *

"I shall remember the king's words," said Joseph, while his eyes flashed with anger. "How did he look?"

"Like the devil in the likeness of an old man," said the peasant. "His voice is as soft as that of a bridegroom ; but his words are the words of a hangman, and his eyes dart fire like those of an evil spirit. Even his own men have nothing good to say of him. His generals call him a selfish old man, who wants to do every thing, and knows nothing. He has not even appointed a general staff, and has no one to attend to the wants of his army." †

"Further, further !" cried Joseph, as the man paused.

"I have nothing further to tell, sire. As the king and his people left my house, it was growing dark, so I slipped out. The curates were in the churches with the women and children, and we men ran to the next village, where the people gave us horses ; and I have come to entreat the emperor not to let the King of Prussia take us, as he did Silesia."

"I give you my word that you shall not be given over to Prussia. Remain true to your country, and oppose the enemy whenever and wherever you can. Go back to your village, greet your friends for me, and promise them my protection. Count, be so good as to see that these men get some refreshment before they start."

The adjutant bowed, and, followed by the villager, left the room.

"Lacy," cried the emperor, "the time for deliberation has gone by. The hour for decision has struck, and I am free to give battle. It is Frederick who has thrown down the glove, and I too, shall emerge from obscurity, and prove to the world that others besides the King of Prussia are worthy to lead their men to victory. It would be dishonorable to refuse the challenge he has sent through his invasion of Bohemia. Let orders be given to march to Jaromirs. We shall await the enemy there ; and there at last I shall measure swords with the greatest captain of the age !"

CHAPTER CXXIV.

SECRET NEGOTIATIONS FOR PEACE.

AFTER the departure of the emperor for the seat of war, the court of Vienna became supremely dull. All the state apartments were closed, the gentlemen and ladies in waiting went about silent as ghosts, the archduchesses were pale and sad, and the empress, disconsolate, spent all her days in the solitude of her own apartments.

Not only at court, but in the city were all sounds of joy hushed into speechless anxiety. Above all, since it had become known that

* Frederick's own words. Dohm's Memoirs, vol. i., p. 130.
† Historical. See Dohm, vol. i., p. 133.

Frederick had invaded Bohemia, the Viennese were in a state of painful excitement, convinced as they were that the warlike king would never stop his marches until they brought him to the gates of Vienna.

Finally the panic reached the palace. The rich were conveying their treasures to places of security, and the archduchesses and ladies of honor were importuning the empress to leave Vienna, and remove the court to Presburg.*

Maria Theresa turned a deaf ear to these entreaties. Her eyes, which had grown dull through weeping, flashed with defiant courage as she replied: "I remain here in Vienna, and if the King of Prussia lays siege to my capital, I shall die like an empress in imperial panoply. I have never known what it was to fear for my life, and if now my heart throbs with uneasiness, it is for my people, it is not for myself. I mourn for my subjects, should Heaven, in its wrath, permit Frederick to prevail. For this it is that my life is spent in seclusion and prayer. Come, my daughters, come, ladies all, let us betake ourselves to the house of God."

And leaning upon the arms of the Archduchesses Elizabeth and Christina, the empress proceeded to the chapel. Behind them, with downcast eyes and reluctant steps, came the ladies of the court, all of one mind as to the weariness of too much godliness and too much praying.

"When will the empress's private chapel be completed?" whispered one of the ladies to another. "When will this daily martyrdom cease? Is it not too bad to be forced to church five times a day?"

"You may thank fortune for your headache yesterday. It was my turn to accompany the empress to the chapel, and we stayed so long that the Archduchess Elizabeth told me that toward the end her senses began to fail her, and she was scarcely able to utter the responses. How is the Archduchess Marianna to-day?"

"Her highness," whispered the first lady, "is too sensible to recover in a hurry. The wound in her cheek has reopened, and she really suffers a great deal at present. But she bears her pain with great fortitude. Yesterday the English ambassador was paying her a visit of condolence, and as he was expressing his sympathy, the archduchess interrupted him with a laugh. 'Believe me,' said she, 'for a princess of forty, who is an old maid, even a hole in her own cheek is a godsend. Nothing that varies the dull uniformity of my life comes amiss.' "†

Both ladies tittered, but perceiving that the empress was turning her head, they resumed their sanctimonious faces, and folded their hands.

"Was it you, ladies," said Maria Theresa, with severity, "who were interrupting our solemn silence by friovlous whisperings?"

"Yes, your majesty," replied the first lady of honor. "We were preparing ourselves for prayer by edifying conversation."

The empress smiled kindly upon the speaker. "I know that you are inclined to religion," said she, "and I am glad that you have had so good an influence over the Countess Julia, for she is not wont to be too zealous at prayer. I will remember you both for your

* Dohm's Memoirs, vol. i., p. 137.

† The archduchess's own words. See "Courts of Europe at the Close of the Last Century," by Henry Swinburne, vol. i., p. 342.

piety, dear children, and will see that you are both well married. There is the young Baron of Palmoden and Count—"

But the empress, who, in her darling schemes of marriage, had forgotten for a moment whither they were going, suddenly crossed herself, saying, "Forgive me, ladies; let us hasten our steps."

On this day the empress remained for three hours in the chapel, and while her attendants, worn out by *ennui*, were some sleeping, or others whispering to keep themselves awake, Maria Theresa, before the altar, was on her knees, praying with all the fervor of her honest and believing soul. As she prayed, she heaved many a sigh, and many a tear fell unheeded from her eyes upon her tightly-clasped hands.

Certainly her prayers proved consolatory, for when they were ended, she rose from her knees, calm and resolved. As she reached the door of her own room, she turned to her favorite daughter.

"Is your heart still disconsolate, Christina?" said she, with a look of supreme tenderness.

"How can it be otherwise, my mother?" said Christina, sobbing. "Has not my cruel and avaricious brother forced my husband into this wicked war? Oh, dearest mother, if you would but speak the word, Albert might be relieved from the disgraceful contingency of appearing in arms against his native land! He has no alternative—he must either become a traitor to his own country, or perjure himself by deserting his colors. Oh, your majesty, have mercy upon your subjects, and force the rapacious emperor to forego his unjust claims, and obey your imperial commands!"

"Dry your tears, my daughter," replied the empress, kissing her tenderly; "I have prayed so fervently for wisdom in this matter, that I feel as if my prayers had been answered. What He has commanded I will do, and may His grace strengthen and guide me! Hope for the best, my child, and do not speak so unkindly of your brother. He is not as cruel as you represent him; he has always been a dear, obedient son, and I trust, I may find him so to the end. Go, now, Christina, and remember that God directs all things."

The empress dismissed her daughters, and entered her room, passing rapidly to the place where hung the portrait of the Emperor Francis. For a long, long while she looked at it without any thing but a vague yearning to be united to her adored husband. Finally, as was her custom, she began to speak to it.

"Franz, I have prayed from my soul for light. It seems to me that God has spoken, but, oh, my darling, if what I am about to do is unwise, whisper me one word of warning, and I shall be passive. Sometimes I think that you visit me, beloved, and whisper words of angelic sweetness in my ear. Speak now, my Franz, speak if I am wrong—I will obey your voice."

She clasped her hands, and looked imploringly at the picture. Finally she sighed. "Your dear face still smiles upon me," murmured she, "and I must believe that I have decided for the best. I will act."

So saying, she rang her bell, and a page answered the summons.

"Send hither my private secretary, and let a carriage be dispatched for Baron Thugut. I wish to see him immediately."

A few moments afterward, Koch made his appearance, and in half an hour after a page announced Baron Thugut.

"Baron," said the empress, "I wish to put a serious question to you. Remember that God hears you, and answer me without reservation."

"Your majesty has forgotten," replied Thugut, "that I have been so long in the kingdom of unbelief that I am an unbeliever myself. I do not know whether God hears me or not; but as I know that your majesty exacts of me to be candid, I shall obey your commands."

"Then, tell me what is your opinion of the war of the Bavarian succession. Do you think it an equitable one?"

The baron's small black eyes turned from the empress to the secretary. Maria Theresa understood the glance.

"Speak without reserve; Baron Koch is loyal, and knows all my secrets. Do you think, then, that our claims to Bavaria are just?"

"Just, your majesty?" repeated Thugut, in his sharp, cutting tones. "Their success or their failure must decide that question. He who wins will have proved his right. If we succeed in holding Bavaria, Germany will uphold us—for Germany never raises her voice against a *fait accompli*. Should Frederick unhappily defeat us, not only Germany, but all Europe will cry out against the greed and injustice of ambitious Austria."

"I do not wish to expose myself to this contingency," replied the empress. "I must have peace with God, the world, and my conscience, and you must come to my assistance, Thugut."

An ironical smile played over Thugut's face. "With God and your majesty's conscience, I would be a poor mediator," said he, "but toward the world I am ready to serve your majesty in any shape or form."

"Then you shall mediate between myself and Frederick."

"Between your majesty and the King of Prussia!" said Thugut, astonished.

The empress nodded her head, and, just then, the door opened, admitting a page who handed two letters on a golden plate.

"The answer of Prince Gallitzin," said he, bowing and retiring.

Maria Theresa opened the letters, which were unsealed, saying:

"Now we have every thing requisite. Here is a passport for you as private secretary to the Russian ambassador; and here is a letter which you are to bear from Gallitzin to the king. This is the pretext of your visit to Frederick."

"And the real motive is—"

"You will find it in the letter which I shall intrust to you for him. Read my letter aloud, Koch."

The secretary read as follows:

"From the recall of Baron von Reidsel and the marching of your majesty's troops into Bohemia, I perceive with profoundest sorrow that we are on the eve of another war. My age, and sincere love of peace, are known to all the world, and I can give no greater proof of this love than I do by writing to your majesty. My maternal heart, too, is sorely grieved with the thought that I have two sons and a beloved son-in-law in the army. I have taken this step without the knowledge of the emperor, and whatever its result, I exact that it shall remain a secret between us. It is my desire to resume the negotiations which were broken off by my son. Baron Thugut, who will deliver this into your majesty's hands, has received my instructions, and is empowered to treat with you. I trust that your majesty may deem it consistent with our common dignity to meet my wishes in this matter, and hope that you also correspond to the earnest desire which I cherish for a continuation of friendly relations with your majesty. With this hope I remain,

"Your majesty's affectionate sister and cousin,

"MARIA THERESA." *

"Your majesty wishes me to bring about a peace. But what sort of peace?" asked Thugut. "A conditional one, or peace at any price?"

Maria Theresa's eyes flashed fire.

"Is Austria so weak that she should crave peace at any price?" cried she, proudly.

"No, indeed, your majesty. She seems, on the contrary, so powerful that she undertakes war at any price. But Bavaria is well worth a war with Prussia. Allow me one more question. What is the emperor to do with his army, while we negotiate?"

"They must await the result. I have written to Leopold to use all his influence to reconcile Joseph, for he will be indignant when he hears what I have done. But until it becomes evident that we cannot treat with Frederick, the emperor and his generals must remain passive. Should I fail, my son may then give battle, while his mother intercedes for him. If the medicine of diplomacy fails this time, we shall have to resort to the knife to heal our political wounds."

"Your majesty is right," said Thugut, with a heartless laugh. "When medicine fails we use the cold steel; and if that is not enough, fire is the last resort. What are your majesty's conditions with Prussia, medicine, iron, or fire?" †

"Balsam, I trust," replied the empress. "Koch has drawn out my propositions. And now go, and make your preparations to depart, for I long for peace with the whole world."

CHAPTER CXXV.

FRATERNAL DISCORD.

VERY different were the preparations making by the empress's warlike son. In company with Lacy and his staff, he had reviewed his troops for the last time, and had ridden from one end of their encampment to the other, that he might personally inspect the condition of his army. He had found it cheerful, spirited, and eager for the fray, the officers assuring him that their men were impatient to meet the enemy, and end the campaign by one decisive blow.

Even Lacy himself ceased to preach caution. He saw in the triumphant smile and flashing eyes of Joseph that counsel would be worse than useless, and warning would only drive him to some deed of mad daring, which might peril his life, or the safety of his army. The emperor himself had planned the attack, and his generals had approved his strategy.

On the other side of the Elbe was the King of Prussia, afraid to cross, lest the Austrian army, from their secure heights on the op-

* This letter was written in the French language, and is to be found in Gross-Hoffinger's "Life and History of the Reign of Joseph II.," vol. iv., p. 39.

† Thugut's own application of the old-fashioned method of cure. See Hormayer's "Contributions to the History of my Fatherland."

posite shore, should annihilate his troops as they attempted the passage.

But what Frederick hesitated to undertake, Joseph was resolved to accomplish. He had determined to cross the Elbe, and force the king to give him battle. His columns were to move under cover of night, to ford the river below, and, by rapid marches, to reach the Prussian army at break of day.

"We shall be victorious, I feel it," said the emperor to Lacy, on their return from the encampment. "I have a joy within my heart that is the forerunner either of victory or of death."

"Of death!" echoed Lacy, with surprise. "Does your majesty mean to say that man can encounter death joyfully?"

"Why not?" said the emperor. "When a man dies, has he not won the long and bloody battle of life?"

"These are disconsolate words to fall from *your* lips, sire. To you life must present a bright array of hopes and useful deeds. None but an old and decrepit man should take such gloomy views of the world."

"I have suffered as much as older men, Lacy," returned the emperor, laying his hand upon his friend's shoulder "But all my sufferings are forgotten in the anticipated joy of the morrow. Let the dead past bury its dead—the birth of my happiness is at hand. I shall no more rest my title to the world's homage upon the station to which I was born. It shall know at last that I am worthy to be the friend of Lacy and of Loudon. All the years that have intervened have never yet sufficed to blot out the remembrance of that fearful day on which the empress recalled the consent she had given for me to meet Frederick in the field. I have never looked upon my mother since without feeling the wound reopen. But to-day I can forgive her. I can even forgive the hated priests who were the cause of my misfortune. Lacy, I love the whole world, I—"

The emperor interrupted himself to stare with astonishment at the figure of a man, who just then had opened the door.

"The Grand Duke of Tuscany!" exclaimed Lacy.

"My brother Leopold," murmured Joseph, in a low, tremulous voice, but without rising from his seat, or offering his hand.

A cloud passed over the pale, sickly face of the grand duke, and the smile vanished from his lips.

"Your majesty does not invite me to enter?" asked he, reproachfully. "You do not bid me welcome?"

The emperor gazed upon his brother in silence, and Leopold shrank from the keen and searching glances of Joseph's inquiring eyes.

"My brother," cried the emperor, suddenly, "you have come hither to bring me some evil tidings."

"I have come to greet your majesty, and to enjoy a few hours of family intercourse with you," replied the grand duke, while, without awaiting the courtesy which Joseph would not extend, he closed the door, and advanced into the room.

"No, no," cried the emperor, "that is false. We are not such a pair of loving brothers that you should seek me for affection's sake."

And approaching Leopold as he spoke, he stopped just before him, and continued:

"I implore of you be generous and tell me what you want. You have letters from the empress, have you not?"

"I have. I have not only letters from our imperial mother to deliver to your majesty, I am also the bearer of verbal messages, but—"

"But what?" cried Joseph, as Leopold paused.

"But I must request of your majesty to grant me a private interview."

"With his majesty's permission, I shall withdraw," said Lacy.

Joseph inclined his head, and, as Lacy disappeared, he turned his eyes once more upon the pale, embarrassed countenance of his unwelcome relative.

"Now we are alone," said he, breathing fast. "Now—but no. Give me one moment to collect my strength. My God! what evil has the empress in store for me now, that she should select you as the messenger of her cruelty? Peace—I do not wish to hear your voice until I am ready to listen to its discordant sounds."

"I await your commands," replied Leopold, with a respectful inclination.

The emperor crossed the room several times forth and back. His cheeks were blanched, his mouth quivered, while quick and gasping came the breath from his heaving chest.

"Air, air!" said he in a stifled voice. "I shall suffocate!" He approached the window, and leaning far out, inhaled the cold winter blast, whose icy breath was welcome to his hot and fevered head. After a while, he closed the window and turned to his brother, who, with folded arms, still stood near the door.

"Now," said Joseph, gloomily, "I am ready to hear. Speak out your infernal errand!"

"I must first beg pardon of your majesty if the intelligence which I am compelled to communicate is unwelcome," began Leopold, in a deprecating voice.

Joseph cast a rapid, searching look athwart the perplexed face of his brother. "You are forgiven," replied he, contemptuously. "Your message seems to be punishment enough of itself, if I judge by your countenance. Let us be quick, then, and be done with one another. Give me the letter, and say at once what you have to say."

The grand duke took from his coat-pocket a sealed dispatch which he delivered to the emperor.

"Here are the letters of the empress, but she ordered me to accompany them with a few words explanatory of her motives. She commissioned me to tell what she found it difficult to write."

"She was afraid," muttered Joseph.

"Yes, she was afraid to commit an injustice," returned Leopold. "She was afraid to offend her Maker by continuing a war whose object was to break one of His holy commandments—"

"Oh, my brother!" interrupted Joseph, sarcastically, "you are yourself again—I recognize the dutiful son of the priests who denounce me because I would disturb them in their comfortable Bavarian nest. I see plainly that if I should be so unfortunate as to fall to-morrow on the battle-field, you will throw yourself into the arms of Frederick and of that frantic amazon, the Duchess Clemens, beg pardon for my sins, and hand over the fairest portion of Germany to pope and Jesuits. Oh, what a favorite you would become with the black-coats! Doubtless they would give you absolution for all the sins you are accustomed to commit against your wife. But, my virtuous brother, I shall outlive the morrow, that I promise you, and shall gain such a victory over Frederick as will astound you and the whole popedom."

"You were about to give battle to Frederick?"

"I am about to do so," replied Joseph, defiantly.

"Then it was time for me to come!" exclaimed Leopold, solemnly. "The mercy of God has sent me to stop the carnage! My brother, the empress earnestly entreats you, by the tears she has shed for your sake, to desist from fighting! As your empress she commands you to sheathe your sword until you hear the result of the negotiations now pending between herself and the King of Prussia."

The emperor uttered a cry of rage, and the angry blood darted to his very brow. "The empress has opened negotiations without my consent!" cried he, in a voice of mingled indignation and incredulity.

"The empress requires the consent of no one to regulate her state policy. In the supremacy of her own power, she has reopened negotiations with the King of Prussia, and hopes to terminate the war honorably without bloodshed."

"It is false, I will not believe it!" again cried Joseph. "My mother would not offer me such indignity, when she herself placed in my hand the sword with which I seek to defend my rights. It is a priest's lie, and you have been commissioned to be its interpreter. But this time your pious frauds will come to naught. Take back your packet. It is not the empress's handwriting."

"It is that of her private secretary."

"I am not bound to respect his writing, and I have no time to listen to your stupid remonstrances. Wait till day after to-morrow. When a man is flushed with victory, he is generous and ready to pardon. When I have beaten Frederick, I shall have leisure to inquire into the authenticity of your papers. Remain with me, not as the emissary of priests and Jesuits, but as the brother of the emperor, who to-morrow is to win his first victory and his first budding laurels. Give me your hand. On the eve of a battle, I am willing to remember that we are brothers."

"But this is not the eve of a battle, your majesty. The empress commands you to await the result of her efforts to end the war."

"I have already told you that I see through your intrigues."

"But I have the proofs of my veracity in these papers. You will not read them?"

"No, I will not!"

"Then I shall read them myself," returned Leopold, breaking the seal. "The empress commands you, and it is your duty as her subject to obey."

"I shall obey when I am convinced that the empress commands. But in this case I am convinced that it is not my mother, the high-spirited Maria Theresa, who intrusts you with such an abject commission."

"You surely will not deny her handwriting?" returned Leopold, extending an open letter to his brother.

Joseph looked imploringly at his brother's calm face.

"You are resolved to show me no mercy," said he. "You will not understand my refusal to believe. Listen to me, Leopold. Show that you love me for once in your life. Think of my joyless youth, my sorrowing manhood, my life of perpetual humiliation, and give me one day of independent action."

"What does your majesty mean?" asked the grand duke.

The emperor came up to him, and putting both his hands upon Leopold's shoulder, he said in a voice of deep emotion: "Majesty asks nothing of you, but your brother entreats you to serve him this day. See, Leopold, it is too late, I cannot retract upon the very eve of battle. The army knows that we are about to engage the enemy, and my men are wild with enthusiasm. The presence of Frederick upon Austrian soil is an indignity which I am pledged as a man to avenge. If I allow him to retreat from his present disadvantageous position, my name is gone forever, and all Europe will cry out upon my incapacity to command. Remember, Leopold, that it concerns not my honor alone, but the honor of Austria, that this battle should be fought. Rescue us both by a magnanimous falsehood. Go back to the empress. Tell her that you lost her letters and that I would not take your word. Meanwhile, I shall have humiliated the enemy, and Maria Theresa will have been forced to submit to an event which she cannot recall. Let us burn these papers, Leopold," continued Joseph, passionately clasping his hands, "and God will forgive you the innocent deception by which your brother shall have won fame and glory."

"God will never pardon me for sinning so deeply against my conscience," replied Leopold, unmoved. "You require of me to burn those papers and consign thousands of your own subjects to death and worse than death—the lingering agonies of the battle-field. Never! Oh, my dear brother, have pity on yourself, and bethink you that you peril your own salvation by such thirst of blood—"

"Peace!—and answer my question," cried Joseph, stamping his foot. "Will you do what I ask of you?"

"No, Joseph, I will not do it. The empress desires to spare the blood of her people, and we must obey her just demands."

"I *will* not obey!" cried Joseph with such violence that his face was empurpled with passion. "I am co-regent, and as a man and a commander, it is my right to defend the honor of the crown. I will not read those letters, and I choose to assert the superiority of my manhood by doing that which they forbid. In your eyes and those of the empress, I may be a rebel, but the world will acquit me, and I shall be honored for my just resistance. You will not destroy the papers as I implored you to do?—then give them to me, and so satisfy your tender conscience."

"No," replied Leopold, who had replaced the dispatches in his pocket, "for I see that you intend to destroy them."

"That need not concern you. Give me the letters."

"No, Joseph, I will not give them."

The emperor uttered a hoarse cry, and darted toward his brother with uplifted arm.

"Give me the papers!" said he, with his teeth set.

"What! you would strike me!" said Leopold retreating.

"Give me the papers!" thundered the emperor, "or I fell you to the earth as I would a beast!" and he came yet nearer.

Pale and panting, their eyes flashing with anger, the brothers stood for a moment confronting each other.

"Refuse me once again," hissed Joseph in a low, unnatural voice, "refuse me once again, and my hand shall smite your cowardly face and disgrace you forever; for, as God hears me, you shall never have satisfaction for the affront."

Leopold was silent, but with his eyes fixed upon Joseph, he retreated, farther and still farther, followed by the emperor, who, still with uplifted hand, threatened his brother's face. Suddenly Leopold reached the door and, bursting it open, rushed into the anteroom. With a tiger-bound he sprang forward to Lacy who had remained there in obedience to the emperor's orders.

CHAPTER CXXVI.

THE DEFEAT.

"FIELD-MARSHAL LACY," said the grand duke, "I claim your protection—the protection of a man whom the empress has honored, and who has sworn to obey her as his lawful sovereign."

"Even unto death," added Lacy solemnly.

The emperor groaned aloud, and his upraised arm fell powerless to his side. A triumphant smile flickered over the pale features of Leopold. He thrust his hand into his pocket and drew forth the dispatches of the empress.

"The empress charged me," said he, "in case the emperor refused to read these letters, to deliver them to you, Marshal Lacy, and to bid you, in my presence, read them to him. Come, then, your excellency, let us obey the commands of our sovereign."

Lacy bowed, and followed the grand duke in silence. The emperor retreated to his cabinet, and, sinking upon a sofa, buried his face in his hands. Nothing interrupted the stillness save the measured footsteps of Lacy and the grand duke, who entered and closed the door behind them. A long pause ensued. The grand duke retired to a window, where, with his arms folded, he awaited the development of affairs with recovered composure. Joseph still sat with his face hidden by his hands, while Lacy with military decorum stood at the door with his letters, silent until the emperor should signify that he might read. Finding that Joseph would not speak, Lacy took a few steps forward. "Does your majesty allow me to read the letters which, in the name of the empress, his imperial highness, the grand duke, has delivered to me?"

"Read," said Joseph hoarsely, but without removing his hands. Lacy approached the table, and from the various documents which he unfolded and examined, selected the letter which was in the empress's own hand—

"MY DEAREST EMPEROR AND SON: As co-regent and heir to my throne, I hasten to advise you of the negotiations which have just been renewed between the King of Prussia and myself. I have every hope that they will terminate to our satisfaction, and thus not only save the lives of many of our subjects, but relieve my heart of the pangs it has endured during the absence of my beloved son. The King of Prussia has promised that, pending our diplomatic correspondence, he will not attack our armies. I therefore hope that you, my son, will concede as much, and scrupulously avoid all collision that might interrupt our negotiations. I send you copies of our correspondence, and will continue to do so regularly. Hoping that God in His goodness will restore to me my imperial son, I remain now as ever, your affectionate mother and empress,

"MARIA THERESA."

A deep sigh that was almost a sob was heaved by the emperor. Slowly his hands fell from his face, while with tearful eyes he turned to Lacy, and said, "Is it really so? Are my hopes of glory all frustrated?"

Lacy answered with another sigh and a slight raising of the shoulder.

"Read on, Lacy," continued the emperor, mildly; "my eyes are dim and I cannot see."

Lacy continued reading the correspondence: first the letter of the empress; then the reply of the king, in which he promised that Maria Theresa should have nothing to fear for the life of her beloved son.

When the emperor heard this he started; the color mounted to his face, then faded away and left it pale as before. His lips moved, but with a convulsive twitch he closed them again, and listened in silence. Two more letters followed, full of mutual and distinguished consideration; then came the propositions of the empress and the comments of the king.

Maria Theresa pledged herself, from that portion of Bavaria of which Austria had possession, to retain only so much as would yield a revenue of one million, offering to cede the remainder to the elector palatine, or to exchange with him for territory situated elsewhere.

Then followed Frederick's conditions. He stipulated that Austria should renounce all pretensions to Bavaria, contenting herself with a small portion of Upper Bavaria, and recognizing and upholding the claims of Charles Theodore, as well as those of his heir, the Duke of Zweibrücken.

"Further, further!" exclaimed Joseph, as Lacy paused.

"There is nothing further, sire; the correspondence ceases there."

"And to these disgraceful propositions we are not permitted to make the only answer of which they are deserving—that is, to wipe them out with blood! Oh, Lacy, Lacy, is it not fearful to be compelled like a schoolboy to submit to the punishment which my tormentor judges fit to inflict?"

"It is a painful duty, sire; but it *is* a duty, and your majesty must submit."

"I must not submit!" exclaimed Joseph in bitter anguish, while he sprang from the sofa. But suddenly his eager, fluttering glances were turned toward the window where stood the grand duke quietly surveying his movements.

"Have you not gone?" asked the emperor. "I thought that your mission being fulfilled, your imperial highness had nothing more to do here."

"I await your majesty's answer," replied the grand duke.

"Oh, you wish to mock me, do you?" cried Joseph, trembling with passion, "for well you know there is but one answer to the empress's commands, and that is—obedience. But since you are anxious to take a message, here is one, and mark it well. Say to the empress that I sumbit as becomes her subject, and so long as it suits her without my knowledge and behind my back to hold conferences with the enemy, I will abstain from engaging him in battle, although by so doing I shall ruin my reputation forever. Tell her furthermore that should she accept the dishonorable proposals made by Frederick and conclude a peace upon the basis of his conditions, she need never expect to see me again in Vienna. I never shall go near her so long as I live, but shall take up my abode in Aix la Chapelle, or in some other free city, as it was once the custom of the Emperors of Germany to do." *

"Oh, sire!" exclaimed Lacy, shocked, "retract those words, I implore of you!"

"I will not retract them," replied Joseph, imperatively; "I order the envoy of the empress to repeat them faithfully."

"I shall obey your majesty, the co-regent of the empress," said the Grand Duke of Tuscany. "Has your majesty any other commands?"

"Yes!" shouted the emperor, fiercely. "When you shall have accomplished your mission in Vienna, go home to your priests in Tuscany, and bid them say a mass for the repose of your brother's soul, for from this day you have lost him who was called Joseph. He is dead to you forever."

The grand duke returned his brother's look with one of equal hatred. "I can scarcely lose that which I have never possessed," replied he with composure. "Had the affront which your majesty has put upon me to-day come from a brother, we should have measured swords together before the sun had set upon the insult. But he who stands before me is my emperor, and of him I am prohibited from demanding satisfaction."

"Our paths in life lie apart, and I trust that we shall never be forced to look upon each other again," said Joseph in reply.

"Since we can never meet as brothers, I am compelled to echo the wish," returned Leopold. "Farewell!"

"Farewell—and let it be farewell forever!"

The grand duke crossed the room and opened the door, while Joseph watched his disappearance with glaring eyes and stormy brow, and Lacy in anguish of heart looked first at one brother, then at the other. The door closed, and the jar it made caused Lacy to start. He recovered himself and hastened to the emperor's side.

"Call him back, sire," implored he. "Call him back. He is your brother and the son of your mother. He is also the hope of those who tremble with apprehension of your majesty's reign."

"Oh, yes—he is the leader of my enemies, the head of the pious conspirators who have cursed my life by their diabolical opposition. But a day will come when I shall crush the whole brood in their owl's nest, and put my house in order. In that day I shall remember this interview with the Grand Duke of Tuscany." †

"Sire," insisted Lacy, "I entreat of you, recall him—if not as your brother, as the envoy of your sovereign. Before it is too late, retract those fearful words, which in a moment of—"

"Lacy!" interrupted the emperor, in a loud, angry voice, "I have this day lost a brother and a battle. Am I also to lose a friend?"

The tears rose to Lacy's eyes. "Sire," said he in a voice of

* Joseph's own words. See Dohm's Memoirs, vol. i., p. 143.

† The two brothers never met again. Although Leopold was next heir to the crown, Joseph would not allow him to receive the title of King of Rome, but bestowed it upon Leopold's son and heir, Francis. Even upon his death-bed the emperor refused to see his brother. By his explicit commands, it was only when his death had taken place, that a courier was sent to inform Leopold of his accession to the throne.

emotion, "forgive your truest friend if he has presumed to oppose you. I have no kindred to love; my heart is bound to you, and if I lose your regard, I am desolate and alone in the world!"

"You shall not lose it, my dear, dear friend," exclaimed Joseph, throwing his arms around Lacy's neck. "O God, you do not know how I suffer! I feel as if I had lost some beloved friend. And is it not so? Have I not buried to-day the hopes of a whole life? The hopes which from my youth I had cherished of winning glory and fame through Frederick's humiliation!—I would give years of my life to have measured swords with him, for—let me tell you a secret, Lacy—I hate that man as much as I once fancied that I loved him. He is the cause of every misfortune that has befallen our house for forty years past. His fame is our shame, his splendor our obscuration. I might forgive him his robbery of Silesia, but that he has reduced me to the *rôle* of an imitator, I can never forgive! Every thing on earth that I imagine, he executes before me. If I desire to free my people from the dominion of the clergy, he has already liberated his; if I seek to advance art, literature, or manufactures, he has just afforded them protection in Prussia; if I recommend toleration, lo! he has removed the disabilities of the Jews, and has pronounced all sects equal before the law. Would I excel in music, or yearn for military glory, the world has long since pronounced him a hero, and his flute was heard before I learned the violoncello. Oh, I hate him, I hate him, for his greatness is the rock upon which my originality is fated to split; and his shadow projects forever before me and my unborn deeds. He forces me to pass for a counterfeit of his true coin, and yet I feel that my individuality is as marked as his! He is the evil genius of my destiny, vanquishing me even in that which I would have done for the good of my subjects and the advancement of the world!"

"Your majesty goes too far," said Lacy, smiling. "There is one thing which Frederick has never dreamed of doing, and it is precisely there that you are destined to eclipse him. He has never sought to do any thing for Germany. A German prince, the ruler of a German people, he is the patron of foreign industry, literature, and art. The most insignificant writer in France is better known to him than Lessing or Winklemann; and while he is perfectly familiar with the composers of Italy, he has blundered into depreciation of Gluck's inspired music. There is the great and glorious contrast which your majesty presents to Frederick of Prussia; and the German people, whom he has despised, will look up to you, sire, as to the Messiah of their decaying greatness."

"He will foil me there as in all else," replied Joseph, disconsolately. "Has he not already guessed my plans in Germany, and has he not torn my banner from my hand to flaunt it above his own head, as the defender of German liberties! And Maria Theresa, too, is deceived by his infernal logic. Oh, Lacy! I hate him beyond expression. I hate him for the letter wherein he promises to spare her son, a man whom he loves, although he differs with him on the subject of German nationality.* The cowardly remnant of a warrior! He takes refuge under my mother's hooped petticoat, and whispers in her credulous ear that this war is a great sin. Do you really think that I am bound to sheathe my sword at the *ipse dixit* of my mother?"

* Gross-Hoffinger, "Records of the Life of Joseph II.," p. 41.

"Your mother is the reigning empress, sire, and it is for you to give to her other subjects an example of loyalty and obedience."

"Ah," sighed Joseph, "I must still the throbbings of my bursting heart, and suffer in silence!"

For a while he paced the room with hasty, uncertain steps, murmuring inaudible words, and darting despairing looks toward the window, whence gay throngs of soldiery were to be seen preparing to leave the encampment, while they sang their martial songs, and speculated together upon the events of the morrow. Suddenly the emperor turned his heard toward Lacy, and said:

"Field-marshal, I withdraw my plans of battle. The empress-queen has spoken, it is for us to obey. Apprise the army of the change. We remain where we are."

"Sire," exclaimed Lacy enthusiastically, "your victory has been won to-day. A victory over self!"

The emperor raised his eyes with a sad, weary expression, and shook his head: "It was harder to win than could have been that which I contemplated for to-morrow. Go, Lacy, go, we must still hope and pray—pray God to grant that at some future day we may be revenged."

CHAPTER CXXVII.

THE REVENGE.

LACY had assembled the generals and the staff-officers to communicate the decision of the emperor; while the latter, overcome by this supreme disappointment, was pacing his cabinet with heavy and measured step. Then he stood at the window, and watched the movements of his soldiers.

"They have heard it now," thought he, "and the word has gone forth, 'The emperor is afraid to meet the old hero.' Yes, my brave soldiers, I know full well that you despise me! Your songs have ceased—your spirit is crushed, and, ah, mine also! This unfought battle is worth a victory to Frederick; for the army will think that my courage failed me, and the King of Prussia will still remain in their estimation the invincible foe of Austria! Oh, when will the hour of retribution sound?"

At this moment a knock was heard at the door, and an adjutant announced to the emperor that a hussar, belonging to a Galician regiment stationed directly opposite to the Prussian encampment, wished to communicate something of importance.

"Admit him," said Joseph, wearily.

The adjutant bowed, and returned, accompanied by a stalwart figure, attired in the fanciful and becoming costume of a Galician hussar. The emperor returned his salute with a slight bend of the head, and motioned him to approach. The adjutant withdrew, and Joseph was alone with the man.

"Now speak," said the emperor, "and if you have important tidings, let me hear them."

The soldier raised his head, and spoke. "I have come to do your majesty a service, but first you must promise to reward me as becomes an emperor."

"If your service is great, your reward shall be in proportion."

The soldier bowed. "I am on picket duty immediately on the banks of the Elbe. As I have lain among the bushes, I have more than once seen the King of Prussia just opposite to me, taking a survey of our strength. Little thinks he, as he reins in his horse, that a sharpshooter's ball is not too far off to bring him down. But I have thought of it."

"You have thought of WHAT?" exclaimed Joseph, shocked.

"I have thought that my ball has never yet missed its man, and what a rich man I might become if I were to free Austria from its worst enemy. I was turning this over in my mind yesterday, when here comes the king on his gray horse, and halts directly in front of me. He held a cane in his hand, and pointed with it toward our encampment, and beat the air with it, as though he were showing his officers how he was going to thrash the Austrian army. When I saw this, my blood began to boil, and I rose half up, and cocked my gun. Many a Bosnian have I brought down with it."

"Go on," said the emperor, as the soldier paused, and threw an admiring glance upon his musket.

"Yes, sire, I raised my gun, and took aim, when I began to reflect that—"

"That what?" exclaimed Joseph, upon whose forehead great drops of sweat had begun to gather.

"That it would be better first to ask the emperor's permission, and get the promise of a reward," said the hussar, with a salute.

"Ah!" cried the emperor, breathing freely, "that was a lucky thought of yours!"

The soldier bowed low. "I put down my musket, and when the hour came round for me to be relieved, I asked leave of my captain to come here to see an old acquaintance. And, indeed, your majesty, I was not telling a lie, for you once slept under my father's roof, and paid him so well for the night's lodging, that he was able to buy some land to settle me upon it, and thereupon I married my sweetheart. So that I *did* come to see an old acquaintance; and now, your majesty, I have a firm hand and a sharp eye, and if you say so, Frederick shall bite the dust before this day week."

"What said your captain to such a proposal?"

"Does your majesty suppose that I am such a fool as to give another man the chance of stepping in my shoes?"

"It follows thence that I am the only person in your confidence," said Joseph, much relieved.

"The only one, sire, and I believe that you will not misuse it."

"No, I will not, and as a reward for your trust in me, here are two gold pieces."

At first the soldier smiled as he received the gold, but presently his brow darkened, and casting a dissatisfied look at the emperor from behind his bushy eyebrows, he said, "Is the life of the King of Prussia worth but two ducats?"

"It is worth more than all the gold in my imperial treasury," replied the emperor, with energy; "and no man on earth is rich enough to pay for it. I gave you these ducats to repay what you spent in coming from your camp hither. But I shall reward you still further if you will promise not to divulge what you have confided to me. Not only that, but I will also give you your discharge from the army, send you home, and give you a situation as imperial huntsman. If you break your promise, I will punish you with death."

"Sire, I promise, and I shall never break my word."

"Swear it in the name of God and of the Blessed Virgin."

"I swear," said the soldier, raising his right hand to heaven. "And now, your majesty, that no one is to know it except us two, when shall I shoot the King of Prussia, and return to my home?"

The emperor looked sternly upon the unconscious hussar. "Soldier," said he, in loud and solemn tones, "keep the gold I have given you in remembrance of the warning which your good angel whispered, when you forbore to murder the King of Prussia. I hope and believe that every man among you would risk his life in battle to take him prisoner, but God forbid that any one of you should stoop so low as to become his murderer!"

The man stared at the emperor in utter bewilderment, and not a word of reply was he able to make to this incomprehensible harangue.

The emperor continued: "I pardon your evil thought because it did not germinate into an evil deed. But had you followed your impulse to murder the king, I would have hung you without giving you time to see a priest. Thank God for your escape, and let us dismiss the disgraceful subject forever. You can remain here for the night."

"But I have only six hours' leave of absence, sire."

The emperor looked distrustfully at the soldier. "I have discharged you from the service, and will see that you are not molested."

"And I am really to go home?" cried the man, overjoyed. "And the emperor really means to fulfil his promise in spite of the dreadful reprimand I have received?"

"Yes, I mean to fulfil my promise. But you also must swear to live a peaceful life, and never try to kill another man save in open fight, were he even a Bosnian."

"From my heart, I swear," replied the soldier, solemnly.

"Now you can go."

The emperor then rang his bell, when the door opened, and Günther entered the room.

"Günther," said he, "give this man his supper and a bed in your room, and, while he remains here, see that his wants are attended to."

Günther bowed, and retired with the hussar. The emperor followed the gigantic figure of the soldier until the door closed upon him, then he raised his eyes to heaven with a look of unspeakable gratitude.

"Lord," said he, "I have suffered cruelly since the sun rose today, but oh! how I thank Thee that Thou hast preserved my name from eternal infamy! How would the world have spurned me, if, refusing to give him battle, I had taken the life of my enemy through the hands of an Austrian soldier! My God! my God! the life of Frederick has become more precious to me than my own—for *his* life is one with *my* honor.

"But what, if another should execute what this Galician has conceived?" continued the emperor, shuddering. "What if, in his ignorance, another one of these wild huntsmen should deem it his duty to take the life of Frederick?" The emperor grew pale with the thought, and his hand was lifted as if to protest against the crime. "I must find means to shield myself from such disgrace, for his safety and my honor are cast on the same die."

Far into the night Günther heard the tread of his imperial master, and he waited in vain to be called in to attend him. He watched until the dawn of day, and when, at last, unable to contain his anxiety, he opened the door of the cabinet, he saw the emperor asleep in an arm-chair. He was in full uniform, and the rays of the rising sun lit up his pale face, which, even in sleep, wore an anxious and painful expression.

Günther approached, and touched him lightly.

"Sire," said he, in a voice of tender entreaty, "let me assist you to undress. This is the fourth night that your majesty has slept in your uniform. You must lie down, indeed you must."

Joseph opened his eyes, and looked at Günther.

"Ah!" sighed he, "during three of these nights I might just as well have slept in my bed as any respectable burgher who has nothing to trouble him but his growing corpulence. But last night I dared not undress, for I have much to do this morning. Good Heaven! Günther," continued the emperor, suddenly remembering the hussar, "what has become of the man whom I gave into your custody last evening?"

"Your majesty's second valet is in the same bed with him, and they are both asleep. The door between our sleeping-room and the anteroom has been open all night, so that, while I sat there awaiting your majesty's call, I had the hussar directly under my eyes. He seems to have pleasant dreams, if I judge by his smiles and snatches of songs."

"Let him sleep, Günther, and when he awakes, allow no one to hold any conversation with him. Now give me a glass of fresh water for my breakfast."

Günther hastened to obey, and returned in a very few minutes. The emperor emptied the glass at a draught.

"Oh!" exclaimed he, refreshed, "how delightful it is! I have not a cook in my palace capable of brewing me such a beverage."

"And yet the meanest of your subjects, sire, would grumble if he had nothing better than a glass of water for breakfast."

"No doubt of it, Günther. Men set no value upon that which is easily obtained. If I were to close up the fountains, and forbid them to drink water for breakfast, they would raise a howl, and protest that they could drink nothing else. And if I desired to give them a taste for assafœtida, I would have nothing to do but forbid its use. Once forbidden to the multitude, the multitude would go mad for it. But see, the sun has sent a ray through the window to bid us good-morning, and to warn me that it is time to depart. Order my horse to be saddled. Tell some of the staff to prepare to accompany me, and then go to Field-Marshal Lacy, and request him to go with me this morning on a tour of inspection."

"Lacy," said the emperor, as they galloped off together, "you must prepare yourself for a long ride. We had anticipated an early start to-day, and we are punctual. To be sure, we are minus an army, and neither our hearts nor our trumpets are sounding triumphant blasts of victory. Ah, friend, what miserable puppets we are in the hands of Almighty God! Yesterday I was gazing exultingly upon the heaven of the future, so clear, so blue, so silver-bright—when lo! the rustling of a woman's dress is heard, and the sky of my destiny grows black as night. Yesterday I fancied myself a man—to-day I am a schoolboy in disgrace upon my knees. Oh,

Lacy, those weary knees ache me so, that I could sob for pain, were it not laughable for a commander-in-chief to put his handkerchief to his eyes.

"Good God! Lacy," shouted the emperor, suddenly, while he reined in his horse until the animal almost fell upon his haunches, "why do you not laugh? You see that I am doing my best to divert you."

"I cannot laugh, sire, when you yourself are suffering almost to madness!"

The emperor made no reply, but rode on, relaxing his speed until his horse ambled gently over the road. "Lacy," said he, finally, "I am unreasonable when I murmur against destiny, for yesterday Providence was most benign toward me. Some other time, you shall hear in what manner. Let us quicken our pace, for to-day I must visit all the outposts. I have an order to promulgate to the pickets, of which I shall explain to you the reason when we return."

Shortly after the emperor had spoken, they reached the front. Joseph sprang forward to the very edge of the river-bank, and looked earnestly toward the opposite shore. Nothing was to be seen, save far away on the horizon, a few black specks which showed the outposts of the enemy. The emperor signed to the officer on duty to approach.

"Do the Prussians ever venture any nearer?" asked he.

"Yes, sire. They seem to be officers of high rank making a reconnoissance, probably with a view to finding a crossing for their army. They sometimes approach so close that the sharpshooters, who have eyes like telescopes, recognize the King of Prussia in the group."

"It is quite possible that in the excitement of a survey, the king may approach the shore. In the event of such an accident, I have a command to give to your men. As soon as they recognize the king, they shall present arms, and remain thus until he is entirely out of sight. I desire, through this courtesy, to expess the respect due to a crowned head, a great general, and a personal friend of my own. This order must be strictly enforced by the officer of the day." *

The emperor then inclined his head, and rode off with his staff. At each outpost the order for presenting arms to Frederick was repeated, and the officers charged with its execution to the letter.

Late in the day Joseph returned from his long and tiresome visit of inspection. But so far from suffering fatigue, he sprang from his horse with a light bound, and his countenance was as free from gloom as it had been before the arrival of the Grand Duke of Tuscany.

"Lacy," said he, taking the arm of the field-marshal, "I am about to explain to you the cause of my over-politeness to my abhorred enemy. You must have been astounded at the orders I have been giving to-day."

"To tell the truth, I was surprised. But I thought that in the nobleness of your heart, sire, you were proving to me that you had relinquished all thoughts of revenge."

"Nevertheless, Lacy, my hate is unappeased and I have kept my word. I have already had my revenge. I have saved the King of Prussia from the bullet of an assassin." †

* The emperor's own words. See Gross-Hoffinger, i., p. 431.

† This whole chapter is historical. See Riedler's archives for 1831, and Gross-Hoffinger, i, p. 427.

CHAPTER CXXVIII.

A LETTER TO THE EMPRESS OF RUSSIA.

WITH flushed face and panting bosom, Maria Theresa paced her cabinet, sometimes glancing with angry eyes at the heaps of papers that covered her *escritoire;* then wandering hastily to and fro, perfectly insensible to the fatigue which in her advancing years generally overwhelmed her whenever she attempted to move otherwise than leisurely. The empress had received bad news from every quarter; but worst of all were the tidings that came from Bohemia. For more than a year the Austrian and Prussian armies had threatened one another; and yet nothing had been accomplished toward the settlement of the Bavarian succession.

Maria Theresa, shocked by the threat which Joseph had made to her through the Grand Duke of Tuscany, had broken off her negotiations with Frederick, and had sacrificed the dearest wishes of her heart to appease the fury of her imperial son. Notwithstanding this, no battle had been fought, for Frederick was quite as desirous as the empress could be, to avoid an engagement. He had declared war against his old adversary with the greatest alacrity; but when it became necessary to manœuvre his army, the hero of so many fights was obliged to confess in the secrecy of his own heart that his gouty hand was impotent to draw the sword, and his tottering limbs were fitter to sink into an arm-chair than to bestride a war-horse.

Irritable, crabbed, and low-spirited, his campaign had proved a disastrous failure. Instead of planning battles, he had planned pillaging and foraging expeditions, and his hungry and disaffected army had converted the rich fields of Bohemia into a gloomy and desolate waste. At last succoring winter came to the help of the oppressed Bohemians, and both armies went into winter quarters.

Maria Theresa had employed the season, which forced her ambitious son to inactivity, in new negotiations for peace. Count von Mercy had sought for intervention on the part of France, and Baron Thugut had made new proposals to Prussia. Until to-day the empress had indulged the hope of terminating this unhappy and ridiculous war; but her hopes had been frustrated by the dispatches she had just received from France and Bohemia. Count von Mercy wrote that so far from accepting the *rôle* of mediator, the French king expostulated with him upon the injustice of the claims of Austria, and earnestly recommended their total relinquishment as the only road to peace.

Another courier from Joseph announced that the winter season having almost closed, he hoped that he might now be permitted to prosecute the war with firmness and vigor. Circumstances were favorable to Austria, for General Wurmser had succeeded in surprising the Prince of Philippsthal, and in driving the Prussian garrison from their stronghold. The emperor, therefore, declared his intention of giving battle to Frederick, that he might at one stroke free Bohemia from the presence of a tyrannical and merciless enemy.

These were the tidings which had flooded the heart of the empress with anguish.

"I must have peace," thought she, as, perfectly unconscious of the fact, she still paced the floor of her cabinet. "I cannot go to my grave burdened with the crime of an unrighteous war. Peace! peace! Heavenly Father, send us peace! Something I must do, and that at once; and if my son still vituperates his unhappy mother, I know that my subjects, the people of Germany, and all Europe, will sustain me by their approbation."

Filled with the idea, she approached her *escritoire*, and again her eyes rested upon the papers and pamphlets that lay there. Her cheeks flushed and her eyes flashed fire, as lifting from the desk a heavy package, she threw it down with violence, exclaiming:

"Has that Schrötter been printing another absurd pamphlet, braying to the world of our rights to Bavaria? I must stop that man's mouth, and teach him discretion!"

Here the empress rang and gave two messages to the page who answered the summons. "Let Prince Kaunitz be informed that I would be happy to see his highness as soon as possible. Send a messenger to Counsellor von Schrötter, and let him be here in an hour."

So saying, the empress, who at last began to feel that she was exercising her limbs beyond all power of endurance, sank into an arm-chair and continued her reflections. They were any thing but consolatory. She could not humble herself to make any more proposals to Frederick. He was so arrogant that he might answer in such a way as to make war the only alternative for Austria. But where to go for a mediator? France had refused, and Marie Antoinette had with difficulty obtained from her husband a promise not to sustain Prussia.

"I have a most disobliging son-in-law in Louis," thought the empress, "and if Marie Antoinette were not in a condition where anxiety of mind might be fatal to her life, I should very soon speak plainly to the king, and let him understand distinctly how little I care for his approval or disapproval! But I must be patient for my daughter's sake; and if she gives birth to a dauphin, I shall be too happy to quarrel with her stubborn king. I had reckoned upon France, however, and I am disappointed and grieved."

So saying, the empress bent once more over her papers, and this time she opened a dispatch from her ambassador at St. Petersburg. She began to read:

"The King of Prussia is asking succor from Russia. The empress is quite ready to grant it, and has already marched an auxiliary force into Galicia. But she exacts that her troops shall act independently of Frederick, and requires of him for the prosecution of her war with Turkey, a subsidy of two million of thalers. The king is indignant at her exactions, so that the opportunity now offers to dissolve this dangerous alliance. If the empress-queen could bring herself to pen a letter to Catharine requesting her intervention—"

"No," exclaimed Maria Theresa, interrupting herself, "to such degradation I cannot stoop! It would be too base!" She threw down the letter, and frowning leaned her head upon her hand. "How," thought she, "could a virtuous woman write to that abandoned wretch who degrades the divine birthright of royalty by a dissolute life? How could Maria Theresa so humiliate herself as to ask succor of such a Messalina!"

The entrance of a page interrupted the empress's meditations. His highness Prince Kaunitz regretted that he was unable to obey her majesty's commands, as he was sick and not able to leave his room.

The empress dismissed the page, and frowned anew.

"I know perfectly well the nature of his malady," thought she. "Whenever he desires to consult with the emperor before seeing me, he falls sick. Whenever danger is ahead and affairs look stormy, he retreats to his hole like a discreet fox. I wish to Heaven that I too could take to my bed and shut my eyes to all that is transpiring around us! But no," continued the empress with a pang of self-reproach, "I have no right to retire from the post of danger. I must act, and act quickly, or Joseph will be before me. Oh, my God, help me in my great need!"

She re-read the dispatches from her different ambassadors, and each one breathed the same spirit. From every court in Europe came disapprobation and blame. Every one of the great powers counselled peace—speedy peace, lest all should be drawn into the strife, and Austria left to the humiliation of struggling single-handed against every other nation in Europe.

The tears of the empress flowed fast. She could see no help on earth, and how could she feel otherwise than resentful toward the minister and the son who had brought her into this mortifying position? Suddenly she dried her tears and once more took up the dispatch from St. Petersburg. The silence in that little room was broken only by her sighs, and the rustling of the papers which she held in her hand. She paused, and those trembling hands fell into her lap. She threw back her head as if trying to make a difficult resolve.

"There is one way--but oh, how disgraceful!" murmured she. Again the gathering tears were dashed from her eyes, and she tried to read.

"It must be," sighed she, as she replaced the paper on the desk; "and if so, it must be done quickly. Oh, my Creator! Thou alone knowest how fearful to my heart is this sacrifice of womanly pride; but thou willest my humiliation, and I submit! Let me drink the chalice!"

She took up her pen and began to write. Often she hesitated—threw aside her sheet, and took another. Sometimes she read aloud what she had written; then starting at the sound of the words, resumed her writing in silence. At last the task was accomplished, and her eyes scanned the concluding paragraph:

"With the conviction that my honor could be intrusted to no abler hands, I leave it to your majesty, in conjunction with France, to make such propositions as you may esteem best calculated to promote peace. In this trust I remain,

"Your majesty's true and devoted sister,

"MARIA THERESA." *

As she read these words, the cheeks of the empress crimsoned with shame, and, burying her face in her hands, she sobbed aloud. When the paroxysm of her grief was over, her face was very pale and her eyes dim and swollen.

* This letter of the empress is yet in the archives of St. Petersburg. Coxe, who copies it word for word, saw it there himself. See Coxe's "History of the House of Austria," vol. iv., page 392.

"I must complete the humiliation," thought she; then folding the letter, it was directed "To Her Majesty the Empress of Russia."

She took up a tiny gold bell, and ringing it so that it gave out but a few strokes, a *portière* was raised, and Koch entered the room.

"Take a copy of this letter, and send a courier with it to St. Petersburg. I have at last yielded to the wishes of my counsellors, and have written to the Empress of Russia. Peace, Koch—not a word!—my heart is not yet strong enough to bear the grief and shame of this hour."

The private secretary had scarcely left the room, when the page reëntered, announcing Counsellor von Schrötter.

"Ah," said the empress, "he comes at the right moment. I am just in the mood to castigate those who have displeased me."

CHAPTER CXXIX.

THE GRATITUDE OF PRINCES.

THE message of the empress had been received by Counsellor von Schrötter with rapture. His heart throbbed so joyfully that its every beat sent the quick blood bounding through his veins. The hour for acknowledgment of his long-tried services had arrived. For years he had lived a life of labor, research, and patient investigation. Among the deeds, parchments, and dusty green tables of the chancery, his youth had faded to middle age, and of its early hopes had retained but one single earthly ambition: it was that of taking a place among learned men, and becoming an authority of some weight in the judicial world. His pamphlets on the Bavarian succession had lifted him to fame, and now among his countrymen his name was beginning to be quoted as that of a great and accomplished jurist. Nothing was needed to complete the measure of his simple joys, save the approbation of the court, and some acknowledgment on the part of his sovereign of the fidelity with which he had labored for so many years in her behalf.

This precious tribute he was called upon to receive. He was to speak himself with the Empress of Austria. So excited was he by the thought, that the strong man trembled from head to foot; he was even more agitated than he had been twenty years before, when he had received his diploma as doctor of laws. Pale, but inexpressibly happy, he stood upon the threshold of the empress's cabinet, and awaited her permission to approach and kiss her beloved and honored hand.

Maria Theresa saw him and spoke not a word. She sat immovable in her arm-chair, darting lightning glances upon the unconscious counsellor, and growing every moment more enraged at the thought of his impertinent researches, until the storm burst with all its fury upon his head. The empress clutched the pamphlets which lay near her upon the table, and rising from her chair, strode through the room to the door where the unhappy author stood.

"Did you write these *brochures?*" asked she.

"Yes, your majesty," said Von Schrötter with a happy smile.

"Read the title-page."

Von Schrötter read: "The rights and measures of her imperial, royal, and apostolic majesty in reference to the Bavarian succession."

"Now read the title of your first pamphlet."

"Impartial thoughts on the various questions arising from the succession of Maximilian Joseph."

"You acknowledge the authorship of these two *brochures?*"

"I am proud to acknowledge them, your majesty."

"Whence it follows that you are proud to be the cause of the unholy war which now rages throughout Germany," said the empress in a voice of indignation. "It is you, then, whose pen has metamorphosed itself into a sword wherewith to take the lives of thousands of good and honest men! What right had you to publish 'impartial thoughts upon the Bavarian succession?' I suppose you had an idea that in so doing, you were proving to the world what an important part you play in the affairs of the nation!"

"Your majesty," stammered Von Schrötter, utterly at a loss to understand his crime—"your majesty, through Prince Kaunitz, conveyed to me your entire satisfaction with my researches into the imperial archives, and the emperor himself requested me to write the second pamphlet."

"I am in no wise indebted to you for your complaisance," replied the empress; "for your ink has changed itself into blood, and your stupid vagaries, hatched in the comfortable quiet of your own room, have driven my poor soldiers from their homes, out into the pitiless storm of hardship, danger, and death. What right had you to meddle with the difficulties of the succession? Did you expect that, in gratitude for your valuable services to the crown, I would reward you with a title and an estate in Bavaria?"

"No, your majesty," replied Von Schrötter, blushing, "I was but doing my duty as a jurist and civil officer of the crown."

"And do you suppose you have succeeded in proving any thing with your rubbish?" asked the empress, scornfully. "Do you imagine that any one woud take the trouble to read your balderdash?"

"In defending the claims of the crown, I was performing an act of sacred duty toward my country," replied Von Schrötter, emboldened to reply, by a just sense of the indignity offered him.

"Oh, yes, I know something of the vanity of authors," said the empress. "They imagine themselves to be Atlas, each one with the world upon his shoulders, which must certainly fall, if they are not there to uphold it. I, however, take the liberty of judging that if they were all to be blown to atoms, nobody would be the worse for their disappearance. What has come of your writings? A paper war of such dimensions, that I think the foul fiend must have plucked all the geese in Avernus, and have thrown their quills at your heads. What with your imbecile pens, nobody knows who is right!"

"But, your majesty," remonstrated Von Schrötter, "discussion is indispensable to the discovery of truth, and as I am sure that I have contributed to this discovery, I cannot regret what I have done."

"Ah, indeed!" exclaimed the enraged empress. "You think you have contributed to the discovery of truth! I will tell you to what you have contributed, sir: you are the cause that the emperor became so headstrong on the subject, that sooner than give up Bavaria, he has involved me in war; you are the cause that the whole world has had something to say on the subject of our claims; whereas, had you held your tongue, they might have passed for what they are not—just. You are the cause that my days are spent in sorrow, and my nights are sleepless; that in the despair of my heart, I have been reduced to write to a woman whom I despise! Yes, of all this you are the cause, and more than this—you will be guilty of my death; for I repeat to you that this war has broken my heart, and will be the last nail in my coffin.* When my people, then, mourn for my death (and I hope that they will regret me), you may boast of having compassed it yourself; and from my grave I shall arise to—"

"No more, your majesty, no more! Spare me, in mercy," sobbed he, "if you would not see me die at your feet!"

"And I presume you would consider it a great misfortune for Austria if you were no longer able to unsheathe your goose-quill in her defence. There is no danger of your dying from the wounds inflicted by my tongue; but I am resolved that you shall carry their marks to the grave with you. This is all I had to say to you; you are dismissed."

"But, your majesty," replied Von Schrötter, "I have something to say—I must defend myself."

"You must defend yourself!" cried Maria Theresa, surveying him with a look of ineffable disdain. "Defend yourself to God—I am not disposed to listen to your defence."

"But, your majesty—"

"Peace!" thundered the empress. "Who dares speak when I have ordered him from my presence? Go home, and ponder my words."

So saying, she walked back to her seat. But seeing that Von Schrötter's lips were parted as if in an attempt to say something, she snatched her bell, and rang it so loud that in its clang his words were lost.

"Counsellor Von Schrötter is dismissed," said she to the page. "Open the doors, that he may pass."

Von Schrötter gasped out a convulsive sigh, and scarcely knowing what he did, turned one last sad look upon his cruel sovereign, and bowing his head, left the room.

When his tall, majestic form had disappeared from her sight, the empress said:

"Ah!—that outburst has done me good. And now that I have driven away humiliation by anger, I shall go and pray to God to bless the sacrifice I have made to-day for the good of my people."

She rang the bell, assembled her ladies of honor, and with them entered the private chapel which had lately been added to her own apartments. She knelt before the first *prie-Dieu* that presented itself, and her attendants knelt around her.

Whilst the empress was praying, Von Schrötter returned to the home, which an hour sooner, he had left with a heart so full of hope and ecstasy. He had not a word for his old house-keeper, who opened the door to admit him; and motioning away the servant who would have shown him into the dining-room, he ascended the staircase with slow, uncertain steps, his hands clinging to the balustrade, his head so heavy that he scarce could bear its weight. The servants stood below in sorrowful amazement. They had never seen their master so agitated in his life before; they could scarcely believe that this ghastly being was the dignified and stately man who had left them but an hour before. Suddenly they started, for surely they heard a loud laugh from the study, but what a laugh!—so wild,

* Maria Theresa's own words.

so unearthly, that it sounded like the dreadful mirth of a madman! —Then all was silent. Presently there came the sound of a heavy fall.

"That is our master! Some misfortune has befallen him," cried the servants, hurrying up the stairs and bursting into the room.

On the floor, surrounded by the books which had been the pride and solace of a harmless life, lay the counsellor weltering in his blood.

"He has broken a blood-vessel!" cried the house-keeper, with a sob, while the other servant ran for a physician. The old woman raised her dear master's head, and his bloody lips parted with a ghastly smile.

"This is the gratitude of princes!" murmured he almost inaudibly. "Such is the reward of him who loves his country!"

"What is it, my dear, dear master?" faltered the faithful servant, in vain seeking to penetrate the meaning of his words. "Why do you stare at me so horribly? What has distressed you?"

He moved as though he would have raised his head. "This is Austria's gratitude!" cried he in a loud voice; then, forth from his lips gurgled the purple stream of life, and his words died into hoarse, inaudible mutterings.

The physician came in, followed by the valet, and together they raised the sufferer and placed him upon his bed. The doctor then felt his pulse and his chest, and bent down to catch his breathings. He shook his head mournfully and called to the weeping servants.

"He is dying," said he. "Some fearful shock that he has received has induced a hemorrhage, which in a few hours will end his life."

Maria Theresa rose from her prayers, comforted and light of heart. And as she left the chapel, the man whom she had crushed to the earth by her unjust anger, drew his last sigh.*

CHAPTER CXXX.

FREDERICK THE GREAT.

KING FREDERICK and his Prussians were still encamped at Wildschütz. His army was weary of inactivity, and every morning the longing eyes of his soldiers turned toward the little gray house at the end of the village where the king and his staff were quartered, vainly hoping to see their Fritz in the saddle, eager, bold, and daring as he had ever been until now. The men were destitute of every thing. Not only their food was exhausted, but their forage also. Bohemia had been plundered until nothing remained for man or beast. The inhabitants had fled to the interior, their villages and farms were a waste, and still the King of Prussia insisted that his army should subsist upon the enemy.

The men were in despair, and the officers began to apprehend a mutiny, for the former were surly, and no amount of conciliatory words could appease their hunger or feed their horses.

"We must see the king, we must speak to old Fritz!" cried the malcontents; and with this cry a crowd of artillerymen made their way to headquarters.

* This whole chapter is historical. Hormayer "Austrian Plutarch," vol. vi.

"We must see the king! Where is old Fritz? Has he ceased to care for his soldiers?" repeated the crowd.

"No, friends, I am ready to listen," said a soft voice, which, nevertheless, was heard above the din, and the king, clad in his well-known uniform, appeared at the window.

The soldiers received him with a cheer, and at the sight of the well-beloved countenance, they forgot their need, and shouted for joy.

"What is it?" said Frederick, when the tumult had died away.

One of the men, as spokesman, stepped forward. "We wanted to see our old Fritz once more; we can scarcely believe that he sees our wants and yet will do nothing to relieve them."

"You see *mine*," said Frederick, smiling, "and, as you perceive, I am scarcely better off than yourselves. Do you think this a fit residence for a king?"

"It is a dog-kennel!" cried the soldiers.

"And is that all you have to say to me?"

"No, sire, it is not. If our king can do nothing for us, at least let him rescue our horses from starvation. We are men, and our reason helps us to bear privations; but it is a sin to keep our horses here without food. We beseech your majesty, give us forage for our horses!" And the others repeated in chorus: "Forage, forage, give us forage for our horses!"

Meanwhile, the king had closed his window and had retired to the other end of his house. This made the soldiers frantic, and they screamed and shouted louder than ever:

"Give us forage for our horses!"

Suddenly the voice which had so often led them to victory, was heard at the door:

"Peace, you noisy rebels, peace, I say!"

And on the steps before his wretched cabin, stood Frederick, surrounded by the principal officers of his army.

"Sire," said one of the king's staff, "shall we disperse them?"

"Why so?" replied Frederick, curtly. "Have my poor soldiers not the right to appeal to me for help? Speak, my children, speak without fear!"

"Forage, sire, forage—our horses are dying like flies!"

"You see," said the king to his officers, "these poor fellows ask nothing for themselves. Why is it that they have no forage for their horses?"

"Sire," replied the officers, deprecatingly, "as long as there remained a hay-stack or a storehouse in this part of Bohemia, your majesty's army was fed by the enemy. But the country is stripped of every thing. The inhabitants themselves have been obliged to fly from starvation."

"Starvation!" echoed the king. "I will warrant that, while the horses of the privates are suffering for food, those of the officers are well provided."

"Your majesty!"

"Do not interrupt me, but let all the forage belonging to the chief officers of the army be brought at once, and placed before these men. They can wait here until it comes, and then divide it between them. Are you satisfied, my children?"

"Yes, yes," cried the men, shouting for joy at the prospect of the abundance about to be vouchsafed to them.

The officers, on the contrary, were deeply humiliated, and beheld the proceedings with gloomy discontent.

Frederick pretended not to perceive their dissatisfaction. He stood with his hat drawn down over his brows, leaning for support upon the crutch-cane which, of late, had been his inseparable companion.

Occasionally, when a soldier came up with his bundle of hay, the king glanced quickly around, and then looked down again. The artillerymen gradually ceased their noisy demonstrations, and now, with anxious, expectant faces, they looked at the king, the officers, and then at the very small amount of forage which was being placed before them.

Just then an adjutant bowed to the king, and announced that the last bundle of hay had been set before his majesty.

Frederick raised his eyes, and sadly contemplated the miserable little heap of forage which betokened with so much significance the destitution of his brave army.

"Is this all?" said he.

"Yes, sire, all—"

"It is well. Now," continued he to the artillerymen, "divide this between you. Had my officers been more selfish, your horses would have fared better. But you see that my generals and adjutants are as noble and self-sacrificing as yourselves; and unless you manage to forage for us all, we shall all starve together. I have called for this hay to prove to you that your officers were not revelling in plenty while you were suffering for want. Take it, and do not ask for that which I cannot give you."

The artillerymen looked almost ashamed of their clamor, while the faces of the officers brightened, and their eyes turned with love and admiration upon the man whose tact had so entirely justified them to their men.

The king pretended to see their delight as little as he had feigned to see their mortification. He seemed wholly absorbed watching the soldiers, who were now striving together as to who was to have the remnants of forage that was far from being enough to allow each man a bundle.*

Finally Frederick withdrew to his cabin, and, once alone, he fell into the leathern arm-chair which was the only piece of furniture in the room besides a bed and a table.

"This will never do," thought he, sorrowfully. "We must either retreat or advance. This war is a miserable failure—the impotent effort of a shattered old man whose head is powerless to plan, and his hand to execute. How often since I entered upon this farcical campaign, have I repeated those words of Boileau:

'Malheureux, laisse en paix ton cheval vieillissant
De peur que tout à coup essouflé, sans haleine,
Il ne laisse en tombant, son maître sur l'arène.'†

Why did I undertake this war? Why had I not discretion enough to remain at home, and secure the happiness of my own people?"

The king sighed, and his head sank upon his breast. He sat thus for some time in deep discouragement; but presently he repeated to himself:

* Dohm's Memoirs, vol. i., p. 158.
† Frederick's own words.

"Why did I undertake this war—why?" echoed he aloud. "For the honor and safety of Germany. How sorely soever war may press upon my age and infirmities, it is my duty to check the ambition of a house whose greed has no bounds, save those which are made for it by the resistance of another power as resolute as itself. I am, therefore, the champion of German liberties, and cannot, must not sheathe my sword. But this inactivity is demoralizing my army, and it must come to an end. We must retreat or advance—then let us advance!"

Here the king rang his bell. A valet entered, whom he ordered to go at once to the generals and staff-officers and bid them assemble at headquarters in fifteen minutes from that time.

"Gentlemen," said the king, "we cross the Elbe to-morrow."

At these words every countenance there grew bright, and every voice was raised in one long shout:

"Long live the king! Long live Frederick the Great!"

The king tried his best to look unmoved.

"Peace! peace! you silly, old fellows," said he. "What do you suppose the boys will do out there, if you raise such a clamor in-doors? Do you approve of the move? Speak, General Keller."

"Sire, while out on a reconnoissance yesterday, I discovered a crossing where we may go safely over, without danger from the enemy's bullets."

"Good. Are you all of one mind?"

A long shout was the answer, and when it had subsided, the king smiled grimly and nodded his head.

"We are all of one mind, then. To-morrow we engage the enemy. And now to horse! We must reconnoitre the position which General Keller has chosen, and part of our troops must cross to-night."

CHAPTER CXXXI.

"THE DARKEST HOUR IS BEFORE DAY."

A FEW moments later the officers were mounted, and the king's horse stood before his door. Frederick, coming forward, with something of his youthful elasticity, tried to raise himself in the saddle; but he stopped, and with an expression of great suffering withdrew his foot from the stirrup.

The old hero had forgotten that the gout was holding him prisoner. His face flushed with disappointment, as he called his lackeys to his help. But once in the saddle, the king struck his spurs with such violence into his horse's flanks, that the animal leaped into the air, and bounded off in a swift gallop.

Whether Frederick had intended to prove to his officers that he was as bold a horseman as ever, or whether he had yielded to a momentary impulse of anger, he suffered keenly for his bravado; for at every bound of the horse, his agony increased. Finally he could endure no more. He came to a complete stand, and requested his suite to slacken their pace. They rode on in perfect silence, the officers casting stolen glances at the king, whose lips quivered, while his face grew every moment paler with suppressed anguish. But he bore it all without a sigh, until they had reached the point for which they started. Having accurately surveyed it, Frederick turned his horse's head, and rode back to his quarters.

This time he had not only to be lifted from his horse, but to be carried to his room. Once there, he signed to his attendants to leave him. He felt the imperious necessity of being alone with his afflicted mind and body. He leaned his head back, and murmured:

"*Malheureux, laisse en paix ton cheval vieillissant!*"

Then, closing his eyes, he quoted the sacred Scriptures for the first time in his life without irreverent intention.

"The spirit is willing," sighed the wretched unbeliever, "but the flesh is weak."

He remained pondering over those truthful words for several moments; then casting his eyes over the various objects that lay upon his table, they lit upon the little leather-covered box, which contained his flute. For some time past his perplexities had been so great that he had held no intercourse with this object of his life-long affection; but now he felt as if its tones would be consolatory. And with trembling, eager hands he unfastened the case, and raised the instrument to his lips. But alas! the flute, like its adorer, was superannuated. Wearily came its feeble notes upon the air, each one hoarse as the wind whistling through a ruined abbey.*

Frederick had played but a few bars of his adagio when his hands fell slowly, and the flute rolled upon the table. He contemplated it for a while, then his eyes filled with tears, which fell rapidly down his cheeks. A mournful smile flickered over his countenance.

"Well," said he, in a low voice, "I suppose there is nothing disgraceful in the tears of an old man over the last, faithful friend of his youth."

With these words he replaced the flute in the case, and locked it, murmuring:

"Farewell, forever, my life-long solace!"

Just then, a thousand voices shouted:

"Long live the king! Long live old Fritz!"

"They are rejoicing over the approaching battle," thought Frederick. "But their hopes, like mine, are destined to be crushed. Instead of crossing the Elbe, we must retire to Silesia. Old age has vanquished me—and from such a defeat no man can ever rally.

"Well, well! We must take the world as it comes, and if I can neither fight nor play on the flute, I can still talk and write. My eulogy on Voltaire is not yet completed—I must finish it to-day, that it may be read before the Academy at Berlin, on the anniversary of his death." †

Selecting from among his papers the manuscript he wanted, Frederick took up his pen and began to write.

Gradually the songs and shouts of the soldiers ceased, and the king was consoling himself for the loss of music by flinging himself into the arms of poetry, when a knock was heard at his door, and his valet announced the secretary of Count Gallitzin.

Frederick's heart throbbed with joy, and his great eagle eyes were so strangely lit up, that the valet could not imagine what had caused such an illumination of his royal master's features.

* It was during the war of the Bavarian Succession that Frederick found himself compelled to give up the flute. His *embouchure* had been destroyed by the loss of his front teeth, and his hands trembled so that he could scarcely hold the instrument.

† Voltaire died in May, 1778, and Frederick, while in camp in Bohemia, wrote a poem on his death.

"Thugut," cried the king; "is Thugut here again? Admit him immediately."

By the time that Baron Thugut had appeared at the door, Frederick had so forced down his joy, that he received the envoy of the empress-queen with creditable indifference.

"Well, baron," said he, with a careless nod, "you come again. When the foul fiend comes for the third time, he must either bag a man's soul, or give it up forever."

"I feel flattered, sire, by the comparison your majesty makes of me to so great and powerful a potentate," replied the baron, laughing.

"You believe in the devil, then, although you deny the Lord."

"Certainly, sire, for I have never yet seen a trace of the one, and the other I meet everywhere."

"For an ambassador of Maria Theresa, your opinions are tolerably heterodox," said Frederick. "But tell me what brings you hither? You must not expect me to continue our interrupted negotiations. If the empress-queen sends you to claim ever so small a portion of Bavaria, I tell you, beforehand, that it is useless to say a word. Austria must renounce her pretensions or continue the war."

"Sire, I come with new propositions. Here are my credentials, if your majesty is at leisure to examine them, and here is a letter from the hand of my revered sovereign."

"And what is that?" asked Frederick, pointing to a roll of papers, tied up with twine.

"Those are my documents, together with the papers relating to the past negotiations."

"I think that I have already refused to go over these negotiations," said Frederick, sharply; and without further ceremony, he broke the seal of the empress's letter. While the king read, Thugut busied himself untying his roll and spreading his papers out upon the table.

"This is nothing but a letter of credentials," observed the king, putting it down. "The empress refers me to you for verbal explanations. I am ready to hear them."

"Sire, the empress-queen, animated by a heartfelt desire to restore peace to Germany, has called upon France and Russia to settle the difficulties which, to her sincere regret, have arisen between herself and your majesty. These two powers, having responded favorably to my sovereign's request—"

"Say, rather," interrupted Frederick, "that these two powers having given to her majesty of Austria the somewhat peremptory advice to relinquish her pretensions to Bavaria—"

Baron Thugut bowed, and resumed: "That the two powers may have the opportunity of conducting their negotiations without any new complications from military movements, her majesty, the empress, proposes an armistice, to begin from to-day."

Up to this moment the king's eyes had been fixed upon Thugut; but as he heard these few last words, he dropped them suddenly. He was so overjoyed, that he was afraid to betray his raptures to the diplomatist. He recovered himself in time. "Did you come through my camp?" said he to the baron.

"Yes, sire."

"You heard the shouts and songs of my brave Prussians. Were

you told that I intend to cross the Elbe, and offer battle to your emperor to-morrow?"

"Yes, sire, I was told so."

"And at the very moment when I am prepared to fight, you come to me with proposals of armistice! You perceive that I could only be brought to consent to a truce through my consideration for the empress, provided she offered sound guaranties for the conclusion of an honorable peace. Let us hear your proposals."

The interview between the king and the secret envoy of the empress was long and animated. When the latter was about to take leave, Frederick nodded condescendingly, saying:

"Well! I consent to make this sacrifice to the wishes of the empress. You can inform her, that instead of giving battle to the emperor, as I had hoped to do on the morrow, I shall retreat to Silesia, and retire into winter quarters."

"And your majesty promises equitable conditions, and will consult with the Russian ambassador?"

"I promise, and the empress-queen may rely upon me. Farewell." The envoy turned to depart, but before he reached the door the king called him back.

"Baron," said he with a significant smile, "you have forgotten something." Here he pointed to the twine which had fallen on the floor, and lay near the baron's chair. "Take what belongs to you; I never enrich myself with the possessions of others."

When the door closed, the king raised his eyes to heaven. "Is it chance, or Providence, that has succored me to-day?" thought he. "Which of the two has vouchsafed me such honorable deliverance in my extremity?"

CHAPTER CXXXII.

THE EMPEROR AND HIS MOTHER.

It was a day of double rejoicing in Vienna, at once the celebration of peace, and of Maria Theresa's sixty-second birthday. For three months the seven envoys of Austria, Prussia, Russia, France, Bavaria, Zweibrücken, and Saxony, had been disentangling the threads of the Bavarian succession. For three months Joseph had hoped and prayed that the debates of the peace congress might come to naught, and its deliberations engender a veritable war. But he was destined to new disappointment. The love of peace had prevailed. Austria had renounced all her inheritance in Bavaria, save the Innviertel, and had declared her treaty with Charles Theodore to be null and void.

The people of Vienna were overjoyed. They, like their empress, preferred peace to increase of domain; and they hastened to offer her their sincerest congratulations. All the European ambassadors were in full uniform, and Maria Theresa was seated on a throne, in all her imperial regalia.

She was radiant with smiles, and happiness flashed from her still bright eyes; but on this day of rejoicing there was one void that pained the empress—it was the absence of her eldest son. Since his return to Vienna, three months before, there had never yet been a word of explanation between Joseph and his mother. He had studiously avoided being alone with her, had never made his appearance in council, and when documents had been presented to him for signature, he had no sooner perceived the sign-manual of the empress, than he had added his own without examination or comment.

It was this cold submission which tortured the heart of Maria Theresa. She would have preferred recrimination to such compliance as this; it seemed so like aversion, so like despair!

When the ceremonies of the day were over, the empress sent a messenger to request the presence of her son, in her own private apartments. The messenger returned, and a few moments after, was followed by the emperor.

He entered the room, and his mother came eagerly forward, her two hands outstretched to greet him. "Thank you, my dearest child," said she, affectionately, "for coming so promptly at my request. My heart has been yearning for my son, and I have longed all day to see my co-regent and emperor at my side."

She still held out her hands, but Joseph, affecting not to see them, bowed with grave ceremony. "I am neither emperor nor co-regent," replied he; "I am but the son and subject of the empress, and as such I have already congratulated your majesty with the rest."

"Were your congratulations for my birthday, or for the restoration of peace, my son?"

"The birthday of my empress is, above all others, a day of gratulation for me," replied Joseph, evasively.

"Then peace is not agreeable to you?"

"Pardon me, I have every reason to be satisfied. Have we not exchanged compliments with all the powers of Europe, and have not the people of Vienna sung ninety-nine thousand *Te Deums* in honor of the peace of Teschen?"*

"I see that you do not approve of it, Joseph," said the empress, who was anxious to come to an understanding on the subject.

"I was under the impression that I had signed all your majesty's acts without giving any trouble whatever," was the cold reply.

"But you did it unwillingly, I fear, and thought of your mother as a weak and timid old woman. Is it not so, my son?"

"When I signed the treaty I thought of my ancestor, Charles V. After a disastrous campaign in Africa, he was obliged to return with his fleet to Spain. He sailed, it is true, but he was the last man to go on board. So with me—I signed the articles of peace, but was the last one who signed."†

"Have you nothing more to say on the subject? Are you not glad that there is to be no bloodshed?"

"A son and subject has no right to sit in judgment upon the actions of his mother and empress."

"But you are more than a subject, you are an emperor."

"No, your majesty; I am like the Venetian generals. In war, they commanded the armies, and received their salaries from the republic. When their campaigns were over, their pensions were paid, and they sank back into obscurity."

"Oh, my son, these are hard and bitter words," exclaimed the empress, pressing her hands upon her heart. "I see plainly that you

*Joseph's own words.
†Ibid.

are displeased because I have exchanged a doubtful war for an honorable peace."

"I am not so presuming as to be displeased with your majesty's acts, and if you have obtained an honorable peace, I wish you joy of it."

Maria Theresa sighed heavily. "I perceive," said she, disconsolately, "that you are resolved not to let me see into your heart."

"Oh, your majesty," cried Joseph, with a bitter smile, "I have no heart. Where my heart once was, there stands an open grave; and, one by one, my hopes have all been buried there."

"I think it strange that the future Emperor of Austria should speak of buried hopes."

"I said nothing of an emperor, your majesty, I spoke of poor Joseph of Hapsburg and of his personal wishes. As regards the future emperor, he of course has many hopes for Austria. First among them is the wish that the epoch of his reign may be very far off! Second, is his desire to serve his country. As we are now to enjoy the blessings of peace, and I am on the list of your majesty's pensioned officers, I should like, if it do not conflict with your views, to receive an appointment as minister to some foreign power."

"Oh," exclaimed Maria Theresa, sorrowfully, "would you leave me so soon again?"

"Yes, your majesty, I desire a long leave of absence."

"Whither would you then journey, my dear child?"

"I desire to visit the Empress Catharine."

"The Empress Catharine!" echoed Maria Theresa, starting and coloring violently. "You would visit that woman?"

"Yes, your majesty. I would visit that woman as Baron Thugut did the King of Prussia; with this exception, that I do not go secretly—I first consult your majesty."

Maria Theresa would not notice this thrust of her son. She contented herself with replying: "What object can you have in going on a mission to Russia?"

"I propose to win the friendship of the empress."

"The friendship of that degraded woman! I do not covet it."

"And yet your majesty was the first to request her mediation in our affairs with Germany. As you have raised the foul fiend, and he has come at your call, you must abide the consequences, and accept him as a friend. Since Russia is to have a voice in German politics, it is better that she speak for us, than sustain our enemy, Prussia."

"But she has long been the ally of Prussia," objected the empress.

"So much the more incumbent is it upon us to disturb the alliance. To do this, is the purpose of my journey to Russia. I repeat my request for your majesty's consent."

For some moments Maria Theresa contemplated her son with inexpressible tenderness. At length she said with a sigh, "You really desire, then, to go to Russia?"

"Such is my wish, your majesty."

"Well, my child, since you desire it, I consent; but I do it unwillingly. I wish to prove to my son how gladly I gratify him, when I can do so without conflicting with my duties as a sovereign."

The emperor bowed, but spoke not a word. Maria Theresa sighed again, and an expression of deep pain crossed her face.

"When do you expect to start?" said she, sadly.

"As soon as possible; for if I am not mistaken, the time is now propitious for stepping in between Prussia and her beloved ally."

"Then I am to lose my dear son at once?" asked the mother, with tearful eyes. "I fear he leaves me without a pang; and will seldom bestow a thought upon the mother whose anxious heart follows his every movement with love."

"I shall bestow my thoughts upon my sovereign, and remember that I am pledged to obtain for her a powerful ally. But I have much to do before I start. Above all things I must see Prince Kaunitz. I beg therefore of your majesty the permission to retire."

"As the emperor pleases," said Maria Theresa, with quivering lip.

Joseph bowed, and without a word or look at his mother's sorrowing countenance, turned toward the door. Up to this moment the empress had controlled her distress, but she could master her grief no longer. She looked at the emperor with dimmed eyes and throbbing heart; and in the extremity of her maternal anguish, she cried out,

"Oh, my son, my precious boy!"

The emperor, who was opening the door, turned around. He saw his mother, her tears falling like rain, standing close by with outstretched arms. But he did not respond to the appeal. With another ceremonious bow, he said, "I take leave of your majesty," and closed the door behind him.

Maria Theresa uttered a loud cry and sank to the floor. "Oh," sobbed she, "I am a poor, desolate mother. My child loves me no longer!"

CHAPTER CXXXIII.

PRINCE POTEMKIN.

Prince Potemkin was just out of bed. In front of him, two pages, richly dressed, bowed down to the floor as they opened the door for him to pass into his cabinet. Behind him, two more pages held up the train of his velvet dressing-gown, which, all bedecked with jewels, came trailing behind his tall, graceful figure. Behind the pages were four valets with breakfast and Turkish pipes.

And in this wise Prince Potemkin entered his cabinet. He threw himself upon an ottoman covered with India cashmere shawls, and received from a kneeling page a cup of chocolate, which was handed to his highness upon a gold waiter set with pearls. Then, as if the cup had been too troublesome to hold, he replaced it on the waiter, and ordered the page to pour the chocolate down.

The page, apparently, was accustomed to the order, for he rose briskly from his knees, and approaching the cup to Potemkin's lips, allowed the chocolate to trickle slowly down his princely throat. Meanwhile the three pages, four valets, and six officers, who had been awaiting him in his cabinet, stood around in stiff, military attitudes, each one uncomfortably conscious that he was momentarily exposed to the possible displeasure of the mighty favorite of the mighty Czarina.

Potemkin, meanwhile, vouchsafed not a look at any one of them. After he had sipped his chocolate, and the page had dried his mouth with an embroidered napkin, he opened his lips. The valet whose duty it was to present it, stepped forward with the Turkish pipe, and depositing its magnificent golden bowl upon the Persian carpet by the ottoman, placed the amber mouth-piece between the lips of his master.

Again a dead silence; and again those stiff forms stood reverentially around, while Potemkin, with an air of *ennui* and satiety, watched the blue wreaths that rose from his pipe to the ceiling.

"What o'clock is it?" asked he moodily.

"Mid-day, your highness," was the prompt reply.

"How many people in the anteroom?"

"A multitude of nobles, generals, and lesser petitioners, all awaiting your highness's appearance."

"How long have they been there?"

"Three hours, your highness."

His highness went on smoking, impelled probably by the reflection that three hours was too short a time for the court of Russia to wait for the ineffable blessing of his presence.

After a while he became weary of the pipe, and raised his head. Three valets rushed forward, each with an embroidered suit, to inquire whether his highness would wear the uniform of a field-marshal, that of a lord-chamberlain, or the magnificent costume of a Russian prince. Potemkin waved them off, and rose from the ottoman. His long brown hair, which flowed like the mane of a lion around his handsome face, bore here and there the traces of the down pillow upon which he had slept; his open dressing-gown exposed to view his slovenly under-garments; and his pearl-embroidered slippers were worn over a pair of soiled stockings which, hanging loosely around his legs, revealed his powerful and well-shaped calves.

In this *néglîgé*, Potemkin approached the door of his anteroom. As soon as he had been announced, a hundred weary faces grew bright with expectation; and princes, dukes, and nobles bowed before the haughty man who was even mightier than the empress; for *he* bent before no mortal, while she was the slave of one will—of Potemkin's.

Silent and disdainful, Potemkin walked through the lines of obsequious courtiers that fell back as he passed, here and there condescending to greet some nobleman of wealth or influence. As for the others who raised their imploring eyes to his, he affected not to know of their insignificant presence, and returned to his cabinet without having vouchsafed a word to anybody.

"Is the jeweller there?" asked he of the officer at the door, and as the latter bowed his head, Potemkin added, "Admit him, and after him the minister of police."

With these words he passed into his cabinet, and his valets began to dress him. While his long mane was being combed into order, Potemkin amused himself playing like a juggler with three little golden balls, while the pale and trembling jeweller stood wondering what new robbery awaited him now.

"Ah, Artankopf, you are there?" said the prince, when his toilet had been completed. "I have an order for you."

The jeweller made a salam, and muttered some unintelligible words of which Potemkin took no notice.

"I saw a magnificent service of gold yesterday in your show-case."

"It is an order, your highness," said Artankopf, quickly.

"Then I cannot buy it?"

"Impossible, your highness."

"Then I order one exactly like it, above all in weight. The statuettes which ornament that service are exquisitely moulded. How much gold is there in it?"

"Sixty thousand rubles, your highness."

Potemkin's eyes sparkled. "A considerable sum," said he, stroking his mane. "I order two services of the same value. Do you hear? They must be ready on this day week."

"And the payment?" Artankopf ventured to inquire.

"I shall pay you in advance," replied Potemkin, with a laugh. "I appoint you first court-jeweller to the empress."

The jeweller did not appear to appreciate the mode of payment; he seemed terrified.

"Oh, your highness," said he, trembling, "I implore you not to make such fearful jests. I am the father of a large family, and if you exact of me to furnish you a service worth a fortune, the outlay for the gold alone will ruin me."

"You will be irretrievably ruined if you do *not* furnish it," laughed Potemkin, while he went on throwing his balls and catching them. "If those two services are not here on the day, you take a journey to Siberia, friend Artankopf."

"I will be punctual, your highness," sighed the jeweller. "But the payment—I must buy the gold."

"The payment! What, the devil—you are not paid by the appointment I give you! Go; and if you venture to murmur, think of Siberia, and that will cure your grief."

With a wave of his hand, Potemkin dismissed the unhappy jeweller, who left that princely den of extortion a broken-hearted, ruined man.

The robber, meanwhile, was counting his gains and donning his field-marshal's uniform. "One hundred and twenty thousand rubles' worth of gold!" said he to himself. "I'll have the things melted into coin—it is more portable than plate."

The door opened, and Narischkin, the minister of police, entered.

"Out, the whole gang of you!" cried Potemkin; and there was a simultaneous exodus of officers, pages, and valets. When the heavy, gold-bordered silken *portière* had fallen, the tyrant spoke.

"Now let us hear your report," said he, seating himself before his toilet-mirror, where first he cleaned his dazzling white teeth, and then pared his nails.

The minister of police, in an attitude of profound respect, began to go over the occurrences of the past two days in St. Petersburg.

Potemkin listened with an occasional yawn, and finally interrupted him. "You are an old fool. What do I care for your burglars and bankrupts! You have not so much as a murder to relate to me. Can you not guess that there are other things of which I wish to hear?"

"Doubtless your highness wishes me to report the doings of the Emperor of Austria."

"You are not quite such a dunce, then, as you seem to be. Well, what has the emperor been about these two days past?"

"He leads the same life as he did in Moscow," said Narischkin. "He goes about as Count Falkenstein."

"He comes as his own ambassador," cried Potemkin, laughing, "and he could not have chosen a worse one than Count Falkenstein.* What a wretched country Austria must be when its emperor travels about like an ordinary Russian gentleman!"

"He arrived in St. Petersburg with one servant carrying his portmanteau, and engaged two rooms at a hotel."

"Oh, yes, I have heard of his passion for living at hotels. It all proceeds from avarice. Were he the guest of the empress, he would be obliged to make some imperial presents here and there. When our great czarina invited him to Sarskoe-Selo, he accepted, on condition that he should be allowed to lodge at an inn. Now there happens to be no inn at Sarskoe-Selo; so the imperial gardener has hung out a sign, and the little Count of Falkenstein is to take up his lodging with him. He never will be the wiser, and will fancy himself at an inn. So that in trifles, as in matters of state, the czarina shall befool Austria, and lead him by the nose. Tell me something more of his eccentricities. Have you dazzled him with a sight of our wealth?"

"He is not to be dazzled, your highness. Even the homage he has received seems to give him no pleasure."

"Ah! Has he, then, been the object of so much consideration?"

"Her majesty ordered it, and she has even devised some delicate compliments wherewith to surprise him."

"Ah!—she seems to be inclined toward this little emperor," muttered Potemkin. "She indulges in fanciful projects of aggrandizement with him, and forgets—. Well—what were the surprises which the czarina prepared for his countship?"

"Day before yesterday, he visited the Academy of Sciences. An atlas was presented to him; and when he opened it, he found a map of his own journey from Vienna to St. Petersburg, with engravings illustrating the various details of the journey."†

"Pretty good," sneered Potemkin, "but unfortunately not original, for the little count received a similar compliment in Paris. Go on."

"Then the emperor visited the Academy of Arts, and there he found a portfolio of engravings, among which was an excellent portrait of himself with this inscription: '*Multorum providus urbes et mores hominum inspexit.*'"

"Who wrote the inscription?" asked Potemkin, hastily.

"Her majesty's self," replied Narischkin, with a deep inclination at the name. "But the emperor greets every thing with a quiet smile. When he visited the mint and saw the enormous piles of bullion there, he merely said: 'Have you always as much silver in the mint as there is to-day?'"

Potemkin laughed aloud. "That was a sly question, and shows that little Falkenstein has been peeping behind the scenes and has discovered that we were prepared for his coming."

"Yes, your highness. It would appear that Count Falkenstein does not quite believe in our enormous wealth; for after seeing the mint, he put on that mocking smile of his, and asked whether the Imperial Bank was in a condition to redeem its issue."

"What was the answer?"

"'Yes,' of course, your highness."

* Potemkin's own words.

† Theodore Mundt, "Conflicts for the Black Sea," p. 141.

"It was a masterpiece of effrontery then, and I shall take the opportunity of testing its truth. Go to the bank, Narischkin, and say that I need one hundred thousand rubles for an entertainment I propose to give to the czarina. I must have it in coin. Quick—begone."

"I fly, your highness, but first be so kind as to give me the imperial order. You well know that no coin can leave the bank without the signature of the empress."

"I should like to see whether they will dare to return *my* signature," cried Potemkin, fiercely.

He wrote the order, and handing it to Narischkin, said: "Take this to the bank directors; and if they ask for the signature of the empress, tell them she will send it to-morrow, but I must have the money to-day."

Narischkin bowed lower than he had ever been seen to do toward the son of the empress himself, and left the room on reverential tiptoes.

CHAPTER CXXXIV.

THE PRUSSIAN AMBASSADOR.

When Potemkin felt himself quite alone, he leaned back in his arm-chair with an ugly frown.

"Something is going on to my disadvantage here," muttered he. "I saw it yesterday in Panin's exulting countenance. How I hate that man! Almost as much as I do Orloff! It is a blessing for me that both are not here to plot together. Singly, I do not fear them; but together—Orloff is the loaded cannon, and Panin the lighted match, and if I am not wary—"

Here, as though he had felt the shock of the ball, Potemkin sprang from his seat, and swung his hands above his head. But presently he sank back into his chair, and continued his meditations. "I must spike Orloff before he destroys me. But to spike a cannon, one must be able to reach it; and Orloff is far away on his estates, like a spider in her wicked web. Oh, if I could but reach it, I would soon tear it to pieces! But where are its threads? How shall I find them?—Panin, too, is getting intimate with the grand duke, and so, is currying favor with the empress. Yesterday when I entered the parlor without saluting him, Paul called after me with an oath, and turned to his mother with a complaint of my insolence. And the empress did not utter one word of reproof, although she saw me near enough to hear. That is significant—it means that Catharine fears me no longer. But, by the eternal God! she shall learn that she has a master, and that her master is Potemkin!

"How dare she take Panin into her confidence? He it is who inclines her to the King of Prussia. This fancy for Prussia is the only thing she has in common with the grand duke. Love of Frederick is the bridge which Panin has built to unite them. I must try to lead her into another road of policy, and so remove Orloff and Panin. Orloff hates Austria, and if—pshaw! Why is that Joseph so niggardly that one cannot feel the slightest interest in him? If after refusing all other invitations he had paid me the compliment of accepting mine—but, no!—this haughty Austrian treats me with as little consideration as he does the rest of the world; and forces me, in spite of myself, to the side of Frederick. But there I find Orloff and Panin, and we cannot work together. They must be disgraced, and Catharine made to follow me. How shall I commence? What shall I do?"

A knock at the door put an end to his communings.

"His excellency the Count von Görtz, ambassador of his majesty the King of Prussia," said the officer, who announced the visitors of Potemkin.

"Show his excellency into the little parlor," said the latter, carelessly, "and tell him that I will receive him there."

"Ah!—Count von Görtz," thought Potemkin. "That signifies that my enemies have not yet triumphed, and that the King of Prussia thinks me powerful enough to conciliate. Well—I must have time for reflection."

And without the slightest regard to the station of his visitor, Potemkin sat for half an hour, revolving in his mind what sort of reception he should give to Frederick's overtures. In spite of the slight, Count von Görtz came forward with a gracious smile, as Potemkin, slightly nodding, passed on to a seat, and waved his hand for the count to take another.

"I am commissioned by my sovereign, the King of Prussia, to request an interview of your highness," began Von Görtz.

Potemkin nodded, but said nothing.

"His majesty has intrusted me with a most flattering commission," continued the ambassador.

"Let us hear it," replied Potemkin, with indifference.

Count von Görtz bowed, rose, and drew from his bosom a rich velvet *étui* which he handed to the prince.

"His majesty, my august sovereign, in acknowledgment of your highness's great and glorious deeds, wishes to convey to you a token of his admiration and friendship," said Count von Görtz, solemnly. "He has bestowed upon your highness the order of the Black Eagle, and I have the honor to present it to you with the insignia."

Potemkin took the *étui* and without opening it laid it on the table beside him. "Ah," said he, with a shrug, "his majesty sends me the Black Eagle. I am much obliged to him, but really I have so many orders that I have nowhere left to wear them, and how to dispose of this new one I scarcely know. See for yourself," continued he smiling, and pointing to his breast, which indeed was covered with crosses, "do I not look like a vender of orders, carrying about his samples?" *

"If I may be allowed to use your excellency's words, you carry about samples, not only of your treasures, but of your heroism and statesmanship. It would be a pity if among them, you should not wear a decoration of my august sovereign."

"Very well, then, to oblige the King of Prussia, I will wear the cross, and I beg you return him my thanks. Have you any thing more to say, count?"

Count von Görtz cast a searching glance around the apartment, especially upon the heavy velvet window-curtains.

"Get up and look for yourself, if you suspect the presence of anybody," said the prince.

* All Potemkin's own words. Dohm's Memoirs, vol. i., p. 413.

"Your highness's word is sufficient. Allow me then to speak openly and confidentially."

"In the name of your sovereign?"

"Yes, your highness. You know that the treaty, which for eight years has allied Russia and Prussia is about to expire."

"Is it?" said Potemkin, carelessly. "I was not aware of it, for I take no interest in minor politics."

"Your highness has in view the great whole only of the field of diplomacy," replied the complaisant minister. "But for Prussia this alliance is a most important one, and my sovereign has nothing more at heart than the renewal of his alliance with Russia. He knows how much his interests here are threatend by the visit of the Emperor Joseph; and he desired me to ask of your highness whether it would be advisable for him to send Prince Henry to counteract it."

Potemkin replied to this question by a loud laugh. "What a set of timid people you are!" said he. "What formalities about nothing! When the emperor was about to visit us, the czarina must know whether it was agreeable to the King of Prussia; now the king wishes to know from *me* whether the visit of Prince Henry is expedient."

"Yes. His majesty wishes advice from your highness alone, although there are others who would gladly be consulted by him."

"Others? you mean Panin—have you, then, asked counsel of no one, count?"

"Of no one. My sovereign wishes to consult with no one excepting your highness."

For the first time Potemkin betrayed his satisfaction by a triumphant smile. "If your king comes to me exclusively—mark me well, *exclusively*—for advice, I am willing to serve him."

"Your highness may see that my sovereign addresses himself to you alone," replied the minister, handing him a letter in Frederick's own handwriting.

Potemkin, without any appearance of surprise, took it and broke the seal. The king began by saying that he had every reason to believe that the object of Joseph's visit to Russia was to alienate Russia from her old ally. Then he went into ecstasies over the genius and statesmanship of Potemkin, and besought him to uphold the interests of Prussia. Furthermore he promised his interest and influence to the prince, not only for the present, but for the future, when it was probable that he (Frederick) could serve Potemkin substantially.*

A long pause ensued after the reading of this letter. Potemkin threw himself back, and in an attitude of thoughtfulness raised his eyes to the rich pictured ceiling above him.

"I do not entirely understand the king," said he, after some time. "What does he mean by saying that he will try to make that possible which seems impossible?"

"His majesty has learned that your highness is desirous of being created Duke of Courland. He will use all his interest with Stanislaus to this effect, and indemnify the Duke de Biron, who would lose Courland, by augmenting his possessions in Silesia. The king also means that he is ready to find a bride for the future Duke of Courland among the princesses of Germany."

* This letter is historical, and is to be found in Dohm's Memoirs, vol. i., p. 412.

"Really," said Potemkin, laughing, "the mysterious phrase is significant. But the king lays too much stress upon that little duchy of Courland; if I wanted it, I could make it mine without troubling his majesty in the least. As to the bride, I doubt whether it would be agreeable to the czarina for me to marry, and this matter I leave to herself. What does the king mean by a proffer of friendship for the future?"

Count Görtz leaned forward and spoke scarcely above his breath. "His majesty means to promise his influence with the grand duke, so that in the event of his mother's death, your highness would be secure of your person and property." *

This time the prince was unable to suppress his real feelings; he started, and a deep flush overspread his face.

"How?" said he, in a whisper, "has the king the power to read my thoughts—"

He did not conclude his sentence, but sprang from his seat and paced the room in hurried excitement. Count von Görtz also had risen and contemplated him in anxious silence.

"Did the courier from Berlin bring any letters to the czarina?" asked Potemkin, as he ceased walking and stood before Von Görtz.

"Yes, your highness, and I shall deliver them, as soon as I receive the assurance of your influence with the empress."

"Very well, you have it. I will go to her at once. Meanwhile go to Count Panin, to whose department this affair belongs, and induce him to lay before the czarina a proposition for the renewal of the Prussian alliance. Then ask an audience of the empress and present your credentials. You see that I am in earnest, for I work in conjunction with my enemy; but before I make one step, you must write out the king's last promise to me, adding that you are empowered to do so by his majesty of Prussia and having signed the promise, you must deliver me the paper."

"May I inquire the object of these papers?"

Potemkin approached the count, and whispered in his ear. "It is a matter of life and death. If the grand duke should come to the throne, from the unbounded regard which he has for the King of Prussia, I know that this paper will protect me from his vengeance."

"Your highness shall have it."

"At once? For you understand that I must have some guaranty before I act. Your king's words are not explicit."

"I shall draw up the paper, and send it to your highness before I ask an audience of the czarina."

"Then the King of Prussia may reckon upon me, and I shall serve him to-day, as I hope that in future he will serve me. Go now, and return with the paper as soon as it is ready."

"I believe that Prussia means fairly," said Potemkin, when he found himself once more alone. "But that only means that Prussia needs me, and that," cried he, exultingly, "means that I am mightier than Panin, mightier than the grand duke—but am I mightier than Orloff?—Oh, this Orloff is the spectre that forever threatens my repose! He or I must fall, for Russia is too small to hold us both. But which one? Not I—by the Eternal—not I!"

Just then there was a knock at the door, and Potemkin, who was standing with his fist clinched and his teeth set, fell back into his seat.

* Raumer's Contributions, etc., vol. v., p. 485.

"How dare you disturb me?" cried he, savagely.

"Pardon me, your highness, but this is your day for receiving the foreign ambassadors, and his excellency of Austria craves an audience?"

"Cobenzl? Is he alone?"

"Yes, your highness."

"In ten minutes, admit him here."

CHAPTER CXXXV.

THE AUSTRIAN AMBASSADOR.

TEN minutes later the door was opened, and Count Cobenzl, on the point of his toes, tipped into the room. Potemkin, on the sofa, was looking the picture of indifference; his eyes half-shut and his tall form stretched out at full length, he seemed just to have awakened from sleep. But during those ten minutes he had been doing any thing but sleeping. He had been decorating himself with the cross of the Black Eagle, and had allowed the broad ribbon to which it was attached to trail upon the carpet.

"It is well, Count Cobenzl," said Potemkin, greeting the minister, "that you did not come five minutes later, for you would not have met me at all."

"Pardon me, I should then have had but five minutes to wait in your anteroom," replied Cobenzl. "I detest anterooms, and wish that I had come ten minutes later, that I might have been introduced to your presence at once."

"You would not have seen me at all, I tell you; for I am about to have an audience of the empress."

"Ah, indeed!" cried Cobenzl. "That accounts for all these brilliant decorations, then."

"You certainly did not suppose that I was wearing them in honor of *your* visit, did you?" asked Potemkin, with quiet insolence.

"Oh, no, I thought it a mere *mise en scène.*"

"Ah, Count Cobenzl is still mad on the subject of the drama," replied Potemkin, laughing. "What new comedy are you about to get up at the Austrian embassy, eh?"

"A very pretty thing, just from Paris, your highness. It is called, 'The Disgraced Favorite, or the Whims of Fortune.'"

Potemkin's eyes flashed fire, but he controlled himself, and said, "Where is the scene of the drama laid?"

"I do not precisely remember. In Tartary, or Mongolia, or—"

"Or in the moon," interrupted Potemkin, laughing. "But come—be seated, and let us be serious." So saying, Potemkin threw himself back again upon the divan, and pointed to an arm-chair, which Cobenzl quietly accepted. The chair happened to be close to the spot where the ribbon of the Black Eagle was lying. Cobenzl seeing that it was under his feet, picked it up, and presented it to the prince.

"You know not what you do, count. You raise your enemy when you raise that ribbon. It has just been sent to me by the King of Prussia. I am quite in despair at being obliged to wear it, for it takes up so much room. The star of the Black Eagle is very large. Do you not think so?"

"Yes, your highness, and I congratulate you upon its possession, for the close King of Prussia does not often give away his diamonds."

"It would appear that diamonds do not abound in Prussia," replied Potemkin, with a gesture of slight toward the cross on his breast. "These brilliants are rather yellow."

"Do you prefer Austriàn diamonds?" asked Cobenzl, significantly.

"I have never seen any," answered Potemkin, with a yawn.

"Then I am happy to be the first to introduce them to your notice," said Cobenzl rising, and taking from his pocket a turkey-morocco case. "My august emperor has commissioned me to present to you this little casket."

"Another order!" said Potemkin, with affected horror.

"No, your highness. Orders are toys for grown-up children. But you are a great man, and a toy for you must have some scientific significance. My emperor has heard that your highness has a costly collection of minerals and precious stones. His majesty, therefore, with his own hand has selected the specimens which I have the honor to present in his name."

Potemkin, whose indifference had all vanished as he listened, opened the casket with some eagerness; and an exclamation of rapture fell from his lips, as he surveyed its costly contents. There were Indian diamonds of unusual size and brilliancy; Turkish rubies of fiery crimson; magnificent sapphires; turquoises of purest tint; large specimens of lapis-lazuli, all veined with gold; and translucent chrysoprase of bright metallic green.

"This is indeed a princely gift," cried the covetous Potemkin, perfectly dazzled by the magnificence, and intoxicated by the possession of all these riches. "Never have I seen such jewels. They blaze like the stars of heaven!"

Cobenzl bowed. "And this sapphire!" continued the prince, "the empress herself has nothing to compare to it!"

"The czarina looks upon your highness as the brightest jewel in her crown—as her incomparable sapphire. But observe this turquoise; it is one of the greenish hue so prized by connoisseurs, and its like is not to be purchased with money."

Suddenly Potemkin, ashamed of his raptures, closed the casket with a click and pushed it aside.

"You can tell your emperor," said he, "that you were an eye-witness of the gratification I have received from this superb addition to my scientific collections. And now, count, without circumlocution, how can I serve you, and what does the emperor desire of me? Such gifts as these indicate a request."

"Frankly, then, the emperor seeks your highness's friendship, and wishes you to further his majesty's plans."

"What are these plans?"

"Oh, your highness is too shrewd a statesman not to have guessed them, and not to understand that we merely shift the scene of the war. We pitch our tents at St. Petersburg with the object of winning Russia to our side."

"But here Prussia holds the battle-field; you will have to fight against superior numbers."

"Not if Prince Potemkin be our ally," replied Cobenzl, courteously. "True, Prussia has Orloff, Panin, and the grand duke—"

"And who tells you that Prussia has not Potemkin also?" cried the prince, laughing. "Do you not see that I wear the Black Eagle?"

"Yes; but your highness is too wise to be the ally of Prussia. You are too great a statesman to commit such a *bévue*. Orloff, who has never forgiven you for succeeding him in Catharine's favor, Orloff asks no greater triumph than that of harnessing your highness to the car of *his* political proclivities."

"He shall never enjoy that triumph," muttered Potemkin.

"Not if the emperor can prevent it; and, therefore, his majesty hopes that your highness will sustain Austria."

"But what are Austria's plans?"

"Austria wishes to occupy the place which Prussia now enjoys as the ally of Russia. Prussia, while wooing the czarina, ogles the grand duke, and it is her interest to bring them together. I know that the matter was thoroughly discussed yesterday between Count Panin and the Prussian ambassador."

"The Prussian ambassador was yesterday in conference with Panin?"

"Not only yesterday, but to-day, I met him coming from Panin's with his order of the Black Eagle, and a letter for your highness from the king."

"Truly your spies are great detectives," cried Potemkin.

"They are well paid," was the significant reply.

"And what, for example, were the proposals of Von Görtz?"

"Von Görtz stated that as Panin, the grand duke, and himself were not a match for the emperor and your highness, you were to be won over by flattery, orders, and promises."

"True!" cried Potemkin. "Your spies are right. What else?"

"Another powerful friend of Prussia has been recalled from his estates, and summoned to Petersburg."

Potemkin sprang from the sofa with a howl of rage.

"What! Orloff summoned by Von Görtz; he who—"

"Who was enticing your highness with vain promises, had suggested to the czarina the imperative necessity of recalling Orloff, with the express intention of holding you in check."

"What an infernal plot! But it bears the stamp of Panin's treachery upon its face," muttered Potemkin, while with hasty strides he walked up and down the room.

Cobenzl watched him with a half smile, and taking up the ribbon of the Black Eagle, he passed it through his hands by way of pastime.

After much going to and fro, Potemkin stopped, and his countenance was expressive of courage and resolve.

"Count Cobenzl, I know what are the plans of Austria, and they shall be sustained. Your interests are mine, for it is no longer a question of Austria or Prussia, but of Potemkin or Orloff! You see, therefore, that I am sincere; but Austria must sustain me, and we must tread our political path together."

"Austria will go hand and heart with your highness."

"Austria must sustain me, I say, and our password shall be, 'THE CONQUEST OF TURKEY.' That is the spell by which I rule the czarina. My enemies often fill her mind with distrust of me, but that great project shields me from their weapons. Still I am in danger; for here in Russia, we look neither to the past nor to the future; the excitement of the hour reigns absolute. A good subject never knows how to regulate his conduct. If I were sure of blame for doing evil, or of approbation for doing good, I might know what to expect from the czarina. But when a sovereign is the slave of her passions, all ordinary modes of deducing effect from cause fall to the ground.* I live in a whirlpool, from which I can devise no means of escape; but, by the grave of my mother, this life shall cease! I shall resume my power over the empress, and I shall trample my enemies underfoot, were they to take shelter under the throne itself!"

While Potemkin spoke thus, he clinched his fist, and his herculean arm was raised as if to fell his invisible enemies.

"Whosoever be the foe, Austria will be at your side," said Cobenzl.

"I believe you," replied Potemkin, with returning calmness, "for it is your interest to be there. I know what you desire. First you supplant Prussia with Russia, and that entails a coolness with France, Prussia's dearest friend. Then you also dissolve with France, and we both court the alliance of England, so as to isolate France and Prussia from European politics. The plan is good, and will succeed if you are discreet."

"How discreet?"

"You must weigh well your behavior toward the czarina. I dare not advise the emperor, but let me advise you. You have often occasion to see the empress. Before you see her consult with me as to the topics of your discourse with her, and so we shall always be enabled to act in concert. Avoid all dissimulation; let her perceive that you leave craft to the lovers of Prussia. Flatter as often as you see fit; flatter Catharine, however, not for what she is, but what she ought to be.† Convince her that Austria is willing to further her ambition, not to restrain it, as Prussia has always done. Do this, and in a few months Austria will have changed *rôles* with Prussia, and your enemies and mine shall be overthrown together."

A knock was heard at the door, and an officer entered.

"How dare you interrupt me?" cried Potemkin, stamping his foot.

"Pardon, your highness. The private secretary of the Emperor of Austria has orders from his sovereign to hand a note to Count Cobenzl in your highness's presence."

"A very singular order. But we will gratify the emperor. Admit his majesty's messenger."

Günther was introduced, who bowed low to Potemkin, passed on, and delivered his note.

"From his majesty's hand," said he. "Your excellency is to read it at once. It requires no answer." Then, bowing deeply, the secretary backed out of the room, and the discreet *portière* fell, preventing the transmission of the slightest sound.

"Read," said Potemkin, "for doubtless the emperor has good reason for his haste."

Count Cobenzl broke the seal; but instead of a note for himself, a sealed dispatch within, bore the address of the prince. The count presented it at once, and Potemkin eagerly tore it open. He seemed electrified by its contents; so much so that Cobenzl started forward to his assistance, exclaiming: "Gracious Heaven, what has happened? Your highness is ill!"

* Potemkin's own words. Raumer, vol. v., p. 573.
† Ibid.

"No, no," said Potemkin, "but read this, that I may be sure I do not dream."

Cobenzl took the letter and read:

"'MY DEAR PRINCE: To win your friendship, I have neither flattery, decorations, duchies, princesses, nor promises for the future; convinced as I am that your highness is able to reach the summit of your desires without help from other mortals. But I have something to impart which will prove the sincerity of my intentions toward you. An hour ago, Count Orloff arrived in St. Petersburg, and he is now in secret conference with the czarina.

"'JOSEPH.'"

"I was right; it was not my secret apprehensions which conjured those spectral letters," cried Potemkin; "they are really the writing of the emperor, and Gregory Orloff is here."

He sprang forward like a bull rushing to the attack.

"Gregory Orloff is with Catharine, and I cannot slay him at her feet! But stay," exclaimed he, exultingly, and then his words resolved themselves back into thought. "My key—my key—I will force her to hear me. Count," continued he aloud, "I beg of you to excuse me, for I must go at once to the empress. Tell the emperor that if I weather the storm that is bursting over my head, I will prove to him my eternal gratitude for the service he has rendered me this day. Farewell! Pray for me; or if you like better, go home and get up a fine drama for the day of my burial."

"Nothing less than Voltaire's 'Death of Julius Cæsar' would suit such an occasion; but God forbid that your highness should come to harm! I hasten to do your bidding."

Potemkin, trembling with impatience, stood watching Count Cobenzl, as with his mincing gait he tripped out of the room, and turned again at the door to make his last bow. Scarcely had the *portière* fallen when he sprang across the room, and darted toward his sleeping-chamber. Near his bed stood an *escritoire*. He flung it open and taking thence a casket filled with gold chains, diamonds, and other jewels, he turned out the contents with such violence that they flew over the room in every direction. He found what he sought; it was a little secret compartment. He pressed the spring and it opened, revealing nothing but a key! But Potemkin snatched it up, and, unheeding the treasures worth a million, that lay scattered about the room, he passed into a little dark anteroom, thence into a corridor, up and down staircases, forward, forward, rapidly forward!

Finally he reached the end of a long, narrow corridor. Nothing here was to be seen save a blank, white wall, which separated Potemkin's dwelling from the palace of the czarina. But in the corner of this wall was a scarcely perceptible recess. He pressed it with his finger, when the wall parted, revealing a door—the door which led to Catharine's own private apartments. Potemkin's key unlocked it, and he darted through the opening—on, on, until he reached another door, which also yielded to his key; and then, breathing freely, he looked around the cabinet of the czarina, and exclaimed, "I am saved!"

CHAPTER CXXXVI.

THE EMPRESS CATHARINE.

THE magnificent state-apartments of the empress were silent and empty, for she had given out that she needed solitude to work, she would hold no levee to-day. But she was not alone; she was in a cabinet which led to her bedchamber; and with her was Count Orloff, her former lover and the murderer of her husband.

The empress lay half buried in the depths of a crimson velvet couch; and her large blue eyes were fixed with an expression of tenderness upon Orloff, who sat opposite to her. In spite of her fifty years, Catharine was a very handsome woman. Age had respected her fair, imperial brow, and the fingers of time had relented as they passed over it. Her eyes were as bright and beautiful as ever; her lips as red, and their smile as fascinating, as in the days of her youth; and in her bosom beat the passionate, craving, restless heart of a maiden of seventeen. This heart was as capable of love as of hate; and her graceful person as fitted to inspire love as it had ever been. Just now Catharine was anxious to please. She thought over the golden hours of her youthful passion, and tried to win a smile from Orloff's stern face. She forgot in him the man who had placed a bloody crown upon her head, she saw but the paramour who had wreathed her brow with the myrtles and roses of requited love.

They had spoken of indifferent things, but Catharine had grown silent, and the silence was becoming embarrassing to Orloff.

"Your majesty commanded my presence," began he.

Catharine raised her beautiful white arm from the cushion where it lay, and motioned him to approach.

"Hush, Orloff," said she, in a low voice. "No one hears us, do not call me majesty."

"My revered sovereign," stammered Orloff, "I—"

"Sovereign! Do I look as if I were your sovereign, Orloff? No, no, I am here as the woman who is not ashamed of the love we once cherished for each other. The world says that I am not pious, and verily I believe that Voltaire has corrupted me; but I have one steadfast faith, and I cling to it as fanatics do to Christianity. My religion is the religion of memory, Gregory; and you were its first hierophant."

Orloff muttered some unintelligible words; for truth to tell, he did not quite comprehend the vagaries of his imperial mistress. He was a man of deeds, fit for action and strife; but there was neither imagination nor poetry in his nature. He saw, however, that Catharine smiled and beckoned. He hastened forward, and bending the knee, kissed her hand.

"Gregory," said she, tenderly, "I sent for you to talk of the prospects of your son."

"Your majesty speaks of Basil Bobinsky?" asked Orloff, with a smile.

"Yes," replied Catharine, "of your son, or rather, if you prefer it, of *our* son."

"Your majesty acknowledges him, and yet you have thrust his father from your heart. You sacrificed me to a man whom I hate—not because he is my successful rival, but because he does not deserve the love of my empress; because he is a heartless spendthrift, and a wretch who is ready to sell his sovereign's honor at any moment, provided the price offered him be worth the treachery. Oh! it maddens me when I think that Gregory Orloff was displaced for a Potemkin!"

Catharine laid her jewelled hand upon Orloff's lips. "Hush, Orloff, do not vituperate. I have called for you to-day to give me peace. I do not wish the two men who share my heart to stand forever glaring at each other in implacable hatred. I wish to unite you through the sweet influences of a young couple's love. I beseech you, Gregory, do not refuse me the boon I crave. Give your consent for Basil to marry the Countess Alexandra, Potemkin's niece."

"Never!" thundered Orloff, starting to his feet, and retreating like an animal at bay. "Never will I consent for my bastard to marry the wench of such a contemptible fool as Potemkin!" *

Catharine rose from her couch with a look of tender reproach. "You will not grant my heart's dearest wish?" said she.

"I cannot do it, Catharine," cried Orloff, wildly. "My blood boils at the very thought of being connected to Potemkin. No, indeed! No tie shall ever bind me to him, that hinders my hand, should you one day ask of me, to sever his head from his body."

Catharine again put her hand before Orloff's mouth. "Hush, you fulminating Jove!" said she. "Must you be forever forging thunderbolts, or waging war with Titans? But you know too well that in your godlike moods you are irresistible. What a triumph it is to win a boon from such a man! Invest me with this glory, Orloff; and I give up my plan for a marriage between Basil and Potemkin's niece."

"Niece," echoed Orloff, "say his mistress!"

"Not so," exclaimed Catharine. "So treacherous, I will not believe Potemkin to be!"

"Nevertheless, Alexandra is his mistress, and the whole court knows it."

"If I find it so, Potemkin shall feel the weight of my vengeance, and nothing shall save him!" cried Catharine, her eyes darting fire. "But I tell you it is not so. He has his faults, but this is not one of them."

"Then you confess that the great Potemkin *has* faults, do you?"

"It was precisely because of his faults that I sent for you!"

"*Me!*"

"You—Gregory Orloff, the truest of the true! You have done me good service in your life; to you I am indebted for my crown, and you are its brightest jewel. But I have a favor now to ask of you which concerns my happiness more than any thing you have ever done for me before, my Gregory."

"Speak, my empress, speak, and I will die to serve you;" replied Orloff, inspired by Catharine's earnestness.

She laid her white hand upon his shoulder, and said in her most enticing tones: "Be the friend of Potemkin. Let him learn by your example to be more careful of the great trusts which he holds from me; more conciliating, and more grateful. For, indeed, in return for all the favors I bestow upon him, he makes my life one long martyrdom. For God's sake, Orloff, be friendly with Potemkin, and try to rescue me from the tempests which daily and hourly

* Orloff's own words. Raumer's Contributions, etc., vol. v., p. 412.

burst over my devoted head."* She leaned her head upon his bosom, and looked imploringly into his face.

"Your majesty," said Orloff, warmly, "you know that I am your slave. If Potemkin is obnoxious to you, speak the word, and I annihilate him. But my reputation will not permit me to consort with a man whom I despise, and whom I should be forced, nevertheless, to regard as the first subject of the empire. Pardon me if I cannot grant your majesty's petition."

"Go, then, cruel man, and leave me to my fate," said Catharine in tears.

"Since your majesty desires it, I retire." And Orloff bowing, turned to leave the room, but Catharine threw herself upon the sofa with a sob and he returned.

"Do you weep for Potemkin?" said he. "Spare your tears. He loves no one but himself, and his only aim in life is to enervate and weaken *your* mind, that he may reign in your stead."

"Oh, Orloff, be merciful!" said Catharine, clasping her hands.

But Orloff continued: "Potemkin has essentially damaged your fleet; he has ruined your army; and what is worse, he has lowered you in the estimation of your subjects, and of the world. If you are willing to be rid of so dangerous a man, my life is at your disposal; but if you must temporize with him, I can do nothing to further measures which are to be carried out by flattery and hypocrisy."

"I believe you, unhappily I believe you," said Catharine, weeping. "Potemkin deserves all that you say of him, but I have not the heart to punish him as he deserves. I cannot bid you destroy the giant whose shadow darkens my throne. You see, Orloff, that I am a poor, weak woman, and have not the strength to punish the guilty."

"I see that your majesty prizes the oppressor of my country far more than that country's self; and since it is so, I have nothing more to do here. Farewell, Catharine—I must return to Gatzchina."

He kissed the hand of the empress, and passed into the adjoining apartment. He went slowly through the magnificent state-rooms, through which he had to pass to the corridor, and with weeping eyes Catharine followed his tall form from door to door. She would have leaned for support upon that strong man, but he refused to shelter her, and she felt a sense of desolation which seemed to her a presentiment of evil.

"Orloff, Orloff!" cried she, imploringly; and she hastened after him. He was passing out into the corridor, when he heard her voice, and saw her coming fleet as a dove toward him.

"Orloff," said she, panting for breath, "do not leave St. Petersburg to-day. Remain for three days, and, perhaps, in that time I may gather courage to accept your help, and rid myself of this man."

"I will await your majesty's decision," replied Orloff; "and if then my sword is not required in your service, I shall leave St. Petersburg forever."

He bowed, and the heavy *portière* fell behind him as he passed from the czarina's sight. Slowly she returned to her cabinet, murmuring, "Three days he will wait to know if—"

But suddenly she started, appalled at the sight of an apparition

* Catharine's own words.

that occupied the divan on which she was about to repose her weary limbs. She uttered a wild scream of terror, for on this divan sat—Potemkin.

CHAPTER CXXXVII.

THE CZARINA AND HER MASTER.

WITH flashing eyes, folded arms, and pale, stern, face, sat Potemkin, and his glance seemed about to annihilate the terrified woman, who had neither strength to call for help nor self-possession to greet her unwelcome visitor. He rose, however, and came forward. Catharine trembled and shuddered as he passed her by, locked the door and put the key in his pocket.

The empress looked around, and in deadly fear saw that there was no hope of rescue. She was alone with Potemkin, entirely alone!

Not a word had yet been spoken, but this fearful silence affrighted her more than a tempest of angry words would have done.

At last Potemkin stood directly before her, and spoke. "If Potemkin is obnoxious to you, speak the word, and I annihilate him."

"Oh!" screamed Catharine, "he knows all."

"Yes, I know all—I heard Orloff offer to be my executioner. Pray, why did you not accept the offer at once?"

He had come so near, that Catharine felt his hot breath upon her brow, like the blast from a furnace.

"I ask you again," said he, stamping his foot with fury, "why do you not let the axe of your executioner fall upon my neck? Answer me!"

Catharine was speechless with fright, and Potemkin, exasperated at her silence, raised his clinched hand, and looked so fierce, that the czarina fell backward almost upon her knees, murmuring—

"Potemkin, would you kill me!"

"And if I did," cried he, grinding his teeth, "would death not be the just punishment of your treachery? Your treachery to me, who have given you my heart, my soul, my life, while you—betray and accuse me, not face to face, as would an honorable woman, but behind my back as becomes a coward and a hypocrite! Look at me, and answer my question, I command you!"

Again he raised his hand, and his deep voice rolled like angry thunder in her ear. Catharine, against her will, obeyed his voice, and raised her eyes to his. She saw his lofty brow, like that of an angry demi-god, his dark, dangerous, fiery eyes, his glistening teeth, his magnificent frame, lithe, athletic, and graceful as that of

"The statue that enchants the world,"

and a sensation of shuddering ecstasy flooded her whole being. Forgotten were her fears, her terror, her dream of vengeance; and, regardless of the hand which was still raised to threaten her, she cried out, in tones of mingled love and anguish:

"Oh. Alexandrowitsch, how preter-human is your beauty! You stand, like an avenging god, before me; and I—I can only worship and tremble!"

With faltering steps she approached, and folding her arms around his stalwart form, she laid her head upon his breast, and wept.

"See," murmured she, "I am here to receive the stroke. Let me die by your hand, Gregory Alexandrowitsch, for since you love me no longer, I am weary of life!"

Potemkin heaved a sigh, and freeing himself from Catharine's arms, fell back upon the sofa, buried his face in his hands, and sobbed convulsively.

"Why do you weep, Potemkin?" said Catharine, hastening to his side.

"Why I weep!" exclaimed he. "I weep because of my own crime. Despair had well-nigh made of me a traitor. Why does not this hand wither, which was uplifted to touch the anointed of the Lord! Why does not Heaven smite the wretch whose misery had tempted him to such irreverence of his sovereign!"

And Potemkin flung himself at Catharine's feet, crying out:

"Kill me, Catharine, that I may not go mad for remorse of my treason!"

Catharine smiled, and tried to raise him up.

"No," said she, tenderly, "live, and live for me."

But Potemkin still clung to her feet.

"No, let me lie here as the sinner lies before the altar of the Most High! I am a traitor—but despair has made me criminal. As I stood behind the tapestry, and heard how my empress accused me, I felt that the spectral hand of madness was hovering above my brain. Oh, Catharine, it is you whom I adore, you who have made of me a lunatic!"

Again he buried his face in Catharine's robes, and wept. She, perfectly disarmed, leaned over him, caressing him with her hands, and imploring him to be comforted.

"Let me lie here and weep," continued her Alexandrowitsch, "not for me, but for my Catharine—the star of my life! She, whom my enemies would deceive; that deceiving they might ruin her, when her only friend is lost to her forever!"

"Of whom do you speak?" asked the czarina, frightened.

"I speak of those who hate me, because I will not join them in their treachery toward my empress—of those who hold out to me gold and diamonds, and who hate me because I will not sell my loyalty for pelf. Oh, I was flattered with orders and honors, promises and presents. But I would not listen. What cared I for future security? What mattered it to me that I was to be the victim of Paul's vengeance? I thought of you alone; and more to me was the safety of your crown than that of my worthless life! I was loyal and incorruptible!"

Catharine had listened with distended eyes and lips parted in suspense. When Potemkin named her son, her whole bearing changed. From the love-stricken woman she leaped at once into the magnificent Czarina.

"Potemkin," said she, imperiously, "I command you to rise and answer my questions."

Potemkin rose with the promptness of a well-trained slave, and said, humbly:

"Imperial mistress, speak—and, by the grave of my mother, I will answer truthfully."

"What means your allusion to the Grand Duke Paul? Who are the enemies that sought to corrupt you? What are their aims?"

"The grand duke is weary of his subordinate position, and yearns for the crown which he thinks it is his right to wear."

Catharine's two hands clutched at her head, as though to defend her crown.

"He shall not have it!" she screamed. "He will not dare to raise his impious hands to snatch his mother's rights away!"

"He will find other hands to do it; for you well know, Catharine, that the crime from which we recoil ourselves, we transfer to other hands, while we accept its fruits."

Catharine shuddered, and grew pale.

"Yes, yes," murmured she to herself, "yes, I know it—well I know it, for it has murdered sleep for me!"

"And the grand duke has accomplices, Catharine. Not one, nor two—but half of your subjects mutter within themselves that the crown you wear has been Paul's since his majority. Russia is one grand conspiracy against you, and your enemies have pitched their tents at the foot of your throne. They may well hate the only man who stands between you and destruction. Their arrows have glanced harmlessly from the adamantine shield of his loyalty, and there remained but the alternative of calumniating him to his empress. Oh, Catharine, my angel, beware of Paul, who has never forgotten how his father lost his life! Beware of Orloff, who has never forgiven you for loving me! Both these traitors, with Panin to truckle to them, are in league with Von Görtz to force you into a league destructive of Russian aggrandizement. Oh, my beloved! sun of my eixstence! mount into the heaven of your own greatness, and let not the cloud of intrigue obscure your light. And when safe in the noonday of your splendor, you think of this day, let one warm ray of memory stream upon the grave of the man who died because his empress ceased to love him!"

At the conclusion of his peroration, Potemkin knelt down and passionately kissed the hem of Catharine's robe. Then, springing up, he clasped his hands, and turned away. But the empress darted after him like an enraged lioness, and, catching his arm, gasped:

"What! you would leave me, Alexandrowitsch?"

"Yes—I go to Orloff, to receive my death! The empress has willed it, and she shall find me obedient even unto my latest breath."

"No, Gregory," said Catharine, weeping profusely, "you shall remain to shield me from my enemies."

So saying, she put her arms around his neck, but he drew them away.

"No, Catharine, no! After what I have heard to-day, I do not desire to live. Let me die! let me die!"

"Potemkin," cried she, struggling to detain him, "I shall never, never mistrust you again. And I promise you that Gregory Orloff shall never pass this threshold again."

"How? Do you promise to sacrifice Orloff to me?" cried Potemkin, eagerly, cured in a thrice of his desire for death.

"I do, Gregory, I do. There shall be but one Gregory to reign over my court and my heart, and he shall be Gregory Potemkin!"

"You swear it, Catharine?"

"My imperial word thereupon. Now will you remain and protect me?"

"Yes, I remain, to confound your enemies. It shall not be said that I am flown in the hour when your noble head is endangered. I shall remain for your sake, for the peril is very great, Catharine!"

"Gracious Heaven, Gregory, what danger threatens me?"

"You ask me such a question while Paul lives, and has Orloff and Panin for his accomplices, and Frederick for his friend?"

"Oh, no, dear Gregory, your anxiety leads you into error. I know that Paul hates me, but I do not believe that Prussia is his ally; for it is clearly the interest of Prussia to conciliate me, and he is too wise to entangle himself in such conspiracies just at the expiration of our treaty."

"Oh, you noble, unsuspecting woman!" cried Potemkin, ardently, "you know nothing of the egotism of the world. You believe in the honesty of Frederick, while he speculates upon the consequences of your death!"

The empress grew pale and her eyes flashed with anger. "Prove it to me," said she, imperiously.

Potemkin drew from his bosom the letter he had that morning received from Frederick. Catharine read it, and then said, "Much flattery, and many mysterious promises. What do they mean?"

"Count von Görtz was so good as to explain. The king offered to make me Duke of Courland, to give me a German princess in marriage, and to secure me the favor of your successor."

"That is not possible!" exclaimed Catharine, "those were idle words."

"Oh, no, your majesty, I will prove to you that they are not, as soon as Von Görtz is announced."

The empress looked at the clock, which pointed to two.

"It is exactly the hour I appointed to receive him," said she. "He must be in the anteroom."

"Have I your permission to go to him?"

The empress nodded, and Potemkin, drawing the key from his pocket, unlocked the door and disappeared. Catharine looked after him, and heaving a bitter sigh, said: "No more hope of rescue! He rules over me like irresistible destiny!"

In a few moments Potemkin returned with the paper. Catharine having looked over it, returned it with a smile.

"I thank the King of Prussia for this," said she, gently, "for my last hours will no longer be embittered by anxiety for your safety, Alexandrowitsch. Preserve this paper with care."

Potemkin took it from her hand and tore it to pieces.

"Are you mad?" cried Catharine, "that you tear this promise of protection from Paul?"

"When Catharine dies, I no longer desire to live, and I hope that Paul may release me of life at once—I shall die rejoicing."

"Oh, Gregory," exclaimed Catharine, again moved to tears, "I shall never forget these words! You have sacrificed much for me, and you shall have princely reward; on my word you shall! Let the grand duke be careful to utter no inconsiderate words, for the steppes of Siberia are as accessible to the prince as to the peasant; and every traitor, were he the heir of the crown itself, is amenable to justice before me! And Panin, with his eternal pratings of honesty and frankness, let him, too, beware, for he wavers on the edge of a precipice!"

"And Prussia?" asked Potemkin, with a significant smile.

Catharine smiled in return. "I cannot chide *him*, Potemkin, for he would have befriended *you*."

"And the treaty? Do you intend to renew it with this wise, far-seeing prince?"

"I cannot say. It depends upon the offers he makes. Stay in this room, Gregory; and I will receive Von Görtz in the next one, where you can hear what passes between us."

CHAPTER CXXXVIII.

A DIPLOMATIC DEFEAT.

THE empress entered the small audience-chamber adjoining her cabinet, and ringing a bell, gave orders that Count von Görtz and Count Panin should be admitted. Then she glided to an arm-chair, the only one in the room, and awaited her visitors, who, conformable to the etiquette of the Russian court, bowed three times before the all-powerful czarina. Panin's salutation was that of a serf who is accustomed to kiss the dust from his tyrant's feet; Von Görtz, on the contrary, had the bearing of a man of the world, accustomed to concede homage and to exact it.

"Well, count," said the empress, graciously, "what pleasant news do you bring from Sans-Souci? Has your accomplished sovereign recovered from his indisposition?"

"The king has recovered, and will be overjoyed to learn that your majesty takes so much interest in his health."

"Oh," exclaimed Catharine, "the great Frederick knows how much interest I feel in his life—perhaps as much as he has in my death!"

Count von Görtz looked in astonishment at the smiling face of the empress. "What! Your majesty says that my sovereign has an interest in your majesty's death!"

"Did I say so?" said Catharine, carelessly. "It was a slip of the tongue, my dear count. I should have said *takes*, not *has;* for many people fancy they have what they would like to take. I should have said then, that the king cannot *take* more interest in my death than I do in his life."

"The king, your majesty, is much older than you, and war has added to his years."

"If war adds to our years," replied Catharine, laughing, "then I certainly must be superannuated."

"I trust that the time has arrived when their majesties of Russia and Prussia may sheathe the sword, and enjoy the unspeakable blessings of permanent peace," said Von Görtz, with emphasis.

"Are you of the same mind, Panin?" asked Catharine, quickly.

"I know from my sovereign's noble heart that she would gladly bestow peace upon the world, and I believe that the time has come when that is possible," replied Panin, evasively.

"It is true, we have for the moment no pretext for war. The troubles between the Porte and myself were settled at the last peace convention, and he will take good care not to provoke a renewal of hostilities. We have no reason to apprehend any breach of peace in Poland, and our relations with the other European powers are equally friendly. England, Holland, and France seek our good-will; Prussia is our firm ally; and Austria, by sending her emperor himself, has given the most flattering proof of her consideration for Russia. It would appear that we enter upon an epoch of universal concord."

"And to give stability to this great blessing," replied Von Görtz, "it is the duty of all sovereigns to fuse their separate interests into one great alliance, whose watchword shall be 'Peace!' In presence of those who are bound together by the tie of one common policy, no ambitious enemy will venture to disturb the great international rest."

"I think we are already able to present the scarecrow of such an alliance to covetous princes, for we have a firm ally in Prussia, have we not?" said Catharine, smiling.

"Our treaty was but for eight years, your majesty," interposed Panin, "and the eight years have expired."

"Have they, indeed?" exclaimed Catharine, surprised. "Well—certainly years do fly, and before we have time to think of death, our graves open to receive us. I feel that I am growing old, and the King of Prussia would be wise if he were to direct his new negotiations toward my successor, and make him the partner of his magnanimous schemes for universal peace."

"Your majesty is pleased to jest," said Von Görtz, reverentially. "But to show you how heartily my sovereign desires to cement his friendship with the mighty Empress of Russia, I am empowered by him to make new proposals for a renewal of the eight years' treaty."

"Are you acquainted with these proposals, Panin?" asked Catharine.

"No, your majesty. I only know from Count von Görtz that his proposals are merely preliminary, and not until they obtain your majesty's approbation, will the king present them formally."

"Very well, count, let us hear your preliminaries," said Catharine.

"My sovereign desires nothing so much as a permanent alliance with Russia, which shall give peace to Europe, and deter over-ambitious princes from trenching upon the possessions of other crowns. To secure this end, my sovereign thinks that nothing would be so favorable as an offensive and defensive alliance, with a guaranty of permanent boundary-lines between Russia, Prussia, Poland, and Turkey. Such an alliance, in the opinion of my sovereign, would give durable peace to Western Europe. If the conditions be acceptable to your majesty, my sovereign will make like propositions to Poland and Turkey, and the treaty can be signed at once; for it has been ascertained that France approves, and as for Austria, the very nature of the alliance and its strength will force her to respect the rights of nations, and give up her pretensions to territorial aggrandizement."

The czarina had listened to this harangue with growing displeasure. Her impatience had not escaped the eyes of Panin, and he saw that the scheme would be unsuccessful. He had promised to second the proposals of the Prussian minister, but the stormy brow of the empress was mightier than his promise, and he boldly determined to change his front.

When Count von Görtz ceased, a silence ensued; for the czarina was too incensed to speak. She looked first at the Prussian ambassador, and then at her minister of foreign affairs, who was turning over in his mind what he should say.

"And these are the proposals of the King of Prussia?" cried she, when she found breath to vent her indignation. "Instead of a simple renewal of our mutual obligations, you wish to entangle us into alliances with Turkey! Count Panin, you are my minister. I therefore leave it to you to answer the Prussian ambassador as beseems the dignity and interest of my crown."

She leaned back in her arm-chair, and bent a piercing glance upon the face of her minister. But he bore the test without change of feature, and turning with perfect composure to his ex-confederate, he said:

"As my sovereign has commanded me to deliver her reply, I must express my surprise at the extraordinary preliminaries presented by your excellency. His majesty of Prussia proposes an alliance of Russia with Turkey. The thing is so preposterous that I cannot conceive how so wise a prince as your sovereign could ever have entertained the idea!" *

"Good, Panin!" said Catharine, nodding her head.

Panin, encouraged by the applause, went on: "Peace between Russia and Turkey can never be any thing but an armistice; an alliance with the Porte, therefore, is incompatible either with our policy or with the sentiments of my revered sovereign." †

"In this case," replied Von Görtz, bowing, "my sovereign withdraws the proposal which was merely thrown out as an idea upon which he was desirous of hearing the opinion of his august ally, the empress."

"Then you know my opinion upon this 'idea,' " cried Catharine, rising from her seat, and darting fiery glances at the ambassador. "Count Panin has expressed it distinctly, and I desire you to repeat his words to the King of Prussia. And that the great Frederick may see that I make no secret of my policy, he shall hear it. Know, then, that my last treaty of peace with Turkey was but a hollow truce, whereby I hoped to gain time and strength to carry out the plans which I shall never abandon while I live. The king has guessed them, and therefore he has sent me these unworthy proposals. Russia has not reached the limit of her boundaries; her ambition is co-extensive with the world, and she means to grow and prosper, nor yet be content when Poland bows her neck to the yoke, and the crescent has given place to the Greek cross!"

So saying, the czarina bowed her head, and haughtily left the room. When she raised the *portière*, there sat Potemkin in the fulness of his satisfaction, ready to greet her with his most beaming smiles. Catharine motioned him to follow, and they returned to the cabinet. Once there, the czarina threw herself upon the divan and sighed:

"Shut the door, Potemkin, close the *portière,* for in good sooth I know not whether I am about to laugh or cry. I feel as if I had been hearing a fable in which all my schemes were transformed into card houses, and were blown away by the wind! But indeed I must laugh! The good King of Prussia! Only think, Gregory, an offensive and defensive alliance with Turkey. Is it not enough to make you laugh until you cry?"

"I cannot laugh at such a disregard for the sacred rights of man," replied Potemkin. "This proposal of Prussia is an outrage to the

* Panin's own words. "Dohm's Memoirs," vol. i., pp. 400, 401.
† Panin's own words. "Dohm's Memoirs," vol. i., pp. 400, 401.

faith of the whole Russian nation, and a challenge to you, my noble sovereign, whose bold hand is destined to tear down the symbol of the Moslem, and replace it with that of the Christian!"

"And believe me, dearest friend, I am ever mindful of that destiny," replied Catharine.

"And the treaty between Russia and Prussia—"

"Will not be renewed."

"Check to the king, then," cried Potemkin, "and checkmate will soon follow."

"Yes, the king is old, and would gladly end his days in a myrtle-grove; while I long to continue my flight, higher and higher, till *I* reach the sun. But who will go with me to these dizzy heights of power—"

"His majesty, the Emperor of Austria," said the loud voice of a gentleman in waiting, who knocked at the door of the cabinet.

"The emperor!" exclaimed Catharine. "You know I granted his request to come to me unannounced; but I have given orders to the sentries to send the word forward, nevertheless, so that I always know when he is about to appear."

"Farewell, Catharine," said Potemkin. "The crow must give place to the imperial falcon. Why am I not an emperor, to offer you my hand, and be your only protector?"

"Could I love you more if you were an emperor, Gregory? But, hush! He comes, and as soon as his visit is ended, return to me, for I must see you."

Potemkin kissed her hand again and again, and vanished through the tapestry by a secret door, which led to a small corridor connected with the czarina's private apartments. But instead of crossing this corridor, he turned into a little boudoir, through which the emperor would have to pass and there awaited his appearance. He came, and seeing Potemkin, looked surprised, but bowed with a gracious smile.

Potemkin laid his finger upon his lip, and pointed to the cabinet. "Sire," said he in a whisper, "I have anticipated you. Prussia has received an important check, and the treaty will not be renewed. It rests with your majesty now, to improve the opportunity and supplant the King of Prussia. Be sympathetic and genial with the czarina—*above all things* flatter her ambition, and the game is yours. Depend upon my hearty co-operation."

"A thousand thanks," whispered Joseph in return. Potemkin made a deep and respectful salutation, and left the room. As he closed the door noiselessly behind him, the emperor crossed the threshold of the imperial cabinet.

CHAPTER CXXXIX.

THE CZARINA AND THE KAISER.

When Joseph entered, he found the empress reclining with careless grace upon the divan, perfectly unconscious that he was anywhere within her palace walls. But when she saw him, she sprang up from the cushion on which she lay, and, with protestations of delighted surprise, gave him both her hands. He bent over those soft white hands, and kissed them fervently.

"I come to your majesty because I am anxious and unhappy, and my heart yearned for your presence. I have bad news from Vienna. My mother is ill, and implores me to return home."

"Bad news, indeed!" exclaimed Catharine, sadly. "The noblest and greatest woman that ever adorned a throne is suffering, and you threaten to leave me? But you must not go, now that the barriers which have so long divided Austria from Russia have fallen."

"Your majesty may well speak of barriers," laughed Joseph, "for we were parted by a high Spanish wall, and the King of Prussia walked the ramparts, that we might never get a glimpse at each other. Well! I have leaped the walls, and I consider it the brightest act of my life that I should have journeyed thither to see the greatest sovereign of the age, the woman before whom a world is destined to succumb."

"Do not give me such praise, sire," replied Catharine, with a sigh; "the son of Maria Theresa should not bestow such eulogium upon me. It is the Empress of Austria who unites the wisdom of a lawgiver and the bravery of a warrior with the virtues of a pure and sinless woman! Oh, my friend, I am not of that privileged band who have preserved themselves spotless from the sins of the world! I have bought my imperial destiny with the priceless gem of womanly innocence!—Do not interrupt me—we are alone, and I feel that before no human being can I bow my guilty head with such a sense of just humiliation as before the son of the peerless Empress of Austria!"

"The Empress of Austria is still a woman, reigning through the promptings of her heart, while Catharine wears her crown with the vigor of a man. And who ever thought of requiring from an emperor the primeval innocence of an Arcadian shepherdess? He who would be great must make acquaintance with sin; for obscurity is the condition of innocence. Had you remained innocent, you had never become Catharine the Great. There are, unhappily, so many men who resemble women, that we must render thanks to God for vouchsafing to our age a woman who equals all, and surpasses many men."

"You have initiated a new mode of flattery, sire," said Catharine, blushing with gratification; "but if this is your fashion of praising women, you must be a woman-hater. Is it so?"

"I would worship them if they resembled Catharine; but I have suffered through their failings, and I despise them. You know not how many of my bold schemes and bright hopes have been brought to naught by women! I am no longer the Joseph of earlier days—I have been shorn of my strength by petticoats and cassocks."

"How can you so belie yourself?" said Catharine. "It is but a few months since we had good proof that the ambition of the Emperor Joseph was far from being quenched forever."

"Ah! your majesty would remind me of that ridiculous affair with Bavaria. It was my last Quixotism, the dying struggle of a patriotism which would have made of Germany one powerful and prosperous nation! And it was *you* who opposed me—*you* who, of all the potentates in Europe, are the one who should have understood and sustained me! Believe me, when I say, that had Catharine befriended me there, she would have won the truest knight that ever broke a lance in defence of fair ladye. But, for the sake of a dotard, who is forever trembling lest I rob him of some of his withered bays, the bold Athené of the age forgot her godlike origin and mission, and turned away from him whom she should have countenanced and conciliated. Well! It was the error of a noble heart, unsuspicious of fair words. And fair words enough had Frederick for the occasion. To think of such a man as *he*, flaunting the banner of Germany in my face—he who, not many years ago, was under the ban of the empire as an ambitious upstart! He thought to scare me with the rustling of his dead laurel-leaves, and when he found that I laughed at such Chinese warfare, lo! he ran and hid himself under my mother's petticoats; and the two old crowns fell foul of one another, and their palsied old wearers plotted together, until the great war upon which I had staked my fame was juggled into a shower of carnival *confetti!* Oh, you laugh at me, and well may you laugh! I am a fool to waste so much enthusiasm upon such a fool's holiday!"

"No, I do not laugh at you," replied Catharine, laying her arm upon his. "I laugh for joy, to see how lustily you hate. A man who hates fiercely, loves ardently, and my whole heart glows with sympathy for such a being. So, then, you hate him soundly, this King of Prussia?"

"Hate him," cried Joseph, clinching his hand, "ay, indeed, I hate him! He has instigated Germany to oppose me; he wrested Bavaria from me, which was mine by right of twofold inheritance; and I destest him the more that he is so old, so gouty, and so contemptible, that to defeat him now would not add one hair's breadth to my reputation as a general."

"It is true," said Catharine, thoughtfully, "Frederick is growing very old. Nothing remains of the former hero but a dotard, who is incapable of comprehendng the march of events—"

"And, yet, is ambitious to legislate. Oh, Catharine, beware of this old king, who clings to you to support his own tottering royalty, and to obstruct your schemes of conquest. But he will not succeed with you as he has done by me. You have no mother to thrust you aside, while she barters away your rights for a mess of pottage! I see your eagle glance—it turns toward the south, where roll the stormy waves of the Black Sea! I see this fair white hand as it points to mosques of Constantinople, where the crescent is being lowered and the cross is being planted—"

Catharine uttered a cry of ecstasy, and putting her arms around Joseph's neck, she imprinted a kiss upon his brow.

"Oh, I thank you, Joseph!" exclaimed she, enthusiastically. "You have comprehended the ambitious projects which, identified as they are with my existence as a sovereign, I never yet have dared to speak above my breath!"

"I have guessed and I approve," said Joseph, earnestly. "Fate has assigned you a mission, and you must fulfil it."

"Oh, my God!" ejaculated Catharine, "I have found a friend who has read my heart."

"And who will aid you, when you call him to your side."

"I accept the offer, and here is my hand. And so, hand in hand, we shall conquer the world. God be praised, there is room enough for us both, and we will divide it between us. Away with all little thrones and their little potentates! Oh, friend, what joy it must be to dwell among the heights of Olympus, and feel that all below is ours! I am intoxicated with the dream! Two thrones—the throne of the Greek and the throne of the Roman emperors; two people so mighty, that they dare not war with one another; while, side by side, their giant swords forever sheathed, they shed peace and happiness upon the farthermost ends of the earth! Will you realize with me this godlike dream?"

"That will I, my august friend, and may God grant us life and opportunity to march on to victory together!"

"To victory," echoed Catharine, "and to the fulfilment of the will of Peter the Great! He enjoined it upon his successors to purge Europe of the infidel, and to open the Black Sea to Christendom. In Stamboul I shall erect the throne of my grandson, Constantine, while in Petersburg, Alexander extends the domains of Russia in Europe and in Asia. You do not know all that I have already done for classic Greece. From his birth, I have destined Constantine to the Greek throne. His nurses, his playfellows, and his very dress are Greek, so that his native tongue is that of his future subjects. Even now, two hundred boys are on their way from Greece, who are to be the future guards of the Emperor Constantine! As the medal which was struck on the day of his birth prefigured his destiny, so shall his surroundings of every kind animate him to its glorious fulfilment. Look—I have already a chart on which Constantine is to study the geography that my hand is to verify for him and for his brother."

The empress had risen and approached her *escritoire*. From a secret drawer within another drawer she took a roll of parchment which, after beckoning to the emperor, she placed upon the table. They unrolled it, and both bent over it with beating hearts.

"Observe first the marginal illustrations," said Catharine. "Here stands the genius of Russia, leaning upon the Russian shield. To the left you see arrows, horses' tails, Turkish banners, and other trophies—here at the top, you see the Black Sea, where a Russian ship is in the act of sinking a Turk.

"Here in the centre, are the empire of Greece and the Archipelago. Take notice of the colors on the map, for they show the boundaries. The yellow is the boundary-line of the Greek empire. It begins in the northwest by Ragusa, takes in Skopia, Sophia Phillippolis and Adrianople as far as the Black Sea. It then descends and includes the Ionian islands, the Archipelago, Mitylene, and Samos. That is the empire of Constantine, whose capital is to be Constantinople. The red lines show the future boundaries of Russia. They pass through Natolia, beginning in the north by Pendavaschi, and end with the Gulf of Syria."

The emperor, who had been following Catharine's jewelled hand with anxious scrutiny, now looked up with a significant smile.

"Your majesty's map reminds me of an incident among my travels. In the beginning of my unhappy regency, I was inspecting the boundaries of my own empire. In Moravia I ascended a steep mountain whence I had a view of the surrounding country. 'To whom belongs the pretty village?' said I. 'To the Jesuits,' was the reply. 'And this tract with the chapels?' 'To the Benedictines.' 'And that abbey?' 'To the Clarissarines.' 'But where then are *my* possessions?' said I."

"And your majesty would put the same question to me," interrupted the czarina. "Look at the colors of the map. We have appropriated the yellow and the red, but there is another color to be accounted for."

"I see a boundary of green, which includes Naples and Sicily," said Joseph, looking down upon the map with new interest.

"Those are the boundary-lines of new Austria," said the empress, with a triumphant smile. "As I hope for the reëstablishment of empire in Greece, so must your majesty accomplish that of Rome. Since you have no objection to give me the Black Sea, I shall make no opposition to the extension of your empire to the shores of the Mediterranean. Italy, like Germany, is a prey to petty princes. Rescue the Italians from their national insignificance, sire, and throw the ægis of your protection over the site of the old Roman empire. Do you not bear the title of King of Rome? Give to that title, meaning and substance. Yours is the south and west, mine is the east, and together we shall govern the world."

Joseph had listened with breathless attention. At first he grew pale, then a flush of triumph suffused his face, and he took the hand of the czarina and drew it to his heart.

"Catharine!" cried he, deeply moved, "from my soul I thank you for this inspiration! Oh, my heart's interpreter, you have read my secret yearnings to be in deed, as well as in word, 'King of Rome!' Yes—I would free Italy from the oppression of the church, and lead her on to greatness that shall rival her glorious past! God is my witness, I would have done as much for Germany; but Germany has rejected me, and I leave her to her fate. For the future I remain Emperor of Austria; and my empire shall be so vast, so prosperous, and so powerful, that Catharine of Russia shall esteem me an ally worthy of the greatest woman of modern times."

"Two faithful allies," exclaimed Catharine—"allies bound by one common policy, whose watchword shall be 'Constantinople and Rome!'"

"Ay," returned Joseph, with a laugh, "though while *you* raise the standard of the cross in Constantinople, *I* shall overturn it in Rome. As soon as my shackles fall, I shall set to work!"

"I see that you have faith in my plans," cried Catharine, joyfully.

"Such faith that I would aid them from my heart, were they even to require the coöperation of Frederick." *

"I shall have no coöperation but yours," was the reply. "Besides, I know that you owe a grudge to Turkey."

"I do; for she has taken Belgrade, and I must retake it. The Danube is my birthright, as the Black Sea is yours. I give up Germany, to concentrate my forces upon Turkey and Italy."

"Let us await the proper time, and when I see it, I shall call upon you to come with me and crush the intrusive Moslem."

"Look upon me as your general, and upon my army as yours," replied Joseph, kissing the hand which the czarina extended. "And now," continued he, "I must say farewell, and I fear it is for a long separation."

"Indeed!" cried Catharine. "Must I lose you so soon?"

"My mother is sick, and yearns for my presence," said Joseph. "The emperor parted from her in displeasure; but the son must not slight the call of a mother, who perchance is on her death-bed. I start for Vienna to-day; and before I leave, at the risk of being ac-

* Raumer. Contributions, etc., vol. v., p. 444.

cused of flattery, I must express to your majesty the admiration, respect and love which I feel for the noblest woman I have ever known."*

The empress, overcome, put her arms around Joseph's neck, and folded him to her heart.

"Oh, were you my son!" whispered she, "I might thank Heaven for the gift of a noble child who was soul of my soul! Were you mine, I should not be the victim of courtiers' intrigues, but with my proud arm within yours, I might defy the world."

As she spoke these words, Catharine raised the emperor's hand to her lips.

Joseph uttered a cry, and sinking on his knees, kissed the hem of her robe. Then rising, as if reluctant to break the solemnity of their parting by a sound, he turned and left the room.

Catharine looked after him with tearful eyes. "O God, he has left me! I have found a noble heart, only to grieve that it can never be mine. I am alone, alone! It is so dreadful to be—"

Suddenly she ceased, for a deep, melodious voice began to sing. Catharine knew that the voice was Potemkin's, and that he was calling her to the secret apartments which she had fitted up for her lover.

The song awakened bitter memories. Potemkin had written it in former years, and she had shed tears of emotion when she heard it—tears which at that time were as precious to him as were his finest diamonds to-day.

The music ceased, and two tears which had gathered in the czarina's eyes stole down her cheeks. As if drawn by an invisible hand, she crossed the room, and, stooping down, pressed a tiny golden button which was fastened to the floor. A whirr was heard, the floor opened and revealed a winding staircase which led from her cabinet to the room of her favorite.

As her foot touched the first step, she raised her eyes with a look of despair to heaven, and her trembling lips murmured these words, "Catharine once more in chains!"

*The emperor's own words. Raumer, vol. v., p. 552.

THE REIGN OF JOSEPH.

CHAPTER CXL.

THE OATH.

MARIA THERESA was no more. On the 29th day of November, of the year 1780, she went to rejoin her much-loved "Franz"—him to whom her last words on earth were addressed. In her dying moments, her pale countenance illuminated by joy, the empress would have arisen from the arm-chair in which she sat awaiting her release. The emperor, who had devoted himself to her with all the tenderness of which his nature was capable, held her back. "Whither would your majesty go?" asked he, terrified.

Maria Theresa opened her arms, exclaiming, "To thee, to thee, I come!" Her head fell back, and her dying lips were parted once more. Her son bent his head to catch the fluttering words, "Franz, my Franz—"

Maria Theresa was no more! The tolling of bells, and the roll of the muffled drum, announced to Vienna that the body of their beloved empress was being laid in the vault of the Capuchins, and that after so many years of parting, she rested once more by the side of the emperor.

The iron doors of the crypts were closed, and the thousands and tens of thousands who had followed the empress to her grave, had returned to their saddened homes. The emperor, too, followed by his confidants Lacy and Rosenberg, had retired to his cabinet. His face was inexpressibly sad, and he paced his room with folded arms, utterly forgetful of his friends, whom nevertheless he had requested to follow him, and who, both in the embrasure of a window, were silently awaiting the awakening of the emperor from his dumb grief.

At last he remembered their presence. Directing his steps toward the window he stood before them, and looked anxiously first at one, then at the other.

"Was I an undutiful son?" asked he, in a faltering voice. "I implore you, my friends, make me no courtier's reply, but speak the plain, unvarnished truth, and tell me whether I was an ungrateful son to my noble mother. Lacy, by the memory of your own mother, be honest."

"By the memory of my mother, sire," said Lacy, solemnly, "no! You bore the burden of your filial duty with exemplary patience, and bowed your will to the will of your mother, even when you knew that she erred in judgment."

"And you, Rosenberg?" asked Joseph, with a sad smile.

"My opinion, sire, is that you were a noble, all-enduring son, whose heart was not hardened against his mother, although from your childhood it had provocation to become so. Your majesty bore with more than any other man would have done whose lips had not been locked by filial tenderness."

"I was silent but resentful," said Joseph, mournfully. "I bore my burdens ungraciously, and Maria Theresa was aware of it. I have often been angered by her, but she has often wept for my sake. Oh, those tears disturb my conscience."

"Your majesty should remember that the empress forgave and forgot all the dissensions of by-gone years, and that in her last illness she expressed herself supremely happy in your majesty's care and tenderness."

"You should remember also, that with the sagacity which is often vouchsafed to the dying, Maria Theresa confessed that she had unwillingly darkened your majesty's life by her exactions, and in the magnanimity of her regret asked your forgiveness."

"I have said all this to myself," replied Joseph, "I have repeated it over and over in these wretched, sleepless nights; but still the dagger of remorse is in my heart, and now I would gladly give years of my life, if my mother were living, that I might redeem the past by cheerful submission to her every wish."

"Let the great empress rest in peace!" exclaimed Lacy. "She was weary of life, and died with more than willingness. Your majesty must cherish *your* life, mindful of the vast inheritance which your mother has left you."

"You are right, Lacy," cried Joseph, warmly. "It is a noble inheritance, and I swear to you both to cherish it, not for my own sake, but for the sake of the millions of human beings of whose destinies I shall be the arbiter. I swear to be a good sovereign to my people. By the tears which my mother has shed for me, I will dry the tears of the unfortunate, and the blessing she left me with her dying breath, I shall bestow upon the Austrians whom she loved so well. If I should ever forget this vow, you are here to remind me of it. And now that my reign begins, I exact of you both a proof of your loyalty."

"Speak, sire," said Lacy, with a bright and affectionate smile.

"Put me to the test," cried Rosenberg, "and I shall not flinch."

The emperor laid his hands upon the shoulders of his friends, and looked at them with unmistakable affection. "Happy is the man who possesses two such friends. But hear what I exact of you. I stand upon the threshold of a new order of things. I am at last an emperor, free to carry out the designs which for so many long years I have been forced to stifle in my sorrowing heart. I am resolved to enlighten and to elevate my subjects. But if in my zeal to do well, I should lack discretion, it is for you to check and warn me. And if I heed not your warnings, you shall persist, even if your persistence becomes offensive. Will you promise me to do so, dear friends?"

"We promise," said both with one breath.

"God and the emperor have heard the promise. Give me your honest hands, my best and truest friends. You, at least, I shall never doubt; I feel that your friendship will be mine until the day of my death!"

"Your majesty is the youngest of us three," said Lacy, "and you speak as if we would outlive you."

"Age is not reckoned by years," replied the emperor, wearily, "but by wounds; and if I count the scars that disappointment has left upon my heart, you will find that I have lived longer than either of you. Promise, then, to be with me to the last, and to close my eyes for me."

"Your wife and children will do that for you, sire," said Rosenberg.

"I will never marry again. My nephew Francis shall be my heir, and I shall consider him as my son. The Empress of Russia has consented to give him her adopted daughter in marriage, and I trust that Francis may be happier in wedlock than his unfortunate uncle. My heart is no longer susceptible of love."

"And yet it beats with such yearning love toward mankind!" exclaimed Rosenberg.

"Yes—my heart belongs to my people, and there is nothing left of it for woman. For my subjects alone I shall live. Their souls shall be free from the shackles of the church, and they shall no longer be led like children by the hands of priests or prelates! You have tranquillized my conscience, and I have received your vow of fidelity till death. With two such mentors to advise me, I may hope, at last, to do something for fame!"

CHAPTER CXLI.

PRINCE KAUNITZ.

For three days Prince Kaunitz had not left his cabinet. No one was allowed to approach him, except the servant who brought the meals, which the prince sent away almost untouched. His household were sorely troubled at this, for no one had as yet ventured to communicate the tidings of the empress's death. Still he seemed to know it, for precisely on the day of her demise, Kaunitz had retired to his cabinet, whence he had not emerged since.

To-day the tolling of bells and the dull sound of muffled drums had doubtless revealed to him that the funeral was at hand. Still he had questioned nobody, and sat in stupid silence, apparently unmindful of the tumult without. Even when the procession passed his own house, he remained rigidly in his chair, his large eyes glaring vacantly at the wall opposite.

Baron Binder, who had noiselessly entered the room, and had been watching the prince, saw two large tears rolling slowly down his face, and the sight of these tears emboldened him to approach the solitary mourner.

When he saw Binder, his lips quivered slightly, but he made no other sign. Binder laid his hand upon the shoulder of the prince, and felt a start.

"Take compassion upon us who love you," said he, in a low, trembling voice. "Tell us what it is that grieves you, dear friend."

"Nothing," replied Kaunitz.

"This is the first time that I have ever known your highness to speak an untruth," cried Binder, boldly. "Something grieves you; if not—why those blanched cheeks, those haggard eyes, and the tears that even now are falling upon your hands?"

Prince Kaunitz moved uneasily, and slowly turned his head.

"Who gave you the right to criticise my behavior?" asked he, in a freezing tone of displeasure. "Does it become such as you to measure or comprehend the sufferings of a great mind? If it pleases you to parade your troubles, go out and ask sympathy of the contemptible world, but leave to me the freedom of sorrowing alone! My grief is self-sustaining. It needs no prop and no consolation. Attend to your affairs of state, and go hence. I wish no spies upon my actions."

"Ah!" said Binder, tenderly, "'tis not my eyes that have acted the spies, but my heart, and—"

"Baron Binder," interrupted Kaunitz, "you are not under this roof to dissect my sentiments, or to confide to me your own; you are here to assist me as a statesman. Go, therefore, and confine your efforts to the business of your office."

Binder heaved a sigh, and obeyed. It was useless to offer sympathy when it provoked such stinging resentment.

The state *referendarius* had scarcely reached his study, before the folding-doors of Prince Kaunitz's entrance-rooms were flung wide open, and the valet in attendance announced—

"His majesty the emperor."

A shudder was perceptible through the frame of the prince, and he clutched at the arms of the chair in an attempt to rise.

"Do not rise," said Joseph, coming forward; "I have intruded myself upon you without ceremony, and you must receive me in like manner."

Kaunitz sank back, and inclined his head. He had not the power to make a reply. Joseph then motioned to the valet to withdraw, and drew a chair to the prince's side.

There was a short silence, and the emperor began: "I bring you greetings from my mother."

Kaunitz turned and gazed at the emperor with a look of indescribable anguish. "Her last greeting," said he, almost inaudibly.

"You know it, then? Who has been bold enough to break this sad intelligence to you?"

"No one, your majesty. For three days I have received no bulletins. When they ceased, I knew that—Maria Theresa was no more."

"Since you know it, then, my friend, I am relieved from a painful task. Yes, I bring you the last greetings of a sovereign who loved you well."

A sigh, which was rather a sob, indicative of the inner throes that were racking the statesman's whole being, burst from his heart. His head fell upon his breast, and his whole body trembled. Joseph comprehended the immensity of his grief, and made no ineffectual attempt to quell it.

"I know," said he, "that you grieve, not only for her children, but for Austria."

"I grieve for you—I grieve for Austria—and, oh! I grieve for myself," murmured Kaunitz.

"You have been a faithful friend to my mother," continued Joseph, "and the empress remembered it to her latest hour. She bade me remind you of the day on which you dedicated your life to Austria's welfare. She told me to say to you that the departure of your empress had not released you. It had increased your responsibilities, and she expected of you to be to her son what you have ever been to her, a wise counsellor and a cherished friend. Do you accept the charge and transfer the rich boon of your services to me?"

The prince opened his lips, but not a sound came forth. For the

THE EMPEROR JOSEPH II AND HIS GENERAL OFFICERS.

From an engraving published in 1780 by Fielding & Walker, London.

second time an expression of agony fluttered over his face, and no longer able to control his feelings, he burst into tears. The sight so moved the emperor, that he, too, shed tears abundantly.

Kaunitz gradually recovered himself. With an impatient movement he dashed away the last tears that had gathered in his eyes, and dried his moist cheeks with his delicate cambric handkerchief. He was himself again.

"Pardon me, your majesty," said he, respectfully inclining his head. "You see how grief has mastered me. I have behaved like a child who is learning his first difficult lesson of self-control. Forgive this momentary weakness, and I promise that you shall never see me so overwhelmed as long as I live."

The emperor, with an affectionate smile, pressed the old statesman's hand. "I have nothing to forgive, dear prince. I have to thank you for permitting me to view the penetralia of a great man's heart. And still more have I to thank you for the sincerity with which you have loved Maria Theresa. I accept it as a pledge of your obedience to her last wishes. May I not?"

Kaunitz looked up, and answered with firmness, "Sire, this is the hour of unreserve, and I will speak the unvarnished truth. I have been expecting the last greeting of my empress, and had I not received her command to serve your majesty, I should have known that Austria had need of me no more, and ere long I would have followed my peerless mistress to the grave."

"How! you would have laid violent hands upon your life?"

"Oh, no, sire—I would simply have starved to death; for I never could have tasted food again, had I once obtained the conviction that I had become superannuated and useless. Your majesty has saved my life, for I have eaten nothing since she—went; and, now, since I must still live for Austria, let me implore you to forget what you have seen of me to-day. If I have ever served Austria, it has been in virtue of the mask which I have always worn over my heart and features. Let me resume it then, to wear it for life. Had we worn our political mask a little longer, Frederick would not have foiled us in our Bavarian projects. We must beware of him, old though he be, for he is a shrewd, far-seeing diplomatist."

"Oh, I do not fear his prying propensities!" cried Joseph. "Let him watch our proceedings—and much good may it do him. He will see a new order of things in Austria. Will you stand by me, prince, and lend me a helping hand until my stately edifice is complete?"

"Your edifice, above all things, will need to be upon a secure foundation. It must be fast as a mountain, behind which we can intrench ourselves against the stormings of the clergy and the nobility."

The emperor gave a start of joyful surprise. "You have guessed my projects of reform, and I have not yet uttered a word!"

"I had guessed them long ago, sire, I had read them more than once upon your countenance when priests and nobles were by; and I triumphed in secret, as I thought of the day that was to come, when you would be the sole arbiter of their destinies."

"The day has come! it has come!" exclaimed Joseph, exultingly. "Now shall begin the struggle in church and convent, in palace and castle; and we shall shake off ambitious prelates and princes as the lion does the insect that settles upon his mane!"

"Let the lion beware, for the insect bears a sting, and the sting bears poison!"

"We shall rob it of its sting before we rob it of its treasures. And whence comes the sting of these troublesome gnats? It resides in the *riches of the church* and the privileges of the nobles. But the noble shall bow his haughty head to my laws, and the church shall yield up her wealth. The lord of the soil shall come down to the level of his serf, and by the eternal heavens above me, the priest shall be made as homeless as Christ and His apostles!"

"If your majesty can compass this, your people will adore you as a second Messiah."

"I will do it! I will free my people from bondage, and if I am made to die the death of the cross, I shall exult in my martyrdom," exclaimed Joseph, with flashing eyes. "The internal administration of Austria calls for reform. The empire over which I am to reign must be governed according to my principles. Religious prejudices, fanaticism, and party spirit must disappear, and the influence of the clergy, so cherished by my mother, shall cease now and forever. Monks and nuns shall quit their idle praying, and work like other men and women; and I shall turn the whole fraternity of contemplatives into a body of industrious burghers."*

"Oh, sire," exclaimed Kaunitz, "your words affright me. Bethink you that you throw the brand of revolt among a numerous and influential class."

"We will strip them of their armor, and so they shall become innoxious."

"Gracious Heaven!" ejaculated Kaunitz, "your majesty will—"

"Capture the convents, and carry off the booty."

"But that will be tantamount to a declaration of war against Rome!"

"Exactly what I propose to bring about. I desire to teach this servant of God that I am absolute monarch of my own dominions, and that his—"

"True, sire, true, but be cautious, and go warily to work."

"I have no time to temporize," cried Joseph. "What is to be done shall be done at once. So much the more quickly that this question of stripping the convents is not only one of principle but of expediency also. They abound in objects of value, and my treasury needs replenishing. The state debt is large, and we must retrench. I shall not, like my gracious mother, require a budget of six millions. I intend to restrict myself to the expenditure which suffices for the King of Prussia. Of course, I shall not, like the munificent Maria Theresa, dispense ducats and smiles in equal profusion. My people must be satisfied with a greeting that is not set to the music of the chink of gold. Neither shall I, like my imperial lady-mother, keep two thousand horses in my stables. Moreover, the pension-list shall be decreased—let the retrenchment fall upon whom it may. But all this will not suffice to straighten my financial affairs. I need several millions more. And as they are to be found in church and convent, I shall seek them there."

Prince Kaunitz had listened to this bold harangue with perfect astonishment. Several times in the course of it, he had nodded his head, and more than once he had smiled.

*This whole conversation is historical. The expressions are those of the emperor. See "Letters of Joseph II.," p. 48.

"Sire," said he, "you have such an intrepid spirit that my scarred old heart beats responsive to the call like an aged war-horse that neighs at the trumpet's note. Be it so, then. I will fight at your side like a faithful champion, happy, if, during the strife, I be permitted to ward off from my emperor's head a blow from his adversary's hands. Remember that we go forth to fight thousands. For the people are with the clergy, and they will cry out even more bitterly than they did at the expulsion of the Jesuits."

"And they will cease to cry, as they did on that ocassion," exclaimed the emperor, with a merry laugh. "Courage, Kaunitz, courage! and we shall prevail over Rome and all monkdom; and when we shall have utilized their treasures, the people will return to their senses, and applaud the deed." *

"So be it then, your majesty. I will help you to pluck the poisonous weeds, and sow in their places good secular grain."

CHAPTER CXLII.

THE BANKER AND HIS DAUGHTER.

THE beautiful daughter of the Jewish banker was alone in her apartments, which, from the munificence of her wealthy father, were almost regal in their arrangements.

Rachel, however, was so accustomed to magnificence that she had lost all appreciation of it. She scarcely vouchsafed a glance to her inlaid cabinets, her oriental carpets, her crystal lustres, and her costly paintings. Even her own transcendent beauty, reflected in the large Venetian mirrors that surrounded her, was unheeded, as she reclined in simple muslin among the silken cushions of a Turkish divan.

But Rachel, in her muslin, was lovely beyond all power of language to describe. Her youth, grace, and beauty were ornaments with which "Nature's own cunning hand," had decked her from her birth. What diamond ever lit up Golconda's mine with such living fire as flashed from her hazel eyes? What pearl upon its ocean-bed ever glittered with a sheen like that of the delicate teeth that peeped from between her pouting coral lips? When she wandered in her vapory white dresses through her father's princely halls, neither pictures nor statues there could compare in color or proportion with the banker's queenly daughter herself.

She lay on the dark silk cushions of the divan like a swan upon the opalline waters of the lake at sunset. One arm, white and firm as Carrara marble, supported her graceful head, while in her right hand she held an open letter.

"Oh, my beloved!" murmured she, "you hope every thing from the magnanimity of the emperor. But in what blessed clime was ever a Jewess permitted to wed with a Christian? The emperor may remove the shackles of our national bondage, but he can never lift us to social equality with the people of another faith. There is nothing to bridge the gulf that yawns between my beloved and me. It would kill my father to know that I had renounced Judaism, and I would rather die than be his murderer. Oh, my father! oh,

* Joseph's own words. See Letters, etc., p. 49.

my lover! My heart lies between you, and yet I may not love you both!—But which must I sacrifice to the other?"

She paused and raised her eyes imploringly to heaven. Her cheeks flushed, her bosom heaved, and no longer able to restrain her agitation, she sprang from her divan, and light as a gazelle, crossed the room, and threw open the window.

"No, my lover," said she, "no, I cannot renounce you! A woman must leave father and mother, to follow him who reigns over her heart! I will leave all things, then, for you, my Günther!" And she pressed his letter to her lips; then folding it, she hid it in her bosom.

A knock at the door caused her to start slightly, and, before she had time to speak, the Jewish banker entered the room.

"My dear father!" exclaimed Rachel, joyfully, flying to him and putting her arms around his tall, athletic form.

Eskeles Flies stroked her dark hair, and pressed a kiss upon her brow. "I have not seen you for two days, father," said Rachel, reproachfully.

"I have been absent inspecting my new factories at Brünn, my daughter."

"And you went away without a word of adieu to me!"

"*Adieu* is a sorrowful word, my daughter, and I speak it reluctantly; but a return home is a joy unspeakable, and you see that my first visit is to *you*, dear child. To-day I come as a messenger of good tidings."

Rachel raised her head, and a flush of expectation rose to her face.

"Do the good tidings concern us both?" asked she.

"Not only ourselves, but our whole people. Look at me, Rachel, and tell me wherein I have changed since last we met."

Rachel stepped back and contemplated her father with an affectionate smile. "I see the same tall figure, the same energetic, manly features, the same dear smile, and the same—no, not quite the same dress. You have laid aside the yellow badge of inferiority that the Jew wears upon his arm."

"The emperor has freed us from this humiliation, Rachel. This burden of a thousand years has Joseph lifted from our hearts, and under his reign we are to enjoy the rights of men and Austrians!"

"The emperor is a great and magnanimous prince!" exclaimed Rachel.

"We have been trampled so long under foot," said the banker, scornfully, "that the smallest concession seems magnanimity. But of what avail will be the absence of the badge of shame? It will not change the peculiarity of feature which marks us among men, and betrays us to the Christian's hate."

"May our nation's type be ever written upon our faces!" exclaimed Rachel. "The emperor will protect us from the little persecutions of society."

"He will have little time to think of us, he will have enough to do to protect himself from his own enemies. He has decreed the dispersion of the conventual orders, and as he has refused to yield up the goods of the church, his subjects are becoming alienated from a man who has no regard for the feelings of the pope. Moreover, he has proclaimed universal toleration."

"And has he included us among the enfranchised, dear father?"

"Yes, my child, even we are to be tolerated. We are also to be permitted to rent estates, and to learn trades. Mark me—not to *buy* estates, but to rent them. We are not yet permitted to be landed proprietors.* But they cannot prevent the Jew from accumulating gold—'yellow, shining gold;' and riches are our revenge upon Christendom for the many humiliations we have endured at its pious hands. They have withheld from us titles, orders, and rank, but they cannot withhold money. The finger of the Jew is a magnet, and when he points it, the Christian ducats fly into his hand. Oh, Rachel! I look forward to the day when the Jews shall monopolize the wealth of the world: when they shall be called to the councils of kings and emperors, and furnish to their oppressors the means of reddening the earth with one another's blood! We shall pay them to slaughter one another, Rachel; and that shall be our glorious revenge!"

"My dear, dear father," interposed Rachel, "what has come over you that you should speak such resentful words? Revenge is unworthy of the noble sons of Israel; leave it to the Christian, whose words are love, while his deeds are hate."

"His words to the Jew are as insolent as his deeds are wicked. But I know very well how to exasperate and humble the Christians. I do it by means of my rich dwelling and my costly equipages. I do it by inviting them to come and see how far more sumptuously I live than they. The sight of my luxuries blackens their hearts with envy; but most of all they envy the Jewish banker that his daughter so far outshines in beauty their Gentile women!"

"Dear father," said Rachel, coloring, "you go to extremes in praise, as in blame. You exaggerate the defects of the Christian, and the attractions of your daughter."

Her father drew her graceful head to him, and nestled it upon his breast. "No, my child, no, I do not exaggerate your beauty. It is not I alone, but all Vienna, that is in raptures with your incomparable loveliness."

"Hush, dear father! Would you see me vain and heartless?"

"I would see you appreciate your beauty, and make use of it."

"Make use of it! How?"

"To help your father in his projects of vengeance. You cannot conceive how exultant I am when I see you surrounded by hosts of Christian nobles, all doing homage to your beauty and your father's millions. Encourage them, Rachel, that they may become intoxicated with love, and that on the day when they ask me for my daughter's hand, I may tell them that my daughter is a Jewess, and can never be the wife of a Christian!"

Rachel made no reply; her head still rested on her father's bosom, and he could not see that tears were falling in showers from her eyes. But he felt her sobs, and guessing that something was grieving her, he drew her gently to a seat.

"Dear, dear child," cried he, anxiously, "tell me why you weep."

"I weep because I see that my father loves revenge far more than his only child; and that he is willing to peril her soul by defiling it with wicked coquetry. Now I understand why it is that such a profligate as Count Podstadsky has been suffered to pollute our home by his visits!"

* Ramshorn, "Joseph II.," p. 259.

The banker's face grew bright. "Then, Rachel, you do not love him?" said he, pressing his daughter to his heart.

"Love him!" exclaimed Rachel, with a shudder, "love a man who has neither mind nor heart!"

"And I was so silly as to fear that your heart had strayed from its duty, my child, and that the tears which you are shedding were for him! But I breathe again, and can exult once more in the knowledge of his love for you."

"No, father," said Rachel, "he does not love me. He loves nothing except himself; but he wearies me with his importunities."

"What has he done to you, my daughter?"

"During your absence he came three times to see me. As I denied myself, he had resort to writing, and sent me a note requesting a private interview. Read it for yourself, father. It lies on the table."

The banker read, and his eyes flashed with anger. "Unmannerly wretch!" exclaimed he, "to use such language to my daughter! But all Vienna shall know how we scorn him! Answer his note favorably, Rachel; but let the hour of your interview be at mid-day, for I wish no one to suppose that my daughter receives Christians by stealth."

"I will obey you, father," replied Rachel, with a sigh; "but I would be better satisfied to thrust him, without further ceremony, from the door. I cannot write to him, however, that would be a compromise of my own honor; but I will send him a verbal message by my own faithful old nurse. She knows me too well to suspect me of clandestine intercourse with a wretch like Podstadsky."

"Why not send the girl who delivered his letter?"

"Because I discharged her on the spot for her indiscretion."

"Bravely done, my precious child! You are as wise and as chaste as Israel's beauteous daughters have ever been. I shall reward you for despising the Christian count. But I must go. I must go to double my millions and lay them all at my Rachel's feet."

He kissed his daughter's forehead, and rose from the divan. But as he reached the door he turned carelessly.

"Has the emperor's private secretary visited you of late?"

"He was here yesterday," said Rachel, blushing.

"Did you receive him?"

"Yes, dear father, for you yourself presented him to me."

Eskeles Flies was silent for a while. "And yet," resumed he, "I believe that I was wrong to invite him hither. In your unconscious modesty, you have not perceived, my child, that Günther loves you with all the fervor of a true and honest heart. He may have indulged the thought that I would bestow my daughter upon a poor little imperial secretary, whose brother enjoys the privilege of blacking the emperor's boots. Athough I laugh at this presumption, I pity his infatuation, for he is an excellent young man. Be careful —or rather, receive him no longer. You see, Rachel, that toward an estimable man, I do not encourage coquetry; on the contrary, I plead for poor Günther. He must not be exposed to a disappointment. It is understood, then, that you decline his visits."

He smiled kindly upon his daughter, and left the room.

Rachel looked after him with lips half parted, and face as pale as marble. She stood motionless until the sound of her father's footsteps had died away; then sinking upon her knees, she buried her face in her hands, and cried out in accents of despair:

"Oh, my God! I am to see him no more!"

CHAPTER CXLIII.

THE COUNTESS BAILLOU.

THE beautiful Countess Baillou was about to give a ball. She had invited all the *haut ton* of Vienna, and they had accepted the invitations. And yet the countess had been but four weeks in the Austrian capital; she had no relations there, and none of the aristocracy had ever heard her name before. But she had come to Vienna provided with letters of introduction, and money; and these two keys had opened the saloons of the fashionables to the beautiful stranger.

Her splendid equipage had been seen in the parks, and her magnificent diamonds at the theatre. All the young men of fashion had directed their *lorgnettes* toward her box, admiring not only her extraordinary beauty, but the grace and *abandon* of her attitude, as she leaned back in her velvet arm-chair. She had not long been seated when the door of the box opened, and a young man entered whom the lady greeted with a cordial smile. Every one knew the visitor to be Count Podstadsky-Liechtenstein, the richest, haughtiest, and handsomest cavalier in all Vienna. Podstadsky was the son of a distinguished nobleman, high in the emperor's favor; he had just returned from his travels, and all the Viennese gallants were eager to imitate him in every thing. To see him in the box of the beautiful stranger was to fire the ambition of every man to know her; the more so that the haughty Podstadsky, instead of accepting a seat, was standing in an attitude of profound respect, which he maintained until he took his leave.

Podstadsky, of course, was assailed with questions in relation to the countess. He had known her in Italy as the wife of a wealthy old nobleman to whom her parents had sacrificed her before she was eighteen. She had been sincerely admired in Rome, not only on account of her beauty, but of her wit, goodness, and above all of her admirable behavior toward her repulsive old husband. Her conduct had been so exemplary that she had been called "*La contessa del cuore freddo.*" * Podstadsky confessed that even he had been desperately in love with her, but finding her unapproachable, had left Rome in despair. What then was his delight when, a few moments ago, he had learned from her own lips that she was a widow, and had come to spend a season in Vienna!

The consequence of this recital was that Podstadsky's young acquaintances were clamorous for presentation to *la contessa.* He stepped into her box to inform the lady of their wishes, but soon returned with the unwelcome tidings that the countess would receive no male visitor unless he came in the company of a lady. This, of course, increased the longing of the gallants tenfold, and the next day when her equipage was seen coming in the park, it was followed by many an eager horseman, jealous beyond expression of

* The countess with the cold heart.

Count Podstadsky, who was admitted to the blessed privilege of riding near the lady of their thoughts.

Some days later the young countess left her cards and letters of introduction, and as they were from Orsinis, Colonnas, and other grandees of Rome, her hotel was crowded with elegant equipages, and she was admitted into the charmed circles of the first society in Vienna.

As for the furniture of her hotel, it surpassed anything in the city. Her orders of every kind had been princely. Her sofas and chairs were of embroidered satin; her tables of inlaid wood and *verde antique;* her carpets the richest Persian; her paintings and statuary of rarest value. She had bespoken several services of gold, and jewellers were revelling in her orders for *parures* such as princesses would have been proud to possess.

One quality which the Countess Baillou possessed gave her unbounded popularity with those whom she patronized. Her purchases were all promptly paid in new Austrian bank-notes, and tradesman vied with tradesman as to who should have the privilege of her custom.

Finally, her palace was furnished, and the day of her ball had dawned. Every invitation had been accepted, for the world was curious to see the splendors of her fairy abode, and to behold the fairy emerge from the retreat wherein she had buried herself up to the date of this grand reception.

And now the long suites were lit up, and room after room was one blazing sea of light, gold, crystal, bronze, and marble. Here and there were charming boudoirs, where those who were weary of splendor could retire to converse in the soft, subdued light that was shed upon them from veiled lamps. The whole was closed by magnificent conservatories, where flourished the flowers and fruits of every clime; where tropical birds were seen fluttering among the branches of the orange-trees, or dipping their beaks in the classic basins of the fountains that were gently plashing there.

The countess had just emerged from her dressing-room. Her dress for the evening was of white satin, and the coronal of brilliants which flashed among the braids of her black hair was worthy to be the bridal-diadem of a queen. The Countess Baillou was tall and stately in her beauty; hers was the fascination of the dark-eyed Italian, united to the majesty of a daughter of ancient Rome, and the union was irresistible. Her throat was slender, her head small, and her classic oval face was of a pale, pearly hue, without a tinge of the rose, which, while it lends animation to a woman's face, detracts from the camelia-like purity of genuine patrician beauty.

The countess glided across the room, and throwing back her head took a critical survey of her apartments. They presented a combination of taste with magnificence, and their mistress was satisfied.

She turned to her steward, who was breathlessly awaiting the result of his lady's inspection. "Not bad," said she, in a rich, melodious voice. "I am quite pleased with your labors."

"Will my lady walk through the rooms to see the conservatories?" asked the steward.

"Why so?" replied she, with indifference. "I have no doubt that all is as it should be; I am too weary of splendor to take much interest in it. See, however, that the tables are spread with every luxury that can tempt the palates of my guests."

"I hope your ladyship will be satisfied. The two cooks from Paris profess, the one to have learned his art under the Prince de Soubise, the other to have received his receipts for pastry from the Duke de Richelieu?"

"Let them both do their best," said the countess, languidly, "and remember that expense is to be no obstacle to the carrying out of my orders."

With these words she dismissed the steward, and sank back into the recesses of an arm-chair. But when he had fairly left; and she knew that she was alone, her aspect changed. She rose quickly from the chair, and walked through her rooms, surveying their splendor with visible exultation.

How peerless was her beauty as she swept through those empty rooms, her diamonds reflected from mirror to mirror, her rich dress falling in heavy folds about her form! He who had seen her there would have taken her for the princess who had just awakened from her hundred years' sleep, looking around her palatial solitude to see who it was that had broken the spell of her enchanted trance. Her face was lit up with triumph as she went, and at times, when something of rare value met her eyes, in the ecstasy of her pride she laughed aloud.

Suddenly the stillness was broken by the sound of a man's footstep. The laugh of the countess ceased, and she drew on her mask of indifference. She turned slowly around, and dropped it again—for the intruder was Count Podstadsky.

Just in the midst of the dancing-room, under the blaze of a crystal chandelier, they met. The countess gave him her hand, and he grasped it in his own, looking earnestly at her fair, bewitching face. She returned the glance with her large, flashing eyes, and so they stood for a time together. There was a secret between those two.

The countess spoke first. Her mouth relaxed into a scornful smile. "Count Carl von Podstadsky-Liechtenstein," said she, "you are a man, and yet you tremble."

"Yes, Arabella, I tremble, but not for myself. As I look upon you, in the fulness of your incomparable beauty, my blood freezes with terror, and a voice whispers to me, 'Have mercy on this woman whose beauty is so akin to that of angels! You both stand upon the edge of a precipice: shield her at least from the ruin which threatens you!'"

The countess raised her snowy shoulders. "German sentimentality," said she. "If you mix sentiment with your cards, we shall lose the game, Count Podstadsky. Hear, then, what I have to say to you. It is true that we stand upon the brow of a precipice; but we must contemplate it fearlessly, and so we shall grow accustomed to our danger, and learn to escape it. Why do you wish to rescue me, Carl? I do not wish to be rescued. I like the giddy brink, and look down with defiance into the abyss that blackens the future before me."

"Give me some of your courage," sighed the count. "Let me drink confidence from the depths of your fearless, flashing eyes, my angel."

"Angel!" said Arabella, with a mocking laugh. "If so, call me your fallen angel; for when I took the unfathomable leap which leads from innocence to guilt, your arms were outstretched to receive me. But pshaw! what bootless retrospection! *I* am here, Carl, true as steel; ready to stand or fall at your side. Feel my hand, it is warm—feel my pulse, it beats as evenly as though I had never slept a night out of Eden."

"You are a heroine, Arabella. The magnificence around us affrights my cowardly soul; while you—surely I heard your silvery laugh when I entered this room awhile ago."

"To be sure you did, faint-hearted knight of the card-table! I laughed for joy when I thought of former misery; and compared it with present splendor; the more so, that I am the bold architect who raised the edifice of my own fortune. We need not be grateful to Heaven for our luck, Carl, for we are not in favor with the celestial aristocracy; we have no one to thank for our blessings but ourselves."

"And will have no one to thank but ourselves when ruin overtakes us."

"Possibly," said Arabella, with a shrug. "But remember that we have already been shipwrecked, and have not only saved ourselves, but have brought glorious spoils with us to shore. So away with your misgivings! they do not become the career you have chosen."

"Right, Arabella, right. They do not, indeed! But promise me that I shall always have you at my side to share my fate, whatever it bring forth."

"I promise," said she, raising her starry eyes to his, and clasping with her small, firm hand his cold and clammy fingers. "By the memory of Rome, and the dark-rolling waters of the Tiber, from which you rescued me that night, I promise. And now let us pledge each other in a draught from the depths of the Styx Look around you, Carl, and realize that all this magnificence is ours, and to-night I play the hostess to the proud aristocracy of Vienna. But one question before the curtain rises. How goes the affair with the banker's lovely Rachel?"

"Gloriously! She loves me, for she has consented to receive me day after to-morrow, during her father's absence."

"Go, then, and the blessings of your fallen angel go with you! Play your game cautiously, and let us hear the chink of Herr Eskeles Flies' gold near the rustling of our fragile bank-notes. And now go. Return in half an hour, that I may receive you in presence of our fastidious guests. They might not approve of this *tête-à-tête*, for you are said to be a sad profligate, Carl!"

She kissed her little jewelled hand, and while her Carl disappeared through a secret door on one side of the room, she glided forward with grace and elegance inimitable, to receive the high-born ladies who were just then passing the portals of her princely abode.

CHAPTER CXLIV.

THE EXPULSION OF THE CLARISSERINES.

THE stroke so long apprehended by the church had fallen. Joseph had thrown down the gauntlet, and had dealt his first blow at the chair of St. Peter. This blow was directed toward the chief pastors of the Austrian church—the bishops. Their allegiance, spiritual as well as temporal, was due to the emperor alone, and no order emanating from Rome could take effect without first being submitted for his approval. The bishops were to be reinstated in their ancient rights, and they alone were to grant marriage dispensations and impose penances.

But this was only one step in the new "reformation" of the Emperor Joseph. He dissociated all spiritual communities whatever from connection with foreign superiors, and freed them from all dependence upon them. They were to receive their orders from native bishops alone, and these in their turn were to promulgate no spiritual edict without the approbation and permission of the reigning sovereign of Austria.

These ordinances did away with the influence of the head of the church in Austria, but they did not sufficiently destroy that of the clergy over their flocks. This, too, must be annihilated; and now every thing was ready for the great final blow which was to crush to the earth every vestige of church influence within the dominions of Joseph the Second. This last stroke was the dispersion of the religious communities. Monks and nuns should be forced to work with the people. They were no longer to be permitted to devote their lives to solitary prayer, and every contemplative order was suppressed.

The cry of horror which issued from the convents was echoed throughout the land, from palace to hovel. The people were more indignant—they were terror-stricken; for the emperor was not only an unbeliever himself, he was forcing his people to unbelief. The very existence of religion, said they, was threatened by his tyranny and impiety.

Joseph heard all this and laughed it to scorn. "When the priests cease their howls," said he, "the people, too, will stop, and they will thank me for what I am doing. When they see that the heavens have not fallen because a set of silly nuns are startled from their nests, they will come to their senses, and perceive that I have freed them from a load of religious prejudices."

But the people were not of that opinion. They hated the imperial freethinker who with his brutal hands was thrusting out helpless women from their homes, and was robbing the very altars of their sacred vessels, to convert them into money for his own profane uses.

All this, however, did not prevent the execution of the order for the expulsion of the nuns. In spite of priests and people, the decree was carried out on the 12th of January, of the year 1782. A multitude had assembled before the convent of the Clarisserines whence the sisters were about to be expelled, and where the sacred vessels and vestments appertaining to the altars were to be exposed for sale at auction!

Thousands of men were there, with anxious looks fixed upon the gates of the convent before which the deputies of the emperor, in full uniform, stood awaiting the key which the prioress was about to deliver into their hands. Not far off, the public auctioneers were seated at a table with writing-materials, and around them swarmed a crowd of Jewish tradesmen eagerly awaiting the sale!

"See them," said a priest to the multitude, "see those hungry Jews, hovering like vultures over the treasures of the church! They will drink from the chalice that has held the blood of the Lord, and the pix which has contained his body they will convert into coin! Alas! alas! The emperor, who has enfranchised the Jew, has disfranchised the Christian! Unhappy servants of the Most High! ye are driven from His temple, that usurers and extortioners may buy and sell where once naught was to be heard but praise and worship of Jehovah !"

The people had come nearer to listen, and when the priest ceased, their faces grew dark and sullen, and their low mutterings were heard like the distant murmurings of a coming storm, while many a hand was clinched at the Jews, who were laughing and chattering together, greatly enjoying the scene.

"We will not permit it, father," cried a young burgher, "we will not allow the sacred vessels to be bought and sold !"

"No, we will not allow it," echoed the people.

"You cannot prevent it," replied the priest, "for the emperor is absolute master here. Neither can you prevent the expulsion of the pious Clarisserines from the home which was purchased for them with the funds of the church. Well ! Let us be patient. If the Lord of Heaven and Earth can suffer it, so can we. But see—they come—the victims of an unbelieving sovereign !"

And the priest pointed to the convent-gates through which the procession had begun to pass. At their head came the prioress in the white garb of her order, her head enveloped in a long veil, her face pale and convulsed with suffering, and her hands, which held a golden crucifix, tightly clasped over her breast. Following her in pairs came the nuns, first those who had grown gray in the service of the Lord, then the young ones, and finally the novices.

The people looked with heart-felt sympathy at the long, sad procession which, silent as spectres, wound through the grounds of the home which they were leaving forever.

The imperial commissioners gave the sign to halt, while, their eyes blinded by tears, the people gazed upon the face of the venerable prioress, who, obedient to the emperor's cruel decree, was yielding up the keys and the golden crucifix. She gave her keys with a firm hand ; but when she relinquished the emblem of her office and of her faith, the courage of the poor old woman almost deserted her. She offered it, as the commissioner extended his hand, she shrank involuntarily, and once more pressed the cross to her quivering lips. Then, raising it on high, as if to call upon Heaven to witness the sacrilege, she bowed her head and relinquished it forever.

Perhaps she had hoped for an interposition from Heaven ; but alas ! no sign was given, and the sacrifice was complete.

The priest who had addressed the crowd, advanced to the prioress.

"Whither are you going, my daughter?" said he.

The prioress raised her head, and stared at him with vacant, tearless eyes.

"We must go into the wide, wide world," replied she. "The emperor has forbidden us to serve the Lord."

"The emperor intends you to become useful members of society," said a voice among the crowd. "The emperor intends that you shall cease your everlasting prayers, and turn your useless hands to some account. Instead of living on your knees, he intends to force you to become honest wives and mothers, who shall be of some use to him by bearing children, as you were told to do when your mother Eve was driven from *her* paradise."

Every head was turned in eager curiosity to discover the speaker of these bold words ; but in vain, he could not be identified.

"But how are you going to live?" asked the priest, when the murmurs had ceased.

"The emperor has given us a pension of two hundred ducats," said the prioress, gently.

"But that will not maintain you without—"

"It will maintain honest women who deserve to live," cried the same voice that had spoken before. "Ask the people around you how they live, and whether they have pensions from the crown. And I should like to know whether a lazy nun is any better than a peasant's wife? And if you are afraid of the world, go among the Ursulines who serve the emperor by educating children. The Ursulines are not to be suppressed."

"True," said some among the crowd; "why should they not work as well as we, or why do they not go among the Ursulines and make themselves useful?"

And thus were the sympathies of the people withdrawn from the unhappy nuns. They, meanwhile, went their way, chanting as they walked:

"*Cujus animam gementem, contristanten et dolentem pertransivit gladius.*"

While the Clarisserines were passing from sight, the people, always swayed by the controlling influence of the moment, returned quietly to their homes.

Three men with hats drawn over their brows, pressed through the crowd, and followed the procession at some distance.

"You see," said one of the three, "how a few words were sufficient to turn the tide of the people's sympathies, and to confound that fanatic priest in his attempt to create disturbance."

"Which he would have succeeded in doing but for your majesty—"

"Hush, Lacy, hush! We are laboring men, nothing more."

"Yes," growled Lacy, "and you put us to hard labor, too, when you embarked in this dangerous business. It was a very bold thing to come among this excited multitude."

"I was determined to watch the people, and counteract, if possible, the effect of the sly blackcoats upon my subjects. Was it not well that I was there to rescue them from the miseries of revolt?"

"Yes. I think there was danger at one time that mischief would result from the pious comedy of the prioress."

"To be sure there was," cried the emperor. "But this time I won the field through a few well-directed words. And now let us go and see the show at the two other convents. Perhaps we may come in time to send another well-directed arrow in the midst of the sisterhoods."

CHAPTER CXLV.

COUNT PODSTADSKY'S ESCORT.

"You promise that he shall remain but five minutes in my room, father?" said Rachel.

"I give you my word that he shall stay just long enough for me to complete my preparations to escort him home."

"What mean you, dear father? At least tell me what you intend to do."

"I merely intend a jest, dear child," said Eskeles Flies, laughing. "A jest which shall announce to the people of Vienna that the Jewish banker has no desire to receive the visits of the Christian count. Ah, eleven o'clock! The hour for your interview. Farewell, my daughter, your lover comes."

The banker disappeared through a tapestry-door, and scarcely had he closed it when Count Podstadsky was announced.

Rachel had so unconquerable an aversion to Podstadsky that, instead of going forward to greet him, she actually stepped back and raised her hand as if to ward him off. But the count was not easily repulsed.

"At last, my angel," said he, "my hour of happiness is here—at last you are mine. And I am the happiest of mortals."

"Who tells you that I am yours?" said Rachel, still retreating.

"Yourself, my houri, when you consent to receive me alone. How shall I prove to you the extent of my adoration?"

"Oh, you can easily do that," said Rachel, "by becoming a Jew for the love of me."

At the idea of his becoming a Jew, Podstadsky burst out into a fit of laughter; but Rachel affected not to hear it.

"You know that by becoming a Jew," continued she, "you would be at liberty to marry me, and inherit my father's ducats."

At mention of her father's wealth Podstadsky felt that he had laughed too soon. The thought of the banker's millions made him feel rather grave. They were worth any thing short of such a *lèse noblesse* as apostasy.

"What to me are your father's ducats?" cried he, vehemently. "I love nothing here but his daughter, and my love is sufficient for me. I ask nothing but the priceless treasure of your heart. Come, sweet one, come!"

"Away with you!" cried Rachel, unable to endure his insolence longer. "If I have permitted you to sully the purity of my home with your presence, it was that I might tell you once for all how I despise you! Now, begone, sir."

"And allow me to accompany you home," said a mocking voice behind; and as Podstadsky turned with a start to see whence it came, he met the fiery black eyes of Eskeles Flies, who approached with a tall wax-light in his hand.

The count trembled inwardly, but recovering his self-possession, he asked, with a haughty smile: "Are we in the carnival, and do you represent the Israelitish god of love?"

"Yes, count," said the banker, "and his torch shall light you home, lest you stumble on your way, and fall into the pit of dishonor. Come and receive the ovation prepared for you."

So saying, Eskeles Flies opened the door, and the count looked out with dismay.

The long hall was lined on both sides with the liveried servants of the banker, each holding in his hand a wax-light, whose yellow flame flared to and fro, as the air from the open door below came in fitful puffs up the wide marble staircase.

"Come," said the banker, advancing with his flambeau. Podstadsky hesitated. If his sense of honor was dead, his vanity was not; and it winced at the slightest touch of ridicule. Was there no escape from this absurd escort? He looked around and saw no hope of rescue. Behind him Rachel had locked the door, and the servants were so closely ranged together that it was vain to attempt a passage through that living wall of fire. He had no alternative but to laugh derisively and step into the ranks. The procession moved on, and gathered strength as it moved; for on the staircase, in the lower hall, and at the front of the house, they were joined by throng after throng, each man of which, like the commander-in-chief, was armed with a flambeau. This was bad enough of itself, but the count's body-guard were all in a titter, and every man enjoyed the jest except himself.

By this time they had reached the street, and what was the rage and mortification of the proud Austrian grandee, when he saw that curiosity had drawn thither a concourse of people, who kept up with the procession, wondering what on earth could be the meaning of it! *

"See," cried one, "Herr Eskeles Flies has caught a marten in his hen-roost and is lighting him home."

"And the marten is the fine Count Podstadsky-Liechtenstein," cried another. "I know him. He rejoices in the title of 'woman-killer.' Only look how he sneaks along as the tribe of Israel are dogging him home!"

"The Israelites are escorting him home," jeered the multitude, and the procession moved on, never stopping until it reached the count's own hotel. Once there, Eskeles Flies, in a loud voice, bade him adieu, and requested to know whether he should accompany him farther.

"No," replied Count Podstadsky, trembling with passion, "and you shall answer to me for this outrage. We shall see whether the unbelieving Jew can mock the Christian with impunity!"

"Accuse me before the public tribunals," answered the banker, "and I shall enter *my* complaint against you."

"Indeed!" said Podstadsky, contemptuously. "The Jew will be allowed to accuse an Austrian nobleman, will he?"

"Yes, by the God of Israel, he will," replied Eskeles Flies, so loud that his voice was heard by the people around. "Yes, thanks to the emperor, his subjects before the law are all equal, and Jew and Christian are alike amenable to its judgments. Long live Joseph the Second, the father of his people!"

"Long live the father of his people!" shouted the fickle multitude; and glad that the attention of the crowd had been diverted from himself, Count Podstadsky-Liechtenstein slunk away to ruminate over the mortifying occurrences of the morning.

CHAPTER CXLVI.

THE LAMPOON.

THE emperor, with his confidential secretary, had been at work through the entire night. Day had dawned, and still he wrote on, nor seemed to be conscious of the hour. In his restless zeal, he felt no fatigue, no exhaustion, nor yet any excitement, and not until the last document had been read and signed, did he rise from his chair

* This scene is historical. See "Letters of a French Traveller," vol. i., p. 405. Friedel's "Letters from Vienna," vol. ii., p. 30.

to take a few turns around the room, while Günther was sorting the papers, and placing them in a portfolio.

"Günther," said the emperor, "what is the matter? You look pale and suffering."

Günther raised his head, and smiled. "Nothing, sire, is the matter, but want of rest. A few hours' sleep will restore me."

"Not so, Günther; you belie yourself when you say so, for never in my life have I seen such an indefatigable worker as you. Ah! you look down, so that I know you are not frank with me. Come, have you no confidence in me?"

"Oh, sire, I have the most unbounded confidence in your goodness; but since you force me to speak, I am uneasy about yourself."

"How so, Günther?"

"Because, your majesty strides forward in your projects of reform without the least apprehension of the danger that attends such changes. You rush through the flames without ever dreaming that they may some day consume you."

The emperor shrugged his shoulders. "Always the same song—an echo of Lacy and Rosenberg. I have no time to temporize as you would advise me to do. Who knows how long I shall live to carry out my own free will?"

"Certainly, if your majesty works as you have done of late, your chance for life is not very great. You seem to forget that mind is subordinate to matter—not matter to mind—that physical nature must have her rights, and no man can withstand her exactions. Pardon me these bold words, sire, but if I speak at all, I must speak the truth. You have begun a gigantic edifice, and if you die, it must remain forever incomplete."

"For that very reason, I must complete it myself; for, indeed, Günther, you are right—when I die, I leave no man worthy to succeed to my stupendous undertakings. I shall, therefore, live until I have accomplished them all."

"Then your majesty must work less," exclaimed Günther, warmly. "You do not believe that in pleading for you, sire, I give one thought to myself, for nothing is too laborious for me when I work for my emperor."

Joseph laid his hand softly upon Günther's shoulder. "I believe you, Günther. I esteem you as one of my best friends, and well you know that from you I have no political secrets."

"I would sooner die than betray your majesty, even unwittingly," said Günther, looking with his large, honest eyes into the emperor's face.

"I know it, Günther; but as you enjoy my confidence without reserve, you ought to know that I have too much to do to think of rest. Oh, it would be dreadful for me to die before my structure is complete! Günther, Günther, the priests would transform my fairy palace into a gloomy church; and from its towers, in lieu of the noble clock which is to strike the hour of reformation for my people, would frown the CROSS that is the symbol of the unenlightened past. Oh, let me not hear in my dying moments the crash of the temple I would rear to Truth!"

"Then recreate your mind, sire, with literature or art. It is long since the speaking tones of your violoncello have been heard in the palace."

"Very true, Günther, but I cannot invite the Muses into my

study. A prince has no right to associate with such frivolous ladies, for he is not on earth to pass away time. The King of Prussia heads a royal sect who devote themselves to authorship. The Empress of Russia follows after him with Voltaire in her hand. I cannot emulate their literary greatness. I read to learn, and travel to enlarge my ideas; and I flatter myself that as I encourage men of letters, I do them a greater service than I would, were I to sit at a desk and help them to weave sonnets.* So let us eschew Apollo and his light-footed companions; I aim to be nothing but an imperial statesman. But," continued the emperor, frowning, "I get little sympathy from my subjects. Counsellors, nobles, burghers, priests, all heap obstacle upon obstacle in my path, and the work advances slowly. The revenues, too, are inadequate to the state. The financial affairs of the crown are disordered, and it is only by the strictest economy that I am able to sustain the army. The people call me a miser, because Maria Theresa's prodigality of expenditure forces upon me measures of retrenchment, and necessitates unusual expedients for the raising of funds."

"Which unhappily were extorted from convents and shrines."

"Unhappily! *Happily*, you mean to say. The treasures which were wasted on convent-chapels and shrines, have saved us from bankruptcy; and God will look down with favor upon the sacrifice which dead superstition has made to living love, and will bestow a blessing upon the work of my hands! True, those heroes of darkness, the monks and priests, will cry Anathema! and the earth will be filled with their howls."

"Like that which greeted Alcides, when he stormed the gates of Tartarus," said Günther, smiling.

"You are right. The work is worthy of Alcides, but with the blessing of God it shall be done. Little care I for the wail of nuns or the groans of priests; let them shriek and tear their hair, or, if they like it better, let them vent their spleen in lampoons and caricatures. See, Günther, what a compliment I received yesterday."

And the emperor drew from his *escritoire* a paper which he unfolded. "Look at this. It takes off one of my great crimes. You know I have deprived the court of the privilege of living in the palace, and I have given them wherewith to find lodgings in the city. Here go the ladies with their bundles under their arms, and the lord high-steward has a broom sweeping after them as they go. This charming individual in the corner with a hunting-whip is myself. And here is the pith of the joke. 'Rooms to let here. Inquire of the proprietor on the first floor.' † What do you think of it?"

"Abominable! Inconceivable!" ejaculated Günther. "As unjust as it is stinging."

"It does not sting me. I have a sound hide. When it itches it is cured by scratching.‡ Here is another pasquinade. It was thrown before my horse's feet as I was riding in the park."

"'*Joseph Premier, aimable et charmant: Joseph Seconde, scorpion et tyran.*'"

"How can your majesty laugh at such unparalleled insolence?" cried the indignant secretary.

* The emperor's own words. "Letters of Joseph," p. 57.
† Hubner, i., p. 190.
‡ Joseph's own words.

"No one can deny that I have stung priests and nuns," said Joseph, laughing, "so they are welcome to roar, since their tongues are the only weapons wherewith they may revenge themselves upon their tyrant. As I have proclaimed freedom of speech and press, you see they take advantage of the privilege."

"Well, if your majesty takes so magnanimous a view of these insulting lampoons," said Günther, drawing a paper from his pocket, "I must show you one which yesterday was posted on the wall of the Königskloster."

"So the Königskloster irritates the servants of the lord, does it?" laughed Joseph. "They cannot forgive me for selling it to the banker Flies, to transfigure into a Jewish palace!—Well, let us see the pasquinade!"

"Sire, my tongue refuses to pronounce the words," replied Günther, handing it to the emperor.

"Nay, you must accustom your tongue to pronounce them, for we are likely to have many more of the same sort to read. So go on, and speak out boldly."

The emperor threw himself into an arm-chair, and making himself comfortable, prepared to listen.

The lampoon denounced him as the persecutor of the brides of the Lord, and the enemy of the church. It accused him of having converted a holy temple into the abode of sin, that he might gratify his greed for money.

When Günther had concluded, he cried out impatiently, "This time at least your majesty will show your enemies that forbearance has its limits, and that the liberty of the press shall not degenerate into license."

"By no means. That would look as if I were afraid. I commission you to have the lampoon reprinted and to expose it for sale in the bookstores at six kreutzers a copy, the proceeds to be given to the poor." *

"Oh that your majesty's enemies were here to sink with shame at your feet, and beg your forgiveness!" cried Günther.

"Hush," said Joseph. "Were my enemies to hear you, they would liken me to other princes, who make a parade of their good qualities so that flatterers may immortalize them in laudatory dithyrambics.—But the time for chatting and resting has expired," continued Joseph, rising from his chair. "The labors of the day call me. I must go to receive my petitioners, who must be weary with waiting, for I am a quarter of an hour behind the time."

CHAPTER CXLVII.

THE PETITIONERS.

THE wide corridor in which Joseph was accustomed receive his petitioners was crowded. People of all ages and conditions were there, waiting with trembling impatience the appearance of the emperor, who received the applications of his subjects every day from nine o'clock until twelve. Suddenly a commotion was perceptible among the crowd, and a pressure was felt toward the door which led to the cabinet of the emperor. The ears of those who

* Historical.

have suits to urge are keen; and every one of that motley throng heard the footsteps of him who held their destinies in his hand.

The door opened, and Joseph was before them. At once every hand that held a paper was eagerly stretched forward. The emperor went from one to another, and, while he collected their petitions, entered into friendly converse with the applicants.

The last petitioner was an old man in the garb of a Hungarian peasant. His white hair fell in locks from beneath his wide-brimmed hat of dark brown, and the cloak which was thrown carelessly over his stalwart shoulders was embroidered with shells and silver spangles. His sun-burnt face was free from the Runic characters which the slow finger of Time is apt to trace upon the brow of the human race; and but for the color of his hair, he would have been mistaken for a man in the prime of life.

The emperor was favorably struck with his bearing, and smiled with more than usual benignity.

"Whence come you?" said he.

"From Hungary, sire," replied the peasant, with a smile that revealed two rows of regular, white teeth. "I was one week on my journey; at night the open field my bed, and by day a drink of water more than once my only breakfast."

"You must have had important business in Vienna."

"Yes, sire. I was sent with this petition to your majesty."

"It must be urgent, to have induced you to travel so far."

"Urgent, indeed, sire. I promised the peasants of our district to give it into your majesty's own hand. It has the name of every man in the district; but if I had had time to go around with it, I might have brought with me the name of every peasant in Hungary. It was arranged that I should present the petition this morning, and now, while we stand here, every man, woman, and child at home is praying for my success."

"What can I do for you? Speak, and if possible, I will grant your petition."

"Then, your majesty, read it aloud, that I may say to my brethren, that our cry of distress has reached the imperial ear."

Joseph smiled, and opening the paper, read aloud:

"Compassionate emperor! Four days of hard labor as socmen; the fifth day at the fisheries; the sixth day following our lords in the hunt—the seventh day is the Lord's. Judge, then, whether we are able to pay our taxes."

"Yes, yes," murmured the man to himself, "he cannot say that if we are oppressed, he knows nothing of it."

"I will not say so, my friend," said the emperor, with emotion. "The whole history of your wrongs is written in these few touching lines. I know that you are oppressed, and that, when you sink with exhaustion at your tasks, you are roused with the lash. I know that you are treated like cattle, that you have neither property nor rights, and that agriculture suffers sorely from the obstacles which your masters place in your paths. I know all; and by the God above us, to whom your wives and children are even now at prayer, I swear to free the Hungarian serf from bondage!"

"To free the Hungarian serf!" shouted the peasant. "Do I hear aright? Does your majesty promise freedom to the Hungarian serf?"

"As God hears me, I will free him," replied the emperor, solemnly. "Servitude shall cease, and free socage shall replace villeinage. Your tax-bill shall be revised, and your rights guaranteed by the crown. If, after this, you are oppressed, come confidently to me, and your tyrants shall be punished; for under my reign all men shall be equal before the law."

The peasant sank on his knees and looked up with glistening eyes. "Oh, my lord and emperor," said he, "I had heard of tears of joy, but, until to-day, I knew not what they meant. I have been scourged for refusing to kneel to my lord; but I bend the knee to you, for I feel that you are a mighty sovereign and a merciful father to your people. God bless you for the words by which you have recognized our right to live and to be free!"

He bent down and kissed the emperor's feet; then rising, he said "Farewell, gracious lord of Hungary. I must return home."

"Will you not remain a day or two to see the beauties of Vienna?" asked the emperor.

"No, your majesty. I carry too much joy with me to tarry on my way; and what could I see in Vienna to rival the snow-white mountains that mirror themselves in the blue lakes of Hungary?"

"Then, at least, take this purse to defray your expenses."

"No, your majesty, I cannot take gold to defray the expenses of a holy pilgrimage. Farewell! And may the blessings of a grateful people be echoed for you in heaven!"

The emperor laid his hand upon the peasant's shoulder.

"Tell me the name of my Hungarian friend!"

"My name? It is Horja,* sire."

"Farewell, then, Horja; let me hear from you."

CHAPTER CXLVIII.

THE PETITIONERS.

As the door closed behind Horja, the emperor continued his rounds, but no more petitions were presented. Here and there, however, was heard a request for an audience, which Joseph granted, and then retired to his cabinet, leaving the door open.

"Have the goodness to walk in," said he to the lady, who was in advance of the others. She obeyed, and the emperor, closing the door, took a seat at his *escritoire*.

"Now, madam, I am ready to hear you; but, as there are nine persons to follow, I must request you to be brief. What is your name?"

"I am the widow of the President von Kahlbaum."

"He was a worthy man. Have you any children, madam?"

"Yes, your majesty; I have two daughters and a son."

"Two daughters? I once had a little maiden of my own, but she is dead," said the emperor, sadly. "How can I serve you and your children?"

"Oh, sire, the fearful ordinance by which the pensions from her late majesty's privy-purse were withdrawn, has ruined me. I beseech of you, sire, restore to me my pension extraordinary."

"Are you not aware that the pensions extraordinary are abolished?"

* Unhappy Horja! This sentimental interview cost him his life.

"Yes, sire; but through your majesty's liberality, I hope to retain the pension I held from the empress. The loss of it heightens my grief for the death of my husband, and makes life unendurable. Without it I should have to part with my carriage, with a portion of my household, and live in complete retirement. I am sure that your majesty's own sense of justice will plead for me."

"Justice is the motive power of all my actions, madam," replied the emperor, curtly, "and for that very reason you cannot retain your pension."

"Sire, I am sorely stricken. The merits of my husband—my position—"

"Your husband's merits have earned you the pension you already receive from the crown; and as for your position, that can in no way concern me. I grant that your loss is great; but your special pension will maintain three poor families, and I cannot allow you to receive it longer."

"Alas!" cried the lady, "what are my daughters to do?"

"They can become good house-keepers or governesses, if they have received good educations."

"Impossible, sire. My daughers are of noble birth, and they cannot descend to the humiliation of earning a living."

"Why not? I am sure I earn my living, and earn it by hard work, too. No one is too good to work; and since the aristocracy cannot shield their children from want, it is clear that they cannot free them from the necessity of labor."

"Then, your majesty, have mercy upon my son—the only son of a man of noble extraction."

"What profession has he chosen?"

"He wishes to be an officer in the army; but he was so severely dealt with in his examination, that he has not been able to obtain a commission. Oh, your majesty, I beseech of you, grant him a command in the infantry!"

"Madam," cried the emperor, impatiently, "a man may be the son of a distinguished father without having the slightest claim to serve as an officer. As your son was not able to stand his examination, he must content himself with being the 'son of a man of noble extraction.' Excuse me, but time is limited. I regret to refuse your requests, but justice compels me to do so."

The lady burst into tears, and making her inclination to the emperor, left the room. The latter, following her, said, "Let the next petitioner advance."

This was an old hussar, a captain of cavalry, with lofty bearing and snow-white beard. He came in, making a military salute.

"What can I do for you, my friend?" asked Joseph.

"I come to ask of your majesty not to deprive me of the pension extraordinary which the empress of blessed memory bestowed upon me from her privy purse," said the old soldier, bluntly.

"Oh, another pension extraordinary!" said the emperor, with a laugh. "That cannot be, captain. The privy purse of the empress, which, in the goodness of her heart, was thrown indiscriminately to all who asked for alms, this purse exists no longer. It has a large hole in it, and its contents have all run out."

The old hussar gave a grim look to the emperor, and raised his peruke. Pointing with his finger to three wide, purple scars upon his head, he said:

"Sire, my head is somewhat in the condition of your privy-purse, it has several holes in it. They were made by your majesty's enemies."

"To stop such holes as those is my sacred duty," said Joseph, smiling, "and enough remains yet in the bottom of the privy-purse to satisfy the wants of a brave officer, who has served me to his own prejudice. Forgive my refusal. The petition which you wear on your head is more eloquent than words, and your pension shall be returned to you."

"I thank your majesty," said the captain; and with another stiff salute, he marched out.

The emperor looked after him, laughing heartily.

As he disappeared, a pale, delicate woman came forward, accompanied by several young children, two of which were hiding their heads in her skirt. The group filled up the door like a picture, and the children clung so to the pallid mother that she could not advance a step.

"As you cannot come to me, I will go to you," said the emperor, contemplating them with a benevolent smile. "Give me your petition, madam."

"These are my petitions, your majesty," said the woman pointing to her children. "My husband served for many years in the twelfth regiment, and died of the wounds he received in the Bavarian war. He left me nothing but these orphans."

The emperor looked kindly at the little golden heads that were peeping from among the folds of their mother's dress, and a cloud came over his face. "You grieve for your poverty, poor woman," said he, "and know not how I envy your riches. How many millions would I give if one of those children were mine! Children are a great blessing."

"Yes, sire, when they have fathers to work for them."

"I will be their father," said Joseph, and at the sound of these loving words, the children raised their bashful heads, to steal a look at the speaker. "Come, boys," continued he, offering his hand, "will any of you be soldiers?"

"Yes, yes," replied the two eldest, standing erect and making the military salute.

"That is right. You are brave fellows, and if you behave well, you shall belong to my body-guard.—Come to-morrow," continued he to the mother, "and the lord-chancellor will attend to the maintenance and education of your four eldest. Meanwhile, you shall have a pension for yourself and the youngest. In a few years I will do as much for the little one there. Be punctual in your visit to the chancery. You will be received at ten o'clock."

"God reward your majesty!" faltered the happy mother. "Oh, my children, my dear children, the emperor is the father of the orphan! Reward your gracious sovereign by being good, and pray for him with all your hearts!"

With these words the woman courtesied and withdrew, and the audience for that day was at an end.

"And pray for him with all your hearts," whispered the emperor. "May God hear the petitions of these innocents! Perchance they may weigh against the curses of others. They are the little roses which I sometimes find beneath my crown of thorns. But away with sentiment! I have no time to indulge in heart-reveries. My vocation is to work. Here is a portfolio filled with petitions. Günther must help me to examine them."

He rang the bell, and Günther seated himself and went to work. Meanwhile, the emperor had taken up one of the papers and was reading it. Suddenly he put it down and began to laugh.

"Listen, Günther," said he, "listen to this touching appeal. One of the discharged counsellors orders me to give him a larger pension that he may live in a manner befitting his position. Now hear the conclusion of the petition. 'Our emperor is a poor callow mouse.' " *

"And your majesty can laugh at such insolence!" exclaimed Günther, coloring wih indignation.

"Yes, I do," replied Joseph. "Nothing can be franker and more to the point."

"And I, pardon me, sire, think that the writer of this insolent letter should be severely—"

"Nay," interrupted the emperor. "You would not have me punish him for being man enough to say to my face what thousands say of me behind my back, would you? Now, I am so disinclined to punish him that I intend to increase his pension just because he is an honest, plain-spoken fellow. You need not make such a grimace, Günther. If you feel badly, console yourself with your work."

The emperor seated himself at the table and went on looking over his petitions, occasionally murmuring to himself, "Our emperor is a poor, callow mouse!"

CHAPTER CXLIX.

THE LADY PATRONESS.

THE days of the Countess Baillou glided away in one continued round of pleasure. She was the cynosure of all eyes at concert, ball, or festival. Even women ceased to envy the conquering beauty, and seemed to think it just that all mankind should succumb to her unparalleled attractions. The emperor had shared the common enthusiasm, and, at a ball given by Prince Esterhazy, had danced twice with the countess. Those therefore who, through their rank or station, were ambitious of the emperor's presence at their entertainments, hastened one and all to issue pressing invitations to the enchantress of whom their sovereign had said that she was the most fascinating woman in Vienna.

Count Podstadsky-Liechtenstein was about to give a ball, and the Countess Baillou had consented to receive his guests. It would perhaps have been more natural that the mother of the count should play the hostess on this occasion, but it was known that the old couple were at variance with their only son; and the more lavish he grew in his expenditure, the more penurious became his parents. The avarice of the latter was as well known as the extravagance of the former, and whenever there was a new anecdote current, illustrative of the prodigality of the son, another was related to exemplify the increasing parsimony of the father.

It was no wonder, therefore, that the bewitching countess should

* Hubner, i., p. 199.

have been selected to preside over the ball given by her aristocratic friend. Everybody was delighted. The emperor was to be there, and it was to be the most magnificent entertainment of the season. Long before the hour fixed for the arrival of the guests, the street before the count's palace was thronged with people, eager to obtain a glance at any thing appertaining to the fairy spectacle. While they were peering through the illuminated windows at a wilderness of flowers, mirrors, silk, and velvet, a carriage drawn by four splendid horses came thundering down the street, and drew up before the door of the palace. Two footmen in sky-blue velvet picked out with silver, leaped down to open the door, and in a trice the large portals of the palace were thrown open, and a rich carpet rolled to the carriage-door, while six liveried servants ranged themselves on either side.

And now from the carriage emerged the lady patroness, resplendent in silver gauze, and diamonds that glittered like a constellation just fallen from the heavens. The people, enraptured by the beauty of the countess, gave vent to their admiration without stint. As she reached the top of the marble steps, she turned and smiled upon her worshippers, whereupon they shouted as an audience is apt do at the appearance of a favorite prima donna.

In the midst of this applause, the lady entered the hotel, and until the door closed and shut out the enchanted scene within, the crowd watched her graceful form as it glided along followed by a train of lackeys. Count Podstadsky came forward to meet her with ceremonious courtesy. They entered the gay saloons, but, as if led by one common impulse, both traversed the long suite of apartments in silence, and approached a door which led into a small boudoir evidently not lit up for the occasion. Once within, the door was closed, and the purple velvet *portière* was dropped before it.

"Do not be afraid," said the countess, with a bewitching smile, "we are alone. You are at liberty to congratulate me upon my appearance, for I see by your eyes that you are dying to tell me how beautiful I am."

"Neither eyes nor tongue could give expression to a hundredth part of the rapture which my heart feels at your approach, Arabella," replied Podstadsky, gazing upon her with passionate admiration. "Surely every woman must hate you, and every man be intoxicated by your charms."

"They *are* intoxicated, Carlo," replied she. "They are such fools! To think that they are willing to commit any deed of folly for the sake of a fair face and two bright eyes."

"And you, my angel, are cruel to all, and for me alone has the proud Countess Baillou a heart."

"A heart!" ejaculated the countess, with irony. "Do you believe in hearts, silly Carlo? My dear friend, I at least am without such an inconvenience. If I love any thing it is gold. Its chink to my ear is sweetest harmony, its touch thrills through my whole being."

"How you have changed, Arabella! The time was when your lips murmured words of love and despair, too?"

"Ay, Carlo! But the woman who murmured of love and despair —she who believed in innocence and loyalty, is buried in the Tiber. She whom you rescued thence has received the baptism of shame; and you, Count Podstadsky, were her sponsor. You taught me the art of lying and deceiving, and now you prate to me of a heart!"

"It is because your maddening beauty will not suffer me to forget that mine is still susceptible of love," replied Podstadsky.

The countess laughed, but there was no mirth in her voice. "Podstadsky," said she, throwing back her superb head, "you have about as much heart as a hare, who runs from a rustling leaf, taking it to be the clink of the hunter's rifle."

"And yet, Arabella," replied Podstadsky, with a sickly smile, "I am here, although sometimes I *do* start, and fancy that I hear the hunter's step behind me."

"Hare-like fright," said Arabella, raising her shoulders. "I wonder at you, Carlo, when you look upon what we *are*, and reflect upon what we have *been*. Everybody in Vienna admires and envies us. The highest nobles of the land are our willing guests, and the emperor himself (*dit-on*) has fallen in love with the Countess Baillou. Oh, Carlo! Is it not enough to make all the gods of Olympus laugh?"

"You are right," replied Podstadsky, encouraged. "The emperor's visit here to-night will silence the clamor of my creditors."

"Creditors! What of them? Was there ever a nobleman without creditors! They are one of the appendages of rank. And, then, Carlo—if your creditors annoy you, what prevents you from paying them?"

Podstadsky shuddered. "Do you mean—"

"What is the matter with the man?" asked Arabella, as he paused, and she saw how ghastly he looked. "Of course, I mean you to pay as you have paid before. Pay, and pay promptly. Then when every thing—furniture, plate, jewels, horses, and equipages are ours, we sell out, and realize our fortune in *gold*—(no bank-notes, Carlo)—and, then, we take up our abode in the city of cities—Paris! Gold—gold! There is—"

A light knock was heard at the door. The countess disappeared, and the count put out his head. It was his steward, who announced that a lady, closely veiled, wished to speak with Count Podstadsky on urgent business.

"Show her into the anteroom. The Countess Baillou will do me the favor to receive her."

"My lord," said the steward, "the lady wishes to see you alone."

"Indeed? Then show her in here."

The steward retired, and the count stepped into one of the lighted rooms. The countess came forward, smiling.

"I heard it all," said she playfully, threatening him with her finger. "I am not going to allow you to have a *tête-à-tête* in the dark. No, no, my Jupiter, your mysterious beauty shall be received just here under the light of the chandelier, and I shall watch you both from the boudoir. That will be safer for all parties. I suspect a certain dark-eyed beauty of this stratagem, and I long to see the haughty prude."

"Do you suspect Rachel Eskeles?"

Arabella nodded affirmatively. "Doubtless she comes to implore forgiveness for her father's insolence, and to deny all complicity with the old Jewish dragon. Here she comes, Carlo, but mark me! if I see danger ahead, I come to the rescue."

The countess, like a graceful gazelle, then bounded into the boudoir, while the count advanced to meet the veiled visitor.

CHAPTER CL.

MOTHER AND SON.

WITH the bow and smile of a veritable libertine, Count Podstadsky offered his arm to the lady, whose face was completely hidden by a long black veil. The accommodating steward retired in haste, and the lady, looking around with anxiety, murmured, "Are we alone?"

"Entirely alone, my charming sphinx," replied Podstadsky. "The god of love alone shall hear the secrets which are to fall from your coral lips. But, first, let me remove this envious veil, my mysterious charmer."

The lady stood perfectly still, while Podstadsky, by way of exordium, embraced her affectionately. Neither did she offer any opposition to his daring hands, as first they removed her long mantilla, and then threw back her black crape veil which had so faithfully concealed her features.

When he saw her face, he started back with a cry of remorse.

"My mother, oh, my mother!" exclaimed he, covering his face with his hands.

Behind the *portière* there was the faint sound of a mocking laugh, but neither mother nor son heard it. They heard naught but the insufferable throbs of their own hearts; they saw, each one, naught but the death-like face of the other.

"Yes, it is your unhappy mother—she who once vowed never again to cross your threshold—but maternity is merciful, Carl, and I come hither to pardon and to rescue you, while yet there is time for flight."

The young count made no reply. At the astounding revelation made by the dropping of that black veil, he had retreated in mingled shame and surprise. He had accosted his own mother in the language of libertinism, and he stood gazing upon her with looks of sorrow and regret. He had scarcely heard her speak, so absorbed was he in self-reproach, and now as she ceased, he murmured:

"Is that my mother? *My* mother, with the wrinkled brow and the white hair!"

The countess returned his gaze with a mournful smile. "You have not seen me for two years, Carl, and since then sorrow has transformed me into an old woman. I need not tell you why I have sorrowed. Oh, my child! Whence comes the gold with which this fearful splendor is purchased? Your father—"

"My father!" echoed the count, recalled to self-possession by the word. "What am I to him, who cursed me and forbade me his house! Tell him," cried he, fiercely, "that if I am lost, it is he who shall answer to Heaven for my soul!"

"Peace!" exclaimed the mother, in a tone of authority. "Nor attempt to shift your disgrace upon him who has been, not the cause of your crimes, but their victim. Why did he curse you, reprobate, tell me why?"

The count was so awed by her words and looks that he obeyed almost instinctively.

"Because I had forged," was the whispered reply.

"Yes—forged your father's name for a million, and forced him, for the honor of his house, to sell all that he possessed. We are so poor that we have scarcely the necessaries of life; nevertheless, we have borne in silence the contumely of the world that scorns us as misers. And now, although you have nothing to inherit, we hear of your wealth, the magnificence of your house, of your unbounded expenditure!"

"Yes, mother," replied the count, beginning to recover from his shock, "it is plain that I have discovered a treasure—somewhere."

"Then you will have to explain the nature of your discovery, for your father is about to reveal the state of his affairs to the world."

"If he does that, I am lost!" cried Podstadsky, in tones of despair.

"Ah!" gasped the unhappy mother. "Then we were right in fearing that your wealth was ill-gotten. Oh, Carl, Carl! look into the face of the mother who bore you, and has loved you beyond all things earthly—look into her face, and say whence comes this magnificence."

The count tried to raise his eyes, but he could not meet his mother's glance. Alas! he remembered how often in childhood, after some trifling misconduct, he had looked into those loving eyes, and read forgiveness there!

The mother trembled, and could scarcely support her limbs. She caught at a chair, and leaned upon it for a moment. Then, with faltering steps she approached her son, and raised his head with her own hands. It was a touching scene, and Count Podstadsky himself was not unmoved by its silent eloquence. His heart beat audibly, and his eyes filled with repentant tears.

"Tell me, my child, tell me whence comes your wealth? I will not betray you, for I am your unhappy mother!"

"You can do nothing for me, mother," sobbed the count. "I am lost beyond power of redemption."

"Alas! alas! Then, you are guilty! But, Carl, I will not ask you any questions—only let me save you from public disgrace. Your father is inexorable, but I can save you, my beloved child. I will leave home—country—name—every thing for your sake; even the husband of my life-long love. Come, my son, let us go together where no one shall ever hear your story, and where, with the grace of God, you may repent of your sins and amend."

The strength of her love lent such eloquence to the words of the countess that her son was borne away by the force of her pleadings.

"Oh, my mother! if I could—if I could—" but here his voice faltered, and the tears, which he had been striving to keep back, gushed out in torrents. He covered his face with his hands, and sobbed aloud.

His mother smiled and made a silent thanksgiving to Heaven. "God will accept your tears, my dear prodigal child. Come, ere it be too late. See, I have gold. My family diamonds have yielded enough to maintain us in Switzerland. There, among its solitudes—"

A clear, musical laugh was heard, and the melodious voice of a woman spoke these scornful words:

"Count Podstadsky a peasant! a Swiss peasant! Ha! ha!"

The old countess turned, and saw, coming from the boudoir, a vision of such beauty as dazzled her eyes. The vision came forward, smiling, and, Podstadsky dashing away his tears, passed in one instant from the heights of saving repentance to the unfathomable depths of hopeless obduracy.

The two women, meanwhile, faced each other: the one laughing, triumphant, beautiful, alas, as Circe; the other pale, sorrowful as the guardian angel of the soul which has just been banished from the presence of God forever!

"Pray, Carlo, introduce me to your mother," said Arabella. "You are not yet a Swiss peasant. Pending your metamorphosis, be a little more observant of the conventions and courtesies of high life!"

"She has been eaves-dropping," exclaimed the Countess Podstadsky, contemptuously.

"Yes," said Arabella, with perfect equanimity. "I have enjoyed the privilege of witnessing this charming scene. You, madame, have acted incomparably, but your son has not sustained you. The *rôle* you have given him is inappropriate. To ask of him to play the repentant sinner, is simply ridiculous. Count Podstadsky is a gentleman, and has no taste for idyls."

"Who is this woman?" asked the old countess.

Her son had regained all his self-possession again. He approached Arabella, and, taking her hand, led her directly up to his mother.

"My mother, I beg to present to you the Countess Baillou, the lady-patroness of the ball I give to-night."

The old countess paid no attention to Arabella's deep courtesy. She was too much in earnest to heed her.

"Will you come, Carl? Every moment is precious."

"My dear lady," exclaimed Arabella, "you forget that not only the aristocracy of Vienna, but the emperor himself, is to be your son's guest to-night."

"Do not listen to her, my son," cried the wretched mother. "Her voice is the voice of the evil spirit that would lure you on to destruction. Carl! Carl!" cried she, laying her vigorous grasp upon his arm, "be not so irresolute! Come, and prove yourself to be a man!"

"Ay!" interposed Arabella, "be a man, Carl, and suffer no old woman to come under your own roof and chide you as if you were her naughty boy. What business, pray, is it of this lady's, where you gather your riches? And what to the distinguished Podstadsky are the clamors of two unnatural parents, who have long since lost all claim to his respect?"

"Carl! Carl!" shrieked the mother, "do not heed her. She is an evil spirit. Come with me."

There was a pause. Arabella raised her starry eyes, and fixed them with an expression of passionate love upon the count. That simulated look sealed his fate.

"No, mother, no. Importune me no longer, for I will not leave Vienna. Enough of this tragi-comedy—leave me in peace!"

Arabella flung him a kiss from the tips of her rosy fingers.

"Spoken like a man, at last," said she.

For a while not a word was heard in that gorgeous room, where the chandeliers flung their full red glare upon the group below—the white-haired mother—the recusant son—the beautiful enchantress—whose black art had just sundered them forever.

At length she spoke, that broken-hearted mother, and her voice was hollow as a sound from the grave.

"Thou hast chosen. God would have rescued thee, but thou hast turned away from His merciful warning! Farewell, unhappy one, farewell!"

She wrapped her dark mantle around her, and concealed her face again in the veil.

Her son dared not offer his hand, for evil eyes were upon him, and he allowed her to depart without a word. Slowly she traversed the scene of sinful splendor, her tall, dark figure reflected from mirror to mirror as she went; and before the receding vision of that crushed and despairing mother the lights above seemed to pale, and the gilding of those rich saloons grew dim and spectral.

Farther and farther she went, Podstadsky gazing after her, while Arabella gazed upon him. She reached the last door, and he started as if to follow. His tempter drew him firmly back, and calmed his agitation with her magic smile.

"Stay, beloved," said she, tenderly. "From this hour I shall be mother, mistress, friend—all things to you!"

He clasped her passionately to his heart, sobbing, "I wish for nothing on earth but your love, the love which will follow me even to the scaffold!"

"Pshaw!" exclaimed Arabella, "what an ugly word to whisper to these beautiful rooms! Look here, Carl, the diamonds we own in common are worth half a million. We must do a good business to-night. When the emperor has retired, the hostess will have a right to preside over the faro table, and you know that my cards never betray me."

"I know it, my enchantress," cried Carl, kissing her. "Let us make haste, and grow rich. I would go anywhere with you, were it even to Switzerland."

"But not as a peasant, Carl. First, however, we must have our millions. Now, be reasonable to-night, and don't play the Italian lover. Colonel Szekuly is desperately enamored of me, and he will be sure to sit next to me at the faro-table. The place he covets shall cost him a fortune."

At that moment the steward entered the room.

"A message from the emperor, my lady."

"What can it be?"

"His majesty regrets that he cannot keep his engagement this evening with Count Podstadsky."

"This is a disappointment. What else?" asked the countess, as the servant still stood there.

"Several other excuses, my lady. The two Princesses Lichtenstein, Countess Thun, and Princess Esterhazy also have sent apologies."

"Very well, Duval. Go, for the guests will be coming."

The steward went, and the pair looked at each other in anxious silence. Both were pale, both were frightened.

"What can it mean? What can it mean?" faltered the countess.

"What can it mean?" echoed the count, and he stared, for again he thought that he saw his mother's shadow darkening the splendor of those princely halls, whose lights were flickering as though they were about to be extinguished and leave the guilty accomplices in irretrievable darkness.

"Arabella, something threatens us!" whispered Podstadsky.

"Nonsense! Our guests are arriving," said she, rallying. "Courage, Carl, courage! A smooth brow and bright smile for the aristocratic world, Count Podstadsky!"

The doors opened, and crowds of splendid women, accompanied by their cavaliers, floated in toward the lady patroness, who received them all with bewitching grace, and won all hearts by her affability.

CHAPTER CLI.

THE TWO OATHS.

"ALREADY, beloved? Think that for three long weeks I have not seen you, Günther! It is so early: no one misses me in the house, for my father returns from his bank at nine only. Who knows when we shall meet again?"

"To-morrow, my Rachel, if you will permit me to return, and every morning at this hour, I shall be here behind the grove, waiting for my angel to unlock the gates of Paradise, and admit me to the heaven of her presence."

"I will surely come! Nor storm nor rain shall deter me. Here, in this pavilion, we are secure from curious eyes. God alone, who blesses our love, shall see into our hearts!"

"Oh, Rachel, how I honor and love your energetic soul! When I am with you, I fear nothing. But away from the influence of those angelic eyes, I tremble and grow faint."

"What do you fear, Günther?"

"The pride of riches, Rachel. Your father would laugh me to scorn were he to hear that his peerless daughter is loved by a man without rank or fortune."

"But whose heart has a patent of nobility from God!" exclaimed Rachel, with enthusiasm. "And besides, Günther, are you not a confidential friend of the emperor?"

"Yes," said Günther, bitterly. "The emperor calls me 'friend,' and in 'grateful acknowledgment of my services,' he has raised my salary to three thousand florins. But what is that to your father, who pays twice the amount to his book-keeper! Why are you the daughter of a man whose wealth reflects discredit upon my love!"

"No one who looks into your noble face will suspect the purity of your love, dear Günther. But, alas, my lover! there is an obstacle greater than wealth, to part us—the obstacle of your cruel faith, which does not permit the Christian to wed with the Jew."

"If you were poor, my Rachel, I would try to win you over from the Jewish God of vengeance to the merciful God of the Christian. Would I could bring such an offering to Jesus as that of your pure young heart!"

"My father would die were I to renounce my faith," said Rachel, suddenly growing sad. "But before he died, he would curse me."

"How calmly you speak, and yet your words are the death-warrant of my hopes!" exclaimed Günther, despairingly.

"I speak calmly, because I have long since resolved never to be the wife of another man," replied Rachel. "If I must choose between father and lover, I follow you. If my father drives me from his home, then, Günther, I will come and seek shelter upon your faithful heart."

"And you shall find it there, my own one!—I dare not call you, beloved, but oh! I await with longing the hour of your coming—the hour when, of your own free will, your little hand shall be laid in mine, to journey with me from earth to heaven! Adieu, sweetest. I go, but my soul remains behind."

"And mine goes with you," replied Rachel. He clasped her in his arms, and over and over again imprinted his passionate kisses upon her willing lips.

"To-morrow," whispered she. "Here is the key of the gate. I shall be in the pavilion."

Again he turned to kiss her, and so they parted. Rachel watched his tall, graceful figure until it was hidden by the trees, then she clasped her hands in prayer:

"O God, bless and protect our love! Shelter us from evil, but if it must come, grant me strength to bear it!"

Slowly and thoughtfully she returned to the house. Her heart was so filled with thoughts of her lover, that she did not see the stirring of the blind, through which her father's dark, angry eyes had witnessed their meeting. It was not until she had entered her room that she awakened from her dream of bliss. Its splendor recalled her senses, and with a sob she exclaimed:

"Why am I not a beggar, or a poor Christian child? Any thing—any thing that would make me free to be his wife!—"

She ceased, for she heard her father's voice. Yes, it was indeed he! How came he to be at home so soon? His hand was upon the door, and now he spoke to her.

"Are you up, my daughter? Can I come in?"

Rachel hastened to open the door, and her father entered the room with a bright smile.

"So soon dressed, Rachel! I was afraid that I might have disturbed your slumbers," said he, drawing her to him, and kissing her. "Not only dressed, but dressed so charmingly, that one would suppose the sun were your lover, and had already visited you here. Or, perhaps you expect some of your adoring counts this moning—hey!"

"No, father, I expect no one."

"So much the better, for I have glorious news for you. Do you remember what I promised when you consented to let me punish Count Podstadsky after my own fashion?"

"No, dear father, I do not remember ever to have been bribed to obey your commands."

"Then, I will tell you my news, my glorious news. I have become a *freiherr*."

"You were always a free man, my father; your millions have long ago made you a *freiherr*."

"Bravely spoken, my Jewess," cried Eskeles Flies. "I will reward you by telling you what I have bought for you. A carriage-load of illuminated manuscripts decorated with exquisite miniatures, that you may enrich your library with Christian Bibles and papal bulls of every size and form."

"My dear father, how I thank you for these treasures!"

"Treasures, indeed! They are part of the library of a convent. The emperor has destroyed them as the Vandals once did the treasures of the Goths. I bought them from one of our own people. And that is not all. I have a communion-service and an *ostensorium* for you, whose sculptures are worthy of Benvenuto Cellini. I purchased these also from a Jew, who bought them at one of the great church auctions. Ha, ha! He was going to melt them up—the vessels that Christian priests had blessed and held sacred!"

"That was no disgrace for him, father; but it is far different with the emperor, who has desecrated the things which are esteemed holy in his own church. The emperor is not likely to win the affections of his people by acts like these."

"Pshaw! He wanted gold, and cared very little whence it came," cried Eskeles Flies, with a contemptuous shrug. "His munificent mother having emptied the imperial treasury, the prudent son had to replenish it. True, his method of creating a fund is not the discreetest he could have chosen; for while teaching his people new modes of financiering, he has forgotten that he is also teaching them to pilfer their own gods. What an outcry would be raised in Christendom, if the Jew should plunder his own synagogue. But I tell you, Rachel, that when the lust of riches takes possession of a Christian's heart, it maddens his brain. Not so with the Jew. Were he starving, he would never sell the holy of holies. But the Jew never starves—not he! He lays ducat upon ducat until the glistening heap dazzles the Christian's eyes, and he comes to barter his wares for it. So is it with me. My gold has bought for me the merchandise of nobility."

"Are you really in earnest, father? Have you thought it necessary to add to the dignity of your Jewish birthright the bawble of a baron's title?"

"Why not, Rachel? The honor is salable, and it gives one consideration with the Christian. I have bought the title, and the escutcheon, as I buy a set of jewels for my daughter. Both are intended to dazzle our enemies, and to excite their envy."

"But how came it to pass?" asked Rachel. "How came you to venture such an unheard-of demand? A Jewish baron is an anomaly which the world has never seen."

"For that very reason I demanded it. I had rendered extraordinary services to the emperor. He sent for me to repay me the millions I had lent him without interest; and I took occasion there to speak of my thriving manufactures and my great commercial schemes. 'Ah,' said he, putting his hand affectionately upon my shoulder (for the emperor loves a rich man), 'ah, if I had many such merchant-princes as you, the Black Sea would soon be covered with Austrian ships.' Then he asked what he could do in return for the favor I had done him."

"And you asked for a baron's title!"

"I did. The emperor opened his large eyes, and looked knowingly at me. He had guessed my thoughts. 'So,' said he. 'you would like to provoke the aristocracy to little, would you? Well—I rather like the idea. They are in need of a lesson to bring down their rebellious spirit, and I shall give it to them. You are a more useful man to me than any of them, and you shall be created a baron. I shall also elevate several other distinguished Jews to the rank of nobles, and the aristocracy shall understand that wherever I find merit I reward it.'"

"So then it was your worth, and not your gold, that earned for you the distinction!" cried Rachel, gratified.

"Nonsense! 'Merit' means wealth, and I assure you that titles cost enormous sums. I must pay for my patent ten thousand florins, and if I should wish to be a count, I must pay twenty thousand. But enough of all this. Suffice it that I shall prove to the nobles that my money is as good as their genealogical trees, and now we shall have crowds of noble adorers at the Baroness Rachel's feet. But be she baroness or countess, she is forever a Jewess, and that parts her eternally from any but a wooer of her own faith. Does it not, my Rachel, my loyal Israelitish baroness?"

"Do you doubt me, my father?" asked Rachel in a faltering voice, while she averted her face.

"No, my child, for if I did, I would curse you on the spot."

"Dear, dear father, do not speak such fearful words!" cried Rachel, trembling with fright.

"You are right, child. I am childish to indulge the supposition of my Hebrew maiden's treachery. She is pure before the Lord, loyal and true to the faith of her fathers. But we must be armed against temptation, and before we part for the day, we must both swear eternal fidelity to our creed. These wily Christians may come with flattery and smiles, and some one of them might steal my Rachel's heart. I swear, therefore, by all that is sacred on earth or in heaven, never to abandon the Jewish faith, and never to enter a Christian church. So help me God!"

Rachel gazed upon her father with blanched cheeks and distended eyes; her muscles stiffened with horror, until she seemed to be turning to stone.

"Did you hear my oath, Rachel?" said he.

She parted her lips, and they faltered an inaudible "Yes."

"Then," said he, gently, "repeat the oath, for we both must take it."

She raised her head with a quick, convulsive motion, and stammered, "What—what is it, father?"

"Swear, as I have done, never to leave the faith of your fathers, never to enter a Christian church."

Rachel made no reply. She stared again as though her senses were forsaking her. She thought she would go mad. Her father's brow contracted, and his mien grew fierce as he saw that his daughter's heart had gone irrevocably from him. There was a long, dreadful pause.

"Are you at a loss for words?" asked the baron, and his voice was so savage that Rachel started at the ominous sound.

"Repeat my words, then," continued he, seeing that she made no answer, "or I—"

"Say, on, my father," replied the despairing girl.

Baron Eskeles Flies repeated his oath, and the pale victim spoke the words after him. But at the end of the ordeal she reeled and fell to the floor. Her father bent over, and raising her tenderly, folded her to his heart. His voice was now as loving as ever.

"My precious child, we are truly united now. Nothing can part us, and your happy father will surround you with such splendor as you have never beheld before."

"Oh, my father!" exclaimed she, "what has splendor to do with happiness?"

"Everything," replied her father, with a careless laugh. "Misfortune is not near so ugly in a palace as in a cottage; and I do assure you that the tears which are shed in a softly-cushioned carriage are not half so bitter as those that fall from the eyes of the houseless beggar. Wealth takes the edge from affliction, and lends new lustre to happiness. And it shall shed its brightest halo over yours, my daughter. But I must leave you, for I expect to earn a fortune before I return, when I hope to see you bright and beautiful as ever."

He kissed her forehead and stroked her silky hair. "The Baroness Rachel will be a Jewess forever! Oh, how can I thank you for that promise, my adored child! What new pleasure can I procure for my idol to-day?"

"Love me, father," murmured Rachel.

"What need you ask for love, you who are to me like the breath of life? To show how I anticipate your wishes, I have already prepared a gratification for you. I have remarked how much pleasure you take in the gardens and little pavilion yonder. Since my Rachel loves to take her morning walk there, it shall be changed into a paradise. The brightest fruits and flowers of the tropics shall bloom in its conservatories; and instead of the little pavilion, I shall raise up a temple of purest white marble, worthy of the nymph who haunts the spot. For a few weeks your walks will be somewhat disturbed, darling, for the workmen will begin to-morrow; but they need not be much in your way, for while the walls are down, I shall set a watch at every gate to make sure that no one intrudes upon your privacy. In a few months you shall have a miniature palace wherein to rest, when you are tired of roaming about the grounds. Farewell, my child. I shall send the workmen to-morrow—early to-morrow morning."

"He knows all," thought poor Rachel, as he closed the door. "The oath was to part me from Günther; the changes in the garden are to prevent us from meeting."

For a long time she sat absorbed in grief. But finally she made her resolve.

"I have sworn to love thee forever, my Günther," said she. "When the hour comes wherein my choice must be made, I go with thee!"

CHAPTER CLII.

NEW-FASHIONED OBSEQUIES.

THE emperor's horse was saddled, and he was about to take his daily ride. But as he was leaving his cabinet, a page announced Field-Marshal Lacy.

"Admit him," said Joseph, and he hastened to the anteroom to greet his favorite.

Lacy received the cordial greeting of the emperor with a grave, troubled expression.

"Sire," said he, "may I beg for an audience?"

"Certainly, my friend," replied Joseph. "I am just about to ride, and you can accompany me. We can converse together in some of the shady alleys of the park. I will order a horse for you at once."

"Pardon me, sire, our interview must be here. I saw your majesty's horse in readiness for your ride, but that did not prevent me from coming, for the matter which brought me hither is one of supreme importance."

"And you cannot put it off until we take our ride?"

"Sire, my first request is that your majesty will relinquish the ride altogether. You must not be seen in the streets to-day."

"Bless me, Lacy! you speak as if I were Louis of France, who is afraid to show himself in public, because of the murmurs of his discontented subjects."

"Sire, assume that you are Louis, then, and give up the ride. Do it, if you love me, my sovereign."

"If I love you!" repeated Joseph, with surprise. "Well, then, it shall be done." And he rang, and ordered his horse to be put up. "Now speak. What can have happened here, that *I* should be threatened with a discontented mob?"

"Sire," began Lacy, "you remember the day on which we swore to speak the truth to your majesty, even if it should become importunate, do you not?"

"Yes, I do, Lacy; but neither of you have kept the promise up to this time."

"I am here to redeem my word, sire. I come to warn your majesty that you are proceeding too rashly with your measures of reform."

"And you also, Lacy!" cried Joseph, reproachfully. "You, the bravest of the brave, would have me retreat before the dissatisfaction of priests and bigots."

"The malcontents are not only priests and bigots, they are your whole people. You attempt too many reforms at once."

"But my reforms are all for the people's good. I am no tyrant to oppress and trample them under foot. I am doing my best to free them from the shackles of prejudice, and yet they harass and oppose me. Even those who understand my aims, place obstacles in my path. Oh, Lacy, it wounds me to see that not even my best friends sustain me!"

"I see that your majesty is displeased," replied Lacy, sadly, "and that you reckon me among your opponents—I who am struck with admiration at the grandeur of your conceptions. But you are so filled with the rectitude of your intentions, that you have no indulgence for the weakness and ignorance of those whom you would benefit, and you make too light of the enmity of those whom your reforms have aggrieved."

"Whom have I aggrieved?" cried Joseph, impatiently. "Priests and nobles, nobody besides. If I have displeased them, it is because I wish to put all men on an equality. The privileged classes may hate me—let them do it, but the people whom I befriend will love and honor me."

"Ah, sire, you think too well of the people," said Lacy. "And mindful of my promise, I must say that you have given cause for dissatisfaction to all classes, plebeian as well as patrician."

"How so?" cried Joseph.

"You have despised their prejudices, and mocked at customs which in their superstitious ignorance they hold as sacred. They do not thank you for enlightening them. They call you an unbeliever and an apostate. Do not be displeased, sire, if I speak so plainly of things which the stupidity of your subjects regards as a crime. I come as your majesty's accuser, because I come as the advocate of your people, imploring you to be patient with their blindness and their folly."

"What now? Is there any special complaint against me?"

"Yes, sire. Your majesty has issued an edict which has wounded the people in those relations which the world holds sacred; an edict which is (forgive me if I speak plain)—which is—so entirely free from prejudice, that it trenches almost—upon the limits of barbarism."

"What edict can you mean?"

"That which concerns the burial of the dead, sire. I beseech you, revoke it; for the people cry out that nothing is sacred to the emperor—not even death and the grave! Leave them their cemeteries and their tombs, that they may go thither and pray for the souls of the departed!"

"That they may go thither and enjoy their superstitious rites!" cried Joseph, indignantly. "I will not allow my subjects to seek for their dead underground. They shall not solemnize the corruption of the body; they shall turn their eyes to Heaven, and there seek for the immortal spirit of the departed! They shall not love the dust of their forefathers, but their souls!"

"Sire, you speak of an ideal people. To bring mankind to such a state of perfection would require the reign of a Methusaleh! It is too soon for such edicts. The people, so far from appreciating, abhor them."

"Are you really in earnest, Lacy?" exclaimed the emperor, with flashing eyes.

"Yes, sire, they are indignant. Yesterday the first burial, according to your majesty's edict, took place, and since then the people are in a state of revolt. To-day there are of course other bodies to be interred. There is not a vagrant in the streets that does not utter threats against your majesty. From the burgher to the beggar, every man feels that his sacred rights have been invaded. They feel that the prohibition of coffins and burying-grounds does not reach the rich, who have their hereditary tombs in churches and chapels, but the people, who have no such privileges."

"The people for whose sakes I would have converted the mould of the burying-ground into fertile fields, and spared them the cost of a useless coffin, which, instead of rotting in the ground, would have been so much more wood to warm them in winter, and cook the food for their hungry, living bodies!"

"But, your majesty, they are not sufficiently enlightened to comprehend your ideas. Revoke the order, sire—in mercy to their ignorance, revoke the order!"

"Revoke it!" cried Joseph, furiously. "Never will I make such a concession to stupidity and malice!"

"Then," said Lacy, gravely, "it is possible that the flames of a revolution may burst forth to consume this unhappy land. Oh, sire, have mercy upon the poor people, whose eyes cannot endure the light of reform! Preserve yourself and your subjects from the horrors of a revolt, which, although it would be ultimately quelled, might cost bloodshed and misery! I have never seen such excitement as prevails throughout the streets of Vienna. Thousands of men and women throng the quarter where the body lies."

"When does the funeral take place?"

"At three o'clock this afternoon, sire."

"In one hour, then," said the emperor, glancing at the clock.

"Yes, sire; and it may be an hour of tribulation, unless your majesty has the magnanimity to prevent it! To discourage idle assemblages, your majesty has forbidden the people to follow funerals. The effect of this prohibition is, that the poor woman who is to be buried this afternoon will be followed, not by her friends, but by thousands who have never seen or known her. The police have done their best to disperse the rioters, but so far in vain."

"Then there is already a revolt," cried the emperor.

"But for this I never should have presumed to deter your majesty from enjoying your ride to-day."

"Do you suppose that I would retreat before my own subjects?"

"Sire, the wrath of the populace is like that of a tiger just escaped from its cage. In its bloodthirstiness it tears to pieces every thing that comes in its way."

"I am curious to witness its antics," replied the emperor, touching the bell.

"Sire," exclaimed Lacy, staying Joseph's hand, "what would you do?"

"Mount my horse, and go to the funeral."

"What! To exasperate the crowd! To endanger yourself, and drive these poor, half-frantic creatures to desperation! Oh, by the love you bear us all, I beseech you, have mercy upon those whose only possession on earth is oftentimes the grave! You would deprive their children of the only comfort left them—that of praying over the ashes of the departed. You would deprive those who are condemned to live like brutes, of the comfort of dying like men. You would have their bodies sewed in sacks and thrown into ditches where they are not even allowed to moulder, but must be destroyed by lime. No tombstone permitted over their remains, nothing to remind their weeping relatives that they were ever alive! Oh, this is cruel! It may be a great thought, sire, but it is a barbarous deed! I know how bold I am, but my conscience compels me to speak; and were I to lose the emperor's favor, I must obey its faithful monitions. Revoke the edict, sire! There is yet time. In one hour it will be too late!"

The emperor looked despondently at Lacy's agitated countenance. Then, without a word, he turned to his *escritoire* and hastily began to write. His writing concluded, he handed the paper to Lacy, and commanded him to read it aloud. Lacy bowed and read as follows:

"As I have learned that the living are so material in their ideas as to set great store upon the privilege of having their bodies rot and become carrion after death, I shall concern myself in no way as to the manner of their burying. Let it be known, therefore, that having shown the wisdom of disposing of the dead after the manner described in my edict, I shall force no man to be wise. Those who are not convinced of its expediency, are free to dispose of their carcasses as they see fit." *

When Lacy had read to the end, the emperor called imperatively for Günther. He obeyed the summons at once.

"This letter to the lord high chancellor, Prince Kaunitz," said he. "I wish this writing to be printed and posted at the corners of the streets. Then hasten to the Leopold suburbs, where any one of the police will show you to the house whence the funeral is to take place. Go within, and tell the relatives of the deceased that I give them permission to bedizen their corpse in whatever style they may

* Hubner, "Life of Joseph II.," vol. ii., p. 525.

choose, and to bury it in a coffin. Take a carriage and drive fast."

Günther bowed and turned to leave. "Stop a moment," continued the emperor. "Go to the chief of police, and tell him that the people must not be disturbed in any way. They must be allowed to disperse at their pleasure. Now, Günther, be quick."

With a look of unspeakable affection Joseph gave his hand to Lacy. "Lacy," said he, "if I have made this great sacrifice to-day, it is neither from conviction nor fear; it is to show you what influence your words have over me, and to thank you for the manliness with which you have ventured to blame my acts. Few princes possess the jewel of a faithful friend. I thank God that this jewel is mine!" *

CHAPTER CLIII.

THE POPE IN VIENNA.

A REPORT, almost incredible, was obtaining currency in Vienna. It was said that the pope was about to visit the emperor. Many a German emperor, in centuries gone by, had made his pilgrimage to Rome; but never before had the vicar of Christ honored the sovereign of Austria by coming to him.

Pius VI., confounded by the headlong innovations of Joseph, and trembling lest his reforms should end in a total subversion of religion, had resolved, in the extremity of his distress, to become a pilgrim himself, and to visit the enemy in his own stronghold.

To this intent he had dispatched an autographic letter announcing his intention, to which the emperor had replied by another, expressive of his extreme anxiety to become personally acquainted with his holiness, and to do him all filial reverence. Furthermore, he begged that the pope would relinquish his intention of taking up his abode at the nuncio, and would consent to be the guest of the imperial family.

The pope having graciously acceded to this wish, the apartments of the late empress were prepared for his occupation. Now Joseph was quite aware that these apartments abounded in secret doors and private stairways, by which Maria Theresa's many petitioners had been accustomed to find their way to the privy purse of the munificent empress, and so had diminished the imperial treasury of several millions.

The emperor, dreading lest these secret avenues should be used by the friends of the church to visit the pope in private, caused the stairways to be demolished, and all the doors to be walled up. He allowed but one issue from the apartments of his holiness. This one led into the grand corridor, and was guarded by two sentries, who had orders to allow nobody to enter who was unprovided with a pass

* The burial edict was as follows: "As the burial of the dead has for its object the speedy dissolution of the body, and as nothing hinders that dissolution more than the casing of the corpse in a coffin, it is ordained that all dead bodies shall be stripped of their clothing, and sewed up in a linen sack, laid in an open coffin, and brought to the place of interment. A hole shall be dug six feet long and four feet wide, and the corpse being taken out of the coffin, shall be put into this grave, strewed plentifully with quick-lime, and covered with earth. If more than one corpse is to be buried, the bodies can all be put in the same grave."—Gross-Hoffinger, "History of the Life and Reign of Joseph II.," vol. ii., p. 146.

signed by Joseph himself. He was quite willing to receive the pope as a guest; but he was resolved that he should hold no communication with his bishops, while on Austrian soil.*

Meanwhile, every outward honor was to be paid to the head of the church. Not only had his rooms been superbly decorated, but the churches, also, were in all their splendor. The vestments of the clergy had been renewed, new altar-cloths woven, and magnificent hangings ordered for the papal throne erected for the occasion.

Finally, the momentous day dawned, and Vienna put on its holiday attire. The houses were wreathed with garlands, the streets were hung with arches of evergreen. A hundred thousand Viennese pressed toward the cathedral, where the pope was to repair for prayer, and another throng was hastening toward the palace, where the pope and the emperor were to alight together. In their impatient curiosity the people had forsaken their work. No one was content to remain within doors. Everybody said to everybody, "The pope has come to Vienna;" and then followed the question:

"Why has his holiness come to Vienna?"

"To bless the emperor, and approve his great deeds," said the friends of Joseph.

"To bring him, if possible, to a sense of his sacrilegious persecution of the church," said his enemies.

This question was not only verbally agitated, but it formed the subject of thousands of pamphlets, which fluttered from many a window toward the crowds who, in breathless anxiety, were awaiting the advent of Pius VI.

"The Arrival of the Pope."
"Why has the Pope come to Vienna?"
"What is the Pope?"

These were the titles of the *brochures* which were converting the streets into a vast reading-room, and preparing the minds of the readers for the impressions it was desirable to create on the subject.

At last the deep bells of St. Stephen's opened their brazen throats. This signified that the pope and the emperor were at the gates of the city. The consent of the latter having been asked in the matter of the bell-ringing, he had replied to Cardinal Megazzi: "By all means. I wonder you should ask me the question, when bells are the artillery of the church."†

The people received the tidings with such wild joy that, in their eagerness, several persons were trampled to death. But on they rushed, seeing and hearing nothing until eight lives were sacrificed to the fierce curiosity of the mob.

And now the iron tongues of every bell in Vienna proclaimed that the pope had entered the city. The crowd, who, up to this moment, had laughed, sung, and shouted, suddenly ceased their clamor. Nothing was heard save the musical chime of the bells, while every eye was fixed upon a small white spot which was just becoming

* It was to Joseph's manifest advantage that the pope should not reside outside of the palace; and the emperor showed his ingenuity in the various strategic movements by which he defeated the purpose of his visit. One of the pope's most zealous adherents was the Bishop of Görtz. When the pope left Rome for Vienna, he would pass through Görtz. Joseph summoned the bishop to Vienna, and so prevented a meeting between them at Görtz; and on the day of the pope's arrival in Vienna, the bishop received peremptory orders to return to his diocese. He was not allowed to communicate with the pope, not even to see him as he passed. —Friedel's "Letters from Vienna," vol. i., p. 223.

† Friedel's Letters, vol. i., p. 213.

visible. The point grew larger, and took form. First came the outriders, then the imperial equipage drawn by eight milk-white horses caparisoned with crimson and gold. Nearer and nearer came the *cortége*, until the people recognized the noble old man, whose white locks flowed from under his velvet cap, the supreme pontiff, Antonio Braschi, Pope Pius VI.

Never, throughout his pontifical career, had the pope beheld such a crowd before. And these hundreds of thousands had assembled to bid him welcome. A smile of gratification flitted over his handsome features, and he raised his eyes to the face of his companion.

The countenance of the emperor wore a satisfied expression; by some it might have been regarded as derisive.

He had seen what the pope, in the simple joy of his heart, had not observed. The people who, in the presence of the high dignitaries of the church, had been accustomed to kneel and ask a blessing, were standing, although the prelate who stood in their midst was the sovereign pontiff himself; and Joseph, as he contemplated his subjects, exulted in secret.

The *cortége*, impeded by the throng, moved slowly toward the imperial palace. When it drew up before the gates, Joseph, springing from the carriage, assisted the pope to alight, and accompanied him to his apartments. Occasionally Pius raised his mild eyes to the emperor's face and smiled, while Joseph, in nowise discomposed by the honor of receiving the chief pastor of Christendom, walked proudly by his side.

They passed through the magnificent state apartments designed for the occupation of the pope; but not until they had reached his private sitting-room, did the emperor invite him to rest after his fatiguing walk.

"It has not fatigued me," replied Pius. "It has interested me, on the contrary, to traverse a palace which has been the residence of so many pious princes. I esteem it a great privilege to inhabit these rooms whose deceased occupants have each in his turn received the benediction of my honored predecessors—"

"But who never were blessed by the love of their subjects," replied Joseph, interrupting him. "To my mind, this is a blessing better worth striving for than a papal benediction; and it is the aim of *my* life to deserve it."

"Doubtless your majesty will reach your aim," replied the pope, with courtesy. "I have confidence in the rectitude of your majesty's intentions, and if I have made this pilgrimage to Vienna, it is because, relying upon your honesty of purpose, I hope to convince you that it has been misapplied. The visit of the pope to the Austrian emperor is a concession which I cheerfully make, if by that concession I can induce him to pause in a career which has sorely wounded my heart, and has been the occasion of so much scandal to our holy mother the church."

"I fear that your holiness has been mistaken in your estimate of me," replied Joseph, turning his flashing eyes upon the imploring face of the pope. "However I might be moved by the pathos of your words, a sovereign has no right to listen to the pleadings of his heart. 'Tis the head that must guide and influence his conduct. I fear, therefore, that your holiness will be disappointed in the result of your visit here. I accept your journey to Vienna as a distinguished mark of your papal good-will, and am rejoiced to have it in my power to show all possible filial reverence to your holiness. Neither I nor my subjects will deny the consideration which is due to the *spiritual* head of the church; but he on his part must refrain from touching with his consecrated hand the things of this world which concern him not."

"It is my duty to attend to all the affairs of holy church, whether spiritual or temporal," replied the pope, gently.

"The temporal affairs of the church concern your nuncio and my minister," said Joseph, with impatience. "And as your holiness has entered at once upon a controversy with me respecting my acts toward the church, I declare distinctly to you that I shall not recede from the least of them; and that your journey to Vienna, if its object is to influence my policy as sovereign of these realms, is already a failure. The reasons for my conduct are satisfactory to me, and no power on earth shall move me from the position I have taken." *

"I will not altogether give up the hope I have cherished of moving your majesty's heart," replied the pope, earnestly. "I shall continue to pray that it may be my privilege to convince you of your errors, and lead you back to the path of justice and of religion."

"Which means that you expect me to retract!" cried Joseph, impetuously. "Never will I retract what I have said or done, for I act from conviction, and conviction does not slip off and on like a glove! But let us speak no more on this subject. If your holiness will write down your canonical objections to my proceedings against the church, I will lay them before my theologians for examination. My chancellor shall reply to them ministerially, and the correspondence can be published for the edification of my subjects. Meanwhile, I shall endeavor to deserve the good-will of your holiness by acting toward my honored guest the part of an obliging and hospitable host. This reminds me that I have already trespassed upon your time, and have deprived you of the repose which a traveller always craves after a long journey. I hope that your holiness will overlook this intrusion, and pardon me if my great anxiety to enjoy your society has caused me to forget the consideration due to my tired guest."

With these words the emperor retired. The pope followed his retreating figure with a glance of profound sadness.

"I fear," thought he, "that Joseph is indeed irreclaimable." Here he raised his soft dark eyes to heaven, and continued in a low murmur, "For a time the Lord endureth with mildness, but His might overcometh the blasphemer, and he vanisheth: while holy church remaineth unchangeable forever!"

CHAPTER CLIV.

THE FLIGHT.

"YOU persist in your refusal?" cried Eskeles Flies, in an angry voice. "You dare to oppose the will of your father?"

"I persist in my refusal," replied Rachel firmly, lifting her dark, tearful eyes to her father's excited countenance. "I must rebel against your authority, my father, for you would compromise my

* The emperor's words.—Hubner, i., p. 119.

earthly happiness and my salvation. Oh, dear father, do not harden your heart against me! In mercy heed my prayers!"

With these words Rachel would have thrown herself upon her father's bosom. But he thrust her from him.

"'Tis you who have hardened your heart against the law of God which bids the child obey her father," cried he.

"I cannot recognize my father's authority when he oversteps his rights, and trenches upon mine as a human being," urged Rachel. "I cannot perjure myself by accepting, as a husband, a man whom I do not love. He is a coarse, illiterate creature, who honors nothing but wealth, loves nothing but gold!"

"He is the son of the richest merchant in Brussels, and the emperor has made a nobleman of his father. He is your equal, or rather he is your superior, for he is richer, much richer than we."

"He my equal! He cannot understand me," cried Rachel.

Her father laughed. "Not your equal, because he does not go into raptures over young Mozart, and does not indulge in speculative theology, but worships God after the manner of his fathers!—a Jew, in short, who hates the Christian and glories in his Jewish birthright!"

"Yes," said Rachel, shuddering, "a Jew in feature, speech, and spirit. Not such a noble Israelite as you, my father, but a man possessing every repulsive peculiarity which has made the Jew the pariah of the civilized world. Oh, father, dear father, do not barter me for gold! Let me remain your child, your darling; living and dying in the home which your love has made like Eden to my girlhood!"

"I have promised your hand to Baron von Meyer," was the curt reply.

"I will not give it!" cried Rachel, frantically. "You force me to disobedience, by requiring of me that which is impossible."

"I shall force you to obedience, rebellious girl, for our laws invest the father with absolute authority over his child, and I shall use my right to rescue you from dishonor. I read your heart, Rachel, and therein I see written the history of your perfidy and shame."

"Then you have read falsely," exclaimed Rachel, with indignation. "Up to this day I have kept the oath I made to remain a Jewess! And no mortal, were he ten times my father, has the right to couple my name with perfidy or shame!"

"You dare look me in the face and deny your disgrace!" said her father, trembling with anger. "You, who at early morning in my own garden have listened to the vows of a false-tongued Christian! You who have sworn to be no man's wife, if not his!"

"Ah, you know all!" cried Rachel, in accents of supreme joy. "God be praised, there need be no more concealment between us! Yes, father, I love Günther, and if I be not permitted to become his wife, in the might of my love I would not scorn to be his handmaid! I have loved him since you first brought him hither, and proudly presented him as the emperor's favorite. Oh, my father, we were not rich then!"

"No—and he would have scorned to ask you to wed him. Now he would degrade the heiress of my wealth by seeking to make her his wife."

"Degrade me!" echoed Rachel, with a blush of indignation. "I should be honored by bearing his name, not because he is the emperor's favorite, but because he is worthy of my love."

"And yet, God be praised, Rachel Eskeles can never be the wife of a Christian!" shouted the banker, triumphantly, "for she has sworn by the memory of her mother to die a Jewess!"

"She will keep her oath unless her father release her," replied Rachel. "But oh!" added she, falling on her knees and raising her white arms above her head, "he will have pity upon the misery of his only child; he will not condemn her to despair! Have mercy, have mercy, dear father! Be your generous self, and take me to your heart. Release me, and let me become a Christian and the wife of my lover! He cares nothing for your wealth, he asks nothing but my hand!"

Her father glared at her with a look that seemed almost like hate. "You are a Jewess," hissed he, "and a Jewess you shall die!"

"I am no Jewess at heart, father. I have been educated in a Christian country, and after the manner of Christian women. And you, too, have renounced your birthright. You have eaten and drunk with the Gentiles; you have cut your hair, and have adopted their dress. Nay, more! You have parted with your name, and have accepted a Christian title. Why, then, have you not the manliness to abjure the God of revenge and hate, and openly adore the Christian God of love and mercy?"

"I will live and die a Jew!" cried the banker, choking with rage. "I swear it again, and may I be accursed if I ever break my oath!"

"Then, father, release *me* from the lie that follows me like an evil shadow, blasting my life here and hereafter. Give me to my lover. Keep your wealth to enrich your tribe, but give me your blessing and your love!"

"You shall remain a Jewess!" thundered her father.

"Is this your last word?" cried Rachel, springing to her feet. "Is this your last word?"

"It is," replied he, eying her with cold cruelty.

"Then hear my determination. I have sworn fidelity to Günther, and if I must choose between you, I give myself to him. I will not become a Christian, for such was my oath; but I will abjure Judaism."

"And become a Deist?"

"Call it what you will. I shall adore the God of love and mercy."

"A Deist! Then you have never heard what punishment awaits the Deist here. You do not know that the emperor, who affects toleration, has his vulnerable heel, and will not tolerate Deism. The gentle punishment which his majesty awards to Deism is—that of the lash.* So that I scarcely think you would dare me to accuse you of *that!* But pshaw! I go too far in my fears. My daughter will recognize her folly, and yield her will to mine. She will be, as she has ever been, my adored child, for whose happiness I can never do too much; whose every wish it shall be my joy to gratify."

"I have but one wish—that of becoming the wife of Günther."

Her father affected not to hear her. "Yes," continued he, "she will verify my promise, and take the husband I have chosen. This marriage will be a fine thing for both parties, for I give my daughter one-half million of florins, and Baron von Meyer gives his son a million cash down. Then the father-in-law gives three hundred

*Gross-Hoffinger, ii., c. 160.

florins a month for pin-money, and I seven hundred; so that Rachel has a thousand florins a month for her little caprices, and of this she is to render no account. That is a pretty dower for a bride. I give my daughter a *trousseau* equal in magnificence to that of a princess. Upon her equipage, the arms of our two houses are already emblazoned, and to-morrow four of the finest horses in Vienna will conduct the Baroness von Meyer to her husband's palace. I congratulate you, baroness. No Christian woman in Vienna shall have an establishment like yours."

"I shall never be the Baroness von Meyer," said Rachel, calmly, but an icy chill ran through her veins, for she loved her father, and felt that they must shortly part forever.

"Yes, you will be the Baroness von Meyer to-morrow. I have anticipated all your objections. The rabbi that is to marry you is a Pole. He will not understand your reply, and the young baron has magnanimously consented to overlook any little informality of which your folly may be the cause; for he likes money, and is too good a Jew not to aid me in rescuing my heiress from disgrace. You see that your poor little struggles will all be in vain. Resign yourself, then, and accept the brilliant destiny which awaits you."

"I will sooner die than consign myself to misery and disgrace!"

"Be easy on that subject. God will shield you from misery, and your father's watchful eye will see that you do not consign yourself to disgrace," replied the banker, coldly. "But enough of words. Night sets in, and I have yet a few preparations to make for to-morrow. It is proper that you pass the last evening of your maiden life in solitude, and that you may not spend it in weariness, I have ordered your drawing-rooms to be lighted, and your *trousseau* to be laid out for your inspection. Go, and gladden your heart with its magnificence. Good-night."

So saying, Baron Eskeles Flies left the room. Rachel heard him turn the key in the lock, and withdraw it. She then remembered that the drawing-rooms were lighted. Perhaps her father had neglected to fasten some of the doors leading thence into the hall. She sprang to the door of communication, and flung it open. The rooms were brilliantly illuminated, and the sparkling chandeliers of crystal looked down upon a wilderness of velvet, satin, flowers, lace, and jewels—truly a *trousseau* for a princess.

But what cared Rachel for this? Indeed, she saw nothing, save the distant doors toward which she sped like a frightened doe. Alas! they, too, were locked, and the only answers to her frantic calls were the mocking echoes of her own voice.

For a few moments she leaned against the wall for support; then her glance took in the long perspective of magnificence which was to gild the hideous sacrifice of a whole human life, and she murmured, softly:

"I must be free. I cannot perjure myself. I shall keep my vow to Günther or die! My father is no father—he is my jailer, and I owe him no longer the obedience of a child."

She went slowly back, revolving in her mind what she should do. Unconsciously she paused before a table resplendent with trinkets, whose surpassing beauty seemed to woo the young girl to her fate. But Rachel was no longer a maiden to be allured by dress. The exigencies of the hour had transformed her into a brave woman, who was donning her armor and preparing for the fight.

"Günther awaits me," said she, musing.

But why—where? that she could not say. But she felt that she must free herself from prison, and that her fate now lay in her own hands.

At that moment she stood before a large round table which was just under the principal chandelier of her superb reception-room. Here lay dainty boxes containing laces, and caskets enclosing jewels. Not for one moment did she think of their contents. She saw but the gilt letters which were impressed upon the red morocco cases.

"RACHEL VON MEYER" was on every box and case. In her father's mind she already bore another name.

"Rachel von Meyer!" said she, with a shudder. "My father denies me his name! Who, then, am I?"

A flush of modest shame overspread her face, as scarcely daring to articulate the words, she knelt, and murmured:

"I am Rachel Günther. And if such be my name," continued she, after a pause of rapture, "I have no right to be here amid the treasures of the Baroness von Meyer. I must away from this house, which is no longer a home for me. Away, away! for Günther awaits me."

And now she looked with despair at the locked doors and the lofty windows, so far, far from the ground.

"Oh, if I had but wings!—I, who am here a prisoner, while my heart is away with him!"

Suddenly she gave a start, for deliverance was possible. She looked from the window as if to measure its height, and then she darted through the rooms until she saw a table covered with silks. She took thence a roll of white, heavy ribbon, and, throwing it before her, exclaimed joyfully:

"It is long, oh, it is quite long enough. And strong enough to support me. Thank Heaven! it is dark, and I shall not be seen. A gold ducat will bribe the guard at the postern—and then I am free!"

She returned to her sitting-room, and, with trembling haste, threw a dark mantle around her. Then, looking up at her father's portrait, her eyes filled with bitter tears.

"Farewell, my father, farewell!"

Scarcely knowing what she did, she fled from her room, and returned to the only object which possessed any more interest for her there, the long, long ribbon which, like a gigantic serpent, lay glistening on the floor where she had unrolled it. She stooped to pick it up, and trailing it after her, she flew from room to room, until she came to the last one of the suite which overlooked the park. She opened a window, and listened.

Nothing was heard there save the "warbling wind," that wooed the young branches, and here and there a little bird that ventured its note upon the night.

Rachel secured the ribbon to the crosswork of the window, and then let it fall below. Once more she listened. She could almost hear the beatings of her own heart, but nothing else broke the silence of the house.

She gave one quick glance around her beautiful home where lay all the splendor that might have been hers, and grasping the ribbon firmly in her hands, she dropped from the window to the ground.

CHAPTER CLV.

THE MARRIAGE BEFORE GOD.

GÜNTHER had returned from the palace to his own lodgings in the city. Here, the labors of the day over, he sat dreaming of his love, wondering whether she thought of him during these dreary weeks of their forced parting.

He had stretched himself upon a divan, and, with his head thrown back upon the cushion, he gave himself up to thoughts of that love which was at once the greatest grief and the greatest joy of his life.

"Will it ever end?" thought he. "Will she ever consent to leave that princely home for me?"

Sometimes a cloud came over his handsome, noble features, sometimes the sunlight of happiness broke over them, and then he smiled. And on he dreamed, happy or unhappy, as he fancied that Rachel was his, or was parted from him forever.

The door-bell rang with a clang that startled him. But what to him was the impatience of those who sought admittance to his house? He had almost begun to fancy that Rachel was before him, and he was vexed at the intrusion.

Meanwhile, the door of his room had been softly opened, but Günther had not heard it. He heard or saw nothing but his peerless Rachel. She was there with her lustrous eyes, her silky hair, her pale and beautiful features. She was there.

What! Did he dream? She was before him, but paler than her wont, her dark eyes fixed upon him with a pleading look, her lithe figure swaying from side to side, as with uncertain footsteps she seemed to be approaching his couch. Good God! Was it an apparition? What had happened?

Günther started to his feet, and cried out, "O my Rachel, my beloved!"

"It is I," said she, in a faltering voice. "Before you take me to your heart, hear me, Günther. I have fled from my father's house forever—for he would have sold me to a man whom I abhor, and whom I could never have married, had my heart been free. I bring neither gold nor jewels. I come to you a beggar—my inheritance a father's curse, my dowry naught but my love and faith. So dowered and so portioned, will you take me, Günther?"

Günther looked upon his love with eyes wherein she must have read consolation for all her trials, for her sweet lips parted with a happy smile.

"My treasure!" was his reply, as he took her little trembling hand, and pressed it fondly within his own. "Come, my Rachel, come and see how I have longed for this day."

He drew her forward, and opened a door opposite to the one by which she had entered.

"Come, your home is ready, my own."

They entered together, and Rachel found herself in a drawing-room where taste and elegance amply atoned for the absence of splendor.

"Now, see your sitting-room."

Nothing could be more cheerful or homelike than the appointments of this cosy apartment, lighted like the drawing-room by a tasteful chandelier.

"There," said Günther, pointing to a door, "is your dressing-room, and within, your chamber, my Rachel. For six months this dwelling has awaited its mistress, and that she might never enter it unawares, it has been nightly lighted for her coming. I was almost tempted to despair, beloved. You have saved me from a discouragement that was undermining my health. Now you are here, and all is well. When shall the priest bless our nuptials? This very night, shall he not, my bride?"

"He can never bless them," replied Rachel, solemnly.

Günther turned pale.

"Never? You have not, then, come to be my wife?"

"I cannot be your wife according to human rites, Günther, for well you know that I have sworn never to become a Christian. But I am yours for time and eternity, and knowing my own heart, I accept the world's scorn for your dear sake. Earth refuses to bless our nuptials, but God will hear our vows. Günther, will you reject me because I am a Jewess?"

Günther imprinted a kiss upon her forehead, and sank on his knees before her.

"Rachel," said he, raising his right hand to heaven, "I swear to love you for better or for worse, devoting my life to your happiness. On my knees I swear before God to honor you as my wife, and to be faithful and true to you until death does us part."

Rachel then knelt at his side, and laying her hand in his, she repeated her vows. Then they kissed each other, and Günther, taking her in his arms, pressed her to his throbbing heart.

"We are husband and wife," said he. "God has received our vows, and now, Rachel, you are mine, for He has blessed and sanctioned your entrance into my house!"

CHAPTER CLVI.

THE PARK.

THE first days of a smiling spring had filled the park with hundreds of splendid equipages and prancing horsemen. There was the carriage of the Princess Esterhazy, with twenty outriders in the livery of the prince; that of the new Prince Palm, whose four black horses wore their harness of pure gold; there was the gilded, fairy-like *vis-à-vis* of the beautiful Countess Thun, its panels decorated with paintings from the hands of one of the first artists of the day; the coach of the Countess Dietrichstein, drawn by four milk-white horses, whose delicate pasterns were encircled by jewelled bracelets worthy of glittering upon the arm of a beauty. In short, the aristocracy of Austria, Hungary, and Lombardy were there, in all the splendor of their wealth and rank. It seemed as though Spring were holding a levee, and the nobles of the empire had thronged her flowery courts.

Not only they, but the people, too, had come to greet young Spring. They crowded the footpaths, eager to scent the balmy air, to refresh their eyes with the sight of the velvet turf, and to enjoy the pageant presented to their wondering eyes by the magnificent turn-outs of the aristocracy. Thousands and thousands filled the alleys and outlets of the park, all directing their steps toward the centre, for there the emperor and his court were to be seen. There the people might gaze, in close proximity, at the dainty beauties, whom they knew as the denizens of another earthly sphere; there they might elbow greatness, and there, above all, they might feast their eyes upon the emperor, who, simply dressed, rode to and fro, stopping his horse to chat, as often with a peasant as with a peer.

The emperor dismounted, and this was the signal for all other cavaliers to dismount and accompany him. The ladies also were compelled to rise from their velvet cushions and to tread the ground with their silken-slippered feet. Their equipages were crowded together on one side of the square, and around them the horses, now held by their liveried jockeys, were champing their bits and pawing the ground with restless hoofs.

The crowd was so dense, that the patrician and plebeian stood side by side. The people, in their innocent enjoyment of the scene, broke several times through the ranks of titled promenaders, who, vainly hoping to find some spot unprofaned by the vicinity of the vulgar herd, were moving toward the centre of the garden.

The emperor saw the lowering brows of his courtiers, and knew that their angry glances were directed toward the people.

"What is the matter with you, my lords?" asked he. "You are the picture of discontent. Pray, Count Fürstenberg, speak for the court. What has happened to discompose your equanimity?"

"I do not know, your majesty," stammered the count.

"And yet you frown terribly," laughed Joseph. "Come—no concealment. What has vexed you all?"

"Your majesty commands?"

"I do."

"If so, sire, we are annoyed by the vulgar curiosity of the populace, who gape in our faces as if we were South Sea Islanders or specimens of fossil life."

"True, the curiosity of the Viennese is somewhat troublesome," replied the emperor, smiling; "but let us call this eagerness to be with us, love, and then it will cease to be irksome."

"Pardon me, your majesty, if I venture to say that under any aspect it would be most irksome to us. If your majesty will excuse my freedom, I think that in opening all the gardens to the people, you have made too great a concession to their convenience."

"You really think so?"

"Yes, sire, and I beg you to hear the request I have to prefer."

"Speak on, count."

"Then, your majesty, in the name of every nobleman in Vienna, and, above all, in the name of our noble ladies, I beseech of you grant us the exclusive privilege of *one* garden, where we may meet, unmolested by the rabble. Give us the use of the Prater, that we may have some spot in Vienna where we can breathe the fresh air in the company of our equals alone."

The emperor had listened with a supercilious smile. "You desire to see none but your equals, say you? If I were to indulge in a similar whim, I should have to seek companionship in the crypts of the Capuchins.* But for my part I hold all men as my equals, and my noble subjects will be obliged to follow my example. I shall

* The emperor's own words.—Ramshorn's "Life of Joseph II."

certainly not close any of the gardens against the people, for I esteem and love them." *

The emperor, as he concluded, bowed and turned to greet the Countess Pergen.

"Welcome, countess, to Vienna," said he, bowing. "You have been away for some time. May I inquire how you are?"

"*Très-bien, votre majesté,*" replied the countess, with a profound courtesy.

The emperor frowned. "Why do you not speak German?" said he, curtly. "We are certainly in Germany."

And without saying another word to the discomfited lady, he turned his back upon her. Suddenly his face brightened, and he pressed eagerly through the crowd, toward a pale young man, who met his smiling gaze with one of reciprocal friendliness.

Joseph extended his hand, and his courtiers saw with surprise that this person, whose brown coat was without a single order, instead of raising the emperor's hand to his lips, as was customary at court, shook it as if they had been equals.

"See," cried Joseph, "here is our young *maestro*, Mozart. Did you come to the park to-day to teach the nightingales to sing?"

"Heaven forbid, your majesty; rather would I learn from the tuneful songsters whom God has taught. Perhaps some of these days I may try to imitate their notes myself."

The emperor laid his hand upon Mozart's shoulder and looked with enthusiasm into his pale, inspired countenance. "Mozart has no need to learn from the nightingale," said he, "for God has filled his heart with melody, and he has only to transfer it to paper to ravish the world with its strains. Now for your 'Abduction from the *Auge Gottes*'—nay, do not blush; I am a child of Vienna, and must have my jest with the Viennese. Tell me—which gave you most trouble, that or your opera '*Die Entführung aus dem Serail?*' " †

"Truly," replied Mozart, still somewhat embarrassed, "the abduction from the *Auge Gottes*, sire. I had to sigh and sue until I was nigh unto despair before I was successful."

"But you concluded both works on the same day."

"Yes, sire. First, that which lay in my head, and then that which was nearest my heart."

"I congratulate you upon the success of both. '*Die Entführung aus dem Serail*' is a charming opera. Charming, but it contains too many notes."

"Only as many as were necessary, sire," said Mozart, looking full in the emperor's face.

Joseph smiled. "Perhaps so, for you must be a better judge of the necessity than I. For that very reason," added he, lowering his voice to a whisper, "I have sent you my *sonata* for revision. Like all inexperienced composers, I am anxious to know my fate. Tell me, what do you think of my *sonata, Herr Kapellmeister?*"

* When the emperor opened the park to the people, he caused the following inscription to be placed over the principal entrance: "Dedicated to all men, by one who esteems them."

† On the day of the representation of the opera "*Die Entführung aus dem Serail,*" in Vienna, Mozart ran away with his Constance. He conducted her to the house of a common friend, where they were married. This same friend brought about a reconciliation with the mother of Constance. The house in which the widow and her daughter lived was called "*Das Auge Gottes,*" and the Viennese, who knew the history of Mozart's marriage, had called it "*Die Entführung aus dem Auge Gottes.*"—Lissen's "Life of Mozart."

Mozart was silent, while the emperor waited anxiously for his reply. "Why do you not speak?" said he, impatiently. "Tell me, what do you think of my *sonata?*"

"The *sonata*, sire, is—good," returned Mozart, with some hesitation; "but he who composed it," added he, smiling, "is much better. Your majesty must not take it ill if you find some of your passages stricken out."

The emperor laughed. "Ah!—too many notes, as I just now remarked of your opera—only that from your judgment there can be no appeal. Well—give us a new opera, and let it be comic. Music should rejoice, not grieve us. *Addio.*" *

He then returned to the group which he had left, none of whom seemed to have been much comforted by the familiarity of the emperor with a poor little *kapellmeister*.

"My hour of recreation is over," said Joseph, "but as you know that I am no lover of etiquette, let no one retire on my account. I know where to find my equerry, and prefer to find him alone." With these words he turned away.

Suddenly he was seen to stop and frown visibly. With a quick motion of the hand he signed to Count Podstadsky-Liechtenstein to approach.

As Podstadsky was about to make a profound inclination, the emperor interrupted him roughly. "No ceremony—we have no time to be complimentary. What are you doing in Vienna?"

The count saw that his sovereign was angry. "Sire," replied he, "I spend my time just as it happens—"

"That is, you ride, walk, gamble, and carouse, when you are doing nothing worse. I thought you had left Vienna. You had better go upon your estates and attend to the welfare of your vassals. Idleness is the parent of crime, and I fear that *if you remain another day in Vienna*, you will bring disgrace upon your father's name. Go at once." †

Count Podstadsky looked in wonder after the emperor. "Is this accident or design? Does he suspect something, or is he only trying to induce me to work, as he does every nobleman? Ah, bah!—I must see Arabella, and hear what she thinks of it!"

CHAPTER CLVII.

THE PARTING.

THEY sat together in the little boudoir which had so often rung with their laughter, and where they had so often sneered at their titled dupes in Vienna.

There was no laughter to-day: the beautiful features of the Countess Baillou were contracted with alarm, and the frivolous Podstadsky was thoughtful and serious.

The countess was superbly dressed. A rich robe of velvet, embroidered with gold, fell in heavy, glistening folds around her graceful figure; a diadem of brilliants sparkled like a constellation

* This interview is strictly historical.—Lissen's "Life of Mozart."

† The emperor's own words to Podstadsky.—"Anecdotes, etc., of the Emperor Joseph II."

upon the blackness of her luxuriant hair, and her exquisite neck and arms were covered with costly gems. She had just completed her toilet for a dinner given by the Princess Karl Liechtenstein, when Podstadsky had met her with the alarming intelligence which had obliged her to send an excuse.

For one whole hour they had been considering their situation—considering those words of the emperor; now planning one method of escape, now another.

"Then you do not believe that the danger is imminent?" said Podstadsky, after a long, anxious pause.

"I do not," replied the countess. "The emperor has always been fond of advising other people, and of humbling the Austrian aristocracy; above all, when the people are by to hear him, and he can make capital out of it to increase his popularity. I suppose his rudeness to you was all assumed, to make an impression upon the foolish populace. That is all."

Podstadsky shook his head. "The tone of the emperor was so pointed—it seemed as though some special meaning lay in his words."

"That, my dear Carlo, simply means that fear caused you to interpret them significantly."

"The words themselves were significant enough; and his look!—Oh, Arabella, we are in danger! Dearest, let us fly, fly at once!"

He had risen, and, in his anguish, had tried to draw her to himself. She put him quietly away, and contemplated him with a sneer. "No folly!" said she. "Even if the emperor had meant to warn you, his warning came too late to save you from the watchful police of Vienna."

"No, no, Arabella. I tell you that the emperor will facilitate my escape for my parents' sake. Oh, why did I not obey, and mount my horse at once, and fly to some sequestered vale where I might have found refuge from dishonor?"

"And where you might realize your mother's touching dream of becoming a boor, and repenting your sins in sackcloth and ashes! That maternal idyl still troubles your poor, shallow brain, does it? For my part, I think no spectacle on earth is so ridiculous as that of the repentant sinner. It is the most humiliating character in which a man can appear before the world, and it is unworthy of you, Carlo. Hold up your head and look this phantom of danger in the face. It is but a phantom. The bright, beautiful reality of our luxurious life is substantially before us. Away with cowardice! He who treads the path which we have trodden, must cast all fear behind him. Had we been scrupulous, or faint-hearted, you would have been to-day a ruined nobleman, dependent upon the pittance doled out to you from parental hands, or upon some little office pompously bestowed by the emperor; and I—ha! ha!—I should have been a psalm-chanting nun, with other drowsy nuns for my companions through life, and a chance of dying in the odor of sanctity! We were too wise for that; and now the structure of our fortunes is complete. Its gilded dome reaches into the heaven of the most exclusive circles; princes, dukes, and sovereigns are our guests. In the name of all for which we have striven, Carlo, what would you have more?"

"I am afraid that the structure will fail and bury us under its ruins," said Carlo, shivering.

"Better that than inglorious flight. Stay where you are; show a bold front, and that will disarm suspicion. Why do you gaze at me so strangely?"

"I gaze at you because you are so beautiful," replied he, with a faint smile, "as beautiful as was that fallen angel who compassed the ruin of man!"

"I *am* a fallen angel," returned she, proudly, "and you know it. Together we fell, together we have risen. So long as we smile, we shall compass the ruin of many men; but if once we frown, we shall be known as evil spirits, and our power is at an end. Smiles are the talismans that insure victory; so smile, Carlo, smile and be gay."

"I cannot, I cannot. My veins are chilled with vague terror, and ever before my eyes comes the pale and anguish-stricken face of my mother! Arabella, if you will not leave this accursed spot, let us die. Better is death than the dungeon and disgrace!"

He threw his arms around her, and pressed his hot, parched lips to hers. Again she disengaged herself, and her musical laugh rang out upon the stillness—clear, merry, silvery as ever. "Die! Are you tired of pleasure? I am not. I shall yet have many an intoxicating draught from its golden beaker. Die! As if we knew what came after death! But come; I pity your state of mind, and since you can no longer be happy in Vienna, we shall travel. Mark you! I say *travel;* but there shall be no flight."

Count Podstadsky uttered a cry of wild joy, and pressed the hand she gave him to his lips. "When shall we travel? Now?"

She shook her head. "That were flight. We start to-morrow."

"To-morrow!" cried he, exultingly, "to-morrow, at dawn of day?"

"By no means. To-morrow at noon, in the sight of the whole world."

"Be it so, then," sighed the count. "We go by different roads, and meet at Neustadt."

"Yes, at Neustadt. And now go, Carlo. We both have important arrangements to make before we leave."

"*I* have very little to do," laughed Podstadsky, who had already recovered his spirits. "My valuables all belong to the usurers. For some time past they have stationed an agent of theirs in my house as steward. He watches over their property; I have no interest in it."

"Why don't you pay them with your nice new bank-notes—hey, Carlo?"

Carlo grew troubled again. "I did try to do so, but they refused. They had given me gold, and must have gold in return."

"So much the better. Your bank-notes will meet with a better reception elsewhere," said Arabella, hurriedly. "But come, let us go to work. Burn all indiscreet papers, and take every thing that you can secrete. And now away with you! I must be alone, for I have enough to do to keep me up this livelong night. Clear your brows, my Carlo, and sleep free from anxiety. To-morrow we leave Vienna, and your trials will be at an end. *Addio, caro amico mio, addio!*"

He kissed her hand, and she accompanied him to the door. He closed it behind him, while she stood breathless, listening to his retreating footsteps. Now he was on the staircase. The heavy street door closed—a moment's delay, and his carriage rolled away. Yes, he was off at last. Thank Heaven, he was off!

CHAPTER CLVIII.

COLONEL SZEKULY.

ARABELLA listened—listened until the sound of the wheels had died away; then she laughed. "He thinks me fool enough to share his disgrace! As if I had not long ago foreseen that this was to be the end of that hair-brained fool! In expectation of *his* fate, I have been countermining with Szekuly, and his foolish old hands have flung up shovelfuls of gold as we went along—bright, shining ducats, which shall go with me to Paris. Now I am free, free from my dangerous accomplice, free from my tiresome old adorer, whose love for me so nearly approaches insanity that it may lead him to compromise himself in more ways than one. But he must not compromise *me!* For the world, as yet, I am the modest, virtuous Countess Baillou, chaste as I am beautiful!"

While she soliloquized thus, the countess walked hurriedly through the room, with folded arms, fiery eyes, and on her lips a smile—but what a smile! Alone in that gorgeous apartment, with her sinister beauty and her angry, flashing jewels, she might have been mistaken for a malign spirit who had just left her kingdom of darkness to visit the earth with ruin!

"It is evident," said she, musing, "that the emperor meant to warn him; and it follows that as he has not fled to-day he is lost! And he *shall* be lost, for I must be free. I cannot afford to share my hardly-earned winnings with him. He must away to prison; it is my only chance for freedom.

"But if, after all, the emperor should connive at his escape! Or if he should be seized with a fit of suspicion, and return! Good Heaven! now that fortune favors me, I must snatch security while it lies within my grasp."

Here she rang so violently, that the valet, who was in the anteroom, almost precipitated himself into her presence.

"If Count Podstadsky-Liechtenstein calls, say that I am not at home. Apprise the other servants, and add that he is never to find admittance into this house again. Whosoever, after this, admits him even to the vestibule, shall leave my service. Away with you!

"And now," continued she, as the valet closed the door, "now to work." She went toward a mirror, and there unfastened her diadem, then her necklace, brooch, and bracelets. With her hands full of jewels, she flew to her dressing-room and deposited them in their respective cases. Then she opened a large, brass-bound casket, and counted her treasures.

The first thing that came to light was a necklace of diamond *solitaires*. "These three stars of the first magnitude," said she, contemplating the centre stones, "are the involuntary contribution of the Princess Garampi. I borrowed her bracelet for a model, giving my word that it should not pass from my hands. Nor has it done so, for I have kept her brilliants and returned her—mine. She is never the wiser, and I am the richer thereby. For this string of pearls, with the superb ruby clasp, I am indebted to her highness the Princess Palm. One evening, as I welcomed her with an embrace, I made out to unfasten it while I related to her a piquant anecdote of her husband's mistress. Of course she was too much absorbed in my narrative to feel that her necklace was slipping, for I was not only entertaining, but very caressing on the occasion. There was music in the room, so that no one heard the treasure fall. The necklace, a perfect fortune, lay at my feet; I moved my train to cover it, and signed to Carlo, who, I must say, was always within call. He invited the princess to dance, and—the pearls found their way to my pocket. What a talk that loss made in Vienna! What offers of reward that poor woman made to recover her necklace! All in vain, and nobody condoled more affectionately with her than the charming, kind-hearted Countess Baillou. This sorrow—but, pshaw! what a child I am, to be gloating over my precious toys while time passes away, and I must be off to-night!"

She closed her boxes, replaced them in her strong, well-secured casket, and, having locked it, hung the key around her neck. "Here lies the price of a princely estate," said she, "and now I must attend to my ducats."

She stood upon a chair, and took from the wall a picture. Then, pressing a spring behind it, a little door flew open, revealing a casket similar to the one containing her jewels. She took it down, and, placing it on the table, contemplated the two boxes with profound satisfaction.

"Twenty thousand lovers' eyes look out from this casket," said she, with a laugh; "all promising a future of triumphant joy. Twenty thousand ducats! The fruits of my savings! And dear old Szekuly has made economy very easy for some months past, for one-half of these ducats once belonged to him. To be sure, I gave him in return the deeds of an entail which I own in Italy, and which he can easily reconvert into money. At least he thinks so. Well—I owe him nothing. We made an exchange, and that is all."

After this edifying monologue, the countess exchanged her elegant costume for a simple travelling-dress, and as she completed her toilet the clock struck eight. Every thing being ready, she returned to her boudoir and rang once. This signified that her confidential valet was wanted. In a few moments the door opened, and an old man, whose dark hair and eyes marked his Italian birth, entered noiselessly. The countess bade him close the door and approach. He obeyed without the least manifestation of surprise, muttering as he went, "Walls have ears."

"Giuseppe," said his mistress, "are you still willing to follow me?"

"Did I not swear to your mother, my beloved benefactress, never to abandon you, signora?"

"Thanks, *amico;* then we leave Vienna to-night."

"I heard the order forbidding Count Podstadsky the house, signora, and I made ready to depart."

"Good and faithful Giuseppe! Since you are ready, nothing need detain us. Go at once and order post-horses, and come with the travelling carriage to the corner of the street above this."

"*Si, signora;* I shall leave the carriage there, and return for the two caskets; you will then go out by the postern, and having joined us, we are off. Is that your will?"

"Yes, Giuseppe, yes. Go for your life!"

"Be ready to leave the house in one hour, signora, for you know that I am a swift messenger."

The old man bowed and retreated as silently as he came. His

mistress looked after him, saying, "There goes a jewel which I have neither borrowed nor stolen: it comes to me by the inalienable right of inheritance. Now I can rest until he returns."

With a deep sigh of relief, she threw herself upon the divan, and, closing her eyes, gave herself up to rosy dreams. She had not lain long, before the door opened and a valet announced "Colonel Szekuly."

"I cannot receive him," exclaimed she, without rising.

"You must receive him, countess," said a voice behind her, and starting from the divan, she beheld the tall form of her "tiresome old adorer," enveloped in a military cloak, with his plumed hat drawn far over his brow. Before she had time to speak, he had dismissed the valet and closed the door.

"You presume strangely upon your influence," cried Arabella, half amused, half angry. "Because you reign over my heart, you aspire to reign over my domestics, I perceive."

"Peace!" cried the colonel, imperatively. "I have not come hither to suck poison from your honeyed lips. I have already had enough to cause my death. Though you have cruelly deceived me, I come to give you a last proof of my love. Do not interrupt me."

"I will not breathe," said she, with a smile so bewitching, that Szekuly averted his eyes, for it maddened him.

"You know," said he, and the old man's voice faltered as he spoke, "that the director of police is my friend. I had invited him to dine with me. He came but half an hour ago to excuse himself because of an arrest of some importance. Do you guess whose arrest?"

"How should I guess?" said she, still with that enchanting smile. "I have no acquaintance with the police."

"God grant that you may never make their acquaintance!" ejaculated he, hoarsely. "They have just now arrested Count Podstadsky."

Not a feature of her face changed, as she replied: "Ah! Count Podstadsky arrested? I am sorry to hear it. Can you tell me why?"

"For forging bank-notes to the amount of a million of florins."

"I suspected as much; I have several times been the victim of his thousand-florin notes."

"The victim, countess? Is that an appropriate expression?"

"I think it is," replied she, quietly. "Is that all the news?"

"No, countess. The count is taken, but his accomplice—"

She breathed quickly and her mouth quivered, but she rallied and made answer. "He had accomplices?"

"He had an accomplice, and—hush! we have no time for falsehood. Every moment is precious to you. Perhaps the director of the police came to me because knowing how—I have loved you, he would rescue you from shame. Let us hope that he did, for he told me that he had orders to arrest the Countess Baillou."

"When?" asked she, almost inaudibly; and now her face was pale as death.

"At dusk, that you might be spared the curiosity of a crowd."

Arabella sprang from her couch. "It is already night!" cried she, her voice rising almost to a scream.

"Yes," replied her lover, "but I hope we have time. I have prepared every thing for your flight. My carriage and postilions await you in the next street. Be quick, and you may escape."

"Yes, yes," exclaimed she. "Give me but one moment." She

flew to her dressing-room, and tried to carry her two boxes. But the ducats were too heavy.

"I must leave the jewels," said she; and climbing up again with her casket, she concealed it in the wall, and replaced the picture. "It is, at all events, perfectly safe, and Giuseppe will come for it."

"Come!" cried Szekuly from the drawing-room.

"I come," answered she, while she wrapped a cloak about her and with trembling hands tied on her travelling-hat.

"Give me your box," said Szekuly, "it will impede your movements."

But she held it fast, and said: "No—they are my jewels, now my only riches."

"And you are afraid to trust them with me?" asked he, with a bitter smile—"to me, who will die of your treachery!"

"People do not die so easily," said she, trying to smile; but her teeth chattered, as she flew rather than ran down the grand staircase, and arrived breathless before the door. The porter opened it in wonder. The night-air blew into her face, and revived her courage. Now she might breathe freely, for she was—

But no! From the dark recesses of the stone portico emerged three muffled figures, and one of them laid his rough grasp upon the delicate arm of the countess and dragged her back into the vestibule.

"Too late, too late!" murmured the colonel, passively following, while his heart bled for the treacherous woman whom he would have died to save.

"Countess Arabella Baillou," said one of the figures, "I arrest you in the name of the emperor."

She looked defiance at him. "Who are you that dare arrest me?"

He took off his hat and bowed derisively. "I am the director of police, countess, very much at your service. Here is my authority for your arrest."

He would have shown her the emperor's signature, but she dashed away the paper, and fastening her angry eyes upon Szekuly, who was leaning against a marble pillar, she said:

"That is your dear friend, is it? You have been playing the detective, have you? Inducing me to fly, that my flight might expose me to suspicion!"

The colonel cried out as though he had been wounded. "By all that is sacred in heaven, I would have saved you!" sobbed he.

"And for your attempt I am obliged to detain you also, my poor, unhappy friend," said the director of the police. "But you will soon be able to prove your innocence. Let one of these men accompany you home, and there remain under arrest until you hear from me. Now, madame, follow me, if you please."

"Allow me first to speak a word of consolation to my generous protector," said the countess.

"Certainly, madame."

Arabella bowed her beautiful head and approached Szekuly, who was scarcely able to stand, so great was his emotion.

"Colonel Szekuly," said she, in a whisper, "you lent me fifty thousand florins upon some Italian securities of mine. They are all forgeries. I forged them myself, as well as all the fine letters of introduction with which I befooled the aristocracy of Vienna."

Szekuly stared for one moment at his tormentor, then hastily, pressing his hand to his heart, he sank with a low sigh upon the marble floor.

The countess laughed out loud. "He has fainted!" exclaimed she. "Contemptible world, wherein men act like women, and women like men! Come, gentlemen, I am ready to follow you; but my innocence will speedily be reëstablished, and the emperor, then, will owe me an apology for his want of courtesy."

CHAPTER CLIX.

THE POPE'S DEPARTURE.

THE people of Vienna were enraptured to the last with the visit of the pope. Whenever he appeared, they sank upon their knees, as, with his bewitching smile, he gave them his benediction. But these accidental meetings did not satisfy the zeal of the Viennese; they longed to receive a formal and solemn blessing, pronounced in the cathedral from the papal throne.

High upon his throne sat the holy father in his pontifical robes, his triple crown upon his head, and the diamond cross of his order upon his breast. His canopy was of velvet, richly embroidered with gold, and around him were grouped the princes of the church. But the pope, his large expressive eyes fixed upon the altar, seemed isolated from all ecclesiastical pomp, mindful alone of the God whose representative on earth he was. And when he rose to give the papal benediction, the handsome face of Pius Sixth beamed with holy inspiration, while the people, filled with love and joy, knelt to receive the blessing which had been transmitted to them in uninterrupted succession from the holy Apostles themselves.

But however the loving heart of the pope might rejoice at his reception by the people, there were two men in Vienna who resisted him with all the pride of individuality and all the consciousness of their own worth and consequence.

The first of these was the emperor. He had sought continually to remind the sovereign pontiff that although the head of Christendom might be his guest, he, Joseph, was sole lord of his own domains. He had ordered that all ecclesiastic ordinances, before being printed, should receive the imperial *exequatur*. The pope had desired during his stay to issue a bull in relation to the newly-erected church of St. Michael. The bull had been returned for the signature of the emperor.

Other humiliations besides this had been endured by the head of the church. Perhaps in the two solemn benedictions which he had given—the first in the palace-court, the second in the cathedral, Pius had hoped to appear in public with the emperor as his spiritual vassal; but Joseph was careful not to allow him this gratification. He had no sooner learned that the throne of the pope in the cathedral was being erected higher than his own, than he ordered the imperial throne to be removed, and excused himself from attendance at high mass upon the pretext that he was suffering from severe pain in the eyes, and dared not encounter the blaze of light. It was an obstinate case of ocular malady, for it had already prevented him from appearing in the palace-court, when decorum would have exacted of him to walk behind the pope.

The other man who had completely ignored the pope's presence in Vienna, was Kaunitz. In vain had his visit been expected; he never came; and finally the day of the departure of his holiness arrived. He had received the adieus of the nobles and had taken leave of the clergy. At two o'clock he expected the emperor, who was to accompany him as far as Mariabrunn. It was now eleven, and he had, therefore, three hours of leisure.

He rang for his valet and bade him send a messenger to Prince Kaunitz, apprising him that in half an hour the pope would visit him. A few moments after this, the door reopened and the papal master of ceremonies entered the room. Pius received him with a friendly smile. "I know why you are here," said he. "You have heard from Brambilla that I contemplate a visit to Prince Kaunitz, and you come to remonstrate with me."

"Yes, I entreat your holiness not to take this step which—"

"Which is beneath the dignity of the head of the church," interrupted Pius. "You can well imagine that I have already said as much to myself. I know, that in going to visit this proud man, I humble myself. But if humility becomes any one of the servants of God, it becomes the successor of Peter, and I have no right to shrink from personal humiliation, when, perchance, it may win something from haughtiness in favor of the church of God. Perhaps the advances I make to Kaunitz may move his cold heart, and teach him to do unto others as others have done unto him."

"But if your holiness intends to bestow such an unheard-of honor upon the prince, you should at least have given him a day wherein to make suitable preparations for your coming."

The pope smiled. "Dear friend, I see farther into this man's heart than you. I have taken him unawares, precisely because he would gladly have added to my humiliations by neglecting the hint which such an announcement would have conveyed. It was, therefore, better to forestall the slight by making it impossible for him to offer it as a matter of choice."

"But why does your holiness confer upon this disdainful Austrian an honor which he is unworthy to receive?"

"Why? Because I feel it my duty to leave nothing undone which can be conducive to the interests and glory of our holy mother, the church. Who knows but that the Lord may have sent me to convert an erring sinner from his ways? Go, my friend, go, and send my messenger. I must see this man who, from youth to old age, has defied the Lord of heaven and earth!"

A half an hour later an imperial state carriage was before the palace of Prince Kaunitz, and the pope, followed by his chaplain, entered its lofty vestibule.

The prince had been diligent, for there, in their richest liveries of state, were his whole household, and at the foot of the staircase, over which a rich Turkey carpet had been spread for the occasion, stood the young Countess Clary in full dress, who knelt, and in soft, trembling accents begged of his holiness a blessing.

He laid his hand upon her head, and then extended it that she might press to her lips the ring of St. Peter. He then raised her, and begged her to accompany him to the presence of her uncle, the prince.

As they walked together from one magnificent apartment to another, the countess was apologizing for her uncle who, not having left his room for some weeks, was unable to come out to receive his holiness from dread of encountering the cold air of the halls.

The pope bowed, and followed the countess until she stopped before a closed door, and said:

"In this room, my uncle awaits the gracious visit of your holiness."

The pope entered, but he was not met on the threshold as he had anticipated. No, indeed. Far from the door, with the entire length of the room between them, close to the chimney where a huge fire was burning, stood Kaunitz. He was in an undress coat, with his hat upon his head,* and so absorbed in thought that he was quite unaware of the entrance of his guest, until the Countess Clary, in a loud voice, said:

"His holiness the pope."

Kaunitz moved, and measuring his advance by that of Pius, he managed to meet him just half way, and, as he bowed, he at last condescended to take off his hat.

Pius returned the bow, and, as is customary with all independent princes, extended his hand to be kissed.

Kaunitz, with an assurance almost inconceivable, took it within his own, and giving it a hard shake, after the English fashion, exclaimed:

"*De tout mon cœur! de tout mon cœur!*" †

At this familiarity an expression of pain flitted over the handsome, noble features of the pope, and the smile died upon his lips. But he had expected humiliation, and had armed himself to endure it.

"I have come to visit your highness," said he, mildly, "because, although you have not asked it, I would fain leave with you the blessing of the church."

"I thank your holiness for the consideration you are pleased to show me," replied Kaunitz. "But before all things let me request your permission to resume my hat. The cold air is injurious to my weak head." ‡

And whether to ward off the cold air or the blessing of the church, the old sinner replaced his hat without waiting to hear the pope's reply.

Pius could only affect not to perceive the rudeness, while he seated himself, and invited the prince to be seated also.

There was a pause. Kaunitz took the chair, and then looking full into the eyes of his guest, awaited with perfect indifference the opening of the conversation.

The expression of pain deepened upon the face of the pope; but again he recovered himself, and made a second effort at conciliation.

"I have come to give to your highness a proof of my esteem and consideration," said he.

Kaunitz bowed stiffly. "I am so much the more surprised at this mark of consideration, that I have never been able to see in your holiness's state-papers the least recognition of my claims to statesmanship."

"Perhaps we may have misjudged one another. I have desired, in visiting Vienna, to heal all misunderstandings, and to afford to

* Gross-Hoffinger, iii., p. 38.
† Historical.—See Gross-Hoffinger, iii., p. 39.
‡ The prince's own words.—See Bourgoing, "Pius VI. and his Pontificate," p. 225.

my son in Christ, the emperor, every facility for his reconciliation to the holy church. I have also prayed to Almighty God to touch the heart of your highness, that you also might turn your steps toward the 'one fold.' "

"I hope that I have never strayed from the path of right. The object of my life has been to make Austria great and independent, and to aid my emperor in freeing his subjects from foreign dominion. To-day no earthly potentate has a voice in Austria, save Joseph; he is absolute master here, and as all his acts have been for Austria's good, she has entered at last upon a career of indisputable prosperity. But there is nothing wonderful in this, when he had me as a coadjutor."

Pius looked with profound sadness at this haughty statesman, who had not a thought beyond the present world.

"You speak of things that are of the earth, earthy. And yet your hair is white as snow, and *you* an old man hastening to the grave! At your advanced age it would become your highness, who have done so much for your sovereign, to do something now to reconcile yourself to your Maker." *

Kaunitz grew deathly pale; not all the paint that besmeared his wrinkles could conceal his pallor. His forehead contracted, and hung in heavy folds, while his breath came fast and gasping. The pope had spoken of THE GRAVE, and the vulnerable heel had received a wound.

It was some time before he could recover his self-possession—some time again before he could force down his fury, and so remain master of the situation. At last the victory was won, and he spoke calmly.

"I hope," said he, "that having done nothing to offend my Maker, it is unnecessary for me to seek reconciliation with Him. I have done all that I could for *religion;* it is not my fault if her interests are not identical with those of the church. But pardon me that I should have strayed to themes so unbecoming to my character as host, and yours as my guest. Let us speak of science, art, life, and its multitudinous enjoyments. Your holiness, I know, is a distinguished patron of the fine arts. And as you are fond of painting, allow me to offer you a sight of my pictures. You will find them quite worth your inspection."

With these words, Kaunitz rose, and, without waiting for the pope's consent, stepped as hastily forward as his infirmities would permit, and opened the door which led to his picture-gallery. The pope followed him leisurely, and after him came the chaplain, the Countess Clary, and Baron Binder.

Kaunitz did the honors, passing with visible haste from one painting to another. "Here," said he, "is a masterpiece of Murillo, which the Vatican might envy me—Murillo, who was equally successful, whether he tried his hand at Virgin or vagabond. Just look at this! Did ever the earth bestow upon longing man a more voluptuously-beautiful woman than this dark-eyed Madonna!"

"It is a beautiful picture," murmured Pius, approaching with the hope of being spared any more such comments on art.

"But your holiness has not the proper light," cried Kaunitz, familiarly. "Come a little more to the left."

And, in the excitement of his enthusiasm, the prince was so for-

* The pope's own words to Kaunitz.—See "Pius VI. and his Pontificate," p. 226.

getful of the rank of his visitor as to catch him by the arm, and drag him to the spot he advised. Pius started, and for one moment his eyes darted fire, for, to the very depths of his soul, he felt the indignity: but he remembered his resolve to "bear all things," and stood quietly contemplating the picture until his tormentor spoke again.

He, on his part, affected not to perceive that he had done any thing amiss; and with an apperance of great *empressement*, he followed the pope from picture to picture, dragging him first to one point, then to another, as he pretended to think that the best light for seeing his paintings was to the right or to the left.*

The pope made no resistance, perhaps because he was astounded at the insolence of the proceeding, perhaps because he judged it best to affect unconsciousness of the insults which were being heaped upon his head. But he was wounded to the heart, and raised his eyes to his chaplain, who, indignant at the contumely offered to his beloved pontiff, at once came forward to his relief, by reminding him that the emperor would shortly visit his rooms.

"You are right, my friend," said Pius. Then turning to Kaunitz, he continued: "I must go, and cannot have the pleasure of completing my survey of your paintings. Had I known that you possessed so many treasures, I would have come earlier, that I might have been allowed to visit them a little more at my leisure. I am under many obligations to you for your politeness, and for the very unusual courtesies which I have received at your hands."

He took the arm of his chaplain, and left the room. At the door he was met by the Countess Clary, and as she knelt a second time before him, he laid his hand upon her head, with a gesture full of nobleness and grace.

"I leave you my blessing, my child, and I leave it to all who inhabit this house. May those whose hearts have been hardened by sin, return in humility to the Lord; for humility is the crown of Christian graces, and he who hath it not can never aspire to life eternal."

He went on without ever turning his head or seeming to know that Kaunitz was behind, excusing himself from going farther with his holiness, by reason of the danger to which he would be exposed, etc., etc.

At the portal of the palace the pope was received by his master of ceremonies, who accompanied him to his cabinet. One glance at his pale countenance had revealed to him the inutility of the condescension of the supreme pontiff, who with a weary sigh sank back into the depths of an arm-chair.

"You were quite right," said he, after a pause, "and I was wrong. I ought never to have gone to this man. God has punished me for my vanity, and has used him as an instrument to remind me that I am but a poor miserable creature, full of projects, but empty of results! Ah, Battista! with what bright hopes of touching the emperor's heart I started upon this pilgrimage to Vienna, priding myself upon my humility, and building thereupon my trust! Nothing has come of my efforts—nothing! I have learned one thing, however, of the emperor. He is no Christian, but he is not a bad man. I really believe that he acts from a sense of mistaken duty."

*Bourgoing, "Pius VI. and his Pontificate," p. 227.

The master of ceremonies shook his head, and was about to reply, when there was a knock at the door, and the emperor asked admittance. The master of ceremonies retired to the anteroom, where the suites of the pope and the emperor were awaiting the signal for departure. Joseph approached his holiness, and gave into his hand a case which he begged him to accept as a souvenir of his visit to Austria.

Pius, bewildered by all that he had endured on that day, opened it in silence. But he was astonished when he saw the magnificence of the gift. It was a large cross of pure, white brilliants, upon a bed of dark crimson velvet.*

"I beg of your holiness," said Joseph, "to wear this in remembrance of me."

Pius raised his head, and looked anxiously into the smiling face of the emperor. "Oh, my son," said he, "would this were the only cross I was forced take back with me to Rome!"

"Your holiness must be content to take with you my love and regard," replied Joseph, evasively; "and I would gladly give you another pledge of them before we part. Will you allow me to bestow upon your nephew, Luigi Braschi, the title and diploma of a prince?"

Pius shook his head. "I thank your majesty; but my nephew cannot accept the honor you would confer upon him. It was not to advance the interests of my family, but the glory of the church, that I came to Vienna.† Your majesty would make a prince of my nephew, and yet you seek to humble his uncle, who is the vicar of Christ on earth."

"What have I done, your holiness?"

"You have suppressed the order of the Mendicant Friars, and you have called Cardinal Megazzi to account, because he printed one of my bulls without submitting it to you for your approbation."

"I consider that the Mendicants lead a contemptible life, and we have no use for them in Austria. As to the bull, no law is permitted to go forth in my dominions unless it is approved by me, for the laws of my land must be subject to no power but my own."

The pope heaved a sigh, for it was useless to argue with Joseph. "Is it also true that your majesty has confiscated and sold all the property of the convents and churches, and that it is your intention to give salaries to the clergy?"

"Yes, that is my plan; I may as well be frank with you, and avow it. But I am very far from its accomplishment; I have taken nothing but the property of the convents as yet."

"And woe to your sacrilegious hand that you have done so!" cried Pius, rising to his feet and confronting the emperor. "I cannot conceal from your majesty that your conduct has inflicted a serious wound upon the church, and has scandalized all good Christians. The robbing of the church is an error condemned by ecclesiastic councils, and execrated by the fathers of the church. Shall I remind you of the words which John, the patriarch of Alexandria, spoke to a sovereign who would have robbed the clergy of their temporal goods? 'How canst thou, a perishable mortal, give unto another that which is not thine own? And when thou givest that which belongs to God, thou rebellest against God himself. What man endowed with reason will not pronounce thine act a transgres-

*This cross was valued at 200,000 florins.—See Hubner, i., p. 128.

†Pius's own words.—See Gross-Hoffinger, iii., p. 46.

sion, a signal and sinful injustice? How can a man presume to call himself a Christian who desecrates the objects consecrated to Christ!' Thus has God spoken through the mouth of His servant, and his words are appropriate to the acts of your majesty!" *

The voice of the pope was choked by tears, and in the excess of his grief he sank back upon the chair and leaned his head upon his hand.

The emperor had listened with profound indifference. It was not the first time he had seen the pope thus moved, and he was perfectly aware that it was better to make no reply until the violence of his emotion had exhausted itself

"Your holiness goes too far in your apostolic zeal," said he, after a pause of some length. "I shall neither quote the Scriptures nor the Fathers in my defence; for you and I would not be apt to interpret them in the same sense. I shall content myself with observing that, in spite of all your anger, I shall hearken to the voice of my own conscience, which tells me that my acts are those of a wise lawgiver, and of a faithful defender of religion. With this voice, my own reason, and help from above, I am not afraid of being in error. † At the same time, I assure your holiness of my sincerest regard. You may not have attained the object of your visit, but I hope that you carry away at least the conviction of my honesty and integrity of purpose. The interests of state and church may be at variance, but we need not be personal enemies; and over the gulf which separates us as princes, we may join hands as friends, may we not?"

With these words, the emperor extended his hand, and the pope did not refuse to take it.

"It is time for me to be going," replied he. "This cross, which in the prodigality of your friendship, you have bestowed upon me, I shall wear for your sake, and it shall remind me to pray daily that God may enlighten you, and lead you back to the Way, the Truth, and the Life. For in the church alone is true peace to be found. He who strives against her, strives against Christ. Farewell, and may He mercifully bring you to a sense of your errors!"

CHAPTER CLX.

THE REPULSE.

THE aristocracy of Vienna were in a state of extreme excitement. It was whispered from one noble to another, that the Aulic Council had condemned Count Podstadsky-Liechtenstein for life to the house of correction, and he was to sweep the streets in the garb of a common criminal. ‡ This was not all. Another fearful announcement had fallen like a bolt upon the heads of the most illustrious families in Vienna. For some weeks past, Count Szekuly had been missing. His servants had given out that he had gone to visit his relatives in Hungary; but they seemed so embarrassed and uneasy, that no one believed them. Colonel Szekuly had many powerful friends. He was an intimate associate of all the Hungarian noblemen in Vienna, and had long been a welcome guest wherever the fashionable world

* This harangue of the pope is historical.—Hubner, i., p. 285.
† Joseph's own words.—Hubner, i., p. 287.
‡ This was in accordance with the new Josephine code.

had assembled. Moreover, he was the adorer of the most admired woman in Vienna, the lovely Countess Baillou.

She, too, had disappeared. Where could they be? Was it accident, or had she responded to his love, and left a world of worshippers, to live for him alone?

Finally the mystery was solved. A few days after the arrest of Podstadsky, Szekuly also had been arrested. It was now well known that Podstadsky had forged notes; but it was impossible to suspect a man of Szekuly's unimpeachable character of any connection with a crime of that nature.

Unhappily, however, though less in degree, the accusation against Szekuly was similar in kind. He was a defaulter; and from the coffers of his regiment (which were confided to his care) sixty thousand florins had disappeared.

The Countess Baillou was his accuser. She had been charged with being a party to Podstadsky's fraud, but he, as well as Szekuly, had loudly declared her innocence. Both had avowed themselves to be her lovers, and it was ascertained that her household had been maintained at Podstadsky's cost. As his mistress, she had received many of his bank-notes, but he protested that she knew nothing of his forgeries. He confessed his own guilt, but firmly upheld her innocence. So far from being his accomplice, Podstadsky declared that she had been his victim.

But a coffer containing twenty thousand ducats had been found upon the person of the countess. This money had not been given her by Podstadsky, since he had nothing but forged notes to give. The countess, when questioned, answered unhesitatingly, that one-half the sum she had won at play, and the other half she had received as a present from Colonel Szekuly. It was well known that Szekuly had not the means of bestowing such princely gifts; yet, when informed of the countess's charge, he had grown pale, but replied that the countess had spoken nothing but truth.

Suspicion was aroused; the strong box of the regiment was examined, and found empty! Von Szekuly acknowledged that he had taken the money, believing in good faith that, by the sale of certain deeds in his possession, he would be able to replace it at short notice. But where were these papers? They could not be found, and Szekuly refused to give any account of them. He was guilty, he said, and must submit to his fate. Colonel von Szekuly, a Hungarian baron, under sentence for theft! This was a blot upon the escutcheon of more than one illustrious family. But the emperor, in framing his severe code, had reserved to himself the right to pardon; and this right, it was hoped, he would exercise in favor of the high-born criminals. It was not possible that he intended to humiliate the nobility of Austria so cruelly as to condemn two of them to the pillory, to the sweeping of the streets, to be chained to two common felons for life!*

No!—this was an outrage which the emperor would never dare to perpetrate, for it would arouse the bitter animosity of the whole aristocracy. Still it would be better to petition him at once, and warn him of his peril.

He was petitioned, but his invariable reply was, that the law must decide. It was known, however, that the sentence was not signed, and there was still hope. But how to reach the emperor?

* Hubner, ii., p. 383.

Since the council had pronounced judgment on the criminals, Joseph had granted audience to no one; he had avoided all proximity to the nobles, and to secure himself from importunity, had ceased to ride in the park, contenting himself with a daily drive in his *cabriolet*. Finally the petitioners remembered the "*Controlorgang*," and thither they repaired early in the morning. Ladies, as well as lords, came on foot, that the emperor might not be warned by the sound of their rolling equipages to deny himself again. They were the first to enter the palace on that day, and were so numerous that no other petitioners could obtain entrance. On that occasion, then, they were among their peers, and the *canaille* would never know how count and countess, baron and baroness, had humbled themselves for the sake of their caste.

As soon as Günther opened the door, they rushed into the small room which was called the *Controlorgang*, and there, with beating hearts, awaited the entrance of the all-powerful emperor.

He came, and when he saw who were the petitioners of the day, his countenance expressed astonishment; but he did not depart from his usual habit, and walked slowly down the middle of the room, extending his hand to receive the petitions.

"How?" said he, when he had reached the last person, "Count Lampredo, you have nothing to present! You all desire to speak with me? I fear that my time is too short to gratify you."

"Sire, we have but one petition to make," said the count, speaking for the others. "One common misfortune threatens us all—"

"What can it be?"

"Oh, your majesty," cried he, fervently, "have mercy upon Count Podstadsky and Baron von Szekuly!"

"Mercy, sire, mercy for Podstadsky and Szekuly!" cried the noble petitioners with one accord, while all knelt before the astounded emperor.

He surveyed them with an angry frown. "Rise, all of you," said he. "Have you forgotten that kneeling has been abolished here? The Spanish customs which were once so popular in the palace, are unbecoming in this room, where all who enter it are nothing but petitioners seeking justice at my hands."

"And mercy, sire!" added Count Lampredo, imploringly.

"And mercy which can be conceded only so far as it is perfectly compatible with justice."

"Mercy, gracious emperor, mercy for Podstadsky and Szekuly!" reiterated the petitioners.

"You ask for mercy which wounds justice, and I repeat that I cannot grant the one without the other. Count Podstadsky, through his frauds, has ruined thousands of my subjects; Baron von Szekuly has stolen sixty thousand florins, and both these men have disgraced their births and titles."

"Allow Szekuly to be tried by a military court, sire. They at least would shield him from dishonor, for they would sentence him to death."

"He has committed a vulgar crime and he shall be punished according to the burghers' code. That code ignores capital punishment."

"But its punishments are more fearful than death, sire. A man is thrice dead who has lost liberty, honor, and name. The man who in manacles sweeps the public streets, or tugs at the car, is a thousand times more to be pitied than he who lays his head upon the block. Oh, sire, it cannot be that you would consign a nobleman to such contumely!"

"No, I honor the nobleman too much to brand him with such infamy," replied the emperor, hastily. "But if a cavalier commits a crime, I disfranchise him at once; and, stripped of name, title, and privileges, I hand him over to the law which regards him exactly as it does any other base-born villain.* Be comforted, then. These criminals are no longer noblemen, and have nothing in common with you."

"Oh, sire, do not say so; for their shame is reflected upon us all!"

"How?" exclaimed Joseph, with affected surprise, "are you all thieves and forgers?"

"No, sire; but our honor suffers through their dishonor. Oh, your majesty, in the name of the illustrious families who for centuries have been the loyal subjects of your house, save our escutcheons from this foul blot!"

"Save us, sire, save us from infamy!" echoed the others.

"No!" exclaimed the emperor. "He who is not ashamed of the crime, will not be ashamed of the disgrace. If, for the sake of his rank, a man is to have the privilege of being a villain, where, then, is justice?† Not another word of this! My forbearance is exhausted; for I have sought by every means to convince you that, as a sovereign, I shall show partiality to no order of men. Podstadsky and Szekuly shall suffer to the full extent of the law, for the worth of their ancestors cannot wipe out their own unworthiness."

The emperor withdrew, and when the door closed behind him, many an eye there flashed with hatred, and many a compressed lip told of meditated vengeance for the indignity suffered by a powerful order at his hands that day.

"Our humiliation, then, has been of no avail!" muttered Count Lampredo, "and the nobles of Austria must suffer disgrace because of the obstinate cruelty of the man who should uphold them."

"But we will be revenged!" whispered Count Hojada, a near relative of Szekuly's. "The sovereign who, like Joseph, heaps obloquy upon a nobility, some of whom are his equals in descent, is lost! The emperor shall remember this hour, and rue it also!"

"Yes," said another, "he shall repent this day. We are all of one mind, are we not, friends?"

"Ay," muttered they, with gnashing teeth. "He shall pay dearly for this!"

CHAPTER CLXI.

THE COUNT IN THE PILLORY.

CROWDS of people gathered around the street corners to read the large hand-bills posted there. The bills announced that Count Podstadsky-Liechtenstein had been condemned to three days of pillory, to public sweeping of the streets, and ten years' detention in the house of correction. Colonel von Szekuly to three days of pillory, and four years' detention.

* Joseph's own words. See Hubner, ii., p. 432.
† Ibid.

The guilt of the Countess Baillou not having been fully established, she was pardoned by the emperor. But she was ordered to be present at Podstadsky's exposition in the pillory, and then to leave Vienna forever.

The people read these fearful tidings in dumb amazement and vague apprehension of evil to themselves. Never had they so completely realized the new order of things as at this moment. One of the privileged, whom they had hitherto beheld at a distance in splendid equipages, on elegant horses, in brilliant uniforms around the person of the emperor, one of these demi-gods was to be trailed in the dust like a criminal from the dregs of the populace. A count, in the gray smock of the felon, was to sweep the streets, which, perchance, his aristocratic foot had never trodden before. A proud Hungarian nobleman, a colonel of the guard, was to be exposed in the pillory for three days. These were terrible and startling events. Not a trace of exultation was upon the gloomy faces of the multitude; this abasement of two men of illustrious birth to an equality with boors, seemed an invasion of the conservative principles of society. It was an ugly dream—the people could not realize it.

They must go to the spot where the sentence was to be executed, to see if indeed Olympus had been levelled to the earth. Hurried along by one common impulse, the silent multitude wound in a long stream through the streets, until they reached the market-place where the sentence was to be carried out. Neither idle curiosity nor malice had led the people thither; it was a pilgrimage to the new era which at last was dawning upon the world.

There, in the centre of the great open square, was the throne of infamy upon which an Austrian nobleman was about to bid adieu to name, honor, family, and the associations which had surrounded his boyhood, and to be thrust into the revolting companionship of robbers and murderers!

Not a smile was seen upon those appalled faces; men whispered to one another that the count was the only son of one of the proudest families in Hungary; and that the countess, his mother, had died of her son's shame. The eyes of the women filled wth tears, and, for the sake of the martyred mother, they forgave the guilty son. The weeping of the women deepened the sympathies of the men; and they began to murmur against the heartless emperor, who degraded an illustrious subject, and sent a noble countess broken-hearted to the grave!

And now appeared the criminal. Culprit though he was, his beauty and air of distinction were indisputable.

"Poor young man!" murmured the women, sobbing.

"He will not long survive his disgrace," said the men, sorrowfully. "He looks like a ghost, and the emperor will soon have to bury him by the side of his mother."

No one remembered that this man had committed an infamous crime; no one thanked the emperor for having bestowed upon the Austrian people the inestimable gift of equality before the law. The commoner himself felt aggrieved at the monarch who had treated a nobleman no better than he would have done a serf.

Count Podstadsky was still in the elegant costume of the day. Graceful and distinguished in his bearing, he leaned his weary body against the stake that supported the scaffold on which he was to suffer the last degree of public infamy. But now the executioner approached, holding a pair of large glistening shears. He gathered the soft brown curls of the count in his rough grasp, and very soon the glossy locks fell, and there remained nothing but the shorn head of the felon. This done, the executioner drew off the gold-embroidered coat which became the young nobleman so well, and threw over his shoulders the coarse smock, which, henceforth, was to designate him as a miscreant.

How changed, alas, was the high-born Carlo! How little this chattering creature, disguised in serge, resembled the cavalier who had enlisted the sympathy of the multitude! He was no longer a man, and name he had none. His number, in scarlet list upon the left sleeve of his smock, was the only mark that distinguished him from his brethren—the other malefactors. But the fearful toilet was not yet at an end. The feet and hands were yet to be manacled. As the handcuffs clicked around those delicate wrists, the executioner looked up in amazement. Heretofore he had been accustomed to hear the jeers and loud mockery of the multitude, as they applauded the completion of the felon's toilet; but to-day there was not a sound! Nothing to be seen but pale, sorrowful faces—nothing to be heard but sobs and murmurs of sympathy.

Still one more torture! The executioner gave him the broom, the *bâton* of his disgrace, and he grasped its handle for support. He could scarcely stand now!

At this moment, in fiendish contrast with the behavior of the people, a loud, mocking laugh was heard. Shudderingly they looked around, wondering who it was that could add the weight of a sneer to the supreme misery which was rending *their* hearts. It came from above; and every face, even that of the wretched Podstadsky, was uplifted in horror. He caught at the stake, and his vacant eyes rested upon the house whence the cruel laugh had issued. There, on a balcony, guarded by several men in black, stood a beautiful young woman. She it was who had dealt the blow. In the hour of his agony her rosy lips had mocked him!

"Arabella!" shrieked the despairing man; and with this cry he sank insensible to the earth.*

While all this was transpiring at the market-place, an imperial state-carriage had been hurrying through the streets until it stopped before a gloomy house, of which the doors and window-shutters were all closed. A footman, in the imperial livery, was seen to ring, and then an old man in faded black livery opened the door. A few whispered words passed between them; then a cavalier, in an elegant uniform, sprang from the carriage and entered the house. The old butler went before, and showed him up the creaking staircase, and through a suite of mouldy rooms until they reached one with closed doors.

"So please your majesty," said the old man, "Count Podstadsky-Liechtenstein is in there."

The emperor nodded. "Do not announce me," said he, and he knocked at the door. A feeble voice from within responded to the knock, and the emperor entered without further ceremony. A tall,

*Count Podstadsky did not long survive his disgrace. His delicate body soon sank under the hardships of his terrible existence. One day while sweeping the streets he ruptured a blood-vessel, and died there, with no mourners save his fellow-criminals.—See Hubner, ii., pp. 583-591. "Characteristic and Historical Anecdotes of Joseph II." Friedel's "Letters from Vienna," vol. i., p. 68.

venerable man in deep mourning came forward and looked at him with hollow, staring eyes.

"The emperor!" exclaimed he, recognizing his unexpected guest.

"Yes, Count Podstadsky, it is I," said the emperor, bowing, as he would have done before a mighty monarch. "I come to express my profound regret for the great misfortune which has lately befallen you. No man knows better than myself what grief it is to lose a beloved wife. And yours was such a noble, such a devoted wife!"

"Devoted!" echoed the old count, sadly. "Alas, sire, there was something on earth which was nearer to her heart than I, else she had not died and left me alone. I loved nothing but her, and in losing her I lose all that made life endurable. I would wish to die now; but I have still a principle to defend—the honor of my family."

"We both have a principle to defend!" replied the emperor, deeply moved at the excessive grief of which he was a witness. "The principle of honor and justice—let us both teach the world that justice attacks the individual criminal and not his family; and that the honor of a family requires that justice should be satisfied. The name of Podstadsky-Liechtenstein has ever been an illustrious one, and I desire to prove to you my regard for your race. Give me your hand, count, and let us be friends."

He extended his hand, and with quiet solemnity the old count took it and looked up into his sovereign's face.

"I thank your majesty," said he, after a pause. "Your conduct toward me is noble and magnanimous, and I shall be grateful for it to my latest breath. You have acted as became a sovereign who has no right to set at defiance the laws he has made. Had I been his judge, I should myself have condemned the criminal who was once my son, and to-day is the murderer of his mother. Years ago I sat in judgment over this transgressor and when I did so, I lost my only child. As for the man who to-day has suffered the penalty of his crimes, I know him no longer."

"And *your* honor is unspotted," said the emperor. "Give me your arm, count, and let me conduct you to my carriage. It is a lovely day. We will take a drive together, and then dine at Schönbrunn. Come—I am resolved that you shall spend this whole day with me. Give me your arm."

"Sire," whispered the old man, hesitating and looking gloomily toward the window, "the day is so bright and the sun shines so fiercely, I fear that my eyes cannot bear the glare. I beg of you allow me to remain at home."

The emperor shook his head. "Nay, your eyes are not weak. You can bear the fullest light of day; you have no need to hide your honored head from the gaze of the world. Take courage, dear friend, and think of what we both have said. Have we not our principles to defend? And must we not both assert them courageously?"

"Your majesty is right," cried the old count. "I am ready to follow you." *

And while Carl Podstadsky, awaking from his swoon, looked up into the face of the malefactor, who from henceforth was to be the companion of his sleeping and waking, and the witness of his despair—while one of a long train of outlawed felons, he dragged his misery through the hot, dusty streets, his father drove with the em-

* Hubner, ii., p. 391.

peror to Schönbrunn, and among all the brilliant guests who dined with him on that day, to none was the emperor so deferential in his courtesy as to the old Count Podstadsky-Liechtenstein.

CHAPTER CLXII.

THE NEMESIS.

MEANWHILE where was the siren who had lured Szekuly to destruction? Where was she for whose sake Carl Podstadsky had precipitated himself into the waters of obloquy? When the waves had engulfed him, she had disappeared, and the last sounds that had rung in his ears were the sounds of her cruel mirth!

Was there no punishment in reserve for such atrocity? No punishment for this woman without heart, without pity, without remorse? Would no hand unmask this beautiful fiend?

The hand is ready, but it is invisible; and Arabella, in her new-found security, is dazzled at the magnitude of her own good fortune. "Whom the gods wish to destroy they first blind." True, she had lost her gold, the price of Szekuly's good fame; but she was not poor; her jewels were worth many such a coffer of ducats. Once in possession of her casket, she was again rich, happy, and courted. Not a creature, save Giuseppe, knew the whereabouts of this precious casket, and with it they must away to Paris!

It was dusk, and Giuseppe, with a travelling carriage, once more awaited his mistress at the corner of the street. There remained nothing to do now but to remove the coffer from its hiding-place, and that was the work of half an hour. Arabella had the key of the little postern, and there was no danger of spies, for the house was empty. Having avowed herself to be the pensioned mistress of Podstadsky, the law had placed its seal upon her effects, and they were all to be sold for the benefit of the count's creditors.

The night was dark, and the street lanterns were propitiously dim. Here and there was heard the step of a solitary foot-passenger, and from time to time the monotonous tramp of the patrol. One of these patrols had just passed the garden-wall of the hotel, of which the Countess Baillou had been the presiding goddess. He looked up at the darkened windows as he went, wondered whither the goddess had flown, and walked on. When the echo of his step had died away from the pavement, and the last beams of the lantern were flickering out, a dark, slender form emerged from one of the pillars of the wall, and glided toward the little side-door, which opened on that narrow street. The key was in the door, it clicked in the lock, and the figure disappeared within. All was quiet.

"I am safe," thought she; "not a sound is within hearing. Now for my treasures, and away! away from this hateful city forever!"

"Whom the gods would destroy, they first blind."

Arabella never suspected that, under cover of darkness, others besides herself were lurking in that garden; and now as she advanced toward the house, two tall figures approached the postern, and stationed themselves on either side of it.

"She is caught," whispered one.

"Yes," replied another, "the bird has come of its own accord into the net. We must wait now until we receive further orders."

Arabella, meanwhile, looked exultingly at the dark clouds which overhung the sky, and almost laughed. "Thank you, fair moon," said she, "for withdrawing your splendor at my behest. To morrow you shall shed your soft beams upon my flight, for then I shall need your friendly light. Far away from Vienna, I shall be rich, happy, and free!"

Now she was at the servants' entrance. Oh, how the hinges creaked, as she opened the door! But what of it? No one was there to hear the sound. How foolishly her heart was beating! Now she was inside, and, with spasmodic haste, she bolted herself within. The darkness was intense. She could not see her hand before her, and in spite of herself a cold chill ran through her frame, and her knees trembled with vague terror. What if, through this black expanse, a hand should suddenly touch hers! and—"Oh, how dreadful is this darkness!" thought she. "I might die here, and no one could come to my help! I feel as I did once before, on that night of horror in Italy!"

She shuddered, and, almost swooning with fright, cowered under the shelter of the marble balustrade, to which she had by this time groped her way. And now, before her terrified soul, swept phantom after phantom, all from the miserable spirit-land of the past. Once more she lived through a night dark as this, when a wretched, betrayed, dishonored girl, she had slunk through the streets of Rome in search of death—death and annihilation in the black waves of the Tiber. She felt the waters engulf her, she heard her own death-cry, the last protest of youth against self-destruction; and then she felt the grasp of Podstadsky—Podstadsky who, in restoring her to the world, had laid a new curse upon her life. Until then she had been luxurious, frivolous, pleasure-loving; but in the Tiber she had found a new and terrible baptism—the baptism of crime. Without love she had consented to become Podstadsky's mistress, and so became the partner of his guilt. Together they had planned their bold schemes of fraud, and, oh, how successful they had been until this last misfortune! At all events, her connection with Podstadsky was at an end. The pillory had liberated her, and now—now she would lead a blameless life. No more fraud—no more theft. Crime was too dangerous; she saw that it must inexorably lead to shame. She would be satisfied with what she had, and become a virtuous woman. She was quite rich enough to be good, and it would be such bliss to live without a guilty secret!

She laughed, and then shivered at the sound of her own voice, and a supernatural terror took such violent hold of her imagination, that she could no longer bear the darkness. She *must* see, or she would die of fear. Giuseppe had provided her with a dark lantern, a vial of phosphorus, and some matches.

"How delightful it is to have this new invention!" thought she, as, touching the phosphorus, she struck a light. With this light she felt a little reassured, but could she have seen her blanched, terror-stricken face, she would have screamed, and fancied it a spectre!

Hush! Was there a muffled sound behind her? She paused and listened, her eyes glaring as though they would start from their sockets. Pshaw! it was only the rustling of her own silk mantle as it went trailing up the marble staircase. Nothing in human shape was there, save two pale statues, which stood like dead sentinels at the head of the stairs. As she passed them she shuddered, and almost fancied that they had stepped from their pedestals to follow her. Giving one quick glance behind, she sped like a hunted doe through those halls, of which so lately she had been the pride, and arrived breathless at the door of her boudoir. She darted in, and there, safe in its place, was the picture.

This gave her courage. But she must have rest after her fearful pilgrimage through that dark, empty house. She sank upon her satin lounge, and abandoned herself to the joy and security of the hour. She had just come to the end of a perilous journey. Night and danger were behind, the rosy morning of safety was about to dawn. She was so full of joyous emotion, that scarcely knowing what she did, her lips began to move in unconscious prayer!

Prayer! She had no right to such a privilege as that; and starting from her seat, lest she should falter in the purpose of her visit, she quickly removed the picture, touched the spring, and the precious coffer stood revealed.

No, no, she could never give it up! She stretched out her arms, and pressed it to her heart, as a mother does her only child. Trembling with eager joy, she placed it on the table, and opening it, contemplated her treasures on their beds of crimson velvet.

How they sparkled! How they seemed to burn with splendor as the rays of the little lantern coquetted with their beauty! She was repaid for all her terrors, she was happy and secure!

"Whom the gods would destroy, they first blind."

She was so absorbed in the magnificence of her diamond necklace for which she had been indebted to the Princess Garampi, that she did not hear the footfall of the men who were close behind her. They smiled, and pantomimed one to another as they watched her toying with her flashing jewels.

Then suddenly springing forward, as if they feared she might escape through the secret opening in the wall, they grasped her with their powerful hands, and she was once more a prisoner.

"The emperor can no longer defend his beautiful countess," said the one who seemed to direct the others. "We have caught her in the act of robbing Count Podstadsky's creditors. And, unless I am mistaken, we shall find among her booty all the jewels that were missing at last winter's entertainments; for, as I had the honor of reminding his majesty, the Countess Baillou was at every ball where jewels were lost. I told the emperor that if he would give you freedom, I engaged to find something more than a mare's nest when I tracked you hither. I was sure you would come, and my spies have been within, waiting for you since this morning."

"What reward was promised by the emperor for my detection?" said Arabella, now self-possessed.

"Five hundred ducats," was the reply.

"Five hundred ducats?" repeated she, tossing back her beautiful head. "A beggarly reward for the person of a lady of rank like me! Take this necklace, and divide it between you. Each one will then have more than the frugal emperor has promised to all. Take it and give me my freedom. Your generous act will never be known."

"How, lady! You would bribe us, as you have bribed so many noble cavaliers? No, no. Your game is at an end, and if ever you appear in public again, it will be as a criminal. You must come with me. You, men, take up this coffer."

She strove no longer. Without another word she took the arm of the police-officer, and went firmly forward.

Her lips moved, and she murmured: "Alas he is right. My career is at an end." *

CHAPTER CLXIII.

HORJA AND THE REBELLION IN HUNGARY.

FOUR years had gone by since Joseph had reigned sole monarch of Austria. For four years he had devoted himself to the Austrians, having but one object, that of making them a free, enlightened, and happy people, emancipating them from the influence of the church, and breaking the fetters of serfdom; granting them equality before the law, and enriching them by his encouragement of manufactures and the privileges he accorded to merchants.

What was his reward? Dissatisfaction and opposition from every class of society; ingratitude and ill-will from all parties.

The nobles disliked him because he had sought every opportunity of humbling them before the people; the clergy opposed him, because of his sequestration of church property, and his assumption of spiritual authority. But his bitterest enemies were the *bureaucratie*. He had invaded all their customs, discharging every man who had not studied at the university, and requiring constant labor from the first as well as the last of the employés. He was the terror of all aspirants for civil office, and the whole body hated him, embarrassed his steps, and ruined his plans by voluntary misconception of all his orders.

As yet, there was no outburst of dissatisfaction. The discontent was latent, and Joseph still indulged the hope of outliving opposition, and proving to his subjects that all the innovations which they had so ungratefully endured were for the ultimate good of the Austrian nation.

He was therefore ill-prepared for the news which reached him from Hungary. He had freed the people from slavery and taxation, and had exacted that the nobles should pay their share of the imperial taxes. He had instituted a general conscription, and the most powerful Magyar in Hungary was bound to serve, side by side, with the lowest peasant. Finally he had forbidden the use of any other language in Hungary save the German.

A cry of indignation was heard from every turreted castle in the land. They were wounded in the rights hitherto guaranteed to them by every emperor of Austria. And above all other oppression, they were to be robbed of their mother tongue, that they might lose their nationality, and become a poor Austrian dependency. †

But Joseph's enactments were detested not only by the nobles, they were equally unwelcome to the people. The latter were horror-

* This beautiful woman, "the ornament of the most elegant circles in Vienna," as she is called by the chroniclers of the times, was condemned to three days of pillory, the same punishment as that suffered by the victim of her wickedness and coquetry. She was then sent guarded to the confines of Austria, from whence she was banished for life.—See Hubner, ii., 392. Gross-Hoffinger, iii.

† That was precisely Joseph's object; and yet he wondered that this people did not love him.

stricken by the general conscription, and fled by thousands to take refuge among the mountains from the conscribing officers.

One of their own class, however, succeeded in drawing them from their hiding-places. The loud voice of Horja rang throughout every valley, and ascended to every mountain-summit. He called them to liberty and equality. He asserted that nobility was to be destroyed in Hungary. There were to be no more castles, no more magnates of the land. The emperor had promised as much in Vienna. He had sworn to free the Hungarian peasantry, and to bring the proud noble down to an equality with his serf.

The hour for fulfilment had arrived. All the new laws regarded the nobles alone, they had no reference to the peasantry whom the emperor had promised to make free, happy, and rich. He needed the help of his Hungarians. They must complete what he had begun. The peasant was to be free, happy, rich.

This was the magic song which attracted the boor from his thatch under the hill, and the goat-herd from his hut amid the mountain-peaks.

Horja was the Arion who sang—and now to his standard flocked thousands of deluded beings, all eager to complete the work which the emperor had begun. Joseph had made them free—it remained for themselves to plunder the nobles, and appropriate their long-hoarded wealth. It was the emperor's will. He hated the Magyars, and loved the peasantry.

If ever any of those poor, ignorant wretches held back, Horja showed them a massive gold chain to which the emperor's portrait was attached. This had been sent to him by Joseph himself, and in proof thereof he had a parchment full of gilt letters, with a great seal attached to it, which made him Captain-General of Hungary. They could all come and read the emperor's own writing if they chose.

Poor fellows! None of them knew how to read, so that Krischan, a friend of Horja and a priest of the Greek Church, read it for all who doubted.

This brought conviction to the most skeptical. That a Greek priest could read a lie, never once entered the heads of these simple children of nature.

Now commenced the carnage. The nobles were imprisoned and murdered, their castles burned, and their fields laid waste. The aristocracy of the borders, whose territorial domains the insurgents had not yet reached, armed themselves, and having captured some of the rebels, put them to death under circumstances of exaggerated cruelty, executing them by the power which the Magyar possessed of administering justice as an independent prince.

These executions, unsanctioned by the emperor, raised the indignation of the people to ungovernable fury, and they now demanded the entire extinction of the nobles. They were summoned to resign their titles, and, until the coronation of Joseph, the rightful King of Hungary, they were to obey their lawful ruler, Horja.

The nobles, not having condescended to take any notice of Horja's summons, the people began to pillage and murder with redoubled fury. They spared every thing, however, belonging to the emperor—the only nobleman who, for the future, was to be suffered to own land in Hungary.

Joseph could no longer turn a deaf ear to the remonstrances of the

Magyars. He had hoped to be able to quell the rebellion by lenity, offering a general amnesty to all offenders with the exception of Horja, for whose capture a reward of three hundred ducats was offered.

But the poor, deluded peasantry, having faith in no one but Horja, thought that the offer of pardon was nothing but an artifice of the enemy. The emperor, then, was obliged to march the imperial troops against the people, and to bring about with musket and cannon what he had hoped to accomplish through moral suasion.

Horja, finding that he had nothing more to hope from the clemency of the emperor, tried to induce the disaffected nobles to accept his peasantry, and rebel against Joseph. But they rejected the offer with disdain, and gave their support to the imperial troops.

Thousands delivered themselves up, imploring mercy, which was granted them. Thousands fled to the mountains, and thousands were taken prisoners. Among these latter were Horja and Krischan. Both were condemned to death. Horja pleaded hard to be allowed to see the emperor, alleging that he had something of importance to communicate to him, but his prayer was not granted.

Perhaps Joseph suspected that Horja would prove to him, what he already dreaded to know, namely, that the nobles had connived at this insurrection of the peasantry to frighten him with the consequences of his own acts.

Horja was not permitted, then, to see his sovereign. He was broken on a wheel on the market-place at Carlsburg, and two thousand of the captured insurgents were forced to witness the cruel spectacle.*

Thus ended this fearful outbreak, by which four thousand men perished, sixty-two villages and thirty-two castles were consumed; and the deluded peasantry, instead of freedom, happiness, and wealth, found threefold oppression at the hands of their masters.

The magnates and nobles, meanwhile, stood upon the ruins of their castles, and cried out:

"This is the work of Joseph! These are the fruits of his insensate reforms!" †

CHAPTER CLXIV.

THE JEW'S REVENGE.

THE emperor paced his cabinet in unusual agitation. Contrary to his daily habits, the *Controlorgang* was closed, and his secretaries had been ordered to remain in the chancery, and do their writing there.

The emperor had been weeping; and he wished his anguish to be hidden from any eye save that of God.

A great sorrow had befallen him. Günther, his indefatigable co-laborer, the trustiest of counsellors, the man whom, next to Lacy and Rosenberg, he loved best on earth—Günther had betrayed him! He had sold a secret of state for gold!

There, before him on the table, lay the reports of the secret police, whose duty it was to open all letters passing through the

* On the 3d of January, 1785.

† Hubner, i., p. 273. Gross-Hoffinger, iii., p. 135. Ramshorn, p. 138.

post, and to present such as looked suspicious.* Among these letters was one which strongly inculpated Günther. It was written by Baron Eskeles Flies to a commercial friend in Amsterdam. It stated that he (Eskeles Flies) had just received a communication of such vital importance that it was worth much more to him than the thousand ducats he had paid to his informer. The emperor, tired of his contention with Holland regarding the navigation of the Scheldt, had agreed to accept the ten millions offered by Holland in return for his guaranty that she should still preserve her right to demand toll of all ships passing through that portion of the river which was within the Dutch boundaries.†

Eskeles Flies besought his Amsterdam correspondent to procure him this loan, which he was ready to advance to the republic in four instalments. He bound his friend to strict secrecy, for the information he imparted was not to be made public for twenty-four hours, and the possession of this secret gave them signal advantage over all other bankers.

Now Günther alone had been intrusted by the emperor with this secret of state. With the exception of Prince Kaunitz, not another man in Austria knew that Joseph intended to accept the proffered indemnity.

It was clear, then, that Günther was the traitor, and yet his imperial master would not believe. He clung to the hope that something might yet occur to exculpate his favorite, though how or whence exoneration was to come, he could not conceive.

The banker had been summoned, and the emperor awaited his coming. In the impatience of his heart he had sent a courier, and after the courier his own carriage, for he could not endure his suspense one moment longer than was unavoidable.

Often as he paced the room, his heart throbbing violently, he paused to listen, and then glanced again and again at the clock to see if the banker could be nigh.

"If it be true," thought he, resuming his agitated walk, "I never shall trust man again. I believed that Günther's heart was as noble as his face. Is it possible that such a countenance should lie? Günther, the generous, disinterested Günther—can it be that he has sold my secrets? I cannot, will not believe it. I must see himself, and hear his defence from his own lips."

Hurried along by this magnanimous impulse, the emperor approached the door. But he paused, and shook his head.

"No, no. Conviction must come from testimony, not from assertion. Men are all actors, and often have I seen how skilfully they wear the mask of innocence. I have been too often deceived. Ah! there at last is the banker."

Yes, it was he. The page flung open the door, and announced:

"Baron von Eskeles Flies."

The baron entered the room. He had grown old since Rachel's

* "The Emperor Franz and Metternich: a Fragment." (From Hormayer, p. 79.)

† Joseph had claimed from Holland the right to navigate the Scheldt and the canals dug by the Dutch, free of toll. These latter refused, and the emperor forthwith marched his troops into Holland. He had expected to be sustained by the other maritime powers of Europe, but they protecting the Dutch, Joseph was obliged to withdraw his troops. But he claimed an indemnity for the expenses incurred by putting his regiments upon a war-footing, and demanded twenty millions. He then agreed to take fifteen, but was finally obliged to be content with ten, which was all that the Dutch would allow him. Whereupon Frederick the Great said that Joseph had cried out for a great sum, but had been obliged to come down to a "*pour boire.*"

flight. Scarcely a year had elapsed since then; but in that year her father's raven locks had become white as snow, and the stalwart man of fifty had grown old and feeble.

The emperor came forward, and extended his hand.

"Look at me, Eskeles," said he, in his quick, eager way; "do not bow so ceremoniously, we have no time to waste on formalities. Look at me, and let me see whether you are an honest man scorning falsehood, even though it might shield a fellow-creature from harm."

The banker looked the emperor full in the face, and bore the scrutiny of his searching eyes without wincing.

"I see that you can look me in the face," said Joseph. "You will speak the truth."

"The Jew is forbidden by his religious code to lie," was the reply.

Joseph crossed the room quickly, and taking a letter from his *escritoire*, gave it to the banker.

"Is this your writing?"

Eskeles lifted his eyes slowly to the paper, and seemed surprised.

"Yes, that is my writing. I posted this letter yesterday. How, then, do I find it here? Its detention is a serious inconvenience to me."

He said this with the demeanor of a merchant whose mind is upon his business, and who has no idea that it can concern any other person.

"The letter was sent to me by the secret police," said the emperor.

The banker looked up in astonishment. "Ah!" exclaimed he, "then the tales which are told of the opening of all our letters by detectives, are not fables!"

"No—they are not fables, and I am justified in the scrutiny. Men are so corrupt that our only defence against treachery is *espionage*. It is a pity that it should be so; but as long as the people are base, their sovereigns must stop short of no means to foil them."

"But I have never sinned against your majesty. Why, then, is my letter open to suspicion?"

"Every man is suspected by the secret police," replied Joseph, with a shrug. "For that reason they had orders to stop every letter addressed to Holland. The precaution had been made imperative by our misunderstandings with that country. And you see yourself that your letter betrays a secret of state."

"Betrays!" repeated the banker. "We betray that which we are expected to bury within the recesses of our own heart. But this news was to go out into the world, and was a subject for percentage. I should have made at least half a million had my letter not been unluckily detained by your majesty."

"I shall not prevent you from earning your percentage," replied Joseph, scornfully. "Your letter shall go to-day, and my dispatches shall be detained until to-morrow. In that way you can still make your half million."

The banker bowed. "I thank your majesty for your exceeding condescension," said he.

"I will do you this favor, but you must do me a service in return."

"It is not necessary for your majesty to concede me the right to earn half a million, to buy my services," said Eskeles, with a slight shade of reproach. "I hope that I have always been ready to serve your majesty, even when no percentage was to be gained thereby."

"And I have recognized it, *Baron* Eskeles Flies. But I do not speak of pecuniary services to-day. I ask a favor of another nature. Tell me, then, without reserve, who is the man that receives a thousand ducats for revealing a secret of state to you."

The banker started as if he had received a shot, and glanced inquiringly at the emperor. "Was that in the letter?" asked he.

Joseph gave it into his hands. Eskeles perused it eagerly, and then, murmured in a voice of exceeding contrition, "Ay, it is there. I was indiscreet." Then, as if overcome by his fault, his head sank upon his breast.

"I await your answer," said the emperor. "Who betrayed me to you for a thousand ducats?"

The banker raised his head as if making a difficult resolve. "Your majesty, that was an idle boast of mine to enhance the value of my news."

"Mere evasion, baron!" replied Joseph, angrily. "Even if you had not written the words in that letter, I should still ask of you, who it is that betrays my secrets?"

"No one, sire," replied Eskeles, uneasily. "I guessed it. Yes, yes,"—continued he, as though a happy idea had just struck him—"that is it—I guessed. Every one knows of your majesty's difficulty with Holland, and I might well guess that you would be glad to end this strife by accepting the ten millions, and so save your subjects from the horrors of war."

"You are not the truthful man I had supposed. There is no logic in your lies, Baron Eskeles. You might guess that I would accept the ten millions, but as you are not omniscient, you could not say positively that I had written my dispatches yesterday, and would sign them to-day. Your inventions are clumsy, baron, and I must say that they do you honor; for they prove that you have little experience in the art of lying. But the truth I must have, and as your lord and emperor, I command you to speak. For the third time, who betrayed my secrets to you?"

"Oh, sire, I swore not to betray him," said Eskeles, in a faltering voice.

"I absolve you from the oath."

"But the God of Israel cannot absolve me. I cannot speak the name of the man, but—your majesty can guess it."

He was silent for a few moments, then raising his head, the emperor saw that his face had become deadly pale. In a low, unsteady voice he continued: "Your majesty knows that I once had a daughter."

"HAD? You *have* a daughter, baron."

"She is dead to me," murmured Eskeles so inaudibly that the emperor scarcely heard him. "She left me a year ago for a man whom she loved better than her father."

"But she left because you would have married her to a man whom she hated. Günther told me so."

"Yes, sire. I had no idea that my unhappy child would go to such extremity. Had she entreated me as she should have done, I would have yielded; but her lover had hardened her heart against me, and she abandoned me—not to become the honorable wife of any man, but to lead a life of shame and reproach. Rachel is not married, she is the mistress of that man."

"This, too, is your fault, baron. You made her swear never to become a Christian, and by our laws she could not marry him. But he considers her as his wife. You see that I know all. Günther, to justify himself, confided to me the whole history of his love."

"He did not tell the truth, sire. My daughter herself is unwilling to become a Christian."

"Then she is a conscientious Jewess?"

"No, sire, she does not attend the synagogue."

"What is she, then?" asked the emperor, astonished.

"She is a Deist; and precisely because I required of her to profess either Judaism or Christianity, she fled to that man whom she cannot be made to believe is the suitor of her wealth and not of herself."

"Do you think, then, that Günther is interested?"

"I know it, sire. He offered for a hundred thousand florins to renounce Rachel and deliver her up to me. Here is his letter; your majesty can see it."

The emperor took the letter, and read it. "It is his writing," murmured he, sorrowfully; "it is too true."

"I refused," continued Eskeles. "I would not buy my daughter back. I therefore waited to see what would follow."

"What followed?"

The banker was silent for a moment; then sighing, he said, in low, trembling tones: "Not long after, I received another letter. He said he was straitened in means, that Rachel was pampered, and required so many luxuries that she had exhausted his purse. As I would not listen to his first proposition, he had another to make. I would give him a certain sum, and he would do me a substantial service."

"He offered a thousand ducats, did he not?"

"I do not remember. The sum is stated in the letter. Here it is, your majesty." And with these words Eskeles drew a paper from his bosom.

"It is, it is," said the emperor, in a voice of anguish. "I can no longer doubt his treachery."

Eskeles Flies returned the paper to his bosom. "I keep this on my person," said he, "because when Rachel returns to me, it will cure her of her love for such a villain."

"Günther, then, received the money?" said Joseph.

"He did, sire."

"Then you no longer deny that *he* was the Judas."

"Your majesty can remember which of your secretaries was charged with the copying of your dispatches."

The emperor sighed. "I know, I know," murmured he; "and yet it pains me so to believe it, for I have loved him sincerely."

"And I have loved my daughter," returned Eskeles. "This man stole her from me, and has converted my child into a Deist."

"She shall be returned to you, and Günther shall receive the punishment of his crimes," cried Joseph, in a loud and angry voice. "No mercy for *him!* I shall know how to act as becomes a wronged and outraged sovereign."

"But that will not restore my child," said Eskeles, disconsolately. "What good is it to me that this wretch is to suffer? It will not bring back Rachel. And even if she should be forced to seek my protection, what comfort can I derive from one who is a Deist—a creature who mocks at religion?"

"She will be obliged to become one thing or the other, if she would shield herself from the fearful consequences of her skepticism."

"That is it," cried Eskeles, joyfully. "Your majesty has found the remedy. Rachel must be threatened with the disgrace of legal punishment, and then she will repent, and return to her father. Sire, I accuse her of Deism. I exact that she be brought to judgment."

"To judgment!" exclaimed the emperor. "Do you know the punishment for her offence?"

"Fifty lashes on the offender's back! But fear will save her. My Rachel will never dare avow herself a Deist."

"Perhaps not; but I, as a Christian, cannot allow you to force her back to Judaism."

"Then try to make a Christian of her, sire Oh, I beseech you, lend yourself to my paternal stratagem for her restoration to honor! Act upon my accusation; have her imprisoned in her home; and for four weeks, let a priest visit her daily to instruct her in your majesty's faith. Then let her decide whether she will become a Christian or remain a Jewess."

"Bethink you that if she should prove contumacious, I cannot rescue her from punishment. If you persist in your accusation, remember that the law must take its course."

"I persist, and demand investigation."

"It shall be granted you. And now here is your letter. Post it to-day, and it will still be twenty-four hours in advance of mine. We must both perform our duty, you as a merchant, I as a sovereign; and, believe me, you shall have revenge for the wrongs inflicted upon you by the double traitor who has betrayed his emperor and his mistress!"

"I care nothing for his punishment," repeated Eskeles, wearily; "all that I ask is my daughter."

The emperor gave his hand, and the banker, pressing it to his lips, backed out of the cabinet. Joseph looked after him with sympathizing eyes. "Poor man! Grief has made him old. Sorrow lengthens days to years, and wrinkles many a brow which time has never touched."

But without, Baron Eskelies Flies had changed his mien. No longer bowed down with grief, he stood triumphantly reviewing the success of his strategy.

"I am revenged!" thought he. "Short-sighted emperor, you do not dream that you are the tool wherewith the Jew has wreaked his vengeance upon the Christian! Go on, and ruin your faithful friend! Go on, hot-headed judge; punish the man who loves you, without giving him a hearing; and imagine yourself to be administering justice, while you inflict the grossest injustice. It is so Christian-like. Follow the instincts of your love and hate, your passion or your pleasures, ye children of the moment, while the calculating Jew plays upon your credulity!—And now, God of my fathers, let the Christian priest but irritate my child with his importunities, and she will seek refuge from his persecutions in the synagogue!"

CHAPTER CLXV.

THE FAVOR OF PRINCES.

THE emperor thrust open the door which led from his cabinet to the chancery. There at the long, green table, immersed in their business, sat the four imperial secretaries; and next to the arm-chair, which was surmounted by the Austrian crown, sat the unconscious Günther. Had Günther seen the look with which Joseph regarded him as he sat quietly writing, his heart would have grown chill with apprehension. But not an eye there was raised. One of the emperor's most stringent orders forbade the secretaries, when in the chancery, to raise their heads on any account. They were to take no note of the entrance of Joseph himself; they were co-workers, and no time was to be wasted in ceremonial.

Joseph seated himself in silence, and taking up a pen, wrote a few hasty lines upon a sheet of paper. He then rang, and delivered the paper to a page.

"Take this to the colonel commanding the recruits," said he, and his voice trembled as he spoke these few words. There was a long silence; the secretaries continued to write, and Günther, always obedient to orders, had not once raised his head. His countenance was as tranquil as it had ever been.

"Günther," said the emperor, in an imperious tone, "begin a new sheet, and write what I shall dictate."

Günther bowed, and prepared to obey. The others went on with their work. Had Joseph not been so blinded by indignation against his private secretary, he might have seen how one of the others raised his head and glanced furtively around; how his face was pale, and his lips were twitching; and how his hand was so tremulous that he was scarcely able to hold his pen. No one observed it. The other secretaries were writing; the emperor, in his wrath, saw nothing but Günther.

And now with flashing eyes, he called upon Günther to write.

"To his Eminence, Cardinal Megazzi:

"It has come to my knowledge that the absurd sect which originated in Bohemia, is spreading its pernicious tenets even to our capital. A heart-broken father has this day come before me to accuse his daughter of Deism. To what extremes the Deists go in their imbecility, is shown by the fact, that this girl, who has defied Heaven, the laws of her country, and the authority of her father, has left the paternal roof, and is now living a life of shame with her paramour. She must either profess some faith, or be punished as the law directs. To this end, your eminence wll commission an intelligent priest to visit and instruct her in the tenets of Christianity. From this day she is a prisoner in her own house; but as she is of Jewish birth (and I do not wish to have it said that we have forced her into Christianity), a Jewish rabbi can also have daily access to this unhappy infidel. I give to both priests four weeks to convert her. If, at the end of that time, she continues contumacious, she must be punished as the Josephine Code directs, with fifty lashes." *

* Gross-Hoffinger, iii., p. 116.

The emperor had dictated this letter in sharp, biting tones, while Günther, nothing apprehending, had written it. Once only, when the accused had been designated as a Jewess, his pen faltered, and his handsome, noble face was contracted for a moment by pain. But the pang had been sympathetic and momentary.

"Have you written?" asked the emperor, striking the table with his clinched hand.

"I have written, sire," replied Günther, in his fine, sonorous voice, whose familiar tones, in spite of himself, stirred the innermost depths of his misguided sovereign's heart.

"Now, answer me one question," continued Joseph, hoarsely. "Have you ever received a thousand ducats from Eskeles Flies?"

Again the head of one of the secretaries was furtively raised, the hands shook like aspen-leaves, and the eyes gave one rapid glance toward the side of the table where Günther sat.

The emperor, as before, was too blinded by passion to see any thing save the innocent object of his wrath. Günther was surprised at the tone in which the question had been asked, and seemed at last to be aware that it was one full of significance. But his reply was prompt and calm.

"Yes, sire, I received that sum yesterday. Not for me, but for a lady whose name is well known to your majesty. It was a legacy left by her mother."

Joseph laughed scornfully. "Give me the note to the cardinal," cried he. Günther presented it, and having signed it, the emperor gave it into the hands of the secretary opposite. "Fold and address the letter," said he. "But stop—write first the address of the person who presumes to avow herself a Deist in the face of my laws. Her name is Rachel Eskeles Flies."

A cry of anguish burst from Günther's lips, and in his madness he would have snatched the horrid missive from the secretary's hands. But he recollected himself, and turning his blanched face toward the emperor, he exclaimed:

"Mercy, gracious sovereign, mercy for my Rachel! You have been wickedly deceived."

"Ay," cried Joseph, "I have been wickedly deceived; but he who has dared to betray me, shall be made to suffer for his crime. Rise from this table and leave this room. You are dismissed from my service as a false traitor!"

"What, your majesty!" cried Gunther, in tones that were proud and defiant. "You defame me without so much as telling me of what I am accused! without allowing me the right of justification! Tell me—what have I done?"

"Ask your own conscience, if you have one, and find an answer there!" cried Joseph, furious at the lofty bearing of his victim.

"If your majesty refuses me that poor boon," continued Günther, "I appeal to the laws. My legal judges will be bound to hear me publicly accused, and to listen to my defence!"

"I am your accuser and your judge—your only judge," replied Joseph, with concentrated passion. "I have already found you guilty, and have already sentenced you."

"But why, why?" cried Günther. "If you would not drive me mad, tell me why?"

"I shall do nothing but carry out your sentence," cried Joseph, ringing a bell. "Are the men without?" said he to the page who answered his summons.

"Yes, your majesty. A subaltern of the third regiment is without, with four soldiers."

"Show them in!" The page opened the door, and the men entered.

"You march to Hungary to your new garrison to-day, do you not?" said the emperor.

"Yes, sire—we march in one hour," was the reply.

"Take this man with you as a recruit."

Günther started forward, and with an exclamation of horror fell at the emperor's feet. "Mercy! mercy!" gasped he.

"No mercy, but justice for all men!" cried Joseph, stamping his foot. Then motioning to the soldiers, he said: "Take him away and watch him closely, lest he escape. Equip him and put him in the ranks. Away with you!"

The men advanced, and Günther, seeing that any further appeal was vain, suffered himself to be led away in silence. The door closed behind them, and the emperor was alone with his three secretaries. There was a long, fearful pause, through which the retreating steps of the soldiers and their victim were heard. When the echoes had died away, the emperor spoke in hard, cold tones:

"Günther was a traitor, who betrayed the secrets of the state for gold. I discovered his treachery, and have punished him accordingly. Take warning by his fate!"

So saying, he passed into his cabinet, and once more gave vent to his bitter grief.

"I could not do otherwise," thought he. "I, who would not spare Podstadsky and Szekuly, could not spare this traitor, though he has been very dear to me indeed. He must suffer, but I shall suffer with him. Mercy is so much more natural to man than justice! Still, mercy is the prerogative of Heaven alone. I am here to be equitable to all."

An hour later the third regiment left Vienna for Szegedin, their new garrison. A few wagons followed with the luggage, and the sick men who were unable to encounter the hardships of that formidable march to Hungary. In one of these wagons lay the new recruit. His eyes glared with delirium, and his lips were parched with raging fever. For a moment he seemed to awake from his dream of madness, for he raised himself a little, and murmured, "Where am I?" No one answered him, but a flash of memory revealed to him the horrors of his situation, and falling back with a shudder, he cried out, "Rachel, my Rachel!" and then relapsed into delirium.

The same evening, Baron Eskeles Flies left his hotel on foot, and hastily traversing the streets, stopped before a house where, ascending to the second story, he rang the bell. A richly-liveried servant opened the door at the head of the staircase.

"Is the imperial secretary Warkenhold within?" asked the baron.

The servant did not know—he would see; but the banker saved him the trouble by putting him aside, and entering the little vestibule.

"Show me the way," said he; "you need not announce me. A rich man is welcome everywhere."

The servant obeyed, and conducted the banker through a suite of apartments whose splendor he contemplated with a sneer. "Now go," said he, as the servant pointed to a *portière*. "I shall announce myself."

He drew the *portière* and knocked. Then, without waiting for an answer, he entered the room.

"Eskeles Flies!" cried the occupant, who was lounging on a sofa, and was no other than the secretary that had been so disturbed by the emperor's words in the morning. "Eskeles Flies!" repeated he, springing from the sofa, and hastening forward.

"Yes, Baron Eskeles Flies," replied the banker, proudly.

"But what brings you to me?" cried Warkenhold, terrified. "Your visit exposes me to danger."

"Nobody knows of my visit, for I came on foot; and let me tell you, Herr Warkenhold, that my presence in your house is an honor which is not apt to endanger you."

"Only to-day, only at this time," murmured Warkenhold, apologetically.

"Then you should have come to me for your money. You said you were in great want, having lost every thing at cards, and so I hasten to acquit myself of my debt. Here is a draft for one thousand ducats."

"Hush, for the love of Heaven!" whispered Warkenhold. "What can I do with a draft? I never would dare present it for payment, for you know that the emperor keeps spies with a hundred eyes to track his employés. And suppose I go to your office, I expose myself to discovery."

"Not at all," interrupted the banker, laughing. "Who should betray you? Not I. And no one but us two are in the secret. Who, then, should tell the emperor that you were hidden behind the door while he dictated his dispatches, and that you are such a skilful imitator? I swear that Günther himself would have been staggered had he seen those letters! They are capital, and I congratulate you. You are a genius."

"Great God! must you annoy me with repetition of all that I did?" cried the secretary, with asperity. "Is it not enough that I am already wretched, as I look back to the terrible scenes of the morning? I cannot banish the image of that unhappy Günther from my mind. I felt at one time as if I must confess and save him."

"Ha, ha! did you? Then it was terrible, was it? He thundered like another Rhadamanthus, did he, that sapient emperor? And forced poor, innocent Günther to drink of the chalice we had prepared for him? Oh, rare, far-seeing judge!—Tell me all about it, Warkenhold."

Warkenhold, shuddering, repeated what had taken place. When he spoke of the question relating to the thousand ducats, Eskeles Flies interrupted him.

"And of course he had to say yes. Günther is of knightly veracity, and I invented the story of the legacy, in anticipation of that question. Oh, how admirably my calculations have been made! Let me hear the rest."

Warkenhold went on, and when he had concluded his woful narrative, the banker nodded and said:

"You are a genius. You narrate as well as you eavesdrop and forge! Upon my word, you have entertained as well as you have served me! My success in this affair is entirely owing to you. You are as skilful as your great Christian ancestor, Judas; but as I hope you are not such a fool as to go out and hang yourself, here are fifty ducats above our bargain. They are for your mistress."

He drew out his purse and counted the gold.

"I thank you," said Warkenhold, almost inaudibly. "I must take the money, for I am sorely pressed; but I would give my right hand not to have been forced to do this thing!"

"Pray say the left. Your right hand is a treasure not lightly to be parted with," said the banker, laughing. "But a truce to sentiment. It is useless for you to drape yourself in the toga of honor or benevolence. Our business is at an end. You have nothing more to claim, I believe?"

"Nothing whatever; I am—"

"Then," said the banker taking up his hat, "we have nothing further to say to each other. You have been the instrument of my righteous vengenace; but as I have an antipathy to villains, let me never see so much as a glance of recognition from you again. From this hour we are strangers. Adieu!"

CHAPTER CLXVI.

THE DEPUTATION FROM HUNGARY.

In the great reception-room of the imperial palace, a deputation of the most illustrious magnates of Hungary awaited an interview with the emperor. For one whole year the Hungarian nobles had withdrawn from court; but now, in the interest of their fatherland, they stood once more within the walls of the palace; and in their magnificent state-uniforms, as the representatives of all Hungary, they were assembled to demand redress for their national grievances.

When the emperor entered the reception-room, he came alone, in a plain uniform. He greeted the deputies with a smile which they returned by profound and silent inclinations of their aristocratic heads. Joseph looked slowly around at the brilliant assemblage of magnates before him.

"A stately deputation of my loyal Hungarians," observed he. "I see all the proudest families of the kingdom represented here to-day. Count Palfy, for example, the son of him whom the empress was accustomed to call her champion and father. Count Batthiany, the heir of my favorite tutor. I rejoice to see you, and hope that you are here to-day to greet me as ever, in the character of loyal subjects."

There was a short pause, after which, Count Palfy, stepping a little in advance of the others, addressed the emperor.

"Sire, we are sent by the kingdom of Hungary to lay our wrongs before your majesty, and request redress."

"Does the count represent your sentiments?" asked the emperor, addressing the delegates. A unanimous affirmative was the reply, and Joseph then continued: "Speak on. I will hear your complaints and reply to them."

Count Palfy bowed and resumed: "We have come to remind your majesty that when, in November, 1780, you ascended the throne of Austria, we received a written declaration from your imperial hand, guaranteeing our rights under the national constitution of Hungary. Nevertheless, these rights have been invaded, and we come before your majesty's throne in the hope that our just remonstrances may not appear offensive in the eyes of our king." *

"But what if they do appear offensive?" cried the emperor, chafed. "What if I should refuse to hear those complaints which are nothing but the fermentation of your own pride and arrogance?"

"If your majesty refuses to hear us to-day," said Count Palfy, with firmness, "we shall return to-morrow, and every day; for we have sworn to present the grievances of the states to your notice, and must keep our oath."

"I am quite as well acquainted with the grievances as you, and to prove it to you, I will state them myself. First, you are aggrieved because I have not gone to Hungary to be crowned, and to take the constitutional oath."

"Yes, sire, we are; and this grievance leads us to the second one. We venture to ask if, secretly and without the consent of the states, the crown of St. Stephen has been removed to Vienna?"

"Yes, it has been removed," cried Joseph, with increasing irritation. "It has been brought to me, to whom it belongs; but I shall return it to Ofen, when the structure which is to receive it is completed."

"That is an unconstitutional act," said Count Palfy. "Is it not, my friends?"

"It is," cried a chorus of Magyars.

"I have never taken the oath to the constitution," was Joseph's reply. "Hungary would have to undergo signal changes before I ever go there to be crowned as your king. You are not content with reigning over your vassals; you desire, in your ambitious presumption, to reign over me also. But I tell you that I am no royal puppet in the hands of a republic of aristocrats. I am lord and king of all my provinces. Hungary has no claim to a separate nationality, and, once for all, I shall no more take the coronation oath there, than I shall do it in Tyrol, Bohemia, Galicia, or Lombardy. All your crowns are fused into the imperial crown of Austria, and it is proper that I, who own them all, should preserve them with my regalia at Vienna. All strife and jealousy between the provinces composing my empire must cease.† Provincial interests must disappear before national exigencies. This is all that I have to say to the states; but I will say to yourselves, that when I find myself absolute lord of Hungary, as well as of Austria, I will go thither to be crowned. And now, Lord Chancellor of Hungary, what other grievance have you to present?"

"Our second grievance, sire, is, that to the great humiliation of all Hungary, our native tongue and the Latin language have been superseded by the German. This, too, is unconstitutional, for it has shut out all Hungarians, in a measure, from public office, and has placed the administration of our laws in the hands of Austrians, perfectly ignorant of our constitution." ‡

"To this I have to say that German shall be the language of all my subjects. Why should *you* enjoy the privilege of a national language? *I* am Emperor of Germany, and *my* tongue shall be that of my provinces. If Hungary were the most important portion of the empire, its language, doubtless, would be Hungarian; but it is not,

* These are the words of the Hungarian protest.—See Hubner, ii., p. 265.
† The emperor's own words.—"Letters of Joseph II."
‡ The words of the Hungarian protest.—Hubner, ii., p. 267.

and, therefore, shall you speak German.* I will now pass on to your third grievance, for you see that I am well posted on the subject of your sufferings. I have numbered and taxed your property, and that, too, in spite of your constitution, which exempts you from taxation. In my opinion, the privileges of an aristocracy do not consist in evading their share of the national burdens; on the contrary, they should assume it voluntarily, and, for the weal of the nation, place themselves on an equality with the people, each class striving with the other as to who shall best promote the prosperity of the government.† I cannot exempt you, therefore, from paying taxes."

"But, sire, this tax violates our rights and our constitution," replied Count Palfy.

"Has Hungary a constitution? A tumultuous states-diet, privileged aristocracy, the subjection of three-fifths of the nation to the remainder—is this a constitution?"

"It is the constitution of Hungary, and we have your majesty's written promise that you would respect it. But even had we received no solemn declaration of the sort, upon the security of our national freedom depends the Austrian right of succession to the throne of Hungary." ‡

"You dare threaten me?" cried Joseph, furiously.

"No, sire, we do not threaten; we are in the presence of a truth-loving monarch, and we are compelled to speak the unvarnished truth. We have already borne much from your majesty's ancestors. But, until the death of Maria Theresa, our fundamental laws remained inviolate. True, in the last years of her life she refused to allow the states-diet to assemble; but she never laid her hand upon our constitution. She was crowned Queen of Hungary, and took the coronation oath. Charles the Sixth and Joseph the First did likewise. Each one guaranteed us the right of inheritance, and our national freedom."

"There is no such thing as national freedom in Hungary. It contains nothing but lords and vassals, and it is vassalage that I intend to abolish."

"Does your majesty think that the general freedom of the state is promoted by your conscription laws?"

"Ah! here we have grievance the fourth," exclaimed Joseph. "Yes, the conscription is a thorn in your sensitive sides, because it claims you as the children and servants of your country, and forces you to draw your swords in her defence."

"We have never refused our blood to the country," replied Count Palfy, proudly throwing back his head, "and if her rights are intact to-day, it is because *we* have defended and protected them. We have fought for our fatherland, however, not as conscripts, but as freemen. Our people are unanimous in their abhorrence of the conscription act. When we weigh the motives and consequences of this act, we can draw but one inference from either: that we, who were born freemen, are to be reduced to slavery, and to be trampled under foot by every other province of Austria. Rather than submit to such indignity we will lay down our lives, for we are of one mind, and would sooner die than lose our liberty!"

* The emperor's own words.—See "Letters of Joseph II.," p. 76.
† The emperor's own words.—See "Letters of Joseph II.," p. 95.
‡ The words of the Hungarian protest.—Hubner, ii., p. 263.

"And I," cried Joseph, his eye flashing and his face scarlet with passion, "I say to you all, that you shall live, for I, your king and master, command you to do so."

An angry murmur was heard, and every eye looked defiance at the emperor. "Ah," said he, scornfully, "you would ape the Polish diet, and dispute the will of your king! You remember how the King of Poland succumbed to dictation! I am another and a different man, and I care neither for your approbation nor for your blame. It is my purpose to make Hungary prosperous, and therefore I have abolished the feudal system which is unfavorable to the development of the resources of the country. You Magyars would interfere with me. You have a constitution at variance with my laws, and for the sake of a piece of rotten parchment three hundred years old, Hungary must be suffered to remain uncivilized forever! Away with your mediæval privileges and rusty escutcheons! A new century has dawned, and not only the nobly born shall see its light, but the people who, until now, have been thrust aside by your arrogance! If enlightenment violates your ancient privileges, they shall be swept away to give place to the victorious rights of man! And this is my answer to all your grievances. Go home, ye Magyars, assemble your peers, and tell them that my decision is unalterable; and that what I have done with deliberation I shall never revoke. Go home and tell them that the emperor has spoken, and they have nothing to do but to submit!"

With a slight inclination Joseph turned his back; and before the magnates had time to recover themselves and to reply to this haughty harangue, the emperor had disappeared and closed the door.

In speechless indignation they glanced at one another. They had expected difficulty; but such insulting rejection of their petition they had not anticipated. They remembered the day when, with this same Joseph in her arms, Maria Theresa had appealed to their fathers for succor; they remembered, too, how in the enthusiasm of their loyalty they had sworn to die for Maria Theresa, their king!

"He never revokes!" muttered Palfy, after a long silence. "You heard him, Magyars, he never revokes! Shall we suffer him to oppress us?"

"No, no!" was the unanimous reply.

"So be it," said Palfy, solemnly "He has thrown down the gauntlet; we raise it, and strip for the fight. But for Hungary this man had been ruined. To-day he would ruin us, and we cast him off. Henceforth our cry is—'*Moriamur pro rege nostro constitutione!*'"

"'*Moriamur pro rege nostro constitutione!*'" echoed the Magyars, every man with his right hand raised to heaven.

CHAPTER CLXVII.

THE RECOMPENSE.

For four weeks Rachel had been a prisoner in her own house; all persons, with the exception of a Catholic priest and a Jewish rabbi, having been refused access to her. But at the expiration of this time a deputy from the imperial chancery was admitted, who had a long interview with the poor girl, and at dusk another visitor presented himself at the door of that gloomy abode. This last one was Baron Eskeles Flies.

The sentinels had allowed him to pass, and the guards in Rachel's anteroom gave way also, for the baron's permit to visit his daughter was from the emperor. With a respectful inclination they presented the key of the prisoner's room and awaited her father's orders.

"Go below, and wait until I call you," said he.

"Of course, as we are commanded in the permit to obey you, we follow the emperor's order."

Herr Eskeles thanked them, and putting a ducat in the hand of each, the men departed in a state of supreme satisfaction. They had scarcely left, when the banker bolted the door from the inside, and crossed the room toward the opposite door. His hand trembled so that he could not introduce the key to open it, and he was obliged to retreat to the sofa, and there recover himself.

"How will she receive me?" thought he. "They say that she is sadly changed, and that her father would scarcely know his beautiful child again. Oh, my child, will I be able to bear the sight of your grief without falling at your feet, and acknowledging my guilt? But pshaw! She is safe now. I shall take her home; and for every tear that she has shed, I will give her a diamond bright as a star. She shall have gold, pearls, riches, and be once more the envy of all the women in Vienna. Yes, my Rachel, yes—gold, diamonds, and happiness!"

He turned the key, and the door opened. Not a sound greeted his entrance into that dismal room, wherein four funeral-looking wax-lights were burning at each corner of a square table. Even so had the lights burned in the room where Rachel's mother once lay dead. The banker thought of this, as between those flaring lights he saw the pale, wan figure on the sofa, that seemed as rigid, as motionless, and as white as a corpse.

Was it indeed Rachel? Those pinched features, those hollow eyes; that figure, so bowed with sorrow, could that be his peerless daughter? What had diamonds and pearls in common with that pale spectre?

The banker could scarcely suppress a cry of anguish as he gazed upon the wreck of so much beauty. But he gathered courage to cross the room, and stood before her.

"Rachel," said he, in a soft, imploring voice, "do you know me?"

"I know you," replied she, without moving; "do you know *me?*"

"My beloved child, my heart recognizes you, and calls you to itself. Come, darling, come and rest within you father's protecting arms. See, they are open to receive you. I have forgiven all, and am ready to devote my whole life to your happiness."

He opened his arms, but Rachel did not stir. She looked at him, and when he saw the look, his hands dropped nerveless to his side.

"Where is Günther?" asked she. "What have you done with him?"

"I, my child?" exclaimed Eskeles. "The emperor has detected him in some dishonorable act (I know not what), and has sent him as a recruit to Hungary."

"I have heard this fable before," said Rachel, with a glance of scorn. "The priest who was sent to convert, has tried to console me for my loss, by dinning in my ears that Günther was a traitor; but

I know better. He is the victim of a Jew's revenge. It is you who have accused him with false witnesses, false letters, with all that vengeance can inspire, and wicked gold can buy. You are the accuser of my noble Günther!" By this time she had arisen, and now she stood confronting her father, her wasted finger pointing toward him, and her sunken eyes glowing like lights from a dark, deep cave.

"Who says so? Who has dared accuse me?" said he.

"Your face accuses you!—your eyes, that dare not encounter mine! Nay—do not raise your hand in sacrilegious protest, but answer me. By the faith of your ancestors, are you not the man who denounced him?"

He could not meet her scrutinizing glance. He averted his face, murmuring: "He who accused him is no better than himself. But it is the emperor who condemned him."

"The emperor is miserably befooled," cried Rachel. "He knows not the subtlety of Jewish revenge. But I am of the Jewish race, and I know it. I know my father, and I know my lover!"

"In this hour of reunion we will not discuss the innocence or guilt of the emperor's secretary," said the banker, gently. "I am thankful that the dark cloud which has hidden you so long from my sight is lifted, and that all is well with us again."

"All is not well, for between us lies the grave of my happiness, and that grave has sundered us forever. I cannot come to you, my father: the memory of my lover is between us, and that memory—oh, do not call it a cloud! 'Tis the golden beam of that sun which has set, but whose rays are still warm within my breaking heart. I say nothing to you of all that I have endured during these four weeks of anguish; but this I can tell you, my father, that I have never repented my choice. I am Günther's for life, and for death, which is the birth of immortality!"

"He is a dishonored man!" said Eskeles, frowning.

"And I, too, will be dishonored to-morrow," replied Rachel.

Her father started. He had forgotten the disgrace which threatened her.

"Rachel," said he, with exceeding tenderness, "I come to rescue you from shame and suffering."

"To rescue me?" echoed she. "Whither would you have me fly?"

"To the house of your father, my child."

"I have no father," replied she, with a weary sigh. "My father would have forced my heart, as the priest and the rabbi would have forced my belief. But I am free in my faith, my love, and my hate; and this freedom will sustain me to-morrow throughout the torture and shame of a disgraceful punishment."

"You surely will not brave the lash!" cried her father, his cheeks blanched with horror at the thought. "You will be womanly, my child, and recant."

"I must speak the truth," said she, interrupting him. "The doors of the synagogue, as well as those of the church, are closed against me. I am no Jewess, and *you* forced me to swear that I would never become a Christian. But what matters it?" continued she, kindling with enthusiasm, "I believe in God—the God of love and mercy; and to-morrow I shall see His face!"

"You would destroy yourself!" cried her father, his senses almost forsaking him.

"No. But do you suppose that I shall survive the severity and humiliation of the lash which it is the pleasure of tne emperor to inflict upon me? No, my father, I shall die before the executioner has time to strike his second blow."

"Rachel, my Rachel, do not speak such dreadful words!" cried Eskeles, wringing his hands in despair. "You cannot be a Christian, I know it; for their belief is unworthy of a pure soul. How could you ever give the hand of fellowship to a race who have outlawed you, because you scorn to utter a falsehood! But confess yourself a Jewess, and all will be well with us once more."

"I shall never return to the Jewish God of wrath and revenge! *My* God is all love. I must acknowledge Him before the world, and die for His sake!"

There was a pause. Rachel was calm and resolute; her father almost distracted. After a time he spoke again."

"So be it, then," cried he, raising his hand to heaven. "Be a Christian. I absolve you from your oath, and oh, my Rachel! if I sought the world for a proof of my overweening love, it could offer nothing to compare with this sacrifice. Go, my child, and become a Christian."

She shook her head. "The Christian's cruelty has cured me of my love for Christianity. I can never be one of a race who have persecuted my innocent lover. As for you, the cause of his martyrdom, hear my determination, and know that it is inflexible. I am resolved to endure the punishment; and when the blood streams from my back, and my frantic cries pierce the air until they reach your palace-walls;—when in the midst of the gaping populace, my body lies stretched upon the market-place, dishonored by the hand of the executioner,—then shall your revenge have returned to you; for the whole world will point at you as you pass, and say, 'He is the father of the woman who was whipped to death by the hangman!'"

"Alas!" sobbed the father, "I see that you hate me, and yet I must rescue you, even against your own will. The emperor has given me a pass to Paris. It is himself who allows me to escape with my poor, misguided child. Come, dear Rachel, come, ere it be too late, and in Paris we can forget our sorrows and begin life anew!"

"No! he has made the law, and he must bear the consequences of his own cruelty. He need not think to rescue himself from the odium of his acts, by conniving at my escape! I hate that emperor, the oppressor of my beloved; and as he dishonored Günther, so shall he dishonor me. Our woes will cry to Heaven for vengeance, and—"

But Rachel suddenly ceased, and fell back upon a chair. She had no strength to repulse her father, as he raised her in his arms, and laid her upon the sofa. He looked into her marble face, and put his lips to hers.

"She has swooned," cried he in despair. "We must fly at once. Rachel, Rachel, awake! The time is almost up. Come, we must away!"

She opened her eyes, and looked around. "Come, my daughter," said her father, kissing her wasted hands.

She said nothing, but stared and smiled a vacant smile. Again he took her hands, and saw that they were hot and dry. Her breath, too, was hot, and yet her pulse was feeble and fitful.

Her father, in his agony, dropped on his knees beside the unconscious girl. But this was no time for wailing. He rose to his feet again, and darting from the room, offered a handful of gold to the sentry, if he would but seek a physician. Then he returned to Rachel. She lay still with her eyes wide, wide open, while she murmured inaudible words, which he vainly strove to understand.

At length came the physician. He bent over the patient, examined her pulse, felt her forehead, and then turning to the banker, who stood by with his heart throbbing as if it would burst—

"Are you a relative of the lady?" asked he.

"I am her father," replied Eskeles, and even in this terrible hour he felt a thrill of joy as he spoke the words.

"I regret, then, to say to you that she is very ill. Her malady is typhoid fever, in its most dangerous form. I fear that she will not recover: she must have been ill for some weeks, and have concealed her illness. Has she suffered mentally of late?"

"Yes, I believe that she has," faltered the banker. "Will she die?"

"I am afraid to give you any hope—the disease has gone so far. It is strange. Was there no relative near her to see how ill she has been for so long a time?"

Gracious Heaven! What torture he inflicted upon the guilty father! At that moment he would have recalled Günther, and welcomed him as a son, could his presence have saved the child whom himself had murdered!

"Doctor," said he, in husky, trembling tones, "doctor, you must save my child. Ask what you will—I am rich, and if you restore her to me, you shall have a million!"

"Unhappily, life cannot be bought with gold," replied the physician. "God alone can restore her. We can do naught but assist Nature, and alleviate her sufferings."

"How can we alleviate her suffering?" asked Eskeles humbly, for his spirit was broken.

"By cool drinks, and cold compressions upon her head," said the physician. "Are there no women here to serve her?"

"No," murmured the banker. "My daughter is a prisoner. She is Rachel Eskeles Flies."

"Ah! The Deist who was to have suffered to-morrow? Poor, poor child, neither church nor synagogue can avail her now, for God will take her to himself."

"But there is a possibility of saving her, is there not?" asked the father imploringly. "We must try every thing, for—she *must* be saved!"

"*Must?*" repeated the physician. "Think you because you are rich that you can bribe Heaven? See, rather, how impotent your wealth has been to make your beautiful child happy (for I know her story). And, now, in spite of all the gold for which you have sacrificed her, she will die of a broken heart!"

Just then Rachel uttered a loud shriek, and clasping both her hands around her head, cried out that her brain was on fire.

"Cold compressions—quick," exclaimed the physician imperatively; and the banker staggered into Rachel's dressing-room (the room which Günther had so daintily fitted up), and brought water and a soft fine towel, which his trembling hands could scarcely bind upon his poor child's head. Then, as her moaning ceased, and her arms dropped, he passed into an ecstasy of joy, for now he began to hope that she would be spared to him.

"We must have female attendance here," said the physician. "She must be put to bed and tenderly watched. Go, baron, and bring your servants. I will see the emperor, and take upon myself the responsibility of having infringed his orders. Before such imminent peril all imprisonment is at an end."

"I cannot leave her," returned the baron. "You say she has but a few days to live; if so, I cannot spare one second of her life. I entreat of you, take my carriage, and in mercy, bring the servants for me. Oh, listen! she screams again—doctor go, I entreat! Here—fresh compressions—water! Oh, be quick!"

And again the wretched man bent over his child, and laid the cloths upon her head. The physician had gone, and he was alone with his treasure. He felt it a relief to be able to kiss her hands, to weep aloud, to throw himself upon his knees, and pray to the God of Israel to spare his idol!

The night went by, the servants came, and the physician, examining his patient again, promised to return in a few hours. Rachel was carried to her bed, and, hour after hour, the banker sat patient and watchful, listening to every moan, echoing every sigh; afraid to trust his precious charge to any one, lest the vigilance of another might fail.

A day and another night went by, and still no sleep had come over those glaring eyes. But she wept bitter tears, and when he heard her broken, murmured words of anguish, he thought he would go mad!

But sometimes in her fever-madness she smiled and was happy. Then she laughed aloud, and spoke to her beloved, who was always at her side. She had not once pronounced the name of her father; she seemed to have forgotten him, remembering nothing in all her past life save her love for Günther.

Often her father knelt beside her, and with tears streaming from his eyes, implored a look, a word—one single word of forgiveness. But Rachel laughed and sang, heedless of the despairing wretch who lay stricken to the earth at her side; while the lover whom she caressed was far away, unconscious of the blessing.

Suddenly she uttered a wild cry, and starting up, threw her arms convulsively about. Now she invoked the vengeance of Heaven upon Günther's murderers and at last—at last, was heard the name of her father! *She cursed him!*

With a cry as piercing as that of the poor maniac, Eskeles Flies sank upon his knees, and wept aloud.

Gradually Rachel grew more tranquil; and now she lay back on her pillow with a happy smile on her lips. But she spoke not a word. Once more she sighed "Günther," and then relapsed into silence.

Into a silence that seemed so breathless and so long, that her father arose, frightened, from his knees. He bent over his smiling child, and her face seemed transfigured. Not a sigh stirred her bosom, not a moan fluttered from her lips. But that smile remained so long unchanged, and her eyes—surely they were glazed!

Yes!—Rachel was dead.*

*The sad fate of Günther and of his beautiful Rachel is mentioned by Hormayer in his work, "The Emperor Francis and Metternich: a Fragment," p. 78.

CHAPTER CLXVIII.

THE REBELLION IN THE NETHERLANDS.

THE Emperor Joseph was in the Crimea, on a visit to the Empress of Russia. Here he witnessed a great triumph prepared for Catharine by Potemkin. It was her first greeting at Sebastopol from that navy which was to confer upon Russia the dominion of the Black Sea.

Potemkin invited Catharine and Joseph to a dinner served in a pavilion erected for the occasion. The festivities were interrupted by the clash of military music; and as the Russian empress and the Austrian emperor stepped out of the pavilion, the fleet, arranged in line of battle, was before them, and greeted them with a salute of a hundred guns. As they ceased, Potemkin turned to Catharine, and cried out in tones of joyful enthusiasm:

"The voice of the cannon proclaims that the Black Sea has found its mistress, and that ere long the flag of Russia shall wave triumphant over the towers of Constantinople!" *

On another occasion, Joseph was sailing around the bay of Sebastopol, in company with the empress, Potemkin, and the French ambassador. As they neared the fleet, Potemkin, pointing out the five-and-twenty vessels-of-war, exclaimed:

"These ships await my sovereign's word to spread their sails to the wind, and steer for Constantinople!" †

As Potemkin spoke, Catharine's eyes were turned to the south, where Stamboul still defied her rule, and ambitious aspirations filled her heart. Joseph, however, looked down upon the foaming waters, and no one saw the curl of his lip, as Catharine and Potemkin continued the subject, and spoke of the future Greek empire.

For Joseph had lost all faith in the brilliant schemes with which Catharine had dazzled his imagination at St. Petersburg.

The enthusiasm with which he had followed her ambitious vagaries, had long since died out, and he had awakened from his dreams of greatness.

All the pomp and splendor which Potemkin had conjured from the ashes of a conquered country, could not deceive Joseph.

Behind the stately edifices which had sprung up like the palaces of Aladdin, he saw the ruins of a desolated land; in the midst of the cheering multitudes, whom Potemkin had assembled together to do homage to Catharine, he saw the grim-visaged Tartars, whose eyes were glowing with deadly hatred of her who had either murdered or driven into exile fifty thousand of their race.

Nevertheless, he entered with his usual grace and affability into all Catharine's schemes for the improvement of her new domains. Not far from Sebastopol she proposed to lay the foundations of a new city, and the emperor was invited to take a part in the ceremonies.

Amid the booming of cannon, the loud strains of martial music, and the cheers of her followers, the empress laid the first stone of the city of Caterinoslaw, and after her, the emperor took up the

* See "Conflict for the Possession of the Black Sea."—Theodore Mundt, pp. 253, 255.

† Ibid.

mortar and trowel, and laid the second one. He performed his part of the drama with becoming solemnity; but, about an hour later, as he was taking his customary afternoon walk with the French ambassador, M. de Sigur, he laughed, and said:

"The empress and I have been working magic to-day; for in the course of a few minutes we built up an entire city. She laid the first stone of the place, and I the last." *

But in the very midst of these festivities, a courier arrived with letters for the emperor from Prince Kaunitz. The prince besought him to return at once, for the discontent which had existed from the commencement of his reign in the Netherlands, had kindled into open rebellion, which threatened the imperial throne itself. Joseph took hasty leave of Catharine, but renewed his promise to sustain and assist her whenever she put into execution her designs against Turkey.

On the emperor's arrival at Vienna, he found new couriers awaiting him, with still more alarming intelligence. The people were frantic, and, with the clergy at their head, demanded the restoration of the "*Joyeuse Entrée.*" †

"And all this," cried the emperor, "because I have summoned a soap-boiler to Vienna for trial!"

"Yes, your majesty, but the *Joyeuse Entrée* exacts that the people of Brabant shall be tried in their own country," said Prince Kaunitz, with a shrug. "The Brabantians know every line of their constitution by heart."

"Well, they shall learn to know me also by heart," returned Joseph, with irritation. "Brabant is mine; it is but a province of my empire, and the Brabantians, like the Hungarians, are nothing but Austrians. The Bishop of Frankenberg is not lord of Brabant, and I am resolved to enlighten this priest-ridden people in spite of their writhings."

"But, unhappily, the priests in Belgium and Brabant are mightier than your majesty," returned Kaunitz. "The Bishop of Frankenberg is the veritable lord of Brabant, for he controls the minds and hearts of the people there, while your majesty can do nothing but command their ungracious obedience. It is the Bishop of Frankenberg who prejudiced the people against the imperial seminaries."

"I can well believe that they are distasteful to a bigot," cried Joseph; "for the theological course of the priests who are to be educated there is prescribed by me. I do not intend that the children of Levi shall monopolize the minds and hearts of my people any longer. This haughty prelate shall learn to know that I am his emperor, and that the arm of the pope is powerless to shield where I have resolved to strike."

"If your majesty goes to work in this fashion, instead of crushing the influence of the bishop, you may irretrievably lose your own. Belgium is a dangerous country. The people cherish their abuses as constitutional rights, and each man regards the whole as his individual property."

"And because I desire to make them happy and free, they cry out against me as an innovator who violates these absurd rights. Oh, my friend! I feel sometimes so exhausted by my struggles with

* Masson, "Mémoires Secrètes sur la Russie," vol. i.

† The "*Joyeuse Entrée*" was the old constitution which Philip the Good, on his entrance into Brussels, had granted to the Belgians.

ignorance and selfishness, that I often think it would be better to leave the stupid masses to their fate!"

"They deserve nothing better," replied Kaunitz, with his usual phlegm. "They are thankless children whom he can win who feeds them with sugar. Your majesty, perhaps, has not sufficiently conciliated their weakness. You have been too honest in your opposition to their rotten privileges. Had you undermined the *Joyeuse Entrée* by degrees, it would have fallen of itself. But you have attempted to blow it up, and the result is that these Belgian children cry out that the temple of liberty is on fire, and your majesty is the incendiary. Now, had you allowed the soap-boiler to be tried by the laws of his own land, the first to condemn and punish him would have been his own countrymen: but your course of action has transformed him into a martyr, and now the Belgians are mourning for him as a jewel above all price."

"I cannot make use of artifice or stratagem. With the banner of Truth in my hand, I march forward to the battle of life."

"But, with your eyes fixed upon that banner, you may fall into the precipices which your enemies have dug for you. I have often told your majesty that politics can never be successful without stratagem. Let your standard be that of Truth, if you will, but when the day looks unpropitious, fold it up, that fools may rally around it unawares."

"Perhaps you are right," sighed the emperor; "but all this is very sad. I have meant well by my subjects, but they misinterpret my actions, and accuse me of tyranny. I go to them with a heart full of love, and they turn upon me as though I were an enemy. But I will not relent! I must be free to act as seems best to myself. The *Joyeuse Entrée* is in my way. 'Tis a gordian knot which must be unloosed before Belgium can be truly mine; I have no time to untie it—it must be cut in twain!"

Just then the door of the chancery opened, and one of the secretaries came forward.

"Sire," said he, "a courier has arrived from Brussels, with dispatches from Count Belgiojoso to his highness."

"I had ordered my dispatches to be sent after me, your majesty," said Kaunitz, taking the papers, and motioning the secretary to withdraw. "Does your majesty allow me to read them?"

"By all means. Let us hope that they bring us good news. I gave stringent orders to Belgiojoso to see that my will was carried out in Belgium. I bade him inform the people that they should not have their precious soap-boiler back; that he was my subject, and I intended to have him tried here. I told him, moreover, that, like all my other subjects, the Belgians must pay new taxes without expecting to be consulted as to the expediency of the measure."

"Belgiojoso has obeyed your majesty's commands," remarked Kaunitz, who had just finished the first dispatch. "And the consequence is, that the good people of Brussels broke his windows for him."

"They shall pay dear for those windows," cried Joseph.

"He told them, furthermore, that in spite of the eighth article of their constitution, they should pay extraordinary taxes; whereupon they answered him with the fifty-ninth article."

"What says the fifty-ninth article?"

"It says that when the sovereign violates, in any serious way, the rights guaranteed by the *Joyeuse Entrée*, the people are released from all obligations toward him."

"That is the language of treason!" cried Joseph.

"And treason it is," returned Kaunitz, folding the second dispatch. "The poeple collected in the streets, and the burghers, arming themselves, marched to the palace of the governor-general, and demanded admittance."

"And he, what did he do?"

"He received them, sire," said Kaunitz, despondingly.

"And what said he to the insolent demands of the rebels?—You are silent, Kaunitz, and I see in your countenance that you have bad news for me. I know my brother-in-law, Albert of Saxony, or rather, I know my sister Christina. From her youth she has been my enemy, forever crossing me in every purpose of my life! Christina was sure to prompt him to something in opposition to my wishes."

"It would appear that you are right, sire," replied Kaunitz. "The burghers exacted of the governor-general that they should be reinstated in all the rights of the *Joyeuse Entrée*, without exception whatsoever."

"Their *Joyeuse Entrée* is nothing but a mass of impertinent privileges, which Christina herself could not desire to concede," cried Joseph. "I am curious, then, to know how my brother-in-law crept out of the difficulty. What was his answer?"

"He asked time for reflection, sire—twelve hours. It was eleven o'clock in the morning when the burghers came to him."

"Did they go quietly home then?"

"No, sire. They surrounded the palace, their numbers continually increasing until the place was filled with armed men, supported by thousands of insurgents, who rent the air with cries of 'Give us the *Joyeuse Entrée!* The *Joyeuse Entrée* forever!'"

"Kaunitz, the answer of the Elector of Saxony must have been a disgraceful one, or you would not be at such pains to describe the clamors of the rebellious multitude. Tell me at once what occurred."

"Sire, when the twleve hours had expired, the burghers forced the palace doors, and two hundred armed men rushed unannounced into the presence of the duke."

"Well—well!" cried Joseph, breathing heavily.

"The governor was obliged to yield, and to promise them that their constitution should be reinstated."

The emperor uttered a cry of fury, and grew pale with rage. "He reinstated the *Joyeuse Entrée!* He presumed to do it! Did I not tell you that Christina was my enemy? She it is who has brought this humiliation upon me! She has dared revoke what I had commanded!—Oh, how those vulgar rebels must have laughed to see that with their pestiferous breath they had power to blow away my edicts like so many card-houses!"

"Not at all, sire," said Kaunitz, with composure. "There was no jesting among the people, although they were very happy, and passed the night in shouts of joy. Brussels was illuminated, and six hundred young men drew the carriage of the elector and electress to the theatre, amid cries of 'Long live the emperor! Long live the *Joyeuse Entrée!*'"

"'Long live the emperor!'" cried Joseph, contemptuously. "They treat me as savages do their wooden idols. When they are unpropitious, they beat them; when otherwise, they set them up and adore them again. Those over whom I reign, however, shall see that I am no wooden idol, but a man and a monarch, who draws his sword to avenge an affront from whomsoever received. Blood alone will extinguish the fire of this rebellion, and it shall be quenched in the blood of the rebels."

"Many a throne has been overturned by the wild waves of human blood," said Kaunitz, thoughtfully; "and many a well-meaning prince has been branded by history as a tyrant, because he would have forced reform upon nations unprepared to receive it. The insurgent states have some show of justice on their side; and if your majesty adopts severe measures toward them, they will parade themselves before the world as martyrs."

"And yet I alone am the martyr," cried Joseph, bitterly—"the martyr of liberty and enlightenment. Oh, Kaunitz, how hard it is to be forever misunderstood!—to see those whom we love, led astray by the wickedness of others! I must crush this rebellion by force, and yet the real criminals are the clergy."

"If you think so," said Kaunitz, shrewdly, "then be lenient toward the misguided people. Perhaps mildness may prevail. Belgium is united to a man, and if you enforce your will, you must crush the entire nation. Such extreme measures must be resorted to only when all other means shall have been exhausted."

"What other means do you counsel?" asked Joseph, irritated. "Would you have me treat with the rabble?"

"No, sire, but treat with the people. When an entire nation are united, they rise to equality with their rulers, and it is no condescension then on the part of the sovereign if he listen to their grievances and temporize with the aggrieved. You have not yet tried personal negotiations with your Netherlanders, sire. Call a deputation of them to Vienna. We shall thereby gain time, the insurgents will grow more dispassionate, and perhaps we may reason them into acquiescence. Once get as far as an armistice with your rebels, and the game is yours; for insurgents are poor diplomatists. Let me advise your majesty to dissimulate your anger, and send conciliatory messages."

"Well, well," said the emperor, with a deep sigh, "be it so. I will do as you like, but I must for ever and ever yield my will to that of others. Call a deputation of the provinces, and cite the governor-general and his wife also to Vienna. I will investigate as a father before I condemn as a judge. But if this last proof of my goodness should be of no avail, then I shall strike; and if blood flow in torrents—upon *their* heads and not mine, be the sin." *

CHAPTER CLXIX.

THE IMPERIAL SUITOR.

A HALF year had passed away. The deputation from the Netherlands had visited Vienna, and had been deeply impressed with the affability of the emperor. They returned home, taking with them his assurance that their time-honored usages should be respected, and that Joseph himself would be the guardian of their ancient

* Joseph's own words. See Hubner, ii., p. 454.

rights. He merely desired to free them from "certain abuses which in the lapse of time had crept into their constitution." To this end he promised that an imperial delegation should visit Brussels to consult with the states.

The two envoys publicly sent by the emperor were Count von Trautmannsdorf and General d'Alton. But to these he added a secret envoy in the person of Count Dietrichstein, the former marshal of Maria Theresa's household.

"I know that my two ambassadors will find a wise mentor in you, count," said Joseph as Dietrichstein was taking leave of him. "I thank you for sacrificing your pleasant home with its associations to my interest; for no man so well as you can enlighten public opinion as to my character and intentions."

"Your majesty knows that not only my comfort but my life are at the disposal of my emperor," replied the count. "I deserve no credit for this; it comes to me as a proud inheritance from an ancestry who have ever been the loyal subjects of the house of Hapsburg."

"I wish that I knew how to testify my sense of your loyalty, and to prove to you that the Hapsburgers have grateful hearts," exclaimed the emperor.

"Sire," said Count Dietrichstein, solemnly, "it is in your power to do so. If your majesty really thinks that my family are deserving of it, you can confer upon us a very great favor."

"Speak, then," replied Joseph, eagerly—"speak, for your wish is already granted. I well know that Count Dietrichstein can ask nothing that I would not accord!"

"I accept your majesty's kindness," said Dietrichstein, in the same solemn tone. "My request is easy of fulfilment, and will give but little trouble to my beloved sovereign. It concerns my daughter Therese, whom I shall leave behind in Vienna."

"You leave Therese?" said Joseph, coloring.

"Yes, your majesty. My daughter remains under the protection of her aunt."

"Ah! Therese is to be left!" cried the emperor, and an expression of happiness flitted over his features.

Count Dietrichstein saw it, and a cloud passed over his face. "I leave her here," continued he, "because the mission with which your majesty has intrusted me might possibly become dangerous. Unhappily, however, for young girls there is danger everywhere; and for this reason I scarcely deem the protection of her aunt sufficient."

While Count Dietrichstein had been speaking, Joseph had seemed uneasy; and finally he had walked to the window, where he was now looking out upon the square. The count was annoyed at this proceeding; he frowned, and, crossing the room, came directly behind the emperor.

"Sire," said he, in a distinct voice, "I wish to marry Therese."

"With whom?" asked Joseph, without turning.

"With your majesty's lord of the bedchamber, Count Kinsky."

"And Therese?" asked Joseph, without turning around. "Does she love the count?"

"No, sire, she has never encouraged him. She affects to have a repugnance to marriage, and has continually urged me to allow her to enter a convent. But I will not give my consent to such a ridiculous whim. Count Kinsky is a man of honor; he loves Therese, and will make her happy. Therese is the true daughter of my house, sire; a wish of your majesty to her would be a law. I therefore beg of you, as the greatest favor you could bestow, to urge her to accept Count Kinsky."

The emperor turned hastily around, and his face was scarlet. "How?" said he, in a faltering voice. "You exact of me that I should woo your daughter for Count Kinsky?"

"It is this favor, sire, which you have so graciously promised to grant."

The emperor made no reply. He gazed at the count with gloomy, searching eyes. The latter met his glance with quiet firmness. A long pause ensued, and the emperor's face changed gradually until it became very pale. He sighed and seemed to awake from a reverie.

"Count Dietrichstein," said he, in a trembling voice, "you have pointed out to me the means of serving you. I will do your behest, and urge your daughter to be the wife of Count Kinsky."

"There spoke my noble emperor!" cried the count, deeply moved, while he pressed the hand, which had been extended by Joseph, to his lips. "In the name of my ancestors, I thank you, sire."

"Do not thank me, my friend," said Joseph, sadly. "You have understood me, and I you—that is all. When shall I see your daughter?"

"Sire, I leave Vienna this evening, and I would gladly leave Therese an affianced bride. The marriage can take place on my return."

"Very well," said Joseph, with a smothered sigh, "I will go at once. Is the countess in the city?"

"No, sire, she is at the villa near Schönbrunn. But I will send for her, and when she arrives, she shall have the honor of an interview with your majesty."

"No, no," said Joseph, hastily; "let her remain at the villa, and enjoy one more day of maiden freedom. I myself will drive there to see her. I shall be obliged to renounce the pleasure of your company thither, for I know that you have important business to-day to transact with Prince Kaunitz."

A distrustful look was the reply to this proposition. The emperor divined the cause, and went on: "But if you *cannot* accompany, you can follow me with Count Kinsky; that is, if you really think that I can persuade the countess to accept him."

"I know it, sire. Therese will be as docile to the wishes of your majesty as her father. As I am ready, at your desire, to renounce the happiness of accompanying you to my villa, so she, if you speak the word, will renounce her foolish fancies, and consent to be Kinsky's wife."

"We can try," said the emperor, moodily. But he smiled as he gave his hand to Count Dietrichstein, who, perfectly reassured, went off to his affairs of state.

When the count had left the room, the expression of Joseph's face changed at once. With a deep sigh he threw himself into an arm-chair, and for some time sat there motionless; but when the little French clock on the mantelpiece struck the hour, he started up, exclaiming: "Eleven o'clock! Time flies, and my word has been given. Alas, it must be redeemed!—An emperor has no right to grieve; but oh, how hard it is, sometimes, to perform one's duty!—Well—it must be:—I am pledged to fulfil the motto of my escutcheon: '*Virtute et exemplo.*'"

A quarter of an hour later, the emperor was on his way to the villa, which was situated in the midst of a fine park, not far from the palace of Schönbrunn. Joseph drove himself, accompanied by a jockey, who stood behind. The people on the road greeted their sovereign as he passed. He returned the greeting, and no one saw how pale and wretched he looked; for he, like his mother, was fond of fast driving, and to-day his horse sped like the wind.

CHAPTER CLXX.

THE LAST DREAM OF LOVE.

THERESE VON DIETRICHSTEIN was alone in the little pavilion which her father had built expressly for her. It consisted of a parlor and a boudoir. The parlor was fitted up without magnificence, but with great elegance. Herein Therese was accustomed to receive her intimate associates. But no one ever entered the boudoir without an express invitation; for it was her sanctuary and studio. There the countess was transformed into an artist; there she studied music and painting, in both of which she excelled. Her father and her very dear friends knew of her great proficiency in art, but her reputation went no further, for Therese was as shy as a gazelle, and as anxious to conceal her talents as many women are to parade them.

At her father's hotel, Therese received the distinguished guests who visited there, with the stately courtesy befitting a high-born countess; but in her little pavilion she was the simple and enthusiastic child of art. Her boudoir contained little besides a harp, a harpsichord, and an easel which stood by the arched window opening into a flower-garden. Near the easel was a small marble table covered with palettes, brushes, and crayons. When Therese retired to this boudoir, her maid was accustomed to keep watch lest she should be surprised by visitors. If any were announced, Therese came out of her boudoir, and, carefully closing the door, awaited her friends in the parlor.

To-day she sat in this boudoir, feeling so secure from visitors that she had raised the *portière* leading to her parlor, and had flung wide the casement which opened upon the park. The sweet summer air was fanning her brow as she sat at the harp, singing a song of her own composition. She had just concluded; her little white hands had glided from the strings to her lap, and her head rested against the harp, above the pillar of which a golden eagle with outstretched wings seemed to be keeping watch over the young girl, as though to shield her from approaching misfortune.

With her head bent over her harp, she sat musing until two tears, which had long been gathering in her eyes, fell upon her hands. As she felt them, she raised her head. Her dark-blue eyes were full o sorrow, and her cheeks were glowing with blushes.

"What right have I to weep over a treasure which is as far from me as heaven is from earth?" said she. "I will not repine, so long as I am free to dream of him without crime. But what if I should lose that freedom? What if my father should wish to force me into marriage? Oh, then, I should take refuge behind the friendly portals of a convent!"

"Why take refuge in a convent?" said a soft voice behind her.

Therese sprang up with such wild agitation, that the harp, with a clang, fell back against the wall. Too well she knew this musical voice—it was the voice which spoke to her in dreams; and as its tones fell so suddenly upon her ear, she felt as if a bolt from heaven had struck her heart, and knew not whether she would die of ecstasy or fright.

"Joseph!" exclaimed she, all unconscious of the word, and she sank back into her chair, not daring to raise her eyes. With one bound the emperor was at her side, taking her hands, and pressing them within his own.

"Pardon me, countess," said he, tenderly, "I have startled you. It was wrong of me to send away your maid, and to present myself unannounced. In my selfishness, I would not wait for form, and forgot that my visit was totally unexpected. Say that you forgive me; let me read my pardon in your heavenly eyes."

Slowly Therese raised her head, and tried to speak. She longed to say that she had nothing to forgive; but had not the courage to meet the glances of those eyes which were fixed upon her with an expression of passionate entreaty, and seemed to be gazing into her heart, reading its most cherished, most consecrated secrets.

Did he understand the language of her agitation? "Look at me, Therese," whispered he. "It is an eternity since we met, and now—one more look at your angel-face, for I come to bid adieu to it forever."

She started, repeating his words, "Bid adieu—adieu!"

"Yes, sweet one, adieu. Some wiseacre has guessed the secret which I had fondly imagined was known to God and to myself only. And yet, Therese, I have never even told myself how passionately I love you! My eyes must have betrayed me to others; for since that happy day at Schönbrunn when I kissed the rose which had dropped from your hair, you have not been seen at court. I never should have told you this, my best beloved, but the anguish of this hour has wrung the confession from me. It will die away from your memory like the tones of a strange melody, and be lost in the jubilant harmony of your happy married life."

He turned away that she might not see the tears which had gathered in his eyes and were ready to fall. As for Therese, she rose to her feet. For one moment, her heart stood still—the next, her blood was coursing so wildly through her veins that she thought he must surely hear its mad throbbings in the stillness of that little room. The emperor turned again, and his face was grave, but calm. He had mastered his emotion, and, ashamed of the weakness of the avowal he had made, he determined to atone for it. He took the hand of the countess and led her to a divan, where he gently drew her down, while she obeyed, as though her will had suddenly been merged into his. She was conscious of one thing only. He was there!—he whose name was written upon her heart, though she had never uttered it until that day!

He stood before her with folded arms, and contemplated her as an enthusiast might look upon the statue of a saint.

"Therese," said he, after a long silence, "why did you say that you would go into a convent?"

Therese grew pale and shivered, but said nothing. Joseph, bending down and looking into her eyes, repeated his question.

"Because my father wishes me to marry a man whom I do not love," replied Therese, with a candor which yielded to the magic of his glance as the rose gives her heart's sweet perfume to the wooing of the summer breeze.

"But, Therese," said the emperor, mindful of his promise, "you must obey your father. It is your duty."

"No—I shall never marry," returned Therese, eagerly.

"Marriage is the only vocation fit for a woman," replied Joseph. "The wife is commanded to follow her husband."

"Yes, to follow the husband of her love," interrupted she, with enthusiasm. "And oh, it must be heaven on earth to follow the beloved one through joy and sorrow, to feel with his heart, to see with his eyes, to live for his love, or, if God grant such supreme happiness, to die for his sake!"

"Therese!" exclaimed Joseph, passionately, as, gazing upon her inspired countenance, he forgot every thing except his love.

She blushed, and her eyes sought the floor. "No," said she, as if communing with herself, "this blessing I shall never know."

"And why not?" cried he. "Why should one so young, so beautiful, so gifted as you, cast away the ties of social life and pass within the joyless portals of a convent?"

Therese said nothing. She sat ashamed, bewildered, entranced; and, in her confusion, her beauty grew tenfold greater. The emperor's resolutions were fast melting away.

Again he besought her in tender tones. "Tell me, my Therese; confide in me, for I swear that your happiness is dearer to me than my life." He bent closer, and seized her hands. His touch was electric, for a tremor took possession of them both, and they dared not look at each other. Joseph recovered himself, and began in low, pleading tones: "Look at me, beloved, and let me read my answer in your truthful eyes. Look at me, for those eyes are my light, my life, my heaven!"

Therese could not obey. Her head sank lower and lower, and deep, convulsive sighs rent her heart. The emperor, scarcely knowing what he did, knelt before her. She met his glance of intoxicated love, and, unable to resist it, murmured:

"Because I love—thee."

Had he heard aright? Was it not the trees whispering to the summer air, or the birds cooing beneath the eaves? Or had an angel borne the message from that heaven which to-day was so radiant and so silver-bright?

He still knelt, and pressed her trembling hands to his lips, while his face was lit up with a joy, which Therese had never seen there before.

"Have I found you at last, star of my dark and solitary life?" said he. "Are you mine at last, shy gazelle, that so long have escaped me, bounding higher and higher up the icy steeps of this cheerless world? Oh, Therese, why did I not find you in the early years of life? And yet I thank Heaven that you are mine for these few fleeting moments, for they have taken me back to the days of my youth and its beautiful illusions! Ah, Therese, from the first hour when I beheld you advancing on your father's arm to greet me, proud as an empress, calm as a vestal, beautiful as Aphrodite, my heart acknowledged you as its mistress! Since then I have been your slave, kissing your shadow as it went before me, and yet not conscious of my insane passion until your father saw me with that rose—and then I knew that I loved you forever! Yes, Therese, you are the last love of an unfortunate man, whom the world calls an emperor, but who lies at your feet, as the beggar before his ideal of the glorious Madonna! Bend to me, Madonna, and let me drink my last draught of love! I shall soon have quaffed it, and then—your father will be here to remind me that you are a high-born countess, the priceless treasure of whose love I may not possess! Kiss me, my Therese, and consecrate my lips to holy resignation!"

And Therese, too bewildered to resist, bent forward. Their lips met, and his arms were around her, and time, place, station, honor —every thing vanished before the might of their love.

Suddenly they heard an exclamation—and there, at the *portière*, stood the father and the suitor of Therese, their pale and angry faces turned toward the lovers.

The emperor, burning with shame and fury, sprang to his feet. Therese, with a faint cry, hid her face in her hands, and, trembling with fear, awaited her sentence.

There was a deep silence. Each one seemed afraid to speak, for the first word uttered in that room might be treason. With dark and sullen faces, the two noblemen looked at the imperial culprit, who, leaning against the window, with head upturned to heaven, seemed scarcely able to sustain the weight of his own anguish. The stillness was insupportable, and it was his duty to break it. He glanced at the two men who, immovable and frowning, awaited this explanation.

Joseph turned to Therese, who had not yet withdrawn her hands. She felt as if she could never face the world again.

"Rise, Therese, and give me your hand," said he, authoritatively.

She obeyed at once, and the emperor, pressing that trembling hand within his own, led her to her father.

"Count Dietrichstein," said he, "you reminded me to-day of the long-tried loyalty of your house, and asked me, as your reward, to advise your daughter's acceptance of the husband you have chosen for her. I have fulfilled my promise, and Therese has consented to obey your commands. She promises to renounce her dream of entering a convent, and to become the wife of Count Kinsky. Is it not so, Therese? Have I not your approval in promising these things to your father?"

"It is so," murmured Therese, turning pale as death.

"And now, Count Dietrichstein," continued Joseph, "I will allow you to postpone your mission to Brussels, so that before you leave Vienna you may witness the nuptials of your daughter. In one week the marriage will be solemnized in the imperial chapel. Count Kinsky, I deilver your bride into your hands. Farewell! I shall meet you in the chapel."

He bowed, and hurried away. He heard the cry which broke from the lips of Therese, although he did not turn his head when her father's voice called loudly for help. But seeing that the countess's maid was walking in the park, he overtook her, saying, hastily, "Go quickly to the pavilion; the Countess Therese has fainted."

Then he hastened away, not keeping the walks, but trampling

heedlessly over the flowers, and dashing past the lilacs and laburnums, thinking of that fearful hour when Adam was driven from Paradise, and wondering whether the agony of the first man who sinned had been greater than his to-day, when the sun was setting upon the last dream of love which he would ever have in this world!

CHAPTER CLXXI.

THE TURKISH WAR.

THE bolt had fallen. Russia had declared war against Turkey. On the return of the emperor from his unfortunate pilgrimage to Count Dietrichstein's villa, three couriers awaited him from Petersburg, Constantinople, and Berlin. Besides various dispatches from Count Cobenzl, the courier from Petersburg brought an autographic letter from the empress. Catharine reminded the emperor of the promise which he had made in St. Petersburg, and renewed at Cherson, and announced that the hour had arrived for its fulfilment. The enmity so long smothered under the ashes of simulated peace had kindled and broken out into the flames of open war.

The Porte himself had broken the peace. On account of some arbitrary act of the Russian ambassador, he had seized and confined him in the Seven Towers. Russia had demanded his release, and satisfaction for the insult. The sultan had replied by demanding the restoration of the Crimea, and the withdrawal of the Russian fleet from the Black Sea.

The disputants had called in the Austrian internuncio, but all diplomacy was vain. Indeed, neither Russia, Turkey, nor Austria had placed any reliance upon the negotiations for peace; for while they were pending, the three powers were all assiduously preparing for war. In the spring of 1788, the Austrian internuncio declined any further attempt at mediation, and hostilities between Russia and Turkey were renewed.

Joseph received the tidings with an outburst of joy. They lifted a load of grief from his heart; for war, to him, was balsam for every sorrow.

"Now I shall be cured of this last wound!" exclaimed he, as he paced his cabinet, the dispatches in his hand. "God is merciful—He has sent the remedy, and once more I shall feel like a sovereign and a man! How I long to hear the bullets hiss and the battle rage! There are no myrtles for me on earth; perchance I may yet be permitted to gather its laurels. Welcome, O war! Welcome the march, the camp, and the battle-field!"

He rang, and commanded the presence of Field-Marshal Lacy. Then he read his dispatches again, glancing impatiently, from time to time, at the door. Finally it opened, and a page announced the field-marshal. Joseph came hurriedly forward, and grasped the hands of his long-tried friend.

"Lacy," cried he, "from this day you shall be better pleased than you have been with me of late. I have seen your reproving looks—nay, do not deny it, for they have been as significant as words; and if I made no answer, it was perhaps because I was guilty, and had nothing to say. You have sighed over my dejection for months past, dear friend, but it has vanished with the tidings I have just received. I am ready to rush out into the storm, bold and defiant as Ajax!"

"Oh, how it rejoices my heart to hear such words!" replied Lacy, pressing Joseph's hand. "I recognize my hero, my emperor again, and victory is throned upon his noble brow! With those flashing eyes, and that triumphant bearing, you will inspire your Austrians with such enthusiasm, that every man of them will follow whithersoever his commander leads!"

"Ah," cried Joseph, joyfully, "you have guessed, then, why I requested your presence here! Yes, Lacy, war is not only welcome to you and to me, but I know that it will also rejoice the hearts of the Austrian army. And now I invite you to accompany me on my campaign against the Turks, and I give you chief command of my armies; for your valor and patriotism entitle you to the distinction."

"Your majesty knows that my life is consecrated to your service," replied Lacy, with strong emotion. "You know with what pride I would fight at your side, secure that victory must always perch upon the banners of my gallant emperor."

"And you rejoice, do you not, Lacy, that our foe is to be the Moslem?"

Lacy was silent for a while. "I should rejoice from my soul," replied he, with some hesitation, "if Austria were fighting her own battles."

"Our ally is distasteful to you?" asked Joseph, laughing. "You have not yet learned to love Russia?"

"I have no right to pass judgment upon those whom your majesty has deemed worthy of your alliance, sire."

"No evasions, Lacy. You are pledged to truth when you enter these palace walls."

"Well, sire, if we are in the palace of truth, I must confess to a prejudice against Russia and Russia's empress. Catharine calls for your majesty's assistance, not to further the cause of justice or of right, but to aid her in making new conquests."

"I shall not permit her to make any new conquests!" cried Joseph. "She may fight out her quarrel with Turkey, and, so far, I shall keep my promise and sustain her. But I shall lend my sanction to none of her ambitious schemes. I suffered the Porte to cede Tauris to Catharine, because this cession was of inestimable advantage to me. It protected my boundaries from the Turk himself, and then it produced dissension between the courts of St. Petersburg and Berlin, and so deprived the latter of her powerful ally.* But having permitted Russia to take possession of the Crimea, the aspect of affairs is changed. I never shall suffer the Russians to establish themselves in Constantinople. The turban I conceive to be a safer neighbor for Austria than the hat.* At this present time Russia offers me the opportunity of retaking Belgrade, and avenging the humiliation sustained by my father at the hands of the Porte. For two hundred years these barbarians of the East have been guilty of bad faith toward my ancestors, and the time has arrived when, as the avenger of all mankind, I shall deliver Europe from the infidel, and the world from a race which for centuries has been the scourge of every Christian nation." †

*The emperor's own words.—See Gross-Hoffinger, iii., pp. 428, 429.
†The emperor's own words.—See "Letters of Jos ph II.," p. 135.

"And in this glorious struggle of Christianity and civilization against Islamism and barbarism, I shall be at my emperor's side, and witness his triumph! This is a privilege which the last drop of my blood would be inadequate to buy!"

The emperor again gave his hand. "I knew that you would be as glad to follow me as a war-horse to follow the trumpet's call. This time we shall have no child's play; it shall be war, grim, bloody war! And now to work. In one hour the courier must depart, who bears my manifesto to the Porte. No, Lacy," continued the emperor, as Lacy prepared to leave, "do not go. As commander-in-chief, you should be thoroughly acquainted with the premises of our affair with Turkey, and you must hear both the manifestoes which I am about to dictate. The first, of course, declares war against the Porte. The second is, perhaps, a mere letter to the successor of the great Frederick. His majesty of Prussia, foreseeing, in his extreme wisdom, that I am likely to declare war against Turkey, is so condescending as to offer himself as mediator between us! You shall hear my answer, and tell me what you think of it."

Lacy bowed, and the emperor opening the door leading to the chancery, beckoned to his private secretary. He entered, took his seat, and held his pen ready to indite what Joseph should dictate. Lacy retired to the embrasure of a window, and with his arms crossed stood partly hidden by the heavy crimson velvet curtains, his eyes fixed upon his idolized sovereign.

Joseph went restlessly to and fro, and dictated his manifesto to the Porte. Referring to his alliance with Russia, and the failure of his attempts at intervention, he went on to say that as the sincere friend and ally of the empress, he was compelled to fulfil his obligations, and reluctantly to take part in the war which Catharine had declared against Turkey.*

"Now," said the emperor, "take another sheet and write 'To his majesty, the King of Prussia.'"

"My Royal Brother—

"It is with feelings of profound regret that I find myself forced to decline your majesty's most friendly offers of mediation with Turkey. I am obliged to unsheathe my sword, and I shall not return it to the scabbard until it shall have won full reparation for all the wrongs sustained by my forefathers at the hands of the Porte. Your majesty is a monarch, and as such, you are acquainted with the rights of kings. And is this undertaking of mine against Turkey any thing more than an attempt to resume the rights of which my throne has been dispossessed?

"The Turks (and perhaps not they alone) have a maxim, that whatever they lose in adverse times, they must win back when opportunity is favorable. By such means the house of Hohenzollern has attained its present state of prosperity. Albert of Brandenburg wrested the duchy of Prussia from its order, and his successors, at the peace of Oliva, maintained their right to the sovereignty of that country.

"Your majesty's deceased uncle, in like manner, wrested Silesia from my mother at a time when, surrounded by enemies, her only defences were her own true greatness and the loyalty of her subjects.

*Hubner, ii., p. 468.

"What equivalent for her lost possessions has Austria received at the hands of those European courts who have blown so many blasts on the balance of power?

"My forefathers were forced at different times to yield up Spain, Naples, Sicily, Belgrade, the principality of Silesia, Parma, Piacenza, Guastalla, Tortona, and a portion of Lombardy. What has Austria taken in return for these heavy losses?

"A portion of the kingdom of Poland! And one of less value than that assigned to Russia.

"I hope that you will not dispute the justice of my resolve to make war upon the Porte, and that you will not hold me less a friend because I may do some injury to the Ottoman. Your majesty may rest assured that under similar circumstances, I should apply the same principles to myself, were I possessed of any of *your* territory.

"I must also announce to you that, for some years to come, diplomacy must give place to war.

"Hoping for a continuation of your majesty's friendship, I am, with highest esteem, you friend and brother, JOSEPH." *

The letter concluded, the emperor dismissed his secretary and threw himself into an arm-chair.

"Well, Lacy," said he, "are you pleased with my letter? Have I convinced the king that it is my duty to declare war against the Moslem?"

"Sire," said Lacy, approaching, "I thank you from my heart for the privilege of hearing that letter. I know not which to admire most, your majesty's admirable knowledge of the history of your house, or the quiet sharpness with which you have made your statements. But this I know, that had you forbidden me to accompany you, I should have been, for the first time in my life, rebellious; for if I had not been allowed to fight as an officer, I should have done so as a private."

"There spoke my Lacy, my own gallant Austrian!" exclaimed Joseph. "To work, then, to work! Promulgate your orders and set your men in motion. In two days we must have two hundred thousand men on our frontiers. We must draw a gigantic cordon from the Dniester to the Adriatic. The main body, however, must go forward to Semlin and Futak. We two follow the main army, and day after to-morrow we must set out, and—no," said the emperor, interrupting himself, while all the light died out from his countenance. "No—I cannot set out for a week yet. I must first bid adieu to the last tie that binds my heart (as a man) to this life! That tie riven, I live as an emperor and a warrior. Once in camp, I shall, Heaven be praised! forget all things else, and be myself again!"

CHAPTER CLXXII.

MARRIAGE AND SEPARATION.

THE eight long, weary days had gone by, the preparations for war were complete, and the emperor was ready to join his army. He had worked day and night, refusing to rest, and answering all remonstrances with a sad smile.

* "Letters of Joseph II.," page 121, and the following.

"I was not born a sovereign to devote my life to my own comfort," said he, "but to consecrate it to my empire. When I become too feeble to do my duty, I shall ask for a pension, and retire to a convent, like Charles the Fifth. I have no taste, however, for the vocation, sincerely hoping to die as I have lived—an emperor."

"But, sire," said the imperial physician, Von Quarin, "your first duty is to preserve your life for Austria's sake. You have a hot fever, and your eyes and cheeks are hollow."

"Give me a cool drink, doctor, perchance it may refresh my burning heart," said Joseph, with sad irony.

"Cool drinks will do no good unless your majesty consents to take some rest. Sleep is the sovereign remedy of which you are in need, sire."

"I do not wish to sleep," replied Joseph, gloomily. "Sleep brings happy dreams, and I hate them because of their falsehood! Who would dream of bliss, to wake and find it all a lie!"

"Your valet told me that you did not lie down last night."

"My valet is a chatterbox, and knows not what he says."

"But, your majesty, I know that you have not been to bed."

"Then I slept in an arm-chair! But no, I will not deny it. I sat up all night, Quarin, for I had an important duty to perform before leaving Vienna. I was making my will."

"Your will!" repeated Von Quarin. "Surely your majesty does not fear—"

"No, I fear nothing—certainly not death," returned the emperor. "It must be sweet to die, and part from the disappointments of life; for man either goes to eternal sleep, or wakes forever to eternal happiness! I am not afraid of death, but I must put my house in order, for bullets respect no man, and they have never yet been taught that an emperor is not to be approached without ceremony. One might strike me on the head and send me to my eternal rest. Why, what a doleful face you wear, Quarin! '*L'Empereur est mort!—Vive l'Empereur!*' I shall bequeath to you a noble young emperor and a beautiful and charming empress. Is not that better than a surly old fellow like myself? Francis is my pride, and his sweet Elizabeth is like a daughter to me. I must then make my will, and provide for my children. Now, doctor, have you forgiven me for sitting up all night?"

"I have nothing to forgive, sire; but I implore you grant me one request."

"You wish to dose me with medicine! It is in your face; you carry an apothecary's shop in your eyes just now."

"No, sire, I wish to ask permission to follow you as your surgeon, that if any thing should happen, I may be there."

"No, Quarin, you must not follow me. I cannot be guilty of the egotism which would monopolize your valuable services. A soldier in the field has no right to be sick, lest he be suspected of cowardice; and as for casualties—why, if a ball should strike me, there are plenty of army surgeons who will dress my wounds as they dress those of my men. Remain at home, then, my friend, and do better service by far than you could render me on the battle-field. Farewell now. In two hours I leave, but before that time I have some important business on hand. First, I must go with my will to Prince Kaunitz."

"Did your majesty hear that he had almost struck the Countess

Clary, and had banished her from his presence for a week, because she had pronounced the word 'testament' in his hearing?"

"Yes, I was told of it, and I shall take good care not to bring down the vials of his wrath upon my head," said Joseph, laughing. "I shall not pronounce the word 'testament,' I shall speak of my treaty of peace with life, and use every precaution to save his highness's feelings. Strange mystery of life!" continued the emperor, musing, "forever changing shape and hue, like the nimble figures of a kaleidoscope! Well, I must use stratagem in this matter of the 'testament,' for Kaunitz must assume the regency of the empire, and then—then—I must attend a wedding. After that, the battle-field! Adieu, Quarin—if we meet no more on earth, I hope that we shall meet above."

One hour later the emperor returned from the hotel of his prime minister, and entered the imperial chapel. He was in full dress, decked with all his orders. It was only on state occasions that Joseph appeared in his magnificent uniform; he had not worn it since the marriage of his nephew to the Princess Elizabeth of Würtemberg. But his face was very pale, and when he perceived the bride, he leaned for one moment against a friendly pillar that saved him from reeling. This weakness, however, lasted but a moment, and he walked firmly up to the altar, where the bridal party stood awaiting the imperial entrance.

The emperor approached Count Dietrichstein, and greeted him cordially; then turning to Count Kinsky he extended his hand. The bridegroom did not appear to see this, for he cast down his eyes, and made a deep inclination, while Joseph, with a sad smile, withdrew his hand.

He had not dared to look upon the trembling bride, who, seated on a chair, and surrounded by her attendants, had just recovered from a swoon. Her aunt, the Countess Dietrichstein, explained that from Therese's childhood, she never had been able to overcome her terror of lightning; and certainly, if this were so, she had every reason for terror now. The whole sky was darkened by one dense pall of heavy clouds; the stained windows of the chapel were fiery with angry lightning, while fierce above their heads the rolling thunder boomed along the heavens, and then died away in low mutterings that made the earth tremble.

There was no time to await the passing away of the storm, for the guests at that hurried bridal were impatient to depart. The carriages of the emperor and of Count Dietrichstein were without, and neither could tarry long in Vienna. At the altar stood Therese's uncle, Count Leopold von Thun, Bishop of Passau, and around him was grouped a stately array of prelates and priests. Count Dietrichstein whispered in his daughter's ear. She rose from her seat, but her light figure swayed to and fro like a slender tree before the advancing storm, and her lovely face was pale as that of a statue just leaving the hand of the sculptor. Therese's fear of lightning was no fiction, and she almost sank to the floor as a livid flash glanced across the form of the emperor, and enveloped him in a sheet of living flame. Unheeding it, he moved on toward the unhappy girl, and without a word or a look extended his hand. Therese, trembling, gave him hers, and started when she felt the burning clasp that closed upon her icy fingers. The emperor led her to the altar; behind came the aunt and father of the bride, and between them Count Kinsky, whose jealous eyes watched every movement of those hands which joined together for the space of a moment, were about to be sundered forever.

Nothing, however, was to be seen. The emperor's eyes were fixed upon the altar, those of Therese were cast down. Neither saw the other. Only the burning pressure of one hand and the clammy coldness of the other revealed to both the extent of the sacrifice they were making to the Moloch of the world's opinion.

Now they stood before the altar. The emperor gave the bride into the hands of the bridegroom, and stepped aside to take his place.

The ceremony over, the bishop pronounced the blessing, and all present knelt to receive it. Joseph and Therese were side by side. With a sigh they raised their eyes to heaven, each praying for the other. The emperor's eyes were dim with tears, but he dashed them away, and, rising from his knees, prepared to congratulate the bride.

A peal of thunder drowned the few words which he murmured. But her heart caught the meaning, and she whispered in return:

"Yes, in heaven."

Then he dropped her hand, and addressed himself to the bridegroom.

"Count Kinsky," said he, authoritatively, "I wish to speak with you in private."

The count, with a scowl, followed his sovereign to the nave of the chapel, where, at a distance from the bridal party, they were in no danger of being overheard.

"Count," said the emperor, gravely, "you love the Countess Therese?"

Count Kinsky was silent for a while. Then, suddenly, he replied in sharp, cutting accents:

"I *have* loved her."

The emperor repeated his words.

"You *have* loved her? Do you, then, love her no longer?"

"No. I love her no longer."

"When did you cease to love her?"

"On this day week, your majesty," said the count, defiantly.

Joseph would not seem to observe the look which accompanied these words. His voice was unchanged, as he replied:

"Count, although you feel resentful toward me, you believe me to be a man of honor, do you not?"

"I do, sire."

"Then I swear to you by all that is sacred to me as man and sovereign, that Therese is as pure in the sight of Heaven as its brightest angel. I swear to you that she is as worthy as ever she was to be loved and esteemed by her husband as his wife and the future mother of his children."

"Your majesty must have formed an intimate acquaintance with the countess, to be able to answer for her purity of heart," returned Kinsky, coldly.

Joseph looked up, pained.

"Ah!" said he, "you are implacable. But you believe me, do you not?"

The count inclined his head.

"I dare not doubt my sovereign's word."

"Then you will love Therese as she deserves to be loved?"

"Love is not to be controlled—not even by an emperor. My love and hate are not to be drawn off and on like a glove!"

"Hate!" cried the emperor, shocked. "Great God! it cannot be possible that you hate the woman whom you have voluntarily chosen, and whom even now, before yonder altar, you have sworn to love. Why, then, did you marry her?"

"Sire, you commanded me to do so just one week ago, and, as a loyal subject, I was compelled to obey. You gave me no alternative, and I married her."

"She will make you happy," replied Joseph, in a faltering voice. "I beseech of you, be gentle with her. Her heart is not at ease, and she needs all your tenderness to restore her to happiness."

Count Kinsky bowed frigidly.

"Will your majesty allow me to ask a favor of you?" said he.

"It will gratify me to do any thing for you," replied Joseph, his eyes lighting up with pleasure.

"Then I ask of your majesty, on your honor, to answer the question I am about to ask."

"On my honor, count, I will answer it," said Joseph, smiling.

"What did your majesty say to the countess just now, and what was her reply?"

The emperor was thunderstruck—he could not articulate a word.

"Your majesty was so obliging as to promise an answer."

"Yes, count, yes," faltered the emperor. "You shall be satisfied. I said, 'Farewell, Therese, I shall claim thee in heaven.'"

"Your majesty was so condescending as to address my wife in this familiar strain? And her reply was—"

"Only these words, 'Yes, in heaven.'"

"I thank your majesty."

They both returned to the company. Joseph cast one last look at Therese, who, pale and rigid, was receiving the congratulations of her unsuspecting friends, and then he addressed her father.

"Well, count, I believe that our furlough has expired, and we must return to our commands. Farewell! and may we both return victorious to Vienna!"

A half an hour later, an imperial *calèche* conveyed him to the army, and to Field-Marshal Lacy, who had preceded him there by several days.

At the same moment, the travelling-carriage of Count Kinsky drove up to his hotel. Count Dietrichstein, before setting out, had accompanied his daughter to her husband's residence, and had bidden her adieu. Therese was now alone. She shuddered as she heard Count Kinsky's step, and wished from her soul that death would release her from the hateful tie which bound them together.

The door opened, and he appeared. She uttered a faint cry, and pressed her hands to her throbbing heart. Count Kinsky answered the cry with a laugh of scorn.

"Are you afraid?" said he, striding toward her, and contemplating her with a face indicative of smothered passion.

Therese raised her eyes, and looked fearlessly into his eyes: "No, Count Kinsky, I am not afraid, nor would I fear, if you had come to kill me."

The count laughed aloud. "Ah!" cried he, in a harsh, grating voice, "you think that I might do like Prince Bragation and the

Duke of Orleans, who strangled their young wives because they suspected them of infidelity! My dear madame, these romantic horrors belong to a bygone century. In this sober and prosaic age, a nobleman avenges his wounded honor, not by murder, but by contempt. I have only intruded myself to ask if you are ready to start?"

"I am ready," replied Therese, wearily.

"Then allow me to accompany you to the carriage."

"My father having given you my hand, I have no right to refuse your escort."

"Before we go, be so condescending as to say which one of my estates you prefer for a residence."

"Select my residence yourself, count; you know that I have never visited your estates."

"Then I choose for you my castle in Hungary, near the Turkish frontier, for there you will have the latest news from the army and its commanders."

Therese made no reply to this sarcasm. She bent her head, and said: "I am ready to submit myself to your decision in all things."

"I hope that the Countess Therese will not long have to live in subjection to her husband," continued he, "and that the journey which I am about to undertake, will result happily for us both. You go to Hungary, I go to Rome. I go to implore of the pope a divorce."

"You are going to sue for a divorce?" asked Therese. "Perhaps you can spare yourself the trouble of a journey to Rome, count, for I have already anticipated your wishes. My petition to his holiness went several days ago, and—"

"His majesty, the emperor, was so obliging as to send it by an imperial courier. Is that what you were about to say?"

Therese continued as though she had not heard the interruption: "My application went through Monsignore Garampi, the papal nuncio, who promised to use his influence in my behalf."

"What an edifying couple!" exclaimed Kinsky, with another scornful laugh. "How congenial! The same wishes, and, unconsciously, the very same deeds! What a pity we must part so soon, for, I leave you to-day; nor shall I have the pleasure of seeing you again until I bring you a decree of divorce."

"You will be most welcome," returned Therese, calmly. "Now be so good as to escort me to my carriage."

"Pray give me your arm. I have but one more observation to make. I hope that you will now be able to prove substantially to the emperor that it was quite useless for him to shelter himself behind the words, 'I shall claim thee in heaven!' But if I may presume so far, I request that you will defer these demonstrations until I return from Rome with my letters of divorce."

Therese had no strength to retort. She hung down her head, and large scalding tears fell from her eyes. Count Kinsky placed her in the carriage, closed the door, and then returned to his own travelling-chariot, which was a few paces behind. The two equipages thundered down the streets together, but at the gates they parted, the one taking the road for Hungary, the other for Rome.*

*This whole story is historical. The "heavenly Therese," as she is called by Hormayer, was really married and thus abandoned by her husband, who persisted in believing that the connection between herself and the emperor was not guiltless. But the count met with no success in the matter of the divorce. The pope refused

CHAPTER CLXXIII.

THE LAST DREAM OF GLORY.

DESTINY was testing the fortitude of the emperor with unrelenting harshness. It would seem that inflexible fate stood by, while one by one this man's hopes of fame, honor, and love were wrested away, that the world might see and know how much of bitterness and disappointment it is in the power of one human heart to endure.

In the Netherlands and in Hungary he was threatened with rebellion. The Magyars especially resented the violation of their constitutional rights; in Tyrol, too, the people were disaffected; and Rome had not yet pardoned him the many indignities she had endured at his hands. This very war, which he had welcomed as a cure for his domestic sorrows, was yielding him naught but annoyance and misery.

Yes, destiny had decreed that nothing which he undertook should prosper. His army, which was encamped in the damp marshes that lie between the Danube and Save, was attacked by a malarious fever more destructive by far than the bloodiest struggle that ever reddened the field of battle. The hospitals were crowded with the sick and dying, and the enfeebled soldiers, who dragged themselves about their camps, wore sullen and discontented faces; a spirit of insubordination was beginning to manifest itself among the troops, and the very men who would have rushed to the cannon's mouth, grew cowardly at the approach of the invisible foe that stole away their lives, by the gradual and insidious poison of disease. The songs and jests of the bivouac were hushed, the white tents were mournful as sepulchres, and the men lost all confidence in their leaders. They now accused the emperor and Lacy of incapacity, and declared that they must either be disbanded or led against the enemy.

This was precisely what Joseph had been longing to do, but he was compelled to await the advance of the Russians, with whom it had been arranged that the Austrians were to make a junction before they marched into Turkey. The Russians, however, had never joined the emperor; for some misunderstanding with Sweden had compelled the czarina to defend her northern frontier, and so she had as yet been unable to assemble an army of sufficient strength to march against Turkey. Joseph then was condemned to the very same inaction which had so chafed his spirit in Bavaria; for his own army of itself was not numerous enough to attack the enemy. He could not make a move without Russia. Russia tarried, and the fever in the camp grew every day more fatal.

Instead of advancing, the heart-sick emperor was forced to retreat. His artillery was withdrawn to Peterwardein, and the siege of Belgrade entirely relinquished. Disease and death followed the Aus-

it, perhaps because he wished to prove to rebellious Austria the power of the church. Years passed by before the decree was obtained. Finally Therese deposed that she was married under compulsion, and that the storm had so terrified her that she had been almost insensible during the ceremony, so much so that Bishop Leopold von Thun also deposed that he had not heard her assent. These declarations proving the marriage to have been invalid, the divorce was granted. After the death of Joseph, Therese married Count Max Meerveldt, the same who in 1797 concluded the peace of Campo Formio with Napoleon.—See Hormayer, "The Emperor Franz and Metternich: a Fragment," page 180.

trians to their new encampment, and louder grew the mutterings of the men, and more bitter their denunciations of the emperor.

They little knew that while they were assailed by physical infirmities, their hapless chieftain was sick both in body and mind. He shared all their hardships, and watched them with most unremitting solicitude. He erected camp hospitals, and furnished the sick with wine and delicacies which he ordered from Vienna for their use. All military etiquette was suspended; even the approach of the emperor for the time being was to be ignored. Those who were lying down were to remain lying, those who were sitting were to keep their seats.

Meanwhile Joseph walked daily through the hospitals, bestowing care and kindness upon all, and no man there remarked that the deadly malaria had affected him in an equal degree with his troops. Heat, hardships, and disappointment had done their work as effectually upon the commander-in-chief as upon the common soldier; but no one suspected that fever was consuming his life; for by day, Joseph was the Providence of his army, and by night, while his men were sleeping, he was attending to the affairs of his vast empire. He worked as assiduously in camp as he had ever done at home in his palace. Every important measure of the regency was submitted to him for approval; the heads of the several departments of state were required to send him their reports; and many a night, surrounded by heaps of dispatches, he sat at his little table, in the swampy woods, whose noxious atmosphere was fitter for the snakes that infested them than for human beings of whatever condition in life.*

One little ray of light relieved the darkness of this gloomy period. This was the taking of the fortress of Sabacz where Joseph led the assault in person. Three cannoneers were shot by his side, and their blood bespattered his face and breast. But in the midst of danger he remained perfectly composed, and for many a day his countenance had not beamed with an expression of such animated delight.

This success, however, was no more than a lightning-flash relieving the darkness of a tempestuous night. The fortress won, the Austrians went back to their miserable encampment in the sickly morasses of Siebenbürgen.

Suddenly the stagnant quiet was broken by the announcement that the Turks had crossed the Danube. This aroused the army from their sullen stupor, and Joseph, as if freed from an incubus, joyfully prepared himself for action.

The trumpet's shrill call was heard in the camp, and the army commenced their march. They had advanced but a few miles when they were met by several panic-stricken regiments, who announced that the Austrian lines had been broken in two places, that General Papilla had been forced to retreat, and that the victorious Turks were pouring their vast hordes into Hungary.

Like wildfire the tidings spread through the army, and they, too, began their retreat, farther and yet farther back; for, ever as they moved, they were lighted on their way by the burning villages and towns that were the tokens of a barbarous enemy's approach. The homeless fugitives, too, rent the air with their cries, and clamored for protection against the cruel infidel.

*In the archives of Vienna is preserved a dispatch of Joseph, written in the open woods on the night before the taking of Sabacz.—Gross-Hoffinger, iii., p. 464.

No protection could they find, for the Austrians were too few in number to confront the devastating hosts of the invading army. They were still compelled to retreat as far as the town of Lugos, where at last they might rest from the dreadful fatigues of this humiliating flight. With inexpressible relief, the soldiers sought repose. They were ordered, however, to sleep on their arms, so that the artilleryman was by his cannon, the mounted soldier near his horse, and the infantry, clasping their muskets, lay in long rows together, all forgetting every thing save the inestimable blessing of stretching their limbs and wooing sleep.

The mild summer moon looked down upon their rest, and the emperor, as he made a last tour of inspection to satisfy himself that all lights were extinguished, rejoiced to think that the Turks were far away, and his tired Austrians could sleep secure.

Joseph returned to his tent, that is, his *calèche*. He, too, was exhausted, and closed his eyes with a sense of delicious languor. The night air, blowing about his temples, refreshed his fevered brow, and he gave himself up to dreams such as are inspired by the silvered atmosphere, when the moon, in her pearly splendor, looks down upon the troubled earth, and hushes it to repose.

The emperor, however, did not sleep. For a while, he lay with closed eyes, and then, raising himself, looked up toward the heavens. Gradually the sky darkened; cloud met cloud and obscured the moon's disk, until at last the firmament was clothed in impenetrable blackness. The emperor, with a sad smile, thought how like the scene had been to the panorama of his life, wherein every star had set, and whence every ray of light had fled forever!

He dreamed on, while his tired men slept. Not all, however, for, far toward the left wing of the army, a band of hussars were encamped around a wagon laden with brandy, and, having much more confidence in the restorative powers of liquor than of sleep, they had been invigorating themselves with deep potations. Another company of soldiers in their neighborhood, awakened by the noisy mirth of the hussars, came forward to claim their share of the brandy. It was refused, and a brawl ensued, in which the assailants were repulsed.

The hussars, having driven them from the field, proceeded to celebrate their victory by renewed libations, until finally, in a state of complete inebriation, they fell to the ground, and there slept the sleep of the intoxicated.

The men who had been prevented from participating in these drunken revels, resolved to revenge themselves by a trick. They crept stealthily up to the spot where the hussars were lying, and, firing off their muskets, cried out, "The Turks! the Turks!"

Stupefied by liquor, the sleepers sprang up, repeating the cry. It was caught and echoed from man to man, while the hussars, with unsheathed sabres, ran wildly about, until hundreds and hundreds were awakened, each one echoing the fearful words—

"The Turks! the Turks!"

"Halt! halt!" cried a voice to the terrified soldiers. "Halt, men, halt!"

The bewildered ears mistook the command for the battle-cry of the Turks, "Allah! Allah!" and the panic increased tenfold. "We are surrounded!" shrieked the terror-stricken Austrians, and every sabre was drawn, and every musket cocked. The struggle began;

and the screams of the combatants, the groans of the wounded, the sighs of the dying filled the air, while comrade against comrade, brother against brother, stood in mortal strife and slew each other for the unbelieving Turk.

The calamity was irretrievable. The darkness of the night deceived every man in that army, not one of whom doubted that the enemy was there. Some of the terrified soldiers fled back to their camps, and, even there, mistaken for Turks, they were assaulted with sabre and musket, and frightful was the carnage that ensued!

In vain the officers attempted to restore discipline. There was no more reason in those maddened human beings than in the raging waves of the ocean. The emperor, at the first alarm, had driven in his *calèche* to the place whence the sound seemed to come.

But what to a panic-stricken multitude was the voice of their emperor? Ball after ball whistled past his ears, while he vainly strove to make them understand that they were each one slaying his brother! And the night was so hideous, so relentless in its darkness! Not one star glimmered upon the face of the frightful pall above—the stars would not look upon that fratricidal stuggle!

The fugitives and their infuriated pursuers pressed toward a little bridge which spanned a stream near the encampment. The emperor drove rapidly around, and reached the banks of the river before them, hoping thence to be heard by his men, and to convince them that no Turks were by.

But they heeded the sound of his voice no more than the sea heeded that of the royal Canute. They precipitated themselves toward the bridge, driving the carriage of the emperor before them to the very edge of the steep river-bank. It wavered; they pushed against it with the butt-ends of their muskets. They saw nothing—they knew nothing save that the carriage impeded their flight!

It fell, rumbling down the precipice into the deep waters which bubbled and hissed and then closed over it forever. No man heeded its fall. Not one of all that crowd, which oft had grown hoarse with shouts at his coming, paused to save the emperor from destruction. But he, calm and courageous, although at that moment he could have parted with life without a sigh, had made a desperate spring backward, and had alighted on the ground.

When he recovered from the violence of the fall, he found himself unhurt, but alone. Not one of his suite was to be seen; in the mad rush of the men for the crossing, they had been parted from him. The little rustic bridge had fallen in, and those who remained behind had rushed with frantic yells in search of some other crossing. The emperor could hear their cries in the distance, and they filled his heart with anguish inexpressible.

With desponding eyes he gazed upward, and murmured, "Oh, that I could die before the sun rises upon the horrors of this night! My soul is weary—my every hope dead. Why did I turn back when death was smiling from the crystal depths of that placid stream? Even now, I may still find rest. Who will ever know how the emperor met his fate?" He paused, and looked around to see if any thing was nigh. Nothing! He made one step forward, then shuddering, recoiled with an exclamation of horror at his miserable cowardice.

"No!" cried he, resolutely, "no, I will not die—I must not, dare not die. I cannot go to the grave misjudged and calumniated by my own subjects! I must live, that, sooner or later, they may learn how faithfully I have striven to make them happy! I must live to convince them that the promotion of their welfare has been the end and aim of my whole life!" *

At that moment there was a rent in the blackened firmament, and the moon emerged, gradually lighting up the dark waters and the lonely woods, until its beams shone full upon the pale, agitated features of that broken-hearted monarch.

"The emperor!" cried a loud voice, not far away. "The emperor!" and a rider, galloping forward, threw himself from his horse.

"Here, your majesty, here is my horse. Mount him. He is a sure and fleet animal."

"You know me, then?" asked Joseph.

"Yes, sire; I am one of your majesty's grooms. Will you do me the honor to accept my horse?"

The emperor replied by swinging himself into the saddle. "But you, my good fellow, what will you do?"

"I shall accompany your majesty," replied the groom, cheerfully. "There is many a horse seeking its master to-night, and it will not be long before I capture one. This done, if it please your majesty, I will conduct you to Karansebes. The moon has come out beautifully, and I can easily find the way."

"I have found *my* way," murmured the emperor to himself. "God has pointed it out to me, by sending help in this dark, lonely hour. Well, life has called me back, and I must bear its burdens until Heaven releases me."

Just then a horse came by, at full speed. The groom, who was walking by the emperor's side, darted forward, seized the reins, and swung himself triumphantly into the saddle.

"Now, sire," said he, "we can travel lustily ahead. We are on the right road, and in one hour will reach Karansebes."

"Karansebes!" mused the emperor. "'*Cara mihi sedes!*' Thus sang Ovid, and from his ode a city took her name—the city where the poet found his grave. A stately monument to Ovid is Karansebes; and now a lonely, heart-sick monarch is coming to make a pilgrimage thither, craving of Ovid's tomb the boon of a resting-place for his weary head. Oh, *Cara mihi sedes*, where art thou?

In the gray of the morning they reached Karansebes. Here they found some few of the regiments, the emperor's suite, and his beloved nephew Franz, who, like his uncle, had been almost hurried to destruction by the hapless army, but had been rescued by his bold and faithful followers. They had shielded the archduke with their own bodies, forming a square around his person, and escorting him, so guarded, until they had penetrated the dangerous ranks of the demented fugitives.†

All danger was past, but the events of that night were too much for the exhausted frame of the emperor. The fever, with which he had wrestled so long, now mastered his body with such violence that he was no longer able to mount his horse. Added to this, came a blow to his heart. The army refused to follow him any longer. They called loudly for Loudon, the old hero, who, in spite of his years, was the only man in Austria who would lead them to victory.

* The emperor's own words.—Hubner, ii., p. 488.
† Hubner, ii., p. 477.

The emperor, stung to the soul by the mistrust of his men, gave up his last hope of military glory. He sent for Loudon; and Loudon, despite his infirmities, came at the summons.

The old hero was received with shouts of welcome. The huzzas reached the poor, mean room where Joseph lay sick with a burning fever. He listened with a sad smile, but his courage gave way, and scalding tears of disappointed ambition moistened his pillow.

"Loudon has come," thought he, "and the emperor is forgotten! No one cares for him more!—Well—I must return to Vienna, and pray that the victory and fame, which have been denied to me, may be vouchsafed to Loudon!"

CHAPTER CLXXIV.

THE HUNGARIANS AGAIN.

DESTINY had broken the emperor's heart. He returned from the army seriously ill, and although he had apparently recuperated during the winter, the close of the year found him beyond all hope of recovery.

Even the joyful intelligence of Loudon's victories was powerless to restore him to health. Loudon had won several battles, and had accomplished that for which Joseph had undertaken the war with Turkey. He had once more raised the Austrian flag over the towers of Belgrade.*

Vienna received these tidings with every demonstration of joy. The city was illuminated for three days, and the emperor shared the enthusiasm of the people. He took from his state-uniform the magnificent cross of Maria Theresa—the cross which none but an emperor had ever worn—and sent it to Loudon with the title and patent of generalissimo.† He attended the *Te Deum*, and to all appearances was as elated as his subjects. But once alone with Lacy, the mask fell, and the smile faded from his colorless lips.

"Lacy," said he, "I would have bought these last superfluous laurels of Loudon with my life. But for me no laurels have ever grown; the cypress is my emblem—the emblem of grief."

He was right. Discontent reigned in Hungary, in the Netherlands, and latterly in Tyrol. On every side were murmurs and threats of rebellion against him who would have devoted every hour of his life to the enlightenment of his subjects. All Belgium had taken up arms. The imperial troops had joined the insurgents, and now a formidable army threatened the emperor. Van der Noot, the leader of the revolt, published a manifesto, declaring Belgium independent of the Austrian empire. The insurgents numbered ten thousand. They were headed by the nobles and sustained by the clergy. Masses were said for the success of the rebels, and requiems were sung for those who fell in battle or otherwise.‡ The cities of

* The conquest of Belgrade was accompanied by singular coincidences. The Emperor Francis (the husband of Maria Theresa) had been in command when, in 1739, the Turks took it from Austria. His grandson, Francis, with his own hand fired the first gun, when it was retaken by Loudon. In 1739 General Wallace surrendered the fortress to Osman Pacha. In 1789 Osman Pacha, the son of the latter, surrendered it to General (afterward Field-Marshal) Wallace, son of the former.—Hubner, ii., p. 492.

† This cross was worth 21,000 ducats.—Gross-Hoffinger, iii., p. 500.

‡ Gross-Hoffinger, iii., p. 289.

Brussels, Antwerp, Louvain, Mechlin, and Namur, opened their doors to the patriots. The Austrian General D'Alton fled with his troops to Luxemburg, and three millions of florins, belonging to the military coffers, fell into the hands of the insurgents.*

Such was the condition of the Austrian empire toward the close of the year 1789. The emperor resolved to make one more attempt to bring the Belgians to reason, and to this end he sent Count Cobenzl to Brussels, and, after him, Prince de Ligne.

The prince came to take leave of the emperor. "I send you as a mediator between myself and your countrymen," said Joseph, with a languid smile. "Prove to those so-called patriots that you, who endeavor to reconcile them to their sovereign, are the only Belgian of them all who possesses true patriotism."

"Sire, I shall say to my misguided countrymen that I have seen your majesty weep over their disloyalty. I shall tell them that it is not anger which they have provoked in your majesty's heart, but sorrow."

"Yes," replied Joseph, "I sorrow for their infatuation, and they are fast sending me to the grave. The taking of Ghent was my death-struggle, the evacuation of Brussels my last expiring sigh. Oh!" continued he, in tones of extreme anguish—"oh, what humiliation! I shall surely die of it! I were of stone, to survive so many blows from the hand of fate! Go, De Ligne, and do your best to induce your countrymen to return to their allegiance. Should you fail, dear friend, remain there. Do not sacrifice your future to me, for you have children." †

"Yes, sire," replied De Ligne, with emotion, "I have children, but they are not dearer to me than my sovereign. And now, with your majesty's permission, I will withdraw, for the hour of my departure is at hand. I do not despair of success. Farewell, sire, for a while."

"Farewell forever!" murmured Joseph, as the door closed behind the prince. "Death is not far off, and I have so much to do!"

He arose hastily from his arm-chair, and opening the door that led into the chancery, called his three secretaries.

"Let us to work," said he, as they entered.

"Sire," replied one of them, in faltering tones, "Herr von Quarin desired us, in his name, to implore of your majesty to rest for a few days."

"I cannot do it," said Joseph, impatiently. "If I postpone this writing another day, it may never be accomplished at all. Give in your reports. What dispatches have we from Hungary?"

"They are most unsatisfactory, sire. The landed proprietors have refused to contribute their share of the imposts, and the people rebel against the conscription-act, and threaten the officers of the crown with death."

"Revolt, revolt everywhere!" exclaimed the emperor, shuddering. "But I will not yield; they shall all submit!"

The door of the cabinet opened, and the marshal of the household entered, announcing a deputation of Magyars.

"A deputation! From whom?" asked Joseph, eagerly.

"I do not know, sire, but Count Palfy is one of the deputies."

* D'Alton was cited before the emperor, but on his way to Vienna he took poison and died four days before Joseph.

† The emperor's own words.—"Œuvres du Prince de Ligne."

"Count Palfy again!" cried the emperor, scornfully. "When the Hungarians have a sinister message to send, they are sure to select Count Palfy as their ambassador. Show them to the reception-room which opens into my cabinet, count. I will see them there."

He dismissed the secretaries, and rang for his valet. He could scarcely stand, while Günther was assisting him to change his dressing-gown for his uniform.* His toilet over, he was obliged to lean upon the valet for support, for his limbs were almost failing him.

"Oh!" cried he, bitterly, "how it will rejoice them to see me so weak and sick! They will go home and tell their Hungarians that there is no strength left in me to fight with traitors! But they shall not know it. I *will* be the emperor, if my life pay the forfeit of the exertion. Lead me to the door, Günther. I will lean against one of the pillars, and stand while I give audience to the Magyars."

Günther supported him tenderly to the door, and then threw it wide open. In the reception-room stood the twelve deputies, not in court-dress, but in the resplendent costume of their own nation. They were the same men who, several years before, had appeared before the emperor, and Count Palfy, the Chancellor of Hungary, was the first one to advance.

The emperor bent his head, and eyed his visitors.

"If I am not mistaken," said he, "these are the same gentlemen who appeared here as Hungarian deputies several years ago."

"Yes, sire, we are the same men," replied Count Palfy.

"Why are you here again?"

"To repeat our remonstrances, sire. The kingdom of Hungary has chosen the same representatives, that your majesty may see how unalterable is our determination to defend our rights with our lives. Hungary has not changed her attitude, sire, and she will never change it."

"Nor shall I ever change mine," cried Joseph, passionately. "My will to-day is the same as it was six years ago."

"Then, sire, you must expect an uprising of the whole Hungarian nation," returned Count Palfy, gravely. "For the last time we implore your majesty to restore us our rights."

"What do you call your rights?" asked Joseph, sarcastically.

"All that for centuries past has been guaranteed to us by our constitution; all that each king of Hungary, as he came to the throne, has sworn to preserve inviolate. Sire, we will not become an Austrian province; we are Hungarians, and are resolved to retain our nationality. The integrity of Hungary is sorely threatened; and if your majesty refuse to rescue it, we must ourselves hasten to the rescue. Not only our liberties are menaced, but our moneyed interests too. Hungary is on the road to ruin, if your majesty does not consent to revoke your arbitrary laws, or—"

"Or?"—asked Joseph, as Palfy hesitated.

"On the road to revolution," replied the deputy firmly.

"You presume to threaten me!" cried Joseph, in a loud voice.

"I dare deliver the message intrusted to me, and, had *I* been too weak to speak it, intrusted to those who accompany me. Is it not so, Magyars?"

"It is, it is," cried all, unanimously.

"Sire, I repeat to you that Hungary is advancing either toward ruin or revolution. Like the Netherlanders, we will defend our

* This was the brother of him who was the lover of Rachel.

constitution or die with it. Oh, your majesty, all can yet be remedied! Call a convention of the states—return the crown of St. Stephen, and come to Hungary to take the coronation oath. Then you will see how gladly we shall swear allegiance to our king, and how cheerfully we will die for him, as our fathers did before us, in defence of the empress-queen, his mother."

"Give us our constitution, and we will die for our king!" cried the Magyars in chorus.

"Yes, humble myself before you!" exclaimed Joseph, furiously. "You would have the sovereign bow before the will of his vassals!"

"No, sire," returned Count Palfy, with feeling. "We would have your majesty adopt the only means by which Hungary can be retained to the Austrian empire. If you refuse to hear us, we rise, as one man, to defend our country. We swear it in the name of the Hungarian nation!"

"We swear it in the name of the Hungarian nation!" echoed the Magyars.

"And I," replied Joseph, pale and trembling with passion, "I swear it in the name of my dignity as your sovereign, that I never will yield to men who defy me, nor will I ever forgive those who, by treasonable importunity, have sought to wring from me what I have not thought it expedient to grant to respectful expostulation!"

"Sire, if you would give this proof of love to your subjects, if, for their sakes, you would condescend to forget your imperial station, you cannot conceive what enthusiasm of loyalty would be your return for this concession. In mortal anxiety we await your final answer, and await it until to-morrow at this hour."

"Ah!—you are so magnanimous as to grant me a short reprieve!" shouted the infuriated emperor, losing all command of himself. "You—"

Suddenly he ceased, and became very pale. He was sensible that he had burst a blood-vessel, and he felt the warm stream of his life welling upward, until it moistened his pallid lips. With a hasty movement he drew out his handkerchief, held it for a moment before his mouth, and then replaced it quickly in his bosom. Large drops of cold sweat stood out from his brow, and the light faded from his eyes. But these haughty Magyars should not see him fall! They should not enjoy the sight of his sufferings!

With one last desperate effort he collected his expiring energies, and stood erect.

"Go," said he, in firm, distinct tones; "you have stated your grievances, you shall have my answer to-morrow."

"We await your majesty until to-morrow at noon," returned Count Palfy. "Then we go, never to return."

"Go!" cried the emperor, in a piercing voice; and the exasperated Magyars mistook this last cry of agony for the culmination of his wrath. They bowed in sullen silence, and left the room.

The emperor reeled back to his cabinet, and fell into a chair. He reached the bell, and rang it feebly.

"Günther," said he to his valet, and now his voice was hardly audible, "send a carriage for Quarin. I must see him at once."

CHAPTER CLXXV.

THE REVOCATION.

When Quarin entered the emperor's cabinet, he found him quietly seated before his *escritoire*, half buried in documents. The physician remained standing at the door, waiting until he should be ordered to approach.

Suddenly Joseph was interrupted in his writing by a spell of coughing. He dropped his pen, and leaned back exhausted. Quarin hastened to his side.

"Your majesty must not write," said he, gravely. "You must lay aside all work for a time."

"I believe that I shall have to lay it aside forever," replied Joseph, languidly. "I sent for you to say that I have a lawsuit with my lungs, and you must tell me which of us is to gain it." *

"What am I to tell your majesty?" asked the physician, disturbed.

The emperor looked up with eyes which glowed with the flaming light of fever. "Quarin, you understand me perfectly. You must tell me, in regard to this lawsuit with my lungs, which is to gain it, myself or death? Here is my evidence."

With these words he drew out his handkerchief and held it open between his wan, transparent hands. It was dyed in blood.

"Blood!" exclaimed Quarin, in a tone of alarm. "Your majesty has received a wound?"

"Yes, an interior wound. The Hungarians have dealt me my death-blow. This blood is welling up from a wounded heart. Do not look so mournful, doctor. Let us speak of death as man to man. Look at me now, and say whether my malady is incurable."

"Why should it be incurable?" asked the physician, faltering. "You are young, sire, and have a sound constitution."

"No commonplaces, Quarin, no equivocation," cried Joseph, impatiently. "I must have the truth, do you hear me?—the truth. I cannot afford to be surprised by death, for I must provide for a nation, and my house must be set in order. I am not afraid of death, my friend; it comes to me in the smiling guise of a liberator. Therefore be frank, and tell me at once whether my malady is dangerous."

Again he raised his large, brilliant eyes to the face of the physician. Quarin's features were convulsed with distress, and tears stood in his eyes. His voice was very tremulous as he replied:

"Yes, sire, it is dangerous."

The emperor's countentance remained perfectly calm. "Can you tell me with any degree of precision how long I have to live?"

"No, sire; you may live yet for several weeks, or some excitement may put an end to your existence in a few days. In this malady the patient must be prepared at any moment for death."

"Then it is incurable?"

"Yes, sire," faltered Quarin, his tears bursting forth afresh.

The emperor looked thoughtfully before him, and for some time kept silence. Then extending his hand with a smile, he said, "From my soul I thank you for the manly frankness with which you

* Joseph's own words.—"Characteristics of Joseph II.," p. 14.

have treated me, Quarin, and I desire now to give you a testimony of my gratitude. You have children, have you not?"

"Yes, sire—two daughters."

"And you are not rich, I believe?"

"The salary which I receive from your majesty, united to my practice, affords us a comfortable independence."

The emperor nodded. "You must do a little commission for me," said he, turning to the *escritoire* and writing a few lines, which he presented to Quarin.

"Take this paper to the court chancery and present it to the bureau of finances. You will there receive ten thousand florins wherewith to portion your daughters."

"Oh, sire!" exclaimed Quarin, deeply moved, "I thank you with all the strength of my paternal heart."

"No," replied Joseph, gently, "it is my duty to reward merit.* In addition to this, I would wish to leave you a personal souvenir of my friendship. I bestow upon you, as a last token of my affection, the title of *freiherr*, and I will take out the patent for you myself. Not a word, dear friend, not a word! Leave me now, for I must work diligently. Since my hours are numbered, I must make the most of them. Farewell! Who knows how soon I may have to recall you here?"

The physician kissed the emperor's hand with fervor, and turned hastily away. Joseph sank back in the chair. His large eyes were raised to heaven, and his wan face beamed with something brighter than resignation.

At that moment the door of the chancery was opened, and the first privy-councillor came hastily forward.

"What is it?" said Joseph, with a slight start.

"Sire, two couriers have just arrived. The first is from the Count Cobenzl. He announces that all Belgium, with the exception of Luxemburg, is in the hands of the patriots; that Van der Noot has called a convention of the United Provinces, which has declared Belgium a republic; her independence is to be guaranteed by England, Prussia, and Holland. Count Cobenzl is urgent in his request for instructions. He is totally at a loss what to do."

The emperor had listened with mournful tranquillity. "And the second courier?" said he.

"The second courier, sire, comes from the imperial stadtholder of Tyrol."

"What says he?"

"He brings evil tidings, sire. The people have rebelled, and cry out against the conscription and the church reforms. Unless these laws are repealed, there is danger of revolution."

The emperor uttered a piercing cry, and pressed his hands to his breast. "It is nothing," said he, in reply to the anxious and alarmed looks of the privy-councillor. "A momentary pang, which has already passed away—nothing more. Continue your report."

"This is all, your majesty. The stadtholder entreats you to quiet this rebellion and—"

"And to revoke my decrees, is it not so? The same croaking which for eight years has been dinned into my ears. Well—I must have time to reflect, and as soon as I shall have determined upon my course of action, you shall learn my decision.

* These are the emperor's words. This scene is historical.—Hubner, ii., p. 496.

"Rebellion in Tyrol, in Hungary, in the Netherlands!" murmured the emperor, when he found himself alone. "From every side I hear my death-knell! My people would bury me ere I have drawn my last sigh. My great ancestor, Charles, stood beside his open grave, and voluntarily contemplated his last resting-place; but I! unhappy monarch, am forced into mine by the ingratitude of a people for whom alone I have lived! Is it indeed so? Must I die with the mournful conviction that I have lived in vain? O my God, what excess of humiliation Thou hast forced upon me! And what have I done to deserve such a fate? Wherein have I sinned, that my imperial crown should have been lined with so many cruel thorns? Is there no remedy? must I drink this last bitter chalice? Must I revoke that which I have published to the world as my sovereign will?"

He ceased, and folding his arms, faced his difficult position. For one hour he sat motionless, his face growing gradually paler, his brow darker, his lips more rigidly compressed together.

At length he heaved one long, convulsive sigh. "No—there is no other remedy. I have toiled in vain—my beautiful structure has fallen, and my grave is under its ruins! O my God, why may I not have a few months more of life, wherewith to crush these aspiring rebels?—But no! I must die now, and leave them to triumph over my defeat; for I dare not leave to my successor the accursed inheritance of civil war. To the last hour of my life I must humble my will before the decree of that cruel destiny which has persecuted me from boyhood! Be it so!—I must clutch at the remedy—the fearful remedy—I must revoke!"

He shuddered, and covered his face with his hands. There had been one struggle with his will, there was now another with his despair. He moaned aloud—scalding tears trickled through his poor, wasted fingers, and his whole being bowed before the supremacy of this last great sorrow. Once—only once, he uttered a sharp cry, and for a moment his convulsed countenance was raised to heaven. Then his head fell upon the table, and his wretcheness found vent in low, heart-rending sobs.

And thus he spent another long hour. Finally he looked up to heaven and tried to murmur a few words of resignation. But the spectre of his useless strivings still haunted his mind. "All my plans to be buried in the grave—not one trace of my reign left to posterity!" sighed the unhappy monarch. "But enough of repining. I have resolved to make the sacrifice—it is time to act!"

He clutched his bell, and ordered a page to summon the privy-councillor from the adjoining room.

"Now," said the emperor, "let us work. My hand is too tremulous to hold a pen; you must write for me. First, in regard to Hungary. Draw up a manifesto, in which I restore their constitution in all its integrity."

He paused for a few moments, and wiped the large drops of cold sweat which were gathering over his forehead. "Do you hear?" continued he; "I revoke all my laws except one, and that is, the edict of religious toleration. I promise to convoke the imperial diet, and to replace the administration of justice upon its old footing. I repeal the laws relating to taxes and conscription, I order the Hungarian crown to be returned to Ofen, and, as soon as I shall have recovered from my illness, I promise to take the coronation-oath.* Write this out and bring it to me for signature. Then deliver it into the hands of Count Palfy. He will publish it to the Hungarians.

"So much for Hungary!—Now for Tyrol. Draw up a second manifesto. I repeal the conscription-act, as well as all my reforms with respect to the church. When this is ready, bring it to me for signature; and dispatch a courier with it to the imperial stadtholder. Having satisfied the exactions of Hungary and Tyrol, it remains to restore order in the Netherlands. But there, matters are more complicated, and I fear that no concession on my part will avail at this late hour. I must trample my personal pride in the dust, then, and humble myself before the pope! Yes—*before the pope!* I will write, requesting him to act as mediator, and beg his holiness to admonish the clergy to make peace with me.† Why do you look so sad, my friend? I am making my peace with the world; I am drawing a pen across the events of my life and blotting out my reforms with ink. Make out these documents at once, and send me a courier for Rome. Meanwhile I will write to the pope. Appearing before him as a petitioner, it is incumbent upon me to send an autographic letter. Return to me in an hour."

When, one hour later, the privy-councillor re-entered the cabinet, the letter to the pope lay folded and addressed on the table. But this last humiliation had been too much for the proud spirit of the emperor to brook.

He lay insensible in his chair, a stream of blood oozing slowly from his ghastly lips.

CHAPTER CLXXVI.

THE DEATH OF THE MARTYR.

He had made his peace with the world and with God! He had taken leave of his family, his friends, and his attendants. He had made his last confession, and had received the sacraments of the church.

His struggles were at an end. All sorrow overcome, he lay happy and tranquil on his death-bed, no more word of complaint passing the lips which had been consecrated to the Lord. He comforted his weeping relatives, and had a word of affectionate greeting for every one who approached him. With his own feeble hand he wrote farewell letters to his absent sisters, to Prince Kaunitz, and to several ladies for whom he had an especial regard; and on the seventeenth of February he signed his name eighty times.

He felt that his end was very near; and when Lacy and Rosenberg, who were to pass the night with him, entered his bedchamber, he signed them to approach.

"It will soon be over," whispered he. "The lamp will shortly be extinguished. Hush! do not weep—you grieve me. Let us part from each other with fortitude."

* This is the revocation-edict, which, promulgated a few weeks before the death of Joseph, caused such astonishment throughout Europe.—Gross-Hoffinger, iii., p. 290.

† Gross-Hoffinger, iii., p. 279.

"Alas, how can we part with fortitude, when our parting is for life!" said Lacy.

The emperor raised his eyes, and looked thoughtfully up to heaven. "We shall meet again," said he, after a pause. "I believe in another and a better world, where I shall find compensation for all that I have endured here below."

"And where punishment awaits those who have been the cause of your sorrows," returned Rosenberg.

"I have forgiven them all," said the dying monarch. "There is no room in my heart for resentment, dear friends. I have honestly striven to make my subjects happy, and feel no animosity toward them for refusing the boon I proffered. I should like to have inscribed upon my tomb, 'Here lies a prince whose intentions were pure, but who was so unfortunate as to fail in every honest undertaking of his life.' Oh, how mistaken was the poet, who wrote,

'Et du trône au cercueil le passage est terrible!'

"I do not deplore the loss of my throne, but I feel some lingering regret that I should have made so few of my fellow-beings happy—so many of them ungrateful. This, however, is the usual lot of princes!" *

"It is the lot of all those who are too enlightened for their times! It is the lot of all great men who would elevate and ennoble the masses!" cried Lacy. "It is the fate of greatness to be the martyr of stupidity, bigotry, and malice!"

"Yes, that is the word," said Joseph, smiling. "I am a martyr, but nobody will honor my relics."

"Yes, beloved sovereign," cried Rosenberg, weeping, "your majesty's love we shall bear about our hearts, as the devotee wears the relic of a marytred saint."

"Do not weep so," said Joseph. "We have spent so many happy days together, that we must pass the few fleeting hours remaining to us in rational intercourse. Show me a cheerful countenance, Rosenberg—you from whose hands I received my last cup of earthly comfort. What blessed tidings you brought me! My sweet Elizabeth is a mother, and I shall carry the consciousness of her happiness to the grave. I shall die with *one* joy at my heart—a beautiful hope shall blossom as I fall!—Elizabeth is your future empress; love her for my sake; you know how unspeakably dear she is to me. And, now that I think of it, I have not heard from her since this morning. How is she?"

The two friends were silent, and cast down their eyes.

"Lacy!" cried the emperor, and over his inspired features there passed a shade of human sorrow. "Lacy, speak—you are silent—O God, what has happened? Rosenberg, tell me, oh tell me, how is my Elizabeth, my darling daughter?"

So great were his anxiety and distress, that he half rose in his bed. They would not meet his glance, but Rosenberg in a low voice replied:

"The archduchess is very sick. The labor was long and painful."

"Ah, she is dead!" exclaimed Joseph, "she is dead, is she not?"

Neither of his weeping friends spoke a word, but the emperor comprehended their silence.

* The emperor's own words.—"Characteristics of Joseph II.," p. 23.

Falling back upon his pillow, he raised his wasted arms to heaven. "O God, Thy will be done! but my sufferings are beyond expression! I thought that I had outlived sorrow; but the stroke which has come to imbitter my last moments exceeds all that I have endured throughout a life of uncheckered misery!" *

For a long time he lay cold and rigid. Then raising himself upon his arm, he signed to Rosenberg to approach. His eyes beamed as of erst, and his whole demeanor was that of a sovereign who had learned, above all things, to control himself.

"She must be buried with all the tenderness and honor of which she was deserving," said he. "Rosenberg, will you attend to this for me? Let her body be exposed in the court-chapel to-morrow. After that, lay her to rest in the imperial vaults, and let the chapel be in readiness to receive my own remains." †

This was the last command given by the emperor. From that hour he was nothing more than a poor, dying mortal, whose last thoughts are devoted to his Maker. He sent for his confessor, and asked him to read something appropriate and consolatory. With folded hands, his large violet eyes reverently raised to heaven, he listened to the holy scriptural words. Suddenly his countenance brightened, and his lips moved.

"Now here remain faith, hope, and love," read the priest.

The emperor repeated the three last words, "faith—hope"—and when he pronounced the word "love," his face was illumined with a joy which had its source far, far away from earth!

Then all was silent. The prayer was over, and the dying emperor lay motionless, with his hands folded upon his breast.

Presently his feeble voice was heard in prayer. "Father, Thou knowest my heart—Thou art my witness, that I meant—to do—well. Thy will be done!" ‡

Then all was still. Weeping around the bed stood Lacy, Rosenberg, and the Archduke Francis. The emperor looked at them with staring eyes, but he recognized them no longer. Those beautiful eyes were dimmed forever!

Suddenly the silence was broken by a long, long sigh.

It was the death-sigh of JOSEPH THE SECOND!

JOSEPH died on the 20th of February, 1790. But his spirit outlived him, and survives to the present day. His subjects, who had so misjudged him, deplored his loss, and felt how dear he had been to them. Now that he was dead—now that they had broken his heart, they grieved and wept for him. Poets sang his praises in elegies, and wrote epitaphs laudatory of him who may be considered the great martyr of political and social enlightenment.

* The emperor's own words.
† Joseph's own words.—See Hubner, ii., p. 491.
‡ Ramshorn, p. 410.

THE END.

COSIMO CLASSICS

Lightning Source UK Ltd.
Milton Keynes UK
UKOW04f1909191015

260949UK00001B/13/P